ALSO BY CHRISTOPHER BUNN

A Storm
In Tormay

by
Christopher Bunn

The Complete Tormay Trilogy

Westly,
May you read
many books, see
many lands, and
some day conquer
the galaxy.

For Jessica, Finn, Jesse & Toby

-LANDS-
OF
TORMAY

A STORM
IN TORMAY

CHAPTER ONE
DOWN THE CHIMNEY

The man raised his fist again.

"No shirking," he said. "If you know what's good for you."

The boy dabbed at his cut lip and then touched the wall. His fingertips were greasy with blood. The alley they stood in was narrow, but the moon shone down from overhead, glimmering on the stones of the wall. The sweet scent of selia blossoms filled the air.

"Hurry up."

"I need to get a feel for it first," said the boy sullenly.

Only a fool would climb without trying to understand a wall first. No telling what would be there. Ward spells woven into the stones. Holds and ledges that were illusions, melting away once your weight was on them. He leaned his forehead against the wall and closed his eyes. The stones were still warm from the day's sunlight. And something else.

"The wall's warded," said the boy. "It's listening to us."

"So be silent."

The boy cinched the knapsack on his back tight and began to climb. He was the best of the Juggler's children. The tiniest edge of rock was a foothold or a handhold to him. If he had been given a wall reaching up to the sky, he could have climbed it. Even up to the stars.

He listened as he climbed. Wavering focus could result in injury or death. Eight feet above the ground, he heard the first whispers of the ward spells contracting, weaving themselves tighter and waiting for the intruder. He froze into silence. He thought of the emptiness of sky, where even the wind blows in silence. He recalled a memory of night, mute with stars and darkness. The wards relaxed, hearing the same silence inside the boy. They became still, waiting for a real intruder, someone of noisy flesh and blood, not this shadow of a boy.

He climbed higher. Perhaps there would be some coins for the night's work. Maybe the Juggler's temper would hold good for a few days. After all, surely this was an important job. More important than purses stolen in the markets, or rings slipped from the fingers of ladies strolling the promenades. How else to explain the presence of the Knife? He was not one to bother himself with the Juggler and his pack of children.

It was a high wall, but it wasn't a hard climb. After a few minutes, he reached the gutter and swung up over it. He crept up to the peak of the roof and peered over. An enclosed garden sprawled below. Moonlight shone on bushes and trees. From what the boy could observe, the house was built along the lines of a large rectangle—three stories in some places, four in others—with a tower that surmounted it all on the eastern end.

He took some rope from his knapsack, tied a loop around the chimney, and tossed the free end down to the alley below. It did not take long for the man to climb up. The boy eyed him as he crept over the side of the roof, hungry for any sign of weakness. But Ronan of Aum had not become the Knife of the Thieves Guild by being weak. The boy shivered and rubbed his palms down the sides of his pants.

Only a fool would have said no to the Knife. But the boy had almost refused when the Juggler had approached him earlier that afternoon. He had felt the *no* trembling in fear on the tip of his tongue. The Knife needs a boy to do a chimney job tonight, the Juggler had said. Up a wall, down a chimney, into a sleeping house. As easy as that. The boy knew he could not say no. Not with the Knife involved.

When did the Knife ever have need for one of the Juggler's children? They were cutpurses and pickpockets. They were the whispers and breezes that ran through the marketplaces and the bustling streets of the Highneck Rise district where the lords and ladies came to shop. They were the children that came home to the Juggler with pockets full of coins and the lace handkerchiefs of ladies and the odd key ring or two. Some were climbers, like the boy, but that was done more in fun than anything else. Lazy afternoons in back of the Goose and Gold when the Juggler was snoring drunk on his bed. Scaling the wall there, with only the stableman to shout at them every now and then.

The Knife. The boy had seen him once before. One of the older children had pointed him out, a tall man walking into the Goose and Gold. The Knife. *More blood on his blade than any man in Hearne. Slide up to you closer than your shadow. Slit your throat and be halfway to Dolan before you even knew you were dead. Steal the regent's eyes right out of his head.*

The boy watched the man creep up through the darkness, up and across the roof toward him. Not creep. Flow. It was as if the Knife was made out of liquid shadow. He flowed. And settled next to the boy against the chimney.

"The wards," said the boy. "They didn't hear you?"

A scornful smile crossed the man's face. He pulled the rope up after him.

"Do you remember everything I told you?" he said.

"Yes, sir," said the boy. How could he forget? The two of them had sat the boy down in a back room at the Goose and Gold and gone over every detail until he could have recited them in his sleep.

"In the room at the top." The Knife pointed at the tower rising from the far corner of the manor roof. "Remember, boy. Don't open the box. If you do, I'll cut your throat open so wide the wind'll whistle through it."

"I won't."

"Good." The Knife paused. "What's your name, boy?"

"Jute, sir," he said. "At least that's what they call me."

"Well, Jute. The night won't wait much longer."

The man tossed the free end of the rope down the chimney. Jute clambered up onto the chimney ledge and then lowered himself into the shaft. Narrow, but not impossible for someone as thin as he was. It was obvious no one had lit a fire below in months, for it was the end of summer now. Only a dusting of soot coated the walls.

Jute climbed down into darkness. Wary. Listening. Tense with the effort of both focusing and trying to ignore fear at the same time. He rested halfway down the chimney, with his back wedged against one wall and his feet pressed against the opposite. The moon peered down at him through the tiny square of sky far above.

Down again.

After a while, the moonlight failed, and he found himself in complete darkness. *The chimney must have jinked,* he thought. *Somehow it bent, and I didn't notice.* For a moment he found it difficult to breathe, but he shut his eyes tight and that made things better. Hand over hand on the rope, feet feeling for stones in the wall to aid his descent.

Down he went, until the chimney widened out and his toes touched the ribs of an iron grate below him.

Jute listened for a while, his eyes closed. But there was nothing to hear, except for the snuffle of a mouse as it skittered along a wall somewhere off to his left. He opened his eyes. He blinked, for the room seemed as light as day after the darkness of the chimney, but it was only the moonlight streaming in through the windows. He tiptoed to the door in the far right corner of the room. Just where the Knife had said it would be. He pressed his ear against the door and listened. Nothing. Except something was behind the door, or somewhere in that direction, listening to him.

He froze. The back of his neck prickled. There was a difference between something— a warding spell, a person—listening for whatever it might hear, as opposed to something listening to him. This thing, whatever it was, was listening specifically to him. That meant it had already identified him.

He had attempted to explain the idea to Lena once, right before she had tried breaking into the bakery in Highneck Rise. Wards are listening spells, mostly. Wards listen all the time. To everything—the wind, the ticking of clocks, people, songbirds, other wards. But a ward can also choose to listen to individual sounds. "Like if you walk through the tavern," he had said. "I can pick out the sound of your feet from among the other sounds. I begin to listen specifically to you because I have identified your sound. Once a ward has identified a sound it listens to that sound for a while, according to whatever rules are woven into the ward spell. If the ward then decides the sound is a threat, then it activates."

Lena had nodded and, later that day, snuck off to Highneck Rise without telling him. The lock on the back door of the bakery hadn't been difficult, but a ward had activated as soon as she had crossed the threshold. Her face was still scarred from the burn.

Jute closed his eyes, listening. The thing somewhere past the door wasn't hostile. Curious, perhaps, and something else he couldn't identify. It was listening specifically to him. Sweat trickled down his back. A tiny voice in the back of his mind suggested turning and leaving. But he couldn't. Turning back meant climbing up the chimney to the man waiting on the roof.

Jute slipped through the door and into a dark hall. *Once inside the hall, the door at the far end and then up the stairs*, the Knife had said.

The door opened and stairs rose before him. They wound around and around, higher and higher. Moonlight filtered down windows cut in the stone walls, softening the darkness into shadow. He was higher than the rest of the manor now. Looking out, he could see the roof stretching away below him. He thought he could make out the dark blot of the Knife crouched beside the chimney.

Up the stairs, boy. Up the stairs and into a small room. That's where the box is.

The sensation of the thing listening to him strengthened. It knew him somehow. He was sure of it. The voice inside his mind suggested again the wisdom of fleeing, but turning away was not an option. The man waiting at the top of the chimney was reason enough, but another reason trembled to astonished life inside Jute. If truth be told, he was not even sure of his own name. To find someone—something—that knew him would be more valuable than the richest purse he had ever stolen.

The stairway curved one more time and came to a door. A warning whispered from the door: a ward woven into the iron handle. He could hear the spell wavering through the air in search of whatever drew near. Instantly, he willed himself into silence, thinking of the quiet moon in her empty sky. The ward subsided back into sleep.

The handle turned under his fingers, and he was inside. Moonlight shone through windows. The city sprawled around him in every direction. Like stars in the night, lamplight gleamed through chinks in the shuttered windows of houses. Overhead, the stars gleamed like lamplight. But Jute had no eye for any of this.

On a table in the middle of the room sat a box.

Somewhere in that room. It isn't a large place, so it shouldn't be difficult to find the thing.

Of course not. There's nothing else here. Only a table, a chair, and a box.

It was the box that called soundlessly to him, so clearly that he turned in fright, thinking someone had spoken his name. Several thoughts floated through his head, reminding him of the Knife, of instructions, of the Juggler, but he quashed them down. His nose twitched like a dog's. The pull was strong. It certainly wasn't a ward. Ward spells never pulled at people—at least, not any ward he'd felt before. Wards pushed people. Pushed them hard in deadly ways. This was like someone tugging at his hand.

It'll be the length of your forearm. Made of black oak and fastened with a catch and hinges of silver. If that isn't enough for you, there's a carving on the top of it. A hawk's head staring at you, with the moon and the sun rising and setting behind him.

The hawk's head gazed at him from the box, the eyes frozen in an unblinking stare. The carving was so lifelike that it seemed the bird was only resting, ready to spread its wings and fly free.

If you open the thing, it'll be my knife in your gullet. Just stow it in your bag, and back up the chimney with you. Don't stop to think, boy. Best not to think.

That was the trouble.

He didn't stop to think. His hand reached out, and the catch flipped up. The lid sprang open. Lying on a cushion of threadbare velvet was a dagger. It was an ugly thing, black and battered. Set within the handle was a gemstone. The stone was cracked and blackened, as if it had been subjected to great heat. It was hard to tell, but Jute suspected it might once have been red.

He shivered. It was the dagger that was aware. A questioning, delicate touch feathered around the edges of his mind. Curiosity, and then something else. Satisfaction.

Jute sat back on his heels in astonishment. How could this thing—this dagger—have anything to do with him, know him?

If you open the thing, it'll be my knife in your gullet.

He touched the blade and snatched his hand away. A smear of blood stained the iron. Surely the edge looked as dull as a spoon! Scarlet welled from his finger. He sucked the salt of it into his mouth. The awareness brushing his thoughts vanished. There was nothing. Only an old, cheap-looking dagger. The stone in the handle was probably just glass. And yet he could have sworn, right when he had felt the sting of the cut, someone had whispered in his ear.

If you open the thing, it'll be my knife in your gullet.

Sweat sprang from Jute's forehead, and he shivered. He shut the box. His hands shook. The hawk no longer looked lifelike. It was a crude carving at best. He stuffed the box into his knapsack. His teeth chattered.

What have I done?

Jute fled from the room. He ran through the doorway and down the dark stairs. Behind him, he felt a soundless wave of menace explode and roll down the steps after him as the ward triggered. He lunged forward. His heart thumped within his chest. Heat surged against his back. He ran so fast that his feet barely touched the stairs. Down and

5

down, curving around and around, until he grew dizzier with each step he took. He risked a glance behind him, but there was only shadow and silence.

Jute crept back into the room with the fireplace. He took one despairing look around the room, but there was nothing to do except climb back up the chimney. The knapsack swung from his back, and the box inside seemed to grow heavier the higher he went. He had to rest for a moment, wedged between the chimney walls, for the dread inside him had welled up until his hands were too weak to hold his weight on the rope. But then his scalp prickled, for a whisper drifted down from above him.

"Jute. Come up, boy. Come up."

Trembling, Jute continued. The opening of the chimney came into view, first as a smudge of night, then widening into a square of sky speckled with stars. The shape of the man's head peered down. Jute could make out the black spots of the man's eyes.

"Do you have it?" said the man.

"Yes," said Jute, trying not to let his teeth chatter. His hands ached on the rope.

"Did you open it?" said the man.

"No!" said Jute, feeling the sweat bead cold on his skin.

"Hand it here."

"Let me come up first," said the boy.

"Hand it up."

The man leaned down into the well of the chimney, one arm extended. He snatched the box up and examined it in the moonlight.

"Well done," he said, turning back. "Come up, boy."

Jute pulled himself up to the edge and a blessed view of stars and the city sleeping around them. He could smell the selia blossom on the breeze. And then, almost carelessly, the man's hand touched his shoulder and Jute felt a sting that dulled into nothing.

Time slowed.

Numb.

A needle gleamed in the man's hand.

"Nothing personal, boy," said the man. "We all have our jobs to do."

And he pushed Jute.

Gently.

He fell.

Down and down.

Down into darkness. Which blossomed with bursts of light as his head struck the chimney walls. Stars in the night sky. His silent sky. And then nothing.

Nothing personal, boy.

The eastern horizon blushed into purple, even though sunrise was another hour away. The moon retreated over the sea to the west, gazing down on the city of Hearne with her silver eye. Another eye gazed down on Hearne. High in the sky soared a hawk. Nothing escaped his attention. The bird circled wider. The wind bore him up. A scream of defiance and exultation burst forth from his beak. He soared higher into the emptiness of the sky.

CHAPTER TWO
LEVORETH CALLAS

Far to the north, Levoreth woke up frowning, tangled in her bedsheets and the thoughts in her mind. She padded to the window. A breeze cooled her brow. Over the mountains in the east, the sky was streaked with rose paling to blue. Murmurs drifted up from the barn below—the stable hands pitching hay for the horses. A boy yawned his way across the courtyard, water slopping from the buckets he was carrying.

She sat down on the window settle and gazed out. She could see all the way down to the ford beyond the cornfields. The road crossed the river there and made its way southwest through the forests of Dolan, and further still, across the plains and, ultimately, to the city of Hearne.

Why was she thinking so much of Hearne these days?

It had been a long time since she had been south. It had been a long time since she had been anywhere. She frowned again. A thought tickled at the back of her mind and then was gone before she could reach for it.

She shrugged into a frock and went downstairs. The scent of bread met her as she walked across the hall and opened the kitchen door. An old woman was bent over the oven, poking with a paddle at several loaves of bread inside. She straightened up, her face red from the oven's heat.

"M'lady Levoreth—it's early for you to be up," said the old woman.

"Nonsense, Yora. The sun's nearly up and the hands are up, and I just saw Mirek ambling across the yard."

"The lazy good-for-nothing. It's a wonder he's awake. He's near as bad as his father who died of sleep, snoring away his life in the sun—M'lady! You'll burn yourself!" The girl had stooped down and pulled a loaf of bread from the oven with her hands. She grinned at Yora and ripped a hunk of bread free. It steamed in her grasp.

"It's quite done. And smells wonderful, too."

"M'lady! You shouldn't be doing such things!"

Levoreth went outside, chewing on her piece of bread. The sun edged up over the mountains. She squinted up into the light and then frowned down at her toes in the dirt.

The stable hands ducked their heads when she walked into the barn. Even the villagers were not as reverent as that with her uncle, Hennen Callas, the duke of Dolan. But the stable hands held her in awe and would never let her forget it. It had been her own fault.

She had been careless one day, two years ago. It had been getting harder to remember, to be careful. But she had forgotten. Perhaps it had been the intoxication of a spring after a long, cold winter. She had hiked out to the upper pasture in search of the first lupines. The previous week to that day, the Farrows in their gaily painted caravans had rolled through Dolan, and Hennen Callas had bought three wild colts off of them. He had happily parted with a purse stuffed with gold, for the Farrows had an eye for horseflesh that was unsurpassed in all the duchies of Tormay. The colts had been turned out into the upper pasture to wait until Hennen had time to break them to bridle.

Not thinking, she had set the colts dancing around her—wheeling away and thundering back at a gallop to stop, quivering, in front of her, pushing their silken noses into her palms. Their minds thrilled against hers, jarring her with impressions of childish delight. She caught images of time blurring into light and back again, shot through with joy and gold and pounding hearts, and the vast spaces of the northern plains racing away beneath their flying hooves. Their thoughts trembled with the solemnity of her name.

Rejoice! Sun and speed and wind. Rejoice!

Something had made her turn. Three stable hands sat on the fence at the end of the pasture, their mouths gaping. They tumbled off the fence and ran off. The colts wheeled and danced around her. Sunlight shimmered in the air, and everywhere there was the perfume of sage and lupine and the freshness of the earth wakening to spring. Wakening for her.

That had been two years ago.

Levoreth swallowed the last bite of bread and whistled. All the horses in the barn stuck their heads out of their stalls and nickered at her. Whispers of horse-thought brushed against her mind: oats, sunlight, and canters through the grasses of the high fields. She smiled.

"You're all just as lazy as Mirek," she said. A roan stretched its neck out and breathed alfalfa on her.

She rode the roan down to the ford and reined him to a halt in the shallows of the river. Sunlight shone on the water sliding over stones. The road curved from the ford and stretched away into the forest. Deep within the forest it split into two roads: one road to the south, toward Harth and Hearne; the other west to Andolan, the ducal seat of Dolan. Hearne. It had been many years since she had been to that city. The thought tickled again at the back of her mind and she caught it this time.

Soon.

"Soon?" she said aloud.

You have slept long enough, Levoreth Callas. You have slept too long. Your time draws near. Not today. Not tomorrow. But perhaps the next. Or perhaps after that.

And she frowned up at the sky and then down at the light sparkling on the water rippling by. The voice was her own.

When she brought the roan to a clattering halt in the yard, Hennen Callas was striding down the manor steps. He was a tall man, with gray hair and kind brown eyes.

"Levoreth."

"Uncle," she said, dismounting and flipping the reins to a hovering groom.

"It has been quite a while, hmm." He stopped and blinked several times.

"Yes?" she said.

"I have it in mind," he said. "I have it in mind to . . ." He trailed off again and gazed across the yard. "Blast those boys. They haven't mucked the mares out yet."

"You were saying?" she said.

"What? Oh. As I was saying, I think it time we paid a visit to Botrell in Hearne."

"Hearne?"

"Been a few years since we've been down to the city," her uncle said, "and every trader coming north says Botrell has a mare, Riverrun's dam, been foaling the best hunters since Min the Morn first set hoof in Tormay."

"Which is an exaggeration," Levoreth said, "as Min the Morn supposedly lived over seven hundred years ago, and the tradition of formal hunting began less than two hundred years ago when your great-great-grandfather broke his neck riding out after wolves. So the story goes."

Hennen blinked. "But there's also the Autumn Fair. Everyone goes who's anybody. Even the royal court of Harth. Your aunt has her heart set on going this fall, and besides, you haven't been since you were a little girl." A puzzled expression crept over his weathered face. She waited and said nothing.

"What's more," he said, "I received a raven last week, with word from Botrell that the duke of Mizra will be attending the Fair this year."

"Yes?" she said, smiling at him. And then words failed her uncle, for he turned and beat a hasty retreat toward the safety of the barn.

CHAPTER THREE
EXPECTATIONS

The Knife strode through the dark streets of Hearne. Houses sleeping still, shuttered windows, bolted doors and gates—he was alone. The box was a comforting weight in the bag slung across his back. Shadows, but he'd be paid well for this night's work. Nearly enough gold to take him far away from this miserable city, up to the Flessoray Islands, off the coast of Harlech. Nearly enough. And there he could lose himself on one of the islands and never be known for who he was, never be found again.

Nearly enough gold.

Night was weakening fast into the dark blues of morning, and he cast the sky one disinterested glance. If he had paused to look more carefully, he might have seen a hawk flying far overhead. He came to the Goose and Gold. The inn was still shuttered against the night. He slipped down the alley that ran alongside the inn and knocked at a door. It popped open and revealed the face of the Juggler.

"Success?" said the fat man.

"As expected," said the Knife, moving past him into the room. The building was silent around them.

"And the boy?"

"Did his job well."

"He was the best I had," said the Juggler, trying to look sad. "I hope our patron takes my loss into account. I'm a poor man who loves his children. They're all I have."

"You will be rewarded," said the Knife. "Enough gold to keep you drunk for a year."

"Ah," said the fat man, rubbing his hands together.

"You will also forget this night. It never happened. If even a whisper of this is heard anywhere from Harth to Harlech, I'll come for you. Understand?"

"Of course." The fat man smiled shakily. "I would never dream of—"

"Don't even dream of it. I'm not fond of killing children. You, however, would be a different matter altogether."

They walked downstairs into the basement of the inn. At the far end of the room were the oak barrels where the innkeeper kept his wine and ale. The barrels were taller than a man and a good fifteen feet in diameter. When he came to the last barrel, the Knife felt along its side until his fingers encountered a tiny catch. The side of the barrel swung out on well-oiled hinges. It was empty. Inside was an opening in the floor. The Knife climbed in and lowered himself down through the shaft. He paused.

"Tell your other children, those children you love so well, that the boy stumbled across a ward. A fire ward or something like that."

"Yes, yes." The Juggler nodded. "The sort that leaves nothing but ashes."

"We can't have them asking questions."

"I'll beat them if they do." And the Juggler smirked.

The other eyed him distastefully and then disappeared down the shaft. The Juggler closed the barrel door behind him. He waited, listening until the faint noises within faded into silence, and then, rubbing his hands together, he padded back up the stairs.

CHAPTER FOUR
WAKING UP

The boy Jute woke by degrees. First, he was only aware of pain—a dull sort that came in waves. He was not sure he had a body any longer. Pain was all he was, an ache that was everywhere. An ache that bloomed into fire.

He gasped. And then he heard a voice.

"There, you see? He's coming to."

Another voice rumbled an answer, but Jute could not make out what it said. He became aware of his body, lying heavy and useless on a mattress.

"He's been out long enough," said the first voice. "We'll get some answers now. Try that philter of yours again. Maybe that'll bring him around properly."

Recollection seeped back into Jute's mind. Images drifted through his mind. The Knife, like a shadow against the moonlit sky, reaching down for him. And then the prick of the needle and the long fall back down the chimney, into a well of darkness. But there had been something before that. He had opened the box. The black dagger. He had cut his finger on its edge.

A bitter odor tickled at his nose. He sneezed and opened his eyes. He was in a room lit by a candle burning on a table near the door. The light blurred in his eyes. Blinking, he tried to focus. He was aware of a figure seated next to him beside the bed. Another man stood at the foot of the bed. The man leaned forward, and the candlelight cast his features into shadowed relief. A hooked nose and a narrow skull gave him the appearance of a bird of prey stooping over its kill.

"Of all the houses in Hearne," said the man. His eyes glittered. "This is the one you should not have broken into. You'd have been safer robbing the regent's castle."

The pain flared down into Jute's bones with a sickening rush. His jaw clenched, grinding his teeth together. A spasm arched him off the bed, and his hand flailed off to the side, grabbing desperately. A warm hand grasped his. The pain subsided as quickly as it had sprung up.

"You're going to kill him, Nio," said the other voice.

"I'll snap him like a stick!" The hawk-faced man glared at the other seated next to the bed. "The box is gone, Severan! It's gone!"

"He's just a boy," said the older man. "I'm sure he wouldn't mind answering a few questions. Would you, boy?"

"No," said Jute, blinking away the tears blurring his sight. But then the candlelight winked out and he sank back down into blessed darkness.

The darkness was warm and complete. The warmth seeped into his bones. The pain receded. He was not sure whether he was awake or dreaming this darkness. Something rustled nearby and then settled into silence—a patient, waiting sort of silence.

Jute coughed experimentally. The silence deepened. He was relieved, however, for he knew that whoever was there was friendly. Someone different from the first two men. How he knew this, he wasn't sure. But there was a comfortable feel to the darkness, not unlike someone drowsing by the bed of a sick friend on the mend.

11

"Excuse me," said Jute.

"I was wondering when you would speak."

"Do I know you?" said Jute. "Your voice sounds familiar."

"Once or twice," said the voice. It spoke in an odd, old-fashioned sort of way. "In dreams. Mostly when you were small."

"Do you know who I am?" Jute asked, his voice eager.

"For a surety," said the other. "It is because I knew you that I've spoken to you."

"Who are you?" said the boy.

There was a pause, and then the voice chuckled. "Enough time for that later. We shall find our explanations when we must, but no sooner. If I were you, I would not say a word about opening the box. To anyone. You're in a difficult enough spot as it is."

"I didn't mean to open it," said Jute.

"Perhaps," said the voice. "There's usually a difference between what one means to do and what one is meant to do. At any rate, this Nio fellow will not be interested in whether or not you meant to open the box. What will interest him is whether you did. Tell him anything except that."

Someone shook his arm then, and he opened his eyes. Jute found himself blinking in the candlelight of the room. The thin-faced man, Nio, was gone, but the old man was still sitting by his bed.

"Could you stomach some food, boy?"

The old man had brought with him bread and a bowl of stew on a tray. Jute ate, and the man watched in silence. He was dressed in grubby clothes that hung loosely on his gaunt frame. His eyes were brown as polished walnut wood.

"What's your name, boy?" he asked.

"Jute, sir. At least, that's what I've been told." He mopped up the last bit of stew with some bread and eyed the old man nervously.

"Well, Jute," the old man said, "It's a name as good enough as another. As for myself, my name is Severan. You seem rather young for robbing houses. Work for the Thieves Guild, don't you?"

"Er, yes," said Jute. "Sort of." He plucked nervously at his blanket.

"Ah," said Severan. "You run with the Juggler's children?"

"Yes," said Jute, startled by him knowing.

The man nodded. "Even dusty old artifacts like me know a thing or two about this city. Guild or no Guild, they can't help you in this house. If Nio deals with you as he'd like, you'll be wishing you broke your neck falling down the chimney. He put a lot of stock in that old box, even though he couldn't figure out how to open it. He swore it held something valuable. Something unusual. Not sure if I ever believed it myself, but, no matter. He's angry, lad. Extremely angry. It never does to cross his sort."

"He's not—" Jute said, faltering as he remembered the fury in the other man's eyes. "Is he here?"

"He isn't here," said the old man. "You're in luck of a sort this evening. He hardly ever leaves this house these days so intent is he on his studies. Reading, researching, that sort of thing. For the moment, though, he's gone. Listen, Jute—you'd do well to tell me what you know. There'll be no harm coming to you if you tell me everything that happened two nights ago."

"Two nights ago?" said the boy in disbelief.

"Aye." Severan reached out and touched Jute's head. "You got a knock there, falling down the chimney. Strange that a clever lad like yourself would miss his step climbing a chimney. Perhaps you were pushed, eh? Perhaps your friend waiting for you at the top?"

Jute's eyes widened. The needle in Ronan's hand gleamed in his mind, gleaming in the moonlight. The old man sat back with a gloomy smile.

"Who can you trust, Jute?"

The candlelight dimmed down, like a golden eye winking at him from the shadows. The room blurred around the boy, and then there was only darkness.

CHAPTER FIVE
DISCUSSIONS DURING SUPPER

The duchess of Dolan had been born Melanor Ayn, only daughter of Rodret Ayn, whose family had held the western foothills of the Morn Mountains for the dukes of Dolan ever since Dolan Callas had built the town of Andolan.

The story Hennen always told Levoreth was that he had been hunting deer in the foothills when a stag led him to the country lodge of Rodret Ayn. A young woman had been hanging out the washing on a line, and she had paused, pegs in her mouth and a damp shift in her arms, when he had ridden up. Love at first sight for both of them, Hennen always solemnly intoned.

Melanor Callas's story, however, was different.

"That idiot tried to set his horse at the holly hedge bordering the garden. Of course the horse balked at the prickles and pitched him over onto his head. Knocked him cold, and blood everywhere. I ruined a good tablecloth wrapping up that knucklehead of his. Wouldn't be the last time, mind you. Fever took him for two whole days, raving out of his mind. When he came to, the first thing he did was propose to me in a most unsuitable way. I refused him, of course, until he had spoken to my father. It's best to keep a man waiting, my dear."

Prompted by meaningful glances from the duchess at supper, the duke broached the subject again. He looked down the table at Levoreth and cleared his throat. She ignored him and concentrated on Yora's mushroom and potato casserole. The steam rose up from her plate and tickled her nose. She chewed thoughtfully. Garlic, crushed pepper, dill.

"Your aunt and I've been talking," said Hennen, refilling his glass out of precaution. "She feels, as do I, that you're old enough now to—"

"Thyme," said Levoreth.

"Um—well, time is a consideration, of course. The fact is, you do so splendidly overseeing this house whenever your aunt is in Andolan." He gulped some wine.

"Fennel," said Levoreth. "But it's not fresh."

"What?" said the Duke.

"She's doing her trick again," said his wife. "Figuring out the herbs Yora used in the casserole. Levoreth, don't be difficult. What your uncle has been referring to with such delicacy is that it's high time you were married." The duchess glanced at her husband, but he was applying himself industriously to his casserole. "Surely you've thought it yourself, my dear. How old are you now? Seventeen, eighteen? Don't tell me you're nineteen!" Melanor waved her hand. "I can never remember such things. No matter. Your age isn't important. What's important is that you're a grown woman. And not just any woman— you're lovely, sensible . . ."

"And bake excellent apple pies," said the duke.

". . . and can run a household without even raising your voice. I don't know how you do it, Levoreth. The maids mind you more than they do me."

"All the stable hands live in adoring fear of her," said Hennen. "Some of the tales they come up with, you'd think they'd been at the hard cider. Just the other day, that idiot Mirek had the nerve to tell me I shouldn't be riding the roan, as it's Levoreth's favorite. I threw him into the pigsty for his impertinence. Melanor, my dear, do you know the spotted sow?"

"No," said his wife. "We aren't acquainted."

"She bit Mirek. Twice on his hind end, before he could make it over the fence. I've never seen the boy move that fast, but that sow was moving faster." The duke shook his head. "Imagine that."

"I fail to see your point."

"The point is, my dear, you'd think a boy would run faster than an old pig."

"Hennen," said the duchess, "have some more casserole."

"Oh, all right," said the duke.

"Levoreth?"

"Yes, aunt?" said Levoreth.

"Would you at least consider accompanying us to Hearne for the Fair?"

"And miss the autumn here? The walnuts won't be picked in time and they'll rot with mildew. The stable hands will pine away for me and forget to muck out the horses. They're useless on their own. What's the Fair to me? Cooped up in Hearne and having to put up with dreary balls and teas and oily princes and lords slobbering all over my hand and telling me how beautiful I am while trying to calculate how much dowry I'd be bringing to their bed."

"Really, my dear," said her aunt.

"What's more," said Levoreth, "Botrell will ogle me shamelessly."

"Botrell'll do no such thing!" said the duke, pounding his fist on the table. "I'll horsewhip him in front of his own guests!"

"Nonsense," said Levoreth. "He's the regent of Hearne. He can do whatever he wants at his silly Fair."

"But if you don't go you won't meet Brond Gifernes!" said the duchess, and then her hand flew to her mouth in alarm.

"Brond Gifernes?" asked Levoreth. "The duke of Mizra?"

For once, Melanor Callas was at a loss for words. She was saved, however, by the door swinging open. Yora entered, bearing a platter of blueberry turnovers.

"Something for afters, m'lord?" asked Yora.

"Thank you, Yora," said the duke. He selected a turnover and bit into it. They remained silent while Yora cleared the dishes. The door closed again behind her.

"You were saying something about the Duke of Mizra," said Levoreth.

"Yes, Mizra!" said the duke, spraying crumbs onto the table. "No reason why we can't say things about the Duke of Mizra every now and then. Why, just the other day, I was talking with the miller down in the village and . . ."

"Uncle."

"Well, the fact is I received a raven from him last week."

"And?"

"And he's asked for your hand in marriage, and why not, I say! You couldn't do much better. He's a duke and you're the niece of a duke, and all the traders say he's got more gold than all the noble houses of Harth put together!" The duke banged his fist again on the table for emphasis and then ruined the effect by looking longingly at the door.

"My dear," said the duchess. "I know this comes as a bit of a shock, but do consider it. At least come to Hearne with us and meet the fellow. There's no harm in that."

15

"I'll think about it," said Levoreth. "Excuse me." She rose to leave the table. As she walked up the stairs, she heard the duke whisper behind her, "Shadows, why does she always make me feel like a little boy?!"

"That's because," said his wife, but then her voice faded and Levoreth did not hear the rest.

She sat on the settle of her window. The moon was rising. The voice whispered again in her head.

You have slept overly long. It is time to wake.

And she knew the voice was her own. It had been so many years. Years of living quietly in the sleepy backwoods of Dolan, days blurring into months and years and lifetimes, all slipping by her. Strange, how time had passed. It was as if she had been asleep for years, drowsing through the days. It was time to wake.

Perhaps for the last time. One last autumn—I can feel it—but not here in this place I've come to love so well, but in Hearne at the center of the duchies. The center of Tormay. At least, what man thinks is the center. For there is no center. Only the four stillpoints. The silence of the depths of the sea. The silence of the wind in an empty sky. The silence of a motionless flame. And the silence of the earth.

My beloved earth. I could sink into this loam and sleep forever. Down below root and leaf, below the spine of the mountain range and the stretch of the plains. I could sleep away the centuries instead of refashioning myself into one Levoreth after another. But this one—poor girl—this Levoreth is the last one I shall be. I can feel it in my bones. I've grown weary.

The moonlight painted the forest silver, etched with shadows. Levoreth let her thoughts drift out across the yard, through the fields and into the trees. She felt a fox trot by, his tongue lolling over sharp teeth, thoughts of chickens in his head. The oaks were mumbling about root rot and the band of noisy crows that had settled into the east forest fringes. A trader slept by the coals of his campfire, far down the woods road, snoring under his cart. His old horse dozed nearby, but her thought woke the animal and it nickered in question, scenting the air for her. She quieted the horse, and it contentedly went back to sleep.

I'm tired. Tired, irritable, and forgetful. I've forgotten so many things. How odd. I can't remember ever having been in the duchy of Mizra.

She turned from the window and gazed around her room. Fresh flowers in the vase next to her bed. A smile crossed her face. Yora looked after her jealously, as if she were the daughter the old woman had never had.

Sometimes I can barely remember who I am.

In the morning, Levoreth walked down the stairs and found the duchess knitting in the sitting room that looked out into the garden. A cat slept in her lap, paws wrapped around a ball of yarn.

"I'll go with you and Uncle to Hearne," said Levoreth.

Her aunt glanced up. The cat woke and jumped down. It rubbed its head against Levoreth's ankles. She scratched behind the cat's ears and it purred in adoration.

"Besides," said Levoreth, "who'll keep you company when Uncle is off talking horses with Botrell and every other half-witted noble?"

"You'll never get married with that attitude." But her aunt smiled. "You only have to meet this duke of Mizra fellow. For all we know, he might be missing his teeth."

The cat nipped Levoreth's finger out of affection and then strolled away. It flopped down in a pool of sunlight and promptly fell asleep.

"To be honest, Levoreth," said the duchess, "I was beginning to think you'd never leave this place—hiding away here like a hermit with no one at all around. Why, you've been here for two years and never once come back to Andolan. The only time we see you is when Hennen drags me out here so he can inspect new colts."

"I was tired of Andolan," said Levoreth. She turned away.

"Anyway," said her aunt, not hearing her. "I'll tell Hennen. He'll be pleased."

CHAPTER SIX
MURDER BY NIGHT

The night lay over the valley. A blanket of darkness was draped over the hills and ravines and stands of pine, over the sleeping houses of the hamlet nestled below the ford. Smoke drifted up from their chimneys. A stream glimmered its way through the valley, down from the mountains and into the larger Rennet valley and the River Rennet itself, which ran for leagues until it reached the far-off city of Hearne and the sea. The air smelled of pine and the scent of heather wafting down from the plain of Scarpe, which stretched away from the top of the rise to the north.

But there was another smell as well. Only the most sensitive of human noses could have noted it, and even then they would have not recognized the scent, thinking it perhaps the whiff of a dead animal, rotting in the thickets that covered the valley slope.

In the valley below, a dog barked, calling a warning to the sleeping villagers. There was fear and anger in the sound.

Wake! Wake! Danger approaches! Wake from your sleep, oh my masters!

But there was no response. No lights flaring in windows, no doors flung open to bloom with firelight and life.

Wake! Wake!

The dog fell silent.

The moon hid behind a cloud. The darkness deepened. It was the third hour after midnight, when the tide of blood is at its lowest ebb, when the soul sinks so low in slumber that the sleeper drifts near to death. The third hour after midnight is the time when dreams and nightmares gain form; the scratching at the door, the tapping at the window, and the stealthy step in the hallway come close to reality.

In the home of the miller, Fen awoke with a gasp. She was nine years old and the miller's youngest child. She had slept poorly for the past three days. Nightmares crowded her sleep, but they faded whenever she woke up so that she could remember nothing except fear and the horrible sensation of something watching her just out of the corner of her eye. She was more sensitive to such things than others. Even as a little girl, she had known things, such as where the ducks hid their eggs in the rushes, or whether there would be ice on the river in the morning, or the fact that milk turned to butter faster and sweeter if you said its true name as you churned: *butere*. No one had ever told her that word. She just knew it, somehow, gazing down at the milk. Her grandmother on her mother's side was a bit of a hedgewitch in her own small way. She wondered about her youngest granddaughter but never spoke of what she thought.

Fen sat up in bed, trembling. Beside her, her sister Magwin stirred in her sleep. Magwin was fifteen and would be married next spring. She never had nightmares. Fen tiptoed to the window and looked out. It was dark outside, but the few stars visible in the sky gave enough light for her to make out the vague, looming shape of the barn and the mill beyond on the bank of the stream.

What had woken her this time? Another nightmare, but something else as well. Something else. A sound. The dog had been barking. That was it. Poor Hafall, cooped up in the barn every night. But he wasn't barking anymore. Silence. Probably smelled the foxes that lived up in the brambles. The foxes were sniffing around the yard, no doubt, hungry for chickens.

Except—the barn door was open.

She did not see it at first, for the building was only a big blot of shadow. But for one instant, the moon peered out from behind her cloud and illumined the open door and the well of shadow within the door. The moon vanished again, and the barnyard plunged back into darkness.

Hafall will be out, she thought. *The foxes will be in. Killing the chickens. Blood on white feathers. Someone forgot to shut the door.*

Fear swept over her until it was all she could do to just stand there, shivering. She thought of her bed and Magwin breathing gently there, but then she turned and trudged out of the room, feeling her way through the darkness of the house. She was her father's daughter, and while he was a kind man, he stood for no weakness from his children.

It was cold outside. Her breath steamed in the air. The night was hushed with a silence, unbroken by anything except the murmur of the stream. The barn loomed up before her.

"Hafall?" she said. "Here, boy." Fen whistled softly, like her father had taught her—two fingers angled together between her lips. But there was no response. No sheepdog running up to lick her face and push his damp nose into her palm. Only silence. The girl stepped through the doorway of the barn and immediately stopped. Her toes felt a warm stickiness. She looked down. The dog lay at her feet. Trembling, Fen knelt.

"Hafall?"

His fur was matted and clumped with blood, but she stroked his coat anyway. A gaping hole had been torn in his throat. She touched his face, the muzzle brindled with gray and the floppy ears that had been attuned to so many years of the miller's children, watching over them with his brown eyes and patiently enduring all the indignations they had lovingly heaped upon him. The eyes were dull and unseeing now. The pain inside Fen was almost too much to bear. It felt as if her own throat had been torn out. She could not breathe.

Something whispered behind her. The slightest of noises. Perhaps it was just the breeze. She turned. The moon peeped out from behind her cloud again and flooded the yard with silvery luminance.

The door!

I closed it!

But the door to the house stood ajar. The moonlight cast the entrance into relief—a thin rectangle of shadow set within white stone walls. And then the shadow grew as the door swung wider. For a moment Fen thought her father was about to step out, but then to her horror she saw that the stone walls were moving. No, something in front of the walls was moving—forms shifting. The moonlight and shadow slid off them like liquid. She blinked and rubbed her eyes. The forms gained definition and color. There was a tall, slender shape that at first she thought was a man, but then it turned its head, and she was no longer sure. The thing's eyes glimmered in the darkness like veiled stars. A long, thin blade curved from its hand. At its feet slunk two dogs, bigger than yearling calves, with massive shoulders and huge heads.

A word surfaced in her mind unbidden. A word she did not know. *Cwalu.* Death.

Again, the moon vanished back behind the safety of her cloud. Shadow reclaimed the yard. The shapes at the doorway blurred and vanished into the house. A scream clawed at

Fen's throat, quivering on her tongue and springing tears from her eyes. But all she could manage was a whimper.

That was enough. The last shadow disappearing through the doorway across the yard halted at the sound. The hound's head swung from side to side, scenting the air. Two red eyes gleamed and fastened on her with dreadful certainty. Fen turned and ran.

Into the darkness of the barn she ran, heart pounding so fast it was a solid blur of agony, gasping, stumbling, arms windmilling. Tripping over a bale of hay to land sprawling. Palms stinging, blood in her mouth. The darkness was like water around her, holding her fast as if she were trying to run through the creek chest-deep, struggling, desperately reaching for the other side that was no longer there.

She heard the scrabble of claws somewhere behind her and a hoarse breathing that shuddered through her. Memory flooded her mind with a rush. Her thoughts drifted by. *I remember now. I've been here before. In my nightmare. I wish I was sleeping still.*

And she slammed straight into a wall. Wood. Stars burst across her sight. She felt splinters in her face, and her left hand burned with a heavy ache. She could not close her fingers. She nearly collapsed with the pain of it, but her other hand caught on the wooden rungs. She had run right into the ladder leading up to the hayloft. Frantically, she began to climb, clinging with her right hand and hooking her left elbow over the rungs.

Up.

Up. The ladder under Fen shook as the animal threw itself against the supports. The thing made no sound except for the harsh breath rasping in the darkness below. Her body cringed in anticipation of claws tearing at her, of teeth pulling her down flailing from the ladder to fall and fall and fall. She found herself over the top, sobbing and face down in the straw that littered the hayloft.

Fen turned and looked down. Below her, a pair of eyes stared up from the darkness. She could make out the shape of the hound—the lolling tongue and jaws of gleaming teeth, the head, the shoulders bunching and tensing. Tensing to jump! She threw herself backward, scrambling in the straw for anywhere, nowhere to hide. Fire shot up her arm as she fell on her injured hand. The hayloft trembled with the impact of the beast. Splinters and straw flew as claws raked the planks at the edge of the loft, scrabbling to gain a hold. Fen could smell the stench of the thing—a musk of decay mixed with a strange, sour damp. With a snarl, the hound fell away. She heard the thump of its body landing on the ground below.

And then only silence. A complete and awful silence. She strained her ears listening, but everything was quiet. That was even worse than hearing the hound, that dreadful breathing from her nightmare. Her thoughts raced through the silence.

Was there another way up onto the hayloft, a way she had forgotten? What was the hound doing? What if the other creature—that strange man with his sword in his hand—what if he was standing in the darkness below? Staring up, silently beginning to climb the ladder?

Fen crawled as quietly as she could to the edge of the hayloft and peeped over. Nothing. Only shadow. She peered out a little farther. And the hound surged up out of the darkness. Fangs snapped in her face. The thing's breath stank of death and blood and sour rot. Claws raked down the side of her arm. She screamed and flung herself back. The beast hung over the side, eyes staring and tongue lolling from gaping jaws. With a tremendous scrambling heave it kicked its way up onto the loft.

For a second there was silence. Fen was caught within the beat of her heart—a knell that paused in the midst of its toll, lingering in the act of being as if there was no need to beat any more. She stared at the beast, and it stared back at her. Saliva gleamed on its lips, illumined by a moonbeam.

The hound leapt.

It would only take a heartbeat. One more heartbeat.

She stumbled backward.

I hope it's quick, she thought.

So it won't hurt.

Please, no.

And then she was falling.

The trapdoor over the haymow. Someone left it open. *Papa will be furious. Magwin fell through here when she was small and broke her leg.* Fire lanced through Fen's thigh. She shrieked. Slammed down on her back. Musty hay. Alfalfa dust choking in her throat. Agony.

Fen looked up. Her vision was dizzy and muddled with white spots blooming in the darkness. Long, thin, curving spikes obscured most of what she saw. Red eyes glared down at her from high overhead. There was intelligence in them, assessing and weighing the situation.

She tried to get up, but the instant she moved her leg, she almost blacked out from the pain. One of the spikes sprouted from her thigh like the tendril of an obscene plant, transformed into steel and slick with blood. She had fallen between the spikes of the harrow. They rose up around her, protecting her, claiming her for their own, anointed with her blood like some strange, ancient altar of thorns.

Dimly, from far away, she heard a whistle. Darkness claimed her and she knew no more.

CHAPTER SEVEN
DARKNESS AND WATER

Jute woke to find himself alone in the room. A candle guttered on the table, melted down almost to its base. As there was no window, he was not sure how much time had passed. An hour? Another day? He tested his limbs. They ached, but no worse than a beating from the Juggler. He sat up and almost passed out. Dizzily, he forced himself to his feet.

Trust no one.

He glanced around, startled. But there was no one in the room, only the voice inside his head.

Trust no one.

"Even you?" he said. "Who are you?"

There was no answer. He tiptoed to the door, pressed his ear to the wood, and listened. Every house has its own sounds: the sigh of wood beams shifting slightly under the onslaught of wind and sunlight and time, the creak of a stone fireplace cooling around embers, the scrape of tree branches against a window, the stately tick of clocks. And then there are the human sounds: voices, footfalls on stairs and hall floorboards, the settle of a body's weight into beds or chairs, and the whisper of knives in the kitchen, punctuated by clattering pots and pans.

But there was nothing at all. Jute strained to listen, but there was only silence. He was afraid, for the silence held an anticipation, not unlike a ward—a coiled expectancy seeking its moment of violent release. He touched the door handle, expecting the tremble of a ward spell infused through the iron. There was nothing. However, the door was locked.

He turned out his pockets, but he did not even have a bit of fluff, let alone a piece of wire. Someone had emptied them. He frowned at that, for he had a habit of keeping his pockets stuffed full of interesting things that he collected: perhaps a polished mouse skull, some walnuts if he felt hungry, a ball of string, the remains of an expired ward that Lena had proudly given him, and always a piece of wire. But his pockets were empty now.

He examined the bed, but it had been made by a craftsman with no love of metal, for there was not a single nail in its frame. The chair Severan had sat in and the table by the door were no better. They looked to have been built by the same hands—notched and grooved with wooden joints.

The candle. It sat on a copper plate. Wax had run down and built up on the metal in draperies. The candle would not come unstuck from the plate when he tried twisting it, and he ended up splashing hot wax on his fingers. The flame went out, plunging the room into darkness.

He did not mind darkness. He never had, even when the Juggler had locked him in the basement for the first time. That had been years ago. He had been smart enough then, as a young child, to pretend terror and tears for the Juggler's satisfaction. Being locked in the dark had become the Juggler's favorite punishment for him. That and beating him. He'd choose the darkness over a beating any day.

Never mind that now. The candle.

He froze, unsure if the voice was sounding within the room or from within his head. The skin prickled on the back of his neck.

"Who are you?" he said.

I told you before, boy. There'll be time for that later.

The voice subsided into silence. Jute shivered, despite the stuffy air in the room. The candle came away from the plate in his hand in one wrench. His fingers found what he hoped for: a metal spike protruding from the center of the copper plate, ideal for impaling candles. Ideal for picking a lock. He bent the spike back and forth until it broke free from the plate.

It took him a while to pick the lock, for his hands were shaking so badly that he dropped the spike twice and had to fumble in the dark for it. But the tumblers of the lock were simple, and the door creaked open.

A glow flooded into the room. He peeked out into a gloomy hallway stretching into shadows on either side. High on the wall hung a lamp glimmering with pale light. The light flickered as if something moved behind the glass. A dark spot appeared on the lamp and then grew outward, no thicker than his finger, wavering toward Jute. He slammed the door shut.

An understandable response, but too late.

"What was that?"

A very nasty spell. Run!

Jute flung the door open and darted out into the hall. He had one glimpse of rippling, black tendrils wriggling toward him, with the lamplight streaming from their midst. But then he was running down the hall and into the shadows. A flight of stairs. His foot slipped on the first step and he caught at the banister to steady himself.

The stairway descended down into a high-ceilinged chamber shrouded in shadows. There was no way to tell whether someone or something lurked below, but Jute didn't care. He hurtled down the steps in panic. He turned at the bottom of the stairs and looked back up. A light shone at the top, and then a dark blotch spilled like fog over the highest stair. With a whimper, Jute plunged away into the darkness.

He tripped over a chair and fell. Bit his tongue and tasted blood in his mouth. He stumbled to his feet, disoriented. Felt the smooth wooden top of a table and skirted it. The shadows were thickening into almost discernable shapes. The moon bloomed through one water-streaked window. It was raining outside. Behind him, the sea of darkness flowed down from the last step and surged forward. Frantically, he looked around for a door.

"Dispel!" said a voice. The darkness vanished and ordinary shadow reclaimed the room. Two quick steps sounded and a hand grabbed Jute by the throat. He found himself staring up into Nio's face.

"How'd you get out?" said the man.

Jute could not answer. Nio's fingers tightened around his throat, choking him.

"I want answers," Nio said. "Now. Tonight. If I have to flay them from your flesh, one by one. I can't wait any longer on the qualms of my tiresome old friend."

Nio dragged him down a flight of stairs into a cellar. Water dripped from the stone walls onto a floor of mud and broken flagstones. The man flung him to the ground.

"The wind blows us where it wills," he said, his voice harsh. "There's no stopping it, no matter how we duck and hide."

He strode to the far end of the room, stooped over the ground, and levered up a grate set into the floor.

"Come here, boy," he said.

Trembling, Jute crept closer. The man grabbed him, once he was within reach, and pulled him to the edge of the hole. It was rimmed in stone and revealed a well of darkness. The noise of rushing water echoed up from far below.

"What do you see?" said the man.

"Nothing," said Jute, his voice shaking. "Darkness."

"Aye," Nio said. "Darkness. And there's water as well. Both restless and both in abundance. A quick lesson in wizardry, boy. Much of it is only the manipulation of what already is, of naming things and calling their essence, their *feorh,* to heel. In air, water, earth, and fire are the four ancient *feorh*—the stuff of creation itself—though there is a fifth of an even more ancient sort in darkness. When any of the four mix with darkness, there is unrest and pain."

The man spoke into the hole, three words of a strange language. The sound of rushing water stilled for a moment and then something rose up from the hole in the ground. It was the figure of a man, a grotesque parody with limbs that moved oddly, as if they had extra joints. It was formed out of water and darkness that swirled together. Gaps opened and closed in it with wet, sucking sounds. A chill exuded from its dark substance.

The man spoke again, a sentence in the same strange-sounding language, and the thing moved. It shambled straight at Jute. The boy stumbled away, scrabbling against the mud and flagstones for balance. The thing did not seem to move quickly, but wherever he turned it was there, sprouting extra fingers and limbs to hedge him in. Nio watched, his face expressionless.

The thing cornered Jute against the wall and descended on him in a dark, watery wave. He screamed, but immediately choked on water. Ice crept into him, soaking into his body. His bones ached with the cold. He could hardly move, even though he frantically strained to thrash his arms and legs. He could not breathe. He was weighed down, drowning. Darkness welled into his mind.

Nio snapped a word, and Jute felt air on his face, as if he had surfaced from being deep under water. He gagged.

"You'll talk, and talk freely," said the man. "This thing is hungry and wishes to feed."

"Yes, yes!" sobbed Jute. "Please take it away!"

"Not just yet." The thing tightened its grip on Jute. It was as if an icy hand held his entire body and was constricting its fingers. His limbs were numb.

"I would learn of you, boy."

Through a haze of pain, Jute heard himself begin to speak. Words tumbled out, one after another. Disjointed phrases gasped. Hissed through clenched teeth. Sobbed. His life was ripped from him, word by word.

Early faded memories of Hearne. The face of a woman who he himself had not even remembered. He clutched at the memory, frantic to examine her face for a second more, but the memory was gone, washed away by the pull of Nio's will. A summer sky with a hawk circling far overhead. The jumble of city streets and alleyways, mapped in his mind into impressions of angles, distance, time. This wall was climbable, this one was not. This door here never locked properly. Shops, taverns, and houses. The passing gilt carriages of the titled and wealthy. Faces of children. Lena and the twins. Dirty, tearful, laughing, cringing in fear. Hungry. Always hungry. Shadows.

Dimly, he was aware of Nio sorting through his memories, pausing on some but discarding most as quickly as they came up. An image of the Juggler floated to the surface—the first time he had met him, running down an alleyway from an irate shopkeeper. Nio seized on the memory. Questions came quickly, and Jute heard himself begin to speak of recent years.

The Juggler. Hunched over his kidney and onions every morning in the Goose and Gold. Stinking like a brewery. Malevolently eyeing his children—his imps if in a good mood, the shadowspawn if in a bad mood, blows and curses if drunk—as they slunk past him for another day of lifting purses in Highneck Rise. Another day in the markets and streets of the city.

The Thieves Guild. A grimace crossed Nio's face.

Careful.

Just as quickly as it had come, the voice was gone.

"The Juggler works for the Thieves Guild?"

Jute could not help himself. His voice continued, numb with hopelessness and the cold. The Thieves Guild. The little man named Smede who came every Sunday afternoon and drank a mug of ale with the Juggler and then took away a pouch of gold and silver. The fear on the Juggler's face. Whispers among the children. Memories of the older ones who left the Juggler's ranks to work for the smashers or the men who ran the docks. Or the few who went higher on the hill. Highneck Rise. Somewhere, it was rumored, somewhere higher on the hill of Hearne, there lived the Silentman, the head of the Thieves Guild. He ruled from a court hidden beneath the city streets. The Court of the Guild.

"Was this job for the Silentman?"

Yes.

Nio's eyes glittered in triumph.

"How do you know that?"

Ronan of Aum. The Knife. The hand of the Silentman. Walking through the door of the Goose and Gold. Silence falling over the room, followed by nervous chatter, glances flicking at the man dressed in black. The Knife. The Juggler's face slack with fear. Sitting at a table with morning sunlight slanting down. The Juggler's hand on his shoulder, forcing him forward. The Knife staring at him, leaning forward. A plate of bread and cheese going stale on the table between them. The details. Gone over again and again. The manor. Up a wall, down a chimney, into a sleeping house guarded by ward spells.

No matter, the Juggler had said. *Jute can handle wards. He's silent.*

"He knew the house," said Nio, grinding his teeth together. "How could that be?"

Once inside the hall, the door at the far end. Up the stairs and into a small room. That's where the box is. Somewhere in that room. It isn't a large place so it shouldn't be difficult to find the thing. Somewhere inside, a box the length of a forearm, made of black mahogany as hard as stone and fastened with catch and hinges of silver. A hawk's head carved on top, with the moon and the sun rising and setting behind. And if you open the thing, it'll be my knife in your gullet. Just stow it in your bag and back up the chimney with you.

Careful.

Nio hissed and spun away from the boy. "By the Dark!" he said. "Who has undone me?!" He turned back to Jute, his face twisted with anger. "Did you open the box?"

Careful.

No. He told me he would kill me if I did. Kill me. He did kill me.

"Did he tell you what was inside the box?"

No.

"What did you do after you found the box?"

Back down the stairs. Step by step by step. Back through the sleeping house. Tiptoeing silent as a mouse. Up the chimney toward the man waiting on the roof. But he wouldn't let me up. Darkness was creeping up the chimney after me. He made me hand the box up first. He took it away from me. And then the poisoned needle. And darkness. I fell.

"You've told me everything, boy?" Nio's face was inches away from his own.

Yes.

Yes.

The man snapped a word and the horrible, cold grip released him. Jute collapsed on the ground and sobbed with relief. Out of the corner of his eye, he saw the darkness of the thing subside beside him. Jute crawled forward. His body ached. The thing beside him kept pace. He could hear Nio stalking back and forth, muttering to himself and sometimes addressing the boy.

"What shall I do with you now?" said the man.

Jute heard his footsteps crunching this way and that on the broken flagstones.

"I realize you were just a tool, but you pose a problem for me. But how could they have known? No one else knew except for my fellow scholars, and it's unthinkable they would consort with the Thieves Guild. Unthinkable! What would the Guild want with it except for money? They must have been hired—but by whom? You know too much, boy, whether you realize that or not. We can't have that. Besides, I think our friend here is hungry, in his own peculiar way. Perhaps that will be best for all involved."

A wet tendril of darkness wavered out from the thing next to Jute and licked at him. He shied away from it, crawling forward mindlessly. His bones ached. A memory of sky faded through his mind. The summer sky of long ago, when he was a small child. His first memory. A hawk floated far overhead, black and remote against the expanse.

"The problem with the Guild," said Nio, "is they consider themselves free of any obligation to Tormay. To any of the lands of Tormay. Do you understand the repellence of that? Those who live in Tormay are obligated to Tormay, and this—this box that you stole—involves obligation of the highest sort. If the Guild was hired, they could've been hired by anyone. Anyone with enough gold to satisfy the Silentman. The fool! The blind fool! Meddling in matters beyond him! But who could have known? A secret uncovered at the cost of many years! Who is my enemy? Is my shadow conspiring against me?"

Jute felt a different sort of stone underneath his fingertips. He inched forward. The darkness in the cellar seemed to be growing thicker. He could not see. The thing shambling next to him muttered damply.

"Our friend grows impatient." The footsteps turned and Nio's voice sharpened. "Boy!"

Jute's fingers reached into space. The hole in the floor. A stench of rotting sewage filled his nostrils. Nio called out a phrase—words that flung themselves through the air. The thing of water and darkness reached out a dripping hand toward Jute. And the boy threw himself forward, down into the hole. Behind him, he heard a wet gibbering and the furious shout of the man.

He splashed down into swiftly coursing water and was swept under. Tumbling around, he banged his head against stone. He bobbed up to the surface, choking and spitting. The roar of the torrent was in his ears. It was all he could do to keep his head above water. The rains, he thought dazedly. All the early rains. Summer has barely ended. Such strange weather.

He almost blacked out when the current slammed him into a stone bulwark that split the flow into two channels. His body spun off into the left-hand channel. The course angled down sharply, and he found himself careening along at a tremendous speed. Years of flow had worn the stonework of the sewers smooth and, even though he tried to slow himself, he could not gain any purchase on the sides of the channel. The current swept him under again.

I'm going to die, he thought.

No. For once, the voice sounded anxious.

Hold on.

Why?

Faster and faster now. There was no time for thought anymore. He fought his way to the surface for a gulp of air, and then the last of his strength was gone. Resigned, he curled himself into a ball, face tucked between his knees and hands laced around his ankles. Lights flared in his head—blots of scarlet and white pulsing with the beat of his heart. His lungs burned.

Hold on.

I can't.

You can.

It's always been like this.

What has?

Life.

Not anymore.

All at once, the sounds changed. Another sort of roar presented itself. The rhythmic surge of the surf. Growing louder. His mind groped to understand. The sea? And then he was tumbling through the air. Air. Rushing around him. His mouth flew open from sheer surprise and he sucked in cool air. He had one instant of a spinning view of the night sky, speckled with stars and ribboned with clouds. The moon stared down, her light gleaming on the sea and trailing off toward a horizon where dark sky and even darker sea met.

He hit the water hard, like a massive slap, and he was under but already fighting up toward the surface. He broke back into the air and treaded water, gasping. The cliffs of Hearne towered far overhead. Moonlight shone on a waterfall spouting from the mouth of the sewer high up on the cliff face. Wearily, the boy swam through the waves to the foot of the cliff and pulled himself up onto the rocks. He found a stretch of sand and, too tired to even feel the wet and the cold, fell fast asleep.

High overhead, a speck of black turned and wheeled against the night sky. The speck grew closer, gaining form as it neared—a hawk. He settled on top of a rock near the sleeping boy with a flutter of wings. Motionless, the hawk stared out at the sea.

CHAPTER EIGHT
NURSEMAID WORK

Ronan added the numbers up in his head. He frowned at his mug of ale. The numbers didn't add up. Not yet, at least. One or two more jobs might do the trick. Well-paid jobs, of course.

Supplies wouldn't come cheap. Warm clothing, furs, and skins, though he could certainly hunt and cure his own. That would take time and it had been years since he'd done such a thing. Line and hooks for fishing. Timbers for building a cottage. There weren't many trees growing on the Flessoray Islands, not as far as he knew. He'd never built a cottage before but he had a fair idea of how to do it. It couldn't be that hard, could it? Timbers for the frame, rocks for the walls—plenty enough of those on the islands—and turf over the top in layer after layer to keep out the wind and the weather. The timbers would have to be sailed over from Averlay. That would be expensive. Perhaps he could build a cottage entirely out of stone.

He sighed and took a drink of ale. A sailboat would be necessary as well. Maybe he could just sail the timbers out to the islands himself. He added the numbers up again in his head. It just wasn't enough. Even with the money coming to him for the chimney job. A dependable sailboat would cost a lot of gold. The sea wasn't his element. Not that he minded taking risks. You just didn't take risks with the sea.

"More ale?" said the innkeeper.

Ronan shook his head. The innkeeper swirled a dirty rag over the countertop and grunted something. It might have been about stingy thieves, or it might have not.

Perhaps if he did some freelancing on the side? The Guild was quiet these days. But the Silentman frowned on his men going off to earn a bit on the side. Thieves didn't obey the laws of Hearne, but they had to obey the laws of the Guild.

Maybe he could tutor a young noble in fencing. That wasn't thievery. Surely the Silentman wouldn't expect his piece of the pie from a swordsmanship lesson. There wasn't a better hand at the sword in the whole city. Except for Owain Gawinn. Perhaps. The Gawinns were known for their swordsmanship. Even his father had thought highly of the Gawinns.

Someone at the table in the far corner called for the innkeeper. The kitchen door behind the counter swung open and the scent of roasting meat wafted through the air. Beef and onions. Fresh bread. His stomach rumbled and he remembered he hadn't eaten yet that day.

"Lunch ready?"

The innkeeper nodded at him as he passed by with a pitcher of ale.

"Just on," the man said.

Stew. He inhaled appreciatively over the bowl when it came. There were still some good things left in life.

"That'll be a copper," said the innkeeper.

"Maybe with a loaf of bread it'll be."

The innkeeper grunted sourly but brought him the bread. It was fresh. Ronan tore off a hunk and dipped it into the stew.

Someone cleared their throat behind him.

Ronan sighed. "Can't it wait, Smede?"

"No, it can't. How did you know it was me?"

Ronan turned. Smede took a step back. He was a little man with a large nose and small hands that were always either rubbing together or investigating the surfaces of his nose, which was understandable as it was the only large thing Smede had in his possession.

"You smell of dust and ink and all the other nasty smells accountants smell of, molding away in your piles of parchments and gold. I'm eating lunch. Go away. The less I see your ghastly face, the better my life is. You disturb my digestion."

"Your words pain me," said Smede. "I've always had nothing but fondness for you, from the first day the Thieves Guild took you in—a wayward lad with an eagerness for fighting and all the sordid activity that carries on in our back alleys."

"Activity that makes you and your betters quite rich," said the Knife. "Blood on my blade is gold in the Guild's coffer."

"Gold offers more serene constancy than anything else in this world, be it noble titles, the love of a beautiful woman, honor at arms. To see it mount up in gleaming piles, to lock it up tight in strongboxes, to let it clink through your fingers, to tot the numbers up in fresh ink—purest joy! I fail to see why songs are not penned in its praise. Love, honor, valor—bah! Show me a bard and I'll show you a babbling fool."

"Why are you here, Smede? My stew is getting cold."

"Ah yes. The Knife is known for getting to the point." Smede wheezed once in honor of his own humor. "Economy of words. Being the Guild accountant, I should appreciate that."

The little man lowered his voice.

"Plainly put," he said, "the Guild has a job for you that must be done immediately. It'll pay well, of course."

"How much?" Ronan spooned up some stew and scowled at the accountant.

"Enough."

"I said, how much?"

"The amount remains to be seen, but it'll be generous. Rest assured. We have found ourselves yet another rich customer." Smede appropriated the stool next to Ronan. "Perhaps I should have a mug of ale? I don't drink the stuff often, but it might help me experience your degraded culture." He signaled to the innkeeper for ale. "Ahh, not bad, not bad at all," said the accountant. He licked foam off his lip with a pale tongue. "Poor man's wine, isn't it? Perhaps I should get away from my desk more, see the sights, take in the culture of our fair city Hearne? I'm sure you, my violent friend, know all the best spots and all the—"

"What's the job?" said Ronan.

"The job? Yes, the job. Let me tell you about this job."

Smede leaned close, whispering between sips of ale. Ronan listened and mopped up the last of his stew with chunks of bread. When he was finished speaking, Smede leaned back a bit unsteadily and gulped down the rest of his ale.

"That's it?" said Ronan.

"That," said Smede, "is it. An' I seem to have run out of ale as well. Mebbe another mug? Innkeeper! S'more ale!"

29

"Why me? If there's good gold in it, I don't mind taking the job, but surely this is something more suited for—for—"

"For a n-nursemaid?" hiccupped Smede. The accountant buried his nose in his fresh mug of ale.

"Yes. A bleeding nursemaid."

"Because you're the Knife," said Smede. He rubbed his nose and peered furtively around the room. "Because you're the best, the absolute best an' our customer wanted the best the Guild has to offer. Silent an' swift! Most importantly on this job—silence! Discretion! Not a word to anyone! The best!" He banged his fist on the table. "The best, I tell you!"

"Right," said Ronan. He shrugged.

"Innkeeper!" bawled Smede. "S'more ale!"

"My friend will be paying for my lunch," said Ronan to the innkeeper.

"Lunch!" echoed Smede.

"Thank you, my friend." Ronan clapped the little accountant on his shoulder. "Have some more ale."

"S'more ale!" hollered Smede.

Ronan turned and left the inn.

He had not realized how far gone the day was. The sun was already past its zenith. There was a chill in the air. He flipped his collar up and strode along, not bothering to mind where he was going.

It was a strange job, to say the least. Definitely not the sort to boast about afterward. However, he could see the wisdom in having the likes of himself doing the job. He, more than anyone in the Guild, understood the need for discretion. Loose lips shed blood. He shook his head. Who'd have thought the regent of Hearne himself would be hiring the Thieves Guild to do his dirty work?

He found himself down on the docks. Waves crashed against the seawall. Gulls circled through the sky. A fishing boat was rounding the breakwater. He could hear its lines creaking in the wind. The sea was alive with light. Something shivered and tightened inside him.

The regent.

Who'd have thought it?

CHAPTER NINE
FEN AWAKE

Fen desperately wanted to stay asleep. It was so much more comfortable in the darkness. The darkness was soft, and she had the notion that waking up might prove to be painful.

It'll be bright, she thought. *The sun in my eyes will be bright and I'll blink and squint like one of those little barn owls caught outside in the daylight. They must hate that.*

The barn.

Something about the barn. Something dreadful had happened in the barn. And then she was no longer able to hold onto sleep. She drifted up through the depths, growing lighter and unbearably lighter with each exhalation. Her body shivered alive with agony. Her leg was burning. She opened her eyes and remembered. A shriek burst from her lips, but she bit down hard the instant it escaped her mouth. She lay trembling and listening. There was only silence. Morning sunlight slanted down through cracks in the wall. Dust gleamed, hanging in the light.

Fen was able to inch her way up by getting her left foot onto the axle of the harrow. She stood up as slowly as she possibly could. The spike slid greasily through the hole in her thigh. Tears ran from her eyes and her teeth chattered. Her body quivered in agony. She could not see for her tears.

She must have blacked out again, for the next thing she knew she was lying face down in the hay. From the slant of the sunbeams she could see it was late afternoon. She looked up. For a moment she thought Hafall was alive, stirring from his nap just inside the barn door. The shape of his body, shadowed by the light outside, moved and seemed almost to rise. Fen limped forward, and the crows stooping over the corpse rose in a flutter of wings. They hopped away, croaking in irritation at her. Sobbing, she stumbled after them, scooping up dust, straw, anything to throw at them. But her left arm was numb and would not obey her. She tripped and fell flat on her face. Behind her, the crows settled back to their meal.

Movement caught her attention across the yard. A pair of rats rocked back on their haunches and stared at her with beady-eyed malevolence. They were crouched over a body lying across the threshold of the miller's house: a tall man with a head of hair nearly white blond in the sunlight. The same color as her hair, but stained and spiked with blood.

She could not breathe. Her heart was bursting, too big to be held within her small chest, and she screamed and screamed and screamed until the world dulled down into gray around her, until there was nothing except the sound of her voice dying away into a whimper of nothing that no one heard, that meant nothing within the darkness falling on what could have been a perfect sunlit day.

CHAPTER TEN
THE EDUCATION OF NIO

Nio stomped up the tower stairs. He slammed the door shut and stalked to a window. From there he could look from his house out over most of Hearne. And beyond. East. Something there had drawn his attention for the past few months. First in a dream and then, whenever he was within the tower, in unconscious habit.

Tonight, though, he glared out over the city. He saw nothing. The stone walls, the brick houses faded by so many summers' suns, the heights of Highneck Rise mounting toward the higher cliffs crowned with the regent's castle, the broken hulk of the university standing in a jumble of spires and towers and turrets huddled in ruins over the secrets they still held. Everything was washed pale in the light of the moon. It was all a blur, for rage does not sharpen sight, as some are wont to say; it merely blinds.

The work of half his life lost in one night. Stolen from this room by a boy. Years of study, of tracking down forgotten tomes to find a single line of text, a casual reference in a book of history moldering in a dusty library. It had taken him three years alone to get into the royal tombs of Harth—forbidden to all but the ruling line and the deaf and dumb servitors that guarded those tombs—just for the sake of one fresco fading into incomprehensibility on the wall of Oruso Oran II's mausoleum.

All lost.

Stolen by a boy.

Stolen by the Thieves Guild.

How had they known?

The boy stared back at him in his memory. Skin white with fear, eyes hollowed with shadow, the gaunt face and even gaunter body. A skeleton. Nio ground his teeth together. His hands curled into fists. The boy would be a skeleton when he was finished with him. He would flay the flesh from him. He would break his bones with his bare hands. He would—

No.

With an effort, he stilled the tumult in his mind. Such thoughts would not serve him now. He needed to think. It had all been so close, just within his grasp. If only he had been able to figure out how to open the box.

He would find them. He would find them all. This so-called Knife, the enforcer of the Guild. The fat man. What had the boy called him? Oh yes—the Juggler. They would tell him everything, once he had found them. They would beg his permission to speak. They would give him more threads to follow, until he had made his way to the center of their web and discovered what was there to be found.

It had begun forty years ago. When he had been a student under Eald Gelaeran in the Stone Tower, far to the north of Hearne, on the Thule coast. There, the last true library of magic existed, preserved since the destruction of the university in Hearne. For the tower was a school of wizards, a secret place not known to many. Those who did know had no cause to share such knowledge with others. The tower could be found only if one already knew it was there. The place was woven about with spells. Travelers who came along the moors tended to find themselves on twisting paths and heading east or south or straight over the cliffs into the sea when they meant to go north.

He had been a quiet boy, even for the Stone Tower. The other students spent their free time playing on the moor or climbing the rocky cliffs there that fell down to the sea. He never joined them, and they, in the unthinking manner of boys, were cruel with their words and actions. But he taught them otherwise with his fists and later with the aptitude he demonstrated in learning magic. It is unwise to bully someone who can enspell spiders and send them swarming over your sleeping body at night.

He learned quickly, much more quickly than he let on to those who taught in the Stone Tower, for there was an innate cunning in him that cautioned against revelations of any kind. When he saw the old wizards were soon reaching the limits of what they were willing to teach, he determined to find his own manner of study. This he did by stealing into the private library of Eald Gelaeran and reading the books there page by page, stolen minute by stolen minute.

One day, Eald Gelaeran set out on a journey to Harth. Nio surmised the wizard would be gone for at least a month, traveling as he did by ship to Hearne and then further south to Harth by horse. On the day the old curmudgeon set sail, Nio crept into his library and stole a book. The book of Willan Run.

He did not know why he chose the book out of all the others.

For thirty days and thirty nights, the book of Willan Run lay open before him. Strange spells worked their way into his memory. Incantations muttered beneath his fingertips. Shreds of forgotten history wrote themselves across the pages: old wars and rumors of wars in far-off lands, countries he had never heard of before that seemed to have no part in Tormay and its eight duchies. Much of what he read he did not understand. He did not concern himself over this, however, for his mind was hungry and he stored the words in his memory.

On the tenth day, he turned a page and heard the sea, smelled the green earth, felt the wind on his brow, and was warmed by the heat of the fire. He read of the four ancient anbeorun—the stillpoints—those beings of power who walk the boundaries of the world of man and beast and keep watch against the Dark. Four words spoken in the first language, in the tongue that is called *gelicnes*.

The four words spoken became the four beings who ruled and held sway over all the *feorh*—all of the essences of what is. Everything was theirs to command, from the creatures of the sky, earth, and sea, to the foundations of stone, wood, water, and flame.

Nio's imagination was caught. He devoured the rest of the book by candlelight at night, or in the afternoons, lying on his stomach and hidden in the tall grasses on the moor. The book went back onto the desk in Eald Gelaeran's library even before the white sail was seen beating its way up the Thulish coast.

He dreamed of the anbeorun. He dreamed of what he did not know. The dreams filled him with a longing for wide open spaces, higher fields, and places from which one may stand and see things more clearly. And he dreamed of power. Thrones and dominions. The heights that ascend above and beyond all else.

But dreams are dangerous things. They are not to be indulged lightly or deemed just the perfume of sleep's flower. In dreams, the sleeping self reaches for things beyond normal life. It ventures through unknown lands and, without realizing, disturbs the thoughts of others who make their home in dreams just as man makes his home in the world. With certain of such creatures it is perilous to draw their attention.

All souls are like dwellings shuttered and locked against the night. If one dreams too much, then a light grows and shines from behind those shutters. That, by itself, can be enough to draw notice from whatever stands outside in the darkness. If one continues to dream, day after day, then perhaps the door of the dwelling creaks open, and the sleeping soul wanders forth into the night, shimmering with the light that is the mark of life. The darkness is wide and the night is complete. Even a little light may draw attention.

So it was that the Dark woke to the existence of young Nio. It considered, watched, and waited.

A month later Nio left the Stone Tower and wandered across the duchies of Tormay. He arrived at the city of Hearne, where most people end up who have nothing better to do with their lives. Even then, perhaps nothing would have happened had he not signed on to a caravan that was heading toward Harth. Who knows? It is foolish to speculate on what might have been if another path had been taken. At the beginning of a life, there are many paths to choose from. At the end of a life, one looks back and realizes there was only one path all along.

The caravan master was pleased with his new hire. Travel and trade were always dangerous. He needed someone conversant with magic, even a fledgling wizard. Goods could be maliciously enspelled and there was always the inconvenience of unfamiliar wards in foreign cities.

Crossing the desert, they stopped on the outskirts of the ruined city of Lascol. Sheepherders kept their winter camp there, and the caravan-master always made a good trade bartering for their wool and fleeces. Bored, Nio wandered into the city ruins and spent several hours wandering about. Stone and fire-blackened timber formed a jagged mosaic around him.

It had happened then.

He found himself standing in a courtyard overgrown with weeds. A crow perched upon the sheared-off top of a pillar. It regarded him with one beady eye. The bird bobbed its head from side to side and fluttered off the pillar and onto the cracked flagstones below. It seemed almost as if the bird knew him. It hopped away and then stopped to look back at him.

The message was unmistakable. Nio followed the crow, not bothering to think why a bird would behave in such a fashion. It led him deeper into the ruins, through hallways choked with rubble, past collapsed walls, and around fissures that gave him glimpses of darkness below. The crow stopped from time to time, teetering on its claws and waiting until he came near. The sun gazed down through the gaps in the broken timbers. The stones shimmered with its heat. Sweat trickled down his back.

The bird halted at the foot of a marble stairway. The steps spiraled up until they ended in midair. The crow hopped up five steps and then pecked under the lip of the sixth step. One eye swiveled back to look at him. It pecked at the marble again.

Nio had known what to do, almost as if someone had spoken the words aloud. Kneeling, he felt under the lip of the step. A catch clicked under his fingertips and the face of the step swung open to reveal a recess. A book lay within the hollow. He heard a rustling flap behind him and turned, but the crow was gone.

Nio gazed out over the city of Hearne. The book. The writings of Willan Run had opened the door—true—but the book from Lascol had opened his eyes to what lay beyond the door. Strange. After all these years, he still did not know who had written the thing. The books of the wizards always had some hint as to which of them had been the writer, some mark or feel of the person reaching forward from the past. But the book from Lascol was different. It was a mystery that had intrigued him for years but was unimportant in the light of other questions. Such as who had hired the Guild, and where was the box? How had they known?

And what was in the box?

Had the thieves managed to open it?

The thought made him grind his teeth together. All the learning of forty years at his command and he had not been able to open the cursed thing. He wasn't even certain what was inside. The enchantment woven about the box had been so beyond him that he had not been able to find the end of the weave, the knot, the last syllable muttered into being that provided the final knit of the spell. What he was certain of, though, was that whatever was inside the box had been instrumental in the death of one of the four anbeorun. He was sure of it.

Hunger rose up in him at the thought.

The book from Lascol was explicit in what it wrote of such an occurrence. *If the life of an anbeorun be taken, and here I speak of the four great wanderers—Aeled, Eorde, Brim, and Windan—then that which hath taken life shall possess it until the blood of another is spilt by that same instrument. E'en death to life be returned by such a blow and with it the essence of the wanderer springs anew. But this be a perplexing matter, for the anbeorun cannot be known in form or custom, for they are not bound to the ways of men. And e'en if thou hath the fortune to encounter one such as these, with what will thou fill thy hand and strike?*

Nio shivered at the thought. Shivered in anticipation of the life and power flooding through him. Which would it be? The strength of the sea? The solidity of the earth? The fury of the wind shrieking through the heights, or the hunger of the fire?

But the box was gone.

Severan and the other three old fools scrabbling in the university ruins had never understood the promise of the box. They had thought it only a curio, an oddity. He had been careful to not dissuade them of this. He had never told them all he had learned. They knew it perhaps contained knowledge of the anbeorun—that was all—another tool to combat the Dark. Knowledge of the anbeorun could be found in other places.

No. They could not be trusted with the whole truth. They were content enough to hunt in the ruins, looking for scraps of the past. Looking for the so-called *Gerecednes*. The Book of Memories. The fabled writings of the wizard Staer Gemyndes. Looking for a book that did not exist.

The box.

Glass shattered as he drove his fist through a windowpane. Far below, he heard shards breaking on the street. The pain of it cleared his head. Blood trickled down his hand. Blood. There was always a use for blood. An idea bloomed in his mind. He turned and went down the stairs.

The house was quiet these days. Originally, the entire party searching within the ruins of the university had stayed in the house. As the exploration progressed, they had determined there were safe areas within the university, and they had moved there to be closer. To be closer to what they might find. And now the house was his, alone.

Well, not quite alone anymore.

Nio lit a candle in the kitchen and went down into the cellar. The candle guttered and shadows danced along the walls. The room was empty at first glance. The stone walls gleamed with moisture and shrouded with the tattered leavings of a thousand generations of spiders. Water murmured from the hole in the center of the floor. The same hole that the boy . . . With a grimace, he focused his thoughts. The room waited. Then, with an effort, he spoke.

"*Wesan.*"

Something stirred in the gloom. Shadow coalesced into a blob that wavered and stretched until it had achieved the semblance of a figure. The wihht. Water beaded on the floor around it, rolled toward the two feet and then vanished, as if blotted up by a dry bit of cloth. The addition of water lent the form definition, but it was hazy and Nio could see through its edges. The creature had lost much of its essence since the night he had spelled it into being. Pity that the wretched boy had escaped. His life would have given the wihht vitality.

"*Neosian.*"

The thing shambled toward him and stopped, several feet away. He could feel the chill rising off of it. A smell of decay filled the air. There was not much strength left in the wihht.

It took a tremendous amount of power to shape the feorh of anything, whether it be remaking wood into stone or a blade of grass into the petal of a flower. Simple things, but they required careful concentration. The crux of such fashionings was in the renaming. The true name of a thing had to be reshaped into a different name. Difficult enough with a blade of grass, but to fashion a wihht was a different thing. Who could mix darkness and matter and bend it to a human will? He doubted even old Eald Gelaeran would have been able to do such a thing.

A voice whispered inside his head that Eald Gelaeran would never have chosen to do such a thing.

Nio bit his lip. The voice died into silence. He had the will to succeed. The book he had found in Lascol had certainly taught him a thing or two. It was dangerous to fashion darkness, but darkness offered certain benefits—yes, *benefits* was the right term to use—that other materials would not give. The water woven into the wihht lent placidity and made the fashioning easier to control.

But it needed a third element to add strength. He held out his bleeding hand. The wihht before him did not move. Portions of its form faded in and out of visibility. Gaps opened up in its torso, so he could see the wall beyond, and then drifted closed again. A drop of blood fell from Nio's hand and plashed to the floor. It beaded into a ball and rolled toward the wihht's foot. The blood vanished.

The thing whispered wetly in satisfaction and then extended its own hand. The two hands—shadow and flesh—melded and became one indistinct mass. Nio felt warmth creeping up his arm and then back down, like a tide moving sluggishly through his flesh. The sensation made him feel sleepy, but he knew better than to close his eyes.

"Enough!" he said, and he took a step back, pulling his hand free.

He was exhausted, but he held himself still. The wihht snarled but did not move. For a moment, there was no change in its appearance, but then it gained form and substance. The limbs took on definition; fingers appeared and divided; the torso thickened, broadening across the shoulders. A head rose up—a thing of clay as if made with clumsy hands—it had only a daub of a nose, a gash for a mouth. There were two holes for the eyes, as if the potter had merely plunged his thumbs into the clay to fashion sockets. These two holes lay under a slab of a brow and, though they were filled with shadow, Nio could detect a point of light in each, fixed upon him. He read intelligence there and nodded in satisfaction. It was good enough for his designs now, despite the startling appearance of its face. Besides, he did not fancy giving it any more blood. It would not do for the thing to develop a taste for him.

"I have a job for you," he said. "In the city. Listening and watching. But first, we'll have to find you some clothes."

CHAPTER ELEVEN
THE HORSES'LL MISS YOU

They left early the next morning, with the sun just up over the Mountains of Morn. Yora refused to leave the kitchen; she sat in a corner with her apron bunched against her face. She only hunched her shoulders when Levoreth kissed the top of her head. Outside, the stable hands stood in a row in front of the barn, caps clutched in their hands. They stared at Levoreth, barely acknowledging the duke's admonitions to look after the horses and to be sure to mind Yora. The youngest, the boy Mirek, stumbled forward after being kicked by those nearest him. He touched Levoreth's stirrup and then snatched his hand away, his face coloring.

"You'll be coming back soon, M'lady?" he said.

She smiled down at him, not trusting herself to speak.

His face brightened. "The horses'll miss you, M'lady." He ducked his head, backing away.

She turned one last time at the river ford. Sunlight shone on the manor's stone walls. The cornfields around it were soft and thick with the gold silk of their tassels. The hills rose beyond in green slopes. The air was still, as if time had stopped at this place, finding nothing to age and content to leave things as it had found them. The dust of their passing hung in the air and gleamed with light. But as the roan clattered down onto the riverbed and splashed across, Levoreth felt the touch of a breeze on her face.

It grew warm as the party rode along. Dolan tended to have long summers. This year was no exception despite the unseasonal rains of the past months. The men-at-arms loosened the collars of their leather jerkins and tipped their helmets back. At the head of the column, the duke rode alongside Willen, the old sergeant. They chatted back and forth, trading thoughts on horses and tactics and whether or not there was any truth to the rumors of wizards returning to Tormay. The duchess rode behind them, sidesaddle on a placid mare. She eyed Levoreth, who had opted for a split skirt and was riding astride.

"My dear," she said, "I'd think you one of those unsavory Farrows if I didn't know better."

"They're the best horsemen in all of Tormay," said Levoreth.

"And the best thieves and killers," returned her aunt. "So it's said."

"So it's said."

"Hmmph."

It was true. In addition to being the best horsemen in the four kingdoms, the Farrows also were acknowledged as being extremely handy at theft and killing. To be fair, the Farrows tended to steal only under great mental duress—such as when confronted with a beautiful horse or a beautiful woman. However, the Farrow men were polite enough to never steal a beautiful woman without stealing her heart first. As for killing, that only happened if the clan itself was threatened, or if someone came along who was stupid enough to steal a Farrow horse or a Farrow woman.

Certain members of the clan had been known to kill for hire, but they were shunned by other Farrows. The most famous of these had been Janek Farrow the Blackhand, who had climbed the tower of Tatterbeg on the northern coast and fought the wizard Yone. Their struggle broke the tower into ruin. Dying, Yone had cursed Janek, that everyone Janek loved would be brought to heartbreak, ruin, and death. Janek fled to the east, determined to forget his family so that the wizard's curse would not come to settle on them. He disappeared and was never heard of again. The other famous Farrow, of course, was Declan Farrow, son of Cullan Farrow, who had stolen his father's sword.

The roan danced under Levoreth, drunk on sunlight and fresh air and the prospect of a lengthy and leisurely outing. Levoreth patted its neck and brooded on Declan Farrow and Farrows in general. Odds were, Declan Farrow was still alive, for the incident that had resulted in his disappearance had happened only fourteen years ago. He would still be a young man. At least, young by her standards, and Levoreth smiled to herself.

The road turned to the west. A few oaks grew in the rolling grasslands. They stood like sentinels of the Lome Forest, which lay miles further to the southeast. Crickets hidden in the grass rasped their music, buzzing cheerfully of the last days of summer. Occasionally, the hooves of the horses stirred them up into sight and then the little creatures would hop lazily away to safety.

Levoreth hummed under her breath, picking up the note of the crickets. Blackbirds swooped by with their wings flashing blue in the sunlight. She borrowed the melody of their song and wove it into her own. She pursed her lips and turned the tune into a whistle.

"Lovely," said her aunt, riding near. "What is that, my dear? A folk song?"

"Just an old tune about the earth. I think they're all based on the same handful of melodies."

"It puts me in mind of green things. Rather like one of those songs the girls sing while out in the harvest."

Levoreth smiled.

CHAPTER TWELVE
THE MOSAIC IN THE CEILING

With a sigh, Nio shut the book of Lascol and rose from his chair by the library fireplace. He put the book back on the shelf. The firelight flickered on his face as he stood a while in thought. A musty odor of parchment and leather filled the air—the scent of books, of time stopped and caught by words.

The book of Lascol contained an index of anything relevant to the subject of the anbeorun. *Aeled, Eorde, Brim,* and *Windan*. The guardians of fire, earth, sea, and wind. The four wanderers who had walked the world since the beginning of time, bulwarks against the Dark so that man and beast could live their lives in peace. It had taken years to track down everything referenced in the book, all the other books, the inscriptions in tombs and castles, even a tapestry in the manor of Duke Lannaslech in Harlech. Shadows, that had been a close one. If he had been discovered there, his life would have been forfeit. The lords of Harlech did not suffer strangers gladly, least of all a thief prowling their halls at night.

Forty years searching, and the final answers still eluded him. The information contained within the book had not proven to be enough. It was silent in several areas. Such as what could kill an anbeorun. Or what the origin of the anbeorun was. But at the end of the day, there was only one question that mattered: *What was in the box?*

A noise drifted up from below in the house. Nio went to the door, opened it, and listened. The wihht had returned. He heard the front door close, and then there was silence.

The wihht was waiting for him in the hall at the foot of the stairs, motionless in the shadows. Only its eyes moved as Nio walked down the steps. The candles in their sconces on the walls flamed to life when Nio muttered a word.

Lig.

Light.

It seemed there was more detail in the creature's face, more pronounced cheekbones and a fuller nose. Odd. He put the matter from his mind. He was honest enough to realize he did not know everything about fashioning something as complex as a wihht. Little was written on the subject, for not many wizards had ever dared to fashion the darkness.

"What did you learn?" he asked.

The thing answered him with a hoarse voice that was strangely soft, as if it had no lungs to breathe with and so make normal speech.

"Many things were learned, master. What would you wish to hear?"

"Tell me about the fat man called the Juggler."

"He cares for a band of children who live and work together. Without father or mother. Orphans. He works for—this group of thieves, this—" It paused, stumbling for the word.

"Guild."

"Guild," repeated the wihht.

"Go on."

"The Juggler controls their lives."

"Ah," said the man. "He would've certainly known more than the boy. Describe the Juggler to me so I'll know him when I see him."

"This one is a short, fat man with a round face. A round face like the smaller sun that lights the night."

"The moon. It's called the moon."

"A round face like the moon."

"Does he have a real name, other than this Juggler nonsense?" asked Nio.

"This was not learned," said the wihht.

"And what of the man called the Knife?"

"Less can be learned of this one."

"Why?"

"He is feared, master."

"Well," said Nio, "there must be something you can tell me of him."

"His name is Ronan and he comes from a town called Aum, in the duchy of Vo. No one believes that. But no one knows better."

"Aum's a ruin, a haunt of jackals and hoot owls. No one's lived there for over three hundred years. He has a past that's not to be found out and everyone be damned if he cares if they try. Arrogant of him. What else did you learn about him? This is of no use to me."

"He is a tall man," continued the wihht. "He is a man with dark features as if he has seen much sun. No one in this city is reckoned his equal with the sword or knife."

"Weapons don't concern me. What else?"

"That is all," said the wihht.

"What? Not even where he lives?"

"No, master. That was not learned."

"Friends, a lover, a favorite inn?"

"No, master. That was not learned."

"Is that all you have to say?" said Nio. "We'll have to start with the fat man. Curse the Guild! They're a stealthy, sneaking bunch, and curse that paltry excuse of a regent for letting them flourish in his city! Speak of the rest of what you saw today. Maybe some trifle will come to light that might be of purpose."

The wihht's hoarse voice mumbled on. A picture emerged of children flitting through the marketplace, of sunlight painful in the wihht's eyes, of small hands filching from barrows and the pockets of unsuspecting passersby. Men in taverns, gossiping over tankards of ale, of hidden things and the long arm of the regent, the Guard of the city and their captain Owain Gawinn. Locks, wards, streets, and doors. Roofs, back alleys, walls, and grappling hooks. The Silentman, rumored to be hidden in his labyrinth of tunnels under the city. Travelers from distant lands. Merchants, traders, noblemen. The Autumn Fair approaching. An inn called the Goose and Gold. After a while, the wihht ran out of words and stood silent before Nio. The moon glanced in through the window over the front door.

"Tell me more about the inn you mentioned," said Nio.

At that same moment, there came a knock on the door. For a second, Nio froze and then he jumped to his feet. His mind feathered forward and he felt a familiar presence at the door—impatience, age, someone tapping their foot and grumbling. Severan and another. One of the other so-called scholars from the digging party in the university ruins.

41

"Quick," he said to the wihht. "Into the closet there. Don't make a sound until I release you!" The creature obeyed and Nio locked the closet door behind it. At the front door again came the knock.

"Coming!" he called.

Severan stood on the threshold. Water dripped from his nose. It was raining and dark outside. A fat little man bobbed up and down behind him.

"Catch our deaths of cold, Nio, waiting for you," said Severan. "It's bad enough breathing dust and mold in that confounded ruin day after day."

"Come in," said Nio, forcing himself to be agreeable. "Ablendan, I haven't seen you for some days. I'm surprised you tore yourself away from your beloved rubble."

"Well worth choking on mold," said the little man, "seeing the find we made today. Amazing! Haven't seen anything like it before. With what we've found, I tell you, we're one step closer to finding the *Gerecednes*! Why do you stay cooped up in this dreary house, poring over your books? You don't know what you're missing."

They clumped into the front hall and hung their cloaks over some pegs on the wall. Severan stopped and turned, his nose twitching.

"What's that smell in here?" he asked. "Almost like mice dying in the walls, but worse."

"It's worse in the cellar," returned Nio. "There's an open drain into the city sewers and I'm afraid the rains have stirred some muck up. You'll get used to it after a while."

"No sign of the boy?"

"He vanished. I can't fathom how he managed it. Clever wretches, these thieves."

Severan shook his head. "At any rate, no one will be able to open that blasted box. Probably just rubbish inside once the thing's open. It's not like it was a book. Now that would've been a loss."

The two arrivals suggested some bread and cheese and maybe a mug of hot ale to take the chill off. Nio agreed with as much goodwill as he could muster. In the kitchen, Severan stuck his nose around the door leading down into the cellar. He sneezed and frowned, but said nothing.

"What brings you out from your beloved ruin?" asked Nio. "And what's this find you speak of?" He sipped from his mug and watched Severan over the rim.

"A mosaic," said Ablendan. "We were digging in the west wing, just past that hallway with all those wretched dog wards—can hardly take a step through the place without some cursed hound appearing and chasing you from here to the moon. We were puttering about there and the floor gave way, revealing a blocked-up stairwell. So down we went, shone the lantern around, and there it was! Covers the whole ceiling."

"There are many mosaics in the university," said Nio.

"Ah," returned Severan. "But this one moves."

"Some kind of warding spell?"

"No," said the other. "The mosaic doesn't pose any detectable danger. Rather, its stones rearrange themselves according to what's said aloud in the room. At first we thought it was just a beautiful but pointless decoration. The stones shifted and flowed around each other as we stood below gazing up and gabbing back and forth all the while in a confusion of talk. It was only after we fell silent that the mosaic ceased its movement. Then, when one of us spoke singly, the stones moved with his speech."

"So stones move to the sound of a voice, like pigeons fluttering around Mioja Square at a child's yell." Nio shrugged. "Interesting, yes. Unique, yes, but hardly worth rushing all the way through the city in the rain to tell me. More cheese?"

42

"No, no," said Ablendan. "Yes, more cheese. The mosaic's much more than that. It shows you what you speak of, as if a mirror of your words."

"Is this true?" asked Nio, turning to Severan.

Severan nodded. "As far as we can tell, the older the tongue, the more precise the picture. I spoke about my cottage, naming the earth beneath it, the moor, and the sea beyond, giving such names as I know are bound into the land, and the stones of the mosaic rearranged themselves so as to show me my old place far up the coast of Lannaslech in Harlech, with moon flowers growing up its walls and onto the roof as I know they must be at this late summer's time."

"Amazing!" said Nio, startled despite himself.

"It shows the exact present," said Ablendan, "for old Adlig, on a whim, described us and soon there we were, gazing up at ourselves, blinking and gaping just as we were doing at the moment. A lot of fools we looked."

"This mosaic could be a powerful tool!"

"It could be," acknowledged Severan. "But the picture it shows is warped, as if seen through a crooked glass. Happily, though, we think you might have the key to this problem. Part of the key, at least."

"My possession of such a key is unwitting. What is this thing you think I have?"

"It's a guess on my part," said Severan. "Only a guess, but one I'm convinced will prove sound. Upon each of the four walls of the room are smaller mosaics inlaid, high up on the wall, just out of arm's reach—one for each of the walls. They are fashioned of the same stones but lifeless and unmoving in their pieces, while the large mosaic shifts at the sound of our voices. Naturally, this drew our attention and we noticed that a border framed each of the four smaller mosaics—"

"That's why!" broke in Ablendan. "That's why we thought you might have the answer! And then, we'll ask it to show us the *Gerecednes*!"

"I'm still confused," said their host. He forced a smile. "Why do you need me for answers?"

He thought of the closet door and wondered if wihhts ever grew restless or out of sorts. He would have some disagreeable explaining to do if the thing decided to emerge.

"You?" returned Severan. "Well, the first of these borders is carved with all kinds of fish, seabirds, and waves. The second has a pattern like flames of fire. The third is covered with trees, plants, and animals. The fourth is carved over with a single, unbroken line that flows—no—rushes about like—"

"—the wind!" said Nio, his eyes widening. "The four anbeorun!"

Severan nodded. "Eorde, Brim, Windan, and Aeled. We think their four separate mosaics awakened might prove the proper unlocking of the larger mosaic. And we were right, for between us we could speak a handful of ancient names related to the earth, to Eorde. The little we knew proved enough, and the mosaic bounded by trees and plants and animals came to grudging life and portrayed a wolf. A great head of black fur with staring, silver eyes. At that moment, the stones in the portion of the huge ceiling mosaic nearest to that wall instantly shifted in subtle ways so that that part of the larger mosaic became sharp and clear."

"A wolf?" said Nio. "Why would it be a wolf and not a horse? How odd."

"Eh?" said Ablendan. "What's that?"

"It's peculiar that Eorde should be represented by a wolf rather than a horse. Many of the legends written about her mention a horse. The men of Harlech claim their own equine bloodlines are descended from this companion of Eorde, the great horse Min the

43

Morn. But maybe the historians have it wrong. Might her companion have been a wolf instead of a horse?"

Severan shrugged. "Who knows the mind of the anbeorun, even Eorde, despite the stories depicting her as friendly to the race of men? At any rate, Nio, we all know you're an expert in such lore. Your knowledge might unlock the three other small mosaics."

"Perhaps," said Nio. An idea bloomed in his mind. "Perhaps."

The three men set out into the rain and darkness. Nio did not worry about the wihht waiting in the closet, and he was right in doing so, though he did not realize why. The Dark is patient, and the wihht was fashioned mostly of shadow by now, as a great deal of the water had trickled out of it in its day of creeping around the city. It had left many damp footprints behind.

Nio's heart quickened as they made their way through the city. The thought of what the mosaic could do was intoxicating. Could the present be revealed, spied upon as it advanced with every clock tick? The box! Perhaps he could discover where it was with the mosaic. And the boy as well. I will be able to see him and so find him. Nio was glad of the rain and the dark and the hood about his head, for his face was so twisted with malice at these thoughts that his companions would have been startled to see him.

They hurried across the cobblestones of Mioja Square. It was deserted at that time of night. Light shone from the windows of the buildings around the square, but the university ruins loomed dark and lifeless. In a trice, they were up the steps and ducking through the little door that opened up like magic—it was magic—tucked away to one side of the real doors, massive things that looked more like the tombstones of giants than anything else.

Severan produced a lantern from his cloak. He muttered a word and it flamed to life. Light flickered on stone walls. Everything was grimed with dust. The floor was strewn with rubble. Their shadows ran along the walls beside them, waxing and waning with the wavering of Severan's lantern. Darkness crowded up on their heels. Anyone else would have been lost after ten minutes in such a place, but the three knew the university ruins well.

"I don't think I've ever been in this part of the west wing before," said Nio. "There's a powerful warding spell here. I can feel it."

They paused within an arch opening into a hall lined with slender clerestory windows. Moonlight and shadow alternated in slices of luminance and gloom.

"As I said before. An impressive spell." Ablendan's voice sounded suspiciously cheery.

"Don't tread on the blue tiles," said Severan. "Though, if you do, the dogs can't pass the far threshold. They're quick brutes, but they need a second or two to materialize and that's enough for a running start."

Near the halfway point it happened. The light was poor, and the pattern of blue, black, and white tiles was bewildering to the eyes. The blue and black tiles were so near in color that they could only be safely distinguished apart in daylight. At any rate, Ablendan trod on a blue tile, and all three heard the feathery whisper of a ward activating.

"Oops," said Ablendan. He took off for the far door, bounding like a child's rubber ball. The others ran after him, though Nio saved a breath or two to curse him as they went. Many other blue tiles came to life in their wake. Paws scrabbled and teeth snapped behind them.

"Safe," called the little man, flinging himself over the far threshold. The other two almost tripped over him, so close behind were they.

"That is not a child's game of tag!" gasped Severan, mopping sweat from his brow. "I'm too old to be playing such a thing, and the beasts want blood if they win!"

"You did that on purpose!" said Nio. He scowled at Ablendan.

"My eyesight is quite poor at night."

They all turned toward the hall. The pack stood just on the other side of the door. They were magnificent brutes, all with fur tinged blue and eyes an even brighter blue that glowed with light. Their teeth gleamed white. Some paced back and forth in agitation, but most stood stock-still, eyeing the three men. They did not bark or growl, but their rasping breath was audible.

"Astounding, aren't they," said Ablendan. "Brilliant spellcraft. Lana Heopbremel of Thule. Apparently, she had a thing for wolfhounds. They'll fade in a few minutes."

They clattered down the stairs. The room below was well-lit with torches. A tall man with a nose as big as a vulture's beak pounced on them as they reached the bottom.

"Where have you been? Half the night gone and I had to give old Adlig a tincture of sluma leaf, so worked up was he. Look at the mosaic. It's moving as we speak. There's Adlig snoring away in bed. At least what you can make out. Confound the thing! If only it were clear. Just imagine if we can coax a glimpse of the *Gerecednes* out of it. Nio, what've you been doing all these days hiding away in that gloomy house? Do you know any of the ancient names for the wind?"

"Peace, Gerade," said Severan. "Give him a moment and we'll see what he can add. The wolves were just chasing us."

Ablendan laughed at that, but Nio stepped forward, ignoring them. The place smelled musty and the air felt heavy, as if it had lain within the stone confines of the room for hundreds of years. He gazed up at the ceiling. Overhead, the mosaic rippled with movement, surging in silent mimicry of the sound of the men's voices. Thousands of tiny stones gleamed in the torchlight—white, black, brown, scarlet, shimmering yellow and glossy green, vermilion, dull gold, and a blue gleaming like the summer sky. His eyes flicked to the smaller mosaics, high up on each of the four walls of the room. Four smaller stars ringing the larger fifth. A strange constellation. The wolf stared down at him with silver eyes from the wall on his right. The other three were blank. Their stones were a uniform, dull brown. Behind him, he heard several impatient coughs. He ignored them.

The wolf in the small mosaic was a puzzle. Four small mosaics. Each one framed with the traditional signs of one of the four anbeorun. It would make sense that each, when revealed, would represent the four corresponding companions of the anbeorun. Unless, of course, they would show things such as actual earth or sky or water or flame. But the earth mosaic containing the wolf disproved that. Perhaps the four little mosaics were intended to reveal enemies? But that was illogical. The wolves were the subjects of Eorde.

According to the legends of the anbeorun, each of the four wanderers had a companion of sorts—an entity that was an extension of themselves, a shadow of their being, an echo of their voice. Only Eorde's companion was identified in the legends with any certainty. A horse named Min the Morn, whose hooves had shattered the earth in the north and formed the hill country of the Mearh Dun. However, the wolf's face staring at him from the little mosaic cast doubt on that.

There was hardly anything known about the companions of sea and sky and fire: a hint in a treatise, a suggestion in an obscure codex, an idea woven into the strictures of an ancient weather-working spell. And then there were the guesses inspired by an excess of learning. For example, some maintained that the companion of fire was a dragon, as no

45

other known creature was better suited to the inherent power of flame. Logical, but logic is only one lens of many through which to examine existence.

"Come on," said Gerade behind him. "Have at it! We've been waiting long enough on this blasted mosaic."

"Well, then, you can wait a bit longer," said Nio.

The mosaic was magnificent. He could sense a weaving of power so delicately designed it was as if he could hear it as music. It was a melody played on the edge of his thoughts. He stood in awe, for the fashioning was beyond his understanding. The blue stones shimmered above him, standing out from the rest. Blue like the sky washed with sunlight.

Sunlight.

"Sunlight," he said. The stones shifted slightly, as if encouraged.

"*Sunne*," he continued. "*Brunscir, beorht*." And the mosaic over them flared into a near white yellow. The room flooded with light. It was so blinding that everyone had to shut their eyes.

"*Sweart*," said Nio, and the radiance vanished as the mosaic went dark.

"Light and darkness," said Severan from somewhere behind him. "You picked the only two things in existence that require no clarity. Blurred or focused, both are the same to our eyes and, I wager, to this mosaic."

"I was only curious to see the stones transform," said the other.

"But what about fire, wind, and sea? Do you know any of the ancient languages that might describe the three?"

"Of fire I know a fair amount," Nio said reluctantly. "And of wind, three words gained at great cost. I am loath to share them. But of the sea? Nothing, for the sea has never been interested in man's affairs. All the books I've read are silent on the subject. The sea remains a stranger and, I think, always shall. The sea is unknowable and unstoppable. She's an alien land of unfathomable depth and distance and darkness. Even the fishermen who venture upon her waters, day after day, even they do not know her. They take their livelihoods from her, yet they know she'll demand their lives one day. Brim, the eldest of the anbeorun, is a mystery to me. And my study has been considerable."

"Yes, yes," broke in Gerade. "Your study is considerable, but my patience is not. So what about fire and wind? Speak, man, and bring some clarity to this confounded mosaic."

"Very well," said Nio.

But he would not speak a word until the other men retreated to the far corner of the room. They grumbled at this, but he was unmoved. His knowledge had come at a price and he was not inclined to share it. He first approached the small mosaic bordered with carved flame on the left-hand wall.

"*Brond, byrnan, sweodol, ond lig*," he said quietly. "*Fyr*." The stones of the fire mosaic shifted slowly and then the dull color of them darkened. The music on the edge of his thoughts changed. The new melody sounded uncertain and ominous.

Would it reveal a dragon? Nio's pulse quickened. "*Bael*!"

The stones adjusted themselves into darkness etched with darkness. Within the absence of color there was the suggestion of a face. A human face. No. Nearly human. There was something wrong with the eyes. Something slightly off. Unbidden, the memory of a sketch in an old book came to him. He gaped at the little mosaic in astonishment. But only for an instant.

"*Undon*," he said, and the image blurred somewhat until the face was no longer recognizable. The others hurried forward. From where they had been standing they had only been able to discern the stones' movement rather than detail. They gawked at the little mosaic.

"What is it?"

"Were your words enough? You brought color to it. That's more than we could do."

"I suppose those are eyes and something of a face, but it's impossible to tell where it begins and leaves off. Perhaps there, right where that deeper shadow—"

"You needn't be so secretive about a few old words, Nio. Why, I'll tell you the thirty-three curses of Magdis Gann in exchange, if you want."

"Much better than our efforts, but is that all you can do with fire?"

"Yes," said Nio.

"Rather like a fire salamander, I'd say."

"What? Are you crazy? Who ever heard of a fire salamander with black scales?"

"Perhaps a black dragon," said Ablendan. "I read somewhere—I can't remember where—that if the gefera of fire is a dragon then it must be a black dragon."

That gave them pause, and they all studied the image uneasily.

"Why black? That doesn't necessarily follow. Might as well be a red dragon. If there actually is such a kind."

"The worst of the lot, supposedly. A black dragon?"

"I certainly hope not," said Gerade. "Surely they've all died out or have fallen asleep. No one's seen a dragon for five hundred years."

"Rubbish, Ablendan. Don't believe everything you read."

"I can't remember where I read it. Anyway, has anyone gone looking for dragons recently? I thought not, so it's illogical to assume there aren't any."

"Who'd be dumb enough to go looking? There might be some left, beyond the northern wastes, but the cold will keep them asleep."

"Theoretically."

"The seventh stricture of dragons states that the heart-flame of a dragon can be dimmed by nothing except death. Therefore, the cold would have no effect on them."

"Nonsense!"

They might have continued arguing had Nio not shooed them back to their corner. He wanted to try some words on the wind mosaic. They complained, but they had no choice. Wizards and scholars were not fond of sharing hard-won knowledge. Basic knowledge, such as what was taught in the Stone Tower on the Thule coast, was shared freely. Anything beyond that was jealously guarded, kept to trade with others for a word here or a newly discovered thread of history there. All of the men in that room possessed knowledge unknown to the others. Though they grumbled at Nio, they understood and would have done the same had they been in his position.

He gazed up at the lifeless mosaic of the wind. He was uneasy now, thinking of what stared down from the fire mosaic. So what lay behind this one? Something else just as disturbing? He knew only three words of the wind, surely not enough to bring much definition to the mosaic stones.

"*Fnaest, rodor, ond styrman*," he said.

The tiny stones sprang into life, flowing around each other and lightening in hue. The little mosaic became a patch of blue sky from which a hawk's head stared down. Black eyes and black feathers tinged with silver. Blurred, but clear enough to recognize. He was

47

surprised that only three words could bring clarity to the wind mosaic, when six had barely done the same to the fire mosaic.

Still, how could you measure the power of one word against another? Some scholars argued that the purer the form of the word in relation to the first language spoken, the more power it contained. Others said words gained power according to how they were used. Some maintained that certain words were influenced over the years by the Dark. Words that had been twisted into a mockery of their original intent. Power flooded through these words easily, but it was power that could only be used for evil. Such words were few and far between, and anyone who discovered one was bound by honor to destroy whatever clues, whatever writings or artifacts led them to the word.

"A hawk," said someone behind him. They had silently advanced while he had stood lost in thought.

"Were you expecting a rooster?"

"It makes perfect sense," said Severan. "A hawk as the companion of the wind. You can see the storm's cruelty in his eyes and the softness of the breeze in his feathers."

"Excellent," said Gerade. "We've made some progress, despite the sea. This hawk, the wolf in the earth mosaic, and our mystery creature of fire. I'm puzzled about the wolf. The anbeorun of the earth, Eorde, has always been friendliest to the race of man. She's always popping up in our history. There's a decent amount known about her. Everything I've read, from Staer Gemyndes on down, suggests that her companion is the legendary horse Min the Morn."

"Perhaps the little mosaics don't represent the four companions?"

"What, are you saying a hawk would be the enemy of the wind? You, my friend, are stupider than you look."

"Enemy or companion. Those seem to be the only logical options."

"Staer Gemyndes must have got it wrong. Unbelievable!"

Severan shook his head. "Even the wisest must be allowed the luxury of failure. Let's see how the mosaic will work now, despite the lack of the sea."

Nio left them then, arguing about what pictures they should call forth, while the huge mosaic overhead swirled with the sound of their voices. He wanted to use the mosaic, but for that he would need the room to himself. He didn't want the others to see what he was interested in. Particularly Severan. He wondered what their reaction would be if they found out he could bring the fire mosaic closer to clarity, and that he knew one word of the sea. One word.

He trudged up the stairs and wove a wisp of fire from some moonlight. The flame lit him through the long hall as he picked his way around the blue tiles. The mosaic would find the boy and the box for him. He would return later—after all was quiet and the old fools were snoring in their beds. Let them dream of finding the lost book of Staer Gemyndes.

When Nio reached his house, he stood a while in the entrance hall, dreading what waited him within the closet there. His mind was tired. He opened the door. The wihht stood within.

"Go down to the cellar," he said. "Wait there until I have further need of you."

Silently, the wihht obeyed him. As it shuffled past, the thing looked at him furtively with one sidelong glance. Nio went up to his room and cast himself onto his bed. He immediately fell asleep.

CHAPTER THIRTEEN
THE HAWK

Jute woke in the gray light of morning. For a moment, he did not know where he was, but then memory flooded back in with the surge of the nearby surf. His clothes were cold and damp against his skin. Pebbles and sand grated beneath him. He sat up and then wished he hadn't. The sky tilted overhead. His head ached.

Careful.

Something moved at the edge of his sight. He turned to see and then scrambled backward, staring, until he was painfully stopped short by a boulder.

Careful. The voice sounded amused. *You have been through enough to kill most people.* The hawk watched Jute with unblinking black eyes. His feathers were a glossy black. Around the eyes and the edge of the cruel ivory-colored beak, the feathers softened to silver.

"You—you're a hawk!" said Jute.

A hawk. That will do well enough.

"But birds don't talk!" said the boy.

To most people, no. We could not be bothered. You are different.

"What do you mean?" The boy leaned forward without knowing it.

Something akin to a sigh escaped the hawk's beak.

There are those fated to fly faster and higher. Those who have always held the sky in their hearts. Some who fly higher than others. And then there is you. You cut yourself on the knife, did you not?

"I never meant to touch it," protested Jute.

At that, the hawk's wings unfurled with a whisper of feathers. A breeze fanned the boy's face. Further down the beach, the surf rolled up the sand toward them.

Do not speak so! Thank the wind, the sky, every star in the heavens. Blessed be the house of dreams that you touched the knife. Knowing what one was meant to do, or not meant to do—this knowledge is beyond the understanding of man, beyond the wizards, beyond you. Even you.

"Who am I?" said the boy.

The hawk sprang into the air with a beat of his wings.

That will be learned one day at a time. Suffice it for now to stay alive. Walk softly, for things wake that should not have been disturbed. You would do well to avoid their attention. Above all else, listen.

"Listen? To you?"

To me, yes. Amusement, once more in the voice. *Listen to the sky. Listen to the wind.*

The hawk mounted into the sky. Morning light gleamed on his feathers.

For now, be content with staying alive, youngling.

"Wait!" he called, but the hawk wheeled away into the blue and was lost in the sunlight.

CHAPTER FOURTEEN
STOLEN APPLES

Arodilac Bridd was the orphaned nephew of the regent and his heir apparent, as Botrell had no offspring in evidence, or any other living relatives. Arodilac was sixteen, a gawky boy, teetering on the brink of manhood. His head was thatched with hair as yellow as straw, and guileless blue eyes blinked from his face. He had the thick wrists of a natural swordsman, but his hands were still awkward, and, at the moment, they were knocking over a mug of ale.

"Oh, sorry," said Arodilac.

Across the table, Ronan hurriedly pushed his chair back. He mopped at his pants and thought about the Flessoray Islands. He had been there, once, when he had been young. His mother's family came from the coast east of the islands. Older cousins of his had taken him out in a boat. The day had been cold and clear, with the light on the white sail and the wave tops so bright they had brought tears to his eyes. On the horizon, the islands rose remote, too far for a day's outing. He had stared at their silhouettes with all the dreaming intent of boyhood. Even now, he still felt the longing. The pale sunlight of the north, serene and gleaming on the lonely sea. Solitude and peace. He sighed.

"Tell me how it happened," he said. "From the beginning. Don't leave any details out, even if it means your honor at stake."

Arodilac fidgeted with a spoon, his face reddening.

"Well, you see—it's Ronan, isn't it?—you see," he said, "it's not just my—"

"Or if it's her honor at stake," interrupted Ronan. "I don't care. I'm a thief and we don't care about things like honor. All I care about is getting the job done and getting paid."

Arodilac glared at him for a moment from across the table and then turned to stare glumly out the window.

They were seated in an anteroom in the servants' quarters of the regent's castle, the door locked and two Guardsmen standing outside to discourage any interest. It wasn't proper for thieves and nobility to be seen together, though many nobles were adept at robbing their people and the odd thief or two managed to be noble on occasion.

Ronan had never been inside the castle before. Normally, he would have been fascinated by the chance, attentive to every detail of how the remote and near-legendary ruler of Hearne lived. As far back as the history of the Thieves Guild reached, there had always been an unofficial truce between the Guild and the regents of Hearne. In return for not stealing from the castle and the families of the regents, the regents refrained from executing thieves except for the most grievous offenses.

This day, however, Ronan would have rather been anywhere else. Anywhere else than sitting across from this slack-jawed idiot who probably didn't even clothe himself and whose wit was evidently in reverse proportion to his family's wealth. True, he would earn a lot of money for the job, but it was all he could do to sit there politely. Well, somewhat politely.

Arodilac leaned forward, one elbow on a filled scone. Blackberry jam oozed out.

"She's like one of those, whatchamacallits," he said.

"That's helpful information," said Ronan.

"Yes," said the regent's nephew. "One of those—what are they?—the tallish flowers with the single white bloom unfurling up, just like her graceful neck—what are they called? My mother used to grow them in her garden."

"Mustard grass? Deadly nightshade?"

"Lilies. That's what they are. White spring lilies. She's like a slender, white spring lily. Lovely as the first day of spring—"

"It usually rains on the first day of spring. A downpour."

"—and as graceful as the best filly the Farrows ever raised."

Ronan, whose eyes had been glazing over, jerked upright. He snorted.

"So what you're saying is she's a flowerlike horse on a spring day."

"That's it!" said Arodilac. "That's her. Why, you said in half as many words what I couldn't say in twice the amount. How did—"

Ronan's fist crashed down on the table.

"Blast it all to the seven walls of Daghoron!" He cursed with all the fluency of a Thulian sailor waking up the morning after the first night home in port. His head was beginning to throb, which lent his words vigor. He had not joined the Guild for this.

"What was that last bit?" asked the regent's nephew. "The part about the jackass and the thingummy? Fascinating stuff—I must confess I've never—"

Mugs and plates jumped as Ronan's fist crashed down again on the table.

"Never mind that," he said. "What's her name?!"

"What?"

"Her name!" said Ronan.

Her name was Liss Galnes, and she was the daughter of Cypmann Galnes, a widower and merchant who, by virtue of his wit and his wealth, was the regent's advisor on matters of trade. The Galnes family lived in a mansion in one of the more secluded streets of Highneck Rise, a stone house surrounded by a walled garden. Liss was an only child, and her father had kept her from the social circles of the court, judging that such a place was no fit environment for a child. This was a view he held privately, of course, for, although he entertained doubts regarding Nimman Botrell's mental capabilities, he did not doubt the regent's capacity for sudden and malicious judgment.

Liss was raised mostly alone, except for her father, a few servants, and a succession of tutors. She learned needlepoint and the history of Hearne, although facts on this subject became sparse, of course, once one reached the Midsummer War and the reign of Dol Cynehad, the last king of Hearne. She learned to play the spinet and how to figure compound interest, though her father grumbled that compound interest was no suitable pastime for women. She read Harthian poetry in its original form—slowly and with much frowning, of course—and she learned how to run a household. She also became an accomplished gardener and grew the best apples in all of Hearne. This was how Arodilac Bridd met her.

"The best apples you've ever tasted," said Arodilac.

"Get on with your story," said Ronan, gritting his teeth.

Cypmann Galnes was in the habit of carrying fresh fruit with him wherever he went, said Arodilac. Even to the castle. The regent, who was given to three vices—horses, women, and food—availed himself of some fruit Galnes brought one day, and, after his appetite was piqued with an apple, inquired where the merchant found such delicacies.

51

"In his garden, of course," said Ronan, eyeing a pewter pitcher and wondering if beating Arodilac over the head with it would, in any way, speed up the storytelling.

"In his garden," echoed the youth. "And then, do you know what happened?"

"No, but you're going to tell me."

"Uncle pulled me aside after dinner, and said there was something he wanted me to get for him. He wanted apple pie for dessert, the next day, and the best apples were to be had from the garden of Cypmann Galnes. And if he didn't have his apple pie, he'd be cross."

"So what'd you say?" asked Ronan, intrigued despite himself by this private side of the regent.

"I told him that, once when I was small, Cypmann Galnes thrashed me for chucking pebbles at his horse."

"Rightly so. I would've done the same."

"He only laughed and told me to get some of those apples."

"Which are in that garden."

"In the garden, yes," agreed Arodilac. "I pointed that out to him, and he told me to steal them."

"What?"

"He told me to steal them."

"So the regent's muscling in on the Thieves Guild? Let the fruit vendors look to their knives, or they'll be paying double in protection."

Arodilac fell into a reverie, gazing out the window. Twilight was falling, and the oak trees that stood alongside the castle wall were dappled with shadow and blurred light.

"The house is at the end of the Street of Willows, and it was one of those trees that I climbed to make my way over the wall. Cypmann Galnes was working at his warehouse down at the docks. I swung over the top and Liss was there, sitting under a tree and doing needlepoint. She didn't say anything. She just watched me. I figured it'd be best to leave with whatever dignity I had left. Of course, it's easier to get into that garden than get out. After watching me slip and fall several times in trying to jump for the top of the wall, she brought me a cup of water. It was a hot day."

"Over such little things have kingdoms fallen," said Ronan.

Arodilac reddened. "She's unlike anyone I've met before. Not like all the girls at court fawning around me, cooing like pigeons, all beady-eyed over my title and not ever seeing me."

"You didn't tell her who you are."

Arodilac looked away. "Not until her father caught us together. He was angry. He went and told Uncle."

"And you intend to marry her?"

He looked up. "Yes! We love each other."

"You're the heir to the regency of Hearne," said Ronan. "Who you marry won't be left up to you. Horses and the nobility. Both bred with an eye for bloodlines. No doubt there's a duke's daughter being groomed somewhere. You'll be foisted on each other, whether you like it or not, for alliance, for blood, and for money."

"I don't care about such things," said Arodilac.

"What you care about doesn't matter," said Ronan. "What I care about doesn't matter. All that matters is that your uncle has hired the Guild to tidy up. So tell me, and with few words, why the regent hired thieves to clean up after his nephew."

Arodilac's eyes slid away from him. "Just some letters I wrote to her. That's all."

"Letters?"

"I promised we would be wed. My uncle would be embarrassed if—"

"Do you take me for a fool, boy? A letter, no matter how idiotic, is not going to matter a whit to the regent of Hearne. With all the beds and mistresses he's worn out, he won't be bothered by his nephew's indiscretions, even if you ran about the city, naked as the day you were born. Tell me the truth."

The boy hung his head.

"I gave her my family ring," he said.

"You did what?"

"I gave her my family ring. I don't know why I did it! Something came over me, but she doesn't know what it actually is. She just thinks it an old ring, only dear because it comes from me."

Wordless for once, Ronan stared at him. The boy winced.

"I know, I know. And it isn't just my old family estate bound into it. Uncle's been teaching me the wards of this castle."

It was customary within the noble families to pass a ring down, from father to eldest son, or whichever heir was to assume the title. All the ward spells guarding the estate were bound into the family ring, so that whoever wore it, anywhere at any time, would always be aware of any dangers threatening the estate. What's more, whoever bore the family ring could safely pass through the wards.

Possession of the family ring of one of the noble houses of Tormay was every thief's dream. With such a ring, one could pass unchallenged into the richest estates of the land. But even though the house of Bridd was reputed for its wealth, this ring was much more valuable. It disarmed the ward spells guarding the regent's castle. Ronan shook his head. He could hardly believe it.

"Are you telling me your uncle's been teaching you his castle wards and then weaving the spells into your ring as he goes?"

Arodilac nodded.

"And she's hidden it? Refuses to give it back?"

The boy nodded again.

"She says she wants something in exchange," he said. "But she won't tell me what."

The words hung in the room, like dust glinting in the sunlight. There was irony in the fact the regent had called in the Guild to solve his problem. A missing ring containing his castle wards was bound to turn up. Such things always did.

A ward-bound object attracted certain kinds of people who came near it. The problem was that most people attuned to such things tended to use their knowledge in illegal activities. Many of them worked for the Guild. Others worked alone. The regent's decision to hire the Guild to find the ring—some of the people who would be most tempted to use it against him—was a clever move. Bound by their own honor code, the Guild would not be able to use that which they had been hired to recover.

"What does it look like?"

"A gold band carved in the shape of a hawk, with rubies for eyes."

"The mark of the wind," said Ronan.

"My family has always honored the wind lord and the sky." His head came up, proud once more.

"Tales for old women."

"Don't hurt her," said Arodilac.

"What do you take me for? The Guild doesn't turn its hand against children."

An image of the boy sprang unbidden to his mind, falling down the chimney into darkness. Ronan got up and pushed through the door, past the two Guardsmen, wooden at their post, and then down a hallway and out into the gloomy evening. The air smelled like wood smoke and coming rain.

CHAPTER FIFTEEN
WHAT THE TRADERS FOUND

Murnan Col hailed from Averlay in Thule. He was a trader who worked the coastal route of villages down to the duchy of Vomaro and all places of interest in between, including, of course, Hearne. Once in Vomaro, he always turned inland to Lura to acquire more expensive items for the return north. That spring, however, a bag of pearls bought off a fisherman convinced him to venture south, down through the desert to the city of Damarkan in Harth.

Harth made him nervous. He wasn't sure why. Perhaps the desert stretching on forever and ever into heat-shimmered distances. Perhaps the odd beauty of the Harthians themselves with their dark skin and their bone-white hair bleached by relentless generations of sunlight. Or maybe it was their courtly grace, their politeness, and the liquid cadence of their speech—all so different from the rougher customs of the north.

He grimaced, shifting in the saddle. Shadows, but it was a long road up from Damarkan. He'd be glad to get back to Averlay and his own bed. Cwen. How long had it been since he'd seen her? Four months? Much too long to leave a good woman idle. No telling what she had gotten up to in his absence. He smiled to himself.

Damarkan had been profitable. The pearls had brought the court chamberlain of Oruso Oran IX stalking through the marketplace, attendants scurrying along at his side. A cold man serving an even colder master, if the stories were true, but he had been fair in his dealings with the trader and he knew good pearls when he saw them.

Murnan turned in his saddle. The pack train straggled out behind him. Four heavily laden mules and the giant Gavran twins bringing up the rear, smiling as ever and singing one of their endless ballads. The sea and death and the melancholy of unrequited love, no doubt. They were young and didn't seem to think about much else.

An hour would see them down into the valley of the Little Rennet River. They had stopped there on the way south. The villagers had been friendly, eager for news and a chance to trade for his iron, wool, and the small kegs of salt so dear to inland folks. He'd promised to buy some cheap silk in Damarkan for the miller's wife. She'd be pleased with the bolt of ivory-colored cloth he'd found—smooth to the touch and full of light. There was to be a wedding in the family. A daughter. He frowned. Perhaps it was high time he married his Cwen.

They smelled the village before they saw it. Faintly at first but then stronger and stronger—the sickly sweet odor of rotting flesh warmed by the sun. The trader's horse shivered under him.

Murnan loosened his old sword in the saddle sheath. "Gann, tie up the mules and stay with them. Loy, come with me." His hand flexed on the sword handle. Not that he was any good with the thing, but you had to try. That was what life seemed to be about.

The stench grew as they rode down the trail into the valley. With each step, the horses grew more restive, trying to sidle off the path and head back up the incline. They came around a bend and a stand of pine. The village lay before them. Murnan reined in.

"The birds," he said.

Below them, among the houses standing together beside the stream, crows rose and settled in flurries of wings. Dark blots clumped into bigger masses as if huddling together for intimate meetings. Here and there, buzzards were visible, waddling about the ground or stooped over the awkward, broken-looking shapes littering the earth.

"Shadows!" cursed Loy.

They galloped down the slope. The birds rose at their approach, sluggish and slow as if so heavy with their meals that they could only struggle up into the uncertain support of the air. Murnan could see Loy turning green beneath his sunburnt skin. Bile burned up inside his own throat. The dead were everywhere: lying in the clay and stone of the pathways between the cottages, sprawled across doorways, crumpled against walls.

They had been dead for perhaps a day, he reckoned. He swallowed, trying to calm his stomach. Even though the bodies were torn by bird beaks, there was enough definition left to suggest recent death. Perhaps even less than a day. *And if we had not tarried another day in Damarkan?* He shuddered.

His horse twisted and he caught a glimpse of a panicked white eye. He soothed the beast with soft words and touch. The horse shuddered and subsided under him.

Loy exclaimed. Murnan turned to look. Further down a path between two cottages stood a girl. She was a skinny little thing, no bigger than a shadow and with white hair tangled around her head. For a moment she stared at them, and then whirled to run. Loy jumped off his horse. It took only several steps of his huge strides to catch her, for the girl ran awkwardly. She screamed once when he scooped her up and then her body went limp.

"What shall we do?" asked Loy. His jaw was clenched in anger. The girl was tiny in his arms. She dangled there like a child's broken doll.

"She's unconscious?"

"Aye. Skin's burning. She's got fever."

"We're four days' ride from Hearne. If we push the mules. Back with her to your brother, and I'll do a quick scout through the rest of the village. Perhaps there are others still alive."

But there weren't any other survivors.

Murnan stood for a while over the body of the miller. The man's eyes were gone, pecked away by the birds, no doubt, and his sockets stared up at the sky. There would be no wedding for his daughter. He turned away.

CHAPTER SIXTEEN
SPYING ON JUTE

Nio returned to the university ruins in the morning.

Mioja Square already bustled with people. Vendors called back and forth, vying for the attention of customers. Nio was so wrapped up in his thoughts as he walked along that he failed to notice Severan hurrying toward him, hand raised in greeting. At the last moment, though, the old man must have somehow thought better of it, for he ducked behind an apple cart. Nio swept past, head down and brow furrowed. Severan stood and looked after him, but then he made his own way in the opposite direction, away from the university and into the city.

As Nio expected, the university was silent within. He double-checked anyway and stood motionless for several minutes, eyes closed and listening to the silence looming around him. He let his awareness drift through the expanse of the ruins. Countless halls, chambers, courtyards choked with rubble, mold, dust, and silence. Towers crumbled in magnificent disarray or still standing proud over the city. Stairways climbing into the sky. Secrets and shadows and old memories soaked into stone, still stained with blood and tears centuries after the living had been brought down into dust. And the slumber of his fellow searchers, floating across his consciousness like dandelion seeds drifting in the air. No one was awake.

Nio frowned. Only three sleepers. The fourth was not in the university ruins.

He came to himself and opened his eyes. It was as he expected. Though the absence of one so early in the morning was a bit surprising. They all tended to stay up late, arguing over discrepancies in this history or that, or quarreling over inflections in long-dead words that had not been uttered out loud in hundreds of years. With such a habit, they all slept until noon every day.

Scholars. His lip curled. All of them hid behind the title scholar, rather than the dubious distinction of being a wizard. Both studied the same kinds of things. A wizard, however, sought to apply his learning to life. A scholar did not, being content to learn, observe, and record. It was a distinction that had arisen after the Midsummer War and the ill repute that conflict had given wizards. These days in Tormay, hardly a wizard could be found in any of the duchies, unless you counted the tame court wizards of Hearne and Harth, who existed only to ply their parlor tricks at parties to amuse the nobility. In truth, it wasn't safe to be a wizard.

Ridiculous.

Things would be different. Someday. He would see to that.

The morning sunlight poured in through the thin clerestory windows of the west wing hall. The blue tiles shimmered benignly, as lovely a blue as a summer sky. He picked his way around them, though he deliberately stepped on a blue tile just before the threshold. Safely on the other side, he turned and watched the dog rise up from the floor. A blue vapor, like steam rising from a kettle spout, thickened until it grew opaque and took on solid form. The creature snapped at him once, but then settled on its haunches not two feet away. They regarded each other silently, the man and the beast, and there was interest on both sides.

It has intelligence woven into it, thought Nio. It isn't just a mindless ward created to strike out blindly. Those eyes are assessing me. Thinking. Planning.

He marveled at the craft, wanting to understand and possess the knowledge that had gone into the making. The dog stared back at him. After several minutes, the thing grew transparent, and then it was only a blue mist that drifted down and vanished into the floor.

He stood in silence beneath the ceiling mosaic for a while. It waited in a meaningless jumble of colors. He wondered what the others had sought from it the night before. The three smaller mosaics were still in the same state as when he had last seen them: the hawk, the wolf, and the red eyes of the fire staring down from within darkness. Only the mosaic of the sea was featureless, secure within its border of carved fish, seabirds, and waves.

First, there was the fire mosaic to restore.

"*Brond, byrnan, sweodol, ond lig,*" he said. The stones shifted, the colors sharpening. "*Fyr ond bael!*"

And then the image was clear. Not as clear as it might have been, had he possessed more knowledge of fire, but clearer than what the others had seen last night. It stared down at him. It was similar to a man, yet not. The face was formed of shadow. The eyes were coals, banked and smoldering behind the lids.

A sceadu.

His heart quickened and his mouth went dry. A sceadu. A being woven out of the true darkness at the beginning of time. According to lore, only three of them had ever existed. No one had ever seen one since the days of Staer Gemyndes, and even he had written guardedly of them in his books. But there had been a sketch of a sceadu in one of his histories. Nio shivered and tried to doubt his own eyes. There was something oddly familiar about the sceadu's face. What was it? The wihht. That's what it was. A hint of similarity between the two.

The wihht, he thought guiltily. But seldom do I exercise such a spell. It is always on behalf of a greater need, when there are no other choices available. I will unmake the wihht once I have no more need for it. Besides, I would never have dealings with such a thing as a sceadu.

What could it mean? The fire wanderer, Aeled, served by a sceadu? But perhaps we had it all wrong. Perhaps these four smaller mosaics signify something different and do not represent the four companions of the wanderers. After all, the three visible are all black in color to some degree. Surely that might represent some sort of tie to the Dark, like the sceadu. Might they all represent enemies of the wanderers? The purpose of the anbeorun is to guard against the Dark, all the histories agree on that, so how could one be served by a creature of the Dark? Also, the earth mosaic should portray a horse, not a wolf. The horse Min the Morn. Were all the old writings wrong?

He pondered on this a while, but he could not come to any conclusion and so turned his attention to the lifeless mosaic of the sea. Sometimes it was better not to think about certain things.

Only one word of the sea. That was all he knew. The memory of its cost was still painful. Even after all these years, he wasn't sure if he had been cheated. Was there value in the word? Or was it merely a lifeless sound? He had never been able to devise a test. He wet his lips with his tongue and then spoke.

"Seolhbaeo."

The word whispered in the air. It sounded like the ocean surf sighing on the shore. Nio held his breath. What sort of creature would be revealed? He was not sure he had pronounced the word correctly. The old man who sold the word to him had refused to say the thing out loud, but had written it out on parchment, which he then burned after Nio memorized it. *Not a safe word, lad,* he had said. *No telling who might hear. Things listen, they do.*

For a moment, Nio was sure he had been cheated. The old man had swindled him. But then the little mosaic came alive. Its stones did not move like the other mosaics. Rather, all of its stones turned blue. A deep, greenish blue the color of the sea. There was nothing else. Just the color. The blue seemed to heave and sway as soon as he looked away, but whenever he stared straight at the little mosaic, it was still.

Elated, he turned his attention to the huge mosaic overhead. He described the box in detail. Black mahogany. Old silver hinges and catch. The lid carved with a hawk's head, the moon and the sun floating behind. Whorls curving in and out of each other on all four sides.

The mosaic sprang into life. The definition of color and shadow was more precise than what he had seen the previous night. The tiny stones shifted around each other. Colors blurred into other colors. Then the mosaic went still. The picture it presented of the box was indistinct. Not because of a lack of focus, but because the box was obviously in a dark place.

Nio cursed out loud. The mosaic was thrown into confusion by his words. The picture of the box vanished into a jumble of color and nonsensical shapes as the mosaic sought to portray what his cursing looked like. He had to laugh at that, and then he restored the original view of the box. When it was once again visible, he studied the picture.

The box was on a shelf in something like a closet or a cupboard. A faint bit of light shone from somewhere, perhaps a crack in the door. The space was lined with shelves crowded with boxes of all shapes and sizes, stacks of books, bulging velvet bags, and a heap of necklaces crammed into one corner and spilling over the shelf's edge like a waterfall of gold. Obviously, the hideaway belonged to someone wealthy. The Guild.

Nio cursed again, but was prudent enough to do it under his breath. There was no self-evident way to shift the angle of view the mosaic presented. If he could see the outer door of the hideaway, then he might gain a clue as to where the thing was. Perhaps if he waited? Did the mosaic maintain its views in the changing immediacy of the present? If true, then he might see someone open the hideaway to take or leave an object. His eyes gleamed at the thought. But what if one of the old men came down the stairs and caught him here? He couldn't risk that.

But what if finding the box was no longer important? What if whatever had been inside was no longer there?

The thought sickened him.

The boy had known where to look in the house. Someone had instructed him how to beat the guardian ward. That indicated magic at work. Ridiculous, to think the boy knew such arts. Someone powerful had set up the theft. That same someone might have known how to open the box. If he could find the boy, then he would unravel him like a thread and find his way, inch by inch, back to whoever had hired him.

The boy.

The frightened face appeared in his mind.

59

"A boy named Jute. Within the city of Hearne, most likely. Slight for his age. About thirteen years old. Ragged, probably. Dirty, I'm sure. Thin-faced. Straight black hair." He wracked his memory, trying to recall details.

"Dark brown eyes. Old bruises on his face, I think. Slender hands. The hands of a thief. A thief. *Oeof.*" He held his breath and watched the mosaic.

The stones shifted. Colors rippled. Lines blurred into being and then rearranged themselves into shapes. A stone warehouse, long sweeps of wharves, the blue stretch of sea and sky behind. Figures bending over crates spilling over with silver. Silver. Fish. The docks. And there in the foreground, a boy clambering up from the beach. It could have been any one of the hundreds of street urchins afflicting the city of Hearne. But then, the boy turned toward him, almost as if aware of his gaze, and the dark eyes and face sprang into clarity.

Nio whirled and leapt up the stairs. He stopped, cursed, and ran back down.

"*Undon,*" he said to the little mosaic of the sea. The blue grayed into dull stone. He muttered a word at the mosaic of fire, and the image of the sceadu lost clarity, devolving into the indistinct mass of darkness and two red eyes that had been there before. He snapped a few words at the mosaic overhead until it swirled into a confusion of color and shape.

He ran for the stairs. There was no time to lose.

CHAPTER SEVENTEEN
THE PERFECT PLACE TO HIDE

Jute made his way along the foot of the cliffs until he came to the sweep of beach curving along the city walls toward the harbor. He hunkered down behind a boulder and thought for a while. At least he tried to think, but this proved to be difficult, as he was shivering with cold and growing hungrier by the minute.

It was some help, though, to think about the hawk. The whole affair was so strange that it diverted his thoughts from his miserable state. He had a memory of someone saying there were certain animals that could talk—beasts that had been enspelled. Perhaps it had been one of the older boys. Some of the Juggler's children had come from privileged backgrounds, children who had run away from families wealthy enough to have afforded schooling.

What had the hawk meant?

Things wake that should not have been disturbed. You would do well to avoid their attention.

Did the hawk mean things like the horrible creature in the cellar? Even though he was already shivering, this thought made him shiver even more. *For now, be content with staying alive, youngling.* He might be able to manage that, if he could somehow get warmed up. Some food would help too.

Several fishing boats were drawn up on the beach. Fishermen were stretching out their nets to dry on the sand. Others carried wicker baskets of fish from the night's catch to the wharves further along the beach. Bigger boats were tied up along the wharves, prows in and crowded for space. Costermongers sold the fresh catch from their stalls. Housewives, cooks from the city's inns, stewards, even the blue-liveried servants from the regent's household prodded and poked and sniffed their way through piles of bass, snapper, and flounder, along with buckets of oysters and baskets of eels twisting about themselves like tangled black velvet ropes. Someone had caught a pair of sharks, and the brutes hung by their tails at the side of a stall, seawater and blood trickling from their jaws.

Past the wharves, an immense pier on stone pilings extended out into the harbor almost to the breakwater that sheltered Hearne's port from the sea. Larger oceangoing vessels were moored along the pier. Slim, double-masted ketches, sturdy schooners from the northern duchies of Tormay, and huge galleons from Harth flying the golden flag of the house of Oran. Even now, a brigantine with square white sails running up was coming about, turning toward the gap in the breakwater and the sea beyond.

Jute stood and discovered his legs were trembling so badly he could hardly walk. Hunger drove him forward, however. He slunk down the beach toward the wooden arch named Joarsway, or the Fishgate, as it was called by the locals. One of the fishers, an old man mending a torn net, called out to him, but Jute flinched away at the sound of his voice.

The Fishgate neighborhood of the city was a warren of inns, shops, and dwellings, built in a hodgepodge fashion of stones and thatch and timbers and plaster. In places, the narrow streets were cobbled, but this was rare. Most streets were merely dirt packed to the hardness of stone by years of traffic and weather. Due to the night's rainfall, the alleys and shadows were slick with mud. Jute made his way through the crowded streets. His stomach hurt.

He did not know the Fishgate neighborhood well. It was one of the poorer parts of the city and the Thieves Guild did not waste time robbing poor people. The Juggler's children never worked the Fishgate streets. It was not that the Guild had sympathy for the poor; rather, they preferred to go where the money was.

Within the shadow of an alley, Jute paused and looked around. The back of his neck prickled as if someone was watching him. But there was no one there. The alley was heaped with rubbish. Other than that, it was empty. Three children ran past the mouth of the alley, threading through the crowd and shrieking with laughter. A stout woman trundled past in pursuit. With a grunt, she lunged and caught the smallest boy by the ear and hauled him off.

"But Mama, I don't want to go!" Jute heard him squeal before the two vanished out of earshot. He felt nauseated and tired. His stomach spasmed. Sunlight angling over the wall fell on his face and he looked up toward the sky. It was empty and blue.

Jute let himself drift out into the crowd. The street opened up into a small market square bustling with life. An open-air butchery stood on one corner, with haunches of beef, pork, and mutton hanging red and fly-speckled from a crossbeam. Links of sausage glistened in looped piles alongside folds of rubbery tripe and stacks of muttonchops. The *thwack-thwack-thwack* of the butcher's cleaver on the chopping block could be heard. At another stall, cabbages and wilted lettuces lay heaped on canvas. Shriveled potatoes sat mounded in baskets. The stink of fish filled the air, and a board slung across two barrels gleamed with piles of their slick silvers and blues and blacks. A small boy sloshed water onto the fish from a bucket and scratched himself, yawning. Flies buzzed around his bare feet.

A spicer stood guard in front of his wares and eyed the crowd. Jute could smell the pepper and cinnamon from where he stood, and he drifted toward the man, his nose twitching. The smell was pungent, even amidst the stench of fish and the butcher's goods. Strings of dried chilies in green and yellow and red dangled from the awning next to braids of garlic. Behind the man were bowls of spice: chunks of rock salt, peppercorns, tiny green cardamom seeds, golden ginger, paprika in dusty shades of scarlet and orange, and brown cinnamon. Jute sniffed, his mouth watering.

The spicer scowled at him. "Are you going to buy my spice or just stand there, smelling it up? Run along, you wretch."

Reluctantly, Jute moved away. At the far corner of the square, a baker did business. His oven exhaled the fragrance of yeast and salt. Jute edged closer and stared. What happened next would have been normally unthinkable for a boy of his abilities. Filching a loaf would have been child's play for any of the Juggler's children, but the past few days had taken their toll. His hand trembled on a loaf of bread and the baker glanced up.

"Thief!" yelled the baker, lunging for him. Flour billowed in the air around him. He missed, but the woman standing next to Jute did not.

The baker beat him soundly with the wooden paddle he used for shifting loaves in the oven. A crowd of people gathered and called out advice. Business picked up, and the baker's assistant scurried about with armfuls of bread. Concerned the paddle would not hold up, the baker dropped Jute onto the cobbles and kicked him. The boy tried to crawl away, but the baker danced around him like a fighting rooster.

"This is what we do to your sort in the Fishgate!"

"Tsk—you'd think Hearne was run by thieves these days. How much are the large ryes?"

"Two for a copper! The baker's assistant waved a loaf in the air. "Fresh an' hot from the oven!"

"That'll teach him!" said a crone.

"Aye, Mistress Gamall," said the baker, his boot connecting with the boy's ribs. "We should be concerned with the schooling of our youngsters." He stepped on Jute's hand and smiled in satisfaction as he heard the bones crack. The boy blacked out and then came to, gasping, as the baker kicked his stomach. He caught a glimpse of sky spinning overhead, empty and blue.

"Hold, baker!"

Dimly, Jute remembered the voice, but he could not place it. He heard a brief, angry exclamation from the baker. And then the sky was blotted out by a face peering down into his own. Brown eyes, faded, dusty clothing, a ragged cloak. The old man. Severan. The crowd drifted around them, the man kneeling next to the crumpled boy. The baker stomped back to his stall.

"Can you get up, Jute?" asked Severan. The boy shivered from his touch.

"I'm sorry for that," said the old man.

"Sorry!" spat Jute. His voice cracked. Tears tracked down his muddy cheeks.

"I can't fault you for judging me on the company I keep," said the old man. "I fault myself! But trust me for now. You must be away from here immediately."

"Back to the house and that basement?" said the boy.

"Darkness take me, boy, if I lie. I didn't intend you any harm and you won't be going back there. Not if I can help it. We've both learned a thing or two these last days."

Jute tried to pull away from him once he was on his feet, but he was too weak and Severan held onto his arm. The old man seemed to know the neighborhood of the Fishgate well and led Jute through a maze of alleys and twisting streets. He moved fast for an old man. The boy was soon stumbling on his feet, barely able to keep up, but the man would not release his hold on him.

"Leave go," gasped the boy. "Let me go. You'd take me back to him and—and that thing!"

Severan hustled him down an alleyway and did not stop until they had rounded a corner. He glanced around before he spoke, but there was no one in sight.

"Hear me out, boy. I mean you well. I never dreamed he would do such a thing. Such sorceries are forbidden!"

"Then you saw it?! That, that—"

The old man shivered. "You can know someone—think you know them—and then in one instant what you hold true is discovered to be false. The mask is peeled away and a strange visage is revealed. A chance trick of the light and suddenly a stranger is looking back at you. Last night, I happened to be at Nio's house. Questions had arisen in my work that only Nio could answer. When I walked in the door, I sensed something strange. A scent in the air made me uneasy. The place quivered with the vibration of unseen magic. Somewhat similar to what you hear, boy, when you are about your thievery and listen for ward spells, but this was a tremble in all material at hand, as if something of the Dark had been recently near. Echoes, if you will. A kind of footprint peculiar to the Dark.

"I had uneasy dreams last night," continued Severan. "When I awoke, I determined to go and confront Nio with my fears. Perhaps the thing, whatever it was, had crept into his house without his knowledge? I would not damn an innocent man with assumptions. But I saw him in Mioja Square this morning. He was oblivious to my presence. Something in his demeanor changed my mind and I did not approach him. What if the evil was in the house by his design?"

"He did it," said the boy, shuddering. "He spoke and something came up out of the sewer in the basement! Darkness and water all mixed together. It felt like ice when it touched me!"

"You should have died there. Luck was on your side. The thing you speak of is called a wihht. The essence of darkness married with some item of our world. Such creatures cannot be created except through an evil will, for they can only be used for evil. This sort of magic is forbidden. It is accursed. When you use the Dark for your purposes, it uses you as well." The old man sighed. "Whatever possessed you to rob that house of all others?"

The image of the Knife stooped over the chimney sprang to Jute's mind and again he heard the whisper floating down through the darkness. *Come up, boy. Come up.* And the long arm reaching down for him. The Guild had a long arm indeed, and it could still reach him in this city. He stared at the old man and did not answer.

"I decided to investigate for myself while the house was empty," said Severan, "for Nio was heading in the opposite direction when I saw him. The place was silent and filled with shadow. All the windows were shuttered. The air smelled of decay. It grew stronger as I entered the kitchen. The door to the cellar was ajar, and I eased it open to look down the stairs."

Jute clutched his hand.

"And you saw it?" he said, his voice shaking. "Did you see it?"

"Not at first. It was dark inside. I crept down a few steps and thought to call forth a flame to aid my sight. I'm not a wizard, but one needn't be a wizard to attempt certain modest things. But at that moment, below me in the darkness, I saw two dim points of light. Perplexed, I thought them a pair of candles. But then, to my horror, they slowly moved my way. I heard a wet, whispering noise as of sodden flesh pressing against stone. A form gathered shape out of the darkness. I turned and ran up the stairs with my heart pounding so painfully in this old chest of mine I could hardly breathe. I did not stop until I was out of the house and halfway down the street. I had to see the thing, to prove to myself—but for you to have been in that house . . ."

"It was a job." A spark of defiance flared in Jute's eyes. "The Guild needed the Juggler's best for that chimney, and I'm the best of his lot."

"But why that house?" Severan shook his head. "I don't know much about wihhts. However, creatures of the Dark all share certain similarities. One is that they do not easily forget a scent. The wihht will remember your smell and it'll sniff its way through this city in search of you."

Jute sat down on a wooden crate. His face was white.

"I'm as good as dead," he groaned.

"Not if we act fast. We have some time, I think. I'm no tracker, but I think any scent would get confused in the Fishgate. The stink of fish is nauseating. Even a wihht, let alone a bloodhound, will have trouble here finding your scent. You'd be a sight safer if you hadn't tried your luck with the baker. People remember that sort of thing. It gives them something to talk about over their ale. Wihhts do have ears."

"But where can I hide?" said the boy. He looked up at the sky. "Where can I hide?" Severan got the odd impression that the boy wasn't speaking to him.

"I have the perfect place," said Severan briskly, "but we must be quick. The more time you spend in the streets, the more chance the wihht will pick up your tracks."

He urged Jute to his feet and they hurried off. They made their way through the back alleys of the Fishgate, avoiding the busy streets. After a while, they came to a narrow passage that emptied out into a crowded square.

"Mioja Square," gasped Jute.

Severan grabbed his arm. "But, look you beyond the square."

"There are so many people! I might escape the wihht, but what if someone from the Guild sees me? They think I'm dead. I'll really be dead then!"

"We'll have to risk it," said Severan. "This is our best chance. You see, just beyond the square? That's where we're going."

Mioja Square teemed with life before them. Market stalls, barrow vendors, jugglers, musicians, a throng of humanity. Looming above it on the other side of the square was a massive edifice of black stone spires, squat towers, arches, and crazily angled roof planes that gleamed ancient green copper in the sunlight, rimmed with balustrades and festooned with every manner of gargoyle, glaring and grinning down at the city.

"That's the old university," said Jute. "No one goes there. It's full of magic and death and all sorts of ghosts."

"True to a point," said the old man, smiling. "However, the place is so steeped in magic that the wihht would have immense trouble finding your scent there. Besides, the Guild would never set foot in the ruins, so we're killing two birds with one stone. We don't need them and the wihht both hunting you. You should be safe within the walls. Reasonably safe. Oh, you needn't look like a frightened sheep, Jute. Most of the stories you've heard about the university ruins aren't true, and the ones that are true—well, you step carefully once inside those walls and you're safe enough."

Here, Severan paused, as if unsure as to how he should proceed. "I'm a scholar of sorts. Some years ago, several of my colleagues and I were granted permission by the regent of Hearne, Nimman Botrell, to conduct a search of the university grounds. It's been unoccupied and locked up since the end of the Midsummer War, more than three hundred years ago."

"Yes," said the boy, remembering stories told late at night by the older boys. "And for good reason!"

"Oh, piffle. Worn-out reasons from long ago. Perhaps in the years following the war—the first hundred or two hundred years—there was wisdom in that. I'll be the first to admit that, er, not just anyone should wander about the university. There are some interesting wards within the grounds that have survived the years intact. Some of the most deadly wards ever spelled. But don't worry, boy," he said hastily, for Jute's eyes were widening. "My colleagues and I are well suited for what we do. If we weren't, the regent would have never given us permission. Besides, he's gambling he'll have his cut out of whatever we find—a greedier man I've yet to meet."

"If I take one step out into the square," said Jute, "the Silentman will know instantly. Half the barrow vendors are in the Guild's pay. Pickpockets and cutpurses everywhere. Worse still, we, the Juggler's children, always considered the square as our play field. They know my face. I'm sure to be seen!"

"Wait here," said Severan.

The old man hurried off across the square and disappeared among the vendors and the crowds eddying about the carts and stalls. The boy hunkered down behind some garbage and stared out at the square. The thought of his old playmates worried him.

65

Would they turn him in for a copper coin and a kind word from the Juggler? He wasn't sure, and the uncertainty was worse than the hunger in his belly. Lena wouldn't squeal on him, but she was only one among dozens. The twins. They probably wouldn't say anything either.

Mioja Square was the proving ground of the Juggler's children. It was where the children honed their skills at picking pockets in hopes of graduating to the richer pickings of the Highneck Rise district. His first lift had been a wallet filched from a fat man inspecting bolts of silk at a draper's stall. But he had been too eager, and the man had whirled around. Jute had sprinted away, the wallet clutched to his chest. The fat man could not keep up for long and stopped, gasping and hurling curses after the boy. Jute had collapsed in a fit of nervous giggles, once safe, and the Juggler had been pleased later. Three gold pieces as shiny bright as butter.

The Juggler.

Shadows.

It felt like a hundred years ago.

The Juggler. The Knife. The man's face swam into his mind and he saw his lips move, forming the words: *Remember, boy. Don't open the box, whatever happens. If you do, I'll cut your throat open so wide the wind'll whistle through it.* He shivered, remembering too well the man's hand drifting down, the needle prick on his shoulder, and the night sky receding away as he fell down the chimney. Something tight and hot congealed within his chest, a point of almost physical obstruction that made him swallow convulsively. And for the first time in his life, Jute hated.

A breeze rustled down the alley and blew across his face, waking him from his reverie. Footsteps sounded and he looked up to see Severan.

"Here," said the old man, handing him a folded up cloak. "Put this on. Pull the hood down over your face."

There was one bad moment when they crossed the square. Right next to Vilanuo's barrow—he sold fried bread—Jute looked up from within the shadow of his cowl to meet Lena's glance. Lena, of all people. She was turning away from the barrow, gnawing on a slab of greasy bread dripping honey. Her eyes flicked up, blue against the ravaged, ward-scarred skin. An uncertain frown drifted across her face, followed by blank eyes and dismissal. But Jute had already turned away, steeling himself from breaking into a run. Sweat trickled down his back. Lena was his closest friend among all of the Juggler's children. *Had been*, said part of his mind. *Trust no one.*

He hurried to catch up with Severan stalking through the crowd. Some beggars sat lazing in the sun on the steps of the old university. They scattered like a flock of ragged starlings as Severan and the boy came toward them, shambling to the outer edges of the steps and down to the square.

"Your precious ruins are safe, scholar," jeered one old man as they passed. "We've been hard at guard."

"Aye," said Severan. "I warrant your smell's enough to do the job."

This elicited a chorus of cackles from the other beggars, and they drifted back to their spots in the sunlight pooled on the steps. The front doors were massive, ironbound affairs, with chains wound through the double handles. They were secured by a rusty lock. As Jute stepped closer, he felt his skin prickle and go cold.

"This is warded," he said. "Heavily warded." He could feel the curious stares of the beggars behind them.

"Yes, yes," said the old man, not paying attention to him. "Ah, there it is."

Jute blinked in astonishment. Where there had only been a stone wall before, a small, dark opening yawned.

"Hurry," said Severan. "It'll only stay open for a moment. We can't have one of these old fellows sneaking in after us. One of them did that several months ago. Never saw him slip inside. Didn't find him until later. What was left of him. He didn't survive much more than an hour."

Jute snorted. "I can be a lot quieter than a beggar."

"I'm sure you can," said Severan. "But an alarming number of the ward spells here aren't attuned to noise. The university isn't a safe place."

"I thought you said it was safe," said Jute, but they were already through and there was only stone behind them where the opening once had been.

"Safe?" echoed the old man. "Did I say that? Well, yes, of course it's safe. In a relative sort of way, perhaps. Safer than the streets of Hearne! The wihht won't find you in here. Er, at least, that's my hope."

It was dark inside after the morning sunlight, and at first Jute was aware only of an echoing space before and above him. As his eyes grew accustomed to the darkness, he saw stone pavement stretching out in front of him for a great distance. Rubble lay scattered across it. Pillars rose up in rows running along either side of the floor. Some of them were shattered and broken off at different heights. Shafts of scarlet, gold, and azure light slanted down through clerestory windows of stained glass. It was a place of shadows, despite the light falling through the stained glass.

"Come," said the old man. "Food and a bed for you, and then later we'll talk of what must be done. For now, however, walk behind me and don't speak unless I speak to you. There are certain wards within this place that are disturbed by the sound of human voices."

The boy wondered why Severan had bothered to say *human voices* instead of just *voices*. At the end of the row of pillars, there was a series of doors. These led into a maze of corridors and stairways so full of twists and turns that Jute was soon hopelessly bewildered as to their direction. Dust lay over everything and stirred in their wake.

From time to time, the old man stopped and mumbled a sentence or two. He spoke so quietly, however, that Jute could never make out what he was saying. But he knew the old man was disarming wards, for he always stopped in places where the air quivered with expectancy, and whenever the old man finished, the quivering sensation was stilled. The expectancy was everywhere—that listening quality every ward has, regardless of its function. The air rustled with it. Jute prided himself on never having yet encountered a ward he could not lull into complacency through his own silence. Here, however, the coiled, listening expectancy of the ward spells was different than anything he had ever known. The back of his neck prickled. He imagined eyes watching from every dark doorway and from behind every pile of rubble they passed. Once, he whirled, sure he had heard footsteps, but there was nothing except the empty corridor behind them.

It seemed as if they walked for hours, through shadows and archways, down long malls and past stairways twisting away in every direction. They picked their way through gaping holes in crumbled walls. They crossed a hall filled with light so bright it made his eyes ache. The roof, high above them, was shattered and open to the sky. The wind moaned through the broken ribs of stone overhead and Jute looked up, thinking of the hawk. They came to a warren of corridors relatively untouched by ruin. Severan opened the door to a room furnished with a bed, a wooden chest, and a table and chair.

"Wait here," said the old man.

When he returned with a plate of bread and cheese and a withered summer apple, he found Jute snoring on the bed. The boy had fallen asleep on top of the blankets. It was chilly in the room, and the old man rummaged in the chest for a woolen blanket. He laid it over Jute and then left, closing the door quietly behind him.

Jute lay on his back under a night sky. He had the strange sensation that he could feel the entire earth pressing up underneath him. Mountain ranges, plains, long ribbons of river shining silver in the moonlight. Distant lands. Deserts chilled and shrouded in darkness. Forests lost in shadows of green midnight. The whole of the earth pushed up against his back, as if he were on the prow of a gigantic ship rushing through the night, propelling him through a vast darkness in which only a few stars gleamed. The wind touched his face. He heard in it the echo of a mighty tempest blowing toward him from an impossible distance away, blowing and howling among the far-off stars and spinning dusts of space.

He wanted to reach the sky, to hurl himself up into it. To unravel into the night until there was nothing left of himself. To be freed from the hold of the heavy earth. The breeze whispered to him of the older winds roaming free, far above the plodding earth. A tremor shook him as he strained upward, but he could not lift a hand from the ground. The blades of grass growing from the earth under and around him held his body fast in their gentle embrace. Stone shifted beneath him like bone scraping on bone. The earth held him close, whispering to him with the sounds of rustling leaves and the mutter of worms as they pushed their patient way through the loam.

No. It cannot have you, said a worm.

No, agreed another.

It has nothing to give you, rustled a leaf. *Nothing except the emptiness of sky.*

Nothing.

You must not forsake the earth.

You will wither like this leaf, said a worm in satisfaction.

Aye, said a leaf. *The best and truest of fates.*

He will wither like you.

Aye, agreed the leaf.

The worms murmured together in lines that moved so slowly and smoothly he thought he could feel the damp earth eaten and left in the wake of their tiny passage.

He will fade into worn hues.

Muted from last year's bold spring.

He will tatter in the wind.

Teeter on a shivering branch.

And lose his breezing balance.

He will fall to drift on down.

And so lay with the whole of earth.

Pressed against his crinkled back.

Aye, rustled the leaf.

"But the sky," he said. "It's so perfect and clear. I wish. . ." He could not say what he wished. The worms had nothing more to say either. The leaf, however, rustled one more time.

Aye. I have seen the sky before. Before I fell.

He cried out in longing and awoke. The dream faded from his mind, as dreams do, and he was conscious only of regret and the memory of sky.

CHAPTER EIGHTEEN
ANDOLAN

The town of Andolan nestled in a valley within the Mearh Dun, or the Horse Hills as they had been known hundreds of years ago, before Dolan Callas had first ridden north during the settling of the lands of Tormay. It was written that Dolan Callas fell in love with the region for three things.

First, for the hills themselves and the prairies stretching from the cliffs in the west on the sea's edge to the Mountains of Morn in the east. Each season was more beautiful than the preceding: lush green in the spring spotted with the scarlet poppies like drops of blood, all of which burned into gold under the summer sun, followed by the rust of autumn and the stark snows of winter.

Second, he was drawn by the wild horses that claimed the hills and prairie of the Mearh Dun as their own. The love of horses runs strong in the blood of every Callas, and Dolan Callas was the first of that line.

Third, and most important, Dolan was caught by the gray-green eyes of a peasant girl whom he saw as he rode along the banks of the river Ciele in the heart of the Mearh Dun. Legend has it the girl was washing laundry at the river's edge. Dolan reined in his horse on the other side. The girl's black hair, bright and dark together as a raven's wing, fell across her face as she bent over her work. She did not look up, even though she must have heard him approaching, for the Ciele is a narrow river. At the nicker of his horse, she finally glanced up. Her name was Levoreth, as so many women of the Callas family down through the years have been named. He built Andolan for her and she bore him three sons. So began the lineage of the dukes of Callas.

The duke's party clattered over the bridge crossing the Ciele and came up the road winding toward the two old towers that guarded the southern gate. Lights gleamed in the town of Andolan, for the sun was lowering in the west. The men-at-arms laughed and talked among themselves. They were glad to be back—good ale and good friends at the castle, the warmth of their homes and wives. The guards at the gate were already standing at attention, for the tall form of the duke was distinctive at a distance.

Children skipped alongside the horses and chased after pennies the duke tossed for them as the party rode through the streets. Men and women called cheerfully from porch stoops and windows and from market stalls shuttering for the night. They tugged their forelocks in respect to the three members of the Callas family. The duke and duchess were loved in Dolan, but especially in the town of Andolan. The dukes of Callas had never forgotten the peasant girl who had become the mother of their line. It was in honor of her that the castle doors were always open to the townsfolk. Equally so, it was just as normal to find the duke sitting outside the local tavern with the old men who had nothing better to do than warm their bones in the sun and swap tall tales.

Grooms ran out to hold the horses' reins as they clattered to a halt in the castle courtyard. Two hounds lollopped up and sniffed dutifully at every horse before making for Levoreth to slobber happily all over her hands. The old steward Radean emerged from the front door and tottered down the steps. Servants peered smiling from lamp-lit windows. The Callases were home.

The days whisked by in a whirl of activity. There was much to do before setting out for Hearne and the Autumn Fair. Melanor decided none of her dresses would do and, catching Hennen at an opportune time when he was sneaking a pork pie in the larder before supper, convinced the duke to part with the necessary gold.

"I think Levoreth could use a few new things, too," said the duchess.

"You women are going to beggar the duchy," said her husband, edging around so that he was standing between the duchess and the remains of the pork pie sitting on the shelf.

"Nonsense," said his wife. "We're the only reason the land hasn't gone to ruin, with you buying up every horse in sight and paying a king's ransom for whatever four-legged creature the Farrows trot through here."

"What?" said the duke, foolishly rising to the bait. "Madame, you speak of things you know nothing of. Horses are the treasure of Dolan. That last colt—she'll be faster than Min the Morn, or I'll eat my best cloak—was worth every penny I paid."

"And how much was that?"

"Er . . ."

"I don't suppose you'll grudge Levoreth and me a few pieces of gold."

"A few pieces? Why, I know that just one of your dresses—"

"Hennen, you have crumbs on your chin," she interrupted. "And we'll need to get some shoes too. Several pairs each."

"Oh, all right," he said.

Levoreth would have smiled if she could have heard them, but she was walking down by the river Ciele. She did not care about new dresses and shoes. The few she had she was comfortable with, for they were faded and known, like old friends. Green and growing things fascinated her: the change of seasons, how the earth accepted the coming of the rain. And the homey parts of everyday life never ceased to tire her: the scent of bread baking, the cooing of a baby, the flicker of a hearth fire at the end of the day. And then there were horses. She was a Callas, through and through, in every best sense of the name. Every Callas loved horses.

One of the hounds had followed her from the castle and now was snuffling among the rocks by the river's edge. Every once in a while, he would stop and raise his head to stare at her, as if to reassure himself of her presence. She sat down on a slab of rock. Light glittered on the water. The sun rode up the arch of a perfect sky. She leaned back, rested her head on her shawl, and slept.

She dreamt of a young girl standing on a savannah of grasses waving in the wind. The girl's face was remote and still. Sadness pooled in the shadows under her gray eyes. Her hair streamed away from her in black tresses. She gazed away into the distance. The girl turned, slowly, to look at Levoreth.

Levoreth awoke with a start. The hound was nosing at her hand. It woofed happily when she scratched its head, and then it flopped down at her feet. She lay back and slept again.

This time, she dreamt of a winter sky. High overhead, a hawk floated on the wind, wings stretched wide. Its cry thrilled through the air, fierce and cruel. Far off across a snowy plain, a figure walked toward her. She could not tell if it were man or woman, as the distance was great. A roaring rose in her ears. Wind howled through the sky and whipped across the snow. A flurry of ice stung her skin. Indistinguishable at first, but then clearer and clearer, a voice called to her from far away.

Levoreth.

I am Levoreth Callas. He stopped for me, and I looked up. I chose to look up. I took his name.

Levoreth.

It is mine. I never wanted much.

This time, she awoke with a hand touching her shoulder. One of the maids from the castle was kneeling next to her. The hound sat up and yawned.

"Miss Levoreth," said the maid. "Milady would like you to come for your fitting."

"All right, girl," she said. "Run back and tell her I'll be along shortly."

"Yes, miss." And the maid scampered across the meadow toward the town walls.

Levoreth sat for a moment, staring down at the river. Its liquid voice sang of the valley, of the heather on the hills graying into autumn, of the mists that rose in the mornings on the plain and melted away under the noonday sun. Through it all was the murmuring memory of rain, of the storms in the Mountains of Morn that brought life to the Mearh Dun.

"And the hope of rain, yet again," said Levoreth out loud. The hound looked at her quizzically. "So it ever goes, and the years are preserved. May it ever be so and may the Dark never wake in Daghoron." She scratched the dog's ears, and it growled with pleasure. "Come, or Melanor will grow impatient and take it out on the poor tailor."

The tailor proved accommodating to Melanor's wishes, even though he sighed at her demand that all the clothes be finished in two days. He was a melancholy man with sad eyes and the air of an undertaker.

"Honestly," whispered the duchess, "you'd think we were being fitted for our shrouds. But he's positively the best tailor north of Hearne. Something terribly sad must've happened to him."

"Or perhaps," said Levoreth, "he has corns and his shoes are too tight."

"You think so?" And the duchess spent the rest of the afternoon scrutinizing the poor man's shoes until he grew so flustered that he jabbed Levoreth with a safety pin as he was measuring her for an evening gown.

CHAPTER NINETEEN
STARTING THE JOB

Ronan spent some time watching the comings and goings of the merchant Cypmann Galnes. He had heard of Galnes even before Arodilac Bridd had told him his story. The man was well-known among the merchants and traders of the city. He was wealthy, powerful, and equally comfortable among the nobility of Highneck Rise and the roughnecks of the docks. It wouldn't do to anger a man who had the ear of the regent. Even if the regent was paying for the job.

Obviously, the man was aware of his daughter's circumstance. And angry. The best thing would be to find out his habits and then rob his house when he wasn't home. There was no need to anger him any further. Strange, though, that his daughter wanted the Bridd family ring for something. What was it Arodilac had said?

She wants something in exchange. But she won't tell me what.

Strange.

It was raining—a chilly downpour, unseasonal but welcome enough to the gardens and greenery parched brown by summer—and this dreariness plunged him into a brooding study. The rain reduced the city to a blur of stone, punctuated by the glow of lights in windows—taverns, shops, homes—all promising warmth and respite from the damp and dark.

Water ran on the cobbled streets; it streamed from cornices and peaks and spouts. It flowed along through the gutters and gurgled down storm drains. In Mioja Square, in the heart of the city, the fountain began to overflow, sheeting water across the square. The vendors had already packed up their handbarrows and stalls and scurried away. Nobody shopped in weather like this.

Cypmann Galnes stalked across the square, oblivious to the rain and oblivious to the shadowy form of Ronan trailing behind him. As far as the thief could tell, they were the only two souls out in the city that morning. He flipped his collar up and shivered. Rain ran down his neck. A curse escaped his lips as he splashed through a puddle.

Normally, such a job would be given to one of the runners, one of the children fresh from the Juggler's pack. Someone with enough brains to follow and keep their mouth shut, stay invisible, and hang about in doorways, waiting for someone else to move, someone else to think, someone else to act. But the instructions Smede passed on from the Silentman had been explicit. The regent wanted no one else from the Guild working on the job, no one else from the Guild even knowing about the job. The potential of embarrassment for the regency was too great.

Ronan smiled sourly to himself. He appreciated the trust that the Silentman obviously thought him worthy of. Still, he'd much rather be sitting in an inn somewhere, a mug of ale in hand.

We all have our jobs to do.

Almost, he stopped to turn around, to see who had whispered the words, but it was only his memory stirring. Darkness filled his eyes and he saw the chimney yawning open underneath him, filled with shadow. He felt dizzy, as if he were teetering on a height. As if he was the one falling. He strode on in the rain, shoulders hunched against the wet and the cold, and against the past.

Nothing personal, boy.

We all have our jobs to do.

Cypmann Galnes owned a warehouse near the harbor. Here, the city continued its hustle and bustle in spite of the rain. Water was a customary part of life, whether in the sea or raining from the sky. Even now, the docks swarmed with fishermen unloading the morning catch. Rain hissed on the swells rising and falling against the pilings. A schooner nosed up against the dock, its mainsail dropping with a clatter. Ronan could hear the calls of the sailors as ropes were flung and made fast. He huddled in an archway and watched as the merchant disappeared through a door down the street. A moment later, lamplight flickered from behind a window. The merchant would be there until late in the day. His routine was predictable. Ronan trudged away.

CHAPTER TWENTY
THE GAWINNS TAKE IN AN ORPHAN

They drove the mules hard. The twins no longer smiled and sang, even though Loy took to crooning wordlessly over the girl. She did not wake from her sleep. Her body grew thinner with each passing hour until it seemed she was only a collection of bones wrapped with skin. From time to time, Loy managed to trickle drops of honey and water between her lips.

"Her skin feels like fire," he said. "And the wounds on her leg stink of rot."

"Tomorrow morning we'll be there," said Murnan.

"Might be too late."

"Aye," said the other twin. "If these lazy mules of yours weren't weighted so heavily, we'd make better time. Be there by nightfall."

The twins both glared at the trader. He tried to stare them down but could not.

"All right!" he said. "Have it your way. It'll mean less for all of us at journey's end."

After a hasty discussion they decided on the copper ingots, as well as a pair of silver cats that had caught Murnan's eye in Damarkan.

"For a wedding," he said to himself. "They'd have been a perfect wedding gift. Cwen loves cats." But then he subsided into silence, for his thoughts turned to another wedding and the miller's face staring up blindly at the sky.

They buried the copper and the cats at the foot of an oak in a dell near the river Rennet. It was beginning to rain. The mules stepped out eagerly, now that their burdens had been lightened.

"Ten hours," said the trader.

It was closer to nine hours and just into night when they reached the gates of Hearne. The horses steamed with sweat in the light of the flaring lamps and the mules refused to move once they clattered under the stone arch. A young officer emerged from the guard tower.

"Sir—"

"I need a physician. Quickly, and the best you know!"

The officer raised his eyebrows.

"Physicians don't just come for anyone, sir. Even in Hearne, only a few practice and they cost a—"

"What's this?" said a voice behind the officer. A man sauntered down the steps of the guard tower. The young officer stepped to one side and saluted him.

"Murnan Col, is it not?" said the man.

"My lord?" said the trader.

The lamplight drew the man's face out of shadow, revealing a bony visage with startling blue eyes and dark hair falling over his forehead.

"You sold me a pair of emeralds a year ago," said the man. "Perfectly matched. Had them made into earrings for my wife."

"Ah!" Murnan's face lightened. "Owain Gawinn! My lord, surely fate has brought you here. I'm sorely in need of your assistance. I know a good physician's hard to find, but not for the regent's Lord Captain of Hearne."

"For yourself, no doubt," said Owain, though he didn't mean it. His eyes had already noted the form cradled in Loy's arms.

"Several days ago, my lord, as we came up from Damarkan, we arrived at a village on a tributary of the Rennet. A little place I've traded at before, pleasant and friendly folk. This time, however, when we entered the village we found a charnel house out of the worst nightmare! Every person slain except for this one poor girl we brought away, and she is gravely wounded. Perhaps it would be a kindness to let her die, seeing her people are gone, but who knows why one is left to live?"

The captain's face had stilled at the trader's words.

"How were the villagers killed?" he asked. His voice was quiet. "Did you take time to notice?"

Murnan's face twisted in disgust. "Their bodies were disfigured by the birds and rats feeding, but it seemed they died in one of two ways. Some had deep wounds, thin and precise as if stabbed by knife or sword. Others had their throats torn out as if by a wild beast."

Owain Gawinn said nothing more after that, except to snap an order to the young officer at the gate. Soldiers dashed out with fresh horses, and in a matter of seconds the trader and the twins found themselves hurried along through the streets of Hearne. The rain and the darkness and the looming walls around them passed by in a blur of clattering hoofs and the muttered talk of the soldiers. Owain rode at their head, but he seemed a shadow flitting through the night, only just in sight and always out of reach.

The street climbed up a steep rise. The houses were larger there, mansions, for the most part, set back behind walls and gardens. The rain rustled overhead in the branches of trees sheltering the street. They came to a gate in a high wall. Owain called out, and the gate swung open. They entered into a courtyard. Light spilled from doorways and windows. Servants came forward.

"Welcome to my house," said Owain Gawinn.

The regent's own physician came and tended to the little girl. He was an old man with a stern face, but his hands were gentle and the girl's labored breathing eased under his touch.

"Her blood's tainted with a strange poison," he said. He bled her with a knife into a stone vial, though Loy scowled and grumbled in the corner so much that he had to be ushered from the room. Owain's four children peeped in through the doorway, all with his blue eyes. Sibb, his wife, swept in and out with hot water and a cool hand that seemed to do just as much good, if not more, than the physician.

Murnan Col left that same night, relieved and heading north to Thule and home. One twin, Gann, went with him, but Loy stayed behind in the house of Owain Gawinn, for, as he said to his brother, he had felt the little girl's life ebb away in his arms over the course of those past days and he wished to see her whole again before he left.

Her fever broke after three days, and the wounds on her arm and leg began to heal. But even though she opened her eyes, she would only stare at her visitors. Not a sound escaped her lips, despite Owain's repeated attempts to question her. Finally, his wife banned him from the room.

"She'll speak when she's ready," she said. "Until then, you'll have to wait. Now go, before I lose my patience."

"Know your place, Sibb!" said her husband. But then he laughed and kissed her. He was a wise man and knew that his wife was wiser still in most matters.

The days passed, and still the girl remained silent. All of them grew used to her grave eyes—Owain, his wife Sibb, their children, the servants, and Loy—though Owain wondered what it was that she had seen. This was not the first tale he had heard of such killings, but it was the first time he had encountered a survivor.

After some time, the girl plucked up enough courage to venture out of her room, but only if Loy was in view. Besides Owain's wife, he was the only one she would suffer to pick her up. But even for him she remained silent and solemn, despite the many ridiculous faces he would make for her benefit. Not a night went by without a nightmare coming to her, and it was only then she made noise—screaming as if she were looking into the darkness of Daghoron itself. The household waited patiently for her improvement and speech. She remained mute, however, and so the family grew to expect nothing more of her, though Sibb wept over her sometimes at night.

CHAPTER TWENTY-ONE
VANISHING STAIRS

There was food on the table when Jute woke up. After he ate, he investigated the room. There was nothing worth stealing. Wool blankets and old books would not bring much from the barrow sellers who bought from the Juggler's children. The room adjoined another room with nothing in it except for a window opening out onto a stone casement. He crawled outside and sat in the morning sunlight. The stone was already warming with the sun. He was at a great height, well above the rooftops of the city. Above him, the university spires towered even higher, up into the clear sky. Far below, the hubbub of Mioja Square drifted up to him. People bustled like ants among the brightly colored awnings of the stalls.

The city sprawled around his vantage point. The sea was a brilliant line of blue to the west. To the east, huddled near the university walls, was the ugly mass of the Earmra slum, where the poorest of Hearne's poor lived and worked. To the north, of course, the rooftops sloped sharply up toward Highneck Rise, at whose highest point rose the gleaming white stone towers of the regent's castle. He had never been inside, or even close, for the castle was so heavily warded it set his ears buzzing if he got within a hundred yards of the place. According to the Juggler, the castle of Nimman Botrell was filled with the most fabulous treasures imaginable.

The Juggler.

His jaw tightened. A breeze blew by his face, prompting him to look to the sky, but there was nothing there—no hawk riding the winds—only the empty blue.

The view from the window only held him so long. By noon, his boredom outweighed his fear of the university and the terrors Severan had hinted at. He opened the door to the hall and peered out. No one was there. The hall was silent. Even better, he could not hear any ward spells whispering in his mind. What was it Severan had said?

An alarming number of the ward spells here aren't attuned to noise.

Then what do they listen to if not noise?

He rubbed his nose and thought hard about this for a moment. He hadn't met a ward yet he couldn't beat. The trick was to be as silent as the sky. Silent and empty, and the spell would reach right through you and find nothing.

Jute crept down the hall.

He tripped his first ward twenty minutes later.

After some time prowling about the warren of hallways, he came upon a marble door carved with whorls that seemed to creep in and out of each other. He pressed his ear against it and listened. There was only silence. More importantly, there was no ward whispering in his mind. He opened the door and found himself standing on a platform jutting out over a huge, gloomy space of darkness. He edged over to the side to look down. He could see nothing below. But surely something was down there. He had to find out.

Happily enough, a staircase curved down from one side of the platform. The steps were visible some distance down in the darkness, reflecting a hidden light source he could not make out. Jute tiptoed down the stairs in silence. However, after some time, he became aware of a noise. He froze. It was the quietest of noises—similar to a finger tapping on stone. Just a simple, peaceful tapping.

Or so Jute thought.

He took another step down the stairs, listening hard. After a few more steps, he realized the tapping increased in rapidity the further he descended. He retreated back up the stairs a way and paused. Sure enough, the tapping slowed back down.

If Jute had understood the history and nature of the university, he would have promptly ran back up the stairs and hurried to the room where Severan had left him. And there he would have waited until the old man returned. But Jute didn't. He was a stubborn boy and he was also a curious thief. It was a combination that didn't always prove healthy.

He tiptoed down the stairs, listening with all his might to the tapping as it increased in tempo with every step he took. He still could not tell where the stairs ended, as no floor was visible below. By this time, the tapping was so fast that surely the next step down he took would result in the tapping becoming a single, unbroken blur of sound. He took one more step and found this to be true.

It was at that moment the stairway began to vanish. The steps below him disappeared, one by one, climbing up toward him. He turned and ran. There was one horrible spot at the end where he felt the step under his foot soften and he looked down to see the thing vanish. He lunged for the platform at the top of the stairs and hauled himself, sobbing for air, up over the edge.

Jute lay on his back, his heart hammering against his ribs. After a while, he noticed with horrified fascination that, far below the platform, the stairway was reappearing. The stairs shimmered into view, one by one, mounting higher and higher. The last stair materialized under his fingertips, and he snatched his hand away as if the cold stone would burn him.

Severan was waiting in his room, perched on the wooden chest.

"Have an apple," he said, waving at a pile of withered specimens on the table. He took one for himself and bit into it. Jute picked up an apple and promptly dropped it on the floor. His hands were shaking.

"Ah," said Severan. "You found Bevan's stairway. I felt it vanish. My colleagues also did. We figured it must have been a large and unlucky rat, though I had my suspicions. No one's ever reached the bottom of those stairs. Alive, that is."

"I can't just stay cooped up in here!" said Jute.

"It's either stay cooped up or have the wihht find you," said the old man. "Or have your neck broken in any number of ways. The wards in this place are deadly. Can you get that through your thick skull?"

"The stairs vanished right underneath me!"

"You shouldn't have been wandering around. I don't doubt you're bored, but, trust me, you were lucky. Those stairs killed a lot of people during the Midsummer War. Bevan was an unusually creative wizard. He was the one who figured out how to mask the warning buzz that wards give off. Once he'd discovered that, it wasn't long before all the best wards in this place were woven for silence. Though—did you hear a tapping noise when you were on the staircase?"

"Of course," said Jute. He bit into an apple. "What do you expect me to do? Sit in here until I grow old and die?"

"Most people would never have heard any tapping, which is how Bevan designed it. However, if you heard it that means you'd probably be able to recognize many of the wards in these ruins, one way or another. So I suppose it would be safe for you to see a bit of the place. Though," he warned, as Jute's face brightened, "you must use your wits, which you obviously didn't do on the staircase."

"I'm alive, aren't I?" said the boy.

"Next time, if you hear noise, no matter how quiet, get away from that place as fast as possible. Furthermore, don't go below the ground level and do not go outside, whatever you do. Some of the entrance wards are strong enough to reduce a house to rubble. The wards in this place are much more sophisticated than the variety people buy in the marketplace for their homes and whatnot. Any noise, any movement, changes in color or temperature, even a change in odor—treat them as signs of a ward listening to you."

"What if it's just a mouse scurrying by?" said Jute.

The old man sighed and reached for another apple.

"A mouse," he said. "How I wish the world was that simple. You obviously know nothing about the Midsummer War. If you did, even the mice in this place would give you cause for concern." He settled back on the wooden chest and began to speak.

CHAPTER TWENTY-TWO
SCUADIMNES AND THE MIDSUMMER WAR

"Long ago," said Severan, "all Tormay was united under a monarchy that ruled from the city of Hearne. The duchies of Dolan, Hull, and Thule in the north and those of Vo and Vomaro in the south all gave their allegiance to the king. Harlech, of course, far to the north, minded its own business, as it has always done and always will. The deserts of Harth, beyond Vomaro, gave their loyalty to no one, though the tribe of Oran was beginning to establish itself in those years by seizing control of the oasis trade routes. The duchy of Mizra did not exist in those days."

"What?" said Jute, blinking. "Mizra, where all the gold comes from?"

"Mizra, where all the gold comes from. There're more important things to know about Mizra than that. The Guild is obviously selective in what it teaches its budding criminals. Mizra, at the time, was a wilderness, east of the mountains of Morn. No one ever went to Mizra and no one ever came from Mizra. Anyway, at the time, the university in Hearne was a center for the study of history and certain other topics. It was a place of wonder, a repository of knowledge so vast that men have never known its like. Students came from every walk of life."

"To learn how to be wizards?" said Jute.

"Not just wizards," said Severan. "It was a place for scholars as well. Besides, no one learns how to become a wizard. You either are or you aren't. Wizardry is just a trait like any other trait. Some people are born with the knack of understanding animals or throwing the perfect clay pot or knowing just when to whisk a cake out of the oven. The university taught how to control and refine the trait of wizardry. The trait itself can't be taught."

"But what about ward-weavers?" asked the boy. "Fat old Arcus in Mioja Square offered to take on Wrin as his apprentice, and Wrin's stupid as a rock. I once gave him a piece of tin and he thought it silver."

Severan waved his hand in the air. "You can teach a dog to do tricks if you're patient and have plenty of bones to keep the rascal happy. Anyone can learn a few bits of wizardry, but it doesn't mean you're a wizard. Most modern ward-weaving is tomfoolery and only fit for keeping out rats and mice. As I was saying, er, what was I saying? Oh, yes. The university! The university was a vibrant place, a marvelous mix of the best minds of Tormay. All dedicated—well, mostly all—to preserving knowledge of Tormay's past and the study of the Dark. For if one does not know the past, one cannot guard against the future."

The day was darkening outside. Severan rummaged in the chest and found a candle. He lit it and set on the table. The light flickered on their faces. Shadows trembled on the wall. The old man settled back on his seat and continued.

"But then an unfortunate thing happened. The old king died. His son, Dol Cynehad, ascended the throne, and the wizard Scuadimnes was appointed advisor to his new majesty. Scuadimnes was the senior archivist at the university, a quiet man of no distinction other than his remarkable memory. It was said that every word in every manuscript of the archive was held within his mind. One need only go to him and ask where might one find a treatise on cloud formations, or hedgetoads, or sicknesses caused by the touch of a lich, and he would select the pertinent work. Plucked, mind you, from thousands of scrolls and scripts and books. No one was sure where Scuadimnes came from originally. Some said Vomaro. Others said that he was a farmer's son from Hull. Still others said that he came from Harlech, though that's unlikely, as few wizards have ever come from that land.

"Scuadimnes set about poisoning the young king's mind against the university and the wizards. Any power not in the hands of those who rule is found suspect by them. This is a dangerous inclination to exploit. Slowly, Scuadimnes twisted the king's thinking until he regarded the wizards with suspicion. And then enmity. And then fear. Edicts were proclaimed, limiting new students to only those approved by the king's council. Taxes were levied on wizards and the practice of the arts on behalf of others. The council of the university did not suspect the involvement of Scuadimnes at the time, for he came to them in those days with honeyed words, protesting his lack of influence over the king and his dismay at the cruelty of the throne."

The old man stared at the candle flame.

"They believed him," he said. "Even though they must have known. They must have! But it's easier to pretend all's well than to awake and confront the Dark."

"What happened then?" said the boy.

"What happened then?" echoed the old man. He sighed. "The Midsummer War is what happened then. It began with murder. The body of Volora Cynehad, the king's grandmother, was found in her rooms. A harmless old woman who was only important by virtue of who her grandson was. Murdered in a hideous manner that pointed to wizardry of a dark and learned sort. The dean of the university was arrested and died in the royal dungeons under mysterious circumstances. Students were beaten in the streets of Hearne. Mobs tried to break into the university grounds. The wizards avoided confrontation at first, but the violence spiraled out of hand. It was only a matter of time before the royal army attacked. And attack they did.

"The deceit of Scuadimnes was then revealed, for many of the younger wizards, students mostly, turned on their peers and masters. Bought long ago by promises of power, they aided the king's soldiers and transformed the university into a raging battleground of sword and spear and the magic arts. The nights of Hearne were lit up by the eldritch glow of the struggle. Three times, the battered remnant within the university threw their attackers from the school. And in the evening after that last time, an awful sight was seen."

"What? What was it?" said the boy. He stared at Severan with wide eyes.

"The gates of the royal castle were thrown open, and out marched the dead, in row upon row. Warriors and wizards alike, woven back to a strange half-life by the arts of Scuadimnes. Fathers and husbands, sons and brothers, brought back from the grave to fight again. Their wounds gaped, and they bled darkness instead of blood. They called to each other in strange, whistling voices as if the wind spoke through them instead of their own breath. Terror fell on the city. The inhabitants fled. They carried word of the horror through all of Tormay. The duchies mobilized in confusion, readying themselves to march on Hearne, but to what end? To save it from wizards, or to save it from the hand of the king?"

"And the wizards here in the university?"

"They died almost to a man," said the old man sadly. "They died not understanding why. To be faced with the greatest puzzle of their lives and to not be allowed even a hint of the answer was a terrible thing. The genuine wizard is not as interested in the exercise of power as he is in discovering answers. Who was Scuadimnes? How was he able to command the dead? What was his intent?"

"His intent?" Jute stirred. "Didn't he gain control of the king?"

"He did, but it didn't seem to be his goal. Scuadimnes disappeared after the university was destroyed. The army of the dead wandered the city streets for days, witless and stumbling on limbs that slowed until they no longer moved. And when the armies of the duchies of Tormay arrived at the city gates, they found only the dead—the truly dead—within. Hearne was as a tomb, the silence broken only the harsh cries of the carrion fowl feeding in the streets. Thus it was that the monarchy of Tormay ended. The king's body was found in the castle. None wasted grief on him, because the land bore a larger grief. A regency was installed in Hearne, and the duchies went their own ways, each seeing to their lands and no longer giving fealty to Hearne. And so the years have come to our times and our own regent, Nimman Botrell."

"But what does this mean for Mizra?" said the boy. "You said the duchy there had something to do with the Midsummer War."

"Excellent. Listening is the first step on a long road."

"The first step on a long road to what?" asked Jute.

"Wherever it is you're going, of course. Ah, Mizra! What a strange land it is! They say a traveler can, in a single day, traverse from icy crags to deep canyons where smoke rises from crevices in the ground and the earth is warmed by the fires smoldering far below the surface. As I said, no one lived there before the Midsummer War. It was considered a dangerous, inhospitable land. After the war, however, some of the king's court found refuge there, and the duchy of Mizra was born. There was a sort of humor to the matter, for it was the king's treasurer, Maom Gifernes, who found gold there in the spot where the city of Ancalon now stands. His family has held sway there ever since. Brond Gifernes rules today in Ancalon. He's an able lord, despite his youth—so they say—but I've never been to his land."

"When I was in the basement," said the boy, "that thing—was it something like the dead warriors of, of —"

"Scuadimnes?" The old man paused, as if reluctant to answer.

"Was it the same? He told me what he did as he fashioned it, calling down into the sewers. He told me it was darkness and water woven together and that anything fashioned with darkness would cause pain. Four things, he said. Any of four things with darkness. Fire and water, earth and air."

Severan nodded. "I don't think Nio capable of the dark arts of Scuadimnes, but the shadow behind such men remains the same. It's always the same. Forcing fire, earth, water, or air to join with darkness can only result in evil. Those four things are the materials of the four ancient anbeorun, the four stillpoints around which all life revolves. They were created to stand against the Dark, so how then can they be forced into union with their enemy? They are a bulwark against evil and have always been beyond the understanding of man. Even the wizards know little of the anbeorun, though certain small things have been discovered. It's said there exists a book called the *Gerecednes*, that it contains knowledge of the anbeorun, but this is only what some believe. Legend says that the *Gerecednes* is a wonder, a book so fascinating that anyone would be content to sit and read it forever." He sighed. "Finding that book is the main reason my fellow scholars and I came to these ruins."

"What about Nio? Does he search here as well?"

Severan nodded reluctantly. "He's a man of letters, a scholar of history and things lost. I can't bar him from this place, for he was one of our original company when we struck our deal with Nimman Botrell, the regent of your city, five years ago. He has the right to enter here. But the university grounds are huge. None of my peers know of this room here and this area of halls. I really wouldn't worry about Nio. The air here is jumbled with the memories and currents of magic. It would be impossible to find the one faint thread that is you in this vast place."

CHAPTER TWENTY-THREE
THE GOOSE AND GOLD

Nio, of course, did not find Jute down by the docks. It had been a foolish idea. In his haste, he had not considered the fact that it took a good half hour to hurry from the university to the docks. By the time he reached the wharf, there was no sign of Jute. This sent him into a rage, and he spent the rest of the day cursing and stamping about his house. It was only later that he recalled what the wihht had told him. There were other avenues to investigate. What had the wihht said? Something about an inn the Thieves Guild patronized. The Goose and Gold. He hurried downstairs, shrugged on his cloak, and slammed out the door.

It took Nio a vexing amount of time to find the inn, for as with Fishgate it also was in an area of the city where he rarely went. He should have had the wihht explain the location with more detail. The inn was situated on a street called Stalu, which was ironic, as the word referred to the business of robbery. Not in one of the ancient languages, of course, but in an old trade language fallen into disuse about two hundred years ago. A wooden sign hung above the inn's door. It showed a golden goose on a black field. The paint was faded and peeling.

How interesting. He could sense the usual confusion of ward spells around him. Weak and badly woven—fitting quality for such a neighborhood. Spelled into doors, windows, gates, and walls. About as sturdy as spider webs and just as easy to brush away. The curious thing was that there was a very powerful ward in one place, hidden behind shabbier wards. Intrigued, Nio let his mind drift out, feathering past the layer of cheaper wards. He ran a mental finger over the closest loop of the ward. Impressive. Old, subtle, and so cunningly woven that he could not find any loose ends in the weaving. It wasn't work he recognized. Not many wizards would be capable of such a thing. He withdrew his mind as soon as the ward woke to his presence—woke—wards weren't sentient the way a man is, but the better wards did seem alive.

He looked about to see where the ward was situated. It was a shabby house, a three-story affair several doors down from the Goose and Gold and on the opposite side of the street. Broken shutters, stone walls grayed and pitted by the years gone by, and a slate roof pocked with missing tiles. Not the sort of place one would think necessary to guard. But someone obviously did and had the money to do so. Nio had been many times to the Highneck Rise district—dinners or soirees put on by bored nobility who thought to amuse themselves with the scholars grubbing about in the university ruins. But even there, in the richest neighborhood of the city, one would not find a ward like the one guarding the old house.

He would return to investigate on another day. He was always hungry to learn. He wondered what demanded such protection. But not today. There was a box and a boy to hunt, a fat man and a master thief to find, and the trail of the Guild to sniff along until it led him to whoever—or a whatever—had commissioned the theft.

A whatever.

Where had that thought come from? The histories mentioned other beings who once lived in these lands—Tormay, and the older countries lost in the east centuries ago. Beings other than the ogres and giants and dragons and such that existed uneasily on the fringes of man's civilization. For some reason, the image of the sceadu staring from the mosaic sprang into his mind.

Nio muttered a few words under his breath, and then opened the door of the Goose and Gold. He had an impression of shadow and odors of food and ale and tobacco, but then his eyes adjusted to the gloom. Men sat around tables, busy at their lunch and busier at their ale. A fire crackled on the hearth. Stairs rose up on one side to a second floor. Lodging available for travelers, no doubt. Grime blackened the timbers in the ceiling. The rumble of conversation lulled when he entered, but it picked up again. He nodded to himself, satisfied. The obscuring worked. It was a minor weaving, but one he had never tested before.

He sat down at a small table in one corner and looked around. From the looks of the clientele, the inn was favored by the rank and file of the Thieves Guild, and not their masters. To Nio's eye, everyone seemed on the oafish side. Pig-eyed, thick-necked dolts with fat hands and small heads. He had trouble imagining anyone in the room burgling a house successfully, let alone stealing their grandmother's eggs.

"What'll it be, love?"

A serving girl materialized at his elbow. She was young enough to be his daughter, but her eyes were much older. Faded brown and looking right through him.

"Ale and—what do you have for food?"

"Beef stew and bread," she said.

"All right, then."

She returned with a platter and a tankard. The ale was decent and the bread was only half stale. He eyed the crowded room while he ate and considered what to do.

An old man lurched up to his table.

"Spare a copper, mister?"

"Perhaps," said Nio. "If you can answer a question."

The old man swayed closer and tried to look knowledgeable. He breathed wine fumes in Nio's face.

"Do you know a man called the Juggler?"

"Aye, I do," said the old fellow. "He's like a son to me. A dear son."

"Bring him to me and you'll have your coin."

"Bring him to you?" repeated the other.

"Yes."

"Maybe a drop of ale first. Just to ease the dryness, you know. It's terribly dry in here."

"Go on."

Nio turned back to his lunch. The old man shuffled away, mumbling to himself. A few minutes later, someone slid in across the table from Nio.

"Here he is, and I'll have my coin."

He looked up. The old sop was standing by and, across the table, sat a fat man. Nio fished a silver piece from his pocket.

"As promised."

He tossed it through the air. But before the old man could grab it, a hand darted out and snatched it.

"Hey there," protested the old man.

85

"You don't rouse me from my drink for nothing, Gally," said the fat man. "Here's a copper. That's enough for some ale. Get on with you."

Grumbling, the old man took the coin and shuffled off toward the counter.

"You shouldn't throw away silver on garbage like that," said the fat man. "No telling what those around here'll do if they catch wind of money."

"I'm touched by your concern," said Nio.

"Right you are," said the other. "I don't like to see folks taken while I'm around. Gives the place a bad name, and we don't want that. Now then, old Gally told me you wanted a word."

"You're the Juggler?"

"Fifteen years and counting. Took over for my father before me, as he'd done for his. It's a family thing. One Juggler after another. Fathers and sons. Tradition ain't a thing to be taken lightly. What can I do for you? You seem a gentleman of distinction—not the sort to frequent the Goose, if you don't mind me saying so. Is it a spot of trouble you're reluctant to bother the city guard with? Need a word spoken in someone's ear? Bits and bobs you want scooped up? Something found, something lost?"

"Something lost," said Nio. His mind feathered out to touch the Juggler's thoughts. But then he stopped and withdrew, for a ward shielded the fat man's mind. It was a cheap one, probably just a bauble carried in the pocket. He could have broken it easily, but such dispelling always generates attention, and he did not want that.

"Well, now," said the Juggler. He turned and signaled to the serving girl. "Lost things don't always want finding. It can take effort and skill. But you've come to the right man, assuming you're a man of generosity, that you're a man of liberality, that your purse is ready to aid me in my search. Why, I've got the cleverest little hands in the city. Just right for finding things."

He waggled his stubby fingers in the air. Nio knew, though, the man was not talking of his own hands.

"The item I've lost," said Nio, "might be difficult to find."

"And why's that?"

"I think other people might be looking for the same thing."

The serving girl materialized at the table and plunked down a tankard of ale. The Juggler took a swig and shook his head happily.

"Other people mean problems, headaches for me, say, if I were to find this missing thing you speak of. Headaches can be expensive. Especially if they're mine. But I know you wouldn't want me to suffer needlessly."

"Of course not."

"Gold has a medicinal quality."

"Naturally."

The Juggler smiled. "I think we're in agreement. Now, what is it you need to find? A chestful of coin wandered into someone else's coffers? Deeds, diamonds, a mortgage paper in need of disappearing?"

"No," returned the other. "Nothing like that. I first need to find a person."

"You refer, sir, to a series of jobs. If there's a first, then there must be a second. Series of jobs are more costly to accomplish. It's the focus that must be maintained, you see. The follow-through. Often I see the young lads setting up shop, thinking to do me out of my business, but I never worry. And d'you know why? The follow-through. They have no follow-through."

"I need to find a man known as the Knife."

The Juggler flinched, but recovered so quickly that Nio was uncertain of the reaction. It had been only his eyes flicking open wide, and a glimpse of something behind them. Fear, thought Nio.

The Juggler leaned forward, his voice quiet. "Why would you want to look for such a man? There are a lot of men in Hearne, but only one Knife. Might be easier to find someone else."

"As you said, there's only one Knife. I've heard he's a unique sort of person."

The Juggler glanced around the room and then back at Nio.

"A city crammed with people and you're bent on finding this one man? Being picky can be hard on your health. Why, I remember when I was a young lad, examining a merchant's storeroom. It was filled with all kinds of wonderful things. Being young and lacking wisdom, I took my time to find only the best, as opposed to grabbing what I could and making a hasty exit. Imagine my surprise, as I knelt there attempting to determine whether a cube of Harthian jade was more valuable than a bolt of gold-threaded silk, when the master of the house barged in. The ensuing unpleasantness would have been avoided had I been content with lesser things. What a valuable lesson!"

"I can always go elsewhere for help."

"No, no," said the Juggler. "I'm sure the man can be found. It's just that . . ." Here, his voice trailed off and he gazed pensively down at the table.

"Money is not an object."

"Ah," said the fat man. "That always helps."

They came to an agreement, though Nio found the fat man as stubborn as a Vomaronish moneylender. But he did not care. The box was priceless in his eyes. He would have been willing to give a fortune for it. Still, it was somewhat irritating to be cheated.

"It just so happens," said the Juggler, "I might know a thing or two about the Knife's habits."

"I expected nothing less of you." Nio slid several gold coins across the table.

"Now I remember," said the Juggler. "There's a house on a street called Forraedan. Heading west, it's the seventh house, past the south market square. The Knife visits there most Thursday nights—a certain young lady. I'll have a word with him beforehand. He'll be pleased to meet a gentleman of your distinction." The Juggler paused and then added, "And the rest of the gold?"

"You'll have it once I've met him," said Nio.

CHAPTER TWENTY-FOUR
OLD RESEMBLANCES

That evening, the autumn feast was held at the castle in Andolan. It was early in the season to celebrate the autumn harvest, but with the duke and duchess soon leaving for Hearne, this could not be avoided. Besides, no one cared. A feast was a feast, and the people of Dolan seized any chance to get together and eat and argue and drink large amounts of wine. All that day, the lords of the holdings scattered throughout the reaches of the Mearh Dun had been arriving with their retinues. The whole town was invited, though it was tacitly understood that children were not welcome.

"It's not that I don't like children," said the duke. He fiddled with his cravat and frowned at himself in the mirror. "They grow up, mostly, which seems to work out. It's just, as children, they do better far from me and, er, vice versa." The duchess smiled and said nothing. She had been doing this frequently in the last two weeks. It made her husband uneasy.

The duke and the duchess went down together to greet their guests in the great hall. Three tables ran the entire length of the hall. At the far end, raised on a dais, was the high table. Candelabras filled the hall with light. A throng of townsfolk and crofters eddied about the hall, threaded through by servants offering mulled ale. The duke and the duchess stopped to chat with villager and holder alike. Here was Weorn the miller, talking oats with Gan Ierling and his three silent sons who farmed on the high plain. Several traders in town from the southern duchies were arguing amiably in one corner about the spring market in Hearne. And there was Slivan Hyrde, the largest sheepholder of the hills, flirting with the young widow of Foren Mallet.

"Already set her cap," said the duke in his wife's ear, "and her man not in the ground thirty days."

"She's merely looking after herself," said the duchess. "I would do no less."

"Oh, you would, would you?" said the duke loudly, outraged.

"Shush, Hennen. I'm teasing you."

A serving boy appeared in a doorway and blew a strangled-sounding note on a horn that startled the hall into silence. He scampered away, and Radean the steward, looking pleased with himself, tottered onto the dais.

"Lords and ladies, gentlefolk," he called, his old voice cracking, "My Lord and Lady Callas bid you welcome to the autumn feast. Please take your places."

The assembly moved toward the tables. Radean steered select guests to the high table. The duke got to his feet, cup in hand, and a hush fell over the hall.

"Friends," he said, "Thank you for attending my lady wife and me this evening. The Callas family lives to serve this land, and you are this land, every one of you. Long ago, when Dolan Callas first rode north into the Mearh Dun, he saw a wild countryside. He saw promise. He saw—"

"He saw a woman!" cackled old Vela Hyrde from the far side of the room. The hall erupted into laughter and the duke grinned.

"That he did. The first Levoreth Callas, your own sturdy Dunnish stock, whose blood runs strong in all our veins and who our family has honored every hundred years by naming so another girl-child." Here, the duke broke off at the sight of Levoreth attempting to unobtrusively edge her way toward the dais and the empty chair next to the duchess.

"And here's my niece, our own Levoreth!" called the duke, raising his cup of wine. "Back with us after these two years!" Heads swiveled, necks craned, eyes stared. Levoreth turned bright red and dropped into her chair.

"To Levoreth!" roared the duke, upending his cup.

"To Levoreth!" roared the hall back at him, raising their cups.

"Is he already drunk and the meat not served yet?" said Levoreth, frowning at her aunt.

"We'll live, my dear," said Melanor. "Besides, you should have been on time."

"Dolan!" bawled the duke, downing another cup of wine.

"Dolan!" echoed the hall.

"More wine!"

"Aye, more wine!"

"Let the feast begin!"

A procession of servants filed in and out, bearing the choicest of summer's end and the beginning of the fall. Grouse and quail, roast boar, trout from the Ciele, and haunches of venison. Baked squash, pickled onions, snap beans as sweet as honey, leeks smothered in dill sauce. Fragrant loaves of crusty bread. White rounds of goat cheese redolent with thyme. Pies, cakes, pastries stuffed with the last peaches of summer, pear and strawberry tarts. And through it all came more and more pitchers of wine: the smooth reds of Harth, the darker flavors of Mizra, and the unpredictable vintages of the north.

Levoreth toyed with some trout on her plate and then set her fork down. She did not have much of an appetite. Some bread and cheese would do. Glancing up, she caught the eye of the eldest son of Gan Ierling staring at her. He had a vacant look on his face. Particularly with his mouth hanging open. Like a sheep, she thought, and she scowled at him. Flushing, he turned away.

"Really, Levoreth," said the duchess. "You shouldn't do that. It's bad manners, and people think you're peculiar enough as it is. Besides, those Ierlings can be muddle-headed. If you glare at him too much, he'll probably fall in love with you."

"Nonsense," said Levoreth.

"How odd," said the duke.

"What's that, dear?" said his wife.

"Have you known Ginan Bly to ever miss a chance at a good meal?"

"No, I haven't. Though I recall he seems fonder of his wine than meat." And here the duchess looked at her husband, for he was in the act of refilling his own cup.

"I'd never noticed." Hennen took a sip. "At any rate, he isn't here."

He would have said more on the subject, but the sight of a roast boar's head teetering by diverted him. Resplendent with apples and plums and a stuffed grouse perched inexplicably in between the beast's ears, it was borne on the shoulders of two servants who seemed just as old as Radean the steward. They maneuvered up to the dais and plonked their burden down in front of Levoreth. She forced a smile but then ruined the effect by scowling and waving the platter away.

"I have it!" said the duke conspiratorially, in what he obviously thought was a whisper directed at his wife. He set his empty wine cup on the table and eyed it suspiciously for a moment before leaning over.

"I have it!" he repeated again. Heads turned in interest from along the high table. "Do you know why, my dear, I always feel like a little boy around our niece?"

"Later, Hennen. Have you tried this peach pastry yet? I must confess that Ada works absolute magic with the—"

"It's because she's the spitting image of my great-aunt! You know, my grandfather Toma's sister, or, er—I can't remember whose sister she was—somebody's sister, I'm sure. I lived in terror of the woman, ever since she caught me smoking cornsilk behind the barn with the stable boys. She came after me with a horsewhip. Wasn't able to sit down for a week! Horrible woman! I think she drowned in the spring thaw when I was twelve. She has the same sort of glare—like she's doing now."

"Within families," said Levoreth, "resemblances have been known to happen. Perhaps it did not occur to you, but that's why you look, sound, and behave like your father—a more pigheaded man I do not recall."

"My dear," said her aunt.

"It came to me," said the duke stubbornly, "quite clearly. While I was drinking my wine."

"Precisely," said Levoreth.

The advent of an enormous trifle, borne by several staggering servants, prevented the conversation from going any further. A collective, drawn-out sigh was heard from the other members of the high table who had been attending the exchange the duke and his niece. Old biddy Clummian, who was standing on her seat down at the second table, snorted in disappointment.

Levoreth looked out across the hall. Ierlings, Hydres smelling of sheep, flaxen-haired Meyrtts and their Wendish cousins. Mallets, Feorlins, Farlins, Ealu Fremman and his six sons. Munucs—pious to a fault, every one of them—solemn Murnans, old biddy Clummian who knew every bit of gossip there was to be had in Andolan and was never loath to pass it along. Sceohs, fat Wynn the cobbler, merry Elpendbans, and the dour Hyrian family. They were all crowded elbow to elbow, eating, drinking, talking, laughing, arguing, red-faced and cheery in the candlelight.

Dolan.

Her people—if something like that could be said. Her heart turned over in her chest. They were a stubborn lot, set in their ways and determined not to see beyond the ends of their noses. But that same quality was also what kept Dolan strong and rooted in the Mearh Dun, right on the edge of the cold north and bounded by the dangerous beauty of the Mountains of Morn.

Levoreth sat on the windowsill of her room later that night and brushed out her hair. Lights shone in the village clustered around the castle. She could smell wood smoke in the air. Two years away. Perhaps she was losing her touch. Falling asleep all the time and dreaming about the past. Dozing off during the day. Getting into ridiculous arguments with the duke in front of half the town. How mortifying! She smiled.

Dreaming about the future, said the voice within her mind. She frowned at that, but then sat for a long time, staring out into the night. Her daydream down by the Ciele. The young girl standing on a windswept plain. Black hair flowing. Gray eyes emptied of everything except sorrow. She looks like me, Levoreth thought, startled.

Precisely.

Like I looked six hundred years ago, when Dolan came riding up the Ciele and I ignored him until he could only sit on his horse, foolish and red-faced, staring like a boy at his first midwinter feast. Maybe I was foolish as well, lingering for thirty years and watching him age before my eyes. But I bound him to this land, another bulwark against the Dark. That was no violation of who he was, for he had already grown to love this place before I strengthened his resolve. I gave him three sons to carry on and sink their roots deep into the Mearh Dun. A fair trade by anyone's lights. It cannot be said I did wrong there. I loved him.

But the girl—I was never that sad when I was her age. How long ago was that? I can't remember. Perhaps I never was young. I thought it was all a lark, a wonderful adventure unfolding. I never realized. Perhaps that's what went wrong. Not badly wrong—but enough. Not realizing. I put down roots of my own without knowing it. The better part of six hundred years spent returning to these hills and inventing yet another Levoreth to weave through the descending generations of the Callas family. That was a mistake, she thought tiredly. Tormay is bigger than just the duchy of Dolan. I have been remiss and must set about fixing that. There is still time. But Min loved these hills. And I never thought I'd fall in love. I never thought I'd love this family so—my children and their children's children continuing on and on. At any rate, there's been no hint of the Dark for so long, besides the news the wolves brought me of the sceadu in the mountains. And even that creature proved to be long gone. It might not even have been a sceadu.

Yes, but have you been hunting these past years?

She lay back on her bed and promptly fell asleep, without even blowing out the candle. The wind wandered in through her window and, after investigating the hanging drapes of her bed, snuffed the candle out. It blew back outside into the night sky and headed south, winging its way toward Hearne, further to the Vornish lands and the deserts of Harth beyond.

For the first time in a long while, Levoreth did not dream.

CHAPTER TWENTY-FIVE
AN ENJOYABLE CRISIS

"You've got that look on your face again."

"I do? What look?"

Owain Gawinn tried to rearrange his features into a pleasant smile but could not. He was not fond of smiling. His wife, Sibb, was sitting by him, knitting a scarf from red wool. The needles clacked in her hands.

"There," said his wife. "You're doing it again."

"Doing what?"

"I know that face, Owain," she said. "That's the same look you got the day you told me you were leading a troop to Vomaro to hunt for Devnes Elloran. Intent, inscrutable, as solemn as an owl, but there! With a bit of glee glinting in your eyes."

"I do not feel glee, as you put it," he said, "due to the distress of others, if that's what you're saying."

"You know that's not what I'm saying. All I mean is you enjoy crises." Sibb softened her words with a smile. "There's nothing more you love than buckling on your sword and riding out the gates with your soldiers behind you."

"Perhaps," he admitted. "But if I'm out in the field, cold and tired and bruised, there's nothing I love more than riding home to you."

"Devnes Elloran!"

A strand of wool snapped in Sibb's fingers. She exclaimed in annoyance.

"That girl was a hussy if I ever saw one," she said. "She got what she had coming to her!"

"Sibb, Sibb—I wouldn't wish ogres on anyone. At any rate, the Farrow lad handily beat us there." Owain shook his head in wonder. "I still marvel at the story after all these years. He must've been the bravest fool in the land to have done what he did. Even with a column of men, I'd be wary of venturing into an ogre's lair."

"So what are you thinking of doing now?"

"Doing now?"

"Don't try that on me, Owain. I know when you've got something brewing in your head."

He smiled and kissed her, but then his face became serious.

"I've been wondering about our little foundling. To my knowledge, she's the only survivor of whatever's been murdering its way across Tormay."

"Murdering its way—what? There've been others?"

"I didn't want to trouble you, my dear," said her husband. "But there have been other incidents reported. Twice in Vo and three times in Vomaro. Mostly isolated farms. The news of them has been trickling in over the last few weeks. The same signs, the same methods of killing. Murder for no reason at all. No reason, at least, I can see."

"What are you going to do about it?"

"Do?" He picked up a ball of wool and turned it over and over in his hands. "I'm not sure yet. It doesn't affect Hearne, but the regency does have obligations. I can't just sit here and do nothing."

She touched his hand.

"No, you can't. No Gawinn would."

He smiled.

She said something else, but it was lost in the sudden shrieks and laughter that invaded the room as their four children burst through the door. Loy was scrambling about on all fours, mooing like a cow and chasing them about.

"Help, Father! Help!"

"My duties don't extend to defending the city against cows," said their father, laughing. But his smile faded when he looked up, for the girl was standing in the doorway. Her face was grave. Her eyes stared at the other children, but Owain had the distinct impression that she did not see them.

CHAPTER TWENTY-SIX
RONAN MEETS HIS MATCH

Some hot ale would do him good.

Ronan paused outside the Goose and Gold and considered. Even though night was approaching, the day still had time enough in it to accomplish what he had to do. Cypmann Galnes would be at his warehouse for at least another three hours. Plenty of time.

Any other inn would have been more to his liking, as the Goose and Gold was a dirty, run-down place, but he was chilled to the bone and the inn was conveniently on the way. A wave of warmth and noise met him, lit by lamplight and the roar of a fire burning on the hearth.

The boisterous chatter lulled as he walked through the door, and then it surged back. He recognized many of the people in the room. Guild members, mostly. Eyes slid toward him and then flicked away. Curiosity on some faces. Fear on others. He was used to it all. He sat down at the bar.

"Mulled ale," he said.

He drank and savored the heat flowing down his throat. He propped his elbows on the bar and shut his eyes. Oats and honey. A memory surfaced in his mind of his mother stirring porridge over a fire. The sun was not up yet and he remembered there had been a sound of horses nickering to someone nearby. Likely his father, bringing them something to whet their appetite before they ventured out onto the moor to crop the grasses. Oats as well, probably. His mother had turned to him and smiled, seeing him wake, and she had spooned honey into the porridge. Ronan took another sip of ale. The taste was like the memory of the taste. Porridge and honey. Oats and honey.

Someone slid onto the stool next to him.

"Go away," he said.

The Juggler tried to smile. He took a pull at his mug of ale and smacked his lips.

"Go away," repeated Ronan, not bothering to look at him.

"I was wondering," said the Juggler, "when I'd be compensated for the loss of my boy." Here, the Juggler almost managed to look sad but ruined the effect by rubbing his hands together.

"Your boy?" Ronan scowled at the fat man.

"Innkeeper, another ale! Ahh, that's more like it!" The Juggler took a gulp of his freshly filled mug. "We were family. Almost like father and son, we were. It pains me to have lost him. It pains me, lemme tell you! To have lost my son! Are you a family sort? I didn't think so. I can tell with most folks—I have a knack for it. You can't imagine the sorrow a father experiences when his son goes missing. A lamb from the fold! Ahh— someone's drunk my ale. Wuzzit you?"

"Innkeeper!" Ronan barked. "Get this man more ale!"

Another mug of ale appeared as if by magic. The Juggler blinked at it.

"Have a drink on me," said Ronan. "Drink and shut up. I don't want to hear another word."

The Juggler drank. He wiped his mouth.

"But where's my money?" he said. "Where's my—"

Ronan grabbed him by the collar and threw him headfirst into a nearby table. Plates and food went flying. The table collapsed in a tangle of legs and curses and spilled ale. The Knife had been moving so fast when he threw the fat man that it was doubtful anyone saw what he did, other than the innkeeper, who had been wiping the counter nearby. Ronan sat back down and took a drink of ale. Behind him, a joyous roar went up and the place descended into chaos.

A pitcher whizzed by Ronan's head and shattered against the wall behind the counter. He turned to survey the room. There was no logic to the brawl other than a willingness on most participants' part to fight whoever came within reach. The Juggler's face surfaced briefly in one spot, long enough for someone to break a plate over his head.

"No blades!" bawled the innkeeper.

A man staggered up against Ronan. The man took a swing at the Knife and then stepped back, aghast.

"Sorry," said the man. "Didn't recognize you."

"Don't mention it," said Ronan. He kicked the man's feet out from under him and sent him flying face-first into the thick of the fight. He sighed and mopped at his shirt. The man had spilled his ale.

"Can't a man drink in peace?" he said, glaring at the innkeeper.

The innkeeper scowled back at him.

Ronan closed the door of the Goose and Gold behind him. The street was quiet after the clamor inside the inn. It was raining. A lamp shone above the door of a pawnshop across the way, but the street was dark other than that. Time to visit the Galnes manor in Highneck Rise. He stepped out into the rain.

"Hey, mister."

The voice came from somewhere on his left. There, in the alley running back alongside the Goose and Gold. He saw some movement. Water streamed down from the eaves.

"Hey, mister."

He kept walking. He had a few hours before Cypmann Galnes would leave his warehouse down at the docks. A few hours to break into the Galnes manor. Time enough to find the missing ring.

"He's still alive, ain't he?"

That stopped him.

It was a young child's voice. High and taut with malice. There, just within the alley, he saw a face. A white blur of a face. He wiped the rain from his eyes.

"I saw him. You didn't kill him, cully."

"Kill who?" But he knew who the child was talking about.

Nothing personal, boy. We all have our jobs to do.

The boy was dead. When he killed people, they stayed dead. That was his job.

"You should know. You're the one knifing people."

But it hadn't been a knife. No. Poison. Enough of it to kill a horse.

Ronan stepped into the alley. The walls were close and high. The stones underfoot were slick with mud and garbage. There was no light at all, but he heard the scuffle of footsteps retreating before him. As quiet as a mouse, but enough for him. He'd tracked animals in the past that made less noise than mice. They were just as easy to kill.

"You saw him? Saw who?"

Abruptly, the alley angled around a corner. He strained his ears but all he could hear now was the rain pattering on the roof and dripping from the eaves.

"Who'd you see?"

The knife slid from his sleeve and into his hand without a sound.

"You know, cully, well as I do."

The voice was closer than where he thought it would be. It was a little girl's voice, he was sure of it. Brave. He had to give her that. Brave, like the boy had been. He paused. The knife felt heavy in his hand. But then he took a step closer and the night burst red with pain. A tremendous blow struck his head. Again and again. Something shattered on the cobblestones next to him. Wood splintered. He staggered, trying to duck and hide but there was nowhere to go. His body would not obey. The world spun. He caught a glimpse of the night sky above him. There were faces in it. No, not in the sky, but leaning out, peering down from above the eaves. Children's faces, wizened and evil, leering at him. A boy heaved over a wood barrel right on top of him.

The world went black.

It was still raining when he came to. He was laying face down in the mud. He tried to roll over and then immediately wished he hadn't.

At least it's still raining, he thought dizzily. I'll be able to wash this muck and blood off. Children. The Juggler's children.

I don't blame them.

Surprised they didn't cut my throat while they were at it.

"How you doing, cully?"

It was the little girl. He opened his eyes.

"Don't feel too good, do you?" she said.

She crouched down, hands folded around her knees, eyes intent on him. Just out of reach. Not that he was in any shape to try anything. The rain had plastered her brown hair against her head. She wore a shapeless brown dress several sizes too large for her, and the sleeves were bunched up in rolls around her arms. A scar lay like a hand slap across the side of her face.

"Felt better," he said. He could taste blood in his mouth. "Give me a few days."

He tried sitting up but he couldn't. The little girl did not move away, but he saw her tense. He heard feet shuffling around him in the darkness. Other children.

"You're the Knife," she said. "The big, bad Knife."

She flipped a blade in her hand, end over end and catching the haft. His knife.

"Jute," she said. "The boy who did the chimney job. He's my friend. The Juggler says he got snaffled by a fire-ward, but you can tell when he's talking rot. Besides, we saw you."

"You saw me?" he said stupidly. His head ached. This was almost as bad as when he got thrown and trampled breaking a yearling when he was a boy. Years ago. He could still remember his father's sudden yell, running toward the corral. Blacking out when the horse stomped on him. He hadn't been much older than this girl.

"Course we did," said the little girl scornfully. "Haro an' I climbed a house close by an' watched the whole thing. Jute went down the chimney, we saw that. An' then we saw you push him down when he tried to come out. We saw it all, cully."

Ronan closed his eyes and saw the boy's face again, staring up at him from within the chimney darkness. The girl stood up. She kicked him in the side. A rib grated against another and he almost blacked out from the pain of it. She crouched down next to his face.

"All that hurt like fallin' down a chimney, cully?" Her voice trembled. "I wish I could kill you, but I can't. I just can't. It ain't in me. I'd like to, for Jute. I'll be keepin' your knife. Maybe I'll grow up one day and change my mind."

He heard her footsteps fade away and then there was only the sound of raindrops dripping on cobblestones. He took a deep breath and pushed himself up to his knees.

Pain wasn't a bad thing altogether. It meant you were still alive.

He scooped up a handful of water from a puddle and tried to clean his face, but the water only ran through his fingers. His side was on fire. Broken rib, he though dully. More than one. He levered himself up to his feet, cursing the day. He was in no condition to attempt the Galnes manor. Maybe tomorrow. Maybe tomorrow would be a better day.

CHAPTER TWENTY-SEVEN
WARDS AND CARELESSNESS

Jute was a boy, and boys are best at forgetting, even if sometimes those things that they forget are important. And so, for a while, he forgot about the wihht and he forgot about Nio Secganon. If truth be told, he even forgot about the hawk, for the university ruins were so strange and marvelous they drove all else from his mind.

Emboldened by familiarity, he took to roaming the ruins. Ten minutes could not pass by without him encountering a ward of some sort, but he became adept at recognizing them, even if their warning was as unobtrusive as a single, warm stone underfoot in a cold hall or a shadow that fell slightly crooked while all others fell straight. Out of youthful curiosity—or simple foolishness—he experimented with wards at random, figuring out how to trip them by tossing stones or by sprinting madly through the danger spots.

This was not always the safest diversion, as Jute discovered a certain ward always produced large dogs that glimmered blue as if lit by strange fire. He also discovered that these dogs ran extremely fast and had sharp-looking teeth. They never barked; the only noise they made was the scuffle of paws on stone. Jute had a suspicion they were illusion, but he was not willing to gamble his flesh to test this.

The first time one such dog appeared, Jute had the luck to be standing near a wall made of roughly hewn stone, perfectly suited for climbing. And climb it he did, in a flash, for his heart nearly jumped up his throat when the dog appeared. The thing roamed about the foot of the wall for about an hour, glaring up at him with enormous blue eyes. And then it had vanished, disappearing like a blown-out candle flame. He stayed clinging high up on the wall with cramping fingers and toes for a good while after. One never knew.

In a hall that must have once been used for ceremonies and the like—for the ceiling, high above him, was festooned with hundreds of elegant chandeliers that he had never seen in any other part of the school – he discovered an unusual ward.

The floor of the hall was tiled with large squares of black and white marble arranged in whorls looping and weaving through each other with no apparent pattern. When Jute came to the center of the hall, he found a circle of blue stone set within the floor. He stood in the middle of it and admired the blue stone for a moment, for it had a lovely gleam and looked, to his eye, valuable and regretfully wasted as floor paving.

To his alarm, however, as soon as he stepped off the circle he discovered that he could not control his movement and marched stiff-legged all around the hall in a nonsensical pattern that would have done justice to a drunkard. At first, he was frightened, for he assumed that some sort of creature or fire or chasm was about to appear. Nothing of the sort happened, however, and he continued marching crazily about the hall, hopelessly caught by the compulsion of the ward.

After about an hour of this, he was cross and tired. By a stroke of luck, though, his wandering path brought him veering toward the blue circle, which had not happened yet in the last hour, so large was the hall. As he neared the blue stone, he felt the compulsion on him lessen and with a tremendous wrench he leapt into the safety of the circle. He sat there panting and mentally cursing all wizards, alive or dead.

Growing hungry, he attempted the floor again but was caught by the same compulsion. He could have wept, so tired was he. This time, however, his fatigue aided his escape, for with drooping head and eyes fixed on the floor he noticed that the compulsion marched him around only on the black stones. Not once was he allowed to step on a white stone.

The next time he neared the circle of blue stone in the center of the hall, he was ready. He leapt into its safety and then ventured back out, careful to step on a white stone. The compulsion did not seize him and he left the hall, stepping from white stone to white stone.

One afternoon, Jute wandered down a hallway lined with old mosaics. Many of them were missing stones, rendering faces eyeless and dragons toothless. A fool grinned at him with seven scarlet balls describing a circle around his patchwork body. A warrior leaned on a bloody sword under a bone-white moon. Horns mutely blaring, a hunt rode through a gaunt and ghostly wood. A fearsome dragon of black-scaled bulk curled its length about the base of a crumbling tower, eyes glinting red and a wisp of flame escaping from the massive mouth. The sun set on the horizon of an ocean that seemed to swell and surge with movement—but when he stepped closer, startled, to inspect the tiny stones of the mosaic, they were only that: tiny stones of varied shades of blue and green. Something stirred at the corner of his eye, and he whirled, fearing a ward. But nothing moved again. There were only long, sloping shadows from the setting sun and the dust motes that turned and glided within the light. For a moment, he thought he heard a voice whisper his name, but then there was only silence. He turned and walked quickly to the end of the hallway, the back of his neck prickling uncomfortably.

Through a door, Jute found himself standing in a high gallery that ran the length of one side of huge hall that was, perhaps, a staggering three stories in interior height. To his recollection, he had never been in this part of the university before. Tall, thin clerestory windows lined the walls, and the late sunlight streamed in, shining on the white stone walls and filling the place with a blinding radiance. Such was the reflective quality of the white stone that he could not see a single shadow cast anywhere in the room. Fragile pillars rose up from the floor below and swept up and up and up into an arched ceiling that seemed to float on the slender columns that lined the walls. At the far end of the gallery he found a winding stair that circled down and down until he stood on the hall floor. Faces were carved into the pillar facades—both men and women, old and young. He counted them as he walked along but soon lost track, for the pillars were not arranged in any particular order but were myriad and rose from the floor like the trunks of trees in some strange, unearthly forest. It was the oddest room he had been in yet, but there was a quiet peace to the place, and it seemed untouched by any of the ravages of the Midsummer War that had marred so much of the university.

CHAPTER TWENTY-EIGHT
A DISTURBING ENTRY ON SCEADUS

The night arrived as the sun slipped down into the ocean. The moon crept up into the sky, but no stars were visible yet. To the east, a dark bank of clouds rolled toward the city.

Nio sat in his library and stared out the window, a book open in his lap. Fynden Fram's *Endebyrdnes of Gesceaft*. The Order of Creatures. He knew the book by heart. There was not much point in reading it, but he was looking for reassurance. Vainly looking, of course.

When he had returned to the house after meeting the Juggler, he had found the wihht shambling about the rooms. It was unsettling, for his command over the thing should have kept it waiting in the basement. Somehow, his control was fraying. The thing had been unwilling or unable to give him much of a reason for its behavior, only mumbling that it was hungry. It needed food. Just some food. Just a taste. A bite. But wihhts didn't need food, like a man or an animal needs food to survive. Wihhts survived on the strength of their maker's will.

At least, that's what he had assumed.

The thing had lurched off to the basement without protest as soon as he snapped out the order. Still, it made him uneasy. There were definitely some things about wihhts he did not know yet.

But Fynden Fram, despite his genius, had nothing to say in his *Nokhoron Nozhan Endebyrdnes of Gesceaft* that Nio did not already know. Wihhts only ate on command of their master, and only then to bring about a modification their master willed. Nio thought uncomfortably about the wihht absorbing his blood. It had wanted to take more than he had wanted to give, hadn't it?—right at the end? That didn't line up with what old Fram had written. No matter. He would unmake the wihht soon. Besides, it would be good to have the thing unraveled and gone before Severan or one of the other old fools might come by the house and stumble on it.

The irritating thing about Fynden Fram's writing was that, despite the wealth of detail, his descriptions of creatures tended to be divorced from historical context. For example, if he wrote of giants, he had nearly nothing to say of their origins, or in what lands or wars they had been encountered. Rather, he provided terse descriptions of physiognomy, habits, and social customs. In addition, there were often details on how a creature interacted with magic or was affected by the same.

The giant, or *oyrs*, can live to ages of over three hundred years, though they reach their full maturity at the first hundred. In death, they are laid out upon the ground where, in some curious interaction of the moonlight, they slowly turn to stone. In appearance, the giant resembles the race of man, though one must be a distance away from a giant in order to notice the similarity. If one gets too close, besides the hazard of proximity, one will find the giant's face so large that it cannot be viewed in entirety; rather, it must be looked on in part—here is the nose, here is a huge, staring eye, over there is a portion of mouth or cheekbone.

The scarcity of historical setting in the entries gave one the unpleasant feeling that all the creatures the old scholar wrote of were still alive.

Such as the sceadus.

A scant page in the book was devoted to details of the sceadus. It was the shortest entry among hundreds of other entries that ran from the next shortest—five pages about cobolds—to the longest—seventeen pages about dragons, a section that made for fascinating, but unsettling reading. Almost as unsettling as what Fram had written concerning sceadus.

The sceadus were not created by Anue. Rather, they were made out of darkness, woven from the feorh of it into forms of their master's choosing. Legend tells that only three sceadus were ever brought into existence, though I am not certain of this claim. Some analogy exists between the making of a wihht and the making of a sceadu. An external will must be brought to bear upon the essence desired as the foundation material for the creature. There, the similarity between the two types ends. A wihht, of course, can be made from nearly anything, combinations of material such as earth, wood, water, fire, or stone. A sceadu, on the other hand, can only be made from darkness, and thus is a thing of pure evil. Certain histories indicate that the sceadus are close in power to the anbeorun themselves. While some have claimed the ability to fashion wihhts of all shapes and strengths, no man has ever had the power to fashion a sceadu. No man ever will—thankfully. This begs the question: if not the gods, then who was powerful enough to have created the three sceadus?

That was the question. Perhaps one of the four wanderers, the anbeorun, could command enough will to shape darkness? But they would never have reason, for the creation of a sceadu meant a level of evil in the creator equal to the abomination created. That made no sense in light of what was known of the wanderers. According to history, the anbeorun existed to guard against the Dark. Yet the mosaic indicated a tie of some kind between the anbeorun of fire, Aeled, and a sceadu.

The entry in Fynden Fram's anthology continued.

A sceadu can take any shape it chooses: stone or shadow, the wind crossing the plain, animals, man, a tree growing in the forest. It mimics the shapes of things that already are, just as its power is merely a reflection of the strength of its maker and the darkness. There is no reliable way to determine the presence of a sceadu, though one account of the death of Allevian Tobry—

Who was Allevian Tobry? Nio had always wondered about that, for he had never come across any other mention of the name.

—records that a stranger appeared at his gates, cloaked and hooded despite the summer's heat, and so brought death to that lord with a touch of his hand. Everyone of his household felt an intense cold emanating in waves from the stranger, as ripples do spread out around a stone tossed into a pool. After the stranger had departed, all fell sick of a lingering fever. The wizard of the household claimed it had been no man, but a sceadu. I cannot vouch for the truth of this account, as there is little other firsthand knowledge of encounters with sceadus. There is no known way of killing the creatures, though they themselves feed on death and will kill for no reason at all. They need death in order to live. This is not surprising, as they are the oldest servants of the Dark.

CHAPTER TWENTY-NINE
LISS GALNES

The following day, Ronan made his way to the Street of Willows in the Highneck Rise district. It was still raining. It had not let up through the night. The gutters ran with water.

The worst of his injuries had faded to dull aches over night. Except for his ribs. He'd have to be careful there. He had always been a quick healer. His mother had said that came from her side of the family.

A sour smile crossed his face. He could only hope the children wouldn't breathe a word of what they'd done. If anyone found out about it, he'd be the laughingstock of the Guild. But those children would be thinking hard on what they'd done. Especially when they were alone. They'd be looking over their shoulders for a long time. He'd been the Silentman's Knife for seven years now, settling matters in alleys and in back rooms where his prey had nowhere left to run to, except into the tired arms of death.

Death. Like a shadow always on his heels, treading closer over the years until it was almost like his own shadow. But they weren't friends, even though he had handed over many souls into its embrace. No, it was a working relationship, begun in distaste and dulling over the years into numbness. He didn't dream anymore. His memories no longer troubled him, for they also had numbed.

But it would be different when he went to Flessoray. It was too late to go back home, but he could go to the islands. If he could get the Silentman to release him from his duties. Maybe he would have to sneak out of the city. The Flessoray Islands were north, off the coast of Harlech. They rose up out of the sea, made of stone and scrub pines. Folk lived apart there, content with their lives and having no interest in the outside world of Tormay. Life was measured by the patience of the sea and by the wind wearing away the days until stone and man alike were scraped clean to their bones. Perhaps then, there, things would be different, and he would let the wind blow through him until he was empty.

The Street of Willows was lined with manors, complacent behind their high walls. Gates were locked against the weather and thieves such as himself. The trees from which the street took its name stood in rows of drooping branches on either side of the cobblestones. He stood underneath one and considered the wall a few yards further down. Water dripped down from the leaves onto his head. Under normal circumstances, without broken ribs, the height of the wall would not have been a problem. He scowled. Children!

Ronan wasn't getting any warmer, or any drier for that matter, so he climbed the wall. Just as Arodilac had said, the tree outside the Galnes wall provided an easy ascent. He crept out onto a branch that reached toward the top of the wall and listened for a moment. But he heard no wards whispering, no rustle of invisible threads tightening, ready to snap around him. And then he was over and down, wincing as his ribs grated, a dark shape in the rain that melted into the darker shadows of the shrubbery.

It was a small garden, filled with bushes and trees that crowded about a patch of grass. The rain had stripped the flowers from the bushes, and everywhere the ground was dappled with white petals. Lights shone in the windows of the manor beyond. And there were the apple trees. He reached out and plucked one. Tart and sweet. Good, but certainly not good enough to warrant this mess. There were better apples to be bought in the city. Something tickled uneasily at the back of his mind, but then he thought no more of it. A job was a job, regardless of the client's reasons.

Ronan paused in the shadows against the manor wall and pressed his ear to the stone. He heard nothing. No wards muttering their hidden menace. Nothing at all. He shrugged and began to climb. The walls were made of granite and offered easy holds. His hands and feet were unerring in their instincts. His ribs twinged in protest but he ignored them.

He stopped at one window, just to the side of the casement. The glass was ajar, and he heard the sound of a lute. The notes bore a strange resonance in them that brought to mind the sea. They sounded singly. One like the wavering call of a seagull, others like wind plucking the rigging of a ship, still others that belled in the low tones of the buoy that swayed at the harbor mouth of Hearne.

He edged closer and peered inside. A girl sat upon a stool, her head drooping over the instrument. He could not see her entire face. But he could see enough. The angle of cheekbone, stark with shadow, a white brow and neck framed by a wing of hair, burnished blue-black like night on water. Her fingers wandered across the strings, slow and blind in their movement, for her eyes were closed. Silently, he eased away and resumed his climb.

A dormer window provided entrance to the house from the top of the roof. Ronan tripped the lock with a length of wire and slipped inside. Immediately within was a small room, dark except for light glowing from beneath a door. He took off his wet jacket and boots and then settled down in a corner.

Anyone can rob a house. But to do the job well takes more than just skill. It takes an instinct for places—being able to walk into a house and let your senses reach out and become aware of spaces, shapes, shifts in temperature, drafts betraying holes and hidden rooms, the creaks of old wood, of water dripping, mice mumbling within walls. No amount of teaching or practice can guarantee this; it's instinctive.

A few notes drifted up to Ronan's ears. The lute. He could smell bread baking—the old cook hardly ever left her kitchen, according to Arodilac. As he listened, he began to sense more: the tick of a grandfather clock, warmth from the kitchen stove rising up a chimney and exhaling into all the floors of the house, the contented creak of beams and boards complacent about the rain outside. There was a comfortable shabbiness to the place, as if many generations had been birthed and lived and died within its walls, leaving their marks in staircases worn smooth, faded paintings, and the ghosts of memories lingering in the place they loved.

Ronan eased open the door and found himself at the top of a staircase. The lute played faintly from several floors down. The steps were silent under his weight—good workmanship and heavy wood. He smiled complacently. He had no fear of discovery within the manor. It was a large place, with surely many hiding spots if someone approached. And he knew—he sensed—there were only two people within: the cook far below in her kitchen, and the girl still playing her lute. Two floors down was his guess. He could sense something else. A touch of power concentrated in a tiny place. The ring.

Far below him, he heard the lute stop.

Footsteps creaked up the stairs. The girl emerged up from the shadows, still carrying her lute. She stopped in front of him, an almost incurious look on her face. The lamplight brought her face alive. He tried to move, but could not.

"There are easier houses in Hearne to rob," she said. He could not answer.

She regarded him for a moment and then spoke again.

"I am mistress of this house." Her eyes turned on his, dark blue as a storm sky. Or gray. Yes—he was mistaken. They were gray. "My name is Liss Galnes."

Whatever held him vanished. He stumbled back and caught himself on the wall.

"It would only take the blink of an eye," he said, furious and shaky with fear at the same time, hand groping for the knife at his side.

"Not in this house," Liss said.

He believed her.

"Come," she said, turning away.

Liss led him downstairs, through room after room and more staircases. Faces stared down from paintings: knowing, secretive looks of men and women; children standing gravely with pet dogs; a mother holding a silk-swaddled infant who seemed to smile at him. Faded furniture, tall casement windows that reached up to the cobwebs of vaulted ceilings. Rain streaked against the glass. They crossed the polished wooden floor of a hall. Mirrors showed a girl who seemed to drift like a feather, followed by the grim-faced man moving heavily in her wake.

"Where are we going?" he said.

She smiled for the first time. "The kitchen. You're hungry."

He was about to deny it, more out of contrariness than anything else, but it was true. Besides the apple in the garden, he hadn't eaten anything that day.

The cook stood chopping parsley at a table in the center of the kitchen. She was an old woman with a face as brown and worn as a walnut. A fire burned on the hearth, pots bubbled, and kettles steamed. Iron pans and ladles hung from brackets on the wall, and a row of windows looked out onto an herb garden.

"Didja catch him?" said the cook, intent on her parsley and not turning her head.

"Him?" echoed Liss. She looked at Ronan. He had the distinct impression she already knew his name.

"My name's Ronan," he said. "Ronan of Aum."

"Sit, then—Ronan of Aum. His name," she said, turning to the cook, "is—"

"I know, I know," said the old woman. "I haven't gone deaf in my old age, though you think me feeble, with all your coddling, trying to do the cooking and whatnot. You'll be the death of me, girl."

Liss smiled.

Ronan sat down to soup, fresh bread, cheese, and a mug of red wine—tired, bemused, and not sure what to think. If anything, there was a pathetic humor in it all, in the fact that the revered Knife of the Guild could not defend himself against a handful of children. That the Knife could not even rob a house guarded by two women. But who would believe that? Certainly not the Silentman. He shook his head.

"What's that, then?" said the cook. "Don't like my soup?"

"No, no," he said. "It's good."

"Hush, Sanna," said Liss. "Leave him to his food. There'll be time enough to bother him later."

"Shaking his head like that," said the old woman, "with a face long enough for a horse. Who is he now, besides a name? Has he come to rob the house or is he another half-wit like young whatsisname, mooning about and eating all the cakes?"

"Hush."

"That's no way to eat the food. He'll sicken with that frown on him, no matter how good the fare. Why, what you'll get from this hearth is better than what even the regent sups on. Him and all his gold plates and—"

"Sanna."

The old woman shut her mouth, but began to clatter pots and pans about in the sink. Liss gazed at Ronan. He noticed that her eyes, even though he had thought them gray, seemed to shade blue or green at times, depending on how the light fell. He pushed his plate away, the bread uneaten. A sniff came from the vicinity of the sink.

"Why did you come here?" she asked.

"I think you already know," he said.

He was tired. None of it mattered anymore. Loyalty to the Guild. Serving the Silentman. Whether or not he could find the boy and prove his own innocence. The islands of Flessoray waiting for him. All the memories uneasy in his mind. The girl from Vomaro—how old would she be now?—surely graying and gone fat with bearing children. They could go to the shadows, every one of them, for all he cared. Besides, he hated the city. He always had. Sleep would be nice. That was what death would be. A dreamless sleep with no end.

"Perhaps," she said. "But I'd like to hear it from you."

Ronan shrugged, not caring anymore. "I work for the Thieves Guild. A job came through several days ago to recover the ring of Arodilac Bridd. You have the ring. Simple as that."

"Ooh, the Guild," broke in the cook. "I always thought if they were foolish enough to break in, they'd come for that sea-jade figurine in the drawing room—nice piece. Fetch a better price than that ring. I'm more inclined to a string of pearls myself. Pity the oysters are always so stubborn about giving 'em up, the grumpy little beggars. Here." She banged down a plate of cakes in front of him. They were tiny and sprinkled with chopped almonds. "Eat."

"Surely there's more to it than that," said Liss. She took a cake, as if to encourage him, and ate it in three neat bites.

Again, he shrugged.

"It doesn't matter if you know. I'm already ruined." He bit into a cake—apple—and almost found the strength to smile. "Nimman Botrell hired the Guild to recover the ring. He doesn't approve of you as wife of the next regent of Hearne. And that ring isn't just any old ring, it's—"

"The regent," said the old woman. "Doesn't approve of my Liss! Why, I'll give him what for, the wretched man! I hear he doesn't like fish at all."

"Of course," said Liss, ignoring the cook. "Of course it isn't just an old ring. Why else do you think I made him give it to me? I knew it wouldn't be long before you came looking for the thing. The tide always brings me what I need."

He almost choked on his apple cake.

"What? Me? Arodilac said that he gave you the ring impulsively. He climbed the wall, fell in love . . ."

Her eyes were unblinking and remote. He could not look away. The gray of them deepened to blue and then receded back to gray, like the surf of the sea washing up and away on a shore. Something ancient and serene gazed out at him, as patient as the tide. She blinked, once, and released him.

"Men can be impulsive. Particularly for love of a girl." She frowned, as if puzzled by the idea.

"It's an unusual ring."

He looked down, unwilling to meet her gaze. Somehow, he knew it would be better—much better—to tell her what he knew, rather than have it taken from him in some other way.

"It's his family's ring, passed from father to heir. It holds the key to the wards of the Bridd castle in Hull."

She waited patiently, displaying no interest in plundering the wealth of the Bridds, saying nothing. He took an apple cake and fumbled it to bits in his hands. It was the last part, of course. The regent didn't care about his nephew. Only a fool would believe that. But a ring that could open up the secret ways into the regent's castle—now that was something to care about. Why did she want him?

"The ring also . . ." Ronan trailed off in to silence. The tide turned within her eyes—gray to blue and back again. Infinitely patient. Water, wearing away the stone. The moon sailing over the sea to its dark, unseen horizon. Endless and inexorable.

"It holds the keys to wards in the regent's castle. Spells that guard his castle. Here, in Hearne." There. He'd said it. Now he could leave. Leave and tell the Silentman of his failure, and then wait for death, however it would be meted out.

She reached for the last apple cake, broke it in half and offered him a piece. She smiled and she was only a girl again. Behind them, scrubbing potatoes in the sink, the cook broke into wordless song.

"For a thief, you're an honest man."

"An honest dead man, mistress," he said. His voice was dull.

Ronan's thoughts drifted. He could creep out of the city at night. Over the south wall where it angled near that hostelry with the conveniently high roof. And then disappear. Forever. It would have to be north. The Guild never went there. There was nothing to steal except ice and snow and, farther north, the treasures of giants—and no one stole from them, even the Guild. Or perhaps he could go east, past Mizra and into the wastes.

"You needn't run," she said, frowning.

"You can read thoughts as well?"

"It's evident from your face." And she slid something across the table toward him. A ring. A gold ring fashioned in the shape of a hawk.

"Take it," she said.

"You'd just give it to me?" He reached out for the ring.

"No, of course not," she said. "Why else did the tide bring you here? You'll do something for me in return."

His hand hovered over the ring. "And that is?"

"In seven days' time, a ball is to be held at the regent's castle in honor of the Autumn Fair. I wish to attend, uninvited though I will be."

She smiled placidly, as if talking of a visit planned to the dressmaker's. "I'm afraid my good Cypmann Galnes has not noble enough blood to be asked to such an affair, else I'd lean on his graces. You will bring me into the castle, unseen, and shall keep me unseen through the evening. I've heard of your particular skills. In return, you may take the ring back to the boy." Her hand flicked in dismissal. "If I have you, then I have no need of the ring. I never intended to use it. That's all."

"That's all?" He gaped at her.

"Yes." Liss smiled at him. A girl with gray eyes. Her eyes were gray now.

"You don't just walk into the regent's castle!" said Ronan. "Do you know what you're asking? Particularly on a night as that. In all of Hearne, there isn't a more impossible place to enter unwanted."

"There is another place more perilous in this city," she said. The color of her eyes was shifting again. Gray washing into blue.

"Where?" He spoke without thinking.

"This house."

And it was back again. Someone—something—ancient looking through her eyes, examining him and weighing who he was. The ring was strangely cold in his hand, as if it had taken none of the warmth of her body. He knew he would not be able to deny her, even though what she asked might prove beyond him. The sea surged within her eyes and she sat before him, a wisp of a girl with her hands folded on the table. He suddenly realized he feared her more than the Silentman himself.

"You aren't Liss Galnes, are you," he said.

The girl said nothing.

"Sakes, dearie," said the cook, turning from the sink with her hands covered in suds. "Liss Galnes died near three years ago now. Caught the influenza and withered up like the flower she was. Just like her mother before her. Inconvenient for her, but timely for my mistress. She needed a place, like a hermit crab needs herself a new shell every now and again."

"Who are you?" His voice sounded hollow. "And how is it that Cypmann Galnes still calls this place home?"

But they said nothing to that. The girl and the old woman merely looked at him, the one with beady, black eyes and the other with eyes like the shifting sea.

CHAPTER THIRTY
TREATIES AND FOUL MOODS

"Enter!" barked Botrell.

The regent was sitting on the end of his bed and contemplating the floor. It didn't seem to be shimmering in such a sickening fashion anymore. He was in a filthy mood, for he had stayed up late with the envoy from the court of Oruso Oran IX in Damarkan. Who would have guessed that blue-eyed icicle would have had such a capacity for wine? But he'd shown him. The man had been scarcely coherent by the time his attendants had carried him off to his rooms.

The court chamberlain peeked in through the door.

"The Lord Captain of Hearne requests an audience, my lord."

"Tell him to come back another day! Next month!"

The chamberlain vanished for a moment and then reappeared.

"He says the matter is urgent and cannot wait another day. He says it involves the security of your people and Hearne and, consequently, the safety of your own lordship. He apologizes most humbly for bothering you in your bedchamber."

"Tell him to come back next year!"

The door closed and then reopened almost in the same instant.

"He says—"

"Good morning, my lord regent," drawled Owain Gawinn. He pushed past the chamberlain and stood smiling.

"Gawinn," gritted Botrell. "It's early. Don't you have a city to watch over? Aren't there soldiers to drill and horses to be galloped about?"

"Fear not, my lord. I watch over Hearne with a jealous and unsleeping eye. So have the Gawinns always served the regents of Hearne, and so do I. A danger has arisen, my lord. It requires your attention, even though, as you've pointed out, the hour is early. Nearly noon, isn't?"

There was ice in his voice and in his smile. Botrell stirred uneasily on the edge of his bed. When he was honest with himself, he had to admit that the Lord Captain of Hearne made him nervous. The man was much too serious about his job.

"Have the old scholars in the university uncovered something dangerous? Pirates threatening our sea trade again? Is the Thieves Guild overstepping their bounds?"

"Nothing like that," said Owain. "The university ruins contain nothing more dangerous than rats, in my estimation. The last pirate to plague our coast died on my sword three years ago. And the Guild? Bah! If you gave me a free hand with them, I'd hang the lot—but, as ever, I defer to your notion that they somehow encourage trade."

"Then what do you speak of?"

"I have reports of strange killings to the east of us. Isolated farms wiped out. Entire villages decimated. All in the last month."

"Old news," said the regent, yawning. "None of our business. The duchies can look after their own."

"The massacres happened in three different duchies as well as in northeastern Harth. Twice in Vo, thrice in Vomaro, once each in Harth and Dolan, and now just five or so days ago again in Vo. All the duchies have been in contact with me, as well as Damarkan's envoy. That was one of the reasons Damarkan sent their man north. According to the old treaty drawn up after the Midsummer War—a treaty, no doubt, you are conversant with, as it outlines the balance of power between Hearne and the duchies of Tormay—when danger threatens multiple duchies, leadership in such a situation is deferred to the regency in Hearne."

"The treaty says that?" Botrell was reasonably sure he had read the old document. Years ago, true, but he would have remembered such a ridiculous and imprudent provision. His head hurt.

"It does."

"Probably just bandits. Unfortunate, but merely part of life."

"No," said Owain. "Bandits steal, even if they sometimes will kill. Whoever is doing these killings isn't interested in gold. Nothing is ever stolen. Except for life. So I ask your permission, my lord, to scout in the east where the massacres happened. It would do us well to learn what we can of this new enemy. Besides the obligations of the treaty, who knows but there might come a day when the killers are within our walls?"

"I suppose there have been no witnesses," said Botrell, mentally cursing whichever addled ancestor had seen fit to sign such a treaty. An expedition of the sort Owain was intending would cost much gold.

"There is one. A girl of perhaps eight or nine years. She was found by a passing trader at the site of the last massacre in Vo."

"Aha! So she saw those involved!"

"Doubtlessly. However, the terror she has been through has struck her mute. She responds to little that is said to her. The only noise she makes is when she screams in her nightmares. I have hopes of her speaking someday—"

"Hmmph."

"—but for now she is in the care of my good lady. What do you say, my lord? Do I have your permission to undertake my duties? I'm confident that you, as ever, are eager to see our laws fulfilled."

Owain took a little of the sting out of his words by smiling, but it was a wintry smile at best. That was all he could manage for the regent. There was silence in the room. Both men thought their thoughts, one smiling and the other scowling, both despising the other.

"Oh, all right!" burst out Botrell. "Hunt and be damned! Just get out of my sight!"

"Thank you, my lord," said Owain, bowing. "As ever, you are a wise and able ruler."

"Just remember to leave someone behind to guard the city," said Botrell nastily.

"To be sure," said the other, and then he was gone.

"Chamberlain!" shouted the regent. "Bring me some wine!"

CHAPTER THIRTY-ONE
A MEMORY OF WOLVES

In the town of Andolan, near the castle, was a small church. It was a tumbledown building made of stone, weathered by the years and grown over with gray-green lichen. The church was older than the castle, even older than the walls of Andolan themselves. It had been built before Dolan Callas ever rode north to the Mearh Dun, when there had been only a hamlet where the town of Andolan now stood. The church was dedicated to the nearly forgotten sleeping god and was watched over by one old priest. He spent most of his days feeding the town cats who regarded the churchyard as their home. He also mumbled his way through mostly unattended vespers once a week and pottered about in the cemetery behind the church, tending the roses and weeding around the headstones.

It was midmorning when Levoreth walked around the side of the church. A rose bush grew at the back of the cemetery, where the oldest gravestones stood near the town wall. The bush had vines as thick as tree branches. They gripped the stones of the wall and climbed upward until they spilled over the top in scarlet blooms. Bees buzzed amidst the growth, and the air was heavy with perfume. The priest, armed with a rusty pair of shears, tottered around the perimeter of the bush, poking at some vines that curled out toward the nearest headstones. It was there, at the back of the cemetery, that the members of the Callas family were buried.

"Here," said Levoreth. "Let me get that for you."

"Thank you, my dear," said the priest, startled at the girl's appearance but happy to relinquish the shears. He blinked in admiration as she clipped the vines back.

"Eh," he said, mopping his brow, "Thought it might be the shears, but perhaps it's just my arms." He blinked at her some more. "Why, it's Lady Levoreth. I haven't set eyes on your pretty face in nigh on five years."

"Two years," said Levoreth. "You remember? I sat up with you for midwinter compline the evening the great snows started falling. No one else came."

"Ah," he said. "The great snows. What a winter that was. My poor cats refused to leave the church, even after they'd caught all the mice. Not that I blame them, with the wolves coming down out of the mountains. It was a wonder we didn't have them wandering about the streets."

"Aye," she said. "It's a wonder." She stepped back and looked up at the rosebush. "This old vine certainly has seen better days." A sparrow rustled its way through the leaves and trilled a burst of song down at her.

"That it has," said the old man. "That it has. Like us all." He sighed in contentment, sat down on a fallen headstone, and glanced about the cemetery. Sunlight lay on the headstones, on the mossed-over paths that ambled between the graves, the crooked back of the church hiding the cemetery from the rest of the town.

"What a pleasant place to sleep."

"I've always thought so," said Levoreth.

And sleep, the priest did—his head nodding forward until his chin was resting on his cassock.

It was remarkable how many Levoreths had been buried in the cemetery. One double headstone in particular drew her. It looked to be the oldest, and it was. Over six hundred years of sun and rain and snow had hollowed out the engravings until the letters were almost illegible. She knew them by heart, however. With one finger, she traced the stone: Dolan Callas. First Duke of Dolan. Levoreth Callas. Beloved Wife and Mother. Her namesake. Her own self. A smile crossed her face. She sat down upon the grass, the headstone at her back, and closed her eyes.

Two years ago. The coming of the wolves. That was why she had left Andolan for the solitude of the country manor in the east. At least, that was the practical reason. She would have left sooner or later, for she could never bear the town that long. Too many memories. The wolves had hurried her decision.

Two years ago, she had been woken in the night by the wind murmuring at her window in the castle. She had leaned against the sill to listen. Normally, she did not trust the wind, for she found it fickle, given to fits of whimsy and equally quick in turning to violence. It was not tamable, at least not by her hand. But that night had been different. She could not ignore the melancholy in the wind's voice. And in its murmur she heard news of an approaching winter, of shadows stirring on the far side of the mountains, and of wolves coming west.

The following night, midwinter's eve, she had heard the howl of a wolf lingering in the wind as she trudged back to the castle after compline. She had stopped, surprised, for there was fear in the wolf's voice. The snow drifted in her hair as she listened. Fear in a wolf was something rare.

And then the reports had started trickling in from the shepherds in the far reaches of the Mearh Dun. Huge timber wolves, the likes of which had never been seen west of the Mountains of Morn. Fierce beasts that terrorized the folds where the flocks were wintering, unafraid of dog and man alike. It had been only days later when the first one was sighted near the walls of Andolan. Children were no longer allowed outside the town. One day, the remains of a trader and his packhorses were found dead in the snow, three miles from the gate.

On that evening, she had wrapped herself in a cloak and slipped out of the town. A full moon was rising, and its light shone on the snow. Her breath steamed in the air. For half an hour she trudged through the snow before stopping. She stood on a hill, bare of anything except the snow and her footprints. In every direction there were only the rolling slopes of the Mearh Dun. There was not a cottage or tree in sight. She stood and listened to the land.

Then she had heard them, far to the north. She sent forth her thoughts and called. She subsided into silence, waiting in the cold, under the night and a scattering of stars like jewel shards and the moon with its pale eye.

They had come in a rush, shadows loping over the next hill, vanishing down into the divide and then hurtling up the hill she stood on. Snow flew through the air from their paws as the pack surged around her, a few daring to brush her hands with their cold noses. Tongues lolled and eyes flashed amber, blue, and polished as wet stone. They stilled their pacing and stood around her—near a hundred, she counted. A black wolf stalked forward. His eyes, gray as a winter sky, met hers, and then he dropped his head to nose at her palm.

Mistress of Mistresses.

"Drythen Wulf," she said. "The Mountains of Morn are the home of your folk, not the Mearh Dun."

Aye. You speak truth.

"What has brought you and yours west? Does your clan entire think to chase the sun?"

He had laughed at that, soundlessly, his yellowed teeth glistening and his eyes half closed. And then his head drooped, and a shiver ran through the watching pack.

Nay, Mistress. We have no heart for legends anymore. We have run away from our land.

We run, echoed the pack. Their voices were doleful.

"What follows after you?"

But his head had drooped lower at her question. She knelt in the snow and took his shaggy head between her hands.

"Drythen Wulf, what follows after you?"

A sceadu, Mistress. A cursed shadow out of our ancient legends. The home of our ancestors has become a haunt of shadows and dread. The mountains are no longer ours. The deer took herself away, and the rock hare vanishes since summer's sun. Our small ones dream of horrors and no longer wake, leaving us to chase the sun. He trembled with anger. His teeth snapped shut on the air.

"Are you sure of this? It has been many hundreds of years since such a one has been seen in this realm. There were three of them from days of old."

The wolf did not speak, but only gazed at her with his gray eyes. She nodded, then, in acceptance of his words. The pack waited in silence around her.

"The Mearh Dun cannot be your home. Your coming has brought great distress to its folk. They are a gentle people and unused to the ways of the wolf."

Are we not also your folk? Does the lady grow to love man more than her four-footed subjects? The nyten of mountain, hill, forest, and plain?

"Nay, nay," she had said, vexed under the eyes of the wolf.

Would have us south, then, into the crowded plains of man and the desert beyond? The north will not have us. Giants walk there in the fields of ice, beyond the realm of man, and they have never been friendly to our folk. Should we run west, into the great sea?

"I would not have you anywhere except the land that bears you love, the Mountains of Morn."

We cannot, Mistress. Unless—and here the wolf paused, unsure at his own daring—*unless we have your company to search out the sceadu and make it safe for our little ones.*

And so was struck the deal that brought Levoreth east from Andolan, bargained under the night sky and far from the sleeping town. The pack bore witness and the wolf brought forth a gawky-legged pup with his own black fur and eyes as silver as moonlight on the sea. It padded about her feet and licked her hand.

My own whelp, Mistress of Mistresses. I would have you name him, for someday he will lead the pack, after the sun has called me to the great chase.

She had named the pup Ehtan, after the great wolf that the Aro had bidden to hunt among the stars, tirelessly seeking after the Dark. She smiled and awoke in the stillness of the cemetery. The old priest was gone. The air was full of light and the sweetness of the rose bush.

"Aye," she said aloud. "This is a place well-suited for sleep." She stood up, somewhat stiffly, and lingered for a moment at the headstone of Dolan Callas before walking away.

CHAPTER THIRTY-TWO
A PLACE CALLED DAGHORON

Jute slept poorly that night.

He dreamt of the darkness. This is a dangerous thing to do, for such dreams are opportunities for the Dark. To dream of the Dark is to bring yourself to its attention. Who knows what may happen then?

It was a night without stars. Cold and breathless. A shadow stretched past Jute out into the expanse of space. If I turn, Jute thought, will I see this thing that casts such a shadow? Or what if it already stands before me, far on the other end of this darkness? For everything is shadow here, and the darkness stands everywhere. It does not need light to cast the shadow of itself.

The shadow gained form as he watched. Battlements rose up. Spires soaring above and below and on either side. Towers and walls that climbed ever upward, dizzying. Endless. The façade was pitted with windows that gaped without glass or light inside.

I could look for a lifetime and find no end to this. But I would find desolation. Who am I to stand here and live?

And in desperation he wished for a small place so he might creep away into it, close the door, and pretend his little room was the only world that was.

Light glimmered by his side.

The hawk.

Do you wish death upon yourself? What brings you to this place?

I do not know. Take me from here!

I cannot. We stand before the gates of Daghoron.

He felt the hawk's wing brush along his arm.

Know you not the words of Staer Gemyndes, with which he began the Gerecednes? "Deep within the darkness, further e'en the void, Nokhoron Nozhan built himself a fortress of night."

I am only a boy. I know nothing of such things.

If men forget such things, then all that is will surely pass away.

The shadow deepened. And moved, ever so slightly. As if that which cast it was beginning to wake. Nightmares stirring from their sleep. Shivering with hunger.

We must be away. Now!

I cannot! You said this yourself!

Not true. I only said I could not take you away by myself.

Then how?

Look down!

He looked down and could not breathe. There was nothing below him except the dizzying emptiness of sky. The hawk hovered next to him on outstretched wings. And he fell, plunging down into the nothingness, his mouth stretched wide in a scream and his arms flailing at the air. Darkness rushed past him like water.

Aye. There was satisfaction in the hawk's voice. *Fear serves its purpose at times.*

Jute awoke and rose from his bed. He opened the window and stood amazed. The university and the city were gone. Below, a plain lay gloomy under a moon colored ivory like bone. Far beneath the window, something gibbered. The thing turned and shambled alongside the tower. The boy rushed to the door and eased it open. Below him, up a winding stair, there came to him the creak of a turning handle. Footsteps shuffled up the stairs. A smell of decay and damp things assailed him and he stumbled away from the door. There was only the window.

He threw himself from it.

And awoke, again, in his bed. Sweating and shivering. A candle burned on the table. Severan sat there and watched him.

"You don't sleep well," he said.

"No," said the boy, but he was glad to see the old man, and he knew he dreamt no longer. There was bread and cheese on the table. Jute rose and ate.

"Have you ever heard of a place called Daghoron?" asked the boy.

Severan shook his head and helped himself to a hunk of bread. But it seemed to the boy that the old man avoided his gaze.

"Or someone named Staer Gemyndes?"

The old man froze.

"Where did you hear that name?"

"In my dream. Someone spoke it."

"Who?" said Severan.

"I don't know."

"Staer Gemyndes was the court wizard of Siglan Cynehad, the first king of Tormay. It is said that Staer Gemyndes wrote a book called the *Gerecednes* at the end of his life—a book that speaks of those events which brought Siglan Cynehad to Tormay, centuries ago. For the king did not come as a conqueror, as most scholars assume, or an adventurer out to win fame and glory for an older homeland. No, he came with his people—all those who are our own forefathers—fleeing some terrible doom. And in that book it is written of these matters. It's said that in the book are the answers to so many questions! But the book's been lost for hundreds of years, and we know only a little."

"And this book is one of the things you hope to find here in the ruins? You told me that before, didn't you?"

"Yes," said Severan. But he would not say anything more on the matter and did not ask again where the boy had heard such names.

CHAPTER THIRTY-THREE
THE WIHHT IS GIVEN A TASK

"The Guild," said Nio. "The Guild and this fellow they call the Knife. Ronan of Aum. Both of them made-up names that tell us nothing of the man, other than his vaunted position in the Guild and his own arrogance."

He was pacing back and forth in the library. The wihht stood silently. Only its eyes moved, slowly shifting back and forth to keep its gaze on Nio.

"I want you to find the Court of the Guild, the court of the so-called Silentman. It's somewhere in this city, that's obvious, and I've heard enough rumor to guess it's underground. A cellar, tunnels, something like that. Find one of these thieves and squeeze the truth out of him!"

"Is it permitted to then end his life?"

"What? Yes, yes—whatever you want. I don't care. Just keep it quiet, d'you hear? The last thing we need is the attention of the Lord Captain of Hearne and his men. And if you hear or see anything of the boy Jute, find him too."

"I remember his taste," said the wihht.

"If you catch him, bring the miserable rat to me. I'll wring his neck myself. Mind you, the Guild's more important now, not that guttersnipe. Find me a key that'll get us into the Guild, and I don't care how many bones you break along the way."

"Ah," said the wihht.

Nio stalked to the window and stared out. Water streaked down the glass. It was raining again. The street below was virtually empty. One solitary figure hurried by, shoulders bent and head hunched against the rain. It was a miserable day. Most of the city would be holed up like rats in their houses, Guild and non-Guild alike. The wihht would have a more difficult job of it.

"Concentrate on the inns," he said. "They'll be crowded, no doubt."

"And the man called the Knife?"

"I daresay you'll have an easier time finding the *Gerecednes* than that man. Find me my key. And I don't care if it's a key made of metal or one of flesh and bones."

The door closed silently behind the wihht.

Nio flung himself down in a chair and picked up a book. *A Concise History of Harlech*, written by some long-dead Thulian duke with aspirations of being a scholar. It was a short and concise book. There was little to know about Harlech, for they did not give up their secrets easily and they were not fond of strangers.

Travel in Harlech is not advisable in the winter due to the harshness of the climate, the frequency of wolves, and the peculiar fact that the roads and paths seem to rearrange themselves at will, particularly for the misfortune of visitors. The towns are few and the inns, while excellent and well-appointed, exist more for local traffic, rather than for travelers from afar. Furthermore, those who live in Harlech tend to be inhospitable unless some happy twist of fate has given one a reason to form an acquaintance, for if they give their friendship, they will remain so until death. If their enmity has been aroused, however, one would be advised to stay far away from Harlech, for they are implacable and feared in all of Tormay for their skill in battle.

Nio tossed the book aside. It made for dull reading. Particularly on a day like today. He got up and again went to the window. Rain. The drops ran down the glass and blurred his sight.

He still remembered her name. Cyrnel. Cyrnel, the farmer's daughter. For several years after he left the Stone Tower, he had purposed to return. To return once he had made a name and a fortune for himself. He would have rode up on a fine horse to the admiring glances of the students. The teachers would have invited him in to hear his tales. And then he would have ridden off south along the coast to the little valley and the farmer's daughter who lived there.

She was probably married and fat now. She probably even had grandchildren by now. He could not remember her face.

CHAPTER THIRTY-FOUR
STILL WAITING FOR GOLD

The Silentman received the return of Arodilac Bridd's ring with pleasure.

"Well done, Ronan," he said, tossing him a purse of coin. "Our client, the regent, will be pleased."

The Silentman was sitting on his stone throne, raised by a dais several steps up from the floor. As usual, his face was blurred and his voice muted by an obscuring charm. His form was shrouded by a cloak of black silk. Standing to one side was the short figure of Dreccan Gor, advisor to the Silentman. Dreccan was known for his wisdom and feared almost as much as the Silentman himself, though this was largely due to the fact that the advisor also served as chief steward to the regent of Hearne. Such an unusual association served the Guild well, as it allowed the Silentman to always stay one step ahead of the regent.

"Easiest job I've ever done, my lord," said Ronan.

The Silentman nodded and Ronan had the impression that the man was smiling. There was no way to tell through the blur. He had his suspicions about who the Silentman was, but no proof. Anyway, it was not healthy to voice such suspicions out loud.

"A question, my lord?" said Ronan.

The Silentman inclined his head.

"If I might step closer?"

Not that there was much chance of anyone overhearing them. The court was crowded and noisy with conversation and music. Besides, no one came near the Silentman unless bidden.

"Approach," said the Silentman. Ronan stepped up onto the dais and lowered his voice.

"Is our client pleased with the chimney job?"

"You want your money, don't you? The client is coming soon to collect. You know the rules of the Guild, Ronan. Satisfaction first for the client, and then you'll get your gold. Don't try my patience."

Ronan bowed and retreated back down the steps.

The court was busy that night—petitioners with grievances and jobs, thieves being given instructions, a trio of musicians jangling through the latest court tunes in one corner. The place was full of torchlight and shadow and the radiance of a fire burning on the hearth halfway down the room's length. A table sagged under the weight of its bounty: roast chicken, ham, breads and cheeses, cold sausage, kegs of ale, and baskets overflowing with fruit. All courtesy of the Silentman.

Ronan slouched against a pillar and chewed on a chicken leg. He fingered the purse in his pocket and added numbers in his head. He would have enough now, once the payment came through for the chimney job. Before the week was out, if the Silentman was to be trusted.

The chimney job.

The little girl. She had said the boy was alive. What had his name been? Jute. But that was impossible. No one survived a dose of lianol like that. Still, she had sounded certain.

Ronan shook his head. It was not possible.

We all have our jobs to do.

The boy stared up at him from within the chimney, falling backward. Vanishing down into darkness.

Just like himself.

Years and years of falling down into the darkness.

The stone ceiling seemed to be lowering. The lamplight swam in his eyes. The air was hot and stifling. Faces blurred by. Voices babbled around him. Ronan flung the half-eaten chicken away from him. His stomach clenched. Someone said something to him. He mumbled a reply, not knowing what the other had said or what he had said in return. He needed to get out.

The doors to the Court of the Guild swung shut behind him and he stood for a moment, breathing in and out and trying to quell the nausea inside. He looked up and down the stone passage. No one in sight. The place was silent. On the edge of his mind, however, he could hear the whisper of the ward that governed passage. It pushed its way into him, examined him, recognized him, and then retreated.

The first time Ronan had walked the underground passage as a novice member of the Guild, years ago, no one had bothered to explain the uniqueness of the ward guarding the passage. He had memorized the twists and turns and counted his steps. When he emerged once more into the sunlight, he retraced the way in his mind as he walked the streets of Hearne. But he found that the path only led him in a circle that meandered back to where he started. Later, it was explained to him that the ward guarding the passage was crafted to constantly manipulate the passage, forever shaping new routes beneath the city. It rearranged itself so that no one ever walked the same way to the Court of the Guild. The passage moved even as people walked within it, hurrying or slowing them on their way to the court. And for those who had no business with the Silentman? Why, they never found their way out of the passage. Ronan had come across such intruders before, but the rats always found the bodies first.

It didn't matter what direction the passage chose. If you were walking away from the Court of the Guild, it would find an exit for you. The only trouble was, the ward spell was so powerful you could never be certain where you would find yourself when you exited. There were numerous places throughout Hearne the ward could choose from. It was irritating to emerge at the opposite end of the city from where you started.

Lamps burned on the wall every once in a while, but flames were so meager and the distances between them were always so great that most of the passage was plunged into gloom. Something scurried away in the shadows. A rat, most likely.

Scurrying away like himself.

Abruptly, the passage turned a corner and ended at some stairs.

"The stables on Willes Street," said Ronan to himself, guessing.

At the top of the stairs was a wooden door. He opened it and shrugged. He was not in the stables, not that he had expected to be. He had never guessed right before. He was in the cellar of the Goose and Gold. He stepped through a door concealed within a wine barrel.

Something crashed and he heard a gasp.

"Now look what I've done!"

It was one of the serving girls. She crouched down onto the floor to pick up some pottery shards.

"Just filled it with ale, too." She scowled at Ronan. "Gave me a turn, you did."

"Sorry," said Ronan. He shut the door behind him. It was built into a fake wine cask that sat at the end of a row of casks. If you didn't know what you were looking for, it was impossible to detect the lines of the door.

The sky was clear and cold when he emerged from the Goose and Gold. The first few stars were emerging in the east. He breathed deeply and smelled the salt of the sea. That steadied him and he strode off, collar flipped up against the cold. He slept well that night and did not dream, even of the girl with poor Liss Galnes's name.

CHAPTER THIRTY-FIVE
A DEATH, A DELAY, AND A WEASEL

They would have left that day for Hearne, but just after breakfast a horseman came clattering into the courtyard of the castle in Andolan. He was only a boy, but by the expression on his face, he bore sorry news.

"Stone and shadow," said the duke. "So that's why he didn't come." He stared down at the ground for a moment and then forced himself to smile—albeit grimly—at the boy.

"My thanks for your kindness. Get yourself to the kitchen and have them feed you there."

"Thank you, my lord," said the boy. The duke turned away, striding toward the castle steps.

"You, lad!" he yelled at a passing man-at-arms. "Find Willen and have him attend me immediately!"

Levoreth and the duchess were in the sunroom adjoining the duchess's rooms. It was a pleasant room suited for silence, and both women liked it for that reason. Melanor was knitting what looked like the beginnings of a blanket. Levoreth was curled up in a chair, intent on a book of poetry written by a long-dead Harlech lord. The door flew open with a crash.

"Hennen," said the duchess, dropping a stitch. "There's no need to be stamping about so."

"Ginan Bly is dead. He, his wife, and their babe. Torn apart by wolves—right inside their house."

"Wolves?" said Levoreth. Her voice was sharp.

"Oh, my dear," said the duchess. Her face whitened. "She was so happy to have borne a child."

"I'm riding north for Bly's farm. Willen and a score of his men will be with me as well. A couple of his lads are good trackers. If there's a trail to find, we'll hunt down the brutes. I don't know how long we'll be gone."

He turned to go.

"But what about Hearne?" said his wife. "We were to set out this afternoon."

"Hearne will have to wait."

"It was not wolves that did this," said Levoreth. But the door was already closing and the duke was gone.

She stared down blankly at the book in her lap. She flung her mind wide, ranging across the hills of the Mearh Dun toward the north and east. Earth and sky blurred through the speed of her thought. Dimly, she was aware of lives flickering by. Men, cattle, flocks of sheep scattered on the hills, dogs, rabbits in the heather, birds on the wing. Nowhere, however, could she sense wolves, even in the tangled weaving of old scents left from weeks past. Nothing. She pushed out farther, drifting up into the foothills of the Mountains of Morn.

"Levoreth!"

She blinked and looked up. Her aunt was looking at her.

"Are you all right? You had such an angry look on your face. I've never seen you so—"

"Ginan Bly was a good man," said Levoreth.

"Yes, yes he was." The duchess blinked back tears.

The duke and his men returned two days later, tired and gray-faced from the hard ride into the north. The duchess hurried down the castle steps to meet him, with Levoreth behind her. He swung down from the saddle and trudged over to his wife. Stubble covered his face and his eyes were bloodshot. His wife touched him gently, running a hand down his arm as if to reassure herself.

"It wasn't wolves, was it?" said Levoreth. It was more a statement than a question.

"No," said the duke. "No signs to track. Nothing at all. I'm half in mind not to go to Hearne now, but don't fret, love—we'll be going still. Ealu Fremman's six sons have promised to ride the borders and there are no better trackers in this duchy than those boys. The best of the men'll be staying on at the castle." He shook his head. "Dolan is in good hands with them, but this is poor timing. Poor timing indeed."

Dinner was a silent affair that night, although the duchess tried to make conversation. The duke hardly spoke at all and Levoreth was even quieter.

"I'm dreadfully sorry about the Blys," said the duchess, putting down her fork. "But they are gone and you do them no benefit by grinding your teeth like that, Hennen. My dears, we needn't go to Hearne. There'll be other times."

"We're going to Hearne," said her husband.

"I meant what I said," returned his wife. "It isn't as if the regent and his Autumn Fair cannot go on without us. After all, what are we to Botrell but uncouth country folk, smelling of horses and going about with straw in our hair?"

"We're going to Hearne!"

"Excuse me," said Levoreth, and she got up and left the table.

"And you're still coming, too!" said her uncle.

"I know that," said Levoreth. She glared at the duke and then slammed the door behind her.

Levoreth had not known the Blys well. She could not even recollect what Ginan Bly looked like, let alone his wife and child. But they were still her people. This was her land.

No.

She forced herself to unclench her fists.

No. All of Tormay was her land. Not just this sleepy little duchy of Dolan.

She locked the door of her room and blew out the candle. Outside, a sickle moon was rising in the east over the Mountains of Morn. The moon was so thin it looked like the sky's weight would snap it in two. There was something in the air. Something—she was not sure. She leaned out the window. Her nose twitched. Heather from the surrounding hills, woodsmoke, the scent of hay and horses in the stables, a guard in the courtyard below smoking a pipe. Apples rotting on the ground in the orchard behind the castle, the musk of a fox sniffing around the chicken coop.

A fox in the chicken coop. Teeth and feathers.

They kill for pleasure sometimes. But there are other things that kill for pleasure as well.

There was something else in the air. Her nose twitched again.

Definitely. Just the barest hint.

Something dark.

There was just enough time. She had to see for herself.

A cloak around her shoulders, Levoreth tiptoed through the hall. The castle was settling into evening. She could hear servants chatting and laughing down in the kitchen. Crockery clinked together. Somewhere on the floor above, her aunt was humming to herself. Levoreth tilted her head to one side and listened. The tune was an old Dolani love song. A smile crossed her face. She wondered if her uncle knew.

Mistress of Mistresses!

Levoreth looked down. A mouse scurried out from behind a chest and stood shyly before her.

"Sir Mouse," she said. "Well met."

Indeed, Mistress! Indeed!

"Can you do me a great favor?"

Aye! What is your wish? We mice will do anything in our power to aid you, even though it cost us our lives! Command us!

"I would have you and yours guard this castle and the town. Parley with the cats, with the hounds, with the horses, and with all that live hereby. Bid them my peace. Bid them that all must be my watch against the Dark."

The Dark!

The mouse squeaked in alarm and its whiskers quivered.

"Aye, Sir Mouse. Can you aid me?"

The mouse bobbed up and down. It reached out one tiny paw and patted the hem of her cloak.

We shall! We shall! Word shall come to you if we see aught!

The mouse scurried away.

The moon was rising high when she made her way from the castle grounds. A small gate in the gardens opened into the street behind the castle. Though, in truth, it was more of a cattle path than a street, full of ruts and mud puddles. Lights shone from the windows around her. A cow lowed in question from a shed nearby.

Hay.

Hay. And grass tomorrow?

She quieted the cow with a touch of her mind and passed on.

Steps were built into the wall here for the soldiers who walked the watches, but no one was in sight. She hurried up to the top of the wall and glanced at the moon. There would be just enough time. Barely enough, and she would be doubtlessly falling asleep in the saddle in the morning when they left for Hearne.

She took a deep breath and jumped off the wall.

Landed already running. She could hear the galloping of horses in her mind. Herself galloping.

The ground flowed away beneath her, earth and stone and trees blurring into one. The wind whipped through her hair and her cloak, tossing them back like a dark mane. She heard the river Ciele murmuring before her, and then she was past it, hurdling it in one stride. The moonlight flashed on the water, and the moon in the sky was the only thing that stayed motionless with her, watching her with the narrow curve of its unblinking eye. Hills rose and fell before her. The dew sprang from the grass at the strike of her feet. Her cloak was drenched in it. Time slowed, but she ran faster and faster.

Oh, Min!

Her heart was full and it seemed to her that if she turned her head she would see the great horse galloping next to her. She was up higher now, up on the plateau that rises in the northern portion of the Mearh Dun hills. She slowed her pace and felt sweat springing cold from her limbs.

The moonlight gleamed on the whitewashed stone walls of a cottage. A barn stood nearby. The ground was hard underfoot. She smelled the oily tang of sheep in the air. Sheep and hay and death.

And the other smell.

It was unforgettable. The Dark. Nausea twisted her stomach.

A memory struggled to life and for a moment she went blind to the cottage and the silent land around her. Shadows were falling from the sky. A mountain range rose like broken teeth into the night. Fires raged on the plain below. She heard the distant shouts and screams of the dying. The battle lines snaked across the plain. Iron clashed on iron. And the shadows fell from the sky.

They fell and they fell.

So long ago.

Long before we fled to Tormay.

But the stench was the same.

Levoreth forced her eyes open. Her head ached. The cottage sat waiting for her in silence. She swallowed and tasted bile.

In the little garden behind the cottage were two fresh graves. They were heaped over with stones and she touched them. The animals would respect her scent. They would not bother these graves. The lock on the cottage door was shattered. The smell was almost overpowering inside. She doubted, of course, that a normal human would be able to smell the scent. A wizard might be able to. Others would merely become uneasy, fearful, or sick to their stomachs, but they would not know why.

Animals, however, would smell it and know it for what it was.

The cottage was a single room that served as kitchen, living space, and bedroom. Just inside the door, moonlight slanted down onto the wood flooring. The wood was stained dark. Someone had kicked dirt over it, but the stain was apparent, ugly and dark red. Broken crockery, torn bedding, and splintered furniture had been piled up in one corner— all that was left of the Blys besides the two graves in the garden.

There was something else in the room. A thread of emotion fast fading away. Terror. And rage.

Ginan Bly had died fighting.

Levoreth nodded. She looked once around the cottage and then walked outside. The stench was all around. It clung to the stone walls and to the grass poking up from the ground. She stalked around the cottage, her head down.

There.

There it was.

The scent led away toward the north.

North. Yet she had no time to go north herself. Something in the city of Hearne was calling her. She cast her thoughts wide, searching across the surrounding land. Nothing. Not even a field mouse to be found. She pushed wider, but there was only a residue of fear. The animals had all fled. But there—there was something. A weasel skittering along the ground, nervous and hungry. She caught at its mind and pulled it toward her, but the animal shied away. She snared it again and soothed it with thoughts of fat mice and crickets. The weasel shivered.

Come.

The animal came, snarling and protesting, hardly able to talk for fear.

Afraid. Evil. Here! It is here! Run! Run away!

It popped its head out of a bush several yards away, its shiny black eyes darting every which way at once, and then it disappeared.

Come.

Run! Run away!

Come.

The bush quivered and then the weasel burst out from among the leaves and scurried across the ground to her. It wrapped itself around her ankles. She could feel the staccato of its heartbeat trembling against her skin.

Peace, little one.

Here! It is here! Everywhere!

Peace.

The weasel poked its head out from under her cloak and stared up at her. The moonlight glittered in its eyes. She felt the animal quiet down, but its thoughts still darted through her mind, tense and afraid.

Mistress of Mistresses. The Dark has been here. Not long ago. Can you not scent it? Humans lived here. They are dead. All dead.

Aye, the Dark has been here, but it is here no more. Peace, little one, and listen to what I shall say. Alone, there is none of you that can stand against the Dark. That is not your place, for it is the duty of those who have been given charge over you. Now, listen, for I would have you do a great thing for me.

Name your bidding, Mistress of Mistresses! Even if it be death, I shall do it!

Go now to all the nyten, all the four-footed folk who call these hills home. Go to the hares, the deer, the mice, and the foxes. In my name, put aside your enmities for a time and bid all to keep watch against the Dark. Do not stand and fight, but wait and watch.

I shall do so, Mistress. Even to the mice! The plump and tasty mice!

And one last thing, little one. A very important thing.

Aye?

Find me a fleet-footed deer and send her to the Mountains of Morn. Give her word for the wolves, that they must come to this place and track the scent of Dark as far as they dare. If the deer keep my name in her mouth, the wolves shall not harm her.

The weasel bobbed its head up and down in obedience. Then, without a backward glance, it scampered away and was soon lost in the night.

Levoreth sighed.

"I know this stink," she said to herself. "Damn you to your endless night, wherever you have gone! But my little ones shall keep watch, and the wolves shall track you to your doorstep, and then I shall unmake you, if it's the last thing I do. If my fate didn't bid me to Hearne, I would hunt with the wolves. I would hunt you to the ends of the earth. Even if it took me back east over the sea."

And with these words, she turned once again to the south. The moon gazed down upon her. The wind sprang up and the sky blazed with stars. As she ran, it seemed that the ghostly shape of a horse ran by her side.

They left the next morning for Hearne. The duke was quiet all that day, causing the duchess anxiety. However, the sunlight and the beauty of the late summer soon proved enough to wrest him from his mood into his usual cheerful self. Levoreth yawned and slumped in the saddle, such that her aunt thought her ill.

"You should've said something, my dear," said the duchess. There's a tea of willow bark and jona flowers I've had splendid success with."

"I'm fine," said Levoreth.

"You look dreadful."

"I'm fine," said Levoreth.

The road wound south, through hills thinly forested with pines. For a time, it followed the east bank of the Ciele, before the river swung toward the west and the great sea. Here, the hill country met the plain of Scarpe, which stretched from the Mearh Dun in the north to the cliffs far to the west that rose above the sea with their rocky heights. The plain of Scarpe extended a good five days' journey by horse to the forests of Lome standing on the western foothills and flanks of the Mountains of Morn. South was a hard week's ride before the plain met the river Rennet and Hearne, whose stone walls loomed over that course's mouth.

The plain of Scarpe was like an ocean of grasses, rippling in the wind toward an endless horizon. In the spring, it was patchworked with wildflowers—the different purples of the allium, the yellow-white spray of saxifrage, and the tiny blood-red poppies. By summer's end, however, the flowers were faded and gone, leaving only the grasses burnished into gold under the sun. Water was a chancy thing at best on the plain, but Willen, the old sergeant-at-arms, knew Scarpe like his own hand, having fought in the Errant Wars that had raged across that land thirty years earlier.

"Besides," he said to Levoreth as they rode along, "you give a horse a chance for his own notions, he'll find a waterhole soon enough. They're smart in that. There be other ways, too—the flight of bees and birds, the mixture of grasses, even the wind if you have the sense to smell it." And he chuckled and laid a finger alongside his own weathered beak of a nose.

Levoreth smiled at him, and the roan under her danced a few steps.

They were a day into the Scarpe when one of the outriders came galloping in toward the party. He reined up next to the duke, spoke with him, and then cantered away. The duke spurred his horse alongside his wife and Levoreth.

"Good news!" he said. "The Farrows! Just half an hour south of us!"

CHAPTER THIRTY-SIX
OWAIN GOES HUNTING

"It'll only be for a few weeks, Sibb. Not long at all."

The Lord Captain of Hearne was sitting with his wife in the garden behind the house. Sibb grew herbs for her kitchen there. The scent of sage and basil filled the air. Around them, the plants flourished in their tiny plots. Morning sunlight crept down the wall. The honeysuckle vines growing along the wall were covered in a profusion of yellow flowers.

Sibb picked up his hand, turning it over in her own. His palms were calloused and his knuckles wealed with scars. A particularly large scar ran between his thumb and finger, reaching almost to his wrist. She ran her finger along the ridge, remembering. A frown crossed her face.

"Three weeks at most," he said.

She said nothing in reply, but only traced the scars on his hand.

"I'm leaving Bordeall in charge at the tower. He'll have near enough the entire strength to command, so Botrell can sleep soundly at night. Hearne will keep safe while I'm gone."

"It's not Hearne I worry about," she said, tracing the scar alongside his thumb. He laughed and kissed her.

"Don't fret, Sibb. With a sword and a good horse, I'll always have the luck to find my way home. Odds are we won't find hide or tail of them, so there'll be no need to worry on that account."

"Them," she repeated.

"Aye." He sighed. "I don't even know what we're looking for. Man, beast, or something in between. I have the feeling it's something in between. At any rate, we'll ride out to our foundling's village and see if we can find some tracks. How I wish she would regain her tongue. Without her knowledge, we'll be hunting blind. Even if we return with only stories of bones and an old slaughter gone cold, it'll be worthwhile, for I want Botrell thinking beyond this city. He's able as regent, I'll give him that, but he forgets that all the lands of Tormay look to Hearne. The other duchies are unsettled about these murders and, so far, Botrell ignores their unease."

"He's an odious man," said Sibb.

"Woman, you forget he is our regent. I'm sworn to protect his city and his personage. In pursuit of such office I'll have to—ouch!"

She punched him in the ribs and they were both silent for a moment. Bees drifted and settled among the honeysuckle vines.

"I'm worried about that girl. I fear she'll never be well."

He frowned. "Would any child who's lost their family at such an age ever become well?"

"I've held her while she sleeps. She's as fragile as a sparrow. Doubtless, she's older than our Magret, but less than half the weight. When she's taken by nightmares, her heart races and she pants as if she is running, as if there's some horror chasing her. I can't help but think the thing is chasing her still, sniffing along her trail. Perhaps, one day, it'll find its way here and so her nightmare and waking day will merge into one. Not just for her, but for all of us."

"Sibb."

She sighed and laced her fingers through his.

"I can't shake the thought from my mind, Owain. Such eyes she has. She's always staring and not noticing anything about her. Perhaps she sees things we cannot see. Sometimes she seems to focus on Loy—"

"Her devoted dog," he said, smiling.

"I can't help but think of our own in her stead."

Her hand tightened on his.

"Find them, Owain. Find them and kill them."

The Lord Captain of Hearne and his men rode out that afternoon. The troop was twenty strong—the best of Hearne. Some of the older ones had seen battle during the Errant Wars, when Owain Gawinn had been but a young sergeant and the forces of Hearne had been commanded by his father, Rann Gawinn.

Their saddles creaked with the weight of their gear and provisions. On their backs they bore spears and quivers bristling with arrows, muffled by their cloaks. They received scant notice from the folk in the streets going about their business—the vendors at their carts, the shoppers sniffing over turnips and fingering bolts of cloth, the drifting rabble, and the urchins—they made grudging way for the troop, action that stemmed more from the need for their own safety from the stamp of hooves rather than from any regard for the regent's men.

This lack of regard was due to no fault of the Lord Captain of Hearne. On the contrary, he had always been pleased by the blind eye the people turned to him and his men. He considered that his job was to allow folk to go about their lives while he dealt quickly and quietly with those who broke Hearne's laws. And he did that job well enough so that he had achieved a kind of facelessness for his men.

When the troop reached the city gates, however, a cheer went up from the soldiers standing watch. Owain reined in under the shadow of the tower, and a man strode forward. His hair was white but his back was as straight as a sapling. He held a spear in his hand.

"Bordeall," said Owain.

"My lord," said the other, touching the spear shaft to his forehead. His voice was deep and raspy.

"Hearne will be in good hands while we're gone."

"Thank you, my lord."

Another soldier came forward and both men turned in some annoyance.

"My lord Gawinn."

"Arodilac Bridd," said Owain. "You would do well to observe the propriety learned under the patience of my sergeants. Did they teach you nothing?"

Arodilac flushed red at the rebuke.

"Forgive me, my lord," he stammered. "I merely wished—is there no chance of—?"

"None," said Owain, cutting him off. "You will remain and serve here. Curb your patience, my young cub. Do not be so eager to rush into battle, though likely we'll see none on our hunt."

"It isn't because of my uncle wanting me kept from danger, is it?"

"No," said Owain, though it had been precisely for that reason. "Bordeall, I'd ask you to see that my household is well. My wife has some womanly fear concerning the

128

foundling we took in. Perhaps send a man by, now and again, to have a word with my doorkeeper and see that the child is well enough."

"Assuredly, my lord," said Bordeall. "Might I not make that Arodilac's duty?"

"Certainly," said Owain, and looked sharply at the young man, for his mouth was opening. Arodilac shut his mouth with a painful click of teeth and backed away.

"The city is yours."

"Thank you, my lord. Good hunting." Bordeall turned away to bellow at the soldiers at the gate. "Present!"

Spears gleamed as they rose in a flourish. With a jingle of harness and the clop of horse hooves on stone, the troop rode out through the gates and onto the road that curved away east, over the bridge and across the river and then down through the long, green reaches of the Rennet valley. The sky was clouding over. It would be raining again soon.

CHAPTER THIRTY-SEVEN
THE JUGGLER'S MISTAKE

Nio tightened his cloak around his throat when he stepped out the front door. It was just past twilight and stars winked down from the dark sky. He was late, but it wouldn't hurt the Juggler to be kept waiting. A cold rain was falling. It had been a strange summer for weather, almost as if the earth was no longer sure of the seasons. He wondered what the fall would bring. An early snow, perhaps. The streets were nearly empty of people, and the only ones he passed hurried along with their heads down, intent on reaching their homes and the warmth and welcome and firelight waiting there.

Once, a long time ago, he had wanted the same kind of life.

Cyrnel. He had loved her—that much he was sure of. But when he tried to recall her face, there was only an impression of beauty and a blur in his memory. He remembered freckles on her arms and a low, laughing voice. She smelled of fresh bread and the sunlight on the wheat fields in the valley east of the Stone Tower in Thule. The school bought their milk and cheese and grain from her father, the farmer. Nio remembered the look of the cheese more clearly than the farmer's daughter: small, white rounds smelling of caraway. The cook had been stingy with that cheese. Nio almost smiled to himself at the thought.

Perhaps he had wanted to marry her. He would have had a home to hurry back to at night. Someone waiting for him, other than the old ghosts sleeping inside the books in his library. But he had chosen the ghosts. Or perhaps they had chosen him. Some days he wasn't sure.

It was dark by the time he reached the south market square—an ugly, cramped plaza hemmed in with shops shuttered against the night. The rain had turned into a mist heavy enough to blur the shapes of buildings and the lights shining from windows. The stars and the moon could not be seen at all. It seemed he was alone in the city, for the mist also had the effect of muffling noise. Even his boots on the cobblestones only whispered.

Nio smelled the butcher's place before he saw it. A cloying scent of offal and blood filled the air, and the mist felt greasy with it. The stones there were stained dark. He turned west and walked down the street called Forraedan. It was narrow enough to be more of an alley than a street. He fancied he could almost stretch out his hands and touch the houses on both sides as he walked. The mist thickened, and close by he heard water dripping.

Seventh house on the left, the Juggler had said. He passed the fourth. The street turned sharply to the right where the fifth house stood, though it was puzzling to make out where one house ended and one began. They were built right up against each other, sharing their walls and a common sweep of roof that loomed overhead. Perhaps he should have been counting doors instead of houses. Fancy a brothel being hidden away in this warren. But then he came to the sixth house and the street ended against a stone wall taller than the houses themselves. A door opened behind him, further back up the street. He turned.

"You're late," said the Juggler. The fat man was standing about twenty feet away. A lantern hung from his hand and cast a glow on the wet cobblestones.

"I was reading and lost track of the time."

"Ah," said the Juggler. "I've never gone in much for reading."

"There's no seventh house," said Nio. His voice was mild. "You did say come to the seventh house, didn't you?"

"I did," said the fat man.

"There's only this wall."

"Yes," said the other, nodding. "There're only six, and then this wall. It's not a house, as you see. It's the back wall of a warehouse where an old man makes candles, he and his family. Candles made of grease, boiled in cauldrons and poured into his molds. Nothing to steal inside. Only thousands and thousands of candles. We leave him alone, we do, and in return—well, he'll use just about anything to make his grease with. Just about anything. We keep 'em well supplied here. It's convenient for us."

"Where's the man called the Knife?" asked Nio.

"Ah, the Knife," said the fat man, laying one finger alongside his nose and looking concerned. "Well sir, I says to him, come on out tonight as there's a gent who wants to talk with you. But he says no, I've got better things to do than that—you go tell him I'll see his gold first before meeting. That's what he says to me. See now, sir, he's a difficult lad, the Knife is—always has been, always will. Won't come to heel when you call him, and even the Silentman knows that."

"That won't do. I'm afraid you've disappointed me."

"Aye, and I'm disappointed the same!" said the fat man. He shook his head sadly. "I begged the lad nicely. Just a few minutes' chat and then you'll have your gold. But he wouldn't have none of it. Tell you what we'll do, sir. Why don't you hand over your bag of gold and I'll see the Knife gets it. That'll put him in a better mood."

"No. I don't think so."

At the words, two shapes materialized out of the darkness behind the Juggler. They were both large men—the sort of brute that Nio had seen in the Goose and Gold. He sighed inwardly. The evening could have been spent in a more pleasant fashion, reading a book in his library and smoking a pipe.

"Tsk," said the fat man. "We'll just have to take it from you, then."

"I don't think so," said Nio.

This seemed to please the Juggler. He smiled, his teeth gleaming in the lamplight.

"Then we'll have to kill you."

The two men behind the Juggler moved forward. Knives appeared in their hands. The darkness and mist blurred their faces so their eyes were only gouges of shadow and their mouths black holes. Skulls, thought Nio. He sighed again. One of them reached for him, a big, bony hand. Moisture gleamed on the skin, and the lamplight picked out scars across the knuckles.

He whispered a word and time slowed. The air thickened around the two men approaching him so that they swam through it. Their limbs were ponderous and weighted. He stepped to one side. Their eyes could barely follow him. The Juggler stood frozen behind them, huddled against the stone wall of the building. The light cast by his lantern seemed to have congealed and turned a yellowish gray. Water dripped from an eave overhead, falling so slowly that he could have plucked them from the air, one by one, like jewels.

The darkness in the street behind the Juggler trembled, and then a wisp of it separated, clotting together to form the shape of the wihht. On unhurried legs, it started forward and reached for the fat man.

"*Na, hie aerest,*" said Nio. The thing obeyed, veering, and made for the closer of the two other men. Shadow closed on flesh and grew, flaring up like a flame leaping into life, but without light or heat—only darkness that surged with quick movements. A scream cut off into silence. The second man was turning, turning slowly until he saw the shadow reaching for him. His eyes widened, and then he was blotted out in a wave of darkness. Only seconds, perhaps, went by. Nio was not sure, for the spell of slowing still held sway within the confines of the cobblestones and walls and dark, shuttered windows that looked on in silence.

The mass of shadow receded until there was only the wihht standing there. The two men were gone, although a few damp rags of clothing fluttered to the ground around the wihht's feet. It turned toward Nio and seemed to smile. He could not rightly tell in the little light there was, but it seemed now that the features of the thing were finer and more human.

"And this other?" it said, voice still hoarse and awkward.

"*Bidan,*" he said. Wait. He bound it into patience with his will woven into the word. Yet, even though the word and his will held, the wihht walked at his heels as he advanced toward the Juggler. The lantern trembled in the fat man's hand, his fingers white-knuckled across the handle.

"You chose poorly," said Nio. The other only stared at him, eyes huge in their sockets. Behind them, the wihht chuckled.

"Though this night has proven disappointing," continued Nio, "as you have brought no Knife, we must talk, you and I. Perhaps you know nothing I would find valuable, but I must make sure. I hope you understand. Now, where is the Knife?"

But the fat man remained silent, frozen except for the lantern trembling in his clutch and his eyes flickering from Nio's face to the shadow waiting behind and then back.

"*Cweoan,*" said Nio. Speak.

"I don't know, my lord!" stammered the Juggler. His face shone with sweat. "He did a big job some nights back. A real big job! Did it with one of my boys. He owes me money now, but the Guild ain't paid up yet!"

"What was the job?"

The words came in a rush, but Nio knew the answer already.

"A box lifted from a rich merchant's house. Just a little box, but it had something valuable in it. It wouldna been so or the Knife wouldna run the job. Usually, those jobs are left to the burglars—and he ain't a burglar, he's the bleeding Knife! I saw the box myself, right after it was nicked. The Knife was carrying it when he entered the tunnel underneath the Goose and Gold—the inn where you and me first met."

Nio said nothing, though it was all he could do not to grind his teeth together.

"The tunnel—it goes to the Silentman's court," gabbled the fat man. "Through the labyrinth. Nice place, all old stone, but strange. I hate going there! The Silentman ain't paid up yet, which means the client ain't got the goods yet. That's standard Guild procedure."

"How many in this Guild of yours know about the box?"

"Er," gulped the Juggler, his eyes sliding past Nio toward what waited behind him, "prob'ly not many. The Silentman's real silent 'bout his jobs an' clients. That's why he's called the Silentman."

"How many?"

"Um, mebbe four at most. The Knife, the Silentman and his advisor fellow, and me."

"What of your boy?"

"Oh, well, he was—he was dead by the time the work was finished."

"Ah," said Nio. "Broke his neck in a fall, did he?"

"No, no! More a matter of tying up loose ends. Another sign of the importance of the job. No need for flapping lips about. The boy was poisoned."

"Poisoned?" said Nio. "What do you mean by that? A strange sort of business, this Guild of yours, if it kills off its employees as they work."

"Just a boy," babbled the fat man. "Nothing personal. As soon as he came up out of the chimney, handed the box over, the Knife jabbed him full of lianol. Out like a blown candle. He wouldn't have felt a thing."

"What?!"

The fat man gurgled like a water fountain, but Nio no longer heard him. Lianol. The poison was lethal. There was no way to reverse it. He had never heard or read of any way possible.

His mind froze. The box. If what he guessed about the box was true—if what he guessed about what was inside the box was true—then that was how the boy had cheated death. Nausea swept over him. The boy had opened the box. The boy had touched what was inside the box. Blood had been drawn.

Nio turned back to the Juggler. His voice shook with rage.

"Who contracted the Guild for this job?"

"I don't know," said the fat man.

Behind Nio, the wihht stirred to life and stepped forward. Out of the corner of his eye, Nio could see the pallid face and the light gleaming in the sockets.

"I don't know! I don't know!" shrieked the fat man. The lantern fell from his grasp and broke on the cobblestones, sending up a brief flare of flame over the pooled oil. Glass crunched underneath the wihht's boot and the flame was extinguished.

"No, no!" sobbed the Juggler. He shrank away and covered his face with his hands.

"I believe you," said Nio.

"You do?" faltered the fat man, peeping at him from between his fingers.

"Yes. By the way, it's nothing personal, but this will probably hurt a great deal."

Nio turned and stalked away down the dark street.

The boy was all that mattered now. Only the boy. But he would make the Guild and its client pay dearly for what they had done. First the boy, then he would see to everything else. Everything! He ground his teeth together in fury. He had been so close. The boy had been within his hands. He could have snapped his filthy little neck. The wihht would find him. It would find him, sniffing its way through the city until it caught the scent.

Behind Nio, a scream choked into a sort of bubbling noise, and then a sigh. The clouds in the sky had frayed away sometime in the last hour, and the moon stared down, pale and white and disapproving.

CHAPTER THIRTY-EIGHT
THE FARROWS

The Farrows had pitched camp within the shelter of a hollow containing a spring, a rarity on the plain of Scarpe. Groundwater was scarce on the plain. Creeks and rivers were nonexistent, apart from the Rennet River bordering the plain's southern edge. About a dozen wagons were drawn up in a semicircle near the spring, and a temporary corral had been put together for the colts. The older horses never wandered far; such was the bond between Farrow and horse.

There were upward of fifty Farrows, and they ranged the gamut from tiny Morn, the four-month-old grandnephew of Cullan Farrow, the patriarch of the clan, to old Sula Farrow, Cullan's widowed mother. Uncles, aunts, cousins, young, and old. The Farrows took their brides from all four corners of Tormay, and every hue of skin and hair could be found within their family, though the thin, hawkish face and gray eyes were seen everywhere.

The duke's party stayed with the Farrows for two days, even though this meant they would be late for the beginning of the Autumn Fair in Hearne. The duchess had words with her husband about this, but he was unrepentant, as there was nothing he loved more than talking horses with old Cullan Farrow. Though he was wise enough not to say this to her.

"My dear," said the duke, "there are two or three colts I'll have to see put through their paces. Cullan bought them in Harlech—bought them, of course—stealing a horse in Harlech! Why, you might as well cut your own throat on the spot. Best bloodlines in all Tormay. A positive gold mine for breeding."

"Imagine that," said his wife.

But she knew a lost cause when she saw one and contented herself with sitting in the shade of one of the wagons—for the Farrows had promptly cleared out of one their nicer covered wagons for the duke and duchess—where she spent hours knitting.

"It's not that I mind," she said to Levoreth. "It does seem to have taken Hennen's mind off the Blys. There's something restful about the Scarpe, the way the wind billows the grasses. It's like the waves on the sea. Even with these Farrows popping up everywhere like dandelions, it's peaceful here—which can never be said about a city like Hearne." And here she glared good-naturedly at several children who were peeping around the wagon wheel. They giggled and scampered away.

"However, I can't allow your uncle to have his way whenever he wants."

"Of course not," said Levoreth, smiling.

"You're laughing at me."

"Yes."

Cullan Farrow was a tall man and as lean and hard as a polished oak spear. His hair was white and cropped close to his skull. His eyes were gray, as cold and hard as a winter sky in Harlech. But he smiled easily, and then the gray warmed well enough.

"Botrell has a nice pair of colts now," he said to the duke. They stood at the edge of the camp, smoking their pipes and watching several yearlings being put through their paces.

"Foaled off of Riverrun's dam, no?" said the duke.

"Aye, so you've heard then."

"The traders have been talking of that line getting good hunters for him."

Cullan nodded.

"There's good blood there, and the newest colts should be proof if they're broken well. Botrell's got some wise lads in his stable."

They were both silent for a moment. The boys on the yearlings called cheerfully to each other as they galloped across the green sward. Sparrows dove and swooped overhead.

"You haven't come across any strange deaths lately, have you?" said the duke.

"What do you mean with that?"

"One of my farmers was killed recently. In the northeast of the Mearh Dun, just up under the foothills of the Morns. He and his family. I thought it wolves when I first heard, for we had trouble with them several years back. With the way you travel about, I figured you might have heard something of the sort."

"Can't mistake wolf," said Cullan. "They aren't shy in how they step."

"The manner of it's a cursed puzzle. They were torn by beasts, but the bites were huge. Bigger than any wolf I've ever heard of. If it had only been those marks, then I might still have been convinced of wolves, but there were cuts as well—thin, deep thrusts as if made with a slender sword. Beast and man killing together."

"Wolves never run with anything but wolves. No tracks for you to pick up?"

"A few signs, but we lost them quickly," admitted the duke. "I'd have given much to have had you there."

"Aye. Farrows don't lose tracks." Cullan smiled crookedly. "Though I wager you'd do as well if you were raised under the sky with no roof or walls withering your senses."

"Then have you heard of any such killings?"

"Not exactly. Though we passed through Vo two months past and heard talk about something odd in Vomaro. Something had the folk there worried. But I didn't bother for details."

"I'll have a word with Botrell when I get to Hearne. Perhaps he knows something. So you heard nothing of the matter in Vomaro itself?"

"We took the road to the east," said Cullan. He squinted up at the sky. When he looked back down, his gray eyes had gone cold. "Farrows don't go to Vomaro."

Levoreth loved the Scarpe. The plain stretched away in every direction. It billowed like the sea, as her aunt had said, with the wind rippling the grasses in waves that rolled on toward the horizon. A sweet, dry scent perfumed the air, wafting from the tiny jona flowers blooming in the grass. A robin trilled through the air, and she answered it absentmindedly, whistling in her thoughts. The bird sang in response, telling of worms and the bright, yellow eye of the sun in the sky that sees all, and three eggs warm in her nest.

Levoreth wandered away from the encampment until the only sign of it was a trail of smoke rising into the sky. The earth was peaceful here, slumbering under the passing of years and the faithful return of the sun. She lay down, with the grasses whispering around her, and fell asleep. The sun was high in the sky when she awoke. Sitting next to her was a girl. She was chewing on a stalk of grass and staring at Levoreth with curious gray eyes. Her face was narrow and browned by the sun. Tangled black hair waved across her brow in the breeze.

"Do you always cry in your sleep?" asked the girl.

"I don't think so," said Levoreth. She stared at the girl's face. Her heart ached, and she put her hand to her breast. "I'm not sure."

"You're the duke's niece—Lady Levoreth—aren't you? Mother said she dreamt about you."

"No need to 'lady' me. What did she dream?"

"She wouldn't tell," said the girl cheerfully. "When I dream, I'm never sure if I'm asleep or awake. Mother says my eyes glaze when she talks to me, that I do it on purpose so I don't remember what she's said. But maybe that's just me dreaming, or maybe that's just me forgetting—I'm good at that." She giggled and twirled the stalk of grass between her fingers.

"Have you forgotten your name also?"

"Oh." She grinned. "I'm Giverny Farrow, Cullan's daughter." Her hands rose and drifted through the air, palms up and fingers stained with earth. "How do you know if what you see is in a dream or in a waking moment?"

"There's more pain when you're awake. You'll learn that soon enough, if you haven't already."

"But you were crying in your sleep."

"Dreams hurt sometimes. But not compared to waking life." Levoreth sat up and plucked her own stalk of grass to chew.

"The wretched bay colt stood on my foot yesterday when I was brushing him. That hurt. Here, look." And Giverny kicked off her sandal to display her foot.

"Ouch," said Levoreth, admiring the blue-black bruise.

"He did it just to be spiteful," said the girl, "because I'd been spending too much time with his sister. Father had the pair from Duke Lannaslech in Harlech—who is terribly stern and scary, even though he gave me an apple and the horses all love him and follow him about like dogs. They're perfectly matched—twins, of course—but the filly is the sweetest colt you've ever seen."

She ran out of breath at this point and lapsed into silence. The sun was perfectly warm and the breeze had subsided to a murmur. Levoreth closed her eyes and felt the Scarpe stretching around her in leagues and leagues of grasses and the light, redolent with the scent of flowers and pollen, laying like gold over it all. The nearness of the girl stirred a memory in her of another girl from a long time ago. The same blithe heart, the same gray eyes, so clear and free of guile, those same fluttering hands expressing every nuance of word and heart. Long ago. Another time and another place. And now those hands were silent and unmoving in her lap.

"That's not what you meant, is it?" said Giverny.

"No. A colt can only kick you or step on you out of its foolishness. Or your own. That's not such a dreadful sort of pain. It's a thing that passes."

Giverny nodded. She inched a bit closer and propped her chin in her hands.

"My brother ran away when I was three years old. I don't remember what he looks like, though Mother says he looks like Father. She won't talk about it much, but everyone knows the story." Here, her voice fell into a sort of singsong tone, for she was telling a tale. Levoreth knew the story, had heard it sung by traveling bards more times than she could remember, but she did not stop the girl.

"Devnes Elloran, the only child of the duke of Vomaro, went riding with her attendants on the eastern shore of the lake. There, they were set upon by ogres. All were killed except for the lady, and she was carried off in great distress."

Here, Giverny made a face. "If it had been me on a horse, no ogre would've caught me. The stupid cow obviously didn't know how to ride."

"Ogres are cunning," said Levoreth. Her voice was mild. "Many wiser than Devnes Elloran have fallen into their hands before. Do not be so hard on her."

"No, maybe not for that," said the girl. "But for what she did later, she should've been boiled and eaten by those ogres!" She paused, frowning, and then continued. "The duke of Vomaro sent word throughout all the lands of Tormay, entreating men of valor to come to his castle at Lura. And they came there, from Hull and hilly Dolan, the coast of Thule, Vo, and Vomaro. Even the haughty lords of Harth came, though not a soul from Harlech—for they have never paid much attention to the rest of Tormay."

"Your Duke Lannaslech," said Levoreth.

"Yes," said Giverny, grinning. "I'd imagine he'd say if she were silly enough to get caught, then she might well deserve an ogre dragging her off. He has a terribly cold voice—all deep and hard. Father never steals horses in Harlech."

She sobered again. "My brother vanished one night, for the duke's proclamation promised the hand of his daughter in marriage for the man who brought her back. He stole Father's sword, so that he might walk with pride." Her chin lifted. "All Farrows take to horse and reading the signs of the earth. And Declan was the best of our family—so I've been told. But his hands lent themselves best to war, as had his father—our father—before him. The sword and the bow and all those other wretched things that take life."

Her own hands fluttered before her as if shaping the words.

"As the story goes, Declan found trace of the ogre trail on the moors south of Lome forest and tracked them through those woods for days. What he found there has never been told, for neither he nor the Lady Devnes Elloran ever spoke of it. On a cold, wet day in March, Declan rode out of Lome forest with the Lady Devnes. And then—and then . . . " Her voice trailed away.

"And then he was betrayed," said Levoreth.

"Yes!" burst out the girl angrily. "I hate it! I hate it all! Oh, he was brave and foolish to run away and think that he could make his way in such a world. I love him for that, for I sometimes feel the same thing inside myself—to see what's beyond the horizon and in far-off lands. I want to know more. I want to know more than just our wagons and our horses. But I hate him for leaving me not even a memory and Father and Mother growing old without him. Yet I hate that duke and his daughter even more for what they did. We Farrows no longer go to Vomaro, nor will we ever! May the Dark take them all!"

"Hush," said Levoreth. "No one should ever wish such a thing, for our lives here are only a breath. That which follows after endures. May we all come safely to the house of dreams and so escape the grasp of the Dark."

"Aye," said Giverny sulkily. "Save the house of Elloran."

"Child."

They sat in silence for a moment. Then, her face averted, the girl said, "That's what you meant about pain, yes?"

"Yes," said Levoreth.

The sun was lowering in the west, down toward the horizon and, past that, the far-off sea. Purple stained the sky in the east, and there a single star gleamed. Levoreth shivered in spite of the warmth left by the sunlight. It would be cold in the Mountains of

Morn tonight. She reached out with her thoughts across the leagues, toward the peaks. The silence within her mind was broken by the howl of a wolf pack. It welled up like a lament, rising from the flanks of the range to the north, where the mountains climb high into the sky with their heights of stone and ice.

Mistress of Mistresses.

Drythen Wulf.

We have hunted along the scent of the Dark.

Where has it brought you?

We ran north from the hills of the Mearh Dun, north across the fields of snow and up into the heights. We found an eyrie, long cold, but the Dark did abide here a while, for the stink is rooted in the rocks and has crept down into the bones of the mountain.

And from there?

The scent did not end there, Mistress.

A hand touched her shoulder, and she opened her eyes to the fading afternoon of the Scarpe. Giverny drew back.

"Are you well, Lady Levoreth?" she asked anxiously. "You had such a look on your face."

"I'm fine. I was just thinking of an old friend." She forced a smile.

They walked back together. The girl skipped along beside her, humming an old Thulian song and darting away now and then to collect flowers that caught her fancy. Levoreth knew the song and she sang the words as she walked along.

"On the heathered downs of Davos bay
where the river meets the sea
the fishers mend their broken nets
upon the sandy lea."

"You know it," said Giverny, surprised, twirling around. She smiled in delight. "My grandmother taught me that one when I was little. She said 'The Girl of Davos Bay' was one of the forgotten treasures of Thule."

"Not yet forgotten," said Levoreth. "Some things are never forgotten. Delo of Thule was the finest bard Tormay has ever known. They say his songs wove themselves into the coast of Thule. If you walk the cliffs there, you can hear his music in the sounds of the wind and the sea, and in the call of the gulls." She continued singing.

"Blues and greens and shadows beneath—
the colors of the sea.
Breathe wind—blow the storm clouds hence
and bring my love home to me."

A brindled old hound loped out to meet them as they approached the camp. It licked at Levoreth's hand before pressing up against the girl's knees.

"Gala, my love," said Giverny, rubbing the dog's head. "That's Lady Levoreth Callas you just kissed. It isn't every day you're hobnobbing with the royalty of Tormay."

"Nay, girl," said Levoreth, laughing. "I darn my own socks."

Mistress of Mistresses.

Gala Gavrinsdaughter. The blood of the wolves flows in your veins. I knew your grandmother well.

Aye. There are days when I hear my mountain-kin calling. The hound turned sad, brown eyes on Levoreth. *Do you come for my little one?*

Levoreth caught her breath sharply. The hound nosed at her palm and whined. Giverny whirled away to pounce on a clump of blue bonnets.

What do you speak of?

Your mark is on her. All the nyten, even the sly jackal and the poisoned serpent, all things living cannot help but love her of instinct within them. The earth protects her, though she has ever been headstrong and foolhardy, even as a tiny whelp. Fate has not touched her for the life of her people. Do you have some design for her days?

Levoreth quickened her pace angrily.

I am not Anue that I would stand in the house of dreams and shape the futures of men. Would you assign to me more might than is my due? Listen well, Gavrinsdaughter! I did not seek my lot in life, for though I am the Mistress of Mistresses, there are powers beyond me that, unseen and unsought, move me to my fate, just as they do you. We are all borne upon the wind blowing from the house of dreams.

The hound padded alongside her, head hanging low. Behind them, Giverny trailed, deaf to their speech.

You speak of legends beyond legends, but you are the only legend we know to be true, for we see you with our own eyes and feel your touch upon the earth. You are our bulwark against the Dark. Do not judge me too harshly, Lady. You are the stillpoint of my people. Can we not help but think the skeins of our fate hang from your hands?

The encampment bustled with people: women washing clothes, children carrying buckets of water to a trough set up just beyond the wagons, where a string of horses was picketed. A fire crackled under an iron pot suspended from two crossed pikes. Levoreth could smell sage and onions and the sweet meat of the roebuck. She inhaled—dried rosemary, wild carrots that must have been plucked from the Scarpe itself, and a sprinkling of pepper all the way from Harth and worth its weight in gold. On the far side of the camp, the Dolani men-at-arms had their own cook fire burning. Night was coming. The hound lingered nearby for a moment and then slunk off among the wagons. Giverny brushed past her and Levoreth found a single blue bonnet in her hand.

The flames from the fire in the center of the encampment flickered sparks up into the darkness. In the east, the moon gleamed a yellow so feeble it seemed the night was about to swallow it up forever. But the stars overhead shone brilliantly within the black expanse. They were like the gleams of countless jewels—some tinged with the ruby's dark wine, others hinted at blue sapphire fire, yet even more gleamed with the incandescence of diamonds. As the darkness deepened, they burned all the brighter.

Someone handed Levoreth a bowl of stew and a hunk of bread. She sat down and leaned back against a wagon wheel. The bowl was warm in her hands. Across the way, she could see the duke talking with Cullan Farrow and several old men. Horses, no doubt. Smoke curled up from the pipes in their hands. She closed her eyes and let her mind drift, listening to the sounds of the night.

Children played at hide-and-seek among the tethered horses of the herd. Someone plucked a guitar, murmuring the words of an old Vornish love song. A mother crooned to her baby. The knitting needles of the duchess clacked quietly together. A young man-at-arms grumbled to the sergeant about having to eat their own food, as the old Farrow woman in charge of the cook pot had beckoned them over. The sergeant explained that their rations were good enough and that he'd break both his arms if he saw him laying a finger on the Farrow women.

Levoreth smiled. The Farrow women were famed through all the lands of Tormay for their beauty. But they were also renowned for their tempers and willingness to stick a knife in any who might offend. They wouldn't be needing any sergeants to defend their honor.

Lady.

Levoreth sighed. The hound lowered herself down beside her.

Gala Gavrinsdaughter.

The night is replete with sorrow. From three hearts it wells.

You would tell me, I think.

Aye. The mother of my little one. I have tasted her dreams ever since her firstborn went away. She is of the blood of Harlech, as you must know, Mistress of Mistresses. She dreams of shadows. Harlech dreams true, do they not?

And the second?

She is you, Lady. I can smell it in the change of season and the scent of the earth. I can—

You presume, hound.

The old dog flattened her head against the ground and was still.

And the third?

But the dog did not answer her and soon crept away into the darkness. Levoreth tasted the stew but it had gone cold. She got up, stiffly, and walked to the fire. Light flickered on the ring of wagons that encompassed it, gleaming on faces. A woman stooped over the cook pot. She straightened and turned. The promise of beauty and grace in the girl Giverny was fulfilled in her. A sheaf of silvering black hair was bound back from her head. Firelight pooled in her eyes.

"Lady Callas," she said.

"I'm only her niece," said Levoreth.

"Still a lady," said the woman. "There's old noble blood in your family line." Her head tilted to one side, her face impassive.

"My stew's gone cold."

The woman took the bowl from her and refilled it.

"I am Rumer Farrow," she said. "Giverny's mother."

"Yes, I know."

"Giverny is all we have left these days, Cullan and I. Ever since our son went away. As you know. As everyone, all of Tormay, knows." There was no bitterness in her voice, only resignation.

"She'll be a great lady someday."

Rumer touched her arm, as if to apologize. "But this I do not want for her. I would only wish her a quiet life, a man to love her just as mine loves me, children to grow up around her like young colts. This is all she needs. This is all anyone would ever need. Is not anything more than this only a burden and chasing of the wind?"

"You speak truly," returned Levoreth. She could not keep the harshness from her voice. "What more could anyone want? May all have such lives and find quiet deaths at their end, surrounded by loved ones and peace. Yet the Dark rises and men ride off to war. Lightning strikes where it will. Do we choose any of this? It chooses us and sweeps us along toward ends we can never see."

The woman bowed her head and, when she raised it, there were tears in her eyes. "I am from Harlech, Lady. We dream true there, for the veil of the sky wears thin in Harlech. I can't help but dream. I see my son's face, my young Declan, returning to me, but of my daughter I see nothing but darkness and the silent earth."

Giverny then appeared from the shadows and twined her arms around Rumer's waist. They stood and looked at Levoreth—the daughter smiling and the mother staring mutely. Levoreth did not dream her own dreams that night. The ground whispered to her of Rumer's sorrow, and she stirred uneasily on her pallet.

The duke of Dolan and his party stayed one more day with the Farrows and then left, with many plans voiced concerning colts and broodmares between Hennen and Cullan, until the duchess rolled her eyes and even Rumer laughed. The Farrows stood and waved goodbye until the vastness of the Scarpe swallowed them up in its horizon of grass, and they were gone.

"Fine people, fine people," said the duke happily.

"To be honest, my dear," remarked his wife, "they are pleasant. Rumer Farrow is a remarkable lady, and her father was the lord of Lannet in Harlech. I'd rather spend the next two weeks with them than having to survive Hearne and that insufferable sop Botrell."

The duke was pleased and startled at this. He suggested that perhaps they should return, as he was beginning to regret not buying a certain broodmare Cullan had shown him.

"Certainly not," said the duchess. "We're going to Hearne and the fair and Levoreth will fall in love, and I shall be polite to Botrell. We'll soon see the Farrows again, I'm sure. Perhaps they'll come through Andolan later in the fall."

"Oh, all right," said her husband.

"Duty, my dear."

"Hmmph."

CHAPTER THIRTY-NINE
FALLING FROM GREAT HEIGHTS

That day, Jute fell from the tower that stood in the center of the university grounds.

The tower stood by itself in the middle of a courtyard. He trudged up the stairs, hoping for a good view of the city from the top. The steps creaked under his feet, old oak worn to a dark, satiny sheen. Up and up they went, until his face was wet with sweat. The stairs ended beneath a trap door, which he pushed up, and he found himself standing on a platform. Hearne stretched around him in a patchwork of minarets, spires with their weathervanes pointing for the west wind, and flat-topped roofs, colorful and flapping with drying laundry. Sunlight shone on brick and stone, thatch and slate, and the green copper roofs of the regent's castle, perched on Highneck Rise. The castle rose up amidst the white stone villas of the nobility clustered on the heights. Its towers were the highest in Hearne, but the tower Jute stood upon was almost as high. Beyond the rooftops, the sea was a streak of blue under an even bluer sky.

A cloud drifted across the sun, and something creaked on the stairs far below him. At first, he thought he was imagining things. But then he heard it again. Wood creaking accompanied by an almost inaudible, wet sort of squish. The sounds came one after the other, climbing up the stairs. It was all he could do to clamp his chattering teeth together and remain silent. Hands trembling, he eased the trap door down and sat on it, thinking. Nothing at all came to mind except the desperate desire to jump up and down and scream.

"Hawk!" he said. "Please. Where are you?"

The cloud hiding the sun thickened and grew into a gray mass that obscured the entire sky. Rain began to fall. Jute scrambled over to the edge of the platform and looked down, hoping for ledges, handholds, anything. However, a master craftsman had his hand in the building. The stones of the tower had been fitted together with perfection. Jute leaned over and ran his fingers over the stone joints, and a groan of despair escaped his lips. They were impossibly smooth.

The trap door slammed open behind him. A stench of corruption filled the air, a stink of damp and rotting things. He had smelled the same odor before—in the cellar of Nio's house. He did not even turn to look but threw himself out into space.

This is going to hurt. Much worse than any beating the Juggler gave. For only a second. Maybe less. I hope.

The cobblestone court rushed up toward him.

A last thought floated by.

One more day would have been nice.

And then the wind caught him.

Softer than silk.

Silent.

Something—a door—eased open inside his mind for a moment, and then, just as gently, closed again. The wind left him standing, bewildered and mouth hanging open, in the middle of the cobblestone court. Around him rose the walls of the university and before him loomed the tower. A damp snarl floated down from high above. He turned and ran.

Jute had no clear thought except that he needed to hide. Somewhere quiet and still. A small space. Small spaces are always safer, but he shivered in doubt and thought about the open expanses of the sky. Hurtling around a corner, he started down a flight of steps. A man hurried into view at the bottom and looked up. Severan. They both stopped, staring at each other.

"What happened, boy?" said the old man. "Was it only a ward that set the air in this place quivering? I'm running out of explanations for my fellow scholars!"

"I don't know," said Jute, his voice cracking. "You tell me—you're a wizard, aren't you?"

"A scholar," said the old man. "Only a scholar. The true wizards all died many years ago. Come. We must talk."

The boy followed him to what was obviously the old man's rooms: a simple cell furnished with a writing desk, several cane chairs grouped around a banked brazier, and an iron-bound chest. Off to one side was a sleeping alcove. Severan stirred the brazier to glowing life.

"It's here," said the boy dully. "That thing. The wihht. It came for me. I was on top of the tower in the courtyard."

The old man's face turned pale. "And you escaped it for the second time? There's more than luck at play here. Who are you, boy? You must trust me."

"Why should I?" Jute's hands curled into fists.

"I was Nio's friend a very long time ago. He was a different man then. I don't know him now. Listen, Jute. I understand why you don't trust me completely. Hopefully in time you will. Perhaps if you understand more of what might happen. Scholars like myself are not just interested in the past. We're interested in the future, in what might happen. In what might become. I think there are other things that might become interested in you. Not just Nio and his wihht."

"What do you mean—other *things?*" asked the boy.

"When you broke into Nio's house, you stepped beyond the everyday world of Hearne. An entire life can be lived in this city without awareness of the larger world behind and beyond it. Anyone who can live this way should thank fortune for such happiness. They'll never face such a thing as you faced in Nio's cellar. But even a wihht pales in comparison to the ancient powers that serve the Dark."

"The Dark? Is there really such a thing as the Dark? I thought it was something made up, a bedtime story."

"Rest assured, it isn't a bedtime story." Severan smiled somewhat. "Unless, of course, you want to give children nightmares. You might laugh, but there's a great deal of truth to be found in bedtime stories and the like. You see, such tales don't just spring up out of nothing. They weave themselves into being out of truth. A whisper in the countryside became gossip in a nearby village. Details were added in the local inn, influenced by candlelight and winter boredom and too many tankards of ale. Traders passing through took the local tales and carried them away to the cities. And as years followed upon years, the stories worked their way into history, or into the delicious bedtime terrors mothers tell their children in hopes of securing their obedience. The very oldest of such stories, however, are as rare as pearls and, I think, even more valuable still."

"What are those stories about?" asked Jute. He drew his knees up to his chin and the old man noticed, for the first time, that the boy's eyes had a peculiar silvery sheen that gleamed in the light of the brazier.

"The very oldest ones are about four words and four mysterious creatures of immense power. Such power that the earth would shatter and reform itself at their bidding, that the wind and sea was theirs to command. The beasts and birds were their servants. They were the four *anbeorun*—the four stillpoints. It was said, though this has only been mentioned once in the single surviving copy of the Lurian Codex, that even the dragons would still their flame for them. The book that the wizard Staer Gemyndes wrote, the *Gerecednes*, surely contains even more knowledge of the anbeorun." He sighed and shook his head. "I'd happily spend the rest of my life looking for that book."

"There are no such things as dragons," said Jute.

"Don't be so quick to presume," said Severan. "There are more terrible things than dragons that walk this earth."

"I suppose so," said the boy doubtfully. "But what does all of that have to do with the four words?"

"Patience. We're coming to that. Most legends are rooted in fact, no matter how thin that fact might be when compared to the legend. Sometimes, the opposite is true. When the armies of Oruso Oran II sacked the city of Lascol, the plunder carried back to Harth included many books from the ducal library. Later, cataloguing the books, a court scribe discovered the memoirs of the wizard Sarcorlan."

"How do you know this?"

"That scribe went on to become one of the greatest historians that Harth has ever known. And if Harth is known for anything, it's known for a rigid attention to details, which has resulted in a highly efficient army, orderly cities, and marvelous historians. When I read the scribe's account of the discovery, I journeyed to Harth to see the memoir for myself."

Severan fumbled a ring of keys from his robe and unlocked the chest in the corner. He returned to his chair with a black book in his hands. He muttered a word over the thing and then opened it.

"Is that the memoir?" said Jute.

"Er, yes," said the old man.

"You're a thief?"

"Do you think thievery is the sole right of thieves?"

"No," said the boy, smiling. "It just seems a bit odd. Especially at your age."

"You shouldn't be so presumptuous. I, of course, don't mind. A dragon might." He turned over some pages. "Sarcorlan was never known for his humility, even on his deathbed. Listen to this, however, for his love of the truth was equal to his pride, as he remarks. 'What I am about to relate is true, for I am Sarcorlan of Vomaro, and all of Tormay has never known a greater wizard than I. My latter years were spent in peace, living in the mountains east of the great forest. A village nearby saw to my wants, which were few.'"

Severan paused in his reading. "I think he's referring to the Forest of Lome, which would have placed his village in the Morn Mountains east of Dolan, though I'm not completely certain. At any rate, there's no village there now." He turned back to the book and continued.

"In the spring after the fall of Ancalon, when the snows had melted in the mountain passes and the roads were open, a caravan of traders came east from Hull. I walked down to the village, as was my wont. The headman valued my presence when strangers came through, and thus we had a private agreement concerning such occasions. Three traders with their horses and pack-mules crested the ridge when I came to the inn. I cast a simple knowing on them, and they were as they appeared: tired traders and overworked, overloaded animals. Something else lingered in the knowing, however—a faint hint of power. Intrigued, I waited until they had arrived at the inn and set about unloading their goods. The whole village gathered around. There was the usual array of stock: knives, axe heads, Dolani wool, sea salt from Flessoray, spices, and a jumble of oddments spilling from a wooden chest.

"While the traders bickered with the villagers over the value of the local copper and opals, I cast a stronger knowing. This time, I felt a spark centered within the wooden chest. It was like nothing I had ever encountered before, and I am, mind you, Sarcorlan of Vomaro. At the bottom of the chest, tucked away in a small sack, I found the pearl. The trader to whom it belonged was reluctant to sell the thing, protesting that he would find a higher price in the markets of Mizra. I am not ashamed to say that I put a compulsion on him, for I gave him three fire opals for the stone, which was better than any price he would have received in Mizra. He did not know what he owned. I did him a favor to take it off his hands, for he was a fool to have been carrying such a thing.

"I did not ask him how he had obtained it, as the furtive look in his eyes proclaimed his association with the Thieves Guild. Still, to be sure, I probed his memory as he cheated Wan the Miller's wife out of several lengths of homespun cloth. There was nothing of import within his mind—just the usual, brutish thoughts typical of most men. As I suspected, he had bought the stone among an assortment of stolen goods from a member of the Guild in Damarkan. A certain Jaro Gossan. Perhaps I shall have to visit Damarkan someday and find this man?

"For thirty days and thirty nights, I studied the pearl. That is, I think it was a pearl. It resembled one, but it was harder and heavier than any pearl should have been. In color, it was dark blue with wisps of green in it that drifted upon the surface of the blue, but only if I were not gazing at the thing. Power lay bound within the pearl, bound in some strange fashion that kept it, I think, sleeping. The peculiar thing about the binding enchantment was that it seemed to be one and the same with that which it bound—a balance I had never encountered before. Despite all my skill, however, I was unable to unlock the enchantment.

"Had it not been for my leaky roof, I would have never discovered the secret of the pearl. A storm arose in the night, and water dripped down onto my table as I sat staring at the pearl. Several drops splashed on the pearl, and it was then I heard the sound of the sea. The surge of surf. The crash of waves on rock. At that moment a geas took hold of me, compelling me up from my chair. I could not muster the necessary strength to fight the compulsion. If truth be told, I was curious enough to see the matter out and where I would go. Pearl in hand, I left my abode and set off into the night in a westerly direction. At first, the geas was content enough to allow me to walk, but after several hours it grew so strong that I took to the winds in the form of a gray kestrel, pearl clutched in one claw.

"I did not wonder at the time why I chose the form of a kestrel, but it made sense after I thought on the whole affair, days later. Gray kestrels are lovers of the sea and do their hunting over the deep. I flew west for two days, over the mountains and across the plain of Scarpe. I crossed the hills of the Mearh Dun and then turned north, following the

145

cliffs along the coast of Thule to the country of Harlech. It was at the bay of Flessoray that the geas pulled me out to sea, toward the islands. The waves were white with foam and the sea looked a cold gray, gray to match the sky and the feathers in my wings. On the barren rocks of Lesser Tor, I settled to the sand and retook my human form. The geas was gentle on my mind, bidding me stand and wait. In my hand, however, the pearl warmed.

"A wind sprang up and whipped the waves into a frenzy of spray. And out of the breakers the girl walked. She was formed of water and foam and shadows. Her skin was shell white, and seaweed twined within her dark hair in glistening strands of purple. A garment of water flowed about her limbs. Her eyes were a blue so dark that I could not discern a pupil within them. It was the unlined face of a child, one who has just woken from slumber and blinks sleepily in the sunlight. But I would not presume to guess her age, for her body was formed of the sea and the sea has existed from the earliest days. She was more beautiful than anything I had ever seen in my life, yet I feared her greatly. She smiled at me and the geas vanished from my mind.

"'Thank you for bringing back my name,' she said, and her voice was like the sighing of the waves. She reached out one pale, foam-colored hand and I placed the pearl within her grasp. I could do nothing else. She smiled again and turned to go, but I found my voice and desperately called after her to wait. At the edge of the waves, she looked back.

"'What is your name?' I said. A frown crossed her face and an ominous calm fell on the sea. Later, thinking back, I realize that the tide had stilled, but I did not recognize it then, so intent was I on her face. She spoke then, and the word was in a language I had never heard nor have ever heard since. I was almost unmade in the sound of that single word she voiced. For in the uttering was all the power and form of the sea itself. The sea roared back in response, waves rising and pounding in an exuberant fury of existence on the shoreline. At my feet, the rocks trembled and instantly became roiling sea. The island was melting away. She had vanished. And my body was dissolving into water. I flung myself skyward, taking the form of a hawk and frantic to escape. It was all I could do to keep that shape, for the word she had spoken still battered and grasped at my being. I strove onward, east, and so arrived on the coast of Harlech, exhausted and spent.

"Never in my life have I been so near death. And not just death. This was unmaking and a way of power long denied to those of us who are wizards, for we cannot tamper with the fabric of life. To unravel one small portion might mean the unraveling of all.

"I made my way back home, still in hawk's form. In my mind was the memory of the word she had spoken. I examined the remembrance. I was able to inscribe the barest hint of the word into good serviceable letters, but I soon discovered that if I delved into the memory deeper to retrieve the complete word, objects around me began to turn into water. Books, my furniture, my cooking pot, the clothes on my back, and, at one point, my entire left arm melted into a puddle of seawater before I was able to wrest it back into flesh.

"I resolved, then, to press the matter no further and sealed the memory with the strongest binding I could muster. I pray it does not reawaken some unexpected hour as I dream on my bed and so change me forever.

"The hint of the word I had already written, however, and this I set about studying. As summer faded into a rainy fall, I came to discover the ancient feorh of water woven within the word. As you know, there is a way to command the simple feorh, or essence, of what water is: *vatn*. This is known and used by most wizards. The girl's word (I only use the term "girl" because I am not sure what she was), however, was proof of a language older than existence itself. The word also indicated the existence of three additional words, as if the four together completed each other as do the sides of a square.

"At this point, I closed my books and stood in the doorway. It was a gloomy afternoon. Rain fell, blown by the wind from an iron-colored sky onto the soggy earth. Behind me, within the cottage, a fire burned on the hearth. Understanding bloomed in my mind. I had read the Lurian Codex when I was an apprentice, thinking it merely an entertaining collection of questionable history and quaint fables—the old tale of four words spoken in the darkness: wind, earth, sea, and fire. The four stillpoints that encompass existence. The four wanderers. The *anbeorun*. As I stood in my doorway, a sudden fear came to me. Fire, for example, is an amoral thing that can be used just as readily for good as it can for evil. A home can be warmed by fire or be destroyed by the same. The power I had seen unleashed at the isle of Lesser Tor could easily unmake the world. Her eyes, though, had been free of guile. They had been the serene eyes of a child. But if her power was turned toward evil, then there was no wizard, no creature in my knowledge, no army that would be able to stand against such might. Even worse, if there are four stillpoints that encompass all that is, then the danger is much greater. For though one might not turn to the shadow, there would still be three others that might fall.

"I am an old man as I set this ink to paper, but she still walks through my dreams."

Severan stopped reading and closed the book. The night sky outside the window was studded with stars. The boy stirred the brazier into flame. They were both silent for a while as they stared into the coals.

"Sometimes," said Jute, "I would run away from working the street and go down to the beach, sit on the rocks, and stare at the sea. I could sit there for hours. The waves going and coming back endlessly. She would have been out there all the time, wouldn't she?"

"If Sarcorlan is to be believed, and I think he is. I'd wager he encountered the anbeorun of the sea. Of water."

"And then the Juggler would beat me for not bringing in enough for the day." The boy shrugged and forced a laugh. "I'd always go back, sooner or later." He looked up. "But what has all of that, words and power and wizards, have to do with me doing my job?"

The old man sighed. "I'm afraid what was a simple job to you interfered with years of work done by Nio. He always was asking questions about the anbeorun. He told us some of his knowledge, grudgingly, for he needed our help in searching the university. We helped him, though we were all looking for different things. Books, words, bits of knowledge hidden in the ruins. He knew what he was looking for. A small wooden box. I daresay he spent years searching for it. I think he had some idea the box contained something to do with the anbeorun."

"You mean no one ever opened it?" the boy asked.

"No. When Nio found the box, he couldn't open it. The spell binding it shut was too strong. And he, mind you, is the strongest of us all. He didn't say anything at first. Later, though, he told us. Reluctantly. He thought, I suppose, that one of us might have some insight he had not divined. The thing's presence drove the servants mad and he's lived in that house, alone, for the past two years, with the box secreted in his tower. We lost interest in it after a while, for we all hoped to find the *Gerecednes* manuscript of Staer Gemyndes. That was always our real goal. Not an old box."

"But I don't understand," said Jute. "How could someone like him not be able to open a little box?"

147

"Just because someone's a wizard, it doesn't mean you can wave your hands and have pigs fly about. Though it would probably be simpler to sprout wings on a pig than to open that box."

"I'm sure someone'll figure it out someday," mumbled Jute.

Severan looked at him curiously, but the boy would not meet his glance. Outside, the wind rattled at the window, as if it wanted to get inside the room.

CHAPTER FORTY
THE CONTENTS OF THE BOX

"Tonight's the night, my good Dreccan."

The Silentman rubbed his hands together.

"Not until the gold's safely in our coffers," said Dreccan Gor.

"Always the cautious one," said the Silentman.

"I'm a Gor, and Gors are always cautious. I'd be that way even if you weren't paying me."

The Silentman and his advisor were hurrying along through the passage leading to the Guild court. Their shadows trailed behind them, for Dreccan was carrying a burning torch in his hand.

"The job's good as done," said the Silentman. "And there's nothing I like more than finishing a job. Unless it be gold. And the gold'll be plentiful for this job. Plenty for everyone. At least for you and me."

"Less a few coins here and there."

"How's that?" said the Silentman.

"Ronan will need his share, as will the Juggler. And Smede, of course."

"I don't grudge Ronan, he's a faithful dog, and we can't do without Smede to manage the books, curse his smelly little soul, but why's that fat oaf getting a cut?"

"Because," said Dreccan, trying to stay patient, "It was one of his boys that did the job in the first place. And then, of course, we had the little fellow done away with."

"Pity we can't do away with the Juggler as well. Why can't we do that? Have Ronan cut his throat."

"The Juggler, as you doubtlessly know, my lord, has proven to bring a consistent profit for us. His children sustain a steady stream of money into our coffers—"

"Then just have the children—"

"—and without his fatherly hand, I suspect that stream would dry up."

"Right, right," said the Silentman irritably. "This person needs that person to tell them what to do, and that other person needs someone else telling them how to do their job. Can't any of our people think for themselves? Perhaps we should have a few murdered, just to keep the rest of 'em on their toes."

They came to the end of the passage. An iron door was set in the wall. It bore a knocker fashioned in the likeness of a horse's head. There was no handle. Dreccan let the knocker fall. A deep bell-like tone rang out and echoed away. It sounded like a funeral knell. The door swung open for them.

"He should be here soon," said Dreccan.

The Court of the Guild was dark and empty, but the lamps high on the walls winked on, one by one, at their entrance. The light slanted across carvings etched into the stone walls and filled them with shadow. The footsteps of the two men were the only sound in the court. The Silentman shivered, and it seemed to Dreccan that the man's face trembled beneath the blur of his obscuring charm.

"Some days, old friend," said the Silentman, "I miss the sunlight. We spend too much time down here in the dark."

"Sunlight's nice," said Dreccan. "But gold is better."

The Silentman sat down in his stone chair on the dais and drew his cloak about his knees. "The cold in this place gets into my bones and aches. I'm getting old. Damn the man, where is he?"

"If our client is a man," said his advisor, frowning.

"What is he? A woman? An under-sized ogre? I don't care what he is, as long as his gold's good. Judging by the down payment, it's very good."

"I'd like to know," said Dreccan. "There was something unnerving about the fellow. Put me off my supper for days afterward."

"Who cares? Hand it to me." The Silentman turned the box over in his hands. "Strange, that such a little thing would command so much money. Have we ever gotten such a price, Dreccan? Never in my memory. It can't be the box itself our client is interested in. Look at this ugly carving. No, it's definitely what's in the box that matters. I wonder what it is? At that price, I can't imagine what it is."

"Magic," said Dreccan. "I'm sure of it. A book, or some object full of spells and power. These scholars and wizards, such as the old fools searching the university ruins, they'll spend their whole lives in search of one word from older days. Whatever's in that box is probably worth a lot more than just one word."

"Dreccan?"

"Yes?"

"You didn't try to open the thing, did you? Because this box won't open. See here? It won't open."

"My lord!"

"I can't help it. I had to try. Ever since I was a boy, I've never seen something locked that I didn't want to open. At any rate, no harm done because this thing won't open. Funny thing is, I can't sense anything magic about this box at all."

"It must have a locking spell on it. That's magic enough for me."

"Not necessarily so," said the Silentman. "Might be a lever built into the wood. Push on the hawk's beak or the like. Ingenious, some of these carpenter sorts. Though I'd have had the fellow whipped for making such ugly carvings."

At that moment, the knocker on the door tolled. Both men jumped. The tone echoed through the empty court and then died away into silence.

"Welcome to the Court of the Guild!" said the Silentman.

There was no answer. The lamps seemed to dim and the room grew even colder than it was. The Silentman shivered and pulled his cloak tightly around his shoulders. The little box was heavy in his lap. He strained his eyes but he could not see anything in the gloom. But then he blinked and there was the figure. Just like before. It stood in front of the dais. He could have sworn, a second before, nothing had been there. Damn Dreccan! The advisor's words had slipped into his mind and taken root. The figure was short and thin, shrouded in a cloak. The face was hooded and covered in shadow.

"Welcome to my court," said the Silentman.

The figure bowed its head but said nothing.

"I trust you've found your visit to Hearne profitable—that is, if you're not from our city? I hope you haven't minded the wait. These jobs can be difficult, you know, arranging all the details and—"

"No apologies are necessary," said the figure. The voice was low and muted. There was something peculiar about the sound, as if it were coming through water from a long way off. An obscuring charm, thought the Silentman to himself. A powerful one, too. Well, I won't grudge him that. After all, I use them myself.

"This is the appointed day," continued the figure. It paused and its head turned from the Silentman to Dreccan and then back. "Where's the box?"

"Right here," said the Silentman. "And our gold?"

"First the box. Was it found where I said it was?"

"Precisely," said Dreccan. "Right where you said."

The Silentman nodded. "A child could've waltzed in and lifted it."

"It took a great deal of skill," said Dreccan hastily, "our best men. And not without danger. Sadly, we lost one on the job."

The hooded face turned to him.

"Was the box opened?"

"Of course not," said the Silentman. "We followed your instructions to the letter. The Guild's about business, sir. When we accept a contract, we keep our word. We're known through all of Tormay for—"

"Put it on the steps."

Feeling somewhat disgruntled, the Silentman placed the box on the dais steps and then retreated back to his chair. The little fellow obviously did not trust them. The figure crouched over the box but did not touch it. The hood lowered until it was almost touching the carved hawk's head on the lid. And then, the figure sniffed sharply. It straightened up.

"What have you done?!" said the figure.

"What do you mean?" said the Silentman. "We've got you your box, haven't we? Where's our gold now?"

"Your gold?" said the figure. "Curse your gold! You've opened the box!"

"You must be mistaken," said the Silentman. "No one's opened the blasted thing."

"The box has been opened, and what was once within is now gone. You'll not get your gold!"

"Here now," said the Silentman. "How do I know you're telling the truth and not just trying to swindle us out of our gold, hey? What about that? I wasn't born yesterday!"

"Fool! I would happily give you the wealth of the entire world for what was once in this box. I would have filled this court with gold. But you have brought your doom upon you. You and this accursed city!"

"Doom?" said the Silentman, alarmed at these words. "What do you mean by that?"

"Death," said the figure. "Death, and something worse. Unless you can do one thing."

"What's that?"

"Bring the person who opened the box. Bring them alive and you yourself shall live."

The Silentman gulped and mopped his forehead. The person who opened the box?

"Certainly," he said. "Anything you want. Anything at all."

"It isn't what I want. My wants are nothing. It's what my master wants. And he is coming."

"Oh, he is? And when do you think—"

"Find the person who opened the box. Quickly, for you do not know what you have done. The power that was inside the box is beyond your imagining, the power to destroy, the power to bring to life in a single breath. The power to preserve. Do you not know that all of Tormay is as dross in comparison to what that box held? Find the person who opened it. My master is coming soon!"

The Silentman opened his mouth to say something—he was not sure what—but the figure was gone. The lamplight flared and the shadows in the court retreated.

"Ronan," said Dreccan, after what seemed like a long silence.

"Find him!" The Silentman pounded his fist on his chair. "Find him now!"

"And what of the boy?" said Dreccan.

"What do you mean?" said the Silentman. "The boy's dead. Ronan killed him."

"But you heard what he said."

"What are you babbling about? I want that gold!"

"The power to destroy." Dreccan's face was pale in the lamplight. "The power to destroy, the power to bring to life in a single breath. The power to preserve."

When the Silentman spoke. His voice was slow and tired.

"Then maybe it isn't just Ronan we need to find."

CHAPTER FORTY-ONE
THE VIEW TO THE EAST

The hawk angled through the night sky on his outstretched wings. The city of Hearne lay far beneath him, pricked with light here and there, but mostly sleeping in darkness on the edge of the sea. The night sky above the hawk had more light to offer than the city, blazing and sparkling with stars in a perfectly clear expanse. The stars seemed impossibly close, and they bent their gaze down to the world and to the hawk flying alone in the night.

There were, perhaps, only four people in all of Tormay, save the hawk, who would have had the wisdom to hear the speech of stars, but they all were asleep. Only the hawk heard.

The stars hastened lower, growing in brilliance and deepening in the colors of their fire. Ruby, emerald, diamond and amethyst, the night grew darker and blacker around them as they burned ever brighter with their gem-like fire.

Hast thou seen? whispered one star.

Hast thou seen and hast thou not heard?

There is one who dreams in the darkness.

But he sleeps still, said another star.

Thankfully, he sleeps.

And thou, little wing, thou must watch and wait.

Watch and wait.

Look ye to the east.

Fly well, little wing, murmured another star.

Aye, fly well, for the house of dreams sleeps not.

Never sleeps but doth watch over all.

Even the stars, added another stars.

Even the stars!

Rejoice!

And with this word echoing in the sky, the voices of the stars grew and rose in liquid song, thrilling through the dark and the bitter cold and the unfathomable distances of space. The sky trembled with the sound. The beauty of it was so sharp and sudden that the hawk faltered in his flight. But then the chorus died away and the stars withdrew to their appointed courses, shining in comfort and sorrow. The two will ever go hand-in-hand, for that is the balance of wisdom. The hawk knew it well, knew it to his own comfort and sorrow.

As he flew, the hawk considered carefully what he had heard. His gaze until this moment had ever been on the city of Hearne, particularly on the dark ruins of the university where the boy Jute slept. Now, however, he turned his beak to the east and looked there. There was no one in all of Tormay, no person, animal, or bird, who had as keen eyesight as the hawk. But even he could not pierce the night with his vision. All he could make out, far across the miles and distance, was the vague, jagged outlines of the

Morn Mountains in the east, their snowy peaks touched here and there with starlight and moonlight.

With a shrug of his wings, the hawk turned and spiraled down toward the city. Hearne slept in an uneasy quiet below him. He could hear the surge and crash of the waves on the beach beneath the wharves. He could smell bread baking as a baker went about his lonely morning duties. His sharp eyes caught a hint of movement in an alley as three cats strolled along, careless and casual in their pursuit of rodents. Despite these tiny signs of life, the city lay in darkness. A deep darkness.

The hawk alighted on top of the tallest tower in the university ruins. He furled his wings. He could feel the whispering of the wards guarding the university. Down and away to his right, in one of the larger and better preserved wings of the complex, he sensed Jute. Sleeping, safe and sound. The hawk nodded in satisfaction at this. The wind blowing past the tower seemed to sigh in agreement.

The hawk turned and gazed to the east. There was nothing to see there except for the night, of course. But that did not matter to the hawk. He waited and watched and he did not sleep. He spent the remainder of the night there, perched in silence on the tower roof. And even when the first faint blush of sunrise crept up into the eastern sky, the hawk was still watching.

CHAPTER FORTY-TWO
A SUDDEN DEMOTION

The Knife drowsed in a chair behind the Stone Crow Inn after a breakfast of fried mushrooms, sausages, and eggs. He tilted the chair back against the wall. The view was not the best, but it was quiet. Several horses gazed at him solemnly from over the stable fence. He could smell hay and manure and the thick, warm scent that was horse. The morning sunshine was the color of honey. He shut his eyes. A memory floated through his mind, of his mother likening him to a lazy cat always seeking sunlight to sleep in. A reluctant smile crossed his face. He hadn't thought of his mother in a long time.

Ronan would have fallen asleep had not someone cleared their throat nearby. It was a polite, apologetic sort of sound. Just out of boot's reach, he reflected to himself. Pity. He opened one eye. Smede took a step back.

Ronan sighed. "Can't it wait until next month?"

"The sun will be here another day," said Smede.

"But I may not. Go away. You bother my digestion. If I were regent, there'd be less Smedes in this city."

"One Smede will suffice," said Smede. "However, as much as we're both fascinated by myself, there's no time for pleasantries. The Silentman requests the honor of your presence. As soon as is convenient for you, which is—"

"At once, no doubt?" said Ronan.

"Of course," said Smede. The accountant followed him from the courtyard, smiling and rubbing his hands together. The horses gazed after them with placid eyes.

Ronan had guessed it was that. Smede hardly ever emerged into the sunlight unless it was for a serious matter. Because he kept the books for the Guild, he was one of the few Guild members who knew, so it was said, the real identity of the Silentman. The Silentman often used him as a messenger when he had something important brewing.

"I know where I'm going, Smede," said Ronan, quickening his pace. "Why don't you trot back to your numbers? Being seen with you won't do my reputation any good. You aren't a fit companion for the dreaded Knife."

"No, no. I don't mind a nice, brisk walk," said Smede, whose own habits rarely required him to do more than lifting his pen to the inkbottle. "Exercise is purported to promote health and long life, so I've read. I myself find that rigorous work cleanses the liver and sharpens the mental faculties so much so that, happily enough, the arithmetic of accounting seems to solve its own puzzles before my eyes. Truly, a blissful state. Though, the application of leeches produces the same effect in me. Do you find this for yourself as well?"

Hearne thronged with people that morning. The city was crowded enough any day of the year, for Hearne was the center, the heart of Tormay, the lodestone that drew travelers and traders from all other lands. It was here that the old seat of power had been, when kings still governed Tormay as one united land. Even though rule had dispersed to the duchies long ago, people still journeyed to Hearne to gawk at the castles and mansions, the spired terraces and manors that wound up the heights of Highneck Rise, the sprawling stone wharves, and the mysterious, ruined grandeur of the once-mighty university that now stood silent, warded and chained shut. And, of course, people came to Hearne for trade. The marketplaces of Hearne bought and sold everything there was to be had in all the duchies of Tormay. If money could purchase the thing, then it could be found in Hearne.

But this morning the streets were even more crowded than usual. For in a month's time, the annual Autumn Fair would begin, when the lords and ladies from all the duchies of Tormay came to Hearne to enjoy the hospitality of its regent, Nimman Botrell. The Fair was when every trader in Tormay came to buy and sell and barter. Magical oddities unearthed from the past, rare weavings and wines, gems and silks, dancing badgers and surly sandcats from southern Harth that could be enspelled into wards and, as such, provided one of the more vicious and effective protections for buildings that gold could buy. In short, the Autumn Fair was a time of celebration of the rare, the beautiful, the valuable, the finest things of Tormay trotted out to impress and astound, to enspell and ensnare. It was a time to make and lose fortunes.

And the Autumn Fair was a gold mine for the Thieves Guild.

The traders had been arriving all that week, carting in their goods by camel, mule, ship, and horseback. They would settle into rented quarters and begin preparations for the upcoming month. Ripe for the picking.

Ronan's fingers twitched in anticipation. A nice job or two with fat pickings, and with what he had coming from the chimney job the other night, he'd have enough to leave the city. He'd go to Flessoray and find himself an island. Fishing and cold sunlight. The sea.

Beside him, Smede plucked at his sleeve.

"What?" he said, palming an apple off a passing cart. He bit into it.

"Let's use the widow Grusan's place," said Smede. "It's the nearest entrance, just down the next alley, and the Silentman doesn't like to be kept waiting."

Various entrances and exits to the Silentman's headquarters were maintained by the Guild throughout the city. Several were in more public places, such as the Goose and Gold tavern, while others were located in private residences like the widow Grusan's house, and, as such, their existence was not as widely known among the lower rank and file of the Guild.

"Oh, all right," said Ronan, not willing to admit that he was ignorant of that particular entrance. The apple, half-eaten, sailed into the gutter. They turned down the alley.

They stopped at a wooden door tucked away in a corner. The door was so small and unobtrusive that the usual passerby would never have noticed it. The accountant knocked, and after a moment the door creaked open. An old woman peered out at them. The place was dank and dark, full of the odor of sour porridge and crowded with rickety furniture that seemed to consist mostly of broken arms and legs. Spiderwebs hung from the ceiling and festooned the furniture and walls with their dirty gray draperies.

"Splendid to see you, Widow Grusan," said Smede. "You look the perfect rose of health. What is it that you do? Exercise, hot tea, regular doses of sunlight, liver soup strained through cheesecloth to remove all the nasty bits of grit? Come, I must know your secret. Tell me all."

"Ale, and plenty of it," she said. The widow Grusan was a collection of bones and wrinkled skin. Wisps of hair straggled out from underneath a knit mobcap. "With two teeth, t'ain't much else I take. Now tell me, little man, where's my silver for the month? The Guild ain't paid me and I'm sitting here, chewing my own gums."

This was, perhaps, the only sort of thing that could send Smede running. He jumped like a startled rabbit at her words.

"Oh my, Ronan, we're late, and we—"

"We're not that late," said the Knife. "How much does the Guild owe you, madame?"

"—certainly don't want to keep, er, *him*, waiting, do we?"

"Five silver pieces," said the old woman. "Little enough to have the rabble tramping through my house all hours of the night, tracking dirt onto my clean floors and putting my pets into panic. It's not asking much to have the silver on time, is it now?"

"Of course not," said Ronan. "You should expect nothing less. The Guild prides itself on its efficient business practices, including the payment of debts. Isn't that right, Smede?"

"Well, yes," said Smede reluctantly.

"Believe it or not, madame," continued the Knife, "my friend Smede here happens to be the chief moneybags for the Guild and, as such, can easily pay you your silver."

"Fancy that," said the old woman. "Don't look much, does he, all pale and nervous-like. Twitchy."

At that point, Smede had no option. He haughtily drew himself up as best as he could and paid over the silver, dribbled from a greasy wallet he pulled from deep within his coat.

The widow Grusan led them to a room, where a large tapestry hung on one wall. The weaving was covered with blue whorls and meandering black lines that wove in and out of each other in a bewildering manner that made no sense to the eye. Probably of Harthian origin, the Knife thought to himself. And it was a ward. He could hear the faint warning buzz, trembling on the edge of his perception. Definitely a ward, but of a strange sort.

The old woman hobbled up to the tapestry and muttered a few inaudible words. The whorls and lines came alive, and, like a tangle of snakes roused from sleep, writhed away from the center of the tapestry until there was only plain, black wool in the middle of the hanging. Smede stepped forward, plunged right through the tapestry, and disappeared.

There was something unsettling about the tapestry, the way those lines had convulsed into life, squirming their way through the woven wool. The darkness of the room weighed on Ronan. He felt old and tired. What was he doing in the cramped, stone-lined life of Hearne? He needed wide open spaces and escape from forever wondering whether the next day would bring his death, with all the ghosts of his past an attentive audience.

"It won't stay open forever."

"What?" he said.

"The door—t'won't last," she said. Her voice was paper-thin, worn down by age. "Forward or back, lovie, that's our lot—we were never intended to stand still on the spot like a dumb ox, for death'll find us quick-like then."

He scowled at her and stepped forward through a soft, clinging sensation. Tendrils trailed over him, and then he was standing in a narrow passage. A torch guttered with cold, blue fire on the wall, only giving off enough light to reveal hints of dusty stonework and Smede's scowling face. Ronan turned, but there was nothing behind him except a blank stone wall.

"Come on, then," said the accountant. "We don't have all day."

It took them almost half an hour of walking through the gloomy passageway to reach the court of the Silentman. They walked in silence, for Smede was grumpy and Ronan didn't like talking with the accountant, even on the best of days. The passage twisted and turned in a fashion that defied logic. At various places, they came to cramped intersections at which other passages plunged away into the shadows. But at such spots, where it would be easy to lose the way, a white hand, painted high up on the wall, always pointed in the direction of the Silentman's court.

The passage ended at an iron door. There was no handle, only a knocker. The accountant glanced expressionless at Ronan and then let the knocker fall. A bell-like tone rang out and echoed away into the darkness of the passage. It sounded like a funeral knell. The door swung open.

Before them was a narrow hall, lined with pillars rising to a low ceiling. Carvings adorned the stone walls, elaborate scenes of the city, all of Hearne—the habitations of the rich and of the poor, the crowded marketplaces, the groves and fountains of Highneck Rise—chiseled in graceful strokes by some long-dead craftsman. There were a number of doors behind the pillars on either side of the walls. The same strange torches that lit the passageway with their cold, blue fire, were the only source of illumination in the hall.

As soon as Ronan stepped through the door, the flesh prickled on the back of his neck. Never, in all his time with the Guild had the court been empty when he had been there. It was always a place of exuberant life, of loud voices and a multitude of conversations jumbled together into the incoherent roar of a family. A sly, devious one that might stab you in the back given the opportunity—true—but still a family.

Now, however, there was only silence. At the far end of the hall there were two people. Standing beside the dais was the short figure of Dreccan Gor—steward and advisor of the Silentman. Slouching in the stone chair on the dais was the Silentman.

"Approach," said the Silentman.

Smede and Ronan walked down the long, lonely length of the hall. The Silentman leaned forward as they neared. His face was a blur of enspelled shadow that went out of focus whenever Ronan looked at him. The torches on either side of the dais limned his stone chair with blue light and lent a sickly hue to Dreccan Gor's face. The shadow shrouding the Silentman drank the light and was not diminished.

"How long has it been, Ronan," said the Silentman, "since you first entered my employment?"

"Thirteen years," offered Dreccan. "Almost to the month."

A trickle of sweat ran down Ronan's back.

"The steward's right, my lord," he said. "Nearly thirteen years."

The Silentman leaned back in his chair. "When I first became the Silentman, the Guild was a feeble construct, a rabble ruled by a meteoric succession of fools unable to see beyond their own lusts. But I've built the Guild into an enterprise stretching as far north as the coast of Thule and south to the bazaars of Damarkan in Harth. I've ruled the Guild with an iron hand—I won't deny it, particularly to the three of you who know more than all the other members taken together—but my severity has been more than balanced by our success. While much of this has been due to my will, some of this success hinged on surrounding myself with capable and extraordinary people—foremost, the three of you. If you would indulge me, the three of you are death, money, and wisdom personified. And I, of course, am power.

"The tedious machinations of money are, in your hands, Smede, a work of art. What were you before I found you—a draper's clerk in Vomaro, totting up bolts of silk? You pluck sense from a hundred different tangled threads of gold that weave their way through Hearne. With you at your books, I can rest easy, for I know your diligence."

"Thank you, my lord," said the accountant. Out of the corner of his eye, Ronan noticed Smede edging away from him.

"And Dreccan Gor, the Guild has profited from your advice. The Gors have always served the house of Botrell well, our thin-blooded line of ruling regents, as you still do today, but I fancy your wisdom does more good for the Guild."

The fat steward bowed.

"We Gors have advised the house of Botrell for nearly two centuries," the steward said. "Our present regent, Nimman Botrell, has proven to be somewhat of a wastrel and lazy hound, but we still have stood by him, my father before me, and now I. We are Gors."

A snarling laugh echoed from the shadows of the Silentman's chair. "And if the regent heard your words, Dreccan?"

"I'd tell him to his face, my lord," said the steward, "if I thought it beneficial for him and Hearne."

"I suspect you would, but you waste your time on Botrell."

Dreccan bowed again. "I serve you better with my ear in the regent's castle, privy to his thoughts."

"As long as there isn't a conflict," said the Silentman.

Ronan had the distinct impression that the conversation was a charade, a delay while the Silentman examined him from the shadows.

"And my Knife," said the Silentman.

A breath of air feathered across Ronan's face. Sweat sprang from his forehead at its touch.

"Thirteen years," said the shadowed figure. "Thirteen years and I've never had cause for complaint. All the hardest jobs, all the delicate matters I couldn't allow into other hands, and all the deaths I've found sadly necessary. I've never enjoyed a fellow Guild member's death—"

"Neither have I," muttered Ronan.

"But always you've proven faithful to the task."

"That he has," said Dreccan Gor. "Dependable. As even-keeled as one of those Thulish cargo boats."

"This is the problem, Ronan," continued the Silentman, ignoring his steward. "When the Guild's hired to do a job, it's my word given as surety that the customer will be satisfied. Our reputation rests on this. When that reputation is tarnished, our profits fall. This, I cannot have."

"I've always given the Guild my complete loyalty, my lord," said Ronan. "What prompts your speech? I confess myself confused."

"The Guild was hired recently to recover a box from the house of Nio Secganon, a member of that group of scholars mucking about the university ruins. They've been searching for ancient manuscripts and whatnot. Trinkets from the past. Botrell is a fool. He should never have allowed them permission. It's always best to let the past sleep. Anyway, the box had previously belonged to our client and then, unfortunately, found its way into the hands of this Nio fellow."

"The box carved with the hawk," said Ronan. "I remember it. I delivered it to your hands in full sight of the steward here, just a few days ago."

"Were all the details of the job observed?"

"Of course."

Memories from that night raced through Ronan's mind. The moonless sky. Listening at the chimney and hearing the stealthy descent of the boy down through the darkness.

159

Waiting crouched on the roof and gazing out over the sleeping skyline of Hearne. Tension in the rope, signifying the boy's return. The tiny, poisoned knife hidden and waiting inside his cloak. And the guilt. Numb as ever, but guilt nonetheless.

"But they weren't," said the Silentman. "The box was opened."

"What do you mean, my lord?" asked Ronan.

"The box was opened," repeated the Silentman. His voice, diminished to a rough whisper by whatever magic masked him, was vicious. "It was the simplest of instructions. What am I to do if my most trusted thief, my ablest killer, doesn't obey me?"

"I didn't open the thing," said Ronan, hating the shadowed figure in front of him. "Did I become the Knife to act like a child, to hear words and then forget them?"

"But the boy's dead, isn't he?"

"Beyond a doubt," said Ronan. "He took enough lianol to kill all four of us. He would've been dead thirty seconds after I jabbed him. I'd stake my life on it."

"I might have to take you up on that."

The words fell into the silence of the room and lay there, heavy and immobile. Torchlight gleamed on Dreccan Gor's face. His fat jowls glistened with sweat. A dispassionate part of Ronan's mind observed this with interest. *He's afraid. This fat old man I thought as sturdy and as unmovable as the hill of Highneck Rise. The unshakable Gor fears something. Something that isn't being said, behind these words and whatever is in the devious mind of our Silentman. Something stands in the shadows behind them.*

I'm afraid too.

"My lord?" said Ronan.

His senses tingled raw, poised for sudden movement. He felt the weight of the knife slung around his neck. One second. That's all it would take to draw and fling the knife. He could already see it buried in the Silentman's throat. He never missed. But he didn't know what kind of magic was guarding the man. His fingers twitched once and then were still.

"The box was opened before it reached this court. Of that I'm in no doubt."

"How do you know this is true, my lord?" said Ronan.

The Silentman waved one hand in irritation. "It was opened. It contained an item of great power and now it's gone. It was gone before you brought the box here."

"But you have only the word of your client on this. Perhaps he's merely—"

"Silence!"

The Silentman rose from his stone chair in fury. Shadow thickened around him, and the torches throughout the hall dimmed as if choked of air.

"You dare question me?" he said. "The box was opened."

"Not by me," said Ronan.

"Someone opened the accursed thing!"

Ronan's thoughts rapidly filled in the answers, the options. There was only one. But it was impossible. The boy's face, bewildered and frightened and knowing all at once, flashed through his mind. Vanishing down into the darkness of the chimney.

"That means," said the Silentman, "one of two possibilities. Either the boy opened the box, or you opened it."

"And," said Dreccan, "if the boy opened the box, he might still be alive."

"But the lianol—"

"The lianol would not have killed him if he had opened the box. Whatever was in the box might have—I'm not sure—protected him. Preserved him, perhaps."

The Silentman pointed a long black arm at Ronan. "One of you opened the box."

As quickly as the Silentman's fury had flared, it was gone, damped down and invisible beneath the shadows wreathing his body. But Ronan could hear it vibrating below the surface of the Silentman's words. Anger welled up within his own mind in answer. His mouth went dry with it and his hands trembled. The anger was tinged with fear. He hated the Silentman, then, as he never had, for having such an effect on him— the Knife, the dreaded enforcer of the Guild.

"There's magic involved," said the Silentman, speaking more to himself now than to the three assembled before him. He shifted restlessly on his chair. Shadow drifted around him. "We still don't know what the box contained. Our client is proving unusually close-mouthed on the subject. There's the possibility something unusual happened to the boy, as Dreccan said. If he opened the box. I won't discount that. You're convinced he's dead, Ronan. But your certainty puts you in a bad spot. For if he's dead, that leaves me with few options. You're hereby stripped of the position of the Knife of the Guild. You'll confine yourself within the city walls. Leave Hearne and your life is forfeit."

"I'll find him," said Ronan, his voice hoarse. "His body, anything—"

"Get out of my sight," said the Silentman. His voice was a monotone, as if his mind were already busy somewhere else.

White-faced, Ronan bowed. He turned and walked away. Smede scurried after him. The torches guttered in the hall as the door shut. The Silentman and his steward were alone.

"What are your thoughts, Dreccan?" said the Silentman. His voice was changing. The forced whisper relaxed to the even tones of a man well-bred. The shadows around his form retreated.

"I can't sleep at night but I hear that thing's voice whispering," said Dreccan. "I jump at every shadow and twitch at the slightest noise, thinking that he—that it—will be standing there when I turn. I fear the Guild chose poorly. Magic's a chancy matter at best, but this thing we're dealing with is probably something from the distant past, something that was old even before the Midsummer War. I don't doubt your pet wizard's capabilities, but this thing is beyond him."

"Maybe so," said the Silentman. "But even he could scry the interior of the box and tell that it once contained great power."

"I think we can assume our client didn't lie. Whoever opened that box also opened a door that would've been best left shut. We don't know what came crawling through. Our doom, perhaps."

"The doom of Hearne," said the Silentman. "It was too much gold to turn down, and you know how empty our coffers are." He laughed sharply, a harsh bark devoid of mirth. "Perhaps my greed has gotten the better of us all."

"I find it hard to believe Ronan had any hand in this. He's been nothing but loyal for thirteen years, and he knows the penalty—as he should, seeing that he's been the one meting it out."

"But there are few options before us," said the Silentman. His fist slammed down on the arm of his chair. "Two people handled that cursed box between the theft and its delivery to us: a boy who could be alive or dead, and a decidedly alive Ronan. What am I supposed to think?"

"We don't have the boy. Alive or otherwise."

"True."

"If Ronan is doing any thinking on this—and I'd bet his entire mind will be grappling with the problem—then he'll find the boy, if he is to be found. The Knife or not, he's still the best the Guild has."

"His salvation is the boy alive, so he must find him. But what will he find?"

"That's the hinge upon which all else turns."

"Have him watched."

"Oh, he'll be watched," said the steward. "Never fear. The dogs are already on his scent."

CHAPTER FORTY-THREE
THE COUNTRY COMES TO THE CITY

The duke of Dolan's party crested the rise on the southern edge of the Scarpe and began their descent down into the Rennet valley. The summer rains had been kind to the valley, and it was a lush vision of greenery. The river Rennet lay like a gleaming silver snake below them, sliding through the patchworked fields of corn, hay, and golden barley. To the west, the valley opened out into rolling hills. The city of Hearne rose there, shining in the afternoon sun. High stone walls, white towers proud against the sea beyond, spires threading the sky like so many slender needles. The river flowed past the city to meet the sea below the south wall. But though the city shone bright, the sea shone even brighter— a glittering expanse of blue light that blurred up into the sky.

The wind was hushed on the valley floor, for the heights on either side were greater than they seemed. Everywhere there was the damp scent of loam and the trill of birds. The music of the river drifted up to them in all of its liquid voice.

They made the gates just after sunset. An officer led them by torchlight through the city streets, winding ever higher toward the Highneck Rise district and the regent's castle towering over all on its cliff. Their horses clattered over the stone bridge that led into the courtyard of the regent's castle. Grooms and footmen materialized around them to take possession of horses and baggage. The regent's steward came bowing down the wide marble steps. Nimman Botrell stood at the top. Torchlight flared around him, pushing back the night.

"Hennen Callas!" the regent called out, smiling. "You and yours are welcome in my house."

He was tall and had a soft and foolish-looking face, a somewhat stout man with delicate, white hands that would have seemed more fitting for a woman than the regent of Hearne. He was dressed exquisitely in silk and velvet. A fop at casual glance. But only those lacking sense would dismiss Botrell carelessly. Even though his appearance did not inspire confidence, he had ably ruled Hearne for more than three decades, strengthening trade and improving relationships with the duchies.

"Always an honor to have you and your husband, m'lady," he said, bowing over Melanor Callas' hand. "It's been too long. The ladies of Hearne fade in the presence of northern roses such as yourself."

"I declare, Nimman," said the duchess. "You do go on."

"Yes, you do," said Levoreth, as the regent transferred his attention to her. His lips brushed against the back of her hand like the flutter of a butterfly.

"Ah, Lady Levoreth. You'll turn the heads of our young noblemen as never before."

"Perhaps their heads will turn right around until they fall off. An improvement for them all, no doubt."

"Such beauty. Such fire." The regent turned to the duke and duchess. "You must be proud of your niece."

"Oh, rather," blinked the duke. His wife mouthed something unintelligible and reproving at Levoreth, who scowled at her from behind the regent.

"My steward will show you to your rooms," said the regent. "Now, if you'll excuse me, I've some matters to attend to. Details and whatnot for the great ball, you know. So delighted to see you after so long. Hennen, we must talk horses in the morning. I've a young colt you should see."

The castle was magnificent. Even Levoreth, who was never fond of buildings in general, was impressed despite herself. It had been a long time since she had been to Hearne, and she had forgotten. From within a vast anteroom vaulted with stone arches curving overhead, hallways and staircases stretched away in every possible direction, all fashioned of white marble polished to a brilliance glimmering with the light of countless lamps. Servants flitted by on silent feet. Somewhere, an unseen fountain splashed. The steward showed them into a suite of chambers that seemed to extend on forever—door after door opening up into more rooms, a solarium with its glassed-in roof revealing the starry sky, and a kitchen where three servants bowed and smiled and bowed again.

"They will see to your needs," said the steward.

The three servants smiled, bowed again, and murmured polite noises.

In no time at all, a fire was crackling on the hearth, candles gleamed, and one of the servants whisked in with a platter of bread, cheese, and fruits.

"Perhaps an omelet?" said the duke, but his wife frowned at him.

"It's much too late," she said. "Your stomach will rumble all night."

"A nice, light omelet—"

"Have an apple."

Levoreth took an apple as well. Her bedroom had a balcony that looked out across the city below. She leaned on the railing and bit into the apple. Lights twinkled in the darkness, past the castle wall. Something trembled in the air, a slight heat and the hush of the wind holding its breath. A storm was coming. She could smell the promise of rain. She closed her eyes. Her thoughts flew far and fast, but there was nothing but darkness and cold and a mist that pressed against her mind.

Something is there. Something evil. Near the mountains. The wolves must hunt alone for a while more. A storm is coming.

Far in the east, thunder rumbled. She went inside and locked the balcony doors.

164

CHAPTER FORTY-FOUR
THE SHADOW AT THE GATE

Lightning fell far in the east. Whips of white flame lashed out of the gloom of clouds and darkness. The sky was scarred with traceries of fire that burned on a man's sight for minutes afterward. The air was thick with heat and the taste of metal and the promise of rain. Thunder muttered. It was the only sound in the sky, for there was no wind. The thunder sounded like the growl of some strange beast stalking through the stars and darkness of the sky.

The city of Hearne was oddly deserted that evening, despite the beginning of the Autumn Fair. A few stalls and carts still stood on the cobbles of Mioja Square, but there was no heart in the vendors as they hawked their wares. No one was buying onions or yarns or pottery or any of the other goods. Thunder rumbled, growing in volume as it neared. The last of the barrows trundled away. Along the streets, the shops were shuttered against the night. Only the inns were impervious to the approaching storm, being more crowded than usual as if there was safety in mirth and wine and numbers.

The animals of the city were behaving strangely. The head groom at the regent's castle walked through the stables, perplexed at the sight of horses stamping nervously in their stalls. One placid old hunter lunged at him over the bars with bared teeth. Down in the Fishgate district, a child's kitten scratched her and then ran yowling from the house. Dogs crept under beds and refused to come out. Cats disappeared into cellars and attics.

In Nio's house, the wihht stood up straight in the silence and darkness of the basement. It turned its head ever so slightly from side to side, nostrils flaring as if it were trying to smell something. Its eyes gleamed with a cold, hungry light. Three stories above the wihht, in the comfort of his library, Nio sat reading by candlelight. He stirred uneasily, but it cannot be said whether this was because of what he was reading or something else. In the university ruins, the old scholars did not notice anything unusual. This was understandable, for the magic was so thick about that place that any outside influence would have had a difficult time making itself known.

There were two people in that city, however, who felt the change in the air and knew it for what it was. Levoreth was right in the middle of tightening the stays of her aunt's dress when she inhaled sharply. For a moment she stood frozen, staring fixedly over her aunt's head. The girl in the mirror on the wall stared back at her. She did not recognize the face. The skin was pale and the mouth was set in a white-lipped gash. For an instant, the eyes had a blank, startled look to them. But it was only an instant, and then the eyes flickered—they flashed with animal savagery and the skin of her face felt tight and stretched, as if a wolf's head was emerging up from the planes of her face and gazing through her sockets.

"My dear," protested the duchess, squirming on the seat in front of her, "that's much too tight."

"Sorry," said Levoreth, and then it was only herself in the mirror on the wall—a tired-looking girl of seventeen.

In the house of Cypmann Galnes, a window was flung open. Liss stared out toward the sea. Far on the horizon, the last sunlight shone, hemmed in by the growing night. Liss turned and went downstairs. Dishes clattered from the kitchen. She opened the door and walked into the warm light and the scent of fresh bread. A fire burned on the hearth. Sanna looked up from the sink.

"It's going to be a fury of a night," said the old woman.

"Aye," said Liss.

She went outside into the garden. It was nearly true night now. The light in the west had faded to a bloody smear of sky. As she watched, it darkened through reds and purples into deep blue-black. Thunder muttered. She stared up at the sky. A frown crossed her face. Her hands curled into fists at her side. The thunder rumbled, nearer and nearer. Abruptly, she flung one arm out, her fingers fluttering open in the air. Then she disappeared back into the house.

It began to rain.

The city seemed to sigh in relief as the rain started to fall, as if it had been holding its breath. The thunder still growled, and lightning flickered, but the menace had subsided. In the inns, the laughter grew more genuine and the ale flowed more freely. Throughout the city, dogs crept out from under beds, looking ashamed. The horses in the regent's stable dropped their heads contentedly to their oats, and in one shabby house in Fishgate, a kitten strolled in through the door, at which point she was promptly scooped up by a small girl, who hugged her tight.

But in Nio's house, the wihht still stood patiently in the cellar, its head moving from side to side, sniffing at the darkness. Up in the regent's castle, Levoreth frowned down at her dinner plate. The talk of a glittering assortment of nobles tinkled around her, but she heard none of it. And in the house of Cypmann Galnes, Liss sat motionless at a window. Rain slashed down against the glass and she pressed her hand flat against it. She stared out at the sea.

Old Bordeall stamped down the steps of the gate tower. The rain fell on his shoulders and his white hair. Torchlight bloomed out of the open doorway behind him.

"I'll leave you to it, Lucan," he rumbled. "Don't know what got into me. Sitting down for a good roast and then I felt my bones go cold. Getting old, I guess." He spat in the mud. "I'll pay for it when I get back home—cold dinner and no doubt my woman will dose me against the flu."

"The men'll be on the walls, sir," said the young lieutenant. "Rain or not."

"Keep them on the lookout. Some foolish noble might come straggling out of the night for bed and board at the castle. Wouldn't do to have them locked out in weather like this."

"Perhaps Lord Gawinn will return tonight," said the lieutenant.

"Perhaps." Bordeall turned and strode away into the rain.

The lieutenant was pleased to have the watch for the night. He was young, just nineteen, and was rarely given the opportunity to command an entire watch. He would have never said it out loud, but he privately thought that he could command a troop just as well as someone like old Bordeall. He imagined Lord Gawinn riding in out of the night on his watch. A smile crossed his face as his men's spears flashed inside his mind—a perfectly executed salute for the Lord Captain of the Guard, protector of Hearne and keeper of the regent's word.

"Bar the gate!" he said. "Secure the city for the night!"

The older soldiers at the gate exchanged grins as they pushed the massive gate shut. The enormous weight of oak and iron groaned on its hinges as it swung around. The gate was easily the height of three tall men, and four horsemen could ride abreast through its stone arch. With a boom, the gate settled against its iron frame. The crossbeams were dropped into place. A couple of urchins watched, sheltering from the rain under the tower overhang.

"Gate's barred, sir," said one of the soldiers.

"Very good," said the lieutenant, and he vanished up the tower steps.

"Go on with you," said the soldier, making a half-hearted run at the urchins. "Get on home to your mothers. This ain't a night to be out in." The children scattered, jeering, lazily evading him and then returning to settle in the dry comfort of their spot.

The night grew deeper. Lightning flashed in the upper reaches of the Rennet valley. The rain fell so heavily that everything was reduced to an indistinguishable blur. The hard-edged shapes of the city—walls, roofs, towers, arches, spires—every corner and line and angle was reduced to impressions of darkness and depth. On the north side of Hearne, the city wall ended at a tower that stood on the heights of the cliffs plunging down to the sea below. A walk on top of the parapet from that tower to the tower beside the main gate at the eastern edge of the city took one hour. Proceeding along the parapet from the tower gate to the third wall tower standing at the southernmost edge of Hearne, looming over the sprawl of the Fishgate district and the outward curved arm of the bay, took another hour. That night, however, as a tribute to the miserable weather, the soldiers of the Guard walked each route in less than forty minutes, hurrying along, shoulders hunched against the rain and flinching at every lightning flash. They did not waste time to gaze out across the parapet's edge. Even if they had bothered to look out across the valley toward the Rennet Gap, they would have seen nothing except darkness and rain.

It happened at the third hour after midnight. The parapet door of the gate tower opened and light spilled out into the darkness. It gleamed on the falling rain and the wet stone. The lieutenant, young Lucan, emerged and looked out. He was looking the wrong way, however, for he gazed out across the rooftops of the city. Smoke curled from his mouth as he puffed contentedly on a pipe. The door closed again behind him. Several lengths down the wall, something stirred in the darkness. The air grew even colder than it already was. It was a dark night, but the thing creeping over the parapet's edge was darker still. If Lucan had remained at the door, if he had turned to look in that direction, he would have been hard pressed to see much beyond a blur of shadow standing on top of the wall. But he had gone inside, content that the city was in his capable hands—content with all the self-assuredness of youth. He was blissfully unaware he had cheated death by several seconds.

The thing on top of the wall stood motionless for a moment. It was the shape and size of a man, but no man could have climbed the outside wall, for it was forty feet in height and constructed of perfectly joined stones. Even the most accomplished thief in the Guild would have considered the city wall beyond his skill.

In one fluid movement, the form jumped off the wall. It fell through the air slowly. If it had been a huge bird with outstretched wings then the peculiar descent would have made sense. But the thing was not a bird and it did not have wings, only a black cloak that drifted about as it fell. The form landed silently on the cobblestones below. It drew the cloak about its shoulders and then strode away into the city, looking for all purposes like a man.

Inside the regent's castle, Dreccan Gor hurried along a corridor. He was sweating and the torch he clutched seemed to dance and tremble with a life all of its own. A sleepy guard slouched outside a door came to startled attention at his approach.

"Sir," said the guard, half in question, half in respect. Gor brushed past him without a word, and opened the door. He locked it behind him and then stood in the darkness, trying to assemble his scattered thoughts and catch his breath.

"Who's there?"

On his best nights, the Silentman slept poorly. He sat up in bed and the torchlight fell across his face, pooling shadow in his eyes.

"Gor, my lord," said the steward.

"I trust there's some reason for this?" A candle flared to life in the Silentman's hands, revealing the hands of an ivory clock on a stand next to his bed. The hands pointed to four hours past midnight. The steward came and stood by the edge of the bed. His face was drawn.

"We have a visitor."

"Oh?" said the Silentman. He did not think much of visitors at four in the morning.

"It's him."

"Stone and shadow," muttered the Silentman. "I was hoping he'd never return. That he'd become another bad memory. Stupid, I know. How did we get into this accursed mess?"

"We took the job," said Gor wretchedly. "We took his gold."

"Aye, we did."

"He seems to be in a bad mood. Worse than last time."

The Silentman dressed hurriedly. He wore a silver chain around his neck, engraved with interwoven whorls. He rubbed the necklace between his fingers and muttered a few words under his breath. The light around him dimmed until a shadow wreathed around his face, hiding his features.

"Send for the Knife," said the Silentman. His voice was roughened to a deep whisper by the concealment ward. "Immediately. If our guest is upset, then I want a scapegoat. Send Ronan word and then join me in the court."

"Very well, my lord," said the steward. His voice was unhappy.

The Silentman walked over to a tapestry hanging on the wall and placed his hand on it. The cloth depicted a hunt—horsemen with spears and bows pursuing a menagerie of beasts. Wolves, bears, and stag ran alongside griffins and unicorns. A dragon encircled the scene with his long tail, threatening both beast and man alike. The hanging quivered, and the depiction writhed into a hideous nonsense of lines. Only the dragon's tail remained, curving and sliding endlessly over itself. The Silentman walked into the swirling cloth and disappeared.

He swallowed hard to dispel the nausea the transfer always induced. The job had been so straightforward. A simple theft from a house that was virtually unguarded. It could not have been easier. And yet the Knife, the ablest man he had in the entire Guild, had fumbled the job. Everything had gone wrong. But who was at fault? Ronan, or the boy, whatever his name was. Whatever his name had been. The Juggler would know, but he had heard the fat man had disappeared.

The Silentman hurried down a flight of stairs. Halfway down, he paused. A door built into the wall swung open at his touch. It opened into a chamber crowded with chests of all sizes. Shelves sagged under the weight of bags bulging with coins and jewels, stacks of old books, and ingots of gold. On the top shelf was the wooden box. The door at the bottom of the stairs opened to reveal torches burning along a passage. His shadow wavered along like an elongated, grotesque caricature. He swallowed. He wished he had a drink. A good, stiff gulp of brandy.

When the Silentman entered his courtroom, he thought for a moment that he was alone. The torches high on the walls burned with their blue fire. Shadow stretched away from the rows of pillars running the length of the hall. The place was silent. But then he knew, somehow, that someone was there. The back of his neck pricked. The air felt colder than usual. He stepped up onto the dais and tried to still the tremble in his hands. The box was heavy in his arms.

"Hello?" he said, his voice shaking. He sat down on the stone throne. The room was silent. "Welcome to the court of the Silentman," he said.

Still, there was only silence. He furtively looked at the door at the far end of the hall. Perhaps Dreccan would walk through at that moment. He'd even be glad to see Ronan, and his fist curled convulsively at the thought. The Knife would pay for this.

"Your court?"

The air in front of him shimmered. Before he could even blink, the figure stood before him—short and stooped, shrouded in a cloak. The torches burning beside the throne threw a long shadow that stretched out behind the figure. The shadow trembled as the torches flickered, but the figure did not move. The Silentman tried to lick his lips but his mouth was too dry.

"You'll rule dust and ruin," said the figure, "if you haven't found the person who opened the box. Where is he? It will go poorly for you if he isn't here."

"He's just coming now," said the Silentman. "Almost here, I'm sure."

"It would be better for you if the wretch were already here. My master has come, and it isn't wise to keep him waiting." The little figure gave a horrible laugh that somehow ended up more as a gasp of pain.

"Oh, he's arrived?" The Silentman could not suppress a shiver. "Is this his first time to Hearne? The weather's been unseasonable lately. Quite a lot of rain. Still, it's a pleasant city. Will he be joining us?"

The figure did not say anything.

"I'm sorry about the wait," said the Silentman, but then he stopped speaking.

The shadow behind the little figure was growing. The shadow stretched and thickened and gained form. It stood up. It was tall, taller than most men. Torchlight fell across thin features that emerged out of the shadow like a corpse surfacing from water. A hand like a pale spider materialized and drifted up to the face. The fingers briefly played across the white skin of its features as if to check if they were all there. The jaws opened in the parody of a smile. They opened much too wide for any man.

"So."

The creature spoke in a hoarse whisper, so quiet that the Silentman could barely hear it. He could not stop his teeth from chattering. The air was cold.

"So, this is the thief lord."

The thing moved forward. It seemed to drift rather than walk.

"Give me the box."

"It was opened," said the Silentman. He could barely speak the words. "It was opened, my lord."

"I know, thief. Give me the box."

The Silentman could not hand the box down to the creature. His limbs ached with the cold. The blue flames of the torches in the hall seemed frozen into strange, sapphire

169

gems carved into the impossible shape of fire. The box fell from his hands onto the dais. The creature did not move, but suddenly the box was in its hands.

"No weight to it," said the creature. "It was opened and the weight inside is gone. But your debt is heavy, thief. Heavier than you will ever know."

Behind the creature, the little cloaked figure stood motionless. Its hood was tilted toward the Silentman but he could see no face within, only darkness. The creature held the box delicately. The Silentman could feel his heart thudding against his ribs. Slowly, the fingers crept across the carving of the hawk. The latch clicked open and light gleamed on the knife resting within. The cracked gemstone set in the handle shone dully. One finger caressed the blade.

"Old iron," said the creature. "Old iron, but an even older stone. Once it was so very old and precious beyond compare. But someone touched it. Someone stole the weight right out of it."

The hall, already cold, grew colder still. The Silentman could not feel his hands or his feet. The box fell to the floor and shattered. The creature turned the knife over in its hands. It looked up at the Silentman.

"This blade drew blood," it said. "Several days ago. I can still smell it."

"W-we have the man," stammered the Silentman.

"There are worse things than death, thief."

To his horror, the Silentman realized the creature's eyes were not like the eyes of a man. They were pits of shadow, as if the sockets of a skull. A red light flickered in the center of each. The Silentman could not look away from that awful stare. At that moment, the door at the end of the hall opened. The creature turned at the sound. Dreccan Gor and Ronan stood there. The Silentman was pathetically grateful for the interruption—abjectly grateful to be out from under those eyes, even for a moment. Ronan's face was a study in bewilderment and suspicion, while Gor looked terrified.

As terrified as I am, thought the Silentman.

The pair's steps lagged as they came closer. The thing waited at the foot of the dais. Darkness deepened in the hall, thickening until it was a presence—a vapor drifting through the air like smoke. It was difficult to breathe. The two men stopped.

"Come closer," said the thing.

Neither of the men moved. The creature raised a hand and beckoned. Both men staggered forward, taking awkward, jerky steps as if they no longer had control over their limbs. Ronan's face was twisted in hopeless effort.

"Closer."

They stumbled to within a step of him and then halted.

"The fat one is nothing, master," said the little figure. "A puppet of the thief lord."

The thin face tilted to one side, examining Gor and then discarded him as unworthy of attention. The strange eyes flicked to Ronan. A hand rose and drifted through the air in front of Ronan's face.

"This one," said the creature.

The cold knifed through Ronan. It felt as if an iron band was constricting around his chest. Surely his heart was about to burst with the pain and pressure. The pulse in his temple slammed like a hammer on an anvil. All he could see was the white hand hanging in the air in front of his face and, beyond it, two wells of darkness staring at him. Reddish gleams glowed deep within that darkness.

A small voice somewhere inside his mind, hidden away from that terrible scrutiny, whispered to him. *This door is not intended for you. Death is a heartbeat away. Listen—*

hear the latch close—you cannot return now to who you once were. This city shall never be the same again. The face of the girl Liss floated through his mind, gazing back at him with her eyes like the sea, and he felt reassured somehow.

"No," said the creature. "This one did not open the box, but he came close to the one who did. I can smell the taint on him." The clamp around Ronan's chest vanished and he could breathe again. He stumbled backward, coughing and wheezing. Tears streamed from his eyes.

"The boy, then!" said the Silentman.

The thing turned to him.

"What boy?"

"The boy who stole the box. He gave it to this man." The Silentman gestured at Ronan.

"Ah." The reddish light in the creature's eyes gleamed brighter. "The bargain still stands, thief. You have taken my gold. You will find this boy. One week. One week and I shall return."

"And if we don't find the boy by that time?" said the Silentman.

The red eyes flared.

"Then I shall destroy this city," said the creature. "One day. I will destroy it stone by stone. Hearne shall become a memory, a curse, a haunt of jackals and owls. I will bury my sword in your heart and feed on your death. This city is not worth what was in that box. One week, thief."

Without another word, it turned and strode down the hall. The little cloaked figure hurried after it. The cold and the darkness retreated with their passage, swept along until the door at the far end of the pillars closed behind them. The torches on the walls struggled back into life.

"What in the name of stone and shadow was that?!" said Ronan.

Neither of the two other men said anything. Gor tottered to the dais and sank down on it, his head in his hands.

"What was that thing?" repeated Ronan. His head ached.

"That—that," said the Silentman. He shrugged helplessly.

"We shouldn't have taken the job," said Gor. His voice was low and quiet, ashamed. "It's too late now, but we shouldn't have taken the job. The strange little fellow in the cloak came first, a month ago. By himself, understand. We thought there was something odd about him then, but we knew nothing about his master."

"The gold was good," said the Silentman. "It was more than should have been paid for a year of jobs and we thought him a fool. We were the fools. But, by the stones of Hearne, the bargain shall be kept. The boy shall be found. You'll find him, Ronan, if it's the last thing you do. Every cutpurse and climber and tosser in this Guild will be looking under every stone in this city. I want every door opened, every lock picked, every chimney plunged. If you find the boy, then I'll reinstate you as the Knife. One last chance, do you understand me?"

"What if—"

"Is that clear?!"

"Yes," muttered Ronan, not trusting himself to say more.

"I don't know what either of those two are," said Dreccan. "I think the small one might be a human of some sort, but the other?" He shuddered. "That was no human."

"One week," said the Silentman.

"Stone by stone," said Ronan. His headache was fading and malice stirred inside of him, viciously glad at the sight of the Silentman terrified on his throne. "How long does it take to destroy a city that's stood for a thousand years?"

"It'll stand for another thousand," growled the Silentman.

"Oh—aye—it will," said the steward, but he did not sound convinced.

CHAPTER FORTY-FIVE
THE LIES OF THE WIHHT

Nio hurried down the stairs and across the hall to the front door. It was his plan to go to the university ruins and try his luck again with the scrying mosaic hidden away in the lower level. He grasped the doorknob and then stopped, puzzled. There was a trace of the wihht on the metal, as if the creature had been through the door recently. He concentrated on the doorknob.

Yes—definitely. Only the day before, but he had not sent the creature out then. He had given it no command. Anger flared within him. The wihht was his creation and, as such, was subservient to his will. His word was its law. Everything there was to be known about wihhts he knew, had read, had studied and committed to memory. The writings of Willan Run, Staer Gemyndes' treatise on the seven orders of fashioned creatures, and the definitive *Endebyrdnes of Gesceaft*, written by the wizard Fynden Fram.

It was unthinkable for a wihht to make a choice of its own will. Unthinkable. Fram clearly said in his chapter on wihhts that "such creatures are physical manifestations of their maker's will." He had not willed the wihht to do anything yesterday, but the evidence of the door handle was unmistakable. It was as obvious as a footprint in the mud. Anger pushed hard at him, and he strode to the kitchen, to the stairs down into the basement and what waited there in the darkness. And yet, uneasiness wriggled like a worm in the back of his mind.

"*Lig*," he said.

A sphere of light bloomed in his hand. The steps creaked underfoot. Moisture gleamed on the stone walls. The wihht stood silently, waiting—easy in its complete stillness as if it had been standing patiently and comfortable in that position for the last twenty-four hours. Nio remembered the final, whimpering cry of the Juggler and the wet, bubbling sounds of the wihht feeding, and the unease in his mind grew.

"You left this cellar last night," said Nio. The creature said nothing in response, though a slightly puzzled expression crossed its face. The brow wrinkled into momentary furrows and then was once again smooth.

"You left this cellar without my command." He watched it closely. Something sparked in the dull pupils. Still, it remained silent.

Furious, Nio muttered under his breath.

"*Brond.*"

The sphere of light grew in brilliance and heat. The wihht blinked and stepped backward.

"Where'd you go yesterday?" the man said. "I command you to tell me."

"I went nowhere," said the wihht, but its voice seemed stronger and clearer than the last time it had spoken with Nio. The unease inside the man's mind quivered into something else. Fear. He clamped down on the feeling.

But how could the wihht's voice have changed unless it had been strengthened somehow? Unless it had fed.

He let his mind drift out toward the wihht, searching for a spark of conscience that he could examine. His consciousness pushed forward, encountering nothing. He pushed a little farther. And felt something that was more than nothing—an absence of being, color, meaning, and form. The emptiness of it pulled at him like a lodestone pulls at iron. A smile drifted across the wihht's face. Nio wrenched his mind back.

"I know you left the house. Don't test my patience. I made you, and I can unmake you. Darkness and water woven together make your flesh, and those threads can be plucked apart and dispersed back into the shadows, back into the drains of this city."

"More than that now," said the wihht. There was cunning in the hoarse voice. "More than darkness and water in me now. There's a bit of this and that. Blood and flesh. Not just yours."

Wordless, Nio stared at the wihht. His hand ached with the remembrance of the blood he had given to the thing.

Given out of his own foolishness.

He backed away, and then quickly walked up the steps. When he reached the kitchen and the door closed behind him, he realized he had been holding his breath. He stared at the shut door. The thought crossed his mind of telling Severan, of confessing his stupidity. Perhaps he knew something about wihhts that he himself did not? No. That would not do.

He wove a binding on the door, working it down through the wood beams into the stone foundation of the house. Three times he sealed the weaving with his own true name. When he was done, he could hardly keep his eyes open, for the binding had been done with all of his will.

He trudged up to his bedchamber. As he fell asleep, a thought crossed his mind. *Not just yours.* That's what the wihht had said. More than just his blood in the thing. Of course. He had witnessed the thing devour the Juggler and his two thugs. But had the thing meant more than that?

Not just yours to command. . .

CHAPTER FORTY-SIX
THE APPARENT BOREDOM OF DUTY

Ever since Arodilac could remember, his uncle had been telling him duty was honorable. Duty is the pursuit of the nobility. Nothing better than duty, my boy.

Duty, however, was boring.

He yawned.

By rights, he should have been allowed to go with Owain Gawinn. He had watched the troop clatter out the gate and canter away, down through the long, green reaches of the Rennet valley. He was seventeen—practically a man—and just as good a swordsman as any of Owain's men. When he had complained to Bordeall, the old man had just handed him a spear and told him to patrol the wall. Tramp the length, up around to the northern tower, all the way down to the southern tower, and then back to the main gate tower.

That had diverted him for a while. The city crowded up to the wall with its labyrinth of stone and brick and shadows drawn by the morning sunlight angling down. On the other side of the wall was the rest of Tormay. The land stretched east for miles and miles through the cradle of the Rennet valley. On either side, the land rose up sharply. To the north, it rose up to the Scarpe plain. It was said that the Scarpe was the inland sea, for when the wind blew, the grasses billowed and rolled like waves of water, and the birds skimmed over the green as if they were gulls over the sea. South of the valley, the land climbed up into the rough, broken hills of the duchy of Vo.

Arodilac gazed out across the wall and imagined an army attacking up the valley. The corn and hay would be trampled underfoot and the green of the grasses blotted out by the silver and gray of armor. Flags waving in the wind. Horns bugling above the neigh of horses and the shouts of men. He would lead a last, desperate charge of cavalry from the gate, spears already dark with blood.

Smiling, he tripped over the spear he was carrying. Shadows, but the thing was heavy. He sighed and limped on. His feet were getting sore. He was bored.

So much for duty, he mumbled to himself. I wouldn't mind it so much if it meant fighting someone. But not with this spear. Give me a good sword and I'm happy enough. I wonder if uncle would give me gold enough to buy a new sword? He's been in a nasty mood lately. Perhaps I'd better try my hand at the Queen's Head and win some gold there.

I wonder how Liss is doing?

With that melancholy thought in mind, he trudged along. The tower at the main gate was near enough. He'd kick off his boots and have some ale in the shade.

"Off to Gawinn's house," rumbled Bordeall.

"I went just yesterday. Besides, I'm tired."

"Get going."

"I fail to see what some little girl having nightmares has to do with being a member of the Guard. I'm a soldier, not a nanny."

"Go. Now."

"Oh, all right," said Arodilac.

He did manage to sneak a tankard of ale in the guardhouse before leaving. The sergeant on watch took the spear and locked it in the armory. The man grinned at him. Oh, they had been polite when he had first joined the Guard. After all, he was the regent's nephew. But that had worn off fast enough.

"Off to take care of babies?"

"Shut up," said Arodilac.

It was a long walk from the main gate to the house of Owain Gawinn. The crowded streets didn't make matters easier, and by the time he reached the garden wall behind the house, he was sweating and feeling sorry for himself.

A wooden gate opened through the stone wall and into a garden. The air smelled of herbs and the honeysuckle massed along the wall. Bees hummed as they darted from flower to flower. Three small boys were chasing each other around a patch of grass. The sun was high and the garden brimmed with light.

Not even a ward, thought Arodilac crossly to himself. You'd think the Lord Captain of Hearne would have more sense that that. Particularly if I'm supposed to waste my time looking after his houseguests.

"Hullo," said the eldest of the boys. He barely came up to Arodilac's knee.

"Hullo," said Arodilac. "Is your mother home?"

"Hullo," said the middle of the boys.

"Do you like bees?" said the eldest boy.

"I'll just let myself in," said Arodilac.

"We have lots an' lots, but they never sting us. Just never."

"Just never," echoed the smallest of the three boys. He smiled shyly.

"But they'll probably sting you," said the eldest boy generously.

Arodilac knocked on the back door and then stuck his head in. It was dark and cool inside.

"Hello? Mistress Gawinn? Hello?"

The three little boys pushed past his legs.

"We'll find Mother," said the eldest boy. They disappeared down the passage.

Soon, he heard the sound of skirts and footsteps and then Sibb Gawinn appeared. She wore an apron and her hands were white with flour.

"Arodilac," she said, smiling, "you needn't hover about the stoop like a stranger. Come in."

He ducked his head in embarrassment. Not that she compared to Liss, but he thought Sibb Gawinn one of the most beautiful women he had ever seen, almost as beautiful as the duke of Dolan's niece—Levor-something or another. He'd caught a glimpse of her in the courtyard when the duke's party had arrived.

"Just dropping by to check on the girl, ma'am,' he said.

"Come in, then. She's in the kitchen with Loy and my Magret. We're baking bread."

The big Hullman scowled at him when he walked into the kitchen, as if to say that he had things in hand, could watch over the foundling himself, thank you. Arodilac was in complete agreement, but that didn't prevent him from scowling back.

Magret was perched on top of a stool next to the table, barely visible behind an apron many years too big for her. Flour rose around her in clouds as she pummeled a mountain of dough with her sharp little fists. Bread baked on the stone hearth. Arodilac's stomach growled as he inhaled the warm scent. Magret giggled.

"I'll have to speak to my husband about your rations," said Sibb. "Here." She sawed off a generous portion of a loaf and then sliced up a tomato to pile on top of the bread.

The foundling girl sat on top of the counter beside the hearth, knees drawn up to her chin and slender hands laced about her ankles. Her eyes shifted from Sibb to Loy and then back. Her face was expressionless.

"Hello," said Arodilac, stepping in front of the girl. Her eyes focused momentarily on his. She frowned and then looked past him.

"Silent as ever."

"Not at night." Sibb handed him the sandwich. "Eat. Every night brings her nightmares and she wakes, screaming and crying. I'd take them on myself, if I could, the poor dear."

"At least she's safe enough here."

Loy shook his head. A knife moved slowly in his hands—unwatched but deft—carving away curls of wood as he whittled a stick. His voice rumbled quietly.

"In Hull, they say that a man lives in two homes. One a house of wood and stone. The other a house of flesh and soul. She might be safe in the one, but not t'other."

CHAPTER FORTY-SEVEN
A DAY OUT

Jute woke up that morning desperately trying to remember his dream. He had been flying with the hawk. Soaring through a night sky without end. Thunder had been muttering in deep, sullen crescendos. Dark columns of clouds riven by white lightning. A storm gathering in the east and hurrying toward Hearne as if whipped along by the malice of some ancient sky god.

But he had been untouchable. He rode on the wind with the hawk soaring next to him. Stupefying speed. The air had rushed through him. His flesh frayed into wind, speed, moonlight. The hawk's eye as black as night. Filled with the depths of the sky, glittering with stars, as if that single pupil was a portal that opened into a larger sky than the one through which they flew.

But he woke and the dream faded.

Jute was instantly depressed. Bored. He opened the shutters of his room and peered out. It had rained the night before. Far below, he could see the puddles on the street. It was early, but Mioja Square was already crowded. He could see quite a bit of the square, for it was just down the street that ran alongside this side of the university. He knew he was too high up for anyone to see him from the street below. Perhaps he might hit someone if he spit. There was a breeze blowing, however, and the wind blew his attempts back into the wall below him.

He was about to swing the shutters closed when he noticed a stone ledge just below his window. Well, not just below. It looked a good fifteen feet down from the sill. Still, what was fifteen feet? He had dropped further than that before. True, if he missed his footing on the ledge that meant there was another hundred feet or so to fall before his descent would be abruptly stopped by the roof of a lower story of the university.

He breakfasted on some bread and a sad-looking sausage and thought about the ledge. It looked like the ledge ran the length of the wall to the corner, at which point it met a copper drainpipe. That made the ledge doubly interesting. The copper drainpipes he had encountered in the past had usually proven to be helpful. He could recall a manor in the Highneck Rise district that had been guarded by wards on all of its doors and windows. They had been very good wards and, being much younger then, he had not had the skill to evade them with silence. But there had been a copper drainpipe climbing right up to the roof. The dormer windows of the attic had not been warded.

For the rest of the morning, he made a valiant effort to put the ledge from his mind. It wouldn't do to think about such things. After all, if he ventured out into the streets of Hearne there was no telling who he might run into. He certainly didn't want to end up in the clutches of the Juggler, or, even worse, Nio and that creature he kept in his cellar. No, he had best remain within the university ruins.

It was noon when he gave in.

He climbed out the window. The sun was high and the light felt warm on his skin. He lowered himself over the side, hanging onto the sill with his hands. Then, after taking a deep breath, he let go and dropped. It was ridiculously easy. The ledge was wider than it had looked from his window, particularly once he was standing on it. He grinned and looked up at the window above his head. And then he realized he had no way to climb back up. He ran his hand over the stone wall. He could not feel a single handhold.

"Shadows," he muttered. But then he cheered up quickly enough, for he was a boy and part of what makes a boy is the faith that problems take care of themselves. At any rate, he didn't have to worry about getting back inside until after he had climbed down and stretched his legs a bit. And that was that.

Jute made short work of the ledge. It was almost wide enough to walk along. The drainpipe was made of stout copper and the brackets were fixed to the walls with large bolts that had survived whatever weather the last several hundred years had thrown at them. In no time at all, he was shinnying down the pipe.

He was so pleased with himself that he made a dreadful mistake once he reached the roof below. It was a gentle slope of slate tiles. Jute figured on walking across the roof and then climbing down the wall to reach the alley below. The roof was fairly high and safe from casual eyes, but the wall would be another matter altogether. Not difficult to scale, of course, but it would have to be done unnoticed.

When he reached the middle of the roof, he began to sink. One moment the tiles were perfectly hard slate, and then the next instant they were like soft clay. He staggered, terrified, trying to grab onto something. There was only the roof. The wall was too far away. He fell forward on his knees and felt them sink into the tiles. Jute could hear a moist, sucking sound as if some horrible child was greedily devouring a peach. He looked down, half-expecting to see the gigantic mouth around his ankles. A scream gurgled up through his throat but he bit down hard and the roof was silent except for the dreadful sucking sound of the tiles.

He was sinking faster now. A terrifying thought struck him. What was below? What was waiting in the darkness below the roof? His mind devised nightmarish creatures. Dozens of arms and claws and eyes on stalks, all craning upwards and ready to grab hold of his ankles to wrench him down into the dark and their feast. He could even hear their noisy hunger now, the clicking of claws and teeth clamoring in his mind. What a wretched, horrible noise!

Noise.

Noise is exactly what you don't need.

Of course, Jute thought stupidly, feeling himself sink even further—he was almost up to his waist now. It's just another ward.

Silence.

He leaned back and looked at the sky. A perfect blue arc spanned his sight. The sun shone down. It seemed the most natural thing in the world to open his mind to the silent watchfulness of the sky, the silence of the blue heights and the light that did not waver in the muteness of its descent. A window in his mind swung open and the light and the space flooded inside. The horror was gone, for there was no more room for such a thing in the midst of the silence. With a damp, disappointed sigh, the roof gave Jute up. Trembling, he rolled over onto his back and closed his eyes. He grinned shakily. He crawled across the tiles until he reached the edge, even though he knew the roof ward would not activate again. The wall under the roof's overhang was simple enough. With no one in sight, he shinnied down a drainpipe to the cobblestones below. Grinning from ear to ear, he scampered down the street.

He was scarcely able to take in the delight of what lay before him—Mioja Square crowded and bustling with people. He had never seen so many people before. Flags fluttered in the breeze. Canopied stalls and barrows were jammed side by side. An incomprehensible hubbub came to the boy's ears. He heard a bewildering mix of every accent of every duchy in Tormay, from Harlech in the north to Harth in the south, every village from the plains and forests, and the mountains of the Morn range. Anyone who had anything to sell, anyone who had the gold or desire to buy or be bought from, was in Hearne. All of Tormay was crowded into that immense square, jumbled and jostling and cheerful in the sunlight. At least, that's the way it seemed to the boy.

There were haughty Vomarone gentry, strutting like peacocks and stooping every now and then to investigate whatever bits of finery happened to catch their inquisitive eyes. The people of Harth were there, aloof and imperious with their eyes as blue as a desert sky and their hair sun-scoured white. Rich farmers from Hull, proclaiming loud, boisterous opinions on everything and everyone to impress their womenfolk they shepherded about. There were even a few men from Harlech, though hardly anyone in that city would have recognized them as such.

Jute forgot everything Severan had said. He forgot the cellar in Nio's house and what waited there in the dark. He forgot the Guild. The sunlight and the colorful clamor of the square were too much for him. It was all too wonderful. Without another thought, he sauntered out of the alley and into the crowd.

At first, Jute contented himself with ambling through the press of people. This could not be done in a straight line, of course, because the vendors had created an impromptu maze in the square. The place was a labyrinth of stalls with their canopies and tented inner sanctums, as well as the barrows that maneuvered about into more advantageous configurations as the day wore on. The placement and ordering of these little shops were delicate feats of diplomacy, guile, bribery, and sometimes downright violence on the part of the merchants and their apprentices. It might be more beneficial for a honeycake seller to be near someone selling pillows and blankets, for the sight of such homely articles tended to encourage people, particularly men, to indulge in sweets. Those who wove wards always tried to locate their stalls next to blacksmiths, particularly those specializing in weapons. There was nothing quite like racks of gleaming daggers to set a goodwife wondering whether or not her home could use an extra protection ward. Any jeweler would be grateful to have a tea brewer nearby, for those most likely to buy an icefire pendant for their mistress or earrings for a daughter were always helped along to their decision by plenty of time and plenty of hot tea.

For a while, Jute wandered along at the heels of two tall men who were clearly from Harth. They conversed together in courtly tones that delighted him, for their speech sounded like the poetry the street storytellers sometimes used when they told their most expensive tales. He considered relieving the two men of their purses, for his own pockets were empty, but decided against it, as both of them walked with the alertness of cats and bore swords on their belts. This was also noticed by a blacksmith's apprentice as the pair proceeded down a row of stalls, small shadow in tow.

"Sharpen yer swords, sirs!" bawled the apprentice. "Copper an edge!" In the stall behind him, a cloud of steam rose as the blacksmith plunged a glowing knife into a tub of water. The two Harthians stopped.

"Only one copper an edge," said the apprentice. He wiped his nose and then rubbed his hands together, sensing a bit of business.

"I fear this blade of mine has no need for the stone," said the taller of the two men. He glanced over the weapons displayed on the planked tables within the stall. The offerings were mostly unimpressive—serviceable blades, bundles of arrowheads, axe heads, and even a helm or two—but there was a collection of three knives that seemed to catch his eye.

"The Hearne air, sir, puts a rust on any iron," returned the apprentice.

"What think you, Stio?" said the man to his companion. "Would my lady sister be pleased by such as these?" He indicated the three knives.

"Has your father's court become so dangerous that gentle ladies would need knives?" said the other. "Faith, my lord Eaomod, her beauty is weapon enough, for keenly do I still bleed from her edge."

Eaomod laughed and picked up one of the knives. It was an elegant weapon, the blade inlaid with delicate whorls of silver. With a careless flick of his hand, the man sent the knife dancing across his fingers. It whirled and spun through the air, though at every moment it seemed the blade must surely draw blood.

"My master's a right hand with the anvil, my lord," said the apprentice. "Just as you surely are a weapon master."

"I doubt you not," said the Harthian. "Yet I fear his anvil did not see the making of this blade."

The apprentice grinned and shuffled his feet. A small crowd of onlookers had gathered, attracted by the sight of the flashing blade. Jute edged closer as well and relieved the apprentice's pockets of two copper pieces. The blacksmith wiped his hands on a rag and stepped up. He cuffed his lad good-naturedly.

"Right you are, my lord," he said. "Someday I might be making a pretty little thing like that. I've many years to live yet before I learn the secrets of such smithying."

"I think you will have to travel to Harlech to learn art as made this," said the Harthian.

He might have said more, but Jute had already moved away. A breeze brought him the scent of raisins and he drifted along its trail, listening to his stomach grumble and jingling the two coppers in his pocket. Never before had he seen the square so crowded. Even on days when such extravagant fairs weren't being held it took quite some time to walk from one end to the other. Now, it would take all day long if he was to see every stall, every barrow, and every delightful oddity being hawked.

And what if he himself was seen?

Jute sobered at the thought, even though he had not seen a single familiar face since he had climbed out the window. Yet he might be spotted without his knowledge. He quickened his pace and slipped down a row of carpet merchants, sash sellers, and handkerchief vendors. Just ten minutes more and then he'd hurry back to the university and safety. He'd investigate a few pockets and then be on his way. No one would be any the wiser, and besides, Severan himself would never know. He hardly ever saw the old man.

A crowd of people had gathered at the intersection of several rows of stalls. Jute could smell the raisins close by, and he slipped through the people, helping himself to pockets as he went. He emerged beside a confectionery's barrow, from which a delicious steam rose. Biscuits studded with raisins and glazed with honey cooled in a wire basket. A griddle sizzled over a brazier glowing with coals. Behind him, a cheer went up from the crowd. He looked to see what had roused them, but he was too short. At any rate, the growling in his stomach rated more attention than a crowd cheering and he turned back to the confectionery.

"Run along with you," said the old woman behind the barrow. She shook her wooden paddle at him.

181

"But I'd like to buy," protested Jute. "I'm not a thief." He jingled the coppers in his pocket and felt virtuous.

"One for half a copper," said the old woman, "and let's see your metal first. I've had enough of you scamps today."

"I'll take two," said Jute grandly, and he tossed a copper piece on the griddle. The old woman scraped the coin off with her paddle.

"All right, then," she said.

"Of course, my good woman," said Jute, trying to recall how the Harthian lord had spoken. She whisked two of the hot confections into a twist of cotton and handed the lot over. Jute ruined the lordly effect by taking an enormous bite and nearly choking on the hot dough. The old woman smiled.

"She's about to start again," she said, unbending a little.

"Who?" managed Jute. He gulped for air and licked honey from his lips.

"The Mornish girl. The singer." The old woman gestured toward the crowd. "Been singing on and off all morning. Got a throat on her like a bird."

The singer started before Jute saw her, for the people were standing toe to heel and it took some doing to work his way through. The voice had a confiding quality to it, as if the singer sang for Jute alone. Each person in that crowd probably thought the same. Despite such intimacy, her notes soared up into the sky.

She sings like the hawk flies, thought Jute.

He edged between a stout couple dressed in the commonsense weaves of Hull. They made grumbling way for him and then closed up behind him like a sturdy wall fed on pork and potatoes. The Mornish girl was no girl, for the old confectionery woman would have regarded any woman under the age of fifty as a girl. The singer had the solid features of the mountainfolk, as those people, when along in years, tend to look like they have been carved from the stones of the Mountains of Morn. But the beauty of her voice overwhelmed all other senses. A man sat on a stool near her feet and played accompaniment on a lute. The singer stood unmoving, her arms at her side. Only her mouth and throat moved, buoyed by the slow bellows of her breast.

"Hanno Col rode from Lascol forth
on the first of summer's day.
The earth was green and tasseled gold,
corn heavy with the rain.
The wind blew him west, along the plains,
toward an unseen shore.
Where the keep of Dimmerdown stood,
the sea knocking on its door."

The air around the singer seemed to shimmer, almost as if the sunlight had been caught by the woman's voice and was coaxed to slow and thicken in attentiveness to her sound. Jute tasted honey in his mouth and was not sure if it came from the biscuit or the song.

An arm clamped around his neck, nearly wrenching him over.

"Jute," said a voice.

He yelped in fright. The arm tightened and a small face insinuated itself against his own.

"Shh!"

And then he recognized the livid burn and the tangled brown hair falling down around her face. She frowned and smiled in delight at the same time.

182

"Lena!"

"Quiet," she said. "That old Demm is standing not three feet away and he's allus been a nasty one." She nodded. A gaunt rail of a man was standing in the front of the crowd. With one step, the man could reach them and grab Jute by the scruff of his neck. But the singer sang on and Demm stared at her with glazed eyes. Sweat slid down Jute's back. Demm was one of the bashers who ran the docks for the Guild.

"C'mon." Lena's hand slipped into his own. They threaded their way back through the audience until they were in one of the less crowded byways of the square.

"Shadows, Jute," she said, rounding on him. "Where you been at?" She stuck her small fists on her hips and glared at him.

"Not here," he said. His heart was beating fast, as fast as the heartbeat of a sparrow he had picked up once. The silly thing had broken its wing and had been flopping about the cobblestones. He had picked it up and felt the tiny hammer of its life knock faster and faster until it was gone and there was only a bundle of feathers and bones in his hands. The heartbeat had been so fast. At that moment, his heart felt the same. Demm had been so close. Almost close enough to touch.

"You tell me, cully!" she said furiously.

"Not here, Lena."

He grabbed her hand and pulled her along. There were too many people, too many twists and turns, too many carts jammed into hodgepodge lines and angles, too many canopies blocking out the sky. He felt as if he could not breathe. He needed empty spaces and silence. Too many hands that might reach for him, too many faces, and too many eyes. Surely they were all watching him. Too much noise and babble hiding the gossip surely being whispered behind hands and stalls and hanging drapes.

They hurried through a fading fringe of people and scattered carts, right on the edge of the square, and dove into the alley skirting the university ruins. The wall loomed up next to them and shrouded the alley with afternoon shadow.

"Jute!" said Lena, "You're hurting me."

"Sorry."

She perched on a pile of rubble and glared at him.

"Now where you been? And this better be good. Better than being dead, for that's what the fat old Juggler was allus telling us. I cried, and he just smiled all over his fat, greasy face."

Jute laughed, for the little girl had twisted up her own face into an approximation of the Juggler's leer.

"Don't," Lena said crossly.

"Sorry." He sat down next to her. She laid a hand on his arm.

"Are you going to have that?"

"No," he said. He handed her the remaining biscuit. He wasn't hungry anymore. Besides, the thing had long gone cold.

"So then?"

Jute was half of a mind to tell her the whole story. After all, he had known Lena for years, ever since she had shown up at the back door of the Goose and Gold, a tiny, frightened girl. The innkeeper had put her to work in the scullery, scrubbing the endless grease of pots and pans. The deftness of her hands had caught the Juggler's eye, and it wasn't long before he had her. She had learned under the tutelage of the older children. Jute had taught her a fair bit himself.

He winced at the memory, looking down at the burn scar blooming on the side of her face. It covered one cheek and reached up into the scalp. Luckily, her hair had grown back.

"I got caught." He shrugged. "There's not much to the story. The job went bad and got me nicked."

"As if you'd get nicked." she said, spraying crumbs. "That'd be the day."

He shook his head, secretly pleased at her praise. "Plenty of things out there that shouldn't be tried for. You know that. No matter how quick you get, there's always a bit that's gonna be quicker. And those are the bits you have to leave be—only I tried for one of 'em."

She scowled, but he saw her touch her face, fingers drifting unconsciously across the burn scar.

"It were for the Knife, weren't it?" she said.

"Aye." And he saw the man's face again, floating pale and ghostly above the chimney's mouth. *Nothing personal, boy.* His hands clenched. Stone and shadow. He hadn't thought of the man for several days now.

She licked her fingers clean of honey and then wiped them on her shirt.

"Ain't no reason to worry about the Knife," she said.

"What do you mean?" he said, startled.

"Oh, nothing," she said, smiling in triumph. "Just that, me 'n the other—we jumped the Knife behind the Goose 'n Gold."

"What?"

She told him, waving her hands about for emphasis and grinning.

"You could've been killed," said Jute, angry and jealous and amazed all at the same time.

"Well, I weren't. What's more, I heard the Knife ain't the Knife any longer. He been kicked outa the Guild or something. All in disgrace, cuz of you, cully. Everyone's talking about it."

"Kicked out?" he said in amazement.

"On his rear. So, what was it? What were you trying to swipe?" she said.

His mind cast about for something suitably impressive. "An old book. Something filled up with magic spells and things like that. Real expensive and rare."

"Must have been a real swoop," she said, "else the Silentman wouldn't have put out such a price on you."

"The Silentman? A price? What are you talking about?"

"Stone," she said, wide-eyed. "You hadn't heard?"

"No. I've been—I've been busy. Tell me then."

"Maybe I'd like another biscuit first."

"Maybe you'll tell me." He poked her in the ribs.

"A hundred pieces of gold." She wriggled away. "Who'd have thought your ugly mug'd be worth all that?"

"A hundred pieces of gold," he breathed. "You should turn me in yourself. You'd be rich."

"There's plenty would turn you in for a lot less than a hundred, Jute. Word's gone out around the city. Every kid in the Juggler's lot is dreaming of gold. Oh, not Wrin and the twins. They'll allus be true as can be. But every member of the Guild has word to take you if they've the chance—alive. The Silentman wants you alive. You've the shadow's own luck to be out on the square today and nobody seen you."

"It was stupid of me." He shook his head in disgust. "I need to disappear. Don't tell anyone you saw me, will you?"

"Course not," she said indignantly.

He stuck his hands in his pockets. "Here, you better take this lot." He forked over his pickings from the square. The remaining copper from the blacksmith's apprentice, a silver coin embossed with the ducal crest of Hull, and an opal no bigger than his thumbnail but black as night. Lena's eyes bulged and she squeaked.

"I won't need 'em," he said. "Not where I'm holed up. Give the opal to the Juggler. That should keep him in a good mood for days."

The little girl looked at him blankly for a moment.

"You don't know, do you?"

"Know what?" he said.

"Bout the Juggler. He's been gone more'n a week now. He must be dead or something, 'cause the Guild's moved a new one in. Old man who just sits and smokes his smelly pipe all day and take our swoop. He's not half bad, an' he don't beat us hard at all."

"The Juggler's dead?"

Joy trembled inside him, but then it was swept away by anger. His vision blurred. Someone else had killed the fat man. He had wanted that pleasure himself—somehow— to watch the life go out of those beady eyes. To extinguish him, just as a wick would be blown out.

A breeze blew down the alley.

What are you doing? Beware your mind, fledgling.

The hawk.

Instantly, his sight cleared. Lena was watching him curiously. He forced a smile.

"I have to go," he said.

She nodded. He grabbed her arm.

"Could you do something for me, Lena?"

"Of course."

"There's a man named Nio who lives near Highneck Rise. An old manor at the end of the Losian Street. A tall garden wall and a tower. Find out if anyone in the Guild is talking about him. But be careful. He's dangerous. More dangerous than the Knife. Quiet as a mouse, all right?"

"But how'll I tell you what I find?" she said.

He wondered guiltily about the hawk and glanced at the sky.

"Three nights from now," he said. "Meet me here at dusk."

"All right," she said, and then she scampered away down the alley, back toward the cheerful clamor of the square.

After a suspicious look around the alley—he was alone except for a little gray cat washing itself in a pool of sunlight—he climbed back up the wall. He swung over the eave and lay for a moment on the edge of the slate tiles. The noise of the day and the memory of the crowd drained from his mind, displaced by the slow warmth of the sunlight and the silence of the sky. And then, when he was still within, he walked across the roof and the slate tiles remained slate tiles.

The copper pipe remained a copper pipe, for that was all it had ever been. He tried not to think about how he was going to get back up to his window as he clambered up the pipe, but it was no good to put off the problem much longer. A fair amount of Mioja Square was visible from where he was and he marveled at how small it had all become.

185

There was an odd enjoyment in seeing the crowd drifting about, eddies of people as tiny as ants all a variety of color but no longer short and tall and fat and thin. They were all tiny. Remote. He wondered if that's how it always was for the hawk—a constant remoteness that never necessitated involvement on its part except for whenever it wanted to fall from the heights and then climb back up with its prey.

Rabbits, probably.

Jute stood a while on the ledge under his window, running a disconsolate hand over the stonework of the wall. It was different up here as opposed to the wall below. Different masons, he thought gloomily. Whoever had fashioned the upper walls had a skill he'd never seen before. Each stone was fitted into its mates as close as heartbeats falling one after the other. There were no gaps. Every stone had been hewn to a flat, smooth face. The wall was unclimbable. If only he could fly.

"What in the name of the accursed darkness do you think you're doing?"

Startled, he stared up at the window ledge. Severan's wispy gray head leaned out. The old man glared down at him.

After some furious words back and forth, they decided upon the idea of sheets knotted together. It started to rain, but the overhang of the roof protected Jute. Severan let down the makeshift rope and Jute clambered up in a trice.

"You," said the old man, "are a lackwit. Of all the things to do, you have to go wandering through the city, smack in the middle of the Autumn Fair."

"I did not!" protested Jute.

"Then why's there honey smeared all over your lying face? I don't recollect seeing any bees in these ruins."

The boy wiped at his cheek and then reddened as his hand came away sticky.

"I was bored," he said.

"You were bored?" said Severan. He threw his hands up in the air, and then sighed. "Look, Jute. We've decided—the other scholars and I—that we're going to finish our work here in one more month. We've yet to find what we hoped would be here, but perhaps the book never existed in the first place, or maybe it was taken away during the war. Some of the wizards escaped, you know. A precious few, but some did. At any rate, one more month and then we'll pack it in."

"So you'll be leaving?" Panic gripped Jute. He clenched his jaw and hoped that he would not cry.

"Aye, but you've no cause to worry. None of us are from this city. I come from the north myself, from Harlech. They're a secretive folk there and keep to themselves. They wouldn't bother noticing one more boy."

"You mean, I could come with you?"

"If you wish. I've a cottage up on the coast of Lannaslech. That's the land of the duke of Harlech himself. Right where the cliffs reach the sea. It's a homely place with enough quiet to give a man space to think, not like this noisy city. The cottage was old before my time. Stone walls and a big chimney, for the winters are cold in the north."

He smiled, more to himself than at Jute.

"Summers are beautiful there. The moon flowers will be blooming still, I think, and I hate to be missing them. Stone and sky and sea and a fire on the hearth—the four stillpoints of the world. You remember what I read you from the memoir of Sarcorlan?"

Jute nodded, wondering what a moon flower was.

"The Guild never comes to Harlech. No one would know you there, and you'd be more than welcome."

"Thank you," said the boy.

CHAPTER FORTY-EIGHT
THE SPELL AT THE TOP OF THE STAIRS

"Rain and more rain," said Levoreth.

She plopped down onto a window seat and gazed out. Rain streaked down the glass. Mist obscured most of the view out across the city. Here and there, however, roofs and spires were visible like islands of brick and stone and slate in an ocean of gray.

"Nothing a coach and a good umbrella can't deal with," said her aunt.

"Are you serious?"

"My dear, you know me better than that. Get your coat on."

"This is weather for frogs and fishes."

"Don't be uncouth. I was having tea with Lady Blyscan, Rudu Blyscan's wife, and she told me of a splendid little dress shop down in the city. Just off the main square—what is that place called?"

"Mioja Square."

"She bought a lovely watered silk there yesterday for a pittance. Harthian, I think. They have such gorgeous silks."

"I'm sleepy," said Levoreth. "I think I'll take a nap."

"Nonsense. All you seem to do these days is sleep. Are you sick? You look healthy to me—"

"I'm not sick."

"—though, my great-grandmother Ella dropped dead at age thirty-one. In perfect health. My great-grandfather was inconsolable. Lost his head and promptly ran off with that dreadful Narnessy woman. They fought like cats and dogs for forty-nine years."

"And were perfectly happy," said Levoreth.

"What's that?" said her aunt.

"Oh, er, weren't they rather happy?"

"Perhaps they were. Get your coat. We have a coach waiting."

It was strange. Ever since they had arrived in Hearne, Levoreth felt an overwhelming desire to sleep. Even when she woke up in the morning, all she wanted to do was go back to sleep. Levoreth buttoned her coat up and suppressed a yawn. A coach harnessed to two horses waited at the bottom of the steps. A footman half-hidden by an enormous umbrella hurried forward. The driver huddled on top of the coach box, the reins dripping in his hands.

"Come, my dear," said her aunt.

One of the horses swung its head around to gaze at them.

Mistress of Mistresses.

I'm sorry, she said in her mind. It's cold and wet and you should be warm in your stable.

Ah, well, said the horse. *Some things cannot be helped. Besides, it is our honor, Mistress.*

It was dry inside the coach.

"That's better," said her aunt. She rapped on the ceiling with her knuckles.

The coach lurched away. Levoreth closed her eyes. The swaying motion of the coach was quite restful. That, and the sound of the rain thrumming on the roof and the clip-clop of the horses' hooves, was enough to put anyone to sleep. She yawned.

"Levoreth, you don't have to take the duke of Mizra seriously. That is, if you don't want to."

"What's that?" Levoreth came wide awake.

"My dear, your uncle and I have no intention of manipulating you into marriage." The duchess leaned forward and patted her niece's knee. "It's just that, well, you're getting older and we worry about you sometime. Marriage can be wonderful with the right person. Mind you, I don't subscribe to this silly idea that marriage must be made only for love, but it can be equally dreadful with the wrong person. So if the duke of Mizra at first strikes you wrong, all I'm saying is that you shouldn't dismiss him. However, if after a while he still doesn't seem right—not that you must fall in love with him, my dear—then smile and walk on."

"Did you marry for love, Aunt?"

"Of course not. I chose to fall in love after we were married, and only when I was sure Hennen loved me. It makes things easier if you wait. It gives you the upper hand. You're laughing at me."

"Perhaps," said Levoreth, smiling.

The coach creaked to a stop and the door opened. Rain dripped off the footman's nose. He unfurled the umbrella with a flourish and held it aloft.

"Thank you," said the duchess.

"Milady," said the footman, bowing deeply but still managing to keep the umbrella over the duchess' head.

"Will you be waiting outside for us?" asked Levoreth.

"Er," said the footman.

"Of course," said the duchess.

"There's a good inn down the street," said Levoreth. She dropped a gold piece in the footman's hand. "Wait there. See that the horses have some oats. We'll send someone to fetch you when we're ready. Have some ale yourself."

"Very good, milady."

The footman ushered them to the door of the shop and then backed away, bowing. He was young and the niece of the duke of Dolan was beautiful. Everyone thought so in the servants' hall.

The duchess shook her head.

"Sometimes, Levoreth, you are much too nice."

The dress shop was alive with light. Lamps hung from the ceiling and their glow reflected from mirrors of all sizes hung on walls and propped in corners. The proprietor appeared out of nowhere, bowing and smiling and bowing again.

"Welcome, maladies. Welcome. Tea?"

"That'd be nice," said the duchess, already drifting toward a flowing blue silk.

"Tea!" called the proprietor.

He clapped his hands together and a small girl hurried up with a silver pot. A second girl, even smaller, followed with a tray of mugs. Steam and cinnamon filled the air. Levoreth found herself holding a mug of tea. A third girl, the smallest of the three, peered up at her from beneath a plate of cookies.

"Gingersnap?" said the little girl.

"Yes, thanks," said Levoreth. She took two.

"My daughters," said the proprietor. "Now, back to work, my dears. Nimble fingers, you see." He bowed to the duchess. "Little fingers make little stitches. They take after their mother."

"You don't say. This blue silk, do you have it in green?"

"Milady has excellent taste. This comes from the loom of the best weaver in Damarkan, Avila Avilan herself. I'm devastated, but I do not have it in green. Purple, scarlet, blue. If I may say so, this blue does marvels with your eyes, milady."

"Pity," sniffed the duchess. "Why is it so difficult to find a good green?"

"The dye's been rare this last year," said the proprietor.

"And why's that?"

"I don't know, milady." The proprietor spread his hands in apology.

"Because the yarrow crop in Vomaro has failed for the last three years," said Levoreth to herself. "Too many gophers."

"What's that, my dear?" said the duchess.

"Nothing."

"You look good in green, Levoreth, but this brown velvet damask would go splendidly with your hair—"

"Absolutely, milady," said the proprietor. "Absolutely."

"—though brown is a difficult color, difficult to pin down into a proper tone, don't you think?"

"Certainly," said the proprietor. "But if it's brown you desire, perhaps milady would consider this silk as well? A lovely, rich earth tone, I might say. Finest Harthian silk."

"It is rather nice. Levoreth, my dear, what about a silk instead?"

"If you don't mind, Aunt," said Levoreth, "I'm going for a walk. It is a bit stuffy in here. I'll take this umbrella."

"But this silk would go perfectly with your—"

"Fine. Buy it. I'll wear it."

Before the duchess could say anything else, Levoreth stepped out the door. She discovered she had crushed a gingersnap in her hand. She flung the crumbs into the gutter. The rain was still falling. It drummed on top of the umbrella and dripped down in front of her nose. She took a deep breath to steady herself. Something was not right.

A yawn escaped her lips. The sensation of wanting to fall asleep was even stronger now. Stronger than it had been in the castle up on Highneck Rise. But she was not tired. She knew she was not. Yet here she was, about to fall asleep on her feet. She stumbled and stepped into a puddle.

"Drat!"

Her stocking felt cold and clammy against her skin. It was horrid, but the sensation cleared her head of any thought of sleep. And in that moment, she felt a gentle push against her mind. The sensation was as imperceptible as the push a blade of grass will exert when growing up beneath a rock. Just as imperceptible, but much stronger.

Instantly, Levoreth filled her mind with the memory of earth and stone. The earth settled her, and she felt the depth and the weight of the dark roots of mountains. Stone rose up within her mind into a wall. She could taste earth in her mouth. She could feel the city huddled around her in the dark and the cold and falling rain. Rain thrummed on top of the umbrella. Her knuckles whitened on the umbrella handle. And then the sensation came again. It was like a worm—a cold, soft worm. It crept across the stone shielding her. The touch pressed against the rock as if it sought entrance.

Levoreth shuddered.

Realization stirred in her mind. She knew this touch. It was the cause of her sleepiness, of her forgetfulness. For so many years. The thing was ancient. It was born of the Dark, a spell of some unfamiliar, powerful sort. Of this, she was sure. And now that she recognized its touch, it would never enter her mind again.

Never.

She blinked. Her head swung from side to side like a dog's, sniffing at the air. A growl escaped her lips. The spell was here. Somewhere in the city.

She glanced back at the dress shop. Light spilled from the window into the falling rain. Beyond the shop, the street opened up into Mioja Square. The gloom and the rain obscured the square, but here and there, she could see lamplight shining from the stalls of the more intrepid merchants. Few people were out in such weather, though, and the afternoon was rapidly turning into evening.

Twilight.

Perfect time for hunting.

Something glinted in her eyes. Her pupils seemed to flare green.

Levoreth strode off down the street, heading deeper into the city. The street grew narrower and the buildings began to look shabbier. Windows were shuttered against the approaching night.

There.

The sensation was coming from the southwest.

She turned a corner. Her nose twitched as she sniffed the air.

The sensation was getting stronger. It wasn't like a worm anymore. It was more like the finger of a dead man trailing against her skin. Gentle, but hard, with bone under the cold flesh. It stank of death.

She shoved back against it with her mind.

And the finger recoiled.

It vanished.

Instantly, she flung her thoughts wide, hunting through the silence and the darkness that exists on the edge of the mind. She was dimly aware of countless lives flickering in the darkness. Tiny stars gleaming in the night. Thoughts floated by, blind to her, but they were only the lives of Hearne's people, heedless of the danger that lurked within their city.

How long had the spell been in existence?

Her thoughts raced through the darkness. Nothing. Another thousand lives flashed by. Candle flames. But their lives would be counted as nothing if such a spell were allowed to continue. How many generations had already spent their lives in sleep under the spell?

Sleep possesses three doors. The first door opens from the day. We walk through into sleep. The second door opens on the other side of sleep into the morning. We walk through into the morning.

And the third door?

The third door opens into darkness. And if a sleeper stayed lost in sleep for too long, then the door would open and the Dark would come in.

Then, just when Levoreth was about to give up, she stiffened. A scent lingered in the darkness, far out on the edge of her thoughts. Almost due south now. The scent was faint but unmistakable. The stench of the Dark.

She ran. Her skirts whipped around her legs, sodden with water. She splashed across a street and darted down an alley. The cobblestones were slick, but she ran sure-footedly, vaulting over garbage piles and dodging around corners. The twilight had deepened into night. The clouds were thickening and the sky was gone. A wind arose, slashing the rain down sideways.

The touch of the spell wriggled frantically in her thoughts, desperate to escape her, but it could not. She held to the scent as surely as a bloodhound, as surely as a wolf tracking its kill across the snow. She furled the umbrella without slowing and tucked it under one arm. Her hair whipped free from its pins, heavy with water.

A couple of men—fishermen, by the smell of them—hurried up the street toward her, their heads bent down under the rain. She ran by, and they did not see her. It seemed she ran in a world of silence, a world of darkness and blurred stone and light hiding secure behind shutters. The rain lashed against her face and she smelt woodsmoke cooling in the air. Somewhere in front of her, somewhere in the city and not far away now, was the spell.

Abruptly, she stopped running.

Before her, a street made its crooked way into the evening. Several doors down was an inn. Light streamed from its windows. She could hear laughter and the sound of voices coming from the inn. The street seemed all the colder and darker because of the cheeriness of the sound and the light. Past the inn, however, and on the other side of the street, was a house.

The house was wedged between what looked like a warehouse on one side and a second house on the other. It was shabby and tall, three stories in total, with a sharply pitched roof underneath the chimneys teetering up into the sky. Every window was shuttered and dark. It looked like an empty house, a house that had not been lived in for many years. A dead house.

But the house was not dead. It was alive.

A ward buzzed on the edges of her mind. It was woven about the house. Her thoughts feathered around it, touching and tasting and smelling. The ward was old. Hundreds of years old. It listened to her, coiled as tight as a snake ready to strike. Behind the ward crouched the house. Within the house was the spell. It stank of malice and ancient intent and death.

How long have you been here, you abomination? She whispered the words in her mind.

Long enough, Mistress. Long enough.

The voice of the spell was dry and dusty, creaking as if it were made up of the sounds of footsteps on stairs, of echoes in empty hallways and the drip of water in a dark basement.

Your time here is at an end. This is my land. These are my people.

You did your people well, you foolish old woman. I have lulled your people to sleep for these hundreds of years. Them and you. It is what I was woven for and I have done my job well. You shall die this night and I shall remain until my master returns once again. My lullaby continues, Mistress, and Tormay sleeps.

Who is your master? Tell me!

But the voice fell silent and would not answer.

The ward triggered when she was about fifty feet away from the house. Instinctively, she flung her mind wide to contain it.

Death darkness death—and the ward crashed into her. It had been woven hundreds of years ago—she could feel the age in it—but it had lost none of its potency. Whoever had woven it had been a master. The blow would have leveled a stone building, would

192

have shattered minds and bodies, but her own mind was filled with the earth. She staggered with the impact, but the earth was heavy and deep and old, and it could not be moved.

The ward coiled back on itself and then lashed out again, humming and buzzing and hissing with malevolence.

Death death death!

Dimly, as if from far away, she could still hear the sounds of laughter and conversation from the inn nearby. She could not see the inn, however, for it was as if she looked down a tunnel, blurred stone and light and the bent lines of walls and chimneys on either side. At the end of the tunnel stood the house, waiting for her. The door was in perfect clarity. Raindrops gleamed on the door handle.

The earth lay silent within her mind. Damp earth, full of patience and stone. Roots reaching down into darkness and weight. The ward slammed against the earth, hungry to destroy, ravenous to kill and shatter and rend, but the earth absorbed it in silence. She could smell loam and moss in her mind and she felt the tickle of grass against her skin.

She found herself standing before the door. The handle broke in her grasp and the door swung open. She stepped within and shut the door. It was dark inside. She whispered a word and three fireflies flew from her hand. They gave off only a tiny glow, but the darkness was so complete that their little light was sufficient.

A hall stretched away before her. Doors on either side stood shut. Halfway down the hall, a staircase climbed up into the darkness. The stink of death filled the air. She blinked, momentarily stunned by the smell. A presence battered against her mind. The fireflies winked out.

"Avert!"

One by one, the fireflies blinked back into life. The presence vanished and the silence of the earth filled in around her mind. She coughed, choking on the smell. On her right was a small room, empty of everything except dust and shadows. She threw open the window and breathed the cold, clean night air that flooded in.

"There," she said.

The stairs creaked under her. The fireflies crowded in close around her head and she had to wave them away.

"Go on now," she said. "You're safe with me."

Reluctantly, they hovered in front of her.

The stairs were covered with dust, but here and there, in the faint light of the fireflies, Levoreth could see footprints. She knelt to examine the steps in front of her. The fireflies floated down. The dust bore evidence of several different kinds of footprints. She frowned. But there was something strange about the marks.

Here was the paw print of a dog. Here was that of a cat. And here was the shoe print of a small human. A child, no doubt. The prints were faint, but it seemed there were many different dogs, different cats, different children. They had not all climbed the stairs at once, but over the course of many years. Many years.

She touched the print of a cat's paw with one finger and realized what was strange about the marks. All of them ascended the stairs, but only one kind of print ascended and descended. It was that of an older child. Or a small human.

"Earth and stone." Her voice trailed away.

She shivered. And understood.

Hoped, desperately hoped she was wrong.

Levoreth hurried up the stairs, not caring that the fireflies could not keep up. The darkness grew, but she did not fear it. Her eyes shone like those of a cat. She muttered under her breath and more fireflies fell from her hands. They trailed behind her like a river of stars. She reached the top of the stairs and another hall lay before her. Doors stood open on either side, filled with dust and silence. She followed the jumble of footprints down the hall to a third set of stairs.

Please, no.

Let it not be so.

Please.

The stairs creaked under her. Fireflies shone in her hair. She reached the top of the stairs and another hall lay before her. A door stood at the far end. She stopped. The house remained silent around her, though she thought she could hear rain pattering on the roof. But something waited in the silence. She could feel it, just past the door at the end of the hall.

"Earth and stone," Levoreth said. She took a deep breath. "For how many hundreds of years has this been so? It is to this place all my uneasy dreams blindly looked, and past this cursed house, past this place to the Dark. I am afraid to open the door."

She took a deep breath and then walked down the hall. The door opened at her touch.

She fell into darkness.

No stars.

No light.

No up.

No down.

Nothingness.

Only sleep.

Endless sleep.

A door opened in the darkness. Memory shone through like light. Drowsing in the cemetery behind the church in Andolan. Afternoon sunlight like honey. Bees drifting in the air. Herself napping next to an old headstone. *Dolan Callas.*

Sleep.

It would be a relief.

The darkness pressed closer.

And another headstone next to the other. *Levoreth Callas.* Beloved wife and mother. Roses blooming on the wall. The scarlet petals ready to drift down and die. When it was their time. It was her time. Her eyes opened. It was not her time. When it was her time, she would go willing. She would go rejoicing, for she was weary. But not now. Not this day.

Fireflies flew from her hands. They winked and shone and flashed, spinning around her, and the darkness fled away. She stood in a room without windows. The air was close and foul. It stank of blood, and there was a tremble of misery and pain and fear in it. Her stomach clenched. Before her was a table on which lay a piece of parchment. She forced herself to step closer.

The words of the spell had been written in a bold hand, in dark ink that was not precisely black but something else. Something dried and flaking. She shuddered. Past the table, in the corner, was a heap of what looked like rags of old clothing, but here and there was a shard of bone. The skull of a cat grinned up at her from beneath a torn shirt.

She screamed.

In fury. Rage. For the sorrow of it all.

They all screamed, said the spell. It chuckled. The whisper of it in her mind was filled with malice.

They all screamed. But no one heard them, Mistress. No one. Not you. Were you not their protector? Were you not their bulwark? Where were you in their last moments? Sweet, all of them, and their blood has kept me strong all these long years. I hold their fear and their pain still. So many years.

"Who wrote you?" she shouted. "Who was your master?!"

Better you never know, sneered the spell. *Better you go down to your grave and never know, for you are weak earth and stone. He will bind you and bring you into the endless night. You will sleep deep. Deeper even than the sleep I gave you these last hundreds and hundreds of years.*

"I'll strip the knowledge from your cursed ink!"

Too late, Mistress.

The parchment collapsed into dust before her hand could touch it.

Her fist slammed down on the table. The dust of the parchment drifted down to the floor. A sigh whispered through the air. She stood for a moment with bowed head over the sad little pile of rags and fur and bones. The fireflies hovered around her.

Levoreth turned and left the room.

The house shivered around her. She could hear the rain still tapping on the roof. The wind blew along the walls and it sounded like someone sighing. A stair creaked under her. She turned, her skin crawling as if someone was watching her. Above her, at the top of the stairs, the shadows seemed crowded with the ghostly shapes of cats and dogs and children. They stared down at her without moving or speaking.

"I'm sorry," she said. "I am so sorry."

Still, they did not move.

"Rest well now. Nothing can hold you to this place any longer."

It seemed like one of the children smiled at her, and then the shadows were only shadows. The house was empty now except for its own memories.

She closed the front door behind her and walked away. It was raining harder now, and she was glad for it. She turned her face up to the sky, eyes closed, and let the rain wash away her tears.

CHAPTER FORTY-NINE
BOOKS CAN BE DANGEROUS

For the past three years, Ronan had kept a room on the second story of a house near the city's south gate. An elderly couple lived in the place and made their living from the husband's work as a scrivener. They were happy to get the silver piece he gave them every month for rent. It was a stiff price for a single room in such a poor part of Hearne, but the place pleased him, as there was access across the roofs, as well as by a set of rickety stairs that mounted up from a walled courtyard behind the house. The old couple gave no heed to his comings and goings but were careful to tell him of any strangers who appeared on their street.

Not that he had much to fear from enemies when he was on his own ground. Only one attacker at a time would be able to manage the stairs and the narrow door. And he'd yet to meet his match in a swordsman. When he slept, and when he was away, one of the cleverest wards gold could buy maintained a tireless watch, spelled into the stone and timbers of his room. Money well spent.

Ronan woke that morning and washed away an uneasy night of dreams with a basin of water. Sunlight angled along the top of the rickety stairs. He perched there a while in thought, letting the light warm his face.

At first, he had been afraid that the creature from the Silentman's court would haunt his dreams, but his sleep, though uneasy with old memories and shadows, was thankfully devoid of the thing's gaunt face. Whenever he thought of that strange meeting in the Silentman's court, he could still hear the thing's whispering voice and feel the invisible band tightening around his chest. He had never been so terrified in all his life. Facing an enemy over blades was never a concern, for he had learned how to fight from the best swordsman in all of Tormay.

He sighed at the thought.

"Sword skill or not," he said, "I'm no longer the Knife."

For a while, he paced about the room, scowling. Not that he cared what the Silentman thought, but to be cast off after so many years of faithful service? The Silentman was a bloodsucking tick. A swamp leech, a drooling idiot, the dullard offspring of a goat. And he owed him money.

Ronan slammed his fist on the table.

He didn't care about any of it at all. Not the Guild, not Hearne, not any of the thieves that he had come to know over the years. All he wanted was his money. Without it, he wouldn't be able to leave the city. To leave and lose himself in the north, in the islands and the sea.

But the Silentman would not let him leave Hearne without finding the boy.

There were two possibilities, other than whatever fate might choose to deal out. The house that had been robbed or the little girl. If the boy was alive then his trail would lead from the house. The scent might be picked up there. Doubtful at best, after all the days that had passed. But it would be instructive to find out who lived in the house. A rich scholar. That's what Dreccan Gor had told him when he had been given the job. An idle scholar with too much money and learning. He had said it with no expression on his fat face, the Silentman gazing on them in silence from his dais. A scholar with the habit of collecting ancient oddities. But there had to be more to it than that. There always was. Usually, it didn't matter, but it might now. Not just a scholar.

Ancient oddities that were no use to anyone. Except the white-faced creature whispering its threats while the three most powerful men in the Guild stood before it in utter terror. The Silentman. Dreccan Gor. And the Knife. Ronan frowned. Except he was no longer the Knife.

The little girl. Of anyone in the whole city, knowledge and luck would be on her side to catch the first glimpse of the accursed boy. If he was still in the city. Shadow take the thought. A city boy raised and schooled in the streets wouldn't be likely to leave the walls. No. Hearne was his world.

How many children were in that fat fool's clutches—two dozen, three, more? He didn't know for certain. But they'd be sharing whatever they had with each other, whether it was food or information, everything used as a common bulwark against the Juggler. And if one had seen the boy Jute, then all had seen him. Though maybe not. Not with a hundred gold pieces on Jute's head. At any rate, the girl was probably his best bet.

He smiled sourly. That would be a trick. She would turn and run, the first sight she caught of him. He would have to win her over somehow. There would be time enough later to wring her neck.

He stood up, checked the ward guarding his rooms with one flick of his mind—it was whispering peacefully to itself—and then hurried down the stairs.

It was still early morning, but the city was bustling. Every tavern, every boarding house and hostelry was bursting at the seams with travelers and traders come for the Autumn Fair. The streets were crowded with barrows, fast-talking hawkers, hucksters cajoling the foolish to their dicing and chance games, vendors buying, selling, and trading. A contingent of the city Guard marched by, stepping smartly and stern in their blue-black cloaks and gleaming armor.

Ronan bought some fried dough from a cart and munched on the honeyed bread. A child ran past; he eyed the boy, but then turned away after he saw him scooped up by a stout matron. He strolled on and came to Mioja Square. He sat down on the fountain's edge, washed his sticky hands in the water, and considered. It seemed as if the entire city was out in force, judging from the busy square around him. But the Fair would not properly start for another three days, and then the city would become even more crowded. In three days. That would be the evening of the regent's ball and when he would have to see to the strange bargain struck with Liss Galnes. He shivered and then glanced around, shamefaced, to see if anyone was watching him.

Throughout the morning and the afternoon, he walked the city, down streets and back alleys, crisscrossing the expanse of the square so many times he lost count. He saw street urchins everywhere, with the knowing, sly look about them marked in their furtive eyes and quick hands. The Juggler's children were out in force. He saw them stealing purses and wallets from traders, prosperous farmers, nobles. Most people from the duchies and lands beyond Hearne were not accustomed to the harsher realities of the city. They were easy marks for the industrious children. Once he almost laughed aloud at the sight of several little boys standing on each other's shoulders to filch a fine saddle blanket from the top of a camel towering over them. The snatch was made with only seconds to spare and then they were pelting off into the crowd with a cursing Harthian merchant in pursuit. The camel looked on in disdain.

As the merchant from Harth quickly learned, the children were not easy to follow in the crowded streets. Even for one as skilled as Ronan, he found he could not trail any of the children for long. He attempted this several times throughout the day and ruefully discovered that even his abilities were not up to the task. The children could move quicker than he among the press of the crowd. They could dart between legs and under carts, while he had to content himself with elbowing people aside. He gave up the idea as impractical. It wouldn't do to collar one of the little wretches in passing, for then the word would be out. Not once did he see the girl Lena.

He skulked around in the neighborhood of the Goose and Gold for a while, hoping to discover where the Juggler kept the children. He was certain the place would be nearby, for the fat man had never stirred far from the tavern before his recent disappearance. But he didn't see any children, though he loitered there for an hour. The day was passing. He moved on, gloomy and lost in thought.

Ronan found himself walking along the narrow street behind the scholar's house—the same street where he and the boy had stood that night. It was a quiet place, a neighborhood for those who had money enough to buy security, far from the bustling quarters of trade or the dirty boroughs of the poor. He could hear the wards woven into the place. They whispered to him as he passed. They were harmless, as long he did not intrude, but decidedly aware of him. He admired them. He could sense the care and cost that had gone into their spelling. And he smiled, for he and the boy had beaten them that night. That was certainly something not many in the Guild would have been able to do.

At one place in the wall, there was a small passageway cut in the stone, closed by a gate of iron bars that rose up into sharp points like spears. He could see through them into a large, enclosed garden. It looked a lovely place—the little he could make out—filled with flowers, bushes, and fruit trees growing in unkempt profusion.

Perhaps it was the boredom and frustration of the day that made him do what he did next. Trying to track slippery street urchins was enough to try anyone's patience, and it had already been a bad enough week as it was. A moment of careful listening, listening with every nerve ending alert, left him certain there was no one in the house, or at least in the half of the house closest to him. Oddly enough, the iron gate only had a rather insignificant ward woven into its pilings and hinges. There was a convenient space between the sharp points and the stone ceiling arching above them.

He touched the iron and willed himself to silence. The ward stirred slightly and then subsided back into dormancy. He hoisted himself up and edged over the sharp points crowning the gate. As soon as one leg was straddled over, the gate came alive. Another ward, he thought frantically, masked by the first. The iron bars were lengthening, the points were shooting up toward the stone above at an alarming rate. With a frenzied heave, he was over and through, sprawling painfully on the ground. He froze, senses prickling and quivering out in every direction. But there was nothing. No footsteps hurrying near. No cries of alarm. Not even the whisper of other wards contracting and focusing on him. He shivered, remembering the iron moving and growing underneath him and the unyielding stone above his head. A bird trilled cheerfully in the garden and, on top of the gate, the iron points retracted to their normal height.

Wetness slid down his arm. His fingers came away sticky with blood. He hadn't even felt the iron point slice through him. It wasn't a bad cut, but it could have been worse. He tore a strip of cloth from his shirt and tied it tightly around his arm.

For a long time, Ronan stayed beside the gate, examining the garden and the inner walls of the house standing around it in sunwashed stone. The bird whistled and sang within the branches of a rowan tree in the center of the garden. Oddly enough, there were sprigs of red berries on the tree, even though it wasn't yet autumn. Selia bushes bloomed around the rowan, and the ground was littered with their white petals. Crickets scraped and sawed in the grass. But beyond their droning and the careless notes of the bird, there was only the silence of an empty house.

The ward in the gate had been beyond his skill. He had been lucky. If there were one such ward, there would be more. But he could not go back. The thought of climbing over those iron points again brought sweat to his brow. He would have to get out through the house. Of one thing he was now sure. No ordinary scholar lived here. The gate ward had been meant to kill, not merely warn off, and wards that killed were expensive and rare.

The bird went silent when he ventured across the garden. The sun was almost overhead. There were no shadows to hide in. Quickly, he walked to a door in the nearest wall and tried the handle. It was unlocked and seemed to have no warding. He slipped inside and, as he closed the door, heard the bird burst into song behind him.

He found himself in a pantry. Shelves lined the walls. Bundles of dried herbs hung from the ceiling. Another door opened into a kitchen. The place smelled unpleasantly dank, as if it had been unused for days. A pile of carrots on the counter was covered with mold. Two other doors led out of the kitchen. When he eased the first one open, he saw stone stairs descending into darkness. Obviously a basement. He considered going down, for basements usually meant some sort of access to the city sewers—a mode of exit and entrance that he had used in other parts of Hearne—but at that moment he heard the soft rasp of something dragging slowly across a stone floor. He silently shut the door and backed away.

A great horror came over him, for even though the door was closed, he could hear a faint squishing sound, almost as if a handful of wet clay was being pressed repeatedly against stone.

Shhhs.

Shhhs.

Shhhs.

The noise was getting louder. It was ascending the stairs. A slow, shuffling movement.

Ronan turned and almost ran from the kitchen. Out the other door. Into a long hallway, lined with door after door and floored with a thick carpet that deadened his footfalls. No windows. No sunlight. Only shadow. Which way was he heading? Which door? His arm ached and he felt dizzy.

One day, your luck'll run out, said a tiny voice inside his mind.

No. Never.

Soon. You'll break.

Not even when they beat me bloody.

They were going to hang you that morning in Lura.

Yes. That was years ago. I escaped.

Heart racing, he paused in a small anteroom in the hallway. The corridor split into two directions. One to the right and one to the left. They both looked the same and he was disoriented. Shadow in both directions. Not one single window to betray the sky. If he only had the sky. Open spaces, wind, and the sky. A good horse under him.

"Never should've come to this city," he muttered out loud.

The air sighed behind him, as if shifted by a door opening. Ronan dove down the left passageway without stopping to think. He ran up a stairway. At the top, a mahogany door rose up out of the gloom. His hands fluttered over it. A warning buzz tingled in his fingertips. A ward? No. It felt different. But the air whispered again, far back down the stairs and in the passageway. He slipped through the door.

Whatever was woven into the door was not a ward, for nothing happened, and he closed the door behind him. Light bloomed from a curtained window. It was a library. An uncommon thing in Hearne, for books were rare and costly. This room had more books in it than he had ever seen before, even though in more than a decade of thieving he had broken into most of the wealthier homes of Hearne. Every wall, from floor to ceiling, was lined with books. He stopped in the middle of the room, fascinated despite the fear playing icily down his neck. Leather in rich reds, white, and browns. Spines cracked with age. Copper covers mottled green. Huge tomes clasped with wood covers and brass clasps.

There.

Startled, he swung around. Who had spoken? The room was empty.

On the second shelf.

His eyes wavered up and settled on a slim book bound in brown leather.

Hurry.

The door creaked open behind him. The book almost leapt into his hand. He whirled and caught a glimpse of a shadowy form shambling forward. A damp smell of rotting things filled the air. He dove for the window. Glass shattered around him, and then he was falling, desperately trying to grab onto something, anything to slow his fall. But there was nothing to catch hold of, only the book clutched in his hand.

A thought wavered through his head. That voice. It sounded like her.

And then everything stopped.

He must have been unconscious for only a moment, because something gibbered far above him from the window when he struggled to his feet. His vision blurred and all the world ran red with pain, whirling and tilting around him. The stones under his feet were spattered with blood and he regarded it solemnly, professionally. Too much blood. Whoever lost that much was fast on the way out. Poor fool. He staggered away down the narrow street. Time to leave.

The voice had been hers.

Pain. Everywhere, he thought to himself. There must be a way to escape it. Shoulder is the worst of all. But I have the book.

Hurry.

He did not think anymore. There was only a gray fog of pain. Instinct took over, and he staggered along. At times, he was aware of people passing by. People staring and exclaiming. A hand tugged at his arm once and a voice said something. It could have been anything. An offer of help. But the pain shut all meaning out. There was only movement and, although he didn't realize it, a compulsion that drew him like a broken marionette being walked along by a careless child. He stumbled his way up the shady streets of Highneck Rise and found himself in the Street of Willows. At the end of the street there was no longer anywhere to go, only the high walls that enclosed the manors there. He stood, staring stupidly, and swaying drunkenly. His shoulder was on fire. His head felt disconnected from his shoulders. Ronan staggered up against a wall. Sunlight glimmered in between the leaves of a willow tree. He blinked and could not focus. His knees gave out and he collapsed to the ground. He heard the creak of a garden gate opening. A shadow fell across his face. He could smell the sea. The girl stared down at him. Her face was expressionless.

"I've brought you your book," he said. And then he knew no more.

CHAPTER FIFTY
FOOTPRINTS

They arrived at the village the afternoon of the second day after leaving Hearne. Owain had pushed his men and the horses hard. Every hour lost meant less of a chance of cutting their quarry's trail. He didn't hope for much—hope was a chancy thing in his profession—but even a single print would be more than what he currently knew. And currently, he knew nothing.

The Rennet valley, when heading east from Hearne, devolved into a hilly land covered with heather and small copses of trees and sudden, smaller valleys that branched off the main valley. Creeks veined the land before joining the Rennet River, which flowed west in ultimate pursuit of the sea.

They rode through the valley in the rain and sun, eating cold rations, sleeping as few hours as possible, and making rough bed with their cloaks. The troops did not complain. They were the best soldiers Owain had. Even though the Guard of Hearne was woefully understrength, that did not mean he trained his men poorly. The regent regarded the Guard as a quaint custom from long-dead times that had no real place in the modern society of Hearne. But the Gawinns were fixtures of the city. There had always been Gawinns in Hearne and they had always been the Lord Captains of the Guard. To do away with their office, from the regent's point of view, would lessen the charm of court occasions, balls, and diplomatic functions.

"That fellow there," the regent would murmur to some visiting dignitary. "The one in black, that's the Lord Captain of Hearne. Protector of the city, don't you know. Been Gawinns in Hearne almost as long as my own family. Rather nice uniform, don't you think?"

A rider urged his horse up the path toward Owain and reined in next to him. He was a small man with a face aged by sun and wind and seamed with scars so that it seemed his skin was stitched of leather rather than flesh.

"Another hour," he said.

"Any sign to be had?" said Owain.

"Not w' the weather these days."

The man shook his head. His name was Hoon and he came from the mountains of Morn. At least that's what he'd said twenty years ago when he'd joined the Guard. There was no cause to disbelieve him, of course, but Owain never cared where his soldiers came from, only that they could fight and fight well.

Behind them, a horse blew out a breath of resignation. Harnesses clinked and there came the quiet voices of the troops as they murmured to each other and to their mounts.

"No reason for 'em to've come up this way," said Hoon. "There's a good half-dozen ways into that village. Just see it now, past the pines." Past a stand of pine growing further up the valley, sunlight gleamed on slate roofs.

"Blast the rain," said Owain, but he spoke mildly. There was no reason to worry over the things that could not be shifted. Most of life could not be shifted.

"Aye. Whichever way they came and went, doubt there's sign left with all the rain we been getting."

"Perhaps inside the houses."

"Aye," said Hoon.

Corn and hay grew in plots along the banks of the stream at the bottom of the valley. The corn was unpicked, however, and rotting on the stalk. Mold furred the hay, and grasses were already reclaiming the footpaths winding about the plots. The men rode through the shadow of the pines.

"You hear that?" said Owain.

"Aye," said Hoon. "Nothin' t'all."

"Not a sound here except the stream and the wind in the trees. Not a songbird or even a cricket."

They found the first one just outside of the village, sprawled across the path. The bones were bleached white, polished as clean as a poor man's dish.

"A child," said someone.

"Make camp here, sergeant," said Owain. "Sentry detail and hot food for the men. Stay out of the village lest on my word."

"Aye, m'lord."

Owain and Hoon entered the village on foot.

"Poor enough," said Owain. "But they had themselves a master mason here. Sturdy walls. Good thatch. This village was built to last, but it's not a village now without its folk."

"Graveyard, more like."

The bones were everywhere. Occasionally, they lay together in semblance of a skeleton, but more times than not the bones had been dragged into jumbled disarray.

"Birds and beasts been at 'em," said Hoon gloomily. "No way to treat the dead. Morn, where I come from, you get stuffed inna cave, covered over w' rock. That's the way."

The rain and the sun had beaten the ground into a succession of mud and dust and back again, but even with little hope left by the weather, Hoon methodically quartered the village. He paced between the houses, walking slowly, his face intent on the grass and mud. Owain wandered behind him, careful not to go where the tracker had yet to examine. He stepped around the bones out of a certain sympathy, but mostly out of an unwillingness to hear them snap. A skull grimaced up at him from the foot of a stone wall.

"Someday, the story'll be out," he said to the skull. "Doubt that's consolation to you, seeing how your part's over."

The skull said nothing.

"I wonder if you ever came to Hearne? That's my city—I'm supposed to protect it, like my father did, and his father before him. You see, if whoever destroyed your village isn't caught, then who's to say they won't come to my city one day and try the same?"

Sunlight gleamed in the curve of the skull's eye socket. The light glimmered, as if the skull was winking at him, as if it knew something Owain did not.

"A girl from your village survived. The only one. Maybe you were her father or uncle. Or maybe an older brother. She's safe at my house, with my wife, so don't worry on her account. She's a skinny little thing, not much taller than my Magret. She doesn't talk, just as silent as you. Someday, though, she'll tell her story."

Still, the skull said nothing.

"Then the story'll be out. You'll see."

Hoon straightened up and tossed a clump of mud away.

203

"Ain't nothing worth a cuss."

"Let's try the houses, then," said Owain.

Their luck improved with the third house.

"Dirt floor," said Hoon. He didn't smile, but he came near it. "Keep on the sill here. It'll be trick enough sussing out the sign w'out you clumpin' around."

They both kept to the sill at first, Hoon squatting down on his haunches and examining the ground in front of him. It was one of the smaller houses in the village, having just a single room dominated by a hearth in one wall and a narrow cot beside it in the corner.

"Only one person," said Owain.

"Aye, scattered a bit by what come after. Not enough bones here to go around 'cept once. Woman, by the stretch of that."

Hoon, satisfied by the ground just within the door, took a step forward and continued his perusal.

"Odd," he said.

"What's that?"

"Been crows in here, which don't surprise me none. Nasty birds they are. Like a bit of rotten flesh w' the best of 'em. But this here print's a fox. They ain't carrion eaters, best I know. An' I know."

"Maybe the fox came in afterward. After the crows had come and gone. A curious fox."

"Nope. This fox came in afore the crows. See here? That's crow sign an' it's overlapping this paw print. Old man crow come in after the fox was done w' his meal. Hopping along on fox's tracks. Odd, that. Never seen a fox go for carrion. Lest he gone crazy or somethin'. Mebbe he been bit by one of them skunks and gone foamy at the mouth. Turrible creatures, them skunks."

Hoon crept forward a few more inches. He said nothing for a while. A faded gray apron lay crumpled on top of the bed and Owain wondered if the owner—the skeleton on the floor—had been an old widow living alone. The room was small.

"Ahum," grunted Hoon. "Here 'tis."

"What?"

"Step up an' look over my shoulder. See here? That's a print you've never seen afore. Like a dog, but bigger an' heavier than any dog I know. Been huge cats in the mountains that've prints this big, but this ain't a cat. That's dog."

"A hunting hound, perhaps," said Owain.

"Mebbe so. Mebbe so. Here's t'other bit of the riddle. Look here."

"That's a boot print."

"Ain't no ordinary boot print. First off, the dog an' whoever was wearing this boot, both of 'em were in here at the same time. You gotta boot print over here what the dog stepped on, an' clear over here next t' the skull—that's the dog an' the boot stepped on the same spot later. An' see how the edges are all broke down? Shows the crows an' fox came in long after."

"Hound and master."

"Yep," said Hoon. He sat back on his heels and looked up at Owain. "See anything else strange 'bout that boot?"

"Not specifically. Well, I suppose it just doesn't look right."

Hoon nodded with gloomy satisfaction.

"Aye. It don't look right an' I'll tell you why. Ain't no human wearing that boot. That's a long foot, long as your'n. But here across the ball of the foot, that's too narrow for humans. Ain't no way that was human."

"And it can't be an ogre."

"Ogres don't wear boots much, an' if they did, they've got great big, clumpy feet almost wide as they're long. Asides, ogres are heavy. When they step, they make a print—let me tell you! This fellow here's got a foot long as your'n but he made hardly a print at all. Almost like he weighs close to nothing."

The remaining houses yielded no other clues besides confirmation of the strange prints, and it was only in the poorer dwellings—those with dirt floors—that this was so. After Owain had satisfied himself that there was nothing left to find, he ordered his men to collect the bones and bury them in a large grave they dug at the edge of the village.

"It's the best we can do for them," he said to his sergeant.

"Very good, m'lord." And the man strode away to see to the digging. It was a slow job at best, done with their spears, but they had enough hands and enough hours yet before sundown.

Owain walked through the village and wondered which house the little girl had belonged to. The trader had said they had found her outside.

"Here now."

It was Hoon, who had silently appeared in front of him.

"Summat else turned up," said the tracker.

He held up a tuft of hair and Owain took it from him. The hairs were coarse and colored a dark reddish-brown.

"Where'd you find this?"

Past the village and along the bank of the stream, a path lay among the willows. The two men walked along. It was getting on toward dusk and the sun was dropping fast. The valley was small, but it was deep and, as such, did not possess as much breadth of sky as the plain above. A lantern, however, swung from Hoon's hand.

"At the miller's, you see." Hoon grinned crookedly. "Figured I'd keep outa the way. No stacking bones or diggin' for me."

Owain smiled and said nothing. Hoon was a good fellow—the best tracker he'd ever had—and he liked the little Mornish man. He would never put up with such familiarity from his other men, but he didn't mind it coming from Hoon. The tracker never meant anything by it. Besides, the folk who lived in the Mountains of Morn had little patience with the social contrivances of nobility. Truth be told, Owain had little patience for it himself.

"Millstone ain't gonna turn for a while," said Hoon. The house on the bank was half dwelling and half mill, for a small waterwheel jutted off the side of the house. The wooden shafts and gears were visible through an open shed built against the back wall. The waterwheel was slimed over with moss.

"People will settle here someday."

"Mebbe. Mebbe not. A place gets uneasy-like, when murdering happens. Some folk can sense that. Horses an' dogs can. Shadows move where they shouldn't an' the night air gets a strange taste to it. An' here? Lotta murdering here. This place, whole family got taken inside 'cept one poor soul on the threshold."

"You find the fur in the house?"

"Nope. Fur was in the barn."

205

Across the yard from the house was a barn. Its doors gaped open, but there was only shadow inside. Owain paused in the middle of the yard and frowned. The door to the house was ajar as well, and bones lay scattered across its sill.

For a second there, it had almost seemed like someone had whispered.

Just behind him.

No—it wasn't possible.

He shook his head and entered the barn. Tinder sparked in Hoon's hand and the lantern flared. Bones snapped underfoot. Owain looked down. He had stepped squarely on the skeleton of an animal.

"That's a real dog," said Hoon. He held the lantern high and light filled the barn.

"Where was the fur you found?"

"Right up there." Hoon pointed.

"That's impossible."

They were both looking at the edge of a hayloft. A wooden ladder led up to the loft, but it was a good twenty feet in height.

"Better believe it, an' our beastie didn't climb no ladder. See here on the floor?"

Hoon nudged the straw with one foot.

"Straw, dung, dust—all settled t'gether—but somethin' lunged from here an' kicked the lot loose. Straight up it jumped. Right to the hayloft."

"That's impossible," repeated Owain, looking up. Hoon didn't reply but only began climbing the ladder. Owain followed him. "I could believe a sandcat jumping this distance. Not a dog."

Owain's voice died away as he peered over the top of the hayloft. Hoon scrambled forward and hung the lantern on a chain dangling from the rafters overhead. The planks at the edge of the loft were heavily gouged. The wood was splintered, revealing the yellow grain under the aged exterior.

"It jumped," said Hoon with a certain gloomy satisfaction. "Straight on up. Musta hung on with its front claws, scrabbling like mad to get up and over, ripped this wood to shreds. An' then—here—just past all the splinters, it caught hold. No more grooves, but more like dagger stabs, like it got its claws in good an' proper."

He shook his head.

"I sure would hate to meet this beastie w'out a good brace of swords alongside me."

"My sword would be enough," said Owain. "But why would the thing have bothered to come up? With such determination, it must have been chasing quarry."

"Aye. Right to the trapdoor over the haymow. See here? It lunged forward an' then stopped at the opening."

The two men stared down into the gloom of the haymow below. The lantern's light gleamed on the wicked curves of the spikes beneath them. Light caught on something hanging from the tip of one of the spikes.

"Bring that lantern down," said Owain.

The haymow yielded up its secret easily. The scrap of cloth, once white but now gray with dust and blotched with the dark stains of old blood, lay in Owain's hand.

"Dried blood on the spike, too," said Hoon.

"Aye, there would be. I daresay this is from a child's nightgown." And Owain remembered the wound in the little girl's leg. Part of the puzzle solved at least.

They searched the millhouse before returning to the encampment. Down a hallway there was a small room containing two beds. Owain immediately knew it was the right room. It was a simple space with little in it besides the beds. A skeleton lay tangled in the tattered sheets of one. The other bed was empty. A chest sat in one corner. It contained clothes for the most part, but he did not take them. At the bottom, however, was a doll made of frayed cotton, mended and re-mended with careful, minute stitches. He took the doll and put it in his pocket. Hoon said nothing.

Night had fallen when they left the millhouse. The lantern cast a warm yellow glow around their feet. As they walked away, he heard the whisper again. Clearer now.

Take care of her.

"I will," he said out loud.

"What's that?" said Hoon.

"Nothing."

CHAPTER FIFTY-ONE
THE COUNCIL OF CATS

The regent held a small dinner party that night. Small, at least, by Botrell's standards. Many of the nobility from the duchies had already arrived in Hearne for the Autumn Fair. They were all comfortably represented, except for the duchy of Mizra, whose party hadn't arrived yet, and Harlech, who never bothered to take much notice of the rest of Tormay. Even haughty Harth had sent a contingent: the self-styled king's only son and a small cadre of lords to accompany him. Chandeliers shone above a long table that seemed to stretch on and on through the length of a black marble hall.

Big enough to gallop a herd of horses through, thought Levoreth to herself. Which I would rather be doing than sitting here making polite conversation with a half-witted lordling from Vomaro.

"Must be dull to live so far in the north, Lady Levoreth," drawled the lordling. His name was Dwaes. That was all Levoreth had heard—or had cared to hear—as the scallion pie on her plate was proving more interesting than his conversation.

"What's that?" she said.

Far down at the end of the table, Botrell and her uncle were roaring with laughter. Probably telling horse stories. Or the regent was making another offer for her hand. She scowled down at her plate. The Fair would be tedious enough, fending off whatever ridiculous ideas of marriage the duke of Mizra had. Another admirer slobbering around her and quoting poetry at great length, as Botrell was fond of doing, would be enough to send her around the bend.

"Rather dull, don't you know," bawled Dwaes, inspecting his empty wineglass, "living up in the north where you are, eh?" A servant materialized at his shoulder and filled the glass.

"Oh, extremely," she said nastily. "Most people who visit turn right around and go home. If you're considering a trip, save yourself the bother." Across the table, Aran Maernes, the old duke of Hull, winked at her.

"Right up there next to Harlech," continued Dwaes.

"Umm," she said, realizing that he wasn't listening to her either. Perhaps that was the normal way to converse in these situations. She couldn't remember. It had been a long time, and her head was starting to ache.

"Right up there next to those savages. Uncivilized brutes, Harlech, don't you know," he yapped. "Only interested in horses and fighting. Just like those damn Farrows."

"What?" she said, despite herself. Her aunt smiled at her from far down the table and mouthed something encouraging. Levoreth scowled in response. Probably thinks this weedy lord a potential husband for me, she thought.

"There's some notion the Farrows share lineage with the men of Harlech," offered the duke of Hull.

"Same love of horses and fighting, m'lord," drawled Dwaes. "Probably true. Same ice water in their veins. Not much good for anything else. Can't see why you'd want 'em as neighbors. No reason to have fightin' men around when we have more peace 'n we know what to do with."

"I've met Cullan Farrow a number of times, Lady Levoreth," said old Maernes. "He has a magic hand with horse and sword. Despite the assertion of our young friend here, you'd never know a kinder man. Many a time he's come traveling through Hull. I've sat with him at his fire and he at mine, trading stories until the moon was down. Forgive me, my dear. With your uncle's love of horse, I'd imagine the Farrows would be common enough visitors in Andolan."

"We know another Farrow in Vomaro," said Dwaes darkly.

"That they are," said Levoreth, ignoring the young lord next to her. She returned the old duke's smile. "Every spring, their wagons come rolling along the Ciele. They are well loved in our little duchy."

"In mine as well. My twin sons learned their first turn at the sword under Cullan's tutelage." He smiled, as if remembering. "It was a long, slow summer and his wife had just given birth to a daughter. She had a strange, outlandish name that escapes me."

Levoreth's own smile became forced. "They've only one daughter. Giverny is her name."

"That's it. Cullan was worrisome of the little one's health and so set camp near my town. He'd not take up residence within the gates, though I offered him a fine house. He laughed and said Farrows only stayed alive if they kept out under the sky. Said walls and towns and crowded places with folks all around were enough to blight any soul, though he smiled and asked my pardon for that, me with my stone walls and roofs. Anyway, he came the next day with short swords for my little lads and taught them their first steps, right there in the courtyard. The boys jabbered of nothing else after that and pestered me every day until I arranged lessons with Cullan. He'd more patience than I."

"Anyone who can gentle a horse wouldn't find difficulty in much else. Least of all a couple of boys."

"No," agreed Maernes. The old man lifted his cup and drank. "Though, he'd trouble enough with his own. Wasn't long afterward his boy Declan up and vanished. Lifted his father's best sword and horse and disappeared into the night. And he'd taken a turn or two at teaching my own sons. A remarkable hand with the blade that lad had. Near as good as his father, if not better." He shook his head. "Cullan aged ten years overnight."

Levoreth sensed the young lord beside her stirring to speak. A shiver pricked at the back of her neck and she knew what he would say. A queer foreboding settled on her. The girl again. A thin, suntanned face flashing before her eyes, evoked by the old duke's words. Empty sky and green earth receding away, things older and foreign to the walls and ways of men. There was an inevitability to it all.

"How old be your boys now?" said Dwaes. "Near to twenty?" The duke nodded reluctantly, saying nothing, and the Vomaronish lord smiled with satisfaction. He had a thin, polished quality to his voice that carried well. Conversations quieted around them and faces turned.

"That would be the same summer a Farrow came riding to the court in Lura, eager to join all the other would-be-heroes." He smirked and glanced around, pleased by his larger audience. "I daresay this would be the errant son Declan you spoke of. A brash fool, a thief, as you said, having stolen his father's sword and horse."

"Maybe," grunted the duke. "Still a good boy, I warrant, regardless of all that. Farrows are good folk."

209

"I think not, m'lord," returned the other silkily. "Farrows never show their faces in Vomaro ever since we sent the rascal packing, and that's proof enough. If one proved a scoundrel, then no doubt the trait holds true for them all."

"Would you say the same facing someone of that family over swords?" inquired Levoreth icily, but he ignored her.

Someone called out from further down the table. "Tell us, Dwaes, what was the real story behind that fellow? One hears so many different versions after all these years, there's no certainty to the tale. Aren't you related in some way to the house of Elloran? You Vomarones all seem to be related in some way or another. Goats and all."

A laugh went up, but Dwaes ignored the jibe. He knew he had the attention of those around him. More faces turned and eyes gleamed avidly in the candlelight. It was a shabby, mean story that Levoreth knew well. Probably even better than Dwaes. She selected an apple from a basket offered to her by a servant and began peeling it. The skin fell in unbroken curls from the blade of her knife. She had heard the story for the first time the same summer it had occurred, for the horses would talk of nothing else for days, snorting in disapproval. They behaved grumpily with the grooms for weeks, for the Farrows were legendary among their kind and beloved in the dim way that horses love. And it was precisely because of such stories, such behavior, that Levoreth preferred the company of her four-footed folk to that of humans.

"I am only a distant relation of the house of Elloran," said Dwaes modestly. "My mother being something of a cousin to the duke—"

"Your whole duchy are something of cousins to the duke," said someone, but Dwaes flapped one hand in easy dismissal.

"—and as such, my family spent a great deal of time at the court in Lura. I knew Lady Devnes Elloran, the duke's daughter, rather well, as we shared the same tutor when I stayed with them. She's a true beauty, as all Vomaronish women are, of course, but unusually so, with hair the color of wheat and—"

"Get to the story!" said a fat little man from across the table. He was evidently well in his cups, judging by his flushed face and the scarlet stain of wine across his surcoat.

"Aye, the story," said another.

"And more wine here!"

A quartet, hidden somewhere off in the shadows shrouding the reaches of the hall, launched into an air. The flute trilled over sonorous strings and cheerfully told the story of lost love. Levoreth heard a roar of laughter go up from the far end of the table where the regent sat. The ache in her head increased. The apple fell apart into four sections under her knife. She considered ramming the blade into Dwaes's leg but discarded the idea, as it would only have meant more and louder noise from him.

"The story," said Dwaes, a bit off stride, "does not carry its full weight unless one comprehends the true beauty and virtue of Lady Devnes Elloran—as all Vomaronish women are, of course, beautiful and virtuous—"

"More wine!"

"Aye!" bawled the fat little drunk. "Summat like Thulish cattle, I'd say!"

Dwaes reddened but chose to ignore this, as the rest of his audience was still intact.

"In early May, Lady Devnes went riding with her attendants and several brave men-at-arms along the eastern shore of Lake Maro, as some are wont to do, for there the late spring flowers grow in a profusion that cannot be found elsewhere. While she and her maids were picking flowers, a party of ogres came rushing from the woods and fell upon them! The men-at-arms were hacked to pieces and the maids ravished so that only one survived, and she to die before the week was out. Unhappily, Lady Devnes was carried off, the ogres leaving the one poor maid to totter back to Lura with word of their demand."

"Wasn't the lady ravished too?" called someone raucously.

"Of course not," said Dwaes. "Ogres love gold more than anything else, and the duke's daughter was worth her weight in gold to them. Untouched. They're clever brutes and knew what they were doing. When her father, the duke of Elloran, heard the news, he sent word to all the duchies of Tormay, begging the aid of any lord brave enough to track the ogres and bring back his daughter unharmed, for he feared the ogres would not bother to release his child even if he delivered them their demanded price. Lords and princelings came from all across Tormay, eager to win fame, honor, and much more, for the duke had promised Devnes in marriage and the duchy of Vomaro at his death to whoever brought her back, for she was his only child."

"Two of my nephews," said old Duke Maernes of Hull grimly, "fools that they were, went haring off to Vomaro when they heard the news. I thought the girl already dead. Besides, only an idiot would seek an ogre in its own stronghold."

"Your nephews," said Dwaes, "did not fare so well."

"Aye," said the duke. "Fools, both of them. Dead fools."

"Like many others. It was a grim, sad summer, with every manor and castle in Vomaro flying their mourning flags. And then, on midsummer's day, the Farrow lad came riding on his black horse. Right up to the duke's door, as calm as you'd please, and with coarse and common speech declared he'd come to try his hand at the quest. Oh, the duke knew of the Farrows, and he knew the great iron sword strapped on the whelp's back. He knew who it belonged to. Desperate for his daughter, he would've sent forth anyone who desired. The duke provisioned the young scoundrel, and Declan Farrow rode out in the company of two others undertaking the same quest.

"The trail was cold, but the Farrow lad picked up a trace of it west of the Lome Forest and so followed it with his two companions. I must confess, though he proved to be a damnable scoundrel, he could track the most clever of the woodland animals. Step by step, he made his way through the shadows of Lome Forest until he came to the foothills of the Morn Mountains. There, the trail climbed up into the snowy peaks."

Those at the table near him were silent, eyes fixed on him. They knew the best was yet to come. Levoreth finished her apple and thought morosely about the girl Giverny. The anger on her thin face. She would learn in time.

"The ogres' hideaway was built into the face of a cliff. It could not be approached save by a wicker basket raised up and down on an iron chain. But Declan Farrow climbed the cliff in the night and then lowered the basket so that the other two might come up with him. The mouth of the lair yawned before them, stinking of ogre and darker than the night itself. They ventured in and found themselves looking down into an open hall. A long table was crowded about with ogres, tearing at their meal of mutton and who knows what else. Judging the brutes full of meat and ale and thus slow on their feet, Declan desired to fall on them immediately and try luck and their swords. But his two companions, being of more cautious mind, counseled biding their time until sleep had overtaken the ogres. In his pride, though, the youth scorned them and leapt down into the hall, sword drawn. Fired by his zeal, the two others followed and soon battle was joined. The crows heard the din for miles and came flying to sup on the blood and carnage thereafter."

"Keep to the facts, Dwaes," someone hooted. "Some silkpants bard you're not."

"These are the facts," said Dwaes coldly. "His two companions lived to tell the tale and they are beyond reproach, as I'm sure many of you know them or their families—lord Werian, the second son of the house of Londweard, whose father is the warden of the Eastern Marches of Vo, and Flyg Galaestan, one of the grand-nephews of the duke of Thule."

"A noble name does not guarantee noble blood," said old Maernes. He inclined his head to Levoreth. "Though noble blood can bring about a noble name, as was evidenced in your own family's ancestry, Lady Levoreth."

"Tell the rest!"

"Aye—get to the good bits!"

The good bits. Levoreth frowned down at her plate. She could feel old Maernes' gaze on her from across the table. She wasn't sure, but she thought there had been a speculative gleam in his eyes. Older people. It was the older people that must be treated warily, and she was forgetting that. They were the ones who might have met her before and possibly held memories of a different Levoreth. Next to her, Dwaes droned on, his voice filled with lazy malice. And envy, she thought to herself. He's envious of what Declan Farrow did, for he could never do such a thing. Not many could.

And then Levoreth almost forgot her headache and irritability in a memory that flooded into her mind. Maernes—a young Maernes—not yet the duke of Hull and visiting Andolan for a week of hunting in the hills. When she had been another Levoreth—which one had she been then?—oh yes, the former great-aunt of Hennen Callas. Maernes had chased her around the kitchen table in the castle, cornered her and kissed her for all of two seconds before she had crowned him with an iron pan. She grinned involuntarily and glanced up. Maernes was still looking at her, and she dropped her eyes.

"—of course," Dwaes was saying, "Lady Devnes fainted with joy to be rescued from her cell. Not that the ogres had harmed in her any way. On the contrary, she maintained they'd been the best of hosts, outside of their deplorable cooking and the rather rough manner they'd had with the rest of her party."

"More wine!"

"Get to the good part, you long-winded Vomaronish bit of twaddle!"

"Aye, you sainted donkey!"

Dwaes majestically forged ahead.

"On their journey back to Vomaro they reached an inn on the road leading through the pass from Mizra to the Rennet valley. It was a lonely place, far from any town. There, while his two exhausted companions lay in deep sleep, the scoundrel did his deed. Inflamed by the beauty of the girl and maddened, no doubt, by close proximity to one of such noble blood, he forced his way into her room that night and had his evil way."

There were exclamations of horror around him and people leaned in closer.

"The next morning, the Lady Devnes kept her silence, for the black gaze of the false Declan Farrow was ever on her. She said not a word of what had happened, but bided her time as they journeyed on. The gates of Lura were flung open wide to greet them! The townsfolk cheered at the sight of her, for was she not their duke's only daughter? Trumpets blared their brassy call from the duke's castle. Her father hurried out to meet them, unable to contain his joy. And there, before that great assembly, with tears on her face, she brought her accusation against her rescuer. He said not a word in his defense, but stood as still as a statue. The soldiers took him and he gave no resistance, though he was dragged out into the courtyard, stretched from a post and flayed until the blood streamed on the white marble paving. Still, he spoke no word, as if struck dumb. They tossed the wretch into the dungeon to wait the judgment of Duke Elloran. For my lord is a careful, brooding type and he brings such same traits to his rulings—"

"Aye," bawled the little fat man, "just as he broods over which dish to jab his fork into next!" To better demonstrate his point, the fat man plunged his own fork into a roast chicken and heaved it triumphantly back to his plate. He glanced up and caught Levoreth's chilly gaze on him. This was a mistake on her part, for whenever she happened to again look his way, she found him winking lustfully at her.

"—but that next morning, when the guards unlocked the scoundrel's cell to have him out for hanging. . ." Here, Dwaes paused and took a sip of wine.

"And then?" prompted someone further down the table. Faces leaned in, expectant.

"And then," said Levoreth tonelessly, "they found an empty cell. He had escaped. The great iron sword had been stolen from the guardsroom. The duke put a reward on the lad's head. The girl was found to be with child and her father married her off to some unknown third cousin who was witless enough to put up with raising another's whelp. End of story."

Dwaes choked on his wine. The faces around them glared at Levoreth. The duke of Hull smiled at her from across the table. The little fat man winked at her again, mouth chewing vigorously on chicken. She pushed her chair back and left. Her headache was getting worse. Vaguely, she was aware of people rising behind her, of someone following for several steps, away from the long table and the lights and voices and merriment. Old Maernes, the duke of Hull, she thought. Pity, he's remembering. There's no place to hide from people's memories. Except in death. But even then they remember for a time.

She returned to her room and stood for a while, irresolute, in front of a mirror.

"What would you do if you were me?" she said. The girl in the mirror regarded her gravely and said nothing. Levoreth attempted a smile and her counterpart seemed to wince painfully. They both sighed in unison.

"I worry about her. The young Farrow girl. Giverny. It won't be easy for her."

Her headache was diminishing. Perhaps being away from the noise and clutter of the banquet was healing enough. She put on a cloak and went out onto the balcony. The rain clouds had passed and the night sky stretched overhead, speckled with stars and the watchful moon. It was chilly, so she twitched the cloak closed at her neck.

She then climbed out onto the roof.

Her room was high up under the eaves. A buttress slanted down along her balcony, complete with a sad-looking stone gargoyle perched at its tip. She patted the gargoyle on the head and then walked up the buttress until she was up on the roof. From there, a few minutes' climb brought her to the highest peak of the castle. She sat down and waited.

And waited.

And waited.

And then frowned.

But then the first cat appeared, popping up over a peak further down the roof. It was a little gray thing with brilliant blue eyes. Just short of her foot, the cat stopped, plomped down on its haunches, and began to wash. She could not help smiling. The cat licked her hand once and then resumed its bath. Several other cats padded forward. They settled around her. Others appeared. A chorus of purring rose and fell.

The city sprawled around them. The heights of Highneck Rise sloped down into the shadowed streets. Lights twinkled warmly in windows. The scent of smoke and the day's rain was in the air. West, not a mile away, the sea glimmered with moonlight.

"Well, cat," she said, "where is your elder?"

The little gray cat stopped washing and looked up at her.

Drythen Malkin has seen near fifty years, Mistress of Mistresses. Think you he can run over roofs in haste?

She cuffed the cat for its impudence and then scratched behind its ears. It purred ecstatically.

A large black cat appeared, almost as if the shadows had woven themselves together to make his form. He padded across the roof peak, and the other cats drifted aside before him.

"Drythen Malkin."

Mistress of Mistresses.

The cat sniffed at her hand and then settled down at her side. Even in the uncertain moonlight, age lay heavy on the animal. His whiskers were gray, and old battles had left their marks on notched ears and the weal of a scar arching across his nose.

Your presence brings us honor. Thrice have I seen you. Once as a kit, many years ago, when my sire held sway in Hearne. Then, at his passing. And now, near my life's end.

"You are so sure of your own passing?"

The cat rumbled comfortably.

Death is no stranger, that I would not recognize his scent. Surely, you know him better than I with the few years I possess?

She said nothing to that. The cats around them attended in silence. Only their lord purred.

"I seek news of your city, Drythen Malkin."

The cat inclined his head courteously and waited.

"My sleep has been troubled and my dreams reached blindly to Hearne. Has trouble come to this city? Is there anything in these streets that has gained your notice?"

There was a pause before the cat spoke.

One thing, Mistress. There is one thing that might give you pause, though I know nothing of your dreams. These humans live blindly. They cannot scent death and evil, where a month-old kit could readily mark the trail. Several weeks ago, a sceadu came traveling to Hearne.

"A sceadu?" she said sharply. "Are you certain of this?"

Aye. Our kind bears memory of one such from the old war that ruined this city. A fell creature that did traffic with the evil wizard Scuadimnes. My sire's sire and his sire before him all bore the memory, and so now do I.

"Remember with care, Drythen Malkin, for this is no slight thing."

Though our memory does not run the length of your years, Mistress of Mistresses, it is clear, for darkness does not dim the sight of cats and we do not easily forget.

"Then speak. I will listen."

We caught his scent at the eastern gate and so followed him to a tavern within the city, where he vanished into the tunnels.

"The tunnels of the thieves," Levoreth said. She petted the old cat and he purred.

Aye. This Guild that lusts for gold and ferrets out hidden things for gain. They are fools of the worst kind, for if the sceadu so easily gained the tunnels, then perhaps they do business with it in hope of profit. But I grieve, Mistress, that I cannot tell you what this business may be, for my kind never venture into the tunnels. Danger lurks there that is beyond our ken. The tunnels are woven with magic from centuries ago, when the true wizards still lived.

"And this creature then left the city," she said. "You and yours saw this?"

214

Several hours after the sceadu descended, it emerged again, from this same tavern. It made its way back to the eastern gate and so away. Three of my blood kept pace with the thing until it left the city walls. We thought it the last of the creature, but—

The old cat paused, as if marshalling its words.

"Speak, Malkin."

—it returned.

She knew, as soon as the cat spoke. The thought had been nagging at her mind.

"Two nights ago?"

Then you already know. It was when the strange storm passed over the city. A fear came on my subjects and none ventured out into the night, but in the morning the creature's scent lingered in the streets and near the main gate. If a cat's nose cannot be trusted then there is little left true in this world.

"Aye," she said slowly. "I felt something strange that night but was not certain of its cause, for it has been many years since I've had the misfortune to encounter a sceadu."

The little gray cat inched forward cautiously and spoke.

The thing felt cold, Mistress.

Instantly, the black cat raised a massive paw, but Levoreth touched him.

"Nay. I would hear this."

The old cat sank back and rumbled.

This scamp takes after his dam. Both are quick with their tongues.

"What do you mean, little one? Were you near enough to touch the thing?"

Avert! The small cat shivered. *I would not touch such a thing, for it smelled of an evil worse than death. Only, when it came the first time to the city, it passed down a street before me. I ventured near to know its scent better. A chill like winter's ice breathed from the thing, and I came away sick and trembling.*

"You were foolish to venture so close," she said sternly. "A single touch would have killed a small one such as you." She scratched its ears. "But brave too. Your sire's mark is on you."

The old cat cuffed the little gray fondly. *I beat this litter soundly in their first year, for they all proved scamps and scoundrels, every one.*

The little gray spoke again, emboldened by the praise.

Perhaps one other thing, Mistress.

The old black unsheathed a pair of claws and tapped them impatiently on the tile.

"Speak, little one, before I turn you over to your sire's graces."

I saw a boy climb up into the ruins of the university, said the little cat. *A great height he scaled, up sheer walls that would trouble even a cat. There was something odd about him. No one enters the ruins, Mistress, besides the old humans that work within its confines. They dig and seek for lost things.*

A swift cuff to the head sent the little cat sprawling among the others watching. It yowled once and then shot off into the shadows.

The boy was probably just some witless thief. There are humans looking for that which was lost years ago. Scholars from the Stone Tower. They seek knowledge, not gold. A lost book. They would have no hand in whatever disturbed your dreams, for I myself have hunted the ruins there and scented them. There was no evil in them. Forgive my foolish son.

Levoreth smiled. "Boys and sons are capable of great mischief, but they are not sceadus."

215

They sat for a while without speaking, she and the old black, with all the other cats in polite silence around them. The little gray crept back into the circle and lowered its head meekly.

"I thank you, Drythen Malkin," she said, "for your attendance on me. You have given me much to think on. A sceadu within the gates can only mean the Darkness has bent its thoughts to Hearne. Be certain, though, that you and yours rest within my protection."

The old black rose stiffly and nosed her hand.

We are honored, Mistress of Mistresses.

The cats vanished across the roof and into the shadows. She called after the old black just before it disappeared.

"And the name of the tavern the sceadu entered to gain the tunnels? What is it called?"

The humans call it the Goose and Gold.

CHAPTER FIFTY-TWO
A CONVERSATION OF STARS

After the incident on the roof, Severan tried to be more attentive to Jute. He popped up without warning. Jute would be prowling through a hall, and around a corner would come Severan, trying to appear nonchalant and just as surprised to see Jute as the boy was to see him (though after a while, Jute was no longer surprised to see him). He turned up in the evening without fail, as well as in the morning for breakfast.

"It's rather odd," said the boy, "that you turn up everywhere. I thought you were hard at work with the others, digging things up."

Severan looked somewhat embarrassed. "Well, things have been slow. We struck a bad spot in the lower level. There's a ward proving a vexing puzzle. It's taken days to understand the first thing about it and we're still far from unraveling the cursed thing. The others are down there now, arguing over how to beat it. I decided to take a breather. Besides, I know you could do with some company."

"Rubbish," said Jute. "You've been prowling about just to keep an eye on me."

"If you weren't such a nitwit," said Severan. "Climbing out windows and swanning about the city as if you didn't have a care in the world! You have no idea—"

"I'm bored!"

They glared at each other. The sky outside the window was deepening into purple, flecked with stars emerging at first as suggestions and then, as the purple darkened into velvety blue, gleaming in earnest. It had grown dark in the room. Severan sighed and fumbled in his pocket for a flint and tinder. The candle flickered into life under his hands.

"Why can't you just say something," said Jute. "Say whatever the name is for fire and light it like that? I thought you were a wizard."

"A wizard?" Severan sighed. "No, I'm just a scholar. Besides, there's just as much magic in how a flint works as there is in the true name of fire. A different kind of magic, yes, but magic nonetheless. Look here. You strike a flint and a spark is produced. This can be done with some stones but not with others. If the candle is lit by uttering the true name of fire or by the sparking of flints, a question is revealed behind both actions. How was it ordained that there are two paths to fire, that two disparate means result in the same end? Questions like this are more interesting than using so-called magic or not."

Jute shrugged. "They both work. There's allus more than one way to rob the duchess."

"A dangerous attitude. Just because something works doesn't mean it should be done. If you start thinking like that then, sooner or later, you end up doing all sorts of horrible things to achieve your goal. Nio was not always the man you had the misfortune to meet. Once, he was a good man, but somewhere along the way he must have decided that what he desired outweighed the constraints of what should and should not be done."

"I hope he falls down that hole in his cellar and breaks his neck," growled Jute.

The old man smiled sourly. "If you have to eat, you steal, right?"

"Of course."

"It is said that life—and by that I mean all of everything that exists—is like a mosaic made of countless tiny stones. Each person's life comprises a part of the mosaic, and each person can only see their part of the mosaic. Birth, death, love, and hate—all the pain, sweat, and grief that are the lot of every man—those are the stones man is given power to place. Our choices dictate how our own few stones are laid into the larger pattern of the mosaic."

"But if each person can only see their own part," said Jute, frowning, "then surely the whole mosaic would end up in a mess."

"Perhaps," said Severan. "But if enough people seek to do what is right and true, then the mosaic of their lives is in harmony with the mosaics of all those who choose in like fashion. Some people, however, choose the darkness, even though they do not realize what they have done. There are only two colors of the mosaic: darkness and that which is not darkness, and the two can never exist in harmony."

"Has anyone ever seen the whole mosaic?"

"I've read that it stands in a room within the house of dreams, where no man has ever been, where no man has ever set foot. At least, I hope it's there, for if it isn't, then it is nowhere and life has no meaning."

He paused and eyed the boy for a moment before continuing.

"No one has seen it," he repeated, "but there are those who fly higher than others. The heights afford a better view, and I think such people can see a great deal of the mosaic. Much more than an old man like myself."

"Someone else said that to me recently."

"Who?" said Severan sharply.

"The hawk," said Jute, and then he stopped, appalled at his own words.

"The hawk?"

But Jute would say nothing more. The candle slowly burned down. The wax ran and pooled on the table. Outside, the wind blew through the starry night, smelling of selia blossoms and the sea.

"I've been thinking," said Severan. "For several days I've been wondering. Up until now, I dismissed it as the uneasy dreams of an old man. It began when I first saw you, lying unconscious in Nio's house with him pacing the floor, maddened and muttering, for he had lost something of terrible value in the box you stole. He never said what was in the box, and though he claimed he never could open the thing, I suspect he had a good idea what it contained."

"Did you know also?"

"From what he let slip in unguarded moments, I had a suspicion. As the days went by, I began to think that perhaps what was in the box was no longer there. And now I am more sure of it."

Severan paused, as if expecting a reply from Jute, but the boy said nothing. The old man sighed and continued.

"When I was a boy, I studied at a school far up on the Thule coast. It was a desolate place. A school for scholars and, at times, wizards. The Stone Tower. In the library there I once read an old book. It discussed the existence of the *Gerecednes*, the book written by Staer Gemyndes long ago. He was the first wizard in Tormay. At least, he was the first wizard known in our histories."

"You spoke about him before," said Jute. "That's the book you're trying to find, right?"

"Aye, that I did, and I'll probably speak of him again, for he of all wizards is the least known and it is he that we most desperately need to know better. He and the book he wrote."

"Why?"

"Because the Dark is abroad in Tormay," said Severan. He stood and paced back and forth. "Because the Dark crept back into the land like the fog creeps in upon the shore in the early morning, while folk are sleeping still. It came on silent feet, and no one heard the sound of its passage. This is a terrible thing, for man thinks of war as being won with the loud, sudden violence of swords and battle, but the slow, quiet wars can be lost in peace. It is as if the whole land sleeps. I fear we will awake one day and find that the Dark has crept so close that its face is the face of our neighbor, our loved one, ourselves.

"The most terrible thing of all is that the anbeorun seem to have fallen asleep. The anbeorun are the four great guardians of sea and earth, wind and fire. They are our first and best bulwark against the Dark, but they've vanished out of sight and time these past hundred years. It's almost as if they've ceased to exist. No one knows what happened to them. Perhaps they were taken by death and so returned to the house of dreams from whence they came. Whatever the riddle's answer, their absence is a wound that might prove fatal to Tormay.

"According to all the histories written, Staer Gemyndes possessed a great deal of knowledge about the Dark, for he and his king were at war with it all the days of their lives. Yet no one knows how they succeeded in the struggle. That's what we must discover, and that's why we came to these ruins. That's why we must find his book."

"Maybe he didn't."

"What's that?"

"Maybe he didn't succeed in the struggle."

"Avert," said Severan, frowning. "Of course he did."

"How do you know?" said Jute. "I thought you said you don't know much about him, that most of his writings—that book, whatever it's called—have been lost."

"Aye, the *Gerecednes* was lost, but others wrote of him. Also, some writings of his did survive. I read several pages of his while a student in the Stone Tower. And in those pages, Jute, in those pages. . ."

Severan trailed off into silence.

"It's getting late," said Jute uncomfortably. He wished he hadn't mentioned the hawk. He hadn't meant to. Jute started to get up but Severan stopped him. He had a strange look on his face.

"Sit, sit," he said. "You're right—it is late. I wish I'd said this days ago. Listen—the few pages of Staer Gemyndes I read began with the phrase *there are those that fly higher than others*."

"What?"

"'*There are those that fly higher than others, but none so high as he that is called the wind. The anbeorun of the wind. None so high as the wind and, of course, the hawk at his side.*'"

"A hawk?"

"The wind's a chancy, uncertain thing," said Severan. "One moment stronger than iron, the next moment soft as a child's breath. Strange, but in these last few days I have smelled the sands of Harth, the gardens of Vo, the heathered hills of Dolan, and even my cold stone land of Harlech. I've smelled them all in the wind, as if it has gathered itself from all those far-off places. It's as if the wind's searching for something here."

"It's fall now," said Jute. "It always gets windier in the fall. Winter'll come fast, I reckon."

"Hmm. Perhaps."

Jute did not fall asleep easily that night. His mind would not let him rest. He sat up in bed, not sure if he was dreaming or sleeping. Something stirred in the darkness out of the corner of his eye, and he went to the window, needing to breathe and tasting only dust in his mouth. The casement creaked open and he leaned out. Stars drifted overhead.

"Where are you, hawk?" he said.

There was no answer, of course.

He could hear the faint sounds of the city quieting into night. Beyond Hearne, however, was a deeper silence. It was the silence of the sky, and he realized in that instant that it was also the silence inside of him. He had used that silence for years, wrapping himself up in it to fool wards and to burgle houses. As far back as he could remember, the silence had been there.

The stars continued their slow wheel in the sky overhead. He gazed up at them. They drifted through the night and regarded him with the glitter of their icy stares.

"Have you seen a hawk in your heights?" he said. "A hawk with feathers as black as your sky?"

Thou presumest, said a star.

Aye, said another.

Two questions at such a tender age, while we wait eons to ask even one.

Or perhaps none at all.

Even if none, we shall bide on our paths, content still.

But the stars did not speak unkindly. Rather, there was interest in the sound of their voices. They chimed in the air like the wind passing through bells. Some were light and tinkling like a child's silver bell, some quick and hard like the bells that rang in the harbor buoys swaying on the tide, and others deep and slow, booming like iron bells set in some far-off, ancient tower.

"May I ask only one question?"

Ah, but that is thy third.

"Then I will ask only one: whether you have seen a hawk in your heights. Please."

Aye, that we have.

We have.

Fear not, murmured a star.

Fear not, echoed another.

Their voices chimed in the stillness of the night, calling to Jute in a chorus that rang clear in the darkness.

When the world was still young
When the boundaries of the sea were inscribed upon the shore,
Here and no farther shall thy proud waves come.
When the mountains were raised from the earth
And the valleys cast down to their green depths,
When the flame was kindled in the heart of the mountains
And set to burn in the silence of the earth,
When the winds were unleashed from the house of dreams,
When the winds came rushing to their appointed place,
When the world was still young,
A hawk came flying with feathers black as night.

220

A hawk came flying through the sky
With wings as black as night,
Though they were like fire in the darkness,
Lightning falling through the darkness
When the world was still young.

The ringing of their voices subsided into stillness. Silence reclaimed the sky. The stars gazed down on him from their remote height.

"But what of now?" said Jute. "Surely the world is old now."

No one answered him.

CHAPTER FIFTY-THREE
THE HEALING OF THE SEA

Someone spoke near his ear. The girl. Ronan wished she would go away. She had her book. What more could she want? Someone else could take her to the regent's ball. The town was full of able men. Anyone. As long as it wasn't him. He just wanted to sleep.

Her voice forced his eyes open. She was saying something, but it was only meaningless sound. It could have been the noise of water on rocks, the creak of rigging, a gull's skirling cry. She spoke again.

"You don't have much time left."

Her face was calm, as if his death meant nothing to her. He did not speak. He could not have if he wanted to. A tremendous weight pressed down on his chest. Sunlight shimmered around her hair. She turned to glance over her shoulder.

"It is an ebb tide. Things recede, and that which is already distant drifts even further." Her face turned back, hovering above him. "But the tide is mine, and though your life is ebbing away, I can bring you back. If you wish."

Her eyes gazed down into his. Darkness crept in on the edge of his sight. He could not speak. He could not breathe. The weight was unbearable.

So this is what it's like, he thought. How many lives have I ushered past this point with the edge of my knife? My father never spoke of this. Maybe he did not know. I wish I could speak with him again. I wish I could see his face again.

Ronan stared up at the girl. He could not speak, but there was enough appeal in his eyes for her to read. She took the comb from her hair that held the thick sheaf back and unclasped the pin. A jab at her fingertip and a drop of blood welled out. He felt a touch on his lips and tasted salt in his mouth. A roaring filled his ears as if of the sea pounding on the beach, the crashing of waves rising higher and higher. All the world was drowning, unmade in the fury of the sea, and then he knew no more.

Sometime later, awareness returned to him. The darkness receded until he drifted in a fog. It had a comforting quality of nothingness to it. There was no sound or feel, no cold or heat, only the grayness. He wished it would continue and cradle him there forever.

Wake.

No. Let me drift here.

Wake.

Ronan opened his eyes to a sun-drenched room. Turning his head, he could see the long, thin line of blue that was ocean, past the rooftops of the city and the stone and wood fingers of the docks. And then he realized where he was. There clearly were advantages to living up on the heights of Highneck Rise.

"Rest. You are not yet yourself."

She was sitting on his other side, a book open in her hands. The book.

"You took a grievous hurt, more than I realized at first. You were wounded by a ward, but you also carried a taint on you of something fell, a creature of the Dark that had come close to you. But you are well now, though more sleep will serve you."

"I am well?" he said, beginning to remember.

"Yes."

"Thank you," he said.

"I will have more than thanks out of you," she said calmly, "for you've my blood in you now, and that's something that hasn't been said for over three hundred years."

"What?"

"I had need of you, as I remarked the other day, Ronan of Aum, or whatever name you choose to call yourself. But things have changed more swiftly than I foresaw, and so my plans changed as well. Hence, your rash decision to enter that house and take the book."

She looked down at the book in her hands and a frown crossed her face.

"I confess myself surprised at what you found there. I can only blame it on my rusty knowledge of humans. It has been a long time since I've come to these shores, and I've forgotten much. This book is a thing of great evil. It promises the key to immense power. Men fall prey to such things. Someone has read this book, and thus another door has been opened for the Dark, opened through the greed and ambition of one man's soul."

"Are you telling me you made me enter that house? Who are you?" His voice rose.

She regarded him impassively for a moment and then shut the book. "There's much in the telling and I doubt it can be properly said in the language of man. I doubt much of anything can be said properly in your language. Nevertheless, I will make the attempt."

At this, Liss seemed to sit up straighter in her chair. She frowned a bit, and then began with a sigh. "Long ago, when the Dark first fell from the house of dreams, it roved across the fields of heaven. It sought what it might devour, for the first principle of the Dark is hunger. A hunger that can never be sated. But then those that were called the Aro came, and the Dark fled. It came to the world of man. And the Dark held sway there.

"But then the Aro came hunting. So was fought the first great war, when the mountains were broken and the world wept for pain. The Dark was overthrown, but at great cost. Then Anue stood on the threshold of the house of dreams and spoke four words. They fell like shining jewels, down through the heights beyond the night until they came to their resting place. There, the four eldest of the Aro took hold of the jewels. And so they became the anbeorun: four mighty beings set to guard the paths of the world of men and keep watch against the darkness. To each of them was assigned one of the great *feorh*, the four essences of this world. To the first was given the sea, the waves and all her creatures, the rivers and streams, the lakes and ponds and all that find shelter therein. To the second was given the earth, the green and growing things, mountains, hills and valleys, and all creatures great and small that live under the sun. To the third was given the wind, the storm and lightning, the torrent and blast that beat up against the edges of heaven itself, and every creature on the wing. To the fourth was given the fire, the deep, dark, secret places of the earth where heat and molten rock live to work their magic in gems and gold, and where strange, eyeless creatures breathe their days.

"The anbeorun walked the world and kept watch against the Dark. Centuries passed. There was peace; oh, perhaps not in the world of men, for your kind are ever given to war and the Dark has always left its shadow in your hearts—but in the realms of the anbeorun, there was peace. But the Dark is patient and time means nothing to it. The four anbeorun wandered far and no longer remembered each other, though they had sprang into being together, brothers and sisters. They walked their own separate ways and so disappeared."

Liss fell silent. The room was warm with sunlight, but Ronan shivered under his blankets. Fear gripped him. This was only the beginning of the story and, no matter how strange and fantastic it sounded, he knew for a certainty it was true.

"How do you know all this?" he said. "What has this to do with you?"

She turned blank eyes on him.

"I am the sea."

She stared out the window, looking past the rooftops and houses, gazing at the sea shimmering in the afternoon light. When she spoke again, it was almost in a whisper.

"I fell asleep. I fell asleep and did not wake for I do not know how long. Hundreds of years, I think. But a nightmare came and shook me from my sleep. For in my dream I saw that the Dark, though far from the world, had worked its will and slain one of my brothers. This could not be, but my dreams do not lie. If they lie, then I am untrue, and I cannot be untrue, for I am the sea. I rose from my sleep, troubled and wondering, for if one could be slain, then all could be slain. What terrible magic could have wrought such a thing? And so my path led me from my beloved sea here, to the world of men, to your world. An answer is here in this city and I will find it."

"But surely there's nothing here to stop you," he said. "The wizards are all dead."

She wrinkled her brow dismissively, a slim girl who looked light enough for him to lift with one hand. "You speak of things you know nothing of," she said. "The wizards are not all dead, but they are irrelevant. However, there're other things in this world. Things that hearken back to the times when the Dark walked in openness. Something has come that can lay a hand even on the four anbeorun—on wind, earth, and fire. And on me. It is because of this that I am reluctant to show my hand in this city, for I am not sure who my enemy is. Hence, my need of you."

He dared a last question, though sleep was taking hold of him.

"Which of the four was killed?"

Liss did not answer for a long time, and he could not keep his eyes open any longer. From a long way off, just as he fell asleep, he heard her voice.

"My brother the wind. He was killed with a knife."

CHAPTER FIFTY-FOUR
THE DUKE OF MIZRA

That next morning, in the second week of the Autumn Fair, the duke of Mizra came riding to the gates of Hearne with all his retinue about him. The watchmen on the tower sighted them long before the first outriders came up the long, sloping rise that meets the eastern walls of the city and also marks the mouth of the Rennet valley.

"Ware the gate!" bawled one of the soldiers, and old Bordeall trudged up the stairs of the tower keep. It was a cold, clear day, for autumn had finally arrived. The leaves on the maple and ash were changing colors on the hills of the Highneck Rise district. Down in the valley, the stands of trees blushed with the first reds and golds of the year. Bordeall squinted into the sunlight.

"Mizra," he said. "Nobbut else runs a black and gold banner. Here, you—take a horse from the stable and ride up to the castle. Find the steward. Tell him the duke of Mizra will be at the gate within the hour."

A soldier hurried away at his bidding. Mizra was the last of the duchies to arrive for the Autumn Fair. The other duchies had already sent their delegations, along with the countless traders and merchants and all the other folk, rich or not, who desired to spend the month in Hearne, gawking and buying and selling. And being swindled, more likely than not.

Bordeall spat over the side of the wall. The fair was good for the city, no doubt, but he didn't care for it himself. Too crowded. Too many foreigners. Still, it brought money to the city and, every year, reemphasized the fact that Hearne was still the center of Tormay.

He walked down the wall. The old ash spear felt good in his hands. It hadn't tasted blood since the Errant Wars thirty years ago. He had been a young sergeant then, with more muscle than brain. It was a wonder he had come out of those campaigns alive. He hefted the spear. Still as light as a feather, and his eye was just as keen. He permitted himself a smile. None of the striplings on watch had been able to spot Mizra's colors.

He didn't mind commanding the city. The lads were well-trained and knew their places. Gawinn saw to that. The drill sergeants were good. Nothing much happened that necessitated a stern hand these days. Oh, there were the fights in the taverns every once in a while, but they mostly stopped short of killing folks in such brawls. Besides, the innkeepers kept a lid on such things. The Guild was behaving itself nicely these days as well.

Still, he wished Gawinn was back. It had been almost two weeks now, and there'd been no word from him. One more week and then he might send some riders out. Not that he doubted the Lord Captain's safety. Owain Gawinn was the best man he'd ever seen with a sword, excepting for old Cullan Farrow. Bordeall reckoned there wasn't a man alive in all the duchies of Tormay who knew more about battle than the Captain, and that was a good lot of men who had ridden east with him. All veterans of the Errant Wars. East and a tad south. That was where the village of the little girl was. Toward the rising sun and the Mountains of Morn.

The regent of Hearne was in the stables with the duke of Dolan and several other of the visiting nobility when the news came.

"Beauty, isn't she," said Botrell. A yearling trotted the perimeter of a small enclosure, gently urged on by a trainer who held her traces in one hand and an unused whip in the other.

"I suppose," grumbled Hennen Callas.

"The last of Riverrun's get," said the regent, leaning on the fence. "And the best, I warrant."

"Her lines are drawn in lovely places," said the prince of Harth.

The regent barked a laugh.

"Perfectly said, my lord Eaomod," he said. "It seems that the folk of Harth talk like books."

"Rather," said the prince, smiling gravely, "I think it the books that are written like the speech of Harth, for is not the word first spoken before the scribes set it down to page?"

"A question which has perplexed the wizards since the dawn of time," said old Maernes, "and much too complex for the confines of a stable. For such headaches we need the medicines of wine, comfortable chairs, and full bellies."

"My lord duke of Hull," said the prince, bowing, "surely an hour could not be spent more pleasantly than in such pursuit, unless it be on the battlefield facing a numerous and determined foe."

"Ah," said the old duke. "We are in agreement." The relationship between Hull and Harth would have grown even more cordial, had not a steward hurried into the stable.

"My lord regent," he said. "My lords. The duke of Mizra has been sighted approaching the city."

"Splendid," said Botrell, rubbing his hands together. "Now all the duchies of Tormay are assembled for our fair—"

"Except Harlech, of course," said Hennen, but no one heard him.

"Come, my friends. Let's make haste to the gate to welcome Mizra."

They clattered out of the castle gate and down the winding streets of Highneck Rise, past old manors and stone walls and through the first autumn leaves drifting in red and gold around the horses' hooves. A detachment of the Guard rode before the party, for the regent was fond of their uniforms and the way the silver and blue pennants fluttered from their halberds. The elegance of Highneck Rise soon gave way, descending to the more cramped streets of the city, through rows of tall, narrow dwellings so jammed up against each other that it was impossible to tell where one building left off and the next began. The party made good time, though, for the crowds cleared easily enough for the Guard. They came to the gate of the city, with its tall tower rising to one side. Banners snapped in the wind upon the wall. The massive doors of oak and iron were open and, through them, the vanguard of the duke of Mizra was visible cresting the rise at the top of the valley. A flag fluttered at their forefront—a gold dragon on a black field. Brond Gifernes had come to Hearne.

The trumpets sounded a flourish. The soldiers on the wall snapped to attention and the party of the duke of Mizra came riding through the gate. Nimman Botrell swung down from his horse. A horseman cantered forward and the rider alighted. He was a tall man, young, looking to be barely past twenty years of age, with a long arm and a long face in which reposed a pair of startling green eyes. His hair was shorn closely to his head and it was as gold as the dragon of his banner, both locks and dragon gleaming in the sunlight. He grinned and took Botrell's hand in his own.

"Well met, my lord regent," said the newcomer.

"Brond Gifernes," said Botrell, "welcome to Hearne."

The duke of Mizra and his party were escorted through the city. They were weary with their travel, for the road to Hearne from Mizra was a long one, winding east through the canyons of Mizra and the pass in the Morn Mountains beyond. From there, it was several days' journey, past the southern edge of the Lome Forest and then along the reaches of the Rennet valley. The duke had brought a score of retainers in his retinue, with their horses and pack mules. What's more, there were three hunting dogs in the group—big beasts who trotted obediently at the heels of their handler.

"I'd like to do some hunting here, my lord," said Gifernes to the regent. "Your flatland deer are remarkably swift and I thought to test my dogs on their scent. They're excellent at short bursts of speed, but I'm not sure of their wind for long chases. However, we'll see soon enough. Once they've the odor of a prey, they never forget."

"Of course," said Botrell. "We'll take them up onto the Scarpe in the morning. This evening, however, I have a dinner planned in your honor. Just a small, unassuming affair."

The duke of Mizra laughed. "I doubt it'll be unassuming. The reputation of your board is well known in all of Tormay."

"Horses, wine, women, and a good meal," said Botrell. "There's little else of worth under the sun."

As the duke of Mizra suspected, the small dinner turned out to be anything but small. The great hall in the castle burned with countless candles, glimmering from sconces and the chandeliers that were let up and down by silver chains on wheels. Fires crackled on the hearths. The windows were open to the dark gardens beyond and the sound of the fountains that played invisibly in the night.

An endless procession of servants drifted across the expanse of polished black marble, bearing every manner of delicacy that could be desired. Roast swan with gracefully curved necks swam upon silver platters. Suckling pigs, crisped brown and exuding such a fragrance that it caused tears of joy to spring from the eyes of dedicated trenchermen, slept in splendor upon beds of roast potatoes. Tiny ducklings flew upon skies of sweet rice. Airy fantasies of pastry and quail floated by. Masterpieces of mushroom. Soufflés spun out of audacity fell apart into impossible perfection at the touch of a fork.

The chatter of a hundred different conversations was borne upon the tinkle of gold utensils on gold plates and bowls and buoyed by the sound of a string trio playing up in a balcony overlooking the hall. At the head of the table sat the regent, loud and exuberant and flushed with wine. On his right, in the place of honor, was the duke of Mizra. On the regent's left sat the prince of Harth, honored for his father's sake and, truth be told, the fact that Harth did so much trade with the city of Hearne. For all of his profligacy, the regent was a reasonably practical man. Further along were the other dukes and duchesses present—old duke Maernes of Hull, the Callases of Dolan, the Galaestans of Thule, the Rostannes of Vo, and Elloran, duke of Vomaro, as fat as a pudding and gleaming with sweat as he attacked his overburdened plate. From there, the seating continued on down the table to the hall's end according to relative importance and perceived rank, with each place allotted to the minor lords and ladies, various noble bastards, and rich merchants.

227

Levoreth had ended up in the middle of the table. On either side of her, rows of faces bobbed over their plates and turned from side to side in conversation with their neighbors. Mouths opened and closed on food and words. She had no energy to listen. Her head was aching again. Her aunt smiled at her from further up the table.

A sceadu came traveling to Hearne, disguised as a poor wayfarer.

The old cat's words crept through her mind. The unease within her had been growing ever since they had come to Hearne, but talk of a sceadu from yet another of the lords of the *nyten*, the four-footed kin, was grim news indeed. True, it had been many years ago, but the wolves had spoken of one as well. Such had been her dismay, though she had hidden it from them, that she had agreed to return with them to the Mountains of Morn to hunt the creature down. The hunt had been futile.

Levoreth frowned down at the soufflé on her plate. The worst memories, no matter how old they were, always persisted with painful clarity. Why was it not so with the pleasant memories? There were times when she could not remember Dolan's face, and then the only thing she could do was to look at Hennen Callas until some stray bit of light recast his features into the old, familiar, well-beloved face.

But she had memories of sceadus.

Leaning forward, she could look all the way down the table, past candelabras and fantastic arrangements of flowers, past the faces of the noble houses of Tormay, eyes shining in the candle and firelight. Servants wavered in and out of the shadows, indistinct except for the platters and flagons they carried in their hands. She caught a glimpse of Nimman Botrell and, bent forward in smiling intimacy toward him, the lean, youthful face of the duke of Mizra. Light shone on his hair, and it looked to her as if Brond Gifernes wore a burnished helm of gold.

She took a bite of soufflé. Even cold as it was, it was delicious. But she pushed the plate back. She had no appetite.

"And whaddaya think," brayed a voice near her ear. "Whaddaya think of the regent's hospitality, Lady Levoreth? Do ya—do ya think?"

She did not recognize the lord next to her, but he was young and already unsteady with wine.

"I do think," she said to the young man, and then decided to stop there.

"Yes, yes," he said cheerfully. He sloshed some wine on his shirt. "Couldna said it better myself. Best table there's to be found in all of Tormay. Ain't any better. Been at the best, and this is the best. Bet my life on it."

"You are brave," she said, her head aching even more, "to bet your life on such a thing. After all, you have to be willing to die for something, no?"

At her own words, a wave of homesickness swept over Levoreth for the hills of the Mearh Dun; for the cold waters of the river Ciele wandering down from the Mountains of Morn, flowing west and murmuring of old sea dreams; for the mountains rising up to their snowy peaks; for the forests sleeping under the constant twilight of their branches, letting fall acorn and seed in trust of yet another spring; for the howl of the wolf, the questions of the owl, and the protest of the mouse, the comfortable whicker of the horse, and the dry laugh of the fox; for the earth with its silence and secrets slowly gathered from so many lives drifting down, settling through the grass and roots and soil to find rest.

Levoreth opened her mouth to apologize for the cruelty of her words to the young lordling, for it was not his fault that his life—nay, all the lives of men—was lived in a world of roofs and walls and swift years that did not allow the eye to see beyond. But he had not heard her to begin with. He had already turned, satisfied and smiling, to whoever was sitting on his other side. She heard his words fall and there was less meaning in them for her than the splash of the fountain outside the windows.

No wonder the men of Harlech seldom leave their land, she thought dismally.

The string trio glided into a dreamy air as the dinner ended with more wine. A roar of laughter resounded from the distant head of the table. Botrell was seen weaving about with a bejeweled lady on his arm, her mouth frozen in a smile.

"Lady Devnes Elloran," said the drunk lordling. "The daughter of the duke of Vomaro and a great beauty."

Levoreth pushed back her chair and stood up. She wondered where the Farrows were that night. Probably still out on the plain of the Scarpe, with a bonfire burning in the midst of their wagons and someone playing old love songs on a lute. The girl, Giverny, would be sitting by the fire, dreaming her dreams with the earth under her hands and the flame light on her face.

Levoreth walked through the other guests toward the open garden windows. Her dress whispered on the floor—the delicate brown silk her aunt had been so pleased with. She drew the skirt up into her hands and stepped out onto the veranda. Somewhere on the lawn around the nearest fountain, she lost her slippers. The grass felt cool beneath her bare feet. Light spilled from the castle windows and softened the darkness. The garden spread out around her in groomed terraces that stepped down to the castle wall.

Not the wilds of the north. But earth, nonetheless.

The bushes alongside the fountain rustled and then divulged the narrow face of a weasel, black eyes flicking around suspiciously until they settled on Levoreth. In a quiver of delight, the animal scurried across the grass toward her, daring even to pat at the hem of her dress with a tiny paw.

Mistress of Mistresses! And then the weasel was overcome with excitement and it dashed away, chattering to itself of gods and legends and ancient memories that had been passed down from weasel to weasel. Levoreth smiled.

"There are not such animals in Mizra."

She had not heard him approach. Light shining from a window behind him rimmed his head with the same gold she had seen inside at the table. She could not see his face, though, as it was in shadow. The happiness of the weasel faded into silence as it disappeared into its burrow under the foliage.

"Is there not? I've never been to your duchy," Levoreth said.

"You have not, milady?" There was a hint of amusement in the duke of Mizra's tone. "This is a defect that must be remedied, and doubly so, for if you would deign to visit Mizra then Mizra itself would be happily remedied for the lack of yourself."

"Do you speak thus to all ladies?" she said. "I come from a land of horses and shepherds. They're plain-spoken, though the horses are usually the wiser of the two, as they hardly speak at all. Having grown up around such, I confess myself unaccustomed to the flowery ways of Tormay's courts. We have no such delicacy in Dolan."

He laughed.

"I was warned of your tongue, Lady Levoreth, but I confess your wit would make any edge pleasant. I would not mind such cuts. Rather those than the simpering of the beauties of the regent's court. Their words flutter as weightlessly as butterfly wings. I do not mind a little blood, milady, for pain reminds one of life and all its promises and obligations."

She turned slightly, forcing him to turn as well. His face emerged from the shadows as light from one of the windows fell across it. His green eyes were earnest and clear.

"Need you be reminded of such obligations?" Levoreth said, wondering at his eyes. The greenness of them provoked her. Unreasonably so—she admitted that to herself, though she wasn't sure if she was irritated or intrigued—and she allowed a flicker of thought to waver out toward him and then hastily pulled it back. She blushed and hoped that there was enough shadow on her face.

It was common among the rich and important of Tormay to set wards about their minds, for it wouldn't do to have every hedge wizard and blackmailer probing such people for their secrets. The duke of Mizra, however, had no such ward. His thoughts were as open and as guileless as his green eyes. From that single touch—as delicate and as fleeting as a bee dabbling for pollen—she had gathered the sense of a boyish mind on the cusp of manhood and contentedly grave with his ducal responsibilities. She had also sensed in his mind a keen interest in her. An infatuation, she thought. He's never even met me before.

I hope he's not sensitive enough to realize what I just did.

Apparently, he was not sensitive enough, for his brow was wrinkled in earnest thought at her question.

"But obligation," he said, "must be chosen afresh every day, particularly for those who rule, for the power of the ruler brings with it a temptation to order one's world so that it no longer contains opposition and all the painful weights of duty."

She was about to frown at such a pompous utterance when he grinned and said, "At least that's what my old tutor always used to say. He was fond of lecturing on duty. Bit of a bore, but now that he's gone—he died last year—my castle in Ancalon is too quiet for my tastes. I miss his conversation."

He took a step closer. He looked even more earnest than before. Alarmed, Levoreth wondered if she might convince the weasel to make another appearance.

"I've been thinking lately," continued the duke of Mizra, "at least, that—"

"My Lord Gifernes, I never did get a chance to thank you properly—Levoreth!—oh, how nice, my dear; I confess I thought you already off to bed." The duchess of Dolan stepped out on the veranda.

"Just going now, Aunt," said the girl sweetly. "It's been a long day. I'm rather tired. I bid you good night, my lord duke."

The duke bowed and she left them standing on the lawn in the darkness. Somewhere off in the bushes, she heard the tiny death rattle of a mouse. The weasel, she thought. Her headache had returned, but she could not remember when. She went to her room and fell asleep in bed. In the middle of the night she woke and lay staring up into the darkness.

Strange. I have no memory of Mizra. I have no memory of that land. Perhaps I never have been there.

She turned on her side, and fell asleep.

CHAPTER FIFTY-FIVE
SETTING TRAP FOR MUSKRAT

Owain and his troop left the village early the next morning. The silence of the place was oppressive and the men had become more and more nervous as the night went by. The horses were uneasy and had to be picketed deep within the stand of pine trees, far from the walls and empty windows of the houses.

They rode in a long curving loop that brought them up out of the valley into the rolling hills on the far side and then back down into the valley further to the east. At the end of the day they had completed a wide circuit around the vicinity of the village. Hoon had argued the exercise a waste of time, given the weather. Owain had insisted, but at the end of the day he conceded that the tracker had been right.

"Now if I was a Farrow," said Hoon gloomily, "mebbe then we'd have summat. Those folk are cannier'n foxes, but I ain't a Farrow. I'm just Hoon."

Owain reined in his horse and sat for a while in thought. A hawk sailed by overhead, wings outstretched and motionless. It was heading south. Owain turned in the saddle.

"All right, men," he said. His voice carried cleanly in the cool evening air. "We'll camp here for the night. In the morning, we'll head south for Vomaro. There've been three reports there of such killings as in the village. A couple of days and then back to Hearne."

The guardsmen made camp with good heart on this news and soon a fire was burning, ringed about with saddles and equipment. The horses were hobbled and set to graze. Darkness crept up, but the fire kept it at bay. Long after the others had fallen asleep, Owain lay awake, staring up into the night. A purpled swath of stars stretched across the sky. The moon rose, full and pale yellow. Its eye did not close, but Owain's did and he fell asleep.

They made Vomaro the next day—though, truth be told, there are no real boundaries between the duchies of Tormay. It took a knowledge of old treaties and a good eye for certain hills and river bends and the like to know where one duchy began and another left off.

As they reached the crest of a hill, a lovely view greeted their sight. A lake lay before them, wide and still and shining under the afternoon sun. The farthest shore was not visible. Trees grew along the banks and everywhere there were meadows of late summer flowers like the canvases of some eccentric artist who had daubed on every single color his palette boasted.

"'And to the lake she came to pick her springtime blooms,'" quoted Hoon. "'With her maids not knowing their swift approaching doom.'"

"I never liked that song," said Owain. "Most minstrels are damned fools, writing such tunes to please other fools who happen to have gold. I daresay little of that song is true. Declan Farrow's story will probably never be known. I'd give much to talk with him, if he still lives."

"Probably happened 'round here. More'n likely."

"The eastern lakeshore. Bad enough fighting ogres with good swordsmen, but with just a bevy of maids and some court fops?" Owain shrugged. "It must've ended quickly—look there. We'll make for that hamlet further around the shore."

It was a small village—just a handful of houses built at the water's edge. A dock reached out into the lake. Several fishing boats were drawn up on the rocky beach. A dog ran growling toward them, but a kick from one of the horses sent it shooting off, howling its dismay for any who might care. Children peeped from windows and their elders stood silent in doorways.

Owain reined in his horse, and the troop behind him clattered to a halt. He raised his voice. "Is there anyone here who knows aught of certain strange killings? Where entire villages or crofts were wiped out?"

An old man stepped forward.

"Who wants to know?"

"I am Owain Gawinn, Lord Captain and Protector of Hearne. Word of these things has reached my city and I would seek what knowledge I can find."

"You're far from Hearne, m'lord," said the old man, but he tugged his forelock in respect.

"Hearne must still concern itself with the affairs of Tormay."

"Better'n can be said of our own duke. If'n it's true." The old man spat on the ground. Other villagers nodded. Owain swung down from his horse.

"Why say that, father?"

The old man did not need much encouragement.

"Near two months back now," he said. "That's when it happened. Nonn here, sailed over t' Upper Wen—we're Lower Wen, see? He sailed over 'cause he be courtin' Ganfrey's daughter Gan."

"Aye," said a young man, but that's all he managed. He clamped his mouth shut and turned bright red.

"He found t'whole village dead! Every last one. Man, woman, child. Even the poor dumb beasts. Nonn here, came back straight away an' we all sailed over. It were a terrible sight. Still turns my stomach t' think on it. Course, we sent word t' the duke in Lura, but none came. Things ain't right in Lura ever since she came back."

"Devnes Elloran?" said Owain.

"Herself." The man spat again. "The house of Elloran be cursed, but tain't them that bear it but us poor folk. None to help us, there ain't."

"Perhaps Hearne can be of help. Where is this village, old man, this Upper Wen?"

"Oh, tain't any Upper Wen," said the old man.

"But I thought you said—"

"We burned it straight t' the ground. Every stick of wood an' thatch. Broke the stone walls down an' threw 'em in the lake. You go murderin' folks like they did there an' the spirits linger, you see? An' ain't a while afore they get real mean an' angry that nothing been done about who murdered 'em. We figger it better t' get rid of their houses. Mebbe then they forget where they lived an' just wander off."

"The whole village is gone?"

"Ain't a splinter left," said the old man with some satisfaction.

"Well," said Owain coldly, "that certainly makes an impossible pursuit even more impossible. These killers are faceless and any scrap of evidence, no matter how small, would've been greatly valued. I commend your diligence but not your reasoning."

"Oh, they ain't all that faceless," said the old man.

"What do you mean?"

"Binny here, done seen 'em. Binny!"

A boy shuffled forward, ducking his head in embarrassment.

"Tell the lord what you seen, Binny. You can trust 'em, m'lord. He's my grandson an' allus tells the truth else I take a stick t' him."

"Setting trap for muskrat," said Binny. He mumbled so quietly that Owain was forced to step closer. "Just along the shore near t' the old willow."

"That's close by Upper Wen," broke in his grandfather. "Least, where used t' be Upper Wen."

"Was this during the day?" asked Owain. He tried to keep the excitement from his voice. "Were you able to see clearly?"

"Course not, m'lord," said Binny in indignation. "You allus set trap for muskrat at night. But there was a full moon, so I seen enough." He shuddered. "Lucky for me, I allus been fond of setting 'em in deep water. Just past the bulrushes, up t' my neck an' moving slow an' quiet—see, I was pulling a string of traps behind me."

Binny paused and his eyes seemed to go slightly out of focus, as if he was seeing something else. "You allus gotta be quiet around muskrats. Too much excitement, an' they get t' thinking about moving on t' other parts. That's what musta saved me. I just happen t' look up an' there they were, running along the shore. Heading on t' Upper Wen."

"Who? Who was running?"

"Were a man an' two hounds—only they weren't."

"What do you mean they weren't?"

"They weren't. It looked like a man, but things weren't right. His legs an' arms were all wrong. Too long an' bending too far. He was tall too, taller'n you, m'lord, an' running faster'n a horse. Had him a long, thin face with sick-looking white skin like you'd 'spect on a dead man. An' the hounds weren't dogs, least, no dog I seen. Both of 'em size of a small cow. Big necks an' heads an' eyes all white an' staring like boiled eggs. I thought my heart about t' stop beating."

"But how did you see all this if they were running as fast as you say?"

"Well, they stopped dead, m'lord. Right on the bank, an' me that close. Only the bulrushes between me an 'em. The dogs swinging their heads around. I could hear 'em sniffing like there was a scent t' be had. But water an' mud an' the stink of rotten rushes is a lot t' sniff through. I didn't twitch a muscle, that scared I was, not even t' sink below the surface. You know how it is. Any small move'll draw the eye, even at night."

"I think you came near your death," said Owain. "I'm glad the night turned out in your favor, though it did not for the poor folk of Upper Wen. You are lucky."

"Aye, m'lord, an' right do I know it. But there's more t' my story. The two dogs did their sniffing for a while more an' then the man growled at them. Growled like he knew their tongue an' was telling them something. It were a strange thing. His mouth opened wide, an' it were filled with more teeth 'n any two men have between em'. Made the hair stand up on my neck, it did."

"And then they just left?"

"Aye, m'lord."

Owain nodded. It was a stroke of tremendous luck—luck the lad had survived and luck that had brought him and his men to the little village. Damn the duke of Vomaro. If the incident had been followed up when it had happened, then such details might have made their way to Hearne months ago. At any rate, at least it was known now.

"One last thing, m'lord. I know this might sound strange—"

"Nothing's strange anymore, lad."

"After they were gone, an' I was sitting there in the water, I realized something."

"What's that?"

"It'd been a nice, warm summer night, but everything'd gone cold. Real cold, like close on to ice, an' my bones were chilled so they ached."

CHAPTER FIFTY-SIX
AN UNEXPECTED ALLIANCE

Lena kicked at the door, but it was locked and made of much harder material than her foot. She scowled. Her luck usually wasn't this bad.

True, the time she had tripped the bakery ward in Highneck Rise had been extremely unlucky—unlucky enough to mark her for life with the livid scar on her face—but that had been the exception. Wasn't she the one who had lifted seven purses in a single afternoon in Mioja Square, one of which had contained a perfectly cut ruby as big as a quail's egg and a second that had held a handful of unused guardian wards—wards woven by none other than Bredan Gow, the most expensive ward weaver in all of Hearne? The Juggler had been pleased at that.

And hadn't she beaten Taggity at dice just last week and won a whole jug of ale off of him? Him boasting there wasn't a die in all of Hearne he couldn't roll as crooked as a hanged man's neck. She certainly had set that straight. A dozen rolls and three pairs of eyes. Served him right to boast, the smelly rotter.

She went through her pockets for the third time. Two coppers left over from the swoop Jute had given her the other day, a hunk of stale bread, one handkerchief, and a rag doll she had stolen off a barrow months ago. Not that there was any value to the doll, as far as she knew, but it gave her an odd comfort to have it in her pocket.

But nothing suited for picking locks.

She thought it would have been safe. Surely there wouldn't be harm in asking the other children. After all, they had grown up together, playing and fighting and stealing together on the streets of Hearne. So she had asked. Had they ever heard the name Nio before? Did they know anything about the old manor down on Losian Street, the one with the tall garden wall and the stone tower? They had all said no—no, never heard the name—no, never been near that house. Why would any of us go there? High walls and wards. No. Never heard the name.

But someone had gone and spoken to their new master. The old man. Someone had whispered. They had been pitching pebbles at the blackbirds perched on top of the stable roofs behind the Goose and Gold when she had heard him call through an open window on the second floor.

"Lena!"

The old man had smiled all fatherlike—at least, that's how she imagined fathers would smile like—and she had trotted inside without a second thought. Down the hallway at the top of the stairs. He had held the door open for her, and she had assumed she was going to hear about a job. Perhaps a certain someone to be followed. Someone's pockets to be swooped. But all she had heard was the door slamming behind her and the key turning in the lock. She had yelled and kicked the door until her toes ached. The only response was a whisper from the keyhole.

"Some questions shouldn't be asked."

The room had one window set high in the wall. It was barred, and she grabbed hold of the bottom railing and hoisted herself up. She had enough strength in her skinny arms to hold herself there for a while. The sun was going down and there were afternoon shadows slanting across the yard behind the inn. The rest of the children were gone. She growled in frustration to herself, wondering who had told the old man. The ostler slouched across the yard and disappeared into the stable. Her grip was weakening on the railing and she let go. She would teach them a lesson or two when she found out who squealed.

Her hands balled into sharp little fists, but then she slumped in the corner and cried. *Some questions shouldn't be asked.* She wished Jute weren't gone. It would've been all right if he hadn't gone and gotten himself nabbed. There was no one else she could trust. Certainly not any of the other children. Not even the twins. If only Jute were here.

Don't be silly. He can't help now. You're trying to help him, so pull yourself together.

She wiped her nose on her sleeve and investigated her pockets yet again. Stone and blasted shadow! Next time, she would be sure to carry some wire. But then she remembered she didn't know how to pick locks in the first place.

Jute had promised to teach me.

A slight noise came to her ears. The noise was so quiet she half thought she had imagined it. Perhaps a mouse trotting between the walls. She listened, trying to throw her senses wide—push them out, Jute had always said; let them expand like your cheeks expand when you hold your breath. The explanation had always seemed silly to her. It made no sense at all.

She heard the noise again. It was coming from the door. She tiptoed over and stared at the lock. Dust drifted out of it and she heard metal grating. The handle turned. The door opened and she found herself staring into the face of the man from the alley. The Knife.

She blinked, shocked into silence.

The man from the alley alongside the Goose and Gold. The man who had been bruised and bleeding and face down in the mud when she had left him. Ronan of Aum. The Knife of the Guild.

She opened her mouth to scream, and he instantly clamped it shut with his hand. He nudged the door closed behind him with his foot.

"Not a sound," he said. "Do you understand me?"

She nodded. Felt her heart fluttering faster. Tried to swallow. She nodded again, trying not to cry.

"Good. I'm going to release you and you're not going to make a sound. Is that clear?"

He stepped back from her. She drew a long, shaky breath.

"I'm not going to hurt you, Lena, even though I have good cause. The Guild's a harsh master and it often demands harsh things—things we might not choose to do on our own. Do you understand?"

"Yes," she said, her voice shaking.

"I didn't want to hurt your friend Jute. I was only acting under orders, for I was the Knife and the Knife cannot disobey the word of the Silentman. I've done terrible things, working for the Silentman, things that are shameful even to speak of. But of all of them, nothing was worse than what I was forced to do to Jute. I was forced to do it, Lena, for the Knife must carry out every command of the Silentman. But I'm not the Knife anymore."

"You poisoned him! He did his job and you pushed him back down the chimney!"

She knew, Ronan thought to himself in triumph. She knew what had happened. Poison. More than what could have been learned from spying from a neighboring rooftop that night. Between then and now, she must have talked with Jute.

"I had no other choice, Lena." He kept his voice gentle. "As the Knife of the Guild, my will was never my own. I had to serve my master, just like you served the Juggler. You understand that, don't you?"

She did not answer.

"You do understand, don't you?" he repeated.

"Yes," she said reluctantly, but he had her interest now. He could see it in the way her eyes studied his face.

"I'm no longer the Knife. The Guild cast me out. I don't serve the Silentman anymore. Do you think I'm proud of what I did to your friend? But I'm free now, free to do what I will. I don't lift my hand against children. I'd do anything in my power to take back what I did to Jute. Anything. But what's done is done. Perhaps helping you escape from here will atone in some small way. How I wish I could do more."

He paused to see what effect his words might be having. She scowled down at the floor.

"Anything?" she said.

"Anything. Anything at all."

"Well," she said slowly. "Do you know a man named Nio Secganon?"

"Yes—but not here." Something uneasy turned over in his mind. He remembered the sound in the basement, the shambling figure. "We can't waste any more time here. Your life's already in danger from the Guild for asking questions about that man—that's why you were locked up, isn't it? We must leave now. Later, I'll explain about Nio Secganon."

The hallway was empty, but Lena could hear the sounds of the common room drifting up the stairs at the far end. Laughter, voices, the clink of trenchers and knives. Ronan closed the door behind them. The lock clicked.

"Come," he said.

He walked down the hall and she followed in his footsteps. A lockpick gleamed in his hand and another door opened. It was the innkeeper's own room. She had seen it once, peeking in through the open door while one of the serving girls had been gathering up an armful of bedding. The innkeeper's wife had emerged at that moment from behind a cracked toilet screen, letting her skirts fall down around her skinny legs, and she had seen Lena peeping around the door. What a chase that had been!

"Through there," said the man.

He pointed at the window at the far end of the room. She nodded, wondering if she could climb as well as the legendary Knife of the Guild, the shadow man who could not be stopped by walls or locks or wards. So they said. She scowled down at the fading carpet so that she would not shiver. Jute had taught her to climb, and he had been good enough to have done a chimney job for this man.

The window creaked open. He hoisted her up onto the sill.

"Up," he said, his voice quiet. "Up and over the peak to the right and then lay down on the tiles, still as a mouse."

Lena nodded, fitting her fingers into a promising crevice just above the casement, but he gripped her arm, easing the smart of it with a smile.

"Don't be scampering off now. I'm much faster than you are, girl, and I know these rooftops like the back of my hand."

She nodded again, flustered, for the thought had entered her mind.

238

He was fast, for as soon as she had hoisted herself up over the rise of the roof, he was there behind her. He swarmed up the wall like an enormous spider, all arms and legs and careless speed. For a moment she thought him faster than Jute, but then her old loyalties reasserted themselves and she only sniffed. The rooftops of the city spread out around them like a vast plain of sharply angled hills of red and brown and black. Slate and stone and thatch. Chimneys rose like trees, denuded of their branches and smoldering smoke from their tops.

"You're lucky," the man said quietly.

"No luckier than usual," she said, sullen and unsure whether she should thank him, unsure whether that smile of his was trustworthy.

"Asking questions about Nio Secganon is certain to bring you to the attention of some unpleasant people. I overheard the conversation between your new master and the Silentman's steward and I remembered your name."

"The Silentman's steward?" she gasped.

"I was sitting down the bar from them. They didn't see me, but I heard them. People who get mixed up with Nio Secganon have a habit of coming to unfortunate ends."

If Lena had glanced up at that moment, she would have noticed Ronan eyeing her, as if gauging her thoughts, but she was only concerned with her own misery. She nervously laced her fingers together and then unlaced them.

"Oh, shadows take them," she groaned.

"Someday, perhaps," said Ronan. "Just be thankful you still aren't in that room, for you would've soon been down in the Silentman's dungeons, locked up in the dark with the rats."

She shuddered and furry little horrors with red eyes and twitching claws ran through her mind.

"Thank you," she said.

"It was the only thing I could do," said Ronan. "By helping you, I can repay my debt to Jute. I don't forget my debts." A smile flickered across his face, but she did not see it.

"Though," he continued, "why were you asking about Nio Secganon? There are faster ways to get your throat cut in this city, but not many."

She hesitated and the man held his breath. Far across the rooftops, the sun in the west burned with golden fire. It trailed light across the ocean and he could not see the horizon for the brilliance of it all. He idly wondered if there were other lands across the sea. Other countries and people. Or just waves and endless waves. The shadows lengthened on the rooftops.

"It was for Jute," she said.

"For Jute?"

She told him the whole thing in a rush, relieved to speak and relieved to not have such a burden weighing on her small shoulders. Surely it was important if Jute had asked her, if he was so afraid of his life that he had hidden away. Perhaps the Knife would have an idea. Even if he wasn't the Knife anymore, he still was the legend who had ruled the shadows and byways of Hearne. Why, some of the Guild thought him more powerful than the Silentman himself. More important, he had freed her from that room. He seemed like a pretty decent sort.

"Where'd you say he was?" asked Ronan, half disbelieving her.

"In the old university ruins," she said again. "Jute went there because it was the only place folks don't go to—"

"They sure don't," said the man.

"—all woven about with wards it is. He says there are some real dillies in there that'll fair scare the life out of you, if they don't kill you first. I wouldn't set foot there to save my life, spit on it, but Jute's quieter than a shadow and he knows how to move silent."

"Those ruins are enormous," said Ronan. "They're the perfect place to hide. Even if someone knew he was there, it wouldn't help very much. It would take a hundred men a month to search through properly."

"He's safe enough," said Lena.

"Well, I think we're safe as well. The sun's going down and there won't be much for people to see on these roofs."

He stood and made his way across the tiles, motioning her to follow. Most of Hearne was built in a hodgepodge fashion, buildings jammed up against other buildings, sharing walls and angling roofs wedged onto and under the neighboring slants of other roofs. It was almost possible, if you were brave and skillful, or just plain stupid, to make your way from one end of the city to the other entirely on rooftops and, sometimes, on the tops of high courtyard walls. The one exception to this was the neighborhood of Highneck Rise and the manors of the wealthy and the nobility on the higher ground and cliffs in the northwest of the city. Dwellings such as those were invariably surrounded by gardens, which provided effective barriers against any person who thought to tour the city by rooftop.

The man and the girl flitted from roof to roof, scrambling across peaks and ridges so as not to present profiles to any curious eyes that might glance up. It seemed to Lena, at the speed they went, that this was a quicker way to travel than the more conventional route of streets and alleyways. They were bearing south, for the red gash of the setting sun stayed on their right and its last light threw their shadows past them to lope along the sloping roofs, black and impossibly long-legged.

"Here," said Ronan. "We go down to the street here."

They were perched on top of a warehouse. The yard below was filled with stacks of roughly cut timber. One such stack reached a tremendous height that was almost on level with the bottom edge of the roof. Ronan jumped down and, even though he landed like a cat, the pile of logs creaked beneath him in protest.

"Come on," he said.

Lena crouched on the edge of the roof, her toes in the gutter. A scowl crossed her face. She was tired and in the last few minutes had been starting to think of things like bed and sleep or perhaps merely a pile of hay in a stable somewhere. She wondered if the stack of logs would decide to tumble and roll if she added her small weight to the man's.

"Jump," he said. His voice was patient, and that was enough for her. She jumped and he caught her around the waist and set her down as lightly as a bit of fluff. The logs underneath them groaned and she could feel a slight tremble vibrating up through the soles of her shoes.

"They're going to roll," she said.

"No, they won't. I've done this plenty of times and it's always been safe."

"Not with another person, I bet." She scowled at him, but he was already stepping down the logs like he was walking down a staircase.

"Child, you don't weigh more'n a handful of shadow."

She hadn't been in this area of the city much before, but she figured they were near the south gate. It was a rough area with numerous warehouses and places of trade given over to the simpler needs of mercantile: wax and lumber and iron, the quartz sand from

Harth used by glassblowers for their window-making, hemp and pitch, and the streets of the tanners stinking with grease and rotten fat and acrid lye. The dwellings there were jammed in between the hulking warehouses and among the inns and way houses dedicated to the various guilds.

If she hadn't been so tired at that point, Lena might have tried to run away. Clambering up and down endless roofs was exhausting. Much more exhausting than a day trolling the crowds and having an occasional sprint with a fat merchant in furious pursuit.

But he isn't half bad. Good of him to winkle me out of that wretched room. And he ain't the Knife anymore. He helped me. He wants to help Jute.

And then Lena felt sorry for what she and the other children had done to him. She trotted by his side, feet hurrying to keep up with his stride. Scary face on him, she thought, despite him being rather nice. All hard and thin like an axe head. I wonder how many throats he's cut with that knife of his. She could see the haft tucked away at the side of his belt whenever his cloak billowed out. A thrill shuddered through her.

I'm walking around with the Knife! Wish the other cullies could see me now!

He led her down an alley that zigzagged between high houses crammed so closely together that it seemed the alley was a tunnel, roofed over with the angled walls of the houses and the strip of purple evening sky barely visible past the gutters. Two cats hissed at them from a pile of garbage.

"In through here," he said.

She wouldn't have seen the door if she had been by herself, so perfectly was it fitted within the surrounding wall. It swung open to reveal a modest courtyard and the back of an old house—three stories of dirty gray stone. A rickety wood staircase climbed to a tiny landing clinging to the third story. The Knife paused at the foot of the staircase and muttered something under his breath. The stairs creaked under her steps, and at one point she clutched the railing in panic as the plank beneath her feet shifted.

"It's safe enough," said Ronan. "Though I wouldn't advise trying these stairs when the ward is awake. You'd end up in a nasty fall and, if you somehow jumped and made it past that, there'd be a nice fire at the top to finish you off."

Behind him, she flinched, but he did not see. At the top of the landing there was a door set under the eaves. The Knife mumbled something under his breath and then he opened the door. She saw past him into a room bare of any furnishing except for a bed, a table and chair, and a large chest.

"My castle, milady," he said, bowing slightly.

"What about a chat?" she asked. "Weren't you going to tell me about—?"

"The bed's yours," he said, interrupting as if she hadn't spoken at all.

It wouldn't have been much to many folks, just a cot heaped with threadbare blankets, but it was much nicer than anything Lena had ever had.

"Now see here," she said, trying to sound as severe and as determined as her young years and diminutive height would allow. She looked nervously at the door, wondering if it would have been wiser to have run away while she had had a chance. Some of the older girls had been called to the Juggler's room occasionally during the night, not just the Juggler, but several of the Guildsmen who hung around the Goose and Gold. She remembered the faces of the girls in those mornings after. They hadn't said much, but Lena's imagination was active enough.

But the Knife didn't seem to have heard her, for he wrapped himself in his cloak, lay down on the floor and closed his eyes. Relieved, Lena blew out the candle on the table.

She kicked off her shoes and stretched out on the bed. She wiggled her toes from the sheer pleasure of a real mattress under her and a blanket snug under chin.

"Meant to tell you," she said. "I'll be seeing Jute tomorrow—just at dusk. Mebbe. . . mebbe you could help him some. Like you helped me."

There was no response except for the slow, even sound of the man breathing from across the room. He was already asleep, and then she herself was fast asleep.

CHAPTER FIFTY-SEVEN
THE FIFTH NAME OF DARKNESS

The book wasn't there.

Nio was sure he had not taken the little book of Lascol from the library. Yet, it was not in the library.

He stood in the middle of the room, frowning. An ache was developing behind his eyes. No one had been in the house since Severan and Ablendan had been there several nights before to tell him about the mosaic below the university. At least, as far as he knew, no one had been in the house. Logic forced him to admit there was always the possibility of an intruder. Someone with enough skill to evade the wards set about the place, someone with enough skill to leave no trace of their passing.

But that was not likely.

For the past several nights, Nio's sleep had been broken numerous times. The odd thing was that it always happened right at the third hour after midnight. He would wake and the hands of the copper clock pointed to three. He would fall back asleep for what seemed like hours and yet, when he woke again, the minute hand on the clock would have crept forward only a few paltry minutes. He wasn't sure what was waking him: some slight noise that immediately ceased as soon as he woke, the wind rattling at the window and then tiptoeing away at the first sight of his eyes opening, the shadows slinking by the foot of the bed? His bedroom was so woven about with wards that even the quietest mouse would have had difficulty crossing the threshold. Every night he tested the wards before he went to bed. He was beginning to dread sleeping.

Could the wihht have taken the book?

The thought made him go cold. Obviously, there was more to wihhts than what he had learned from the writings of Fynden Fram and others. The strange, sullen defiance of the thing and the way it seemed to mature in form and intelligence were not explained by what he knew. Perhaps making off with books was another unknown peculiarity of wihhts?

Ridiculous.

But he had to know for sure.

Nio made his way down through the house, down the long hallways, down the staircase into the gloomy parlor with its fine furniture and the fireplace yawning with its cold, ashen mouth. These days, there was never occasion to use the parlor, for the other scholars hunting in the ruins rarely came to the house anymore.

The kitchen door seemed to creak even before he pushed it open. Light sprang into life at a muttered word, and he was grateful for the warmth emanating from the small globe of fire. It floated over his shoulder as he walked down the stairs into the cellar. Shadows, but the place stank. It was much worse than before. A sweet, cloying taste of rotting flesh hung in the air, so strong that he could almost feel the greasiness of it on his tongue. He did not step down onto the muddy stone floor but remained on the bottom stair. The cellar looked empty, but the shadows gathered in the corners seemed to be hiding something.

"*Hie*," he said. The cellar remained lifeless and there was only silence except for the water murmuring from the ugly black hole leading down into the storm sewers of the city.

"*Hie sona*," he said, gritting his teeth and channeling the rush of anger into a focus of power. "*Sona!*"

And there, where nothing had been before, stood the wihht. It gazed at him expressionlessly. Moisture gleamed on the wihht's skin, and the clothes it wore were damp with water. Nio wondered if the creature climbed down into the sewer and so crept about the city, shambling through the passageways and emerging to walk among the unsuspecting inhabitants of Hearne.

"I've a question for you," said the man. "There's a book in the library on the top floor of this house. A small book bound in brown leather, worn and cracked with age. On the front is an inscription in characters from no language known by man. The book's missing. Did you take it?"

The wihht said nothing, but merely stared at him.

"*Cweoan*," said the man.

The force in his command lashed at the creature and it blinked, shifting on its feet.

"I did not take this book," said the wihht in its hoarse voice.

"You speak truth?" the man said.

"I did not take this book," repeated the wihht. It paused and then opened its mouth as if to speak again, but nothing emerged except for a wet, gurgling sort of sound. For a moment, Nio thought that the creature was speaking in some horrible language peculiar to wihhts—yet another detail unknown to Fynden Fram and all the so-called learned scholars of the past. But then he realized the wihht was laughing, and that was even more horrible.

"I have no need to read," said the wihht. It shuffled a step closer. "No need for books. No need. But sustenance I do need. That, I do need."

"On my word and in my time, you will be given it," said Nio coldly.

The wihht subsided into its habitual stillness. Nio eyed the creature and considered. According to the seven strictures of the spoken word, there were ways to test the truth of speech, particularly if one possessed some material of whoever spoke. And he possessed the best of materials—blood—his own blood had been provided to the wihht.

But I'm missing something here.

He gnawed his lip in distracted thought and then he blinked. Perhaps it was due to being so tired—the broken sleep certainly was taking its toll—but it looked as if the wihht was a little closer to him now. It hadn't taken a step, but it definitely looked closer. Or maybe the cellar seemed somehow smaller than before, the walls crowding in and the ceiling lowering, pressing down. The wihht stood as silent and as immobile as ever. It wasn't even looking at him. It was staring down at the floor. He hadn't noticed before, but it seemed as if the creature's arms were slightly too long for its body. They hung down at its sides. The thing's fingers twitched slightly.

Nio turned and hastily made his way back up the stairs. The little globe of fire drifted behind him. When he reached the top step, he looked back down but there was nothing to see. The wihht had vanished, and there was only shadow thickening to darkness. He locked the door and then placed such a binding spell on it that sweat sprang from his forehead. A great weariness took hold of him.

He stood for a moment, irresolute, but then he went upstairs to the library. It was his favorite room in the house and it afforded him more rest than his bed. He sat down in a chair. His head ached terribly.

Perhaps I should not have created the wihht.

What use would a wihht have with a book? The boy could have stolen the book when he stole the box, except he didn't. Whoever knew about the box might have known about the book as well. I wonder what old Eald Gelaeran would say if he knew I was shaping wihhts? It was his fault in the first place—that book he kept on his desk, the book of Willan Run. Too many ideas. Stone and shadow, but I still don't know who wrote the damn thing. Are the anbeorun gods, overseeing the affairs of men as a master puppeteer oversees the strings of his little creatures, or are they men such as myself and, as such, capable of death? The wihht. Fynden Fram was wrong in what he wrote. If he was wrong then who is to say that the little book I found in Lascol is wrong as well? Which words are true and which are false?

The library was lit by a lamp on a table beside Nio's chair. It cast a muted glow around his feet and pooled on the carpet. The warmth of it was comforting. But in the rest of the library, high up in the arches of the ceiling, within the nooks of the shelves and in the corners of the room, shadows grew as the night deepened outside. In particular, the shadows seemed oddly heavy in the alcove on the opposite side of the room. Nio found his eyes returning again and again to that spot. An old painting hung there on the wall. It was of the wizard Scuadimnes, the former senior archivist at the university and advisor to Dol Cynehad, the last king of Hearne. The painting always made him uneasy. The wizard's piercing green eyes always seemed on the verge of blinking to life.

Nio had found the painting the first month the scholars had begun digging in the university ruins. It had been locked away in a vault buried under rubble and bound with such a subtle ward that the vault was all but invisible to the casual eye. Severan had frowned when Nio had uncovered the painting.

"There's a knowing look to him," he said, shaking his head. "I'd be happier burning the thing. Who can tell what happier fate Tormay would've found if he'd never lived?"

"Perhaps," returned Nio, not wanting his find disparaged. "Though I think fate might very well be inexorable. It doesn't alter for the likes of us. If so, then what Scuadimnes did won't matter. The end of the game will always be the same."

"Then we might as well all go home and be done with it. Curse this painting of yours, Nio," the other had said. "And curse its subject. Scuadimnes destroyed this university and the monarchy of Hearne, not to mention utterly disgracing wizardry. No small feat for one man."

"But he possessed more knowledge than any other wizard who has lived, save, perhaps, Staer Gemyndes. And knowledge is merely knowledge, whether it be used for good or for ill."

Severan scowled and did not answer. The painting had gone home with Nio, even though, if he had been forced to be honest, he would have admitted his unease as well. The face was too alive. Light slid greasily over the oil paint and seemed to lend warmth to the flesh. The eyes gleamed. But Nio had hung it in the library. After all, Scuadimnes had been the greatest archivist the university had ever known, despite his treachery.

Something stirred in the shadows in the alcove. The darkness within the alcove was impenetrable, but Nio had the oddest sensation that, if he could see through that dark, he would find the eyes of the painting fixed on him. He shook his head and yawned.

I'll find that boy and I'll wring his neck.

What was in the box?

I wish I could remember her face. She was always smiling.

Nio fell asleep in his chair and dreamed.

There was darkness all around him. The library was gone. He stood up and the chair vanished. He could not see much of anything, but there was an airy noise of wind rushing by him that hinted at a great depth and space. As he stood there, the darkness began to relent, though he could detect no light. The gloom resolved into planes and lines. Before him was a stone wall. It was almost close enough to touch.

The stone of the wall was black and polished to such an impossible degree that it seemed to possess depth just as the darkness of the night sky possesses an almost limitless depth. Nio looked up and saw that the wall rose far above him. It grew into battlements. It mounted up into spires and towers that stood on each others' stone shoulders, higher and higher until they could no longer be seen. The darkness and enormity of the thing seemed vaster than the night itself.

Something drew his eyes back down to the wall directly before him. What had once been unbroken stone now revealed a small, dark opening. The darkness of the hole pulled at his sight, so that he was unable to look away. The shadows around it seemed to bend and slip into the hole. He knew with a sudden, terrible certainty that the hole in the wall reached for a tremendous distance. The wind hushed and the cold deepened. The hole dragged at him. At the far end of it, something stirred. And then whispered.

Nio.

He could not answer.

Thou art welcome in this the third hour.

He could feel the blood in his veins thicken and slow. His heart labored. It seemed as if he had somehow moved closer to the hole. He stared into its darkness.

Once upon a time, there was a jewel that fell from the heights. Its light quenched and it shattered into five shards. The shards fell still, tumbling through a night so long that it hath yet to find its end and they to find their rest.

The hole sighed. There was something of regret in the tone, as if remembering things gone by and long irretrievable. And there was hunger in the sound as well.

"Where is this place?" asked Nio hoarsely.

Here, there are no such things as where. There is only here. All things drift into this night. All dreams wander to these walls. Thy own dreams brought thee here.

"Is this the house of dreams?"

He could not tear his gaze from the black hole cut in the stone wall. Somehow, he knew that the depth of it was so great that, if he fell through, he would fall forever. Tumbling like the five shards in their endless night.

Aye, said the voice.

Aye. Thou hast found the house of dreams. My house of dreams.

Somewhere far away, stars strayed from their paths into unknown ways. Light slowed and dimmed until it was no longer light, but a cold, pallid thing, no longer able to burst forth on its joyous, eternal race across the boundless reaches of space. The light fell, chill and heavy with the sudden awareness of self.

I would have thee accomplish a thing for me.

And he could only say yes.

"Yes. Yes, of course."

Come closer, Nio, for I would speak with thee.

The night pressed against him and he drifted toward the hole. Closer he came, until the thing was a great, yawning gulf without edge or boundary. It was a glooming abyss and, in its impossible black depths, the quiet voice whispered again.

Come closer.

He came closer.

I would have thee accomplish a thing for me.

The voice whispered and whispered until he knew all that it wanted him to do. A small part of him thought to question the thing—some tiny spark still kindled by memories, perhaps, of the stone tower far up on the Thule coast, the grasses that waved on the moors there, and the forgotten face of a girl—but the shadows strangled him into silence with their weight as they rushed past into the abyss.

In return, said the voice, *I will give thee a gift.*

A light winked into being in the darkness before him. It was no stronger than the weakest candle flame, but such was the blackness around it that the light seemed oddly bright. It approached him, steadily growing in size, until there, hanging before him in the mouth of the hole, was a shard of stone, about the length of his finger. The thing was sharp-edged and gleamed with cold light.

Take it.

He could not have stopped himself at that point for anything in the world, for the sight of that light filled him with such a hunger that he had to possess the thing, to grasp the stone in his hand and know it was his.

Take it.

He reached out and took the stone. It burned in his palm with a flare of agony and he closed his fingers around it. Even the pain was beautiful. It bloomed between his fingers like a flower that sought some strange, dark sun. He opened his hand and the stone was gone.

The stone is within thee.

"What is it?" he said.

It is the fifth name of darkness. It is my gift to thee. Use it well, or it shall be taken from thee.

Nio woke. He was still sitting in the chair in the library. The night peered in through the windows. His head ached, but on his lips trembled a strange word he had never heard or known before.

CHAPTER FIFTY-EIGHT
SWALLOWFOOT

Levoreth sat up with a gasp.

The room was silent, which made the beating of her heart hammer that much louder. The vase on the nightstand was filled with flower buds. She reached out. The furled petals were cool to the touch. Her heart slowed. She shrugged a shawl around her shoulders and went to the window. The moon was high. Below, in the city, down past the dark roofs of Highneck Rise, she could see lights in the streets—slow rivers of luminance flowing at a human pace. It was not late.

She lit a candle and then splashed water on her face from a bowl on the dresser. The water trickled through her fingers. It glistened in the candlelight and dripped down like tears.

"Is it the same for you, oh my sister and brother?" she said wearily. "Does the Dark haunt your dreams? There's no rest for me anymore. Perhaps it's a just reward, for I've slept long enough and woke to Tormay in such a sad state. There's blood on our hands now, not just poor brother wind, but all this land, I fear. There's no time left for sleep, for the Dark is in my dreams."

The candle flame did not flicker. The light reflected off the surface of the water in the bowl. All around, though, was darkness.

"Maybe we'll have our rest, someday, but not now. Are you awake, like me? I saw the face of our brother wind in my dream, and he was soaring through the heights. It seemed as if he turned his face and smiled as if he were a child, as he was when the world was still young. But then the darkness took him, like a wave mounting up across the sky. It blotted out the sky and I do not know where he has gone."

Her voice faltered into silence and there was no response.

"I don't know where any of you are gone," Levoreth said. "But he is gone and I do not think he will return."

The darkness chuckled from somewhere behind her. She stiffened for an instant and then turned. The bedroom was filled with shadows and, outside through the window, clouds had hidden the moon.

"You have no part here," she said. "This is an old house. An ancient house that has faithfully served Tormay all these long years. I set my hand upon the cornerstone when it was laid. You have no part here."

Thy hand upon the cornerstone. What do I care for such things? Even thy accursed blood cannot keep me out if the minds of men bid me welcome of their own accord. The darkness chuckled again. *And they have bid me welcome.*

"Then I shall hunt them down," she said, her voice hardening. "I shall hunt them down and spill their blood onto my earth until, blood for blood, the evil is gone and you are banished back to your sleep in Daghoron."

Fret not, little Mistress. Thou hast discourse with my dreams, for I sleep still. It is only my servants that trouble thee and thine. I have set them marching, one puppet stumbling along from one side, another from another. If all do well, then I am glad. But if only one does well, then still am I glad. If they destroy and devour each other, then what do I care? My dreams are warmed and I shall find others. Mayhap one such shall make thy acquaintance.

"I pray the day be soon," she said viciously.

For thy tender sake, I think not, said the voice.

The wood under her feet creaked and lent her the memory of forests and deep woods, strong roots reaching down into the depths to find their strength. The stone walls on all sides groaned and gave her the memory of the mountains towering up into the sky, a ponderous weight redolent with centuries of wisdom and patience. The buds in the vase by her bed broke into bloom and filled the room with their sweet scent.

"I do not fear the servants of the Dark."

Ah, said the voice, *thy brother wind did not fear either, but he did not fare well at the edge of a knife.*

Perhaps the voice would have said more, but Levoreth flung out her arms and, hands shaking, traced the ancient names of stone and wood and earth in the air. They hung there shining and then faded into the walls and floor and ceiling. The room was silent. She sank onto the bed. Her hands stopped shaking after a moment.

"Well, that's that," she said dully. "No use crying now. A hundred years too late, probably. No choice now but to see it out, even if everything falls to ruin."

She wiped her eyes and washed her face one more time. She hurriedly dressed and then left her room. The hallway was quiet and dark. She paused outside her uncle and aunt's room and listened. From within, there came the faint sound of slow, even breathing. She sketched a sign on the door and watched the letters disappear into the wood.

Her awareness drifted five floors down into the depths of the castle, beneath cobwebs and shadows and dusty memories. She sensed the old cornerstone embedded in the bedrock of the cliff. Her name was inscribed upon it, and she could feel the love marked in every character, drawn by her fingertip and still stained dark with her blood.

But there's always another way to open a door, isn't there?

The moon sailed high in the sky. A glitter of stars was thrown across the darkness like splintered light scattered by some ancient hand. She could smell the sea. Glass and copper lamps set on iron poles spilled radiance in pools across the cobbled ground. Three young Vomarone nobles staggered up the steps past her, ale fumes eddying in their wake. Someone said, "Good evening, milady," but she did not stop to smile or see.

How I wish for my wolves.

The castle gates loomed before her. A troop of mounted soldiers clattered past, and as the minds of the horses hurried by, they caught at hers in a swell of wonder and questions and delight. She heard one neigh and the voice of its rider murmuring to the horse, and then the whole troop vanished into the night and down the avenue stretching into the darkness and winding through the trees and stately stone houses of Highneck Rise.

Horses.

She paused and considered. A soldier at the gate came to attention. Moonlight spilled across his helm, across his cheekbones and the bridge of his nose. Shadow welled up in his eyes. It seemed as if he only had a skull instead of a face. Not enough flesh these days.

"Milady," said the skull respectfully.

Levoreth frowned at him, distracted and not even hearing him. The Guardsman reddened and tried to look somewhere else.

Horses.

Horses and wolves.

She turned and strode away.

The stables were on the north side of the castle, past a rambling garden filled with grape arbors and edged with grass. Several mice peeped at her from under the leaves of a bush. Their black eyes shone with starlight and awe.

Mistress of Mistresses.

"Beware the Dark, little ones," she whispered.

They blinked at her, too scared to say anything further.

"Tell your cousins, the vole and the shrew, the rat and the rabbit, the mole and squirrel, that the Dark has come to this city. Beware."

The mice chittered their assent and scampered into the bushes.

She inhaled the warm scent of horse, of oats and hay and contentment. Light shone from the stable windows. The stable was fashioned of oak and stone and was finer than most of the houses in Hearne. The regent loved horses. Levoreth smiled. Botrell was a fool on the best of days, but he loved horses. Inside, a lantern hanging from a hook illuminated straw and wood and the rows of polished leather tack gleaming on the wall. Up and down the corridor, horses poked their heads out of their stalls and stared at her in wonder.

Mistress of Mistresses.

In the stall nearest her, an old man was currying a mare down with brushes strapped to his hands.

"Don't let me disturb you," she said.

The old man did not respond or look at her. The mare swung her heavy head around and blew her breath across the old man's shoulders. He glanced up and saw Levoreth.

"Don't let me disturb you," she repeated.

He touched his ear with one brush, smiled apologetically and went back to his currying.

Mistress of Mistresses.

The mare's liquid brown eyes gazed at her.

The old one has not the use of his ears, silly little hairless things that they are.

And she nibbled affectionately at the old man's shirt. Her own ears flicked forward, attentive to Levoreth's step. Wood creaked as horses leaned against the gates of their stalls. Hooves stamped on straw. She walked between the stalls and touched each silken nose. Thoughts came jumbled and fast at her. Memories poured into her mind, eagerly shared by the horses. Sunlight flooded across open fields. Speed and wind and the arc of the ever-present sky. Joy—fierce, irrepressible, and pounding through their veins like a heartbeat, like the staccato of hooves galloping upon the green earth. They wanted to show her, to run for her out under the sun. The older ones stood stock-still, but the younger ones kicked at the slats of their stalls.

"Peace, children," she said.

What was he like? A foal pushed his head against her hand. Disapproving snorts came from his elders nearby.

"Who?"

Min the Morn! Your steed. The eldest of our kind.

She smiled and stroked the foal's long brown ears.

"He was like the wind."

The wind, the wind! The foal nickered. *Would that I ran like the wind.*

An old bay snorted. *The wind calls to us these days, but we are of the earth. We are yours.*

"Children, I would have one of you do something for me."

Every ear in the stable flicked forward. Every liquid eye gleamed on her. The only sound to be heard was the whisper of the old man's brushes on the hide of the mare. Levoreth plucked up a strand of straw and wound it around her finger.

"Who is the fastest here? Who is the fleetest of hoof and strongest of heart? For I need one who can run without ceasing, through day and night and back into day."

The stable erupted into a clamoring torrent. Thoughts galloped through her mind, flickering in and out of colors and shapes and across an endless expanse of plain. Names jarred into her head like the beat of hooves pounding the ground, stuttered and shouted, each one louder than the last and each one trembling with excitement. Joy.

She could not help smiling.

Peace! The old bay stamped his heavy hoof. *Peace!*

"Thank you," she said.

All here are fast, Mistress. The bay swiveled a wise eye at her. His mane was as smooth as silk under her hands. *All here are fast, for our master has a rough understanding of the way of our folk. He is not a Farrow, but he spends his gold well in the pursuit of our kind. All here are fast, but there is one who is faster than all.*

The bay snorted a sort of laugh. *Aye, faster than all, though our master knows it not. He thinks that yon Seadale is the best of our lot, and we do nothing to dissuade him. But there, Mistress, in the furthest stall, stands one faster and, though I know not what you want, he will do it for you or his heart will fail in the trying, for there is good blood in him.*

A chorus of apologetic assent pattered through her mind. The stable spoke softly now, and even though each head was fixed on her, turning as she walked to the last stall, there was no envy in their voices—pride and eagerness, yes, but it was for the horse who stood before her. He would run for her and he would run for the stable.

"How should I call you?"

S-S-Swallowfoot, Mistress. I am called Swallowfoot.

Swallowfoot ducked his head, abashed. He looked young to her, perhaps two years old at most. His body was a collection of sharp angles and overly long bones, all covered over with a tightly stretched hide of muddy brown.

"Can you run?"

Aye, Mistress. His head came up. *My dam was Evana, she that was the steed of Declan Farrow—*

"The steed of Declan Farrow?" she said.

She was the fleetest of our kin to run the plains. He did a little hop in place, all four hooves bunched together. *Near fast as the wind, she was. She ran for her master and she always told me when I was a colt—"Listen well, Swallowfoot, for you are a child of the Farrows, though you know them not"—that I should wait until I found my own and then I would run and run and run!*

"How did you come to this stable? You are far from the plains and the Farrows." But, even as Levoreth spoke, she knew the answer.

The master of my dam was cruelly used in the south, in Vomaro. Swallowfoot spun around in his stall in excitement and anger. *Cruelly used by evil men, for all men in Vomaro are evil! So said my dam. He was taken from her and she never saw him again.*

251

And there, in that green land which will be ever cursed by my blood, I was born to her after many lonely years.

"Perhaps good will come out of Vomaro someday," she said, her voice gentle. She took hold of Swallowfoot's head in both hands. The horse looked intently at her.

"You will run fast for me. You will run as fast as the wind, and there will come a time, long after we all are returned to dust, when the sons of men remember old days and they will speak of Min the Morn and they will speak of Swallowfoot."

And then she whispered into the horse's ear, whispering for a long while as the horse listened with steady eye and lowered head, and all the stable around stood silent. Behind her, at the end of the row of stalls, the door creaked open and she heard the heavy clip-clop of tired hooves. Someone cleared their throat. The sound was hesitant. She turned and Swallowfoot blew a warm breath of hay over her shoulder.

"Milady Callas."

The Duke of Mizra stood holding the reins of a tall black. The horse's coat was rimed with sweat drying white, and the horse stared at her with shining eyes. The duke dropped the reins, fumbling after them with awkward hands. He never recovered them, for the old man appeared, plucked the reins up from the straw and shuffled away, leading the tired horse behind him. The pair disappeared into one of the stalls and soon there came a tuneless crooning and the whisper of currycombs.

"Milord Gifernes," she said.

"Please," he said, ducking his head. "Call me Brond. I've never been fond of formality, all that bowing and scraping they're enamored with in the south. It makes me want to yawn. I'd much rather be at horse hunting with the dogs than in court, with all the glitter and chattering talk—never know what people mean and if they mean what they say or if they're just saying it because you're a duke—though, it wouldn't be half-bad if it was someone as pretty as you."

Then, he turned red, as he realized what he had just said.

"Andolan is not known for its formality."

Levoreth smiled and was not sure if she did so because of the duke's words or because of memories of the little court that her uncle kept, open to everyone and beholden to none, with the town butcher stomping in to complain about the price of cattle and the little old priest wandering in unannounced and expecting lunch. She closed her eyes and saw children chasing chickens through the courtyard and her aunt sitting in the back garden, knitting with the wool spilling her lap in the sunlight. Her heart lurched.

"Lady Levoreth?"

"I'm sorry," she said, opening her eyes. She shook her head.

"No, I'm sorry. I—I didn't mean to blunder in here and bother you—"

"It matters not," she said, feeling tired and old. He looked even younger than Dolan Callas had been that day, six hundred years ago, when he had reined in his horse across the river Ciele and sat there staring stupidly at her. The expression on his face had been similar to how the duke of Mizra was looking now.

"You aren't bothering me. I miss our horses. My uncle keeps a large stable, near as large as this, and I find their company sorely lacking in the bustle of balls and dinners and receptions that Botrell has seen fit to inflict us with. These long faces aren't the ones I know so well, but they're a comfort still."

The old bay leaned out and blew a warm breath of alfalfa at her.

Mistress of Mistresses.

The duke blinked. He glanced down. A dog had materialized out of the shadows. It pushed its head against his leg, almost like a cat, and then sat down.

"What a large dog," said Levoreth. She spoke involuntarily, surprised, for there had been no awareness of the dog in her mind before it appeared.

How odd, she thought.

She stooped to the dog, though this was hardly necessary as, even sitting, the top of the dog's head came easily to her waist. She let her awareness feather out.

"Careful," said the duke. "I wouldn't want your hand nipped. He's a shy one and doesn't like people much. His name is Holdfast."

"I get along well with most animals."

She stroked the dog's massive head. The hair was a dirty brownish gray. The dog sat motionless and patient under her hand. For a split second her fingers paused, but then she forced herself to continue petting the beast. Her awareness recoiled back into her mind. There was nothing there. Nothing except for a strange monotone of thought muttered over and over. *Find. Hunger, eat, food. Food, hunger, eat. Find. Eat.*

Dogs were always chatty animals, forever gabbling about scents and cats and the best spot of sunlight for snoozing and whether or not that last bone had been buried properly. Every dog she had ever met was like that. Even the stupidest of beasts, even the tiny-minded squirrels and chipmunks, possessed a considerable range of thought. Impressions of light and space and color, memories of tree and nut and leaf, fear of foxes and hawks.

But this was scarcely a mind at all.

"Is he a hunting dog?"

She drew her hand back. The dog watched her with unblinking dark orange eyes, so dark that they almost seemed red in the lamplight.

"The best," said the duke happily. "Never seen his equal. Why, I was just telling your uncle about a hunt we had a month back. I took Holdfast out for deer, and what does he do but run a stag to earth. He pulled the thing down by the neck. A full-grown stag, mind you, probably twice his weight. Once he gets his teeth in, he doesn't let go."

"Hence his name."

"Yes." The duke smiled down at the dog and then looked up at Levoreth. "And he holds fast to the trail as well. He doesn't forget scents. Single-minded, sniffing along. Why, he's been known to cut old sign he's scented before, months before, and follow it down, no matter how faint."

"Admirable."

"Yes, isn't he?" The duke beamed at the dog. "Go on. Say hello, Holdfast. Go on."

The dog lumbered to its feet and sniffed at Levoreth's hand. Its nose was cold. It blinked at her and then sat down.

"There, you're friends."

Levoreth forced a smile.

"I'm afraid I'm the sort that needs a longer acquaintance, milord."

"Oh?" said the duke, and his eyes acquired such a speculative gleam that she ducked her head, murmured an apology about a headache, and hurried out of the stable before he could say something foolish that would have embarrassed them both.

CHAPTER FIFTY-NINE
UNFORTUNATE EXPECTATIONS

Lena grew more and more restless as the day progressed. Perhaps it was the fact she was no longer locked up in the Goose and Gold and needing rescue, waiting helplessly for whatever was to be meted out at the hands of the Silentman's men. Or perhaps it was that she did not trust anyone old enough to be an adult. To make matters worse, Ronan insisted that they both stay cooped up in his rooms until the evening.

"The best way we can help Jute," he said, "is to stay out of sight for now."

"I'm bored," said Lena.

"It won't do for you to be seen," he said. You want me to help him, don't you? As I told you before, I need to get out of Hearne myself. The Silentman's about ready to hand me my head on a platter." Ronan eyed the girl. It would not do to overplay his hand at this point. "I can smuggle Jute past the city walls when I leave tonight. It's the least I can do."

"Ain't there a baker just down the street? I could nip out, lift a few pastries an' be back before you'd count three."

"No," said Ronan. "And that's final. There's no telling who'd see you. Believe me, child, half this city is in the pay of the Silentman." He was exaggerating, of course, but he wasn't that far from the truth. "Why, I know Guardsmen who inform for the Guild. Men in the service of the Lord Captain of Hearne himself, who take the Silentman's gold in exchange for turning a blind eye or whispering a bit of news to the right ears. Maids, merchants, sailors, apothecaries, old matrons stumping about with their baskets of veg. None of 'em can be trusted. None of 'em."

"I ain't afraid of the Guild," said the little girl. "I can slink around this town quieter 'n a cat."

"It isn't just the Guild," said Ronan. "Nio Secganon will be sure to have heard of you by this time. Have you already forgotten what I told you? He's a wizard of the worst sort. He has spells that can wander about the streets like breezes, listening and watching everything said and done in Hearne. Even the Silentman is afraid of him. Why, the Silentman almost refused to take the job Jute did, just for fear of Nio Secganon. We're much safer to stay in until night."

"Oh, all right," said Lena.

She roamed about the rooms as restless as a kitten. There were only two rooms, Ronan's sleeping chamber and a small alcove in which he kept a few chests and a wardrobe. He contented himself with a stick of oak and a knife, idly carving away at the wood.

"Hey!" she called from the alcove. "This wardrobe of yours is locked."

"Yes," he said, not really listening. A curl of wood dropped away from his blade. There was some semblance of a face emerging in the carving.

"Is it warded?"

"No."

She fell silent and Ronan concentrated on the oak, thankful for the momentary quiet and wishing the hours would pass by more swiftly. With a bit of luck, all would be well by that evening. Then he would be gone; he would be quit of the city and its wretched stone streets and the Silentman like a spider in the middle of it all.

The cheekbones of the oak face gained definition. He had not set about the carving with any idea in mind, content to let his hands and the blade feel their way through the wood. But now her face stared up at him from the grain of the oak. He whittled her hair into a frame of waves. The regent's ball. He had given his word to smuggle Liss into the regent's castle for the ball and so take her out again, once she was content with whatever purpose compelled her there.

I won't be able to leave tonight, then. Tomorrow night, after the ball. Shadow take the Silentman. He and those creatures he's been trafficking with. I'd have been long gone if it weren't for his greed.

He swore aloud. Blood welled from his thumb and slid along the knife blade.

"Got it," called Lena from the alcove.

"Got what?" he said.

"Picked the lock, of course. What's this, then—this what all the work gets done with?" She swaggered into the room carrying a sword.

"Give me that!"

The little girl jumped back, but the sword was so long and so heavy that she tripped over it and sprawled onto the floor. He snatched it away from her.

"Serves you right," he said.

"Don't have to be so snappish, cully," she scowled, rubbing her elbow.

"This is no toy," he said. His voice was gruff. He sat back down and laid the sword across his knees. Unconsciously, his hands drifted across the battered sheath and the leather-bound hilt, blackened with oil and age.

"Well, if it's no toy, then you must've done a fair bit with it. Shadows, you're the Knife!"

"Was the Knife," he corrected.

"Poof." One small hand fluttered dismissively. "There ain't no new one yet, so you're about the best there is for now. So g'wan—tell us a story about that thing."

"The only stories in this blade are about death," he said. "A child like you shouldn't be hearing such tales."

"Oh, yes I should. The bloodier the better."

Thoughtfully, he touched the iron guard on the haft. Under his fingertip he could feel a small nick. Lucky, that one. He'd be less a hand if this were any other blade. He had been careless that day.

"This was my father's sword," he said. "And his father's before him. It's been passed down within my family for generations."

"It looks a rubbishy old thing," said the little girl.

"Only a fool trusts to looks," he said, scowling at her. "The Juggler should've taught you that. Now, be quiet or there'll be no story."

"Right you are, sorry."

She crossed her legs, leaned her chin on her palms, and waited expectantly.

"I learned how to handle a sword from my father. I began when I was younger than you, scarcely able to lift the weapon I was given. But patience is the key to any learning, and as the years passed, what was once a burden and a painful duty became my nature.

Never pick up a weapon, child, unless you seek to master it to such a degree that it becomes part of you."

"Even if you're gonna just grab a stick and whack some lug on the head?"

He took some bread and hard cheese from the chest and handed them to Lena.

"Here, occupy your mouth with this."

"Thanks."

"When I turned seventeen, my father gave—gave me this blade and I went to seek my fortune. Youth is foolish. Always. There's no exception to that. I thought myself wise by virtue of my ability with my sword. I went to the mountains of Morn, to seek out some fearsome beast, to hunt down whatever terrible creatures of legend might exist and to defeat them in battle. My mind whirled with thoughts of gold and jewels, treasure beyond compare, but, truth be told, I was more dazzled with glory. Winning a name for myself so that men would be filled with awe, that stories would be told with reverence around tavern tables, that bards would sing of my deeds before noble lords and ladies."

Ronan scowled, eyes gazing at some remembered vista. His hand traced the weave of leather wrapped around the sword's haft.

"So were there?" said Lena.

"Were there what?"

"Wild animals. Wolves an' bears an' ogres an' all."

"Oh, yes," he said. A sour smile crossed his face. "All the legends are true, though I wish they were not. It might give you a pleasant shiver to think about such beasts when you're safe behind city walls, but I'd never willingly come to blows with a bear. And ogres are even worse."

"You killed an ogre?" The little girl stared at him.

"Several," he said. His voice was reluctant.

"What're they like?"

"They look something like a man, but an unusually tall man gone fat, with no neck and huge flabby arms and hands like hams and fingers like sausages."

"Poof," she scoffed, stuffing a hunk of cheese into her mouth. "Fat people are slow as cold honey. I'd run circles around ogres."

"No, you wouldn't. They may be fat, but they're enormously fast and strong. They'd grab you in a trice and I doubt you'd make more than a snack for 'em. Just a bite or two, and they do like their meat fresh, though they aren't choosy and'll sup happily on a body gone rancid, bones and all, for they've got tremendous teeth. An ogre can crunch right through bone."

This thought did not seem to disturb the little girl, for she bit down ferociously on the remaining crust of bread as if to prove that strong teeth did not belong only to ogres. Ronan drew the sword from its sheath. The blade gleamed a dull silver. He took a rag from his pocket and ran it down the edge.

"Three of them I killed with this," Ronan said. "I think they were brothers, but family resemblance is difficult to discern in ogres. They lived in the Mountains of Morn, in a hideaway carved deep in the rock. I crept through the dark of those tunnels, feeling my way over the rusting armor and remains of those who had met their doom in that place."

"Did you search the bodies?"

"Did I what?"

"All those dead warriors," Lena said, flinging her arms out wide. "Allus gonna be good swoop on dead bodies."

"They were a bit further along than just dead bodies. Skeletons—all of them. There usually isn't much to be found on skeletons. Besides, I was there for ogres."

"I woulda swooped the skeletons," she said. "You never know."

"The ogres had plenty of gold," he said. "Even your exacting standards would've been satisfied."

"Ah, that's all right then."

The sunlight was slanting through the windows, casting long shadows. It was close to dusk.

"We should be going," said Ronan. "It's near enough time. The moon'll be rising soon."

"But what about the rest of the story? You haven't killed any ogres yet."

"Later," he said.

She grumbled at that, but cheered up once they stepped outside, for they had been cooped up in the two little rooms all day long. Ronan strapped the sword onto his back. It was nearly invisible under his cloak.

"Right. We're off to see your Jute," he said. "Stick close."

Lena had a hard time keeping up with him, for his long legs covered the ground at such a pace that she was forced to almost run along beside him. They avoided the main thoroughfares of the city, but even the alleys and backstreets thronged with people. The Autumn Fair had begun in Hearne. Every intersection, no matter how small, had sprouted impromptu stalls and barrow carts manned by obsequious merchants. People moved through the cramped streets like water, slowing to swirl around vendors, eddying in the mouths of alleys, and pooling in the tiny squares that graced some of the intersections.

"Don't do that," said Ronan.

The little girl had palmed a muffin off a passing bakery cart. She took an enormous bite and nearly choked. Crumbs sprayed from her mouth as she struggled to chew and breathe at the same time.

"No telling whose eyes'll be drawn if you get caught," he continued, scowling at her. "And we can't have that now. Keep your head down and don't meet anyone's eyes."

"Ah, but I didn't get caught," she said.

It was dusk when Ronan and Lena came to the Mioja Square. Lamps on poles flared golden, standing on the street corners and amidst the peaks of the stalls that filled the square. The towers of the university loomed on the other side of the square, their walls luminous with the light of the setting sun. The square was crowded with people and the air clamored with the sound of voices. Ronan halted as they stood at the mouth of an alley, his hand on her shoulder.

"If I lose you in that crowd, there'll be no finding you again."

They made their way around the perimeter of the square until the outer wall of the university was visible at the end of the street. A contingent of city Guard stepped by smartly, pikes slanting on their blue and black jerkins. Ronan eyed them warily, wondering whether the erstwhile Knife of the Guild was known by face to the regent's men, but the soldiers looked over him blankly and then were gone, swallowed up in the ceaseless flow of passersby.

"Now, where were you supposed to meet him?"

He spoke as casually as he could, but there must have been a touch of excitement in his voice, for the girl squinted at him before she answered.

"Down Weavers Street," she said reluctantly. "In the alley."

"The sooner we get him out of this city, the sooner he'll be safe from the Guild. Won't do to have him waiting out and be seen by some sharp-eyed gabber."

Weavers Street was a crooked stretch of street where many of the Weavers Guild lived and worked and sold their wares. The street was made narrow by the stalls on either side, which displayed all kinds of tapestries, carpets, rugs, blankets, and gossamer-thin shawls woven in every hue the eye of man had ever seen. Apprentices caroled the merits of silk over wool or wool over silk and enticed passersby into shops with trays of hot tea. Lena led the way and she tugged at Ronan's hand, impatiently threading her way through the crowd. She picked the pocket of a passing trader and looked back to see Ronan scowling at her. She grinned and turned down an alley so narrow that he would have walked by without even seeing the opening. The immense wall of the university rose up out of the encroaching night. He could hear the nearly imperceptible hum of wards woven deep within the stonework. There were so many different threads to them that it put his teeth on edge to hear their quiet discord.

Hearne had two places Ronan did not like being near for long. One was the regent's castle on the cliffs above Highneck Rise. The other was the ruins of the old university. Both of them were so wound about with wards that if a person had any level of sensitivity to such things, the sheer number of weavings was bound to produce headaches or dizziness. Some people merely became sleepy. Ronan tended to become irritable, and life irritated him enough as it was.

"Here," Lena said. "Right here." The little girl bounced on her toes. The alley was gloomy with shadows, though the wall, high overhead, was still awash with the fading afternoon sun.

"Perhaps," he said, "it'd be better if Jute didn't see me at first. He might be alarmed. You'd better explain things to him."

She wasn't sure what to make of that, frowned at him, and then glanced up at the wall above her. When she looked back, Ronan had vanished and, though she peered here and there about the alley, the man was nowhere to be seen. She settled on top of a crate and waited. The trader's purse afforded some diversion. Besides the expected handful of silver, it also contained a tiny copper box engraved with grooves that wove endlessly about each other. The box rattled when she shook it, but, try as she might, Lena could not figure out how to open the thing.

"You'll never manage it that way."

She looked up. Jute was grinning at her.

"Jute!" she said, delighted.

"Here," he said. "Let me have a go."

He held the little box loosely in his hands, not even looking at it. His eyes seemed to glaze. The lid of the box sprang open with a click. An opal gleamed inside.

"How'd you do that?" she said.

"Simple. I beat the ward. See all the lines squiggling all over the place? That's the ward. This comes from Vomaro, I think."

"A bad ward?" Her hand drifted up unconsciously to touch the scar on her face.

"Course not," he said. "The ward keeps it locked, that's all. To open it you have to not think about it. Forget you're even holding the box and it'll open right up."

"So why don't the silly thing just open in your pocket any old time?"

"You have to be holding it."

"Ah."

They smiled at each other—the little girl perched on the rickety slats of the wooden crate, the boy rocking on his heels, his hands jammed in his pockets. He seemed taller to her, as if he had grown in her absence or as if she hadn't seen him for a long time—years, instead of a mere handful of days.

"Any scuttle going around on that Nio?" he said, glancing down the alley. It was darker now, and several stars were visible overhead, past the dark edge of the university wall and the houses lining the other side of the alley.

She opened her mouth, thinking of the old man who now ran the Juggler's children. His wrinkled face. His withered mouth. *Some questions shouldn't be asked.* There had almost been a note of apology in his voice when he had whispered through the keyhole. And there, over Jute's shoulder, she saw the face of Ronan materialize out of the darkness.

"Jute," she faltered, bewildered and no longer sure. The man was so silent. The boy turned too late, his eyes widening. In that brief moment, he wheeled on her, his face outraged.

"Lena!" he said. There was such a wealth of hurt and bewilderment in his voice that she would have done anything in the world to have not heard him speak her name like that, to be able to take back what she had done.

The folds of the man's cloak whirled around the boy and he was gone, vanished from before her eyes, and there was only the man standing before her. She hurled herself at him, furious, her fingers crooked into claws. The tears in her eyes conspired against her; he was only a blur, but she felt his hand on her head, holding her away so that her blows flailed through the air or landed on his unyielding iron arm.

"Lena."

He said it kindly, and that only served to make her cry harder and scrabble at the strength of his hand. He said it again, but she did not let up in her efforts. She could not. There was nothing else left for her to do. He sighed and did not say her name again, and a sudden, sharp blow on the back of her head caused her to pitch forward on her face. She blacked out for a moment. She could feel the cobbles under her cheek and she heard footsteps hurrying away.

Lena got to her feet. It was beginning to rain. She wiped her nose on her sleeve and, squinting down the alley, saw the tall shape of a man vanishing into the crowds of Mioja Square. She made off down the alley after the man, dizzy and staggering, but her hands clenched at her side.

CHAPTER SIXTY
HOME TO HEARNE

Owain Gawinn was satisfied. Well, he was reasonably satisfied. After leaving the village of Lower Wen, he and his men had rode northwest, back across the grassland and hills and up into Vo. They had not learned anything else after hearing Binny's tale. None of the villages they encountered had anything to say about the strange incidents plaguing the duchies. Most people had heard of the killings, true, but they had nothing substantial to say. Some thought them the work of bandits. Others declared that ogres must be abroad in the land again, pointing out that it had only been fourteen years since the duke of Vomaro's daughter, Devnes Elloran, had been carried off by ogres. Still others claimed it was the work of wizards needing blood for their spells.

Regardless, Owain was reasonably satisfied. Between Binny's story and the footprints that he and Hoon had seen, he now had something to go on. The mystery had a face. The regent would be forced to take him seriously. More influence would be brought to bear. More gold would be pried loose from Botrell's coffers. More soldiers could be trained. Perhaps several parties could be sent out to scout across the duchies? With Botrell's word behind him, maybe he could even muster support from the duchies.

The Farrows. The best trackers in all of Tormay.

"Hoon," he called.

The little man urged his horse up.

"You think the Farrows would be willing to lend a hand?" said Owain.

"With our friend an' his two beasties?"

"Aye."

"Mebbe so. Never met 'em myself. Folks say they be pleasant enough. Real trouble you'd have is finding 'em in the first place. Farrows are elusive. Howsomever, I reckon if you put word out, they'll hear sooner'n later."

"Think a Farrow could cut the sign of our friend and track him?"

"I reckon so. Back home in the mountains, they tell some tales about Cullan Farrow. About how he tracked a big timberwolf right over the mountains an' out into the eastern wastes until the wolf just got so damned tired of being follered that he up an' heads to Cullan's campfire, plops down an' says 'All right, Farrow, you got me.' Course, there's allus his son, Declan, but they say the lad done vanished for good. Fourteen years back now."

"Now that's a man I'd have in the Guard," said Owain. "I don't know about how he treated Devnes Elloran—if there's any truth in the songs, he's got a wicked streak in him as wide as the Rennet River—but anyone who could track an ogre trail, months old, right into their lair and then cut 'em down by himself. . ." He shook his head in admiration. "I wish I'd been there to see him fight."

"Well, I heard tell you've had some fights yourself, in your time."

Owain grinned.

"Still some time left," he said.

And with that pleasant thought in mind, he turned his horse to the west.

"Lads!" he shouted. "We ride for home and Hearne!"

CHAPTER SIXTY-ONE
HUNGER AND THE WIHHT

Nio woke in the late afternoon, with the sunlight already fading behind the shuttered windows. His dream returned to him in a rush. It seemed as if the fortress loomed unseen behind the paltry reality of his room. If he were only to close his eyes and then open them, the walls would be gone to reveal the stone fastness standing within its unending night sky. Surely that terrible place was the deeper truth than his shabby bedroom. However, when he shut his eyes and then opened them again—chiding himself for being a fool and yet half believing there was a certain wisdom in being a fool—there were only the walls of his bedroom, grimy with neglect and gloomy with shadow.

Nio lit a candle and went downstairs. It had been a long time since he had eaten, but he was not hungry. He did not think he would ever be hungry again. The word stirred in his mouth, and it was meat and drink to him.

The fifth name of darkness.

He marveled at the simplicity of the word. Surely such a sound was self-evident in the shape of shadows, in the creeping dusk, and in the blackness of those rare night skies in which there are no stars. He whispered the word out loud. Instantly, everything around him—the walls, the stone tile of the floor, the copper handles and hinges and keyholes, the mirror reflecting candlelight and his gaunt face—everything began to unravel into shadow. Wood splintered into shadow. The stone underfoot softened. The candle in his hand melted and darkness dripped down his fingers. The mirror reflected nothing except shadow, was shadow.

He laughed aloud. For a moment, he allowed the change to continue, marveling in it and wondering if, left unchecked, it would spread outwards like the ripples caused by a stone thrown into water, until all of Hearne was plunged into darkness. But then he spoke the true names of wood and stone, of glass and copper, forcing his will into the sounds until the original appearance of the hall reasserted itself.

The wihht was waiting at the foot of the stairs when Nio unlocked the cellar door. He was no longer concerned by the thing. It was remarkable how closely it resembled a man. In height and face the wihht could have been his brother. This was probably due to the few drops of blood he had given the creature.

"There's something I need you to do," Nio said.

The wihht did not answer.

"We go to the university ruins this night. I'll introduce you to an old friend of mine. There'll be mutual profit in the acquaintance—he, in adding to his already considerable knowledge and experience, and you, due to your own particular needs."

The wihht smiled.

It was twilight when they left the house. The wihht was cloaked and hooded. It no longer walked in the awkward fashion it had when Nio had first created it. The wihht strode along beside him, head down and silent. He could smell the sour must of the thing, but it wasn't much worse than any poor city dweller who never bathed unless it was by chance of getting caught in the rain. Or perhaps he was merely getting used to the creature's scent.

The streets were busy. They grew more crowded as they neared Mioja Square at the center of the city. Lamps burned along the edge of the square and at intervals throughout the sprawl of carts and tents. The people thronged under the flickering lights. Water shot up from the fountain in the middle of the square and gleamed with firelight. A cheerful babble of conversation, of vendors hawking their wares, of musicians plying their craft in the ale tents blended together into a surging clamor. Under it all, Nio could sense the countless threads of wards humming in wary readiness, guarding a rich merchant here, another there, woven about the tent of a jeweler, spelled into a nobleman's purse, silver whorls hammered into the hilt of a soldier's prized sword.

"Fortunes!" called a boy from the mouth of a tent. "Fortunes told! Fortunes!"

"Who'll buy fine linens? Who'll buy?"

"Wards! Wards for sale!"

"Cakes, cakes, cakeses!"

"Fortunes!"

A mist drifted down upon them as they walked by the fountain. The wihht was silent at his side. The falling water glimmered with dark colors. There were purples and blues quivering within the water and Nio could see the same colors leaping in the flames of the nearest lamp.

"Cakeses!"

And then they were at the steps rising up to the chained doors of the university. The place was a looming mass of stone and shadow hulking on the edge of the square. People sat on the steps, resting from their shopping, their thieving—resting their feet and chattering like the sparrows that made their nests in the eaves overhead. The last few steps, however, were unoccupied.

The little door to the left of the chained entrance opened at Nio's word. The wihht slipped in after him. The door closed and its ward whispered back into watchfulness. They stood in silence in the great entrance hall. Nio closed his eyes and let his mind drift. He could taste dust in the air. There. A spark of life. He caught at someone's thoughts. The slightest touch of surprise quivered in the other's mind and then it was abruptly closed to him.

He opened his eyes and waited.

It was only a matter of minutes before he heard the sound of approaching feet. A glow of light grew far down the passage on the right. The shape of a short little man drew closer, hurrying along with a candle wavering in his hand. He paused at the entrance to the hall.

"Ablendan."

"Nio." The little man's eyes flicked to the wihht and then back. "Did you—were you looking for someone? I felt your mind pass by. Who's this?"

"An old friend visiting the city for the festival. We were students together at the stone tower."

"Ah," said Ablendan. He took a step forward. The candle in his hand seemed to brighten, but the shadows in the hall deepened in response. "Then I imagine he'll be safe enough in here."

"Yes."

At his side, Nio sensed the wihht's body tense. He could feel the creature's hunger—a spark of greed that threatened to burst into ravening lust. He snapped a silent command at the wihht.

No.

And to his surprise, a thought pushed back at him.

But this one will please me.

No.

"Did you say something?" asked Ablendan. He shuffled his feet, eyes again sliding over to the wihht. The candle wavered in his hand.

"No," said Nio, stepping closer. "Is Severan near?" He spoke quickly, for he could see suspicion surfacing in Ablendan's eyes. "I'd like to introduce my friend to him, as they both shared the distinction of solving the yearly riddle Eald Gelaeran set for the students. In my year it was never solved."

"Mine either," returned the other. His face cleared and he grinned. "We always thought old Gelaeran posed riddles without solutions. Ours was that old chestnut—can there be shadow if there's no light?"

"Which has never been answered to anyone's satisfaction. The riddle during my year was supposedly first asked by Staer Gemyndes himself. Where did the men of Harlech come from, and why is it that the ghosts in that land never rest in the earth?"

"I've heard that asked, but not in the stone tower. Hmm—yes, where was it? Was it during the—"

"Is Severan here?" asked Nio again.

"Oh—yes, of course. He's down in the mosaic chamber, trying to find some—something he lost. I'm off to the tower library. I expect you can find your own way."

"Yes, I can," said Nio.

The long hall was dark, despite the windows lining the west wall. Nio could see the moon, a sliver of silver ghosting through the sky. The wihht stirred behind him. Nio muttered a word—light—were light and heat and color always going to be so necessary? Surely the cold space between the stars was lovelier and more interesting than the stars themselves. But for now he still needed light to see with. He spoke the word again and fire arced through the hall, separating into tongues of flame that hung in the air like a line of torches.

"Don't tread on the blue tiles," he said to the wihht.

They stepped through the door at the far end of the hall. Unbidden, the wihht paused and seemed to disappear into the darkness. Light shone deep within the stairwell leading down into the chamber below. Nio let his mind feather out into the stillness. There. He recoiled and then drifted back, testing delicately.

"Severan," he said.

No one answered. He could sense the wihht near him, but only as a hunger, a void that sought to be filled. The silence continued unbroken, but there was a tautness to it that spoke of awareness. The stairwell spiraled around him as he descended the stone steps down toward the light. An oil lamp burned in the middle of the chamber floor.

"Severan."

Nio paused on the last step. In the ceiling above, the huge mosaic shifted with strange colors and shapes that suggested forgotten things teetering on the edge of remembrance. Dreams and nightmares fading at the moment of waking. Words lost on the tips of tongues. The touch of tattered silk draped on dead hands. He could taste the fifth name of darkness in his mouth. The lamplight wavered.

"There's so much memory in this place," said Severan's voice from somewhere in the room. He spoke so quietly that Nio had to strain to hear.

"Farmers, lords, ladies, kings, merchants, craftsmen. They came here for hundreds and hundreds of years—from each duchy of Tormay. Even the men of Harlech."

"And the wizards," said Nio.

"And the wizards. All knowledge was esteemed, whether it was the humble art of the potter shaping clay, the machinations of the king's mind unraveling the fortunes of land and people, or the old languages devolving backward into increasing rarity and power as they approached the language of creation itself."

High above, the mosaic swirled in response to the old man's voice. The tiny stones rearranged themselves around each other and then settled, waiting patiently for whatever might be said next.

"One of the oldest strictures of learning is that all knowledge, no matter how humble, is part of the same whole. Everything learned is another strand to be woven into the tapestry portraying the final truth. Not *the* final truth, mind you, but a depiction. Mortal eye has yet to see it, though surely there's a room somewhere in the house of dreams where the complete tapestry hangs. And past that room, perhaps there are other rooms in which hang other tapestries? But those aren't for us."

"And what of the darkness?" said Nio. He spoke as softly as he could, as if loud words would shatter the quiet into something that could never be mended.

"What of it?"

"Isn't knowledge of the darkness part of that same whole?"

"I don't know," said the other. His voice sounded tired. "Though I'm certain the things of light can be inferred by the darkness, for the shape of shadow only exists out of opposition to the light."

"Not so. The darkness can create. Perhaps, one day, we'll understand that light is only the shadow cast by darkness."

There was a long pause at that point. The lamplight dimmed and the colors of the mosaic dulled into muteness. Then, Severan spoke again.

"I was afraid you'd say something like that."

Now.

The wihht blurred past Nio. It was utterly silent. Part of him was shocked by the speed of the thing. It has grown, he thought. Grown into something I do not understand. But I can control it. I possess the fifth name of darkness.

"*Beorht scir!*"

Severan's voice rang out. Instantly, the chamber blazed with radiance. The mosaic flared white-hot. The light was savage, incomprehensible in its totality. Nio staggered back against the steps, his hands flung to his face, but seared behind his eyelids was the huge red blot of the mosaic like some gigantic sun. Under its merciless light stood the stark, dark form of the wihht stunned into momentary stone. For a second Nio could not think—the light had pushed everything else from his mind—and then he found a word on his tongue, but it was too late. Someone brushed by him. Footsteps clattered up the stairs.

"*Dimnes!*"

The light faded down into shadow. The mosaic darkened and he could see again. The wihht snarled in fury. It rushed past him and up the stairwell. He turned to follow. He was tired. There was no longer any chance for the wihht to catch Severan, not in the labyrinthine sprawl of the ruins. The university was endless. The halls stretched farther than the memory of any man alive.

He reached the door to see the blue dogs rise up out of the warded tiles around the wihht. Jaws gaped and teeth gleamed in the moonlight. The beasts lunged. But instead of torn limbs—how would one tear darkness and water?—the dogs passed harmlessly through the creature, as if the flesh they sought had become only vapor. The form of the wihht wavered in their passing; arms, legs, and torso eddied into a confusion of lines that no longer had much resemblance to a human shape. The dogs skidded on the tiles, scrabbling to gain purchase to turn and lunge again.

Three times the beasts passed through the wihht, jaws snapping futilely, until they learned from their disappointment and contented themselves with circling it, fur bristling across their hackles. It was an odd sight, for as the dogs and the wihht moved further away, they became insubstantial in the pale moonlight streaming through the windows. They looked like a swirl of shadows tinged with blue and flecked at intervals with flashes of white fangs and glaring eyes.

They disappeared into the gloom at the far end of the hall. After several minutes, the dogs came back. The beast in front sighted Nio standing at the door. Its ears pricked up and all the dogs quickened their pace as if their leader had silently communicated to them the prospect of a new quarry. But they had no chance to try their teeth, for they vanished, one by one, like candle flames flickering out. Where each dog had been, a blue vapor drifted down into the tiles below. The room stretched empty before Nio. When he came to the entrance hall, he found the wihht waiting.

"Come," he said.

Outside the university, the city still thronged with people. Never before had Nio seen it so. Mioja Square swayed with movement, as if the sea had overthrown the shore and now flowed through every alley and street. These were not people and barrow carts and the pitched tents of the fair. No—rather, this was a strange tide, the peaks of waves made of sloping canvas angling down into troughs swirling with swaths of heads—white eyes and white teeth gleaming in the lamplight like foam. There—that was no fat, bearded merchant draped in brown velvet, but rather a whiskered seal diving in search of fish. This was no jeweled lady with her gauzy garments but some strange jellyfish glistening with watery colors and tentacles floating around her like a silken shawl.

The voices of the people no longer made sense to him. Words were only formless noises that lapped against each other. He blinked and tried to focus his attention but he still only heard a liquid babble of confusion. He was tired, he knew that, but perhaps he was even more tired than he thought.

And who is to say that this is not how language will end some day? A passage from a book drifted through his mind. *One language marked the beginning, before things began. One language did Anue speak from the house of dreams. From this one language did all languages descend. Do not listen to the fools who say that all things seen descended in this manner. Things seen are only the form of truth, but the one language is truth itself.*

But for how long could languages evolve and further evolve until they lost all meaning? That was the curse of the wizards and scholars, and it only increased with each succeeding generation. As time passed, it became more difficult to discover words from the ancient languages and near impossible to find even a single syllable from the oldest language of all. Perhaps this meaningless wash around him, this inarticulate murmur of the sea that seemed to eddy from the mouths of the crowd around him was the fate of language?

Sharp in the air, he breathed the odor of brine and kelp and all the wet, hidden things of the sea. The scent startled him and the face of the girl floated up through his thoughts—the farmer's daughter. Her name was lost to his memory, but the fifth name of darkness turned within his mind, and that one word was more valuable than all the names and all the words of a dozen lost languages. Her name did not matter anymore. The wihht walked behind him. It did not make a single sound and, for a while, Nio forgot its existence.

The instant the manor doors shut behind them, there was only silence. He could no longer smell the sea. The wihht did not wait for his command but turned and shambled away down the hall, to the kitchen beyond and, past that, to the cellar below. How odd. Not a word about its hunger. Not even a protest about the failed opportunity with Severan.

Nio paused for a moment. Absentmindedly, he commanded the sconces on the wall to light and they flickered into soft glows. I could use a bite myself, he thought. Half a loaf of stale bread sat on the kitchen table. He knew there were onions in the wicker basket in the corner, but the thought of food vanished as quickly as it had arrived. The door to the cellar was open. He tiptoed silently down the steps. Halfway down, he stopped.

The cellar was as dark as usual. Oddly enough, despite the lack of light, he could see quite well. Below, in the center of the floor, was the wihht. The creature was crouched by the drain hole with its head bent down. As Nio stood in silence, there came to his ears a faint sound—a muttering noise of strange words. It was a whisper, hissed in some unknown tongue. There was a tone of supplication in the sound, as if the wihht begged some favor of the darkness within the drain hole. The whisper paused, and Nio found himself straining to listen for an answer to the wihht, but there was nothing to hear except the beating of his own heart. After a moment, the creature whispered again, but the supplication was gone from its voice. Horror fell over Nio and he turned, blundering up the stairs and not caring if the wihht heard the clatter of his sudden retreat.

He fled, not thinking of anything except the dread choking his mind. The house was no longer familiar to him. Passages led in strange directions, angling back upon themselves so that he found himself stumbling through rooms he had just left. Staircases tilted underneath him, and more than once he found himself running down rather than up. He could not find the front door.

I'll unmake this place, he thought savagely. I know the fifth name of darkness. Unmake it into shadow, these stones and wood and walls, until there is nothing here except darkness. There will not be even a memory of this place. I'll walk away. Unmake the wihht. I'll walk away from it all. North. Maybe she's still alive.

He tried to smile. His face was a stiff mask of fear with bared teeth and wide eyes. The fifth name of darkness teetered on the edge of his thoughts. But his tongue would not remember the name. He clamped his mouth shut on the scream threatening to break forth instead, lurched down a hall, and pushed through a door.

The library. This place was familiar. The shelves rose around him in confirmation of all he had studied, all he had learned, all he knew and was. The precious books bought, stolen, begged, traded, and hunted down in every corner of Tormay. The histories written by his predecessors, anthologies of lore and suspect tales, dissertations on arcane subjects and even stranger minutiae, collections of words of power, of dubious power, of no power at all—the works of men and women long dead, fallen to the shadow or safely sleeping within the house of dreams. All of this was his strength.

His breathing slowed.

Nio found himself standing in the alcove, staring at the painting of Scuadimnes, the treacherous archivist of the university. The old wizard's eyes stared back at him.

"Why did you do it?" Nio said aloud.

Why did you?

"It was never a question of why. There was no single moment. It was a progression of events. The little things. They happened."

Ahh. The little things.

"You think a man wakes up one morning and turns his mind to the Dark?"

No. But he wakes up one morning and knows.

"And how did you know?"

The painting smiled.

You would not know the words.

And at that—at that thought of 'word'—the fifth name of darkness sprang back into Nio's mind, as complete as eyes closed in the dead of night.

"I have it!" he said triumphantly.

The painting said nothing but only nodded.

Behind him, a door opened. Nio turned. The wihht stood there. It spoke in a voice that sounded like his own.

"One wizard will do just as well as another."

"I made you," said Nio coldly, unafraid with the name trembling and jittering and shuddering in his mind as if it were impatient for its own articulation. "I can unmake you."

"No." And the creature reached for him with one, impossibly long arm.

The man quickly stepped back and spoke the fifth name of darkness. He spoke it with relief, glad to have the weight of it taken from him, fiercely glad to see the wihht unmade. But the wihht continued to reach for him, still made, still composed of too solid flesh. Its hand reached him and took him by the throat. Nio spoke the name one more time. Shouted it desperately.

"You will be unmade! This is the fifth name of darkness!"

The wihht smiled and spoke, its grip tightening.

"Yes, but my name is older still."

CHAPTER SIXTY-TWO
THE HAWK AND THE OLD MEN

Severan hurried along. A glimmer of light floated above his shoulder, illuminating the corridor. Dust rose in the wake of his passing. As he neared a door, a ward spelled into the handle became aware of him, the invisible strands weaving themselves into defensive readiness. Absentmindedly, he negated the spell without even thinking of the fire that would have met an unwary intruder.

"*Foro.*"

Be still.

Be still. I have no quarrel with this place or the dreams of your long-dead masters. Be still.

He opened the door and passed through. Stairs rose before him, fashioned of once-elegant marble but now so riven by time that each step was a hazard. His attendant light threw his shadow hard against the wall. After some time, he reached what looked like the top of the stairs. If so, it was a sorry destination, for the last stair met a wall of stone that rose up until it passed into shadow and out of sight. The wall was scorched black with the marks of ancient fire, as if many men had sought to pass that way, trying their wizardry and skill upon the façade, and had been turned back by the implacable stone.

Severan passed a hand across his brow and tried to still the thoughts in his mind. His hand shook. He was getting old.

Damn the boy. The rascal was gone again. The city was not safe for him. A whole day and half the night gone and no sign of Jute except for a bed unslept in and the fading awareness of his presence in the ruins.

It's my fault, Severan thought miserably. Over the last week, there had been so much promise in discovering the whereabouts of the *Gerecednes*. The discovery of that one single book might prove—it *would* prove—the key to unlocking the past and the designs of the Dark. They were so close. The thought was intoxicating.

But he had neglected the boy. And the mosaic deep below the ruins revealed only a murky shadow when the name of Jute was uttered. He was hidden.

And now Nio had shown his hand beyond doubt.

Severan carefully cleared these troubling thoughts from his mind. Distractions could prove fatal when unlocking the ward before him. He placed his hands against the stone wall and concentrated on a single name.

Scuadimnes.

He ignored the distaste welling up within him at the thought of that name. The wizard who had caused the destruction of the university and the death of so many of his peers was despised by everyone who studied history. His name was anathema.

But here it was the key to a door and so must be uttered with concentrated thought.

He shaped the word in his mind. Scuadimnes.

Silently, the wall dissolved. The marble stairs mounted up, and Severan had a sensation of a yawning gulf on either side that fell away into darkness and the dust of old bones lying an impossible distance below, further than the foundations of the university.

He hurried up the steps and passed through another door. Three faces glanced up at him. Gerade, Ablendan, and old Adlig, all hunched over their books and manuscripts. The room was a small rotunda lined with shelves and interspersed with windows looking down from a great height upon the university ruins sprawling below.

"You don't seem to fancy our attendant ward, Severan," said Gerade. His nose twitched in amusement.

"What's that?" said Severan sharply.

"The face on you. It's as if you'd been sucking lemons."

"I don't like saying his name. He's the evilest man in all the known history of Tormay, and yet we're forced to parrot his damned name every time we want to get into this chamber."

"None of us are delighted at the thought of him," said Adlig mildly. "But none of these books open outside of this room. If you've another way to do it, let's hear. If I had my druthers, his memory'd perish from the earth."

"I disagree," said Severan. "Despite who he was. Knowledge of the past is the best defense we have."

"Which is why we must find the *Gerecednes*. Imagine what's contained in that book." Ablendan stuck his head out from an alcove in the shelves. "I think we're getting closer, Severan. This evening we found three different references to the book indicating that the university possessed a copy during the time of Scuadimnes. Perhaps the only copy in existence. We have to locate that blasted book—it must be our only objective. Crystal orbs, enchanted keys, and the lost crown of Dol Cynehad? Rubbish. The book must be all."

"In earlier days, I would've been happy to agree with you, Ablendan," said Severan. He sighed. "It was hope of the book that drew me originally to Hearne and these ruins, though I'd some initial interest in that strange box Nio was always harping on. But after the weeks went by—perhaps it was the blasted dust in this place that clouded my mind—I no longer thought about the box, even after Nio found it. And then, of course, it proved an unsolvable riddle and couldn't be opened. But now, as you all know, the box has disappeared. . ."

"So what? Some petty thief has burgled Nio's house, the box is gone, he sits glooming and twiddling his thumbs, and we have work to do. Let's find the *Gerecednes*! Let's find that book. Nothing else matters."

"Oh, but there is something else that matters," said Severan. "There is. Something's come up. There are two things of much greater import for now."

He fell silent, and a strange dread gripped the other men. The room grew stuffy and Gerade opened one of the windows. A breeze blew in from the night and, reluctantly, Severan began to speak.

"When the box was stolen from Nio's house, one of the thieves, a young boy, was left for dead by his fellows. It was a poor trade in Nio's mind—losing the box and gaining a worthless boy. He sought my skill to rouse the lad into consciousness and bade me keep silent on the affair, even from the rest of you, out of some strange embarrassment on his part. I agreed, not thinking much of it. I brought the boy to his senses and both Nio and I questioned him. His name was Jute. He knew nothing of the gravity of what he had done, or whose house he had burgled. However, the damage was done. It was then that I first saw another side of Nio, an odd malignancy that looked out of his eyes when I observed him covertly. He was harsh with the boy and would've killed him, I think, had I not been there."

"Nio doesn't have the best manners and can be abrupt, but killing a lad just for some tomfool thievery? I find that hard to believe."

"Believe it," returned Severan. "For though that's troubling enough, he's done something else. Something of grave evil. He's fashioned a wihht from darkness to be his servant."

"How can you know this?" burst out Gerade. "You make a dreadful charge against his name."

"I know because I just encountered the wihht."

"The other man!" said Ablendan. His jaw dropped. "I chatted with Nio. He had an old friend with him, a fellow wizard from his days at the stone tower. That was a wihht?"

"The same," said Severan. He smiled sourly. "You're lucky they came for me and not you, Ablendan. The wihht was hungry."

Out past the windows, the stars were blotted out, one by one, as ragged wisps of clouds scudded across the sky. The breeze blowing through the room plucked at loose pages.

"This is dark news," said Gerade. "If anyone else had said this, I wouldn't have believed it. But I've known you for years, old friend, and I've never heard you speak anything but truth. A wihht made of darkness. How can this be? In all of Tormay, no one possesses the power for such a fashioning. Where did he gain this evil knowledge?"

"It's an unhappy irony that we're in this room, Severan," said Adlig. "It was Scuadimnes, who took corpses—soldiers, students, and cityfolk alike—and fashioned them into wihhts. That's what they were, weren't they? They destroyed this university."

"The thought occurred to me as I stood on the stairs," said Severan. "It made it doubly hard for me to pronounce his name. His memory has found an acolyte in our Nio. But this isn't all I have to tell. I fear that the wihht has been creeping about these ruins to hunt for the boy Jute."

"The boy? The thief? What do you mean?"

The others stared at him.

"I erred," said Severan. He shook his head unhappily. "I hid Jute here, thinking that he might be safe from Nio in the confusion of old enchantments about this place. But the boy has disappeared."

"Good riddance," snorted Gerade.

The breeze idling through the room kicked up into a wind. Books blew open. The windows rattled.

"Fools."

The word rustled in the air. There was a dusty, creaking sound to it, as if the voice was unused to speaking. On the sill of the open window perched a hawk. Its feathers were as black as night, but its eyes were blacker still, and they gazed at the old men in the room with contempt.

"A talking hawk," marveled Gerade, but the bird silenced him with one sharp click of its beak. Its talons grated on the sill and scarred the stone.

"Did you think Scuadimnes would leave a book such as the *Gerecednes* in this city? No. If it was here to find, he would have found it. You hunt a pearl that is not here, while a pearl of even greater price has been in your presence all the while. Long ago, the wizards were our allies and could be counted on to do their part. But now you are a foolish lot content to muddle about in your books and your stone tower, heedless of what goes on in the world outside your dusty learning."

The old men gaped at the hawk.

"Our allies?" said Severan. "What do you mean? What—who are you, master hawk?"

"The wizards were once the allies of the anbeorun and aided them in their fight against the Dark. Staer Gemyndes was the greatest of them all. They wandered the world as we did, guarding it against the Dark. But no longer is this true, and I fly alone."

"Pardon me," said Gerade hesitantly. "But are you—are you the Wind?"

"Only his shadow, nothing more. Don't you understand what was in that box? It hid the knife that killed the Wind. Due to curiosity, foolishness—fate, perhaps?—the boy Jute opened the box and cut his finger on the knife. Through some mystery, the Wind is now waking in him. He is becoming the Wind. But he does not understand yet. For now, he's more like a breeze." The hawk's eyes gleamed in sudden humor that vanished as soon as it appeared. "But I cannot find him. He's hidden away in the stone of this cursed city, hidden from my eyes. Though it galls me to say so, I need your help. You must find him."

"Find him, my lord?" said Adlig. "But—"

"Find him. He's of more worth than any of the hidden magic in your ruins. He's worth more than all the knowledge in the book of *the Gerecednes* itself. Find him before it's too late. I must hunt the skies, for the dreams of the Dark creep into Tormay and there's no one to stem that coming tide. We were once allies, your forebears and my dead lord. I lay this charge upon you, even if it means your deaths. Find him, for the Dark draws near."

The hawk spread its wings and was gone. The breeze died and the room was silent. After what seemed like a long time, Severan cleared his throat.

"Er," he said, but he did not get any farther than that.

"Did my ears just deceive me," said Gerade slowly, "or did that thing—that hawk—just say that the boy—this Jute—is the anbeorun of the wind?"

"Um," said Severan again. "I think so. Yes."

"And was that the other paltry, insignificant bit of news that you were about to tell us?"

"Yes. I was beginning to have my suspicions."

Gerade's fist crashed down on a desk. "Shadows above and below, Severan. That makes Nio's wihht seem like a rose in a flower garden!"

"It was only a suspicion until recently. Several days ago, the boy fell from the courtyard tower and the wind caught him. That should've been enough right there, but I just couldn't believe my own logic. I concluded it was strange—"

"As strange as a giant sitting at your breakfast table," fumed Ablendan, "eating your children with the morning marmalade."

"—but then it made horrible sense this morning, for I realized that ever since he disappeared, sometime last night, the wind in the ruins has vanished. Surely you must have noticed. For the past several days the boy's been here, the ruins have been filled with breezes and winds eddying around every corner and gusting in rooms with no windows. But now that he's gone, they've gone as well. Don't you see? They came because of him."

"The only thing I noticed," said old Adlig, "is that my rheumatism has been acting up more'n usual."

"Well," said Gerade grimly, "we had better find him. And one of us should ride straightaway for the Stone Tower. They should be told what the hawk said, for who knows what'll come crawling out of the darkness now? Who knows what's already come? Blast it all, Severan! A new anbeorun. Has there ever been such a thing? It's unthinkable.

271

He'll be like—like a gawky duckling—won't he?—and there's no telling what'll happen. Anyone could kidnap him and have in their control a terrible, unpredictable power."

They elected Ablendan to ride out that night for the Stone Tower in Thule. He was the youngest of the four men and more suited to several days on horseback.

"Try the Old Crow," said Gerade. "They have decent horses."

For once, Ablendan did not joke, but made his farewells with a solemn face. The Old Crow tavern was close to the university. Ablendan had the mixed fortune of securing one of the best horses the tavern had for rent. He was fortunate in that the horse was the fastest in the stable. He was unfortunate in that the horse had an iron jaw and a sharp, bony back and Ablendan was unused to riding great distances. He did not consider any of these things, as he was not a horseman. Even though he was not an especially talented scholar, he was a scholar and that was all he was. The stableman, however, considered all of those things while appraising Ablendan's stout form and soft hands with a contemptuous eye. He did not appreciate being dragged from his ale at such a late hour.

Ablendan rode away, clinging to the horse's back and wondering miserably whether it would rain much on the way north and if it were possible to make the journey in less than four days. He clattered through the sleeping streets of the city. A yawning guard swung open the small night gate by the tower for him. He dug his heels in, and the horse set off with a gallop.

As for the others, Severan described Jute to them. They prowled the university ruins and hunted through the night, through the streets and alleys of the sleeping city. And though they searched into the gray hours of the early morning, they found no sign of the boy.

CHAPTER SIXTY-THREE
A HORSE RUNS AWAY

That morning, a curious thing happened. A string of horses had been taken out from the regent's stable for their customary gallop on the meadow north of the castle. The meadow was reached by a path that descended from the castle through a series of switchbacks to a small gate in the city wall. It was customary for the horses to be taken there for a gallop, after which they were walked down to the dunes to cool their legs in the surf.

It was early and the stable lads on the horses were still mostly asleep, heads slumped and bobbing, as the string wended its way down the switchback. Once they came to the meadow, they all awoke, for then it was time to work, and the trainer was a grumpy old fellow who was fonder of using his whip on the boys than on the horses. The regent had ridden down as well, and he sat his horse in the morning sunlight. Several guests were in his company, including the dukes of Mizra and Dolan, as well as the prince of Harth.

"A fine sight, my lord Botrell," said the prince of Harth. "You've horses that beggar all other stables." He himself sat upon a tall sand-colored stallion that seemed to understand its master's words, for its lips curled in ill-concealed contempt. "I wager, though, my own beauty would press them hard."

"Only the best," said the regent. "I buy only the best. I've a good eye for horseflesh, mind you. It runs in the family. My father had a genius for bloodlines. Your steed, my dear prince, is doubtlessly fast, but I've bred some real runners."

"Yes, yes," grumbled the duke of Dolan, but no one heard him. He gnawed his lip in jealousy, for the regent's horses were impressive. He wished he were home in the hills of the Mearh Dun, putting his own stable through their paces.

"Perhaps we should have a match later," said the regent. "What say you, my lords?"

"Your words gladden me," said the prince of Harth.

"I say, Gifernes," said the regent, looking down, "that hound of yours isn't about to trot off and take a bite out of a leg, is he? He's looking rather hungrily at my horses. If he eats one, I shall have to declare war on you."

The duke of Mizra laughed. He was on foot and accompanied by one of his hunting hounds. The dog stood pressed against his knee. There was no denying the regent's words. The creature was staring with undisguised interest at the horses.

"Have no fear, my lord," he said. "You could leave Holdfast here at a baby's crib without worry. He's well trained and will not attack or eat without my word. Your horses are safe."

"I'll take your word for it, but that's a huge brute you have there."

A sharp command came from the trainer and the string broke into a trot heading away from the city wall and across the meadow. Sunlight flashed on their long, slender legs and the ripple of muscle shifting under their skin. The regent smiled.

It was then that it happened. Halfway down the line, a horse began to buck. Startled, the horses nearby shied away until the line was in a shambles. The culprit, a bony-looking two-year-old with an ugly brown coat, plunged and kicked and spun about. The unfortunate lad on top sailed through the air to land on the turf. The trainer let fly an impressive series of oaths and urged his gray forward, but it was too late. The ugly brown broke into a gallop and headed for the distant stand of trees at the end of the meadow.

"That," said the prince of Harth in wonder, "is a fast horse. Exceedingly fast."

"He is, isn't he," said the regent. His voice trailed off, as he wasn't sure whether to be proud or not.

"He's getting away," said the duke of Dolan with gloomy satisfaction.

"He is, isn't he!" howled the regent. "Get him! Catch him, you fool!"

But even though the old trainer whipped and belabored his own horse, there was no doubt of the outcome. With every passing second, the brown galloped faster and faster until he was only a streak of limbs and flying mane skimming across the meadow. In a moment, he would be gone. Faintly, the watching party heard the blurred tattoo of his hooves. The unseated stable lad staggered to his feet and stared after his mount, mouth gaping.

"I fear you have lost a horse, and not just any horse either," said the prince. "Alack and alas. Such a horse only appears once in a lifetime, my dear Botrell, and I would have gladly given a fortune to have that steed for my own. But with such speed comes great heart and will, and if neither choose freely to bend to servitude—nay, even friendship with a kindly master—then there's no hope in keeping the animal. Ah—there—he's gone."

The regent ground his teeth at these words and did not trust himself to speak.

"If you would allow me, my lord," said the duke of Mizra. "I might have a solution."

"What's that?"

"I would send my dog after your horse to bring him back."

"Don't be ridiculous. I don't raise sheep in my stables."

"Sheep and horses can be turned the same, if they hear enough growling and see bared teeth."

"But I don't want that beast of yours biting my horse," said the regent plaintively. "Why, if he caught him—and how could that bow-legged thing catch a horse?—he'd probably take a great chunk out of him or worse."

"Holdfast will not touch a hair on him," said the duke of Mizra. He bent and whispered into the dog's ear and, when he was done, the dog ran off across the meadow toward where the horse had gone, toward the north.

"He's fast," said the duke of Dolan. "I'll give you that, but he's nowhere near the speed of his quarry."

"Ah, but Holdfast can run all day and all night without tiring, and what horse have you known to possess such endurance? He'll track him down, he will, and then herd him back as gently as a sheepdog tending a lamb."

"Min the Morn could've run a month of Mondays and never broken sweat, so the stories say." But the duke of Dolan said this under his breath and no one heard him except, perhaps, the prince of Harth, who smiled slightly at the older man.

"Perhaps," said the prince, "our race should be deferred until the flower of your stable is brought back to hand? I would not want to have you at a disadvantage, my lord."

"Nonsense," sputtered Botrell. "This afternoon. Back here on the meadow!"

And with that, he spurred his horse away.

CHAPTER SIXTY-FOUR
LOOKING FOR CHALLENGERS

Ronan woke up that next morning frowning and smiling at the same time. He was clear with the Silentman. He had not been reinstated as the Knife of the Guild, true, and there was still the matter of payment, but that was nothing to worry about. The Silentman's word was as good as the gold itself. It would only be a matter of time, as soon as the—the creature came to collect the boy.

He shuddered slightly at the thought. The little girl stared at him from across the room, her face reproachful in the thinning shadows of the morning. He sighed, and then she was gone. The shutters swung out to let in the sunlight. There was nothing in the room except for its few bare sticks of furniture. He poured water into a bowl and washed his face. Perhaps it was the water trickling through his fingers, or perhaps it was the sea breeze wandering in through the window, but he smiled.

Tonight was the night of the regent's ball.

Liss Galnes.

It was the night to finish out the bargain she had made with him.

But then he frowned again. Clothing. He didn't have clothes suitable for a regent's ball. Smuggling her into the castle would be one thing, but keeping her safe once inside, safe and mingling with the silkened and bejeweled nobility of Tormay—that would be a different matter. His threadbare clothes would have them as conspicuous as an ogre in a tavern.

Perhaps the Silentman would pay him his money now? No. He'd get the gold sure enough, but not until the completion of the Guild's contract. Not until the creature returned. No use trying to budge the Silentman.

Maybe a generous friend?

He didn't have any friends.

That was the trouble with holding the office of the Knife. Going about leaning on people—quite hard, usually—and killing others every once in a while did not encourage friendships. The Guild was nothing more than a pack of wild dogs, and there was no love lost between the pack and the brute that kept them in line. Not much to show for thirteen years. All he had was scars and a head full of memories.

And then he smiled again, for he remembered it was Saturday.

Ronan slung his knife around his neck, dropping it down his back and under his shirt, and then he was out the door into the white glimmering dazzle of the morning sunshine. It was Saturday and there was gold to be made.

The city was coming alive. It seemed as if there was not room enough for the vast throng in the streets. To Ronan's eye, it looked as if the buildings leaned back from the cobbled thoroughfares to provide more space, more air, more light. Creaking cart wheels, drovers shouting to their oxen, the staccato of hooves striking stone. The cry of vendors rose above the rumble of the city, hoarse from the days gone by and sounding like the greedy voices of seagulls. Awnings flapped in the breeze. He smelled the salt of the sea on the air, distant and sharp above all the other reeks of sweat and dung and spice and cheap perfumes. Three ragged children brushed by him and disappeared into the crowd. He automatically checked his pockets. He bought a loaf of bread at the bakery on the corner. The baker's daughter cut a wedge of cheese for him as well—cut from the family's own stock and not for sale. She smiled at him as she always did, but he did not see her.

The Queen's Head tavern was on the north boundary of the Fishgate neighborhood, close to the streets where the merchants kept their warehouses and counting houses. The tavern drew clientele from around the city. Fishermen drank their ale there. Merchants huddled in meetings, arguing prices and interest and the relative merits of shipping by sea versus an overland caravan. The young sons of the nobility drank there, earnest in their slumming and loud in their bravado, for the heights of Highneck Rise were only a quick canter away—down through cool, tree-lined avenues and stately mansions until the city below came rising up in all of its hard stone and heat. The Guild drank at the tavern as well, for there were deals to be cut with the merchants, foolish lords to be swindled, and drunken fishermen to be sneered at. Besides, the brewer at the Queen's Head was a master with ale and he kept one of the finest wine cellars in the city.

Saturdays, however, were special. That was the day when the Queen's Head did its real business. Behind the tavern, hemmed in by the walls of a stable and two warehouses, was a large, cobbled yard. In the center of the yard stood a raised platform, square and built of wood. The planks were of oak. They were of different ages—some old and bleached by sunlight, some green hewn and freshly replaced. Stains marked them and sand was ground into their grain. And every Saturday, sweat and blood were spilled on that wood, for Saturdays were fighting days. Gold to be wagered and won. Challenges made—soberly, drunkenly, guessing the odds of one man against another. Reputations were made and lost.

It was to the Queen's Head that Ronan had first come thirteen years ago, newly arrived in Hearne without name or prospects. Anyone would fight a skinny boy with an innocent smile. He had made a lot of money back then. Now, though, no one would fight the Knife. Except he was the Knife no longer.

He heard the roar from a street away. The sound was punctuated by the bright, ringing tones of iron clashing against iron. They had started early enough. There was nothing like a good fight in the morning to get your blood going. He grinned, and there was more in that grin akin to the anticipatory snarl of a sandcat as it leapt for a kill rather than the smile of a man.

The sign hanging over the door bore a faded painting of a severed head. Further down the way, between the warehouses flanking the street's end, the stone wall of the wharf was visible, with one pier stretching away on the hard glitter of the sea. Ronan pushed through the door into the gloom of the common room. It was empty except for a potboy scrubbing skewers in the ashes of the fireplace. On Saturdays, no one bothered drinking indoors at the Queen's Head.

The passage at the back led to another door that opened up into the yard and a sudden blaze of sound and sunlight and the smell of sweat. A steep ring of steps circled the perimeter of the yard so that the platform in the center stood comfortably below the eyes of the entire audience. Shouts of derision and cheers rang off the walls. Ronan edged along the top step until he stood in the shadow of the east wall.

It wasn't yet noon, but the yard was already packed. He had never seen it so. Perhaps it was because of the Autumn Fair. Casually, he glanced around the crowd. Here and there were faces he knew. As of yet, though, no one seemed to have taken notice of his entrance. Not that it mattered, but some habits would be forever inescapable.

He nudged the man next to him.

"First fight of the morning?"

"Nay, friend," said the other without taking his eyes from the platform. "Third, and that fool of a Thuleman is about to be taken by the Guardsman. But more fool I to put coin on him."

"Muscle and broad shoulders don't always mean a win," said Ronan.

Light flashed on sword blades as the two men on the platform flung themselves at each other in a flurry of blows. Rather, it was the Thuleman who flung himself forward, using his sword as if he thought it a club with which to bludgeon the other into defeat. He was a good head taller than his opponent, towering over him with a hand's reach to boot and a brawny build that undoubtedly came from hard years of shifting the weights and measures of life. And yet, it was the Thuleman who dripped with sweat that streaked his arms red where the other's blade had already found him. His opponent was only a lad, certainly tall enough, but looking small in the shadow of the giant Thuleman.

Ronan blinked. He'd seen that face before. Of course. Arodilac Bridd. None of the clumsy coltishness was on exhibit now. None of the awkwardness that knocked over cups and saucers.

"I'm afraid the boy's just toying with your Thulish fool," he said.

"Don't I know it," groaned his neighbor. "I thought him just a gangly lad when he took the fight."

"Lad he might be, but he's the nephew of the regent and learned his swordplay under the hand of Owain Gawinn, the Lord Captain of the Guard. Your money's lost."

With a bellow, the Thuleman leapt forward. His sword swung around in a gleaming arc. The other blade drifted up and almost contemptuously deflected the arc from its deadly path. It was the sort of defense Ronan had learned as a child—rote, unthinking skill—easily predicted and easily done. But what was not so easily predicted was the huge fist barreling in from the other side. The Thuleman was not such a fool. Arodilac's eyes widened with the impact and the lad staggered back the length of the platform, arms threshing to keep his balance. The sword clattered free on the wood. A joyous shout went up from the crowd. The sea of faces jammed up around the platform's edge surged. Now this was what they liked. Ronan's neighbor hollered in delight.

"He's got him yet!"

Ronan shook his head. It had been an unforgivable lapse on the lad's part, but Owain Gawinn taught more than swordplay to his soldiers.

"How'd you like that, you whippersnapper!" yelled the giant Thuleman, grinning all over his sunburnt face. He stalked forward, planting one foot on the other's sword. Arodilac did not bother answering, but only smiled. The blade whistled down at him, but he had already launched himself forward, under the sweep of the blade and legs scissoring around the giant's knees. The man toppled over backwards, only to spring upright with an oath. It was too late. Arodilac's sword was an efficient wall of steel that briskly beat him back. He was hemmed in, unable to do more than to feebly block some of the blows and retreat. And retreat he did, until there was no longer any wood underfoot and he fell off the platform's edge like a giant tree cut at the root by the woodman's axe.

Those beneath the Thuleman's fall shouted in surprise, but such was the press of people around them that they had nowhere for retreat and so were also felled by

Arodilac's last blow, crushed under weight of the Thuleman. The crowd howled with delight. Oddsmen worked their way through the press, consulting their slates and collecting or paying out the take. The Thuleman staggered to his feet and slunk off, hunching his shoulders against the blows and jeers that came his way. Cheering and yelling, a group of young nobles mobbed the platform and carried a blushing Arodilac off on their shoulders to the far corner of the yard. Serving girls pushed their way through the throng with trays of ale held high.

"Why, oh why?" moaned Ronan's neighbor. "And I promised the wife, I did. Oh, she has me now."

A bald man, pate shining in the sunlight, clambered up onto the platform. He pulled a slate from the front of his apron, consulted it and then motioned for quiet.

"All right then," he called. "We've got a Vigdis up next. Vigdis?"

The crowd near the platform parted and a man vaulted up onto the planking.

"Ah," said Ronan. He nudged his neighbor. "If you have a coin or two, put it on this fellow, regardless of who challenges."

The man looked at him suspiciously.

"What do you know?"

"It'd be a sure thing. There are only two men in Hearne his better with the sword."

"And what if one of 'em challenge him?" The man drank from his tankard and winked blearily at him. "What then, eh?—then I'd be out my gold, what's left of it. That's no sure thing in my mind."

"It's a certainty," said Ronan shortly. "One of the two is the Lord Captain of the Guard, and he'd never fight in a place as this."

"What about the other, hey? You said two, din'ja?"

"The other's myself."

As soon as the words were out of his mouth, he silently cursed himself for a fool. A drunken sot was no reason for irritation, even one breathing sour ale fumes into his face at such close quarters.

"Right then," called the innkeeper from down on the platform. "Who'll we have to challenge? Who'll we have? Choice of weapons to the challenger!"

The crowd shuffled their feet and glanced around, but no one spoke up. Even the group of nobles lounging on the steps in the far corner kept their silence. The man called Vigdis was too well known for his swordsmanship, among both the common folk and the nobility. Formerly a Guardsman and, therefore, schooled under the eye of Owain Gawinn and his sergeants, he had disgraced himself with the daughter of a particularly grouchy lord. He had drifted into the ranks of the Guild after being kicked out of the Guard. If there was to be another Knife after Ronan, this man would be the logical successor.

"Come on now," yelled Vigdis. "You lazy bunch of cowards! Whoever challenges—I'll cover his wager three to one!"

People grinned uneasily, but still no one responded. Ronan flexed his hands. He hadn't planned on challenging so early on in the day. Larger sums of money were wagered as the hours passed and the ale flowed more freely.

But then the decision was made for him.

"Hi you! Here's your fellow!"

It was his tipsy neighbor. The man was waving his hands over his head and pointing at Ronan. Ale sloshed out of his tankard onto Ronan's shoulder.

"He'll fight! He'll fight y'all!"

Faces turned. The innkeeper squinted up into the sunlight. Vigdis shaded his eyes with one hand. Then, somebody called out from the crowd.

"It's the Knife!"

Ronan sighed.

"All right, my loudmouthed friend," he said. "Put your coin on me."

The man beamed.

The crowd parted around him as he walked down the steps. He heard muttering in his wake. Faces stared at him—some merely curious and some malicious.

"The Knife. . . that's the Knife there."

"Who's this fellow, then?" he heard someone say.

"He's the Thieves Guild killer, he is. Got a history bloodier than all the dead kings of Hearne. Stole the crown right off the regent's head—honest. Wizard with a sword. Sooner hold up the tide then kill him dead."

"He ain't the bleedin' Knife no longer, that's what I heard."

A man spat loudly as Ronan passed, but he ignored him. The sun was just up over the peak of the warehouse standing on the east boundary of the yard. It was nearing noon. He jumped up onto the platform. From there, past the lower wall of the tavern, a stretch of sea was visible. It looked like a hammered sheet of silver, hot to the sight with light and shimmering blue as if it were a mirror of the sky.

"Well, Vigdis," he said. "Is that three to one still good?"

Vigdis grinned and then shrugged.

"Why not?"

The rules at the Queen's Head for fighting were simple. First man to be forced off the platform, or no longer able to lift his weapon, was the loser. No deliberately killing blows. Slightly blunted weapons were provided by the establishment. The innkeeper could stop the fighting at any time. Men were sometimes killed on the platform, though that was a rare occurrence. Everyone knew that Owain Gawinn kept an eye on such entertainment—his own Guardsmen frequently fought on the platform—and he would shut the tavern down fast enough if he deemed it slipping out of bounds.

"What'll it be?" intoned the innkeeper.

"Swords do for you?" said Ronan.

"Might as well."

"Swords!" bellowed the innkeeper. A small boy emerged from the crowd clutching a long wooden box. The innkeeper opened it to reveal two matched blades. They were scarred, nicked, and ugly. Ronan weighed one in his hand. He shrugged.

"It'll do," he said.

"One minute more for wagers!"

The crowd buzzed with excitement. The oddsmakers were mobbed with bettors. Ronan could see his one-time neighbor grinning at him from the top step and waving his tankard. On the other side of the yards, the young nobles were clustered around Arodilac, listening to him and eyeing Ronan.

"All right, then!" yelled the innkeeper. "You know the rules!"

He hopped off the platform and disappeared into the crowd.

The two men circled each other. Vigdis feinted at his shoulder and then lunged low. Ronan batted the attempt away and sighed.

"Did Gawinn teach you anything?"

Vigdis laughed. Pivoted and tested another approach.

"Not going to fall asleep up here, are you?" he said.

"I've often wondered exactly how good he is."

Another lunge, parry. Sunlight flashed on steel.

"Oh, he's good. He never stinted on teaching—drilled us like the terror he is—but he could take any of his Guards, dagger to our swords."

Their swords clashed, clattered, and fell apart.

"That good?"

"Aye. Told us he learned the craft as a lad from two masters. His father, the old captain before him."

The sun was overhead. Underfoot, their shadows sprang together and then whirled away, circling on the wood planking.

"Who was the other? Some graybeard sergeant?"

"No. Man named Cullan Farrow. Head of a horse-thieving clan. The regent buys his horses from that lot, he does. You heard of 'em?"

"A bit here and there. Best thieves in all Tormay."

"Wonder we've never had 'em in the Guild," said Vigdis. Sweat gleamed on his forehead. His blade swept up.

Absentmindedly, Ronan parried, his body sliding through the countless rhythms of the sword. Countless, lad—that's what his father had always said. All to be worked into your body's memory; you'll never cease learning them. The countless rhythms of the sword, just as there are countless rhythms to the way of the hawk on the air, the snake on the rock, and the deer on the plain. And then there's your mother, he'd sometimes say, smiling—you think learning swordplay's hard? Try learning the ways of a woman.

"Heard tell you might be back on the ups with the Guild."

"Where'd you hear that?"

A breeze blew across his face and, for a moment, the sweat stink of the crowd was gone and there was only the salt of the sea. He ducked a blow and watched his blade drift through the air, almost as if it were being wielded by another arm then his own. The edge touched Vigdis' shoulder and then drifted away. The crowd whooped and hollered in amusement.

Touch—you're dead. He heard his father's voice whisper in his mind.

"Dammit, Ronan!"

Vigdis scowled and brought his blade down in a reckless, whistling arc. A stupid blow, as it gave plenty of time for another to duck under and bury their blade in the attacker's ribs. Ronan merely blocked and winced as the shock of the blow rattled his arm.

"Are you even trying?"

"Sorry."

He blinked, shook his head, and then advanced on Vigdis. It was over in a matter of moments. The blade in his hand became a living, darting thing—a steel snake striking repeatedly, lancing past Vigdis' frantic guard. For every rhythm there is a counter rhythm. For man, there is woman. For the day, there is the night. For the sea, there is the land. For the light, there is the darkness, and with each pairing there is a constant ebb and flow, a tide that ceaselessly washes back and forth.

Only the end of time will see where the ebb lands. Perhaps the place is appointed, but who are we to know?

His father's words whispered in his mind.

With one last swing he drove Vigdis off the edge of the planking. He did not hear the mocking cheers of the crowd, for his eyes were blank, his ears dumb. Thirteen years spent silencing that voice, and here it was back again in precise intonation and word.

"Right, then," said the innkeeper. "You want to hold your place?"

Ronan nodded.

"Any challengers?" called the innkeeper. He stood with fists planted at his waist and surveyed the crowd. The faces around them blurred together into one mass in the sunshine. A murmur rose and grew into an angry roar.

"We ain't stupid!" yelled someone. "As if there's anyone could take the Knife!"

"Aye!"

"He ain't the Knife no more!"

"Who cares! He can still fight! Let's see you get up there if you're so brave!"

"Kick him off and let normal folks get back at it!"

"Any challengers?" bellowed the innkeeper.

The crowd fell silent, eyes glaring and shifting restlessly about. The innkeeper turned to Ronan and shrugged.

"I'll challenge!"

Ronan knew the voice immediately. He sighed.

"My lord Bridd," he said, bowing. The lad stood below the edge of the platform, face flushed red.

"I'll challenge," repeated the regent's nephew. He scrambled up and stood in front of Ronan. They were of the same height.

"You've fought already. Perhaps you should rest and—"

"I said, I'll challenge!" Arodilac spoke through clenched teeth.

"Anger and swordplay is a poor mix," said Ronan.

"Swords, innkeeper!"

"Swords!" yelled the innkeeper.

Arodilac fought with a fury and passion that seemed scarcely possible for someone of his age. His initial attack drove Ronan to the edge of the platform, so surprised was he. The crowd bellowed with approval. A hand grabbed his ankle and yanked, but he kicked back and felt his boot connect with someone's face.

How old was the lad? Sixteen—perhaps seventeen. Surely he himself hadn't been able to summon up such anger at that age. But he had. He had been just the same.

"What did you do to her?" said Arodilac. The roar of the crowd and the clangor of their swords was so loud that Ronan had to strain to hear him.

"Who?"

But he knew who.

"She won't see me! She returns my letters!"

"Perhaps she's no longer interested in you," said Ronan.

Their swords whirled, inscribing twin arcs in the air, and met with a resounding clang. Shadows, but the boy had strong wrists. Given enough time and discipline, he'd make an excellent swordsman.

"What did you say to her, you scoundrel!"

Ronan flushed.

"You forget. Your uncle hired me for a job. I cleaned up your mess—that's what I did—so don't press me. I don't take kindly to playing nursemaid for spoiled brats."

Arodilac turned an even brighter shade of red at that. His teeth snapped together with a click audible even over the clangor of their blades.

"Maybe it was just a job to you!" he spat. "And maybe I'm a just child to you—but what of her? Did the job include trampling her heart? What did you say—what did you tell her, curse you! She won't see me!"

"Does Owain Gawinn teach the sword or the art of conversation? In either case, he's failed."

The lad snarled at that and threw himself forward in such a wild flurry of strokes that the onlookers at the platform's edge were forced to dodge the swinging blade.

"Enough," said Ronan.

He reached out and caught the other's sword wrist. His hand moved so quickly that scarcely a person among the onlookers saw the motion. The sword fell free from Arodilac's hand and the boy struggled in the merciless grip—face white with outrage, his mouth gaping, and gone mute. In one quick jerk, Ronan spun him around and ran him right off the platform, heaving him into the air at the edge so that he fell hard, arms and legs sprawling onto the people below. The boy let out a yell as he flew through the air, echoed by those misfortunate enough to be in his path, but they were instantly drowned out by the roar of laughter that erupted from the yard.

The innkeeper clambered up onto the platform.

"Second win for Ronan!" he called aloud. He turned and spoke quietly. "Though not a single bet taken for that round. You'll get no cut from the house and you'll not get another idiot up here soon."

"Try," said Ronan.

The innkeeper shrugged.

"All, right, then!" he shouted. "Who'll challenge?!"

"Might as well grab a sandcat's tail!" someone yelled in response.

"Toss 'im off! He's the bleeding Knife, for shadow's sake!"

"I tell you, he ain't! Not anymore!"

"Well, if you think that changes things, then get up there and take his sword away, you stupid git!"

Ronan held up his hand for silence.

"Ten to one odds," he said. "I'll give ten to one odds for anyone."

The crowd shuffled its feet. Men looked uneasily at each other. Vigdis, slouched in a corner on the top step, grinned and shook his head.

"Well, lad," said the innkeeper. "Ain't no one here going against you."

"Pardon me, good sir, but I would try this man's skill."

As if one creature possessing a hundred heads, the entire crowd turned, all heads swiveling together. Two men stood at the tavern backdoor. The two looked a pair, alike in build, coloring and dress. They had hair like corn silk bleached to near white by a relentless sun. Their skin was the hue of old wood, burnished brown by that same sun and, as if they took all their colors from the heavens, their eyes were as blue as a summer's sky.

"Harthians," said someone.

The two men made their way down the steps. The crowd jostled around them. Already, bets were being taken. The scratch of chalk on slate filled the air as oddsmakers noted wagers. The taller of the two Harthians stepped up onto the platform. He surveyed the yard with bright eyes and then turned to Ronan and the innkeeper.

"I am new to your fair city and, as such, not conversant with your games of skill. If you would instruct me in the rules, I would be grateful."

"Well, m'lord," said the innkeeper awkwardly. "Ain't much to it. No killing strokes. First man to give up or get booted off the planks loses, see?"

"Yes, I suppose I do see. Stio—" This was said to the other Harthian who stood at the platform's edge. "Stio, I think this the tonic to clear my head of dances and dinners."

"May I remind you, Eaomod," said this other, "that we must return to the castle at the hour's end. The regent has promised a race, and you were desirous of testing your steed's mettle."

He spoke calmly and clearly, as if the two were alone. The crowd stared, entranced. The oddsmen paused in their rounds. The serving girls gazed hopelessly at the two. Even the young nobles in the corner blinked, wide-eyed.

"Time enough, Stio. Time enough. Now, good sir," said the Harthian, smiling at Ronan, "I am called Eaomod. I would know your name before we begin."

"He's the bleedin' Knife!" someone yelled from the crowd.

"He's Ronan of Aum!" shouted another.

The Harthian's eyebrows raised. "With Aum a haunt of jackals and owls for how many hundreds of years now?"

Ronan shrugged. "A man has to come from somewhere."

Eaomod regarded the innkeeper's swords with disfavor.

"These, good sir, are barely suited for chopping firewood and it would be dismal sport indeed, waving such crudities about. Have you nothing better?"

"N-nothing, m'lord," stammered the innkeeper.

"Stio. Lend me your blade."

Stio drew a sword from under his cloak. It was a long, lovely, deadly-looking thing, twin to the sword that Eaomod himself produced. He handed them both to Ronan.

"Choose, my friend, and then let us begin."

"Here now," said the innkeeper. "You can't do that. No edges. Blunt weapons, see?"

"Truly?" said the Harthian. "But surely one of your skill, friend Ronan, would not mind?"

Ronan weighed the swords in his hands. They were beautiful weapons, light and graceful and obviously forged by the same master hand. He offered Eaomod's own back to him. As far as he could tell, there was no difference between the two swords.

"No edges," protested the innkeeper. "Lord Gawinn will close my place."

"Let 'em fight!" shouted an onlooker.

"Aye! Get off the planks, you fat plonk, and let 'em have at it!"

The innkeeper threw his hands in the air and clambered off the platform. Eaomod unclasped his cloak and tossed it down to his friend.

"Now," he said. His eyes sparkled.

"Would you care for a wager, m' lord?" said Ronan.

The Harthian shook his head, smiling. "In Harth, it is only for the sake of war or love that we fight. And today, this is for love of the sword. Though, if you throw me into the crowd in such manner as that unfortunate boy received, we shall fight again, but then for the sake of our own private war."

Ronan smiled in turn, swallowing his disappointment.

"First blood?" he said.

"First blood," said the other.

"All right, then."

In that first moment, Ronan knew he faced a master swordsman. The Harthian did not waste a finger's breadth of needless movement. He drifted just out of reach, wavering and insubstantial in the noonday sun. He seemed a thing of dream, moving to some peculiar music whose rhythm only he heard, but the sword in his grasp was sure and swift. Ronan circled around him like a hungry sandcat.

The crowd hushed into silence. A few of the older men there, those who had fought in the Errant Wars, knew what they watched might not be seen again in their lives. And those who were untutored in such skill instinctively knew what they saw was some strange rarity.

Sunlight glittered and flashed on steel. The blades described circles and arcs and angles, creating a myriad of fantastic tableaus that existed in the air over the platform, springing into being one instant, only to be replaced the next instant with another succession of whirls and lines. Here was the perfect, steel-colored circle of a many-spoked wheel throwing off a dazzle of light. Here was the abrupt unfolding of a lady's fan, opening with a clatter and formed of light and air and iron death. And there was a strange flower grown of loops and whorls and deadly clashing petals.

Eaomod's smile grew broader as they fought.

"You fight marvelously well, friend Ronan," he said.

"Thanks."

Ronan parried a bewildering succession of blows. He was not conversant with the style of the other's swordplay and he wondered if it was peculiar to Harth. He had never been to Harth, except as a child.

"I confess myself curious, friend Ronan."

"Is that so?"

"It is acknowledged in all of Tormay that there are nine true masters of the sword. The Lord Captain of your fair city is one of them, of course, though I have yet the pleasure to see his skill. My old teacher is another, even in his dotage and with death his patient attendant."

The blades whistled through the air. Sunlight shone hot and white in Eaomod's hair.

"And who is your teacher?"

"The blademaster of the house of Oran. Lorcannan Nan."

"Ah." Now things were starting to make sense.

"The other seven, naturally, are the seven lords of Harlech, but it is only our elders who have seen their skill, for the lords of Harlech only draw their swords when they ride to war."

"True."

"Perhaps, one day, I shall be so happy as to see their skill, but—alas—I would not wish such a fate on Tormay, even though, since childhood, I have been trained for battle. Most days, peace is better than war. Forgive me, I digress."

"You've named your nine. I've heard of 'em."

The sun was high in the sky and just tipped into the beginning of its downward slide. In the yard, it seemed that only the two men on the platform moved, like bright gods who had stepped down from the heavens and so found themselves darting through the sluggish currents of human time, while all those who stood around them could only gaze in unblinking silence. The gods flickered faster than thought—lunge and parry and wheeling around each other in succession after succession.

"Yes, but I have heard tell of two others."

"I haven't. If war comes again to these lands, then I hope your nine'll prove enough."

"There's a peculiar family that travels the breadth of Tormay, trading in horses and the training of them. They have an ill repute, for it's said they steal their horses if they can't have them for gold."

"Sounds like a dodgy bunch."

"They're called the Farrows. Once, when my old teacher had been drinking and inclined to talk, he did say that no man lives in all of Tormay able to stand before the sword of the head of that family, Cullan Farrow. No man."

"Haven't heard of him."

"No? And he's supposed to have a son that will one day surpass his father's skill. Declan is his name. Even in Harth, the minstrels tell the story of Declan Farrow and how he rescued the daughter of the duke of Vomaro. He was only a boy when he tracked the ogres to their lair and slew them in that dark haunt. Are you conversant with this tale, my friend?"

"I've heard the story. Who hasn't? All minstrels are drunkards and liars."

The blades sang through the air, punctuated by a tattoo of ringing tones—vicious hammer strikes—as sword met sword. Ronan pressed his attack and Eaomod smiled.

"It is time!" called Stio from beside the platform.

Eaomod stepped back and lowered his sword. Ronan paused in mid-lunge. The crowd came alive a surge. They howled in protest.

"First blood! First blood!"

Eaomod bowed slightly and then his hand flashed out, catching hold of Ronan's sword. He held it up. Blood dripped from his palm.

"Here is your satisfaction!"

The crowd howled again, but in delight. A roar of applause went up.

"Poorly done, my lord," said Ronan, laughing. "I've never defeated someone with such a weak cut before."

"Never before has the Prince of Harth been defeated by such a paltry loss of blood."

And the Prince of Harth, for that was who he was, smiled and bowed. Ronan held out his hand. The Prince looked somewhat bemused, but then he gripped the other's hand.

"I am still not fluent in your northern ways," he said.

"Another day, my lord," said Ronan. "We'll have to have another go. It's been a long time since an opponent made me think."

The Prince smiled and said nothing.

"My thanks for the sword," said Ronan, stepping down from the platform and handing the blade to Stio. The man bowed and then, just as bemused as his lord, shook Ronan's still outstretched hand.

"Never before have I seen my sorry steel put to such use," he said.

The crowd jostled noisily around them as they made their way out. To one side, Ronan could see the glaring face of Arodilac forcing a path toward him through the press. He gave the boy no time, however, and ducked through the back door of the tavern. It was dark and cool and silent inside. With a bow, the two Harthians made their farewells, the Prince's eye still speculative. Then they were gone, hurrying off into the busy street.

"For you," said the innkeeper. He thrust a small bag into Ronan's hand. "Half the house take for your fight."

"Ah." The bag was heavy. It clinked with coins.

"You're in luck. Once that sandman got going, the bets came in fast. A lot of the lads were hoping he'd take you."

Ronan slipped out into the street and didn't look back, heading in the opposite direction from Highneck Rise and the regent's castle. The opposite direction from where he knew the two Harthians would be going. Once he was several blocks away, he ducked down an alley. A peek in the bag of coins satisfied him. He had made more than enough to buy clothes suitable for the regent's ball.

The coins were fortunate by themselves, but the contents of his pocket were of more interest to him. He took the two rings out and examined them. They were of plain gold. They bore no stones or markings, but from both of the pair Ronan could hear a faint whisper. Ward rings. And not just any old ward rings. Smiling, he pocketed them and strode on.

The day was proving fortunate.

Never shake hands with a thief.

Ronan wandered down to the wharf. A sloop was gliding out across the breakwater, heading for the open sea. White sails billowed as they rose. Across the bay, he could hear the voices of the sailors as they called to each other. Then, the boat was past the breakwater and heeling over, picking up speed with sails full of wind. Seagulls wheeled overhead. The pound of the surf on the breakwater boomed in the distance. The wind sighed through the timber pilings of the piers. He breathed in the scent of salt, and it was so sharp and sudden that, for one instant, his mind was filled with the blues and greens and blinding sunlight of the sea and sky.

These are the colors of her eyes, he thought.

The tide surged against the breakwater, and spray foamed up into the air, hanging there before subsiding back into the sea. Ronan could hear hunger in the sound of it, for the tide never sleeps, of course, but always returns for what it seeks. He turned away and was not sure if he feared seeing her again, or if he was glad. He was only conscious of the beauty of the day and the hunger of the tide and the silence which, he knew, must lie sleeping in the depths below it all.

CHAPTER SIXTY-FIVE
THE UNFORTUNATE END OF A PAINFUL RIDE

By dusk, Ablendan could go no further that day. The horse seemed fresh enough to continue for many more hours. However, the little man had discovered that his was not a physique suited for riding. What had begun earlier that day as a slight stitch in his side had, as the miles passed, progressed into a searing pain that made him shudder with every jouncing stride. His body was a blur of misery. He had discovered several muscles of whose existence he had been contentedly unaware for so many years, and all of these muscles had conspired to announce their presence in fire and agony. Riding horses, as far as Ablendan was concerned, was for those who detested life and merely wanted another reason to hate it even more.

He slid off the horse and felt his knees begin to fold. He grabbed hold of the bridle.

"A pox on you and all your flea-bitten kin," he said. The horse ignored him.

"If I could shape-change, then there'd be no need for four-footed, traveling torture chambers such as yourself, eh? One word—just one word, that's all it would take. A hawk or an eagle or a gull to wing up the coast. Or even a horse. How would you like that? I'd rather be a skunk than a horse."

The horse blew a sigh that could have been commiseration or disgust, and began to crop the grass.

It was growing dark. The sickle moon gave off only enough light to announce its own form. Ablendan coaxed a fire into life under a tree and then settled down with his back against the trunk to toast some bread. The horse sidled close.

"Go on with you," said the man. "You've done me enough harm this day without stealing my supper as well. I daresay you have designs on this bread and cheese, you wretch, but fair's fair. I can't eat grass and you shan't have any of this."

But he gave the horse a bite of bread after he staked him by the tree. The horse slobbered appreciatively on his coat.

"With some luck, we'll be through Hull by nightfall tomorrow, and then most of another day to reach the tower in Thule. Get some sleep, you wretched beast. We'll both need our strength in the morning."

Ablendan wrapped himself in a blanket and lay down by the fire.

"If I ever wake," he said to himself. The coals winked red at him in the dark. "I wish I were back in Hearne in my bed. I'm not suited for the outdoor life. I wish I had a sausage. At any rate, two more days. That isn't so long. Perhaps the Stone Tower will know what to do? Some of those fellows are as old as the sea. Good gracious—that hawk simply appeared on the sill and began talking. The shadow of the wind. Can you imagine that? It's like living in a story."

He fell asleep.

Sometime after midnight, Ablendan woke. The fire was out but he could smell wood smoke in the air. He was cold. A breeze blew by and, in its wake, he heard a faint sound— the careful placement of a foot, or the slow exhalation of someone who has been holding their breath for a long time.

"Who's there?" he said. He sat up. The horse was an indistinct shape in the darkness, but he could see that it was standing still, head up and staring out into the night.

"Is someone there?"

Abruptly, the breeze shifted and he caught a whiff of something rank, some unclean thing that stank of death and rot. The horse screamed—a strange, bugling shriek of terror—and he saw it rear up. The tether snapped with a twang and then Ablendan heard galloping hooves and the crashing of bushes as the horse blundered off into the darkness. Again, there was quiet except for his own shallow breath and the painful thud of his heart. He struggled to his feet and stood with his back to the tree.

"Show yourself!" he said, trying to speak boldly. His voice came out as a quavering croak. He could see nothing in the night. Thoughts tumbled through his head. What vicious beasts was Hull known for? Ogres? Not in two hundred years. Wolves, perhaps? Yes, of course—wolves! And they did not like fire. His mind stumbled on a word—the second name of fire, which could be used to shape heat and flame. Surely it could be used as a weapon. But what was the stricture that limited its use? He had always been bad with the strictures of use. He could not remember.

He gasped.

A pair of red eyes stared at him from the darkness. Nothing else was visible—only the eyes. They blinked once and came closer, and then he could see the outline of a form. It was a wolf! Relief coursed through him. Just a wolf. Only a wolf. Of course, wolves were bad enough, but at least it wasn't something else. Something he didn't understand. But then the creature took another step forward, and he immediately realized it was not a wolf. It was too big and too broad across the head. The width of its shoulder was enormous. The foul scent grew stronger.

"What are you?" he said. The second name of fire was useless and dead inside his mind.

The creature lunged for him.

Early that next morning, the soldiers at the main gate of Hearne set about opening up the doors, as they always did before sunrise. The timber holding the gate shut was as big around as a fully grown pine tree. It took two men to turn the gears that ratcheted around and around until the timber was levered up and the doors were free. Most days, only one of the gate doors was opened. One was enough, as they were each a good ten strides across.

"All right, lads," said Bordeall.

Two of the soldiers hauled on the iron chains bolted into the wood planks that faced the door. It began to swing, grating in complaint. Bordeall frowned.

"Lucan!"

"Sir?" The young lieutenant hurried over.

"Get some grease on those hinges."

"Yessir." The lieutenant glanced up at the top hinge. It was a good fifty feet high.

"The enfilade slits in the underside of the arch," said Bordeall patiently. "Drop one of the men through on a rope. One of the skinnier men." His eye fell on Arodilac Bridd who, as luck would have it, was leaning drowsily on his spear in the shadow of the arch. He jerked a thumb at the boy. "Him. Use him."

"Bridd? Yessir," said the lieutenant happily.

"And have him grease the portcullis gears while he's at it."

"But it's been working fine. Smoother than a—"

"Do it."

Bordeall turned and stumped toward the tower. The door settled with a booming crash against the inside wall of the arch. People streamed in under the arch and into the city—the poorer traders and peddlers who slept outside the walls rather than pay the prices of the inns. Cart wheels creaked by. A donkey brayed in mutiny at the early hour. The Guardsmen stationed at the far end of the arch stiffened at Bordeall's approach and saluted.

"Stone and shadow!" said the one closest to him.

"What's that, soldier?"

"Sorry, sir," said the man. "I've never seen such a large dog before."

"Dogs are just dogs," said Bordeall, but he turned to look as well.

"Some more so'n others," said the soldier under his breath.

Bordeall opened his mouth, about to rebuke him for his impertinence, but then said nothing. Trotting sedately behind a wagon piled with squashes was the dog. It was more than large—it was enormous, near as big as a yearling calf, with a pelt of dirty brown fur.

"Now that's a dog," said Bordeall.

The creature turned to gaze at him as if it had heard and understood. The orange eyes were expressionless. It was like looking at a pair of flat stones under the sliding water of a stream. A horseman clattered by between them and the dog was gone.

"Sir," said the Guardsman. "You want I should go have a word with that farmer there? Tell him be sure an' keep his beast on a leash?"

"No," said Bordeall. He tried to recollect if there were laws concerning such things. He could not remember. "I reckon he knows what he's doing. Must be expensive squashes to warrant a guardian like that."

"So much for your hound," said the regent sourly. "I don't see my horse. I thought you said he had a nose on him to end all? Well, no doubt his nose has brought him back for his breakfast."

In the stable yard, the regent and a small company of his guests had just settled into their saddles as they were about to set out to tour the more interesting points of the city—interesting, that is, in the regent's eyes. The dog trotted up to the duke of Mizra's horse and sat down. He began to pant. A scandalized-looking footman raced around the corner, followed by several small pages. They skidded to a halt at the sight of the regent and his guests. The dog eyed them blandly.

"Er," said Gifernes, opening and shutting his mouth like a fish. He dismounted from his horse. The dog leaned against his leg and blinked.

"Perhaps," said the prince of Harth, "your errant horse is long-winded as well as being fleet of hoof. Consider, my lord, such a paragon might run at speed for days, no? I knew it in my heart, as soon as the steed galloped away, that, truly, your stable is the finest in all of Tormay."

"Was," said the duke of Dolan.

The regent said nothing to this, but wheeled his horse around and clattered out of the yard. The others followed. The footman hurried across the yard.

"Milord," he said, bowing to the duke of Mizra. "Would you like me to see after the hound? I did not realize he was yours when he came through the castle gate."

"Um, no—no, that's all right. He'll be fine. You may go."

289

"Milord," said the footman, bowing again. He backed away and then cuffed one of the pages.

"So you couldn't catch the horse?" said the duke, squatting down. "I'm surprised at you, Holdfast, quite surprised. I thought you a finer hound than this. But what do we have staining your fur? Looks like you found something."

The dog submitted mutely to his master's hands as the duke ran his fingers through the hair on the neck of the beast. In places, the fur was matted with a dark, dried substance. It flaked away at the duke's touch. His youthful face creased in an uncertain frown. He stood up and dusted his hands.

"Stay here," he said to the dog. "And even if a suckling pig trots up and throws itself onto a platter for you, you'll do nothing. Stay."

The dog lumbered into the shade of the stable wall and sat watching the duke ride away. It rested its head on its paws and then fell asleep.

CHAPTER SIXTY-SIX
LENA'S SACRIFICE

For the seventh time, Jute examined the lock. It was an enormous iron thing forged into the bars of the door. He could get his hand and arm through the bars, but it was hopeless after that. He might as well have tried battering at the iron with his bare hands as shift that lock. He did not even have a bit of wire. The Silentman's men had been thorough, for they were all members of the Guild and there was no trick a boy knew that they did not know as well. The galling thing was that the lock wasn't even warded. It was just a lock.

He huddled in a corner and tried to think. Light glimmered from somewhere further down the corridor. It was scant, but it was enough to relieve complete darkness into mere darkness. The cell was small. The floor was strewn with old, sour-smelling straw. Stone walls rose around him and over him. There was no window. He had a feeling he was deep underground, for the air was still.

Damn Lena!

She had been a silent little thing the first time he had seen her. The Juggler had brought her to the stables in the back of the Goose and Gold one summer evening, where the children would always gather after a day's work. They had stopped at the sight of him—wary of his temper, his cruelty, and his hard fists. The girls swinging the skip-rope in the corner froze, the rope falling across the shoulders of the three jumping in the middle. Several boys teasing the old mare with some rotten apples teetered on the fence, eyeing the Juggler across their shoulders. The horse nibbled the apples from their unresisting fingers. The Juggler had a little girl with him. She stumbled as he pushed her forward. His eyes roved around the yard.

"Here," he had said. "You, Jute. Learn her the tricks. Learn her well or I'll take a rope to you."

Lena hadn't said a word for the first week but just followed him around like a pathetic dog, smiling uncertainly when he had a kind word or a bit of extra food for her and cringing from his frowns and impatience. Picking pockets came easily to her, for she had tiny hands that fluttered as quickly and as gently as butterfly wings. And, in time, she spoke and even smiled. Years ago, that had been—years ago.

Days, she drifted in his wake through the streets, picking pockets and filching from the barrow carts and shops. She would bring her finds to him, more concerned of what he thought than of pleasing the Juggler. Nights, in the cramped rooms jutting off the stable where the children slept, locked in by the Juggler each evening, Lena would always curl up next to Jute, burrowed into an old cloak like a mouse in her nest.

Damn Lena!

Jute sniffled. He wiped his eyes on his sleeve.

I wish I hadn't gone outside, he thought. I wish I had listened to Severan. To the hawk. Are you there? Not with all this stone overhead. I must be deep underground. I can feel it. I can't feel the sky. I wish I had never climbed down the wall. Some walls are meant to be stayed within. As long as there's still sky overhead. I wish I had never met Lena.

After a while, still crying, he fell asleep on the straw.

Later, the jailer shambled by with a hunk of bread and water in a tankard. The boy did not rouse at his call, but lay sleeping with his face turned to the floor, looking like nothing more than a heap of clothing in the corner. The jailer shoved the food through the bars and moved on.

Jute dreamed of the dark sky again.

Below and above him, there was nothing but distance and darkness. There were no stars. Cold crept through his bones. His thoughts drifted through his mind. The words felt heavy, as if the cold and dark made them ponderous, as if the language could not grapple with the idea of a never-ending sky. Weighted with this impotence, words sank into irrelevance and were undone.

Here.

I have been here before.

With the hawk.

But he was alone this time. There was no hawk hovering at his side. The black walls stood before him. They rose up into the darkness, plunged down into the darkness, stretched away on either side, forever and ever and ever. They towered above, below, beyond him with a terrible certainty of being.

Everything ceases here, Jute thought dismally—even words. They are no longer true. Sky and light fail. Even the night ends here, for this darkness is deeper than the night. Even I shall cease here. Things fall apart. They drift on the tide of night and come to rest at these walls.

But then the words of the hawk came to his memory.

Deep within the darkness, further e'en the void, Nokhoron Nozhan built himself a fortress of night.

Even here, there are words.

Something struck him in the back. He turned around. Lena was standing there in the air, rocks in her hand. She threw another one. It hit him in the stomach.

"Stop that," he said angrily.

She did not reply but only threw another stone.

"Stop it!"

Another stone.

"You wretch! Why'd you do it, Lena? I hope they paid you well for selling me. That's what you did—you sold me out. We were friends. I taught you everything I knew! I protected you!"

Her face was pinched with anxiety, but still she said nothing. A stone came whistling at him and he tried to catch it, to throw it back hard at her, but his body would not obey him.

"We were family!" he shouted.

Another stone struck him. It dropped away, tumbling into the nothingness below him. He looked down. It was a long way to fall.

He fell. His mouth gaped open, desperate for the air rushing by.

Jute woke up, gasping for air. He breathed in the odor of straw and remembered where he was. The darkness around him was only darkness, and the stone wall inches from his face was just a stone wall. As if that wasn't bad enough, he thought dismally. Something hit him hard in the back. He yelped and sat up.

"Be quiet!" said a familiar voice.

Lena crouched on the other side of the bars. Jute scuttled across the floor, so furious he couldn't even think. He reached through the bars, grabbed her by the throat. Her little hands flailed at his.

"No, wait!" she said. "Please! He weren't the Knife no more—everyone said so— kicked outta the Guild by the Silentman. Said he did what he did because he was forced to. He only wanted to help now. Said you were in terrible danger. I only thought I could help, that something would work out—Jute, please—I can't breathe!"

His hands were wet with her tears. He let go of her and they both slumped down on either side of the bars. She sobbed quietly.

"Why'd you do it, Lena?"

"I thought I was helping."

"Well, you weren't," he said. This only made her sob louder. "Shush. Or the jailer'll come along and then we'll be both locked up."

"I'd rather be in there than anywhere else."

"I don't suppose you were clever enough to bring a—"

She produced a rusty nail before he could finish speaking.

"It's no good," she said, wiping her nose on her sleeve. "I tried while you were sleeping. The tumblers are so rusty there's no good budging it without a proper key."

"Lemme have it."

She sniffled and handed the nail over. He reached through the bars and around, feeling blind for the lock. The nail rattled in the keyhole. He investigated with his eyes closed, testing the tumblers.

"It won't work."

"Be quiet," he said frowning, but already knowing she was right. He sat back on his heels.

"There's allus another way to rob the duchess. That's what you allus say."

"Aye," said Jute, considering the nail with disfavor. She pressed her face against the bars and smiled uncertainly.

"So how'll it be?"

He told her.

The jailer came yawning down the passage. A torch burned in one hand, but it did little to dispel the gloom, for the fire guttered more with smoke than flame. He paused at Jute's cell and raised the torch to peer within. Two hands shot out from the bars and grabbed him by the coat.

"Help!" yelled Jute.

The jailor shouted in fright and stumbled back, but he was held tight to the bars by the boy's grip.

"Get me out here! Help me, kind sir! Get me out! Help! Help!"

"Leave off!" said the jailer, and he beat Jute about the ears. The boy ducked his head under the blows and doggedly held on.

"Help!" bawled Jute.

The tiny form of Lena materialized out of the shadows and tiptoed forward. Her fingers fluttered at the jailer's belt. Torchlight gleamed on the ring of keys in her hands. She darted silently away.

"Help! Fire! Flood!"

"Here's some help!" said the jailer, and he dealt Jute a tremendous buffet on the side of his head which sent the boy staggering back from the bars.

"Idiot boy." And after tugging his coat straight, the jailer continued on his way. His shadow straggled after him, vanishing into the darkness that thickened as the torchlight disappeared down the corridor.

Instantly, Jute was at the bars.

"Quick," he said.

Lena bobbed out from an alcove, her face pale with excitement.

"Hurry," said Jute. "We haven't much time. As soon as he comes to the next door we're done for if that ring isn't back on his belt."

"Which one is it?" said Lena. The ring was heavy with keys. She tried them, one after the other. They sounded like chattering teeth as they rattled in the lock.

"Hurry up!"

"I am!"

And then the lock opened with such a creak that both of them froze in horror, sure the jailer would be soon hurrying back. The door swung open and Jute popped out.

"In you go," he said. He grabbed the ring of keys from her hand.

"Do I have to?"

"Lay down in the back corner with your face to the wall. He'll think you're me. Whatever you do, don't move or say a word if someone comes. Hurry!"

"And you'll be back for me?"

"Yes," he said, and he pushed her inside and locked the door.

He darted through the shadows on noiseless feet. The jailer stamped along. Jute slipped the keys back onto his belt. It was lucky he did, because the man groped for them not a second afterward and vanished through a door. The lock on the door proved impervious to Jute's nail. He stepped back, frowning, and looked down the passage on either side. Both directions looked identical. Here and there, oil lamps shone, sitting on ledges that jutted out from the wall. The light they shed, however, was so mean and miserable that it only served to deepen the shadows in the spaces between.

"Should just leave her to rot," he said to himself.

It would serve her right. The stupid little beast.

And perhaps Jute would have left Lena, for there's no telling what someone will do when left up to their own thoughts. However, just as he was considering which direction down the passage to investigate, he heard voices. He darted behind a stone arch. The voices slowly approached. There were two voices, and after a little while he managed to distinguish them. The first had a light, complaining tone, as if the speaker had just been roused from his sleep or a good meal and was not taking the interruption kindly. The second was deeper and seemed to spend all his words soothing the first voice.

"That son of a thrice-cursed misbegotten sheepherder," said the first voice. "The gall of him. As if a desert nag could run the legs off one of my beauties."

"Well," said the second voice, "it's difficult to ignore the fact that his horse won."

"Entirely beside the point. Y'have to remember those sand eaters are steeped in magic, up to their noses. Wasn't true speed—wasn't real horse—that won the length. It was magic, I say, magic!"

"Magic," returned the second voice. "I'd give my right hand to be rid of the lot of it—"

"Aye, then we'd be winning some races."

"—for the stuff's been nothing but a torment to us, ever since that cursed creature came knocking on our door. I've heard its whisper in my sleep every night since."

"Gold."

294

"More us the idiots, for I'm thinking it'll be fool's gold before the story's out."

Shadows wavered along the passageway. Jute felt the stone of the wall against his cheek. It was cold and hard and the silence of it seeped into his flesh. The two men appeared in the dim light. They were walking slowly, heads down, and so preoccupied with their conversation that they would not have noticed the boy had there been lamplight shining on his face. Both of the men wore long, draping cloaks with hoods so that Jute could not see much of them other than the shape of their bodies.

"You've always seen the darker side of things, old friend."

"That's what you pay me for," said the second man. "So I'd think it remiss if I didn't look in that direction. But perhaps I'll be proven wrong tonight when the creature returns. After all, we've the boy in hand now, locked up tight."

"Shadow take the little wretch. I knew Ronan would come through. Didn't I say he would?"

"I don't recall your exact words,' said the other politely.

"That'll put us back safely with that—that—whatever that thing is."

"I trust so. I hope so."

"Well, I hope it snaps the boy's filthy neck."

The pair had passed on by this time and Jute, horrified by their words, slipped out and tiptoed along behind them. He knew that the filthy neck they spoke of was his own and, even though his neck was indeed filthy, he did not think it deserved snapping. But necks could get mistaken in the dark, particularly if someone was angry enough. Lena's neck was no bigger than that of a sparrow. It would snap easily. He shivered.

The two men stopped outside the cell and he sidled into an alcove jutting off the passageway. He crouched in the shadows, gnawing his lip and hoping against hope they would not open the cell.

I can run at them, he thought. Scream and shout if they open the door. Enough of a distraction for Lena to dart out and be gone. If only I had a knife. If only I hadn't touched the knife. None of this would be happening.

"So, this is the miserable wretch," said the first man. "Strange to think the mighty Guild could've been brought near to destruction by a child. My father must be writhing in his grave."

The second man sighed.

"I think we were done in by simple curiosity," he said. "What child have you ever known to resist a shut door or a closed box? Doubly so if the child's a thief. And we gave this boy an enticing mystery, for the instructions were to not open the box. If you tell 'em a certain thing mustn't be done, why then they promptly focus all their energies on accomplishing that particular thing. Each of mine was like that."

"One of many reasons why I've never had children of my own," said the other.

They fell silent. Then, without warning, the first man kicked at the bars.

"You there!" he shouted. "On your feet, shadowspawn. Up, and let me see your ugly face!"

Jute flinched at the rage in the man's voice. His lips moved soundlessly.

Don't move, Lena. Please, don't move.

"Do you know who I am? I am the Silentman!"

Don't even breathe.

"I own you! I own your worthless life and I'll do with it what I will!"

No he won't. I'll get you out. It'll be all right—you'll see. It'll be all right.

"Before this night's over, boy, you'll wish you'd never been born. Get on your feet!"

295

A shape passed before Jute's staring eyes. The jailer. He shrank back into the shadows, but the man did not even waste a glance into the alcove.

"My lord." The jailer bowed and tugged at his forelock.

"What is it?" said the first man.

He turned toward the jailer and, for the first time, Jute was able to look within the man's hood. The jailer's torch illuminated the passage, but where there should have been a face there was only a strange blur of darkness that resisted the light.

"Mostly been like that e'er since the Knife brung him in," offered the jailer. "Jus' huddles against the wall."

"Not dead, is he?" said the first man. "It'll be your neck if he is."

"Oh no, my lord," said the jailer. "He ain't dead. Eats his food quick enough, he does, an' today he up and tries to grab me—right through the bars as I was makin' my rounds. You want me to roust the beggar out, my lord?"

The keys gleamed in his hand and jingled against the lock.

"Nay, leave be, jailer. I don't have time."

The first man turned back toward the cell.

"Listen, boy, for I know you can hear me through your shamming. Savor this cell and your stone pillow well, for it's the only pleasant thing you've left to feel. You'll not live out the night."

Still, there was no response from the cell. The man spun away from it with an impatient snarl.

"And you, jailer—the hour after midnight, you be at the stairway door with your keys. You will be so good to hand them over then. Be sure to scrub them well, for I want none of your stench on them."

"Yes, m'lord."

The two men strode away down the passageway. After a moment, the jailer shambled off, and soon there were only the shadows and the stone walls. Jute darted across to the cell.

"Lena," he said.

The shabby heap in the corner of the cell quivered into life. Her eyes blinked, staring and huge, and then she flew at him. Her hands reached through the bars and he caught them in his own. They shook in his grasp.

"Jute!"

"Shh! You'll be out of here soon enough. I'll steal the keys and we'll be out."

"You heard him." Her teeth chattered. "An hour past midnight."

"We'll be out long before then—shh."

"I almost turned when he spoke. I almost screamed an' turned. . ."

He soothed Lena until her teeth no longer chattered and her hands no longer shook. She curled back up in the corner obediently, but the last glimpse he had of her was of two eyes. Then she turned her face to the wall and there was only a heap of ragged clothing lying there.

It shouldn't be difficult, Jute told himself. Just find the jailer. Just find the jailer and you'll have the keys and that'll be it. He's practically deaf and dumb. I could steal the shirt off his back. Not difficult at all.

But the jailer was not to be found.

The passage meandered in both directions for a considerable way. It twisted and turned and digressed into side tunnels and alcoves. It took Jute quite a while to be certain he had covered every foot of the place. The walls were lined with barred cells, but there were no other prisoners. In most parts of the tunnel there were none of the oil lamps that lit the area where Lena was locked up. Jute took one down from the wall and crept about with the hot metal scorching his hand. Cobwebs shrouded the stones. A spider scuttled across the floor and climbed the wall. It was much bigger than any spider he had ever seen. The lamplight caught in its mass of eyes, glittering and shining like a wealth of tiny jewels. He tiptoed past the thing. He shivered and imagined those dozens of eyes watching him, all swiveling at the same time, intent on him.

He did not find any other doors beside the one the jailer had disappeared through, except for one door at the opposite end of the maze of tunnels. It was at the end of a passage well lit with lamps and swept clean of spiderwebs. The door handle turned smoothly and silently under his hand and he stopped, wary of what came easily. He listened to everything around him, but he could hear only the silence of the stone walls. But then he remembered the ward that governed the terrible staircase in the university, and the silence of those steps that had almost sent him falling to his death. He listened again, his eyes shut, and then he heard. Rather, it was what he could not hear. It was not just silence. It was an absence. He could not hear anything through the door. He pressed his ear against the cold iron to be sure, but there was nothing there. Nothing at all.

Jute settled back on his heels and pondered. It had to be a ward of some sort. If so, it was the only ward he had found in the entire sprawl of tunnels. Therefore, whatever lay behind it must be important. And, if one had a dungeon where people were kept locked up in cells, then surely the most important door would be the exit.

He examined the thought and found it reasonable. But even if it was reasonable, the conclusion didn't help him. The door was still warded. However, ward or no ward, he would have to see what lay behind the door. He took a deep breath and filled his mind with the memory of sky, for the memory of sky is composed first of silence, and then of a distance that recedes beyond the reaches of sight. Even there, the wind blows in silence. The sky flooded into his mind, replete with stillness and plucking at his thoughts with the cold, familiar fingers of the wind.

The handle turned under his hand and he pulled the door open.

Just as quickly, he shut the door. Stumbled backwards and crouched there in the middle of the floor, trembling. Sweat sprang from his forehead. He stared at the handle, willing it not to turn.

The door did not open.

Jute sighed thankfully and turned away.

When the door had opened, several inches ajar, he had seen a flight of stone steps mounting up. But, in that brief instant, he had seen a horrifying thing. Several steps up, the stone had shifted—in less than the blink of an eye—hard, flat surfaces becoming fluid, bending and shaping and rising up into the semblance of a gigantic head without eyes or nose or ears but split near in two by a gaping mouth crowded with teeth like shattered rock. The head strained toward him, mouth stretching wider and wider, and then he had slammed the door shut.

Some wards could not be evaded by silence. This was one. Opening the door activated the thing. It was as simple as that. It would take a spell to keep the steps stone and the head in slumber. Perhaps just a single word.

He settled in a dark corner near Lena's cell and listened to her even breathing. She was asleep. Minutes drifted by—each one more valuable than the last. A yawn forced its way from his mouth and he rubbed at his eyes. His head hurt. He hadn't noticed it until he had sat down.

And then he realized something. Right when the door had opened, he had felt a dizzying impression of whispers. It had only been for an instant. The sight of the head welling up from the steps had blotted the impression from his mind.

Jute's headache pulsed with each heartbeat. He knew it was the result of the whispers. The whispers of hundreds of wards all concentrated in one place. Strange. The pain felt familiar, as if he had been in the vicinity of those particular wards before. Where had it been? He couldn't remember.

How much more time until the hour after midnight?

Surely the jailer will come again on his rounds before then.

I'll steal the key, and then—and then. . .

Jute's eyes closed and his head fell forward on his chest. The jailer passed by three times more, but neither of the two saw the other, for the boy was sound asleep and the jailer noticed little even when awake.

CHAPTER SIXTY-SEVEN
THE REGENT'S BALL

The wind blew through the eucalyptus trees lining the lane that climbed up into the neighborhood of Highneck Rise. It moaned in the branches, wandering back and forth as if it were looking for something it could not find. Ronan hunched his shoulders as he walked along. The new coat he was wearing felt stiff around his neck. It chafed his skin. His hands felt cold and his mouth was dry, but that had nothing to do with his new clothing. A cat ran across the lane in front of him. It paused for a moment and stared at him before disappearing into the bushes along a wall.

"Good hunting," said Ronan.

He rattled the two rings in his pocket and wondered how the prince of Harth had explained their loss to the regent or the court chamberlain or whoever it was that saw about such things. At any rate, it was not his concern. Lords and ladies and all that lot could go jump into the sea and be done with, for all he cared, though the prince was a superb swordsman. And a decent fellow, he had to admit that. The rest of them could go drown in the sea.

The sea.

Even if he never saw her again after tonight, the sea would always be there. All the more reason to go north to the Flessoray Islands. Life there was defined by the sea, outlined and delineated just as each island was hemmed about and held by the tide.

He turned down the Street of Willows and pushed through the gate outside the Galnes manor. Light shone in the kitchen window. A door opened and he could see the slim form of the girl.

Her.

The ancient sea.

"You're hungry," Liss said.

He said nothing.

"And it's early yet. Come inside."

The old cook was at the sink again, just like the first time he had been there. She turned and smiled. Her wrinkled skin seemed to waver in the light and he blinked, for he thought he saw a seal, one of the brown seals that were forever sunning on the rocks off the shore.

"I've made a nice casserole of leeks and eggs," said the cook. "You'll have to eat a great deal of it, as I don't eat such things and my lady eats as delicately as a sandpiper fidgeting about the sand."

"And what do you eat?" he asked.

"I haven't fidgeted in five hundred years," said Liss, but she smiled at the old cook.

"Fish, mostly," said the cook, clattering dishes onto the table. "Now, eat."

He ate, and it was good, as he knew it would be. Liss sat across from him and took three bites before laying her fork down.

"What, not tasty enough for you?" said the cook. "I'll have you know I grew those leeks myself in the garden here."

"Hush, Sanna," said Liss. "Two bites would have satisfied me, but I took a third out of appreciation for you."

He glanced up and found her gazing at him. Until that moment, he had not really looked at her. It was the melancholy of the day, perhaps, or the ache in his throat that had kept his eyes from her. Put off the moment, he thought dismally, and then it'll never come. Then it'll never be ended. Then it'll never be past. I should've walked slower.

Liss wore a simple blue gown of a strange material that looked as if it had been woven of foam and water and slow, thick light. It floated around her wrists as though it moved on an invisible tide, and it lapped up around her white neck where it halted at a string of pearls. Her hair was piled on top of her head in a sheaf of heavy, glossy black. She was entirely beautiful and he could not be glad for such a thing, for it only made him more conscious of himself and the dull, tired pain that pervaded his being. He put down his fork.

"How shall you bring me into the castle, Ronan of Aum?" she said.

"That isn't my name," he said bitterly. "Just as Liss is not yours."

"I know."

"Then why do you call me Ronan?"

"You must take back who you are in your own time. There's little of your past that I do not know. Remember, a drop of my blood flows in your veins." She smiled slightly. "The sea is patient. It always returns to the land to see what might be found. Each grain of sand is known and counted, but the future is still of your choosing, even though for the rest of your life you shall feel the tide pulling you its way." Her smile deepened.

He bowed his head.

"Two ward rings."

The two rings spilled from his hand and clinked on the tabletop. Liss picked one up and gazed at it curiously. The ring was too big for her fingers but it settled snugly around her thumb.

"Wearing it will satisfy the wards guarding the castle that you're not an intruder. The regent gives all such rings to his guests and to his servants. It's similar to that—"

"Ah yes," said Liss. "The other ring."

"Which, in your possession, would've easily allowed you entrance to the castle without my assistance. Without this charade." He was conscious of anger pricking at his thoughts. Resentment.

"Yes, I could have. Perhaps." She smiled again and said nothing beyond that.

Liss wrapped herself in a dark cloak that extinguished the glimmer of her gown. Torchlight shone in the street beyond the wall. A horse whickered and the gate swung open under the hand of a bowing driver. The gilded shape of a carriage loomed past him. Ronan took Liss's hand and helped her up the steps to her seat.

"A carriage." She smiled at him. "It's been a very long time."

The driver called to his team, and then they were away as the horses broke into a trot. Moonlight shone in through the windows on either side. The silence and darkness of Highneck Rise slid by, all stone walls and gates and occasional lit windows seen from across the gardens and groves. The road wound higher and higher up through the night and, as they went, the manors grew larger and the walls grew higher. They did not speak as the carriage rolled along. The silence between them filled with the rolling clatter of the carriage wheels and the tattoo of the horses' hooves. Beyond it, Ronan thought he could hear the low boom of the surf surging against the shore. He looked at Liss, but her eyes were closed.

After several minutes, the carriage eased to a halt as the lane turned into a wide drive that curved about a fountain. The door swung open and the driver bowed them out. Liss slipped one hand into Ronan's arm. Water shot up from the mouth of an immense stone fish and splashed down into a pool. The falling water rippled with torchlight, and everywhere there was the liquid gleam of silks and satins as carriages rolled to a halt. The castle gates stood beyond the fountain. Lords and ladies drifted through the gates and past the ranks of Guardsmen standing at attention. The soldiers gazed with unblinking eyes through the nobility as if they were shadows—pleasant wraiths to be dismissed as daydreams. They looked past to the night itself, which seemed to have tiptoed as closely as possible to the windows of the castle as if it might peer inside to learn of balls and dancing and other such wonderments. At the end of the lane, the night plunged down to the city below. Lights glittered there like a thousand stars gleaming through a thousand holes pricked in a tapestry of darkness. The sky above was just the same.

"I'd forgotten the fountain," said Liss. "How lovely."

Ronan twisted the ring on his finger.

"Shall we?" he said.

There was one bad moment when they walked through the gate. Within the courtyard, and at the foot of the wide steps that led up to the castle doors, stood a small contingent of courtiers, smiling and bowing to the guests streaming up toward the castle. Ronan paused and Liss tightened her fingers on his arm.

"That man is the steward of the regent," he said.

A short, squat man stood in the midst of the courtiers. He neither bowed nor smiled with the others but merely inclined his gray head politely to those who passed by. His eyes were watchful.

"His name's Dreccan Gor and, though he's the steward of Botrell, he's also the advisor of the Silentman of the Thieves Guild. He'll know me well."

She said nothing, but merely pressed again on his arm as if to urge him on. He could do nothing except walk forward. He wondered about the state of the regent's dungeons. In his melancholy, he looked down at her shining hair and marveled that she seemed only a young girl, not even reaching his shoulder.

The courtiers bowed and smiled with all the elegance that comes from lives spent doing little else. They inspected Ronan's clothes with sidelong glances. He could feel the pressure of Liss's fingers on his arm. Dreccan Gor stood just past the courtiers. But then, out of the corner of his eye, Ronan saw the question forming on the steward's face. Liss glanced up at that moment—only for a second—and she smiled full at the steward. And then they were past and the steward was shaking his head as if he had just forgotten a pleasant dream. Ronan could smell the scent of the sea in the air.

"I shall not do that again, I hope," Liss said quietly. "Power calls to power, and even the smallest gleam can bring attention. And bye and bye, it brings the contemplation of one unwanted."

"Who would that be?"

She frowned. The tip of her tongue emerged as if to taste the air.

"I don't know," she said. "There's one here, two perhaps. Possibly three. It is strange."

They passed through the marble arch of the doors and into the castle.

CHAPTER SIXTY-EIGHT
A FAMILIAR SCENT

Arodilac Bridd wandered down the corridor. Several footmen whisked past bearing platters. The aroma of roast beef floated behind them. Arodilac's stomach reminded him that he hadn't eaten dinner yet. Lunch had consisted of bread and cheese gobbled down as he trudged back to the castle after Guard duty. He smoothed his hands down the front of his white silk shirt and considered following the footmen to see where they would deposit the platters. But then he thought better of it, for at the far end of the corridor, just visible past a potted fern, was the profile of Bordeall. The old commander was standing with a goblet in hand and a scowl on his face. Beyond him, on the polished floor of the ballroom, couples floated by in blurs of every color imaginable, leaves of silk and satin blown by an invisible wind. They twirled and spun to the strains of an old Thulish air.

Arodilac absentmindedly hummed the song and tried to figure out why he felt guilty. The problem was, at this age, he always felt somewhat guilty. But there was something specific he had forgotten. Perhaps it hadn't been important. Still, it might be wiser to stay out of Bordeall's sight until he remembered what it was.

Now, what had the song been about? Something about coming home after the war? No. Not coming home after the war—that was it. He remembered it now. Most Thulish songs were melancholy like that, but hardly anyone remembered the words anymore. When he had been a child, his governess had been from Thule. She had loved to sing.

The words sprang into his mind. He could almost hear her wispy old voice.

You'll nae find me, my love, for I've left thee a' home.
You'll nae find me, my love, for my bed's laid alone.
Bide thee, my love, thy heart an' thee
For I've ridden to war, my brothers an' me.

You'll nae find me, my love, for I've left thee a' home.
You'll nae find me, my love, for my bed's laid alone.
Sleep thee, my love, thy heart an' thee
Sleep thee by moonlight an' sleep thee by sea.

You'll nae find me, my love, for I've left thee a' home.
You'll nae find me, my love, for my bed's laid alone.
An' if ye would wake an' if ye would search
Ye'll find me my bed laid under the turf.

Arodilac frowned. What a dreary song. It was all well to ride away to war, but it would also be nice to ride back from war. And it would be doubly nice to ride back home to be greeted by a wife and children all standing at the door. Liss and their three sons. Perhaps a daughter or two might be nice as well.

Arodilac sighed.

A heavy hand settled on his shoulder and he jumped.

"Bridd," said a voice. "I've been looking for you."

It was Bordeall. The old man tossed off the last of his wine and then, without even looking, reached behind him and placed his goblet on the platter of a passing footman. He surveyed Arodilac grimly.

"Oh?" said Arodilac. He found himself unable to meet the commander's eye.

"Back early, aren't you?"

"The watch changed at the gate and I came right up here. There's the ball on, you know."

"I'd noticed," said the other.

"After all, I'm the regent's heir." Arodilac warmed to the sound of his own words. The regent's heir had social obligations, didn't he? "It's my duty to dance at the ball."

"If you came straight away here after your watch, then you didn't have time to stop in on Lady Gawinn and the child, did you now?"

"Uh, no."

"That's your duty, not this damn fool ball."

"But—"

"Get going."

Arodilac hurried through the halls. Of all the days to forget. He had never forgotten before. It wasn't fair. By the time he walked all the way down to the Gawinn house, made some polite talk with Lady Gawinn—all women talked overly long—and then returned to the castle, more than an hour of the ball would be lost. Bother it all!

He skidded to a halt. Hang walking. He'd take a horse. Yes! The two-year old he'd had his eye on ever since Uncle had purchased the horse last spring. A splendid black with a bright brown eye and a high step. There'd be some fun in the evening yet. He whirled and ran straight into an unyielding body.

"Steady on, young Bridd," said someone, laughing.

"L-lord Gifernes," he stammered. "I didn't see you. I'm sorry."

"No apologies necessary."

The duke of Mizra stood smiling in the middle of the hall.

"In a hurry for the ball, no doubt?" he said.

"Um, no. I have to see about a—a girl. Just off to the stables now to get myself a mount."

"Aha—women." The duke drew closer and lowered his voice in a confiding manner. "Between you and me, that's one of the main reasons I've come to Hearne. High time to find that certain someone, don't you know."

Arodilac thought of Liss and tried to look as if he did know, but then ruined the effect by ducking his head and grinning foolishly.

"Um," he said.

The duke clapped him on the shoulder.

"I won't detain you any longer. I know how it is. The impatience, the sleepless nights, the waning appetite. Why, I remember when I was your age, I spent a whole month trying to—"

"Milord."

The voice came from behind the duke. It was an odd sort of voice—flat and insubstantial as if the speaker was holding his breath while he spoke so that someone— something—sleeping would not be woken by his words. A tall, thin man stood there. At his feet sat a large dog. Arodilac blinked. How odd that he hadn't seen them until the man had spoken. One of the duke's servants, no doubt. The man was dressed in black, relieved at the collar and the wrists with scarlet. His face was pale as if he did not spend much

303

time in the sunlight. The man's eyes were flat and black. They passed incuriously over Arodilac and then settled on the duke.

"Milord, shall I return Holdfast to the stables? He has not had his supper yet and he grows hungry."

"Eh?" The duke turned. "Oh, of course. Didn't even hear you, Cearu, creeping up like that. Yes, take him away for his bones." He smiled at Arodilac. "Can't have the beast roaming about the castle now, can we? He'll be begging tidbits from your uncle's guests and tripping up the dancing."

The dog yawned and revealed a mouthful of yellowing fangs. Arodilac had never seen a dog less likely to be begging tidbits. If anything, the brute would take its tidbits by force.

"Go on," said the duke. "He won't bite."

Arodilac carefully patted the dog on its head. It sniffed at his hand and then suddenly backed away until it ran into the servant's legs. The hound sat down and stared up at Arodilac.

"If you'll pardon me, sir," said Arodilac, "I'll be off then."

"Best of luck with your lady. I'm off to pay court to one myself. Luck to both of us!"

As Arodilac had hoped, the black was in his stall. The horse blew down his neck and stamped its hoof lightly as he cinched the saddle down. A sleepy groom stumbled up, yawning and knuckling his eyes, but Arodilac waved him away.

For some reason, the horse shied when they clattered out into the yard, but it was a well-broken horse and quickly settled down. The tap of its hooves echoed off the castle wall. Arodilac glanced back uneasily and thought he saw something in the shadow of the stable door. It almost looked like a dog. A large dog. Or maybe it was just a sack of oats leaning against the wall.

The soldiers at the castle gate saluted as he rode through, as befitted the nephew and heir of the regent, but they grinned as they did and the salutes were sloppy, for they all served alongside him. He wasn't the regent's heir to them; he was just the youngest lad in the Guard and an easy target for the worst duties like scouring armor and mucking out the Guard stable.

The night was chillier than Arodilac had thought, particularly with the black trotting along at such a pace. He shivered in his silk shirt and wondered if, when he returned to the castle, he would smell so strongly of horse that no lady would want to dance with him.

Liss.

He sighed and then settled himself comfortably in the saddle to examine his memories of her, like a miser mooning over a handful of coins. It was odd, but he couldn't remember what color her eyes were. Had they been gray? Perhaps blue. Maybe green. Green went nicely with blonde hair. She did have blonde hair, didn't she?

Beneath him, the black two-year-old snorted as if in disagreement. What did hair color or eye color matter? Could the girl run as fast as the wind? But Arodilac did not know the speech of animals, and horse and rider pounded along down the dark streets of Highneck Rise toward the house of Owain Gawinn in friendly and unwitting disagreement. Arodilac was ignorant of the horse's opinions, and the horse, while convinced of the preeminence of such things as speed and four strong legs, might have revised its view if it had known who Liss Galnes was, for even horses dream of the sea.

They rode down further through Highneck Rise, where the streets wind west toward the lower cliffs overlooking the sea. On corners and at some of the gates, lamplight flared gold in the dark. It seemed to Arodilac that he was the only person out that night.

"Everyone up at the ball, no doubt," he said to himself.

That consideration, along with further thoughts of Liss, allowed him to enjoy several more moments of melancholy. The black blew derisively. It had no understanding of what a ball might be—did it taste better than an apple?—and did not care. The horse was pleased to be out of the stable and trotting somewhere. Exactly where did not matter. What mattered was motion.

If either of them had glanced back, they might have noticed a faint movement behind them. The horse would have scented the movement if the wind had been blowing in the right direction, but it was blowing in off the sea and there was only the smell of salt and the rolling boom of the waves from below the cliffs.

The walls of Owain Gawinn's home appeared before them. A fog was thickening in the air. Arodilac tied up the black at the gates and let himself through. He shivered, his breath misting. The horse nickered uneasily after him, but he did not listen. Light gleamed in the windows. A servant opened the door and bowed him inside. He waited in the hallway and closed his eyes. The air was warm with the scent of beef stew and fresh bread. His stomach grumbled. Footsteps whispered down the long hall toward him.

"Arodilac. You needn't be so diligent."

He opened his eyes. Sibb Gawinn was smiling at him.

"Mistress Gawinn." He ducked his head.

"You're missing the ball," she said.

"Well, yes."

"You needn't waste any more time here. She's fast asleep, poor thing."

"If you don't mind, mistress," he said diffidently. "Might I look in at her? Old Bord—I mean, the officer of the watch will ask if I've seen her, and if I say no, he'll probably send me back straightaway."

She nodded. "Come. I'll not have you shunted back and forth between the castle and our home."

The end of the hall opened up into a large chamber lit by an oil lamp hanging high from the ceiling. Arodilac drew a quick breath. He had never been in this part of the house before. For a moment, the ball was forgotten.

"Mistress Gawinn—are these, are these. . .?"

"These worthies spur on my poor husband each and every day."

The walls were hung with painting after painting. They were portraits of men, and in their clothing and in the cracked oil and faded colors, there was evidence of a progression of time spanning hundreds of years. Weapons hung below each of the paintings: a battle-axe with scarred handle but brightly burnished head under a portrait of a stern old man, and, further along, a sword in its leather-wrapped sheath. There were spears with blades as thin and as delicate as paper, braces of daggers, and an ugly-looking morning star with a brutal spiked ball.

"This is all the same family," said Arodilac, looking from face to face.

"All of them Gawinns and all of them Lord Captains of Hearne. All of them dead and buried, from near to distant past. Mostly distant now. Some fell in battle and some were felled by old age itself, cursing, no doubt, the fact that they didn't die on the battlefield.

They've left their weapons behind. Their weapons and their shadows and their whispers to urge on the next son of their house to his duties."

Sibb did not speak bitterly, but smiled about the chamber fondly, as if looking upon the members of a beloved family.

"It is comforting to know we are watched with such good will," she said.

A staircase mounted up from the chamber. The steps creaked under them. Mistress Gawinn took a lamp from a wall bracket and it flared within her hands. Shadows stretched down a hall lined by doors on either side. At the far end, moonlight shone through a window. A door opened and the tall figure of Loy stood there.

"Milady." He scowled at Arodilac.

"Is she sleeping still?"

"Aye. Not stirred a finger."

"We'll just peep in then," said Sibb. "The Guard must be assured that all of Hearne is sleeping safe in their beds."

Arodilac blushed but said nothing.

Loy ushered them into a sitting chamber. A second door opened past that to a bedchamber. Arodilac could discern the form of the girl under the blankets. Her hair spilled about the pillow and gleamed whiter in the lamplight than the cotton sheets themselves.

"I hope she doesn't dream tonight," said Sibb.

Loy shut the door.

"Satisfied?" he said, scowling at Arodilac.

Somewhere nearby, a horse whinnied. The sound was faint, for the walls of the house were of thick stone. The noise came again, and there was a strange, shuddering note of desperation in the sound. It seemed as if it was no longer a horse whinnying but rather a child screaming, thin-voiced and out of breath.

"What in shadow's name is that?" said Loy.

"My horse," said Arodilac.

He turned and sprinted down the hall. Loy ran after him. For some reason, Arodilac stopped at the top of the stairs and crouched down, staring into the chamber below. The light was dim in the space beneath, for there was only the single lamp hanging from the ceiling.

"Why are you—?" said Loy.

"Hush," he said, and in that moment they heard clearly, from somewhere in the house, the sound of glass shattering.

"See after the girl," said Arodilac, his face white. "And bid Mistress Gawinn go to her children."

Arodilac looked frantically around, but there was nothing at hand except for a vase at the top of the stairs. It was filled with dried flowers. He plucked them out and laid them down, rustling, on the floor. The vase itself was scarcely as heavy as the flowers and he grimaced, hefting the thing in his hand. Still, anything was better than nothing. He crept down the stairs. The steps creaked beneath his feet and, with every groaning plank, his heart faltered within his chest.

For some strange reason, the lamp hanging from the chamber ceiling was flickering as if blown by a gentle exhalation, even though the air around Arodilac was as still as if the house itself was holding its breath. Shadows gained form so that ghostly figures glided to and fro on the floor below the stairs. On the opposite wall, light glinted on a spear tip.

It seemed as if the portrait above the spear winked—an old man with a scarred face. Arodilac blinked.

And then he heard it.

It was a quiet sound. A mere rearrangement of weight, as if someone had shifted their balance from one foot to the other. There, the sound came again. Arodilac looked through the railings. His breath caught in his throat. For there, staring up at him, were two red eyes. Two red spots gleaming in the gloom. At least he thought they were eyes. And then he knew beyond any doubt that they were eyes, for to his horror, the two red spots blinked and then blinked again, still staring up at him.

The neck of the vase shattered in his hands. The noise seemed as loud as a thunderclap in the silence of the house. Blood dripped from his fingers where the pottery shards had cut him. He gasped. Below him, claws scrabbled on the floor. The steps creaked and up the stairs hurtled a form made out of shadows and teeth and glaring red eyes. The thing slammed against him and he was thrown against the banister. Wood splintered and he yelled, terrified, for there was nothing beneath his feet. He flailed out and caught hold of a railing, only to have it break, and then he was falling. His fingers grabbed onto something—a smooth horizontal piece of wood—that held, slowed him for a second. The frame of one of the paintings. Then it too snapped, and he heard the sound of canvas ripping.

Arodilac slammed down hard on his back. For a moment he could not breathe and the lamp above him seemed to spin around in circles that left a trail of dull, flaring gold in the dark. He gulped and gulped again until the air came flooding painfully back into his lungs. He stumbled to his feet. Without even thinking, he grabbed hold of the nearest weapon—one of the spears—and wrenched it away from the wall. Then he ran for the staircase.

He was halfway up the stairs when someone screamed. A figure lurched across the hall in front of him, a bundle clutched in its arms. Loy. Hair as white as corn silk flew up against his face and the bundle clutched back at him with desperate hands. The girl. She screamed again. It was a high, ugly sound. The scream of an animal without wits and without hope.

Loy collided with the opposite wall and then stumbled down the hall, away from Arodilac and toward the window at the far end. Lamplight painted a wet red sheen on one of his legs. A shape drifted out of the door after him, a mass of shadow roughly formed in the shape of an immense dog. The dog seemed strangely insubstantial, for one moment part of a leg was there, and then it no longer was—Arodilac could see through it to the oak floorboards beyond—the next moment the head dissolved into shadows and then back. It was as if the beast took on the appearance of whatever was around it— shadows, wood, stone, the weave of a rug. It blended into its surroundings like a sand lizard fading into near invisibility against the backdrop of its desert dune home.

But even though the beast faded in and out of sight, it was easily heard in the creaking steps it took—the floorboards groaned under its tremendous weight—and the sound of its rumbling growl. A stench of decay filled the hall. The thing stalked forward, head lowered and fixed on Loy. It moved slowly, and Loy, even though he staggered along, kept up a quick pace. But the hallway was only so long and Loy was soon at the window at the far end. He untangled the girl's arms from his own to set her down—she fought and clawed to stay in his arms, but she was small—and then, alone, turned toward the approaching creature. He saw Arodilac, but his face was dull with shock and he said nothing.

The dog leapt.

Arodilac shouted and ran forward. But it felt as if he ran through deep water. Surely this was only a nightmare that he was struggling to wake from with the sheets tangled about his legs. The spear felt as heavy as an oak log in his hands. The light in the hallway had been faint enough to begin with, shed by only the flame of one lamp on the wall near the top of the stairs, and now it seemed to be dimming even more so that darkness flooded in around the edge of his sight. All he could see was Loy's face and the white band of his arms clamped around the dog's neck. But the white was slowly blurring into red and the darkness was dissolving the man's face into itself until there was only his eyes blinking tiredly.

"Arodilac."

It was only a whisper. That was all Loy could manage. The moon shone through the window behind Loy and the blot of darkness swallowing him up. Moonlight gilded the spearhead falling through the air so that it looked like a falling leaf. A leaf gone gold with autumn and falling to the earth to die. Then the leaf plunged into the darkness and the darkness seemed to shrink in on itself slightly—it looked much more like a dog now. Its teeth snapped together in front of Arodilac's face.

The window behind Loy shattered around him. He fell out into the night with the darkness still clasped in his arms. It seemed as if he smiled as he fell, his eyes drifting from Arodilac's white face to the even whiter hair of the girl crouched shivering and sobbing below the sill. Desperately, Arodilac tried to hang onto the shaft of the spear but it slipped through his fingers, slick with his own blood.

Light sprang up behind him in the hall and he heard the terrified voices of the servants on the stairs. Footsteps ran by him and Sibb Gawinn was on her knees with the little girl in her arms and there came a thin, faltering voice that fluttered and sobbed and whispered the word *mama* over and over again.

CHAPTER SIXTY-NINE
DANCING AND OTHER ENJOYABLE THINGS

Ronan turned the ward ring around his finger. He had never been inside the castle. At least, except for the time when he had come to meet Arodilac Bridd, but even that time could hardly count as having been inside the castle. He had been whisked through an unobtrusive door all the way around the back. The servants' quarters, probably. Arodilac Bridd. That was one person he did not wish to meet tonight.

He glanced sideways at Liss and marveled. Surely she was only a girl. A slender form capped with a sheaf of shining hair, lips parted, eyes wide and looking everywhere. Just a girl overwhelmed with excitement at her first ball. In the regent's castle, no less. Her hand rested on his arm, lighter than a sparrow's weight.

As light as the foam on a wave.

And Ronan marveled even more. For he knew that if Liss looked at him, he would see in her eyes, past the excitement and the eagerness, something ancient and serene and terrible. He bent his head over her hair and smelled the sea.

"Isn't this marvelous?"

"What?" he said stupidly.

"This. All of this."

"Yes." But he saw none of it, only her.

Her fingers pressed down on his arm, propelling him forward. They drifted across an immense hall, through a throng of people eddying and swirling around them. A thousand lamps dangled high overhead from a thousand gold chains, shedding soft light down and in and over and around everything. The light nestled in white diamonds resting on even whiter throats. Sapphires and emeralds and rubies caught the light and then threw it back into the air, shot through with their blues and greens and scarlets. The light lapped against silks and satins and the impossibly perfect skin of the most beautiful women in all of Tormay. But amidst all of this, the light pooled around Liss until she glowed brighter than the finest diamonds, brighter than the most gorgeous sweep of silk, brighter than the most beautiful duchess. Ronan looked down at her and despaired of his charge. Surely there was no chance to keep her hidden. Surely there were so many eyes on her, covert and calculating and biding their time. He realized he didn't even know what he was supposed to be guarding her from.

Her fingers tightened on his arm.

"We only see what we want to see," she said.

He said nothing, but sweat beaded on his forehead. A servant curveted past bearing a platter of crystal glasses and Ronan claimed two before the man disappeared into the crowd. Liss wrinkled her nose when he offered her one, so he drank them both, thankful for the wine's chill. It swept the bemusement from his mind.

"Who is your enemy here, milady?"

"Do not call me that, thank you."

He steered her past a cluster of courtiers grouped around a young man dressed in what looked like every imaginable color there was to be had, and then some. He was talking loudly and every face in the group around him leaned in avidly. Gems flashed on his fingers as he waved his hands about. A servant with a studiously blank face stood on the outskirts of the group, holding a tray of wine at the ready.

Liss craned her neck, fascinated.

"What is the name of the bird with the enormous tail? It fans out like so—" And she spread her fingers in front of her.

"It's called a peacock. Liss, how can I watch over you if I don't know who I'm watching for?"

"I suppose it is a what, not a who."

"A what?"

"I think I'd like to dance," said Liss. She cocked her head to one side, as if uncertain of her own words and thinking them over. "Yes. I'd like to dance. It has been a long time."

"How long?" he said wearily. He attempted to smile and did not succeed.

She smiled, not needing to attempt it. The lamplight pooled in her eyes. Surely she was only a girl, hardly seventeen years old. But then the light was swept away by a tide of gray, then green, then a blue depth that swayed and settled into stillness.

"Before the dragons fell asleep, the poor things. Before men sailed into the west and found the land of Tormay. Before the Dark came, stooping down from the heights, searching and hunting and so hungry for what it could never have. When the stars sang for joy. When the world was still young."

He understood none of it and could only continue across the marble floor, frowning and wondering. She drifted at his side, attached to him by virtue of her hand on his arm but more distant than the horizon of the sea is to the shore. The throng ebbed and flowed around them, full of richness and light, murmuring with a thousand conversations, a thousand asides and undertones, a thousand bits of gossip carried along like so much flotsam and jetsam. Silver platters bearing goblets and tasty tidbits bobbed along overhead, secure in the hands of servants. A staircase swept up at the far end of the hall. It was wide enough to allow ten men side by side. Up and down its steps flowed a procession of lords and ladies.

Just past an enormously fat woman listening to the solicitous conversation of a rather small man, Ronan caught sight of a familiar face. Smede. The Guild accountant was dressed in faultless black and mooched along with his hands clasped behind his back. Ronan steered Liss away. Odd that Smede would be invited to such an event. Perhaps Dreccan Gor had him to the castle for some reason.

Ronan and Liss came to the staircase and mounted up it. They heard music and entered into an even larger hall than the one they had just left. Here, the walls stretched up and up into an arched ceiling so far overhead and lit with so many hanging candles that it was as if they stood under a starry night sky. Couples twirled and drifted across a black stone floor polished to such an impossible sheen that it seemed more water than stone. Liss turned to him, her face solemn. One hand settled into his and the other came to rest on his shoulder. The music rose up in a swirl of strings and swept them out across the floor.

CHAPTER SEVENTY
STORIES IN THE RAIN

Owain Gawinn reined in his horse and glanced back. The night was dark and the rain made it even more difficult to see. A few shards of moonlight gleamed on leather harness and oilskins. He could hear more than he could see: the creak of saddles, horse hooves squelching through the mud, and the mumble of talk between the men.

They were good men. Well-trained. Hardened under his tutelage. Few of them, though, had proper battle experience. Oh, there had been some skirmishing over the years. Bandits raiding villages and traders. A particularly nasty fight with ogres in the upper reaches of the Rennet Valley. Old Yan Frearen had lost his arm in that one. Not to mention the boy who had been killed. The new recruit.

Owain frowned. He wiped rain from his eyes and squinted ahead. They were nearing the rise at the west end of the Rennet Valley. The eucalyptus trees crowding along the north bank were unmistakable, even in the dark. He could not remember the boy's name. He could remember his face, though. Pale, uncomprehending, eyes widening as if already seeing something more, something beyond Tormay. But even ogres, no matter how vicious they were, could be taken down by sheer strength of numbers. It was a matter of fielding enough swords. The trick with ogres was not to get drawn into fighting in tight quarters with them. Though that wasn't always true. The Farrow lad had proven that. If the story was true.

"River's runnin' high."

It was Hoon. The little tracker materialized out of the night and nudged his horse alongside Owain's mount. He had a length of oilcloth wrapped around his head like a shawl. Water dripped from the end of his nose.

"Runnin' high," repeated Hoon. "Ain't seen it this high in a long time." There was gloomy satisfaction in his voice.

"How high?" said Owain.

"I reckon right up t' the withers at the edge of the ford. Midstream, deep enough to founder a horse. Probably haveta do a little swimming there. Weren't about t' go in just t' find out. Track looks mighty soft where it runs down next t' the bank. Slick clay. 'Spose we could allus turn back an' climb outa the valley. There's a trader's road just south, runnin' up from Lura."

"No. We'll go on," said Owain. He shook his head. "I'm not about to lose half a day backtracking. We're almost home. If needs be, we can swim the ford. Everyone's wet enough already as it is."

Hoon chuckled as if this idea made him happy.

"It'll be easy enough. I do enjoy some good swimmin'."

The two rode along in silence for some time. The entire company had slowed from a canter to a walk, due to the muddy path and the darkness. Owain was not about to push them any faster. A well-trained horse was wise enough to be allowed its own pace in such conditions.

"Hoon?"

"Aye?"

"You've been hunting in the wilds for years. Probably longer than I've been alive, if I guess your age right. What do you think it is we're searching for?"

"Wouldn't rightly want t' say." Hoon spat into the rain and then tugged the oilskin closer around his head. "There be plenty of horrible things in this world, I reckon. Sure enough. Plenty be willing to cut your throat sooner'n say how-do."

"Such as?"

"Well," said Hoon. "You got your ogres an' bears an' kobolds to begin with. Those are bad enough, though them kobolds ain't much for fightin' unless they got no other choice. Then, you watch out. Ogres an' bears—I don't advise tanglin' with neither, but bear steak is good eatin' an' there ain't much like a good bearskin t' keep you warm in winter. Ogre? I'd sooner eat my boots. Nasty, greasy stuff, ogre is."

"I'm not interested in ogres or bears. What of other creatures? You've lived up in the Morn Mountains. Surely you've encountered strange things there that I've only heard about in stories."

The path began to descend. Owain's horse picked its way forward. From up out of the darkness they could hear the murmuring rush of the river below. On either side, the edges of the valley sloped up, reaching higher and sharper until they met with the sky. The wind was cold and brisk and it blew the rain into their faces. High up on the plain, though, Owain knew the wind would be howling.

"Trouble is," said Hoon reluctantly, "stories are most ways true. Makes me wonder if somethin' comes true if enough people say it enough times. Y'ever hear the story about the Lady o' Limary?"

"My sister," said Owain, "bless her heart, used to scare me senseless with that story when I was a little boy. Of course, when I grew older, I realized it was only a story. Things like that don't happen."

"I wouldn't be so sure. Parts of the story might be true. Far as a girl makin' a pact with the Dark to live forever, well, most girls are giddy enough t' try somethin' damn fool like that. But that's aside the point. Truth is, there's a village called Limary, up in the mountains on the northeasterly edge of the Loam Forest. Only, ain't hardly anyone call it Limary anymore on account of no one's lived in the village for more'n two hundred years. Just ruins now. But there're a few folks round abouts that remember. Sheepfarmers, of course."

"What do sheep have to do with the so-called Lady of Limary?"

"Enough, an' I'll tell you why. It happened a whiles back. I weren't much more'n a boy in those days, but I'd struck out from home, making my way hunting an' doing odd jobs. A friend an' I wandered into a village on that same northeasterly edge of the Loam. East of Dolan somewhat. Pretty much nowhere, but right up against the mountains. A farmer hired us to hunt down an old wolf. It'd been makin' off with his sheep. Least, that's what he thought it was."

Owain shifted in the saddle, trying to find a spot that wasn't sore. It had been years since he had been so many days on horseback. The ford wasn't much further now, if his memory served him, and then it would be an hour more to the gates of Hearne. A quick ride in good weather, through the cornfields and meadows of the western reach of the Rennet, but undoubtedly muddy and treacherous this night.

"Oh?" said Owain. "I suspect you're going to tell me it was this Lady of Limary making off with the sheep, and not a wolf."

"Ain't no use tellin' the story," said Hoon. "Ain't no use if you're bound on tellin' it yourself."

"There's surely more to the story than that."

"Well, there is. Much more. I'll tell it, if you let me. We lit out on those tracks, my friend an' I. But the wolf knew a thing or two more'n us, an' we lost the trail halfway up a mountain. Big mountain. Found out later it were called Limary, an' it's had that name long afore any folk lived in those parts. Night was comin' on fast an' it were cold up that high. Cold enough to drive ice into your bones. Luck would have it, just when we were thinkin' about crawlin' our way back down the mountain, my friend sees a light up ahead. Look, he says. I weren't too happy about that light, but I weren't too happy about the cold neither."

"I've heard of the moor lights," said Owain. "Lights far out on the moors that lure travelers to their death in the bogs and falling into sudden crevices."

"Pshaw," said Hoon. "Moor lights ain't nothin' much. Only a fool be taken in by a moor light. Our light, now, was altogether different. We made our way over to it an' found a big stone house built there, right on the mountainside. Light shone out the window. The door opened at our knock an' there stood the loveliest lady you'd never seen. Skin as white as frost on the flowers and lips redder'n blood. She had the prettiest green eyes."

"Ah," said Owain. "The stories are all the same."

"Right they are. That's because they're true. Hadn't you heard me afore?"

"Of course, of course. It's just I've only heard the stories. You've obviously experienced them. So what happened then?"

"Well, I'll tell you," said Hoon, somewhat mollified by these words. "I'll tell you, if you let me talk. The lady offered us shelter for the night. Invited us in. Had her servants give us a dinner—"

"Mutton, probably," said Owain to himself.

"—an' we ate until we were stuffed. Ain't had such good feed in all my life. Real quiet sorts, was her servants. Never said a word. Just all eyes starin' an' silent an' tiptoeing about. She bid us good night an' had us shown to our room. Only one room for the both of us, but she apologized nicely, sayin' it were on account of the weather an' she had other guests already at bed. We was both right tired an' it were late. My friend dropped off like a stone, snoring away. Mebbe it were the racket he were making, but I couldn't sleep straight off. Lay there for a while. The food didn't sit well in my stomach. Just when I were about asleep, I heard this noise at the door. It were quiet enough, but y'understand I were a hunter's son. The sound weren't human, I can tell you. It were a sniffing sound as if some creature were getting a taste of us into its nose. The hair stood up on the back of my neck."

"What happened then?" asked Owain.

"Whaddya expect? About had time to sit up in bed, blink, an' then the door opened. Silent an' slow, but I got a glimpse of green eyes staring at me, huge and flaring like lamps, an' I smelt something like wolf but worse. Tumbled off the bed an' dove into an old wardrobe standing 'longside the bed. Gave a yell enough to wake the dead, but my friend just snored on. Then I was in the wardrobe. Luck would have it, there was slats on the inside an' I held onto 'em for dear life. Somethin' hit the doors, harder'n a mule kick, but it were made of good solid oak. Three times, whatever were on the outside slammed against those doors. I could hear the thing scratching an' snarling. An' then there were only silence. I must've fell asleep in that wardrobe, still clinging to them slats. I woke up shivering the next morning, I were that cold. Except, I weren't in a wardrobe in a room inside no stone house. I were curled up on the mountainside. Just ice an' rock around, an' there weren't no houses in sight. Only thing in sight were my friend, lying there with his throat torn out an' big pawprints in the snow around him. Gave me a right turn."

"And you suppose it was the Lady of Limary?"

"Who else?" Hoon shrugged. "Laugh all you want, but I know what I saw. I know what happened. I was there. You weren't. Point is, ain't much we know. Or want to know. S'far as our murderers, I dunno. Could be any number of creatures we ain't never seen nor heard of."

By this time, the path had descended down to the riverbank. The river rushed through the darkness, and they could hear the rain hissing on the water. The horses behind them halted.

"Going to get wet," said Hoon.

"As long as we're home tonight. That's all that matters."

"All right, men," said Owain. "Swim 'em over. The river's running too high."

Someone mumbled a curse, but Owain did not bother turning. He had not the heart for such discipline, not after a long day's ride in the cold rain. He would have cursed as well, but his thoughts were already full of home and warmth and Sibb. Owain kicked free from the stirrup and stepped down to the ground. His boots sank into the mud. He could feel his men's eyes on him. All grinning, probably. He took a grip on the horse's reins and walked it into the river.

Shadows, but the water was cold as ice. He could feel the stones of the ford underfoot. His mount nickered unhappily. He tugged the horse forward. The flow surged against him. And then he was forced to swim, the reins in his mouth and one hand gripping the horse's mane. The horse lost its footing about midway. The current there was faster than Owain had thought it would be. The flow swept them both along, but the ford was wide and they had not gone more than a dozen yards before the horse struck bottom again. It snorted and surged forward toward the riverbank.

"All right then!" called out Owain.

They swam the ford, one by one. Some grinned at him, dripping with water and smeared with mud, some clambering out, sputtering and cursing under their breath. The horses' breath steamed in the cold night air. Hoon came last, comfortably and impossibly perched on top of his mount, with his boots tucked dry inside his cloak.

"Perhaps my memory doesn't serve me well," said Owain sourly. "Didn't you say we'd have to swim the ford?"

"Can't rightly recollect," said Hoon. "Though I do enjoy swimmin' when it's other folks doin' it. Mebbe it's cuz I'm so small, my horse don't mind the weight."

They made good time riding up through the gap at the mouth of the valley, where the sides were as steep as cliffs. The land fell away down to the fields that sloped all the way to the sea. The river rushed off into the night. It would reach Hearne before them, to curve around the city's southern walls and there find the sea.

Lights winked in the darkness, far off the muddy track, as they passed solitary cottages and hamlets. The rain slackened and then ceased. The wind blew harder. Above them, however, the clouds scudded away to reveal a night sky shining with stars. The horsemen crested a rise and there, still distant but gleaming with more light than the stars themselves, lay the city of Hearne.

"An hour more an' I'll be drinking ale," said someone.

"Bed," said another. "Keep your ale."

Someone else articulated the merits of hot mutton. There was much laughter and good cheer. The horses cantered down the slope.

"Oats and a warm stable," said Owain. He patted his horse's neck. It whickered as if it understood. "Oats and a stable for you. Home for me."

CHAPTER SEVENTY-ONE
LEVORETH UNMASKED

Only a few weeks had gone by since he had been roaming the streets with the rest of the Juggler's children. Only a few weeks. Jute stared into the darkness of the dungeon passage. He chewed on his thumbnail and snuffled once or twice.

It wasn't fair.

When he had been particularly lonely, he had loved to climb up onto the roof of a house several doors down from the Goose and Gold. From there he could see down into the yard behind the house. Most days, if he waited long enough, the mother of the home would come out with the laundry or with a chicken to pluck or to weed the garden. She had four young children, and they usually tumbled after her into the yard, where they would chase each other about—if they could not catch the cat first—until all four turned into a pile of flying fists and happy roaring and, occasionally, an unhappy, bawling face. That was when the woman would straighten up from her laundry or potatoes, or whatever it was, and cuff the children until they were all bawling. And then, invariably, she would go into the house and reemerge with bread and honey to soothe their tears. Jute never tired of watching them.

It wasn't fair. He would have given anything to have been one of those children being cuffed about. Instead, he was in this miserable dungeon. He got to his feet and stretched. His stomach told him it was getting late. No sign of the jailer. There were only shadows and the glow of an oil lamp burning on the wall further down the passage.

Oh, Hawk, he thought miserably. Where are you? If only I hadn't climbed out of my window. If only I hadn't left the ruins. The square was crowded with so many people. Surely I was safe in a confusion of faces and stalls and barrows like that. How was I to know?

But he hadn't been safe in the crowd.

No, agreed the darkness around him.

Jute blinked. For a brief moment, he thought the shadow lying across the far wall moved. Swirled, as water does when it pours down a drain. But now it was still. It was only a shadow.

Safety is found in small places.

Jute scuttled back against the wall.

In small, quiet places in the dark.

"Who are you?" he said. His skin twitched. The voice was quiet. He could not tell if the voice was inside his head or if he was hearing the sound.

Just a memory. Someone asleep, dreaming. Old bones and dust and words. Just someone thinking about waking up and having a bite to eat.

The boy's scalp prickled.

"I-I wouldn't taste good," he managed. "I'm extremely scrawny."

The voice chuckled. There was a sort of damp sound to it, and Jute's imagination trembled into life, inhabited by things with pale eyes that could see in the dark. He remembered the spider he had seen while exploring—hundreds of eyes bulging on stalks and gleaming in the shadows with their own cold light.

There's no telling for some people's taste.

"I wouldn't make more than a mouthful," said Jute.

No, you wouldn't.

"No," said Jute, relieved they had arrived at some agreement.

How are you going to get out, boy? There are two doors in this place, but only one is unlocked and only that one leads out. You've tried it. What did you find?

"Nothing," said Jute, thinking of the stone head rising up out of the stairs. He shuddered. "I'll find a way."

With the little girl also? I heard the two of you whispering in my dreams.

"Of course. I promised."

Jute edged along the wall sideways, one eye on the shadows in the passage. It was unnerving to talk to voices without bodies. What made it even more disturbing was that he wasn't sure if he wished the voice had a body or not. If it had a body, what sort of body would it have? If it didn't have a body, how was it talking to him?

She wasn't much of a help, was she?

"Well, no."

Might be better to leave her, don't you think?

"I promised to get her out of here."

Of course, but there's only the one way out. Up the stairs, and you know what waits on the stairs, don't you?

"I'll figure something out," said Jute.

One second if you're lucky. That's all the time you'll have to get by it. And that's not enough. Especially if you've got a little girl along with you. Listen, I know a word.

Jute crept forward a little from the wall. "A word? What do you mean?"

A word that'll close its mouth. A word that'll put it to sleep, just like me.

"What word?"

I'll give you the word, boy, if you give me something.

"Give you what?" said Jute cautiously.

One little thing for one little word.

Jute crouched down. He stared at the shadows stretching down the passage. There. There it was. A tiny disturbance in the air, like a wisp of smoke on the breeze.

One little thing.

"What's that?"

He stared, fascinated, at the eddy in the middle of the shadows. Certainly there was no wind down here within the stillness of the Silentman's dungeon. Nonetheless, the shadow moved. He inched closer.

The little girl.

"What?"

Turn your back on her. Walk out. Alone.

The shadows thickened. The lamp further down the passage went out. There is no telling what Jute might have said then, but at that moment, right when his mouth opened, there came to his mind a memory of sky—a bright, cold, wide open space awash with light—and there, so far away that it was only a speck of movement, flew the hawk. Jute heard his angry shriek. And that same shriek burst from his lips.

"No!"

A wind sprang up. It blew down the passage in a mighty rush that swept the darkness away. Jute tasted cool, clean air in his mouth. As quickly as it had come, the wind was gone and there were only the normal, gloomy shadows filling the passage. With a quiet pop, the oil lamp sprang back to life. The flame wavered once, as if breathed upon, and then was still.

"Hawk?" said Jute.

There was no response.

Shivering, he hurried off down the passage. Lena peered between the bars of her cell.

"Jute," she said, her eyes wide. "What was that? Something woke me up and then there was a terrible noise!"

"Nothing. You must've been dreaming."

Jute wished he had been dreaming, but it hadn't been a dream. He glanced back down the passage and then nearly jumped when Lena grabbed his hands through the bars. Her fingers were icy cold. He chafed them with his own and tried to think, but nothing came to mind.

"Jute?"

She looked at him anxiously. He managed to smile.

"Don't worry."

Lena curled back up in the corner of her cell, but only after he promised he would stay nearby. He settled into the corner of an arch across from her and tried to think. As far as he could tell, there were only two ways out of the Silentman's dungeon. By key or by magic. Either he had to have the key on the jailer's ring that opened the wooden door he had seen the man go through, or he had to know the magic that commanded the horrible head in the stairs past the stone door. Both of them were keys, despite one being made of iron and one being made of words.

One word.

An idea wormed itself into Jute's thoughts. If all else failed, he could always go back up the passage, around the corner and past the row of empty cells, right to where the shadows seemed to gather against the wall. Perhaps the voice was still there? He hastily squashed down that idea. The trick, obviously, would be to get hold of the jailer's key ring.

Key ring.

Ring.

Jute frowned. There was something he should be remembering, something important to do with rings, but—shadow take it—he couldn't remember. There it was— he almost had it. One of those endless stories Severan had told him (though, if he was honest, he had to admit he had enjoyed all of them). It had been a story concerning the old archivist of the university from hundreds and hundreds of years ago, the evil Scuadimnes. He had a key of some sort.

No. That wasn't it.

Light wavered in the passage and all thoughts of keys and rings fled from his mind. Jute sprang to his feet. Near the door of Lena's cell, the oil lamp flame fluttered. He felt a faint breeze on his face. Someone, somewhere, had just opened a door.

He darted across to the cell.

"Someone's coming!" he said.

"Jute!"

"Don't panic!" He would have done well to heed his own advice, for his heart stuttered and sweat trickled down his back. "Just keep quiet. Pretend you're asleep. Stay in the corner and don't move unless they come in and drag you out."

"Drag me out?" Her voice squeaked in dismay.

"Shush. Don't worry."

Lena scuttled back into the corner of her cell. The oil lamp flame fluttered again. The shadows in the passage swayed with it. He felt the breeze again. It was the gentlest touch on his skin, no more than old air shifting and then settling back into its familiar stone carapace of passageways. And what an odd smell!

Jute backed away into the darkness of a corner arch. The hair on the back of his neck prickled. The air smelled of musty cold things, of damp darkness, dead dreams, and nights without stars. His vision blurred and he could suddenly see the night sky. It was studded with stars flung out across unfathomable distances. Far off, high in the sky, a tiny black spot swiftly grew in mass. As if from far away, he heard the hawk whisper in his mind.

This is the enemy, though only a servant of our ancient foe. Beware, it draws near.

"Hawk!"

The dark spot grew larger and larger, until the stars around it were blotted out. Light was extinguished. The night became blacker than night. Jute realized that the darkness was some sort of body, a creature rushing through the night toward him. The bulk of it was so great that it threatened to cover the whole sky. There was a noise of rushing wind and a howling that groaned through his bones until he could hardly stand up. The hawk shrieked in fury—a terrible, desperate cry—and the darkness abruptly veered away. Jute opened his eyes and he was standing in the passageway again, his back to the wall and his teeth clenched so tightly together his jaws ached.

You see an old memory from him who went before you. But, wait, the servant draws closer.

The hawk's voice rustled in his mind like feathers.

"Hawk," he said.

Hush. I cannot help you. There is too much stone and darkness between us. I am relieved to have found you alive, but you are on your own for a little while yet. Use your wits well, fledgling.

"Hawk!"

But there was no answer.

Footsteps echoed down the passageway. Hurrying footsteps. A jumble of conversation echoed against the stone walls until it sorted itself out into three voices. The first two spoke a lot. They finished each other's sentences, began each other's phrases, and muddled up whatever the other one was saying. Jute knew who the first two voices belonged to—the tall man and the shorter, fat man who had appeared in the dungeon earlier that day—had it only been earlier that day? The third voice hardly spoke at all. But when it did, there was a familiarity to it. A strange familiarity. Jute shivered. The peculiar scent in the air was growing stronger as well. He licked his lips, but his mouth had gone dry.

"Of course, we knew we'd nab the brat," said the first voice. "Didn't waste any time catching—"

"No time lost at all," said the second voice. The shorter man, thought Jute. "So there's no—er—no harm done, my lord. All safe and sound. Safe and sound."

"Yes, yes! Safe and sound. The Guild's never fallen down on a job before, never. And though we might've stumbled a bit on this one, handing over the wretched boy to you will be as good as the knife in the box, eh?"

"Er, you mean the untouched knife," put in the second voice.

"Perhaps," said the third voice. The voice was hardly more than a whisper, yet it seemed to Jute that the speaker stood by him in the shadows and was whispering into his ear. He turned, startled, but no one was there. "Perhaps," the voice repeated. "But we are unhappy with the service you have rendered."

"But all's well now," said the second voice anxiously.

"Exceedingly unhappy," said the other.

"As I am," said the first man. He spoke hurriedly and it seemed as if his footsteps quickened in order to complement the pace of his words. "You can't believe how difficult it is to find reliable help these days. Someone you can trust enough to get the job done, stick the knife in and do it right, mop up the stains afterward, and then show up the next morning with every piece of gold accounted for. Greedy little fingers. That's the problem—everyone's out for themselves."

"I do my own killing," said the third voice.

That seemed to end the conversation for the moment. The only sound left was the footsteps coming nearer, shuffling and echoing off the walls. The echo rustled in the stone corridor like the flapping of wings swooping down from the darkness, settling into a single word that murmured inside Jute's mind.

Beware.

Beware.

Beware.

Three shadows wavered along the corridor floor and advanced up the bars of Lena's cell. The lamp on the wall dimmed. The air grew cold. Three men appeared. Two of the men he recognized. He had been correct about their voices. The tall man and the short man. Yet this time they were both uncloaked and without hoods. Their faces were visible. Velvets and silks shone, even in the weak light. Jeweled rings on their fingers. The face of the taller man stirred Jute's memory. A day at Mioja Square. Surely he had seen this man before.

But before he could pursue the thought any further, the third man turned. Turned into the illumination of the lamp. It was a strangely perfect face. But it was also a terrible face, hard and as implacable as stone. Light gleamed in his eye sockets and Jute realized to his horror that the glow had nothing to do with the lamp. He shivered, for just as the strange scent was familiar to him, so was the man's face. A memory struggled up from within his mind. He knew this man. He had met him before. No. Not met. This man had—had. . .

This man had killed him.

Long ago.

Jute's hand flew to his side. Pain blossomed there as sharp as a knife and hotter than fire. He felt wetness running through his fingers. His life was spilling out.

This man had killed him with a knife.

No.

This man had killed someone else. Someone before him.

His head ached. Feathers drifted through his mind. He could not remember.

"He is here," said the man.

"Of course," said the first man. He spoke with more assurance now. "Piled up there like a bundle of rags. You there! Boy! On your feet! The little brat—he'll hop quick enough."

A key gleamed in the man's hand. The lock on the cell door groaned.

"Dreccan," he said. "Get in there and haul him out."

"My lord," said the short stout man unhappily, but he swung the door open and stepped inside.

"I can smell him," said the strange man again.

"There's rather a stench in here, isn't there? I can barely bring myself to breathe."

At the back of the cell, the stout man bent down and hoisted Lena up by the collar. He marched her forward. She stumbled, her feet dragging on the stone. The cell door creaked and they were through. Light fell across her face, twisted, eyes squinting. One hand fluttered up as if to block out the glow of the lamp, the three faces staring at her, as if to ward away whatever was to come next.

The strange man pounced. He towered over her, his hands gripping her face. He stared down and then, with a snarl, flung her away. She collided with the cell door and then crumpled into a heap, her arms wrapped around her head.

"This is not him!" he spat.

"What?" said the tall man stupidly.

The other's head swung around. His eyes gleamed.

"Near. He's very near."

A knife appeared in his hand. The two other men stepped backwards.

"By the hand of darkness," the man said. His voice was quiet. "By the dream of darkness. By the hunger of darkness I call thee."

The oil lamp on the wall winked out. All light was gone except for the glitter of the man's eyes and the gleam of his knife. His eyes shone like pale stars, and the knife was a gash in the darkness that widened and bled an awful radiance that did nothing to relieve the gloom.

"By the hand of stone. By the dream of stone."

Jute.

"By the hunger of stone I call thee."

Jute. The hawk's voice whispered inside his mind. *You must flee before he finishes the summoning.*

"By the hand of shadow."

He is about to hear my voice. One such as he cannot be guarded against easily. There now! Look—his ring.

His ring?

"By the dream of shadow."

Frantically, Jute strained his eyes in the darkness, trying to see. The man had no rings on his fingers. Not a man—part of his mind whispered—something other, something much older. He heard a rustling in his ears that quickly grew into a hum as if of bees approaching.

"By the hunger of shadow."

The knife in the man's hand was no longer a knife. It was as big as a sword, bigger than a sword, growing up toward the ceiling as if it would split the stones like a tree root. And to Jute's horror, that's what happened. The blade heaved and rippled with its hideous light, struggling to contain something that sought release, and then, finally, it shot up against the ceiling. With a snap, the stone cracked. Fissures zigzagged in every

321

direction. The light crept along the fissures like pale worms that grew longer and longer as they forced their way toward the end of each crack. The ceiling bulged downward, as if something grew within its stone.

The taller of the other two men gave an inarticulate howl.

"Stop, you fool!" he said, his voice shaking. "You'll bring the castle down on our heads! Don't you know where we are?"

"Greater you the fool," said the other, turning on him. "You opened your door to the Dark and we have come. I would rend your castle into ruin to find what my master seeks. I would tear Hearne down, stone by stone and soul by soul, to grasp what we seek. One life, two lives, three lives now, have stood in the gap for this city. You unwitting fool. Your miserable life and your city have been spared so far for the sake of these three meddlers. Sea, wind, and earth—may they all die in the darkness. Now, silence!"

The taller man staggered back and flung up one hand as if to protect his face. Something gleamed on his hand. A ring. The hum pulsed in Jute's ears. It was as if a hundred wards had sprung awake at the same time, all quivering in alarm and waiting for whatever sought to intrude. The ring on the tall man's hand flashed even brighter. Jute's head began to ache from the hum.

Wards!

Your castle.

Wards were coming alive in the stone far above his head. Powerful wards. In the castle. There was only one castle in Hearne. A castle that none of the Thieves Guild ever approached because of the countless wards spelled into its walls. Worse than hopeless to attempt a burglary. Unless you somehow got your hands on one of the ward rings given to visitors. Best of all would be the regent's own ring, which commanded every single ward in the castle.

Jute didn't need any more time to think about it. He darted forward on silent feet. Even though he made no noise, the strange man whirled. The knife in his hand was once more just a knife, but one that whistled through the air at Jute's neck. He slid under it, skidded on the stones, and deliberately collided with the regent's knees. The man exclaimed in surprise and flung his arms out to steady himself.

The regent! That's who the taller man was! The memory of the man's face now made sense to Jute, but that meant. . .

No time to think.

Lena grabbed onto his hand with all the frantic determination of a drowning cat. Behind them, the strange man gave a furious shout. The regent toppled over. His hands reached down, to break his fall or to catch hold of Jute, and it was as easy as that. Jute's one free hand flashed out. A thought crossed his mind and was gone as quickly as it had come. Surely he, of all people, would know better than that.

Never shake hands with a thief, cully.

Jute yanked Lena to her feet and they were off, ducking around the fat man and sprinting down the corridor into the dark. Angry voices sounded behind them. A terrible droning noise filled the air. The ground beneath them shook as if someone—something—impossibly heavy had stamped his foot.

"Jute! Jute!" sobbed Lena.

"Shut up. Just run!"

They ran. Down the passageways twisting and turning through the shadows. One left, the second right, and then straight on to the last turn. Stone and sky! Where was that last turn? It seemed such a dreadful long time in coming. Once, just once, Jute dared to look back and glimpsed a terrifying sight. Pounding around the corner was an immense figure. Something like a man but taller and broader and made of stone and darkness and stray threads of light that wriggled up to the surface of its skin and then sank back again. It had strangely jointed limbs that hinged in more places than could possibly be normal. The thing was awkward looking, but it came at a terrible pace. Behind it ran the man, his eyes shining like lamps in the dark.

"Run, Lena!"

She said nothing, but he could hear her gasping for air. They turned the last corner. It was the right corridor. He had remembered correctly. The walls were lined with lamps. The stones were swept clean of spiderwebs. At the far end of the passage was the door.

"Jute!"

"Don't worry, cully," said Jute. "It ain't locked. Besides, I swooped his ring. Going to be all right."

That, or we're going to be dead.

Jute risked a look at the ring in his hand. A worn gold band, carved into the shape of a hawk's head. Tiny red stones gleamed in the eye sockets. A hawk. He grinned, feeling better. He slipped the ring on his finger.

Then they were at the door. The handle turned. He flung it open and held his breath, but there were only stone steps rising before them. Stone steps that remained stone steps. Lena darted up. Jute glanced back and wished he hadn't. It seemed as if a wall of stone and darkness surged toward him and, in its midst, a pair of eyes shone. He slammed the door shut—there was a key in the hole on the other side! He locked it and dashed up the steps four at a time. Lena stood at the top of the steps, looking bewildered. A gray wall shimmered before her. He grabbed her arm.

"No time to waste," he said. "We have to go. Now!"

"But where are we?"

The wall pulled at them and then they were through. They felt the soft brush of wool against their faces and hands. They blinked in the light. A tapestry hung on the wall behind them, its colors still swirling in agitated movement. They stood in a bedroom. It was immense, big enough to fit the whole Goose and Gold tavern in and still have room for a stable. The ceiling soared up on arches of white marble. Stars shone down through windowpanes high above. Polished wood furniture—dressers and tables and chairs and such an enormous bed—gleamed back just as brightly.

"The regent's castle."

Lena's mouth fell open. "The whosewhat?"

Behind them, somewhere on the other side of the tapestry, the door shook under a mighty blow. They ran. They ran across the bedroom, across a deep, silent carpet and through a door that opened on perfectly oiled hinges into another room of silence and elegance. Everywhere they looked, there was polished wood and marble, doorways and halls stretching in all directions. Copper lamps topped with carved crystal bells shone on the ends of silver chains hanging from the ceiling. Far behind them, they heard a tremendous crash.

"Down or left?" said Lena urgently.

The last doorway brought them to a staircase sweeping down into a vast hall. A blue velvet carpet flowed down the steps onto a marble floor. Pillars reached up and up, curving in to meet each other in an interlacement of stone weaving around glass skylights. The sickle moon and her accompanying train of stars shone down. Jute took a deep breath. It was almost as good as being outside. Left, high along the wall of the hall, ran a gallery.

"Down," said Jute.

They tumbled down the steps. The marble floor was impossibly smooth, and Lena skidded on it until she tripped into a tumble of hysterical giggling.

"Hurry!" said Jute. Above them, the staircase creaked.

"Sorry," she said. He hauled her to her feet. Her hands trembled in his.

"What's all this?"

They turned. A man stood there, hands on hips. He was dressed in servant's livery, in the blue and black colors of the regency of Hearne.

"Beggars sneaking about the castle! I warrant your dirty hands have been doing a bit of thieving, eh? Well, let's have you off to the Guard for a whipping. Come on now!"

But it would have taken someone quicker than a servant to catch those two, especially a paunchy footman who wasn't accustomed to anything more strenuous than chasing the chambermaids in his spare time. Besides, when they had turned, the two children had seen what was coming down the staircase. They fluttered away like birds from the man's hands and were gone.

"Here now!" called the footman. He broke into a run but then thought better of it. He didn't want to muss up his hair, especially as that new maid from Vomaro had started working in the east wing. Shadows, but she was a delectable piece.

Something cold touched his shoulder.

"Here now," he said again, aggrieved at such a liberty. He turned.

Behind them, the children heard a scream that choked off into silence.

"Jute! What was that thing on the stairs?"

"Something real bad. Something worse'n the Juggler on his worst of worse days."

It was then they heard music. They ran down a long corridor, dimly lit and lined with paintings of stern-looking men who all seemed to be frowning at them as they ran by. The music grew louder—the sounds of violins, cellos, flutes, and the curious sliding whistle that is thought much of in the north for its melancholy tones. Jute knew nothing about instruments, but he thought the music sounded nice. With it, there was also the sound of voices. Many voices.

"People!" said Lena, alarmed.

"I'd rather have people than the thing back there! Besides, maybe it'll stop to eat one or two an' waste some time."

"Eat?" squeaked Lena.

The corridor opened abruptly into another corridor, wider and lighter than the previous one and filled with servants hurrying about with platters and pitchers and crystal goblets and vases of flowers. Other than getting a few startled glances, the two children were ignored. The servants were going in one of two directions. Either they exited the corridor by the door at the far end, or they were entering the corridor by the same door, at which point they would then vanish through any one of numerous other doors further down the corridor.

"C'mon," said Jute.

They positioned themselves behind a trio of servants hurrying toward the door at the far end of the corridor. Each one of the three servants bore aloft platters steaming with wonderful fragrances.

"Um," said Lena. "I could do with a bit of supper."

"Shush."

The door was obviously a special door, for it was two doors rather than one. Each had a large silver handle, and each was attended by a white-gloved footman who pulled them open and swung them shut as the occasion demanded. Standing to one side was a fat man with splendid moustaches curling out and up toward his eyebrows. It seemed to be his job to inspect each dish exiting through the doors.

The first of the trio of the servants halted in front of the moustached man and offered his platter for inspection.

"Sweet apples stuffed with cheese, cinnamon—"

"And walnuts," said the first servant.

"Impertinence," said the moustached man, glaring at him. "I was saving the walnuts for last. You may go. Next! Ahh—one of my favorites—baby eels seethed in wild onions and the juice of gently crushed persimmons—"

"Yuck," said Lena.

"Shush."

"—certain to delight the jaded taste buds of even our most bored noble, eh?"

"Er," said the second servant.

"Very good. You may go."

The double doors swung open and the second servant disappeared through them.

"And what have we here?" boomed the mustached man.

The third servant held out his platter.

"What have we here?" boomed the mustached man again, his gaze falling on Jute and Lena. While three servants were more than sufficient to hide behind, one servant was inadequate. The fat man's moustaches quivered in outrage.

"Tiny mutton cutlets," said the third servant. "Baked in a lovely mint sauce, accompanied by baby potatoes, fried golden and—"

"This won't do!" The mustached man produced a bell from his pocket. He rang it vigorously.

"It won't?" said the third servant, pained on behalf of the mutton and still oblivious to the two children behind him.

At that moment, the situation was taken out of the hands of the mustached man and whatever result his bell was designed to produce. Far away, at the other end of the corridor, a scream rang out. Someone shouted and there came a terrific clattering crash as a platter of crystal goblets was dropped on the floor. The mustached man looked up and his jaw dropped. The bell dropped as well from his slack fingers. The two footmen looked up. Their faces whitened.

"Run!" said Jute.

He grabbed hold of Lena's hand. The third servant yelped in outrage as Jute shoved him aside. The mutton went flying and the potatoes followed—one by one—like little falling stars. Jute slammed into one of the doors and they darted through.

For a second, Jute thought they had somehow stepped into the night sky. Into a sky full of stars above and below and on every side, all wheeling in stately grace to the strains of strings and winds. They stood on a floor like polished black glass. It stretched away from them through a vast airy space bounded by columns rising out of the floor toward an unseen ceiling. Clusters of tiny lamps hung high overhead like constellations. These were the only sources of light in the place. They reflected off the floor's expanse and the black curves of the columns. Their light caught in the jewels of the assemblage, glinting in minute gleams of sapphire, emerald, ruby, amethyst, and the white, wintry wink of diamond, for a great throng of people was there, some dancing, some strolling about on the edge of the dance, others standing in conversation by the walls. And the lamps and their myriad reflections twinkled like the stars of the night.

"C'mon," said Jute.

He took her hand in his and they hurried across the floor. Couples swept around them, revolving in circles that spiraled in and spiraled out on the rise and fall of the music. Silk whispered across the glassy floor. Faces spun by, smiling, grave, laughing, intent—dappled with light and shadow and the flash of eyes. No one spared the two children a glance. They crept through the throng, around those dancing, past groups of nobles in tight clusters of discourse, tiptoeing by the servants who floated everywhere on silent feet with their platters and pitchers and their hushed utterances: "Would you care for more wine, milord? May I take that, milady?"

Jute quickened his pace, dragging Lena along with him. His ears hurt, dreading, yet aching to hear the uproar that was sure to erupt behind them at any moment. Something tickled uneasily inside his mind. The back of his neck stiffened.

Don't look!

The hawk's voice exploded into his mind. There was a desperate urgency in the words.

But he had to turn. He had to. Someone was staring at him. Jute could feel the force of the gaze. He stopped, felt Lena's hand pull at him, and turned. Several lengths away, a couple danced under a chandelier. The lamps gilded the lady's neck with light, but her head was tilted away and Jute could not see her face. But her partner was taller and his face was in the light. The light seemed to love him. It burnished his hair into a radiance of gold and it gathered in his green eyes until they looked more like emeralds than simple flesh and blood.

The man stared at Jute. His face was expressionless, but something flickered in those emerald eyes. Something hungry. Jute could not look away. A strange weariness gripped him. Perhaps it's best to just stop running, he thought to himself. Can't run forever. Dimly, he heard the voice of the hawk in his mind, but he could not understand the words. The hawk called again. It was only a harsh, ugly sound. The sound of a bird, angry and raw with fear. He felt Lena tug frantically on his hand.

"Jute!"

That was when the screaming began.

The music faltered to a halt. The stars wandering in their courses froze, stunned into immobility as people halted in mid-step, in the middle of words, in the middle of their dancing, their smiling, their laughter. And then there was a great horrified rush of movement as people turned to run. They floundered, panicked and gasping. The light of the lamps high overhead stayed with them, caught in the spray of amethysts in a baroness's hair, shining in the diamonds on the fingers of a lord, glittering and gleaming on a thousand thousand jewels that fled away in any direction that they could. The stars abandoned their proscribed paths as has never been done before by the stars of the true night, though some have said such a thing will happen at the end of time.

"Jute!"

Lena yanked so hard on his hand that he almost lost his balance, but he could not look away. The emerald eyes held him fast. Not once had the man bothered to glance back at the disturbance. But the woman who had been dancing with him turned, her gaze on the other end of the hall. She was not overly tall, but tall enough so her profile came between Jute and the man. The emerald eyes were gone, obscured for a second by the woman. Jute had a momentary glimpse of her face, of black hair piled up in a glossy sheaf on her head and the slender line of her neck. Jute blinked, released. His head ached horribly.

"Jute! C'mon!"

Lena's voice was shrill with panic. He turned to run but it was too late.

He had an impression of darkness, of something blurring down toward him like a wave of shadow. It blotted out the shining lights overhead and then he was drowning in darkness. Stone crushed him with its cold weight. He could not breathe.

"Stop!"

The angry shout came from somewhere on his right. A woman's voice. She yelled again, the second time louder as if she was approaching. The darkness pressing down around him shuddered at the sound of her voice. It constricted violently, crushing him like a huge fist. He could not move or think or see. Everything was black. He felt stone under his skin, choking his throat, shoving against his eyes until something had to give, something had to burst.

"Stop!"

The shout came a third time. The sound slammed into the stone around him. It hit so hard that Jute felt his body stagger backwards, helpless in the grip of the awful thing that held him. The ground trembled. Abruptly, he was released. He fell to his knees and choked on air.

Jute looked up. Standing next to him was a woman. The woman. The woman who had been dancing with the man with emerald eyes. He saw now that she was young, surely only several years older than himself. She was dressed in a simple gown of brown material that gathered and glowed with the lamplight. Harthian silk, Jute thought tiredly to himself, worth more than a gold piece to the yard. Her fists were jammed on her hips and her chin was up.

The hall was silent. All Jute could hear was the ragged wheeze of his own lungs. He could not see Lena. The great assembly of lords and ladies stood like statues, all crowded far back in fear. A vast open space lay all around Jute and the woman. But they were not entirely alone. Darkness crouched in front of the woman. The darkness was immense, yet formless, without shape or any definable edge. It seemed to blur into the floor on either side. Stone could be seen in it, veiled with shadow, as if that was its heart. The thing did not move.

"Come," said the woman. The anger was bright in her voice. "Come. Let us end this now."

There was some sort of compulsion in her words, for the darkness quivered and then, with a groan of protest as if it already knew its demise, surged forward. It towered up, gaining form. Shadow coalesced into massive legs and arms. A face of stone erupted from the darkness with blunt features and a gaping mouth. Jute cried out, for surely there was no escape from the creature. Surely there was only the darkness.

Aye, said a familiar voice inside his head.

Aye, there is only the Dark. It comes for every man. It is their right and fitting end. As it is yours. Now.

The woman, despite the horror bearing down on her, whirled around as if she had heard the voice as well. Her gray eyes glittered with fury. She snapped her fingers and the voice vanished from Jute's thoughts. And then she turned away. Her hands stabbed in the air—once, twice—and the thing reaching for her staggered and fell back. Her fingers flicked a third time. With a sigh, the creature collapsed. A cloud of dust and shadow billowed out and dissipated in the air until nothing was left.

"L-lady," stammered Jute.

She turned her head slightly but did not look at him.

"Hush, boy," she said quietly. "This was nothing. It was woven in part with stone, and stone is mine. Stone shall not be taken from me. But now the true evil comes."

He saw that her hands were clenched at her side. The light dimmed. The shadows thickened around them. Jute could no longer see anyone else except for the woman standing in front of him. But the hushed sounds of a vast multitude came to his ears—the rustle of clothing, the catch of breath, the muttered undertones. Somewhere, far back in the hall, someone was sobbing.

"Mistress of Mistresses."

The voice was quiet, almost conversational in tone. It floated out of the darkness. A figure followed it, stepping into view as if through a doorway and out of the night. It was the strange man from the tunnels below the castle.

"Hold," said the woman. She raised her hand.

The man stopped. He smiled. There was a dreadful beauty to his face. A blade shone in his hands.

"I still hold these lands, son of darkness." Jute shivered in sudden terror and something akin to delight, for there was an old power in her voice that soothed his heart with strange familiarity. "The earth of Tormay is mine and every stone in this city is known to me. Be gone. Depart into your master's night."

The man barked an ugly laugh. His teeth gleamed.

"I came hunting a pup to blood my blade on, but I find the bitch wolf herself. The Dark will find great pleasure if I take both of your souls."

"I've dreamed of the Dark's demise," she said.

"And did you dream of your brother wind's death, too?"

The woman flinched at the words.

"I thought as much," said the man. He took a step closer. "I have always wondered how closely those such as you are bound to each other. Did you fly with him in your dreams? When curiosity took him east, over the mountains and across the wastes? There, on the shore, he stooped down and found the edge of my knife. The foolish bird alighting to pick at a shiny stone. I knew it would not go unnoticed, but even I did not reckon such as you would bide sleeping still in your hills. What is your pretty hideaway called? Dolan? Mark my words, mistress—when my blade has taken you and the craven cowering behind your skirts, to Dolan the Dark will go to destroy the memory of Levoreth Callas."

"You accursed sceadu," she said. In her voice was the awful weight of the earth. The scent of green and growing things filled the air. Her hands fluttered into the air, shaping it. "I bind you by earth and stone, by oak and iron, by wolf's fang and fox's tooth, by—"

The sword was already arcing through the air toward her head. A tree appeared before him, catching the blade in its branches. The ground buckled. Jute could smell sap and he heard the tree groan in pain. A wolf sprang into being in mid-leap, its jaws snapping shut on the man's arm. A pair of red foxes circled and slashed with their sharp white teeth.

"—by bramble and briar, by bear's paw and horse's hoof!"

An enormous bear lumbered out of the shadows. Briars rippled up out of the ground to bind the man with branch and thorn. There came the thunder of galloping hooves and an angry neigh. The blade whirled in the midst of it all and, wherever it cut, darkness bled. Darkness ate away at the neck of the wolf. Darkness seeped up out of the ground, creeping up the trunk of the oak and the green of the briar. Darkness tore at the flanks of the bear. The woman's hands jerked in the air. Blood ran from her palms. She cried out in pain and rage.

"By wind and gale," said Jute.

He did not know why he spoke the words. He was hardly aware he spoke them. No one heard them except himself, but instantly, there sprang up a wind, a howling wind that whipped through the air, dizzying and inexorable and joyous with being. It felt as if it blew straight through his body—he felt cold and empty inside. The woman in front of him swayed a step forward but did not fall.

It felt to Jute as if everything that was—as if the whole world—was caught up in the rush of the wind. That this was right. That this was the way things should be. The wind blew through him. It rushed forward, and color and line and shape blurred under its blast. The bear had tree branches for limbs now that threshed and swayed under the force of the blast, fraying into the red fur of the foxes, whose jaws grew among the briars and snapped and snarled and bit at wind and darkness alike. Stone encased the wolf in armor, shaped by the wind into shining planes. The man shouted with anger. His blade sang under the fury of the gale—a note rising up and up in shrieking pitch until the steel shattered into dust that blew away on the wind and sparkled under the light of the lamps above like falling stars. The woman called out in words that Jute could not understand and everything vanished. The man was gone. The oak and the briars and the beasts were gone. There was only the hall and the silent, staring assembly. And the wind.

The wind blew and howled. It shrieked high overhead in the arches of the unseen ceiling. It set the chandeliers of lamps spinning and swaying so that everything was dappled with light that fled this way and that and would not be still. People staggered helplessly in the wind's force and some fell, crawling on their hands and knees to find whatever shelter they could. A silver tray whirled by, followed by goblets that shattered into singing shards.

"Call back the wind, boy," said the woman. Her face was tight with anger.

"I can't," said Jute. "I don't know how." A fierce gladness warmed him. He had done this. The wind blew because of him!

She slapped his face. Hard. He could feel the blood on his cheek from her cut palm.

"Call back the wind," she said quietly.

"I-I don't know how," he stammered. He cowered away from the fury in her eyes.

For a moment she stared at him in disbelief, and then she sighed. Her eyes closed. A presence thrust its way into his mind. Shoved him roughly aside—inside—as if he were nothing. He could taste dirt in his mouth. And then the wind died and the presence was gone.

She opened her eyes and blinked.

"Sorry," she said.

"What did you—?" He could not finish the sentence. He felt tears welling up.

"Come on," she said briskly. "Time to go. No telling what'll turn up next if we stay here. I'm afraid this night will be the talk of Tormay for the next five hundred years."

She turned and walked off. Jute stumbled after her. The hall rustled into life around them. Faces stared in shock. People backed away. A babble of excited talk filled the air. They neared a wide arch that swept down in stairs to a hall below, filled with light and torches and the shouts of approaching soldiers. The crowd of nobles near the stairs shrank back. Some averted their eyes from the woman and Jute. Others stared greedily, whispering to their neighbors. An older lady emerged from the crowd. A man followed after her. They approached hesitantly.

"Levoreth," said the lady.

"Aunt Melanor," said the woman.

"No," said the other, hesitant. "I'm not your aunt, am I? I never was."

"No, you weren't, my dear," said Levoreth. "Rather, I'm the great-great grandmother of your husband, though I'm afraid I've left out about a dozen greats in there." She gently touched the lady's face. "We are still family. My blood will run in the veins of your children."

"Children?"

"Yes. Twins. In the spring."

Levoreth turned to the man. Her face warmed in a sudden smile.

"Uncle, take care of Dolan for me."

He could not say anything, but took her hand and brought it to his lips. Tears sprang from his eyes.

"I must go away," she said. "I can no longer hide in my hills. I'm known, now, for what I am. Soon all of Tormay will know and, with it, the Dark. The Dark has come to these lands and it won't rest until it finds what it seeks."

She kissed them both and they were silent. She strode away down the stairs without glancing back. Jute hurried after her.

"Lady," he said, "who were they? Where are we going? And who was—what was that thing?" He paused and then added timidly, "Who are you?"

Levoreth did not answer.

Guards ran up the steps, their officer urging them on hoarsely, but they did not bother looking at the woman and the boy. They walked through another hall. Servants were gathered in clumps, whispering and glancing about them with frightened eyes. It seemed to Jute that he saw Lena peeking around a corner, but he was not sure. Tall doors swung open before them.

It was raining. Horses standing with their carriages stamped and steamed in the torchlight. A contingent of soldiers ran across the courtyard toward the castle steps. An old coachman huddled on his seat called down a question to Levoreth, but she did not stop. Jute had to run to keep up with her. Then they were past the castle gates and walking down through the night and rain, down through the quiet streets of Highneck Rise.

"Lady," said Jute, but she interrupted him.

"Levoreth. For you, I am Levoreth. That's all. No lady this or that."

"Levoreth—"

"Hush. A ways more and then we'll talk. There's not much time, boy, but what time we have might be lost, and lost badly, if we stay too near the castle. No telling what's been woken up by our little spat back there." Levoreth shook her head ruefully. "No use crying over that. What's out is out and that's all there's to it."

She shut her mouth at that and would not speak anymore. Jute trotted along at her side. He thought he would burst from all the questions boiling up inside. He discovered that he was somehow very happy, despite having a lot of bruises and a nervous twitch that had him looking over his shoulder every few minutes in case something terrible was about to come charging out of the night.

Considering your astounding stupidity, you have certainly landed on your feet.

It was the hawk. He sounded relieved. And before Jute could even protest, he heard the rustle of wings, and there, in the rain with the moonlight shining on his wet feathers, was the hawk. He floated down and landed on Jute's shoulder. Levoreth smiled.

Mistress of Mistresses.

"This is a strange night. Faces from the past, both good and evil, but it does my heart well to see you."

The hawk bobbed his head.

As your face gladdens mine. I am beholden to you, Mistress. We are in your debt, this young dolt and I. Thank you for preserving him, for such a task this night would have been far beyond my powers. I cannot stand before a sceadu.

"Wait one minute!" said Jute, his face reddening. He no longer felt all that happy.

"You are not in my debt, old wing," said Levoreth, ignoring Jute. "All this time I have known it my fate to be in Hearne this year, and who knows but it was for this night?"

No. I am in your debt and shall repay it fourfold someday. It is on my blood and the blood of this boy. So be it.

A long, wavering howl broke the stillness of the night. It rose and fell, and then was answered by another same cry.

"What in shadow's name was that?" asked Jute.

"Do not speak by such a name," said Levoreth. "That was a shadowhound."

Another howl keened in the night sky. It seemed to come from somewhere further away in the city.

Three such hounds, I think.

Levoreth's shoulders slumped.

"Have three such creatures ever been seen in Tormay?" she said. Her voice was weary. "We have been given a dreadful night. I don't want to think on what this means, but I fear there's more evil here than a sceadu. But how can that be? The three sceadus were the lieutenants of Nokhoron Nozhan, and there were none mightier than they. We are faced with a peculiar mystery."

The hawk unfurled its wings and launched into the air. Two powerful strokes and it was invisible against the night sky.

A sceadu, Mistress? A sceadu did kill my master.

"I'll weep for your master another day, old wing," she said swiftly. "But for now take your youngling to safety. Keep him alive. Keep him alive so that he may grow in wisdom and power. Hide him in whatever nest you can find. No, I speak hastily. Go north, rather, north to the Duke of Lannaslech of Harlech and command him—command him in my name—to guard the boy, though he spend every drop of blood in his land and Harlech groans with death."

You speak wisely, Mistress. And what of you?

"I'll lead the creatures out of the city, for doubtless they have my scent. They're drawn to power, even over blood. I'm weary this night, but I'll lead them a chase to their deaths."

"What do you mean?" said Jute, bewildered. "What's to become of me?"

"What's to become of you?" Levoreth echoed. She drew close and touched his face with her fingers. Her eyes were sad. "I don't know your name, boy."

"My name is Jute."

"Jute. Know that I grieve for you. I would wish your road on none, but we cannot ordain our days. It is all dreamed beforehand in the house of dreams. Ours is merely to live it well and die. I'd hoped to explain more to you, but the hawk will do so when he sees fit."

She bent down and kissed his brow. Her lips were cold and wet with rain.

"Never forget, Jute," she said. "It is much easier to unleash the wind than it is to deny its power." She touched his face again. "Fly well, little brother."

Then she turned and ran. She ran fast, much faster than Jute had seen anything ever run before, as fast as a horse in full gallop, even faster. Her hair flew out behind her in a heavy, wet mass, almost like a horse's mane. The brown of her dress looked like the sheen of a horse's coat. She vanished into the night, but, even after she was gone, Jute seemed to hear the distant echo of horse's hooves galloping in his mind.

Aye, you see wisely. Once, many years ago, lived a mighty horse and, together, those two kept watch over this land.

"But what of me?" said Jute, feeling rather sorry for himself.

What of you? You are a thief, are you not? Get over the nearest wall here and we shall find some nook in a rich man's house to hide away for the night. The shadowhounds are on the scent of the lady and your skin'll be safe for now.

Jute clambered over the nearest wall and discovered a garden surrounding a large manor. He found an unlocked window and crept along until he found a linen closet that, judging by the amount of dust in it, had not been used for some time. He curled up inside, sniffling and still feeling sorry for himself. Questions jumbled about in his mind, but he was asleep as soon as his head was pillowed on a pile of sheets. The day had been long and he was tired. Just before he fell asleep, however, he remembered the man with emerald eyes. He had meant to ask Levoreth about him.

The hawk perched on the peak of the roof and stared out into the night. Rain fell down. From the street beyond the wall came a faint noise. Something was prowling about, sniffing and growling to itself. The hawk tensed, but then, from far off in the city below, a howl bugled out across the night. It rose and then broke off into a series of excited bays. The scent had been caught. With a scramble and a snort, whatever it was sniffing about in the street padded away. Soon, everything was silent except for the rain tapping on rooftops. The hawk tucked his beak down against his breast, but he did not sleep.

CHAPTER SEVENTY-TWO
LEVORETH RUNS

The rain fell harder and faster than before. The gutters flowed like swollen streams and the cobblestones in some streets were ankle-deep. Levoreth did not mind. She was weary, true, but it was a weariness of mind rather than body. She kilted up her dress above her knees and ran through the night. Buildings blurred by, set with darkened windows and shut doors. Occasionally, though, light shone from a window. Sleep, city, she whispered. Sleep and do not wake. Keep your doors locked. Keep your children safe in their beds. Sleep until I have fled your walls and taken this evil with me.

A bay sounded far behind her, sharp and intent. Another one belled out somewhere on her right. The second was much closer. Levoreth splashed across a street and turned a corner. A shape lunged out of the darkness, mouth gaping with teeth. She swerved. Her hand lashed out, slapping at the air, and the creature skidded over the cobblestones and slammed against a wall. It scrambled to its feet, snarling and shaking its head.

She ran.

The gates of the city loomed before her. A light shone in a window of the Guard tower. Two soldiers leaned on their spears under the gaping archway of the gates. One puffed comfortably on a pipe, and the smoke curled up into the darkness and out into the rain. Immediately, she angled away from the gates. It wouldn't do to lead the shadowhounds straight to the soldiers. They wouldn't have time to see what had killed them until their throats were already ripped out.

Levoreth loped along the road below the wall, listening for the noises behind her. The beasts were close, but not too close. They seemed to run silently once they were within sight of prey. Her ears were sharper than a deer's, however, and she could hear the pad of their paws and their panting. Three shadowhounds. It had been a long time since she had seen such a number. Hundreds of years.

No, whispered her memory to her. Nearly a thousand years ago. Remember? Long before you came to these shores. She stuffed the memory down into the back of her mind and ran on.

The stretch of wall before her looked deserted. The city Guard, apparently, were not dedicated enough to be out in such a night. Levoreth glanced back. Far down the street, spray flew as three dark shapes ran over the wet cobblestones.

She eyed the wall.

Perhaps forty feet high. Easy enough for a mountain cat. She filled her mind with a memory from the previous winter. She had hiked up into the mountains, up through the pine forests on the lower slopes of the Morn range, until she had come out onto the snow fields. They were silent, white expanses angling against the sky, complete and inviolate except for the occasional slab of rock jutting up. A pair of mountain cats appeared then, trotting on wedge-shaped paws across the snow's crust. They were huge beasts, the male standing higher than her waist, and they had pressed their faces imperiously against her hands, demanding to have their ears scratched while they told her of snow and moonlight and the tasty goats that lived on the crags.

She leapt. And landed on top of the wall. A snarl hissed from her lips. Crouching on the wet stones, Levoreth looked down. A rank odor of decay wafted up to her. The beasts below hurled themselves against the wall. They scored the stone in bright gashes with their claws, but they could not leap high enough to reach the top. She waited and watched. The three shadowhounds paced back and forth. Their eyes stared up at her, red spots glowing like coals in the darkness. Then, it happened. The shadowhounds began to fade. Their forms grew insubstantial. The rain fell through them. One by one, they lumbered to the wall—it was more like they were fog drifting over the ground—and then disappeared into the stone.

Levoreth hurled herself off the other side of the wall and was running when she hit the ground. It was turf there, green and thick and soggy with rain, but her feet made no prints as she crossed it. Behind her, the muzzle of the first shadowhound emerged from the wall, moving slowly as if the stone was deep water that must be struggled through. Once clear of the wall, however, the beast regained solidity. In a moment, the two others had joined it. She did not look back again. She went east, down through the darkness of the Rennet Valley and along the river that flowed there. She could smell the cornfields. The rain splashed down on the surface of the river and the patter of the drops blended with the murmur of the flow so that she seemed to hear its voice as she ran.

Down and down, west and west, murmured the river.

Aye, said a passing fish. *We go, we go. We go to the sea.* It blew a string of bubbles that floated up to the surface to be popped by raindrops.

Down from sky, snow, and ice, continued the river, not caring about the opinions of fish one way or the other.

Fog on the field, rain and mist.

Water wends its way.

Splutter, glug, splash, and spray.

Through stone and earth and clay.

In sun and moon and day.

Flies, interrupted a bullfrog. *Flies, flies, flies.*

Down and down—west and west.

"Flow to the sea, little river," called Levoreth, "flow down and bid my sister look to her borders." She was not certain, though, if the river understood her, for water was not her language and neither was it hers to command.

After a while, it stopped raining. The clouds unraveled and revealed the moon. A touch of gray far over the eastern horizon relieved the darkness and hinted of the morning to come. Her breath misted out behind her. The valley narrowed here, while the slope on the north side of the valley rose up steeply toward the plain beyond. A few lights shone in the distance on the river bend. A village. She could smell smoke in the air. Her mind caught at a stirring of life—a baker in the village setting out the dough to rise for the morning's bread, a farmer yawning his way to the barn with milk pails in hand, and a young mother up with a colicky infant.

Levoreth turned her face to the north. It would be an evil morning for the villagers if she led the shadowhounds through their midst. She mounted up the valley slope. Heather and gorse grew there among the rocks. A few trees stood high on the valley wall like sentinels looking out across the plain stretching beyond. And then she had reached the plain itself—the Scarpe. The night wind swept across it, rich with the scent of heather and sweet grass and the perfume of the jona flowers. She breathed in, refreshed.

Levoreth turned and saw, just cresting the rise of the plain, the dark forms of the three hounds. They surged forward and the wind carried the noise of their hoarse panting to her ears. She ran on across the plain. The sky paled into morning. A family of rabbits peeked at her from amidst the grass, but she struck fear into their minds so that they scattered, screaming in high-pitched squeals, darting away in frantic zigzags.

Run, little ones. Evil draws near.

When the sun was peering over the mountains in the east, Levoreth slowed her pace and then stopped. She stood and waited amidst the grass. All the animals had fled—all the rabbits, the field mice, the tomtits and sparrows, the grouse, the quail, and the little red foxes with their quick paws and curious eyes—they had all run away for fear of her and what hunted along her path.

The shadowhounds came. They were long, loping slants of darkness in the morning light. They did not slacken their speed, but rushed at her in silence and gaping jaws. Levoreth stood with her hands folded. Her slim form seemed no sturdier than a blade of grass before their massive bulks. But before they could close with her, she stamped her heel on the ground. The earth shook. It split open in front of her, and the two nearest hounds lunging forward tumbled down into the dark depths. The ground closed up around them with a shivering groan of protest as if it could not stomach what it had swallowed. The third hound checked its rush. It circled her rapidly, belly low to the grass and head turning this way and that, bewildered, to see where its brothers had gone.

Levoreth muttered a word and the grass began to grow. It rippled up from the ground, each blade as thin and as fragile as any other blade of grass, but each blade one of a thousand thousands. The grass caught at the pacing shadowhound. It plucked at the beast's paws until it stumbled and could not stand. Earth flew as it tore at its bonds. The green grass was spattered with dark blood as the creature bit at its own limbs, frantic to break free from the strange chains coiling themselves around and around in ever tightening loops. The grass yanked the beast down onto the ground. More tendrils swayed up into the air and looped themselves about its jaws. Soon, the beast was wrapped up so tight it could not move. Levoreth knelt on the ground by the thing. One red eye stared frantically at her from behind a lacing of green. She placed her hand on its head.

And almost snatched her hand away.

Darkness beat against her mind. Hunger. A ravening emptiness that sought to be filled.

"Who sent you forth?"

The beast would not answer. It could not answer. It was only a clockwork of shadows and bone, hunger, mute instincts and obedience. But in the darkness pooled behind the staring red eye, a separate awareness stirred.

Well met, once again, Mistress of Mistresses.

"You!" she said.

I would have thee as a jewel within my walls.

"Never. Though the sun betray light and plunge the world into darkness, never!"

The voice chuckled.

May that day come. Soon.

"Leave my land—you and your creatures! Tormay is mine and you have no part here!"

Brave words, little Mistress. Brave words, but I am not thine to command. Thou hast been sleeping too long. The years come, the years go, and the Dark comes creeping in. The gate was left unlatched. But peace, child, peace. That is all I wish to give this land.

"If death is peace!" she spat.

Aye, said the voice with satisfaction. It paused and Levoreth saw that red eye between the fur and the binding grass fade into lifelessness. The body beneath her hand convulsed in one last struggle and then fell slack.

Death.

The body of the shadowhound collapsed into dust. The bindings of grass unwove themselves, whispering as the blades rubbed against each other. Radiance rose above the mountains in the east. The sky sprang into blue as the night rushed away into the west. The sun was up. Levoreth could not see for a moment, other than a blur of color that trembled with light, for tears filled her eyes. She blinked them away. Weariness fell over her.

"Old," she said to herself. "I've become old."

She began walking, northwest across the plain. Her limbs ached. The dew on the grass shone with sunlight, blinding bright in the slant of the sun. Levoreth did not see any of the glory of the morning, for within her mind was the face of the boy. He stared at her with questioning eyes.

"You'll find out soon enough, boy."

CHAPTER SEVENTY-THREE
KEEP THE BOY ALIVE

Liss and Ronan left right after the lights flared on in the great hall. The sudden luminance revealed a crowd of white, frightened faces. Wailing was heard from somewhere further back in the hall. The court physician hurried past with two attendants in tow, each one clutching bags of potions and ointments and bandages.

"Come," said Liss.

Her hand settled on Ronan's arm. They drifted through the throng of people. Guards stood at every door, their eyes examining every face that drew near. Ronan tensed. He missed the weight of his sword on his back. Liss's fingers tightened on his arm.

"Peace," she said. "They don't know what they're looking for, but they do not look for you. At least not this night. But as for me, I've seen what I came looking for, and I must go away with many things to be thought over."

"What was that?" said Ronan.

The back of his shirt was damp with sweat. It was the first time he had spoken since the darkness had come stalking out of the crowd. His inclination had been to pull Liss behind him, but she had proved more immovable than rock. He had had to content himself by her side. Never had he felt so much fear.

"Not here," said Liss. A frown crossed her face. "This place is not yet safe. Something is still here. Something hidden and watching."

She paused. The grand stairway before them leading out and down from the hall was choked with people. A mass of nobility surged down its steps. The air trembled with hysteria, voices on the verge of shouting, weeping, and the stridency of strong men unwilling to show that they were afraid.

"Is there another way out? A quicker way?"

"Through those windows on the far side, I think," said Ronan.

Her fingers pressed on his arm, toward the windows.

"There's someone here on the stairs I fear to meet."

"You?" he said in disbelief.

"Me."

Liss looked over her shoulder, but Ronan could not tell who she was looking at. The stairway was so crowded that it could have been one of any number of people. The nobility, he thought critically to himself. The best of Tormay with their airs and their lands and their titles—all as terrified as drowning rats.

Rain streaked down against the windows. They opened out onto a stone veranda. Steps descended from the veranda down into the dark and damp of the castle gardens. Others had the same thought as Ronan, and they passed frightened groups of shadows in the rain. Light from windows fell across shocked faces.

"Scandalous," someone said close by. "And not even hide or hair of Botrell when it happened. Why. . ." The voice faded into the darkness and the slashing rain.

"Your cloak," said Ronan. "We've left it behind and this rain'll have you soaked through in no time."

Liss smiled, shaking her head, and he felt unutterably foolish. And foolish he was, for though he was soon sodden with rain, not a drop touched her. The puddles on the stone veranda shrank back in deference to her slippered foot. Down the long stone steps they went, while the castle rose up alongside them, lights shining from its windows. Then, they were in the dripping gloom of the garden. Oaks huddled over them and the darkness was so complete that Ronan could not trust his eyes.

"There," Liss said, pointing. "There's a gate in the wall."

"I don't see anything."

"Neither do I, but this night is filled with water. Water's mine and it tells me many things."

Sure enough, half-hidden by moss and drooping branches was a little gate of iron bars. It refused to budge when Ronan tried to force it. Liss touched the lock once and the gate swung open.

"Water?"

"Yes," she said.

They found themselves standing in a dark street skirting the wall of the castle grounds. They were alone and nothing could be heard except for the spatter of the rain and the gurgle of a gutter threatening to encroach on the street.

"Will you tell me?" said Ronan. "Or must I plague myself with questions I can't answer?"

"Tell you what that was you saw inside the castle?"

"No. Hang what was inside the castle. Why did you choose me?"

Liss stared calmly at him, her face tilted back. He noticed, then, that the rain did touch her. The drops falling on her skin and in her hair vanished as if she was absorbing them. He took a step back.

"You never needed me, did you? You could've walked right into the regent's castle with all the soldiers in Hearne lined up on either side and none of them would've dared glance at your shadow."

"Perhaps," said Liss. "Power is a chancy thing, even such as mine. When used, it's like a beacon blazing in the night. It draws unwanted attention. This, I must avoid, for I don't know what is waiting and watching. But my need of you isn't confined to what happened this night. Rather, it's just begun."

From somewhere close by, a dog barked. Ronan thought it a dog at the first bark, but with the second bark he thought it more a wolf. Though what would a wolf be doing in the middle of Hearne? The third bark, however, slid into a long howl that wavered up into the rainy sky and then was whipped away by the wind. Not a wolf at all. He had never heard such a noise before.

Liss whirled at the sound. She held out her hand so that raindrops pooled in it. She rubbed her thumb across her wet palm.

"Shadowhounds," she said slowly.

"What?"

"Shadowhounds. Beasts woven of darkness and hunger and dead flesh. I've not seen or heard of their like for hundreds of years. They're hunting this night. We are not the quarry. Rather, I think it my sister and the boy she took with her."

"Your sister?"

Liss turned to walk away, hurrying down the street. Ronan strode after her to catch up.

"Aye. She who watches over the earth and all the furry kin who live there. All those who bustle about on four legs, and some on two. The lady you saw this night stand before the darkness. It did my heart good to see her, for it has been many years since I've come to these shores and I'd forgotten her face, even in my dreams. But the boy was a surprise. I had hoped it was not true, but it is true and real and there lies your task."

"What task? You speak in riddles."

It was raining even harder than before. They were walking through the lower streets of Highneck Rise now. Walls and trees lined the way on either side. Lamps burned at gated entrances, but all such places were barred against the night. The way seemed familiar to Ronan and he realized they had turned onto the Street of Willows. Down at the end of the street was the Galnes house.

"You will find the boy," she said.

Ronan opened his mouth and then shut it. For a moment he did not see the rain and the night, but only saw the darkness of a chimney and Jute's face looking up out of it.

"You will keep him safe. Alive. Even if it costs you everything you are. Even if you lose your life."

"Lady," said Ronan wretchedly. "I killed that boy once. I killed him and then took him a second time to be killed, and now you ask me to guard his life."

"Yes."

"What if I say I can't do such a thing?"

"Water is mine, and you are mine as well, for my blood runs in your veins now. I'll not compel you to do this. If compulsion is not married with choice there is a hatefulness in it that can't help but lead to destruction in the end. I ask you to do it of your own choice, for such a choice will be strong and there's more to you, Ronan of Aum, than a sword."

He did not speak, but bowed his head in assent. They came to the stone wall outside the house of Cypmann Galnes. The willow trees swayed in the windy darkness. The gate creaked and a figure appeared. It was the cook, Sanna, with a leather bag over her shoulder. Liss did not stop walking; without a word, the old woman fell in beside her.

"All I want is to leave this city and go north," Ronan said. "I wanted to build a house in the Flessoray Islands and fish. I didn't want any of this. I should never have come to this city."

"If you live a life as long as mine, then you'll find a great many things aren't wanted but must be done." Liss's voice was sharp, but then it softened. "I will say this, though, there's a good chance you'll build your house someday, but not soon."

Ronan could not help but speak, hating himself for his weakness. "And you—what of you? Will I ever see you again?"

"It isn't my will to see every stream, every brook, every pond and freshet, each drop of water, though they all are mine. Yet each one knows full well it is mine."

Ronan flinched at her words, as if he had been struck. They continued along the Street of Willows in silence. The street ended past the Galnes house where a manor crouched behind a high hedge. A path cut through the hedge and out onto a grassy swale. Liss touched his arm and he stopped. He could taste salt in the rain. Moonlight shone through the clouds. Far below, down through the darkness, phosphorescence gleamed green and white on the wave tops. Surf crashed against the rocks. They were standing on the cliffs where the end of Highneck Rise stood high above the sea.

The old cook handed Ronan the leather bag.

"Had some time on my hands," she said. "Not all folks nitter their nights away dancing with the gentry. Baked some bread and walnut cakes, but such don't keep down under."

She stepped to the cliff edge and it seemed that Ronan saw a seal instead of an old woman, a seal with sleek brown fur and shiny black eyes that winked at him. Then the seal was gone and a dark shape hurtled down into the sea.

"Keep the boy alive," said Liss. There was a heaviness to her words, as if hers was the voice of the tide that always returns for what it wants, forever relentless. Ronan hunched his shoulders under the weight of it.

"For how long?" he said wretchedly.

"You'll know."

Liss pulled down her sheaf of hair. The wind caught at it and the dark tresses fluttered loose. Ronan saw seaweed shining purple in her hair. Her skin was as white as polished shell and gleamed with water. She plucked a strand of hair from her head.

"A boy such as him might be hard to find," said Liss. "Just as it's hard to find the wind, though it blows all around us. Hard to find and easy to lose. This will lead you to him, for all things, in drips and drops, find their way down to the sea."

Ronan said nothing. It seemed as if Liss no longer had any resemblance to a woman, had never had any resemblance to a woman. She was only shell and sand and water and glistening seaweed and her eyes held all the cold darkness of the watery deep.

"And for you, a gift." Liss opened her hand, and there, perfect and blue, was a pearl. "The sea wears away all things with a gentler hand than that of time, and this too will wear away one day. When it's gone, Ronan of Aum, then you'll find what you seek."

She stepped to the edge of the cliff.

"Wait," he said. "What is your name?"

Liss stopped. A slight smile crossed the face of shell and sand and shifting water.

"My name?"

The wind hushed and the boom of the surf below ceased its restless return. Her eyes brimmed with moonlight. She opened her mouth and there came a whisper of sound like music, a strange music breathed through water and light and having nothing to do with human ears or human voices. Pain struck at Ronan. He staggered, desperate for the touch of earth or air, for all he could feel was water pressing around him, heavier than stone. It felt as if his body was dissolving into water. But he gripped the pearl in his hand with all his might and he could feel the strand of her hair wound about his fingers. Those two remained and did not change. The pain vanished.

Liss smiled at him again, somewhat sadly this time. The wind sprang up and her form collapsed into foam that blew off the cliff and drifted away, down into the darkness and the sea waiting below.

CHAPTER SEVENTY-FOUR
HER NAME IS FEN

"'Ware the gate!"

The moonlight shone on faces looking down from the top of the wall. A torch flared into life.

"Who goes there?"

"Lord Gawinn! Open the gate!"

An excited murmur filled the air. Voices called out behind the gates and the portcullis creaked and groaned as it was raised. The gates swung open and spearheads gleamed in the torchlight. A young lieutenant hurried forward, his face beaming. Horse hooves rang on the cobblestones. Owain Gawinn and his men had returned to Hearne.

"My lord," said the lieutenant. "Welcome home."

"Thank you," said Owain. "Have the horses seen to, and hot ale for the men."

"Very well, my lord."

The city was dark as Owain rode through the streets. A great weariness took hold of him. He had not realized how tired he had become over the last days. He'd be glad to have a hot bath and a decent meal. Sibb. The children would all be asleep by now, but she would be awake.

Shadows, but he missed her.

The puddles in the streets gleamed with moonlight. The wind sighed by and brought with it a flurry of rain. The air was cold and sharp and he wondered if winter would come early that year.

"Tracking in the snow," Owain said to himself. His horse's ears went up at the words. "Those are the days you'd much rather be warm in your stable. Believe me."

High above them, on the cliffs overlooking the city, the regent's castle loomed against the stars. Light shone on the towers and castle wall. He thought he heard the sound of music wavering on the wind.

"Dinners and dances," Owain said to the horse. "You see? We've been spared unutterable agony at the hands of the court. Smiling through those endless banquets until your face aches with the pain and pomposity of it all. Limping through the minuet with some fat cow of a duchess, making pleasant conversation while she stamps on your feet with all the delicacy of a stone-fed ogre. Not catching our quarry, sleeping in the mud and cold for days, and saddle sores—courtesy of you, my friend—it was all much more enjoyable."

The expedition had been certainly well worth the trouble. It was a beginning. It had yielded another thread, a thread to be followed in patience until the mystery had been unwound. Botrell would be forced to give the problem his attention now.

His horse's ears again perked up, listening for something. Owain eased back in the saddle. His mount slowed and then halted. Then, he heard the sound of hooves clip-clopping and a figure emerged into view in the moonlight. The horse and rider drew closer.

"Just passing this way myself," said Hoon.

"Oh?" said Owain, trying not to wonder what business Hoon could possibly have in the Highneck Rise neighborhood, let alone why his horse was not being groomed and watered back at the tower stables along with the rest of the company's mounts.

"Got a bit of n'understanding with a girl," said Hoon. He winked. "Works as a cook for one o' these rich laybouts."

"Ah," said Owain, wondering why he felt embarrassed at this revelation while Hoon, as far as he could tell, seemed perfectly unembarrassed.

"Been thinkin' 'bout nothing but her mutton pie for the last week."

"Oh," said Owain. He was at a complete loss for words and would not have said anything past that single utterance, but Hoon raised his hand for silence.

"Hist!"

The little tracker reined his mount in and Owain did the same. Hoon pointed at the horses' ears. Both pairs were upright and rigid and oriented ahead. Hoon stroked the neck of his horse.

"They're not liking what they hear," said Hoon. "Somethin' ain't right."

"We're near my home," said Owain. "Just around the next bend."

He did not wait for any further talk, but urged his horse into a gallop. He could hear Hoon following swiftly behind. And then he heard the first sound of screaming before he rounded the corner. His mouth went dry. The horse slowed, shuddering under him, but he cursed it and whipped at it with the reins until it shot forward. The screaming grew louder. His house blazed with lights from every window. Servants ran to and fro, shouting. Torches burned and sparks rose in the night air. Owain savagely hauled on the bit, yanking his horse to a halt and kicking his boots free from the stirrups. His steed whinnied a terrible, high-pitched squeal and he heard it blunder against the hedge and then gallop away down the street. The cobblestones in front of the gate were slick with blood. What looked like the body of a horse lay mangled to one side of the gate. Owain did not remember drawing his sword, but it was there in his hand. He ran through the garden. The front door was open and his steward, Ognien, stood there with a torch in one hand and a pike in the other. Several of the other men of the household crouched ready behind him, all with weapons in their hands.

"My lord," said the steward, his face grim.

"What's happened here?" said Owain.

"We've sent for the regent's doctor," said the steward, "and for the Guard as well. Your return is timely, my lord."

"Around the side," said Hoon.

He pulled at Owain's arm, but the captain flung him off with a snarl.

"Come!" said Hoon.

There, around the side of the house, among the crushed rose bushes, they found the body of Loy the Hullman. He held a great spear in his arms. The flaming torchlight outlined his broken corpse. The ground was sharp with shattered glass.

"Owain!" Sibb was in his arms, sobbing and gripping his neck. Behind her, he caught sight of the white face of the regent's nephew, Arodilac Bridd.

"Sibb! What in shadow's name has happened here?"

She could not answer him, so hard was she crying.

"My lord!"

It was Hoon. The tracker was crouched on the ground by the dead Hullman.

"My lord," he said again. There was such a terrible urgency in his voice that Owain put aside his wife and went toward him.

"Look here."

Owain snatched a torch away from a servant and raised it high.

"The tracks are the same, my lord," said Hoon. "While we were gone, our murderin' beastie's been here."

Sibb's grip tightened on her husband.

"Her name is Fen," she said, barely audible through her tears.

"She speaks," said Owain, startled.

"Now she does," said his wife. "Now she does." But her gaze was fixed on the crumpled form of the dead Hullman.

CHAPTER SEVENTY-FIVE
WAITING IN THE FOG

Ronan woke up. For a moment, he could not remember where he was. He sat up in bed. His hand was clenched tightly into a fist. With an effort, he relaxed his fingers. A blue pearl and a strand of hair lay in his palm. He remembered and sighed. Somehow, the strand of hair had woven itself about the pearl so that the gem was held within the web of hair. The strand was securely knotted in a loop. Ronan settled the loop around his neck. Instantly, the necklace tugged at him. It was an impatient, almost exasperated tug. He couldn't tell if it was in his mind or merely pressure against his skin.

The boy!

Ronan jumped to his feet. What had he been thinking, sleeping the night away? Less than a minute later, he was hurrying down the staircase into the courtyard behind his rooms. He didn't bother setting the ward spelled into the door. He knew he wouldn't be back. Not ever again.

The morning fog was oddly thick, and his breath misted in the cold air. Summer was certainly gone. Ronan shrugged his cloak around his shoulders and strode off. His sword was a comforting weight on his back. The leather bag from the old cook hung at his side. He reached over his shoulder, eased the sword free an inch from its scabbard, and then let it slide back in. The steel whispered in satisfaction against the leather.

The necklace pulled at him. No, it yanked at him. The fine line of it burned against his skin. The urgency was even stronger, but there was something else as well. Fear. It was then that Ronan heard footsteps. He could not tell from which direction the sound came. First, it seemed the steps shuffled along off to the right, and then the sound came from the left. He touched the haft of his sword. The metal was full of memories of blood. It murmured reassurance to him of the frailty of all flesh. That all flesh would fail, and this steel would help some along the way. But even with that comfort, his heart faltered. Ronan turned and hurried away.

The fog began to unravel. He stood on the outskirts of Mioja Square. He turned and stared into the fog. The street was empty except for the mist drifting across the cobblestones and over the roofs and ghosting around gutterspouts. He shivered and plunged into the labyrinth of the square. Canvas hung heavy with the fog's dew and the gay colors brought to life by night and torchlight were nowhere to be seen. Everything was grimy and gray. The cobblestones underfoot were slimed with mud and the debris of the past weeks.

None of the stalls were open yet—at least, none of those that he passed by. He heard snoring behind the canvas and leather and greasy wool blankets drawn down over the stalls. He saw no one. It was decidedly strange. This was a fair day, and surely it was time to get ready, to inventory goods and finish all the tasks that must be done before the morning onslaught of buyers.

Ronan paused. He had been down this row of stalls before. Surely he had. That tent of blue wool looked familiar. He could not see over the stalls. Their tops were a great deal taller than him. Perhaps down this path to the left? But here was another path to the right, skirting around a heap of garbage. A dog growled at him in warning as he passed the garbage, but then he noticed the animal was looking past him. The necklace tugged at him.

Get to the other side of the square. Now.

Ronan turned. Something moved far back down the row of stalls—a ripple in the air, as if he were looking through water that had been disturbed. He held his breath. The fog was advancing. It spread over the stalls, sliding down greasy tent slopes and reaching around ropes and poles. It flowed toward him as if propelled by a breeze. Perhaps that had been it. The wind eddying the fog. The dog growled again and slunk away.

The necklace pulled at him again. This time it was stronger than before. There was an urgency in the feel of it, as if it were becoming alarmed. Ronan ran through a passage canopied with awnings that sagged and dripped with water. The path twisted, and then, after a dozen yards, there were no more stalls and he was at the foot of some stairs. Stairs that climbed up into the fog. He was at the ruins of the university. The necklace tugged him up the steps. At the top of the steps, the fog was almost nonexistent. The vast walls rising before him stood like an island in a dirty gray lake out of which poked the peaks and tent poles of the stalls in the square below.

Hinges creaked. The necklace shivered warning. His sword felt heavy on his back. In the shadows, past some double doors chained with rusted links, stood a man. He was motionless, his back to Ronan, his hands flat on a small door just to one side of the double doors. He looked as if he would push the door down rather than swing it open.

"Good morning to you, sir," said Ronan.

The man turned. He had a thin, dark face that looked at Ronan without expression. His eyes seemed the only living thing about him, as if the man's face was merely a mask they peered through. Recognition sparked in his eyes, though Ronan was sure he had never seen the fellow before. The pearl hanging on Ronan's chest pulsed cold. Even though the pearl was hidden beneath Ronan's shirt, the man's eyes flicked straight down to it. He flinched and hurried away, down the steps and into the fog. For a while, Ronan could hear the shuffling footsteps, and he knew that it was the same shuffle that had followed him earlier through the streets.

The necklace no longer pulled at Ronan. He prowled about the porch. The huge double doors would never be opened by anyone other than a blacksmith with tools and flame. The chains wound about it were thicker than his wrist. He examined the little door hidden off to one side. He could hear the ward whispering in it and knew it was beyond his skill. After a while, it began to rain, and he settled down in the shadows behind the columns with his cloak drawn about him. Like the necklace, Ronan waited.

CHAPTER SEVENTY-SIX
THE REALITY OF DREAMS

It was a dreadful, howling noise. It yanked Jute out of sleep quicker than the Juggler kicking his ribs. He sat up and knocked his head against the bottom of a shelf. Linens cascaded down around him. The maid screamed again. The scream must have given her an opportunity to collect her thoughts, because it was then she remembered the broom in her hands. She gave another howl. This time there was a warlike sound to her yell. The broom whistled through the air and knocked the last shreds of sleep from Jute's head. He tumbled out of the closet and sprinted down the hall.

"Help! Help!" shrieked the maid. "Thieves! Robbers! Murderers!"

Jute had only a vague recollection of how to get out of the house. Actually, it was a proper manor, with hallways and doors and rooms opening into other rooms into other, endless rooms. If he had the time, he would have exited the manor in a leisurely fashion, collecting a few small objects along the way. It was a lovely place, but Jute wasn't able to appreciate any of it properly. It seemed that with every corner he turned or door he tried, another servant popped out and tried to grab him.

Kindly stop playing about and come outside.

"I'm not playing!" said Jute, dodging a red-faced footman.

"Here now!" bawled the footman.

Two kitchen boys rushed at Jute, hallooing joyously and waving baking paddles over their heads. A stout man waddled along at the rear, shouting threats that seemed directed equally at both the boys and Jute. He yanked an enormous vase over as he ran by. It went down with a crash and he heard the kitchen boys trip over themselves as they tried to avoid the shards.

That'll serve 'em, thought Jute.

As if in answer, a baking paddle whizzed by his head. Jute leapt down the hall and through a set of doors before he had time to take another breath. Morning light filled his eyes. He heard the rustle of the hawk's wings in the air. Someone shouted nearby, but he did not pause to look. He pelted across a lawn and around trees and blundered through a hedge. The garden wall rose up before him: weathered stone spidered with cracks for handholds. Jute clambered up to the top. A gardener brandishing a rake ran down the lawn, followed by the two kitchen boys. Jute waved cheerfully to them, but then, at that moment, something odd happened.

The gardener stumbled into a walk, stopped, and abruptly sat down. His head slumped and he began to snore. Behind him, the two kitchen boys toppled over onto the grass. One turned over to pillow his head on his arm. The hawk fluttered down and settled on Jute's shoulder. The bird's head turned this way and that, as if he were trying to hear something.

Evil awakes.

"What do you mean?" said Jute, looking around uneasily.

Look down into the city, said the hawk in his mind. *Someone has been whispering through the night. Old words of power. Someone has fed an old, evil spell with fresh blood. Nudged it into a design of fresh purpose. And now it falls hard on the city.*

Highneck Rise was like an island rising up out of a gray sea that lay thick and still, without advantage of wave to stir its depths. Fog lay all around them. The only sign of the city below was a single tower like a skeletal hand reaching up out of the water.

"That's the tower in the old university," said Jute. He shivered. "I fell from there."

Aye.

"What is the spell? What is it doing?"

The hawk did not answer, but the nervous pressure of his claws set Jute hurrying down the street. Down toward the city below. It was odd. The sun was rising, but where was the early bustle of the morning, of tradesmen on their deliveries, of servants going about their chores?

They came to a corner where the road curved around a fountain. Water murmured and flowed from a stone urn. An old man sat there on a bench. Jute slowed at the sight of him, for the hawk's claws had tightened again as if the bird saw menace in the aged frame.

"He's asleep," said Jute.

No. It is the spell.

The old man's head rested on his chest. A snore rasped in the air.

"You see? He's just sleeping."

Despite his own words, Jute tiptoed past the old man. The hawk seemed to chuckle inside his mind.

"Are you going to tell me what's going on?" said Jute. "What happened last night? Who was she?"

Levoreth's face formed in Jute's mind as if in answer to his question. But there was an indistinctness to it. The face was a jumble of earth. Stone molded with damp clay, two gray pebbles pressed in as eyes, a bundle of green vines woven about the head to serve as hair. And yet it seemed alive, filled with breath and purpose. The gray pebbles stared back at him.

You see more clearly now. But we will speak of her later. This is not the time for conversation.

"I'm not taking another step until you tell me what's going on."

Stubborn boy. Must I contend with you the rest of my days?

Something dealt Jute a blow on the back of his head. A wing. Feathers as hard as a blast of wind.

We must leave this city as swiftly as possible. The longer you stay here the sooner death will find you. The lady did not draw forth all the poison with her. Something remains within the walls. The telling of who you are will be long, and we simply do not have time.

The weight was gone from his shoulder. With one stroke of his wings, the hawk mounted up into the air. Soon, he was only a speck in the sky that, turning toward the east and the rising sun, became silvered with light until it blurred away into nothingness. There was only sky.

"Wait!"

Get to the gates and then gone. There is sorcery in the air and it compels all to fall asleep. Yet, as they sleep, the Dark is stirring awake.

Jute suddenly heard a noise. It was a soft sort of creak. Apart from the sudden catch of his breath, it was the only sound he could hear. Just ahead, the street descended toward the sprawl of the city below. Down into the fog, and Jute was standing on the edge of it. The creaking sound was coming closer. Jute dashed across the street and crouched behind a tree. He held his breath. A shape began to appear in the fog. It was a hulking mass, as tall as it was wide, creaking on and on as if an endless sigh. But then, just as Jute was about to scream and climb the tree, the thing emerged fully from the fog. It was a cart piled with fresh bread, pulled by a donkey. A baker's lad slept on the cart's seat, head nodding and reins straggling from his hands. The donkey ambled along. As the cart passed by, Jute sidled out and snatched a loaf of bread.

You should not take another man's labor.

"Says who?" said Jute, his mouth stuffed with bread. He turned to watch the cart crawl up the street. Odd. First the old man drowsing by the fountain, and then the baker's lad.

I think this spell does not affect animals. And with humans, this is something different than sleep. Whatever it is, the whole city lies in thrall, between slumber and waking, where the mind is dangerously open in dreams. And through these dreams comes the Dark. What a strange sorcery. I have never seen such in all my years. An odd similarity with the principle of weaving wihhts. . . Run, boy! Into the fog and out of this accursed city. They draw near!

Jute ran.

Right as he plunged into the fog, a figure rose up out of the gray gloom. It reached for him with long hands and even longer fingers. Its mouth snarled open in a face that had no other features. Jute dodged too late. The hands reached for his throat. But at that moment, a blurring arrow of feathers pierced the fog and struck the dark face. The figure staggered back with a shriek.

Run!

Jute ran. Behind him, the hawk surged back into the air. Darkness dripped from its claws. The street descended more steeply into the fog, plunging down into the city. Walls rose up out of the murk. Jute looked back, sobbing for breath. No one was there. But the fog hemmed him in on all sides. A crowd could have been gathered around him, running silent and watching, and he would not have seen them.

Why? I used to be a thief. Just a thief. Steal, keep the Juggler happy, eat, sleep. Live.

Keep yourself alive and I shall tell you your tale tomorrow.

Where are you?

I am near. The hawk's voice was grim. *Run.*

From the sudden levelness of the ground, Jute knew he was no longer in Highneck Rise. He was down in the city itself. He couldn't see for sure, but the odors were different now. Grime, work, the dusty scent of beeswax. He was somewhere near the chandlers' district. Something creaked open in front of him. A door, suspended in the fog. No—set within a wall. Something rushed out of the door at him. Jute screamed and flung himself to one side. The thing came after him in silence. It had too many arms. Jute darted down an alley.

The wind last night. What if I. . .?

No!

Why not?

Luck was with you beyond measure last night. If the lady had not been there, you would have unmade yourself. Yourself and all of this city. The wind is not so easily tamed. Even I cannot do what she did to you. It would mean both our deaths.

Something hissed in the fog before him. An answering call came from behind. He was trapped.

Take to the wall!

Jute hurled himself at the wall on one side of the alley. His fingers slipped on the stone. It was slick with moisture from the fog. But there, just a few steps further, was a gutter pipe. He was halfway up the pipe in no time at all. Maybe the fog wouldn't be as thick higher up on the roof. They wouldn't catch him on the roofs. Whatever they were.

Something grabbed his ankle and yanked down. Jute screamed, sliding back down the pipe. Desperately, he wedged his fingers behind the pipe. He kicked out with his other leg. His heel smacked into something rubbery. The thing glared up at him with eyes like holes gouged in shadow. He kicked harder, furious and terrified all at the same time. The thing fell away with a shriek. Jute scrambled over the edge of the roof.

This way.

The hawk shot past him, appearing out of the fog and vanishing just as quickly, wings outstretched. He ran after the bird.

Most of the buildings in Hearne butted up against other buildings, so that it was almost possible to walk from one end of the city to the other without setting foot on the ground. Jute knew. He had tried it before, he and Lena and a few other children, one summer day when the Juggler had been snoring off a drunken binge in his room. The only problem was that getting across the city in such a fashion meant taking a lot of detours and roundabouts. You couldn't go straight. It also helped if you could see where you were going.

Turn right at this next crest. Hurry! Several of them have gained the roof behind you.

Jute ran along the crest. He could hear tiles snapping under footfalls somewhere behind him and then slate sliding away to shatter in sudden cracks of noise on the street below.

What are they?

I know them now, for I've tasted their blood. Dreams and shadow. The dreams of men twisted into thread and woven with shadow. This is an ancient spell. I would have thought that there was no one in this land with the knowledge. There is dreadful power afoot this day.

They're like that thing in the cellar?

Jute ran down a slope, arms windmilling to keep his balance. Moss grew in the valley where the two roofs joined. He slipped on it and went down hard.

The wihht? Similar, but different. A wihht is held together by the strength of its master. These creatures that hunt you are held together by the malice of men's dreams.

The roof materials were changing from slate to clay tile. Cheaper. And weaker. He put his foot right through one, all the way down to his knee.

Run!

A blot of darkness crawled over the roof peak above Jute. It convulsed and separated into three figures that lurched down the roof toward him. They were skeletal, like limbs broken off a dead tree and reassembled into caricatures of life. Frantically, Jute heaved forward, yanking his leg out. He staggered down the slope. Clay tiles cracked underfoot like eggshells. His body felt too heavy, as if the fog had acquired weight and lay across his shoulders. As one, the three creatures behind him hissed.

You let the fear of them into your mind. This gives them power.

The hawk shot out of the fog. Skimming the roof, the bird crashed through the three creatures. Limbs snapped as if they were dry branches, but the last of the things clutched at the hawk as it fell. Feathers fluttered down. The hawk beat his way back up into the fog. He seemed to stagger through the air.

Leap!

Except there was no next roof.

Leap!

Jute leapt. Out into nothing except fog. His arms and legs flailed and, for a brief moment, it felt as if the air thickened and became thick enough to swim through. The wind rushed past him. He tried to catch it in his fingers, but he fell. Something hit him hard. Everything went black for a second. Jute sprawled face down on the ground. Not the ground. Another roof. He could taste blood in his mouth.

Get off the roof. Use the gable window.

Jute staggered to his feet. The gable window was further down the roof. The casement was not locked. He scrambled over the sill and shut the casement behind, locking himself into a silence stale with the scent of dust. He was in an attic jumbled with rubbish. Everything was covered in dust. There was no door. Something thudded on the roof overhead. Jute looked around frantically. Surely there was a door. Every room had a door. Something scrabbled back and forth on the roof. He stared up at the ceiling. The claws scratched in agitation above him.

You're a thief. Thieves find doors.

There, visible under the dust disturbed by his feet, was a groove in the planking. A trapdoor. But there was no handle. Jute dug at the wood with his fingertips until they bled. The latch on the gable window rattled. The wood shifted under his hands and the trapdoor lifted up. Behind him, glass shattered.

Jute leapt down a stairway into a bedroom, crowded with a rumpled bed and sour with the smell of sleep. The trapdoor fell shut with a crash. Floorboards creaked overhead. The bedroom door opened into a hall. He could smell fried fish and onions. The hall ended in stairs.

Careful.

Jute tiptoed down the stairs. A ward whispered through his mind, spelled somewhere into the house. This was not a rich man's house. And if it was not a rich man's house, then he gambled good odds that the only ward would be the one woven into the main outside door. Behind him, the stairs creaked.

He hurried down a hall and found himself in the kitchen. The air was choked with the scent of fried fish. Coals glinted on the hearth, under a pan full of charred fish. A table stood in the middle of the room. On the far side was a door. Several children sat at the table, slumbering over their bread and butter. A man snored into his greasy slab of fish at the end of the table. His shadow lay across the stone floor. It rippled as Jute stepped through it.

Careful. These creatures that hunt you spring from the dreams of man, and this man dreams.

Something squirmed in the man's shadow. It wriggled up like a water snake lifting its head from a stream. Jute sprang for the door with a shriek. The ward came alive the moment he touched the doorknob. It was an inexpensive ward. The kind bought for a copper and no guarantees. It was designed to guard against intruders coming into the house, not out of the house. But the ward went off with a vengeance when he turned the knob. Jute threw up his hands as he ran out the door, cringing, shoulders tensed for an explosion of flames or something equally horrible. However, there were no flames, no quicksand underfoot, no stone hands bursting out of the ground to grab his ankles.

Instead, the ward howled. It yelled and hollered and shouted. On any other day, Jute would have laughed. Not today.

"Here now!" bawled the ward. "Here nownownow! Heyou! Aouaouaou-arr!"

Unfortunate.

Jute thought he heard the hawk snort inside his mind. Back down the street, the ward continued to yell.

"Heyouyouyou! Yarrr. . .! Thief! Theee-ief!"

Quick. Turn here. A mob of these creatures is hastening up the street toward you, and there are others behind you as well. They do not tire, for the evil dreams of men are never short of hope.

Jute was exhausted and his knee ached. He felt blood trickling down his shin. It was beginning to rain. The cobblestones were slippery underfoot. Either the street curved or it narrowed, for he found himself running an arm's length from the buildings on his right. Lamplight shone from windows, blurred by the fog and the water beading on glass. He caught glimpses of ordinary life: a woman asleep at her spinning wheel, a child nodding over his porridge, an older girl asleep in the act of braiding the tresses of her little sister, fingers caught and unmoving in the skeins of hair.

Shadows take it all, Jute thought to himself. Why me? I wish I was inside somewhere. Inside and asleep over my porridge. I was content being a thief. A beating from the Juggler once in a while wasn't that bad. No hawk. No dreams. No sky. Nothing. I'd rather have nothing. Be nobody.

Beware your mind. Of all dangers, there are two that wield the deadliest swords.

Jute glanced over his shoulder. No one was in sight. There, he thought. I've outrun the wretched things. Hang it all. I know this city like my hand.

Something small hurtled toward him from the fog. A little gray cat. One claw swiped at his ankle. Jute yelped in pain and surprise, turning toward the animal to kick it, just in time to see a dark figure detach itself from the wall and reach for him. Teeth gleamed in a face with no eyes. The cat yowled and shot away down the street, fur standing up on end. Jute darted after the cat, his heart hammering in his throat.

Jute risked a look back and wished he hadn't. The whole street crawled with shadows. They welled up from the puddles, out from the cracks in the cobblestones. They clambered down gutter pipes, sidled out of doors, and winked in and out of view in the falling rain, as if so insubstantial they might hide behind a raindrop. But they were not insubstantial. They were real. Jute could hear their hissing and snarling as they called to each other. He remembered the dark blood on the hawk's beak. Some of the creatures looked like men. Some had extra arms or extra legs. Some had no heads. One had no arms at all but long legs like a spider, with a squat head in the middle covered with an impossible number of eyes.

Hawk!

As I was saying, concerning danger, there are two which wield the deadliest swords. Two which can never be underestimated. One, of course, is the Dark itself.

Where do I go? What should I do?

Follow the cat.

Follow the what?

The cat rounded the next corner, ears laid back flat, and going at a tremendous pace. It was all Jute could do to keep it in sight. Perhaps if he ran a bit faster he'd be able to give it a kick.

Tush, said the hawk. *The second danger is an everyday sort. Commonness renders it invisible, unacknowledged, and unchecked.*

This is no time for lectures, hawk!

The noises behind Jute were getting closer. There was a horrible galloping, pattering, slapping sound to it all, as if dozens of hooves and bare feet and boots were running in concert together. The jumble of sound echoed off the high walls of the houses crowding around and became even more jumbled.

The cat looked back. One blue eye flashed in the gloom, and then the cat bounded away, legs flying and fur matted with water. The rain fell harder. Jute pelted through a small square. A fountain splashed in the center and its pool was overflowing, unable to keep up with the rain. Water sheeted across the cobblestones. Several dark figures jumped up out of the pool at his approach. Jute skidded on the water. The cat yowled and dashed around one outstretched arm.

We are cut off from the gates. You are being herded.

The fog lifted then, up into a dark sky slashing down rain. Jute knew where he was now. The street widened. Shops and stalls and barrow carts were chained to railings. Canvas awnings sagged from the buildings, sodden with rain. Mioja Square. The tangled sea of the fair, of tents and carts and bannered poles, lay before him, huddled in the rain. The cobblestones underfoot were slick with mud. On either side of him, off around the edges of the square, he heard the sound of running feet.

Quick.

Jute plunged into the tents. His skin crawled. Where were the people? Where were the merchants and peddlers and people? He would have given much to see one normal face at that moment. But all he saw was the cat scampering off between the tents, its gray tail flying in the rain.

Courage, Jute.

Beyond the tent tops he saw the ruined walls of the university. His heart rose. There would be refuge behind those walls. Severan would be there. He would know what to do. Jute ran past the stone fountain in the center of the square. Water streamed over its sides. A dead pigeon floated in the pool, bobbing against the stone border. The cat vanished somewhere near the fountain. He didn't blame it, for the hissing and snarling sounds behind him were growing louder and closer by the second. Regardless of the cat leading him through the fog, he would've enjoyed giving the animal a swift kick. His ankle still burned from the clawing it had given him.

The cat saved your life, said the hawk. *The second danger, if you had not yet guessed, is your own self. For every man, regardless of how noble or miserable his life may be, the second danger is his own self. First the Dark, then your self. And in some men, they are the same.*

Jute staggered up the steps of the university. He turned and his heart faltered, for out of the maze of tents came his pursuers. They came forward, slinking and crawling and lurching. They leered up at him through the rain with faces that had no eyes, and eyes that had no faces, shadows with teeth and quick, twitching hands. There was nowhere left to go. The great doors were wound with chains. The stone wall was worn smooth by the centuries. There was nowhere to climb to. The little door Severan had opened buzzed with wards. There was no way through.

"Hawk!" Jute said.

A man stepped out from behind one of the pillars. In his hands gleamed a sword. Jute shied away in terror, but the man moved past him.

"Stay behind me, boy," Ronan said.

The creatures rushed up the steps in a wave, advancing in a crescendo of snarling darkness. Jute cowered back, certain the wave would crash over him. He thought he heard a voice hiss his name from the crowd. But Ronan's sword sang into life, whistling through the air, weaving a wall of steel in front of his eyes. The wave broke on that wall and the sword ran with black blood.

The creatures fell back down the steps and then surged forward. But again they were beaten back. The stones underfoot were slick with their blood. Their bodies fell on the steps to be trampled by their fellows. The dead flesh subsided into mist that drifted down the steps, as if it were heavier than air and sought some low place to rest. The breath grated between Ronan's teeth, and his arm trembled. There seemed no end to the creatures, no matter how many he killed. Perhaps he might have fallen under one more wave had not the hawk stooped down out of the rain. The bird was nearly invisible with his black feathers against the gloom and the dark mass of the attackers. The creatures lifted up their faces to his claws, hissing in fear. Ronan spared the hawk one startled glance and then redoubled his efforts. The wave broke once again.

Where have you been?

Saving your neck, boy, said the hawk. He beat back up into the rain and was momentarily lost to sight. *I went in search of the old man. The sky above the university is warded. I singed my feathers. There is trouble in the ruins, but I would judge us safer within than without. Look to the door.*

And at that word, Jute heard the wards woven into the wall behind him subside into silence. The little door sprang open with a crash.

"Hurry!"

It was Severan. Jute dove for the door. He felt the hawk's wing brush past him. Ronan sprang back, his sword swinging. The door slammed shut and the wards whispered back into life. The door shook under a tremendous blow. The wards buzzed in agitation. Jute could feel them inside his mind. There was almost a coherence to the sound, as if they muttered words from some strange language of rock and dust and earth. His head ached with it.

"Will the door hold?" said Ronan.

Severan touched the door. He frowned.

"I think so," he said. "These wards were woven by one of the wisest professors to ever teach within these walls. Bevan was the master of such magic, and one word from him held more strength than a thousand bolts and locks. It's a strange enemy we have outside, though."

"They bleed well enough," said Ronan in distaste. He turned to look at Jute. "All right, boy?"

"No thanks to you," said Jute angrily. He backed away from him. He would have said more, but the hawk settled onto his shoulder. The claws gripped him hard, and he subsided into silence.

Severan shook his head. "From what I saw, I think him worthy of thanks. And as I bear this boy some affection, despite his pigheadedness, my thanks to you," he said, turning to Ronan. "But come, we shouldn't stay here."

The old man hurried away down the hall. A lamp burned on one wall, but other than that, the place was shrouded in shadow. Behind them, the door shook again under its assault. A hollow booming echoed through the hall.

"Walk where I walk," said Severan. "Touch nothing, and keep silent. Something happened last night, either here in the ruins or close by in the city—we aren't sure—but not all the wards are stable anymore."

There was a trembling in the air, and the light filtering down from the windows high overhead had an oddly tentative quality to it, as if it were nervous of being caught within the stone walls. Pools of water lay here and there, catching the raindrops falling down through holes in the roof.

The wards are awake, Jute thought.

He can hear them too.

Jute scowled at Ronan. The man walked a few paces in front of him. His head was turning from side to side and, every once in a while, his hand strayed to the hilt of his sword.

The hawk's claws flexed on Jute's shoulder.

This man does not deal in magic, but he listens. Perhaps better than you. For now. There is a familiarity to him, a scent I have known from long ago. But surely my memory is from hundreds and hundreds of years past, and this man cannot have lived more than three decades. How strange.

An evil scent, I suppose, grumbled Jute inside his mind.

No, not evil.

He tried to kill me! He left me for dead in that house!

Whatever he did before is done. And though he tried to kill you, he did not. You are the better for it.

And then he kidnapped me and handed me over to the Silentman!

Which would not have happened had you kept safely within these walls. But even disobedience can be turned to good, for there are always greater dreams at work that we cannot see. Within these dreams sleep the smaller reaches of our own dreams.

Jute did not understand this and spent some time thinking about the hawk's words. But no matter how he turned them back and forth, they made no sense to him.

Severan stopped at the end of a corridor that opened into a courtyard. The ground was covered with blue and black tiles in a pattern that confused the eye. The old man squatted down and touched one of the tiles with his finger.

"This is a trap," said Jute. He stared at the tiles with distaste.

"Aye," said Severan, smiling. "You've been in rooms like this before, haven't you? But we've turned the ward here to our own uses. It guards for us now. No one can go where we go without crossing this courtyard, and once entered, it's no small feat to escape these tiles."

"Wards." Ronan spat to one side and hitched up his sword. "I don't care for spells and trickery. Give me an honest blade and as long as there's breath left in my body, I'll meet any foe, wizard or not."

"I'd expect no less from you, for I think I know your name."

"Names don't mean much these days."

"A matter of perspective. Ronan of Aum, isn't it?"

"Aye."

"And Aum a ruin, haunted by jackals and hoot owls. It's been three hundred years since the men of Harth marched north to burn its gates and break down its walls. A lonely place to come from. A place of death. I think, sir, you have another name as well."

There is no telling what Ronan might have said at that point. He opened his mouth to speak, but someone else spoke first.

"Time for talk later, old man." The voice rustled, creaking and quiet, as if little used. "Time enough later."

Jute had never heard the hawk speak out loud before. His voice was similar to how the bird spoke within his mind, but it was odd to hear him with his ears. The sound felt like sunlight and a hot sky and the wind lazing through it all. Of the three, however, Severan was the only one who showed no surprise.

"My apologies, master hawk," said Severan.

"Something seeks to open the outer door," the bird said. "Whoever set those shadows afoot in the city. Your ward won't hold forever against it. Can you not smell the fear in the air? These ruins remember. They remember the day when Scuadimnes opened the door into the darkness."

"Talking monkeys from Harth and now hawks as well?" said Ronan. "I smell nothing except the dust of this place."

"As if you should speak," said Jute angrily.

"Peace, boy," said the hawk. "I remember you now, assassin. I remember you when you were but a child. You broke your father's ash bow, hunting rabbits."

Ronan's face turned pale.

"Quickly now," said the hawk.

Severan muttered a few words and the color of the courtyard tiles dulled. They hurried across, under an arch on whose peak perched a stone gargoyle.

"He'll watch for us," said Severan.

Behind them, stone grated against stone, as if the gargoyle had settled itself more comfortably to wait for whatever might come. After a short time, they came to a door at the end of a corridor. Stone faces lined the walls.

"The forgotten luminaries of this place," said Severan, not bothering to glance at the sculptures. "The founders, the first council, those who began to record knowledge and the histories of men. I doubt there's any man alive who knows all their names."

"No man, aye," said the hawk.

"And him?" asked Jute. He looked uneasily at the stone face over the door at the end of the corridor. The face was by itself. The nearest faces were a good five paces away on either side back down the corridor. There was something odd about the face. It was too thin. The skull was too narrow. The stone of the thing was scorched dark.

"Scuadimnes," said the hawk.

"*Foro*," said Severan to the door.

"Someone should take an axe to him," said Ronan.

Severan smiled sourly. "You would be unpleasantly surprised if you tried such a thing. Scuadimnes wove a ward into the stone that, as far as anyone can tell, merely serves to guard his likeness. There are no hidden secrets in the face. The ward guards his pride, and there has never been any secret to that. People have attempted the destruction of the stone out of hatred of Scuadimnes. The result has always been death."

"By fire?" said Jute.

"Always by fire."

The door closed behind them and they found themselves climbing stairs.

"Watch where you step," said Severan.

"Where are you taking us?" said Ronan, frowning. "I've lost my sense of bearing in this place, and with all the wards buzzing and whispering, I'll be lucky to last the hour without my head splitting open."

"The tower of the library. We've gathered there all the books we've found in these ruins, and it is no small collection. My friends are there already, searching for answers to the questions posed by this day. We will consult on what is best to be done with Jute."

"I don't think you want to be caught in a tower today," said the hawk. "I have wings, but you do not."

"We'll be safe there a while." Severan waved his hand in dismissal. "While there's only one stairway leading up to the tower, there are three other stairways that lead down. Another of Bevan's tricks. Stairs that can only be walked down, and not up. The tower is not a dead end to be trapped in. Besides, the wards in this place weave together in such confusion that I daresay the best tracker in Tormay would lose our trail."

The stairs were marble, cracked in places, missing in others, so that they had to step over gaping holes. The walls rose up with them, sheer on either side, toward such a height that Jute could not see the ceiling. For all he knew, the walls might have been built right up and up until the sky itself was the ceiling. It was dark on the stairs. Jute turned to look back down the steps. He had the uncomfortable feeling that something was down there, just out of sight.

We are alone here. For the present.

Then why is the back of my neck prickling like someone is watching?

The hawk shifted his weight on Jute's shoulder.

Because you are feeling the unease of this place. Something sniffs outside the walls, and old memories wake here within.

What is it? What is outside?

But the hawk did not answer him.

The stairs ended at a blank stone wall. Jute could not see the top of it. The stone was scorched by fire. Severan placed both hands on the wall and closed his eyes.

"An accursed key, old man," said the hawk, his voice sharp.

The wall dissolved in front of them. Stairs rose up beyond in darkness, but light glimmered on the marble steps.

"You're a mind reader as well," said Severan.

"Your thoughts shouted the name aloud," said the hawk. "It would be well not to do such a thing again. These ruins bear ill memories of his name."

"There's no other key," said Severan. "There's no other way to get into the library."

The stairs climbed up through a night without moon or stars. Jute reached his hand out and tried to touch the wall on his right, but there was nothing. Surely there was a wall. His hand trailed through the air. He leaned even farther and a hand closed on the back of his shirt, pulling him back toward the middle of the stairs.

"Careful," said Ronan from behind him.

"I wouldn't do that if I were you," said Severan. "It's a long way to fall."

"How long?"

"No one knows."

The stairs ended and a door opened into the library. The room was octagonal in shape. Books lined the majority of the walls on all sides, from floor to ceiling, and there were lamps glowing in the gloom. Four windows looked out of the room, set opposite and at angles to each other like the cardinal points of a compass. Between each window was a door. Stars shone outside in the night sky.

"It can't be night already," said Jute in astonishment.

"Time behaves oddly on the stairs," said Severan. "We've been climbing all day."

CHAPTER SEVENTY-SEVEN
FOOTSTEPS ON THE STAIRS

Two old men came out of the shadows in the room, silent and staring. It seemed that they looked at the hawk perched on Jute's shoulder, but then he realized that both of them were staring shyly at him. He shuffled his feet and looked down at the floor.

"Is this the boy you spoke of?" said one.

"Later," said Severan. "Have you learned anything about the shadow creatures roaming the streets? Or the spell muttering its way through this city?"

"The wihhts, you mean," said one of the two old men.

The hawk stirred but did not say anything.

"The wihhts?" said Ronan.

He stood near the door, so motionless in his drab cloak that neither of the two old men had even seen him enter the room. They eyed him curiously, but their attention remained on Jute.

"They're wihhts, but they aren't wihhts," said the old man.

"If they aren't wihhts, then they can't be wihhts, Gerade," said Severan.

"There is a similarity," said Gerade. "A similarity in how they're woven into being, I think." He picked up a book from the table. "I found this book tucked away in the back of the fifth volume of Blostma's *Treatises on Flowers*—the fifth volume deals with decorative varieties, you remember—such tedious writing that none of us had bothered to open it until now."

He flipped a few pages in the book.

"Here it is. Apparently, this is the journal of an assistant professor of Naming at the University, and he—"

"An assistant professor at the University?" Severan looked startled.

"Yes," said Gerade. "I haven't figured out his name yet. Probably a wise choice, in light of—"

"So he was alive during the wizards' war?"

"Of course. Hence the pertinence," said Gerade. "What he wrote seems to have bearing on those wretched creatures roaming the city. Now, where was I? Here we are."

Gerade began to read.

"Later that night, those on watch in the lower tunnels reported a strange whisper in the stones around them. It was confirmed in all of the lower tunnels, from the passage that runs the length of the north side to the labyrinth underneath the southern buildings. In the water tunnel, however, from the east wall to the well under the seeing room— which we are in the process of stopping up for other reasons—there was no sound except for the noise of the rushing water. The reasons for this are unclear, but I think it due to the natural unease between water and darkness.

"The whisper droned several words, over and over again. The sound was so quiet it was first only heard by a student who had fallen asleep with his head resting against a wall. He awoke screaming, for there was evil in the words and they had worked their way into his mind. It took three men to subdue him.

"We were unable to determine the exact nature of the words, for they were old and of strange forms that had little in common with the grammars in the library. Besides, we were hampered by the loss of the books Scuadimnes had stolen. The only determination we could make concerned the nature of the spell. It was similar to the weavings that go into the making of a wihht. Also, one of the words drew its meaning from darkness, from *dimnes*."

Jute watched the moon vanish outside the window as clouds drifted across the stars. He was tired and hungry. He did not care about names and words and whether something was a wihht or not. To tell the truth, at that moment he did not care about explanations and what the hawk would tell him—if he ever would, which was highly suspect. All he wanted was some bread and cheese and somewhere to sleep.

Severan sighed.

"*Dimnes*. Scuadimnes. He never tried to hide his nature, did he?"

Gerade continued reading.

"Our knowledge in this matter is not enough to combat the spell. The council is convinced that if the words could be unraveled, their unmaking would also prove the unmaking of the terrible army that batters against our walls. For when these abominations are cut down, they bleed darkness. Their darkness is the same that infuses the words muttering through the stones underfoot. But we have no time to research this, for more and more of us die with every passing hour."

Gerade stopped reading. "It's a variation of the same word, isn't it? Not exactly the same, but reasonably similar to *dimnes*. I heard it this morning. Even Adlig heard it, deaf as he is."

"I'm not deaf."

"But there was another word in the air this morning. *Swefn*. We don't know what it means."

"It means dream," said the hawk. "Those creatures are woven out of shadows and dreams."

"*Swefn*," said Adlig. "I've never heard that word before. Thank you."

"Those things in your book," said Ronan. "They bled darkness?"

"They did, and this was also mentioned in other histories of the wizards' war. Sarcorlan of Vomaro's text on the kings of Hearne, as well as—"

"Save the recitation," said Ronan. Gerade turned red and shut his mouth. "The creatures outside bleed a strange dark substance that seemed to disappear into the air. They sound like those in your histories."

"I daresay we won't come any closer to an answer if the council themselves were not able to," said Adlig. "Surely there's no one alive today who possesses more knowledge than they. But this presents quite an amazing opportunity. Perhaps there's some study we can attempt of these creatures? Could one of them be captured?"

"Spare me from scholars and wizards," said the hawk. "You spend your lives in talk while time steals the days, one by one, like gold from your unresisting hands. Come, we have a grave problem set before us, and these wretched shadows creeping about the city are a paltry trouble in comparison."

Gerade and Adlig blushed like guilty children at the hawk's words, though Severan nodded his head. Jute sat down, leaned against a bookcase and thought about sausages. His head bent forward and he fell asleep. A snore escaped him. Everyone turned to look.

"You speak of the boy, lord hawk," said Gerade.

"Aye," said the hawk.

"He is the. . . he is the—?"

"He is the anbeorun Windan," said the hawk, sighing somewhat.

"The wind lord! Severan said as much, but how could we believe him? He's just a boy. He's so young."

"My old master is dead," said the hawk.

Lamplight gathered in the bird's black eyes and he stared at Jute, but his focus seemed far away as if he looked through the sleeping boy and saw someone else. He rustled his wings and then, with an effort, continued speaking. "The name of the wind is waking in this young one, but it does not waken easily or quickly. The wind will not be in his grasp for many days or even weeks, and I think the Dark knows this. It seeks his life."

"Could such a thing happen?" said Gerade, his face pale. "Has such an evil ever come upon one of the anbeorun? There's no mention of such a thing in any of the histories. The anbeorun have always defended us against the Dark. If the Dark ensnared the wind lord, then what would stop death from coming to the lands of Tormay?"

"Sorrow would come to the world," said Adlig.

"Aye," said the hawk. "It would be the beginning of sorrows."

"What can be done?"

"We must hide the boy, of course," said Severan. He looked around the room. "We have no other choice."

"If we do this," said Gerade, "surely the Dark will come for us as well."

Adlig snorted. "Death comes sooner or later. I've heard it creeping along my trail these past years. Might as well come sooner, for all I care. Never took you for a coward, Gerade."

"I merely think it prudent to consider all potential outcomes. It's the sensible thing to do."

"Rubbish. Stop talking like a pompous scholar."

"We're scholars and, as such, we'd be remiss not to consider all the angles. Perhaps we should form a committee to report back on all history relevant to the situation? The political ramifications should be analyzed as well. The Regent might want a say in this. And the duchies."

Severan's fist crashed down on the table. Everyone jumped. Jute woke up with a start.

"We hide him. We'll worry about the consequences later."

"First," said the hawk, "we must get him out of the city."

"Why?" said Gerade. "What better place to hide than in these ruins? It's a labyrinth in here. Besides, there are more wards guarding these walls than can be found in all of Tormay."

"He must be taken out of the city," said the hawk. "I don't trust these ruins."

"If it must be done, then it can be done," said Severan. "But I don't think he'd get two steps with all those shadow creatures outside."

"I doubt we'd be able to fight our way through them." Ronan tapped the hilt of his sword thoughtfully.

There were many more suggestions. Some bad, some worse than bad. But then Adlig pounded his fist on the table and crowed with delight. His eyes gleamed.

"I have it!" he said. "Just the thing."

"What's that?"

"The well beneath the mosaic."

But before he could say anything further, the hawk turned to stare at the door.

"Quiet," said the bird.

A hush fell over the room. Severan hurried to the door, eased it open, and peered down the stairs. At first, there was only silence, but then, from far below, there came the quietest of sounds. Footsteps. Something was walking up the stairs.

"It could be anything," said Gerade. "Perhaps the manifestation of a ward. A squirrel. There's an infestation of squirrels in the observatorium roof. Right by that old walnut in the courtyard."

"Hush." Severan glared at him.

Jute crept up behind Severan and peeked down the stairway. His nose twitched. There was something familiar in the air. An odd scent. And then he knew. Jute spun away from the stairs, but there was nowhere to run. The room shrank around him. Ronan grabbed his arm.

"What's the matter, boy?"

Jute flung the man's grip off.

"He's down there! The thing! From the basement in the house." Jute backed away until there was no place to go. He felt the wall behind him.

"The wihht?" Severan looked a little pale. "Are you quite certain, Jute? If it made it this far, then it's bound to possess magic of its own. We have Nio to thank for this, blast his soul."

"I don't fancy encountering this wihht fellow," said Gerade. "Despite whatever academic profit might be gained from such a meeting. Quick. The other stairs. One leads down to the conservatory. The second leads to the great hall. And the third leads to the courtyard."

"The conservatory," said Severan. "That would be best. Hurry."

He sprang to one of the doors and grasped the handle. But it would not turn. He tried the other two doors, without luck. He muttered a word, his eyes shut, and then wrenched his hand away with an exclamation of pain. The door shivered but did not open.

"They're locked." Severan's face was blank with shock. "I don't understand it. These doors were built without locks. They aren't supposed to have wards, but there is something in the stone now that keeps them shut. Some sort of spell. The craft of it is beyond my knowledge. Our enemy, whoever he is, plays his hand well. I'm sorry, Jute. I am to blame."

"If only we could fly," said Jute, his voice trembling.

They turned as if one to the hawk.

"I couldn't carry even the lightest of you in my claws," said the hawk.

"Perhaps the boy could call the wind?" said Gerade.

"No," said the hawk. "It would be your deaths once wakened, and such power, if let loose, will waken the Dark itself and it will come to this spot."

"Let's at least shut the other door," said Severan. "The ward will keep the wihht at bay while we figure out what to do."

But, to their dismay, they could not close the door. It shifted slightly in their hands but the air around it felt as if it had turned to stone. Ronan threw his weight against the door and the wood shuddered. Jute gave a cry of fear and clambered up onto one of the window sills. He pushed the casement open and would perhaps have jumped had not Adlig grabbed the back of his shirt.

"Best to stay and fight, boy," said the old man. He smiled. "It makes the last moments worthwhile."

"How much time do we have?" said Ronan. He strode to the window and looked out into the night.

"Not much," said Severan. He and Gerade pushed against the door. It closed perhaps another inch, but it stayed open. There was a chill on the stairs. A greenish light grew, wavering up the walls toward them.

"Buy me a little time and we'll be out of here safely enough," said Ronan. He unslung his pack from under his cloak.

"What are you thinking?"

Ronan pointed out the window. "That other tower, there."

"You must be joking," said Adlig. "We have no wings and I'm no rabbit to leap such a distance. We'll dash our brains out on the stones below."

Ronan pulled a coil of rope from his pack. He turned to the hawk.

"Do you know knots?"

The hawk's eye glinted. "Aye. Ages past, my master and I flew with the seafarers, coming west to Tormay, before this land was settled. They knew their knots."

"Just a knot that'll hold; that's all we need."

The hawk grasped the free end of the rope in his claws and took off from the window in a silent flex of wings. Ronan leaned through the window, paying the rope out as the bird flew. His face was taut.

"Quickly!" said Severan from the door.

"We're going as quickly as we can," said Ronan. The rope slid between his hands. He could see the hawk settle on the roof of the tower opposite them, a little below the height of their window.

"He's there," he said. But the pearl hanging inside his shirt flared with heat. He turned. "Close that door!" he said. The pearl was as hot as a flame. Something was near.

"We're trying." Sweat ran down Severan's forehead. The door was halfway closed now, but the green light beyond it brightened. Shadows leapt up in the room, thrown on the wall, wavering and tinged with green. The air seemed oddly cold. There was a dark figure on the stairs.

"Well now, Severan," said a thin voice. "Is this the reception given to an old friend?"

Severan froze. The figure took another step up.

"Nio!" he said.

The figure paused.

"Aye, that was my name once. Once." Teeth shone in a smile. "It's a good name. I've tasted many names, but that one is good. And fresh. Many interesting memories. But it's no longer my name." The green light deepened, and the shadows grew into darkness. The lamp burning on the table dimmed. The figure took another step up.

"That is your name," said Severan fiercely. "His face is yours. His voice is yours. You were once my friend and no friend of the Dark." Beside him, Gerade shoved against the door with all his might, his lips moving silently. Sweat ran down his face.

"We're almost there." Ronan grabbed Jute by one arm and hoisted him upon the windowsill. "Another heartbeat and the knot'll be tied."

The thing on the stairway laughed and the flame in the lamp went out. Darkness filled the room. The air became chill and their breath misted. A stench of rotting things filled the air. The door swung open wide.

"The lamp," said Severan frantically. "Light the lamp!"

"Jute." said Ronan.

Ronan shoved him out the window. Jute's legs flailed. He cried out, but the man's hand was clamped in the back of his shirt.

"Grab the rope," said Ronan.

Jute grabbed the rope and he found himself sliding away from the casement. The night rushed by him. The rope burned between his hands. Feathers brushed against his face and the hawk whirled away up into the sky on silent wings.

Hold lightly, fledgling.

Behind him, a voice called out, repeating one word over and over. Light flared in the tower window.

The lamp hissed back to life under Adlig's hands, but the flame only guttered uncertainly. He called out again, uttering a word that rang harshly within the room. Fire leapt up and the room was bright with light. The table smoked with the heat. The old man stumbled away, flame dripping from his fingers. But the door slammed shut, and there was a howl of fury from the stairs. The ward in the door whispered into life. Gerade leapt to Adlig's side and beat out the flames.

"Old man!" said Ronan. "Get ready. The boy's almost at the other side."

He was braced with one foot up against the window sill. The rope sang taut against the stone.

"My thanks, Gerade," gasped Adlig. "Three years I worked to learn that word and still I only spoke the first syllable now. I fear the complete word too much."

"You fear it rightly."

"Hurry," said Severan. "The ward won't hold much longer."

The door trembled and the wood groaned.

The rope slackened in Ronan's hand.

"All right," he said. "Next."

Gerade clambered up onto the sill and stepped out into the night. Soon he was just a dark figure receding away toward the lower tower below. A tremendous blow shook the door and beyond it, they could hear a snarling voice. The lamp dimmed.

"Next," said Ronan, winding another loop around his arm. "Quickly!"

"Adlig," said Severan. "You go. Hurry now."

The old man held up his hands. They were blistered by the fire.

"I can't hold onto that rope," he said. "I can't hold onto anything, least of all my life. I'll stay behind to brace the rope for the last trip. Go on now."

"But the wihht will take you!"

"Not if there's nothing of me left." The lampflame reflected in Adlig's eyes. He smiled crookedly.

"Thank you, old friend," said Severan. He turned and stepped through the window. The rope sang tight under his weight. Ronan leaned back against the pull of it. A dreadful whine filled the room.

"What is that?" said Ronan.

"The ward's unraveling," said Adlig.

362

Tendrils of what looked like smoke curled up from the door. But it was not smoke. It was darkness. The lamp on the table was almost out. Adlig crossed to the table in quick steps. He muttered something under his breath and the lamp flared up, but only for an instant. He winced and staggered back. Ronan reached out and steadied the old man. Adlig's flesh was hot to the touch.

"He's close now," said the old man.

"Come," said Ronan. "The rope's free now."

Adlig shook his head. "Tie the rope around my waist and I'll brace you."

Ronan stared at him for a second and then shrugged.

"Wedge yourself against the window frame," he said. "Let the stone bear my weight."

Ronan stepped out onto the casement. He glanced back. The door trembled. A blot of darkness abruptly welled up in its middle, bleeding shadow that crept down the wood.

"Go," said the old man.

The rope tautened under Ronan's weight and he was gone into the night. Adlig gasped at the pain of it, for the rope yanked him hard against the window frame and he could barely move. He could not breathe. It was cold in the room. The heat and pain of the blisters on his hands increased. There was a noise behind him. He turned as best as he could, turning just his head, his jaw scraping against the stone. The wihht stood behind him. The lamp was out.

"Old fool," it said, reaching for him.

Adlig spoke one word. The complete word.

The room surged with light. The scent of dried grass burning under the summer sun. The breath of fire. The char of wood and the slow collapse of steel in the forge. The glaring eye of the sun staring down, engulfing everything. The wihht stood motionless within the wash of light, its darkness inviolate and pure black against the contrast of white.

"Old fool," it said again. "You think such a word can consume me?"

"No," said Adlig. His hair whisked into flame. He could feel the heat of the stone floor underfoot through his shoes. His lungs burned as he took a breath. "But it can me."

The wihht snarled in anger and lunged forward, but it was too late.

Adlig spoke the word again and the room dissolved into white fire.

Ronan was perhaps halfway along the rope when it happened. His hands were looped around the rope, his body dangling down. The courtyard below was shrouded in darkness, but every once in a while, moonlight glanced through the clouds and he could see it shining on the stones far beneath.

"Hold on, old man," he said. "Just a few more seconds. Hold on."

But then the rope abruptly gave way and he was falling, the rope clenched in his hands. The night whistled past his ears. He flailed desperately at the fluttering rope, twisting his arm around it, once, twice. That was all he had time for. He did not even have time to shout. The wall rushed toward him out of the night. Moonlight shone on stone.

And then the world ended.

Ronan came to consciousness slowly. He was first aware of heat somewhere. Where was it? Oh yes, a tiny spot of warmth burning against his chest. It seemed reassuring, and he thought that there was some significance to the thing, but he could not remember what. And then the warmth spread to his whole body as his thoughts struggled to awake. The warmth was no longer reassuring; it was just pain flaring through his flesh. He could taste blood in his mouth. He tried to spit but could not manage to open his mouth. Something definitely was wrong. His left arm hurt horribly. It felt stretched.

No. Yanked.

His left arm was being yanked. His shoulder felt like it was being wrenched out of its socket. Stone scraped down the length of his body. The pain made him open his eyes. He was dangling against the side of the tower the hawk had tied the rope to. The rope dangled slack against his face, but there was a tremendous tightness around his left forearm. He could not feel his left hand. He looked up and saw that the rope was tightly wound around his forearm. His hand was numb and lifeless. Just then, his whole body rose, the stonewall scraping painfully against him. He bit his tongue so he would not cry out. He was not sure how long it took because he seemed to drift in and out of consciousness. The pearl underneath his shirt pulsed. He tried to concentrate on the feel of the thing so that his mind was taken off the pain. He closed his eyes. He felt hands grasping him, pulling him up, and then there was the feel of slate tile underneath.

Someone hissed out loud.

"It's a wonder he held on."

"He didn't," said someone else. The voice sounded like Severan's. "The rope's tangled around his arm. Gently now. It looks like it burned through his skin."

There was silence for a while. Something scraped against his arm. He gasped.

"Careful," said Severan.

"Look. The end of the rope is charred through."

Someone sighed.

"Better that then be taken by the wihht."

"Poor Adlig."

Ronan felt someone touch his face.

"Here," said Severan. "In the strictures of healing, as compiled by Eald Gelaeran—he wrote that when we were still students, do you remember, Gerade?"

"And then he promptly locked the book away in his library."

"Yes, but several of the students from the fourth form broke in one night. We all gathered around and read what we could. In the strictures of healing, the first step is the naming of blood, bone, and flesh. Reaffirmation of being."

"Hurry, master wizard," said the hawk. "What little safety we've found on this roof shall be soon stolen by time."

"The strictures can't be hurried," said Severan somewhat stiffly.

There was a pause, and then Severan spoke again.

"*Blod. Ban. Flaesc.*"

There was a brief silence and then someone cleared their throat.

"It's not working," said Severan. "I don't understand. Perhaps I mispronounced them?"

"Something's standing in the window," said Jute.

"Grief and stone," said Gerade. "The boy's right. Are those eyes?"

With an effort, Ronan opened his own eyes. He was lying on his back on the roof of the tower opposite the library tower. Severan, Gerade and Jute were kneeling around him. However, they were all looking away, staring with horrified faces across the courtyard. He turned his head to look. The library tower rose up black against the night sky. Moonlight etched the vertical edge of stone and the one window at the top. Within the deeper darkness of the window, two points of pale light gleamed down at them. The points of light winked once, as if blinking, and then abruptly went out.

"Haste now," said the hawk. "Thankfully the abomination cannot fly, for the Dark does not have the wind yet, but it will be quick enough. We must be away. Try your spell again, old man."

"It isn't a spell," said Severan. "The naming of blood, bone, and flesh is an affirmation of life, the proper construction of how a body is knit together." He cleared his throat and hunched over Ronan. "*Blod. Ban. Flaesc!* Now, how do you feel?"

"Never worse," said Ronan, his voice barely audible.

"You hit the wall hard," said Gerade. "It's a wonder you didn't burst like a ripe melon."

"I don't understand," said Severan unhappily. "There's something resisting the words. His body won't accept the naming."

The hawk's claws grated on the slate roof. His head bobbed down and Ronan felt the brush of feathers against his neck. The hawk hissed in wonder.

"Little doubt, old man," he said. "An older word has laid claim to this one. It blocks your efforts."

"What then?" said Severan in astonishment.

The hawk did not answer him. High overhead, the moon broke through the clouds and the night sky was revealed stretching away to whatever lay on its other side. Stars shone. Ronan felt the hawk's cold beak touch his ear.

"The sea, the sea," whispered the hawk. "*Brim ond mere.*"

The tide surged in Ronan's blood. His heart quickened. He tasted salt in his mouth, though it was not the taste of blood, but of seawater. The west pulled at him. He felt his bones shifting, knitting, healing. There was a deeper tide, further out, past the tide, running past the horizon, down below the fathoms in the silence. It called to him and promised peace.

"Careful," said the hawk. "Where did you find that necklace?"

"A trinket," said Ronan. "From long ago. I don't remember."

He sat up. They all gaped at him.

"We'd better get off this roof," said Ronan.

Severan looked as if he were about to ask a question, but he seemed to think better of it. The hawk fell silent and sat on Jute's shoulder. Once, Ronan caught the bird staring at him with a speculative look in his black eyes. He said nothing. He could taste seawater in his mouth.

It was easy enough to get off the roof. Ten feet below the roof, a balcony jutted out from the wall, banded by an iron railing. Ronan let himself down the rope and tied it off on the railing. One by one, they slid down onto the balcony.

"Master hawk," said Ronan.

The hawk flew up onto the roof. A moment later, the rope came tumbling down. Ronan coiled it away into his pack.

"Come," said Severan. He opened the balcony door.

"But where?" said Gerade.

"We'll try Adlig's idea. The well under the mosaic. You know just as well as I do what he meant."

"But. . ."

"Do you have a better idea?"

Gerade shrugged and said nothing.

"What do you mean, the well?" asked Jute.

Severan did not answer him. An archway at the bottom of the tower opened out into the courtyard beyond. The hawk floated up into the night and was gone.

"Wait," said Gerade. "We've surely beaten Nio—that thing—down, for the library stairs take much longer than their height, but maybe he did not come alone."

They stood in the shadow of the archway and listened to the night, but there were no sounds other than the labored breathing of the two older men.

Hurry. Time will not wait for you.

"The hawk says we'd better hurry it up," said Jute.

Severan nodded. "Let me go first. Gerade, you take the rear. Put up your sword, master thief. The wards of this place won't be defeated by iron."

Severan walked with his head thrust forward and his eyes darting from side to side. They passed across the courtyard with the moonlight shining down. A breeze ushered them along a colonnade of pillars. The roof of black marble seemed to melt away into the night. They hurried down long hallways, through places that Jute did not recognize from his days of exploring the ruins. He followed Severan closely, and behind him came Ronan, frowning and sniffing uneasily at the air, his hands never straying far from the sword hilt at his shoulder.

"It's everywhere now," said Gerade quietly. The old man glanced behind them. Light glimmered in his hand and it cast long beams back down the hallway. There was nothing there, only dust on the marble floor and their footprints in the dust.

"The smell of the Dark," he continued. "That's what it is. It's creeping through this place and it brings unease to everything it touches. Even the stones are unsettled by it. This place has a long memory and it's still afraid. It remembers another time, centuries ago, when evil walked through these halls."

"Centuries should be enough time to forget," said Ronan.

"Not for stone."

The halls they crossed through were vast places, and the hawk soared overhead.

What is to happen to me?

Jute fixed his eyes on the hawk.

That which is set before you, and only that, fledgling.

That's no help.

Safety first. Safety and silence, for there's much to be said and much for you to hear.

I am the wind.

It was more of a question than anything else. And when Jute said it, he found that he was more conscious than ever before of his tired body, his aching feet, the weight of dread and fear heavy on his shoulders. He glanced up wistfully at the hawk.

Aye, you are the wind, said the hawk.

Then I will fly!

The surge of joy inside him was quickly dampened by the hawk's words.

Truth, you will, but not for a long time. Weeks, perhaps. It is no easy thing to be the anbeorun of the wind. The stillpoint of the wind. It is a burden, no less. I would wish such a path on no one.

But I did not ask for any of this.

We do not ask. We are given, and then it is our task to do well with that which is given. You have been given more than most, and so you must do more than well. Even though it brings you sorrow.

"All I want to be is a thief," said Jute to himself.

"What?" said Ronan from behind him.

"Nothing."

"Hush," said Severan.

He stopped in front of them. They were standing now just within an archway that opened into a hall lined with slender clerestory windows. Moonlight shone through the windows and revealed a tiled expanse of floor that gleamed blue and black and white.

"This room's heavily warded," said Ronan.

"Impressive," said Severan. The old man nodded at him. "I doubt whether one in a thousand would be able to hear the sound of this ward. But it isn't the ward that worries me. If you know its key, then it poses no danger. What worries me is that he was here."

"He?"

"Nio Secganon. The wihht. There's an echo of him here. A recent echo." The old man smiled sadly. "We were friends once, he and I. Old friends. He's easy to recognize."

The hawk settled onto Jute's shoulder and folded its wings.

"Time falls quickly, old man," said the bird. "One grain at a time, but still it falls. We must make haste."

"I'm concerned, master hawk, that he left something here for us in surprise. He was one of the best students the Stone Tower ever saw, and now all that learning is given over to the Dark."

"Better the question before us than the Dark we know behind," said the hawk. He launched himself into the hall with outspread wings.

"Come on then." Ronan stepped forward.

"Careful," said Gerade, catching him by his arm. "Don't step on the blue tiles. If you do, run." And with a mutter and a flick of his wrist, he plucked at the moonlight gilding the clerestory frames and sent it glimmering up over their heads. They could see plainly now and they stepped from white tile to black tile.

"What does the ward do?" asked Ronan, once they had reached the doorway on the far side of the hall.

"Wait a moment and you'll see," said Severan. "We'll wake it and hopefully it'll slow our unwelcome friend, for I fear he'll come this way."

He took from his pocket a round stone and breathed on it. Then, after frowning and mumbling to himself a bit, Severan laid the stone down on a white tile. He snapped his fingers over the stone.

"All right," he said, straightening up. "*Gan.*"

The stone quivered and then rolled away across the tile floor. Not two feet away, it came to a blue tile. Immediately, a vapor rose up out of the tile, thickening and gaining form until the shape of a massive beast stood on the tile. Its fur shone blue in the pale moonlight. The thing turned and saw them. Instantly, it lunged. Jute shrank back, but the beast came to an abrupt halt as if it had slammed against an invisible wall blocking the doorway. It backed away and sat down, staring at them with bright blue eyes. Beyond it, more beasts rose up out of the tiles in the wake of the rolling stone.

Ronan raised one eyebrow. "I once tripped a ward that brought a sandcat to life. But a roomful of dogs?"

"They're wolves," said Gerade stiffly. "Hunting wolves spelled into the stone by Lana Heopbremel of Thule, three hundred years ago."

"They're the smallest wolves I've ever seen."

The hawk launched into the air with an exasperated snap of his wings. They hurried across the room and down a winding stair. Gerade opened his mouth to speak but Severan held his hand up for silence. The stairs ended in what looked to Jute like a dark empty space without windows. Severan walked away into the shadows and came back holding an oil lamp. Flint sparked in his hands and light filled the room. He pointed up at the ceiling silently. Jute stared up and his mouth fell open in surprise. There, on the ceiling, was an immense picture of the tower library. The room was empty and obscured with smoke. Flames flickered from the charred remains of books and from the smoldering table standing in the middle of the room.

"That's how he knew where we were," said Severan grimly.

At the sound of his voice, the picture swirled and was lost in a confusion of color and meaningless shapes. Jute realized that the surface of the ceiling was made up of thousands of tiny stones, closely fitted together.

"It's a mosaic," said Gerade, "a mosaic that shows what is spoken aloud in this room."

"And it'll serve us well now," said Severan. "Hush, and let it hear my voice." He positioned himself squarely under the mosaic and then spoke.

"The mosaic room in the university ruins."

The ceiling above them swirled and rearranged itself into new colors and shapes. Then, they found themselves staring up at a picture of themselves in the mosaic room.

"The sealed well in the mosaic room."

The picture trembled and then seemed to slide over to one side, as if seen through the eyes of someone who had abruptly turned their head. The picture settled on a view of a wall at one side. A deep alcove was set within the wall.

"Aha," said Severan. "So that's where it is."

The alcove was a dozen paces away to the right. The torchlight gleamed on a shroud of spiderweb draped down across the opening. Severan thrust the torch into the web. It caught fire and raveled the web away into nothing. The alcove had smoothly rounded stone walls that curved up to a domed ceiling. However, there was nothing there. The floor was made of flagstone, as perfectly fitted as the rest of the floor of the room.

"Doesn't look like much of a well, if you ask me," said Jute.

"Here," said Severan. "Hold the torch and make yourself useful. Gerade, do you know any of the strictures of opening?"

"Just the first and the second."

"Hmmph. I know those. Go and keep the mosaic occupied with Nio. Watch him."

Gerade hurried out into the larger room. They heard him muttering up at the ceiling. There was a brief silence and then he called back to them.

"It seems confused with his name, almost as if—"

"Did you use his full name?"

"Of course. But I think the mosaic isn't sure who he is."

"Well," said Severan, pausing in his examination of the alcove floor. "I suppose that makes sense in terms of a wihht and how it incorporates portions of those it eats. The Nio that we knew is, probably, only partially in existence. What he is now is mostly wihht. Darkness and the darker parts of Nio woven together, as well as anyone else the thing's eaten."

"Never mind. There he is now. He's on a stairway. I can't tell where. Um, he's running. Down the stairs, of course."

The hawk rocked from side to side on Jute's shoulder in agitation.

"This is no time, old man," he said, "for a discussion of the nature of wihhts. If you do not open that well, then we shall have a wihht in our midst, and a powerful one at that."

"Do you think I need a reminder?" grumbled Severan.

"Between knowledge and action there is a divide," said the hawk.

"Fine!" Severan glared at the hawk and then scowled down at the floor. "Open. No, that's not the right inflection. O-pen! Enter! Be opened! Unlock! Remove!"

Nothing happened. The hawk sniffed audibly.

"Here," said Jute. "The stones are different in this spot. Look, right here."

Severan knelt next to him on the paving stones. The floor was grimy with dust and tattered spiderwebs. Jute ran his fingers along the stone, his nose almost touching the ground.

"They look the same to me," said Severan, wiping away dust with his sleeve.

"You aren't looking close enough," said Jute. "These stones and these stones there are obviously not the same stones. They're the same size and the same color and the same texture, but these stones here—see?—are exactly the same as each other."

"First you say they're not the same, then you say they're too similar," said Severan. "What can you possibly mean? My eyes are too old."

"He's halfway across the corridor leading from the south inner hall to the hall of the wolves," called Gerade from beneath the mosaic. His voice sounded tense. "He's not alone, either. There're some of those shadow creatures with him."

The hawk settled onto the floor and brushed the floor clear of dust with one sweep of his wing. Everyone coughed and sneezed.

"Look closer, man," said the hawk. The torchlight caught in his black eyes. They shone as hard as polished marble. "Look closer. It does not matter if the rest of you die in this wretched room where there is no sky. But it matters greatly if this boy dies."

"Severan, he's reached the hall of the wolves! He's standing at the doorway. There are wolves everywhere, but he hasn't crossed the threshold yet."

A bead of sweat trickled down Severan's forehead, hung on the tip of his nose and then fell. A dark spot appeared on the stone below. Standing beside them, Ronan cleared his throat. They could hear the sound of his fingers tapping on the hilt of his sword, but the man's attention was not on them. His gaze was fixed on the top of the stairs leading down into the room.

"What's the difference between these stones, Jute?" said Severan.

"It's simple if—"

"Maybe to you."

"—if you just look at these two stones—"

"He's entered the hall of the wolves. There's darkness around him like a cloud. The wolves are throwing themselves against it in a frenzy. Severan, he's unmaking them! Blue light is dripping down the darkness and pooling on the floor. The tiles in the floors are cracking, one by one. He's destroying the wards!"

"—they're the same color and shape as the rest of the stones, but they're exactly same as each other. All the stones between here and here. Exactly the same."

"Exactly the same," said Severan. He wiped the sweat from his eyes and peered closer.

"See, they're all chipped on this edge here."

"Severan! He's halfway across the hall!"

The sword gleamed in Ronan's hand. He strode out into the middle of the room.

"Your blade will have no effect on him," said Gerade. "He's a wihht. Darkness and magic."

Ronan frowned at him. "I don't intend to stand about while my throat is cut."

Above them, the mosaic dissolved into a confusion of color and shape at their words.

369

"Nio Secganon," said Gerade. Then, so quietly that Ronan wasn't sure if he heard correctly, "Damn your black heart."

The tiny stones shifted in agitation. Then the colors slowly sharpened into discernible forms. Ronan found himself looking up at a picture of the hall of the wolves. But the picture moved. A dark shape walked across the hall, surrounded by shadows. Bright blue forms—wolves—made quick dashes at the shadows, but they had no discernible effect.

"He's almost at the door," said Gerade. His voice trembled.

"Even the darkness can feel the edge of iron," said Ronan. "Didn't the men of Harlech defeat the shadow that came out of the north? They fought with sword and spear."

"They did. But that was Harlech. Things are never what they seem in that land."

"That's it," said Severan in triumph from the alcove. "Things are never as they seem."

But, at that moment, a strange silence fell on the room. The air grew cold. The torchlight dimmed. High on the stairway, however, a green radiance shone from the open door. Darkness crept in its wake. The tiny stones of the mosaic trembled in agitation on the ceiling.

"It's an illusion!"

"That's not an illusion!" said Gerade. He stared up at the stairs.

"An illusion," said Severan again. "Of course." He seemed to have forgotten the situation they were in, but stared down at the paving, mumbling to himself in abstraction. "Now, what's the word?"

"Old man," said the hawk. "Our time is gone."

The hawk launched himself up into the air. Shadows sidled down the stairs. Behind them, the thin dark figure of a man descended. The air smelled of rot and damp. Ronan quickly moved to the foot of the stairs. His sword blurred in the gloom. The shadows hissed and bled darkness. They rose up around him like waves. The hawk folded his wings and fell from the ceiling. Gerade dashed forward with light streaming from his hands. The shadows quailed and the figure high on the stairs paused.

"*Dyderung!*" said Severan.

The stone paving vanished. Jute pitched forward with a howl of terror, arms flailing madly at the air. He had a brief impression of darkness, of stone walls blurring by, of the air whistling past his ears. He hit water. The impact knocked the breath from his lungs. He choked on a mouthful of water and rose up and up, clawing toward the surface—where was it?—until the air broke cold on his face. He coughed and sputtered. Far above him, up through a shaft of stone, the darkness was relieved by a small square of light. A head appeared.

"Look out below!" the head yelled down. "I'm coming down!" Severan (for that was who the head belonged to) levered himself out over the edge of the well.

"Seal the opening behind you, old man!" said the hawk.

"Severan!"

The old man turned at the well. His eyes widened. Shadows spilled down the stairs and out into the middle of the mosaic room, their mouths gaping black holes. They eddied madly around Ronan and Gerade. The stones under their feet were slick with darkness. Light fluttered in tattered streams from Gerade's hands. Ronan's sword wavered in his grip. The shadows surged around them. Further up the stairs, the dark figure of the wihht descended. The hawk plunged down through the air. Shadows broke beneath him, wailing and yammering and bleeding darkness. But as the bird beat back up toward the mosaic far overhead, the shadows surged forward again. Still, Severan wavered at the well opening.

"Seal the opening!" called the hawk. "Are you deaf and blind? Stay and die if you must, but the boy must not. Seal the well!"

"Help us!" shouted Gerade.

"There's no help for you."

The voice whispered, but everyone heard it in the vast room. Even Jute, shivering in the bottom of the well, heard it. Movement ceased in the room. The shadows congealed into darkness. Ronan's sword hung motionless in the air. Overhead, the mosaic abruptly went black. It seemed as if the ceiling vanished and they stood underneath a night sky without light of stars or moon. Severan's eyes were fixed helplessly on the figure standing at the foot of the stairs. The darkness thickened around it. Vapor plumed in the air.

"All things die. All things end. Such is the lot of man. Peace waits for you in the dark. The peace of the long, cold sleep. Never waking. Never dreaming."

"Lies!" The hawk hung in the air on motionless wings. "There is no peace in the Dark!"

"Ahh." The wihht's sigh slid through the stillness of the room. There was hunger in the sound. "Old feather. I've heard tales of you. You've flown far from the plains of Ranuin. I've heard the ancient stories of you and your windmaster, flying the sky of that battlefield. There are no brave standards here. All have fallen, and their lords gone the way of dust and darkness. There's none to remember them."

"I've kept their memories, shadow, and they are remembered in the house of dreams—"

"The house of dreams," sneered the wihht. "A fool's tale. Stories for old women spinning wool while their own lives are spun out and stretched across my master's hands. Taut for the knife, old feather. Just as your master was taken."

"A knife not wielded by you, shadow." The hawk struggled up through the air. "It took a stronger hand than you!"

"A stronger hand," said the other. "Here's my own, old feather. I've brought you your end. Look what I've been given!"

The wihht opened its hands. No one could look away. A great horror fell on the room, for in the thing's hands was a spot of darkness darker than night. It was an absence of anything that was. It was a hole that sucked in light and life. The air, cold as it was, became even colder. Ice crackled on the walls. The room trembled. Jute looked up from below. His teeth chattered with the cold. The walls seemed to stretch. Jute was no longer sure which direction was up and which was down. He had the horrible feeling he was about fall up.

Things slipped and began to slide. Rocks in the walls quivered. Some shattered and flayed the air with shards that flew toward the wihht's hands to vanish in the darkness. The shadow creatures bent and swayed and then whirled away like leaves blown by the wind.

The wind tore at the room. It ripped at the air. It howled against the stones. There was nothing of the sky in it, no cleanness, no cool emptiness to be drunk like water. The wind stank of darkness and death. It was hungry and it could never be filled. Gerade stumbled across the floor, bent over and blind. The wind threw him staggering toward the wihht. He managed one inarticulate shriek, and then he was gone. The hawk beat his way through the air. His wings seemed to blur in the wind, but he could not gain ground. The darkness reached out for the bird. The blot swelled within the wihht's hands, larger and larger, until it towered high overhead.

Ronan was tossed by the wind, his limbs flailing helpless. But he retained his grip on his sword and that proved his salvation. As he slid across the floor, his sword under him scraping and sparking against the stony floor, a stone loosened and whipped away. And into that hole Ronan's sword hilt jammed. He hung on grimly and tried to right himself, to crawl back around. There was Severan, not ten yards away, wedged in the opening of the well, with ice forming on his hands and in his hair.

Ronan looked back. The darkness had grown at such a rate that there were no walls anymore. At least, no walls he could see. He could look through the darkness. It was a hole. A door. It opened into a night sky scattered with stars that did not shine but were only solitary pinpricks of dead light. Something was behind the darkness. Something so huge that the sky was the shadow it cast. Ronan could see it now—at least he thought he saw an outline. Just a hint. It was a suggestion of stone walls reaching up. Higher than the sky. The dark sky loomed overhead. The mosaic was gone. And with a certainty that froze his blood to ice, Ronan somehow knew somewhere in that endless wall was a window. Behind that window stood someone. Something. It was watching him. Had been watching him.

For years.

Dimly, he was aware of the wihht stepping closer.

"I will bring you to him, man," said the wihht.

The darkness was complete.

Nearly.

Behind him, Ronan heard someone say something. A single word. Repeated over and over again. The voice was weak at first but grew stronger with each repetition.

"*Leoma. Leoma. Leoma.*"

And then, a shout.

"*Leoma!*"

Light blinded Ronan. It tore at his senses with heat and the absence of everything except light. It was worse than staring at the sun. The light was there even when he shut his eyes. Someone shrieked in fury. The wihht. But the shriek was lost in a sudden, shattering noise. It sounded as if every window in the city of Hearne had broken at the same time. Right above his head, light rained down. Shards of light. A thousand thousands of tiny stars. The room was washed in light and there was no longer any hole into the strange sky, no longer any wind, no longer any darkness. Ronan could not see the wihht. He found he could stand. One of the stars brushed against his arm. It was as hot as an ember. But he saw now what it was, for the light was dimming down. It was a small bit of stone, perfectly square and flat. He looked up at the ceiling. The mosaic was gone.

"Hurry!"

It was Severan. He was crouched beside the well.

"Hurry, man!"

"You destroyed the mosaic?" said Ronan.

The old man winced.

"It was already being destroyed. It was never intended to portray the darkness the way it was forced to this night. That was not a simple depiction. That was the true darkness— "

"Hush." The hawk settled onto the stones with a flurry of wings. "The creature stirs." Across the room, by the stairs, a dark form moved. Countless tiny stones twinkled on the floor, but the light was fading fast.

"Down the well," said Severan. "Both of you, now!"

But the hawk had already dove down the well before he finished speaking. Ronan scrambled over the side of the well, hung there for a moment, and then dropped. He fell through the darkness and then plunged down into water. He could not feel the bottom with his feet.

"Up here."

The light was dim but he made out Jute huddled on a ledge beside the water. The hawk crouched on his shoulder. Ronan hoisted himself up.

"Good thing it isn't as tight as a chimney," said Jute, scowling. "You wouldn't have fit down then."

"Hush," said the hawk.

A splash swamped all three of them. Severan bobbed in the water.

"Help!" he gasped. "Quickly now!"

Ronan yanked him out of the water.

"Hurry!" said Severan. "Is the passage—?"

"Give us some light," interrupted the hawk.

Severan muttered something, and a wisp of flame guttered into life in his hand. The flame reflected on the surface of the water and in Severan's eyes. The old man's face looked gaunt.

"Where's the passage?" he said. "We haven't a moment to lose."

"Behind you," said the hawk.

There in the wall was a hole. It was only distinguishable from the shadows in that it was darker. Severan stooped down and crawled into the hole. The others followed behind.

"What did you do?" said Jute. "Where's—where's—?"

"He's gone," said Ronan.

Severan did not answer but only increased his pace. After a few minutes, the passage widened abruptly and they were able to stand. The air smelled of dust. Even though the flame cupped in Severan's hand was small, there was enough light to see stone walls and a roughly hewn floor. The old man stumbled and would have fallen if Ronan had not caught his arm.

"Mustn't stop," gasped Severan.

"Haste," urged the hawk. His claws bit into Jute's shoulder. "Do you hear the stones? It is the noise of rock considering its own destruction. Your diligence, old man, may prove to bury us all. What word did you use?"

They all ran, stumbling together, through the passage.

"I didn't realize," gasped the old man. "I kept that word in my mind for fourteen years without speaking it."

But that was all he had time to say. The flame in Severan's hand flickered. Dust stirred around them. Then the light abruptly went out. The wind hit them like a hammer blow. Jute tumbled through the darkness, arms and legs windmilling. He slammed into a body. Something struck his head, and then the world went black.

Wake.

Let me sleep. It's comfortable here.

The hawk sighed inside Jute's mind.

Sleeping on cold stone? Strange tastes for one such as you. You are a ragged thief no longer.

Let me sleep.

Wake.

Jute opened his eyes. His head ached. He couldn't see anything. He experimented with closing his eyes and then opening them to see if there was any change. Nothing. He couldn't see a thing. Feathers brushed his arm and he almost screamed out loud.

Do you hear?

Hear what? I hear nothing. Except my own heart.

Listen.

Jute held his breath and listened, straining his ears. The hawk pressed against his arm but did not move. At first, there was only a dreadful silence, but then Jute heard it.

Something is digging!

Yes. The wihht.

A scratching noise came from far above them in the darkness. It was a quiet sound, as if muffled by distance and stone, but it was the busy, feverish sound of someone scrabbling and tearing at rock.

It hungers.

Stones clinked in the darkness. Someone groaned. It was Ronan.

"This has been the second worst day of my life."

The man subsided into silence, and then something rustled. Flint rasped on flint. A spark flared. The darkness retreated and Jute shut his eyes.

"The boy's all right, that's something." There was a pause, and then, "You didn't have to bring the whole university down, did you?"

"I didn't."

The flame flickered in Ronan's hand. His face was gray with dust. The light shone on a bloody gash on Severan's forehead.

"I didn't bring the whole university down," said the old man stiffly. "If I had, then we wouldn't be having this conversation, as we're still underneath the university. Underneath the east wing, if I'm not mistaken."

"You brought down more than enough."

Ronan raised his hand and the burning tinder revealed the tunnel behind them. It was choked with rubble. Dust hung in the air.

"Here, I'll bring up some more light," said Severan.

"No you don't," said Ronan. "I've had enough wizardry for the day."

"Ronan's right for reasons he doesn't know," said the hawk. He ruffled his wings, and dust rose around the bird in a cloud. "Have care to keep your words to yourself, old man, for once you're outside the safeguards of the university, such use will garner unwanted attention. Listen. Be still for a moment and listen, for we will soon not be alone here."

"Digging," said Ronan after a moment. "Someone's digging."

"I don't hear anything," said Severan, frowning.

"It's the wihht and those shadows." The hawk hopped onto a fallen timber. "Come. We must be gone before they find their way down."

They went quickly, each with a length of wood guttering flame and each with a prickling at the back of their necks as if something was creeping along behind them in the darkness. Ronan led the way, for Severan declared himself confused by the twists and turns of the passage and the openings branching off here and there.

"I've read of these tunnels," Severan said, staring into one such opening. "They're mentioned in writings in the archives, but I don't remember any of them having adequately conveyed the sheer, the sheer—"

"They go on and on," said Jute.

"Yes," said Severan. "Strange, how the reality doesn't measure up to the written word. Perplexing."

The tunnels looked old. Older than any of the buildings in the city of Hearne itself, which was of interest to Severan, for, as he remarked, portions of the city supposedly dated back to its founding centuries ago.

"How odd," he said, as they paused in a small room formed by the intersection of three tunnels. Ronan advanced several yards into each tunnel and then retreated back to the room. "This style of carving predates the oldest known carvings in this city—the foundations of the regent's castle are what I refer to. As you know, the current castle was built after the old castle was destroyed in the wizards' war. You see here? This oak tree alternated with the boat? You'll find a similar version in the castle foundation. There, however—"

"Hush," said Ronan.

"You needn't be rude," said the older man. "I was merely—"

"I need to listen."

Ronan crouched down in the tunnel that they had just come from, his ear pressed to the ground. He was motionless for several seconds and then sprang to his feet, his face grim.

"What—?"

"Be quiet, please."

Ronan strode into the opening of one of the three tunnels that lay before them. He closed his eyes and turned his face slowly from side to side. He repeated this in the other two tunnels and then shook his head in disgust.

"What is it?"

"That heap of stones you pulled down is still holding them, but not for long. They'll be through soon enough, and I think those shadow creatures can run much faster than you, old man."

"They're fast," said Jute. He thought of being chased through the streets and across the rooftops, and he shivered.

"Then let's go. Let's go!" said Severan. The torch in his hand trembled. "I don't fear the shadows, but I fear the wihht."

"I don't know which tunnel should be ours," said Ronan. "Three tunnels. I'm blind here. I've tracked foxes to their lairs, the serpent on the rock, even a hawk across the sky. But here—no one's passed this way in over two hundred years, I warrant, and there's no trail here."

The hawk stirred on Jute's shoulder.

"I doubt," said the bird, "whether you have ever followed the sign of my kin. Even the Farrows cannot lay claim to the sky."

"Let's choose a tunnel and be on our way," said Severan. "Even a poorly chosen path is better than waiting for death. The first tunnel looks just as ill-favored as the other two. Let's choose it and see where it brings us. Perhaps we'll have the luck to fall down a bottomless hole? Rather that than the wihht."

"Wait," said Jute. "Don't you feel that?"

"Feel what?"

375

The two men stared at him.

"There's a breeze."

"No, there isn't," said Ronan irritably. "Wind is one of the first things I would've sensed. Wind, scent, sign, even the residue of old magic. There's nothing here."

"There's a breeze."

The flames of their three torches burned motionless in the air. Their shadows waited on the walls around them, as still and as silent as they were themselves.

"It's coming from the middle tunnel."

"Remember who this boy is," said the hawk.

Ronan glanced at Jute. His hand strayed up to his neck, and then he strode forward into the middle tunnel. He set a fast pace from there, so fast that Jute had to half run to keep up with him. Severan had the worst of it and stumbled along behind, grumbling until Ronan reminded him of what was hurrying along on their trail.

"They'll have no trouble following us," said Ronan grimly. "The smell of our sweat, the smell of our torch smoke."

At every juncture they came to, Jute indicated which split in the tunnel they should take. He realized that he wasn't precisely feeling a breeze as if it blew against his skin. There was no wind in the tunnels. Rather, it blew within his mind. He could feel it breezing on the edge of his thoughts.

The tunnel widened out into a sort of hall. Pillars lined the walls on either side, carved out of the rock. They rose up like tree trunks into the ceiling, which, upon closer inspection, was carved to resemble a matted expanse of branches.

"Here's the bottomless hole you were hoping for," said Ronan.

The floor was shattered in the center of the hall. A hole plunged down into the darkness below, surrounded by the rubble of paving stones. They skirted around the hole. Severan shuddered.

"Imagine the surprise of those standing here when the floor broke."

"I think the floor was broken from underneath." Ronan crouched down. "Look at how the stones are scattered."

"What could've done something like that?" asked Jute. Fascinated, he stared at the hole. The hawk shifted on his shoulder.

There are creatures in this world unknown to man. Ancient creatures who have crept away from the light, down into the depths and the hidden places of the earth. There are paths in the darkness that should never be trod. Particularly for those of us who love the sky.

Jute realized then that the hawk trembled on his shoulder. That he had been quivering ever since they had entered the passages below the university. He could hear the light, jittering pulse of the bird's heart. With a shock, he became aware of his own heart. Racing, unsteady, and uncertain. Sweat burned in his eyes. He gulped air, but there wasn't enough. The torch shook in his hand and the shadows swayed around him.

Sky.

The ceiling was too low.

The ceiling was lowering.

Have to get out.

Sky.

Jute felt the hawk's beak against his chin. The bird gazed into his eyes.

Peace.

And then, out of darkness, their torchlight shone on a stone stairway. It rose out of sight and past the reach of their light. They ran and it seemed if the stairs would never end. But there was the scent of water. A breeze sprang up and light glimmered ahead of them, higher up.

"It's morning," called out Ronan.

The steps were cracked and broken here. Tree roots reached through the rock in tangled masses. And then the steps ended and light blazed, shining through the roots. They blinked, blinded by it, and scrambled up through a small, choked hole, fighting past roots and feeling the earth crumbling away beneath their feet. The blaze of light was all around them and they could scarcely see for the brilliance of it.

"The sky," said the hawk, and he launched free from Jute's shoulder.

They stood at the base of a huge oak tree growing at the bottom of a steep bank. Brambleberries grew there in profusion, thick with blueberries and sweetly scenting the air. Further down the valley, beyond a tasseled cornfield, the Rennet flowed. Far behind them, the walls of Hearne rose in the west, painted gold and white in the morning light.

"We mustn't rest here," said Ronan.

He shrugged his cloak closer around his shoulders and then strode down toward the river. The others followed him, so weary and so glad that they could not speak.

CHAPTER SEVENTY-EIGHT
OLD FRIENDS IN THE LOME FOREST

It began to rain again that morning.

"Marvelous," said Levoreth. "Drenched as well. What a dreadful day. I imagine it will get worse."

It was difficult to see clearly in any direction. Everything was gray and wet and muddy. She guessed that she was somewhere in the southeastern fringe of the Scarpe plain. She trudged along, her shoes squelching through the mud. After some time, however, the ground began to rise. It was a gentle rise, but a rise nonetheless.

"There aren't any hills on the Scarpe," said Levoreth to herself. "At least, not here."

When she came to the top of the rise, she found herself looking down an incline toward a line of trees in the distance. Beyond them stretched a darker mass that vanished into the rain and the gloom. She had come much farther east than she had thought—right to the edge of the Lome forest. Levoreth shrugged, sighed, and then made her way down the slope. At least there would be some shelter. It was considerably drier under the trees. The rain pattered in the branches and drip-dropped down into the undergrowth. She sat on a fallen branch and did her best to clean the mud from her shoes with a handful of pine needles.

"Drat," she said.

A squirrel peered out of a hole in a nearby oak and stared at her. It disappeared again before she could say anything, but then instantly reappeared with something clutched in its paws. Tail flying, it scampered down the tree and across the ground to her.

A walnut? Levoreth smiled. *Thank you, but I fear the shell too sturdy for my teeth.*

Undeterred, the squirrel popped the walnut into its mouth and bit down.

Eat, eat.

Oh, well. Many thanks.

She picked out the shells and ate the nut. The squirrel hurried away and returned with another walnut.

Your charity becomes you, little one, she said. *But I fear a long winter approaches. You should husband your hoard more shrewdly.*

Nay, nay. Eat, eat.

The squirrel brought her a third walnut.

Do you wish something of me?

Nay, nay.

Surely, said Levoreth. *Surely there is something.*

The squirrel blinked and then bobbed its head.

Aye, Mistress.

What is it? Speak, little one.

The foxes, Mistress. The foxes come when we gather walnuts at the tree. They are quick and cruel and they've sharp, sharp teeth. Quick and cruel, Mistress. Can you bid them leave me and mine in peace? For we love the walnuts!

Nay, she said gravely. *This cannot be done, for I cannot bid a fox be untrue to his nature, just as I cannot bid you to cease loving walnuts.*

The squirrel retreated a few steps and hung its head.

But come, she said, standing up. *Let us go to your walnut tree, for perhaps we shall see a remedy for your trouble. Come.*

Instantly, the squirrel darted off a ways, stopped, ran back to her, and then dashed off again.

Walnuts. Such a tree, Mistress. A giant of trees. My father's father's father and his father before him gathered nuts there. It is a family tree, Mistress. Perhaps a squirrel planted it long ago? Perhaps?

Perhaps, she said, smiling despite her weariness.

After some time they came to a clearing in the forest. The squirrel hopped up and down in excitement. In the middle of the clearing stood a walnut tree.

See? See? Walnuts.

I see, little one. But I also see that you must hurry across the ground to reach the tree. You cannot jump from the nearest tree to the walnut tree. It is surely too far.

Aye, Mistress. Too far. Much too far. So we run across the ground and the foxes catch us. Such sharp teeth, Mistress.

You must remain in the branches.

We cannot. We cannot!

The squirrel hopped about in frustration and then came close. It patted her foot and looked up at her.

Come, said Levoreth. *We will speak with the trees. It is in their power to help you.*

At the edge of the clearing stood an oak. Its branches reached up into the sky but none of them came near the walnut tree. Levoreth placed her hand on the trunk of the oak. It was an old tree, sleepy and preoccupied with memories and long, slow thoughts of water and sunlight.

Peace to you, friend oak, she said.

Earth, murmured the oak. *Deep earth. Deep sky. Suspended between the two. I have grown into both. I shall grow into both.*

And you have. You shall.

Aye, said the oak comfortably. *I shall.*

It became aware of her then, and the bark seemed to shiver under her hand.

Mistress of Mistresses. I remember you. When I was a sapling. When the forest was still young. Before men came to this land. Before the Dark came.

Long years ago, said Levoreth.

I have heard of the Dark, Mistress. I have heard of it whispered amidst the roots and rocks and in the deep earth.

What have you heard?

I have heard that the Dark has come to this land. That it has come here, for this is the last land.

Aye, she said. *This is the last land. The others fell under the Dark, long years ago.*

I have heard that a sceadu walks abroad. That it feeds on death to still its hunger. Fear is struck into the heart of the land like wood rot. I have no memory of such things, Mistress, for this land has ever been yours and your hand has kept it safe.

Levoreth leaned her forehead against the tree trunk and closed her eyes. The squirrel crept closer, and she felt it anxiously patting her foot.

My hand, oak, she said wearily. *Mine and the hands of my sister and brothers. For earth is not alone, but stands with sea and wind and fire. The Dark shall not prevail. I promise you.*

Good, murmured the oak. *Good.*

But Levoreth did not speak again for some time. The rain pattered down through the branches of the oak and dripped on her head. The wind sighed in the tree tops.

I would have a favor of you, she said.

Aye, that I shall. Anything of wood and root.

Stretch out your branch to the walnut. Stretch out your branch so that the squirrels may run to and fro freely.

Ahh, said the oak. *The little walnut. I did not notice her. How fast the saplings grow. I sleep, I dream, and when I wake, a hundred years have gone by. Of squirrels I know nothing, but I shall stretch out my branch. For you, I shall do this thing.*

The oak quivered. Ever so slowly, one branch lowered and lengthened with a great many creaks and groans. The movement was almost imperceptible. The tip of it settled against the uppermost branch of the walnut tree.

It is done, Mistress.

I thank you.

The squirrel hopped up and down in such excitement that it could not speak.

It was raining even harder now. Within the clearing, the rain slashed down. Peering up through the branches, Levoreth could only see a gray, lowering darkness. She leaned against the oak's trunk and tried to think. Her head ached and she was so tired that even curling up to sleep on the muddy ground seemed like a wonderful idea. She sank down to the ground, her back against the tree.

Oh, Min, I no longer know what to do. The Dark has come to Tormay after all these long years, and all I can manage to do is make a squirrel happy. The Dark has come. What had I been thinking? That it would have stayed content beyond the sea? Content in the east and the endless night it brought to those lands? My heart aches, for I still remember the white towers of Corvalea. They haunt my dreams. All I wish to do is sleep.

The squirrel shrieked. It shrieked and made a jump for Levoreth's shoulder, bounding from there up into the branches of the oak.

What—?

And then she smelled them. She would have smelled them before but her mind was heavy with fatigue. The scent was masked by the rain and the damp rot of the undergrowth. The shapes materialized out of the gloom. The wolves. They came loping toward her out of the rain. Their fur gleamed with water. She only saw a few, perhaps half a dozen, but she was aware of them all, a full twoscore, standing silent in the trees around her. The squirrel chattered in fury and threw down acorns.

Mistress of Mistresses.

Drythen Wulf.

We have come. You have bidden us, and we come.

An acorn bounced off the wolf's nose.

Peace, little rat, said the wolf. *My kind does not eat yours.*

Rat?

A hail of acorns showered down.

Peace!

The squirrel muttered angrily from somewhere among the oak branches, but then fell silent.

We have brought your messenger with us, said the wolf. *The northern snows are no safe place for a cub. But we have guarded him for you, Mistress. Though, truth be told, it was most difficult to guard him from ourselves.*

The wolf's jaws opened in a silent laugh.

I thank you, Drythen Wulf, said Levoreth dryly, *for not devouring my messenger.*

Out of the gloom, from under the dripping branches, the horse emerged. The wolves padded restlessly about him, but Swallowfoot ignored them, his ears and eyes on Levoreth.

Mistress of Mistresses.

The horse pushed his nose against her hand.

You have brought the wolves to me.

They thought to eat me at first, said the horse.

The wolf laughed again.

The thought crossed my mind, Mistress, said the wolf. *The snows of the north have little to offer for the hunt. But a closer look at this skin and bones dissuaded us. There's no flesh on him. Truth, Mistress, we could not have caught him. His stride is as fast as the wind.*

You put me in mind of another steed. Levoreth ran her hands through the horse's mane. *One that ran by my side, long years ago. I thank you for what you have done. My thoughts could not reach the wolves, but you went—as quick as thought, did you not?—and brought them here.*

Swallowfoot trembled under her touch. His memories flashed through her mind, flickering from sky to earth, slashed with wind and the drumming of galloping hooves. The vast plain of the Scarpe blurred by. Mountains rose far in the north. They loomed closer and closer. Ice and snow glittered on their slopes with an aching, blinding light. The sun hurried across the sky and plunged down in the west. Stars raced through the night.

The light and the wind slowed, Mistress, said Swallowfoot. *They slowed as I ran to catch them.*

Levoreth smiled.

The wolves crowded around her, sitting under the shelter of the oak's branches. Their eyes gleamed in the gloom, and, out of respect, the older ones did not look at her much, though the younger ones stared avidly. The great wolf stood before her, and at his side was his son, the cub Ehtan that she herself had named years ago.

He has grown, has he not?

Aye, said Levoreth. *He is your shadow now. Faith, I can scarce tell you apart.*

He will lead the pack when I am gone, said the father proudly. *He will bear my memory when I have gone to chase the sun.*

The rain dripped down from the leaves overhead.

Now, Drythen Wulf, you must tell me your tale, for I have wondered for many days where your trail led you from the house of Ginan Bly.

From that house of death it led us, said the wolf. *North we went. North, sniffing along the trail of the Dark. Never has the pack hunted for a prey that it did not want to catch, but this quarry we sought with dread in our hearts.*

And to a mountain eyrie it led you?

A peak towering over its brethren, mantled with ice and snow. The eyrie looked east and west, north and south. The wind rages there in strange fury, and it was all we could do to resist its blast. Its blast is full of death and I think, in time, the wind will unmake that mountain.

381

The young wolf Ehtan stirred.

The wind's voice spoke of murder, Mistress, he said hesitantly. *Murder and loneliness and a terrible sorrow.*

Aye, she said. *For its master was murdered by the Dark.*

We could not enter the eyrie, Mistress. A dread evil sleeps there, and though I set paw in the opening of that place three times, I could not pass the threshold. Fear is a stranger to the wolves, but I knew fear in that place.

That is well, said Levoreth. *I would not have had you step beyond that which you could do. I shall see this place for myself, then. The mountains are mine, and the Dark shall not deny me. Yet, first. . .*

She stopped here, thinking of the boy Jute. The wolves waited patiently around her in the damp and dripping rain. She shook her head, frowning. Jute would have to fare on his own. No, not on his own. He had the hawk.

We go hunting, Drythen Wulf.

And what shall be our prey? asked the old wolf, but the knowledge was already in his eyes.

The Dark.

After some time spent thinking moodily about wolves and other horrible animals that spent all their time trying to eat squirrels, the squirrel scrambled down a few branches and peered around suspiciously. But no one was there. The ground around the oak was crisscrossed with the tracks of wolves and one horse, but the forest was silent. The lady was gone as well. The squirrel scampered down to the ground and sadly sniffed its way around the oak.

Mistress?

There was no answer. The rain dripped down from the branches and leaves overhead. After a while, however, the squirrel remembered the walnut tree and the oak branch reaching across the clearing. This cheered the little animal immensely and it hurried away to tell its family the good news.

CHAPTER SEVENTY-NINE
DREAMING OF THE DARK

He woke and lay staring at the ceiling. The morning was late and he never slept much in general, but the regent had thrown a party the night before that seemed to have never ended. It had been an attempt to raise spirits after the strange happenings at the ball the previous night. Not that it had been successful. Many of the regent's guests had left already, making excuses such as the muddiness of the roads, or the corn harvest, or roofs that needed mending before the winter snows came. The duke and duchess of Dolan had been the first to leave, early the next morning after the ball. They had offered no excuses but left before the castle had even stirred to life. He had seen them leave. The duchess' eyes had been red, as if she had spent the night weeping.

It was raining again. He hated the rain. It somehow obscured what he saw and felt. A lightning storm was different. He understood lightning. The earth cringed under it. The earth shook and trees burned.

Something stirred in the corner of the room.

"Ah," he said. "I was wondering when you'd manage to regain yourself. It was an interesting spectacle. Not too unpleasant, I presume?"

"I endured. A little more blood, a few more deaths, and I will be well."

"I'm sure you can find what you need in this city. At any rate, I thought it best not to intervene. I am still not known in Tormay."

The other emerged from the shadows and stood at the foot of his bed. Its body was vague and insubstantial, as if formed of mist. The thin, white face seemed to hang in the air, and it stared back at him without expression.

"I did not need your help," said the creature. It spoke quietly with a voice that creaked and whispered as if from little use.

"Do you bring news of the hunt?"

"Nothing that will please you."

"Out with it, then," said the man. He sat up and yawned.

"The boy has fled the city."

"You know this for sure?"

"The winds have left Hearne. They came only to find him. They would leave only if he left as well. We have been thwarted. An unknown hand has entered the game and I cannot see it."

The man flung aside the bedcovers and got to his feet.

"You lost him," he said. "He's only a boy. He won't grow into who he is for a great many days yet. The blood on that knife was old and fading in power. Weeks, more likely. You had him within your grasp and you lost him."

"He is—" The creature paused, as if searching for the right word. "He is something more than lucky."

"Your hounds lost him as well, I daresay?"

"They were lured out of the city. Eorde, I think. The old earthwitch. She is a cunning foe, once awakened. The hounds would have been no match for her. Doubtlessly, she destroyed them."

"Doubtlessly," grunted the man, then he gave a bark of laughter. "Shadows, but I never thought that spell would last so long when I first wove it. The weave held for over three hundred years and even caught the anbeorun in its grasp."

"Sleep is a pretty thing, master," said the other. "It has caught us many a tool. Nio Secganon has proven useful. He, also, almost had the boy within his grasp."

"The wihht," said the man in fury. "Wihhts are made to be twitched like puppets, not allowed rein to run free. It came close, like you, did it not? But where's the boy now, eh?"

"What is lost can be found, master," said the thin face hanging in the shadows.

The man did not bother answering, but dressed quickly. He threw open the shutters, revealing a morning sky filled with clouds and rain.

"Come," he said. "I'll tender my thanks to the regent and then we shall leave. Hearne no longer holds anything of interest for me, save pleasant memories of death."

He turned from the window and smiled. The pale light caught in his gold hair and burnished it into flame. And with that, Brond Gifernes, the duke of Mizra, strode from the room, with darkness crowding at his heels.

CHAPTER EIGHTY
NORTH TO HARLECH

They decided to head north to Harlech. The city of Hearne was far behind them now, the walls and towers hidden beyond the rise and turn of the valley. Jute looked back several times as they walked along, remembering the darkness and horror under the city, but there was nothing to see anymore. The wihht. The wihht was gone. Surely gone.

He breathed in deeply, more easily. The morning was bright with sunlight glittering on the dew and the flashing flow of the river winding across the valley floor below them. The scent of grass and the damp earth filled the air. Swallows flew up from the willows along the river, drifted through the sky overhead and then were gone in a gust of wind.

North itself had never been in question. Jute had timidly mentioned the topic of south—perhaps Vo or Vomaro?—even though he knew nothing about the lands of Tormay outside of Hearne and was motivated only by the thought of a winter without snow. Both Ronan and Severan overruled him for various reasons.

"Vomaro," said Ronan, "is fit only for half-witted, inbred sheep."

"Oh?" Severan blinked several times as he considered this. "I've known some pleasant people in Vomaro. I once met a cobbler in Lura who, in the course of stitching boots and shoes and slippers over the years, discovered how to sew together time. He swept it out of the corners of his shop and then stitched it—upside down and inside out, of course—on the soles of his more expensive shoes. They never wore out."

"We aren't going to Vomaro," said Ronan.

"Did I say we should?" said Severan. "The southern duchies are too populous. We need some place where there aren't many people and they aren't fond of talking. Somewhere north, I suppose."

"Harlech," said the hawk. He landed on Jute's shoulder and furled his wings.

"I wouldn't mind going to Harlech," said Severan, "I've a cottage there, up on the coast. Have I mentioned that before? It belonged to my grandfather. But I think we should consider the Stone Tower in Thule. Quite a few wizards still live there, and they should be informed of what's gone on. And the food! The Tower has a wonderful cook. Fish stews, mutton, and mushroom pies that'll make your tongues sing, seed cakes. Er, what's more, Ablendan is sure to have reached the Tower by now and he'll be wondering what's happened in his absence."

"Who's Ablendan?" asked both Jute and Ronan at the same time.

"A fellow scholar of mine. He rode to the Stone Tower with news of—of—well, of you," concluded Severan somewhat lamely.

"I wish I had a horse," said Jute. "I wish I had a mutton and mushroom pie."

"Well, you don't have a horse," said the hawk, "but you have two legs. Walk faster. We must be far from this city before nightfall. The sunlight will keep the wihht at bay, but there's no telling with this weather."

"Sunlight or no sunlight," said Ronan, "walk faster."

They did not stop for breakfast. Ronan produced a loaf of bread from his pack which he tore into three pieces (the hawk declined such food). That, and a hunk of hard cheese, had to suffice as they hurried along. It was not mutton pie, but Jute devoured his portion down to the last delicious crumb.

They struck a path that veered away from the river bank and carved its way up the north side of the valley. It zigzagged back and forth until it disappeared in the gray-green heather that spilled over the top of the valley and ran down the slopes. It was still early, but the air was warm. Bees busied themselves flitting about the heather. Sweat trickled down Jute's back.

"If you keep turning your head this way and that and back again," said Severan, "it's liable to fall right off your shoulders."

"I've a crick in my neck," said Jute with some dignity. "I'm trying to stretch it."

"Crick or not, you're about to walk into a bramble bush."

If truth be told, Jute was overwhelmed and amazed at what he saw. The sky was endless. The land stretched on forever, curving up through the reach of the valley, charged with color and distance and—despite the buzzing of the bees—silence.

The hawk chuckled inside his mind.

You have never been outside the city. . .

Jute did not reply, but it was true. The sky was not hemmed in with rooftops and walls and the stiff stone fingers of chimneys. The blue and the green went on forever.

Wait until we reach the Scarpe. Wait until you reach the sky.

What is the Scarpe?

There was no need for the hawk to explain, for the path made one last turn through the heather and then they were at the top of the valley. A breeze blew past them. Jute's mouth fell open.

"This is the Scarpe Plain, boy," said Ronan.

"It's, it's. . ."

Jute had never seen anything like it. Had never imagined anything like it.

"It's like the sea," said Ronan. His hand drifted up to his neck as if to reassure himself that the necklace still hung there.

The hawk launched from Jute's shoulder and flapped his way up into the sky. He soon was lost in the blue. The sky was immense. But the plain stretching out before them was just as immense. It was a vast sea of green that undulated in waves rolling away under the breath of the wind. The plain had no end to the north, but vanished in a blurred horizon of sky and grass. Looking to the east, almost invisible in the brilliance of the sun and the distance, a mountain range rose in jagged, snow-capped peaks.

"The Mountains of Morn," said Ronan.

"We aren't going there, I hope," said Severan.

Ronan did not reply, but merely hitched his sword up higher on his shoulder, settled his pack more comfortably on his back, and started walking north. Jute and Severan trudged after him. The morning sun mounted higher on their right side, and everywhere there was a bright light and a sweet scent that filled Jute's heart with a gladness he had never known before. Behind them lay the valley and Hearne and who knows what else? But Jute did not look back.

CHAPTER EIGHTY-ONE
THE DUKE AND HIS SERVANT

The party of Brond Gifernes, the duke of Mizra, left Hearne that morning.

"Sorry to see you go, Gifernes," said the regent. "Seems like you just arrived. Seems like everyone just arrived. Still, good times always find their end. It's been splendid having you. Splendid."

"Duty calls, milord," said the duke. "While I'd like nothing more than to enjoy your hospitality, duty is, as you know, duty. I've been away too long and my duchy needs me."

"Yes, yes. Duty." Botrell shook his head and stared around him somewhat blankly. They were standing in the stable courtyard behind the castle. The duke's retinue waited patiently around them. Horses stamped and blew out great breaths of steam in the cold air.

"Duty," repeated Botrell blankly. "Well, yes, it's been splendid having you."

"Are you feeling well, milord?"

"Eh, what's that?" The regent looked at the duke of Mizra, squinted, and then seemed to properly see him. "No, no—never felt better. Just a touch of indigestion. All these feasts. You'll know what I mean when you get a bit older. Rich food, you know. I must have a word with the cooks. Damn their black hearts!"

"And the dancing," said Brond. "The dancing can be wearisome."

The regent shivered. "What was that thing?"

"My lord?"

"Good grief, man, you were there, were you not? That dreadful creature that gobbled up half my kitchen staff and then did its best to slay the duke of Dolan's niece. Right in my best ballroom and right in front of everyone who matters in Tormay." The regent shook his head. "What'll people say?"

"I don't know," said Brond. "I'm afraid I'm still taken aback. It was inappropriate, to say the least."

"Inappropriate?" spluttered the regent.

"As was the behavior of Lady Levoreth."

"Indubitably, indubitably."

"I must confess—and this is purely between you and me, my lord—I had entertained thoughts of wedding her and allying the houses of Gifernes and Callas." The duke of Mizra sighed and attempted to look sad. "Still, whoever—or whatever—she is, her defense of that beggar boy was most admirable. But extremely unladylike. One must have standards."

"Er, yes."

The sun was clearing the Mountains of Morn far in the east when the duke of Mizra's party left the city gates. The contingent of Guardsmen sprang to attention as the duke rode by. Mist hovered on the surface of the Rennet River down in the valley. The stifling smells of the city quickly gave way to the scent of wet grasses as they rode along.

"Curse this city," said the duke to himself as his horse cantered down the road. "May it know fear for the rest of its days. And may the regent never sleep but know the Dark stands watching. May there be terror in his dreams."

"Shall I kill him for you?"

The duke turned in his saddle. To one side and a little behind, rode a figure all cloaked and muffled as if it sought to hide from the sunlight. The hood raised a bit and he saw the thin, white face of his servant Cearu.

"Curse you too," growled the duke. "How could you let the boy out of your grasp? Do you understand the infinite worth in his wretched frame? Doubtless he's far from this city now. Must I take apart this land, stone by stone, to find him?"

"What's lost can be found," said Cearu.

The duke did not respond for a while. Behind them, strung out along the road, was the rest of his retinue. Horse hooves rang on the road's hard earth, bridles jingled, and saddle leather creaked.

"I dreamt last night," said the duke. "I dreamt of a people named Farrow."

"The Farrows," said Cearu. He hissed the name, letting it linger in the air until it died away into a sigh. Farrows. "I have heard something of them."

"They're a clan. A family of wanderers who live on the grace of the earth. The Dark has turned its thoughts to them. The family has a daughter. I dreamt of her and I saw her face. She has the silence of the earth waiting in her eyes, but she knows it not."

"Ahh." Hunger trembled in Cearu's voice.

"Bring her to me, though I think you will not succeed. The old she-wolf is running on the plains. I can smell her scent."

"I would have had her," said Cearu. "I would have had her spitted on my sword, except for the wind. I would meet her again."

"You will," said the duke. "Perhaps she thinks you dead. You were lucky she did not unmake you. The boy diverted her, though he aided her. There was something else in the room that night. Something watching. I would not have lifted a finger to save you."

"What is life?" said the other. "But I am alive, still. I availed myself of another last night and fed well. Enough blood to make me whole."

"Something else was watching," said the duke, not listening to his servant anymore.

Cearu wheeled his horse away. The duke turned his attention back to the road and his own thoughts. The future lay ahead. Heat kindled inside of him. And an old dark hunger.

CHAPTER EIGHTY-TWO
BOTHERING THE REGENT

"For the last time, Owain—it isn't your fault."

Sibb resisted an urge to throw the mixing bowl at her husband. He scowled at her from across the kitchen table.

"If I'd been home," said Owain, "instead of haring across Tormay in search of phantoms, I would've been here."

"No, you wouldn't have. You would've taken me to the castle for the ball and we would've been dancing that night."

They both glared at each other.

"I hate dancing," he said.

"Yes, but you would've taken me anyway." Sibb tried to smile.

"I'm going to have a word with the regent."

"At least have some breakfast first."

But the door had already slammed shut behind him. Sibb tried to focus on the bread dough in the mixing bowl. It just wasn't right. Regardless of what had happened to poor Loy, the Gawinn household could surely stand to be happier. After all, Owain had returned, safe and sound, and little Fen was talking. At least, a few words here and there.

Despite both those blessings, the Gawinn household was not happy at all. Owain had been in a dreadful mood ever since he had returned. All the children had been having nightmares. Sibb had not told anyone, but she had been having nightmares as well. The servants crept around the house with long faces, and one of the maids dissolved into tears when asked to go down to the cellar to fetch a cask of herring. The three boys had removed several of the weapons from the hall and had taken to skulking about the garden, scaring the milkman and a poor old fisherman who had knocked on the back door to sell his haddock. Owain spanked them all soundly—Jonas more than the others, as he was oldest and should have known better—and sent them off crying to bed. Fen, despite having been woken from her silence, could hardly get three words out without bursting into tears. Not that anyone blamed her. At least they knew her name now. That was something.

Sibb punched the dough down in the bowl and tried not to cry.

Arodilac was standing outside the garden gate, his hands jammed in his pockets and his shoulders hunched against the morning chill.

"Let's go," said Owain.

"I haven't slept all night," said Arodilac.

"Get used to it. It's called night duty."

"And I haven't had any breakfast yet."

Owain snorted at that and walked faster.

"I don't see why I have to come as well," said Arodilac.

"You're coming, and that's an order."

They walked along for a while. Arodilac sulked in silence behind Owain. Somewhere up ahead, nearer to the castle, horse hooves clattered on the cobblestone street. The sound died away as if heading down into the city.

"You did well," said Owain.

"Thank you, my lord."

"You didn't lose your head. Combat, whether it's on a staircase or on a battlefield, is a different thing from training in the Guard or tavern matches for money."

"Tavern matches?"

"Don't play dumb with me, boy. I know what goes on at the Queen's Head. I fought there plenty of times when I was your age. That thing that killed Loy, the hound, tell me again what you remember of it."

Arodilac told him. Again, for the sixth time. He didn't think that night would ever fade from his memory. No matter how long he lived.

"It was the horse that probably saved me," Arodilac shuddered. "I can still hear it, my lord. It screamed. It wasn't like anything I'd ever heard before. Otherwise, I would've still been upstairs. The thing would've come up right behind me. But I heard the horse dying. Loy went for Fen, and I went downstairs. I'm sorry about your banister."

"It can be mended."

"The thing wasn't a real animal, my lord, not the way animals should be. When I came back up the stairs with your grandfather's spear, I could see through the thing. Loy was trying to get away. There was nowhere to go, but he was still trying. It was between us, stalking him. I could see Loy through the beast. I could see right through it in spots like it was fading in and out of sight. There must've been magic in it, my lord."

This part of the story had been worrying Owain ever since he had heard it the first time. He didn't like magic. He hated it. No real soldier, in his opinion, should have anything to do with magic. There were enough problems on a battlefield as it were. Magic was a tricky, undependable sort of thing. And in an opponent it could mean for a bloody mess. Owain liked things that made sense, that he could get his hands on, see, and feel. Things he could kill with a sword and not worry about them popping back up like a child's jack-in-the-box due to some cursed spell.

"Well, magic or not," said Owain. "Something strange is going on."

"It was real enough when I ran my spear into it, my lord. But I don't think I hurt it much. The thing turned on me, and I probably would've been done for if the window hadn't shattered." Arodilac gnawed his lip in gloomy distraction for a moment and then said, "There's something else about the beast, something important, that for the life of me I can't remember. Every time I get it on the tip of my tongue, my head begins to ache."

The soldiers at the castle gate came to attention as the two strode through. Owain nodded at them absentmindedly. A curious, strained atmosphere pervaded the castle grounds. There were soldiers stationed at every corner and at every door, something Owain had never seen before. Servants scurried here and there. Lights shone from every window. Inside, a strong smell of soap filled the air.

"Lord Gawinn!"

It was Dreccan Gor. The steward hurried down the hallway toward them.

"Gor," said Owain.

"Did you—have you heard of our unfortunate little mishap?" Gor tried to smile but succeeded in doing nothing more than looking as if he suffered from ulcers.

"Mishap? Eleven servants and one Vomarone lordling slaughtered on the grounds like suckling pigs? A horror straight out of children's bedtime stories and then Lady Callas calling up the wind? If that's a mishap, then I'd hate to hear what you consider real trouble. Where's the regent?"

"In the stables. The duke of Mizra just rode out. Botrell was bidding him farewell. None of the lords have deigned to stay on."

"I can't imagine why not."

Owain turned and strode off, Arodilac hard at his heels. Gor, being short and stout, had to almost run to keep up with them.

"He's in a bad mood."

"So am I," said Owain.

"Quite so," panted Gor. "Quite so. I'd heard news of your own family's rather unfortunate, er—"

"Mishap?"

"Dreadful. Your lady's made of stern stuff, sir, stern stuff. My wife would've expired on the spot from fright. Vapors, tremors, chills, fever—you name 'em—she gets 'em all if you even say 'boo' to her."

"I shall refrain from doing so," said Owain coldly, "the next time I have the pleasure of her company."

The regent was nowhere to be seen in the stable courtyard.

"Probably inside with the horses, my lord," said Arodilac.

"You could always come back later," said Gor. "Probably best, I'd say. The regent has a lot on his mind these days. A new trade agreement under consideration with Harth, the fisher guild is demanding additional slips be built on the wharf, and, with the way the treasury is—"

Owain glared at him and the steward shut his mouth. The regent was inside the stable, leaning over the front of a stall and feeding a carrot to a tall blood bay.

"My lord," said Owain.

Botrell gave a startled yelp and stumbled back. He grabbed a stall post to steady himself.

"My lord," repeated Owain.

"Now see what you've done," said Botrell furiously. "I've got a splinter. A splinter! Look here—it's all bloody."

"It's time we discuss what's going on—"

"What's going on? What do you mean, what's going on? Nothing's going on!"

"—in Tormay, as well as in our own city. I'm not an alarmist in any way, my lord regent, but judging from the events of the past several days, I'm forced to conclude that the Dark has its hand in our distress."

"The Dark," sneered Botrell. "There's no such thing as the Dark. Perhaps your excursion's wearied your mind, Gawinn. Some rest would do you well. The Dark is an old wives' tale, only fit for scaring children into eating their spinach and young girls into the arms of their lovers. We've no problems here save a lack of gold in the city coffers. Look at this splinter, Gor. Just look."

"I would beg to differ," said Owain. "And I daresay several hundred of your guests would beg to differ as well, according to what I've heard of your unfortunate— what was the word you used, Gor?"

"Mishap," said the steward unhappily.

"Mishap. It was a bloody massacre. Twelve people slaughtered in your castle on the night of the grandest ball of the Autumn Fair?"

"Eaten, is what I heard," said Arodilac.

"Be quiet." The regent glared at his nephew.

"Vomaro is demanding an explanation, my lord," said Owain. "It's not often that one of the duke's relatives has the privilege of being eaten alive, and in such exalted company. Will you tell the duke it was a 'mishap'?"

"I'm sure there's a reasonable explanation," mumbled the regent.

"No, there isn't," said Owain. "And neither is there a reasonable explanation as to why something—some creature—invaded my home while I was gone, murdered one of my guests, and nearly did away with one of my children. It was only due to your nephew's quick thinking that the thing was routed."

"Ah, well done for you, Arodilac," said the regent. "Rabid dog, wasn't it?"

Owain grabbed the boy by the arm and hauled him forward.

"Why don't you tell your uncle again what happened? Tell him how the rabid dog faded in and out of visibility."

"Um," said Arodilac.

"Dogs, rabid or not, are not able to become invisible at will. Dogs, my lord, are just dogs and they are not known to kill horses, break into houses, and hunt down their inhabitants."

"Um," said Arodilac again.

"Furthermore, when your nephew plunged six inches of boar spear into the thing's back, it didn't seem to phase the creature one bit. Oddly enough, the prints left by the thing match the prints I found at a village whose inhabitants had all been slaughtered several weeks ago. The prints of the beast were mingled with those of a man. What's even more interesting, my lord, is that, while in Vomaro, I found a young lad who had seen the man. A tall, thin fellow with a long white face and a mouth filled with more teeth than a man should have."

"Oh?" said the regent. "A long white face?" His own face paled at these words and he seemed to find the half-eaten carrot in his hand of more interest than Gawinn's words.

"Not a man at all, I think," said Owain. He eyed the regent narrowly. "Something different than a man. Strange, isn't it, that's the same description of the thing at the autumn ball?"

"Well, appearances are deceiving," said the regent. "My father always said so, mostly in reference to my mother."

"Murder in the countryside, murder in the city. Even this morning, my lieutenant informs me of a dead body close by the city gates. Murdered and left drained of blood. Like a tomato sucked dry. Strange goings-on, are they not? Murder in the castle and in my house. My house—me, the so-called protector of Hearne. What am I going to do about it?"

"Are you saying you need to do something about it?"

"Gold, my lord. I need gold for more men, more horses, more equipment. Gold to pay for messengers to the duchies. They must be apprised of the situation and we must have their support."

"Gold?" said Botrell, more appalled at this than anything else.

"Gold. And lots of it."

"The coffers," said Gor, looking just as horrified as the regent, "are empty. All the guests and feasts and balls, don't you know."

"Sell the crown jewels. Sell your horses. I don't care what you do."

"What?" gasped the regent. "Sell my horses?"

Owain slammed the stable door behind him.

"Your uncle's a fool," he growled at Arodilac.

"He is my uncle," said Arodilac, somewhat stung at these words.

"Hmmph," said Owain, and he stalked off across the courtyard.

His head ached and his stomach growled, reminding him of things like missing breakfast and the bread undoubtedly baking this moment in the kitchen at home. The conversation in the stable turned around in his head. The regent knew something. Right when he had said that the man who had strolled calmly into the castle ball with death in his hands resembled the man sighted by the lad in Vomaro, something had flickered in the regent's eyes. Damn him. Botrell was playing a dangerous game. Something strange was going on. Some sort of connection between the murders happening far off in the Tormay countryside and what had happened in the city a few nights ago.

The Dark.

Not that Owain believed in the Dark. How could you believe in something that could not be seen? But sometimes you were forced to believe. As far as he knew, from what he had heard as a child and as a man, from what he had read in the few books he had come across on the subject, the Dark didn't play games.

It was time he took matters into his own hands. But how?

With this thought moving restlessly through his mind, Owain strode away from the castle, his shoulders hunched and his head down, even though the sun had burned away the mist by this time. Despite everything, it was promising to be a lovely day.

CHAPTER EIGHTY-THREE
THE HOUSE OF DREAMS

They all became more and more silent as the morning passed and grew into day. Severan subsided into a mumble that, as far as Jute could tell, did not consist of any words he had heard before, other than the occasional appearance of the words "cheese," "ale," "nap," and "my feet hurt." The hawk ranged far overhead. The morning began with a clear sky, and with such a background, Jute could usually keep the hawk in sight. However, storm clouds had appeared out of nowhere. One moment, the sky had been a warm blue; the next moment, Jute had glanced up to see storm clouds and no blue at all. The hawk was a dark speck that blurred into invisibility against the gray clouds.

Of all of them—of the three people, that is—Ronan never seemed to tire or slow. As Jute and Severan trudged across the endless plain, Ronan would hurry along at such a tremendous pace that he would vanish in the blowing grasses ahead. At other times, he would go loping back on the trail from where they had come, only to reappear far away on their right or left.

"He hops back and forth like a rabbit," said Jute.

"Do you know much of rabbits?" said Severan, who was not in the best of moods. "I think not, and I suppose Ronan knows a great deal."

"Aye," said the hawk. "I daresay he knows rabbits. Near as much as my own self, and I've killed more rabbits than I can remember. Tasty creatures. I never tire of them."

"He's just another city rat," said Jute, feeling somewhat nettled due to the others' admiration of Ronan. "That's what the Guild is—just a bunch of city rats."

"One cannot be a rat and a rabbit at the same time," said the hawk. "Any fool can see Ronan is not city-bred. This land is his home and there's wisdom in how he walks. Even from a rabbit, you have much to learn, for, up to now, your world's been confined to keyholes and stolen apples and fooling ill-woven wards. You would do well to watch and listen."

"How am I supposed to listen," said Jute, "if no one says anything? And you still haven't explained what's going on. You promised you would."

"True," said the hawk. He shifted from claw to claw on Jute's shoulder. "I did, didn't I? Very well."

Severan, who had been lagging behind Jute, found a burst of energy at these words and quickened his pace until he was walking beside Jute.

"Don't mind me," said Severan. "Fine day, isn't it?"

"No," said the hawk. "If you bother looking at the sky, you might notice a storm is coming. Clouds do mean something. Now, my young Jute, I'll tell you what you want to know, but it'll give you little satisfaction. Knowledge only brings more questions. And, yes, Severan, you may listen, but you'll kindly keep your comments to yourself."

"Of course. I wouldn't dream of anything else."

"I will speak of things that haven't been spoken of for many years. I do not wish to speak, for the past is full of sorrow, and the sorrow sharpens with the telling. But this matters little. The story must be told."

Thunder rumbled somewhere in the east, far across the plain. The hawk tilted his head to one side, as if he was listening to what the thunder had to say. The air was colder now, and it smelled of iron and rain. Then, the hawk spoke.

"Long ago, the world was nothing but a dream in the mind of Anue. He was known as the sleeping god in the old tongue, even though men have forgotten him in this age. Anue spoke and formed many beings. They sprang into existence in the house of dreams, that place which has no beginning or end. They were the Aro, and they are the oldest servants of Anue. The eldest of these was Nokhoron. It was his task to descend from the house of dreams and so observe that which came to be from the words of Anue, for the god had determined to fashion life within the void. The name Nokhoron is akin to 'the Watcher' in the common tongue of men."

Severan opened his mouth as if to ask a question, but the hawk forestalled him with a look. A breeze sprang up, and the grass waved in its passing, bending and pointing to the north. Clouds gathered in the sky.

"Thus, Nokhoron was the first to see the formation of the world as it came into being. A single word echoed into the void from the mouth of Anue as he stood on the steps of the house of dreams. The word fell like a shining jewel into the nothingness and there took shape. Nokhoron saw all this, alone and winging through the heights. He was astonished and marveled at the power of Anue. He returned to the house of dreams. There, he found Anue walking in the silence, his head bent in thought.

"Nokhoron spoke of what he had seen. Anue listened to him, surrounded by the other Aro. Then, without a reply, Anue walked away. His footsteps echoed within the halls and faded into silence. Twilight fell. It was then, in the quiet, that Nokhoron thought again on what he had seen within the void. The jewel fell through his thoughts as it had fallen through the nothingness of the void. And his thoughts darkened as the jewel shone ever brighter in his memory. When Nokhoron had come perilously near the end of his musing, Anue returned. He spoke once again.

"All of the Aro turned aside in deference and honor to him, that they might not see the speaking of the word. But Nokhoron dared to look from behind his hands, opening one eye to see the utterance. Such was the power of the word that it blinded his one eye, searing it with the terrible brilliance of Anue's thought. In agony and horror, Nokhoron stumbled from the house of dreams and found himself in the heights of the void. There, again, he was the first to witness the manifestation of the second word. Great lights flared into being in the void. The distant flames of the stars, the frozen sheen of the moon by night, and the burning globe of the sun by day."

Thunder rumbled again, far in the east, and the hawk again fell silent as he listened to the sound.

"But what has any of this to do with me?" said Jute in bewilderment. "You speak of very strange things. Yet, here we are, in the middle of this plain, running from the city, running for my life from the wihht and the shadows in the streets. The wind whispers in my dreams and my hand aches as it remembers the edge of the knife. I wish to hear of these things. I want to fly."

"You must understand what has gone before," said the hawk, "in order to understand today. You'll not do any flying for a while, if I can help it. You'd be doing more falling than flying, I daresay, and dashing your brains out on the nearest rock. So kindly devote yourself to listening. Now, where was I?"

"The stars," said Severan, trying to not sound too eager. "The stars, the moon, and the sun."

"Ah, yes. The stars, the moon, and the sun sprang into being like flames and ice and fire. And beneath them, turning in the void and warmed by the lights, was the world. Malice awoke in Nokhoron, fueled by his great pain, and he knew hate for the first time. He looked within his mind with his one blind eye and discovered the remembrance of the spoken word of Anue that that eye had seen. He bound his hatred into the memory of the word until it twisted and turned within his mind. A new word formed, and he spoke it forth as his one good eye stared into the void. Both eyes gazed: one in the void and the ruined one in the malice of Nokhoron's mind. The word fell from his mouth and created the darkness. This welled up between the stars and moon and sun. It flowed across the face of the world like water from a spring. It threatened to drown everything in its endless night. The darkness even crept up to the house of dreams, and within that house the shadows deepened wherever Anue was not.

"Anue was troubled at this, for the power within Nokhoron was of a dreadful might. It was not the power to make. Instead, it was the power to unmake, for darkness is the destruction of the light. Anue had not lifted his hand to such a thing within the memory of the house of dreams, and in that house there is no beginning or end to memory.

"The Aro went to war against Nokhoron, their brother and enemy. They called him Nokhoron Nozhan—the watcher in the darkness. He was their eldest and had been beloved by all the Aro. This made his betrayal great. But the love of the Aro was first given to Anue, who stood silent in the house of dreams. They found, however, that the darkness had so filled the void that it seemed limitless, and the Aro feared that, like the house of dreams, the dark had no beginning or end, relieved only by the intermittent stars and the distant, lonely materials of space. They could not find Nokhoron Nozhan, for he had hidden himself away in the deep places of darkness.

"While they hunted, Anue called to himself the youngest of the Aro. Her name was Geronwe, and her brothers and sisters called her the fairest of them, for her eyes were filled with light. She stood before Anue in the house of dreams and he gave her the task of completing the world with all manner of creature. He spoke to her ear new words of power that subsided into expectation within her mind, and he touched her mouth so she might in turn speak them into being.

"But by the whisper of shadow to shadow and thence to deeper shadow, Nokhoron Nozhan heard the quick footsteps of Geronwe as she descended from the house of dreams into the heights of the world. She alighted in the east, where the mountains pierce the sky, and spoke the first of the words Anue had given to her. Thus were the Earmdu created. They are the eldest of the world and greatly hated by Nokhoron Nozhan, for they were created to guard those weaker in the world who have no such means to stand against the Dark. But even then, as the first of the Earmdu came blinking and wondering into the sunlight and the sight of Geronwe, fairest of all the Aro, Nokhoron Nozhan reached out and caught hold of his youngest sister. The Earmdu were helpless before him and fled in terror. Ever since then their race has walked in sorrow, for theirs is the guilt of having fled the anguish of her they call Leoth (life, in the common tongue of men), who brought them forth in the morning of the world.

"Nokhoron Nozhan bound Geronwe and bore her away into the darkness, giving no heed to her entreaties, though she wept and pleaded with him on strength of blood and brotherhood. There, in the dark, he tortured her until her body and mind were broken. So it was he learned from her mouth the remaining words of power Anue had given her. Satisfied that her mind was emptied of this knowledge, he freed her and left her to wander, near witless, in the darkness.

"This was how Nokhoron Nozhan came to possess the words of power Anue had whispered to Geronwe in the house of dreams. He brooded within the darkness and turned the words over in his thoughts, twisting them until they were his and replete with malice. Venturing closer to the world, he spoke the words one by one. They tumbled down through the sky, like jewels that glowed with a dark light, and fell to earth in the region of Ranuin in the north.

"This was how the Dark came to be upon the face of the world. Terrible creatures arose. The races of trolls and ogres were born, those who hunger for flesh and delight in destruction. The people of the cobold rose from the dust and hid themselves deep within the mountains, deep within the secret places. Wights walked in the shadows of the forests. There were other creatures that came to being, awful fashionings that have wandered far down through the years of history, forgotten now but still living within the old places of the world. Most dreadful of all, however, in the ice of the mountains of Ranuin, three sceadus stood in the snow. In them was focused all the malice of their master and they were woven with enchantment. For while the other stolen words had spawned entire races, Nokhoron Nozhan saved the last word to form these solitary three.

"The sceadus stood silent. Their flesh was as cold and as hard as stone, and in their eyes gleamed the dark light of the jewels. Beauty was theirs, even though every other spawn of Nokhoron Nozhan was loathsome to look upon, so twisted were they by his malice. The sceadus were similar to the Earmdu in form, being tall and lean and noble of face. Nokhoron Nozhan, perceiving that even such creatures could not contain the depth of his malice, took his sword in hand and drew its edge along his side. Three drops of blood fell to the ground, and when they touched the snow, steam rose hissing. There lay blood no longer, but three gems that burned with scarlet fire. He gave a stone to each of the sceadus. In the stones was the incandescence of Nokhoron Nozhan's malice. With them could the fair things of the world be twisted and corrupted to the will of the darkness.

"Nokhoron Nozhan was gladdened by what he had wrought, and pride swelled his heart. But as he stood gloating on the heights, the Aro came hunting, filled with wrath, for their sister Geronwe had finally wandered free from the darkness, making her way like a witless beast back to the house of dreams.

"Nokhoron Nozhan, perceiving the Aro were few in number, called forth his armies of ogres and trolls carrying axes, wights riding on swift dowoles and wielding iron spears. The folcstan with stone hammers marched in rank upon rank. The sound of their passing was like the clashing of stone, for they had been formed when the light of the jewels had fallen on the rocks of the Ranuin plain. The sceadus were at the forefront of all. Not even the dowole-mounted wights could surpass them, for the sceadus were fleet of foot and flickered like shadows across the landscape.

"Of all the creatures of the dark, only the cobolds were absent from the amassing on the Ranuin plain. But their efforts were not absent, for the little creatures are the masters of the forge, content to burrow under mountains, mining for ore to feed their smelts and smithies. The armor and weapons of Nokhoron Nozhan's army came from their forges. The top of the northern spur of the Ranuin range was shrouded in smoke, for the cobolds were a crafty folk and cut shafts from deep below the roots of the mountains that rose straight up to the heights. It was through these narrow stone chimneys that the smoke and fume of their furnaces were relieved and guttered into the air.

"The Aro sent Ermannuon and Tanurlin, the captains of the Aro, to parley with Nokhoron Nozhan. Their swords were forged in starfire and they cast no shadow as they walked, so shone their armor and the bright beauty of their visage. The army of the Dark quailed before them and doubt gripped them, though the sceadus stood unmoved.

"Ermannuon called out to Nokhoron Nozhan, to him who had been his elder brother and ever the best and brightest of the Aro. His words fell through the air like music, a shining song of memories and regret. He spoke of the past, of the clean, pure curve of the world, and of Anue standing silent within the shadows of the house of dreams. He spoke with forbearance as, of the Aro, Ermannuon still bore kindness in his heart toward the traitor, for he was next in age to him. But Nokhoron Nozhan answered him with scorn and bade him gaze upon the works of his hands, upon the creatures of his own devising. Then Tanurlin spoke in rage, for the memory of Geronwe weeping within the house of dreams was in his thoughts, and he put his hand to his sword. Thus did the Ranuin War begin.

"The Aro were sorely pressed, for though they were mighty, they were few in number. They swam as if in a sea of darkness, such was the multitude of Nokhoron Nozhan's army that surged against them. It was then that the Earmdu came to their aid, falling upon the flank of their enemies. The ogres and trolls died beneath their swords in scores, for the Earmdu were of strong arm and keen eye and ranged behind them were their archers. An arrow loosed from an Earmdu bow will never fail to find its mark. The enemy retreated before them, as the Earmdu flung themselves recklessly into the fray. They were filled with such sorrow and despair that they cared not for their own lives. The name of Geronwe was their battle cry, and they died in great numbers.

"The tide was turned, however, and the captain of the Earmdu met Tanurlin, he who commanded the Aro, in the midst of the carnage. And Tanurlin, leaning on his bloodstained sword, gave to the Earmdu long life for the deed they had rendered to the Aro. The captain of the Earmdu paled at his words, knowing full well their sentence of grief was lengthened, for there is no Earmdu living that does not carry the sorrow of Geronwe in their heart. But Tanurlin spoke again and gave into their hands the caretaking of the new peoples of the earth, for he revealed to the Earmdu the existence of man within Anue's thoughts.

"The remnants of Nokhoron Nozhan's forces fled away into the mountains and forests of the east in the region of Ranuin. The Aro and Earmdu hunted them all through the long winter but, though many more were slain, just as many escaped into the dark and secret places of the world. The three sceadus hid themselves away and were never found. The hunt was abandoned, for the Earmdu were gravely depleted by their losses on the battlefield and the Aro had already bent their thoughts back to the house of dreams and their sister who wept alone there. Several of the Aro, however, chose to stay in this world, for they elected to watch and wait for the return of the Dark.

"As for Nokhoron Nozhan, no trace of him was found. He fled away into the darkness, gathering it around him like a shroud. From within its depths he slowly recovered his strength and nursed his malice. It was then that he built Daghoron, the fortress of night."

With these words, the hawk fell silent. They walked on for a while. The wind sighed in the grass, as if it remembered, and there was a chill in the air.

"Incredible," sputtered Severan. "Amazing. Fantastic. Do you realize that there isn't a single book that refers to any of this? Not one. At least, no book I've read." He rubbed his hands together in glee. "Just wait until I return to the Stone Tower. No one will believe it. No one."

"But what's this to do with me?" said Jute in bewilderment. "I don't see how it has anything to do with the wind and Hearne and that wretched wihht. You're confusing me, and I think I'm confused enough."

"It has everything to do with you. Remember, young Jute, several of the Aro did not return to the house of dreams." The hawk's voice soft with weariness and something else. "There were four of them. I remember well. They made their pact on the battlefield. One to guard the earth, one to stand as a sentinel in the midst of fire, one to walk the paths of the sea, and one to watch over the wind."

The wind sighed in Jute's ear and he saw in his mind an empty place. No—it was not an empty place, but an enormous plain that stretched away under a night sky. Mountains bounded it on either side, receding to the north. The air was choked with the stench of blood and smoke. The plain's expanse was littered with the wreckage of war. Immense engines of iron and wood and stone lay broken and burning. The dead were there in countless host, and it seemed there was no inch of bare earth that could be stepped upon without instead stepping upon a corpse. Jute saw four figures standing in the midst of a great throng of dead. They were tall and clad in shining armor. One of them turned, and Jute glimpsed gray eyes and a stern face. The eyes widened slightly, as if in recognition. Jute blinked and found himself standing on the Scarpe Plain once again.

"Aye, that was him," said the hawk. "But do not look so deeply into the past, for there are other things there, and they would find you of great interest. Do you not see, fledgling? I scarce can believe it myself. I am too old and weary for such things. One of those four have fallen and you have stepped into his place."

"How can I do such a thing?" said Jute.

"Yes, how?" echoed Severan, looking just as shocked as the boy.

"The how of the matter is done."

"But how? It was that wretched knife, wasn't it?"

"Aye," said the hawk. "It was the knife that killed the wind. In taking his life, the knife drew his essence into itself so that the next blood drawn by the blade would, in turn, receive that essence and so become the next wind. No one knew that such a thing could happen. Perhaps this was of Anue's design, but who can know his mind?"

"The wind," breathed Severan. "It's like something out of a strange tale, a fantastic book no one ever believed, up until now."

"I'm only a boy," said Jute in dismay. He did not understand, but was only conscious of a great horror. His hand ached. "I'm a thief. I'm not the wind. I steal purses and apples and coins from the pockets of fat merchants. It's what I'm good at."

"You may say what you will. The important thing now is keeping you alive long enough so you grow in strength and understanding. The Dark would like nothing more than to find you and cut your throat. The longer you stay alive, the more difficult it will be for that to happen."

"Then we'd better start moving again, and fast, instead of standing here gossiping like a gaggle of old women."

It was Ronan. He had been standing behind them for some time, but no one had heard him approach.

"There's something out there," he said. "Something wrong. The Dark, or whatever wives' tale you prefer. Something strange. It's near, but it doesn't seem to be aware of us. It's hunting someone else. But I'm afraid it might scent us."

"Is it safe enough to continue north?" asked Severan.

"For the moment."

"Perhaps if we veer somewhat west as well," said the old man. "We aren't so far from the sea, are we? The coast road would be close, and there are only a few small villages until Lastane. We might already be north of Lastane. If so, there aren't hardly half a dozen villages north of Lastane until Harlech. We'd be quite safe."

Ronan frowned, considering.

"It'd do us well to have a hot meal and a proper sleep at an inn," continued Severan.

"Yes, please," said Jute.

"Very well," said Ronan. He glanced at the hawk, but the bird said nothing.

Across the blowing grasses they went, with the sky turning darker by the minute. This time, however, they angled away toward the west, and the last bit of light in the sky glowed there in evidence of the sun hurrying over the sea. The thunder muttered nearer as if it was a hound growling along their trail.

CHAPTER EIGHTY-FOUR
FAMILIAR TRACKS

Jute and Severan topped a rise and found themselves gazing down a long slope that fell away to the level plain. High overhead, the hawk teetered from side to side in the sullen sky. The wind rushed by, muttering to itself in words that almost seemed intelligible to Jute. He thought he heard it murmur of the north and stones and the cold. The grass rippled in its passing and pointed north. North. Go north.

Good, said the hawk with satisfaction in Jute's mind. *Your ears are opening. North is where we are going, and north is where we shall stay. There's safety in the north. The Dark doesn't like Harlech. It never has, for it cannot get a foothold there. It tried. Once, a long time ago. A man without a name went there and built a tower, but it was thrown down.*

Below them, a ways off, Jute saw the dark figure of Ronan standing in the grass. He did not move but seemed to be staring down at the ground.

"Maybe he's found some animal tracks," said Severan. He stopped to groan and rub at the small of his back. "A nice, sizzling roast for supper sounds marvelous."

When they reached Ronan, he was pacing back and forth, still intent on the ground. He did not look up.

"Deer tracks, I hope?" said Severan.

"Hardly," said the other.

"Well, I wouldn't mind a rabbit. Do rabbits even leave tracks? They seem so small, so light, but they're still tasty."

"They're horse tracks. Horse and wagons. Some people on foot." Ronan frowned and rubbed a withered blade of grass between his fingers. "Two days ago, I think. Heading south by east. Probably toward Dolan. But we're heading north." He shrugged and then mumbled so only Jute heard him. "No account of ours."

"North. Let's get this wretched journey over with." Severan started off briskly through the waving grass.

"He's going east," said the hawk after a moment.

"He'll figure it out when he glances around. Come on, Jute. We're a long ways from Harlech yet."

They walked along in silence through the late afternoon, aside from Severan grumbling to himself every now and then. He had made a fair distance before bothering to look around, congratulating himself on his stamina that kept him so far ahead. But when he glanced back, the two others were already dark shapes trudging away toward the horizon. He had stumbled after them, puffing and blowing. They had had the grace not to say anything, though the hawk had chuckled out loud.

Are you going to ride on my shoulder all day? asked Jute in his mind.

If you care to remember, said the hawk, *I have been flying for most of the day. At any rate, I enjoy seeing things from down here. It's fascinating to observe from a man's point of view. For a while, at least.*

I will learn how to fly, won't I?

Do birds have wings? Of course.

Well, then, how about now?

I don't think so.

Why not?

The hawk clucked in irritation, sounding like (in Jute's estimation) nothing more than a pompous old hen. *Flying, my overeager fledgling, is not quickly learned. It is painful, for it invariably involves a great deal of falling from heights. This grassy earth is soft enough, but it'll feel like rock when you come hurtling down.*

I could stay low. Just a few feet off the ground.

The real danger is not in falling. The real danger is the Dark. When learning to fly— when learning any sort of thing that involves a great deal of, hmm, you might call it magic or power (though both words do little justice to what goes on)—the process can be messy. We shall wait until we reach Harlech. Harlech is safe. Er, safer.

Messy? Jute looked at the hawk in confusion. *What do you mean? Is it messy like eating a peach?*

No. It's messy in that it scatters power here and there, like cupping your hands around a candle but having the light escape between your fingers. And when that happens, it can be seen. Things take notice.

Things?

Things. Creatures. The Dark.

CHAPTER EIGHTY-FIVE
SMEDE GETS TOO GREEDY

Smede opened the curtains and was surprised to find there was still daylight outside. Twilight, more likely, but it was still daylight of sorts. He had had the curtains made years ago. Time and moths had nibbled holes in the wool, but the folds were so thick that they let no light in once the curtains were drawn. Smede rarely ever opened the curtains, and when he did, it was usually only to see if it was raining or to dislodge the dead bodies of moths that got lost among the folds and never found their way out. He enjoyed seeing them drift down to the floor.

It was not that he actually disliked sunlight. It was that, as the years had gone by, he had grown to consider sunlight fickle. One moment it could be shining brightly, and the next moment it could be sulking behind a cloud. It was not sufficient for his work. He needed a dependable source of light. Candles. Candles were best. He could sit for hours at his desk, scribbling his way through the Guild accounts with a nice fat candle perched on the desk, next to his ledger. Candlelight made wet ink glisten beautifully. And it lent a wonderful glow to gold. But gold on its own glowed enough to be seen in the dark.

"It's the only reliable light there is," Smede said aloud. He took a last disapproving look at the sunlight and the blue sky outside, just visible in slices and wedges past the chimneys and rooftops, and then whisked the curtains closed. There was work to be done and he didn't need to fritter away his time staring out the window. He sat back down at his desk. But no matter how hard he tried, Smede could not concentrate. The numbers before him refused to add up. In a fit of temper, he jabbed his pen so hard against the paper that the nib snapped and flicked ink at his face.

"Bother."

A large chest sat in the corner. Smede's eyes wandered over to it.

"Not that I'd think of doing anything like that," he said to himself. "Mustn't even think of it. Now, where was I? Oh, yes. Three fifties and naught point seven two percent compounded weekly for six weeks is—blast this pen. Nine twenty-eight, carry the remainder. I wonder if he'll come back?"

Smede shuddered and looked everywhere in the room except for the chest.

"Mustn't think of that. Three point seventy-five percent is too low. Four percent would be much more suitable for any merchant. The Silentman is too soft on 'em. That leaves nine two five point three —no—nine two five point two eight. Perhaps he'll never come back? He might be dead."

If truth be told, Smede had a habit of talking to himself. This was born out of a life lived mostly in solitude, a life lived in the sole company of ledgers and candlelight and stacks of gold piled on his counting desk. Smede didn't notice when his thought became speech and his speech became thought. It was a habit that could have been broken by a rigorous regimen of spending one hour a day drinking ale in any pub. The habit, however, had been getting worse over the last several months.

"Yes, he might be dead. Drat this pen. But then the Silentman'll be free and clear. And all that gold. He's got it hidden away, hidden like his face. May the shadow take his black heart. It's our gold. But he doesn't know he's dead, does he? No, he doesn't."

And with these perplexing words, Smede found himself standing at the chest. The ward woven into its wood buzzed once in warning and then relaxed at his touch. He opened the lid.

"He might be dead or he might not. He certainly looked dead. He must be dead. But the Silentman doesn't know that."

The chest was empty except for one thing. At the bottom lay a folded black cloak.

"The Silentman doesn't know everything, does he? No, he doesn't."

Smede settled the cloak around his shoulders. It did not look like much. It was just a shabby old cloak.

"It's our gold," he said. "It's ours and I'm doing him a favor by getting it back. Of course, he might be dead, so I'll have to keep the gold for him. I'll keep it safe. I've always been good, haven't I? I've always done the dirty work."

Smede drew the cloak's hood over his head. Instantly, his face disappeared into shadow. It was peculiar. A mirror hung upon the wall and surely reflected enough light from the candle to see within the hood, but where Smede's face should have been there was only shadow. He twitched at the hood to settle it more comfortably, snuffed out the candle and then touched the mirror. The glass shimmered and Smede stepped through, leaving the room silent and empty behind him.

CHAPTER EIGHTY-SIX
A FAILED GAMBLE

Dreccan Gor's stomach ached.

It must have been something he had eaten for supper. Perhaps the roast lamb with mint sauce. Or the cream of flounder soup. Though the cheese soufflé hadn't been as light as it should have been. It had become a chore by the time he had worked his way to the last slice. Normally, the cook spun soufflés as light as summer clouds.

Dreccan turned uneasily on his bed. Perhaps it had been that last handful of grapes? Yes. He shouldn't have had the grapes. He should have exercised more willpower and said no. Dreccan groaned and rubbed his stomach. A glass of vinegar. That would do the trick. First thing in the morning, he would have a glass of vinegar to settle his stomach. And then perhaps three or four eggs scrambled with some of that lovely spicy sausage from Vomaro. And maybe some fried mushrooms.

Dreccan groaned again.

"You sleep uneasily, human."

The voice came from somewhere in the room. Somewhere in the darkness near his bed. His skin crawled.

"Who's there?"

But Dreccan didn't need to ask. He knew the voice. A figure stood in the moonlight that shone through the window. The creature's servant. Twin points of light gleamed at him from within the thing's hood.

"What do you want?" Gor's voice shook.

"You have something of ours. You and your thief master. We want it back."

"What do you mean?"

"I shall be waiting in your master's court, human. Bring him."

The hooded figure vanished.

Dreccan stumbled down the hall as fast as his legs would carry him. The ache in his stomach grew sharper, deeper, and more determined in its efforts. It was not an ache any more; it was downright pain.

Surely the creature was dead.

Dreccan had spoken with no fewer than five lords, two ladies, and four servants who had all attested to the dreadful events that had taken place at the regent's ball. Eleven conversations adroitly steered by Dreccan so that none of them had thought to ask why both the regent and his advisor had not been at the ball when all the dreadfulness had happened. All their stories had been basically the same. The creature was dead. Killed before the stunned eyes of the nobility from every duchy of Tormay. Killed by Lady Levoreth Callas.

Or whoever she was.

Whatever she was.

His mind shied away from that thought. The problems brought by the Silentman's greed were bad enough without having to grapple with the idea that people you always thought were people might not be people at all. They might be something else entirely.

Such a thought did not fit into a neatly ordered world. And if there was anything the world needed more of, it was order. Neatness. Predictability.

Several guards came to sleepy attention in the hall, bleary-eyed and trying not to yawn. One of them dropped his spear with a clatter. Dreccan hurried by. The night chamberlain was snoring on a couch in the regent's antechamber. His wig had slid down onto his face and fluttered with each snore. Dreccan tiptoed past. He opened the door and eased through.

"Who's there?"

"Shhh!" said Dreccan, closing the door behind him.

"Oh, it's you. What are you doing, wheezing and stomping about like that? You could've given me a heart attack."

A candle guttered into life. The regent was sitting bolt upright in a chair in the corner.

"This had better be good, Dreccan," said Botrell. "Just getting a nice night's sleep and you blunder in like a drunk. Eh? Is that it? You've been at the bottle again?"

"I'm not drunk," said the other stiffly, feeling that such an allegation was unfair, particularly as the bed looked unslept in and a nearly empty bottle of wine stood on the table by the regent's chair.

"Don't equivocate," said Botrell, wagging one finger. "Take your medicine like a man. Drink it down, sir. Drink it down."

With this, he poured himself a generous measure of wine and downed it in one gulp.

"I'd offer you some, Dreccan, but it'd be wasted on your untutored palate. It's a Vomarone. A nice, little Vomarone. Twelve-year old bottling. Velvety, fruity, and notes of, er, something or another. Ahh. Yes—yes. I think I'll have another. Don't mind if I do."

"My lord," said Dreccan, "there's an urgent matter."

"Yes? Excellent. Then it can wait until the morning."

"It can't. He's back."

"What's that? Calm yourself, man. Speak clearly. You babble like an old lady. Get to the point."

The steward ground his teeth together. The pain in his stomach was getting worse.

"He's back. The little creature, the thing who hired us to steal the box."

"Shadows above!" Botrell shot out of his chair like a frightened rabbit. "Counfound it, why didn't you say so before? Is he here? But that's impossible. He's dead. No, he isn't dead. Is he dead? Why isn't he dead too? His master's dead."

"We think his master's dead. We thought his master was dead."

"I was hoping," said Botrell, and then he shut his mouth.

"His master might be dead, but he might not. Who knows what happened that night? Wondering won't do us any good now. He's waiting down in the Guild court."

Botrell shuddered.

"Then let's not keep him waiting any longer."

The darkness in the tunnels seemed even darker than usual. The oil lamps burning on the wall hoarded their meager light to themselves as if unwilling to let it shine down onto the stones below.

"Stop walking so close," said Botrell.

"Sorry."

The steward could feel the man's eyes glaring from within the blurred shadows wrapped around his form. He glanced back down the passage. He had the distinct impression that someone was watching him. Just past the edge of the light. But surely nothing was there. Only cobwebs and a spider or two.

They halted at a turn in the passage. Botrell muttered a few words under his breath and a door yawned open before them. Dreccan gritted his teeth, waiting for the old familiar dizziness. A ward buzzed into life in the door. Nausea swept over the steward. In an instant, the darkness was gone and they were standing in the blue light of the Guild court.

"I hate that spell," said Dreccan. He swallowed, tasting bile.

"It's a long walk otherwise," said Botrell. His voice was barely a whisper.

The court was empty. At least, it looked empty. Shadows crisscrossed the hall from column to column, retreating from the blue flames that burned motionless on the walls.

"He's here," said Botrell. He crept up the dais steps and peered around.

"Silentman."

The voice came out of the darkness, from somewhere within the rows of columns stretching away from the empty throne. Botrell made a convulsive leap for the throne and sat down. The little figure stood before the dais steps, where a moment before there had only been shadow. Twin points of light gleamed within the darkness of its hood.

"You have something of ours, Silentman," said the thing. Its voice was low, but the words echoed in the court, hissing in the quiet like snakes who had come to agree with what was said. "You have something of ours, and my master desires its return."

"Your master? Is he—I mean—where—"

But then the Silentman fell silent, for the hooded thing began ascending the steps of the dais. The drapes of its cloak whispered against the stones. It was unthinkable! No one was allowed so near the throne of the Silentman. It was punishable by death. The Silentman looked over at Dreccan, but his advisor was intently studying the floor.

"Listen to me, and listen well."

The thing came closer until it stood in front of the throne. The Silentman clenched his hands together into fists to stop them trembling. He could smell the hooded thing now, a sour whiff of dust and wax and stale sweat. It was an oddly familiar scent.

"Your Guild has taken our gold, our faith, and our patience. And what has my master in return? Broken promises and a boy that escaped your grasp."

"Here now," said the Silentman. "We got the boy, didn't we? We nabbed him and then your master let him slip through his fingers."

Immediately, as soon as the words were out, the Silentman wished he hadn't spoken. Out of the corner of his eye, he saw Dreccan wince.

"My master?" said the thing. "Hold your tongue, thief! My master returns soon and you shall know his reckoning. For now, however, you will return the gold we paid."

"All the gold?" said the Silentman. "Do you mean all, as in all of it?"

"Every last coin."

"But, but," stammered the Silentman. He thought of all the dinners and dances and guests that had been entertained on the bounty of the regent of Hearne. In reality, they had been entertained on the bounty of the Thieves Guild. Most of the gold was spent.

"I'll return this time tomorrow to collect my master's gold."

The hooded thing turned and descended the dais steps.

"All of it, thief," the thing said over its shoulder.

And then it happened.

The thing tripped on the last step. Perhaps it had stepped on a fold of its cloak or stumbled on the stones, the Silentman could not tell, but the hooded thing sprawled on the floor below the dais. It scrambled to its feet. The hood had fallen back. Light glinted on skin and hair.

"Smede?" said the Silentman in amazement.

"Er," said Smede.

"Smede!" yelled the Silentman, but this time his voice was full of outrage and ferocious joy.

The accountant turned and ran. The Silentman was off his throne in a bound and down the steps.

"Smede! You filthy worm! Traitor! You're a dead man, Smede! Dreccan! Quick, grab him! I'll cut your lousy rotten throat myself, you miserable ink-swilling maggot!"

The door at the far end of the court slammed.

"There'll be no catching him once he's in the labyrinth," panted Dreccan.

"I'll have his head on a pike," said Botrell. He spat on the ground and then grinned in delight. "Did you see his face? He was bluffing us. I know it. Smede. Imagine that. His master's dead and gone, I warrant. He was bluffing us for the gold. He was bluffing. Ha! And he had me. He almost had me, Dreccan. I was already trying to figure out where we'd raise that much gold. Sell the regency jewels, borrow from Galnes and all the other blood-sucking merchants. Sell off my stable. Never!"

"I'll put the word out to the Guild," said Dreccan. "They'll be watching his house, the gates, the waterfront. They'll have him before the day's done."

"And also the city Guard. Make up a story of murder or someone's daughter ravished, I don't care what. Anything that'll withstand Gawinn's scrutiny. Smede'll rue the day he was born when I get my hands on him. I'll skin him alive with a blunt knife. I'll roast him over coals. I'll drown him in his own ink."

"You don't suppose he wasn't lying?"

"What? Nonsense. You're becoming womanish in your old age, Dreccan. You saw his face. He was bluffing or I'm not the regent. Smede's never met a gold piece he didn't love. His master's dead and he was hoping to scoop up all that gold for himself. You have to hand it to him. Imagine that—our accountant a lying, scheming traitor. You can't serve two masters, Dreccan."

The door closed behind them. The court was silent again. Silent and empty and, between the glimmers of blue light, filled with the dark.

CHAPTER EIGHTY-SEVEN
LEVORETH GOES HUNTING

Levoreth and the wolves traveled up through the foothills of the mountains. The air was brisk and clouds blew across the sky in dirty, gray tatters. They were in an area north of the duchy of Dolan and east of Harlech. Neither duchy claimed the land as its own. There was nothing to claim from a practical point of view, for the countryside was inhospitable at best. It was a desolate place of steep, rocky slopes and sudden canyons that dropped down into their depths, cut by years of the rivers running fast and ice-cold down from the mountain heights above. Pine trees grew on the slopes, rising up from the ground dense with dead needles to the treetops above tossing and sighing with the wind. Past them, through the branches and further up still, were the heights gleaming with snow.

"It's winter already, up there," said Levoreth.

Aye, said the old wolf. He loped along at Swallowfoot's side, each stride nearly as long as the horse's. *It's always winter on the heights.*

Do you remember the trail, Drythen Wulf?

Does a wolf ever forget a scent? said the wolf in some indignation. *Would that I could forget such a trail. Would that I had never followed it down, but the wolves shall always live according to your wishes, Mistress of Mistresses.*

They struck the trail later that morning. Levoreth shivered, closing her eyes for a moment. Beneath her, Swallowfoot trembled and stopped stock-still. She took a deep breath and opened her eyes. The scene had not changed. The pale sunlight still streamed down through the pine trees. But in her mind, she could feel the touch of the Dark. The presence was old and faded, but it was there.

We need not follow the trail all the way to the mountaintop, Mistress, said the old wolf. *I think there are other ways to get there.*

Thankfully, she said. *Lead on.*

They climbed past the tree line and up into a region of great rock slabs and a wiry, spiky scrub that had no flowers or leaves but released a sweet scent whenever its branches were broken. The slabs of rock were enormous and they lay in shattered grandeur, like bodies of giants turned to stone, fallen upon a battlefield from some long-forgotten war. Swallowfoot picked his way through the rubble underfoot.

Methinks your horse is descended from a mountain goat, said the old wolf.

Watch your tongue, wolf, said Swallowfoot.

I meant well. Your step is sure and this is no easy, plainsland path we follow. But the old wolf's mouth opened in a soundless laugh, and the other wolves ahead of them on the slope glanced back with amusement gleaming from their eyes and their sharp-toothed grins.

Levoreth remembered, with some surprise, that the last time she had been in the mountains had been with these same wolves. This same pack. Years ago. Hunting a sceadu that had brought death and misery to the mountains and all the wild kin who lived there.

It is in my mind, Drythen Wulf, that this sceadu we trail may be the same creature that brought the Dark to the mountains years ago when I hunted with your pack.

Perhaps, Mistress. But there is a difference. Once we reach the eyrie, you will see. Aye, the sceadu was there, but something else was there as well. Something quite different.

There were different sorts of evil. The evil that men hid in their hearts was one kind. The ancient words of the Dark were another evil, of much greater deadliness than anything a mere man could set his hand to. But words were only words, and they always required someone to speak or read them. There were creatures who had old and abiding allegiances to the Dark, such as ogres and cobolds and sceadus. They were yet another sort of evil. The sceadus were ancient, older, and more terrible than all the works of darkness. They had walked the earth when she herself had still been young. And then there was the Dark itself. The Watcher in the silence.

"Deep within the darkness, further e'en the void, Nokhoron Nozhan built himself a fortress of night," Levoreth said out loud. The wind held its breath at the brashness of her words and then, when nothing happened, it blew into the silence with a relieved sigh.

They walked along a ridge that fell away into the plunging depths below. Swallowfoot shivered beneath her, but she calmed him with a touch of her hand and he stepped along again with assurance. The wolves were strung out before and behind her; some were black against the snow with their dark fur, but many of them were lighter colored and so almost vanished into the glittering white. But the light was fading fast. High above them, past the ridge, was the peak. It waited for them, darkening in the dying light.

We are near, Mistress.

The old wolf came and stood by Swallowfoot's side. The wolf's breath steamed in the air, and she could see the anxiety in his eyes.

A little farther, said Levoreth, *and then I will go on my own.*

No, Mistress. We shall go with you.

They again came upon the trail of the sceadu and were forced to follow it, for there was no other way up. The mountain dropped away into the depths below on one side, down into an awful emptiness. On the other side, a steep rock wall, sheathed in ice, angled up at such a slant that it seemed it would fall over on them at any second.

I would not mind being a mountain goat, said Swallowfoot. *One more look over the side and I shall be dizzy.*

And then, around a corner, they hiked up into a flat space. It was a narrow bowl bounded on three sides by steep rock and on the fourth by the sky and the sheer fall of the mountainside. The bowl was deep in snow.

There, said the old wolf.

But Levoreth already knew. She swung down from Swallowfoot. On the far side of the bowl, where the rock walls came together to a cleft, the opening of a cave was barely visible behind a snowdrift.

Wait for me here, she said.

By the time she neared the cave, the snow was past her waist. Her clothes were stiff with ice. The cold had worked its way deep into her, deep in her bones, but she did not mind. She had once stood on a mountainside in winter for three months, absentmindedly listening to the sounds of the snowfall and the slow, creaking sleep of the earth. She had turned to ice then, but it had not mattered because she was Eorde. She was the earth.

Here, though, something else strove to creep in with the cold. The Dark. Levoreth shut her mind to it, strengthened with the memory of stone and the weight of earth. She wove her thoughts with the green of spring and the long, slow fall of autumn that finds its strength in its inexorable descent. But still, something fluttered against the edge of her mind.

"Avert!" she said.

Levoreth kicked at the bank of snow obscuring the cave mouth until the crust crumbled. The snow collapsed inward. Ice lined the walls of the interior. The cave was silent, but outside she could hear the wind moaning. It was dark inside but Levoreth did not need much light to see. What was sufficient for a cat or an owl was sufficient for her. A rough stairway was carved into the stone at the back of the cave. Whatever waited for her was at the top of those stairs. She began to climb.

And the Dark reared alive. No more than a whisper on the edge of her thought.

It battered at her.

Shadow, deep and dark and heavy as stone.

Thou wilt die.

As all shall.

All flesh is like grass.

Withers and fades.

Into the night without end.

But the earth in her was heavier still. Immovable and fixed. Levoreth hunched her shoulders, staggered a little under the weight of the voice, and then trudged up the stairs. She did not know how long she climbed those stairs. It could have been only a few minutes. It could have been an hour. It could have been a day. She came to the top of the stairs. The darkness lightened to a gloom. Levoreth stood in an empty space carved from the rock. An eyrie. Above her head was a high ceiling of stone, sheathed in ice and stalactites. On all sides, however, openings like windows looked to the north and south and east and west. She moved to one of the windows, the one looking south, and found that the window was large enough to serve as a porch. She stood on the edge of the mountain. Snow blew and swirled around her. She gazed south, and stretching away before her, the peaks of the Morn range stood in all their lonely grandeur, some shining bright in sunlight, some shrouded in darkness and storm.

And in the eyrie was the Dark. It was a memory only. Whatever had been here was now long gone. But the memory was alive and powerful.

"Who were you?" said Levoreth.

The thing lashed at her, striking at her mind with malice as sharp as shattered stone and as cold as ice. But she stood firmly and would not move. She could feel the mountain beneath her, heavy with sorrow and still remembering what it had been forced to harbor for so long.

"Who were you?"

A nobody. A nothing.

The voice was sneering. A voice devoid of life. A voice as thin as the blade of a knife.

"Who were you?"

The thing thrashed on the edge of her mind but it could not escape. It had been in the eyrie for so long that it was rooted to that place.

"Who were you?" said Levoreth. "Speak!"

The rock beneath her shuddered with the force of her words. The mountain shook. Outside, ice shattered and a great mass of snow slid several feet down the face of the crag before pausing. But the pause was only for a second. The snow slid away then in earnest, roaring and billowing down the slope. In the bowl at the cave's mouth, Swallowfoot and the wolves trembled.

We were darkness, said the voice.

We were a word, my brothers and I. We were a jewel that fell through the night sky. We fought wars in the dead lands. We laid waste to those who lived there and brought them to ruin. We were darkness, restless and hungering. Restless, old Mistress. So I left my brothers and came west across the great sea. I came hunting like a dog. I gazed over this land. I stood in the wind and rain, in the tempest and the storm, in the ice and the snow. Watching and waiting. I gazed from this mountain for a hundred years.

"I know you," said Levoreth, shivering. "We fought you in distant lands. Before the land of Corvalea fell into darkness. Three brothers. The three sceadus."

Aye, sneered the voice. *And what else do you hide in your memory? I shall tell you one of mine. I saw the wind one day. I saw the wind one day, stretching his wings from this eyrie. This was his home, as it is mine now. He went flying to and fro in his careless way, as he was wont to do, and a thought settled in my mind that I would be the one to catch him as he fell. I fed his curiosity with a dream. I drew him east. East from the mountains and across the great waste beyond, to the farthest shore where another sea laps. And he came to the sand of the shore so that he might set his hand on the jewel that sparkled there. But there was no jewel to be had. There was only my knife. And there he did die. On my knife. Such a sweet memory.*

"You are a liar," spat Levoreth, "as you and your kind always have been. Your knife did prove his end, but he did not die there. He fled you, did he not? He fled, with your knife in his side, and the Dark has been searching for the blade ever since."

And find it we shall, old Mistress. The dogs are sniffing along the scent. We shall find it and the wind shall be ours.

No. Someone else found it first, thought Levoreth to herself tiredly. She could see Jute's frightened face in her mind. Someone else found it first and you'll have to kill him. You'll have to kill the wind again.

"You are only a memory, a curse on this place. Where did your true self go? Where is the sceadu?"

I am only a memory from my past, said the voice. *When I left this place, my future began. I am only a shadow of the past. I cannot tell you, old hag.*

"But you know. I can feel it in your voice. Tell me."

The thing sought to escape. It tried to hide in the old, fading memories of the past, in what Levoreth had forgotten, in what she wished to forget, but she caught it and held it. And the thing told her. It told her in pictures that flooded her mind. It told her in hatred and darkness and ancient malice that had spied upon Tormay for so long.

My lord sleeps in Daghoron, said the voice, dying away. *But I serve another. There is another and he stands in the shadows. We will rule Tormay. We will destroy as we have always destroyed.* And then the voice was gone, whirled away in a fit of laughter that vanished on the wind. Levoreth released the memory and stood staring blindly. She felt old and tired, unutterably weary.

"Another," she said to herself in a daze. "I do serve another."

Snow was falling when Levoreth emerged from the cave. The wolves were huddled around Swallowfoot to keep him warm. The snow lay across the wolves so that they were only little hills and mounds under it. One of the hills shook itself and cascaded away to reveal a furry snout, ears, and eyes.

The mountain shook, Mistress, said the old wolf.

"The mountain?" Levoreth said, her mind blank. "Oh. I'm sorry."

The other wolves emerged from the snow, sneezing and snuffling and shaking the snow from their coats. Swallowfoot levered himself up. Levoreth ran her fingers through his mane, breaking the ice free and warming him with her touch. She swung herself up.

"Let us go," she said. "A storm is coming."

Above them, the wind blew around the mountaintop, moaning in and out of the eyrie. It sounded forlorn, as if it were searching for an old friend who had gone away and was no longer there.

CHAPTER EIGHTY-EIGHT
THE STONE TOWER

Severan was right in his guess that they had already passed north of Lastane, for early that morning they topped a rise and looked down upon a river gleaming in the sunlight. Willows grew in thickets along the water's edge, and through the dark arms of their branches they could see the gliding flow.

"A river!" said Jute. "Let's go fishing."

"The south fork of the Ciele," said Ronan. "We've traveled farther than I'd hoped."

"There," said Severan. "What did I tell you? We'll reach the coast road and be in Harlech in no time. The road's safe this far north; I'd wager my neck on it."

"Still many a mile to go," said the hawk, "but fresh fish for breakfast would do me no harm."

"I didn't think hawks fished," said Jute. "The seagulls and the pelicans do. I used to love watching them diving in the bay. I thought you hunted mice and rabbits and such."

"Hawks don't hunt mice. At any rate, when you've lived as many years as I have, you learn many things. Among them, a taste for fish. Even the taste of rabbit grows bland after a while."

"I've seen fisherhawks," said Ronan. "In the lakes north of Dolan."

"Aye." The hawk chuckled. "A rough-winged sort. They have a fondness for eels and they claim to speak with the giants."

"Giants," said Severan. "I've never met anyone who has spoken with a giant, let alone seen one. What language do these fisherhawks use when they speak with giants?"

But the hawk did not answer, for he had launched himself from Jute's shoulder and swung steadily away from them into the sky.

"Dratted bird," said Severan. "I know. I know—you needn't look at me like that, Jute. Your hawk is probably the oldest and wisest creature I've ever had the fortune to meet, but he has a habit of ending conversations right when they get interesting."

When they reached the river, they found the hawk perched on top of a rock at the water's edge, busily devouring a fish.

"Trout," said the hawk through a mouthful. "Plenty more, if you're hungry."

"I think I'll have some of Ronan's excellent stale bread," said Severan, turning pale. "That is, if there is any more."

"Pity we don't have a pole and a line," said Jute.

They came to a road an hour after they forded the river. It was more like a carter's track, being just two worn ruts in the grass. It led north and south.

"The coast road," said Ronan. "I can smell the sea."

The others could not, and the hawk eyed him thoughtfully for a while but did not say anything. Being on the coast road put Severan in excellent spirits. He was familiar with the surrounding lands, for he had spent many years in the northern coast duchies.

"You're from Harlech, aren't you?" said Jute.

"Originally." Severan shrugged. "I have an old house there. I told you before, didn't I? It belonged to my father and his before him. High on the headlands past Lannaslech.

More of a cottage than a proper house. It looks down upon the sea. I daresay it would make an excellent hideaway for you, eh?"

"Perhaps," said the hawk. "We shall see."

"A house," said Jute. "That sounds wonderful. I've always wanted to live in a house."

"Thule, however, is where I spent more years. It's similar to Harlech in many ways. Neither has any real cities, just villages and small towns. The duke of Thule himself lives in a simple house out in the countryside. He's a good man, and famous for his hospitality."

"But it was the Stone Tower that brought you to Thule, wasn't it?" said the hawk. "Learning and magic and the pursuit of words?"

"Well, yes."

"I've never seen this Stone Tower," said Ronan. "I've never seen it, though I suppose there's little in any duchy of Tormay I haven't seen."

"Of course you haven't seen it," said Severan. "The Stone Tower's hidden by powerful warding spells. Those who get too close and who have no business there find themselves turned about and heading south if they meant to go north or caught in bogs or walking right off cliffs. It's not a place easily found."

Severan discoursed at length and with great enthusiasm about the Stone Tower. The others listened as they walked along the road, though it was doubtful the hawk listened much, as he spent most of his time flying overhead. When he was not flying, he perched on Jute's shoulder with his head tucked underneath his wing.

"One of the fellows two years senior to me, name of Feldmoru, discovered the third word for oak one day while reading Petersilie's *A Summer in Dolan*. Petersilie's writings were considered light stuff. After all, the book is a recounting of a summer he once spent in Dolan. Lots of detail of walks and suppers at country inns and some hilarious descriptions of the folks he met. There's a superb bit about a gravedigger and an infestation of gophers."

"Then why was the book at the Stone Tower in the first place?" asked Ronan.

"Because of who Petersilie was, don't you know," said Severan.

"No, I don't know."

"You don't? Petersilie used to be the court wizard in Hearne. Hundreds of years ago. Back when it actually meant something. It was always considered odd that he had written something as frivolous as *A Summer in Dolan*. Until Feldmoru came along. Tall fellow with a drippy nose. I remember him well. And his nose. It made a dreadful noise when he blew it."

"Get on with the story," said the hawk. He had been napping on Jute's shoulder, but Severan's voice had woken him.

"It was the names of the people he wrote about, see? Petersilie made up names for them, on the surface because he was much too polite to use actual names, but he was using words from one of the older languages. If he was discussing a shepherd, he would have hidden *sceap*, which is the word for sheep, in the fellow's name. Ansceap or Torsceapan or something like that. People are still analyzing that book and finding hidden words."

"That isn't much of a story," said Jute. "A proper story should have hideous creatures and horrible secrets, and a clever thief. Oh, and descriptions of lots of tasty meals."

"Nonsense," said Severan. "It's a wonderful story."

Jute had something more to say but was stopped by a shout from Ronan. He had quickened his pace in order to avoid Severan's discourse on *A Summer in Dolan* and was farther up the road now, at the top of a hill.

"The sea!" he called.

They hurried up the rise after him. Past the sloping fields before them, bounded by the jagged line of cliffs that marked the edge of the land, was the sea. It was a shining line of light. They could hear the rolling boom of the surf and the faint, thin calls of the gulls. And everywhere there was the salt-smell of the sea.

"Yes, well, that's certainly the sea," said Severan. "It's cold and nasty in these parts. Only fools and fishermen venture out on it—though, down through the years, quite a few wizards have sailed west from the Stone Tower."

Ronan, who had begun to scowl at these words, looked interested.

"What were they searching for?" he said.

"Oh, many things. The end of the world, new lands, a place untouched by the Dark. Some of them were trying to find the anbeorun of the sea. But who knows what they really thought to find? Perhaps only a lost word? No one's ever returned."

The road drew closer to the cliffs. As they walked along, they could see the waves below. There was a freshness in the air that was more than mere purity and light. Jute's heart was glad within him and he watched the flight of the gulls as they swooped and dove across the face of the cliffs.

He loved it here.

Who? said Jute in his mind.

The hawk's eye gleamed in the sunlight.

He who was before you. He often said that the meeting of water, sky, and earth along these coasts was a thing of mystery and beauty, and here in the cold of winter, that mystery became slow and still and clear to sight. He said it reminded him of an older place, when he had been young and that he no longer remembered with such clarity.

I wish we could stop and go fishing. Climb down to the bottom of the cliffs. There must be crabs down there. We could catch them.

"Off the road, quick!" said Ronan.

"What? Why?"

"Get off the road! Is there a way to say it clearer?"

They tumbled off the road and into the bushes beside the road.

"What is it?" said Severan. "Ouch. I fear I've chosen a briar to hide myself in."

"Hush," said Ronan. "Someone's coming along the road behind us."

"I hear it," said the hawk. "A horse and rider, I think."

When the source of the sound came into view, it was a horse-drawn cart. An old woman sat on the seat behind the horse, reins in her hands.

"Well, I'll be," said Severan.

He immediately bounded up from his hiding place and called to the carter.

"Hi, there! I say, stop!"

"What are you doing?" said Ronan.

"It's all right. I know her."

The carter reined her horse in. Severan scrambled up to the road, his face beaming.

"It's Cyrnel, isn't it?" said Severan. He ducked a quick bow.

"Aye, that's me," said the woman on the cart, looking at him warily. She fingered a loop of braided leather around her neck. "And you are?"

"Oh, er, my name's Severan. Do you, I mean, don't you remember me?"

"Sorry, friend."

"I was a student at the tower. You used to deliver vegetables there."

The woman's face eased into a smile. Her hand released its hold on her necklace.

416

"And still do. The students come and go at the tower, but I trot old Apple up there once a week with goods from our farm. The tower's where I'm headed now. If you're going that way, I'll take you along."

"Oh? Thank you. My friends and I'll gladly take you up on that offer."

"Your friends?"

The woman smiled when Ronan and Jute emerged from the bushes. She eyed the hawk perched on Jute's shoulder but said nothing.

"We were hiding," said Severan, turning a little red. "We weren't sure who was coming along the road. There are strange things about these days."

"Oh, I never worry too much," said Cyrnel. "If someone was foolish enough to rob me, why, they'd have the whole of the Stone Tower after them. They like their food, they do. Climb up."

As the cart seat was only wide enough for the woman herself, they climbed up into the back of the cart and found themselves spots among the sacks and chests and casks.

"Careful where you sit," said Cyrnel. "There are eggs in the forward chest. Help yourself to the sack by your knee, boy. It's full of plums."

They bounced along the road, resting in the back of the cart. It smelled of vegetables and the rich, warm scent of fresh milk. Jute could feel something like cabbages in the sack underneath him. He bit into a plum and juice ran down his chin.

"She doesn't remember me," said Severan.

"You don't say?" said Ronan. He winked at Jute.

Severan blushed. In front of them, they could hear Cyrnel whistling and clucking to the horse every now and then. A fine sparkle of dust hung in the air behind them, kicked up by the horse and the cartwheels.

"She delivered food to the Stone Tower when I was a student there," said Severan. "Wheat for our bread, eggs, cheese, milk, fresh vegetables. She and her father would come in his cart. This is probably the same cart. She was just a girl back then. Braids and bare feet and freckles on her nose."

"She's going to the Stone Tower now," said the hawk.

"Er, yes."

"I've nothing against wizards," said the hawk, "other than the fact that they aren't always dependable. Quite a few of them have gone over to the Dark, haven't they? I don't recall discussing a stop at the Stone Tower. Harlech it was. We agreed on that. North to Harlech."

"We're still going north," said Severan. "I can't help it if the tower's on the way. A hot dinner, proper beds, a roof over our heads for the night. That's nothing to sneeze at, if I may say so."

"Oh, please, let's," said Jute. A proper bed sounded marvelous to him.

"I'm not interested in any of your reasons," said the hawk. "I like my dinners warm, if you understand what I mean. The best of beds for me is a tree branch, and the sky's always been my roof. All right, all right, Jute. You needn't make such a face. One night and no more than one night. I'll not rest easy until we've passed into Harlech, and even there I reserve the right to be uneasy whenever I want to."

"I must say," said Severan, "that it would be good to hear an explanation of your comment on wizards and the Dark, master hawk. Wizards are not so easily ensnared."

"Do you think Scuadimnes was the only wizard who fell into darkness?" said the hawk. "He was the only one who found fame with his evil deeds, for it is no little thing to have destroyed the monarchy of Hearne and the university. But there have been others. I

417

think you know one yourself. And how long ago was it, Severan, that your friend Nio began his descent into darkness? When did it begin and why did you not know? It is a quiet thing that cannot be seen. Knowledge alone is not a safeguard against such a fate."

Severan shut his mouth unhappily at that and did not answer. After a while, the hawk flew away from the cart in long, lazy strokes, claiming that the bumpiness of the ride was making him sick to his stomach. The cart descended down into a small valley. The half circle of a bay shone in the morning sunlight. Across the valley, the slopes mounted up to a ridge that fell off into the sea on one end in cliffs and angled away into forested hills on the other. Down in the bay, several boats were at anchor, bobbing in the swell.

"There's the tower," said Severan.

"Where?" said Jute. "I don't see anything."

Severan pointed. "At the foot of the ridge, where the curve of the bay comes around to the cliffs."

Jute still did not see anything that looked like a tower. All he saw was the cliff on the other side of the valley. Slabs of stone angled away from it, looking as if they would fall at any moment. A greenish mass covered the cliff here and there, looking like a strange waterfall of vegetation flowing down from the top.

"I still don't see anything," said Jute.

Severan smiled. "I'd be surprised if you did."

"I can see it clear enough," said the hawk, who had rejoined them on the cart a while ago. "It's very tumbled down for such a famous place."

"It's rather old," said Severan a bit huffily.

"Plums," said Ronan, "don't suffice for lunch." He tossed a pit over the side and reached for another plum.

The cart had reached the floor of the valley. It was warmer now, sheltered by the slopes on either side and the dense, wooded hills to the east. The shore was close there. The surf hissed up onto the rocks and then retreated, leaving behind gleaming foam and long, ropy strands of glistening, purple seaweed. They rolled down a lane of eucalyptus trees. The air was rich with their perfume. The tall trunks rose around them like columns in a stately hall. The cartwheels swished through the leaves on the track. And then the trees were gone and they were under the shadow of the cliff.

"Here we are," said Cyrnel.

She twitched on the reins and the cart came to a halt. They were in a courtyard of sorts, bounded by the trees behind them and the cliff towering overhead. The three travelers tumbled out of the cart.

"Welcome to the Stone Tower," said Severan.

Looking up, Jute could see that the cliff was a great deal larger and taller than it had appeared from across the valley. The waterfall of vegetation he had seen from afar, on closer inspection, was a gray-green lichen that grew on almost every rock surface in sight.

"It's larger than I thought," said Ronan. "Much larger. It's a wonder the entire place doesn't come crashing down."

And then Jute saw it. The cliff itself was the building. The slabs of stone that made up its face, jutting out here and there in fantastic angles and slopes, were hewn into a semblance of walls. Windows looked out from behind the mantle of lichen. Chimneys teetered up to the sky in several spots, bent into grotesque lines like the trunks of trees twisted by the wind. Jute could smell woodsmoke in the air.

"There's a ward spelled into the lichen," said Severan. "It can rearrange itself to conceal the tower. Sometimes, if necessary, the ward conceals the entire valley. Fills it with forest, or even makes it seem as if the sea washes all the way in and there's nothing here but water."

"Magic plants," said Jute. "I would've seen through it soon enough."

"Hmmph," said the hawk. "But do people ever come looking who mean the tower harm?"

"I don't know. If they have, then they've never found it."

A great double door at the foot of the cliff opened, and people streamed out. Soon, the courtyard was filled with people jostling and laughing and unloading Cyrnel's cart. Jute stood to one side and watched, the hawk perched on his shoulder. Many of those he saw were his age or somewhat older. Boys vied to see who could carry the most bags and sacks from the back of the cart. A sack broke and yellow onions bounced and rolled everywhere. Several older men stood at the door.

"Severan," said one of them, making his way across the courtyard. "We've been expecting you. And who are your companions?"

"Friends," said Severan. "Just friends, passing through."

The man smiled and nodded, but Jute noticed him later whispering with his fellows.

In no time at all, Cyrnel's cart was empty and she clucked to the horse, gave them all a friendly nod, and was soon rolling off back down the lane of eucalyptus.

"Well, come in then," said Severan, looking after Cyrnel's departing cart wistfully. "It'll soon be time for lunch."

The entrance hall was spacious. Jute had been expecting a cramped sort of tunnel, but the ceiling inside soared up to ribbed vaults that faded into sunlight. At first, he had a sense of great quiet, but then he heard the whispering of many voices beneath the silence. The words were not intelligible, but they were distinct as words, rushing and falling and murmuring over each other.

The memory of voices, said the hawk inside his mind. *Voices of all kinds. This place remembers those who have passed through this place and speaks of its memory.*

Why does it do that? asked Jute.

I'm not certain. It is the stone of this place that speaks. I think it has gathered in the spells of hundreds of years and so gradually has become more and more awake.

Awake? What do you mean by awake? How can stone be awake?

But the hawk did not answer him, for at that moment, a short fat man bustled up.

"Severan! How good to see you."

"Ablendan!" said Severan.

"I apologize for not sending anyone to help. I was, ah, detained. But, you're well? All in one piece? Come—the council is convening and they wish to speak with you."

"What? Wait. What happened? You left Hearne days ago."

"The truth is," said Ablendan, looking embarrassed, "I only arrived here this morning."

"What?"

"I'll explain later. You're just in time for the council. All of you, especially, er, this is— is this. . . ?" Ablendan's eyes darted to Jute.

They climbed a wide staircase that passed by many rooms and hallways stretching away on either side. The place bustled with life. There were boys everywhere, reading books, huddled together talking, sweeping floors, hunched over manuscripts, running up

419

and down the stairs, talking, yelling, laughing. And, invariably, they all stopped whatever they were doing to stare.

"Sir? Excuse me, sir."

Jute turned to see a small boy. Behind him, several other boys stared avidly, waiting in attentive silence. The first boy glanced behind him at the group, as if to gain courage from them.

"Excuse me, sir," he said again. "Sir, is it true that you're the wind? Everyone is talking of it."

"Um," said Jute, turning red and wishing he were anywhere but where he was. Fury flooded his mind, but it was not his own—it was the hawk's. The bird's talons squeezed painfully into his shoulders. But then Ronan urged him forward up the stairs, brushing by the boy and the onlookers.

"Lunch," he said. "Lunch is more important than questions right now."

And lunch was what they eventually had, in a narrow hall that looked out through windows at the sea far below. A long oak table ran the length of the room. It was surrounded by tall-backed chairs made of woven cane. The room was full of men, mostly old and gray. They were arguing together, some almost shouting in order to be heard over the others, one pounding on the table, several gesticulating wildly with their hands as they spoke, as is the manner of those who come from Vomaro. The moment the door opened and Jute and his fellows stepped through, the room fell into dead silence. But only for a second. Then, it erupted into noise once again.

"Welcome to the—" said Ablendan.

"Severan!"

"Is this youngster the one we've heard of? Why haven't you—"

"I still don't believe it. Not a word of it. Test him. I want to see a test of his powers before we—"

"Food would be appreciated!" bellowed Ronan. "Some of your famed Thulish hospitality!"

There was a moment of startled silence and then a flurry of activity. Several of the younger men in the room hurried out. Chairs were offered. A jug of ale appeared. Bread, cheese, and sausage were whisked in on a platter. A small boy staggered through the door under the weight of a tureen of stew smelling splendidly of beef and spices. Ronan, Severan, and Jute dug into the food with appreciation. The hawk hopped up onto the back of Jute's chair and refused a piece of sausage that Jute offered him. Someone swung open a window, and the sound of the surf could be heard from far below the cliff.

"Honored guests," said an old bald man, inclining his head, "the council of the Stone Tower has been discussing your—this issue, ever since Ablendan arrived from Hearne. I must confess that some of us were dubious of his news, as such a thing has never been heard in Tormay. At least, not in recorded history. But there're ways to determine whether a man is telling the truth, and Ablendan has spoken only the truth to us."

"That's your opinion," said a voice from somewhere in the room. The bald man flushed angrily at this and turned around, but there were only blank faces to be seen.

"Now," said the bald man, trying to smile but only managing to look as if he had stomachache. "Now, there are three questions that must be asked. Two questions aren't enough, and we can't presume on your patience with four. I've been allowed the first. Forgive me for its simplicity. How can the wind die, for it still has been blowing past our tower all these years with never a lull?"

Another stepped forward, a thin man tugging at his beard. "Hedred Hald's book of Naming and Names states that the old languages were made of words that preexisted what they described, that this truth even applies to the four stillpoints of earth, water, wind, and fire, the anbeorun of old. If the name of the wind can be found, then is that word more powerful than the wind?"

A third man spoke, his eyes shut. "The second stricture of death is that it is final. Therefore, if the wind can die, how can it live again? And if it can live again, can it die again?" He opened his eyes and stared at Jute.

The old bald man bowed his head. "We await your answers."

"You'll get no answers from us, old man."

It was the hawk. The bird's voice vibrated with anger.

"My patience was gone before we finished climbing the stairs. Why does even the smallest boy here know who we are? The stones of this place whisper about what has gone on within these walls. And now, we are part of those memories as well. Stone whispers to stone, and beyond them, past them in the shadows, is the darkness. And in the darkness, the Dark listens."

Outside, sunlight glittered on the wave tops and clouds scudded across the sky. Somewhere, outside the open window, a bird whistled. Jute mopped up the last of his stew and tried not to meet anyone's eyes. He could feel stares on him, particularly of the man who had asked the last question. The question about death. Next to Jute, Ronan worked his way through his third bowl of stew, his face blank and uncaring of what was going on around them. The old man stammered an apology, but the hawk interrupted him.

"We'll answer no questions for now," said the hawk, "though we thank you for your hospitality. We've traveled far and would like to rest a while."

The sound of the bird's beak snapping shut on this last word was sharp and final. No one said a thing after that, other than asking if they wanted more stew (which Ronan did) or more ale (which he also did) and murmuring pleasantries about the weather and what a fine time of year it was to travel. After a while, all of the old men left the hall. When they had finished eating, the little fat man, Ablendan, showed them to some rooms. He lingered for a while, trying not to stare at Jute but making a bad job of it.

"Nice rooms, aren't they?" said Ablendan. "They're kept for dignitaries. You know, the duke of this or that, or someone's rich aunt who's considering donating to the school. Lovely view. Look. There's a ship going by. Probably a trader from Lastane."

"I'm not interested in the view," said Severan. "What I'm interested in is how you managed to waste three days riding up from Hearne. Did you detour to go fishing? Stop to take a large number of long naps?"

"Don't be ridiculous. I came straight here. As, um, fast as I could."

Ablendan's voice trailed away and he eyed the door. No one said anything. Jute looked up from the book that he was trying to decipher. He knew his letters and could sound out short words, but anything more than that was a labor. Despite this, he found books to be fascinating things (how peculiar to think you held someone else's thoughts in your hand).

"Well?" said Severan.

"All right," said Ablendan, sighing. "I'll tell you. I was only a day's ride south of here—I came straight from Hearne on the boniest wretch of a nag in existence—when it happened."

"When what happened?"

"I was turned into a mouse."

Everyone considered this for a moment in silence. The hawk eyed Ablendan with interest, as if trying to imagine what a meal of such a mouse would entail.

"You were turned into a mouse," said Severan.

"Er, yes."

The story came out quickly, now that the worst part was over. Or, rather, nearly the worst part.

"I stopped for the night. I made a fire and had a bite to eat. Then, in the darkness on the other side of the fire, I saw a pair of glaring eyes. I choked on my bread and cheese at the sight. It was a huge dog, like a mastiff but even bigger. There was something enchanted about the brute, for I could see right through portions of it. It faded in and out of sight. One second, I could see the trees behind the creature, the next moment it was the horror itself, stalking closer and closer. I didn't know what to do. It was like being turned to stone, waiting for death with all of its glaring eyes and fangs. I tried to think of a spell, anything that would help. But the only thing that came to mind—er, well. . ."

"You turned yourself into a mouse?"

"It worked, didn't it?" said Ablendan. "You should have seen the look of astonishment on the brute's face. I hightailed it down a gopher hole before it could blink. The only problem was, next morning, I couldn't remember how to turn myself back into a man. It was a long walk to the Stone Tower."

"After all our years studying and teaching. The best you can do is turn yourself into a mouse."

"I'm not at all surprised," said the hawk. "All of you so-called wizards are more interested in words than in the actual living of life itself. It weakens the mind. If I had happened along several days ago, I would've eaten you for lunch and you'd have been all the better for it."

This was, perhaps, one of the more tactless things that could have been said at that moment. Ablendan stomped out of the room.

"A mouse," said the hawk. "Words and more words."

"But I thought that words are important," said Jute. "That they shape life."

"They are important," said the hawk. "But you must understand that the shaping of the world is over. The words that were to be spoken have been spoken. There's only danger in them now. They're secrets best left to be forgotten. They should not be sought out."

"What about the Dark?" said Severan. "And the wihht? Creatures like that will find all the secrets first if no one else does. I can't agree with you. Every word must be sought and found."

"Didn't you hear your fellow scholars?" said the hawk. "Some of them don't even believe in the Dark. While you're scrabbling after a word here and there, the Dark comes creeping in. It gains strength from the unbelief of men. I would feel much more kindly about wizards if their search for wisdom was chiefly to aid the battle against the Dark." The hawk hopped up onto the back of Jute's chair. "We should leave. Now. We should've never come here. No bath or bed, I'm afraid, but you've had a good meal, so that's something."

"I don't mind about baths," said Jute, "but I would've liked a proper bed. My back feels like a knotted rope from sleeping on the ground. Must we leave? They don't seem all that bad. Just old. The stew was very good."

"Old?" Severan bristled at him. "Old? I'll have you know that there are only three in the Stone Tower who are older than myself."

"Exactly," said Jute, who did not mean to be unkind.

Severan scowled and strode to the door. "All right, though I think this place would be just as safe as Harlech. I'll see about some supplies."

The door slammed behind him.

"Touchy," said the hawk.

"He's been a good friend," said Jute.

"I'm not saying he hasn't, but the important thing is getting you to a safe place, not preserving the feelings of our pet wizard. And this tower is not safe."

"What do you mean?" said Jute. "It seems safe to me. All these wizards, and a great stone building like this out in the middle of nowhere. Why, I couldn't even see the place because of that warded plant—"

"Lichen."

"—and besides, even if something did show up here, I'm sure they could just turn it into a frog or something, couldn't they? After all, they're wizards."

"Wizards or not," said the hawk, "I don't like this tower. Secrets can't be kept in this place. All the boys here already know who you are, Jute. Obviously, that fat fool Ablendan could not keep his mouth shut. Turned himself into a mouse. That's all his learning's good for. Besides, there's too much noise here. The whispering in the stone. It makes me nervous."

"I agree," said Ronan. He paced back and forth, his brow furrowed. "We shouldn't have stopped here. There's plenty of food and shelter in the hills. Even when I was a boy, I knew enough to survive out in the wild. No need to worry on that regard."

"Oh, all right," said Jute. "I don't mind." He had been looking forward to a proper bed. However, if he had to sleep out in the heather, then that was that. He was finding himself much in awe of Ronan, despite the memory of chimneys and being pushed down them and left for dead.

"Let's be off," said the hawk. "At least you've had a good lunch. We'll thank the council, or whatever they call themselves, collect Severan if he desires to continue on to Harlech, and we'll be off. Back to the open sky."

But when Ronan set his hand on the door, it was locked.

"Confound the old man," he said. "He's locked us in."

"I'm sure it was an accident," said Jute. "Here, I've got a bit of wire."

"I know how to pick locks, thank you." Ronan crouched down by the door and fiddled for a while with a thin blade.

"Well?" said the hawk.

Ronan's face was red. "It's an odd lock. I can't find any tumblers."

"I'll have a go, then," said Jute in a pleased tone of voice.

But he could not pick the lock either. It was infuriating.

"Let me have a look," said the hawk.

"What are you going to do?" said Jute. "Pick it with your beak?"

"Don't be silly. Just hold me up to the lock so I can touch it. A bit higher. Aha. As I suspected."

"What?"

"It's magic, of course. What else would you expect? I doubt there are any of those tumblers you mentioned, whatever they are."

"Well, then say a spell or something."

"I'm a hawk. Not a wizard. I don't know any spells."

Ronan ran his hand over the door. "Oak. Too stout to break." He shrugged. "There's always the window."

The hawk fluttered over to the sill. "Would you be so kind as to open it? Thank you. Right, then. Let's be off."

"There's one problem."

"What's that?" said the bird.

"Neither the boy nor I happens to fly."

"True. It's a pity about you, but I think in a pinch the boy can."

"I can?" said Jute. "No, I can't. You were going to teach me, but you never did. It's a bit late for that now, isn't it?"

"There's nothing to it. Just jump."

"Just jump? That's it?"

"Luckily, we're high up. The wind will notice and catch you. Look, if it's a matter of life and death, the wind will know what to do."

Jute leaned out the window and glanced down. They were extremely high up. He could see several people down in the courtyard at the foot of the cliff. They looked tiny. "I'm not going to jump."

"Of course you are," said the hawk. "The wind won't let you fall."

"I don't know that. I'm not jumping."

"Well," said the hawk, eyeing Ronan thoughtfully.

"No. I know what you're thinking. I'm not about to toss him out the window." Ronan leaned out of the window also and looked down.

"You'd better not," said Jute. "It was bad enough when you chucked me down that chimney."

"Oh, hush," said the hawk. "If you aren't willing to try jumping out the window, then you'll have to climb out and up the cliff."

"Now that," said Ronan, "can be done."

But he spoke too hastily, as he soon discovered, for the surface of the rock was so smooth that he could not get a handhold on it. The lichen itself instantly crumbled into dust at the slightest touch.

"I still think it was just a mistake," said Jute. "Why don't we hammer on the door until someone comes and lets us out?"

"It wasn't a mistake," said the hawk. "That door was deliberately locked with a spell. I'm not saying Severan's responsible, but it's locked. Come now, Jute. Just jump out the window. There's nothing to be afraid of."

"That's all right for you two if it works," said Ronan. "But I don't think the wind will catch me, will it?"

"I'm afraid not," said the hawk. "But rest assured that you've been a great help so far."

"Look," said Jute. "There's a carriage driving up the lane. I could yell and get their attention. Why don't we do that?

"I've a better idea," said Ronan. He would have explained what his idea was had not Jute shot away from the window like a scalded cat.

"It's him!" Jute's face was white.

"What do you mean, it's him?" said the hawk.

"The wihht!"

Ronan peered over the window casement. Far below, a grand carriage pulled up in the courtyard. It was drawn by four horses and, even at that distance, he could see that they were stamping and blowing, their dark coats streaked with sweat. Someone—the coachman, perhaps—was soothing the lead horse. A cloaked figure stood speaking to several of the older men from the Stone Tower. Ronan could almost make out the faces of the older men—at least, the tops of their balding heads—but he could see only the hood of the cloaked man.

"It's odd to be going around cloaked and hooded on a sunny day," said Ronan. "But that doesn't mean he's your wihht."

"He's not *my* wihht and it certainly *is* him," said Jute. He crept over to Ronan's side and peeked down. "I can feel it. It's him, I tell you."

As if he had heard these words, the cloaked figure looked up at that moment. Even at that great distance, there was no mistaking the pale features of the man who had once been Nio Secganon. It was too far to tell, but it seemed as though a smile crossed the man's face. He and the other men disappeared from view as they entered the Stone Tower.

"Burn the crows," growled the hawk. "How'd he find us here? The Dark's at work, and there's no mistake about that. Jute, you'll have to jump and that's all there is to it."

"But I can't," said poor Jute. "What if it doesn't work? What if he's waiting down below?"

"What if? What if?" said the hawk. "What if the stars fall from the sky and land on your head?"

"I've another idea," said Ronan. "Quickly now!"

Ronan's plan didn't seem much more reassuring than the hawk's. It involved dangling Jute out the window via two knotted together sheets. "And then," said Ronan, "I'll swing you back and forth until you grab the railing of that balcony down there. Then you can find your way back up here and open the door for us from the outside."

"Not a bad idea," said the hawk. "Assuming the spell's only to keep the door locked from the inside. I still think throwing him out the window is the best plan."

"But what if the balcony's locked and I can't get in?"

"We'll have to chance that," said Ronan.

"But what if I get lost and can't find my way back up to this room?"

"Oh, stop complaining."

In no time at all, Jute was dangling out the window at the end of the knotted sheets. Above him, Ronan's face slowly turned red with the strain of trying to get Jute swinging.

"Don't drop me!" said Jute.

"Don't tempt me. Kick your legs out at the end of each swing. No! Blast it! Not now! Wait until you're nearing the end of the arc. Good. That's better."

The balcony grew closer with each successive swing. However, it became apparent that it was just out of reach, even at the end of the widest swing, and Ronan's arms were growing tired.

"You're going to have to jump!" he called down.

"Yes, and perhaps you'll miss," said the hawk unkindly. "That'll teach you a thing or two, despite your unbelief."

"All right then," said Jute, gulping hard. "On the next swing. No, the next. One, two, here I go!"

Jute let go of the sheet and went sailing through the air. For one sickening second, he thought he had misjudged the distance and that he was about to discover the truth, or lack of truth, in the hawk's claim. But then he grabbed onto the railing, wrenching his arms badly, and dangled for a moment from the side of the balcony, gasping and sweating.

To Jute's relief, the balcony door was not locked. He opened it and found himself in what looked like someone's study. At any other time, he would have been delighted at being in such a place, for it was full of interesting things just waiting to be stolen. A desk in one corner was piled with books and the shelves were crammed with more books, odd-looking skulls, boxes carved of bone, silver candlesticks, and bottles and jars of all sorts of substances. Several paintings leaned in one corner, covered over with a blanket. The outside one, however, was not completely covered, and he glimpsed a face staring from behind the blanket. A nasty looking face. Its eyes were staring at him.

"I'm not bothering you," said Jute, but the skin on the back of his neck prickled.

He eased open another door into a gloomy passageway lined with other doors, all closed. For the life of him, he wasn't sure whether to go left or right. Footsteps pattered down the passage and Jute shrank back into the doorway. A figure bobbed into view and he saw that it was the small boy from the stairs. The boy was hurrying along with his head down and didn't see Jute until he was quite close.

"Oh!" said the boy, jumping back. "It's you." He looked nervously over his shoulder.

"Can you show me the way up to the next floor?" said Jute. "I'm afraid I've lost my way."

"I shouldn't talk to you," said the boy. "I got in heaps of trouble for talking to you before. I've been told to go dust the attic and no one can abide doing that. I hate it. I had to do it once before when I broke a window. It's full of ghosts, you see."

"I'm sorry I got you in trouble, but I do need help."

"Very well," said the boy, who was the sort that didn't need much persuading, particularly if it meant breaking the rules. "I'll show you the stairs. They aren't easy to find up here. They're not always there, you know. Quick, I mustn't be seen with you or I'll really catch it. My name's Lano."

They hurried along, though Lano glanced back occasionally as if to assure himself that Jute was following him. He led Jute a bewildering, twisting, and turning way. They passed through a series of dark hallways, relieved here and there with doors and the occasional painting. Jute was careful not to look at the paintings. He was sure they all had eyes and were watching him.

"What is this place?" he said to the little boy.

Lano blushed at this question. "Oh, er, this is where the professors have their studies."

"Isn't there just a staircase that goes to the attic?"

Lano managed to turn even more red.

"I, um, borrowed a book."

He showed Jute a book he had tucked under his shirt. Jute did not say anything, but perhaps his face betrayed a sort of encouragement. After all, he was a thief.

"I love to read," said Lano. "I've read all the books in the library and I saw this one on Master Tosca's desk. I'll read it quickly and then return it before he'll even notice it's missing. You won't say anything, will you?"

"Of course not," said Jute.

They came to a landing. A stairway rose up past them.

"Here you are," said Lano. He paused, fidgeting a bit, and then said, "I don't suppose you'd do a wind spell, would you? Maybe call up a zephyr or a breeze to do your bidding?"

"I'm afraid I don't know any spells," said Jute, wishing that he did. Being able to call up a zephyr or a breeze to do his bidding sounded like a lot of fun.

"You don't know a single one?" said the little boy in disbelief.

"Not one."

"I suppose you can fly though, can't you?"

"Um, no."

"Worse and worse. I can do lots of spells. Nearly as many as a second year. Some of the second years aren't all that bright."

Lano hurried up the stairs with him, still chattering away. "I got into the Stone Tower because I could shape-shift and talk to animals. Farm animals, mostly. My pa's a farmer and so was his before him. They could all shift, but they did it mostly to herd the sheep and such. Cows and chickens are the easiest, even though chickens don't like talking about much besides food and who can lay the biggest egg and endlessly retelling the legend of the giant, blood-sucking fox and when's he going to return. I can shift to most farm animals. Goats are chancy, of course. They can tell if you aren't a goat and just go ahead and butt you or trample you and they'll yell stuff like, 'Take that, you stupid git!' or 'Get outta my way!' I don't like goats."

They came to the door. Jute tried it. It was locked and the handle stung his hand.

"It's locked," said Lano helpfully.

"Yes, I know that." Jute frowned and then thought of something. "I don't suppose you know how to undo a locking spell, do you?"

Lano touched the door handle and winced.

"I don't know," he said. "If you get these things wrong, they can be messy."

"Oh well, never mind. I suppose it's the sort of spell that only second year students learn."

"I didn't say I couldn't do it," protested Lano. "Here, let me see."

His hands hovered over the door handle and he muttered a few unintelligible words to himself.

"I'm afraid this is a good spell."

"What about the hinges?"

"Oh? Oh, right. Um, I might be able to convince the pins to undo themselves. What's the word? Aha. Um. . . that's it. No—drat it. That's not it. They won't listen to me. They're iron. Iron's tricky."

"You can't do it," said Jute.

"Uh, no."

"If we only had something to knock the door down," said Jute, glancing around the hallway. "The wood surely can't be all that thick. If I only had an axe or something like that. You don't happen to know a spell to create an axe, do you? No. I didn't think so."

"But I might be able to knock it down," said Lano.

"How would you know a spell to knock it down, if you don't even know a spell to unlock it?"

"No, I meant *I* might be able to knock it down."

"How?"

"I'll shape-shift into a goat. Just stay out of my way or I might feel inclined to butt you. You wouldn't want that."

Jute ducked into an alcove off the hall and then peeped out in time to see a small, mangy-looking goat gallop by. There was a stunning crash. The goat staggered away from the door and shook its head.

"Did it work?" said Jute.

The goat glared at him and looked as if it were considering having a go at him. Jute ducked back into the alcove. Once again, the goat galloped by. This time, the crash sounded splintery. There was another crash and more splinters as Ronan kicked out the hole in the door from the other side. He forced his way through. The hawk hopped after him.

"Where on earth did you find a goat?" said Ronan.

"That's not a goat," said the hawk.

There was a ripple in the air around the goat. It vanished, and Lano stood in front of them.

"Ow," groaned the little boy. "I'm going to have a headache for a week."

"Hurry, now," said the hawk. "He'll not be long in finding us."

No one had to ask who the hawk meant by this, though Lano looked at him in wonder. Being able to talk to animals in their own tongue was one thing, but encountering an animal that spoke the language of man was a different matter.

They hurried to the stairs and looked down. From far below, they heard the sound of hurrying footsteps and voices. No one was visible on the stairs, but it seemed like the gloom deepened and was ascending toward them.

"He's coming," said the hawk, "and he isn't alone. What has happened to this place? The Dark has some secret foothold here, I fear. A pox on all wizards!"

"Boy," said Ronan, turning to Lano. "Is there a way out of this place other than down the stairs?"

"Well, there's the back stairs. They aren't used much except by the servants and us boys. You have to go all the way up to the attic to reach them from here—as far as I know—and then they only go halfway down to the sixth floor."

"And then how do you go from there?"

"Well, the main stairs, of course."

They dashed up the stairs. The stairs narrowed and narrowed until they came to a small, cramped landing. They found themselves before a shabby door that looked as if it had not been opened in a long time.

The attic was not like any other attic Jute had ever seen, and Jute had seen quite a few attics during his days as a thief. Not that such occasions had been a part of belonging to the Juggler's band, as their official duties had always been restricted to pickpocketing, thieving from the market barrow carts, and other such things. However, he and Lena and several other children had sometimes spent their free time breaking into houses. He had spent many a happy hour investigating the contents of unfamiliar attics.

The attic of the Stone Tower, however, was a different affair. A gloomy light illumined the place, though it was difficult to say where the light came from. It seemed imbued in the wood planking and the beams that ran through the ceiling like the ribs of some gigantic animal. The attic was enormous. It stretched away in all directions. Jute could not see any walls in any direction.

"It's best not to talk to the ghosts here," said Lano.

"Why's that?" said Ronan.

"Even a single word. It gives them the right to follow you. My friend Gewose once made the mistake of asking a ghost up here if it knew the time. It followed him after he left the attic. Wouldn't leave him for days. Stayed up all night by his bed telling him stories about dust and moonlight and how much space there is between the end of one minute and the beginning of another. The conversation about the minute went on for two days, but it was mostly one-sided."

"Right," said Ronan. "No talking to ghosts."

Dust rose in the air with their footsteps. The space was filled with odd stacks and shapes: old boxes piled high until they towered and teetered overhead, gaunt outlines of furniture stripped away by time until they resembled more the skeletons of strange beasts rather than couches and wardrobes and armoires and bookcases.

The ghosts began to appear. At first, they looked like a trick of the gloom and shadows, but then they resolved into shapes as if heartened by the presence of the living. They seemed to be mostly old men, though Jute did glimpse two boys crouching over what looked like a game of marbles.

"Splendid day, isn't it?" said one ghost, drifting closer to Jute.

"They'll never answer," said a second ghost. "It's most uncouth."

"Where's that staircase?" said the hawk.

"I'm not sure," said Lano. "I know it's up here somewhere."

"Everything is up here somewhere," said a ghost. "Everything. Depending on your point of view."

"That's just perfect." The hawk scowled at the little boy. "You might've mentioned that before. We could spend the next hour searching this place and never be wiser."

"What's one hour when they're free for the taking?" said a ghost.

"The answer's simple," said Ronan. "I'm surprised, master hawk, you haven't thought of it yourself."

"Oh?" said the hawk. "How's that?"

"Yes," agreed another ghost. "Do tell."

"We'll ask a ghost."

"That's what we shouldn't do," said Lano hastily.

"Capital plan," said a ghost. "Don't listen to the little squit. He's obviously inbred. Looks suspiciously like a goat, too."

"Excellent," said another.

"Brilliant bird," said a third. "Sound thinking. I almost like him."

"But who's going to ask?" said Jute. "I don't want a ghost following me around for the next week. Things are strange enough as they are."

"Things can always get worse," said a ghost. "Why, I could tell you a story that would curdle your blood like rancid milk on a hot summer day. By the way, what is milk? I've forgotten."

"I think our little friend should ask," said the hawk. "After all, we're guests under his roof."

"You think so?" said a ghost. "Not that I've anything against this young twit, but he doesn't strike me as a decent conversationalist, if you know what I mean. Probably all screaming and wailing and rushing about with his eyes bugging out whenever you come popping up from under the bed. That's how he'll behave, I daresay. It's enough to put anyone off. Now yourself, or this tall fellow with the sword, you both look like you've some staying power."

"Excellent idea," said Ronan, ignoring the ghost. "Let's have the boy ask."

"I won't!" said Lano, crossing his arms and trying to look stern.

"You will," said the hawk urgently. "Look, boy, death is coming up the stairs. If we waste more time here, several of us'll be dead before the hour's out, including you."

"And I suppose one of us could die a bit sooner," added Ronan. He tapped thoughtfully on the hilt of his sword.

"It isn't fair," said Lano in despair. "Oh, very well." He gulped and then addressed a scrawny old ghost hovering nearby. "Excuse me, sir?"

"Yes, what's that?" said the ghost, startled on being singled out.

"Um, do you know where the stairs are that lead down into the servants' quarters? My friends—" Here, Lano shot a dirty look over his shoulder at the rest of them. "My friends and I need to find them in a hurry."

"Of course," said the ghost in delight. "My dear boy, nothing could be simpler. I'll take you there myself. The back stairs, you say? Come to think of it, I haven't been down those stairs in a hundred years. I might have a jaunt and come along with you."

"I was afraid you'd say that," groaned the little boy.

"Stairs, you know, exciting stuff," said the ghost. "Rise and run. Rise and run. Rise and run. Or is it run and rise? All depends on where you start first, I suppose. For the life of me—between you and me, I'm not all that alive—I can't remember who invented stairs. It's one of those puzzlers that keeps you up at night, just thinking about it. Did one fellow invent the rise and then some other fellow, unconnected to the first fellow, invent the run?"

"We have yet to move from this spot," said the hawk. "Advise your ghost that time is of the utmost importance."

"He's not my ghost," said Lano, but he then sternly addressed the ghost. "Sir, we need to get to those stairs. Time's running out."

"It is?" said the ghost. "I had no idea. Upon my soul. This bears some consideration. Do you know how much time is left?"

"Don't be a nitwit," said another ghost. "It's not an issue of how much is left. Time itself is running out, don't you see? It's running out the door, but whether it's a dog or a man or something else entirely, I don't know. Interesting problem, though. What do you think?"

This last question was addressed to Jute who, feeling dizzy from all this talk, unthinkingly opened his mouth to reply.

"I don't know," said Jute.

"That's torn it," said Ronan. "Now we have two of 'em."

"I'm sorry!" wailed Jute. "I wasn't thinking!"

"Precisely," said the hawk.

"Oh, I don't know about that," said the second ghost, greatly pleased at this turn of events. "Admitting that one doesn't know a thing is the mark of a genuine thinker. In my career as a professor in the Stone Tower—at least, I think I was a professor. Perhaps I was the cook?—I found that my worst students were those who thought they knew the answers. The best students were those who admitted their ignorance and then allowed me to correct the handicap. Not that such handicaps are always correctable, mind you, for youthful ignorance is a condition that isn't easily reversible."

"I think," said Ronan, "that I will soon prefer death to this babbling. Where are those blasted stairs?"

"My dear sir," protested a fat ghost, "you malign death with such a remark. It isn't such a bad state of affairs. You should try it sometime. The company, of course, leaves a bit to be desired."

"Shut yer trap, fatty," said another ghost.

"Where are the back stairs!" shouted Lano.

"You needn't bellow so," said the scrawny ghost. "I heard you the first time. You don't think just because I'm ghost that I have a bad memory, do you? With some ghosts, you'd be correct. But that's due to the fact that as you are in life, so you are in death."

"Tell him to show us the stairs before I wring your neck," said Ronan.

"The stairs!" said Lano.

"Right this way," said the scrawny ghost. "You won't mind if I accompany you, will you? Of course not. Despite your youth, I think you'll prove a splendid conversationalist."

The scrawny ghost led them through the gloomy darkness of the attic. Behind them trailed a whole crowd of decidedly grumpy ghosts—grumpy, of course, because it had not been any of them who had had the good fortune to coax a response out of one of the living. Their guide stopped beside a pile of moldy fur skins.

"What a stench," said Jute.

"Otter pelts," said his ghost, and he launched into a discourse on the differences between the ocean otter and its smaller cousin, the freshwater otter.

"Here it is," said the scrawny ghost. And there it was. A trapdoor set into the planks. It was so covered with dust that they certainly would not have found it on their own. Ronan wrenched the door up to reveal stairs vanishing down into the darkness.

"Jute and I'll go first," said the hawk. "Hurry. We've wasted too much time."

"All right then. Liven it up."

But even as Ronan spoke, something changed in the air in the attic. There was a chill to it that had not been there before. The meager light dimmed until it was nearly gone. The shadows deepened. Even the crowd of watching ghosts seemed somehow changed. Their forms thickened and there was menace in their stares.

"Not all of us thought so poorly of the Dark," whispered someone in the crowd.

"Aye," said another. "The Dark wouldn't have chained us to this place. It would've let us go free. It would've wanted us to be free."

The chill deepened. The trapdoor felt impossibly heavy in Ronan's grip. Somewhere far off in the attic, there came the sound of footsteps and creaking planks.

"Jute!" said the hawk.

Jute dove down the stairs with the hawk clinging to his shoulder. Behind him, he could hear Lano stumbling along. Even their two ghosts had fallen silent, though he could see them by the strange pale light that they shed. Part of his mind realized, in a pleased fashion, that this was why the attic was lit. It was the ghosts. The rest of Jute's mind, however, gibbered in frantic panic. The wihht! The trapdoor closed softly overhead and Ronan hurried after them on silent feet.

"It doesn't matter how quiet you are," said the hawk. "The wihht doesn't need to hear to follow our path."

"Then run!" said Ronan.

And run, they did. Clattering and jumping down the stairs. Strands of cobwebs broke across their faces. The stairs were dusty and dark and so cramped that they had to proceed in single file.

"What's following us?" gasped Lano.

"A wihht," said Jute.

"What's that?"

"What sort of question is that?" said the scrawny ghost. "Why, if you were my student, you'd be writing out twenty pages on wihhts. I'm shocked at such ignorance!"

"If you're so clever," said Lano, "then why don't you tell me what a wihht is."

"Very well," said the ghost. "There'll be a test on this later. Pay attention and don't shirk your note-taking."

"Tell your ghost to be quiet!" said the hawk.

They clattered down stairs that, judging from the dust and the sheets of cobwebs that hung spun from wall to wall, had not been used for years. Jute caught a glimpse of something scuttling away into the shadows. It looked uncomfortably fat and furry with many horrid legs scrabbling about (many more legs than a spider). What did such things trap and eat, so far up here in the dark? Surely there were no flies buzzing about there.

The scrawny ghost paid no attention to the hawk and launched into a lecture on wihhts. "There's a lot written about 'em that's pure rubbish," it said. "Especially the more modern writers. Rubbish. Not worth the paper they're written on. Some claim you can create wihhts out of neutral material, but there are two problems with that. First off, there's no such thing as neutral material. Everything has a bent this way or that, see? Second, the sort of savage twisting and reshaping required to create a wihht automatically precludes anything good coming of the thing. It naturally will adhere to the Dark."

They had descended at least four flights, if not more. The stairs turned and wound around themselves at sharp angles. There was not any particular method to the turns. Sometimes, they came after only five steps, or twelve, or even as many as twenty-one. Jute's lungs burned and he had a painful stitch in his side.

"How many stories in all," said Ronan, "including the attic, are in this place?"

"Oh, thirteen," said Lano. "I think."

"Fifteen," said Jute's ghost. "One of the strictures of teaching is that boys know nothing. As expected, this boy knows nothing. In my days as a professor here, it wasn't uncommon to have boys in class that knew even less than nothing."

"Seventeen," said the other ghost.

"Quiet," said the hawk. "Be quiet all of you, for one moment!"

They stopped and turned to look up the stairs. Jute could not hear anything and he could tell from the frown on Ronan's face that he heard nothing as well.

"He's on the stairs," said the hawk. "And he isn't alone. I don't think this Stone Tower will be a safe place from now on, for I fear he's freed some of the ghosts, just as they wished. Those who would be naturally inclined to the Dark. We must hurry now."

"As I was saying," said Lano's ghost, "before I was rudely interrupted, wihhts are always created with a binding of the Dark. That is, the Dark in some form (whether it be a strand of shadow or death or nightmare, or something of that kind) is woven together with some sort of natural material. Earth, wood, stone, flesh (dead flesh works best if it's fresh), various plants, water. Water, however, is a chancy material for wihhts. It has to be dark water. That is, water that's spent a great deal of time below ground."

"Oh, hush up," said the other ghost.

Lano's ghost, startled at this betrayal, subsided into a mumbling grumble as he trailed behind them down the stairs. They came then to the bottom of the stairs. It was a wide landing stacked with wooden chests and old furniture. They had to clear their way to a door at the far end.

"Servants' quarters through there," said Lano. "I think." He darted an apprehensive glance at his ghost, but it was sulking and not paying attention.

It was the servants' quarters. There was a smell of laundry and fresh bread in the air. They passed startled looking faces in a drawing room of sorts—some resting over their tea, some gossiping quietly in their corners. The hallway was narrow and shabby, but it was swept clean and well lit.

"Not done in my day," said Jute's ghost primly. "We didn't mix with the servants."

"This will help us," said the hawk.

"What do you mean?" said Ronan.

"More lives." The hawk glanced at an old lady who curtseyed as they passed her. "More lives around us will obscure the trail for the wihht. Rather like footprints from many people walking down the same path. It'll have to stop and determine which belong to us. Which footprints belong to Jute."

They rounded a corner into a wider hallway. Windows opened out to the west and they saw sunlight and the shining water down in the bay. There were many boys here.

"Hey, Lano's with the wind lord!" someone yelled.

"It's the wind lord!"

Other boys took up the shout, and soon the hallway was filled with boys smiling and cheering and trying to catch Jute's eye. It was embarrassing, and Jute was not sure what to make of it.

"One side!" bellowed Ronan. "Let us through!"

The boys surged along with them. Lano smiled and nodded grandly at acquaintances.

"To the stairs!" called Lano.

"What's the occasion?" yelled a boy, sticking his head out of a door, a book in one hand and a quill in the other.

"The wind lord's going to call up the wind and we're going to see some real spells. None of this boring old reading."

"What about the professors? We'll catch it—"

"Boo on the professors!

"And boo on schoolwork!"

"To the stairs!"

The boys cheered, for they were glad of any excuse to abandon their studies. There were several dozen of them. They were on the stairs now and there were furious shouts from two old men stationed there. Jute caught a glimpse of angry eyes with something dark and deadly sliding behind them. Something that knew him. But then the face was gone, pushed away by the crowd of boys hurrying down the steps around him.

"The wihht has help within these walls," said the hawk in Jute's ear. "It is well, I think, that these lads are bent on an impromptu holiday. Once we're under the sky, we'll be safer. And there're several hours between now and sundown."

The entire procession came to the bottom of the stairs and into the entrance hall. Oddly enough, not a single professor was in sight. This did not seem to give any of the boys cause for concern. They threw open the front doors and poured out into the courtyard, talking and laughing. A breeze blew through the eucalyptus trees, carrying leaves and the scent of the sea and the trees with it. It eddied through the courtyard and spun the boys surging around Jute and Ronan so that the boys, too, seemed like leaves to Jute.

Aye, said the hawk inside his mind. *You begin to see the way you are meant to see. They are indeed like leaves, and just as quickly will they fall to the ground.*

What do you mean? said Jute, not understanding the bird, but understanding the touch of the wind on his skin and in his hair. He wanted the sky. *How can they be like leaves?*

"We must get away from this place," said Ronan. "But how? There are no horses, and it looks like quite a climb to the top of the valley."

"If I might suggest something."

It was the scruffy ghost, the one that had attached itself to Lano. In the bright sunshine, it wavered in and out of sight as if the light was too much for the definition of its form.

"Speak on," said the hawk, addressing the ghost. "Speak on, but quickly."

"Thank you for looking at me," said the ghost, somewhat abashed. "I remember you, master hawk. Somewhere in my memories. When I was alive and young, and you were already old. Now I'm dead but you still live."

"We all have our appointed time to die," said the hawk. "But what would you say?"

"I think," said the ghost, "that I have a memory. I think I once read that wihhts fear the sea."

"If that's true, then we're in luck," said Ronan. "Look, there're several small boats at anchor in the bay."

"Thank you, ghost," said the hawk. "Though you're dead, you might've saved many lives today if your words are true."

"Don't mention it," said the ghost, looking embarrassed.

They were under the shadows of the eucalyptus lane now. Leaves and the hard pods of the trees crunched underfoot. The boys ran with them, but more quietly now, for Lano must have whispered what he knew to his friends. Many a backward glance was given as they hurried along, back at the bright, sunlight-splashed clearing at the foot of the cliff and the blank windows carved into the rocks.

"A mouse!" someone called, and a small boy pounced. He crowed triumphantly and stuck the mouse in his pocket.

"And there's another," said someone else, but then an older boy frowned and said, "Hush now." They all felt it, and they bunched uncomfortably near Ronan and Jute.

"Never mind," said the hawk to Ronan's glance. "As long as they don't slow us. It's better for them all to be out of that place."

"Look!" said someone.

Everyone looked back down the lane to see a strange darkness come flowing out of the open doors of the Stone Tower. It had no form. It was like a fog that grew and drifted across the ground. They all stared, fascinated and horrified, even the hawk. The fog wavered, as if in indecision, and then it thickened until, out of it, strode the figure of a man formed out of darkness. Behind him, other shapes flickered: Shadows cast by no bodies, sliding across the stones and the hardened earth of the clearing, heading straight for the lane and all those who stood entranced watching. A hissing snarl filled the air.

"Run!" screamed someone.

"Excellent advice," said the hawk. "You did say there were boats down in the bay, didn't you?"

"Yes," said Ronan.

Lano overheard this and promptly shouted out that everyone should run for the bay and the boats there. This did not result in any modification in what was happening, as everyone was running pell-mell already down the lane between the eucalyptus trees, which headed toward the bay itself. Beyond the trees and over a grassy meadow, Jute could see the tops of several masts swaying back and forth. A rickety looking fence made of split rails stood at the edge of the meadow. Over this they scrambled and then fled across the meadow. The grass underfoot gave way to sandy earth and then the pebbled strand that lay before the lazy waves. Four boats bobbed at anchor some distance out from the shore. A skiff was drawn up high on the beach. A mob of boys fell on the skiff and wrestled it into the water. Fists flew as they all sought to scramble in. The skiff sank lower and lower as more boys clambered aboard. There was a sense of hysteria in the air.

"That's torn it," said Ronan. "They're bound to sink. We'll have to swim. Aim for the last boat on the left. Jute, can you swim?"

"Of course," said Jute scornfully.

The hawk flapped by overhead.

"Hurry!" the bird called.

Jute plunged out into the water. A wave smacked him in the face and he sputtered and gasped. Several yards away, the skiff sank to the accompaniment of a chorus of yells and screams. The boys scattered from it, some swimming strongly and others paddling along like dogs. The boat was anchored further out than Jute had thought. Things like that always looked different from the shore. The hawk landed on the railing of the boat and settled his wings.

"Right," said Ronan from somewhere nearby. "Over the side, but be careful not to tip it."

Jute clambered up over the side of the boat. It lurched a bit, but not much, for it was a stout little boat with a wide beam and a deep keel, perfect for sailing the rough seas of the northern coast. Ronan followed him over and immediately drew his sword to dry it with some rags he found in the boat.

"At least we left the ghosts behind," said Jute.

"Don't worry," said his ghost cheerfully. It was sitting on the railing beside him. "I'm still here. I thought I'd forgotten how to swim, but I just floated along. What a lovely day it is. The sun's on the bright side, though, don't you think?"

Soon there was a second ghost, as Lano and two other boys swam up and hauled themselves into the boat. Ronan frowned but did not say anything.

"Look," said the hawk.

A figure stood on the shore. Darkness lay about him like a cloud that the sun could not pierce. Shadows hovered around him. The figure did not move but stared straight out at them. There was a distance of perhaps a hundred yards between them and the shore, but even this did not seem enough to Jute.

"Can't we go?" he said nervously.

"We're safe enough for now," said the hawk, "though we shouldn't stay here long. There's no telling what else might turn up, and some servants of the Dark aren't so bothered by the sea as others. But for the moment, we're in no better spot. Well done, ghost."

"Oh?" said the ghost, startled at being complimented again. "Thank you."

"Have any of you ever sailed a boat before?"

The hawk looked around expectantly. It turned out that no one had ever sailed a boat before, though one of boys said his family lived next door to a fisherman who had drowned at sea many years ago.

"I've never sailed a boat," said Ronan. He paused and looked out at the sea as if he saw something there that no one else did. "I've never been in a boat before, but I think I'll be able to sail this one."

"I daresay you're right," said the hawk.

And Ronan was able to sail the boat. He set about it unerringly, even though, as he had said, he had never sailed a boat before. There was an old sail, heavy with oil and veined with much stitching, rolled in a compartment below the tiller. He soon had this raised and flapping from the mast.

"Jute," he said. "Pull up that rope there."

"What you're pulling up is called an anchor," said his ghost helpfully.

Jute crawled out onto the prow and hauled up the rope, slimy and green with algae. This prompted his ghost to launch into a long-winded discussion of the health benefits of freshwater algae versus saltwater algae, but Jute paid no attention, although from the argument that ensued as he pulled up the rope, it sounded as if Lano's ghost was outraged by the first ghost's claim that saltwater algae was a key ingredient in the remedy for indigestion.

The anchor rope proved too heavy for Jute after he had taken in the slack, and Lano and the two other boys heaved along with him until the anchor came up. The boys seemed to have forgotten the fright of running down the lane of eucalyptus with the darkness behind them. They seemed to have even forgotten what still stood motionless on the shore, but the hawk did not once move his gaze from that figure.

The sail bellied with the wind and then snapped tight. Ronan eased the tiller over and the boat crept out across the bay. Behind them, the three other boats had gotten underway in various states of shouting and argument, but there was obviously on each craft at least one boy who knew enough of boats and sailing.

"They'll follow us," said Ronan. "I don't have the heart to forbid them. If they turned about to shore now, I think I know what would happen to them."

"No," said the hawk. "And it matters little at this point. It isn't as if we're moving in secret, and it'll be no great guess on the wihht's part that we're heading north. I'll be less concerned with what that thing knows, the further north we get. The closer we get to Harlech, the more chance we have to move about freely and safely. There's power in that land and it isn't friendly to the Dark."

"We'll try along the coast as far as we can go. Averlay might be too far for this boat, but there are other towns closer." Ronan fell silent for a while and then spoke again, more to himself than to anyone else. "There's logic in how this moves, the push of the wind and the waves, and the feel of the tiller. It's almost like riding a horse."

"I don't doubt it," said the hawk. He paused and then spoke again, his voice quiet. "She doesn't give gifts lightly."

"No," said Ronan, and his hand strayed to the necklace under his shirt.

They were out past the bay and sliding past the headland that formed the northern arm of the bay. A slow, easy swell was running and the wind blew steady from the west. One of the two other boys proved to be the lad who had caught a mouse while they had been running through the eucalyptus trees. He pulled the mouse out of his pocket and amused himself by dangling the poor creature by the tail over the sea.

"One shouldn't play with one's food," said the hawk.

Abashed, the boy placed the mouse back in his pocket.

"Wait," said the hawk. "That's not a mouse."

With a sneeze and a wriggle, the mouse vanished, and a fat little man sprawled on the bottom of the boat. The boys gave a yell of alarm.

"My word," said one of the ghosts. "It's a fat man."

"Master Ablendan!" said the boy who had been playing with the mouse. "I didn't realize what—"

"Blast and burn it all!" shouted Ablendan, rubbing his backside. "Twice a mouse in one week. It's enough to make you weep!"

"I'm sorry, master," said the boy, greatly frightened. He and the other boys shrank back from the angry little man.

"No matter," said Ablendan. "No matter. You couldn't have known, and I couldn't unwind myself from that dratted spell until someone said out loud that I wasn't a mouse. That picked the knot free. Thank you, sir." This he addressed to the hawk.

"You're welcome," said the hawk.

"I hope there're no more mice on this boat," said Ronan. "We're riding low enough as it is."

"I shall loathe cats all my days," said Ablendan. He heaved himself up to the rail and looked back toward the bay. The cliffs were disappearing from sight and the Stone Tower could no longer be seen.

"Well," he said, sighing. "That's the end of that."

"What do you mean, sir?" said Lano timidly.

"Speak, wizard," said the hawk. "There's a story in your voice."

"I mean, that's the end of the school. Nio was not alone in his wickedness. The lads here know him, I'm sure, for he taught their class on the fundamentals of naming last year. I'm afraid that two of the other professors, Facen and Tosca, have proved to be his compatriots."

There was a collective gasp from the boys, as Tosca had been popular with them, being the professor who taught most of the classes on animals and animal languages. Lano turned pale, for he was a great admirer of Tosca.

"They tricked us all. Facen called a meeting of the professors after you, master hawk, and your friends went up to rest. And then, when we were in the conference hall, he turned us all into mice, except for Stow and Perl." Ablendan shuddered. "He turned them into cats. I saw Stow gobble down three mice before I had time to find the nearest hole in the wall. And Facen towering over us all like a giant, leering and laughing!"

"But, surely," said Jute, horrified and yet fascinated as well, "surely this Stow fellow would've remembered who he was and what they were."

"No," said Ablendan sadly. "It's difficult to keep one's mind clear when shifting shape into an animal. It's even more difficult when someone else turns you into an animal without a second's warning. The transformation is overwhelming. All your thoughts are consumed with the basic instincts of whichever animal you've become. My mind for the first hour was entirely devoted to terror and cheese. Dreadful."

Ablendan lapsed into gloomy silence and would not talk, but sat huddled against the railing of the boat, wrapped in his cloak. The ghosts pestered him with questions, which he did not answer. Ablendan's mood prevailed over the three boys and they fell silent as well, lost in their own thoughts that, doubtless, concerned the Stone Tower and the life they had known there.

CHAPTER EIGHTY-NINE
HARLECH MUST WAIT

Levoreth and the wolves came down from the mountains in the hills of the Mearh Dun. She knew this land better than she knew her own face in a mirror. The hills were beloved and familiar. She had spent years ranging across them, but they were no comfort to her now. They were only a distraction and an ache.

The wolves went hunting early that morning.

Daylight is not for the hunt, said the big wolf. *Daylight is for sleeping, but we run with you, Mistress. The pack is hungry and I scent meat close by. The little plains deer. Their flesh is sweet.*

Go your way, Drythen Wulf, said Levoreth. *Swallowfoot and I shall continue. But make haste with your hunt and hurry along our trail.*

The wolf growled his assent, and the pack rushed away. They shone black and brown and gray and then were gone across the grasses and vanished from sight.

Wolves, said Swallowfoot.

Levoreth laughed out loud. The first time in many hours.

We can't all eat grass. She patted the horse's neck.

Her mind would not rest. Again, the voice of the sceadu whispered through her thoughts, just as it had first done in the mountain eyrie.

I serve another.

Who? Who was her enemy?

Levoreth examined her memory, sifting through hundreds of years. There had been innumerable faces of evil down through the ages. All the lords of darkness with their might and magic and malice brought to bear against the children of men. Their names and faces flickered through her thoughts. But there had never been any more powerful than the three sceadus. None save Nokhoron Nozhan himself. But he slept in Daghoron. The sceadus had been his most dreadful creation. His supreme mockery of life.

I serve another.

She would have to enlist aid. At once. Lord Lannaslech in Harlech. And then? Who else would be trustworthy and not compromised by the Dark? Owain Gawinn in Hearne, of course. He was a sensible man, and though he was hampered by his allegiance and responsibility to that fool of a regent, he might prove clever enough to handle Botrell. But who else besides Harlech and Owain Gawinn? The dukes of Dolan, Thule, and Hull were capable men of good families. Levoreth sighed at the thought of Hennen Callas. She would not want his blood on her hands and be the making of his widow.

But the preservation of Tormay was more important than considerations of widows and orphans. Still, she would leave that to Lannaslech. He and the other lords of Harlech could easily ride to their neighboring dukes and explain. If Harlech and Hearne rode to war, then all of Tormay would follow suit.

Except for Harth, of course. The self-styled king of Harth was not a charitable fellow and it was doubtful whether he had ever forgiven the rest of Tormay for not coming quickly to his aid so many years ago, when Sond Sondlon had sought to overthrow the kingdom of Harth. Not that that reluctance had been any of Levoreth's doing.

They topped the last hill and the Scarpe Plain lay once again before them. The sun was mounting up over the Mountains of Morn in the east. The plain stretched out under the light and everywhere there was the scent of heather and the trill of birds. Swallowfoot's hooves drummed on the turf. The wind whipped the horse's mane back. Levoreth half-closed her eyes, dreaming in the morning sun.

How I wish I could return to Dolan. That nothing had happened. Go home.

And she thought of the cemetery behind the church in Andolan. *Sunlight and roses and my old love sleeping in the earth. But I think I shall never again rest beside the headstone there.* Levoreth shook her head at the thought, and the wind tangled her hair and Swallowfoot's mane until they were one and the same.

I hope the boy is safe. To think, the Wind has been born anew. The hawk will know what to do. The hawk will keep him safe until he grows into who he is meant to be. But I must call Tormay to war.

Has this whole land been sleeping as have I?

Her eyes flashed in anger and Swallowfoot quickened his gallop.

The sceadu stalking across the ballroom floor in Hearne was a dreadful evil. The house in the city huddling silently with its memories of sleep and death had rent her heart with its malevolence. But the memory of the thing in the eyrie had entirely different implications.

My strength is not equal to the task.

The plain flowed past them. Swallowfoot galloped faster and faster. The sun mounted higher in the sky. Levoreth whispered to the horse, and the earth and the sky became one, both blurring past like the wind, and the wind itself could not keep up with them. But as they rode across the plain, she heard a strange sound, faint at first, but clearer with every step Swallowfoot took. The earth shivered with it. Levoreth cried out and the horse trembled beneath her.

Mistress of Mistresses! Swallowfoot's eye swiveled white in panic at her. *What walks upon your earth?*

South! We must ride south! Harlech must wait!

Swallowfoot turned his face to the south. The sun was at their side and their shadows raced along with them. She flung her thought wide and found the wolves in the hills to the north. Their minds were full of blood and bones and the taste of flesh. She felt the old wolf raise his head from over the broken body of a deer.

We have not eaten our fill, Mistress. Not yet.

Come!

He did not question her again. The wolf pack rose as one from their kill and rushed across the hills, far off but nearing her, nearing and running toward the plain.

CHAPTER NINETY
THE DEATH OF THE FARROWS

"You've got a good hand with these colts, lass."

Giverny's father smiled up at her. She grinned in delight at his words. The horse beneath her caught her mood and danced a few steps.

"He seems to read my thoughts, Pa," she said. "I don't even have to nudge him, and he'll stop dead for me. Swerve, step back—see?"

"All right," Cullan said, laughing. He stepped out of the way as the colt whirled around in place. "Peace, little one, peace." The horse stilled itself and pushed its nose against his hand.

"Now how'd you do that?"

"I've been speaking their language for a long time now, Giverny. Longer'n three of your lives, but I reckon you'll be speaking it better 'n me when you're my age. I'd stake my life on that."

"Well, I'd stake my life on that being breakfast I smell. C'mon, Pa."

The Farrows were camped in a hollow on the Scarpe Plain. The plain stretched flat and green and windblown in every direction. The view was deceptive, however, for the Scarpe was a rolling plain full of little valleys and dells and gentle rises. It swarmed with wildlife, and through it all were many springs and seasonal streams. The Farrow wagons were circled about one such spring. The hollow was deep enough to shelter them from the wind and, when they stood down at the bottom by the spring, also deep enough to cut off the view of the surrounding plains.

Several cook-fires crackled in the encampment. Some women were hard at work over their laundry beside the spring. A dead buck hung by its hind legs from the top of a wagon wheel. Three dead rabbits dripped blood from a step. Two men knelt around another deer, their skinning knives busy. The morning hunt had already returned.

"Not bad, then?" said Cullan.

"Not bad," said one of the hunters. He shrugged. "Coulda been better. Somethin's got the animals spooked. Mebbe a storm coming."

"Mebbe."

Rumer Farrow straightened up from over the flames and smiled at her husband and daughter.

"There's porridge and honey," she said.

Up on the ridge above the hollow, the colt they had left behind raised its head. Its ears pricked forward and it stared south. The wind was blowing from the north, however, and the colt could not smell anything except porridge and honey and other horses and Farrows, of course—all the smells that meant home to the young horse. After a while, it resumed cropping the grass.

"We're running short on honey," said Rumer.

"There's a farmer up near Lastane," said her husband. "Keeps his bees in an apple orchard."

"Hearne's surely a day closer."

Giverny made a face.

"Let's not go there."

"Why not?" said her mother.

"It's too big." Giverny shivered. "The walls are too high. I don't know. I don't like it."

"The regent's reason enough to avoid the place, even though he pays good gold for horses. Other than that, the man's a scoundrel, an' that ain't a bad reason for keeping clear of Hearne." Cullan shrugged. "Still, there's more to Hearne than Nimman Botrell."

"But the honey's better in Lastane."

Her father laughed.

"Aye, better 'n cheaper."

He stiffened and stood up.

"Cullan?"

"Hush," he said.

Something was wrong. He could feel it. All around him, life proceeded as normal. Down by the spring, the women were chattering and laughing over their laundry. He could hear the rumble of talk from the hunters, who had moved on to skinning the second deer. Somewhere in the camp, in one of the wagons, a mother was singing to a sick child. Further along, other children were playing hide and seek, darting under the wagons. Their voices sounded like the twitter of birds. Up on the slopes above the spring, the clan's herd of horses cropped the grass. Cullan frowned, eyeing them thoughtfully.

"Pa, what is it?" said Giverny.

"I don't know," he said. "Mebbe it's nothing. The horses ain't bothered."

But right when he said those words, the herd of horses raised their heads as if one, staring across the hollow toward the south. Cullan swore under his breath. The horses swung around and surged up the slope, galloping to the top of the rise and streaming over the skyline.

"Weapons!" shouted Cullan. His sword appeared in his hand. Giverny hadn't even seen him draw it. She hadn't even noticed he was wearing it.

"The horses!" someone yelled. "The horses!"

"Later!" Cullan grabbed a burning firebrand in his other hand. "Weapons!"

Someone screamed. Figures seemed to rise up out of the ground, out of the long morning shadows. Metal rang on metal. Several attackers darted forward, angling at Giverny and her mother crouched before the fire. Cullan's sword blurred in the sunlight. The men reeled back. Still, others came. The Farrow clan fought grimly and they fought well. They were skilled swordsmen, every one of them. But even great skill cannot stand for long before a more numerous foe, and the Farrow clan was small in number and caught unaware. Flames billowed up from a wagon. Storm clouds loomed, racing across the sky from the east, driven by a faraway wind. The sun could not rise fast enough to keep up with the coming storm. And the Farrow clan died, one by one.

"Well met, Cullan Farrow."

A tall, gaunt figure emerged from the smoke and burning timbers of the wagons. Swords curved from each hand. The blades were thin and oddly insubstantial, as if forged of some material that had more in common with water or flame or shadow than iron. The man smiled, and his mouth shone with sharp, terrible teeth in his narrow face. Teeth that surely were not human, were of something entirely else.

"Well met, indeed. Over blades and blood." The thing smiled again. "This morning almost makes my heart glad, if such a thing were possible."

"Mine'll be glad with my sword in your heart!" said Cullan.

"I have not come for you, Farrow. I have come for your daughter. Give her to me and perhaps I'll permit your sorry life to hurry on for another day's death."

"I'll die first."

Cullan hurled the firebrand in the creature's face. His sword blurred through the air, but his arm was too slow, despite his skill, despite his famed speed. The creature drifted to one side, almost lazily and with the dreadful smile still on his face. The two swords rose and fell, and Cullan fell with them. Rumer cried out. Silence filled the hollow, unbroken except for the harsh scrape of Rumer's breath and the crackle of the flames. Giverny made no sound at all, but stood frozen as if turned to stone.

"Woman," said the thing, turning toward Rumer. "You have old blood in you. Old, cursed blood. Older than you know. But your daughter is older still. She bears the mark of the earth. Do you know this? Do you know who she might become one day?"

"Leave her," said Rumer hoarsely. "Leave her. Take me instead."

"I'll take you both, but you in death."

Rumer reached out her hand, but it could not be said whether she sought to stop what was promised or to grasp it. The swords rose and fell and again there was only silence except for the crackle of the flames.

"Come, lady." The thing seemed to incline its head to Giverny, as if out of respect. Behind it, other dark figures stood waiting. Giverny said nothing. She did not move. Her face was white.

"Come."

Soon the hollow was empty except for the guttering flames, the blackened beams of wagons, and the motionless shapes strewn about the ground. Here, a child lay huddled in death by his mother. There, an older couple slumped together in their last embrace. The bodies of the hunters sprawled among the corpses of their rabbits and deer. The spring ran dark with blood. Far to the north, the herd of horses galloped across the plain, their eyes staring white and their mouths flecked with foam. Thunder muttered in the east.

CHAPTER NINETY-ONE
MICE AND SAILBOATS

They sailed north, with a west wind against their beam. Ronan kept the coast in sight on the horizon's edge. The further they traveled north, the wilder and more rugged the coast became. Oddly enough, Jute discovered that even at such a distance, he could clearly see the details of the shore. The rocky faces of the cliffs, the stunted bushes growing in impossible stubbornness, the spray and billow of foam as the waves surged against the stony shore below—all of this he could see with clarity. Behind them, surging along with their sails angled low against the sky, came the three other boats. They were too far away to communicate with, but there was no doubt they were determined to follow them to whatever landing Ronan sought.

"We must make land before nightfall," said Ronan. "We have no food or water, and I don't want to be at sea tonight, for the wind's picking up. I think a storm's coming."

"Aye," said the hawk. "And it'll blow until morning."

"It's more'n two days sailing to Averlay," said Ablendan. "Once you near the islands, the sea can be as wicked as an ogre with an empty larder. But there's a little harbor this side of Averlay. It's the only one between Averlay and the Stone Tower. The town of Ortran. I've been through there before, and they're good folk. Fishers mostly."

"That sounds like what we're looking for," said Ronan. "Can you recognize it from this far out?"

"I doubt I'd see it if we were a hundred yards offshore. The cliff juts out and conceals the harbor from the sea. There is, however, a ridge of rocks that reaches up from the sea beyond the cliff. They're visible at low tide, but at high tide they're only white water. This coast is a graveyard."

"True," said one of the ghosts, who thought he was being helpful. "There're old bones beneath the water here, buried in the sand, remembered only by the fishes. Perhaps we'll join them if you don't keep a sharp eye out? That is, you'll join them. I'm already dead."

"If we see the inlet, we'll see it," said Ronan, scowling at the ghost. "If not, then we'll have to chance finding a beach under the cliffs."

Without a word, the hawk launched free from the boat and flapped off toward the coast. Soon, he was skimming over the waves and then mounting higher and higher up into the sky until he blurred into the blue and was gone.

The boys had recovered their spirits by this time, despite Ablendan's melancholy. They chattered about things that Jute knew nothing about. Classes, books, night excursions to the moor to hunt for frogs (as these frogs could be put to excellent use with a spell that caused them to inflate until they popped with a splendid noise), and the carter's niece who sometimes accompanied Cyrnel on her trips to the Stone Tower. Jute wanted to be part of their talk. But in addition to knowing nothing of their world, he found himself silenced by the respectful glances they aimed at him whenever they thought he was not looking. Whenever he tried to join their conversation, they fell quiet and attended to him with such respect that he could only stutter into silence. After a while, Jute gave up and made his way back to the stern of the boat, where Ronan sat at the tiller.

"That hawk of yours seen anything yet?" said Ronan.

"No," said Jute gloomily. "I don't think so. He hasn't spoken."

Ronan squinted up at the top of the mast. Sunlight reflected off the taut sail, as white and as blinding as the light shining on the sea. He smiled.

"I can't remember how many times I've ridden the coast from Hearne to Harlech, looking out at the sea but not seeing it. Things look much different from out here."

"I've never been out of Hearne in my life," said Jute. "Except for now. Running away and trying not to get my throat cut. What fun."

Here. The hawk's voice sounded thinly in his mind. *The inlet is here.*

Jute could see the hawk hovering in the sky. It was a while before anyone else in the boat could see the bird as well, but Ronan steered at Jute's direction. The cliffs looked foreboding, high and carved away at their bases by the waves so that the sunlight could not relieve their shadows unless at sunset. The waves pounded against the face of the cliff with a roar. Spray surged into the air.

"High tide," said Ronan.

And it was, for the reef guarding the opening of the inlet was submerged and only revealed itself in the white water foaming above it. The inlet was not visible until they sailed so close to the cliff that Jute was nervously considering swimming through the breakers to the cliff beyond. But then the cliff opened up and they were through, plunging forward on the face of a wave. The wind died and they floated in a tiny, placid bay.

"Get the oars out," said Ronan.

Jute paddled awkwardly on one side of the boat, until he discovered the rhythm to it. On the other side, the three boys fought over the second oar until Ronan barked at them. The boat drifted across the bay toward the dock. Past the dock, a path zigzagged up the cliff until it reached the town. Happily, though, the cliffs inside the bay were not as high as those fronting the sea. The town clustered at the top of the cliffs with houses perching on rocks like birdnests. Boats bobbed at anchor near the dock.

"Not a word of the wind, d'you hear?" The three boys nodded their heads at Ronan and looked both obedient and guilty, as if they had already disobeyed him. "Jute, you be careful with what you say. No telling who's around here."

"Just so," said the hawk.

"There. The others have made it through as well," said Ablendan. He sighed. "At least that's something salvaged from the day."

Jute glanced back to see the last of the other boats sliding in through the gap in the cliff. He thought he heard the faint sound of cheering, but the bay was loud with the echoing boom of the waves and he could not be sure. His back ached horribly, but he paddled on. It would not do to slack off in view of the three boys. Or Ronan, for that matter. Sweat trickled into his eyes.

The hawk settled onto the railing next to him.

"Nothing like hard work to grow a man's soul," said the hawk.

"All right," said Ronan. "Stop paddling."

The boat bumped against the side of the dock. Ronan leapt onto the dock and tied them off. He then strode off to the end of the dock, where the three other boats were coasting in. Ablendan and Jute followed him. The boys from the school gathered around them.

"Not a word, d'you hear?" said Ronan. "If I catch any of you spouting off about wind lords or the Dark, I'll be talking with you myself. That goes for ghosts as well." Ronan tapped the hilt of his sword at this. The boys nodded and looked suitably impressed. The two ghosts looked less impressed.

"Upon my word," said Ablendan. "A mouse!"

And there, perched on a boy's shoulder and peeking out from behind his collar, was a gray mouse.

"Where'd you get that mouse, boy?"

"Er, found it skittering along the stairs back at school," said the boy. He looked guilty as boys do when questioned, even when they have nothing to be worried of.

"Give it here."

"But it's mine," said the boy.

"Give it here," said Ablendan. "Gently! For your sake, I sincerely hope you've treated this mouse well and haven't been dangling it about by its tail. For, you see, this isn't a mouse."

With those words, the mouse vanished and there on the dock stood Severan. He looked furious.

"Severan," said Ablendan, smiling for the first time all day. "I was hoping it was you."

"Nitwit! Blockhead!"

Severan aimed a blow at the boy's head, but the lad proved quicker than the old man. He ducked and vanished into the group of schoolboys. They all stared goggle-eyed at Severan.

"Do these lackwits learn nothing that we teach them? I spent half the trip doing sign language, humming Thulish folk songs, and dancing around like a fool! But did that get any attention? No. Did that prompt any of these idiots to wonder whether, perhaps, the mouse wasn't a mouse? No!"

"At any rate," said Ablendan cheerfully, "all's well that ends well."

"If I ever get my hands on that son of a louse." Severan spat into the water. "Blast him to darkness!"

"Facen, eh?" said Ablendan.

"Of all things, a mouse. Before I had time to collect my thoughts, I had a cat after me. I can still smell the stench of the brute's breath."

"Probably old Perl. He's always been fond of garlic."

"At least you're safe," said Jute, smiling. "I'm very glad to see you again."

"Sir, if we can't return to school," said one of the boys, "how shall we get home, and what shall we tell our families?"

"Mumble something about the flu," said Severan. "I wouldn't have you lie to your parents, but there's a great thing at stake here. No, don't look like that. We'll figure something out. First, though, I think we all need a good, hot meal, but it had better not include cheese."

CHAPTER NINETY-TWO
THE SORROW OF THE EARTH

A wind blew across the plain from the east. A strange half-light filled the sky. Dark clouds hurried across the face of the sun.

The wind bears an evil scent, Mistress, said the big wolf. *The same scent we tracked into the mountains.*

Aye.

Swallowfoot had been galloping for hours. His pace did not slacken. Levoreth felt the horse's heart pounding beneath her. The wolves streamed out around them like a ragged drapery of shadow rushing in their wake.

The sceadu. They were riding in pursuit of the sceadu. A voice inside her mind whispered uneasily. What if the boy had not unleashed the wind in the regent's castle? What would have happened then? Would she have been able to stand alone before the sceadu? She might very well have died. Doubt crept into her mind. She had not killed it in the regent's castle, even with the boy's help. What would happen here?

Somewhere far off on her left, a wolf howled.

The trail is struck, said the big wolf. *It leads south across the plain. A company of men and a terrible evil. They smell of death.*

Levoreth brought Swallowfoot to a halt with a touch of her mind. The horse shuddered beneath her, blowing and stamping on the grass. The wolves milled around them. Far away on the horizon, she thought she saw a smudge of smoke staining the sky. She could feel the sorrow in the earth. It sighed in the ground and the grass bent over in sadness.

"I'm sorry," Levoreth whispered. "I'm too late for you."

Mistress?

We will follow, said Levoreth grimly. *We will follow and many of your pack will die this day, for we hunt a sceadu.*

The wolf bowed his head.

So be it.

The plain rushed away on either side of them. Before them were the scent and track of their quarry. Grass lay trampled by the passage of many horse hooves. The stench of the Dark lay heavy on the track.

They travel not overly fast. I think their horses are weary.

Aye, Drythen Wulf, said Levoreth. *It will not be long now.*

The wolf pack ran all through the morning and into midday. Even though the sun was surely overhead, the day was as gloomy as if it was already twilight. But the wolves and Swallowfoot were not disheartened, for Levoreth called aloud to them as they ran, naming them one by one so that they knew she held each of them close within her mind. They topped a rise and there, far below on the plain, was a dark and moving mass of horses and men. Levoreth could feel the drum of galloping hooves echoing and pounding within the earth. Even from such a distance she saw a white face turn back toward her from the middle of that company, and she saw the girl's brown hair blowing in the wind. But by the girl's side rode a dark figure.

"Giverny!"

The scream tore from Levoreth's throat. It was unbidden and unchecked. The earth quaked at her cry. Below them, the company of horses was thrown into confusion. Riders were tossed from their saddle. The wolves around her stumbled and fell. Only Swallowfoot stood sure-footed beneath on the tremoring ground.

Mistress! Keep us in your care!

The great wolf lay flat on the ground. His son Ehtan sprawled beyond him. The wolves stared at her, their eyes flashing wide in panic.

I would split the earth! she raged. *I would split the earth to save this youngling's life! Get up! Get up and kill!*

The pack rose and rushed howling down the rise and across the blowing grasses. The men struggled to regain their mounts. The dark figure in their midst called out in a dreadful voice. Thunder crashed overhead in answer to him. Lightning fell in the east, drawing closer. The horsemen wheeled around, cursing and whipping at their mounts. The wolves fell on them like a terrible wave, and at the crest of the wave rode Levoreth. The horsemen reeled back before them. They were pulled down by the jaws of the wolves. Swallowfoot lashed out with his hooves. Over the clash of weapons and the screaming of the horses, Levoreth's voice keened in fury. A helmeted face dissolved into blood and ruin before her. An arrow hissed by her ear and she kicked free from Swallowfoot's back to land beside the old wolf.

Mistress! he snarled, his jaws streaked with blood, and then he lunged forward to rip a horse down by its neck.

Levoreth stamped on the earth and it shook and split around her. The wolves leapt over the chasms, but horses and riders tumbled down into the depths. A man swung an axe at her, but she snapped her fingers and the weapon collapsed into a handful of withered flowers. The man cursed and she saw the Dark glaring from his eyes, and then that was gone in a blur of wolf fangs and Swallowfoot's hooves. She ran forward. The wolves surged on either side. But the day's gloom deepened, and out of the darkness emerged the figure of a man. He was cloaked in a deeper darkness that seethed and flowed about his body like living shadow. From one hand curved a sword. The other held a knife, and on its handle a stone shone in blood-red color.

Bicce wulf!

His voice rang inside Levoreth's mind like stone on stone. She staggered under the blow.

Well met, once again, Mistress of Mistresses.

His teeth flashed in the gloom. They were sharper than his sword. Around him, the horsemen rose up. Spears flew in the darkness. Somewhere on her right, a wolf howled as it died.

I killed you!

Nay, Mistress. Blurred, like shadow fouled with the light. Unraveled like a rotten weave. But the wind is not with you this time.

Her fingers stabbed at the air. The earth shuddered. She called out, her voice hoarse. The grass thickened into brambles as gray and as hard as stone. They thrust their way up into the air. Iron thorns clutched and stabbed at the horsemen. But the sword flashed and fell amidst the brambles. The blade whistled through the air at her. A wolf flung itself into the blow and fell. She saw scarlet coursing over black fur. The knife in his other hand slid toward her.

Swallowfoot. The horse blotted out her sight, rearing up before her. Tall, magnificent, mane flying, and neighing in fury. But then he was gone. The dark figure stepped over the horse's body. And then the sword fell again. Sunlight glanced through a rent in the clouds. The blade fell along the angle of the light. And the light slowed. The blade fell slower than a feather. Light gathered on its edge and flowed down, hanging forever from its point in one gleaming drop.

It will fall. The thought floated through Levoreth's mind, slower than the light. *All things fall. Someday.*

The sunlight was gone.

And the blade kept falling.

It lanced straight toward her chest. But her flesh was as hard as oak, her body wavered into branches and deep roots. The sceadu could not wrench his blade free. The sword was imprisoned within the heartwood of herself. The sceadu could not let go, and branches grew out around him. The sword shattered in a clear, bell-like tone. Levoreth felt the earth waiting beneath her, heavy and expectant. The knife in his other blurred toward her. The stone in its hilt burned red with malevolence. Her heart faltered, for her memory was caught by the stone, striving to remember. Despite this, the branches caught and held his wrist. He could not break free, though he twisted and thrashed. Shadows fluttered like rags before her. She heard a wailing cry that faded into nothingness. A mist wavered away across the ground. The horsemen fled with it, but one of the riders checked in flight and the mist rose to settle behind him on the saddle. And then they were all away with a thunder of galloping hooves and the snarls of the wolves in pursuit.

But as the riders fled, the misty form turned in the saddle. Something went whipping through the air, tumbling end over end. The red stone blazed in the heart of the darkness. She remembered now, while time slowed around her. *On the slopes of the mountains of Ranuin. In the silent snows. Nokhoron Nozhan took his sword in hand and did cut his side. Three drops of blood fell to the ground. And there lay blood no longer, but three gems that did burn with scarlet fire. To the sceadus he gave each a stone. In the stones was the incandescence of Nokhoron Nozhan's malice.*

Levoreth blinked, and the knife slammed into her just below her breast. She could not breathe with the pain of it.

All things fall.

Even me.

Levoreth opened her eyes to find herself gazing up at a clear blue sky. The sunlight was warm on her face. The big wolf stared down at her. He whined. She tried to touch his muzzle but she could not lift her hand.

Where is the girl? Does she still live?

She is here, Mistress, said the wolf.

Two wolves gently urged Giverny forward, nudging her with their noses and their heavy shoulders. The girl stumbled to Levoreth's side and knelt down. Her face was white and streaked with tears.

"Lady Callas," said Giverny. Her cold fingers closed on Levoreth's hand.

"Just Levoreth, girl. Help me sit up."

"I don't think that's a good idea." The girl's voice trembled.

"Help me, Giverny."

Levoreth must have passed out then, for when she opened her eyes again, she was sitting up in Giverny's arms. Her body felt numb. It felt as if she were slowly turning into stone. Before her, past the huddled forms of the dead, the plain stretched out green under the sunlight. A breeze blew by and the grass rippled along its path. Levoreth smiled.

"How beautiful it is here."

Mistress of Mistresses.

Drythen Wulf. I thank you.

Your thanks are not needed, Mistress. Does the sun thank the candle for the radiance it sheds?

But the wolf hung his great head and would not meet her eyes.

What troubles you, old friend?

My son.

On the ground, beside his sire, lay the body of the young wolf Ehtan. The black fur was matted with blood and the silver eyes were closed. Beyond him sprawled the larger bulk of Swallowfoot.

The old wolf raised his head.

Can you give him his life back, Mistress?

Levoreth looked away past the wolf, gazing past the grass and the horizon. Four days' journey over the horizon would bring her to Dolan. To the river Ciele and the hills of the Mearh Dun. To the cemetery behind the church in Andolan filled with sunlight and the scent of roses and the bees buzzing at their work.

The wolf waited patiently.

I shall.

The wolf's eyes flared in hope.

I shall, Drythen Wulf, but not a life such as yours. Not a life you would know. Your cub will never lead the pack. He shall never run with the pack again.

Is this a life? said the wolf dully. *You do not speak of a wolf.*

He shall run with the guardian of the earth. He shall wander the world for many long years, even after you and your cubs have gone to chase the sun. He shall pass into legend. He shall be the shadow of the Mistress of Mistresses.

The old wolf stared at her, and then he bowed his head.

"Pull me closer, Giverny. Pull me closer to the dead wolf."

"Lady," stammered Giverny.

"Do it."

The pain of it made Levoreth almost lose consciousness. Her vision swam. She closed her eyes. Her fingers brushed the wolf's fur. Her mind drifted. The wolf was gone. Only cooling flesh and bone and fur remained. Her mind pushed farther. Farther west, toward the edge of sea and sky. Farther and past. And there, across the blue, she saw two figures running fast toward the light. Side by side. A wolf and a horse.

Wait, she called.

The wolf paused and turned, but Swallowfoot galloped on until he diminished and faded into the light.

Wait. Your time here is not done.

Across the distance, the wolf gazed back at her.

A task awaits you. Return.

I go to chase the sun, Mistress, said the wolf. *It is a better thing.*

Aye, she said. *But another time. Another place.*

The wolf was silent.

Return.

Levoreth felt movement under her hand. She opened her eyes. The young wolf struggled to his feet. He nosed at her hand. Awareness sparked in his eyes. Around him, the other wolves backed away.

"Giverny."

The sunlight was dimming. It was certainly only midday, but surely the light was dimming. Levoreth blinked. She struggled to keep her eyes open.

"Giverny. You must do a last thing for me."

"What is it?" The girl's voice trembled.

"Pull out the knife."

"What?"

Giverny's face hovered over her own, but it was lost in darkness and Levoreth could not distinguish her features.

"Pull out the knife."

"Levoreth—I can't!"

"You must," said Levoreth gently. "It is a hard thing, child, but it must be done."

Even though she spoke softly, all the weight of the earth was in her voice and Giverny could not deny her. The wolf Ehtan loomed behind Giverny, his silver eyes expressionless. He did not blink when the knife came free. The stone in the handle no longer shone vibrant red, but was dull and clouded, as if with age and sudden heat.

"Now," gasped Levoreth. "Give me the knife."

It was the last of her strength. She closed her fingers on Giverny's hand. The blade sliced across the girl's palm. She cried out.

"I'm sorry," said Levoreth. "Don't forget that, Giverny. I'm sorry, for I wouldn't wish this on anyone, least of all you. We didn't realize, when we chose so long ago."

"What do you mean?" said Giverny.

But Levoreth did not hear her. The sun passed its zenith and fell toward the west. Giverny laid Levoreth back down on the grass. The older woman smiled.

"Ehtan shall watch over you until your time is full."

"Who is Ehtan?" said the other, her face bewildered.

"Listen to him, for the memory of the earth is in him now. He shall guard your way from the Dark, for it shall be many days before you find your strength. He will be your shadow, your right hand, and your comforter. Do not be afraid."

Levoreth smiled again, though her eyes no longer saw the sky overhead or the girl's frightened face or the watchful eyes of the wolf Ehtan. Beneath her, the earth pressed up against her back.

"Now," she said. "Let the memory of Levoreth Callas fade, for I have done what I was meant to do."

She shivered within Giverny's arms. Her features blurred. And then there was nothing at all in the girl's grasp, only the dry earth crumbling down into the grass. Giverny stood, weeping. The wolf Ehtan brushed her hand with his nose.

Mistress of Mistresses.

The voice was soft inside her mind. It had a deep, rough quality to it, comforting and oddly familiar.

"Who said that?" said Giverny.

The wolf's silver eyes gazed up into her own.

You are the Mistress of Mistresses.

And then other voices joined his.

Mistress of Mistresses.

The wolves around her bowed their heads. She walked through their midst, her steps slow and halting. Ehtan followed at her heels. A breeze blew by her, paused as if startled, and then whirled away.

Next spring, poppies grew there that had never been seen before on the Scarpe or, for that matter, anywhere in Tormay. Their petals were red as blood. In the years afterward, the flowers bloomed further and further across the Scarpe and were later found flourishing throughout the hills of Dolan. It is said that the scent of those flowers brings healing and guards against the Dark, but that is only an old tale from long ago.

CHAPTER NINETY-THREE
JUTE'S CHOICE

The townsfolk of Ortran received them with no fanfare and little surprise. They did not seem interested at the sight of the hawk riding on Jute's shoulder. They ignored the ghosts. They were a quiet, reserved people. They were mostly fishermen, with a few vintners who grew a hardy grape on straggling vines that clung to the rocky slopes beyond the town. The single inn of the town perched on top of the cliff. Its windows looked west, across the bay and over the cliffs that fronted the sea. The last light of the departed sun gleamed on the sea.

"Fish stew," said the innkeeper. And then, inspired to further eloquence, he added, "Halibut." But when he returned to their table, it was more than fish stew. It was loaves of fresh bread, butter, and a crock of pickled onions. The stew arrived in a pot that breathed out a steam of fish and potatoes.

"Ahh," said Severan. "Thulish hospitality. Silent but ample."

They were silent as well for a while as they did justice to the stew. Jute yawned over his bowl. The ghost drifted around the room, inspecting the whalebone carvings hanging on the walls. The hawk fidgeted on the back of Jute's chair.

"We must leave early in the morning for Harlech," said the hawk. "I'd prefer to leave now, but I think a night's sleep would do you well. These are kindly folk in this town and I'd not want their misfortune on my conscience if we tarry. The Dark will come sniffing, sooner or later, and this is no place to defend, though the sea laps at their doorstep."

"Is Harlech so safe, master hawk?" said Ronan. "They might be better with the sword and have some strange legends told of them, but there are fewer of them than in other duchies. Besides, what can men do against the Dark?"

"Strange," said Jute's ghost, seating itself in the empty chair next to the boy. "I seem to remember reading peculiar things about Harlech. All in one book. A very old book. For the life of me, perhaps I should say for the death of me, I can't remember."

The hawk chuckled.

"There's more to Harlech than meets the eye, Ronan, though I daresay they themselves might have forgotten. But the Dark hasn't forgotten. No, the men of Harlech are more than just ordinary men, just as you are more than a thief. They come of an old people."

"A failed thief," said Ronan lightly. "That's what I am."

"If I may say something," said Severan. "This is excellent stew. Not that that was what I wanted to say. Ablendan and I have been discussing the schoolboys. I trust they're all safe in their rooms and not out wandering the village."

"What was the name of that book?" said the ghost.

"Doubtless, we'll have to save the village before the night's out," said Ablendan. "And there's no scullery duty or stair-scrubbing or attic-dusting to punish the scoundrels."

"We've decided," continued Severan, "it would be best if Ablendan and I saw to the schoolboys." He frowned down at his stew. "I don't know who survived at the Stone Tower, but I can't assume any of the other professors are left. We must at least see to it

452

that the boys return safely to their families. Though I fear Lano's family won't appreciate his return, as he'll be bringing a ghost to lodge."

"What's that?" said Jute's ghost, startled out of its pondering.

"You won't be going with us to Harlech?" said Jute.

"Oh, I shall," said the ghost. "Never fear."

"No," said Severan. "I'm afraid not."

"But what about your cottage? You were going to show me the ruins of the tower, you remember, the one the lords of Harlech destroyed. I wanted to see that."

"Don't scowl so, Jute," said Severan. "You'll see the ruins, and the haunted keep of Lannaslech and everything else. I'll only be a month or so behind you."

"A haunted keep?" said the ghost. "Brr. Sounds dreadful."

"I don't fancy shepherding the boys all over Tormay to their homes," said Ablendan. "Why, there's two that hail as far as Vomaro. A pox on duty."

"We'll leave in the morning," said the hawk.

Severan nodded at Jute, but did not speak, and the boy did not trust his own voice to say anything in farewell.

They left before first light. A heavy fog lay about the town and Jute heard water dripping from the eaves as he woke in his bed. Ronan sat on the other bed, packing his knapsack. A second knapsack, bought from the innkeeper's wife for Jute, waited bulging and ready beside it. A mug of hot ale steamed on the table. The ghost eyed the ale mournfully.

"As you're both awake," said the hawk. "We might as well leave. I've never liked fog."

"It's only the breath of the sea," said Ronan.

The fog hung in the streets. Their footsteps sounded muffled. Here and there, lights shone in windows. Jute hitched up his cloak, also bought from the innkeeper's obliging wife, and wished he was still asleep in bed. The street became a carter's track that headed out into the moors. The village vanished in the fog behind them.

"The coast road again," said Ronan. "It'll take us to Averlay, and then on to Harlech."

"Harlech," said the ghost. "Did I mention I once read something odd about Harlech?"

"Yes," said Jute. "I'm sure you did."

"Rest assured that I'll tell you what it was in detail. Once I remember what it was."

"Is there no way, ghost," said the hawk, "that I can convince you there are other things you could do rather than journeying with us? I'm grateful for what you've done for us. The advice about the sea and boats was timely, but, well—"

"I don't need convincing on that account," said the ghost. "I know full well there're other things I could be doing. I simply choose not to do them. I like you. I like you all. Besides, it's been about six hundred years since I've had a stroll in the country."

"Is there no way to make you leave?" said the hawk mildly.

"Yes, of course there is. The fifth stricture of the causality of ghosts."

"And what is that?"

"Oh, don't worry," said the ghost happily. "I won't tell you."

"Never mind," said Ronan. "I'm sure he'll keep his mouth shut when he needs to, won't you?"

"Sir," said the ghost. "I am the perfect painting of discretion."

The fog burned away as the morning progressed. They were on a moor that, except for the sea far below on their left, stretched away on every side. The air smelled of the sea and of heather and it did more to clear one's head than a mug of hot ale.

"We should leave the road," said Ronan. "It meanders too much if we mean to make haste."

"Aye," said the hawk. "I was thinking the same myself."

They headed straight off across the moor. Jute found the springy turf pleasant to walk on. The apparent flatness of the moor was deceptive, for there were deep ponds looking up at the sky with their clear, stony gazes and sudden gullies full of bulrushes and trickling streams. A covey of quail burst out of the grass at their feet and fled away. The hawk surged into the air and climbed high. Then, he dove.

"Quail'll make a nice break from rabbit for him," said Ronan. "I wouldn't mind some myself for lunch."

"Barbaric," said the ghost. "I could never bring myself to eat a defenseless little bird."

"Do you remember the last meal you ate?" asked Jute.

"What do you mean?" said the ghost. "Are you inferring I might've eaten something like that poor quail, which is, no doubt, being dismembered as we speak?"

"I meant no such thing," said Jute, even though this was what he had meant. "I just wondered whether you remembered things like that."

"I don't remember things like that," grumbled the ghost. "I've so many more splendid and worthwhile things to remember that I don't waste time on inconsequential memories."

"I'd differ from you, ghost," said Ronan. "It's the little things that are worth remembering. A woman's smile, the smell of porridge in the morning. The mane of a horse flying out in gallop."

"I don't remember porridge," said the ghost. "I'm sure it's nasty stuff."

"My mother cooked porridge most every morning when I was a child. Porridge and honey."

The moor gave way to low hills. Looking back from the top of the first one that they crested, the sea was visible in the distance as a strip of dark blue.

"You'll always be uncomfortable when the sea isn't near," said the hawk.

"What?" said Ronan. He turned red under his tan.

"What?" said the ghost. "What's what?"

"I don't recollect any human before you with the blood of the sea in his veins. Oh, don't scowl like that, my friend. The mark of the sea is difficult to hide from anyone who has known her well, and I knew her well, many years ago."

Ronan was silent as they walked along, though the ghost plied both him and the hawk with questions about the sea that they both ignored.

"Fair's fair," said the ghost indignantly. "I've shared my knowledge with you. You appreciated my discussion of toads and their predators, didn't you? So why won't you share with me?"

They descended into a little valley and the sea was no longer in sight. It was nearing time for lunch, and Jute's stomach, along with the position of the sun in the sky overhead, confirmed this. They ate, sitting under the shade of an oak. The hawk tucked his head beneath his wing and dozed.

"Hmmph," said the ghost, who had been maintaining a huffy silence for the last few minutes. "I don't care if you're all going to behave selfishly. Anyway, I probably know more about the sea than any of you."

"I fell into the sea once," said Jute.

This thought made him scowl, and he eyed Ronan, but the man was intent on his bread and cheese and paid Jute no attention.

"Very interesting, I'm sure," said the ghost, "but I daresay you know nothing about things like the Dark, eh? Let me tell you, I know plenty. Why, I could tell you stories about horrible creatures such as shadowhounds and kobolds and dropsies. Scare you to no end, I imagine."

"What are dropsies?" asked Jute. He didn't like the sound of them.

"A dropsy," said the hawk, popping his head out from under his wing, "is something rather dreadful. I hope you never have the misfortune to meet a dropsy. I doubt you ever would, for there weren't many dropsies and I think most of them were killed a long time ago."

The discussion of dropsies went on for some time, with the hawk doing most of the talking. The ghost occasionally offered its own ideas, but it was apparent it did not know what it was talking about and gravely made ridiculous claims and assertions that had nothing whatsoever to do with dropsies and had everything to do with the fact that the ghost liked to hear the sound of its own voice.

Dropsies, explained the hawk, were one of the earliest servants of the Dark. Not as old and as powerful as the sceadus, but terrible enough. They were creations of the Dark. Though the important thing to understand was that the Dark could not create of its own power. It could not make something out of nothing. Rather, it could only remake and twist things that already existed into shapes of its own device.

"The Dark is only a warped reflection of what is good in this world," said the hawk. "Think of it like this: you cast a shadow as you walk along this path; the shadow cannot cast you. However, if the Dark somehow gained control of you, then it would slowly work its will in you until you were only a reflection of who you once were—a dim, ugly reflection."

The ghost disagreed with this, pointing out that no one knew what things looked like from a shadow's point of view, and perhaps they viewed people as being their shadows. The hawk snorted and did not bother responding. The ghost took this as a sign of capitulation and launched into an incomprehensible discourse on light and darkness and whether or not they were merely substances such as water or socks or cheese.

"If they are," said the ghost, "then we must figure out what sort of container can hold them. If we can do that, why, we can corner the market. A hundred gold pieces for a pound of light. Twenty silvers for a swallow of darkness. We'll be rich!"

"I don't think anyone," said Jute, "will pay for a pound of light when you can go outside and have as much sunlight as you want."

"Oh?" said the ghost. "I hadn't thought of that. Sunlight is free?"

The sunlight, free or otherwise, shone on them. Down in the defiles between the hills, there was not a breath of wind and the air was warm. On every hilltop that they reached, however, they could feel the breeze, and the scent of the sea was still borne on it.

"When are you going to teach me how to fly?" said Jute to the hawk.

"When we get to Harlech, and only then. I would've considered it sooner, but not with such an unpleasant creature as a wihht on our trail. The power let loose in teaching you to fly would be like waving a flag and yelling, 'Here we are!'"

"If I knew how to fly then we needn't be trudging through these hills," said Jute.

"Ah," said Ronan. "And then I'd be left here with our ghost."

"I'm not enthused about the arrangement either," huffed the ghost.

"No one's flying except me," said the hawk.

They came to the border of Thule and Harlech late that afternoon. At least, Ronan said it was the border as far as he knew. It was not a specific line such as the fence a farmer might put around his lettuce patch to keep the deer out. The hills sloped down into a valley that, as it stretched west and north, opened into a wide bay. The sea sparkled in the late sunlight.

"The northern end of the Scarpe Plain," said Ronan. "It ends here at Averlay. Can you see the town? There, on the furthest curve of the bay."

Far away but just visible along the furthest edge of the shore, Jute could see a town. Smoke hazed in the air overhead. A wharf reached out into the water, crooked around itself, and boats rocked at anchor within the shelter of the breakwater.

"A town," said Jute happily. "Hot dinner!"

"You can't see them at this distance," said Ronan, "but straight out from the bay are the islands. The Flessoray Islands. Only a few fisherfolk live on them."

They made their way down the last hill. The grasses of the plain were golden with summer days and the long autumn that had followed afterward to burnish them brighter and sharper. The wind was in their face, blowing in off the sea. They could hear the sound of the waves, even though they were still far from the shore. It was because of this, because of the wind's direction, that they did not hear the horses until the herd was nearly upon them.

"Watch out!" called the hawk. He launched himself from Jute's shoulder into the air.

They heard the gallop of hooves. The ground trembled. Around the edge of the hills thundered a herd of horses. They were galloping fast.

"Get out of the way!" shouted Ronan. He ran for the hill they had just descended. Jute scrambled after him. The horses were upon them. Jute smelled the tang of horse sweat. There was dust in the air. He was suddenly aware of how small he was in comparison to the huge horses. Ronan grabbed him by the collar and yanked him off his feet, up onto a rock slab. The horses split around them, not slackening their speed.

"Where'd they come from?" gasped Jute.

Ronan did not answer at first. The man stared tensely at the horses. His face looked shocked.

"I know them," he said. "I know these horses. There's the old gray with the blaze on his forehead. Surely he would've been dead of old age years ago. And the dappled mare. I'd know her anywhere. Her colts were as sure-footed as cats, and the duke of Dolan always bought them whenever we came to his court."

Ronan made as if to step forward, to plunge off the safety of the rock and right into the path of the horses, but he flinched at the sight of a tall black stallion galloping at the rear of the herd.

"That's his horse," he said, insensible now to Jute's presence. "I rode it when I was a child. Wynlic! Wynlic, don't you know me?"

But the stallion pounded by in a flurry of hooves and mane. The horses were gone now, past them and veering across the plain and toward the hills along the bay, rising higher and more cruelly broken than the hills to the south.

"What's going on?" said the ghost, who, for once, looked startled and unsure of itself.

Ronan jumped down from the rock and stood staring after the horses. They were lost to sight in a cloud of dust that drifted across the plain. The hawk landed on Jute's shoulder in a flutter of wings. Ronan turned around, his face blank.

"I must go," he said.

He walked away, stumbling at first but then moving more steadily as he went. He walked among the trampled grass and torn earth of the horses' trail, heading south in the direction from where the horses had come from.

"He can't just leave," said Jute. "Wait! Ronan! Where are you going?"

Panic rose in him. The panic shocked him. It was not a reaction Jute could have foreseen. He despised Ronan. Despised and feared him. He could still see the square of moonlight at the top of chimney receding as he fell into the darkness. Still could smell soot and dust and spiderwebs. But watching him walk away sent panic choking at his throat. A whisper in the back of Jute's mind reminded him he'd already be dead three times over if it weren't for Ronan.

"Come back, you!" shouted the ghost. "Don't worry, young Jute. That should do it. People always listen to me. It's all in the voice."

"Patience," said the hawk. "He'll be back."

The hawk was right. Ronan did not walk more than fifty paces before he stopped. His shoulders hunched and he did not move. Then he turned and walked back, his steps slow and dragging.

"I can't go," he said desperately. "You must release me."

"We didn't bind you," said the hawk. "She did."

"Jute!"

The agony in the man's voice made Jute flinch. He could not meet Ronan's eyes.

"The boy can't release you either," said the hawk.

"Jute. I must go. I must." Ronan's voice halted as if he were choking on his words. He shuddered. "Those were my—my family's horses. They're part of my family. They would never leave, unless—unless. . . Something must have happened. I must go."

"I never had a family," said Jute. It was the only thing he could say. He did not know if he understood the anguish in Ronan's face, but he wished he did. He wished he did with all his might.

"I ran away from my family fifteen years ago," said Ronan, his voice shaking. "Fifteen years, and I've not seen them since."

And Jute could not say no. He could not say no, even though he could still close his eyes and feel himself falling down the chimney. Even though the hawk's claws bit into his shoulder so fiercely that he felt blood spring from his skin. The bird's anger beat against his mind.

His family is not important. They are not important in comparison to your life. Do you understand? We must keep you safe.

I never had a family.

Greater things are at stake here.

I never had a family.

At that, the hawk's voice abruptly went silent. Ronan stood, frozen, waiting, his eyes on Jute's face. The boy took a deep breath and then nodded. Ronan turned without a word. The way was easy to follow because of the scarred ground left by the flight of the horse herd. They traveled mostly in silence that was broken only occasionally by the ghost who, being a ghost, was not particularly sensitive to those who still lived.

"I once had the good fortune to see Min the Morn," said the ghost. "Now, that was a horse. One blow from his hoof could split the earth in two. There was an old story that he shattered the northern ranges by galloping across the mountains. Of course, you might think a horse is only a horse, of course. Just because you think you have all the facts, and perhaps you actually do have them all, doesn't mean you have the answers."

The hawk was growing more and more restive in his surliness on Jute's shoulder. With a grunt of disgust, the bird launched into the air. It was then that he saw the smoke.

"Look!" The hawk's voice came down clear and thin to them. "Look there!"

Smoke stained the horizon. It was difficult to discern against the dimming of the early evening sky. Ronan's face turned pale.

"A campfire, I daresay," said the ghost. "Perhaps they'll have a hot supper for us?"

"You don't eat," said Jute. "Besides, they might not be friendly."

"Nonsense. We're in the duchy of Thule, aren't we? Hospitable folk. No one ever goes hungry in Thule. I remember having had excellent meals in this duchy."

With those words, the ghost started off toward the smoke. Ronan and Jute trailed after it. Above them, the hawk soared higher.

"Mutton," continued the ghost. "Sizzling over the flames. Fresh bread. You haven't tasted bread until you've had it baked hot in coals. You'll understand when you're old, boy. There aren't many pleasures left in life at my age. Oh, don't get me wrong—scholarly work is my one true pleasure. There's nothing like hunting down an ancient word and discovering its sound, its letters, its meaning, but a good meal's a close second."

Hurry. The hawk's voice keened through Jute's mind. *One is still alive!*

"We must hurry!" said Jute. "There's someone still alive!"

He began to run, for he could hear the urgency in the hawk's voice and the sound of the wind. The wind knew. He could feel it blowing through his thoughts. The ghost hurried along at his side. Behind them, Ronan faltered, his face white and strained, as if he was reluctant to discover what lay ahead. Thunder rumbled overhead. Jute felt a drop of rain on his face, and then it began to rain in earnest. It was a dreary sort of rain that painted out the sky and plastered the grass onto the ground.

Jute could no longer see the smoke anymore, or the hawk, for that matter. But he could still feel the wind in his mind, blowing his thoughts forward. How odd. It almost felt like the wind was pushing his thoughts forward into the haze. Pushing them forward so that he could see with them. But not with his eyes. It was the strangest sensation. The wind inside his mind blew harder as if in agreement. Jute pushed with his own mind, pushing his thoughts forward to see past his eyes, to see past the obscurity of the rain. A picture formed in his mind. Flames hissing and dying in the rain. The blackened ruins of wagons.

Stop that.

The hawk's voice was sharp.

Why? said Jute, bewildered. *Every time I do something, you tell me to stop.*

Seeing with one's mind is a dangerous thing. Unless you are skilled at it, and you are not, then it is like lighting a fire in the darkness. It attracts unwanted attention. And right now we do not want any such attention.

The wind subsided to an apologetic murmur in Jute's mind. He could smell smoke in the damp air. The ground fell away in a gentle slope, down past a trampled sweep of grass to a hollow. A spring lay in the middle, edged by bushes and cattails. Smoke guttered up from dying flames. The charred timbers of wagons stood gaunt in the rain, skeletons of what they once had been. And there were bodies.

Jute swallowed hard. Beside him, the ghost gasped. They both paused at the top of the rise, but Ronan gave a hoarse cry and stumbled past them. He staggered like a drunken man. The rain hissed on the last of the flames. Ronan howled, his face raised to the sky like a dog. He swung around, looking this way and that, his eyes blank and his head shaking from side to side as if in confusion. Bodies sprawled everywhere: Men and women. Young and old. Here, a girl had been cut down at the water's edge, a spilled armful of laundry around her trampled into the mud. There, an old man lay tangled in the shattered steps of a wagon. The wind gusted through and blew embers out onto the surface of the spring where they died, sputtering and snapping. The hawk swept down.

One is still alive.

"One's still alive!" blurted out Jute.

There. By the cook-pot.

"Here!" said Jute.

An older woman lay crumpled on the ground, her hands outstretched as if she was reaching for something that was gone. Ronan stumbled past Jute and fell to his knees at the woman's side. Hands shaking, he brushed her hair back from her face. Her eyes opened. She stared up at the sky and then her gaze fell on Ronan's face. A smile trembled on her mouth and then was gone.

"Declan," she said.

He said nothing, could say nothing. Her hand crept out to grasp his.

"They took her." Her fingers tightened on his, impossibly strong. Her knuckles whitened. "Find your sister."

Still, he could not speak, though his tears fell on her face. She stared straight up at his face, but she saw him no longer. It was as if she gazed past him into some other sky that was not the gray, rainy sky of Tormay.

"Ever since I was a girl I've dreamt of it," she said. But she did not speak of what she had dreamed, and then she was still.

They carried all of the bodies to a wagon that had not been burned as badly as the others. Jute had seen dead bodies before. Once, an old drunk had fallen out the second-story window of the Goose and Gold and broken his neck on the street below. The Juggler's children had gathered around to gawk and giggle nervously, daring each other to touch the dead man's hand. And then there had been the winter when a horrible bleeding cough had made its rounds of the city. It had restricted itself mainly to the poorer neighborhoods of the city, particularly Fishgate and south of it. Jute could still remember the carts rolling by, filled with corpses like cordwood. But he had been more fascinated than horrified. Now, however, his stomach turned over with nausea. He was only strong enough to carry the lighter bodies, and these were the children. His eyes blurred, and it was Lena's head lolling against his arm.

They set the wagon alight and let it burn.

"Can't let the scavengers get them," said Ronan dully.

Two of the bodies still lay by the spring: the woman and an older man found fallen nearby. Ronan began digging with his sword in the muddy earth. The other two tried to help him, but he turned on them, his face twisted in fury.

"Come away, Jute," said the hawk. "This isn't our place."

The boy climbed up to the top of the rise on the other side of the dell. The ghost drifted after him. Behind them, smoke billowed up as the flames rose higher. But the wind was in their face, blowing out of the northwest, and they could not smell the stench of burning flesh. The hawk settled on Jute's shoulder and furled his wings.

"They were his family," said Jute after a while.

"Yes," said the hawk.

"I never knew my family. I don't remember." Jute paused, staring down at his fingers. They were filthy with dirt and soot and something that looked like blood. He ripped up a clump of grass and scrubbed at his hands.

"What sort of land is Harlech?" Jute said, looking up. He swallowed hard. His stomach felt empty and he found himself missing Lena and the other children. "I've heard Harlech's a dreadful place, where everyone's a wizard. That the land itself's alive. No one from Harlech ever comes to Hearne."

"On the contrary," said the hawk, his voice gentle. "It's a beautiful land. Moors and hills and deep valleys dark with forests. The sea there's cold and the cliffs of Harlech are as sharp as knives, honed by the waves and the wind. As for wizards, I think there're no more wizards in that land than could be found in any other duchy."

"I've never met anyone from Harlech," said Jute.

"Of course you have. The old man, Severan."

"Severan? You're right. I'd forgotten that's where he came from."

"I think I've even seen the house he spoke of. Once, when I was flying along the coast. It's more of a cottage. It perches on a cliff overlooking the sea, about as far from Hearne as a man can get."

"Hearne," said the ghost thoughtfully. "I have some memories of that place. Now, where did I put them?"

The hawk's claws suddenly tightened on Jute's shoulder. His head swiveled this way and that.

"What is it?" said Jute.

"Nothing," said the hawk. "I just thought I heard something strange for a moment. It was nothing. I must've been mistaken."

Ronan trudged up the slope below them. His shoulders were bowed.

"I must leave you here," said Ronan. "Please. Release me."

"But I can't," said Jute helplessly. "I have nothing to do with what binds you."

"He wasn't the one who bound you," said the hawk. "The sea doesn't give her gifts lightly. There's always a price. You know that."

"Don't you understand?" shouted Ronan, turning on them in fury. "That's my family down there! Those bodies burning on the pyre. My father and my mother—" His voice broke. When he spoke again, his tone was quiet. "Only my sister's left, and she's been taken. The tracks lead away from here. I can follow them. I can find her. She's all I have."

"If that's your family," said Jute, "then who are you?"

"My name's Declan Farrow," said the man who had been Ronan. He said the words slowly. The name came reluctantly, as if he had not spoken it for many years. "My name's Declan Farrow, though I haven't been called that for more than fifteen years. Fifteen years I threw away. I can't even remember my sister's face. She was a tiny girl when I left."

"Declan Farrow!" said the hawk softly. "I should've known."

"Release me, Jute. You hold my life in your hand. Let me go."

"I have nothing to do with this," said Jute in great bewilderment.

Declan groaned out loud. "I'm bound fast. I can't willingly desert you, for I'm compelled by a power that cares nothing about what happens to me. But you can help me. Come with me to find my sister."

"No!" said the hawk, alarmed at these words. "I'm grieved by your misfortune, Farrow, but your sorrow and the death of your family truly mean little in light of what lies before us. I'd see all of Tormay dead to save this boy from the Dark. And you're bound to this same purpose, are you not?"

"Yes," said Declan, choking on the word. "I'm bound fast and my will isn't my own. Jute, listen to me. I turned my back on my family years ago. I was a fool and gave them up

460

for what I thought were better things. Fame and fortune won by my sword. But they're worthless in comparison to what I once had. And now there's only my sister. Would you have me turn my back on my family once again?"

"Er," said Jute, thinking of Lena taking his place in the Silentman's cell.

"You chose to leave your family," said the hawk angrily. "Would you have us pay for that choice?"

"I only want one last chance."

"We all want one last chance," said the ghost. "All of us have regrets. I can't remember mine, but I'm sure I've got 'em."

Declan's hand went to his throat. Something lay there—a length of wire or fine chain gleaming against his dark skin. Light shone on a smooth round stone. A pearl. He pulled at the wire as if it choked him, but when he saw Jute's eye on him, he twitched his cloak closed to hide what lay around his neck.

"Just one more chance," Declan said. He spoke more to himself than to anyone else.

"Well, boy?" said the hawk harshly.

The wind blew this way and that, as if saying it would be happy going anywhere. Anywhere that Jute went.

"We aren't far behind them, are we?" said the boy.

Declan looked up, hope in his eyes.

"No," he said. "No, we aren't."

"This is a bad choice," said the hawk. "The only thing that matters is preserving Jute's life, the life of the anbeorun. If the Wind falls into the hands of the Dark, then Tormay will surely be lost."

"What's the difference between one or many?"

"If one falls, then so be it, if many shall be saved," said the hawk.

The hawk spoke angrily and the words rang in the air and in Jute's mind. But even as the boy considered this and the unpleasant thought of falling into the hands of the Dark, he felt the wind blow through his mind. It seemed pleased. Excited. And curious. As if it wished to see where the hunt would go.

The hawk snorted in annoyance.

"We shouldn't waste any time, should we?" said Jute.

The rain eased then, subsiding to a drizzle and then a mist. Oddly enough, the wind shifted until it was blowing out of the southeast.

"Perfect," said Declan. He tried to smile, but could not. "We'll catch their scent and they'll not have ours."

"Hmmph," said the hawk, and Jute could feel anger in the grip of the bird's claws on his shoulders.

They headed southeast with the wind in their faces. Declan moved along with a fast loping stride and it was all Jute could do to keep up with him. His side ached and his lungs burned. He could hear the ghost nattering on about toads and other ingredients dictated by an ancient recipe for invisibility.

"Of course," said the ghost, "with that combination of ingredients, if you get either the burdock or the toad juice out of ratio, you're either dead or paralyzed."

Jute, stop panting like that, said the hawk.

It was the first thing the bird had said in over two hours.

I can't help it.

Yes, you can.

I'm tired.

461

The shadow of the hawk slid across the ground in front of Jute, who looked up to see the bird sailing through the sky overhead.

Does the wind ever tire?

CHAPTER NINETY-FOUR
THE VINDICTIVENESS OF CATS

Smede shivered in the alley across the street from his house. It was raining again and he was cold. His teeth chattered. Something rustled behind him in the alley and he shrank back in the shadows. He groped in his pocket for his knife, but then relaxed. It was only a cat. A bedraggled little cat hurrying by, dodging raindrops and downspouts. The cat gave him a cross look as if to say it had no regard for humans stupid enough to be out on such a night. The cat trotted around a corner and was gone.

Smede gnawed his lip and stared across the street at his house. With the rain and the general state of disarray he was in, he looked like a shapeless lump of shadow. He blinked and then squinted. There. A hint of movement in the window across the street. The third-story window. It had been the merest of movements. Smede whimpered, thinking there in the dark. All that gold. Locked away in his strongbox. So close and so far away. He dared not go up to his rooms. Surely a blade and death waited for him there. The Silentman had put the word out. The Guild was on the lookout. Death stalked him on the streets of Hearne. His master was gone.

"Curse them all," muttered Smede to himself. "Oh, what'll I do? I'm all alone. Where shall I go?"

If he left the city, surely he could find safety in the south. Somewhere far away. Vomaro, perhaps. Harth. The Guild did hardly any business in Harth. But he couldn't leave his gold. He couldn't.

And then Smede's thoughts turned to the house on Stalu Street. Where he had first met his master. His master was gone, but he could find solace there. Sanctuary from the Guild. The wards still held around that house, though the ancient spell was broken.

An idea sparked in his head.

Smede grinnned, his head bobbing up and down. A downspout trickled onto his head but he did not notice. He chuckled nastily to himself and then made his way down the alley, scurrying like an oversized rat. Behind him, the cat cautiously stuck its head around a corner and watched him go. It scrubbed at its nose with one paw as if it sought to rid itself of a bad odor. Then, with one last careful look around, the cat followed the little man.

There was a chill in the air that hinted of winter. The sleeting rain shivered as it fell, as if it were considering such matters as ice and snow. The inns were doing a roaring business. Light and laughter spilled out into the streets, escaping through quickly opened and shut doors and from behind windows steamed blind with the potent brew of conviviality, roaring fires, and hot ale. It was the perfect night in which not to be seen, particularly if one kept to dark alleys.

It was not long before Smede reached Stalu Street. He paused at a corner, hugging the wall. The one drawback of the house's location was its proximity to the Goose and Gold tavern. Too many of the Thieves Guild in and out of that inn. But the drawback had always had a benefit as well. The Juggler's children. There were always plenty of children in the vicinity.

Smede was about to cross the street when a sudden clamor made him shrink back. The noise grew louder, and then its source came into view. A group of men staggering up the street. Drunk, bellowing out a song about a goatherder from Vomaro. The men slipped and splashed through the puddles, oblivious to the cold rain. Smede recognized one of them. A dock enforcer. From memory, Smede summoned up a page from his accounting book. Cod Harston. Twenty coppers a month from the Guild. And, no doubt, whatever else Harston could skim from his work.

"One more!" bellowed Harston, interrupting the song. "One more. My throat ain't up to all this singing. I'm dried out somethin' terrible."

"M'woman'll be waiting up, see," said another man.

"An' a heavy hand she has."

"Aye. S'another round t' bolster you. Take yer medicine afore, that's what I say."

"Aye. Back t' the Goose!"

"Good ol' Goose."

Cheering this idea, the men turned and staggered back down the street.

Smede sneered as he watched them go. Fools, all of them. Like every poor soul that lived in the city. From the regent on his throne down to the lowliest beggar in the gutters of Fishgate. All fools. None of them knew of the strings that trailed from their lives down into the darkness. Strings ready to be twitched. Or snapped in two.

Smede skulked along in the men's wake. Behind him, unseen, crept the cat. The door of the Goose and Gold was flung open with a crash. Light and noise spilled out into the street. Smede froze, shrinking back against a wall. Something in him yearned toward the light and the warmth and the friendly cheer of that place, but then he scowled. He knew something even better. The group of men crowded through the door, which then slammed shut. The street was quiet again except for the rain and the wind moaning in the rooftops. Smede scurried past the inn. The house came awake at his approach. It knew him. Had known him for many years. The warding spells came to life, but they quieted at his whisper and coiled themselves back into sleep. The door eased open and closed behind him.

The little cat stopped on the threshold of the neighboring house. Its fur was plastered flat against its scrawny body by the rain. To all appearances, the cat should have been the most miserable cat in all of Hearne, particularly in view of all the wonderfully dry and warm cellars, basements, and attics that were accessible through drains, broken windows, and the kindness of people. But the cat's eyes were bright with interest and it studied the house that Smede had entered. After a moment, it hurried away into the night.

Smede paused inside the entrance hall of the house to wring out his cloak. He sneezed and wiped his nose on his arm. Shadows, he was cold. But he'd show them, yes he would. He'd show them. He was an accountant. He remembered things. He remembered numbers and figures and letters. He wrote them down. And if he saw them, he could write them again. It might not be one of those things that was pleasant to remember. But sometimes a little unpleasantness was necessary.

Smede took a deep breath and hurried down the hall. And up the long stairs. So many stairs. He opened the door at the end of the long hall on the third story. There was only silence inside. The ancient spell was gone. Its voice was no more. The parchment that had sat on the table for so many hundreds of years was only dust now.

"But perhaps I can write you again," Smede said out loud. "And then some fresh blood. That'll do the trick."

The table was covered with dust. He delved into one pocket and came up with a quill. A sharp, iron-nibbed quill. He brushed the dust off the table. He could almost see the words in his mind. There had not been many of them. But they had been perfect. The script had been an elegant scrawl. The writing of a learned man. Smede frowned, trying to concentrate. Surely he knew them. He had read them aloud countless times over the years.

"Darkness below," he said. "Are my wits lost?"

And with that, the first word came to him.

Smede wrote it on the table. The next word appeared in his mind, and then the next. The iron nib bore down heavily and scored the wood. His writing was cramped and neat, not like the old elegant scrawl. But the words were the same. He wrote faster and faster. His eyes shone. The sentences formed on the table, one after the other. The old sounds of them formed in his mind. His lips shaped them silently. Four more words left. Three more. Only two more. He giggled out loud. The last word floated into his thoughts and he bent back to the table, his face triumphant. But then there was a sound behind him. It was a quiet sound, but even a quiet sound can be loud if heard in a silent house. Smede turned. There, within the doorway, stood a little cat. A gray cat with bright blue eyes. The cat did not move but regarded him steadily.

"Well now," said Smede. "By the shadows above and below, I don't know how you got in, but what a stroke of fortune. You'll do nicely."

He took a step forward to grab up the cat. But then he stopped, astonished. A second cat strolled into view and stood next to the little gray. They both stared at Smede.

"Upon my soul," said Smede.

A third cat appeared. And then another. And another. In no time at all, the open hallway beyond the door was crowded with cats. They stood in silence and stared at Smede.

"Here now," said Smede, clutching his pen and wishing he had a cudgel or a burning torch. "Shoo. Scat! Go on with you!"

He stamped on the floor to encourage the cats, but this had no effect. They continued staring at him. It was disconcerting. Smede tried another method. He bent down and stretched out his hand to the little gray cat.

"Here, kitty," he said. "Here, kitty-kitty. Nice kitty."

The cat hissed.

Smede snatched his hand back.

The cat snarled, revealing sharp teeth. The two cats on either side of it snarled as well. Other cats began snarling. Their eyes shone in the shadows.

"Nice kitty," said Smede, beginning to tremble.

The cats leapt forward as one.

Outside, it was still raining. Across the street, muffled merriment could be heard from inside the Goose and Gold. Smoke drifted up from the inn's chimney, gilded here and there by stray moonlight and riddled with rain. The moon, drifting overhead on her bed of clouds, peered down through the darkness.

Some time later, if a passerby had glanced to one side as he walked down Stalu Street, he might have noticed a strange thing. But there were no passersby, so what happened next was seen by no one except the moon and several foraging rats, who ran off as fast they could in the opposite direction.

A little gray cat with brilliant blue eyes appeared in the open window at the ground floor of the old, three-story house just down the street from the Goose and Gold Inn.

There seemed to be blood on the cat's muzzle. It jumped down to the ground. Another cat appeared in the window and followed it. And then another and another. A whole stream of cats jumped out of the window and vanished away into the night. The little gray cat remained standing in the alley below the window until all the rest of the cats had disappeared. Then, the cat strolled away, tail held high. The rain washed away the blood from the cat's muzzle. By the time it reached the end of the street, the cat was decidedly wet. Wet, but clean as well.

CHAPTER NINETY-FIVE
ON THE TRAIL OF GIVERNY FARROW

They made camp that evening, long after the sun had set and the moon had risen to survey the dark plain with her mournful eye. Declan was all for pushing on into the night, but the hawk would have none of it.

"Jute's about to fall asleep on his feet," said the hawk. "We'll make camp here. This spot is as good as any other on this blasted plain."

Declan reluctantly agreed, and the hawk, attempting to be fair despite being in a foul mood, pointed out that even a Farrow would have difficulty keeping to a trail in the dead of night.

"Might I add," said the ghost, "that I'm feeling tired myself. These old bones aren't what they used to be."

"Ghosts don't get tired," said Declan.

"It's a choice," said the ghost primly.

They ate a cold supper of stale bread and sausage. Then, wrapped in their cloaks, they lay down in the blowing grasses. The last thing Jute heard before he fell asleep was the ghost muttering about books and ogres.

The next day dawned with a chill, leaden light. The sun rose like a silver disk that had more in common with the night and the moon than daylight.

"Bah," said the hawk. "This is no sky for flying. Even a butterfly would fall to earth today." But despite these words, the hawk took to the air in slow strokes of his wings, as if he had to feel his way up through the currents and winds onto the safety of higher ground.

Halfway through the morning they found the bodies. The hawk fell out of the sky and Jute could hear the wind whistling through his wings. He settled onto the boy's shoulder and stared ahead.

"What is it?" said Jute.

The hawk would not answer, but Jute could feel the bird's claws trembling as they gripped his shoulder. Declan called out from far ahead. Jute ran to him and found himself looking down a slope. He caught his breath. On the plain below them lay dark shapes. The bodies of men and horses and beasts. And what looked like enormous dogs.

"Wolves," said Declan. "Mountain wolves."

"Nonsense," said the ghost. "This is a plain. Do you see any mountains nearby?"

"Stay behind me, Jute," said Declan. "Don't step where I haven't stepped."

The ground was trampled, the grass torn, revealing the earth in dark brown gashes. Everywhere there were dark stains of blood. Flies buzzed in the grass and on the silent shapes of the dead.

"I don't recognize this armor," said Declan. He spoke softly, as if he thought his voice would wake the dead from their sleep. "Few fight with spears like these. The soldiers of Harth sometimes do, but these faces aren't from the desert land."

"There are more men and horses dead than wolves, aren't there?" said Jute. He did not like the look of the wolves. They were nearly half the size of a full-grown horse, and their jaws looked large enough to engulf his head in one bite.

"I wish I'd been here." Declan shook his head. "I'll bless and curse these wolves all my days, for their fangs did my job. They killed well. But the dead men here are only soldiers and there's surely more to this evil than them."

"Aye," said the hawk. "There's much more to this place than dead men and wolves. The earth is full of sorrow here. Something very odd happened here. I think—" But the hawk abruptly shut his beak and would not finish whatever it was that he was about to say. Jute marveled at the hawk's eyes. He was not sure, but it seemed as if there was fear in them.

"I can't track sorrow, master hawk," said Declan. He paced the ground slowly, his head down. "But I can track most anything else. Several men on horseback fled this place. Three at most. Three horses running weary. They'd been running long before the wolves attacked them. And here, look here. This is peculiar. The wolves weren't alone. They had companions. This one horse, whose tracks I noted before and, I think, a young man or a woman. I'm not certain which. Whoever it was didn't weigh much, for the prints are light and already the grass is springing back up. But this is strange. See here?"

"I find nothing strange about any of this except for one thing," said the ghost. "Where are the ghosts? I died from choking on a bit of beef, or was it because of a spell gone wrong? I can't remember. At any rate, I ended up a ghost drifting about the Stone Tower for hundreds of years. It's not fair."

"You see?" Declan knelt down in the grass. "That one person stood here and fought for some time, for the bodies of the soldiers lie thickly around. They tried to overwhelm him but they couldn't prevail. And here. . ."

His voice trailed away into silence.

"What is it?" said the hawk.

"Here he fell," said Declan slowly. "But his body is gone. Perhaps he was only wounded, or perhaps the wolves bore him away? That makes no sense." His voice sharpened. "I've found her!"

To Jute's eye, Declan had found nothing. The grass was trampled and bloodstained. Bodies lay like trees felled by a storm and around them were scattered their shattered branches: swords and spears and arrows. It was a horrible confusion, and he could see none of the tracks apparent to Declan. Jute picked up an arrow and frowned at it.

"How do you know you've found her?" said Jute. "How can you tell from this? One footprint's just as good as another."

"Footprints are as different as faces," said Declan. "This one's small and narrow and barely indents the grass. A girl's foot of slight weight, carrying no weapons or armor. The stride is about what I'd expect of someone roughly your height. Giverny would be not much older than you this year."

"I once knew a girl named Giverny," mumbled the ghost.

Jute suspected the ghost said this more to have something to say, rather than because it was true. But, with ghosts, saying something is halfway to believing the thing to be true, and the ghost embarked on a story about a girl named Giverny whose father had a peach orchard in Vomaro.

"This can only end badly," said the hawk.

"Nonsense," said the ghost. "If you must know the end before we get there, she married the third son of a minor lord and lived happily ever after. They had five children."

"Quiet! I wasn't talking to you, you wisp of vapid vapor!"

"You needn't be so rude," said the ghost. And with that, it vanished.

"Aha," said the hawk. "The pest is gone. An unanticipated but happy circumstance. At least there's one bright spot in this wretched day."

"I haven't gone far," came the ghost's voice. "I'm merely taking a nap in Jute's knapsack. Hmm. I can almost feel a pun coming on."

"Look at this!" said Jute.

He had been wandering about, trying to find a sword small and light enough for him to carry. He was envious of Declan's sword and thought it high time he had one of his own. After all, they might find themselves in a fight for their lives or some other dreadful situation. It wouldn't do to be unprepared. The others came around and looked at what Jute had found. A dagger lay on the ground. It was a plain thing, with a sharp and serviceable blade. In the hilt, however, was a stone. A dull, cracked stone. Jute knelt down beside the dagger. The hawk alighted on the ground beside him.

"I wonder who this belonged to?" said Jute. "What an odd-looking stone. It reminds me of something, but I can't recall what. There's a great deal of blood on the blade."

"I think," said the hawk, his voice oddly shaky, "that this is just a worthless old blade now."

"Come, we should be on our way," said Declan, frowning, looking at both of them and wondering.

They set off. Both Jute and the hawk were silent for a long time. Declan ranged far ahead of them. The wind blew the scent of grass and rain into their faces and Jute breathed deep. It was good to be away from the dead bodies. He quickened his pace to catch up with Declan, but the man had stopped about a hundred yards in front of them. When Jute came to him, he was staring down at the ground.

"This," he said, "I don't understand."

"What don't you understand?" said the hawk. "This is a bad day, doubly bad. That's what I understand. Worse than you could ever imagine." And the bird's claws tensed again on Jute's shoulder, clutching in agitation.

"She's not alone."

"What?" said the hawk.

"Giverny. My sister. She's not alone."

"What do you mean? Who's with her?"

"A wolf. They're walking side by side."

They all thought about this in silence for a moment, though the ghost made noises in Jute's knapsack as if it were clearing its throat in preparation for a long speech. But perhaps the ghost then thought better of this, for it said nothing.

"A wolf with the girl," said the hawk. "A wolf? Now, why would that be? Why on earth?" The bird abruptly shut his beak with a click.

"What would she be doing with a wolf?" said Declan in bewilderment.

"Wolves are strange beasts," said the ghost. "There's no telling for their tastes. I once heard a tale of a crofter family who lived high in the foothills of the Morn Mountains. Bandits murdered them all save a child of not even one year of age. The tale said that wolves found the child and raised him as their own."

"I doubt this is a similar circumstance."

"There's no way to know for sure," said the hawk, rousing from silence. "But we're wasting time. The wolf isn't harming your sister, no? They're walking together. No need to bother wondering why for now. If we're going to find your sister, then let's do it, and do it quickly."

Declan needed no more encouragement than this and did not question the hawk about his sudden enthusiasm, other than giving him one startled glance. He walked along at a loping stride that forced Jute to run along behind him.

I don't understand, said Jute inside his mind to the hawk. *One moment you're growling about going to Harlech and the next moment you say we must hurry south to find this girl.*

Precisely, said the hawk. *Find the girl and then hurry off to Harlech as fast as we can.*

Does this have something to do with that old dagger I found? You looked rather strange when you saw it.

Perhaps. The hawk's voice was reluctant.

Jute stopped walking. "What do you mean?"

"What I mean," said the hawk out loud, "is that you need to hurry and catch up with Declan. You're far behind as it is."

"Not until you tell me."

"Tell you what?" said the ghost, popping out of Jute's knapsack. "Whatever it is, I need to know."

"What's going on?" called Declan. He strode back to them. "Are you arguing about flying again? I'm sure there'll be plenty of time for that later. Come on. I don't want to lose a minute of daylight."

"We're not arguing about flying," said Jute. "Hawk won't explain about your sister and the dagger I found. He knows something and he won't tell."

"Very rude of him," said the ghost.

"It's not that I won't explain," said the hawk stiffly. "I'm just, well, I'm still thinking about it. I'm considering. It's not always best to blurt out everything that crosses one's mind. Like some people I know." Here, the bird shot a dirty look at the ghost.

"At least I'm honest," said the ghost.

"If it has something to do with my sister," said Declan, "then I have a right to know."

"She's not just your sister anymore," snapped the hawk.

There was a moment of silence at this. Even the ghost looked shocked by what the hawk had said.

"What did you say?" said Declan quietly.

"I, uh, well. . . " The hawk looked at the man and then hunched his head miserably down into his feathers. "I don't even want to say it out loud. I thought something dreadful had happened yesterday, I thought I heard something in the wind, but I dismissed it. I didn't want to think about it. I didn't want to contemplate the possibility."

"What do you mean?" said Jute "Stop talking in circles."

The hawk heaved a sigh. He was silent for a moment, but then he spoke, slowly and reluctantly. "The earth died yesterday. At that battlefield we found. She died there."

"You mean the lady who—the lady who rescued me in the regent's castle?" An ache and a darkness seemed to open up in Jute's stomach. He could still see her face. The way she had kissed his brow. "She's dead?"

"It was in the scent of the grass and in the voice of the wind yesterday, but I was blind to it. The clouds were hurrying across the sky to conceal the sight. When we reached the battlefield, then I was forced to recognize what I had been willfully blind to. I've not known such sorrow since the day my old master the wind was murdered. But the earth

470

didn't die alone. Someone was by her side. Your sister, Farrow. Do you remember the dagger Jute found on that battlefield?"

"The one with the ugly stone in its handle," said Jute. "For the life of me, I still can't remember where I've seen something like that before."

"But it was the life of you," said the hawk. "Think back to the knife you stole from Nio's house. A knife with a gemstone in its hilt."

Jute's eyes widened. "The same stone?"

"Rather, both pieces of the same stone. They are sister stones. You saw them as lifeless gems, cracked and worthless. But they were ancient things. Nokhoron Nozhan himself gave three stones to his three servants, the sceadus. Long ago. Centuries ago, high on the mountains of Ranuin. They were supposedly as large as a man's fist. Sharp-edged and burning with fire. Three stones born from three drops of his own blood, full of his malice. Enough malice to take the life of the anbeorun themselves. Barely enough. And now, like the knife that Jute stole, whatever power was stolen by that stone is now gone. Gone with your sister, I think."

The hawk looked at Declan. "I do not know what design Levoreth Callas had in this as she died, but I doubt it a mistake your sister was there at that moment. I'd wager everything I know, the earth waits to be born anew in your sister, just as the wind stirs within our Jute here. You've lost your sister, but Tormay will soon gain a powerful protector against the Dark. If, and only if, the girl can survive long enough for the winter inside her to turn to spring. I can do nothing but try to find her while keeping this fledgling safe as well, for the wind and the earth were brother and sister long ago, before the stars fell, before the ancient wars when the world was still young. Both must live or all shall die. And I gave my word to her, I did," But these last few words the hawk spoke quietly, as if only to himself.

Declan's hand clenched on the hilt of his sword. His face was white.

"I've lost all my family," he said. "But now I must lose my sister as well? My loss for Tormay's gain? I've lost enough already."

The hawk did not answer. Declan turned without another word and strode away. The others followed him in silence, and all around them across the plain, the wind mourned as it blew through the grasses.

They hurried along through the day. The sun gleamed across the sky, silvering through the blowing clouds. The light felt chilled from the wind and the spattering rain. The cold of the day worked its way into Jute's bones until he could not tell where the warmth of his body ended and the cold air surrounding him began.

Just so, said the hawk. *That's the first step if you would learn to fly.*

I'd rather have some hot stew, said Jute. But then he thought better of it, for he did wish to fly. He imagined it would be a lot less tiring than stumbling across the ground, forever trying to keep up with Declan.

I know about flying, said the hawk, *but I cannot cook stew.*

What do you mean by the first step?

It took Jute a while to get the hawk back into a better mood. But after a great deal of flattery and declarations of admiration for birds in general and hawks specifically, the hawk relented. He explained that the first step in learning how to fly was to forget about one's self and assume that one was part of the sky.

Which, of course, is not true, said the hawk. *The sky is the sky, and you are you. But thinking otherwise helps, all the same.*

Why should it?

Because it convinces you to forget about yourself. There's nothing more disconcerting than remembering that you're made of all too solid flesh, particularly when you're high in the sky. Start thinking like that and you'll convince yourself to drop like a stone.

Does that happen to birds?

Birds? The hawk snorted in amusement. *Of course not. We have wings.*

The second step in learning to fly was keeping hold of the wind. This, according to the hawk, was not unlike keeping hold of the yarn while knitting. The hawk confided that he had never done any knitting himself, as his claws were not suited for it, but he imagined the two were similar.

"And then what?" panted Jute out loud. "Declan, slow down!"

"What, what?" said the ghost from inside his knapsack. "What do you mean bellowing like that while I'm asleep?"

"I wasn't talking to you."

"Immaterial, my dear boy. Immaterial, just as I am." The ghost appeared and drifted along beside him. It examined him with interest. "You look wan. Pale and sweating. Do you suffer from fever? Your frequent gasping for breath might signify something serious. Consumption, perhaps? It can be fatal."

"What's the third step?"

"The third step," said the hawk, "is just that. A step. You step off the ground."

"That's ridiculous. I can't step off the ground. What would I be stepping onto?"

"Take hold of the wind and step off the ground."

"Ah," said the ghost. "Learning how to fly, eh? Flying is for birds, not boys. You're much too heavy. You'll get up there and then fall like a stone. That'll be the end of you."

Jute made no progress as the afternoon wore on, but the one good side effect of the endeavor was that it diverted his mind from the fatiguing pace Declan set. The hawk coasted overhead on outstretched wings, calling down advice to Jute. The ghost drifted next to him and spent its time listing all the people it knew who had died of falling from heights. The list was long, and the ghost explained the deaths in gruesome detail.

"I remember reading an interesting case," said the ghost cheerfully. "A self-educated wizard who lived in a village in the Morn Mountains, east of Andolan. His name, as far as I recollect, was. . . er. . . hmm. Ah, yes. His name was Dillo. He owned two old books of magic his grandmother had traded off an illiterate peddler. He knew how to read and he had those books—a dangerous combination. He learned how to mend iron pots with just a word, and he learned how to grow the sweetest corn in all of Tormay. If Dillo had stuck to iron pots and growing corn, he would've had a peaceful life. Dull, yes, but peaceful."

The hawk continued to encourage Jute and pretended to ignore the ghost's ramblings. It must be pointed out, however, that the hawk had nothing more specific to say about learning to fly than what he had already said, except for one last bit of advice.

"What do you mean, it'll just happen?" said Jute. "That's no help."

"It'll happen. Trust me."

"Besides all the trifling whatnot of corn-growing and pot-mending and weaving wards to fend off gophers, root blight, and mothers-in-law, Dillo only managed to learn two legitimate spells of power," said the ghost, eyeing Jute and the hawk sternly, for they did not seem to be paying proper attention to his story.

"The first was a spell that divided time. An elegant idea, but difficult in execution. The essential idea is that any measure of time—whether it be an hour, a minute, or even a second—can be divided in half, and then one of those halves divided again, and so on.

Take a second, for example. Divide it in half. Divide one of those halves in half. Divide one of those halves in half. You see what I mean, eh? It leaves you, of course, with the fact that there are an infinite number of halves to be traveled through before you get to the next second. Therefore, you'd never arrive at the next second. Brilliant, eh?"

No one bothered answering. Jute was concentrating on the wind. What did one do if the wind died away? His feet were still touching the ground and felt depressingly heavy. The hawk was muttering under his breath and gliding along beside Jute on motionless wings. Far ahead of them, Declan turned and frowned. He did not say anything, however, but slackened his pace.

"Don't concentrate so hard," said the hawk.

"I can't help it."

"The second spell," continued the ghost, "was, of course, a flying spell. Now, in my opinion, flying spells should never be attempted unless by those with an exceedingly superb education, such as myself, or any number of students I've taught over the years. Such spells always involve the wind and the wind's a tricky, sly sort of thing. Oh, I don't doubt Dillo managed to get a few feet above the ground—more than can be said for you, young Jute—to waver about like a weathervane and impress the chickens and his wife. I'm sure I could've done the same and better in my day. But one afternoon, Dillo got the idea into his head that what this flying thing needed was some stiff encouragement—the proverbial leap of faith. So he climbed up to the falls behind the village and leapt off the cliff there."

The ghost paused here and looked at them expectantly. Jute took the bait. He could not help himself.

"What happened? Did he fly?"

"Ah, no," said the ghost happily. "No, he didn't. I'm sad to say he dropped like a rock. Plunged straight down. Dillo would've hit the bottom if it weren't for the other spell. The spell that divided time. I daresay he must've been frantic, screaming and hollering and trying to figure any way out of his own foolishness. That was when he got the bright idea to divide time. If he could only slow time down, then he would have more time to start flying and not end up a smear on the rocks below. About ten feet short of those rocks, Dillo divided time. And time kept on dividing."

"What do you mean?" said Jute. "What happened?"

"What I mean," said the ghost, "is that Dillo cast his last spell a little too effectively. Sheer terror can do that for you. If you go to the falls above that town, you'll see the skeleton of poor Dillo hanging in the air about ten feet above the rocks, for time's still happily dividing away at that particular spot."

"That's absurd," said the hawk, unable to keep his beak shut any longer. "Of all the ridiculous stories you've told, that's the most ridiculous story yet. Time can't be stopped."

"I don't tell ridiculous stories," said the ghost. "I tell only serious stories that illustrate the wisdom gained from years as a professor."

"Will you all pipe down?"

It was Declan. He stalked back toward them.

"Traveling with a herd of bleating sheep would be quieter than you lot." He scowled and even the hawk looked abashed at his rebuke. "The light's failing and there's no telling what the night'll bring. We don't need your caterwauling catching the attention of whatever's out there. By the way, Jute?"

"What?"

"You're floating."

Jute looked down and felt his stomach lurch. He was floating about a foot above the ground. His arms shot out in order to catch hold of something, anything. He overbalanced and fell flat on his face. He heard the ghost and Declan laughing and the chuckle of the hawk. And somewhere off in the distance, perhaps in his mind, he heard the airy laughter of the wind.

CHAPTER NINETY-SIX
ANOTHER USE FOR DEAD DEER

The duke of Mizra's party camped that evening on the edge of the forest. The trees loomed in the twilight like an impenetrable swath of darkness. A hundred yards away, the Rennet River flowed west toward Hearne and the sea. The water shone with moonlight, and the liquid sound of its passage was the loudest thing to be heard, for the duke's men set up camp in silence. Several fires soon were burning and the shapes of tents heaved themselves up from the ground. The duke of Mizra sat in a chair by the fire before his tent. He stared into the flames. They flickered before him, gaining color and definition as the evening grew darker. Fire needed the darkness in order for its true color to be revealed.

"My lord?"

It was one of the chamberlain's assistants. A son of a minor lord. The duke could never remember their names. They all looked the same to him. Pale, blurred faces with short lives that guttered out like candles.

"My lord?"

"What is it?"

Brond made an effort to stretch his face into the semblance of a smile. A grimace.

"The hunters have brought back deer and geese, milord. Would you prefer one or the other for supper?"

"Both will do."

The boy bowed and vanished back into the twilight.

Not that he needed food. Once, he had gone without food or water for a year and it had not affected him in any way. But eating was still one of several small pleasures that life afforded him. Particularly fresh meat.

Brond stared out at the forest. Not many people knew why it was called the Forest of Lome these days, but he did. He remembered. A dragon had lived there once. A dragon named Lome. The creature had lived in a cave in a spire of rock in the middle of the forest. The spire was still there, but the dragon had been dead for hundreds of years. Killed by a young man named Dolan Callas, who had later gone on to found the duchy of Dolan in the north. The forest had grown dark and thick since the death of the dragon. Brond scowled, remembering the heat of the dragon's breath and the flames. The old trees in the forest remembered too, and he no longer went into the forest if he could help it.

He felt a shift in the air behind him. A sudden chill in the breeze.

"You were unsuccessful," he said, not bothering to turn.

"The bitch wolf intervened."

The voice was quiet and thin, so quiet that Brond had to strain his ears to hear. He saw what looked like a disturbance in the air, a bending of the light. It drew closer.

"Again, she defeated you," he said. "Despite the strength I lent you."

"She's dead."

The duke stared at the fire and did not answer. "Dead," he said to himself, almost in disbelief. After a while, he grimaced and then shook his head, as if clearing an unwanted thought from his mind. "But you didn't secure the means of her death."

"No. It was all I could do to keep myself alive. I was forced to kill the remainder of your soldiers and their horses. Even they were barely enough to sustain me."

"Do you know where the girl is?"

"I don't know. Wandering the plain. She was mute as stone when I took her. Even when I slaughtered her father and mother before her eyes, she did not cry out."

"An old, proud line," said the duke. "But she'll bend, she will. The Dark has been dreaming of her. We need to find her."

"I must go," said the sceadu. "My death is upon me unless I can feed. There's a village not far from here, on the banks of the river."

"You'll stay and tell your tale," said the duke, and though the sceadu strove to evade him, he caught at the few thin strands of life left and bent the thing to his will. It told him its story, of the death and fire it had brought to the Farrows, of the silent, white-faced girl and the galloping ride back across the plain. It spoke of the onslaught of the wolves, of the death that they had brought to the duke's men, and of the broken earth.

"Two shards of my jewel, set in two knives," said the sceadu. "I've carried them for countless years. They were my heart. That's how I slew the wind, and it did for the wolf as well. But my heart is diminished now. I have little left."

"I would've given much to have that knife." The duke's voice was quiet, but it trembled with anger. "First the wind and now this. I'm not sure whether to praise or curse you."

"I would've had it," said the sceadu, "but my life was running through my fingers and now it's nearly gone."

"Then go," said the duke.

He turned back to the fire, but his eyes did not see the flames. He saw her again, smiling and moving lightly across the ballroom floor in the regent's castle. Had she known? He could still feel her beauty like an old wound in his memory. There had been an echo in her eyes of starfire and impossible distance and the silence of the house of dreams. With a snarl, he forced the memory from his mind. Finding the sceadu's knife and the girl were the important things now. Just as important as finding that accursed thief boy. A thought came to him. He stood up and paced back and forth. The fire crackled and sent sparks up into the night.

Of course!

No wonder the Dark wanted the girl. No wonder his dreams had been troubled with her face. He had puzzled over that for days. But the Dark had known what the future held for her. Brond smiled, his teeth bared. There would be no need to find the sceadu's knife now. Only the girl. And after her, if it was possible, the boy. With the two of them, he could rule the world.

"But how to catch her?" the duke said out loud. "My poor hounds are gone, and the sceadu will be no use to me for days. If I don't act now, she might wander far away."

He snapped his fingers and the fire roared up in response.

"Boy!" he shouted.

The chamberlain's assistant came running out of the darkness, wiping his hands on his apron.

"My lord?"

"Has the deer been gutted and cleaned already?"

476

"Yes, my lord," said the boy. "It's roasting on the spit now with the geese. Your supper shall—"

"Never mind that," said the duke. "Bring me the skeleton and hide."

"B-but the offal's been buried."

"Dig it up."

"Aye, my lord."

In no time, the boy returned with his arms piled high with a dirty mess of hide and bones. The duke took it from him and the boy stood there, gaping, until Brond snarled at him. The duke strode away from the camp and the firelight. The darkness of the plain settled around him, waiting. The hide was already in tatters. He slashed it into three piles with his knife. He snapped the bones into pieces. The skull shattered under his boot. He scattered the bone shards on the three piles and stood back.

Brond did not speak, but frowned, concentrating. The darkness crept closer and, high overhead, the moon hid itself behind a cloud. The piles of bone and hide twitched and then, abruptly, heaved themselves up on slender, gangly legs. Darkness wove in and out of the gaps of hide and attached itself to bone, weaving sinew and flesh from shadow. Shards of bone flashed in their mouths like teeth and a red light glinted where their eyes should have been.

"Listen well," said the duke. "I've a task to be done."

CHAPTER NINETY-SEVEN
THE END OF THE HUNT

Giverny was not aware of the day passing by. She only knew a dull, heavy grief that blinded her senses. Her body worked on its own, without needing her thought. Her legs walked on, even while she saw nothing, and the sun neared its completion of the day.

She could not see or smell or hear what was around her—the Scarpe plain at twilight—but the senses of her memory were sharp. Unbearably sharp. She could smell oatmeal steaming over a fire. She saw her mother's face intent over the fire, sweat gleaming on her brow from the heat. From somewhere close by, she could hear her father whistling to himself. The tuneless whistle meant he was whittling or braiding a halter or polishing a weapon, any number of things he did with his callused hands. And then she saw Levoreth's face smiling before it dissolved into earth.

There is another way to mourn the dead.

The voice was deep. Giverny had heard it before inside her mind. It had a strange but reassuring sound to it. A furry sound. That was it.

The wolf.

The shock of the thought caused her to truly see. Beside her, so close she could have stretched out her hand to touch his fur, paced a wolf. His fur was black and his eyes were silver. She shivered away from him.

I would never hurt you.

"How can you speak inside my mind?" she said. "What are you?"

A wolf.

"Can all wolves speak like this?"

The wolf chuckled.

To you? Aye, all wolves can speak so.

The wolf opened his mouth and she glimpsed sharp white fangs.

"But if mindspeech troubles you," he said, "I can speak out loud. And this, other wolves cannot do."

Giverny was not sure what frightened her more—the sound of the wolf's voice in her mind, or the sight of him speaking out loud. She could not answer the wolf for a while. She was shy of him. The wolf was content to pace in silence beside her. Far off on the horizon, the jagged line of mountains shone in the afternoon sun. The sun was dipping down in the west, and Giverny's shadow wavered across the grass.

"What did you mean?" she said. "What did you mean about—about—"

"About mourning?" said the wolf, when Giverny could not finish her sentence. "When death comes to a wolf it is a gift, a good thing. The chance to chase the sun and join the great hunt which courses beyond the stars. Those who remain behind should not mourn such a thing. They should live joyously in honor of the departed."

"I can't live in joy," faltered Giverny.

"Perhaps not now, but when time has passed? For now, the important thing is that you shall live. Only that. For if you die, then the Dark shall tighten its grasp upon this land."

She did not understand what he meant. She was not sure if she wanted to understand.

"Who are you?" she said.

"I am the companion of the Mistress of Mistresses, her paw and her fang. I am the memory of the Earth. I am he who stands at the side of Eorde against the Dark."

"And who am I?" said Giverny, her voice shaking.

"You are the Mistress of Mistresses. The guardian of the Earth and bulwark against the Dark."

"No! That can't be true. I'm just a girl."

The wolf did not say anything, but he regarded her with his silver eyes. Giverny fell to her knees on the grass. The grass was cool and reassuring against her hands. Tears sprang from her eyes. She lay on the ground and pressed her face against the grass. And the earth spoke. She could hear it murmuring to her. Wordless impressions of stone and silence and peace. It spoke of mountains and forests and the dry and thirsty desert of the south. It spoke of trees and hills and rocks. It spoke of the animals that found their home in and on the earth. And it spoke her name.

Giverny did not know how long she lay there. When she sat up, the sun had set and there was only a purpling radiance on the horizon in the west. Stars pricked their way into life in the eastern sky, one by one, in faint points of promised brilliance. The wolf sat by her.

"I'm sorry," she said. "I think I fell asleep. But I don't think I'm tired anymore. I don't think I'll ever be tired again."

"Once," said the wolf, "I used to be an ordinary wolf."

"I know," said Giverny.

The wolf nodded in a satisfied fashion, as if he had remembered something he had almost forgotten.

"My name," he said, "is Ehtan."

They made their way quickly then, for Giverny found that she could run along with a loping pace that did not tire her. Every time her foot struck the earth, it seemed as if life flowed up into her from the ground.

"We should journey east for now," said Ehtan, running by her side. "We're near the forest of Lome and that's a friendly place for our kind. I do not want to be out on this plain at night, for I do not trust the sky. It's for your safety. Consider that a seed needs careful nurture as it sprouts. It is only later, when it has become a tree, that it can withstand the storm. You are that seed and I fear that a storm draws near to Tormay, for the Dark is in this land. We must find safety for a while, and the forest shall give it."

It was darker now. A cold wind rose out of the evening and brought with it the scent of rain and the smell of wood and leaves and the damp rot of the forest floor.

"We're close," said Ehtan. "Noses are better than eyes."

And he was right. As they ran on into the night, Giverny felt her senses come alive, but none more so than her nose. A musky, peppery odor blew by, and with a thrill she realized she knew what it was. A fox. A fox intent on the hunt, and there was the scent of its prey—the sweet, warm smell of a frightened rabbit. She could smell the jona plant, stripped of its summer bloom by the weeks of cold weather. Grass and earth and stone and the faint whiffs of worms and beetles and grasshoppers. And beyond it all, the deep old damp of the forest.

The forest loomed up out of the dark. It was just in time, for the rain began to fall. The girl and the wolf paused under the cover of the trees at the forest's edge and looked back. The leaves above them rustled and dripped with water. The light was failing and the darkness rolled across the plain toward them.

"What is it?" said Giverny. "I can feel unease in your mind. I can smell it."

"I do not know yet. I might be imagining things." The wolf's teeth flashed in what looked like a smile. "You are my first and only charge and I am perhaps overly anxious of my duty. I wish the wind was blowing toward us."

They made their way deeper into the forest. Besides the rain pattering on the leaves overhead, the place was silent to the ear. But Giverny was starting to discover there was another way to listen than with her ears. She turned to the wolf, delight on her face.

"Can all animals listen like this?"

"Listen like what?" said Ehtan.

"This murmuring in my thoughts! Oh, it's not in my thoughts. Rather, it waits politely on the edge of my thoughts, waiting for me to turn to it, to choose to listen to it."

"Most animals can, to a degree. But nothing such as what you are able to do."

"Why's that?"

"Because," said the wolf, "you are the Mistress of Mistresses."

The wonder of being able to listen to the speech of animals was so great that, without realizing it, Giverny's grief fell away. She would have walked straight into tree trunks and stumbled over bushes, so intent was she on listening, were it not for Ehtan patiently nudging her this way and that as they walked deeper into the forest.

A badger chiding her son.

Eat your supper now, there's a good boy.

But I don't like grubs.

They're good for you. Don't you want to grow up nice and strong? Besides, grubs'll make your fur shiny smooth. See, your pa eats his grubs right up.

A mouse telling a bedtime story to his six children.

Once upon a time, there lived a mouse named Cheesetwig. He lived in a hole beneath an old willow tree. One day—

Father?

Yes, son?

I know what a twig is, but I don't know what a cheese is. What's a cheese?

I don't rightly know, son, but I've heard it is something wonderful. Now, don't interrupt. As I was saying, one day, Cheesetwig packed a lunch and set out to see the world.

Father?

Yes, son?

What did he pack for lunch?

Two squirrels curled up in a hole in an oak tree.

Walnuts. Let's see. One for you, one for me. One for you, one for me. One for you, one for—

You gave me the same walnut twice.

No, I didn't.

Yes, you did.

All righty! All righty! We'll start over. Walnuts. One for you, one for me. One for—

That's an acorn.

No, it isn't.

Yes, it is.

Giverny smiled. And then realized there were other voices besides the animals. Quieter, slower voices.

Sweet water. Sweet water deep down here. Deep down.

Aye, deep down. Beneath the rock. But your roots have already broken a way. I thank you, friend oak.

It is nothing. Nothing, little willow. You are still young.

"The trees," said Giverny. "I can hear the trees."

"Hush," said Ehtan. "Something is not right."

The wolf stopped in his tracks and turned his head from side to side. His lip curled in a snarl.

"Can't you smell it? Something comes near. Something of the Dark."

"What do you mean?"

Giverny only had the vaguest of notions of the Dark. Her father had told her tales when she had been a child, but they had been only that to her, just tales. Deliciously frightening stories that sent children to bed with the shivers.

"I don't think I've ever believed in the Dark." But her voice was shaking, for she could now smell something strange in the air. It was the faintest of odors, a whiff of decay and blood and something even more dreadful than those.

"Believe, Mistress," said the wolf. "The Dark believes in you."

"What shall we do?"

Ehtan glanced around. He shook his heavy head.

"The old oak there, Mistress. Climb as high as you can. Find a place in the branches to wait in stillness and silence for my return. The oak will hide you in its quiet. I shall find the creature and slay it before it draws near to you."

"Let me come with you!"

"No. Remember, climb high and then await me there in silence."

With that last word, the wolf disappeared into the dark trees. Giverny scowled and stamped her foot, but then she shivered. She ran to the oak and began to climb. The branches were wet with rain, but it seemed as if the tree shifted ever so slightly beneath her so that her hands and feet always found a secure hold. She settled into the fork of a branch high within the foliage and listened. Other than the dripping of the rain, the forest was silent. The murmur of the animals within her mind had ceased. Instead, there was only a breathless expectancy, a stillness, and dread. Giverny strained her eyes, trying to see through the darkness to the forest floor below, but the night had grown so complete that she could see nothing save her own hands and the leaves in front of her. A thought formed in her mind.

Cats.

They see at night, don't they?

Giverny growled, deep in her throat, and then stopped, shocked. Where did that come from? She blinked. And then discovered that she could see much more clearly. How strange. Through a gap in the leaves, she could see the ground below.

She heard Ehtan howl somewhere to the north. It was a sharp bay, the call of the hunter that means the prey has been sighted and the chase is on. The howl came again, but it was fainter and further away this time. Giverny thrilled with the sound of it. Her fingers flexed. Surely she was safe now. Ehtan had headed off the intruder and, no doubt, he would pull it down to the kill. But he had told her to stay in the tree until he returned. She frowned. And then climbed down several branches. The wolf's howl wavered through the air a third time. It was so far away now that it was barely discernible. Giverny climbed down another branch and then froze.

The smell.

It was back.

Decay and death. The smell was so strong it made her eyes water. The skin on the back of her neck pricked uncomfortably. It felt as if someone was watching her. She peered down at the ground below. Nothing stirred. Rain dripped down her neck. And then the branch broke beneath her.

Giverny didn't have time to scream. She fell, grabbing at branches and only getting handfuls of leaves. Something whipped past her face and she felt a burning line of pain on her cheek. The ground rushed up fast. It was far to fall. But she landed lightly on her feet like a cat. For several seconds she crouched there, her heart beating wildly. The forest was still silent. Nothing moved. But the stench was stronger now. Blood trickled down her cheek. Something rustled in the bushes next to the oak. It was the quietest of noises, but it was appallingly loud in the silence. Giverny backed away.

Something stepped out of the bushes. It was a creature straight from a nightmare. Moonlight gleamed on bare bones and dangling shreds of hide. Its breath steamed in the air, stinking with decay and death. The thing stared at her for a moment. And then it lurched forward.

Giverny screamed and ran. She blundered through bushes and tumbled down sudden embankments. Briers scratched and tried to hold her. Her heart pounded painfully in her breast. Her lungs could not gasp in enough air and she was drowning in the darkness. She did not dare look behind her, but she could hear the strange, staggering run of the creature, crunching across the leaves on the forest floor.

She did not know where to run, only that she had to get away from that thing. Ehtan! If only she could get to him, then she would be safe. He had gone north. Something in her mind nudged at her. North was *that* way. She turned and stumbled down what seemed like a long avenue of trees leading away into the darkness. But a blot of shadow shambled out from the trees ahead of her. It was the creature. No—a second one, for the first one still followed in her wake.

With a sob, Giverny angled away from them both. Trees loomed up out of the darkness. Oaks and willows and ash. For a moment, she could hear voices—old, deep, and slow—murmuring anxiously on the edge of her mind. But the frantic beat of her heart drowned out the voices and she blundered on. She came to the edge of the forest. The trees thinned and the rain fell down in earnest. She tried to turn back, but she could not. The two things hemmed her in on every side except toward the plain. Whimpering, she ran on.

The stars were hidden and the plain stretched out into the night. The two creatures drew closer and Giverny could hear the harsh, greedy rasp of their breath. With a frantic gasp, she ran faster and, for a while, it seemed as if she were outstripping her attendant nightmares. It was then she saw the light in the distance. A tiny smudge of radiance in the darkness. She wiped rain from her eyes, uncertain whether she were only imagining the light. But no, it was there. She ran toward it.

The light grew brighter as she ran. It was a fire of some sort. A campfire. Giverny sobbed out loud with relief. People would be there. Behind her, she heard a hissing snarl and the two creatures increased their speed, stumbling along on their long, grotesque legs. It was a campfire. She could see the flames dancing up from the ground. The firelight gilded the outlines of several tents grouped near the fire. Figures were visible in the encampment.

"Help!" she screamed.

She was nearer now. Near enough to see faces turning toward her. The flames of the campfire roared up as if in response to her scream. But behind her, the creatures snarled and lunged forward.

"Help me, please!"

Several men ran toward her. The firelight glinted on the edges of swords. A tall man with hair as bright as polished gold charged past her. She heard a hideous shrieking noise. Giverny stumbled past the first tent and was in the warm wash of the campfire. Someone wrapped a blanket around her. Voices spoke but she heard nothing of what they said. Her body shook uncontrollably. Hands gripped her shoulders and she found herself looking up into the face of the man with golden hair. He was extremely tall. He said something, his face tight with concern, his eyes intent on hers. He spoke again, more slowly this time.

"They're dead, girl," he said.

"Th-thank you!" Giverny stammered.

"You need not fear them anymore, though such strange beasts as they were—I haven't seen their like in Tormay."

He led her to a chair set beside the fire. A young man hurried up with a mug of steaming broth. She was aware of other faces watching her from across the flames and in the edges of the shadows.

"Drink," said the golden-haired man. "With some of that in you, you'll feel better in no time."

"Thank you," she said again, clutching the blessedly hot mug in her hands and breathing in the steam.

"I bid you welcome to the camp of Brond Gifernes, the duke of Mizra," he said. He bowed and smiled. "And, as I am he, be assured you're safe here."

Giverny drank deeply from the mug. The heat of the broth flooded through her. She could not keep her eyes open. The last thing she saw was the man watching her.

CHAPTER NINETY-EIGHT
SIBB ENCOURAGES THIEVERY

"Come in, come in," said Botrell.

Owain Gawinn entered the room and eyed the regent warily. He could remember only one other time when he had seen him in such a cheerful mood. That had been when Harl Nye of Vo had died from choking on a fishbone. Nye had owned the third best stable of horses in all of Tormay. Nye's widow had sold the horses to the regent two weeks after her lord's death.

"Gawinn, my dear fellow. How are you?"

"Tolerable," said Owain.

"Good, good. Glad to hear it. And how's your lovely wife and the children? Er, you do have children, don't you, Gawinn? I don't know what we'd do without children. Can't stand the little rotters myself, but that's the way life is. A man's big enough to see beyond his personal likes and dislikes. That's me."

The regent smiled and gazed into the mirror. He swiveled around and eyed himself over his shoulder.

"How d'you like this cloak, Gawinn?" he said. "Nice, isn't it, the way it hangs. Splendid silk, just arrived from Harth. Sent courtesy of the prince as thanks for our hospitality."

"I don't have an opinion on silk, my lord," said Owain coldly.

"Oh, come now. We all know that boys play at soldiers only for the uniforms."

"My lord?"

"Haha! Just a joke. You should see your face, Gawinn, you old prune. Ho there! You, boy!" The regent hollered at the page standing in the anteroom. "Where's my breakfast?"

"Coming, my lord!" And the page scuttled away.

"Care for some breakfast, Gawinn?"

"I've already eaten, my lord—"

"Then eat again."

"—and I must return to the barracks. New recruits. It's for that reason I must speak with you. My lord, we're sorely in need of—"

Owain was abruptly shouldered aside by a procession of pages and footmen, led by a fat man with an enormous moustache. A white silk cloth fluttered out onto the table, cutlery appeared as if by magic, a candelabra winked into flame, and three covered platters were whisked forward, each borne aloft by a different footman. The regent sat down and rubbed his hands together.

"No," he said. "Whatever it is, Gawinn, the answer's no. There isn't a problem too great that can't be answered by a sensible, straightforward, resounding no! Living like that is refreshing. I recommend it. Are you sure you won't have a bite to eat? Ahh. What have we here, chamberlain? Smells delicious."

"A quiche of quail eggs, m'lord, baked with a medley of tender wild mushrooms and Vomarone ham and imbued throughout with the fragrance of freshly bruised thyme," said the chamberlain. He stroked his moustache as he spoke and beamed at everyone in the room.

"You haven't heard what I was going to say," said Owain.

"Mmm. Quail eggs. So light and fluffy. You can almost feel the promise of their little feathers tickling the palate. Delightful."

Owain gritted his teeth. "My lord, it's high time we increased the ranks of the Guard. My coffers are empty, the armory's filled with old weapons, and the horses in our stable are even older."

"Horses, eh? Nothing like an old horse for wisdom."

"Furthermore, my lord, for the last time, I can't stress enough the urgent situation our city finds itself in."

"You're casting a blight on my breakfast, Gawinn. A pall!" The regent eyed Owain sourly and then turned his attention back to the next dish as the chamberlain whisked off the cover. "What's this?"

"Wild boar sausage, my lord. Roasted to a delightfully juicy crisp. Flanked by fresh potatoes sliced as thin as parchment and smothered in goat cheese and mountain-grown fennel."

"Hmmph. Mountain-grown fennel? A likely story. And the last dish?"

The chamberlain almost swooned at this question, but he recovered enough to twitch the cover off the third dish.

"Crepes, m'lord," he trilled. "Crepes teased into draperies as delicate as lady's lace, drenched with clover honey, stuffed with the ripest of strawberries, and fried in butter."

This news seemed to cheer the regent up. The chamberlain backed away, bowing repeatedly. Behind him, the other footmen and pages bowed as well.

"As I was saying, my lord," continued Owain doggedly. "Hearne's in a dire situation. Strange murders are taking place in the duchies. Whole villages slaughtered. It falls to Hearne to lead the defense of Tormay when more than one duchy is threatened by a common enemy. It falls to us, my lord."

The regent laid down his fork and glared at Owain.

"What is it that you want?"

"Gold, my lord."

"Well, you aren't getting any," said the regent. "And that's final. Now, get out! My crepes are getting cold!"

Owain felt his face turning red. The footmen and the pages were all staring at the floor. The chamberlain smirked at Owain and twirled his moustache. The regent returned his attention to the crepes and attacked them with his knife and fork.

Outside the castle, a groom was waiting with his horse at the bottom of the steps. Owain grabbed the reins from him and swung up onto the horse.

"Gawinn! Just the man I wanted to see."

It was Dreccan Gor. He hurried across the cobblestones toward Owain.

"What do you want, Gor?"

"I'll need young Arodilac released from his duties all next week."

"Why?"

"The duke of Vomaro's paying us a visit. The regent would like his nephew to be available for the, uh, social niceties. Conversation, ladies to dance with, formal dinners, all that sort of thing."

"No."

"What?" The fat little steward goggled up at Owain.

"You heard me. Arodilac joined the Guard. A soldier he is, and he'll do his duty, just like any other man. No time for prancing about in silks. Good day, Gor."

"No, wait!" said Dreccan, dancing to one side as Owain swung his horse around. "Next week shall be important for Hearne's future. Arodilac has other duties than marching to and fro on the walls. He's the regent's nephew, for shadow's sake."

"The answer's no." And Owain urged his horse away.

There was small comfort in the exchange, but enough to make Owain smile grimly for a moment. Botrell would hear of it soon. But that didn't matter. A Gawinn had always been the Captain of the Guard, and a Gawinn always would.

Owain idly considered why the duke of Vomaro was visiting Hearne. He had met the man once—a long time ago at one of those dreary dinners the regent was so fond of giving. An immense, fat man with a decidedly bitter wit. The dinner had not been pleasant. He had heard strange things about the court at Vomaro. Strange things that had occurred after the duke's daughter had been rescued from the ogres who had kidnapped her. Much of it was obviously nonsense. But one never knew for sure.

The sun shone brightly, but it was a cold day. Autumn had arrived in Hearne, and surely winter was following closely behind. Leaves swirled in the horse's wake, gold and scarlet and brown.

It was true. He had new recruits. But only three, and one of them old and toothless. The Guard was woefully undermanned. He'd be damned if the numbers didn't increase. And soon.

He could hear Bordeall's voice long before he reached the barracks. His voice and the clash of sword on sword. Good. The recruits would be sweating. Owain murmured to his horse and soothed it into a walk. The houses here by the city wall were narrow and tall, built jammed up against each other and, more than likely, jammed just as tightly inside with families and grandparents and aunts and uncles and cousins all living together, cheek by jowl. Hearne was bursting at the seams. At least down here on the flat. Perhaps it was time to consider building outside the city? Extending the walls? No regent had ever done that.

"Must ya start yer shouting an' clashing so early in the morning?"

Owain turned in the saddle, startled.

"What's that?" he said. "Oh. Good morning, Missus Gorlan."

An old woman stumped along beside the horse.

"Tain't a good morning," she said. "Before the sunup, yer lads out there, shoutin' an' bangin' them swords together. It woke the baby. He's colicky an' it ain't easy gettin' him to sleep. We ain't so fond o' the Captain an' his precious Guard in our house."

"Yes, well," he said.

"Ye keep yer lads quiet when honest folks are tryin' to sleep, ya hear me?"

"Noted, madam," said Owain through clenched teeth.

The old woman shouted something else, but he nudged the horse along a bit faster and tried not to listen. Regents and old busybodies. The depressing thing about it was that Missus Gorlan was not the worst of the lot. One fat old cow who lived at the end of the street was forever urging her neighbors to complain to the regent about the barracks. Too much noise at night. Soldiers galloping their horses too quickly down the street. Too much light from the gate torches in the evening. Too much smell from the stables. Too much tax spent on the precious Guard. As if she knew. Complaining was a privilege enjoyed by complacent windbags. They didn't know what lurked outside the city walls.

Owain turned in through the gate. The two soldiers on either side saluted, but he just frowned. A groom hurried up to lead the horse away.

"Find Bridd," he said at a nearby soldier.

"Yes, sir!"

Owain stalked over to the edge of the drill ground and stood watching. A high wall ran around the perimeter, but it was not high enough to prevent the neighborhood children from climbing it. Several of the little wretches were perched on top at the moment. Out on the drill ground, Bordeall barked orders and criticism in a voice loud enough to rattle windows. The three recruits battered away with blunted swords at practice posts. Sweat gleamed on their faces, but the oldest man—a short, wrinkled fellow with a head as bald as a scrubbed potato—swung his sword with vigor, while the other two puffed and staggered about.

"Keep your wrist in it!" hollered Bordeall. "What are you? Men or mice?"

The three recruits surged forward at the posts with renewed vigor. Chips of wood flew. The little old man seemed to be hollering something as he swung his sword, but Owain could not make out the words.

"Mice, more like."

Owain turned. "Keep your tongue in your mouth, Bridd. That'll be extra night duty for you."

"Sorry, sir," said Arodilac.

The lad fidgeted unhappily next to Owain for a while. The children perched on top of the wall jeered and hooted at the three recruits. One of the children threw a well-aimed apple core. It bounced off the head of a recruit, and the man turned, swearing.

"Back to the post!" bellowed Bordeall. "You let something like that distract you, an' you'll be dead your first battle!"

"Ya heard 'im!" yelled the apple-thrower. "Back to yer post or yer dead!" The other children screeched with laughter.

"Sir," said Arodilac, looking outraged, "would you like me to—"

"No," said Owain.

An attempt to deal with the children, regardless of how irritating they were, would end poorly. The children could drop down on the other side of the wall in a trice. Taking their parents to task, if they could even be found, would result in more hard feelings in the neighborhood. No. It would be more prudent to ignore the little wretches. Besides, it would do the recruits no harm to be laughed at.

"Bridd."

"Yes, sir?"

"I'm assigning you to oversee the watch duty of our new recruits, effective this Saturday."

"Thank you, sir!"

"They'll be rotating shifts as I won't have three raw men on the wall at the same time. That means you must remain on active duty. You'll bunk here at the barracks and I won't tolerate slipping out to taverns or up to the castle, do you hear me?"

"Yessir! Thank you, sir!"

Owain did not know what to say after this happy acquiescence. He wasn't sure what he had been expecting, but it wasn't this. Arodilac beamed at him.

"That will be all."

"Yessir!"

He watched Arodilac march away. There was too much jauntiness in his walk. Owain frowned. Perhaps he had done the wrong thing. The three new recruits trooped past him, saluting raggedly. Bordeall strode over to Owain.

"They'll do," said Bordeall. "Given enough time. That old feller, Posle, he's an interesting one. Hasn't got but three teeth in his head, but he's as wiry as a weasel. Handled a weapon before, that's certain. Not much grace, but he's got strong wrists and some knack."

"Bordeall," said Owain, "would you know why Bridd would be happy to pull extra duty next week?"

"I do," said Bordeall. A rare grin split his face. "The lads've been talking about it. Apparently, there's some lord coming to Hearne with his daughter in tow. Bridd ain't so keen to be caught, if you know what I mean."

That made sense. The duke of Vomaro. Only it probably wasn't his daughter. The duke had only one daughter and she was married. Or had been. Perhaps there was a granddaughter?

"Ah," said Owain, trying not to smile. "Well, I don't blame him. Now, Bordeall," he said, clearing his throat, "I'd like to discuss something with you."

"Of course, my lord."

They walked along as they talked and, without plan, they found themselves climbing the stairs behind the barracks up to the city wall. It was cold in the shadow of the wall, but the sunshine was warm at the top. The sky was pale with a thin, bright light. The fields were sun-beaten by the summer, the last stands of corn hammered into gold. The river wound away to disappear between the narrow divide of the gap at the far end of the valley.

"Corn'll be done in a few weeks," rumbled Bordeall. "Seems a quieter, easier place outside the walls than inside. Most days."

"Don't you believe it," said Owain grimly. "There're things out there worse than nightmares. And the Guard's in no condition to defend this city if it came to that. Oh, I can't imagine we'd ever find ourselves in an all-out war. But lately I've been thinking about a cadre for fast actions. Swift response and quick, brutal fighting. Sturdy horses. Training for archery at the gallop. Do you think we can put together such a force?"

"That's how the men of Harlech fight. But we don't have the horses." Bordeall shook his head. "The stable's at half-strength, an' most of the horses are old. We've no one handy enough to instruct, and I've my doubts as to how many of our men'd be suited for such fighting. It'd take months to train 'em up. Course, if we had the gold for it, we could hire away, but we've barely enough to pay the men and keep them in gear and housed. It comes down to gold. Plain and simple."

"Gold!" Owain spat over the wall.

Both men were silent for a while.

"No luck, I take it," said Bordeall, "with the regent?"

"None."

"Well," said Bordeall, after a long and gloomy silence, "perhaps there's another way to find our gold."

"What do you mean by that?"

"The Thieves Guild. Doubtless, they've plenty of coin, and they don't pay tax. Maybe it's time they start paying."

Owain returned home late that evening. A cold wind had arisen with the moon and it chased him through the streets. He hunched in the saddle and pulled his cloak tighter around his neck. A door banged open down the street and three men stumbled out of the light. He could hear them laughing and calling back. The tavern sign over their head swung drunkenly in the wind.

"A load o' herring," laughed one of the men. "Can ya believe it? Lifted a load o' herring!"

The tavern door slammed shut and the men staggered down the street, arms around each other's shoulders for support.

"Reckon the ol'—the ol' sh-shilentman'll pay for fish? Fish! Here, fishy, fishy!"

The three men dissolved into laughter again. They had almost drawn level with Owain, and one of the men looked up, squinting in the evening gloom.

"Whassis? Whosis, eh?"

"Looky here," said another of the men. Moonlight glinted on a silver tooth in his sudden grin. "We got ourselves a fancy-lookin' feller. Hey there, feller! Hi! We're poor folkses an' we're takin' up a collection, shee, for other poor folkses."

"Yesh," hiccupped the third man. "We sez poor folkses cuz thash ush." He attempted to bow and fell flat on his face.

"Gettup," said the first man. "Gettup, I sez! Yer an embarrash—an embarrashment to all us poor folkses! Gotta keep yer chin up afore these rich folkses."

"Which is you," said the second man, swaying on his feet and addressing himself to Owain's horse. "So hand over your purse, or I'll stick ya, shee?"

He produced a knife and waved it about in the air. The first man, who had almost succeeded in hoisting his fallen comrade to his feet, dropped his charge and plucked a club from his belt.

"Yesh," he said, sidling forward. "Or I'll stick ya too!"

"A club, you fool, is a blunt weapon," said Owain coldly, "and thus incapable of sticking, as you so claim." He kicked the man in the face and nudged his horse with his knee at the same time. The horse stepped forward and trampled the man with the knife. It was a warhorse and did not appreciate weapons being waved about under its muzzle.

"Idiots," said Owain to himself.

But what the drunkards had been discussing stuck in his head. The Silentman. Someone had stolen a cargo of fish and attempted to sell it to the Silentman. To the Thieves Guild. His thoughts drifted back to Bordeall's suggestion. Owain had been thinking of little else all day long. He had laughed off the suggestion at first, but he had been unable to get the idea out of his mind.

The Thieves Guild would have plenty of gold. It was what they did. They stole it. And the regent had always decreed a lax hand as far as the Guild was concerned. Anything short of murder was his policy. Anything short of murder, my dear Owain, and you needn't waste your time following it up. After all, it's a safe assumption that the Guild's spending their money in Hearne, and that's good, isn't it? What if a window or two gets broken? It gives more business to the glaziers, and more business is what we need.

Owain scowled.

He had never liked the regent's reasoning. But the regent's word was law.

The lantern at the gate shone bright and clear in the night. He swung down from the horse. A servant took the horse's reins and led it away. A few lights gleamed in the windows, but most of the house was dark. The front door swung open and he saw the silhouette of his wife in front of the light. He kissed her and she shut the door behind them, smiling.

"Sibb," he said, frowning, but she stopped him with a hand at his mouth.

"Not until you get some food in you," she said. "I know that look. Not a word more."

He ate at the kitchen table. The house was quiet around them. Sibb lit a candle and placed it in the middle of the table. She propped her chin in her hands and gazed at him as he ate.

"Well," said Owain, pushing the empty plate aside, "I didn't marry you for your cooking, but I would've eloped sooner had I known about this stew."

"You forget," said Sibb. "I was a dreadful cook then. My mother despaired of me. Don't you remember the bread?"

"I always thought we could've made our fortunes by selling them as bricks. Or we could've changed the tactics of siege warfare forever with the introduction of the catapultable loaf."

"Stop it!"

A servant peeked in the kitchen and then tiptoed away, smiling. It was always good to see the master and mistress laughing.

"Now," said Sibb, "What's on your mind?"

Her husband frowned.

"Gold is what's on my mind."

"My jewels," said Sibb promptly. "I could sell them. I never wear them, anyway, and none of the girls are likely to care about that sort of thing. They're more interested in horses and swords."

Owain laughed. "I need a lot more than what your baubles could bring. The Guard's in sad shape. We're short of men, equipment, horses, but the regent won't open his coffers for us. He's adamant about it."

"And yet you have an idea. I can hear it in your voice."

"I do, though it's not my idea. Bordeall suggested it, and even though my first inclination is to ignore his advice, I'm starting to think there might be something in it."

"And the idea?" she said patiently.

"Bordeall wants to rob the Thieves Guild."

Night had arrived in completeness now, and nothing could be seen through the kitchen window other than a few splashes of moonlight on the rock wall in the garden. The candle on the table between them illuminated the worn wood of the tabletop, the curve of the plate, and their faces. They stared at each other, both of them intent and frowning, for Sibb could scowl just as fiercely as her husband when her mind worried upon a matter.

"The regent's always discouraged the Guard from prosecuting the Guild. He seems to think they bring business to Hearne. Business enough to excuse their excesses."

"Business?" said Sibb angrily. "The Guild brings the business of mending broken windows, of buying stronger wards to keep them out, mastiffs for the garden, and higher prices in the shops. That's not business."

"At least, it's not the sort of business we should be proud of."

"No, it isn't."

Sibb pushed her chair back from the table. She returned with an apple and a knife. The fruit fell apart in neat sections under her hand.

"Here, eat."

"At any other time," said Owain, "I'd grumble and obey the regent's wishes without another thought, but there's something strange in the air these days. Something dark has come to Hearne, even to this house. Maybe it's gone for now, which is well, but I fear it'll return in some unforeseen form. The Guard's woefully undermanned and I'd like to build them up into a force more akin to what my father had when he was in command. But I can't do it without gold."

"Then steal it."

Sibb glared at him so fiercely that he had to smile.

"In truth, my dear, I'd rather face a warrior on the field than you in your kitchen. A rolling-pin is a deadly weapon."

"I'm serious." His wife leaned forward into the glow of the candle. Her eyes filled with light. "Steal it! I detest the regent. I loathe him. He's a spineless shadow of a man. If he can't rule, then the ruling must be done for him. Why, only last week, Marta, our old charwoman, told me her son was beaten at the docks by a couple of Guild enforcers. And for what? Because he refused to pay for protection."

"I wish you'd told me that sooner, Sibb."

"I only just remembered now. Our recent excitement made me forget."

"How's she doing?"

Sibb's face softened and she smiled.

"Better. I think her nightmares are fewer. She's been playing with the girls lately, but she still won't talk much."

"She's our girl now," said Owain.

"Yes."

They sat for a while more in silence. Owain closed his eyes and listened to the house. Outside, the wind moaned about the eaves and peeked in the windows, but all the locks were latched and the curtains drawn against the night.

"I'll try my hand at thievery," he said.

Sibb nodded, but did not say anything.

CHAPTER NINETY-NINE
OSTFALL

"Tracking isn't so difficult," said Declan. "Once you know what to look for. Now, you see? Giverny stepped here, perhaps a day ago, I'd say."

He knelt down on one knee and touched a broken and withered blade of grass. Jute peered over his shoulder.

"It doesn't look like much of anything at all," he said. "That could've been a rabbit. Or one of those hedgepigs."

"They're called hedgehogs, and it wasn't either."

"If it'd been a rabbit, then we could've tracked it and had it for breakfast," said Jute.

He was not in a good mood that morning and, as far as he was concerned, he had reason. To begin with, he was still smarting over an incident that had occurred the evening before. Despite the hawk's warning, he had ventured higher into the air than he ever had. Floating up, his feet had been higher than Declan's head. But then he fell. It knocked the wind out of him and he could only lie there, wheezing in pain, while the other three laughed.

To make matters worse, the ghost had sat up half the night, perched by his head and telling tales about people who had died of chest ailments. "Wheezed just like you did," said the ghost. "It reminds me of old Booley's death. An, airy, whistling sort of rasp. Not an unpleasant sound, mind you. Sometimes, there was an interesting gurgle in it, particularly right before he died."

And then, in the morning, there had been only some stale bread and an onion for breakfast. Jute could still taste the onion.

Declan sighed. "If we hurry, we can hunt later in the day. Meat for dinner. But for now, we're still too far behind on her trail."

"What's that?"

Declan looked where Jute was pointing. Far off on the horizon, a thin dark line was visible.

"Your eyesight's improving," said Declan. "I can barely see that."

"Of course it is," said the hawk.

"What? I don't see anything," said the ghost.

"It's the forest."

As they hurried along, the dark line grew rapidly until Jute could see the trees. He had seen trees before, as there were some in Hearne, of course, behind the walls of the rich manors in Highneck Rise. And there had been trees on the coast when they had journeyed north, pines and little, twisted cypress. But the trees of this forest were different.

"They're enormous," said Jute, forgetting for a moment that he was determined to be grumpy until he had a decent meal. "And the forest—does it go on forever? The sky, the sea, this plain, now the forest. Everything's so big."

On his shoulder, the hawk chuckled.

"There're things in this world bigger than all of those."

The trail of the girl and the wolf drew them closer to the forest. The trees loomed higher, and beyond them, pale against the sky, were the snow-covered tops of the mountains.

"Wait," said the hawk. His head turned this way and that.

"What is it?" said Declan.

"I'm not sure what it is. Something strange. Something of the Dark, perhaps. Something that should not be."

Declan touched the hilt of his sword. He frowned. "My nose tells me nothing, master hawk, but if I'd have known if we crossed such a path. If an enemy's in sight, then I fear we've already been seen. This plain is no place to hide, so let's continue on our trail. Doubtless, it'll lead into the forest and either the trees will hide us or something waits in its shadows."

"The Forest of Lome," said the ghost. "Hmm. I recall something distinctly unsavory about the place."

"What?" said Jute nervously. "What do you remember?"

He was not sure whether he liked the look of the trees. The edge of the forest stretched away on either side further than he could see. Even though the sun was high in the sky, deep shadows lay beneath the treetops. It seemed to Jute as if they awaited the departure of the sun so that they could spill out from among the trees and join the night.

"I don't remember. At least, not precisely."

"Ogres? Bloodthirsty bears? Murder?"

"Probably all those and much more. Undoubtedly."

"Must you be giving Jute notions?" said the hawk. "Kindly restrain yourself."

"Very well," grumbled the ghost. "As no one appreciates my conversation, I think I'll take a nap. Wake me up when someone says something intelligent." And with that, the ghost vanished. Jute felt a quick, cold breath against his neck and heard the ghost mumbling to itself inside his knapsack.

Declan shook his head. "I'm afraid he'll pipe up at the wrong moment when silence is our best defense. There must be some way of keeping our unfortunate friend quiet."

"I heard that," said the ghost angrily.

They reached the edge of the forest. Jute touched the trunk of a tree and gazed up. The trees were taller than he had thought. He could hear the wind murmuring in the tree tops. The shadows were cool and still. Dry leaves crunched underfoot.

"The Dark was here," said the hawk, his voice quiet. "Not so long ago. I'm sure of it now."

"I don't have your nose for such things, master hawk," said Declan, "but I trust your word. Walk in my footsteps, Jute, and keep your voice low. And ghost, for once, keep silent."

"I heard that," said the ghost from inside Jute's knapsack, but it whispered as if, for once, it understood what might be at stake.

Declan loosened his sword in its sheath and then plunged deeper into the forest. He walked with his head forward, turning from side to side, eyes flicking down to the ground and then back up, searching through the gloom and the trees for whatever was there and whatever had been there. Jute hurried after him. Even though he was smaller and lighter than the man, he made more noise as he walked: twigs snapping, leaves crunching, and bushes rustling as he sought to thread his way through. Declan turned and frowned at him.

"I'm trying!" said Jute. "Really, I am."

"Try harder."

The trail led them deeper into the forest. The silence and the shadows grew as they went. Jute could hear the ghost mumbling to itself inside his knapsack. In front of him, Declan halted.

"What is it?" said Jute. He sniffed the air. It smelled odd. Somehow wrong.

"Something evil's come this way," said Declan quietly. "You're right, master hawk. The Dark has been here. Not so long ago. A strange track. This print here looks like a deer, yet the next step is something different. And the stride's too long."

"The smell of it's fading," said the hawk. "A day ago, perhaps. How odd. It's a mix of blood and darkness and something else. Stop quivering, Jute."

"Sorry."

Jute clamped his mouth shut. He was afraid his teeth were about to start chattering. He had the feeling that something was watching him. Something in the darkness, a shadow standing behind a tree. Something perched in the branches overhead and staring down through the leaves.

"Did someone say blood and darkness?" said the ghost, popping its head out of Jute's knapsack.

"And look here," said Declan, kneeling on the ground. "These are Giverny's prints. I think this thing, whatever it is, was tracking my sister."

They made greater speed then. Declan ran, one hand steady on the hilt of his sword and the other keeping his cloak close about him. Jute was hard pressed to keep up. The hawk flung himself from the boy's shoulder and flew through the darkness. Jute was sure the bird would crash into a branch at any moment, for the trees grew close together and their branches wove together with those of their neighbors into an impenetrable and continuous thicket. But the hawk flashed in and out of the branches and for periods of time vanished deeper into the forest, ranging far from them on either side, only to appear once again in a silent flurry of wings. They came to a clearing in the forest, wide enough so that the gloom was relieved by sunlight. Overhead, blue sky was visible. The hawk flapped his way up toward it and was gone. Declan stopped below an oak.

"She was here. Up in this tree." He stepped back, looking up into the branches. "Whatever's tracking her was here too."

"There's a broken branch on the ground," said Jute.

"And blood," said the ghost. It reappeared and crouched down on the ground. "Ooh. Look at that—though, not much, I'm afraid."

"Where?" said Declan. "Move! You'll disturb the mark."

"I'm a ghost. I don't disturb anything. I can't."

"Human blood," said Declan after a while. His face looked pale beneath his tan. The hawk landed on the ground and settled his wings.

"There's a storm advancing from the east," said the hawk. "Dark clouds over the mountains. It'll be on us before the evening and you'll lose the trail, yes?"

"Perhaps," said Declan.

"Let's hurry, then."

And so they went on, following the trail through thickets and brambles and through the shadows beneath the treetops. It grew darker as they went. The hawk settled back onto Jute's shoulder and swayed there as the boy hurried after Declan.

"Can we stop to eat?" said Jute. "It's past lunchtime. At least, that's what my stomach says. There must be plenty of rabbits about here. You can have one yourself. My legs are getting tired. It's not much fun being the wind. I'd rather just be a thief back in Hearne."

"Must you always be interested in your stomach? I doubt there's a rabbit within a mile of us." The hawk shut his beak with an angry click and then took a deep breath. When he spoke again, his voice was measured and patient. "The presence of the Dark tends to drive animals mad. They lose their minds. The scent of whatever it was that passed this way probably sent the animals in the vicinity fleeing."

The ghost stuck its head out of Jute's knapsack. "In my teaching days, I had the misfortune to teach some boys whose minds were perpetually lost. I remember one boy. He got hauled into the head professor's study for various acts of skullduggery: transforming other boys' pillows into piles of slugs while they slept, setting fire to the snow in the wintertime, convincing the tower mice that there were islands made out of cheese just over the horizon. The mice stole a fishing ketch one day and sailed away in great excitement. The cats were furious."

"You're the most infuriating ghost I've ever met!" snapped the hawk.

"Be quiet," said Declan. "I don't mind a snapped twig or a noise here and there, but we might as well give up now if you're all going to continue bickering like this, do you understand?"

The ghost vanished with a snort, and the hawk took to his wings without a word. After a while, the trees thinned before them and Jute saw that they had reached the edge of the forest. The plain stretched away into a gathering gloom. The air was cold and Jute could smell the coming rain.

Declan spat to one side and cursed.

"Nearly back to where we started," he said. "Not a half hour's walk south of where we first entered the forest. I'd bet my life on it. Shadows take it. If we'd just come south instead of wasting time in the forest, we'd have cut hours off the chase. Still, there's no use crying now."

And south they went, with the man intent on the trail. The path led them along the edge of the forest, and the trees seemed to lean forward as if they sought to watch what they did. It began to rain. This only spurred Declan on to greater speed. Jute hunched his shoulders in misery against the cold and wet and hurried after him.

"Oh, how hungry I am," he said out loud. "I wish I had a leg of roast chicken, or one of those dumplings stuffed with onions and cheese that the deaf lady in Mioja Square sold. How tasty they were." He licked his lips at this thought and did some more groaning.

"Stop that," said the ghost from inside his knapsack. "You sound like a sick cow. Get a hold of yourself."

"I'm hungry."

"There seems to be something in here. Bread, I think. Why don't you eat that?"

Jute, groping around in his knapsack, found an overlooked piece of bread. It was stale, but it tasted wonderful.

The hawk coasted by on motionless wings. Raindrops glistened on his feathers. The air rustled with the sound of the rain on the grass and the wind blowing across the treetops. After a while, the ground descended and they found themselves on the uppermost slopes of a valley. Far off at the bottom of the valley, a line of trees was visible.

"The Rennet River," said Declan.

The valley floor looked as if it was heavily farmed. Stands of cornstalks stood in shabby graying yellow, stripped of their produce and ready for the fire. Stubbled fields of

495

cut hay alternated with plots of recently plowed earth turning to mud under the rain. Here and there, hedgerows and stonewalls straggled between the fields. Declan halted at the edge of a grassy field. The grass was trampled flat before them and in the middle was a large scorched area.

"What happened here?" said Declan. "A fire blazed here so hot that it devoured the grass and blackened the wet earth. And, unless I've forgotten everything my father taught me of tracking, this is where our strange creature's trail ended. It seems as if it was burned in the fire."

"You're right," said the hawk, landing on Jute's shoulder.

"But what happened to my sister? A company of people camped here, with tents and horses and even some wagons. A wealthy party, for these were large tents with heavy carpets put down on top of the grass."

"There's a road beyond that rise," said the hawk. "The old road that runs west to Hearne through the Rennet Valley. The king's road, as it was once called. Many travelers use this road—anyone journeying between Hearne and the duchy of Mizra, or any of the villages in between."

"Perhaps she fell in with some kind folk," said Declan. The rain dripped off the end of his nose. "Who would want to harm a poor girl?"

"If you ask me," said the ghost, peeking out of Jute's knapsack, but the hawk glared at it and the ghost shut its mouth.

Jute stood in the rain with the hawk perched on his shoulder. The ghost peered over his other shoulder. All three of them watched Declan crisscross the field. He walked back and forth, his head bent toward the ground. Sometimes he halted and crouched down, his nose twitching like a dog's. He circled the field in wider and wider sweeps until he made his way back to the other three.

"She went with them," said Declan. "I'd bet my life on it. On a horse or in one of their wagons. East on the road."

"East," said the hawk. He shifted uneasily from claw to claw on Jute's shoulder. "The land east of here isn't such a safe place, until one gets to the duchy of Mizra."

"I know," said Declan. "I've heard the stories."

"I haven't," said the ghost, perking up. "Or perhaps I have, but I'd like to hear them again."

"But we have no choice," said the hawk, his voice reluctant and resigned. "We must find her."

They followed the road because, as Declan reasoned, the travelers that had so kindly taken his sister under their wing would probably leave her in the care of the first habitation they came to. And, as far as he remembered, there was a village several miles down the road.

"Ostfall, I think it's called," he said. "I've never been there myself, but I think it's the last village before the foothills. Perhaps they left Giverny there."

"Perhaps," said the hawk.

Twilight had fallen and it was raining hard by the time they saw the lights of the village. Jute smelled wood smoke in the air. The sides of the valley had been growing higher as they walked, higher and closer together, as the valley narrowed and deepened at the same time. The road angled up a rise and, at the top, they found themselves looking down at the gleaming lights of what was undoubtedly a village.

"She might be there this moment," said Declan.

"We could get a hot supper!" said Jute.

496

The hawk did not say anything, but only hunched his head deeper into the feathers of his chest, eyes closed against the rain. The road led them down through the darkening twilight. It was rutted with the passage of carts and horses and livestock from over the years. But the ruts now ran with water, and the hard-packed dirt of the road was slick with mud. Through the black shapes of trees, they saw the river coursing past. Rain hissed on its surface. A small covered bridge straddled the river. They paused for a moment under its shelter. Jute shivered. His clothes were drenched and he was cold. The rain drummed above them on the roof of the bridge.

"It'd be best, I think," said the hawk, "if I were not seen. But I don't fancy flying around in this weather, trying to find a dry roost."

"How about my knapsack?" said Jute.

"Your knapsack?" The hawk blinked.

"It's nice and dry inside, isn't it, ghost?"

"Yes," said the ghost. "Very nice and dry, thank you. What? I'm not sharing my knapsack with a bird. I'm allergic to feathers."

"It's not your knapsack."

Jute lifted the flap of the knapsack and the hawk hopped inside. It was true. The interior of the knapsack was nice and dry. The ghost sneezed.

"You see? Feathers make me sneeze. I'll break out in spots. My nose is swelling up. I can't breathe. Go find your own knapsack."

"Ghosts don't need to breathe," said the hawk. "You're dead, in case you forgot."

Past the bridge, the road ran along with the river on one side and a stonewall on the other. The wall was broken in places, and beyond it, dim in the rain and the darkness, the scraggly branches of an orchard were visible.

"Apples," said Declan. "A great deal of the apples in Hearne come from this area."

Jute became aware of a new sound. A dull roaring noise that was, at first, barely discernible over the sound of the wind and rain. It grew louder as they hurried down the road. It was a liquid, crashing roar that reminded him of the waves of the sea below the cliffs of Hearne. And then the stonewall rose higher and the road ended at the wall. A wood gate stood there, wide enough to admit an ox and cart. The gate was locked, and they could hear the sound of a chain rattling on the other side when Declan pushed against it. He stepped back and glanced up at the top of the stonewall.

"Looks climbable, doesn't it?"

"Anything is," said Jute.

He touched the wall and listened. The rain ran down his face and he wiped at his eyes. He shivered, remembering another time when he had listened to a wall. Another time when Declan had asked him to climb a wall. It had not been so long ago.

"There aren't any wards here," he said.

"Aye," said Declan. "It's silent enough."

But the silence was broken by a voice on the other side of the gate.

"Who's there? Name yerself, or by all, I'll set the hounds on ye!"

"Just some travelers," said Declan. "We're passing through."

"We don't want no strangers here." The voice paused to hiccup. "G'wan with ye! Ain't but an hour back t' Rowanbell. Ye go there fer the night. We don't open the gate 'tween sundown an' sunup. Now, git!"

Jute heard a growl and the scrabble of paws against the gate.

"Dogs," he said. "He'll set them on us."

Declan shook his head and then raised his voice.

"Listen, friend. We're tired and hungry. All we want is a hot meal and a good mug of ale. Unless there's no ale to be had in this village."

There was a pause and then the man on the other side of the gate spoke again.

"A good mug of ale," said the voice mournfully. "That's a precious thing."

"The best," said Declan, winking at Jute. "It warms the bones on a cold night. Keeps the heart stout."

"That it does," said the voice. "That it does. Here, now. . ."

The voice trailed off, and then the gate swung open to the accompaniment of many grumbles (from the old gatekeeper), growls (from his two dogs), and creaking groans (from the gate hinges, which were obviously in need of oiling). The old man peered at them, clutching a rusty pike. An oilskin hood on his head streamed with rain. The two dogs pushed past him and sniffed at Jute and Declan, tails wagging.

"Git down, Flurry! Git down, I say! Off, Digger. Don't ye fear, son. They ain't gonna harm ye, not less I sez."

"I'm not afraid of dogs," said Jute with some dignity. He petted both of the dogs and then wiped their slobber off on his pants when the old gatekeeper was not looking.

"I ain't one to complain," said the old man, "but I get chilled out here, right down to my socks. An' there's them that don't appreciate what I do, if you know what I mean. It's the little things that mean much. A good mutton sandwich, a hot mug of ale. Ale, that means something."

"It does," said Declan.

"Got the best brewer in the Rennet Valley," said the old man. "Right here in our town. Name of Esne. Now, jest hurry along, an' afore you've set down for yer supper, tell her ta send the potboy with a bottle. It's terribly dry out here."

"We'll do that," said Declan.

"Mebbe two bottles. Thank ye."

"By the way, did a party traveling to Mizra pass this way recently? Quite a large group, I'd imagine."

"Don't recollect," said the old man, drawing himself up. "I just keep the gate, see? You send them bottles along, you hear?"

And with that, he ducked into a shed by the gate and slammed the door shut.

"Thank goodness he's gone," said the ghost from inside Jute's knapsack. "I thought he'd never shut up. I hate it when people babble on."

"You don't suppose," said Jute, "you don't suppose it'd be better to go to Rowanbell?"

"Rowanbell? No. It's in the opposite direction of where we want to go. Half a day's journey."

"But he said it was only—"

"People say all sorts of things. Especially old drunkards."

Past the town, an indistinct, dark mass of cliffs loomed against the night sky. The strange sound Jute had noticed before seemed louder now, and he thought he could see movement on the face of the cliffs.

"Sounds like a waterfall," said Declan. "I think the Rennet comes down from the heights somewhere near here. It's a cold, fast river in the mountains."

Jute thought the town a mean and miserable place in comparison to Hearne. The main street was a muddy track pocked with puddles and the fragrant leavings of livestock. The shabby houses crowded together as if seeking warmth from the rain and the cold.

Smoke blew from chimneys, shredded into tatters by the wind. Behind a few shuttered windows here and there, light glimmered.

"I'm glad I don't live here," said Jute. "It stinks of cows."

"Well, it's home to these folks," said Declan. "A roof over your head and a way to make a living are good things. I expect they don't mind the smell. That must be the inn. We'll have supper and perhaps hear word of Giverny."

A faded and peeling sign over the door displayed what looked like a huge man carrying an axe. The windows were shuttered against the night, but they could hear the sounds of laughter and voices inside.

"I can't make out what it reads," said Declan, "Probably the Executioner's Inn or something equally morbid. These rural spots seem to enjoy being morbid. Now, both of you, master hawk, and you, ghost, don't make a sound. We're strangers enough here without the added weight of a talking bird and a ghost. And Jute, no talk of the wind or the Dark or what we're about. It's best to keep your mouth shut around folks you don't know."

Declan pushed open the door and they entered. Conversations paused and then resumed. Jute was aware of faces turning toward them, blurred in the gloom, glancing and then looking away. A fire crackled on the hearth. The delightful smell of ale and roasting meat filled the air. But of even more interest to Jute was the warmth that worked its way through his damp clothes and into his body. They found an empty table in one corner. Jute untied his sodden cloak. His fingers were stiff and cold. He shoved his knapsack under the table.

"Careful," said a voice. He wasn't sure if it was the ghost or the hawk.

"What'll it be?"

A woman stood by their table, a dirty apron around her waist and a platter tucked under one arm. Her graying hair was tied back in a ponytail and her pinched face was smudged with flour.

"What do you have?" said Declan.

"Stew. Roast pork. Mulled ale or a cheap red outta Vomaro."

"Stew and ale. For both of us. And a bottle of ale for the old fellow at the gate."

She scowled. "He's already had his for the night. I don't brew ale just to keep him pickled."

She threaded her way back through the crowded room.

"That must've been Esne," said Jute. "I hope her ale is sweeter than her face."

"I would appreciate some air," said a voice under their table.

"Sorry," said Jute. He bent down and undid the front of the knapsack. He straightened up and, as he did, he noticed three men crouched around a table near the fireplace. They were whispering and furtively looking over at them.

"Declan? Those men near the fireplace are watching us."

"Aye. I saw them. Always take notice of those around you before they take notice of you. They're probably harmless, just curious about strangers. Or they might be interested in robbing us. In either case, we'll be fine. There's nothing like a good fight after a hot meal."

"We heard stories about the fights you were in. About the people you'd killed. The Juggler told us, so that—so that. . ." Jute reddened and shut his mouth.

"So that you'd behave?" Declan smiled, but his eyes were cold. "Behave, work hard for the Juggler, or the Knife'd come one night to slit your throat? Was that it? I never set out to work for the Guild. When I was your age, all I ever dreamed about was being a hero. Fighting dragons and monsters. Defeating evil wizards. Discovering lost treasure and rescuing fair maidens. All those things from the old stories. I wasn't much older than you when I set out on my first adventure. But real adventures aren't like those in the stories. They're hard and painful, and they usually end badly. Mine did."

"Here ye are."

The woman Esne plunked down a covered tureen, two bowls, and a loaf of brown bread. She put her hands on her hips and surveyed Declan.

"Just passing through, stranger?"

"As you say," said Declan. He twitched the top off the tureen and sniffed appreciatively. "Let's have at it, Jute." He ladled out two bowls. The stew was in reality soup, consisting of broth in which floated a few chunks of potato and carrot, as well as some infrequent bits of beef. Jute did not care. It was food, and it was hot.

"Ye ain't been in Ostfall afore," said Esne. "I reckon. I don't forget faces. There isn't cause for strangers in these parts."

"Our first time." Declan smiled at her. "I'm sure the area has much to offer by daylight. Excellent stew. By the way, did a party ride through earlier today? Horsemen, a couple of wagons?"

"Aye, they did. Right passel of 'em. But he didna stop. He never does."

"He?"

"The duke Mizra. I'll be back w' yer ale." She nodded and left.

Declan tore the loaf of bread in two and handed half to Jute. The bread was hard, but it softened well enough when dunked in the stew.

"The duke of Mizra," he said.

They ate in silence, bent over their bowls, which were replenished several times each from the tureen. Hot ale arrived in tankards. The room around them filled with more people as the evening went on. A potboy fed the fire with an armful of wood and the flames spat and crackled with pine pitch. Jute watched him as the boy tossed on one log after another. The fire roared up. The boy turned his head and, for a moment, his eyes met Jute's. There was something wrong about the shape of his head. It seemed as if it had been crudely made out of clay and had dried misshapen. But perhaps it was only a trick of the flickering firelight. The boy's eyes slid away, and he scuttled back into the kitchen.

Jute shivered. And then sneezed. He could feel his clothes drying out. His legs ached. He sneezed again.

"I think it wise we stay the night here," said the hawk from beneath the table. "The health of my charge must be weighed against the concern of our hunt."

"But we might lose them," said Declan into his bowl.

"Perhaps. But we know what direction they're going. We'll be hard on their heels again in the morning."

"Please," said Jute. "I'm tired."

"I can't pretend to understand why the duke of Mizra would keep a poor waif with him, unless—" The hawk fell silent.

"Careful, Jute," said Declan quietly.

"What?" said Jute.

"Where ye from, strangers?"

It was one of the men from the table by the fireplace. He stood behind Jute's chair, swaying slightly from side to side, a tankard clutched in one hand. He took a drink and wiped his mouth.

"Good evening," said Declan.

"I asked ye a question now, didna? Where ye from?"

"Oh, no place in particular." Declan bent his attention back to his supper.

"Well, I shorely dinna take that as a friendly answer. Seein' how yer strangers an' all, that ain't right. But I'm a forgivin' sort, so howsabout ye buy the house a round an' we'll be all right? Howsabout it?"

"Driveling idiot," said a voice from under the table. It sounded like the ghost.

"Whassat?" said the man, glaring at Jute. "Ye talkin' ta me, boy?"

"No sir," said Jute. "I mean, yes, sir! I mean—"

The man clouted Jute on the back of his head. Declan tensed.

"I suggest you go back to your friends," he said. There was a peculiar edge to his voice. To Jute, it did not even sound like a human voice anymore. It seemed as if he was listening to the scraping of steel being drawn from a sheath.

"An' if I didna?" jeered the man. "Whatcher gonna do? Throw yer spoon at me?" The man raised his hand again, but the woman Esne jostled against him, a platter of tankards in her hands.

"On the house," she said. "An' that's the last for ye, Ollic, or I'll be talkin' ta yer wife in the mornin' next. Go on with ye."

The man Ollic snarled and grabbed one of the tankards. He stumbled back to the table by the fireplace. The other two men laughed. The firelight gilded their faces and, when one of them turned his head, it seemed to Jute that his eyes glinted yellow like that of an animal. The man sniffed and wiped his nose with the back of his hand.

"More ale?" said Esne. She offered the platter to Declan and Jute.

"Why'd you do that?" said Declan.

She looked at him for a moment, her face expressionless.

"I don't know who you are, stranger," she said, her voice quiet. "But I know a killer when I see one. Your dinner's on me. Now, eat up and maybe ye should travel on."

"The hospitality of Ostfall is unstinting and admirable," said Declan dryly.

Esne scowled at him. "I have ta live here. Not ye. There's more ta this town than meets the eye, an' it ain't all good. That old drunk Ollic is a pighead fool an' he dinna like strangers. But he's a neighbor, an' I gotta get along with my neighbors, whether I like 'em or not. Besides, everyone's related here, one way or the other."

"My apologies. We're in your debt. And I think we must intrude even further on your patience. Is there a room for us here tonight?"

She took a deep breath and then nodded reluctant.

"I wouldna turn a dog out on a night like this. But one night only, ye hear? And ye'll be away first thing in the morning."

Esne gave them a room at the end of the hallway on the third floor. She lingered at the door, as if she wanted to say something more. But, after a moment, she nodded good night to them and hurried away. A small window looked out through iron bars onto the roof of the inn's stable below. The rain slashed down outside. Declan locked the door and then, after wrapping himself in his cloak, stretched out on the floor in front of the door. The hawk emerged from Jute's knapsack and set about smoothing his feathers.

"Disgraceful," he said, and then tucked his head beneath his wing and fell asleep.

"Yes, wasn't it?" said the ghost, appearing.

"And you," said Declan, levering himself on his elbow. "You'll keep your mouth shut when I tell you, do you understand? You'd think you'd learn a thing or two after how many hundreds of years."

"What?" said the ghost. "What did I do? Are you casting doubt on my intelligence, sir? Well, I'll have you know that—"

"Oh, hush," said Jute, who had curled up on the one bed in the room (it could hardly be called a bed, as it was only a lumpy pallet of straw) and could barely keep his eyes open by this time. "I'd like to get some sleep."

"Very well," said the ghost. "I, er, I'm sorry about your head, Jute."

"That's all right. I've been hit harder."

After a while, the room was quiet, the silence disturbed only by the sound of breathing and the rain tapping on the window. The ghost drifted about the room.

"It's not that I mean to talk all the time," it said to the sleeping hawk.

"I just can't help talking," it said to Declan. "I just can't." The man's hands twitched in his sleep, as if he were grasping a sword or someone's neck.

The ghost wandered over to Jute's bed. The boy was frowning as he slept.

"The thing is," whispered the ghost, "I forget that I'm alive unless I'm talking. Otherwise, what am I? Just a wisp of nothing. Not that I'm alive now. But I was alive, wasn't I? Sometimes I'm not sure."

Jute turned uneasily on his bed. He pulled the blanket up to his neck. The ghost sighed.

"You have plenty enough to worry about without bothering over an old ghost."

The ghost gazed out the window for a while, but there was nothing much to be seen in the dark and the rain. Outside, the wind whispered against the grimy glass, running its fingers through the thatch on the roof and along the cracked gutters.

"A broken heart, that's what it was," said the ghost sadly. "I remember now. At least, I think I do. Wars, wizards, kings and queens. The Dark hunting down my trail, desperate to get its hands on that blasted book. Why did I ever write the thing? Despite all of that, it was a broken heart that did for me. She bore him three daughters. My fault entirely, I suppose. I can't remember her face anymore. Oh, well. No use drinking from empty cups."

The ghost looked around the room, sighed, and then seeped out through the keyhole.

Declan awoke instantly but did not move. The room was dark. Something had woken him. A slight noise. Something out of the ordinary. He could hear the beat of rain on the roof and pattering against the window, but it had not been that noise. He could hear the rasp of the hawk breathing and, over on the bed, Jute stirring in his sleep, mumbling to himself. No. It had not been any of those sounds. Something else.

And then the sound came again. Right in his ear.

"Declan!"

It was the ghost.

"Blast you, ghost," Declan said. "If you ever do that again, I swear I'll—"

"There're people coming up the stairs," said the ghost. "Bad people. They don't look nice. If I wasn't dead already, I'd be worried."

"How many?"

"At least three, four, maybe more. They're on the first flight. I got scared and ran."

"You're dead. You shouldn't be scared."

"I was scared for you," said the ghost with dignity.

Declan knelt by Jute's bed and gently shook the boy's arm.

"Jute. Wake up."

The boy's eyes opened wide.

"Quiet," said Declan. "I think we have unwelcome visitors."

"Who is it? Is it the wihht?" Jute grabbed for his knapsack and tied it shut with shaking fingers.

"I don't know yet. Hurry. Get your coat on."

"The wihht?" said the ghost. "I don't think so. I hope not. Just men. I think. There was something strange about some of 'em, though."

"Men can be evil enough on their own," said the hawk. He shook himself once, and then hopped down to the floor. He paused by the door, his head tilted to one side, listening. "A little time left, I think," said the hawk. "What'll it be, Farrow? The door or the window?"

"The only one fitting through that window would be you, master hawk."

"If you please. I don't fancy trying my wings in these cramped walls."

Declan pushed the casement out and the hawk hopped up onto the window ledge and was gone.

"Now," said Declan.

He eased the door open and peered out. No one was there. They tiptoed down the hallway with the ghost drifting after them. The air was sour with years of slovenly housekeeping. When they came near the top of the stairs, Declan crouched down and sidled forward. He crept back to Jute and shook his head.

"They're at the bottom of the stairs."

"What do we do?" said Jute. "That's the only way down."

Declan did not answer. He tested the handle of the nearest door. It was locked. He produced a piece of wire from his pockets and stooped over the handle. The door eased open silently. He motioned Jute and the ghost inside. The smell of sleep and stale air filled the room. The door closed silently behind Declan, but not silently enough. Perhaps a shift in the air, perhaps the click of the latch locking again; whatever it was, it was enough to wake the sleeper in the bed. The man managed a gasp, which ended abruptly as Declan lunged across the room.

"You didn't have to hit him that hard," said Jute.

"Better once than twice," said Declan.

He stood at the door, his ear pressed to the wood. They waited for what seemed like a horribly long time. Jute expected the door to be broken down, to hear the splintering of wood and shouts and blades glinting in the darkness.

"Stop grinding your teeth together," said the ghost.

"Sorry."

"I wish I had teeth," said the ghost.

Declan turned and glared at both of them. He mouthed something, which was probably "Be quiet, you fools," but to Jute's nervous state of mind it looked more like "I'll cut your throat if you don't shut up."

Out in the hallway, a board creaked. They heard a sniffing sound, as if made by someone whose nose was running. A soft sort of snuffle just outside the door. Declan's hand drifted up to his shoulder, fingers closing around the hilt of his sword. But then there was another creak and the sound of footsteps receding away down the hall.

Declan nodded at Jute.

"All right," he said. "Out the door and down the stairs. There's something odd going on here. Odder than just a couple of night marauders. Get out of the inn as fast as you can. Don't wait for me. If we get separated, I'll meet you outside of town, at the foot of that waterfall we heard. Ghost, you stay with Jute and keep your mouth shut."

Declan eased the door open. Further down the hallway, several figures were stealthily creeping toward the room at the end of the hallway. One of them carried a hooded lantern that cast a faint gleam on the floor. It was not much light at all, barely enough to relieve the darkness, but it was enough for Jute to see their knives. He tiptoed away, shoulders hunched and the back of his neck prickling.

Surely they would turn and see him. And the sound. He knew the sound that would happen: the whisper of a knife as it flipped end over end through the air. Surely he would hear it now. But there was only the drum of his own heart in his ears, and Jute slunk down the steps, down into the safety of deeper darkness. He stumbled at the bottom of the stairs, expecting another step, and reached out to steady himself on the wall.

"Careful," whispered the ghost.

It was impossible to see. Jute had a vague memory of a landing at the second floor. Several doors on the right. Or were they on the left? Where was the staircase leading down into the inn's common room? And where was Declan?

Jute crept along the wall. One door. A second door. Someone snoring behind it. A third door, and then an empty space. The stairs. Behind him, something creaked. He froze. The creak was unbearably loud in the silence. He strained his ears, listening to the inn. It was a quiet building, as far as buildings went. Houses built of wood tended to sigh and creak continuously, particularly at night, but stone buildings were mostly silent. The inn was built of stone with a slate roof.

Jute waited for the pounding of his heart to subside. The slight sounds of the inn came whispering to him. The sounds of sleep. Someone turning uneasily on their bed. The wind sighing in the eaves outside, sighing and waiting for whatever it was that would be coming that night. And then, right when he had breathed a sigh of relief, there came a sudden thump of running feet from upstairs, a thud and a shout, and then the ringing clash of steel against steel on the stairs. Jute turned and stumbled down through the darkness, feeling his way step by step.

"Watch out!" said the ghost.

"What?" said Jute, and then he tripped over something (a mop and bucket) and, with a tremendous clatter, fell flat on his face at the foot of the stairs. He jumped up. A dim light shone from the embers in the common room fireplace. A figure appeared in the kitchen door, wrapped in a dressing gown. Esne. She said something—her mouth opened and he saw her eyes filled with shadows and sleep—but he did not hear her, for he was already dodging around the tables and running for the door.

The handle whispered under his hand. He flung himself to one side as the ward in it quivered into life. There was a brief, soundless flash of light and heat and then the room was plunged back into shadow. Jute blinked and rubbed his eyes. Glaring white spots danced before his vision.

Something rolled thumping down the stairs and came to rest in a dark clump on the floor. Esne shrieked. A man leapt down the stairs with a sword in his hands. Declan. He whirled and beat back a wave of figures that dashed down the stairs after him. Iron shone in the dim light.

"Get the boy too!" shouted someone. "Esne! Get him, if ye know what's good for ye!"

"Oh dear," said the ghost.

Esne strode across the room, her nightgown flowing out behind her. But her face was weary and she clutched at Jute in a half-hearted manner. He ducked under her hand and darted into the kitchen. The glowing coals on the hearth revealed the face of the potboy yawning on his bed of rags by the fire. His eyes widened at the sight of Jute, and he fumbled for the poker hanging on the hearth wall. Jute hurtled past him. The poker hissed through the air behind him.

Jute cringed as he grabbed the handle on the back door, but it wasn't warded; it was only stiff with rust. He flung it open and shot out the door. Footsteps splashed toward him across the muddy yard behind the inn. He did not wait to see who it was (or *what* it was, a voice in his mind pointed out) and darted away through the night and the rain.

For a sickening moment he was disoriented. There was only the rain and the darkness and the muddy streets twisting in and out of the jumbled houses. A dog barked close by. But then Jute heard the rumble of the waterfall somewhere further away in the night. The footsteps pounding along behind him did not slow up. They sounded as if they were gaining on him. Jute ducked down an alley and then clambered up a stonewall and out onto a roof. He peered over the edge. A man ran along the alley. As he passed by Jute's hiding place, he slowed. It was one of the men from the inn. Not the drunk Ollic, but one of the other men from his table. The one with yellow eyes. He crept down the alley, stopping every few steps to examine the ground. Not that there could be anything to see in the rain. The alley was practically a stream sluicing between the stone walls on either side. But still, the man bent his head low over the mud and water. He had a large, strangely shaped head. Long and stretched. And there was also something peculiar about how he moved. His stance was more like that of a dog sniffing for the scent of its prey.

Jute froze.

The man was sniffing!

Sniffing and snuffling, his head lower and lower until he was so bent over that he had to steady himself with one hand in the mud. After a moment, though, the man straightened up and hurried down the alley, disappearing into the night.

"Was he trying to smell you?" said the ghost from inside Jute's knapsack.

"I don't know. Yes, I think so."

"Wake me up when this is all over," quavered the ghost. "My nerves can't stand it anymore."

"Ghost aren't supposed to be afraid," said Jute.

"Shows how much you know about ghosts."

For some reason, this cheered Jute up. True, he was lying on top of a roof in a strange village in the cold rain in the middle of the night, and Declan and the hawk were nowhere to be seen. The day (rather, the night) was turning out badly. But the fact that the ghost was afraid was, oddly enough, an encouraging thought.

Jute wiped rain from his eyes and inspected his surroundings. He was on top of a stable behind a house. A muddy yard separated the two. Light glimmered in one of the windows of the house, but then vanished. Further on his right, past a rubbish pile, loomed the back of another house. From what he could see, squinting in the dark, he did not have much choice other than the alley, unless he wanted to start climbing over roofs. He scowled.

It would be much simpler if I could fly.

Hawk! Where are you?

But there was no answer. There was only the patter of the rain and the moan of the wind. Jute hitched his knapsack up more securely on his shoulders and then climbed back down the wall to the alley below. He slunk through the darkness. The moon was down. Not a single star could be seen. His senses felt raw, quivering, and desperate to hear and smell and feel danger before it found him. He sidled up the end of the alley and peered out.

Further down the street, visible only as a dark shape, walked the figure of a man. The man stopped at the first house he came to and tapped on the door. The door opened and Jute saw the blur of a face in the opening. He could not hear their conversation. They were too far away. The door shut again and the man went to the next house. Again, he knocked softly on the door. The scene was repeated. The door opened, and a face peered out and then disappeared again behind the door after their conversation.

The man moved onto the third house. This time, however, the house was uncomfortably near where Jute was hiding across the street. He could easily see the face peering out of the door, a candle clutched in one hand. The light illumined the face of an old man in a nightshirt, knuckling sleepily at his eyes. The first man quickly reached out and extinguished the candle, but not before Jute saw his face as well. It was the drunk from the inn. Ollic. And despite the wind sighing around the chimneys and through the eaves and the hiss of the rain around him, Jute could hear their conversation.

"Put that out, ya old fool," said Ollic.

"Whatter ya doin' here?" said the old man. "Tain't but after midnight. Go on w' ya afore my wife wakes. Go on." He tried to shut the door, but Ollic stuck his foot in the way.

"Nay, listen here. There're strangers in town an' the man himself has sent word he wants 'em. He wants 'em trussed like chickens fer the spit. A man an' a boy. An' he wants every one o' us out lookin' to catch 'em. They ducked through his lads' hands at the inn, but us'll get 'em for him."

"I'm too frail to be trampin' around in the cold," quavered the old man.

"Get yer boots on. You don't want him comin' down the mountain, crackin' our skulls, do ya? Do yer duty."

Grumbling, the old man closed the door and Ollic went on to the next house. Jute shrank back into the alley. His teeth chattered and he clamped his hand over his mouth to still them. What did the man mean? Trussed up like chickens for the spit? And who was the man Ollic had been talking about?

Jute shuddered. He did not want to find out. Chickens on spits were nice, but only when they were proper chickens and he was eating them. He scurried away through the alley, darting from shadow to shadow, hoping the moon would not breach the clouds and lend her unwelcome light to his steps. He could hear the slight noises of people in the streets, of doors opening and closing, and the rustle of voices. But then he was past the last house and running through the darkness. The rain slashed down around him. It was so dark that he might as well have shut his eyes and blundered along, but he could hear the river flowing on his right, some yards away, and up ahead was the gradually increasing roar of the waterfall plunging down into the pond below.

But then Jute came to the last house and found himself facing a wall. It rose up in the night. Timbers lashed together. Of course. The wall. It went all the way around the village. How could he have expected anything less? The wall was quite high. He scrabbled at it to gain some hold, but the timbers were each a slim tree trunk adzed straight and clean of any vestige of branch. To make matters worse, the wood was slick with rain. He tried wedging his fingers in between the timbers to secure a grip, but it was no use. Perhaps there was a tree near enough to the wall that he might climb it and gain the top of the wall that way. A tree or even a house situated nearby. He stared about, but there was neither.

Hawk! Where are you?

Jute flung all of his desperation into the call. Shouting inside of his mind. The hawk did not respond. However, something else did. Something growled in the darkness nearby. And then the rain let up. The wind tore a rent in the clouds and the moon shone through. A shadow rounded the corner of the nearest house. Moonlight gleamed on teeth and staring eyes and the strangely shaped head. The man from the alley. Only he was not a man. His head was too long. It was changing as Jute stared. The jaws pushed out, narrowing and lengthening. The thing dropped to all fours and loped forward. Jute could not move. He was frozen at the sight.

"Jute!" screamed the ghost.

Jute turned and ran, slipping in the mud and clawing his way back to his feet. His heart hammered in his throat. Behind him the creature rushed. Mud flew from its paws and he could hear the whistle of its breath.

Why can't I fly?

And the wind blew past him, lightening his feet so that he teetered up through the air, catching at it, gulping it down, as if swallowing it would make him lighter. He ran up through the air like he was running up stairs, sobbing with relief. Something slammed into the wall below him. Jaws snapped at his feet. The creature fell away, snarling. Jute's stomach lurched and his legs windmilled through the air. He began to sink, but his hands flailed out and caught hold of the top of the wall. He pulled himself up and tumbled down over the other side of the wall. Crashed down into the mud so hard that he couldn't breathe. The wall shuddered behind him under the impact of a heavy blow. A body, hurling itself against it. Once, twice, and he heard the creature growling on the other side of the timbers. Then, there was only silence.

"Quickly, quickly," said the ghost, its voice trembling. "It'll find us. It knows this place. It'll know where to get past the wall."

"What was that?" gasped Jute. He staggered to his feet and ran.

"You don't want to know," said the ghost. "I don't want to know. I wish I didn't know! I've read of such creatures, or maybe I wrote about 'em? I can't remember. The shifters. *Awendans*, in the old tongue. Men who have given themselves over to their evil natures time and time again so that, one day, they're able to take on their honest form."

"A wolf? That thing was a wolf! What man would have a wolf inside of them?"

Jute ran through the dark. The waterfall was a thunderous roar now. He could hear it cascading down into the pool. The air seemed full of water. Not just the rain, but a thick, flying mist that was surely the fault of the waterfall. He was drenched through and through. There was nothing to be seen behind him. Only rain and darkness and the horrible sense that there were things out there, just on the edge of sight, waiting to pounce once his back was turned.

"Men who murder," said the ghost, its voice shaking. "Men who kill the innocent until they do it for the sheer joy of death. But a shifter who becomes a wolf isn't a true wolf. No, they're something evil and cruel. Real wolves will kill, but only for hunger."

Jute saw a glimmering in the darkness, a ghostly column of light cascading down and down but never going anywhere. The waterfall. It was higher than the tallest tower of the regent's castle in Hearne. Far above, on either side, was the immense blackness of the cliffs. The dark shape of a building huddled near the bottom of the falls. A water mill. It perched on the side of the river, half leaning out over the water so that it seemed as if the building would topple over at any moment. He heard the dripping and splashing of water and a creaking sound.

"What's that noise?" said the ghost from inside the knapsack. "It gives me the shivers. Maybe it's the ghost of a murderer. They always groan like that."

"Stop it. Please! All this talk of murderers and wolves and ghosts is going to make me scream."

"I'm a ghost," said the ghost, but it subsided into silence.

Jute tiptoed closer to the water mill. He saw, then, that the strange creaking noise came from the waterwheel. It turned on the side of the building, water dripping from its scoops. Moonlight glimmered on water and wet wood. The windows in the water mill were dark. Jute crept across the muddy ground until he came to the wall of the mill. The overhang of the roof sheltered him from the rain. He crouched there, feeling miserable. Adventure was all well and good, but not when you were wet and cold and running away from all sorts of horrible creatures that wanted to kill you.

The one good thing about the rain was that it was certain to hide the scent of his trail. At least, that's what he had always thought. Animals had trouble following scents over water. And there was plenty of water on the ground. Jute scowled and regarded his muddy condition with disfavor. Where was Declan? And where was the hawk, for that matter? He edged along the side of the mill until he came to a window. He couldn't see anything through the glass, for it was just as dark within as it was without.

"What's that?" said the ghost, appearing next to him.

"What's what?" said Jute. But then he heard it as well. A sniffing sound. It came from somewhere out in the dark. Somewhere in the rain, back toward the village. His blood ran cold.

"Oh, help!" said the ghost, sounding as if it were about to break into tears.

Jute didn't bother answering. He hurried around the mill, his eyes staring every which way at once. Could wolves, or whatever that creature was, see in the dark? What if it found his footprints?

The door to the water mill was at the top of three stone steps. Rotting and blackened bushes grew on either side of the door. Water sheeted down from the mossy edges of the eaves. Across the yard from the door stood a barn with leaning walls and a collapsed roof. The barn doors gaped open, sagging on their hinges.

Jute slunk up the steps to the door of the mill and touched the handle, willing himself into silence and listening. But there was nothing there. Only a handle. No ward whispering on the edge of his mind and tightening into life within the iron and wood. He turned the handle, expecting it to be locked, but it was not. The door opened silently and he slipped inside.

It was dark and the place had a musty, sour smell of rotting milk and closed up, hidden things. Jute could hear the creak of the waterwheel turning outside; the sound was quieter now, but, at the same time, deeper. The noise trembled in the timbers of the floor as if the entire house was some strange musical instrument. Reaching out his hand against the wall, his fingers brushed against something cold and hard. A key. Hanging on the wall. He could not believe his good luck. He tried it in the door. The key turned grudgingly and then the lock shot home with a click.

"This isn't a good idea," said the ghost. "Aren't we supposed to meet Declan near the waterfall? How's he going to find us in here if you've locked the door? What if there's something much worse inside than what's outside?"

"Don't be silly. In case you forgot, that thing, that shifter, is outside somewhere. What could be worse than that? We can wait for him in here."

"Yes," said the ghost unhappily, "I suppose you're right."

Moonlight slanted in through a window and Jute saw stars shining through the dirty glass. The rain must have stopped, he thought. The light, weak though it was, brought out the details of the room and deepened the shadows that lay in between. Stairs angled up along the back of the room. A table stood against the wall, piled with everything from dishes and dirty clothing to dismantled tools, old grain sacks, and an untidy coil of greasy rope. Beside it sat a chair with two broken legs that had been fixed by propping the stumps on stacked bricks. There were more grain sacks on the floor, empty and full. White dust coated everything, everywhere. Flour. Jute sneezed. The sound was appallingly loud.

"My nerves," moaned the ghost. "I can't take this."

Jute tiptoed forward. The flour on the floor stirred in puffs with each step he took. His fingers twitched and he eyed a cupboard thoughtfully. Even in the shabbiest looking houses there was usually a thing or two of value to be found. He blinked and shook his head. This was no time to be thinking of such things. He should be keeping a sharp lookout for Declan.

Jute peeped out of the window. The moonlight was bright now. Far in the west, he could see a bank of clouds painted gray by the moon, but the rest of the sky was a velvety black, speckled with stars that looked brighter and harder and closer than they had looked in the night sky over Hearne. The river rushed past, shining and eager to be on its way. A field sloped toward the village. He could see chimney smoke rising in sluggish streams from roofs. The field was black with shadows and the few lonely stalks of corn left standing by the autumn's harvest. Nothing moved.

Jute realized he had been holding his breath. He let it out in a sigh and sagged down against the wall. He closed his eyes. And opened them in time to see the handle on the front door turn. It turned slowly, to be sure, but it was turning. Jute stared at it, mesmerized. The handle turned the other way. It turned faster until it came to the end of its revolution with a jerk. It spun back the original way, turning faster yet, as if whoever was on the other end had come to the end of his patience.

And then the entire door shook under the impact of a blow. The wall vibrated with the force of it. Dust floated down from the ceiling. Again and again, the blows came. They made a deep booming noise and, in between the rhythm of that sound, Jute fancied he heard the snarl of the shifter. He scrambled to his feet, his heart hammering. The stairs creaked.

"Here now!" called a voice.

Jute shrank back into the corner beside the cupboard. The door shook under another blow.

"Here now!" bawled the voice. "Stop yer blasted racket! I'm coming, d'ya hear?"

Footsteps shuffled on the stairs. Light wavered into life through the banisters. An old man teetered down the stairs, breathing heavily and looking as if he would topple over at any moment. He carried a lantern in one hand and leaned on a knobby stick in the other. The door shook again. More flour dust drifted down from the ceiling.

"Hold yer horses, ya durn fools!" hollered the old man. And then he said to himself, "Addled, I tell ya. Roustin' out a man from his bed this time o' night. T'ain't right, I tell ya. T'ain't right."

Jute sneezed. He couldn't help it. The sneeze had been gathering force for several minutes, assisted by the flour dust and his damp and chilled state.

"Who's there?" shouted the old man, stumbling back. He glared around the room, holding his lantern high. "Come out, I tell ya, or by all, I'll brain ya, I will!"

He shook his walking stick in the air in a threatening manner, but the effect was ruined by the fact that he was frail and the stick was heavy. He toppled over and only managed to save himself by dropping the stick and grabbing hold of the table. Jute peered at the old man over the top of the table.

"Who's that? Who're ya? Don't come any closer!" The old man grabbed at his fallen stick.

"Please sir," said Jute, trying to keep his voice low, but not succeeding on account of his terror. "There's something chasing me. It's a wolf! Not a wolf, it's a man who turned into a wolf!"

"You don't say," said the old man, clutching his stick even closer. "One o' them manwolfs? Or a wolfman? I heard tell of 'em. Turrible creatures!"

"It's right outside your door!"

As if to emphasize this point, the door shook again under a heavy blow. The old man jumped and almost dropped his stick again. Jute crept closer to him.

"Please, sir," he said, his voice shaking. "What'll we do?"

"What'll we do?" echoed the old man. The door shook again.

"Turrible creatures," he said. "An' the worst thing is, lemme tell ya, boy."

The old man turned, and the light from the lantern wavered in his eyes.

"They shed all over the place. It's turrible!"

Jute stared at him, not understanding. But then he did understand when the old man's stick whipped through the air. It moved much faster than it should have. Much faster than a doddering old man should have been capable of. There was no time to duck.

Pain burst in his head. Vicious and complete, and he felt the floorboards slam up underneath him. Jute saw the old man's face above him fading into darkness, peering down. Then, there was only darkness. Right before he went unconscious, however, he heard the old man cackle, "But they ain't so bad if ya don't mind the shedding."

CHAPTER ONE HUNDRED
A SATISFACTORY THEFT

"Several of the lads heard Posle talking to a fellow," said Bordeall. "A Thieves Guild enforcer. Posle'd had a bit too much to drink and they were at a table nearby."

Owain and Bordeall were walking along the top of the city wall. The morning sun was edging up over the eastern horizon. Shadows stretched long on the ground, and all the houses huddled close by the wall were still deep in its shadow. The stone walk was dappled with puddles, for it had rained heavily that last night. The scent of the damp earth filled the air, temporarily overpowering the more pungent smells of the city. There was a cold, crisp look to the sky.

"An old friend?" said Owain.

"Perhaps." Bordeall shrugged. "Lucan heard him. Him and two of the sergeants. They were in the Fallow Field having some ale after the evening shift. It's dark in there, darker than most inns on account of how the windows face right into the—"

"I've been to the Fallow Field. A guildsman, eh?"

They walked along in silence, Owain frowning and considering, and Bordeall gazing out over the parapets at the beauty of the morning. The dew on the grasses below the wall shone like silver under the sun's eye.

"Have Posle brought to the armory," said Owain suddenly. "Let's have a chat with him. He might be the thin edge of the wedge we need."

"Aye, he might."

Posle trotted into the armory behind the young lieutenant Lucan.

"Here he is, my lord," said Lucan, saluting.

"Thank you. You may go."

Posle stood at attention before them—at least, in what he obviously thought was the proper stance. His eyes wandered about the room, examining the spears stacked in their sheaves, the shields hanging on the walls, the oak chests black with age, and the oil that had slowly seeped out over the years from the swords stored inside. He looked with interest at the stone steps leading down to the forge below, at the old flags hanging from the ceiling overhead, and the iron chandelier of candles chained up high over all, shrouded in dust and cobwebs. His gaze returned to Owain and Bordeall. He grinned in a friendly way, revealing several gaps in his teeth.

"Attention!" said Bordeall.

The smile vanished. The little man's chin shot up and he stared in the air somewhere above Owain's head.

"Yes! I mean, yes, sir!"

"Posle, isn't it?" said Owain. "That's a Vomarone name, if I'm not mistaken."

"Er, yes, my lord."

"Well, Posle, as commander of the Guard, I always like to get to know the new recruits. I like to know where they've come from. I like to know of any talents or associations they have that might benefit the Guard. Sensible, don't you agree?"

"Yes, my lord."

A slight sheen of sweat shone on Posle's forehead.

"Now, what was it you did before joining the Guard? I don't recall being told. Perhaps I've forgotten."

"I was a dockhand, my lord," said Posle. And then, unwisely, he decided to add to his story: "Sixteen years on the docks."

"Sixteen years? That's a long time. Your hands don't look like they've done sixteen years on the docks. Yes, you've calluses enough, Posle, but a dockhand has hands made of leather. Smashed fingers, scars, rope burns. What do you have to say, man? Speak up."

"I, er, well, my lord, um. . ."

"A little rat told me you worked for the Thieves Guild. No, don't deny it, man. The question is, do you still belong to the Guild? If you do, then we have a problem. Divided loyalties is what I'd call it. On the other hand, if you don't work for the Guild anymore, how am I supposed to believe that?"

It was surprisingly simple from there. Posle turned as white as a lady's handkerchief. His mouth opened and closed without making a sound. When he was able to speak, his words came out in an incoherent, gabbling rush.

"It weren't my idea, my lord! Honest! They made me do it. Said if I didn't, they'd break my woman's legs. Just wanted to keep an eye on the Guard. Interested in what you were up to. Oh please, my lord! No harm done in it, no harm! I won't tell 'em anything. There's nothing to be told. Just marching around and drilling."

Posle attempted to smile, but he only managed to look sick.

"A thief and a spy. Well, Bordeall, what'll we do?"

"Hang him, my lord," rumbled the older man. "There's nothing like a good hanging to put the iron in a man's spine. It'll do our lads good to see."

"Mercy!" bawled Posle, falling to his knees. Tears sprang from his eyes. "No! No! Have mercy, my lord!"

"Shall I go see about a rope, my lord?"

"Mercy!" shrieked Posle.

"Yes, Bordeall. Thick hemp. I don't want it breaking like last time."

"No! Please don't kill me!"

"Very good, my lord." And Bordeall strode from the room.

Owain regarded the little man groveling on the floor. A spy. He wondered what his father would have done if he had found himself in such a situation. His father had been a more decisive man in certain ways. More impatient. The older Gawinn probably would have drawn his sword and killed the man on the spot. Oh well. Such things were frowned on these days. The regent would be outraged, and the nobility would twitter like pea-brained hens behind their scented handkerchiefs and their manicured hands. Not that he cared what they thought.

"Posle."

The man was wailing so loudly that he did not hear Owain.

"Posle! Stop that. Get a hold of yourself, man. Maybe I won't have you killed. At least, not today."

Posle left off his wailing and looked up. He scrubbed at his nose.

"My lord?" he quavered.

"I have a job that needs doing. It needs just the right man to lead it, and I think you're the man."

"Anything, my lord. Anything!"

Of course, once Owain had explained what it was that he wanted, Posle wailed just as loudly as he had before. If the Guard wasn't going to execute him, then the Thieves Guild would surely murder him someday. A knife in the back in a crowded inn. Bludgeoned to death in an alley. Strangled and dumped in the bay for the sharks. But he quieted down once Owain pointed out that the Guard would hang him if he didn't comply and, if he did comply, that the Guild might not necessarily find out. If they did, well, Tormay was a big country. Posle could pack up his woman and go hide in a quiet corner of one of the duchies.

"What would I do there?" said Posle. "Er, my lord," he added, as an afterthought.

"Raise cabbages. Steal cabbages. That sort of thing. Whatever it is that thieves do in the country. You'll figure it out. Now, Posle, tell me. Where does the Guild keep all its gold? Where are we going to do our stealing?"

"Well, er, the Silentman's got the gold, I suppose. He's the one we work for. The thing is, my lord, no one knows who he is or where he lives. No one." Posle looked relieved at this thought.

"Obviously, the gold ends up in his coffers," said Owain. "But surely it starts somewhere else, doesn't it?"

"I suppose you're right, my lord." Posle scratched his head. "We gathers it up, each one who works for the Guild, an' then it gets scooped in dribs an' drabs by the accountant, an' then I guess he somehow gets it to the Silentman."

"Ah," said Owain, nodding. "Now we're getting somewhere."

After some discussion between Bordeall, Posle, and Owain, they decided to visit the accountant that same night. Bordeall's plan was to march up, surround the building, and then pull it to pieces, stone by stone, until they had found every last gold piece there was to be found. Posle's opinion was that they should spend several weeks spying— he blushed when he said the word—on the accountant's house in order to learn his habits, who visited him, whether there were guards, and anything else of interest. Owain's view, and decision, was that they should go that night.

"Six men," he said. "Tonight. An hour after midnight. Six men in ordinary clothing and masks. It can't be known that the Guard is thieving. I wouldn't mind a war with the Silentman, but now isn't the time. We don't want him to know who the culprit is."

"And what about weapons?" said Bordeall. "Knives?"

Owain shook his head. "No need to shed blood. Cudgels will be fine."

"Cudgels!" Bordeall spat in disgust on the ground.

"Both of you will go, of course. Bordeall, you're good with wards, aren't you? Get Hoon too. He has ears sharper than a cat, and if there's any need of finding a hidden panel or whatever sort of nonsense these thieves use to hide their gold, he'll find it. And we should have another strong arm or two for cracking skulls."

Owain threw open the armory door and stuck his head outside.

"Lucan!" he bellowed. "Get over here!"

"Yes, my lord?"

"Who's loafing about right now?"

"Young Bridd, of course," said Lucan, pleased to be able to point this out. "He's always loafing and I think—"

"Tell him he's needed for a special job tonight. Vital for the Guard. And find Hoon and—hmm."

513

"How about old Varden?" suggested Bordeall. "He's meaner and quicker than an alley cat. Stronger than any of the lads, despite his gray hair. Knows how to keep his mouth shut too."

"Just the man. Find Hoon and old Varden. Tell 'em the same. They're all to be on duty here at the tower, midnight sharp. Tell 'em to keep their mouths shut, and that goes for you too."

"Very well, my lord."   Lucan stalked away, the stiffness of his back radiating displeasure at the thought of Arodilac Bridd being able to help with anything that was vital to the Guard. And why wasn't it he, lieutenant Lucan, who was being appointed for the job? Whatever the job was.

"Who's the sixth?" said Bordeall.

"Me. Don't scowl like an old woman, Bordeall. I wouldn't miss this for all the gold in the regent's treasury. I've always wanted to do something about the Guild. Posle, you look ill. Perhaps you ate something rotten for lunch. Be sure and have a nap before we go. I can't have you falling asleep on the job."

"Of course, my lord," said Posle weakly.

To Owain's satisfaction, the fog drifted in off the sea that evening. It flowed through the streets, creeping up on the barrow carts, the children playing in the gutters, the old men puffing at their pipes on street corners, and the women hurrying along with their bags and bundles. They all bobbed along on the fog, drifting on its gray tide to whatever ports they called home. Doors and windows disappeared beneath its mist. The fog lapped up under eaves. Soon there were only chimney stacks and roof peaks visible above its gray blanket, rising up into the darkening sky like a strange forest of stone, slate, and brick. Everywhere, there was the sound of water: of dripping and trickling and pattering as it fell from eaves, gurgled down gutters, and sluiced out of downspouts. Somewhere overhead, hidden and unseen, the moon and its attendant stars shone down.

Owain paused at the bedroom door and looked back. The room was too dark to see much, but the curve of Sibb's hip beneath the blankets and the spill of her hair on the pillow were visible. Or perhaps he simply felt them as warmth in his mind. She sighed in her sleep. He closed the door softly.

The hallway creaked under his feet in all the old, familiar places. Outside the bedroom door of the girls, something stirred in the shadows. The dog. He had bought the dog, a wolfhound, on Sibb's urging after Loy's death. The dog was young and had months to go before it would reach its full size, but it was already fiercely loyal to the children, most of all Fen. It tolerated him and Sibb with poorly disguised animosity and was the terror of the servants. The children, after much heated discussion, during which the boys had been defeated by the impassioned logic of the girls (which had involved a bribe of cake), had named the dog Honey. Never, in Owain's estimation, had a name been so inappropriate. Honey curled its lip as he passed by, eyes unblinking. Saliva gleamed on a fang. A growl trembled in its throat. Owain tiptoed past the dog and down the stairs.

It was cold outside. He settled his cloak around his shoulders and set out. It took him a half hour of brisk walking before he reached the barracks. Bordeall's tall form loomed out of the fog. Behind him, Posle fidgeted unhappily. Hoon leaned against the wall, cleaning his fingernails with a knife. He nodded at Owain, grinning, but did not say anything. Old Varden appeared out of the fog like a ghost, yawning and grumpy, but clutching in his bony hands a cudgel that looked suspiciously more like a stone block laced onto a wood grip as opposed to its more humble and purely wooden cousin. Owain sighed and decided not to look any closer.

"Where's Arodilac?" he said.

"Right here, my lord," said a voice.

Owain turned around. Arodilac stood behind him.

"Masks," rumbled Bordeall.

He held out a fistful of what looked like lengths of dark cloth. On inspection, the lengths of cloth proved to be old and immensely stretchy socks with holes for eyes and mouths that Bordeall's wife had cut in them.

"A sock?" said Arodilac in disbelief. "Is this a sock?"

"That'll do," said Owain. He glanced at Bordeall. "I trust these are sufficiently clean."

"They're clean. My woman's a stickler for scrubbing and scouring. You set foot over her threshold with dirty ears and she'll wash them for you."

"First time ah worn socks this year, cap'n," said Varden. "It jest don't feel right. Tain't winter yet."

They set off into the fog. Thick as it was, it grew thicker as they went, until Owain could barely see the form of Hoon slouching along in front of him. Beyond the little tracker, Posle was somewhere up ahead in the mist.

"Don't lose sight of him," said Owain quietly. "I don't want a last-minute change of heart."

"No worries." Hoon turned and grinned lopsidedly at him.

They turned down an alley. Water dripped from the eaves overhead. The stones underfoot were slimy with mud, and the air stank of rotting garbage. Owain fingered the club tucked away under his cloak—it was just a length of oak split for the fire (a toy in comparison to Varden's monstrosity)—and considered the regent. He didn't doubt for a minute that the regent would hear of the night's work. Owain wasn't sure how Botrell managed it, but he maintained an effective network of eyes and ears about the city. Sooner or later, the regent always found out. It didn't matter if it was a dispute over market stalls in the Fishgate or a scullery girl gone missing from a manor in Highneck Rise. He always found out. The question was, would he also find out the Guard's role in the robbery?

"We're here, m'lord," said Posle. The thief looked at him nervously. Sweat trickled down his forehead. "Jest past the end of the alley now. The house with two chimneys."

Dimly, through the fog, Owain saw a narrow house built of the gray stone so common to Hearne. The house huddled between its neighbors on either side. The roofs drooped together to join in an ugly hodgepodge of mismatched slate.

"All right," said Owain, turning back to the others. "I want two of you up on the roof. In through the dormer window. Hoon?"

"Easy enough," said Hoon.

"Are wards a trouble for you?"

"Nah. Me old gram did some ward weaving. She spelled plenty of 'em. I know the tricks."

"Good." Owain nodded. "Take Arodilac with you. How much time do you think you'll need to make the roof?"

Hoon shrugged. "Ain't much different'n climbing a tree, these old houses. All knobby stone. We'll try, mebbe four, five houses down an' then come back over the roofs. Twenty minutes, if young Bridd here don't fall an' break his neck."

"I won't fall!" said Arodilac.

"And remember," said Owain, his eyes narrowing. "Anyone inside, I want them out cold. No noise. Don't forget your masks."

Hoon chuckled and nodded. Arodilac sighed. The two walked away into the fog.

Owain settled down on his haunches against the alley wall and tucked his cloak around him. "Twenty minutes. With luck, the fog'll break enough for us to see them on the roof, and then we'll go in. Varden, I'll want you to slip around the back. If there's a door, anyone coming out, tap 'em on the head. If there's no backdoor, then just keep an eye on the front."

"All right, cap'n. Tap on the head it is." Varden permitted himself a sour smile.

From time to time, the moon peeked down on them as a breeze blew the fog into wisps. The moonlight threaded through in quick gleams and glances, idling on a chimney pot, gliding across the stone steps leading up to a door just across the way, water trickling down from a gutter in ribbons that fluttered in and out of the pale light in silver and dark and again sudden silver before ending in a splash on the darkness and stone below.

"The lads are on the roof," said Bordeall.

And so they were. Two dim shapes crouched next to the dormer gable. Owain thought he saw one of them wave down at them. He was not sure. The breeze died away and the fog was thickening again.

"Off we go," said Owain.

The socks fit surprisingly well and, after a moment of holding his breath, he was relieved to discover they did not smell at all. Varden nodded at them and then ambled off down the street. They followed in his wake. By the time they reached the house, he had already vanished. Bordeall paused on the steps and cocked his head to one side as if listening. The door handle was a massive, rusty knob of iron. He touched the handle with one fingertip, hesitated for a moment, and then nodded.

"There's a ward there, sure enough," he said to Owain. "Doesn't feel like much. It's a bad weave. Poorly done, or old and getting rotten."

"And?"

"We'll give it a go."

But the ward was not badly done. Nor was it old and rotten.

It blew out toward them in a silent, invisible wave of heat. Owain could not breathe. Eyes shut tightly, he felt himself knocked back off the steps. He could smell scorched clothing. His cloak was on fire. He reached out one hand, flailing, to grasp at anything that might break his fall, caught at the iron railing alongside the steps and immediately snatched his hand away. The railing burned with heat. And then he tripped and sprawled on the cobblestones at the foot of the steps. Bordeall landed on him with a painful whoosh of pent-up breath. He heard Posle whimpering off to one side.

"Sorry," rumbled Bordeall.

They huddled under a downspout the next house over until their clothes were no longer smoldering. Owain gave his lieutenant a sour look.

"What were you saying about that ward?"

Bordeall had the grace to look embarrassed.

"Guess I misheard the blasted thing."

"Must be a good ward," Owain said, "if it can pass itself off as poorly woven."

"Only the best, m'lord," said Posle. "The Guild wouldn't spare coin on such as that."

"Aye, but now we've no choice other than to go in fast. If anyone's inside, they're sure to be alerted now."

Bordeall nodded. "Leave it to me. It won't be pretty, but it'll work."

516

He doused himself under the downspout stream one more time and then, dripping wet and with a fold of cloak wrapped over his nose and mouth, he charged up the steps. The door shattered with a crash. Owain rushed up the steps after him, hauling along a reluctant Posle. Bordeall sprawled on the wreckage of the door in a small entrance hall. Flames licked at the man's cloak, and the smell of charred wood filled the air. The two other men fell to their knees and beat out the flames. Bordeall groaned and opened one eye.

"I'm getting too old for this," he said. "My wife's going to have my neck."

"Watch out!" yelped Posle.

A sword hissed viciously through the air. Owain flung himself back against the wall. He felt the blade rip through his cloak. He kicked out hard, connecting with someone's leg. The man cursed. Someone shouted in alarm further back in the house. Owain threw his cudgel at the man. He staggered back, dropping his sword, and then Bordeall surged to his feet and slammed his fist into the man's face.

"Thank you, Posle," said Owain.

"Ain't nothing, m'lord," said Posle.

The house was a dark, cramped sort of place, with narrow passages and doors that let into several rooms that looked uncared for: a dirty scullery piled with crockery and garbage, a room filled with what looked and smelled like sacks of dried fish, and several others in various states of disarray. They only spared these a hasty glance, for it seemed that no one was on the ground floor.

"Quickly now," said Owain.

They rushed up the stairs and found themselves standing in a hallway. Arodilac grinned at them from the other end of the hall. A figure lay slumped at his feet.

"Pull that sock down," said Owain.

"Sorry."

Hoon knelt at the keyhole of a door, a bit of wire twisting in his fingers. Two other doors stood flung open, revealing stairs up to an attic through one and a smelly bedroom through the other.

"In here," said Hoon. "Fat man. Dodged in quicker'n a pig on market day. I couldn't get my hands on him, blast it. The lad got this one smart enough, but I think what we wants is behind this door."

"Break it down," rumbled Bordeall.

Hoon shook his head. "Nice oak, this. Built more'n thick. You'd need a proper axe an' a good sweat at it. Stone frame an' lintel too. This ain't normal house construction here. Someone's gone to trouble."

He bent back to the keyhole, but with no luck.

"Er, if I could have a go."

Posle plucked the wire from Hoon's fingers and knelt beside him. He scrubbed at his face beneath the sock and then probed at the keyhole. Behind the door, there came a faint noise. It sounded like wood scraping together. Something heavy grating against the floor.

"Hurry!" said Owain.

And then metal clicked in the keyhole. The knob turned and they flung open the door, trampling poor Posle in the process. A fat man glanced up, sweating, his eyes wide and his mouth gaping. He was in the process of dragging an enormous chest across the floor toward a large mirror hanging on the wall.

"You can't—you can't!" gasped the man.

"Get him!" said Owain.

It was probably due to the fact that they all reached for him at the same moment—except for Posle, of course, who had only managed to sit up by that time and wonder dizzily what had fallen on his head—but they got in each other's way, and the fat man, evidently deciding that the chest was not worth it, hopped backward and dove through the mirror. At least, that's what it looked like. There was an odd sort of ripple in the glass and the next moment the fat man was gone. The air whispered.

"A warded gate," gasped Posle, having got his breath back. "It's how we—it's how the Guild guards the entrances to the Silentman's court. I don't know how to use 'em, my lord. I don't— bless my heart—I don't! Only the real Guild toffs know, an' they ain't many of them."

"Stone take it!"

Owain rapped on the mirror with his knuckles. It seemed hard enough. Glass. Just a mirror. His eyes glared back at him through the holes in the sock. "With luck, though, what we came for is in the chest. Our fat friend certainly seemed determined to take it with him. But we've no time to fiddle with locks. Bordeall, you and Posle get that chest back to the barracks on the double. The rest of us'll have a quick look around before the Guild turns up in force. Arodilac, go downstairs and get Varden."

But other than a small leather sack of coins—triumphantly discovered in the bedroom closet by Arodilac—there was nothing else to be found in the house in the remaining minutes Owain allowed. They found dust and a great deal of grime. Varden was convinced the walls had something to hide and began knocking holes in them with his cudgel.

"There's gold in these walls here, cap'n," said Varden, bashing another hole. "Can't you jest smell it? I can smell it."

"That's enough," said Owain. "We need to go. We're out of time."

The four men slipped away into the fog. The streets were silent and, if any of the neighbors had heard anything, they had chosen to remain silent in their beds. No lights shone in any of the windows, although at one window across the street a curtain twitched slightly and then was still.

"No trouble in the back, Varden?" said Owain, as they hurried through the fog.

"Weren't nary a bit, cap'n," said the old man. "Jest one nervous sort. Came hopping out like a durned rabbit, but I gave 'im a tap on the head like you advised. Calmed him down."

They walked in silence that was broken only by the whisper of their footsteps and the occasional yawn from Arodilac. But as they turned down the street that led up to the barracks gates, a dog howled somewhere nearby. Hoon shivered.

"Somethin' strange about that house," he said.

"What's that?" said Owain.

"Not rightly certain. Somethin' jest not right there. It didn't tell on me until a while. I know ya don't put much stock in such things, cap'n, but I'd say the Dark's had a hand in that house. It were the smell, I think, an' a bit else. It put me in mind of a thing or two I've run across in the mountains."

"What sort of thing?" said Arodilac, his eyes wide. "What do you mean by the Dark? That's just an old wives' tale, isn't it?"

"That'll do," said Owain, and they said nothing more.

They parted at the barracks. Arodilac wanted to ask a question or two—and it was in the other men's eyes as well—but he shut his mouth when Owain glared at him.

518

"My thanks for the night's work," said Owain. "You'll not mention it to anyone. That's all. Go wake the cook and have a bite to eat. Tell him to bring out a bottle of wine."

"All right, cap'n," said old Varden. He nodded and shuffled off. The two others followed reluctantly.

Bordeall was waiting for him in the armory. The chest stood unopened. Owain locked the door and nodded. Three blows with an axe was all it took. The lid shattered and the lamplight caught within, glittering between the shards of wood. The chest brimmed full of gold and silver coins. Owain grinned in relief.

"I feel a lot more kindly toward the Guild," he said.

CHAPTER ONE HUNDRED & ONE
THE HOUSE OF STONE AND HUNGER

At first, Jute thought he was still curled up in bed at the inn. But then he realized that blankets did not feel like this, no matter how rough the wool. He awoke and became instantly aware of pain. His head ached and throbbed, centered on a point at the top of his skull that threatened to drive itself down in a sharp spike of fire. His back felt as if a fat person in iron-nailed boots had spent the last few hours trudging back and forth across it. But it was his hands that were the worst. Jute could not feel them for a few seconds, and then they burned to life in utter agony. He gasped and opened his eyes. Blinked, and wished he could somehow go back to sleep. Never wake up. Memory swept back in a rush. The old man in the water mill. The shifter growling at the door. The village shrouded in night and rain.

"I wish I were back in Hearne," groaned Jute. "Oh, hawk! Where are you? Ghost, are you there?"

But there was no answer.

As his eyes grew accustomed to the dim light, Jute saw that he was in a cellar of some sorts. It was a gloomy place with crudely hewn stonewalls. Moisture oozed from the stone and moss grew in patches of slimy green. The air stank of rot. A staircase at the end of the room disappeared up into darkness. Behind him, he could hear the drip-drip-drip of water plopping down into a pool or basin. It was the only sound in the cellar.

Jute tried to turn, to see the basin, and immediately wished he hadn't. His back shivered into agony, and his hands—well, he had no words to describe his hands. They were tied up high over his head, stretched out so that his shoulders and back ached abominably. Most of his weight hung dangling from his hands, but by arching his back and standing on his toes, he was able to relieve the stress a bit. By doing that, he was able to slowly turn. And to his relief, Jute saw he was not alone in the cellar.

Declan. The man hung motionless from a length of chain, his hands tied over a hook on the end of the chain. His head was slumped forward and his eyes were closed. Dried blood caked the side of his face. Beyond him, several other chains dangled from the ceiling. They all ended in rusty hooks.

"Declan!" said Jute.

The man did not move.

"Declan, wake up! Please!"

But it was no use. Jute groaned. This was the end. He was going to die in this dreadful place. He was going to die, far from his old life in Hearne, far from home. He had never had a home. It wasn't fair. All he ever wanted out of life was a home. Tears trickled down Jute's face.

"I'm going to die," he moaned.

"Probably," said a voice from close by. "Yes. It's likely."

"Ghost!"

The ghost wavered into view. It looked terrified.

"Ghost! I'm so glad to see you!

"Likewise, likewise," said the ghost. "There's nothing more I enjoy than conversation with an old friend, but we don't have the time for that. You have to get out of here, Jute. Now. Quickly. Hurry up!"

"I'd like nothing more, but I can't."

"Oh? Ah. I see what you mean. Er, well. . ."

The ghost drifted up into the air to examine the chain.

"Nonsense," it said, popping back down. "Quite simple. Your hands are tied together and the rope's looped on a hook. Nasty-looking hook, but no matter. All you have to do is inch your way up the chain a bit so you can get the rope over the hook. Easy as that. Grab the chain and start climbing."

"Easy enough for you to say," said Jute furiously. "I can't feel my hands, let alone get a grip on the chain!"

"You don't understand." The ghost stuck its face near Jute's and lowered its voice to a trembling whisper. "This is a bad place. An evil place! Do you understand the meaning of the word evil? We're going to die if we stay here. Well, not me. I'm already dead, but you certainly will. Oh, my poor heart. I can't stand the tension. My nerves! Why won't you listen, you stupid boy? I should've never become a professor. I should've listened to my father and stayed at home. Raising chickens is an honorable occupation."

"What do you mean?" said Jute. "What do you mean, this is an evil place?"

"This place," said the ghost, gulping and turning paler than it already was. "This place is the—"

But at that moment they heard the sound of a door opening and footsteps on the stairs. The ghost vanished. And down the stairs came a monstrosity. A bulk that moved from step to step with all the slow deliberation of living stone. The shadow slid off the flat planes of face and neck, off the massive hands hanging at the figure's sides. It seemed the thing was made of stone. Gray stone pitted and cracked with age until the flesh looked more like the weathered crags of a mountainside, rather than a living creature. Stubble grew on its scalp like dead hay.

A peculiar clicking and clacking sound jittered in the air. Stone creaked. And settled to stillness before Jute. Eyes like pebbles gazed down at Jute. The mouth yawned open and revealed a cavern lined with enormous teeth like gravestones. The face was so large that Jute could not look at it all at once. He could only take in a bit here and a bit there. It was a strange, disjointed landscape of rock and shadow, planes and hollows, crevices and standing stones.

"Boy," said the creature.

The word slid slowly out of the mouth, deep and dusty and reluctant, as if the creature had been a stranger to speech for so long that it was unsure of words and unsure of its own voice. Somewhere, further back in the cellar, Jute thought he heard the ghost whimper. Or perhaps it was his own whimpering he heard. The dead eyes studied him and, for a moment, it seemed as if something stirred beneath their flat surface. Curiosity.

Jute heard the clicking sound again. It sounded like small stones knocking together. And then he saw the source of the noise. A rusty rope of iron lay around the thing's neck. Skulls hung on it, the size of a man's head but looking as tiny as children's baubles in the shadow of that great head. They stared at Jute with their empty sockets and grinned at him with their toothless jagged jaws. Every once in a while, the skulls stirred on the iron strand and knocked against their neighbors.

"You are strange, boy," rumbled the creature. "There's something old in you. Older than your simple flesh. But not as old as stone. No. Not as old as stone. Nothing's old as stone. Your bones'll still make my bread. I'll grind 'em into flour. Seven wizards came creeping to these heights to try my hand and they all ended on my spit. Heroes with their bright swords. They died in my dark hall and I ground their bones to make my bread. I roasted 'em. Meat and bread. You'll taste just as well, boy."

"Heroes," echoed a skull. At least, to Jute's horrified eyes and ears, that's what seemed to have spoken. "Heroes. Why, I was one of 'em. Head full of sunlight and dreams."

"And me," chimed in a nearby skull. "I was a hero."

"And me!"

"Don't forget me," said a skull. It twisted on the iron strand and Jute could hear the grate of metal against bone. "I was a hero as well. I'd a horse and a sword."

"You'd nothing," sneered the skull beside it. "Can you remember a single thing in that empty head of yours? You'd a nag and a broken blade that did better service chopping firewood than necks. You were better as bread."

"Weren't we all," said the first skull. But then it laughed, and it bared its jagged jaw at Jute. "It ain't the bread that's important, boy. It's the teeth that bites it. He chews, he does, like boulders smashing on boulders. Got quite the gnashers, he does."

"Quiet," said the creature, and the skulls fell silent, though Jute could feel their eye sockets staring at him. The figure stared down at Jute, not moving or blinking.

"Fine as dust," said the creature after a while.

Then the massive head turned toward Declan.

"What have my dogs brought me?"

The voice came alive with sudden hate, though it still whispered in tones so quiet that Jute had to strain his ears to hear.

"Farrow. . ."

The enormous bulk of stone shifted one step forward. The face lowered until it almost touched Declan's, but the man did not move. He hung there, apparently lifeless and insensible. The skulls clicked together in excitement.

"I had three sons. Three sons of stone I raised on this mountain. The wind wore away the crags and time wore away the sons of men into countless generations of death. But my sons grew strong. I fed them on blood and flesh and the bread of dead men's bones. We lived on this mountain when the Rennet River was birthed high in the peaks, when the deep springs dug their way up into the light, when the river flowed down into the plain below and carved its valley to the accursed sea. We were old then, my sons and I. This land was ours. Ours, from the cold crags where the dragons sleep beneath the ice to the sands blowing in the south. Even to the shore we held sway, though there were eyes in the sea always watching. I hate the sea."

The ogre paused and Jute thought he saw the thing shiver. The smallest of trembles, like an earthquake so slight that it might have been no more than the ripple of grass on a hillside, so slight that only a mouse would have pricked his ears at it.

"The sea," said the ogre, not even looking at Declan anymore. "Wearing away my stone without my leave. Stealing it from me and grinding it into sand. May the darkness take the sea. All of Tormay was mine, and yet it is stolen away in little bits. Licked away by the sea, worn by the wind, thieved by those dirty little men crawling about like ants. I'll kill them all. Death was our servant once, and it'll be again. Aye, once again. It'll all be mine, once again."

"It'll be yours," chimed in a skull.

"Aye, yours," cackled another.

"We've heard! We've heard the voice in the dark. Promise this. Promise that. Whisper, whisper, whisper! Busy as bees, ain't we?"

"Silence," said the creature.

The room was silent again, except for the dripping water. Jute tried to breathe shallowly, willing the stone monstrosity not to turn its lifeless face back toward him. He couldn't stand another glance from those eyes.

"My sons wandered south, Farrow. They carved their place under the mountains. And you brought death to them, so many years ago. The shadows told me. I heard them dying, whispers and echoes from mountain root to mountain root until it came to me here. My three sons. My foolish three sons. Who knew iron could cleave stone? But I've a stone knife that needs sharpening. It'll cleave flesh. It has before. I've been saving it for you. I've been waiting."

The thing turned without haste, shambling toward the stairs. Jute shut his eyes tight and listened to the sounds of stone creaking on stone, dust drifting down from the steps, the horrible clicking of the skulls, and then blessed silence.

"Oh, mercy," said the ghost. "Mercy, my poor nerves. I can't stand this. Knives and cleaving. There's bound to be a great deal of screaming. Oh, woe is me. How I wish I were back in my snug little attic. Why oh why did you ever speak to me? A curse on all curses!"

"It's all well for you," said Jute. "You're already dead! What was that thing? It's going to kill me! Help!"

"Bread, specifically," said the ghost. "You're going to be baked into bread."

"An ogre," said a voice. "That was an ogre."

Jute turned in a thrill of delight, swinging on his chain. Declan! The man's voice was weak and his head was still slumped down on his chest, but he had spoken, nonetheless.

"You're alive!"

"Barely," said the man. He took a deep breath and raised his head. One eye opened to fix Jute with a bloodshot stare. "Listen to me. You've little time left. Ogres don't play with words. They never lie. They can't be untrue to their nature, just as a stone can only be a stone. He's going to kill us and grind us into bread. Roast us on his fire. You have to escape. Listen to the ghost. Save yourself. Perhaps he won't chase you. He has good reason to hate me, not you."

"I can't," said Jute. "I can't feel my hands."

"You must." Declan's head slumped forward again.

"You must!" chorused the ghost. "It's quite simple. Grab hold of the chain and climb. You're a thief, aren't you? Aren't thieves always climbing things such as, I don't know, drain spouts and walls and gates and trees, whatever it is you climb. A chain can't be any more difficult. Climb, you lazy boy. Climb!"

"I can't."

"You can and you will!"

Grinding his teeth together against the pain, Jute tried to grasp the chain with his swollen fingers. He pushed up on his tiptoes. Willed his fingers to close. Agony lanced down his arms. Clenched on the chain with one hand, inched the next hand up higher. Willed his fingers to clench once again.

"You can do it!" urged the ghost.

But he couldn't. His fingers refused to cooperate, and he slid back down the few, hard-won inches and jounced with a sickening jolt on the hook.

"It's no use," gasped Jute.

He closed his eyes. Dimly, he heard the ghost wailing at him. The darkness in the cellar grew deeper. It was as heavy as the stone of the ceiling and walls. Weight pushed down on him. There was nothing left to do but die. He was empty inside. And yet there was something. A breeze stirred in the back of his mind. It blew the dust from his thoughts. The coolness of its touch soothed his pain. His mind cleared. The weight lifted, reluctant at first, insisting that stone was stone and it could not be moved. But it could be moved. The breeze blew harder now, filled with the memory of sky and endless light, regardless of night and clouds and blindness.

Jute opened his eyes. The breeze picked him up as gently as a feather. The hook swung free. He fell to his knees, sobbing with relief. He tore with his teeth at the rope binding his wrists. It was to no avail, but the breeze plucked the rope free strand by strand, as delicately as a girl's braid separated one hair at a time. Jute stumbled to his feet. He tried to lift Declan up and off the hook, but he could not. The man's body was a dead weight.

"Hurry!" implored the ghost. "Hurry, oh hurry, hurry!"

The breeze swirled around Jute. It lifted his arms, lifting Declan until the man fell free onto the floor. His eyes were closed and his breath rattled between his teeth.

"Wake up!" said Jute.

"Leave him," said the ghost. "He's dead already. No need to lug around dead bodies. No need to upset the ogre any more than he already is!"

"You'd desert him so easily?" said Jute.

He strained to lift Declan. The breeze came to his aid again. Pushing at him from behind, tugging at his collar, propping him up. This time, however, there was a nervous urgency in its touch. Jute found himself on his feet—he was not sure that his feet were touching the ground at times—dragging Declan's impossible weight up the steps. They emerged into a long, gloomy hallway of stone. It stretched off in either direction.

"Which way?" said Jute.

"I don't know," said the ghost. "How am I supposed to know? Why am I supposed to know everything? Just because someone's a professor, it doesn't mean they know everything about anything. I know too much about ogres! I know spells for getting rid of warts and giving 'em, and I know all seven of the best recipes for roast goat to be had in the Mountains of Morn, but I don't know which way we should go down this hallway. I don't, I tell you! I don't!" Here, the ghost, obviously overcome by the situation, burst into tears and stamped up and down, wailing all the while.

"Shh," said Jute, horrified at this. "The ogre'll hear you."

"Ohh-h!" wailed the ghost. "The ogre! He'll slice your throat with his knife, chop you up into a thousand bloody bits, and bake you into bread, all because of me. I'll be the death of you. It'll be all my fault. Oh, how can I live with myself? I can't stand it!"

"Will you be quiet?"

And the wind came to Jute's aid once again. It blew past him, heading down the passage, and he thought he heard the sound of grass waving in its movement, of branches bending in a breeze, of sky and space and an end to the crushing weight of stone.

Come away outside,

Outside and out from under the weight of things.

Where things neither wither nor fade

And the emptiness is full of light

And again you shall see the sky.

Come you away.

Rejoice!

Despite the dreadful gloom of the ogre's haunt, Jute could hear joy in the wind's voice. Joy and laughter and a sense of sky that started as a speck of blue in his mind. The blue grew wider and wider as if it rushed toward him (or he was rushing toward it) to engulf him in the sheer unending delight of the sky. Of a horizon that curved past itself into colors so fantastic that they could not be described.

Jute followed the wind, was carried by it, as he himself carried the slack weight of Declan's body. Was it he who carried the man, or the wind? No, surely it was the wind. They rushed down the dark and noisome corridors of stone, past iron doors and caverns filled with countless years of evil. Armor and weapons rusted in piles, shrouded in dust and the tangled threads of spiders who had long since moved on to livelier spots—all that were left of hero after hero who had braved the Morns in hope of fortune and fame. Heaps of gold and silver shone, even in that ill light, though the metal gleamed with muted and ill-concealed malice, as if the touch of ogre hands had forever contaminated it. Nowhere in all those twisting passageways was there a bone to be seen, but everywhere there was a fine, white dust. It had little to do with stone but everything to do with the skeletons of hopeful young men who had come to this mountain on the strength of their dreams. The dust stirred in the wake of the wind and Jute's hurried footsteps. It clung to him and would not be dissuaded by either his sudden nausea or the sneezes he tried to muffle against his sleeve.

"Shh!" said the ghost, deciding to momentarily return to its senses. "Do you want to get us killed?"

Stone steps led up into a faltering light, clearing and brightening somewhat. Jute's spirits rose. The wind chuckled in his mind. They were now in an enormous cavern, its ceiling blackened with soot and its walls hung with tattered banners in moth-eaten disarray. Some of them were no more than threads and dust, held together by spiderwebs. A fire smoldered on an open hearth in the center of the cavern. Coals stared from deep within the pile of ashes. A spit hung suspended over the fire, skewering a strange, contorted mass that had been charred into oblivion. Jute shuddered and looked away. Perhaps it was only a deer.

"Hush," said the ghost. "What's that noise?"

They both stopped, though the wind tugged nervously at Jute. It already knew what the noise was. It was a quiet grating sound. A rasping grind that came and went in odd intervals. And in the spaces between the grating, Jute could hear a different sort of sound. A humming croon. A deep voice that sang of stones and blood and slow, sharp things and death. And quieter beneath it all was the punctuation of clicking skulls.

"Save us!" said the ghost, trying not to scream. It stuffed its hands into its mouth and trembled.

A red light shone from a door, and through it Jute could see the massive form of the ogre, back turned and bent over a spinning stone wheel. It held a blade in its hands and sparks flew from the edge. The flames of a forge burned beyond the ogre. Slabs of iron ore lay in piles beside the burning pit, but, massive as the ore was, more massive still was the creature bent over its brightening blade.

"Look there," said Jute. "Just inside the door, leaning against the wall. That's Declan's sword, isn't it?"

"One sword looks like another," said the ghost. "Anyway, no time to stop and dawdle. This is not a nice neighborhood. Hurry up! Hurry up!"

"No, wait."

To the ghost's horror, Jute set down Declan's inert body (rather, the wind set down the body) and crept over to the doorway leading to the forge. He was confident in his own silence. He would not make a sound, and the wind fell silent around him, holding its breath and watching. The ogre's back was like the back of a mountain, cast into shadow by the light of the forge on its other side like the red setting sun. The sword was within reach now. It was Declan's sword. Jute recognized the battered leather sheath. It leaned against the wall, propped beside a sheaf of rusting spears. He reached out his hand and, as he did, heard a rasping sound that set his teeth on edge. The sound of bone scraping against iron.

High up on the slopes of the ogre's shoulder, beside the towering pile of its neck and head, a tiny skull inched its way around the iron strand. The eye sockets peeked down at Jute, and it seemed as if they were filled with the red light of the forge.

"Oh, master," said the skull. "I spy a mouse. A sneaking, thieving mouse!"

The ogre turned.

"Run!" screamed the ghost.

Jute grabbed the sword and fled. In that one instant, there had been time to see the ogre's awful eyes glaring down at him, the forge spitting out sparks and heat, and the blade in the ogre's hand shining blue along its edge. The floor shook under him. He could hear the pounding of the ogre's feet.

"Run, run, runrunrun!" shrieked the ghost.

"Run, run, run!" giggled the skulls. "Run, little mouse! Run as fast as you can!"

The ogre did not say anything, and Jute, of course, did not say anything either, for he had no breath for anything other than running and trying not to scream. Something whipped through the air behind him. And then the wind picked him up. His feet left the ground, still windmilling madly. Dust blew past him. Dimly, out of the corner of his eye, he saw Declan's body tumble head over heels, bounce painfully off a stone outcropping— well, it looked painful to Jute, but it was doubtful whether the man felt it, as he looked decidedly unconscious—and then fly past him to go sailing up a flight of stairs.

The ogre bellowed in fury.

"Death take thee!"

The stairs shook. Rocks tumbled down from the ceiling. Sudden light blazed across Jute's sight. It was so bright he could not keep his eyes open. The brilliance burned past his eyelids with dazzling images of red and white and sunbursts of gold. He had a glimpse of a mountainside falling away into nothingness, of a blinding expanse of snow, of sky and the dark line of trees marching across the slopes below like the advancing guard of an army. The wind surged up into a howling roar. Jute fluttered in its grasp, as helpless as a feather. The wind blew through his mind. The mountain shook, and he heard the thunderous crash of rocks falling and the dull boom of the earth sliding away.

And then the wind set Jute down as a gently as a mother would lay down a sleeping infant in its cradle. He opened his eyes and sat up. The sun shone down from a clear sky. He felt its heat on his face and radiating from the stone beneath him, but the shadows of the forest and the deep crags below him looked dreadfully cold. Snow lay all around. The hawk settled next to him in a flutter of wings.

"That was rather close," said the bird. He nipped at a crooked feather and then nodded in satisfaction. "I was beginning to think it was the end of you. And of Tormay."

"Where were you?" said Jute, furious and happy at the same time.

"Oh, here and there," said the hawk. "Here and there. Don't splutter like that. You look like an outraged infant about to spit up its mother's milk. You figured it out. The wind woke, didn't it?"

"Yes," said Jute, still spluttering, "I suppose. But—"

"But that's precisely the point. You can't always be depending on me, regardless of the severity of the straits you find yourself in. Although I must admit, being in the clutches of an ogre (one of the oldest ogres in all of Tormay) is a severe strait. You have to learn to do with what you can do, and that includes the wind. We should've done better by avoiding Ostfall. Nasty place. I remember now, better late than never, ogres used to hold sway over a great deal of the western Morns. Villages would pay tribute to them, and there were quite a few instances of peculiar offspring among the people. But that was long ago."

"I could've been killed!" shouted Jute.

"Tush."

"But—!"

"Bosh!"

"When you're done shouting at each other," said the ghost, popping out of a nearby snowdrift, "what are you going to do about Declan?"

The boy and the hawk both turned, shamefaced. The rock was larger than Jute had first noticed, for it stepped below him to a shallow ledge and then beyond that into a sweep of stone that fell away down the mountainside. Declan lay sprawled on the ledge. Jute scrambled down toward him. The wind blew past him, and he heard impatience and excitement in its tone.

"He looks cold," said Jute, forgetting his anger at the hawk. He touched Declan's hand and it was indeed cold.

"Cold he may be," muttered the hawk. "And cold he is, but the sea is even colder still."

"What do you mean by that?"

"Yes," said the ghost. "What do you mean by that? What has the sea to do with us? Brr! Wretched sort of cold, that is. I remember a day spent fishing for flounder or, er, some kind of fish. Who cares? It was fish! Started out fine and dandy, as all stories do that end horribly, and then up came black clouds and wind and the surf pounding away I caught a miserable cold." The ghost sneezed in evident enjoyment of its memory.

"Never mind what I mean," said the hawk, "for it isn't mine to explain." And the bird bent over the man's head to whisper in his ear. Both Jute and the ghost edged closer to listen, but they were not close enough to hear.

The wind hushed its voice, for it heard what the hawk said. Out across the horizon, two days' journey to the west, a wave surged higher on the shore than the surf had gone in many a day. Fishermen mending their nets on the sand were caught unawares by its advance and came up sputtering in the foam, to the amusement of their drier and safer fellows.

Declan stirred. He opened his eyes and sat up.

"I was dreaming," he said.

Declan looked around him in sudden and dawning dismay, at the fields of snow and the mountain slopes that stretched away on either side. His hand reached to his collar to feel at the necklace there. He sat in silence and gazed west, but the eyes of man are not strong enough to look over such a distance to see what he wished to see. If the hawk had

527

mounted high into the sky over the highest peak of the Mountains of Morn, even his keen eyes would not have reached the sea.

"I was dreaming," he said again.

"But are you well?" said the hawk.

Declan gazed at his hands unhappily. The gray pallor of death was gone from his face and his skin was already burned red by the cold and the wind.

"Well enough," he said.

"All well indeed," said the ghost. "And what if, one day, we find ourselves in similar sorry straits without you conveniently nearby, master hawk? What then? Shall we just sit by and watch the poor man die? At least teach young Jute here the words. The full power of language doesn't seem to work with ghosts. It's our lack of definition, our ghostliness, I suppose."

"Your point is taken," said the hawk somewhat sourly. "Here, then, it's a simple thing. The mere mention of the sea will prove a powerful tonic for whatever ails Declan, but it must be said in an older tongue. *Brim ond mere*. Will you remember those words? I warn you, they mustn't be spoken with careless intent."

"*Brim ond mere*," said the ghost greedily. "Delightful. I think I knew these words once, yes, it's coming back to me now. Of course, of course. Careless intent? Never. Now, you try it, Jute."

"*Brim ond mere*," echoed Jute.

"No," said the ghost. "More emphasis on the last word. *Brim ond mere*!"

"*Brim ond mere*!"

"Silence!" said the hawk.

The snow shifted in creaking groans around them, drifts warming and collapsing down into water to reveal the real and awful depths of the white fields. The rock on which they sat trembled. A bank of snow on their left slid away in a whisper that grew in tumbling fits and sudden, soft thunder to a rumbling roar as it bounded down the mountainside, growing and gathering to itself more and more snow as the avalanche careened toward the tree line below.

"If that had happened above us," said Jute. He did not finish his thought but looked higher up the mountain in alarm.

"Words are dangerous," said the hawk, glaring at the ghost. "None more so than the older tongues, for they reach back to the eldest tongue of all, in which language a word defines the nature of a thing, rather than the thing defining the word. Once the word's known, the thing itself is controlled, and this is a terrible danger."

"Yes, yes," said the ghost in sulky tones. "The strictures of naming. I taught that class many times when I was alive. I could teach it in my sleep."

"Then you'd do well to remember," said the hawk. "Asleep or otherwise."

"It was Jute who said it," mumbled the ghost. "I'm just a ghost. There's no power in a word when I say it."

Happily, they discovered that the wind had kindly deposited not only Declan's sword on the rock slab, but also both their packs and a bewildering assortment of treasure. The sun shone brightly on the silver and gold, so brightly that the flash could be seen from miles away, for the wind had scoured the trove clean of the dust of hundreds of years.

"The ogre will be missing his baubles, I think," said the hawk, and then he added sadly, "the wind always did have an eye for shiny things."

"We can't just leave it all lying here," said Jute. He scrambled over the rock to sit on his haunches by the shining sprawl. "Someone's bound to take it."

"Squirrels?" jeered the ghost.

"I reckon this'd go for a nice price in Hearne." Jute picked up a red stone laced about with gold filigree as fine as spiderweb.

"Leave that be," said the hawk. "There's no telling when an ogre gets its hands on something. It changes, and never for the better."

"Aye," said the ghost. "Leave it for the squirrels. They'll crack it like a nut."

After some discussion, mainly between the hawk and Declan, they decided it would be quicker to head up the mountainside rather than backtrack down into the Rennet Valley and so find the pass to Mizra. It was bitter, cold work, trudging up those snowy slopes. Jute fell into a daze as he followed in the path that Declan trod. The crags rose around them as they climbed, for the Mountains of Morn reached up like the points of spears into the sky and their peaks were unscalable. Dimly, as if from a distance, Jute heard the hawk and the ghost arguing about the history of the duchy of Mizra and finer points, such as whether or not the city of Ancalon predated that of Hearne, and the degree of autonomy of the mountain hamlets on the eastern slopes of the Morns. The cold worked its way deep into Jute's bones. It would be a fine thing to fly over the mountains and be done with the journey. What good was being the wind—what on earth did it mean: being the wind?—if he could not fly about when he wanted? Jute tried to step into the air as he had done before, but his legs felt as if they were made of lead.

Well, then why don't you just carry me? he said to the wind, but the wind just chuckled in his ear and blew past in a flurry of snow.

Much later in the day, their way began to descend. Jute wasn't sure when, but he was only aware of a new and more agonizing pain in his legs (going down a hill is always worse than going up a hill), and the sunlight vanished behind the crags to the west. It grew colder. Ice covered the snow, undiscernible in the shadows. Jute slipped and fell. He could not feel his hands.

"I don't know how much longer the boy will be able to go on," said the hawk.

"Best to keep moving," said Declan without turning around. "Two more hours and then we'll stop. Down under the lee of the mountain. Below the tree line."

"I can't feel my toes," said Jute, his teeth chattering.

"Can't stop now. Nothing to build a fire with here. We'd freeze and die."

"Precisely," said the ghost, cheering up at these words. "You'll freeze and die. Death by freezing is fascinating. Your blood turns to ice. Your skin turns blue. Your hair gets as brittle as old women's finger bones and then just snaps off, strand by strand, until you're bald. Your eyes freeze into pebbles rattling around in your skull until they pop out and go bouncing across the ground. Your stomach fills up with wind and you'll find yourself thinking thoughts of ale, hard cheese, and witches with long noses."

"That's ridiculous," said the hawk.

"Yes, but true. Many people who've frozen to death have reported similar experiences. The truth is often strange, my fine-feathered friend, but it's still the truth."

"I don't even know why I bother," said the hawk.

Jute didn't hear the rest of their conversation, for his mind was filled with thoughts of ale and cheese. This alarmed him. Perhaps it meant he was freezing to death? But then he realized he had only started thinking about ale and cheese after the ghost had mentioned them. After all, he wasn't thinking about witches with long noses, and for several minutes he had to concentrate hard to avoid thinking about witches. He could do with some ale and cheese. Mulled ale, steaming hot. And bread fresh from the oven to go with the cheese.

529

They continued for what seemed much longer than two hours. It was an endless, dull stumbling through darkness and cold that grew darker and colder with every step Jute took. Thoughts of ale and cheese congealed into ice and fell away, too heavy to carry even as hope.

Pine trees rose up from the icy slope, singly at first like sentinels of an army; past them were the thicker groves of the battalions standing at attention for the return of the sun. Above their snow-bowed heads, the moon skated across the frozen expanse of the sky.

"We'll stop here for the night," said Declan.

Somehow, in the gloom and the deeper swaths of shadows cast by the trees, he had noticed a ravine a short distance away from their path. They hiked across and found it sheltered from the wind. An overhang of rock had preserved a clearing dry and free of snow. Declan disappeared for several minutes and then returned with an armful of branches.

"That won't burn," said the ghost. "It's frozen."

"It'll burn," said Declan.

He arranged the branches in a pile at the base of the overhang.

"It won't burn." The ghost drifted closer. "Ice, you know. Frozen right into the wood."

Declan knelt down. He muttered something over the wood and a flame sprang into life. The hawk, who had been drowsing on Jute's shoulder, raised his head.

"Careful," said the bird, his voice soft. "Careful, man. There's no telling who might be listening in this night."

"Amazing," said the ghost, its eyes popping. "A genuine word of power. From a backwoodsman, no less. Upon my soul, what did you say? Was it the name of fire? Or wood? I suppose you could've remade the nature of wood by naming it. Was it that? No, it couldn't be. Otherwise there'd be no more wood to burn. It would've all been transformed. It must've been a name of fire."

Declan did not answer. The flames spread among the branches until a little fire danced merrily on the ground. Jute crouched down and held out his hands. The hawk hopped off his shoulder and unfurled his wings, shaking snowflakes from the black feathers.

"There're six names for fire," said the ghost, "that is, if you take Olar Olan's treatise on the naming of essences seriously. I can't remember if I did. But that's not important. What's important is that you, an uneducated country bumpkin, possess one of the names of fire. What has the world come to? You wouldn't care to share it with us, would you?"

"I'll get some more wood," said Declan, scowling at the ghost. "Jute, keep an eye on the fire."

He disappeared again into the darkness.

"For your information, there're more than six names for fire," said the hawk. "There are nine. I doubt the wisdom of knowing any of them. They'd be dangerous for even a man such as Declan, who seems admirably lacking in the vices that typically succumb to fire's allure."

"Nine," said the ghost, eyes wide. "Nine names!"

"He's not a country bumpkin," said Jute. "He's the Knife. He was the Knife. The executioner of the Guild." He shivered, despite the warmth of the fire. "He's killed more people than anyone knows. Bodies in alleys and backrooms and on the waterfront, with him as cold as a fisherman gutting fish."

"Hmmph," said the ghost. "That's not any sort of recommendation that impresses me."

Declan returned with another armful of wood, as well as three dead rabbits draped on top of the branches.

"A hot meal'll do us good," he said.

"Would it ever," said Jute. His stomach rumbled in anticipation as Declan spitted the rabbits. "How did you manage?"

"Old trapping secret," said Declan. A smile flickered over his face and then was gone. "I'll show you some day. I was lucky enough to stumble on a burrow. Rabbits aren't the smartest sorts. Not like wild boar. Boar tastes better than rabbit, too, but rabbit'll do for now. Quick to catch and quick to cook."

The rabbits sizzled over the flames, dripping fat and exuding a marvelous odor. Declan shoved more branches into the coals. Around them, the night settled in, and the moonlight gleamed on the snow. The hawk scratched together a pile of dried needles and then sat down on his bed with a sigh of satisfaction. The ghost, after a last attempt to persuade Declan to share his knowledge of fire, vanished in a sulk.

"That's a dangerous word you carry," said the hawk after a while.

"I use the thing sparingly, if ever," said Declan. "Farrows never did place much faith in magic. It's a chancy business and better to be left to those who don't mind risking their lives and limbs. But when you're caught in the winter, far from shelter and the only wood to be had frozen with ice, that one word can be the divide between life and death. It's the only word of power I know, master hawk, and it's the only one I care to know, so you can settle your feathers. My father taught it to me, and his taught it to him before. I've no love of wizards and their endless grasping after words. Here, the rabbits should be done."

Jute burned his fingers on the meat and then burned his tongue as well, but it tasted delicious. In addition, there was bread in their knapsacks, stale and hard, but it toasted well enough on the hot stones at the fire's edge. The hawk pecked at a morsel of roast rabbit.

"Not bad at all," said the hawk. "But raw is better."

A branch collapsed down into the coals. Sparks drifted up. Jute leaned back against his knapsack and closed his eyes. Impossibly and oddly enough, he felt happy. It didn't matter that he was out in the middle of nowhere, on a mountain range in the snow, far from any place that was familiar. What mattered was that his stomach was full and he was warm. He did not need to think beyond that. He could hear Declan and the hawk talking quietly. Snowflakes swirled past, further down in the ravine, but here he was safe. At least for a time, for one night. Jute closed his eyes and fell asleep. Thankfully, he did not dream.

CHAPTER ONE HUNDRED & TWO
FARMERS AND TRADERS

The morning dawned in silence, revealing a world of snow and a sky so drained of blue that it seemed simply a continuation of the snow's white up into the horizon. The fire had burned down into ash.

"I've heard there's an old trader road somewhere below the eastern edge of the mountains," said Declan. He frowned and shook his head as if trying to clear it of cobwebs. "I've never been to the duchy of Mizra before. Farrows never came here."

"And neither to Vo as well," said the ghost, but only Jute heard him.

They hiked down through the hills, through the thinning trees and the melting snow. It was slightly warmer down here in the foothills. However, despite the sunlight and the decrease in altitude, there was no mistaking the fact that winter had arrived in Tormay. At least the snow was not so deep, giving way to stretches of mud in places. They reached the road at midday, when the sun was high in the sky. When they crested the last of a series of lower and lower hills, they finally saw the road. It was a muddy track carved by years of hooves and boots and cart wheels that had passed that way.

"This mud is just as bad," said the ghost.

"I don't know why you get to complain," said Jute. "It's not as if you have any feet."

"Just because you can't see something," said the ghost, "doesn't mean it doesn't exist. For example, I can't see your brain, but that doesn't mean it doesn't exist. Although there's different evidence about that which makes me suspect otherwise. Poor example for my argument, I suppose."

"What?" said Jute.

"Never mind," interrupted the hawk. "What's important right now is the girl and you, too, of course, Jute. For the time being it'd be wiser if we dispense with any flying practice. It's strange, but I find that my memories about this duchy are hazy. There's no telling who or what might be living here. Anyway, we'll swoop in, find the girl—"

"My sister," said Declan.

"—and swoop out. Shouldn't be too hard."

"Swooping in and swooping out," said Jute. "Sounds like a lot of flying to me. Particularly when you've just told me I shan't be doing any flying at all, and right when I was starting to get the hang of it."

"The only thing you were getting a hang of," said the ghost, "was falling flat on your face."

"As for you, ghost," said the hawk, "you'd do well to stay out of sight, with your mouth shut, whenever we're in company. Ghosts make people nervous and they start asking questions."

"And what about you? If we're trying to avoid attention, I doubt a large, talking hawk will do much for the cause."

It was a country of broken hills and sudden, deep valleys through which the track plunged down into gloomy shadows and stands of trees huddling beside the road as if waiting for some long-anticipated guest. There were few houses in evidence and hours passed by without sighting any sign of life. Happily, though, they came to a farm as twilight fell. The farmer allowed them the shelter of the barn for the night on the agreement that they do a little work for him. This meant Declan splitting a pile of logs into kindling and Jute mucking out the pig sty.

"Here," said the farmer, dumping a bucket of corncobs into the pig trough, "Bend with your knees when you get your shovel in. Whoops, don't mind the old sow, son. Ah, well. Mud don't bother nobody."

The farmer laughed and stumped away. Jute clambered back to his feet and glared at the sow who, in her eagerness to get to the corncobs, had knocked Jute off his feet in her rush to the trough.

"Fat slob!" said Jute to the sow.

The sow twitched one ear at him but reserved her attention for the corncobs. The mud was much more than mud, which became apparent to Jute's nose. It was one thing to be standing in the stuff. To have it smeared all over your clothing was a different matter.

"Thank goodness I don't have a sense of smell anymore," said the ghost.

"Wash up, lad," called the farmer. "Dinnertime."

The farmer's wife was as small as he was big, a cheerful bird of a woman who flitted around the kitchen table, banging down pots and plates and platters piled high with more food than Jute had ever seen at one time in his life. The farmer had three daughters and one baby boy of indeterminate months who sat strapped in a high chair, observing the scene with a solemn and indulgent eye.

"Eat up," said the farmer. "Them that's shy don't get any."

The girls giggled and whispered to each other behind their hands. Jute ignored them, though his ears turned red. There was a pot of stew; a platter piled with potatoes, golden and fried, that rolled off onto the table and scattered themselves obligingly by every plate; carrots and leeks; pickled cucumbers spicy enough to send Jute into sneezing fits (which made the girls giggle even more); a bowl of butter that shone in the candlelight; and loaves of fresh bread. Declan put his head down and plowed through, hardly pausing to breathe.

"Quite a trencherman, ain't you," said the farmer.

The farmer's wife bustled up to the table with a platter.

"Fresh trout," she said. "Jesi and Juna caught them down in the oak pool this afternoon, they did."

"Did you now," said the farmer. "Fancy being so clever."

"And Juna hooked the old carp too," said one of the girls. "Pulled her right in. Shoulda heard her holler." All the girls giggled.

"Eat, eat," said the farmer's wife.

"Somethin' sweet?" said the farmer.

"Of course!" His wife looked offended.

After the girls cleared the table and whisked the baby off, the wife brought out an enormous blackberry pie.

"Now then," said the farmer, cutting himself a wedge. "Off to Ancalon, are you?"

"Aye," said Declan. "The boy and I, we got some cousins there. Family business."

"Quite a trip to come across the mountains this time of year. Not many folks attempt that, even for family, I reckon. It only gets worse as the days pass. Soon enough, winter'll close the gap toward Hearne. No getting in or out of the duchy until the spring thaw."

"Every winter?" said Declan.

"Without fail. Gets mighty cold this side of the Morns. Mind you, Ancalon's always cold."

"What do you mean by that? Surely you have summer here."

The farmer shrugged his shoulders and paused on a mouthful of pie. "I ain't one for talking poorly of folks, especially my own duchy, but Ancalon ain't the friendliest of towns. People there're a bit stiff, snobbish. None too fond of strangers. Gotten worse over the years. I suppose that's why most country folk never go to Ancalon. Send in our goods with one of the traders for barter. Salt, iron, a bolt or two of cloth for the missus. Fact is, old Birt should be stopping by in the morning on his way south. Pick up a load of beef an' corn."

"Must be trustworthy traders you have here. I wouldn't want another man handling my gold."

The farmer grinned. "A slippery trader gets known soon enough in these parts. The truth'll out. Have some more pie. You too, laddie."

It was still dark that next morning when old Birt came rolling up to the farm, his wagon creaking across the field.

"Wake up. Wake up," called the farmer, stumping into the barn. A lantern swung from one hand. "Can't sleep away the day. Yawn wide enough, laddie, and the mice'll be using your mouth to piddle in. Lend a hand here, now."

Jute shut his mouth with a snap and brushed the straw from his hair. Icicles hung from the eaves, and the air smelled of woodsmoke. Declan was wrestling barrels and sacks up onto the trader's wagon. Four mules stood in their traces, glaring around at everything in general and nothing in particular. A silent rush of wings fluttered over the peak of the barn and disappeared into the morning gloom. The hawk. No one noticed except for Jute. Besides the barrels of salted beef, there were sacks of corn stitched up in burlap, as well as stone jars of honeycomb packed in crates stuffed full of wool to cushion the journey.

"Be sure an' get a dear price for that honey, Birt, you hear me?" said the farmer's wife. "Raised them bees myself. Clover and honeysuckle. Sweeter'n anything them cityfolk've tasted. A good price, you hear me?"

"I hear you, I hear you. I heard you now, didn't I?"

The old trader was a withered stick of a man, bundled up in a coat large enough to double as his tent. Despite his age, he bustled about with greater energy than both Declan and Jute, heaving sacks and barrels up into his wagon and periodically hopping up to rearrange the goods stowed there.

Birt agreed to give them a ride south in exchange for their company. "The company of your sword," he said, cackling a bit. "Times ain't what they used to be these days."

"And the boy?" said Declan.

"Don't look like he weighs much. Mules won't mind. 'Sides, he can scarper after wood for the fire an' make himself useful, no doubt, or we can beat him."

"Why, no one's—" said Jute, outraged.

Hush.

The hawk's voice floated through his mind.

The old man is fond of talking. Perhaps we can learn something from him of Ancalon and what goes on there. Traders hear much. Do not allow him to remember you more than he should.

The farmer's wife hurried back out with a bulging sack for them.

"A bite for the road," she said. "Eat the pie first, else it go bad. Watch that Birt, though. He's a greedy lout."

The old trader laughed and swung up behind his mules.

"Giddup there."

A line of sunrise bloomed into light in the east, but the morning was still dark around them as the wagon pulled out of the farmyard. The mules grumbled to themselves.

"Anytime you're by this way, lads, you're welcome," called the farmer. "Plenty of work here."

Jute waved back at him. He sighed. It would be nice to stay in one place for a while. With a family. Not that he had to be part of the family. That wouldn't be necessary. Just to live in the barn, perhaps. He could learn how to farm. He could learn anything. Despite three giggling girls.

And what if the wihht comes sniffing along your trail? How long would that last? He would slay the lot of them. And you would live with the memory of their deaths. Jute could hear the hawk's wings rustle inside his mind. The bird sounded sad. *Some things must be left behind.*

The wagon was stuffed full of goods. Barrels smelling deliciously of salted beef, fish, and other things Jute could not put a name to. Sacks and boxes and chests tied down this way and that with a perfectly crazed weaving of ropes. Stone jugs wedged into whatever nooks Birt considered safe enough for their travel. Crates of beets and carrots and potatoes, muddy onions and withered apples. It was a wonder that four mules were enough to pull such a load.

"Don't sit on the cheeses, son," said old Birt. "Now, what about that pie?"

The miles rolled away through the day. The sun rose and disappeared into a gray sky that spat down a sleeting rain. Jute wormed himself down into a gap between a sack of wheat and a crate of apples. He pillowed his head on his knapsack, pulled his cloak around him, and stared up at the sky. From time to time, he saw the hawk float by overhead. The ghost mumbled to itself inside the knapsack. At the back of the wagon, the top of Declan's head was visible beyond a barrel.

It was a lonely land that they traveled through. The road, which was more of a stony, rutted track than a proper road, never went straight but veered and climbed and dropped with fatiguing regularity. The wagon rolled down through canyons choked with pine forests that plunged them into even darker gloom than the day itself. Ice sheathed the tree trunks, and the wind moaned among the branches. The road climbed back up through hills until the travelers found themselves on a high moor. The ground was pocked with pools scummed over with ice and the broken remains of reeds that rattled like old bones as the wind passed by. There were almost words in the rattle of the reeds, if listened to close enough—a rattle and a whisper and a rustling broken by cracks and snaps as the reeds bent under the wind's breath. The words came in a tumbling confusion of thoughts, a hundred different voices: all similar, but still different enough to discern each reed. There was a whistling quality to their voices, as if the wind blew across the open hollows of their broken joints like a hundred little flutes.

Vole's been gnawing and sawing at my roots again.

Oh, my poor, aching back.

Blood's gone to ice and then it snaps—crack!

Curse this wind.

The vole...

Curse this wind and the vole.

Hush, hush! No cause to complain.

Mud and muck and stone. Clack and snap and groan.

Perhaps it'll rain?

Rain? Never, you fool. Just more snow. . .

Old Birt kept up a tuneless whistle that whipped away into the wind. The mules clopped along, heads down and ears flicking back every once in a while to hear the encouragement of their master. Jute must have fallen asleep, for he woke with a sour taste in his mouth and an ache in his neck. The day had grown considerably colder, and he rubbed at his nose. It felt like ice. His stomach growled and he groped for the bag of food from the farmer's wife.

"Here," said Declan, handing it to him. "There's even a wedge of pie left."

"Pie?" said old Birt, looking back over his shoulder. "Did someone say pie?"

After some argument, Jute surrendered the last piece of pie and contented himself with investigating the rest of the bag. The sack was stuffed with all sorts of victuals, for the farmer's wife was used to people who ate in large quantities and, doubtless, she could not imagine any other way to think about food.

"That's fish, hey?" said the ghost, poking its head out of the crate of apples.

"Yes, shh."

"You don't have to be snippy," said the ghost. "I was only curious. Smoked fish, no doubt. I can't remember the last time I ate fish. Hundreds of years ago. That's a long time to go without fish. And does anyone care? No."

"What's that?" said old Birt. The ghost vanished back into the crate of apples.

"Nothing," said Jute. "I was just eating this fish."

"Hand some up, laddie. Hand some up."

"Do you trade in Ancalon a lot?" asked Declan.

"Aye, fair amount."

"I suppose it's like other big towns. Hearne, Lura, Damarkan even."

"Can't say I've been to Lura or that there Damarkan. Too many foreigners for my taste. But I've been to Hearne. Fine city, fine city. Why, there were a lady singing in a tavern there. Sang and danced and clanged little bells on her fingers. Wiggled her hips faster'n a woodpecker tapping for grubs. Done it all at the same time." Birt shook his head in admiration. "It were a wonderful sight. Fine city."

"Not much different than Ancalon?"

"I wouldn't say that," said Birt slowly. He shifted back and forth on his seat as if trying to find a more comfortable spot. "Ancalon's a quiet city. Peaceful, I suppose. Always a good price for food, aye. It's a wonder how much they buy." And he refused to say more on the subject.

The evening brought them to the edge of a valley. The moon shone fitfully through the clouds and the sleet was thickening to snow. Some lights gleamed down in the valley, cheerily enough, but they also served to heighten the darkness around them.

"Pigtown!" called out Birt with some satisfaction.

"Pigtown?" said Jute.

"Aye, laddie. Ain't much of a place, but they got plenty of pigs. We'll stop there for the night."

The presence of pigs asserted itself long before the wagon reached the town. The air thickened with their scent. Jute pulled his cloak around his nose. Old Birt produced a pipe and proceeded to puff out clouds of smelly black smoke that would have stank horribly in any other situation but now seemed almost refreshing. The road descended into a pinewood, silent with snow and night. The mules quickened their pace, anticipating food and rest. Pigtown really wasn't a town at all. Half a dozen ramshackle houses huddled together at the edge of the pinewood. Light shone from windows. Beyond them, further out on a fenced and snow-covered field and barely visible in the darkness, stood several barns, sturdy and in good repair.

"Plenty of pigs," said Birt. "Whoa, now." He hopped down and began to unharness the mules.

A door creaked open somewhere beyond them, and a man stumped out of the dark, lantern in hand. He was tall and had a long beard that gathered snowflakes.

"Eh, Birt," said the man. "Expected you yesterday."

"Nice to see you too, Doyl," said Birt. "Road ain't so good up north."

Doyl nodded and turned away. Birt followed him, leading the mules. Snowflakes swirled down. Jute looked longingly at the cheerily lit windows of the houses nearby. Smoke curled up from their chimneys. He shivered.

"Are we just supposed to sit here?" said Jute.

"Patience," said Declan. He got down from the wagon and began to walk around, swinging his arms back and forth and stamping his feet on the ground. "Always see to your beasts first."

Birt reappeared soon enough.

"All right, then," he said. "Time for some shut-eye."

"Out here?" said Jute in disbelief. "We'll freeze to death!"

"Freeze? This ain't cold, laddie. Bracing, I call it. You wait until winter's here. Now that's a proper cold." The old man cackled out loud. "Poke your nose outside and—snap—ice. Off it comes."

He produced some wool blankets from beneath the wagon seat and, taking one for himself, crawled beneath the wagon, rolled himself up in his blanket and promptly began to snore. Declan shrugged, grinned, and then did the same.

"But what about sleeping inside?" said Jute.

The light in the windows of the nearest house went out at that moment. As if on some silent cue, any other lights that were visible also went out, winking out one by one as if eyes closing to sleep. The snow fell thicker and faster.

I do not think these folks friendly except to their pigs. Get some sleep. You shan't freeze.

"Oh, all right," said Jute. "If I wake up frozen dead, it'll be your fault."

The hawk chuckled inside his mind and then fell silent.

Jute grabbed the last blanket and scrambled underneath the wagon. He wrapped himself up, tucked his knapsack beneath his head, and promptly fell asleep. Sometime in the middle of the night, he awoke with a start, shivering not from the cold but thinking of wihhts and shadows and the wind blowing in silence through some faraway place. The snow lay so deeply now that it had piled up past the sides of the wagon. They were entombed. The air beneath the wagon, trapped as such, was somewhat warm and pleasant. Jute stretched out his hand and touched the bank of snow and then fell back asleep.

They left early in the morning, before the sun rose. Moonlight shone through the pine trees, and everywhere, despite the dark sky, there was a sort of shabby radiance reflecting from the snow and ice. The villagers had their own wagon packed and ready to go, piled with barrels of salt pork, smoked hams, sausage, and brined trotters. A tall, gloomy man who looked like Doyl, but younger and without a beard, sat knock-kneed on the buckboard, dangling a whip over his team of oxen.

"Ox ain't so good as mule in this weather," said Birt. "Y'should consider mule. I recommend 'em highly. Eat on anything, anytime, anywhere. Eat on your salt pork, if'n you let 'em."

"Ox'll do," said Doyl. "Doyl's cartin' corn for 'em. Get a good price on that pork, y'hear me?"

"I hear you, Pa. I hear you."

"Doyl?" said Jute.

"Named all his sons Doyl," said Birt. "All six of 'em."

"Saves time, boy," said Doyl. "Time's money."

The snow had stopped falling sometime during the night, leaving the countryside deep and white with its passing. Gray clouds scudded across the sky. The wind whipped through the trees, blowing snow off branches and along the top of the drifts below.

"Cheer up, laddie," called old Birt over his shoulder. "We'll make Hager's Crossing tonight. Hot ale and a bit of shut-eye, and then Ancalon tomorrow. If y'freeze solid, we'll sell you fer statuary." He snorted and cackled. Declan laughed as well.

"Very funny," said Jute, but he cheered up at the thought of hot ale.

"I must concur," said the ghost from inside Jute's knapsack. "He's somewhat humorous. Though, if you do get sold for statuary, I've no desire to moon about a garden, or wherever they install you, for the rest of my life."

"The rest of your death, you mean."

"You, my young friend, are not humorous."

They made good time despite the deep snow covering the road. The mules trotted along, heads down and grumbling but oblivious to the drifts they trudged through. At noon, after much berating from Birt, Doyl reluctantly agreed to take the lead with his team of oxen.

"After all," said Birt, "your pa says they're as good as mule, don't he?"

"Sure enough," said Doyl gloomily.

The hawk sailed through the sky, almost invisible against the dark clouds. Jute could always pick him out. His eyes instantly found him, wherever he was. Jute reached out with his mind.

Isn't it much colder up there?

The hawk sniffed. *At my age, one is not bothered by such trifles.*

I'd like to try flying again.

You shall do no such thing. Not here, not now.

Of course not, said Jute hastily. *Not with these old carters gawking. Maybe in the evening? If we get to wherever we're going and it's not too late? I'd like to fly. I'm sure I've almost got the hang of it.*

No, said the hawk. *Most assuredly not. You should not be alarmed, but I think something hunts along our path. It isn't close, so do not look so frightened. Rather, consider it solemnly, for caution should guide your actions. As I have told you before, the use of power draws attention like a lantern in a dark night. You would burn like a great light if you truly flew. Like a star. We could not weather such attention. There is something odd about this land we travel through that does not comfort me greatly.*

All right, all right.

CHAPTER ONE HUNDRED & THREE
ESCAPE ACROSS THE ICE

The road wound through the afternoon. The sun emerged from behind the clouds for brief intervals of blinding light that glittered off the snow and transformed the world into a blur of brilliance. However, most of the day was as dark and as cold as a winter evening. Despite the weather, old Birt was in a good mood, chuckling to himself through the smoke streaming from his pipe. Jute suspected his cheerfulness was due to the fact that Doyl's team of oxen was proving considerably slower than the mules in breaking through the fresh snow on the road.

"Will we get to wherever it is we're going before nightfall?" asked Jute.

"Hager's Crossing? Surely, laddie, surely, despite these clubfooted, sway-backed cows leading the way. Afore sundown, or my name's not Birt. The Hartshorn keeps a good table and you'll be soon tipping back an ale there, never fear."

The sun broke through the clouds as it began to drop beyond the edges of the mountains in the east. It was as if a cold red eye surveyed them between the two lids of clouds and mountain range. One last slow blink closed in finality on the day and then Birt called out.

"Hager's!"

He followed up his exclamation with a great deal of muttering about cows and those who see fit to cart about behind cows, all of it uncomplimentary, but only Jute heard him.

The road bumped down an icy incline toward a village. Hager's Crossing was a proper village, in Jute's estimation. It looked large enough to be interesting in terms of things to buy (or steal) and see and do. There were a great many buildings, all dipped in shadow on their eastern side and painted red on the opposite, with their roofs and chimneys and western walls gilded with the remaining rays of frozen sunlight. Past the town, a river curved through the snowy fields. Woodsmoke scented the air, and after such a cold day, that was a comforting smell indeed. The Hartshorn Inn was on the banks of the river, but to get to it, they had to wind their way through the town, down streets deep in muddy slush and between houses huddled against the descending night. The wagons rolled to a stop in the inn's yard. The mules and oxen blew out great breaths of steam, satisfied and already smelling the hay in the barn.

"A warm bed for the night," said Jute.

"Eh, what's that?" said old Birt. "No inn beds for us, laddie. It'll be the wagons and sleeping with both eyes open. Don't trust a soul, that's my motto. But you can pop in for a bite to eat first. Go on with you. Doyl an' me'll see to the beasts."

The inn was crowded with people and warmed by the fire crackling on the hearth. It seemed quieter than most other inns Jute had been in, but it smelled of ale and roasting meat and, for one moment, Jute imagined he was back in Hearne. Surely if he stepped outside, he would find himself on those familiar cobblestone streets. Lena and the other children would dash by with an outraged merchant in pursuit. Perhaps he had just stepped into the Goose and Gold. But then he blinked and he was standing where he was, far from Hearne and far from home.

Hearne was never your home, said the hawk inside his mind. The bird's voice was surprisingly gentle. *Don't fret, fledgling. You'll find it one day.*

"Move it," said Declan quietly. "We're attracting enough attention as it is."

And they were. People turned to watch them thread their way through the room as they tried to find an empty table. The stares were not unfriendly, but neither were they friendly. Declan and Jute sat down at the end of a long table occupied by a group of men leaning over their tankards, talking in low voices and occasionally calling for more ale. Jute squeezed into a chair. There was barely enough room between the edge of the table and wall. Behind him, a window exuded the night's chill.

Ah. A barn. The hawk's voice ghosted through Jute's mind. *I think I'll find myself a roost in the barn.* After a moment, the boy heard him snort in disapproval. *I shan't be sleeping now. Owls. Empty-headed feather dusters!*

"Evenin' to you. Supper?"

A fat old woman in a dirty apron plonked down two tankards of hot ale in front of them. Declan took a swallow of ale and nodded appreciatively.

"Aye, and what do you—?" But before he could finish his sentence, the old woman had bustled away. She returned soon enough with a platter.

"That'll be two silver bits for the pair of you."

"Two silver—?" said Jute, but he shut his mouth when Declan kicked him under the table.

"Here you are, mistress." Declan handed over the coins.

"Two silver bits?" said Jute, once the old woman had gone. "That's thievery. I could eat for a week in Hearne on less than one silver."

"I'm not about to squabble with an old woman about money. Strangers seem to attract attention around here, so keep your head down and eat." And with that, Declan took his own advice and turned his attention to the platter.

The dinner would have proved unsatisfactory to Jute in most other circumstances, but he was hungry enough to finish two bowls of onion soup (which made him hiccup so much that Declan again kicked him under the table) and several slices of gristly beef.

Jute wiped his nose on his sleeve and took a furtive look around the room. As far as he could tell, no one was paying them any attention. The mood in the inn, however, struck him as odd. It was not like the boisterous inns of Hearne he was accustomed to— the Goose and Gold, or the Queen's Head where one of the potboys had a fancy for Lena and snuck them pasties and apple turnovers and other wonderful things. This inn was too quiet. Too subdued. The back of his neck prickled uncomfortably.

"Something's not right," said Jute.

"What's that?" said Declan quietly.

Jute! Stay out of sight! Declan too! The hawk's voice quivered in his mind.

What is it? asked Jute, sinking down in his chair. Declan stared at him.

We're working on it, said the hawk grimly, and then his voice went silent before Jute could ask him any more questions, such as: who was the "we" he referred to, what were they working on, and why?

The door of the inn flew open. Jute glimpsed three men standing in the door, cloaked and hooded, their shoulders dusted with snow. Something unpleasant slid along the edge of his thoughts, a questing, inquisitive touch of cold. The room went silent. Which was immediately broken by shrieks coming from somewhere. The kitchen. The strange presence at the edge of his mind abruptly disappeared. Everyone jumped to their feet. The three men at the door hurried across the room. Armor gleamed beneath their cloaks.

The shrieks sounded again, louder, more frantic. The old woman burst from the kitchen door, followed by several scullery girls.

"Help! Murder!" yowled the old woman. "Blood an' doom! Doom!" The scullery girls shrieked. "Doom!"

The three men vanished into the kitchen.

"Now's our chance," muttered Declan.

He wasn't the only one thinking this. Several others were edging their way toward the door. The room rang with the clamor of voices and excited talk. A knot of patrons surrounded the old woman, who was still howling at the top of her lungs. One of the scullery girls fainted and fell to the floor with a thud. Jute and Declan sidled to the door.

Right as Jute stepped across the threshold, he glanced back into the room. He should not have. He knew he should not have, but he could not help himself. The fire blazed up on the hearth, roaring in an instant from sullen coals to crackling flame. Firelight flickered into every corner of the room, illuminating the edges of faces and tankards. Shadows deepened behind tables and chairs. The old woman was now waving her arms about to accompany whatever tale she was telling, and the knot of men clustered about her grew. But at the kitchen door, a face shone palely, turning just as Jute did. One of the three men in cloak and armor. His eyes locked onto Jute. Something sparked in them. Recognition.

"That's torn it," said Jute, and he darted out the door and into the night. Snowflakes whipped down from a moonless, starless sky. The wind whistled across the roofs, blowing up swirls of snow and stinging ice. Horses stamped impatiently in the street. Declan grabbed Jute's arm and pulled him into the shadows along the wall.

"Soldiers," he said. "But we need to get past them to the barn. My sword. Our packs."

"One of 'em saw me inside. I think he was looking for us. We need to go!"

Declan sighed. "Right. After me, then."

Past the inn, the street ended at the river in a hodgepodge of rickety sheds and a dock that leaned out from the bank on pilings standing frozen in the ice. They ran between the sheds, the snow crunching underfoot. A voice called out from somewhere behind them. It was a curiously flat sound, dispassionate, disinterested, yet intent.

"They'll follow our footprints in the snow," said Jute. He looked down in dismay at the prints he was making.

"Exactly. Quick. Out onto the ice!"

They ran down the bank, slipping and sliding down the slope until Jute could no longer keep his footing and tumbled end over end to land in a heap on the ice.

"Aha," said Declan in satisfaction. "Give me a hand here."

"What?"

"Here!"

Drawn up on the bank and sheltered beneath the dock was a rowboat turned upside down.

"I don't understand," said Jute, but Declan interrupted him.

"No time now. I'll explain later."

They wrestled the rowboat over and slid it out onto the ice. There were two oars tied up on hooks beneath the gunwales. They pushed and pulled until the boat was a good ways across the river, skidding it across the ice perhaps a hundred yards. The wind whipped along the surface of the ice and drove the snow before it in flurries of stinging flakes. Jute felt his hands going numb.

"Get in."

"What?" said Jute.

A shout rang out from the riverbank behind them.

"Get in the boat."

Jute scrambled in and peered over the boat railing at the dark figures of the soldiers slipping and sliding down the bank. Several of the soldiers skidded and fell as soon as they reached the ice, but there was little consolation in that, as the men were now much closer.

"Declan? Is there something I'm missing here?"

"Wait. Just wait." Declan stepped into the boat and the entire craft settled over on one side, teetering on its keel. "Untie that oar there."

"They don't look friendly."

"No, they don't. I think they're planning on taking us prisoner or perhaps killing us. Your teeth are chattering."

"What if they are? It's freezing out here!"

The hawk swooped down out of the swirling snow to land on the boat's gunwale. "What are you doing?" he said. "Are you both idiots? Sculling along the ice? There's death and dark magic getting closer by the second, not to mention quite a few swords. A thing not quite a man is in that company. Run, you fools!"

"Patience, master hawk," said Declan, looking at the soldiers drawing near. There were a good dozen of them, cloaked against the cold but in armor that jingled and rang as they ran. Jute could hear the sound of it in the clash of their mailed boots on the ice and in the rasp of gauntleted fist as swords sang free from their sheaths.

"Patience?" said the hawk, but then Declan spoke, whispering the same word over and over, his voice louder and louder and faster and faster until the night and the frozen river and the blowing snow seemed to ring with the sound of it. It was a hard word, an edged sound, a brisk, sharp thing that hurt the ears just to hear it. Jute snatched his hands away from the gunwale, for the wood railing had grown hot. The air was strangely warm.

"Stop!" said the hawk, but it was too late. The word was out.

The ice around them shattered. Lines zigzagged away in every direction, slabs of ice collapsing into water to reveal the dark depths below. The boat settled into the water. The soldiers had almost reached them by then and, after the first horrifying moment, Jute shut his eyes, for he could not bear to watch. The strange thing about it was that he expected yells and screams as the men went through the ice, but the men were oddly silent as they fought to hang onto something, anything—chunks of ice floating by, scrabbling and clawing at each other as if a body encased in heavy armor would prove to float—but they all plunged down into the sudden water. Jute looked up to see the last man balancing on an ice floe bobbing in the current. It was the same man who had seen him in the inn. Even through the darkness, Jute could see the man's eyes as if they gleamed with a faint light. His face was expressionless. And then the ice floe collapsed and the man vanished into the water.

"Paddle!" said Declan. "Not like that! Put your back into it and dig down!"

"Do you realize what you've done?" said the hawk, his voice vibrating with anger. "This word you spoke, your campfire word. It's a dangerous word from a long dead tongue. Speaking it is like lighting a fire in the darkness, a blazing light that draws eyes from near and far. But the way you used it this time, this was not a whisper. No! This was more like a shout! Didn't I warn you before? The evil might outweigh the good here!"

"It was the only thing I could think of at the time," said Declan. "Better than having our throats cut, wasn't it?"

The river was free of ice now, and it bore them along on its swollen tide. Rain lashed down instead of snow, but the air was growing cold again. They made for the bank just past the town. Willows stood along the water's edge, with branches stripped of leaves and dangling their slimy black fingers down into the water. It was a nasty business to pull the boat up out of the water, for the bank was deep in slush that quickly churned into mud.

"I'm going back to get our things," said Declan. He frowned, wiping mud off on his pants. "I suppose you'd better come along rather than wait here, if only to keep moving and stay warm."

"I'd like to find some new clothes," said Jute, for he had fared much worse than Declan in hauling the boat out. His pants and coat were a stinking mess of black mud.

"Find?"

"Uh, steal."

Snow began falling again as they crept through the town. The streets were silent and the windows were dark on the outskirts, but there was the sound of voices calling to and fro further within the town. Jute stopped outside a promising looking house, larger than its neighbors, standing tall and sturdy in its stone walls and with two stories capped in thatch and snow.

"I'll try this one," said Jute.

"Be quick about it," said Declan. "I'll meet you back at the boat."

"Both of you be quick about it," said the hawk crossly, "for there's no telling who hurries along our trail due to your foolishness."

All three parted at that point, all in bad humor, and all in silence: Declan loping down the street back toward the inn, Jute skulking along the side of the house to investigate windows and doors, and the hawk flapping up to perch on top of the roof.

Jute was in luck, for he found an unlocked window at the back of the house. He had to scrape the sill clear of snow first. The window swung open with a screech loud enough to wake the entire neighborhood. Jute stood there with his nerves jumping and his ears straining to hear any stir of sleepy and outraged life. But there was nothing, not even a barking dog. He clambered over the sill and dropped down into the silence of the house. His fingers twitched in unconscious and happy anticipation. It had been a long time since he had stolen anything and he was looking forward to a good browse.

You should know better, scolded the hawk inside his mind.

What?

Take only what you must, and leave a coin or two in place.

Jute found himself standing in the kitchen. Coals glinted red among the ashes on the hearth, and he warmed his hands for a moment. It would have been nice to stay there a while, but he moved away reluctantly. There was work to be done. He explored the ground floor of the house but did not find any clothing, as it consisted only of the kitchen (as it was a large room and was probably used for everything from cooking, eating, sitting about the fire, and whatever everyday activities the family pursued) and a storage room crammed full of sacked foodstuffs (which proved to be mostly potatoes and turnips, upon closer investigation).

Hurry up, said the hawk.

I am.

Jute tiptoed up the staircase. A chest in the largest of three bedrooms contained what he wanted. The clothes were too large and the boots standing at the foot of the bed would need a few scraps of cloth stuffed into their toes in order to make them fit properly, but they would do just fine. A man snored in the bed beside his wife, and Jute cast them an envious glance. A quilt, a bed, and a roof to keep the night out. He shrugged his shoulders. Ah well. It was not to be for now. He rummaged some more through the chest and found a thick coat, worn and ragged in the cuffs, but much nicer than what he had now.

Footsteps shuffled in the doorway and Jute froze. Out of the corner of his eye he saw a small child in a nightgown trudge to the bed. He heard the sleepy mumble of the child and the soft-voiced response of the mother, and then the child climbed up into the bed. Covers were rearranged and the room was silent again except for the unbroken snore of the man. Jute tiptoed away, the clothing and boots clutched in his hands. He left his old clothes piled up by the hearth, with several copper coins on top. Then, with the pockets of his new coat stuffed full of potatoes, he let himself back out into the night.

Declan was waiting for him at the boat, along with the ghost.

"Thought we'd seen the last of him," said Declan, "but I found him skulking about our packs. Guarding them, he says. And it seems we have him to thank for causing that ruckus in the inn. It was him that did it."

"A brilliant strategy," said the ghost modestly. "Genius, if I may say so. Why, only a mind as keen as my own, adept in military tactics and—"

"I seem to recollect," said the hawk, "that it was my idea."

"The execution was nothing short of inspired. I hid in the pot of stew, lurking beneath the lid until just the right moment, right when the old biddy lifted it off to stir. I then burst out, wailing and gnashing my teeth and chanting 'Doom, doom, doom!' I've never thought myself an actor, being more the intelligent type and far too handsome, don't you know, to put on a convincing performance as a horrible-looking creature, but I did it. I was superb."

"Yes," said the hawk. "Now, let's get moving."

"How she screamed," said the ghost happily. "The ladle went one way, stew flying the other way, one of the scullery girls was scalded. Marvelous."

"Marvelous. Just marvelous," said the hawk.

"I saved your lives, didn't I?"

"I guess you did," said Jute, smiling. "Thank you."

"Get moving," grumbled the hawk.

Ice was forming again on the river, but only in patches, for not enough time had passed yet to sheath the entire stretch. They paddled the boat across, fending off ice floes and trying not to become too irritated with the ghost. The moon had come out, and it was no longer snowing as hard as it had been before.

"There'll be light enough to walk by," said Jute.

"And light enough for us to be tracked by," said Declan. "Go up to the front—"

"It's called the prow, you ignorant landlubber," said the ghost.

"—and bash away at the ice with your paddle. It's starting to form up too fast for us to get through."

"Do you think they'll track us?" said Jute. "Who are they?"

"There were more soldiers back at the inn when I got there. A larger troop on horses, lathered and winded as if they had ridden hard and just arrived." Declan dug in hard with his paddle to propel them the last few feet to the riverbank. Ice grated against the side of the boat. "I suppose they're soldiers of the duke. Can't imagine anyone else in a duchy able to afford that kind of a following."

"But surely they aren't after us," said Jute. "They wouldn't know who we are, and why would they be interested in us?"

"I wouldn't be so sure," said the hawk.

"Don't fret," said the ghost. "Leave these soldiers to me. I'll take care of them. I have a new routine all thought out. It'll be a grand performance. I draw my inspiration from our recent encounter with the ogre and shall call it: Bulging Eyes Ravenous for Flesh and Meaningful Conversation. No, no—you needn't thank me now. The screams of the soldiers as they flee in terror will be thanks enough."

"I'm sure we'll be grateful," said Declan.

The boat ground to a halt in the shallows against the bank. The river had carried them away from the town, which was only visible in a few small lights far off in the night. They dragged the boat up on shore and hid it in some bushes.

"An hour more and the snow will have covered it up," said Declan. "Now, let's be on our way."

They hitched up their packs and set off. It was well past midnight now. The snow was slicked over with ice in spots and Jute slipped and slithered along behind Declan. The older man seemed to have a knack for where to step and never once slipped.

"How far are we going tonight?" panted Jute. "I don't suppose there's another town nearby?"

"No. If our luck doesn't worsen, we'll make Ancalon by midday tomorrow. I had a quick word with old Birt when I slipped back for our packs. Claims it was Doyl who tipped off the soldiers to what we looked like when they came marching up to the inn. Says any of the Doyls would sell their grandma in a wink for gold. Anyway, Birt says we should reach the city early tomorrow if we make good time."

"If you don't freeze to death first," said the ghost.

And it was exceedingly cold. The snow had stopped falling, but this was no consolation, as the wind blew all the more harder, chasing the snow about the ground in clouds and sudden flurries that got into their collars and down their necks.

Sorry, but I must be about my business, the wind seemed to whisper to Jute. *It's what I do. I howl and rush and blow and bother and worry away at everything that is. You'll learn. You'll learn.*

"At least our tracks'll be covered over by this wretched wind," said Declan.

"There are other ways to follow a path than mere footprints," said the hawk. "I remember, long ago, in a different land, my old master and I tracked a sceadu across mountains and valleys without benefit of footprints or such sign as you would find in broken branches and bruised leaves, for a sceadu can travel without touching the ground, so light is their step. But we kept on the creature's trail by following the glance of the moon and by hunting where the deepest shadows lay."

"You don't say," said the ghost, all agog at hearing this. "How does one determine the moon's glance? I'm sure I knew once, but I must've forgotten."

"Sounds like a better way of tracking than looking for prints," returned Declan, "but I can't interpret the moon, let alone fathom that she takes such an interest in men that she'd glance down on our lives."

"But what happened then?" said Jute. "Did you find the sceadu?"

The hawk might have said more, but he did not, for at that moment there came a long, drawn-out howl from somewhere far behind them. It came from far away, but the sound was clear in the cold night sky.

"A dog," said the ghost. "A bloodhound. No doubt already on our trail. It was a valiant effort, but now we're all going to die. And just when I was becoming rather fond of all of you."

"That's not a dog," said the hawk.

"I've heard that sound before." Jute tried to swallow but his mouth had gone dry. "Back in Hearne. She called them shadowhounds. I didn't see them, but I remember the sound of their howl."

"Shadowhound, aye," muttered the hawk.

"Hounds, shadowhounds, whatever you call them, I don't care," said Declan. "Any beast can be killed."

"Not these. Your sword wouldn't suffice. Hiding your trail within a city is the best option. Other than that, the only way to defeat such a beast is with magic, and none of us are skilled in such arts."

"They don't fly, do they?" said Jute, thinking back to that dreadful and wonderful night in Hearne. It seemed long ago now. "You can fly. I can fly!"

"Thank you very much," said Declan. "That would leave me to sort things out by myself."

"I wouldn't leave your side," said the ghost. "Yours will be a brave death, no doubt, and I shall be honored to witness it."

"Never fear." The hawk bobbed his head. "Flying might be an option if the boy didn't always fall flat on his face the moment his feet leave the ground. He wouldn't get far that way. No. We must think of another way to lose the beast."

But they could not think of a way, no matter how much they discussed the problem as they hurried along. They did not hear the howl again, but no one doubted for a moment what followed on their path. They came to the edge of a valley that yawned open before them. The moonlight shone on cliffs sheathed in ice, frozen in folds and draperies and waterfalls halted by winter's hand in their downward plunge but still falling away to the depths below.

"That's not a descent I'd like to make," said Declan. "Even in daylight with ropes and axe. We'll have to skirt it west until we find a better spot, or even further to where the trader's road must surely find its way through." He shook his head. "If we had wings, master hawk, this would be no problem."

"If we threw Jute over the side," said the hawk, "he'd learn to fly fast enough, but I can't vouch for you. Men aren't made to fly and there's only trouble if they try."

"No one's throwing me over the side," said Jute.

They hiked along the top of the cliffs in growing dismay, for there seemed no end to them. The ground was treacherous with ice, and they kept a distance from the edge of the cliffs for fear of slipping and plunging over. Pine trees grew there in ever-increasing frequency until they found themselves walking through a forest. The trees were heavy with snow and the drifts were deep. The moon shone down in shreds and tatters, wherever it could find a way through the tree branches.

"Snow down my neck, in my boots, in my socks," said Jute. "Winter was never so cold in Hearne. Why would anyone want to live in this duchy? I suppose I wouldn't mind being a farmer. He had a nice family, didn't he? Too many girls, though."

"Shh." Declan stopped and turned, his face intent. He tilted his head this way and that, eyes shut, as if he might by such slight positioning hear more of what the wind had to say.

"Something's coming," said the hawk.

Before they could do anything, whether that would have been climbing the nearest tree or drawing a weapon, a quiet scuffling sound came from the bushes nearby.

"It's just a couple of rabbits," said Jute, his voice shaky with relief.

There were two of them. Two small rabbits with fur so white they were almost invisible against the snow. Their ears were the only part of them that moved, twitching back and forth, for the rabbits sat motionless in the snow and stared at the travelers. They had red eyes.

"Is it just me," said the ghost, "or has anyone else noticed these things are only looking at Jute?"

There was an uncomfortable silence after this, during which everyone considered what the ghost had said. He was right. The rabbits were staring at Jute.

"Rabbits are harmless, aren't they?" said Jute. "You don't think they know we've eaten a lot of their relatives, do they?"

"Speak for yourself," said the ghost. "I'm sure I never ate a rabbit in my life."

One of the rabbits yawned, revealing an unusually large mouth filled with unusually sharp-looking teeth. It shut its mouth with a snap.

"I think," said Declan quietly, "that we had better—"

It was then that it happened. The rabbits grew and stretched and elongated until what stood before them were no longer rabbits but two enormous dogs. Shadowhounds.

"Jute! Run!"

Jute was already running. Declan's sword sang through the air, and the hawk flung himself forward, slashing with beak and claw. The hounds lunged forward to meet them. Jute ran through the snow, stumbling to keep on his feet as he staggered through the drifts. He could not see where he was going. It was too dark. Branches whipped against his face and he tripped, falling to both knees. Somewhere behind him, something large and heavy crashed through the bushes. Jute staggered back to his feet. And realized he stood on the edge of the cliffs. Darkness and the sense of a great emptiness falling away lay before him. He turned around. Something ran out from among the trees and stopped in the moonlight. A shadowhound!

No.

Something worse. A huge beast with glaring silver eyes and jaws big enough to swallow him whole. Its fur was so black it was darker than the night around it, a terrible blot of shadow against the snow. Further back among the trees there came a sound of growling and then a sharper, more triumphant howl. The beast before Jute leapt forward.

Perhaps it will be quick, thought Jute. He raised his hands, hopeless and helpless. *Perhaps I won't feel a thing.*

And then, right when he felt the beast's hot breath and could smell the rank odor of the thing, he thought, absurdly pleased: *at least if I'm dead I won't be cold anymore.* But the beast did not kill him. Instead, it slammed into him with one heavy shoulder, knocking the wind from his lungs and off his feet. Jute's arms windmilled through the air, desperate to grab onto something, for he knew what was behind him. His fingers closed on nothing, and then he was falling. The cold and the wind whipped by him. He tumbled down, end over end. One second the moon was overhead, and the next second it was gone. The cliffs were a solid wall of darkness. Or was that the sky? Or perhaps it was just the ground, rushing closer and closer to bring him to his final and abrupt end. Oddly enough, he wasn't afraid.

Life seems to be mostly about falling, doesn't it? Falling down.

The wind chuckled in his ear. *Or falling up.*

And just as Jute expected, though he hadn't realized it until the moment it happened, the wind caught him. It spun him around a few times, merely for the fun of it, and then bore him high up, high into the sky until the cliff and forest below shrank away into the darkness of the night.

Here, said the wind, forming its words in gusts and sighs and the tumbling torrent of its passage, *we shall see. Shall we not?* It blew against the clouds until they unraveled like rotten thread. They frayed apart and then vanished, rolled up on the horizon like dirty garments waiting for the rain and their washing. The moon shone down.

Far below them, beneath the cliffs, a snowy valley stretched away to the south. Further down the valley, miles and miles away, the lights of a city sparkled in the night. Wall upon wall and tower upon tower rose to a pinnacle so lofty that it was a wonder Jute and the wind were higher still. Jute's eyes sharpened. It seemed that he could see across the land if he wanted to, across the mountains and even to the sea if he wanted. But the lights of the city drew him.

Aye, said the wind. *We've always been drawn to bright things. You and me. Shiny baubles. Pretty bits of this and that. Careful now. Some are sharp!*

I think that's the city we must go to, said Jute. *Ancalon.*

But then he remembered Declan and the hawk. And the ghost. He could not forget the poor old ghost. And the shadowhounds.

Let us go, said the wind. *We can whirl and blow and dance. Knock over chimneys! Steal the laundry and throw it in the mud. Break windows. What fun we shall have!*

You must set me down near the cliffs.

No. The wind's voice sounded petulant. *I want to play. I want to break windows!*

You must set me down. Please.

Hmmph!

The wind whisked him across the sky, grumbling in a voice that sounded like thunder on the horizon. The stars rushed by overhead and the clouds blew like streamers around the moon. The air was as cold and as thick as water. Snowflakes stung Jute's face. And then he was on the ground, stumbling with the sudden weight of his own self. The wind whirled around him, mumbling and disconsolate. He floundered through the snow. The cliff rose up high above him. Moonlight shone on ice and crag. Icicles hung down in clusters, sharp as spear points, from the overhanging rocks. He heard a howling on the wind.

"Well, we're in tremendous luck." The hawk swooped down out of the darkness and settled on Jute's shoulder. "Superb luck, for such a terrible day and an even worse night."

Before Jute could say how delighted he was to see the bird, something huge and dark hurtled over the top of the cliff. The shape seemed to fly down the face of the cliff—no, not fly—rather, the thing was running down the cliff. Ice fell in sharp and sudden shards. Jute's mouth fell open.

"Get out of the way!" said the hawk.

Snow showered up around them. And there, standing before them was the terrible creature from the top of the cliff. Its jaws gaped open to reveal teeth as sharp as knives. Jute stumbled backwards.

"Help!" he shouted.

He would have shouted a great deal more than that, none of it flattering to himself and the ideal of courage, but at that moment Declan appeared. Rather, he peered over the creature's head. The creature was so enormous that Jute hadn't seen Declan sitting on the thing's back.

"Ah, Jute," said Declan. "There you are. Hop on."

"Did you say hop on?"

"As in: get on, mount up, jump on, ascend, clamber up," said the ghost, appearing from somewhere behind Declan's head.

"This is no time to throw about words," said the hawk. "Quickly now. He's our friend."

Friend? Jute looked over at the hawk. *What is he?*

I am a wolf. The voice filled Jute's mind. It was deep and growling, but there was a hint of laughter in it. The wolf's tongue lolled out of his mouth in a grin. *Get on. We do not have much time. Do not worry. I shall not eat you, little one. You would be exceedingly tough and stringy.*

This did not encourage Jute, but a sudden howl from high above them on the cliff did, and he jumped for the wolf as if someone had filled his boots with hot coals.

"Climb up," said the wolf. "Plenty of room for all. Caught hold? Good. Now, we are off."

The night surged around them. The wolf ran as fast as the wind. Snow flew up from his paws, shining with moonlight and sparkling like tiny stars in their wake. The countryside blurred past in a confusion of ice-bound trees, of darkness pooled in defiles, and of expanses of snow. The stars glided overhead, their fire frozen into shards of light studding the sky. The moon tumbled by from cloud to cloud. Near them, in the darkness, the hawk flew as fast as an arrow, but even he could fly no faster than the speed of the wolf. They fled through the night, but behind them in the darkness there sounded the belling of the shadowhounds.

The city rose up like a swath of night sky, speckled with lights like stars. As they drew closer, its aspect hardened into towers, battlements, and walls, spiked with chimney spires trailing smoke from their smoldering tips. The city sprawled at the mouth of the valley, out of whose expanse swam a river that hugged the northern edge of the city before curving away to the west. Bridges spanned the water in several places. Torches burned holes in the darkness, along the walls, atop towers, and at the heads and tails of the bridges.

The wolf stopped his headlong rush in a stand of trees halfway down a ridge descending to the valley below. Declan and Jute tumbled off and stamped around to awaken their aching muscles.

"We're nearly there," said the hawk. "Why stop now? You, more than us, surely know what's hidden behind those walls."

"I know full well, old wing," said the wolf. "I've approached this city, from south and north, east and west, and every time I'm stopped in my tracks. There's a strange, dark magic guarding this place and it listens for such as you and I. Each time, the gates opened and a company rode forth on my trail. Shadowhounds, ravens with iron beaks and iron claws, men on steeds and themselves ridden by magic, and other such almost men, but not men, full of death and darkness. This accursed city is shut to me, even though my heart is there." A growl escaped his throat. "She's there. I know it."

"I wouldn't regard ravens as much," said the hawk. "Ugly, smelly birds not good for anything except pecking dead flesh."

"These aren't precisely ravens," said the wolf. "But time's passing us by now. The hounds are still on our trail and shall not rest until they find us. You and Jute must make your way into the city alone. Find my mistress—find your sister—and free her from whatever holds her fast, for I can sense her presence somewhere behind those walls. I'm balked by darkness, for there is too much magic in me, but in you it shall find none and so shall be blind to you. If we can, we shall delay the hounds, the hawk and I."

"But how'll we find her?" said Declan. "Ancalon looks near as big as Hearne and I've never set foot in this city."

"You will find her," said the wolf, his voice grim. "And we shall await you."

He drew near to both Declan and Jute and breathed on them. There was a scent of earth and green growing things in his breath. And with it they gradually became aware of a delicate tug in their minds, almost as if a vine had wrapped its tendrils around them and began to pull with the slow yet inexorable strength of its growth.

"What about me?" said the ghost. "I expect you think I'm going to stay here and mumble among the trees while you're gallivanting around. And this after I saved your lives back in that wretched inn. Hmmph."

"On the contrary," said Declan, eyeing the ghost thoughtfully. "You'll come with us. You might prove useful before the night is out."

"Oh?" said the ghost. "Well, I—"

But it did not get to say more than this, for at that moment there came from behind them on the ridge a sudden sharp howl. The wolf wheeled around.

"Quickly now," he said. "We'll attempt to draw them off. But the shadowhounds have your scent, and they're not known to give up easily." And with that, the wolf and hawk vanished into the darkness.

"Well, that's that," said Jute. He glanced nervously back toward the ridge. "We should go, shouldn't we?"

"Yes," said Declan.

"I suppose," mumbled the ghost.

They plunged down the snowy slope. Pines grew in miserable and twisted states, hunched over themselves under the weight of their icy branches and the fact that winter had many months before it would relent into spring. Jute's side ached. His lungs burned. His mind felt numb with cold and weariness.

If only I could fly. Or at least lighten my feet.

His thoughts groped for the sensation of weightlessness, of air and emptiness and sky. Sky. The pale, scraped-thin, gossamer nothingness of sky. Caught and held onto nothingness. He felt his body lighten. His boots glided across the snow. The wind pushed him forward. He could breathe easily again. And then the hawk's voice whispered into his mind.

Stop. You'll draw unwanted attention.

As quickly as it had appeared, the hawk's voice was gone. Jute plunged back into the snow. Floundering knee-deep. Gasping. Chagrined. He knew better. Declan glanced back at him, eyebrows raised.

"I'm all right," panted Jute. "We'll be there soon enough."

"Aye." Declan frowned and shook his head. "Searching for a pebble on the shore. Unless this pull, this thing." He did not finish the sentence but shook his head again.

But they could both feel it. The delicate tug inside their minds pulled at them ever so gently. It aimed straight across the snowy valley floor, across the frozen black ribbon of river and right at the city walls. And surely once they were within those walls, it would pull them on until they found her. Jute wondered what Ronan's sister was like. Sometimes she looked like Lena and sometimes she looked like the lady in the regent's castle. Vines and leaves wove through her hair, rippling around her neck and dangling down to the ground. Her legs grew into the earth, or was it that the earth rose up and became her?

"What's her name?" said Jute.

"Giverny." Declan paused and then spoke again, more to himself than to Jute. "I can hardly remember her face. She was a tiny thing when I left. Three years old, if that. Toddling around, always getting under the hooves of the horses, though they never stepped on her. The horses and the hounds, they all loved her. Even the wild animals. Foxes, hares, the squirrels would come eat bread from her hand." His face twisted, though Jute could not tell if it was in anger or in wonder. "Was her path already laid out for her then? Is it like that for everyone?"

The city grew as they approached. It was difficult to tell in the darkness, but to Jute's eyes Ancalon seemed as large a city as Hearne. Towers mounted up toward the sky. The massive walls stretched away on either side, bounded by the frozen expanse of the river uncoiled below. Three bridges spanned the river, leading to three gates, each flanked by towers with crenellated battlements.

"The gates are shut," said Jute. "I don't suppose they'd be opening to a pair of poor travelers in the night."

"Even if they did, we wouldn't want that. I don't think this is a friendly place to strangers."

"No," said Jute unhappily. He shifted from foot to foot in the snow, wishing he were sitting in front of a warm fireplace with a tankard of ale in one hand and the night safely shut outside. But he could feel the invisible tug within his mind, gently pulling, insistent and insensible to such concerns as fireplaces and hot ale. "We'll have to climb the blasted wall, won't we? Besides, we can't wait here for the shadowhounds."

Declan nodded. For a moment, however, he looked just as unhappy as Jute felt.

"Shall we climb?" said the ghost from somewhere inside Jute's knapsack. "I love climbing. What are we climbing?"

"The city wall."

They crossed the ice at the foot of the wall. Beneath their feet, the river flowed silent and black below the glassy surface. They clambered up the snowy bank. The city wall stood before them at the top of the rise, tall and dark and foreboding. Declan stopped and looked behind them.

"What is it?" said Jute, staring at the wall and wondering how they could make it up the ice-covered stone. Impossible. It looked impossible.

"Hush."

Something growled on the riverbank behind them. It was answered by another growl further along the river toward the nearest bridge.

"Oh," said the ghost. "I don't like the sound of that."

Declan and Jute ran for the wall. Jute's heart pounded in his chest. He didn't need to see what was behind them. He knew. He scrabbled up the slope, hard on Declan's heels. The snow there had hardened into ice, probably due to being in the shadow of the wall throughout the day. He slipped and fell face-first in the snow.

"Get up!" said the ghost frantically. "Get up! Getupgetupgetup!"

Jute flung himself at the wall and, trembling, he began to climb. Declan was a shadow slightly above and to one side of him.

"All right?" called the man down.

"All right," said Jute, barely able to manage the words.

The back of his neck prickled. He was sure at any moment now there would be a howling and baying behind him. That he would be ripped down by fangs. That he would be—

"Climb! Climb! Climb!" said the ghost.

"I am!"

Jute looked down and was relieved to see he was already a good distance above the ground. No hound, magical or not, would be able to leap that high. He reached up and worked his fingers into the next stone fissure and then felt for a foothold. Something slammed into the wall beneath him. Claws scrabbled on stone, right beneath Jute's feet. He gave out a half-stifled shriek and climbed even faster. There was a muted growling below him. It was a horrible sound. It had more in common with rocks grating together than the growl of a dog.

"Good gracious me," said the ghost. "Why, if I weren't so terrified, I'd say that was fascinating."

"What?" gasped Jute.

"The shadowhound is dematerializing. Astounding."

"What does that mean? Dema—demater—?"

"Dematerializing. It means that the creature's substance, its flesh, is vanishing."

"That sounds like the only good news of the day."

"Will you two be quiet?" said Declan from somewhere above them.

"Good news? No, I don't think so. You see, my poor young Jute, the shadowhound is dematerializing and moving through the stone of the wall. Doubtless, it intends to meet us on the other side. And that's bad news."

"Be quiet!"

They reached the top of the wall. Jute caught his breath, gasping. His hands ached with cold. Lights gleamed here and there in solitary windows, and moonlight shone down. It was enough to reveal the rooftops stretching away from them, divided by troughs of darkness that plunged down between buildings to the streets and alleys below.

"That way," said Declan, pointing. "I can feel it." Far off across the rooftops, a tower stood tall above the city. "The duke's castle. I'd bet my life on it." There was a terrible starkness in the line of the tower. It had nothing in common with the majestic sprawl of the regent's castle in Hearne, or the homey manor of the duke of Dolan. The tower looked like a spear plunged into the earth, haft first. The blade pierced the sky and the night was caught upon it.

"Should we go by rooftop?" said Jute.

As if in response, a snarl floated up from somewhere in the darkness of the street below.

"Rooftop it is," said Declan.

"Until you're deeper within the city," said the ghost. "I recall our friend the hawk mentioning something about a high concentration of lives confusing the trail. The scent gets lost. The footprints muddled. Of course, I knew that already, as I was one of the foremost experts on shadowhounds during my days. I taught a class titled 'On the Evasion of Magical Beasts.' It was a favorite with the—"

"Declan," said Jute. "Look."

Further away on the wall, past where it angled along the curve of the river, torches wavered in the darkness.

"Guards. Making their rounds."

As luck would have it (and they sorely needed some luck that night), the wall loomed above a huddle of buildings standing a scant twenty feet from the wall's edge. The roof of the nearest building was lower than the top of the wall. It looked a good twenty feet lower to Jute, which did not bode well for a comfortable landing.

"Can you manage that distance?" said Declan, frowning. "It'd be easy if we had a rope and a grapple. There's a chimney there that would prove a good hold. Maybe we should try further along and find a shorter jump?"

"No choice," said Jute. "Look there. More guards."

Further down the wall on the other side of them, another knot of torches flickered in the night. The group was too far away to see Declan and Jute, but they were drawing closer. Luck was a shaky thing that night, for it had begun to snow again, with the first flakes drifting down as Jute spoke. Declan cursed under his breath.

"Jump for it, then," he said. "Sooner than later."

Retreating to the parapet on the far side of the wall, Declan made a running start and flung himself out into space. For a moment, it looked as if he would fall well short of the rooftop below, but he did not. He landed with a crash of slate shattering and falling away to clatter with even more noise in the street below. Jute winced. The sound was horribly loud in the quiet of the night. Someone was sure to hear it.

"Was it just me?" asked the ghost, "or did someone just throw a wagonload of pots and pans off the side of the wall? Subtle. I would advise landing lightly."

Jute launched himself off the side of the wall. The night rushed past him. The rooftop below looked dreadfully far away. What had they been thinking? He was sure to fall to the street. Where was the wind when he needed it? He landed hard, the breath knocked from his body. Slate snapped beneath him. Somewhere behind him, high up on the wall and still at a distance, there were shouts of alarm. He scrabbled at the tile beneath him. He was slipping amidst the wreckage of shattered slate. A hand grabbed his arm.

"Come on," said Declan. "One of those blasted dogs is right below us, staring up with eyes like saucers—and an even bigger mouth, no doubt. We've got to get out of here."

"And, no doubt, you've woken the neighbors," said the ghost.

Thankfully, Ancalon was similar to Hearne in that most buildings shared common walls or, at the most, were separated by alleys. It was not difficult to cross the rooftops, as long as one did not slip on the ice or step on a loose tile or plunge down into the sudden abysses of the alleys. The snow was falling thickly now. Soft, fat flakes blanketed the roofs. They hurried along, up and over roof after roof, slipping and sliding and clinging with icy hands, their feet numb in their boots.

"One of us is going to break an ankle," said Declan.

"Not me," said the ghost cheerfully.

They found a dormer window a few roofs further from where they were. It opened silently under Declan's hands and they let themselves in.

"What about the hound?" said Jute.

"Haven't heard a sound in the last ten minutes," said Declan. "I think he's lost our scent."

"For now," said the ghost.

The house they found themselves in was exceedingly dark due to the night outside and the fact that all of the windows were covered by drapes. The place smelled sour, as if it had never been aired out, and surely, if one looked, there was mold growing in the walls and mushrooms in the cellar.

"If I could still smell things," said the ghost, "I'd be sneezing." But then he looked startled at his own words. "Wait a minute. Am I smelling things?"

"Shh," said Jute, who was himself trying not to sneeze.

Stairs angled down through the darkness. The floorboards creaked beneath their feet with every step.

"I'd hate to have to burgle this house," said Jute.

"Shh," said the ghost.

They let themselves out into a little courtyard, deep in snow and ringed about with icicles that hung from the eaves above like the slender teeth of some peculiar beast. The streets were silent around them. The city, now that they were deep within it, seemed strange and less and less like Hearne the longer they walked the streets. The buildings had been built tall and close together so that it looked like they were about to topple over at any moment. Looking up, there was little sky to be seen. Even the ghost was cowed by the mood of the place, and he vanished into Jute's knapsack.

"Have you noticed," said Declan, "there aren't many lights showing. It can't be that late in the evening. Strange. You'd think there'd be folks out and about. Isn't too late for inns."

They made their way along a street. There was little snow on the ground in some places, because of the narrowness of the streets and the height of the walls, and then, in other places, due to a turn and the wind blowing straight down a passage, they found the snow piled high into drifts waist-deep.

Declan was right. Most of the windows they passed were shuttered and dark. In Hearne there were always lights, a bustle and hustle regardless of the time. Wagonloads of fish hauling in from the docks, dripping seawater and trailing a stream of covetous cats. A merchant and his staff scurrying in and out of their warehouse, shouts and curses ringing out as they unloaded a delivery of silks from Harth, stone from Thule, any number of things from any number of places in Tormay. In short, Hearne was always alive.

Ancalon was dead.

But not entirely.

A sharp command cut through the night somewhere further down the street. Somewhere out of sight. There came the sound of ringing bootsteps marching in quick double time. Bootsteps marching in rhythm. Another command. The sounds were coming closer.

"In here," said Declan. "Quick."

A locked door opened under the point of his knife. Declan shut the door behind them and they crouched in the darkness, listening to the approaching sounds and listening just as intently to the silence of the house around them. The marching bootsteps clattered past them, echoing down the street. After a while, the sound died away.

"Let's go," whispered Jute. "Something about this house is making me nervous. Something's not right."

They were standing in a gloomy space. It was too dark to see properly. The air was cold and silent. Dust turned to mud under their boots as the snow on their soles melted. Jute had a brief and horrifying vision of stairs that led up and up into the house. Of long hallways where the floorboards creaked at every step. Of a bedroom muffled in molding velvet drapes and an old, withered couple that lay upon the bed, never sleeping but staring motionless with unblinking eyes into the darkness. Eyes that were slowly turning in his direction.

"It's not just this house," said the ghost.

"But we're in this house now."

"No, not just this house," said Declan. "The ghost is right. We're in this city, and that's the problem. The city. There's something extremely odd about this city." He frowned and touched the necklace beneath his shirt. Then his hand drifted up to the sword hilt above his shoulder. It was an absentminded movement, as if his body were checking on things while his mind attended to other matters. "I wish we were far away from here, but. . ."

"But there's your sister."

"Aye, my sister."

The city huddled under the snow in silence. Here and there, the stars shone down from rents in the dark clouds drifting below an even darker sky. The shadowhounds. They were back there in the night. Somewhere. Jute knew it. He could feel it in the nervousness of the wind, in the way the wind whispered around his neck and prodded him on with its icy fingers. He did not have to urge Declan on with his fear. It was all he could do to keep up with the older man. They hurried through the streets, flitting from doorway to doorway and avoiding every patch of moonlight. Twice more they were forced to turn aside for a troop of soldiers that marched out of the night. It was not difficult, as they heard the ring of their bootsteps long before the soldiers came into view, echoing off the walls of the houses and the stone streets.

The tug in their minds grew stronger. They rounded one last corner, and there before them in the middle of an enormous cobblestone square stood the tower. The tower was awful and immense, a gaunt finger of black stone pointing up at the sky as if forever accusing. It loomed over the city and it seemed that everything shrank away from it, thankful for the night and the snow, that they might draw those twin blankets over themselves and hide from the tower.

Declan and Jute retreated back around the corner. As bad luck would have it, the clouds had chosen that instant to unravel, and moonlight shone down in unwelcome abundance.

"Excellent visibility," said the ghost cheerfully. "Clear as day. You're obviously not going to turn an ankle running across that square. Though it'll be all the easier for the crossbowmen on the walls to put a bolt through you."

"Are there crossbowmen?" asked Jute, alarmed at this thought.

"I doubt it," said Declan, after a moment of peering around the corner. "I don't see any guards. I don't see anybody at all."

"Maybe they don't need guards," said the ghost. "Maybe there's something else. Something horrifying."

"She's there."

"Yes," said Jute. He could feel the pull on his mind even stronger now. Precise and focused and urgent. "Somewhere near the top."

"This place reminds me of something. An old story my mother used to tell me when I was a child. There was a dark tower on a moor. A tower without a door built by a man without a name. It happened a long time ago in Harlech."

"What happened?" said Jute.

"I don't know. I don't remember."

They skulked in the shadows until the moon hid again behind the clouds. It was a dreadful wait, as Jute whirled around a dozen times or more, certain that something was standing further down the street, watching them.

"Let's just go," he said. "We can chance it."

"Wait a bit," said Declan. "The moon's about to go behind a cloud. I don't fancy running across that square with all those windows staring down. We need some darkness first."

There were a great many windows in the tower walls. Not a single one was lit, but they were visible enough, pricked out by the moonlight and looking uncomfortably like empty eye sockets.

"We should go," said Jute, much more urgently this time. "Hang the moonlight. There's something down the street, coming this way. It's no use looking for it. I can feel it. Somewhere on the edge of my mind, and it knows about us. It isn't the hounds. It's something else. I'd much rather have a go at the tower then stay here and let it find us."

Declan didn't say anything. He glanced back down the street. There was nothing to see except shadows and snowdrifts piled up against walls and the tightly locked houses shivering on their doorsteps. But he nodded, and then nodded again. The walk across the cobblestone square seemed to take forever. Declan whispered that running would attract more attention than walking. And attention they did not want. They walked gingerly across the empty square, with their necks pricking as if eyes gazed from every window. But there was no outburst, no sudden cry, no torches flaring up. They stopped beneath the wall of the tower and crouched in the deep shadow there.

"Careful," said Jute urgently. "Don't touch the wall."

"What?" said Declan, who had been about to do just that.

"Don't touch the stone. It's guarded with just about the worst ward I've ever come across."

"I can't hear a thing."

"I know. I can't either. But I can—I suppose I can hear it through the wind. It's like the wind is hearing it and then putting the impression into my mind. The thing's woven out of darkness, mostly. I think." Here, Jute frowned, concentrating and listening intently. He suddenly backed away, looking alarmed. "Shadows above and below. This is a new one. It traps you. The whole wall's alive. It's full of people caught by the ward."

"Not how I'd like to spend the rest of my life," said Declan, taking a step back as well. "I'm disliking this city more and more with every passing moment. I've always despised wards. I'd much rather have to deal with swords and someone trying to cut my head off. Let's find a door. Something. Anything."

They crept around the base of the tower, skulking through the darkness and examining the wall as they went. The snow blew and whirled down around them. The cobblestone square stretched away on their side and the city hunched down on its foundations on the edges of the square in frozen and abject silence. The windows of the buildings stared across at the creeping progress of the two interlopers. Above them, the tower loomed up, vanishing into the darkness of the clouds and the falling snow.

"There aren't any doors," said Declan after a while. "I'm sure of it. We've been around more than once. That's the street we came from originally over there. How on earth do you get out or in? There aren't any doors."

His question was answered immediately—so immediately that it almost proved their undoing. The side of the tower a few feet in front of them vanished. A yawning open hole appeared, wide enough for a horse and wagon to ride through. The air rang with bootsteps. Declan yanked Jute to the ground, and they lay motionless in the thin blanket of snow. A column of soldiers marched out of the opening. They moved as one. Each man's leg stepped out at the precise second as his neighbor. Each chin was held at the same stiff level, each back as straight as a spear. Their eyes stared ahead unblinkingly. Jute lost count of the soldiers. They emerged from the opening in the wall in their perfect files until the column stretched from the tower across the square like an elongated snake, the head disappearing down a street on the far side of the square. The opening in the wall closed up again right behind the last row of soldiers, instantly and silently and solidly. The last of the soldiers marched across the square and vanished.

"Well, now we know," said Jute, getting up and brushing snow from his clothes.

"Not that it does us much good. We'll have to climb and find a window suitably high up. I suppose complete silence will be the only way to beat a guardian ward like the one in this wall. Did you ever do such a thing? Fooling wards with absolute silence in your mind?"

"Of course," said Jute, somewhat irritated that Declan would question his capability. "I only wonder whether you're able to do that as well. I don't think I'd be able to help if the ward took you."

"Don't worry about me." Declan's hand drifted up to the necklace threaded beneath his collar. He spoke somewhat absentmindedly as if he were no longer aware of Jute, or even of where they stood. "The silence beneath the sea is greater than that of stone. Greater even than your sky, I imagine."

With that, Declan began to climb.

"Poetic," said the ghost from inside Jute's knapsack.

"Greater than the sky?" muttered the boy to himself. "Hmmph."

And Jute filled his mind with the memory of sky, of his dreams of flying with the wind far above the earth in the silence of the endless space there, of the absolute stillness of height and depth and distance. He set his hands to the wall and began to climb.

In one way it was not such a difficult thing to climb that wall. The stones were roughly hewn and of many different sizes so that it was easy to find a handhold here and a convenient toehold there. But in another way, it was the hardest wall Jute had ever tried. The thing was horribly alive. He could sense it swirling restlessly just beneath the stone. Hundreds of different lives were locked within, held captive by the powerful weaving of the spell. He could feel sorrow and desperation and the bitterness brought about by the death of hope. He willed himself to not become aware of them, to not listen and feel, for if he did, then his concentration would be lost. He would be pulled in to become one of them. Imprisoned within the stone and darkness. He climbed on.

557

The tower was taller than it looked. From the ground, Jute had thought it no taller than the main tower of the old university ruins in Hearne. But surely he had already climbed that far. Glancing down, the rooftops below looked like a child's patchwork quilt, tiny and mismatched squares jammed together and fading beneath the falling snow. He craned his head back to look up. Above him, the tower stretched up into the night and vanished.

If Jute had looked down again, he might have seen the figure of a dog, deceptively small at such a distance, lope out of a street opening onto the square. The same street that they had come down. The dog headed across the square toward the tower. It stopped at the base of the wall and gazed up. The dog began to fade and after a few seconds the beast resembled nothing more than a shadow. It drifted to the wall and then slowly moved through it like water seeping through dry earth.

Jute came level with Declan. The man had paused climbing and hung motionless, suspended from his fingers and the tips of his boots.

"The windows move," whispered Declan.

"What?"

"They slide away as soon as we draw near. Even though the ward still sleeps, the tower's aware of us. Somehow."

"What we want is much higher up," said Jute quietly. "We might as well climb to the top. There's sure to be a door of sorts up there.

"The top? You're sure about that?"

"After all the houses I've robbed? I'm sure. There's always a door at the top."

They both lapsed into silence, for the stone seemed to tremble as if it were becoming aware of them. A nearly soundless whine trembled in the air. The ward. Coiling on itself like a snake. Ready to wake and strike. Jute closed his eyes and ignored his own exhaustion, the cold, the trembling promise of cramp in his legs. His stomach growled, but he ignored that too. He could not afford any distractions.

Even lovely shiny things? said the wind in his ear.

Even lovely shiny things.

The ward quieted and they climbed on. Forever, it seemed. The horizon in the east lightened imperceptibly. Jute's limbs ached and trembled with exhaustion. The chill of the stone and the continuous pressure on his fingers produced a slow, spreading numbness that worked through his hands and wrists. Each successive hold and pull up was beginning to become something akin to torture. He found himself alongside Declan again. The man was staring up the tower, toward the point where the darkness of the stone and the darkness of the sky blended together until there was only night. Sweat trickled down his forehead.

"I don't think this tower is meant to be climbed," said Declan quietly. "It isn't only the windows moving away from us. The tower itself moves. It's growing above us. We aren't gaining much ground, if any."

"Then what do you suggest?" said Jute.

"I don't know."

"Why don't you ask the wind?" whispered the ghost.

"The wind?"

And Jute asked the wind, wondering why he had not bothered before with this and any other question that had crossed his mind.

Why should I tell you? said the wind somewhat pettishly. *Don't want to play, don't want to knock down the chimney pots and fling roof tiles. Don't want to come flying with me.*

Yes, I do. It's just that the hawk won't let me.

And you don't like shiny, pretty things!

Snowflakes whirled around them as the wind blew back and forth, grumbling in irritation. The ward in the wall coiled in on itself, waking up more than it had before, sensing and listening and focusing. The faint whine became a buzz and the buzz grew until it was as loud as the hiss of an angry snake.

Wind! Please. You're waking the ward. Quickly, before it's too late.

If I must. But promise you shall come flying.

I promise.

Soon?

Yes!

Simple. Go through the wall.

Through?

Go through the wall.

Jute pushed his hand against the wall, wondering and disbelieving. The wall felt like a wall. Hard stone. Not the sort of thing one went through. But then, all of a sudden, the wall softened under his touch. There was no other word for it. One second hard stone, the next second a sort of wavery feel. Like water. It was like wading through water. A strange, heavy, thick sort of water. He could not see. The stone—was it stone anymore?—was all around him. A murmur filled his ears, not unlike that which happened when he put his hands over his ears to try and simulate the sound of the sea. Jute reached back behind him, out into the cold air, and felt Declan's hand grab onto his. He pulled him in and felt the stone ripple outward in response. He could no longer feel Declan's hand and was not sure if he had let go or if they still maintained contact. All he could feel was the pressure of the stone around him, moving him, swimming him slowly forward. The murmur altered somewhat, clarifying and focusing into separate sounds.

Voices. Voices all around him, muttering and grumbling and whispering and moaning. There were so many of them that it seemed impossible to discern what they were saying. They were like countless different streams of water splashing down into the one same sea so that words were jumbling together into confusion. But then the voices clarified further and sharpened into distinction.

Why didn't he kill me?

Never knew nothing but hunting. Deer and them little mountain sheep. Sold the meat down in the lowlands. Nothing but hunting. That's all.

Should've stayed home that day. It was wet out. Slashing down rain. Muddy road. Ford was most likely washed out. Never saw him afore it was too late. Should've stayed home.

Sunlight. I miss the sunlight.

He should've killed me. I wish he had killed me. I'd rather be dead.

What was her name? The girl with long black hair and green eyes. The woodcutter's daughter.

Stitching. Stitching and sewing. Got paid in goat's milk. Made my own cheese from that milk. Strained my eyes working nights by candlelight. Tiny stitches. Best in the village and worth my pay, I was. Got paid in goat's milk.

That fellow had teeth like knives. Ogre blood, I reckon. Knew it the moment he walked into my tavern. If I had locked up early, things might've been different. Things might've turned out different. Wonder if Bess still keepin' the old place open? She were a good girl, were Bess. Had a wrist as strong as an oak branch.

Deer meat sold best in the fall. They cured their winter's lot then. Smoke and salt and hung high in the rafters.

The woodcutter's daughter.

I can't remember her face.

The voices meandered around him, each lost in its own misery and remembrance. At first, they did not seem aware of Jute and Declan in their midst, but slowly and surely the voices trailed off into silence. In their place, there grew a feeling of puzzlement so strong that it was almost a color, a taste, a sensation of some sort that could surely be experienced just as heat was felt from the flame or pain from the edge of the knife.

Jute swam through the stone, still blind, but pushing his arms forward and questing for the end of the wall. Surely they had come far enough. No wall could this be thick. But there was only darkness and the soft, heavy push on all sides.

Who are you?

It was one of the voices. He could not remember which. Perhaps the innkeeper or the hunter.

Who are you?

Another voice. A woman's this time.

You're alive.

Alive.

He's alive.

And we are not. Neither dead nor alive. Something in between. Caught here.

How can I leave this place? said Jute. *Help me, please.*

Help him, he says. Whoever helped us? We're caught here forever. Not a chance of decent burial and some rest.

Please, said Jute. The stone seemed endless about him. And surely there was a hint of thickening in the feel of it. It was getting more difficult to move.

Please. He says please. At least he's got some manners.

That's something.

No, it ain't. Won't buy you ale.

We have to rescue a girl trapped inside the tower, said Jute, his voice desperate. *We're her only hope. You must help us. Surely if you're trapped you wouldn't wish that on someone else. She's young.*

Don't mind if everyone were trapped in here along with us, said a voice. A woman's voice, spiteful and bitter and as sharp as curdled milk. *Reckon if we have to suffer, other folks can, too.*

No, said another voice. *Think on this, now. Helping someone. Now that's a memory we could all use. A new memory. Something fresh to remember.*

Ahh. It was the hunter, his voice full of mountains and the sun on rocks and pine trees. *A good idea, but I've one better. Make him pay with a memory. A good, rich one for his release.*

Aye. An excellent idea. A new memory for us all.

More voices chimed in, falling over each other into a confusion of excited noise. A memory. A new memory to leaven the dark, dreary, and unending tedium of their imprisonment.

A memory. Give us a memory, boy. One of yours. Something with sunlight and summer, for it's dark and cold in here an' most of us, we've forgotten the light.

A picture blossomed in Jute's mind. An old memory from the summertime. He spoke without realizing it, and the unseen audience expectant in the darkness around him listened with avid attention.

Listen, said Jute. *I'll tell you about a day.*

Afternoon sun on the roof, on the slate tiles blinding hot and white, with shadows deep along the eastern wall. The sharp, sweet scent of apples in the air. Lena asleep on the second-story balcony of the old house. Skinny legs and arms burned brown by the sun. Sprawled in a tangle on a dusty rug. Flies crawling about an apple core. Jute and the twins, Moro and Mana, sitting on the edge of the balcony, legs dangling through the wooden railings, crunching apples. Stolen apples. Juice on their hands and chins. Pitching cores down at a dirty white goat in the yard below. The goat, busily happily contentedly munching on apple cores, but still rolling an occasional yellow eye up at the children as if to say it would remember them and deal harshly if they ever came within reach of its horns. Sudden, soft noise inside the house. The owner returned home long before he should have. He should've still been drinking at the inn. He always did. Stayed late. Startled alarmed glances from the twins. Jute nudging Lena into yawning wakefulness. The balcony door flung open and the astonished, angry face of the owner, mouth agape, shouting something, some blur of words Jute hadn't even bothered to hear. The children evading his outstretched hands with practiced ease, giggling and shrieking, hearts thumping, jumping up onto the roof overhang, and scrambling away across the hot tiles. A few tiles kicked free and sliding down with a skittering, scraping sound to shatter in powdery red shards around the man on the balcony. Him shaking his fist at them in rage. The goat still crunching apple cores, not caring. A handful of coins, as gold as fresh butter, heavy in Jute's pocket, scooped from a chest inside the house. The sun drifting down toward the shining surface of the sea as they scampered off across the rooftops. Sunlight, sky, water, and life.

Ahh. A good memory.

I like the goat.

Thank you, boy. Our own memories are tired.

Thank you.

And now? said Jute. His throat was tightening. He struggled to breathe. He could feel the stone around him hardening more. *Your end of the bargain. How do we get out of the wall? How do we get inside the tower?*

Let's keep him. Him and the silent one behind him. They must be full of memories.

No. We made a bargain. And that's a second new memory for us as well. We keep our end. Listen, boy. It's easy enough. Just step forward. We won't keep you any longer.

Jute stepped forward. His legs could only move slowly now. The darkness and stone pressed in around him as if to say, no, we won't let you go.

Ever.

But then the voices were behind him, fading into the distance, and he found himself standing in a bare, gloomy room bounded by stonewalls. He stumbled due to the sudden absence of stone pressing around him. His legs trembled and he almost could not stand. There was a whispering sort of noise and then Declan stood next to him. Behind them, in the wall, Jute thought he heard a sigh.

"I don't want to go through that again," said Declan, his face pale. "Couldn't hardly breathe toward the end there."

"No."

"Just wake me up when it's over," said the ghost from inside Jute's knapsack, its voice shaking and growing louder with every word until surely it was about to break into a shriek. "Just wake me up when—"

"Hush."

"We must go higher up," said Declan. "I can feel it."

Stairs led up from the middle of the room to the ceiling above, curving around a stone pillar. There were no windows in the room, nor were there torches, yet it was lit with a dim light that came from either the stairwell opening in the floor, as there were also stairs leading down to the floor beneath, or from the stairwell opening in the ceiling. Both Jute and Declan did not move for a moment, as if both were reluctant to find what waited higher up the tower. Declan roused himself with a shudder.

"Right. No use standing about. Up the stairs."

"I'd much rather be anywhere but here. That smell. It's horrible."

"Something dead, I suppose. Rats caught in the drains."

"I don't think so. It's magic, I think. It reminds me of a smell from the university ruins. An old spell."

"I'd rather not bother with any more spells for the moment."

The stairs wound around and around, and they walked higher and higher, treading in silence, ears pricked for any sounds. But the tower was quiet around them. The stairs continued their spiral up through room after room. The rooms were identical. Each a bare, gloomy space stretching out into the shadows. Each dimly lit with a poor, unpleasant sort of light that did not come from window or torch. There were no furnishings. No rugs or chests or wardrobes. No tables or chairs or tapestries to hide the stone. No rusty old spears and axes hanging on the walls. Nothing at all. Just stone and dust and the cold silence. Just empty rooms.

"Almost as if nobody lives here," said Jute.

"Lives," said Declan grimly. "Maybe there are things that dwell in a place but don't necessarily live. A strange man, this duke of Mizra, if this is his castle. I don't want to meet him. I suppose his hospitality wouldn't be to our liking. But if we do meet him then it'll be with my sword in my hand."

And then they found her. It happened matter-of-factly, as these things do. They trudged up another flight of stairs and there she was. The air, as cold as it already was, grew even colder. The stairs took another turn around and they found themselves out in the open air. They had reached the top of the tower. It was a flat, wide-open space of black stone, hard and slick with ice and blown clear of snow by the wind. The night stretched around them and the sky seemed uncomfortably close, full of darkness and only relieved in spots by the frozen glitter of stars. The city was so far below that it seemed to be a mirror image of the night sky, with the scattered lights in windows shining like distant stars.

Near the edge of the roof was a girl. She hung motionless in the air, several feet above the roof. Her hands were at her sides and her head slumped on her breast. A strange, blue-tinged fire crept about her body in sluggish coils, the tongues of flame flickering like the leaves of a tree in a breeze. Declan ran to her, stumbling on the ice. Jute followed. Her head lifted and she looked at them.

"No," she said, her voice quiet. "Don't touch me, or you'll die. These flames are my prison. They do not harm me, but their touch would be your death."

Declan recoiled, for he had been about to take her hand.

"Giverny. Don't you remember me?"

She gazed at him, expressionless at first. There was a silence in her stare that stilled him, a silence that seemed to pool around them, despite the wind howling about the tower heights. And then something struggled to come to life in her eyes.

"Giverny," she said slowly. "I remember that name. I think it was mine, once. Long ago. I can't remember."

"It still is your name," he said fiercely. "It'll always be your name."

"Who are you to tell me this?"

"I'm your brother Declan."

She blinked. Snowflakes spun and twirled, swirling down out of the dark sky. "Declan," she whispered. "Declan?"

He could not answer.

"They're dead." Her eyes were wide, no longer seeing him, but staring away into the darkness. The wind blew her hair about until it half-covered her face in tangles. "You should've been there. You should've been there to save them! Where were you?" Her voice rose to a scream. Tears ran down her cheeks. "Where did you go? You weren't there!"

"I wasn't there." He bowed his head, but then he raised it. "But I can save you."

She laughed. The sound was flat and dreadful and without mirth. "You cannot save me. I'm imprisoned by fire and I'm cut off from the earth. Bound here in the air, so high above the ground. He keeps me far from from my beloved earth. I can't even touch this poor stone below my feet. I can't draw its strength into me." She looked past Declan at Jute. "And you, brother sky—yes, I know you—you can't help me either. Darkness holds sway here, and it'll rule all of Tormay some day if it's left unchecked. You can't save me. But you can warn the duchies. Go, before it's too late. He's raising an army. And behind him stands the much deeper darkness."

"Who?" said Declan, despairing. He half raised his hand as if to touch her arm, but then drew back. "Who do you speak of?"

"Have you forgotten the old stories of Hearne?" she said. The wind whipped her words at them. There was weariness and sadness in her voice. "The kingdom was destroyed by an army of the dead, led by a man with no past. A man with darkness in his eyes. He disappeared from Tormay, but he never died. Time means nothing to him. He's had many names over the centuries, and he changes his face like the earth changes through the seasons. Now, he wears the guise of the so-called duke of Mizra. He looks again to the west, to Tormay and all that we hold dear. He serves destruction and death and the darkness, and the unknown ends of its design. But flee this place before you're discovered. Warn the duchies. They will listen to the wind and the last of the Farrows. They've a little time yet, for not even the duke of Mizra can take an army through the winter snow of the Morn passes. Earth is still mistress there, even though I'm a captive in this place." Her tears froze into ice on her cheeks.

"And what of the wolf?" Declan said, the words choking from his throat. "What do we tell the wolf?"

"The wolf?" she said. "Tell him—"

"Shadow and stone. Who have we here?"

The voice came from behind them, thin and sneering. Jute heard the ghost whimper in his knapsack. Two men stood beside the open well of the stairs. Jute recognized one of them at once. The gold hair, the youthful, handsome face, the bright eyes. It was the man from the regent's ball in Hearne. The duke of Mizra. A dog sat at his feet, silent and watchful with massive shoulders and paws. It was the other man who had spoken, however. With a shudder, Jute realized that he recognized the man as well. Not a man at all. The gaunt shape, the thin white face, the sharp teeth. It was the sceadu. The being from the regent's castle who had pursued him and Lena through the tunnels. Up into the castle and across the ballroom floor. People dying. And then the woman, Levoreth, rescuing him.

Jute took a step backward. His hands trembled. He was painfully aware of the space behind him, the edge of the tower unbounded by any wall or parapet. Just the edge and the long drop to the cobblestone square far below. Snow drifted down. The wind was nowhere to be felt. He could not even feel its presence in his mind. Out of the corner of his eye, he could see Declan standing close by the hanging body of his sister. The man's face looked frozen into stone. His eyes stared straight ahead, wide and unblinking.

"The thief-boy and. . ." The sceadu's attention centered on Declan. He laughed, his teeth gleaming. "Another Farrow. Truth, I'd thought I'd killed the lot of you, but I can finish the job now. No matter. But look at the boy, my lord. I wager he's not come into his own, else the wind would be tearing this tower down."

The duke did not speak, but his eyes focused on Jute, sharpening in something akin to weary amusement. His eyes seemed like holes, holes torn in the fabric of existence. They revealed a horrible, endless darkness, deeper even than that which lay between the stars of night. The duke's voice flickered into life on the edge of Jute's thoughts, as quiet as a single flame.

The blood on that knife had been dry many a long year before you nicked your finger. Slow to come back to life, no doubt. The wind has not wakened in you yet. Not like our beauty here. She came alive with a start, with the blood of the old mistress fresh and bright on her hands.

Jute could not breathe. Something constricted around his chest. Darkness welled up on the edge of his sight, tinged with scarlet pain. He could feel his heart beating faster as if trying to run away. He was going to die.

Peace.

The wind stirred inside Jute's mind, and he was suddenly free. The duke's expression did not change. His eyes were empty holes. Snowflakes drifted down and gathered in his shining hair.

"No matter." The sceadu stepped forward. "He'll die quick enough." A knife appeared in his hand. "And then you shall have this blade to bring another wind to life, as you will. A puppet on your chain."

The darkness in the duke's eyes pulled at Jute.

I found a riddle in the darkness, long ago. What does the death of the anbeorun mean? Do you know how many centuries it took to discover the answer? I came west. Through the dead lands. Across the sea. I came west in the shadows of the waning moon until I stood upon the shore. I walked through the memories and dreams and nightmares of the university and found the pieces, one by one. Shards that recreated the hidden form. A thought here. A memory there. A mouthful of words. Books. Aye, books, even though I never found the Gerecednes. *I gathered it all, and so discovered the truth. The house of dreams does not give up its knowledge easily. And then you came three hundred years later and undid all my efforts in one night.*

The duke paused. Snowflakes drifted down and began to pile up across the icy stone of the tower roof. The sceadu moved closer to Jute. The knife in its hand lifted. Jute looked around wildly. There was nowhere to run. The wind was gone. He could jump. Into the air. It was just air, and the wind was gone. If he jumped, he would fall to his death on the cobblestones below.

You have listened to the darkness, have you not? It whispers in your dreams. Look into my eyes and you shall see it more clearly than you have ever before. You shall see the truth.

The darkness welled up within the duke's eyes. It grew until there was only one spot. It was blacker than blindness in the dead of winter's longest night. A night without stars. A night Jute had seen before in his nightmares. It was an endless darkness that stretched away in every direction, into the past, into the present, into the future. And somewhere in the darkness, though he could not see it, he knew there was a single window. Something was watching him from behind that window. Had been watching him for years. A presence even darker than the darkness itself. A negation of what was.

Emptiness.

Annihilation.

An old hatred born before the starfire came to be.

A thing deeper than death.

The duke's eyes bored into his.

My master waits for you.

Jute's vision trembled. Things began to bend, to creep toward the blot of darkness. He felt himself pulled forward. The stones underfoot seemed to quiver as if they were about to break loose and go flying through the air. Giverny's hair streamed away from her head toward the blot of darkness as if blown by the wind. Snowflakes swirled wildly by, caught in the vortex whirling down into the darkness. But there was no wind.

"Darkness is the end of all things, boy," said the sceadu. "It's your end. My end. The end of Tormay."

The darkness pulled at Jute. He knew that if he were to go slipping and sliding across the snowy ice of the rooftop, he would end up on the sceadu's blade. The darkness in the duke's eyes sucked at the night. It seemed almost as if the night was as light as day in comparison to that hole of utter blackness. Something waited in the darkness.

End, said a small voice inside his mind.

"Never!" cried Jute.

He turned, barely able to move, muscles screaming in protest. He staggered and collided with Declan. The man's body felt as immovable as a statue. His eyes were staring and unseeing. Jute's fingers caught the sword strap running down Declan's back. He pulled hard and felt Declan rock on his heels. The sceadu shouted in fury. Jute teetered on the edge of the roof, looking down into nothingness. There was no wind.

And then he fell.

Jute didn't jump. He just fell. It was all he was capable of. His fingers were still hooked in Declan's sword strap. It seemed as if they fell from the edge of the roof in slow motion. As if the darkness welling from the duke's eyes pulled at them and sought to hold them back from falling. But it could not hold them, and they fell. Jute twisted as he fell. He managed to look back and caught a glimpse of the girl still hanging there motionless, bound in flames.

She smiled at him.

And then Jute and Declan were gone, tumbling down through the air. Limbs flailing end over end. The side of the black tower rushed by in smooth stone. Far below, the ground waited. Jute could see rooftops. I didn't realize we climbed that high, he thought in a daze. It only means we have farther to fall.

565

CHAPTER ONE HUNDRED & FIVE
AWAY WITH THE WIND

As Jute fell, the air felt like water around him. Cold and rushing. Like a stream plunging past. He opened his mouth and drank it in. Tried to fly. Reached out with his mind to catch hold of the wind, to lighten his body and rise up. But he could not. There was no wind. He was as heavy as stone. Encumbered with his body. He was imprisoned by its thick, unwieldy mass. He could not shed it, could not rise above the air like a swimmer on a wave. He was drowning in weight.

Wind? Where are you?

But there was no answer.

Jute shut his eyes.

I am tired of falling, he thought. But this will be the last time. Please, let it be the last time.

He fell and fell. Blurring through the night. An impossible height. Dimly, he was aware of Declan's body falling somewhere near him. A black shape blotting out the stars.

The stars.

The stars have come out. That means the clouds are gone. That means the wind has blown them away.

The wind. . .

And the wind caught Jute, chuckling and laughing to itself. There was a rush of air, a frigid blast that enveloped his body. He dangled as helpless as a child in the wind's grasp. The city turned beneath him. Stone and darkness and death. Rushing away from beneath him. He could see the top of the dark tower as clear and as sharply as if his were the eyes of a hawk. The two figures standing and the motionless form of the girl.

Becoming a habit, catching you. Like a mother bird and her foolish chick tumbling from the nest before his time.

It's not my fault.

You must learn to fly, regardless of what that old wing of a hawk says. You must, for I shan't be at every drop and cliff to catch you. Someday, I shan't be there and you'll have to either fly or fall on your own.

Declan!

The other? Fret not. I have him safe.

Jute glanced back and saw the body of Declan blowing along through the sky a good distance from him. He could not tell if the man was awake or still in whatever insensible state the duke had plunged him into.

There are some that would seek to make our acquaintance.

What do you mean?

Look back.

A dark cloud boiled up behind them, rising higher and higher from the tower. The cloud surged into the sky, ragged as a poor man's shirt, shreds and tatters of filth winging their way through the sky after them. Crows. Hundreds and thousands of them.

I don't suppose you could do something about them? said Jute nervously.

Not I, said the wind. *I would not like to touch them. Dirty, nasty bits of death. They have the Dark in them, more than anything else, and that's not something I care to deal with. That is your domain. Not mine.*

Mine? But, I don't know what to do. They'll catch us.

Oh no they shan't, said the wind gleefully.

With a howling rush, the wind blew them higher and faster and quicker until it was all Jute could do to breathe. The ground whirled away at a tremendous rate, far beneath them in a blur of snow and the shine of the ice on the river winding back and forth no thicker than a length of thread, so far below it was. The clouds had vanished and the sky was empty except for the moon and stars. Ancalon was gone and the crows were only the suspicion of a smudge on the rapidly retreating horizon.

They shan't, chanted the wind.

They shan't.

They can't.

They won't.

We will!

The ground rose beneath them, though not because the wind let them down. Rather, the land was climbing in hills and steeper slopes to meet the first few angles of the mountains. The Morn Mountains. Their peaks, dark and indistinct at first, caught fire with the first rays of the morning sun. It was a blinding white blaze of light and Jute could hardly look at it for its brilliance. Far behind them, the eastern horizon blazed with the edge of the sun. The stars retreated and the moon faded in polite abeyance.

"Is it over yet?" said the ghost from somewhere inside Jute's knapsack.

"Yes!" shouted Jute, the wind whipping his words away.

But he knew it wasn't over. It was far from over.

The mountains rose as they approached. Shrouded in snow, peak upon peak jutting up into the paling sky. There was not a hint of what was assuredly earth and rock and tree beneath their gleaming white slopes. There was only snow and ice. The mountains marched away to the north and to the south in close rank, shoulder to shoulder, immovable and unscalable for leagues upon leagues.

The memory of the soldiers in Ancalon returned to Jute's mind. Rank upon rank as endless as the mountains, marching in even more perfect order. Surely they would not be able to cross these peaks. At least, not with the snows so heavy on the slopes. Not yet.

As if to underscore the matter, the wind swooped them down in a heart-stopping drop. Jute's stomach felt like it leapt up his throat and into his mouth. They skimmed across the surface of the snow, angling up along the mountainside until it opened into a pass deep between two peaks, a narrow cleft that looked as if it had been made with a blow from some gigantic axe. Snow billowed up in their wake, shining and flashing in a cloud of whirling flakes.

Here. Here it is. The Pass of Rone.

They were flying so low now that Jute could almost kick at the top of the snow with his feet. He could not tell how deep the snow was in the pass, but judging from the angles of the slopes on either side, it would not be much deeper than the top of a wagon wheel. The pass wound about through the mountains like an uncertain snake, turning this way and that and never going straight for very long. No sunlight fell here, and the snow glimmered blue with shadow.

"I'm going to be sick," moaned the ghost. "All these twists and turns. Can't this fool wind fly straight? This is worse than a drunk carter on a Saturday night. Oh, my poor stomach."

Wind? said Jute somewhat anxiously. *You will put us down sometime soon, won't you? Not that I mind how you fly. I'm concerned about Declan. He's all right, isn't he? Perhaps he's still frozen like a statue. Something happened to him back there.*

Oh, his heart's still beating, said the wind carelessly. *Isn't that enough?*

No, I don't think so. We should stop and—

But at that moment there came a terrible rumbling behind them. Behind them and higher up on the mountainsides.

Mustn't stop now, said the wind.

The wind was right. It would have been extremely unwise to have stopped, for the mountains were falling down. At least that's what it looked like to Jute when he glanced back. The slopes on either side of the pass were collapsing. Hurtling down in crashing waves of white. Slabs of ice catapulted through the air. Snow exploded up in fountains of sparkling powder as the avalanche slammed down into the pass. The mountains thundered with the sound of it all. Booming and echoing and calling.

"It's the snow," said Jute out loud.

One of my favorite tricks in winter, said the wind smugly. *Better than toppling chimneypots.*

And it'll fill the pass even deeper. That'll keep his army back for a while. Well done, wind!

I was planning it all along.

The pass opened out into the west-facing slopes of the mountains, which descended from crag to crag and then from hill to ever-lower hill until they were swooping over the deep divide of a familiar-looking land.

"The Rennet Valley," said Jute in great excitement. "Wind! Please, please put us down. We must see to Declan. At once!"

No. There are still miles to go. Places to see. Chimney pots to blow down!

Put us down at once.

No!

At once! Do you hear me?

You needn't shout, said the wind. *Though, where is the rhyme to your wishes? First you are burbling with delight at being whisked away from that tower, overflowing with joy that those smelly little ravens did not catch you, and deliriously happy at my brilliance in bringing down the avalanches. Now you desire I desist and place you on the ground. The ground, of all places! Inexplicable.*

It's not that.

I know when I'm not wanted. On the ground. At once!

With a breezing *hmmph!* the wind set them down. It dropped them from several feet up so that Jute and Declan fell in a patch of icy mud. The wind blew away in a grump and left them in silence. Jute dragged Declan by the arms out of the mud. The man was a dead weight, his eyes shut and his face white.

"Wake up!" said Jute. "Wake up! Oh, stones and shadows. It's no use. He's asleep, though how anyone could have slept through being blown halfway across Tormay is a mystery to me. What'll we do?"

"A fire and a bite to eat sounds good to me," said the ghost, poking its head out of Jute's knapsack. "Not that they'll do me any good, but I'll enjoy watching them do you some good."

"Good idea, ghost. Maybe a fire will warm Declan and wake him up."

"That's me," said the ghost somewhat mournfully. "Full of good ideas, but mostly for other folks."

The wind had set them down on the upper slopes of the valley, just on the edge of a forest. It was cold, and the morning sunlight was weak and pale and did nothing to dispel the chill lingering from the night. Jute dragged Declan a little ways farther until they were under the pines. The snow was only a dusting beneath the shelter of the trees, and there were plenty of dead branches and pine needles lying about for fuel. Jute heaped together a pile and set a spark to it. The flames leapt up and crackled merrily.

"Looks like it feels warm," said the ghost. "Warm and comfortable. You've been up all night. Feel tired, don't you? Eyelids heavy? I imagine you'll nod off to sleep now and the forest will catch on fire. You and Declan along with it. Burned to a frazzle. Where'll that leave me? Alone. Alone, I tell you, and friendless in an unfriendly world."

"Don't be so gloomy. Declan will wake up, you'll see. We'll have some breakfast and then we'll be off."

Jute rummaged about in his knapsack. All he could find was an onion and some stale bread. Not the most inspiring meal, but he wasn't about to say anything to that effect, for the ghost was watching him closely.

"Onion and bread," said the ghost.

"It tastes delicious," said Jute stoutly.

Declan woke just when Jute was finishing the last few bites of onion.

"Onions?" said Declan, levering himself up on one elbow.

"Not you too," said Jute, but he grinned, delighted.

Color ebbed back into Declan's face. He held his hands out to the fire.

"How long was I out?" he said.

"A couple hours."

"More than three hours," said the ghost. "I was counting. It was either that or do a lot of screaming."

Declan reached inside the collar of his shirt and fished out the necklace. The pearl nestled in his hand, warm and glowing with the light it caught from the fire and the few meager rays of sunlight that pierced the branches above them. The ghost drifted closer to him and gazed avidly at the pearl.

"I think this saved my life." Declan touched the pearl with one finger. "I could feel him at the edge of my mind. The duke. I couldn't move. Could hardly breathe. It was as if I were surrounded by an abyss. Right on the edge of nothingness. And he was about to push me off. But this held me fast. He didn't like that. And he knew what it was. I could feel it. He hates the sea."

"The sea gave you that?" said Jute somewhat shyly.

"A gift and a burden at the same time. Twice the sea's saved my life now, so I can't deny her wishes. She's kept me bound to your path. Wherever you go."

"I'm sorry for that—but thank you."

Declan looped the necklace back under his collar and let it slide out of sight. "I owe it to you. I don't usually murder children, so I suppose that particular guilt will last the rest of my life. Besides, you took my part against the hawk's advice." He paused, and then said in a rather flat voice, "We didn't rescue her, did we?"

569

"No," said Jute.

"Decidedly no," said the ghost.

"I can't remember all of what happened, particularly after the duke appeared." Declan fell silent, staring down at the embers of the fire.

"Well, there's nothing left to do, is there?" said the ghost briskly. "No reason for long faces. We tried our best. Didn't work. Clean conscience and all that. We should just run along home—er, do either of you have a home?—and settle down to a life of peace and quiet. Put in a garden, grow some tomatoes, argue with the neighbor about his blasted goat that's always eating the dahlias." The ghost rubbed its hands together. "Right. Let's be off. After all, those crows might show up."

"Yes, let's be off. To Hearne first, I suppose. We need to warn the regent, and then the duchies."

"What?" said the ghost, looking disgusted. "What about the tomatoes and some peace and quiet?"

"What about the hawk and the wolf?" said Jute.

Declan got to his feet. For a moment he looked as if he was going to topple over. His face whitened and he swallowed hard several times. "I don't fancy explaining to that wolf how we managed to not rescue Giverny. I don't suppose you could call up the wind and just whisk us off to Hearne?"

"I don't think so. I thought about that while you were still asleep. The wind's gone. I think it's irritated with me and pretending I don't exist. We'll have to walk."

They made decent time as the day progressed, for there was less and less snow the further west they went. The ground was frozen in most places. They crossed an ice-bound creek and found a narrow carter's path. The wind must have dropped them a good deal south of the village of Ostfall. Habitations in this part of the valley were few and far between. Ostfall, of course, would not be an option for them, Declan pointed out, but any other village, or even a house, would be welcome, as they needed food.

"And horses," said Jute.

Later in the afternoon, they did come to a house. A small house built of thatch and stone and tucked away in a canyon. A thin-faced woman answered the door, held it open a crack, and cautiously inspected them. Three children clutched her skirts and also inspected them, but from a much lower angle.

"Don't have much use for coin," she said. "Seein' how we trade with mutton an' wool. My man'll be back any moment now from the fold. He ain't in good humor these days, what with the foxes an' all."

She made as if to shut the door, but Declan said, "Perhaps double, mistress? Might be a rainy day when some silver'll come in handy."

"Double?" She nodded at that, but shut the door on them anyway. A shutter swung open on the window beside the door and two small faces peeped over the sill and continued their inspection. A third small face made a brief appearance but then quickly disappeared in a wail and what sounded like a chair falling over.

"Garn," said one of the remaining small faces. The second small face agreed, but in words even less intelligible. Evidently, some conclusion was then reached, for both faces smiled benignly down upon Declan and Jute.

"Well, one less thing to worry about," said Declan. "Though I've found it a good policy not to turn one's back on children, even if they seem friendly, for that's when the rotten fruit starts flying."

"Oh?" said Jute somewhat guiltily. He could recall quite a few instances when the Juggler's children, he among them, had climbed up onto roofs to pelt passersby with rotten vegetables. It was just something one did when boredom set in.

The door opened again.

"Where's the silver then?" said the woman.

The sun was overhead by that time, and they continued along the carter's path as it followed every rise and fall of the valley's edge. It was still cold. The wind blowing along beside them did not help matters much, for it got under their collars and put a chill in the sunlight. Jute tried talking to the wind, but it would have none of him, regardless of how he cajoled and pleaded. They would have to keep on walking. Thankfully enough, their stomachs were full of the cold mutton and cheese the woman had packed for them, and the memory of the dark tower was not so stark anymore, though Jute often noticed a grim expression on Declan's face.

"We'll have to steal some horses," said Declan. "Otherwise, it'll be days to Hearne at this rate."

"I don't condone theft," said the ghost primly.

"All right, then. You can stay behind while we gallop off on our stolen horses."

"I don't condone it, but I never said I wouldn't enjoy the fruits of it. Besides, you'll need me along to instruct you on morals and virtues, seeing that you're sadly deficient. I recall a lecture I once gave on the subject, titled 'Why Boys Must Behave.' Or maybe it was called 'The Breakdown of Society Caused by the Common Boy.'"

"I wasn't the one to suggest stealing horses," said Jute.

"If you're patient enough, I'll remember both lectures. Doubtless, you can't wait to hear 'em."

"We can't wait," said a voice from somewhere above them.

"Hawk!" said Jute.

The bird swooped down and landed in a flutter of wings on Jute's shoulder. He hunched there, his feathers in disarray, head down.

"You didn't rescue her, obviously," he said gloomily, "I would've known from the earth if you had, but the earth has been silent. Tell me what happened."

They told him as they walked along the frozen ground.

"This isn't what I expected," said the hawk when they had finished telling him their story. "Though, to be honest, I'm not sure what I was expecting, other than some vain hope that you might rescue her. We had to try. We had to try!" He repeated the words angrily, but almost as if he spoke to himself alone.

"But did I hear you correctly," continued the hawk, "that this so-called duke of Mizra said he was hunting for an answer to what the death of the anbeorun meant? At the university? There's only ever been one university in all of Tormay, and that, of course, in Hearne. And then he said that you came three hundred years afterward?"

"I don't think he said what their death meant. Rather, what their death could do. What could be done with their death."

"At the university," said the hawk. "He was at the university. Three hundred years ago. Three hundred years? Goodness gracious me. Could it be?" His claws bit into Jute's shoulder and the boy yelped out loud.

"What?" said the ghost. "What is it? You've remembered something? A clue? A lost word? A recipe for delicious roast duck?"

"The duke of Mizra must be the same person as the wizard Scuadimnes. It makes a sort of dreadful sense."

"Scua-who?" said the ghost.

"Scuadimnes," said Jute, pleased to know something that the ghost did not. "He was a professor at the university in Hearne. He was in charge of the archives, and they say he was also responsible for the destruction of the university."

"Correct," said the hawk, nodding approvingly. "I daresay you heard the tale from Severan? Good, good. You do listen sometimes. Scuadimnes was a servant of the Dark. He had no history, no past, nothing that might identify where he came from, for if you can discern the path upon which a man has trod, you can then predict where he will walk in the future. But when Scuadimnes appeared in Hearne three hundred years ago, no one knew him. He taught at the university for years without bringing attention to himself, other than the odd fact that he had an encyclopedic memory for words. The anbeorun paid no attention to him. There was no reason to. We were concerned more with watching the borders of Tormay, for there were rumors of a coming Darkness in those days. The sea in the west, the earth ranging up and down the length of the Morn Mountains and wandering out into the wastelands beyond, my master the wind blowing about the icelands in the north. Fire we had not heard from in many long years, as he had always been preoccupied with journeying far beneath the surface of the earth, down in the deep, dark places where the older mysteries of the world sleep. We paid no attention to Hearne and the comings and goings of a solitary professor at the university."

"But why did he destroy the place?" asked Jute. "Why did he kill the king? I always wondered about that when Severan first told me the story. There seemed no reason for it."

"Oh, but there's an excellent reason. The Dark cannot create. It never could and it never can. Therefore, it hates everything that is with an everlasting hate. It cannot abide life. All the servants of Nokhoron Nozhan follow in his path and, like their master, they delight in killing and stealing and destroying. That is the sign of the Dark. However, my master always suspected that the destruction of the university and the death of the king—the destruction of Hearne itself—were not the chief objectives of Scuadimnes. Perhaps they camouflaged his true objective?"

"So what was the real objective?" said the ghost, all agog at the hawk's words. "I, er, have an idea already myself, but it's always nice to hear someone else's opinion. Professional courtesy."

"I wasn't aware of such an obligation," said the hawk dryly. "Your recent encounter on the tower, young Jute, lends weight to my old master's suspicion. You see, the main purpose of the university, of wizards down through history to a man, has always been the hunt for hidden knowledge—whether it be a single lost word from an ancient language, a forgotten book, a song, or a poem. My master suspected that Scuadimnes came to the university to find something extremely important. Something dangerous. A deadly secret. Obviously, the *Gerecednes* would be the prime candidate, for it was rumored to hold lore reaching back to the founding of the world. Thankfully, it sounds like he did not locate the book. If the duke and Scuadimnes are one and the same, though, then perhaps he ultimately did find what he was looking for. Bits and pieces of knowledge. Words. Clues that he cobbled together. I daresay his search had something to do with the anbeorun. That would seem likely from the duke's own words. And from the fact that he holds the earth captive in his tower and seeks to end Jute's life. The death of the anbeorun. What would it mean? Well, I think we know what it means, and I suppose that the duke, whoever he is—whatever he is—knows as well."

"The *Gerecednes*," muttered the ghost thoughtfully. "What an odd name. There's something about it that makes me nervous. But what about the girl? I don't suppose she can hold out for long. Must be having a tough go of it, I'd imagine. Horrible! That dark tower was a nasty place." But then it abruptly stopped talking, for it saw the expression on Declan's face.

"She isn't lost yet," growled Declan. "You don't know Farrows. At any rate, she told us what to do, and that's what we're going to do." Declan lengthened his stride until Jute was forced to half-run in order to keep up, the ghost drifting along in their wake.

"As you say," said the hawk. "You and the young wolf think alike. I left him prowling about the walls of Ancalon, though he had harsh words for you. She'll survive, we can only hope, and we go to kick the duchies awake. Of course. Of course." The bird shook his head sadly. "I see no other path at the moment. If I must die, then I'll die fighting on a battlefield. But that doesn't hold for you, young Jute."

"Thank you," said Jute, who had no desire to die on a battlefield, or anywhere else.

"You're the only one of the anbeorun left in the world of men. The guardian of the sea has rarely left her depths since the days when Tormay was young, when the first king ruled from Hearne, and who knows where her allegiance lies? She's an inscrutable lady of devious designs and has never shown much interest in the affairs of men. The master of fire has not been seen for hundreds of years. Perhaps he's still wandering the secret ways far under the mountains? And the earth? We could not rescue her."

"I wouldn't be so sure about the sea," said Declan quietly.

CHAPTER ONE HUNDRED & SIX
RECRUITING FOR THE GUARD

The man in the tavern doorway paused to give more effect to his entrance. He was dressed in the blue and black of the Guard of Hearne, a satchel over his shoulder and a pennoned spear in his hand. The hubbub inside died away and heads turned toward him. The herald, for that is what he was, drew himself up and cleared his throat.

"Hear ye, hear ye," he said.

"We're hearing ye," said an old man sitting nearby.

"Be it known that the Lord High Captain of the Guard seeks brave young men for enlistment in the ranks of the Guard. Adventure, excitement, romance! Excellent pay, the best of training guaranteed to turn even the most cowardly weakling into the epitome of manhood."

"I'd like to see one o' them Guard fellers do a day behind the plow," called out a burly farmer. Laughter filled the tavern. The herald frowned and then raised his voice once again, determined not to be done in by a roomful of country bumpkins.

"A wage of two silvers a month with possibilities of bonuses and danger pay, plus a silver on the occasion of the regent's birthday. Now, who could turn such an offer down, particularly"—and here the herald smiled in what he thought was a sympathetic fashion—"particularly when the price of corn is what it is these days."

There were some grumbling at this, but several of the younger men in the room, fourth or fifth sons in large families burdened with many uncles and older cousins, nodded thoughtfully.

"What better way to spend your youthful years than in service to Hearne and our glorious regent?" said the herald.

"Oh, stow your gab!" hollered the tavern keeper from behind his bar. "Have a pint of ale and let decent folks get back to drinking!"

The herald opened and closed his mouth like a gasping fish, momentarily discomfited by this attack from an unexpected quarter, but then he rallied. "Ale? Of course!" he hollered back. "A round for the house on the purse of the Guard!"

A roar of approval went up, and the herald's back was slapped by many a callused hand as he made his way up to the bar. He ensconced himself there with a foaming tankard of ale in each fist. As the evening wore on, a succession of farmers' sons sidled up to him to talk in whispered tones.

And so it went in those days, while the skies grew colder and the days shorter. The heralds rode their horses from village to village along the Rennet Valley east of Hearne, as well as among the fishing villages up and down the coast. They spun their stories well, their pitches and pleas, and, if they judged their audience meek enough, their browbeatings and stern hectoring. They spoke glowingly of the regent, of Hearne's tall towers and majestic walls; they confided over glasses of wine about that most awesome of figures, Owain Gawinn, the Lord Captain of the Guard, even though in reality they had probably never themselves had the privilege to speak much with such an august personage, unless it had been things such as "No, sir!" and "Yes, sir!" and "Right away, sir!"

"Forty-seven," said Bordeall.

"Forty-seven?" Owain frowned and leaned back in his chair. "I'd been hoping for closer to a hundred. Two hundred. Bah."

"I'm pleased enough with forty-seven," said the other. "It's forty-seven more than we had before, and that's nothing to sneeze at. Even one man can be enough to turn the tide of battle. You know that."

"You're right, you're right."

Outside the window on the practice ground, the air rang with the shouts of the sergeants and the gasps of the recruits as they panted for air. Sword clanged on sword, or more dully against the rows of battered wooden posts standing in the center of the grounds. As always, several neighborhood children were perched on top of the stonewall rimming the practice ground, yelling advice and shouting insults. The autumn sun shone down, not providing any heat to the proceedings, but that was fine as the recruits were sweating due to their exertions.

"Not too bad," said Owain grudgingly. "They'll be dreaming of swords rather than plows and fishing nets soon enough. Now, tell me, old friend, is there any gossip on the street about our recent exploits?"

"Nothing as of yet."

"Knowing nothing makes me nervous. I'd much rather know my enemy was out stalking me than know nothing at all. Frankly, I'm disappointed with the Guild. I thought them capable of more than this inaction. Don't they have a dread enforcer, some cold-blooded killer from Aum—"

"Aum's a ruin," said Bordeall mildly. "Has been for over two hundred years."

"I know. But the idea of coming from a ruined city lends mystique to the legend, doesn't it? A murdering ghost of a man from a dead city? That's probably enough to put the fear of the Dark into any self-respecting thief."

"They call him the Knife, is what I've heard. An assassin. A man conversant with any weapon at hand."

"Just the sort who should be in the Guard."

"No." Bordeall shook his head. "Not such a man. He wouldn't bend easy to orders. If he did, men as him are the sort who go off and do horrible, needful things that no one else can do. And then, when the danger has been defeated and men live in more peaceful times, such a man is shunned, an embarrassment to his country and to his fellow man. Times of peace don't care to remember the times of blood."

Owain laughed. "I didn't take you for a philosopher, Bordeall. Have a care. Otherwise you might end up in the salons of Highneck Rise, entertaining the lords and ladies with fine words."

The afternoon afforded Owain a certain amount of irritation. After two hours of inspecting a string of horses from Vomaro and arguing prices with the trader, Owain was left with the nagging suspicion that the blackguard had bested him. True, the horses were of good stock and well-broken, but surely he should not have paid so much gold.

"An' another herd to be finished breaking next month," said the trader. He patted his fat stomach and eyed Owain blandly. "Any interest, my lord?"

"Interest enough," growled Owain.

He had always prided himself on his well-shuttered face, but somehow the trader had discerned that the Guard needed the horses. Needed them badly. And there was something dishonest in the man's eyes. Smiling, the trader bowed himself out of Owain's presence, and Owain stomped off, up the stone steps behind the armory to the top of the wall, where he strode back and forth and contented himself with the thought that it was the Guild's gold he was spending and not his own. Still, he did not like being made a fool of. Curse the man. Curse all Vomarone swine with their fawning, foppish ways. But the horses were well-broken. They would take easily to the drill.

Owain stared out across the green slopes of the Rennet Valley and frowned.

The Farrows.

They trained the best horses in all of the duchies of Tormay. Even the regent would admit that. But it had been a long time since the Farrows had come to Hearne. He had heard no word of them. Cullan Farrow was fair in trading. He drove a shrewd bargain, but he was an honest man. All of Owain's favorite steeds in the Guard stables had come from Farrow stock.

It began to rain—a cold, driving rain that seemed to slant down from every possible direction so that it was no use attempting to hide under the narrow overhangs of parapet and tower and wall. Owain retreated back down the steps and sought refuge in the armory. The rain hammered against the window, turning the view of the city into a muddle of vague gray shapes. He sat at his desk and fiddled at his ledger in distraction, not thinking about the numbers and succeeding only in spilling ink on the paper and staining his shirt. Sibb would have something to say about that.

A knock sounded on the door.

"Enter," barked Owain.

Bordeall stuck his head in.

"They've returned," he said, his face expressionless. And before Owain had time to ask who "they" were, Hoon and Posle popped into the room, Hoon with a smirk on his face and Posle looking positively ill.

"You smell like a brewery," said Owain.

"Money well spent, guvnor," said Hoon. He navigated his way to the only other chair in the room, examined it for a moment as if to make sure it wouldn't try to escape, and then flopped down. "Money well spent. Had to do a spot of mixing with the locals. Do as they do, that sort of thing. Was Posle's idea, and not half bad. Sharp little feller. Puts away the ale with the best of 'em. A tankard clutched in each fist. He stood 'em down. Brave as a soldier on the field, he lifted first the one then t'other. Drained 'em dry to the last drop, and then what'd he do? Why, he hollered for another round. Fill 'em up, cully, sez he, an' I won't have it any other way."

"I'm not interested in hearing about your drinking," said Owain. "Pull yourself together, man. Any news of our theft?"

"Theft? Oh, aye. Our theft. Listen close, guvnor." Hoon leaned forward, laying one finger alongside his nose in a confiding manner. A wave of ale fumes washed over Owain. "The word's on the street. Guild's put out the mark on ye. Well, not ye specifically, guvnor, for they don't know who did the dastardly deed, so they can't say it's ye that did it, if ye follow my reasoning. But whoever did the deed, that's who they want. A hundred pieces of gold for news that leads to your door, an' two hundred for your skin."

"The Silentman's furious," said Posle. "Dead or alive, he wants you." The little man gulped and considered his words. He wrung his hands. "Us. Dead or alive, he wants us. That means me!"

"Aye," said Hoon. "It were all they were talking about down in the taverns of Fishgate. Guild an' no Guild alike. Enterprising folks we have here in the city. Many of 'em already discussing how they'd be spending the gold. Mebbe the posh folks in Highneck Rise are talking of it, too? Never met a rich folk yet that weren't grabby for more."

"A hundred pieces of gold." Bordeall's eyebrows went up. "I'd turn you in myself for money like that, but there's the problem of my own guilt. Stones and shadows. That's more money than most honest men see in a lifetime."

"Well, now we know the news is out," said Owain. "But no word of our particulars? That fat man who wriggled out of our hands? Nothing to tell from him of our looks or voices or anything like that?"

"Nothing we heard, guvnor. Nobody said a thing about that."

Owain nodded. "Can't say I've ever had a price on my head. At any rate, keep your mouths shut, particularly when you're at your ale. It wouldn't do for the Guild to be looking to the Guard for its culprit. We'll ride this out, and then—" He banged his fist down on his desk. "—And then, by stone, we'll cut their purse again."

"My lord," said Posle. "If I could, er, have a word alone?"

"No need. We're all comrades here." Owain chuckled. "Comrades in crime. Speak up, man."

"My woman an' me, we've been talking, my lord, an' we feel maybe it's high time we see other parts of Tormay. City life ain't all it's cracked up to be, an' I'm hankering after some land in the country. Put our roots down. It's old age, you see. Maybe grow some of them cucumber trees and tomatoes. Some goats for milk an' cheese—"

"No," said Owain.

"No?" said Posle, looking crestfallen.

"No. And cucumbers don't grow on trees. So, definitely no."

Owain arrived home that evening in good humor, despite the rain growing colder as the sun fell behind the curtain of clouds and the edge of the sea. He shut the gate behind him and walked up the path. It was quiet inside, but he could smell dinner. He followed the scent into the kitchen and found his wife there.

"Feels almost like snow," he said, kissing Sibb on the cheek.

"Early winter?" she said.

"If we're unlucky." He paused here and scowled. "I think this year is not proving to be the luckiest of years. How're the children? How's the little one?"

"Quiet, which makes me nervous. They've been down in the basement, rummaging about, and then up in the attic for most of the afternoon, doing something with wood and rope and an old pulley. I didn't want to look too closely, as they seemed extremely pleased with themselves, and no one's come running in tears or streaming blood, so that's all right."

"A pulley," said Owain, mystified.

"Yes, a pulley."

"I suppose it's better I don't know. As long as they don't break their necks, or someone else's neck, for that matter."

He wandered over to the stove and twitched the lid off a pot.

"Stewed chicken? With dumplings?"

"Get your fingers out of there. It's far from done yet. You're looking smug. What have you been up to?"

"Up to? My dear, you wound me."

Realization sparked in her eyes. "You robbed the Guild. Tell me."

He told her. In great detail. She was, after all, his wife.

"And that's why, my love, the coffers of the Guard are full. The Thieves Guild is more generous than the regent. And they're generous in their bounties, as well. I've one on my head for a hundred piece of gold. Though, the Guild doesn't know it's me, of course."

"For that kind of money," said Sibb, "I should turn you in myself."

CHAPTER ONE HUNDRED & SEVEN
CONVINCING OWAIN GAWINN

They stole horses from a prosperous-looking farm early the next morning. Rain slashed down, so cold that it teetered on the edge of freezing into sleet. A light shone in the window of the farmhouse on the other side of the yard from the barn.

"You're sure there's no dog?" said Declan.

"If there is, he's asleep in the house," said Jute. He tilted his head to one side, trying to listen more closely to the wind. "Definitely no dog outside."

"No dog," said the ghost, drifting up out of the rain. "I just checked. Assorted chickens, two roosters, cows, pigs, and—yes—there are several horses. For the life of me, I can't understand why I'm aiding and abetting your criminal activity. Low company begets low character, I suppose."

The chickens managed a few sleepy clucks when Declan and Jute crept into the barn. The place was deliciously dry and warm with the scent of livestock, hay, and oats. One of the cows rolled an irritated eye at them, stamping a bit.

"They need to be milked," said Declan. "And soon. The farmer'll be out in less than ten minutes, I'd bet. Quickly now. That gray for you and the sorrel for me. Not the best of horses, but we can't be choosy. Ah, there's bridles and blankets hanging on that wall. I like this fellow. He keeps an orderly place."

"Are we, er, leaving money for him?" said Jute. "Or are we stealing these horses? Let's leave some money."

"It's still stealing," said the ghost.

Declan placed two gold pieces on top of a railing in the sorrel's stall.

"But at great profit to the farmer," he said.

They reached the top of the Rennet Gap that afternoon. The rain had continued through the day, sometimes mixed with sleet and hail. Jute's hands were numb on the reins, and he could not feel his nose and ears. The wind came at them hard at the top of the gap, howling through the oak trees and bending what little grass there was over until it lay flat along the ground. Jute tried several times to speak with the wind, but it must have still been in a bad temper, for it refused to answer.

"We'll make Hearne by nightfall," said Declan. "Not bad for a farmer's nags."

"If we aren't attacked by bandits or wolves or washed away by a flood," said the ghost darkly. "All quite likely, judging by our luck so far."

Jute did not say anything, but he looked back as they stood for a moment at the top of the rise. All of the Rennet Valley to the east was invisible to the eye, misted with rain, silvery gray, dense, and impenetrable. He could have been looking out over a great abyss, the edge of the world, rather than across the slopes of a valley. There was something out there. He was sure of it. Something deep within the mist. Something coming closer. He shivered and turned away.

The horses kept up a good pace, despite having run all day, and Declan urged them along with care. They stopped for a quick rest and a bite to eat in a copse of oaks, more for the sake of the horses than for themselves. The horses cropped eagerly at the meager grass poking up through the muddy earth. Rain dripped down from the branches overhead.

"Ah, onions, cheese, and stale bread," said the ghost, sniffing the air. "An intriguing meal. Gourmet, robust, and pleasing to the palate. Pleasing, that is, if one has no sense of taste."

"Hurry," said the hawk grumpily. "Food! We have no time for such things."

The horses struck out with renewed vigor. They passed through fields of blackened cornstalks protruding from the ground like fingers flayed of their flesh and frozen by the winter into death. The rain seemed to be falling horizontally now due to the force of the wind. Jute hunched his head down into the sodden folds of his cloak and tried not to think about how miserable and cold he was. He wondered where Severan was. Perhaps back at the Stone Tower. Or maybe further north at the old cottage he had spoken about.

Somewhere deep inside of Jute, hope flared like a tiny, warming flame. A cottage. It sounded like a lovely sort of thing. A bed, his own bed, made of wood and having a mattress stuffed fat with feathers, not straw or hay. A fireplace with a spit mounted over the grate. Perhaps a chair or two. Several chests full of marvelous things such as woolen blankets, a pair of boots for the winter months, a fishing pole (he had never fished with a pole before, but he had always thought it a wonderful idea). And, of course, one entire chest devoted to food, with a couple of well-waxed cheeses stinking deliciously, a string of sausages, a side of bacon wrapped in oilcloth, turnips, potatoes, and withered winter apples. And onions.

Jute's stomach growled. He still wasn't tired of onions.

The moon was high in the east and the sun was long sunk into its sleep when the walls of Hearne came into view. The walls were washed pale by moonlight but the countryside around them was lost in darkness. Torches flared above the main gates. The Rennet River murmured and flowed below the wall, swollen with its winter weight and riding high beneath the bridge that crossed over to the gates.

"Hello the gate!" called out Declan. They clattered over the bridge and pulled the horses to a halt beneath the wall. There was only silence in response. He yelled again, but still there was no answer.

The wind tickled at Jute's ear. It tickled him again, harder. He turned.

"Look at the mist," he said, frowning.

"Ah, mist," said the ghost. "Frequently seen hovering above bodies of water, moors, marshes, and other terrain features. Most people don't know this, but mist is caused by the—how can I say this delicately?—digestive habits of flocks of birds during certain key hours of the early morning and late evening. I often lectured about this phenomenon. Mist occurs when—"

"The mist is moving."

"Yes," said the ghost. "It does that when blown by the wind. You are even more uneducated than I previously believed, aren't you?"

"The wind is blowing the other way, you nitwit."

"Really!" huffed the ghost.

"He's right," said the hawk. "It's moving this way and it shouldn't be. Declan!"

"Travelers at the gate!" yelled Declan.

He urged his horse up against the gate and kicked savagely at the wood, but the noise was inconsequential, lost in the clamor of the river below them and the wind moaning against the wall. Behind them, further down the river, the mist grew and gathered. It shone a dirty gray under the moonlight. The mist surged forward, even though the wind and rain blew against it.

"Open the gate!" said Jute frantically. He knew what was inside the mist. He could feel it by the prickling of the skin on his neck and the trembling in his hands.

A face stared down at them from the top of the wall. The torchlight gleamed on an iron helm and the shaft of a spear.

"The gates don't open until the morning," said a voice. "It's the law of the city. Go away."

"Open the blasted gate!" said Declan.

"Can't. It's the law. You mustn't break it. That's why it's the law. Go away, I say."

The hawk flew up to the top of the wall and settled onto the parapet near the soldier. "Open the gate now, little man," said the hawk. "Or I'll gut you like a rabbit." The man gaped at the bird and then abruptly disappeared.

"The mist is getting closer," said Jute.

"Moving faster, too," said the ghost. And with a strangled moan it dove into Jute's knapsack and vanished. The mist had reached the bridge. It boiled up and reached out gray arms along the timbers. Tendrils of vapor crept along the planking of the bridge toward them. Jute's horse tossed its head, prancing uneasily in place, foam dripping from its jaw. Its eyes rolled whitely.

"Keep your reins tight," said Declan. "Ghost, you'll stay out of sight and keep quiet. Do you hear me?"

"Why is it," said the ghost, his voice muffled inside the knapsack, "that I'm the one who must always be staying out of sight? I feel like an unwanted child. The ugly stepchild kept locked up in the cellar with nothing to eat but stale crusts and water. I'm the toad of the party, that's me."

"Stop whining. You're a secret asset. A hidden weapon. That's why you have to stay concealed."

"Ah," said the ghost happily. "I knew it. I'm a hidden weapon."

And then the gates swung open. They urged the horses through. Jute could not bear to look behind him. Torches flared around them. The gates boomed shut. Spears shone in the firelight and he was aware of faces staring at them. A young man strode forward, cloak swirling around him. He stopped in front of Declan. His eyes widened.

"The Knife!" he said. His face darkened and his hand dropped to his sword.

"Bridd," said Declan coldly.

"I should have you thrown into jail, you murdering, double-crossing thief!"

More soldiers appeared out of the darkness, closing ranks behind the young man. A strange smell seemed to grow in the air—an odor of stagnant water, of mud and decaying things. The hawk settled onto Jute's shoulder, wings outstretched to flex and then fold closed. The bird seemed bigger than usual, monstrous almost in the wavering shadows and light of the torches.

"Arodilac Bridd," said the hawk, "son of Tenac Bridd and Dylas, sister of Nimman Botrell. The wind knew you when you were a child, stealing plum wine from the cellar of your father's manor and so causing the dismissal of his steward. That was poorly done. Shall I remind you of other such matters?"

Arodilac's mouth fell open. He stared at the hawk.

"Wh-who are you?" he stammered.

"Take us to your captain!" said the hawk.

"No need for that," drawled a voice.

A man strolled out of the darkness and into the torchlight. The soldiers, Arodilac included, sprang to attention. The man was tall and lean, his black hair closely cropped to his head. His gaze rested for a moment on the hawk before settling on Declan.

"Owain Gawinn, at your service," he said. "Though I'm afraid I can't be at your service. Things are busy here. I'll overlook your untimely entrance, as it's a matter of Guard discipline, a lack thereof, rather than anything to do with you. Welcome to Hearne. Good evening."

He made as if to go, but Declan stepped forward.

"My lord Gawinn," he said. "Hear us out. We've journeyed all the way from the duchy of Mizra to see you."

"Mizra, you say?" The captain nodded politely, as if to acknowledge the length and rarity of such a trip. "Come see me in the morning, then. I'd be pleased to hear any news you have of the eastern lands."

He began walking away into the darkness. The strange smell in the air intensified and what little light there was from the torches was beginning to shrink, its edges damped and drowned by the growing mist.

The pearl inside Declan's shirt warmed. A thought nudged at him, and then he knew what to say to gain the captain's interest.

"It's been a long time since the Farrows have come trading horses to Hearne," he called after the captain. "Has it not?"

Owain Gawinn paused in his tracks and turned.

"What's it to you?"

"My name's Declan Farrow," said Declan.

They were shown into the captain's study, a spartan room on the second floor of the gate tower. The door swung shut behind them, and Owain waved them to chairs. He sat down behind his desk. A fire burned cheerily on the grate.

"Declan Farrow, eh?" said Owain. In the bright light of the study, his face looked tired. Despite that, curiosity sparked in his eyes. "I've heard the stories. Who hasn't?"

"Stories can sometimes be just that: stories. Badly told, half told—"

"I've got it," interrupted Owain. He snapped his fingers. "You're that Knife fellow. One of my soldiers with a bit of Guild connection described you, and it's been bothering me ever since I clapped eyes on you. From Aum. Yes, that's what it was."

"And Aum in ruins for three hundred years," said the hawk coldly. "A haunt of owls and jackals. We didn't come here to discuss the Guild or the tales of Declan Farrow."

Owain stared at the hawk. He opened his mouth and then shut it.

"I don't work for the Guild anymore, my lord," said Declan. "But, regardless of how I've been known, I've always been Declan Farrow. The last of the Farrows, save one, for the Farrows are all dead."

"Dead? I was hoping you could tell me where they were. I need horses for the Guard. Dead, you say? That's terrible news!"

Jute stirred nervously in his chair. He got up and went to the one window. There was nothing to be seen outside except the dark bulk of the wall angling away into the night. The glow of torchlight illuminated the span of the gate below. But mist was drifting over the top of the wall, and the light began to blur into pearly translucence with its approach. The skin on the back of Jute's neck prickled uncomfortably.

"Murdered, every one of them."

The pearl warmed against Declan's skin. He blinked, no longer seeing the study. He could see the face of the creature from the top of the tower in Ancalon. The sceadu. The blade in its hand. The scene from his memory abruptly changed and he saw the regent's ballroom. Crowded with fear. Screams and staring faces. The sceadu stalking across the floor. Candles and jewels shining in the darkness. The young woman standing alone in the middle of the ballroom.

"They were murdered by a man who isn't a man. A thin-faced man who kills for the love of killing."

A frown crossed Owain's face. "This man, does he hunt with hounds? Massive beasts?"

"The same."

Owain jumped to his feet and strode to the door. He yanked it open.

"You there, sergeant. Find Bordeall and send him up."

He slammed the door shut and flung himself back down in his chair.

"What do you know of this creature?"

"He serves the Dark," said the hawk. He fluttered up onto the back of Jute's chair. "He is a sceadu—a shadow, you would say in your younger tongue. A thing of ancient evil who must murder in order to live. He feeds on death. But he himself is only the emissary of a much more dreadful being."

Owain scowled at the hawk. "There are strange things in the world. A hawk that can speak is one of them. There are evil things, too; I'll readily admit that. Things we don't understand. Bears and ogres, wights and ghosts. I've heard stories of peculiar goings-on in the Morn Mountains and further north. Men themselves are capable of great evil. I've seen their handiwork. It's my job. Murder? Men take to it easily. Too easily, I'm afraid. But the Dark? I'm not sure I believe in the Dark. An old wives' tale, as far as I'm concerned. Scare the children into behaving. That's what I've always thought."

"I don't care what you think," said the hawk coldly. "And I doubt the Dark cares either. Things are what they are, regardless of what we believe or do not believe about them. Your opinion, pleasant as it may be, has no bearing on reality. The Dark has a purpose and an intent, and its servants walk this land. They have recently been within the walls of Hearne. Quite recently, captain, and this you know, if you are an honest man. Recall your memory to what occurred during the regent's ball."

The door opened and a burly, older man entered the room. "Ah, Bordeall," said the captain. "These fellows have just arrived from the east. They've some news of our nighttime marauders, and—"

The hawk interrupted him.

"You believe what I say, Gawinn. I can see it in your eyes. Don't waste words with me any longer. We've come to warn Hearne, to warn Tormay of the coming darkness. The sceadu and his hounds murdering in the night was only a herald of things to come. Behind him stands a much deadlier foe. His gaze has been on Tormay for many years and he's gathering an army in the east, beyond the Morn Mountains. Only the winter snows hold them back. The passes are blocked, but come the thaw, his army will march. They'll come to Hearne first, and Hearne will fall unless the duchies of Tormay stand with her."

"Shadows!" burst out Owain. "Yes, maybe I do believe in the Dark, or whatever you want to call it. But you're spinning quite a yarn. I suppose I'm to mobilize the Guard and warn the duchies just on the strength of a story from a talking bird." He snorted in disgust. "The regent'll laugh me out of the castle. And yet, hang it all. You've got me."

"Something's at the gate," said Jute nervously. He was still standing by the window, peering out into the night.

"Traders, most likely," rumbled Bordeall. "Queuing up for the morning."

Jute shot him a withering look.

"If there are any traders at the gate, then they're probably dead by now."

"And who are you?" asked Bordeall mildly.

"He's the reason why we're here," said the hawk. "He's the anbeorun Windan, the stillpoint of the wind, the lord of the sky, and one of the four guardians of Tormay."

There was a brief silence in the room, broken only by the crackling of the fire on the hearth. Owain slammed his fist down on the table.

"The stillpoint of the wind," he said, his face reddening. "The anbeorun? Yet another old wives' tale. Where am I? Back on my mother's knee, dribbling porridge? That's even sillier than the Dark. The guardian of the wind, my dead aunt. Huffing and puffing about the sky like a magic watchdog. You had me believing before, but now, Farrow or not, I've a mind to throw you out on your ears."

And at that point, the wind gusted down the chimney in a roar. The fire went out, showering sparks and coals through the darkness. The wind howled about the room. It hurled Owain's desk against one wall with a splintering crash and knocked him flying into a heap against another. Bordeall went tumbling, head over heels, hollering and cursing. A knife that had been lying on the desk whipped through the air and plunged into the wall planking with a quivering, belling note. Through it all, however, Jute, Declan, and the hawk remained where they were, with not a hair or a feather out of place. As abruptly as it begun, the wind died down. The room was silent. A few coals smoldered on the floor.

"You appear to be bleeding from your forehead," said the hawk politely. "What was that you were saying?"

Owain Gawinn took them straight to the regent's castle without any further ado. Guardsmen brought out horses for them, clattering across the stable yards beside the tower. Torchlight gleamed on bits and bridle iron. The horses stamped and tossed their manes, peevish at being rousted out of their warm stalls into the cold night.

"What did you mention about the gate?" said Owain, frowning at Jute. "Someone—something outside?"

"It's not there anymore." Jute could only smell the usual and familiar odors of Hearne: the thick scent of the horses, hay, manure, woodsmoke cooling in the air, and all the mixing stink of countless dinners that had recently been cooked and eaten in the surrounding neighborhood. His stomach mumbled in reminder that it had not had its dinner. "At least, I don't think it is."

"Not there?" said the hawk. "Then it—whatever it is—is somewhere else."

"Obviously," said the ghost from inside Jute's knapsack. "Aren't we a genius?"

"What did you say?" asked Owain.

"Nothing. Just, er, coughing." Jute coughed a few times. "Cold night air."

"Bordeall, double the watch on the wall." Owain swung up on top of his horse. "Send a patrol through the streets. Check the docks. Down through Fishgate and up to Highneck Rise. Every two hours. Better safe than not. Right. We're off to see the regent."

They clattered off through the dark streets of the city. Jute's horse proved to have an even bonier back than the farmer's old gray he had been riding. He hung on grimly and tried not to think unkindly of the creature. Happily enough, he was diverted as he looked about, his eyes falling on old and familiar places. Houses he had burgled. Walls he had climbed. Roofs he had clambered across. Streets and alleys he had wandered through with the other children of the Juggler's gang. With Lena, the twins, Wrin bumbling along with a smile on his fat, good-natured face. If only the children could see him now. It was good to be home.

584

Home.

As if he even knew what a home was like. Perhaps he could visit Severan at his house someday? The cottage on the coast. A fireplace and a view of the sea. A bench out in the garden, drenched in sunlight. It sounded restful. Peaceful and quiet. The attractiveness of the thought startled him.

"I must be getting old," he said to himself.

"What was that?" said the ghost suspiciously from inside the knapsack.

"Shh."

The mansions of Highneck Rise rose around them as the road wound higher through the city toward the castle towering against the sky. The night was clear and cold, and a full moon painted the edges of the castle towers with its light, creating in brushstrokes of luminance a skeletal construction of darkness and light. Here and there, the rectangles of windows spilled even brighter light out into the night. But beyond the castle, the shadows lay full and dark. Jute shivered. The last time he had been here, he had been running away. Running away through the darkness, hurrying to keep up with the lady. Levoreth Callas. The guardian of the earth.

Grooms appeared in the castle courtyard, silently and swiftly materializing from the shadows to take their reins. A page, nose high in the air, scurried down the steps and hurried over to Owain Gawinn's side to bow several times, bobbing his head like a bird, before trotting back up the steps and disappearing. Somewhere nearby, a fountain was flowing. Jute could hear the murmur of its water.

It was warm and quiet in the great hall. A fire burned in an enormous hearth at the far end of the hall. Its flicker illumined the sweep of stairs rising up on either side of the hearth, wide enough for five men to easily walk side by side. Jute remembered those stairs. They led up to the ballroom. He had come down the stairs at a tremendous pace. He remembered the shocked faces. The screams. The sceadu stalking across the polished expanse of the ballroom floor.

"Bit different this time," said Declan, as if he had read Jute's mind. He winked at the boy with something akin to sympathy on his face.

A steward floated silently across the floor toward them, bowed disdainfully to Owain, appeared to possibly notice Declan and Jute, and raised one eyebrow at the hawk perched on Jute's shoulder.

"The Lord Captain of the Guard and, er, associates," said the steward. He smoothed one hand down an impeccable suit of satin. "Always a pleasure for the regent. Always a pleasure, but he is not disposed to receive anyone at this hour. In the morning, my lord. That would be better. Perhaps sometime after eleven? After lunch would be even better."

"We'll see him now," said Owain, "or I'll wring your neck."

"Very good, my lord," said the steward, bowing again. "Shall I inform his grace that you will see him in the morning?"

"Your neck. Do you hear? I'll snap it like a twig."

"Very well, my lord." The steward managed to look both alarmed and honored at the prospect of being strangled by the Lord Captain of the Guard. "Perhaps we might just. . ."

"Immediately."

"Very good, my lord. If you would please leave your weapons here. . ." He snapped his fingers and several pages scurried over, their hands already reaching out to receive.

"We'll do no such thing," growled Owain. "Now, lead on at once and shut your mouth, or I'll box your ears."

"Very good, my lord."

Jute found all of his old urges awakening as they were led through the castle. His fingers twitched and his nose wiggled. There were so many lovely things. Shiny pretty things, whispered a voice inside his mind that sounded suspiciously like the wind. Gold and silver candelabra sprouting tapers of beeswax candles tipped with flame, rows of paintings with frames encrusted with gems hanging along every corridor they walked down (surely just one painting would not be missed), tapestries heavy with gold thread and pearls worked in like shining little eyes. He glanced through an open door to see an immense room lined with shelf after shelf full of books, a sight that made him lick his lips. A book in good condition brought a tremendous price at the dealers on Smara Street.

Stop that, said the hawk inside his mind.

Stop what?

You're not a thief anymore. You are the anbeorun Windan. The guardian of the wind. Be yourself.

Fine for you to say, said Jute. *You still haven't taught me how to fly. I'm more likely to fall flat on my face than soar. Who's going to be impressed with that? Some guardian I am.*

The steward led them down hallways that opened into anterooms and observatories and miniature gardens vaulted over with glass that revealed the night studded with stars. They walked down yet more halls, each more gorgeous and magnificent than the last, until Jute, who prided himself on maintaining an excellent sense of direction while investigating strange houses, was thoroughly lost. Doors opened into yet more halls and waiting rooms; they trudged up a flight of stairs and stepped carefully through a gallery wet with soap and water and cluttered with drudges industriously scrubbing on their hands and knees.

"Do you even know where the regent is?" said Owain. "Are you lost? Is this your first day on the job?"

"Very good, my lord," said the steward, keeping a wary eye on the captain and increasing his speed just enough to keep him out of range. "Almost there, my lord."

A marble hall opened before them. Their footsteps whispered on the polished stone. They came to a final door and the steward opened it with a deep bow. Multicolored lights glimmered from candles set behind sconces of stained glass. Tucked out of sight in an alcove, a trio of musicians wove music that gently filled the room. A pair of glass doors opened out onto a balcony. White roses climbed the pillars of the balcony and then fell back down in abandon. On the balcony, faces turned toward them from around a table, blurred in the moonlight.

A short fat man stood up and hurried to Owain's side.

"Gawinn, always a pleasure to see you," he said, trying to smile but only succeeding in looking as if he had a stomachache. "But what are you doing here? This isn't the best time."

The man's gaze settled on Declan and Jute. His mouth fell open.

"I don't care what time it is, Dreccan Gor," said Owain. "I'm not in the best of moods. We need to speak to Botrell now. Now, do you hear me?"

"Yes," said Gor, still staring at Jute.

"Gawinn, my dear fellow," called a voice from the table. "Lovely to have you drop in like this, but why don't you run along now? There's a good man."

Owain pushed past the fat man and strode to the table, motioning Declan and Jute to follow him. Candles lit an array of wine bottles, glasses, and plates piled with fruits and cheeses, all crowded across a white silk tablecloth. There were several people sitting around the table, but only one of them commanded attention. The regent. Nimman Botrell. He sprawled gracelessly in his chair. His face was slack and his mouth wet with wine, but his eyes were sharp and attentive. They flickered over to Jute and Declan. His eyes widened for a split second—Jute did not notice, for he was looking hungrily at the cheese—and then his face smoothed, became bland.

"My Lord Captain of the Guard," drawled the regent. "Must you forever be plaguing me? No, you needn't say a word. I'm sure you've come to ask for more money. That's it, isn't it? Always money. So tiresome. Isn't there more to life, I ask you, such as this splendid little red from Thule? I'd offer you some, Gawinn, but it'd be wasted on your untutored palate. Soldier, don't you know." This last comment was made to the others sitting around the table. They tittered politely.

"My lord," said Owain through gritted teeth, "I wouldn't dare intrude on your precious time unless I thought it of vital importance to the safety of our city. This is such a time."

"Doubtlessly. Such a bore, I'm sure." The regent yawned. "Impending doom, a tidal wave, some sort of dreary plague decimating the commoners. They can all wait until the morning. Now, who are these, er, guests of yours?" He sat up a bit straighter and peered at them. "Shadows above. That's a hawk. Didn't notice at first. Tame, eh? Quite a big fellow."

"They're the reason why I'm here. Allow me to introduce Declan Farrow." Here, Declan stepped forward and bowed. "The hawk, of course. He can talk. And this is Jute." Jute stepped forward as well and made an awkward bow in imitation of Declan.

"Charmed, I'm sure," said the regent. "I had a talking magpie when I was a youngster. It said things like 'cake' and 'die.' Farrow, Farrow—that name means something. Just can't bring it to mind."

"Horses, my lord," said one of the other people at the table.

"Oh, yes. Horses. Are you one of those Farrows?"

"A long time ago, my lord," said Declan.

The hawk's voice whispered in Jute's mind.

Careful. Something is not what it seems here. This regent fellow bears a ward that is more than just a ward. It guards him, yet it examines everything around him. More than examine. I think it seeks to intrude on your thoughts.

Even as the hawk spoke, Jute became aware of a gentle pressure on the edge of his mind. It was as soft as a feather, drifting in and out of his awareness. The regent's eyes settled on him and the pressure increased. Jute pushed back in his mind, hard, and the regent dropped his wineglass. It broke in a spatter of glass on the marble floor of the balcony.

"Shadow take it!" said the regent.

"Another glass, my lord," said one of the ladies at the table, but the regent waved it away.

"What was it you were saying, Gawinn?" he said. "Get to the point, man. You've already ruined my evening, but you needn't ruin it much longer."

"Hearne is under threat of attack, my lord. An army is massing in the east. Beyond the Morn Mountains. I want you to invoke the writ of sovereignty so that I can demand the mobilization of the duchies, from Harlech to Harth, so that Hearne might be defended, and with it, all of Tormay."

The regent stared at him for a moment, astonished. Then he let out a bray of laughter. "For a moment I thought you said an army. Beyond the Morns. The only place beyond the Morns is the duchy of Mizra. Fine fellow, the duke of Mizra. Fine fellow, indeed! He has manners, don't you know. Just had him here to visit. Good taste in horses. Excellent clothing, too."

"I did say beyond the Morns, my lord. Yes, the duchy of Mizra." Owain ground his teeth together and then unclenched his jaw, forcing himself to continue. "Hearne will be attacked by Mizra once the spring thaw sets in. A matter of weeks, at most. I need the writ of sovereignty."

"Bosh, man! Absurd. Nonsense. On what do you base these ridiculous claims?"

"The words of these two."

"And they are experts, scholars, renowned for their wisdom?" The regent yawned. "More wine! Give me a fresh glass. Ah, yes. Thank you, my dear. You're too kind."

"This boy is the wind guardian, my lord. The stillpoint of the wind."

"The wind guardian? Isn't that some kind of silly bedtime story for children?"

But he believes. The hawk's voice was puzzled in Jute's mind. *He believes what Owain Gawinn says. I can feel it on the edge of his thoughts. Careful, now. A strange game is afoot here and I do not see how it will play out.*

"He speaks the truth, my lord," said Jute.

Those around the table examined him with interest. Just on the edge of his sight, he saw that the fat man was shifting from foot to foot. Sweat gleamed on his bald head.

"Oh?" The regent leaned back in his chair and took a sip of wine. He smacked his lips. "Now, boy, who exactly are you again? Right, of course, you claim to be the guardian of the wind. That's what he said, Gor, is it not?"

"Yes, my lord," said the short fat man. "Perhaps he, er. . ."

"Perhaps he might be the guardian as he claims? Is that what you are saying, Gor? You hear? My own chief counselor, my sage advisor, thinks you might be the wind guardian. Who am I to gainsay him? I'm merely the regent and. . ." Here, he stared down into his empty wine glass and frowned. ". . . And I've drunk a lot of wine this evening. Quite a lot."

"But not enough, my lord," said someone at the table, leaning forward with a bottle.

"Thank you. Not enough. Never enough. Yes, well, it's not every day we have the guardian of the wind in our castle. Rare day, indeed. A historic day for Hearne. I suppose it's incumbent upon us to extend our hospitality. To you and this, this Farrow fellow. And your pet hawk too, don't worry." The regent focused blearily on the hawk and raised his glass. "Always been fond of birds of prey. Devotee of the hunt, that's me. Go on and say something, my dear bird. Something, anything? No? But you must understand, Gawinn, I can't commit to this idea, this idea of our young friend being the wind guardian, without a little interview on the part of the court wizard. Merely a formality. Check credentials, you know. First thing in the morning. I'm sure he's sound asleep at the moment. Wouldn't want to bother him. First thing in the morning, however. No writ of sovereignty until then."

"My lord," said Owain, grinding his teeth together, "while I appreciate your startling kindness to my guests, I think it vital that—"

"No writ until then," repeated the regent, wagging one finger.

He only plays at being drunk, said the hawk in Jute's mind. *There is more going on here than we can see. Do not trust this man.*

"Find you a nice room to sleep in, my dear boy," said the regent. "I'm sure you'd like a bath, too. You look rather grimy. Gor! Call for a couple dozen of our best footmen and get them on it, straight away." He yawned. "Getting late. Perhaps we should say good night for the night. Ha! That's not bad."

"Very good, my lord," said Gor.

Doubtless, there is a different thought in his mind than what he says. I do not understand the currents here, but there is a hidden thing here and it runs dark and deep. Look at his hand.

Jute glanced down and saw that the regent's hand, the one on his thigh and half hidden by the folds of the tablecloth, was clenched so hard that the knuckles were white with the force of his grip. A bead of sweat trickled down the line of the man's jaw.

"My lord," said Declan, "that won't be necessary. While we're grateful for your hospitality, we're unpolished folk and would be comfortable in the Guard barracks."

"They're welcome at the barracks," said Owain.

"I insist." And though the regent was still sprawled in his chair, wine slopping from his glass, his eyes were hard and cold.

They were shown to a suite of rooms, well-appointed and looking out into the night over the lights of the city. A footman and an indeterminate number of pages (they were always coming and going, thought Jute, like a flock of swallows) bowed them through the door. Several of the pages hurried over to the fireplace, and in no time at all, flames crackled from a pile of logs. Others, wielding glowing tapers, scurried from table to sideboard to mantel, lighting candle after candle.

"If you need anything, my lords," said the footman, "you've only to ring." And he indicated a silk rope hanging discreetly in one corner.

"Never mind ringing," said Jute. "Could we have some dinner? Roast chicken, or something suitable?"

"Very good, my lord." Several of the pages sprinted away. "Would there be anything else? No? Good night, my lords." Preceded by the remainder of the army of pages, he bowed himself out through the door.

Owain Gawinn lingered for a moment in the hallway, scowling and looking embarrassed at the same time.

"Stubborn mule, that's what he is," he said. "Refusing to sign the writ. I suppose a few more hours won't do much harm. Not that anyone's going to ride out for the duchies in the dead of the night." He stepped closer and his voice lowered. "Watch yourselves. It might be more comfortable in the castle than the barracks, but those who are wise are never certain about Nimman Botrell. I'll see you first thing in the morning."

With a final scowl that was not directed at them but in grumpy vagueness at their surroundings, he turned and strode away.

Close the door and do not speak, said the hawk inside Jute's mind. *Bid Declan the same.*

Silently, Jute did as he was told. Declan nodded wordlessly and sat down in one of the plush chairs by the fireplace. The hawk hopped down from Jute's shoulder and prowled about the room.

"Finally, a place with some class," said the ghost, appearing.

"Shush," said Jute.

"Look at that vase. Probably worth a hundred pieces of gold."

Tell that fool to shut his mouth. The hawk glared back over his wing at the ghost.

"Hush."

The ghost made a face at Jute and then drifted over to the window. Jute noticed with pleasure that the two open doorways on either side of the room revealed two bedrooms, each with its own bed. He was tired. A bed. He could not remember the last time he had slept in a bed. It seemed like he had been sleeping in a succession of dreadful places that never involved beds: the ground in various degrees of rockiness, beneath a wagon in the middle of the snow, a barn. The barn had been the most comfortable of all those spots. Hay, despite its knack of working its way under clothes and manifesting itself in scratching and itching, wasn't all that bad.

Ah. The hawk sounded grimly pleased.

What is it?

As I suspected. Do you see the painting over the fireplace mantel? It is not just a painting. It's a ward. An interesting ward. As far as I can tell, it's activated by sound.

But then it's already active.

Jute had not noticed the painting before. It was a large oil set in a silver frame. A man stared from the painting, an old-fashioned ruff of black velvet knotted at his neck. There was something sly and nasty in his expression. His ears dangled from the sides of his head like those of a donkey, but his eyes were filmed over with the milky white patina that signified blindness.

Ears of a blind man, said the hawk in Jute's mind. *Such are much sharper than normal. The painting listens to us. Whisper to the ghost that he must mind himself. I hope that his outburst went unnoticed. The ghost could prove an invaluable asset, but only if unknown to others. At least, if he thinks that, it might keep him quiet and so save our nerves.*

The ghost, looking startled, drifted over to the painting and stared hard at it. Jute yawned, trying not to look in the direction of the painting. Even though the man was sightless in it, he had the uneasy feeling that the blind eyes followed him. Someone knocked on the door.

"Dinner," said Declan.

Two pages tiptoed in bearing platters larger than themselves. They eyed the hawk with a mixture of alarm and interest.

"Is it true, my lord," said one page, "that the hawk speaks?"

"What's true," said Declan, "is that he's fond of raw human flesh. Particularly liver. For breakfast, lunch, and dinner."

The pages fled and the room was once again left in silence. Jute hitched his chair closer to Declan and whispered through a mouthful of cold chicken.

"The painting above the fireplace is a ward. Hawk says it's listening to us." And then, in a normal voice. "Good chicken, isn't it?"

Declan nodded. "Excellent chicken."

With the candles out and the fire collapsing into subdued embers on the hearth, they retired to their rooms. Jute lay in the bed and stared up at the ceiling. The bed was extremely comfortable, the most comfortable bed he had ever had the good fortune to encounter. But he could not sleep. Things were too silent. Much too silent. He turned over on his side, punched the pillow into a more agreeable shape, and shut his eyes.

CHAPTER ONE HUNDRED & EIGHT
A NARROW ESCAPE FOR SOME AND NOT FOR OTHERS

The last of the guests had departed, unsteady on their feet and escorted by solicitous pages who veered and zigzagged with them in sympathetic harmony. A door closed somewhere behind them, and there was silence. A breeze wafted out of the night and breathed across the balcony, batting at the candle flames burning on the table. The regent hunched his head down in the collar of his fur coat and poured himself a glass of wine. He took a swallow and shook his head.

"Shadows above and below," he said. "Can you believe the luck of it? Our little thief shows up unannounced, out of the blue, along with the Knife. Who turns out to be Declan Farrow, of all people. Did you know that, Gor? I never did. I never bought his I-come-from-Aum line, of course, but I never imagined him a Farrow. Not just any old Farrow, but the legendary Declan Farrow himself. I daresay he could tell me a thing or two about horses."

"And ogres," said Gor, shivering a little.

"Right. And ogres. Regardless, we've been handed two juicy plums. At least, they were plums. When we still had a client."

"It looks that way, my lord."

"And claiming to be the guardian of the wind. Ridiculous. An absurd story, yet they somehow hoodwinked Gawinn with it. I wouldn't have thought him susceptible to such nonsense. He must be getting foolish in his old age. Too many whacks to the head on the practice ground. At any rate, what's important is that they're here. In my castle. Ha! What do you advise, Gor?"

"I've been considering nothing else, soon as I clapped eyes on the boy." Gor trailed off into silence and fidgeted with a piece of bread.

"So what've you been thinking? Out with it."

"There's something down there, my lord."

"Down there?" But the regent knew what he referred to.

"Down in the Court of the Guild." Gor's voice sank to a whisper and he seemed to shrink in his chair as if there were eyes watching from the night around them and he sought to evade notice. "I went down there this evening to meet with some of the district enforcers to see what news there was of the robbery. There was something down there. Something watching. It felt like him, if you know what I mean, or something horribly similar to him. Even the others were aware something was wrong. They couldn't wait to get out of there, and I ran back up the passage, expecting to feel a hand on my shoulder at any second."

Botrell shuddered. "I don't like where you're going with this, Gor."

"Neither do I, my lord, but a problem doesn't go away by ignoring it."

"No, it doesn't. Need you be right?"

"I suggest we go down to Court of the Guild and—and tell the thing there. Tell it the boy's here. That we have him."

591

"You suggest we tell the thing? But the creature's dead. Whatever it was. Levoreth Callas killed it right in the middle of my harvest ball, in front of every noble from every duchy of Tormay. And that wretched worm of a traitor Smede is gone too."

"It doesn't matter, my lord," said Gor doggedly. "Something's down there. Waiting. It might be him. We had best be safe."

"All that lovely gold," mourned the regent. "Maybe he'll still want it back, even if we deliver the boy. Oh, hang it all. You're right. You go down there and tell him. Report back here to me when you're done."

"I'm not going alone."

"Get going. That's an order."

"No," said Gor. "I won't."

"Coward!" The two men glared at each other for a moment.

"For the life of me," said the regent, throwing his hands up in the air, "I can't see why you aren't willing to do your job. Don't I pay you enough? Whatever happened to duty and diligence? Whatever happened to the creed of the Gors?"

"We've never had a creed."

They tiptoed down the stairway, leaving the comforting light of the regent's rooms behind them and exchanging it for the gloom of the passages leading to the court of the Silentman. There was something disturbing about the darkness. The warren of passageways beneath the castle and the city had never been a reassuring place, but it was worse now. The darkness had a waiting quality to it, a hushed expectancy. There was something oddly hungry about it. The regent shivered and drew his cloak around him. The familiar blue flames hung motionless on the walls, casting their meager light on stone and dust and shadow. He turned a ring around his finger—once, twice, and then back again—and felt the masking ward come to life around him, blurring his features and his voice. It did not make him feel safer.

"What did they say?" he said.

"Who?"

"The enforcers."

"Nothing. No news. Whoever robbed us must be sitting tight on the gold. But the Guild has an eye on every inn, every chandler, every merchant, every trader passing through, anyone doing business in the city. Any suspicious spending will be noticed. We'll catch whoever did it."

"Good. Well thought, Gor."

The massive double doors to the Court of the Guild stood before them. The passageway led off into darkness on their right. Complete darkness. Behind them, further back up the passage, the last torch in sight wavered and seemed to grow dim.

"The torches," said the regent, his voice quiet. "Will you look at that? What's going on? They've gone out here. That's impossible. The first Silentman had them spelled into being after the wizards' war, when the Guild first gained control of the labyrinth. The torches have burned ever since."

"Not anymore," said Gor nervously. "They were lit just fine when I was down here earlier."

They stood for a moment in front of the door, neither wanting to go in. Dark enough as it was, it was growing even darker. And then, to make matters worse, the only torch still in sight (it was about a hundred feet away, back up the passage) guttered and went out. A faint luminance still clung to the walls. The regent's teeth chattered and he clamped his mouth shut, hoping Gor had not heard. There was an odd, damp sort of feel to the air.

"Almost feels like fog," said Botrell.

"What's that?" said Gor.

"Nothing. Just open the blasted door."

Thankfully, the torches within the court still burned, but the strange sensation of dampness was even more pronounced inside than it had been in the passageway.

"It wasn't like this before," said Gor. "Look at the walls."

Moisture beaded and trickled down the walls. It gathered on the floor in dark patches. Somewhere nearby came the sound of water dripping. Something seemed to move in the darkness in the furthest corner of the room, something slow and stealthy.

"Hello?" called the regent, his voice loud in the quiet. "Hello? Is someone there?"

Nothing responded.

"Gor, be a good fellow and, er, check on the torches. I'd like to know if they're in decent condition. Those out in the passage looked feeble—"

"Feeble? They were dead."

Botrell chose to ignore this remark, as, in his opinion, it was an attempt by Gor to inject hysteria into the discussion. "—and I don't want these in here to wind up in the same state. You needn't look like a stuffed frog, Gor. Here, I'll check the ones along this side, and you check the ones along the other."

Botrell sidled away before Gor had a chance to respond. He ducked behind a pillar. Not that he wasn't brave enough to investigate the far side of the court—he was convinced that something was there—it was the fact that Gor was his chief steward, and in such capacity, it was proper for him to behave as the regent's emissary.

He peeked around the pillar. Gor was no longer in sight. He thought he heard a shuffling footstep. Somewhere on the other side of the court. Obviously, poor old Gor scuffling around. The regent shivered. Partly in unease, partly in pleasure. He wasn't looking forward to seeing that wretched thin-faced fellow again, if he was still alive. At the same time, if he could get the Guild back into the fellow's good graces, perhaps there'd be more jobs down the road. More of that gold. Lovely gold. Beautiful, gorgeous, ravishing gold.

"Nimman Botrell."

The regent shouted in alarm and jumped back. Which wasn't far, as the pillar stopped him cold. His heart leapt in his chest and hammered down, hard and gasping for blood. Something shifted in the shadows.

"Who's there?" he quavered.

"Nimman Botrell."

The voice was husky and creaky, as if it had not been used for a while.

"How do you know my name?" said Botrell wildly. He could see nothing except shadows. Shadows and stone and the cold blue light of the torches. But he could smell something. A rotten, damp stench.

"How do I. . .?" The voice trailed off in amused perplexity. "Ah, you're warded. You think it guards you. But what is a ward? Just another skin to be peeled back, scraped off. Gnawed away."

Something moved again in the shadows. A slow, shuffling footstep. A figure emerged from the darkness. The figure of a man. But then Botrell felt his skin begin to prickle and crawl. There was something dreadfully wrong with the man. The arms hung down, slack and inert. The head lay hunched down in the shoulders as if he lacked the energy to hold it erect. Water dripped from his fingers, and Botrell realized with a shudder that this dripping was what he had heard before. The smell grew stronger. The man took another slow step forward and Botrell saw something else. The man's flesh faded away into nothingness here and there, into shadow. Into wet shadow. As if he were made of some terrible mix of flesh and water and shadow.

"Darkness," said the man, smiling a bit. His teeth seemed overly long. "I'm woven of flesh, water, and darkness. It's an uneasy mix and it makes me hungry. It's been a while since I have eaten."

"How can you read my mind?" Botrell gasped. "Who are you?"

"I read your mind? I didn't realize. I'm full of spells, and I breathe them in and out like air. There's no telling what might happen." The man paused here and tilted his head to one side as if listening. Water ran off the edge of his jaw and spattered on the floor. "Nimman Botrell, regent, Silentman. I think you have my master's gold. Yes, that's it. That's what he's thinking. Sometimes I can't tell. Sometimes, I think, he's forgotten me. What do you have for him? Speak."

The man shuffled a step closer. And then another. Much too close.

"The boy!" gabbled Botrell. "He's here!"

"The boy?"

The man leaned forward, as if to peer more fully into Botrell's face. He gazed for a moment. His eyes caught the regent's frantic stare, and Botrell found that he could not look away. It felt as if he were being pulled forward, like being caught in the steady suck of quicksand. Wet and strangling and choking. Inescapable. Surely he would be pulled down. He would drown.

The man sighed and released him. It was a soft, hungry sigh.

"And the man!" said Botrell. "Declan Farrow. He's here too. Both in the castle. They arrived just this night."

"Ah. Both of them." The man nodded. He smiled slightly. His head tilted to one side as if he was listening to something. Water dripped from his fingertips. From the end of his nose.

"My lord," said Gor, hurrying around the pillar. He froze at the sight of the man standing before them. The man's gaze slid to Gor and then back to the regent.

He nodded, more water dripping. "You were wise to come down here. My master is pleased."

"I have a question about the gold," said Botrell. But then he shut his mouth, because the man took another shuffling step forward.

"You'll take me to them," he said. "Now."

Jute woke up with a start. He sat up in bed, not sure where he was for a moment. Then he remembered. Moonlight slanted in through the window. The night was silent. But something had jarred him awake. Perhaps a dream. His mind felt thick and slow with sleep. The room lay around him in perfect repose: the columns of the bed, the table bearing its mug and pitcher of water, the wardrobe in the corner. But something was different.

Something.

The smell.

A stench of wet, decaying things. For an instant he was back in the cellar. So long ago. Back in the cellar, on his knees and staring down the hole in the floor. Darkness and water and the cold touch of the wihht.

The wihht.

Jute jumped out of bed. He tripped over his knapsack and grabbed his boots. The hawk came awake on his perch above the wardrobe.

What. . .?

The wihht! Jute shouted in his mind. Not caring what was listening. *The wihht! Somewhere close! And getting closer fast!*

The hawk was motionless for one second. *Get out! Get out now!* His voice hammered in Jute's mind. The bird hurled himself off the wardrobe and through the half-open windows with one beat of his wings. Out into the darkness before the dawn. Jute stumbled after him. But the windows were closing. Swinging shut. Slammed shut with a bang.

"Help! Oh, preserve us!" The ghost appeared in a glimmer of light.

"Hush," whispered Jute. "Go wake Declan. Immediately."

"First you tell me to hush. Then you tell me to go wake up Declan, which will undoubtedly involve noise. I don't—"

"The wihht's here."

"Mercy!" The ghost vanished.

Jute crept out into the common room. He touched the handle on the door leading to the hallway. Turned it gently. It was locked. The door to Declan's room swung open.

"The wihht?" said the man.

"Yes. And the door's locked. And the windows."

Get out! Get out now!

We're trying, said Jute furiously in his mind. *Easy for you to say!*

"Glass can break," said Declan. "It'll make a tremendous sound, but that doesn't matter now."

"No." Jute eyed the painting over the fireplace. It was barely visible in the weak morning light, but it seemed as if the old man had a much nastier smile on his face than before.

In one swift movement, Declan drew his sword and slammed the hilt against the window. The noise was appalling. It resounded in the room like a stone giant clapping his hands. But the window did not break. Declan spun away from it, wincing and almost dropping his sword.

"It's warded," he said. "A binding ward. There's no way I could break that."

Get out!

What do you suggest? The door's locked and warded. The windows are locked and warded!

There was a moment of silence, and then the hawk answered.

The fireplace.

Jute dove for the fireplace like a rat bolting for its hole, with Declan hard on his heels. The coals in the grate were still hot. The insides of the fireplace were thick with soot. But the interior of the chimney was wide. Thankfully wide. Jute reached up, scrabbling for a hold where the chimney narrowed. It was too high. Just beyond his fingertips.

"I need a leg up," said Jute.

Behind them, in the room, they heard the creak of a handle turning.

"Climb!" screamed the ghost from somewhere above them, his voice echoing in the chimney. Jute stood on Declan's knee, jammed his elbows against the sooty bricks, and hoisted himself up. He reached down and Declan grabbed onto his hand. Hauled up, his joints popping, he felt skin scrape off against brick, and then they were both wedged in the chimney. Jute began to climb. Quickly. As fast as he had ever climbed. Up through the choking darkness. Up through the soot flaking off under his boots, his hands, his elbows. He could scarcely breathe, gagging on the stink of old burnt feathers and soot. He could hear Declan several feet below him.

What if it's too narrow at the top? said a voice inside his mind.

Shut up. Shut up shut up shut up!

He almost screamed it out loud, but stopped himself, clenching his teeth. Trying not to think of the chimney narrowing. Shrinking. Strangling. Closing in like a tomb. Far below them, down in the darkness of the room, Jute heard a footstep in the coals of the grate. The coals crunching into powder. He knew there were eyes down there looking up. He heard a trickling sound as if water was pooling in some place. Filling up. Rising higher. Lapping against the bricks. Rising up the chimney.

Soot fell away on either side of him. His fingers slipped on greasy brick, scrabbling to find holds in the cracks. His arms ached.

"Faster," said Declan from below, his voice tight and brittle. "There's something coming up the chimney after us."

Jute didn't bother responding. He didn't trust himself to speak. He knew he'd probably end up screaming or crying or gibbering like a lunatic. He tried to remember what floor their rooms were on. How many floors did the castle have? How far did they have to climb?

They climbed in complete darkness, clinging to the fact that up meant freedom and that any slackening in their speed brought the wihht closer. The air became colder as the seconds flitted by, and it no longer smelled of soot but stank of damp, rotting things. It smelled of the wihht. He was down there. Climbing, or somehow rising with the water or the darkness that welled from his body as if from some dark and dreadful spring.

"Jute."

The voice was horribly familiar. It wavered up from below. "Falling down chimneys again. Down into the Dark. You stole my knife. It belonged to me. It belonged to the Dark. But it's no good now. You took the death in it and made it your life. But we'll take your life and make it death. You aren't the anbeorun yet, boy. You never will be. The wind hasn't woken in you. I'll have your blood and your eyes before that happens. Your eyes in my hand. I'll have you blind in the dark."

Jute whimpered and climbed faster, desperate for air, the sky, the wind on his face. Desperate to get away from the voice and what must assuredly be darkness and water rising higher and higher in the chimney beneath him.

"Darkness is a place, boy. A nightmare. A word. Darkness was a star falling from the house of dreams. Darkness is the taste in a dead man's mouth. Darkness is the watcher in the dark."

Unbidden, the hawk's words rose in Jute's memory.

Deep within the darkness,
Further e'en the void,
Nokhoron Nozhan built himself a fortress of night.

But then the darkness was not so dark anymore, and there was a cleaner taste to the air. Something stirred against Jute's face. A slight touch. The breeze. He looked up and, half-crying, almost laughing in astonishment, he saw a small square of dark blue speckled with tiny shards of light more beautiful than diamonds. Stars. He burst out into the fresh air, into the cold touch of the wind, out into the last hour of night before the morning. He tumbled over the side of the chimney and slid down to the roof a few feet below. Declan jumped down after him in a shower of soot and then they ran. Away from the chimney. Away from the darkness creeping up toward the top. They stumbled along the ridge of the roof. Past other chimneys and the stone walls of towers and turrets rising here and there from the long, squat body of the castle. Behind them, they heard a hissing snarl. Jute glanced over his shoulder as he ran and saw an inky darkness billowing up out of the chimney. Tendrils unfurled from it, wavering into the sky. It looked like a hideous, giant hand, and in its palm as it reached for them, two eyes stared.

"Run!" screamed Jute.

"Extraordinary," said the ghost, appearing. "The view up here is extraor—" It turned and saw the hand of darkness stretching out of the chimney, groping along the top of the ridge toward them at a terrible speed. "Runrunrun you fools!" screamed the ghost.

Tiles snapped and clattered beneath their feet. The walls fell away on either side, down three stories to the castle gardens below. Several guards trudging along a path beside the wall looked up with astonished faces.

"We're out of roof," said Declan.

And there was the end, an end to the ridge, to the tiles, and instead of more roof to sprint along, panting and gasping, the cream-colored stone walls descended to what looked like a rose garden planted around a fountain.

"There's ivy growing up the wall," said the ghost. It was floating several feet out from the edge of the roof and was able to see from this vantage. Declan flung himself on his stomach and peered down.

"So there is. Thank you, ghost."

Declan went first, lowering himself from the eaves until he could grab hold of the thick vines of the ivy. He swarmed down, with Jute right after him. The boy craned his head back, sure the enormous hand was about to curl its fingers over the eaves and come walking down the wall toward them. A crow exploded out of the ivy beside him, cawing and complaining. Jute clambered down, grabbing for new holds on the ivy without looking. Fumbling through the vines. Sweat ran cold on his body.

"Stop where you are!" shouted a voice.

They dropped the last ten feet down to the ground. Guards hurried up out of the morning half-light, out of the mist hanging among the roses, hands reaching for them. Declan punched the nearest in the face and tripped another so that he fell over the low rock wall surrounding the fountain and tumbled into the water.

"Run!" said Declan.

They ran, without looking back, as the sun came up in the east and lit the day with its slanting rays. High above them, the hawk teetered through the air on motionless wings. The soldiers at the castle gates fell back before Declan's sword. And then they were pounding through the quiet, tree-lined streets of Highneck Rise and down toward the city.

On top of the castle, the morning light fell on the strange cloud of darkness trailing along the peak of the roof. The darkness retreated from the light as if it were pained by its touch. It shrank, unraveling a bit, and then dissipated until only a remainder wavered from the top of the chimney. And then even that was gone, diving back down the chimney toward whatever waited below.

The man at the mantel stood with his head bowed, one arm inside the fireplace. Inside the fireplace? That did not make sense. Botrell could not properly see from where he stood. They had been standing there for so long. His back ached, but he daren't move. The room was silent. Out of the corner of his eye, he could see Gor shifting from foot to foot. The man turned. Water dripped from his nose, from his fingertips. A puddle spread out slowly from around his feet.

"They have escaped," he said, almost gently, as if he were reluctant to tell them the bad news.

"Oh?" said Botrell, feeling that he had to say something. "I'll put the word out. The Guild, you know. We have our eyes and ears everywhere in this city."

"I am—my master is greatly displeased. He doesn't like being displeased. He's been patient with you, Silentman."

"For which I'm grateful, let me assure you. The Guild aims to deliver on its contracts. A man's word is his bond. After all, if you can't stand by your word, what do you have? Confusion, ill-will, and anarchy." Botrell felt rather good about that last bit. He often lectured Arodilac on a similar theme. He cleared his throat. The man seemed to be listening to him, his head tilted to one side. "And if anarchy reigns, then what's left to man but to live like a beast, rending and tearing the necessities of life from his fellow man?"

The man smiled. He couldn't be such a bad fellow after all.

"Just a mild setback," continued Botrell. "We'll catch the wretch for you. Gor, get the word out to the Guild. Raise the Guard as well. Tell Owain Gawinn to put every man of his into the city on patrol."

"That won't be necessary, Silentman."

"No?"

"I've grown hungry and I must eat before I do anything else. It is a pressing need, to say the least."

"I'll ring for some breakfast, then. I've a marvelous cook."

"No." The man smiled again. He did have large teeth. He shook his head. "You'll do just fine."

In that one frozen moment of silence, the man smiled even wider. It was not that he had large teeth, but that there were too many of them. Too many packed inside his mouth. He reached for Botrell with one hand, his arm stretching, growing longer and longer as if it were made of water and darkness that had no limit to it but could flow and grow and rush into whatever emptiness it might find. Botrell screamed and turned to run. He stumbled over Gor. They both scrabbled at the door handle. The man chuckled behind them.

CHAPTER ONE HUNDRED & NINE
RAISE THE DUCHIES

Owain Gawinn frowned and fiddled with the ink pen on his desk. The numbers added up tolerably well. Enough gold left over from the theft to finance two hundred more recruits, including all equipment and several years of upkeep. Of course, that didn't address the more fundamental problem of finding recruits. Perhaps Harth? His heralds had never ventured that far south. The men of Harth were good fighters and excellent horsemen. Not as good as those of Harlech, of course, but he doubted anyone from Harlech would ever consent to serve in the Guard.

Owain tossed the pen onto the desk. It was a dark, cold morning outside his window. Not even morning yet, but just that indeterminate time before the sun lightened the eastern sky. Most of the city still slept, and he envied them heartily. The thought gave him pause. Early mornings, sleepless nights, long days in the saddle, grinding sword-work for hours on end in the exercise yard, night duty on the wall—all of that had been food and drink for his soul. Perhaps he was getting old. Nonsense. He grinned wolfishly. He could still wield a sword with the best of them and outride even the younger soldiers. He locked the study door and hurried down the steps to the bottom of the tower. His breath plumed in the chill air. A Guardsman snapped to attention. A cadre of recruits straggled across the practice ground in weary formation.

"You there!" Owain called to a passing soldier. The man turned. "Ah, Bridd. Saddle a horse for me. Quickly, now."

Arodilac dashed off toward the stable. The recruits on the practice ground had divided into pairs and were practicing the first sets of swordplay. Lunge, parry, counterattack, recover, circle. The movements were stiff and stylized, and wildly impractical on an actual battlefield, but their memorization provided a foundation for the split-second improvisation that battle required. Owain watched for a while, listening to the clash of swords and the bark of the sergeant. He nodded. Quite a few had strong wrists and decent sensibilities.

"Here you are, my lord."

"Thank you, Bridd."

Owain was about to mount, but then he stopped and frowned. It was not the best of light, being still the murky hour before dawn, but he noticed a man walking by the gates to the Guard compound. A man hunched over against the cold. A man he had seen before.

"Bridd."

"Yes, my lord?"

"Careful how you look, but do you see that fellow walking by, just outside the gate?"

"Yes, my lord."

"After I ride out, I daresay he'll try to follow me."

"My lord?"

"Stop gaping at me like that, Bridd. He was loitering on a street corner near my house this morning. The odds of him being there and here, all within the same half hour, are too small for any good explanation. It might have something to do with our burglary. Take several men and arrest him, once I've ridden out. On second thought, are Posle and Hoon on duty?"

"Posle is, my lord, not Hoon. But Varden just came on."

"Good. Take the two of them, and keep it quiet from the other men, do you hear me? Make up a story if you have to. I'll wait about here until you're ready."

"Very well, my lord." Arodilac dashed off.

Owain stroked the horse's neck and murmured wordlessly to it. Perhaps he was being too cautious, but he had definitely seen the man earlier that morning. There was no mistaking the way he walked: a slow, easy saunter. It might be coincidence, but he was willing to bet a great deal of gold it wasn't. And he didn't want to be taking chances on coincidences where the Guild might be concerned. The Guild was not so delicate in how it handled its affairs. He had heard plenty of stories and he had run across enough evidence in his years in the Guard to realize there was more truth than fantasy in those stories. And the mystery surrounding the identity of the Silentman. Posle turned positively green whenever asked about the elusive leader of the Thieves Guild.

"Ready, my lord."

"All right, Bridd. I'll be at the castle, but back soon enough."

Owain eyed him critically. The boy's face was bright with anticipation, grinning with pleasure at the chance of something different from drills and Guard duty. Action. Even if it only meant collaring a quarry who might prove to be some innocent fellow out for a morning stroll. Bridd reminded him of himself at the same age. He'd do, given a few more years. Owain urged the horse around and clattered out of the gate, not bothering to glance down the street toward where his shadow had gone. There were more important things to pursue this morning. The writ of sovereignty. He would secure that from Botrell, even if it meant wringing it out of his cowardly neck. And then a frank discussion with Jute and the hawk. And Declan Farrow. If he had three of that man, he could whip the Guard into true fighting form and defend Hearne from any sort of enemy.

Owain knew something was wrong as soon as he rode in through the castle gates. Not just wrong, but dreadfully wrong. The guards sprang to attention, but their faces were white and staring and they glanced back at the castle in fear.

"What is it?" he said, reining his horse in. The mount's withers quivered. The horse could feel it, too. Its ears pricked forward uneasily.

"My lord," said one of the soldiers, grounding his spear. "Not sure, my lord. It's just that, well—"

"Get on with it, man."

"The screaming, my lord. Not a few minutes afore you rode up. Surprised you didn't hear it, my lord. Ain't heard nothing like it myself, other than once."

"And that was?"

"The night of the regent's ball, my lord. I was on duty then. When the—the thing ate all them people."

Owain cursed under his breath and spurred the horse across the grounds to the castle steps. He kicked free from the stirrups and shouted at a page standing in frozen shock at the top of the steps.

"Hold my horse!"

The great hall was silent. Here and there, servants stood like statues, faces turned toward the majestic flight of stairs rising up toward the higher floors. Owain drew his sword and took the stairs at a run. It was not difficult to discern the way. He merely followed the horrified stares of the servants, peering out of doorways, standing motionless with arms full of linen, crouching over the shattered pottery they had just dropped. They gaped at him, cringed away from his face and the gleaming steel of his sword.

But the way was unmistakable. Up another flight of stairs. Along the grand hall of yellow marble to the east wing. Precisely where he had left Jute and Declan last night. He slowed, uncertain now. He knew himself a brave man, but he was not a fool either. He stopped and sniffed the air. There was a strange stink to it. A damp funk of rot. The hall was silent. No, that was not true. He could hear a faint, indistinct sound. A sort of bubbling sound. He advanced slowly, the sword held low and ready by his side. The door to the suite stood open. Cautiously, he stepped forward. The room was empty, but the smell was even stronger. A loose pile of rags lay on the floor. Wet rags. Wet with blood. He heard the sound again. Somewhere behind him. Back in the hall. He sidled back into the hall, his mouth dry. The sound was coming from the door across the way. A quiet, bubbling sort of cry. Like that of a child. He reached out with his left hand and eased the handle. The door swung open.

"Don't kill me!" shrieked Gor. "Have mercy!"

The fat little man was curled up on the floor, hidden under a pile of blankets in a linen closet. His eyes were shut and one fist was half shoved in his mouth as if to stifle his distress.

"Shut up!" said Owain.

He grabbed the steward by the arm, yanked him to his feet, and hurried him down the hall. Fast. He did not look back. He knew that if he did, he might see something that he did not want to see. Something emerging from the door and following them. They did not speak until they reached the second floor. Their footsteps echoed after them. Gor breathed in quick gasps. Owain slammed his sword back into its sheath.

"What happened?" he said, tightening his grip on the steward's arm.

"It ate him!" sobbed the little man.

"What?"

"The thing! It ate Botrell. Ate him like an egg. Sucked everything right out of the shell until it just collapsed. Skin and clothes. Caught him before we could get out the door." The steward's hands waved in the air, and he trembled, jerking, trying to wrench free from Owain's hold.

"And you?"

"It just laughed at me. Laughed and said his master was coming to tear this city down. He'd find me then. He'd find me then! He'd find us all!" The steward was almost shrieking by now.

"What was it?"

"What?"

The steward stared at him blankly. Owain grabbed him by the shoulders and shook him. Shook him hard.

"What was it? Why were you in the boy's room? Tell me, blast you, or I'll wring your wretched little neck!"

"It. . . it. . ."

Owain shook him again, rattling his head around back and forth. The words came fast then, babbling and gabbling like a bewildered child.

"We had a contract. We took gold to steal a knife. Steal it and deliver it. About a month ago. Just an old knife in a box. The Guild takes contracts from whoever has the gold to pay. And these people paid, oh, they paid! But the boy stole the knife. He stole the magic right out of it. Something worse than magic, I think. So we had to deliver the boy instead. We had him once, but he escaped during the regent's ball. And when you walked in last night with him, why, it was the best of luck. But it didn't work out." The steward looked as if he were about to burst into tears again. "The boy escaped again. Right up the chimney."

"The Guild?" Owain stared at him, his mind trying to make sense of what the steward was saying. Trying to make sense and yet refusing the implication. "Did you say the Guild?"

"They were willing to pay our price. More than our price. And the Silentman said it was worth the risk. We needed the gold. We always needed the gold. All those feasts, the guests, the horses. And now he's dead!" The steward ended his words with a wail.

"He's dead," repeated Owain. And then the meaning sank in. He stared at the steward. "The Silentman's dead," he said, nodding slowly. The steward nodded along with him, his eyes as wide as those of a child.

"Dead," said the steward. He grabbed hold of Owain's hand. "Dead, like we're all going to be. We're all going to die!"

Footsteps sounded on the polished marble floor behind them

"What's this? Who's going to die?"

Owain and Gor both turned as if one. There, standing before them, was the regent.

"Gawinn, my dear fellow. You look unwell. Is it you who are going to die? Gor, on the other hand, always looks unwell. It's the diet, all in the diet. You are what you eat, don't you know." And Botrell smiled. It was a dreadful smile, all white and shining teeth. "Now, where is that boy? What was his name? I've already forgotten."

"Jute," said Owain. Out of the corner of his eye, he could see Gor standing to one side. The little man's mouth was opening and closing, opening and closing, but not a sound did he make.

"Ah, yes. Jute. How could I forget? Where is he? He seems to have vanished without even thanking me for my gracious hospitality. Rude, I'd say. Manners are a thing of the past. Where is he, Gawinn? I'd like to have a chat with him."

The regent's smile seemed strained now, the teeth bared and ready to snap shut. Cold unease bloomed in Owain's stomach. He wanted nothing more than to be away from the regent, away from that place. And he knew that if he turned to walk away at that moment, it would be with trembling legs, the hairs on the back of his neck standing up, and his ears straining to listen to whatever it was that might be walking up soundlessly behind him.

"I don't know, my lord," said Owain, striving to keep his voice steady. "I was given word that he left the city. Travelling north, I think. To Harlech."

"To Harlech." The regent's face went blank. For a split second, something unutterably old and vicious seemed to look through his eyes. Owain took a step back. But then the moment was past. The regent smiled again. "Harlech! Ice and rock and snow. He's a foolish boy to go to such a place. I'd like to see him again. He impressed me greatly. Notify me immediately, Gawinn, when you hear of his return. Do you hear me?"

This last command was delivered almost in a shout. Owain took another step back.

"Immediately! Do you hear me? Now, Gor, I need to have a word with you. A quick word about lunch. Come. We shall find some privacy in my council chamber."

And Gor, shivering and silent, scuttled after the regent as he turned to walk away down the hall. The fat little man looked back once at Owain; his face was white and staring and hopeless.

The horse was lathered and winded by the time he had descended from the heights of Highneck Rise, but Owain drove him on mercilessly. The city was awake. The sun shone across the eastern sky, dulling the sharp cold edge of the night. Owain spurred his horse through the streets, ignoring the outraged shouts of tradesmen rolling their barrow carts along the crowded way. Someone cursed at him, but he did not hear, his mind intent on what must be done. The horse screamed and faltered in its stride.

"Shadows!" swore Owain, reining it in. "You! I had hoped to see you."

The hawk perched on the horse's neck, digging his claws into the poor beast's neck to maintain balance, wings half-spread.

"There are shadows walking your city today," said the bird. "Shadows in treaty with men, Gawinn. What did you find in the castle?"

"I saw something," said Owain slowly. "I saw the regent, but I don't think he's Nimman Botrell any longer. You did well, all of you, to flee that place. He wants the boy."

The hawk nodded. "He wants the boy's death. He wants the power in the boy's blood. We'll meet you at the city gate. My friends make their way there now. The castle belongs to the Dark, but neither is this city safe."

The hawk lifted off from his perch with one powerful beat of his wings. Owain spurred the horse on.

"So that's it, then," said Declan. "The regent is no longer just the regent anymore."

They were sitting around the captain's desk again in the Guard tower. Jute paced back and forth, unable to sit down. His hands were trembling. Declan slouched in a chair with his eyes half closed.

"A husk, perhaps," said the hawk. "A creature of the Dark, perhaps the wihht himself now? Wihhts have the ability to take on the likeness of people they eat. They're dreadful things, and this particular wihht is quite powerful. Your Botrell was a nasty sort of person, no doubt, but I don't think he deserved the death he found."

"Not only that, but he was the Silentman." Owain shook his head in disbelief. "The Silentman. I always wondered whether someone from the Highneck Rise district was the Silentman. One of the lords of court, or one of the older families. But the regent? I never imagined such a thing. I can hardly believe it now."

"Irrelevant," said the hawk. "Except to prove the point that humans are capable of tremendous greed and folly. What's important is the Dark's attempts to capture Jute. Intrigue has failed them, and I daresay the Dark has been forced to realize this long before the wihht's latest attempt. When intrigue fails, war is the next chapter to be played in the game. I fear, captain, that your Hearne will be the first battleground."

"I don't doubt you, master hawk," said Owain. "I am the Captain of Hearne and my first priority is to defend this city. Let war come. We'll be ready. I can't foresee what'll happen with the regent, though, with the thing wearing his face. I'll have to keep a watch on him so that he doesn't compromise Hearne's safety."

"Keep watch, but don't get too near him," said the hawk. "There are wihhts and there are wihhts. This one is full of dark magic. I'm sure there's a key to his destruction, but I don't know what it is. I wouldn't want you dead at his hands. You must live, for you are the strength of Hearne now. This city must not fall. If Hearne falls, then the duchies will fall as well, one by one. Tormay will become a wasteland of darkness and death. Harlech might stand until the end, but then they will fall as well. Only Jute and the sea will be left. This cannot happen. There's no strength apart, only together. The duchies must lend you their strength."

"You're a comforting sort, master hawk," said Owain dryly. "I can't leave this city now. Someone else will have to make my request to the dukes. But we have no writ of sovereignty."

"When's the last time anyone's seen this writ thing you speak of?" asked Declan.

"About three hundred years ago."

"Then forge the blasted thing. I reckon most of the dukes are smart enough to figure what's what, without needing some fancy piece of paper with the regent's signature on it. Well, maybe not Vomaro."

The door flung open and Bordeall strode in.

"My pardon, gentlemen," he said, nodding to them. "Captain, pardon my interruption, but the rat's out of the trap."

"What? The word's out about the regent?"

"The regent? What do you mean? No, we broke the fellow young Bridd nabbed this morning. You were right. He's Guild. That milksop Posle recognized him, turned whiter than a bucket of goat's milk. Varden batted the fellow about, has a knack for that sort of thing, and the man started talking. The Guild knows all about you and the theft. They're figuring to take you today."

"Let them try," said Owain. "I'm in no mood to fool about with a mob of purse-cutters."

"They've some good swordsmen in that lot," said Declan mildly.

"I'd welcome the chance to test their skill."

"All the more reason for you to stay in Hearne. Stay and keep a hand on things before the Guild complicates this mess." It was Jute who had spoken, standing by the window and gazing down at the morning bustle in the street running alongside the wall. Traders urged their oxen in through the gate, whips cracking. Cartwheels creaked and clattered across the cobblestones.

"We'll go," he said. "Hawk, Declan, and I. We'll go for you. To the duchies."

The hawk tilted his head at the boy. It was difficult to tell, but it seemed as if the bird was smiling.

"We can travel fast," said Jute. "Besides, we are responsible. For all of them."

He whispered the last sentence so that no one heard except the hawk. He turned back to the window and looked down. The street was crowded and bright with sunlight, cheerful, busy with life. A cart full of apples rolled by, a boy not much older than himself perched on the seat and dangling a willow stick over the back of a pair of donkeys in the traces.

Aye. We are responsible for them. The hawk's voice sounded gentle in his mind. *I think the wind is waking more fully in you. You are becoming the anbeorun in truth.*

"I agree," said Declan. "We can ride fast. Give us letters of introduction. There's no duke in Tormay that'll easily ignore the demands of the Lord Captain of Hearne."

Owain slammed his fist down on his desk. "Bordeall, saddle the fastest horses in the stables for them. Eight mounts. We'll send some Guardsmen with you."

"No," said Declan. "Maybe with the boy, but I can ride faster alone."

"One horse only." The hawk hopped onto the desk and settled his wings. "One horse for Declan."

"But what about Jute?"

"He'll fly," said the hawk.

CHAPTER ONE HUNDRED & TEN
HULL AND THULE

They stood on the top of the tower at the gate. It was the highest structure in Hearne, other than the main tower in the university ruins, not counting the Highneck Rise district and the castle, which were higher merely by virtue of being built on the cliffs and slopes of the city's north side. The trapdoor clanged shut behind them and they were alone: the hawk, the boy, and the ghost. The sky trembled with a pale blue light that spoke of the coming winter and the cold heights above the clouds. The ghost wandered about the top of the tower, muttering to itself.

"It's not that I don't want to fly," said Jute. "I do. I don't think there's anything more I want in the whole world."

He stared down at the ground. A hodgepodge of houses pushed up against the wall of the Guard compound. He could see down into a tiny yard shared by several of the houses. A woman stood at a clothesline, hanging up linens. They waved gently in the breeze. Several children ran about in the shelter of the yard. He could hear the sound of their laughter. He looked away, back to the sky and the north.

"It's what I want," said Jute. "I want it with all my heart. But I've never flown before. All I can do is float a few inches above the ground and then fall flat on my face. Or I can fall off buildings and get caught by the wind. I don't call either of those flying."

"Chickens fly better," mumbled the ghost.

"You're right," said the hawk. "You haven't flown yet. But becoming the anbeorun is not about flying, and I think you've finally begun to understand that."

"How do you know the dukes will listen to me? They're dukes."

"You forget who you are, Jute. You're no longer the street urchin, thieving to live. You've become something more. Someone who can see into the past, shape the future, and stand against the Dark. Any duke would gladly honor you."

Jute moved restlessly, leaning on the parapet and staring down again at the children in the yard.

"I still feel as heavy as a body should," he said.

"Regardless, you have changed. You're no longer one of them." The hawk nodded at the children far below. "But you're responsible for them. That is the purpose of the anbeorun. That's why they chose to stay, so long ago."

"What did they give up?"

The hawk laughed at that, an odd, chirruping sound. "There are no words in this language to properly answer your question. They put aside the true heights for this sky. They turned their backs on the light for this humble sun. They gave up much, yet they gained much as well." He sidestepped a few feet away on the parapet and spread his wings. "Come. Time does not wait, so we must fly."

The hawk launched himself off the tower, beating his wings until he mounted higher into the sky. Jute put his hand up to shade his face. The hawk diminished to a dark speck against the blue.

I can't fly.

You can. And must. And shall.

So Jute flung himself from the tower, because he was tired of waiting and wondering, tired of the weight of his body and looking to the sky. He wondered if the children in the yard near the foot of the tower were looking up at that moment, watching. But then he forgot all that, because when he flung himself from the tower, he flew. The wind chuckled, lifted him, and became something else. Became almost like a liquid that he could slide through. His mind caught hold of it and he hurtled forward. He sliced through the air, his hair rippling back from his forehead, with arms, hands, and fingers spread wide with the wind running through them like strands of water. He flew further and higher until the sky was as cold as ice around him and the earth was a distant patchwork of greens and browns and grays and the swath of the sea was a deep blue on his left that stretched away almost as far as the sky.

"You're flying!" yelled the ghost. It sounded like it was perched on Jute's back, but he was not sure. He could not see the ghost. "You're flying. And about time, if I may say so."

The hawk slid into place beside him. His outstretched wing almost touched his fingertips.

North.

I'm flying!

Ribbons of clouds streamed past them. They flew blind in gray mist, water shooting past them in a hundred thousand stinging droplets. And then burst up into the purity of the clear blue sky. Blinding light. Sunlight shone on the bird's feathers. Glossy black like wet stone. The air was clean and cold and scarcely seemed breathable, so thin was it.

Of course. We were ever waiting for you. The sky, the wind, and me.

They flew up the coast of Hull. The sun shone on the sea flashing below them, shining on the spray crashing against the rocks. The smell of salt filled the air. Far out to sea, a ketch beat its way north. Its sails were taut and bellied with wind, as white as a gull's wings. But soon it was only a speck on the horizon behind them, for the hawk and the boy flew as fast as the wind.

It seemed as if his flesh frayed into nothingness as he flew, faded into the insubstantiality of air and then back again to plain, normal flesh. He could look through his hands; he could note the faint outlines of them but then see right through their blur to the sky and earth beyond. The change did not disturb him. It felt right. It was right. He laughed out loud.

The wind, said the hawk in his mind. *You are the wind.*

They neared the town of Lastane in a driving, slashing rain. The sky had gone gray and the sun was lost high in its own solitude of light, somewhere beyond the clouds. Jute could smell woodsmoke in the rain and he was aware that he was hungry and cold and wet. The hawk chuckled.

Old things, fledgling. Old needs. As you grow and learn, you shall discover that such complaints of the flesh need be no longer heeded. My old master once wandered north, beyond the abode of the ice giants, and tarried with the winds there, talking of snow and ice and the frozen night. A full year and more, he was, and did not taste food or sleep or warmth.

Well, I'm not him, and I'd like a bite to eat.

Lastane was much smaller than Hearne. It huddled in shades of gray stone at the mouth of a river that rushed out into the sea, turning the bay there into a roiling mass of muddy water. Further out, waves crashed against a breakwater guarding the bay. The tallest roof in Lastane belonged to an old manor perched on a rise overlooking the wharfs.

607

Smaller houses crowded up against it, as if its taller eaves would somehow protect them from the rain and weather. Smoke streamed up from chimneys, whipped away by the wind into the gray sky.

The manor, said the hawk.

Why, that isn't a castle at all.

Most of the dukes are nothing at all like the regent, said the hawk in some amusement.

They came to rest on the steps of the manor, blurring down out of the rain and in a swirl of wind that flung raindrops so hard against the front door that it sounded like the pounding of dozens of tiny fists. Jute walked up the steps, the hawk balancing on his shoulders. The door opened and the doorkeeper looked out.

"Can I be helping you, lad?" he said.

Maernes. Duke Maernes.

"I have a message for Duke Maernes."

"Very well," said the man mildly. "He's just finishing lunch. Come in. You look as if you've taken a plunge into the sea."

The doorkeeper let Jute in, closed the door against the rain, and disappeared. It was warm inside. He was standing in a hall. He wasn't sure how a duke's house should look. Whatever it should look like, he would not have imagined it would look like this. A pair of worn hip boots stood in comfortable collapse in one corner, a fishing pole and wicker bag leaning alongside them. A pegged board ran the length of one wall, sporting an assortment of walking sticks, umbrellas, and cloaks. On the opposite wall hung a painting of an old woman. She looked out on the shabby room with good humor, her gray hair wound around her head, her blue eyes snapping with life.

"My wife, Maeve."

Jute turned to see an old man standing in one of the doorways. He was thickset and sturdy and as gray as the stone of the town. He limped forward and stood beside Jute. They both inspected the painting.

"She looks nice," said Jute, not sure what to say.

"Aye, she was. Nicest thing ever happened to me. Caught a cold one winter, three years back. The wind blows off the sea something fierce. Nothing can stand before it. That was the end of my duchess." He shook his head and smiled. "Still, we had our years and I'm nothing but grateful. Tush, lad, I'm an old gander to be maundering on like this. What've you to say? Are the yellowfin running again off the cliffs?"

"No, sir. It's not that. I've come—"

"You look familiar, lad." The old duke stared at him. His eyes flicked to the hawk and widened, as if he had just seen him for the first time. "And a black hawk. Now that's a rare sight. Only one I've seen before."

"Sir, I've a message from Owain Gawinn," said Jute, stumbling a bit on the words. "He invokes the writ of sovereignty. He bids the duchies remember their old allegiance to Hearne and send what soldiers they can."

"A black hawk," said the duke, still gazing at the hawk and looking as if he had not heard a word Jute had said. "Now I remember. Not twenty years old I was. Hadn't been duke but a few months. Wind been blowing out of the east all fall, and then one day it changes. He came walking into town with a black hawk on his shoulder. The wind lord." His gaze switched back to Jute. "I remember you now. You were at the ball. With Lady Callas. When the wind arose."

"He is the wind," said the hawk. "He is the guardian of the wind." His voice sounded harsh in the quiet hall.

The duke did not say anything for a while, but then he nodded slowly.

"I should've known. There was a different feel to the rain this morning, and I could tell the land was waiting for you, lad. I know my duchy well, well enough to tell when one of the anbeorun come calling at my door. You do us honor." But the duke sighed as he said the words.

They left shortly after that, with the old duke standing in the cold rain at the top of the steps. But even before they had lifted above the roofs, with the wind rushing to meet them, the duke stumped back into his house, voice raised. Hull would ride south to Hearne. Old allegiances would be honored on the strength of Owain Gawinn's word. And on the strength of the word of the guardian of the wind. It was only until they were high above the clouds that Jute realized he had forgotten about lunch. It didn't matter. He no longer felt hungry.

The weather grew worse as they flew farther north. The sky darkened to nearly black, blowing with snow and towering with clouds. The air was so cold that it seemed he would surely die from it, that his lungs would freeze with the next breath. But this did not happen, of course. The cold merely blew through him and he found it was no better or worse than sunlight on a summer day. Jute discovered that he delighted in the fierceness of the sky. The blasts and blows of the wind, the splinters of ice arrowing down through the gloom, the clouds boiling and massing together on the howling currents of the wind, the snow lashing against his face in shattered bits of flakes. The height and depth of it all. It was beautiful, marvelous, enthralling. He could stay up in the sky forever. Flying north through the storms. Learning the different voices of the winds until they were as familiar as his own. Forgetting the earth.

Aye. It would be easy enough. The hawk shot past him, snowflakes tumbling from the tips of his wings. *And that is a danger.*

Far below them, the coast road meandered along the cliffs above the sea. The Scarpe plain stretched away into the distance, looking just as vast as the sea itself. They passed over a valley opening out onto a rocky beach and a bay beyond.

"Look," said the ghost. "The Stone Tower! Except. . . except. . ."

Except there was no Stone Tower.

Jute could not see a single sign of the tower. The cliff where the tower had stood appeared bare and lifeless, falling away to the meadow below—the meadow that they had run through toward the boats and the sea, with the wihht coming after them like a black cloud blowing along the shore.

"It's gone," said the ghost. "It should be right there. Right against the cliff. Past the eucalyptus trees. Er, you don't mind if we stop and look about, do you?"

"We don't have the time," said the hawk.

"Sorry," said Jute.

"Never mind," said the ghost sadly. "It was only my home. That's all. Nothing important."

Further north, they veered inland. The Scarpe plain rose up to a series of hills, rough with brambly scrub and broken by outcroppings of stone. The hills ascended in leaps and bounds until they leveled out into a moor. It was a wild, lonely-looking country. They were well into Thule by now, according to the hawk, the duchy that lay between Hull to the south and Harlech to the north. They flew over a herd of cattle strung out across the

609

moor, dotted between the occasional pool of water, oblivious to the rain and the snow, heads down, grazing on the withered grass.

Averlay is the only town in Thule, said the hawk. *The duke has a house there but he is most likely in the country.* The hawk chuckled. *Which means all the rest of Thule.*

Then how'll we find him? Will we have to fly back and forth until we spot him? That could take days.

I will find him easily enough. You shall learn how, given time, but dukes are unusual people. They've the land in them, somehow, and the land will always point the way, if a duke does not mind being found. And I think that Galaestan will want to speak with us.

The day darkened toward twilight. There was no evidence of the sun, and the sky could only offer gray clouds and the rain and snow that, more and more, was becoming just snow. Jute flew along in a bliss of awareness—the wind, the tumble of snowflakes past him, the slight variations of colors and textures of the moor far below, the ever-changing shapes of the clouds as they surged across the sky—all of this existed for him in vivid detail. Even a field mouse nosing about in the grass was visible to him. But it was not just his eyes that had sharpened; his mind seemed able to reach out around him, to smell and touch and taste and hear with such clarity that it was almost as if the sky and the wind and the weather were right inside his mind.

A flock of geese winged their way toward them. They veered abruptly at the sight of the hawk, but then straightened out again in renewed confidence. Jute could hear them chanting as they flew.

South by south, lads! So we fly
from winter's blast and snowy sky.
Lake on lake, ho! We shall feed
on little trouts and tender weeds.
Little trouts, ho! And tender weeds!

The geese were past them, wings beating slowly and powerfully. They bent their necks to Jute as they passed, but they did not pause in their flight or their chant. Even when they had diminished to specks against the gray sky and the falling snow, the faint call of their chant could be heard.

Little trouts, ho! And tender weeds!

"Trout, I understand," said the hawk. "But weeds? Disgusting."

"What's that?" said the ghost. He did not understand the language of geese and had only heard what sounded like a cacophony of passing honks. "Trout? Are we going fishing? How peculiar."

And then Jute could smell woodsmoke in the air. It was faint, blurred almost into nothingness by the wind, but woodsmoke nonetheless. He looked about eagerly. The snow swirled down under the blast of the wind. But then he saw the fire far below them. It was still far off, and it winked in the gloom like a friendly eye.

"There's a fire down there!" he called to the hawk.

"I daresay that's where we want to go."

The fire burned in a hollow, sheltered by a thicket of bramble and a tumble of tall standing stones leaning on each other in weary decline. Snow lay piled in a drift against the other side of the brambles and provided an excellent break against the depredations of the wind. Two horses stood patiently, scraping at the snow with their hooves and cropping the withered grass they uncovered. A length of canvas stretched over a pole frame provided shelter behind the fire. Jute landed in a swirl of snow, the hawk settling on his shoulder. An old man looked up from the fire. He was crouched there, gutting a rabbit, flicking the entrails from his knife into the flames. He was a gaunt, rawboned-looking man.

"Sit down by the heat," he said. "Rabbits'll be ready in no time."

He finished gutting the rabbit and then added it to a spit already heavy with several other carcasses. The fat hissed in the fire. A young man walked out of the darkness, carrying an armload of wood. He dumped it by the fire and turned as if to go again.

"That's enough," said the old man. "Ain't all that cold. I ain't an old woman."

The young man grinned, shrugged, and sat down.

The old man turned the spit.

"I reckon I know you," he said to the hawk.

"Duke Galaestan," said the hawk, nodding. "It's been many years. And your son, no?" The bird hopped down from Jute's shoulder and settled under the shelter of the canvas.

"My youngest, Eldon. We're riding the moor from Averlay to the Mearh Dun hills. Check on the stockmen. Draw up lists for their winter supplies. Take accounting of the herds. Besides, I figure it's high time Eldon learned the difference between a cow and a sheep."

Eldon grinned but didn't say anything.

"You, I don't know," said the duke, eyeing Jute. "But it ain't just anyone that flies with the hawk. Kinda scrawny, but you're welcome in Thule, long as you don't eat us into the poorhouse."

Jute ducked his head, embarrassed. "Thank you," he said.

"Scrawny?" The hawk paused in his inspection of his feathers and chuckled. "This boy is the guardian of the wind."

"Oh?" The duke winked at Jute. "I hope you don't mind roast rabbit. Well, I was just teasing. Teasing and tall tales. That's my downfall."

"Sends ma crazy, most days," said Eldon.

"I figured there was something different about you, lad. You don't be a duke for forty-three years without learning a thing or two. I can feel things. I ain't a wizard, never had a hand for spells, but I can read my land and I can read the wind. I knew when things went bad. The wind changed. That was years ago. Years ago. And then, the end of this summer, the wind changed again. Seemed to cheer up."

"But that's not all that's changed in recent days," said the hawk.

"Nope." The duke spat into the fire. "Couple weeks back, the earth shook. Real uneasy-like. It ain't been the same since. Something's wrong. Not just here in Thule, but all of Tormay, I reckon. The land's waiting for something now. Or someone. I expect you know more'n me about that."

"We found the place where she died," said Jute, shivering despite the warmth of the fire. "Out on the Scarpe plain. Dead men and wolves. Blood everywhere. She died there."

"She?"

"The mistress of the earth," said the hawk.

"The mistress of the earth!" said the duke, staring at Jute. "Stone the crows. That ain't welcome news, master hawk. About the worst I've ever heard. She had nothing but kindness for us, here in Thule. Nothing but kindness."

The duke abruptly got to his feet and paced back and forth.

"Mind you, I ain't so old as I can't track the trail from here," he said sadly. "I was hoping things'd keep staying quiet. Folks live their lives in peace. Duchies behave as good neighbors should. Fish a little, hunt some deer. Winter, springtime, summer, and harvest.

The Dark don't like those things. It has its hand in, don't it? The Dark's come back to Tormay."

"Truly," said the hawk. "But the Dark's been in Tormay for many a year now. Perhaps it never left."

"Well, if it's here or not, ain't much you can do except what comes to you. That's the best any of us can do, whether a duke or a youngster mucking stables. And I imagine you're here to tell me what that is."

"The regent would've done well to hire you as his advisor, Galaestan," said the hawk.

"Instead of that fat fool Dreccan Gor? No, master hawk. I can hardly stomach a day of Hearne, let alone years on end. Walls and towers? No, thank you. This is my home, as poor and scrape-by as it is. I know this land like the back of my hand, and you don't get too far from your own hand now, do you? Here, try some rabbit, lad. Eldon, help yourself. I ain't your ma and I ain't gonna serve you. Take more than that, boy. Put some meat on your bones! Sorry. My apologies. It takes some doing to think of you as the guardian of the wind."

"I have trouble with it myself," said Jute, smiling, but then he sobered quickly. "We have a simple message for you. It isn't ours, but Owain Gawinn's. He requests the duchies send what soldiers they can by his—what is that thing called?"

"The writ of sovereignty," said the hawk. "The kings of Hearne created that right, and it was never revoked, even after the monarchy was destroyed."

"And the reason?" asked the duke, looking rather sour. "It'd better be solid gold. I don't fancy calling up my men and marching them off to Hearne. Leave the cattle, the fishing boats, the farms. Gawinn's a good man, but the writ of sovereignty? Never been invoked in my lifetime."

"The Dark is the reason," said the hawk. "The Dark is coming to Hearne. When the snows thaw in the passes of the Mountains of Morn, then the Dark will come marching. If Hearne falls, then the duchies will fall as well, one by one."

"Blast!" said the duke.

"My lord duke," said the ghost, appearing by the fire, "do you, er, have any news of the Stone Tower?"

"Eh? What's that? Ah, you're a ghost. My great aunt Gavaris ended up a ghost. Choked on a fish bone. It's a wonder she hadn't choked years earlier, the way she ate. Haunted my great uncle's house until he got fed up and went to sea. I expect he would've gone to sea even if she had lived. Ghosts can't stay on the sea for long. It's the tides. They keep washing 'em back to shore. But the Stone Tower?" The duke slid a rabbit off the spit and took a bite. "There's enough wards woven around that place to make my head spin. Besides, I don't pay attention to wizards. As long as they don't bother me, that's all I care about."

"Oh," said the ghost, looking crestfallen.

The duke's son threw more wood onto the fire. It flared up, pushing back the night. Snow swirled down, appearing as the flakes journeyed from darkness into light, hissing in the fire. The horses dozed, stamping occasionally in sleepy patience.

"The mistress of the earth dead, the Dark creeping about Tormay, Gawinn calling us to arms." The duke shook his head. "Eldon, I expect your ma'll have an earful to say about this. Well, might as well get one peaceful night's sleep afore she hears it. I'm turning in. Plenty of blankets in the saddlebags if you don't mind the horse smell."

CHAPTER ONE HUNDRED & ELEVEN
A CHANGE IN THE WEATHER

"Two hundred barrels of salted mackerel, eighty wheels of Thulish cheese—that's the cartwheel size, my lord—four hundred kegs of ale, another two hundred kegs of cheap Vornish red wine, twenty dozen sacks of onions, forty dozen sacks of potatoes, thirteen dozen sacks of turnips, and eight dozen sacks of garlic." The quartermaster glanced up from his notes to make sure that Owain was paying proper attention. "Three hundred hams, the same again of bacon, six hundred loaves of twice-baked bread. . ."

"Hard as rock," rumbled Bordeall.

"One hundred seventy sacks of grain, milled, and three hundred sacks of grain, unmilled," continued the quartermaster, choosing to ignore the comment. "Ten blocks of sea salt and thirty-three kegs of olive oil. As to livestock, my lord, we're currently bursting at the seams. I've rented additional space down in Fishgate. Two warehouses for five silver coins a month and three coins a month, respectively. Not a bad deal, if I may say so."

"Yes, yes," said Owain, trying not to fidget in his chair. "Just tell me what the final tallies are."

Rain slashed down outside the window of his office. It had been raining all night and it gave no sign of letting up. Bordeall stood at the window, staring out gloomily at the city wall. The quartermaster cleared his throat with an accusative sort of sound. He was determined to do his job well. He rustled his papers as if to underscore the fact that there were a great many papers covered over with a great many notes, and that he still had a great deal to say about bushels of nails and baulks of timber and other things that could be counted and recounted.

"As I was saying, my lord," continued the quartermaster, "that has greatly expanded our livestock capacity. An increase of threefold over our previous capacity. Fourteen hundred bales of hay, half that of alfalfa, and six hundred bushels of feed corn. I'm not happy about the alfalfa stock, my lord, but there was mildew in the crops this summer. Though, I think that, er, oh yes—the livestock." He began to speak a great deal faster, as it was impossible to ignore the fact that Owain was glaring at him. "Three hundred seventy-five head of cattle, four hundred twelve head of sheep, two hundred pigs, three hundred eighty chickens, and that's giving us about two hundred fifty eggs a day, give or take a few dozen."

"Not enough," said Owain. "We'll be out of meat in no time. Particularly with Harlech having arrived last night."

"Those boys eat a lot of meat," said Bordeall. "Like a pack of wolves."

"Lannaslech mentioned he thought Hull and Thule were only a day's march behind him. That's a lot of extra mouths."

"That's a lot of extra swords," said Bordeall.

"Furthermore," said the quartermaster, feeling that the conversation was wandering away from his lists and numbers, "I have it on the best authority that three herds of cattle shall arrive this afternoon from Vo. An emissary from the duke's court rode in this morning, with the duke's compliments. And there's the fish."

"The fish?"

"Haddock and cod," said the quartermaster. "Excellent catches they're having right now. Almost swamped a boat yesterday, so I was told. The fishing guild said they've never had such a season. Very peculiar, they said."

"At least something's working out these days," said Owain. "We're about to be attacked, but there's plenty of haddock and cod. Bordeall, do you think fish could be used as a weapon?"

"I almost choked to death on a fish bone once," said Bordeall.

"It wouldn't be surprising to me in the least if it started raining fish." Owain got up and walked over to the window. "Almost two days straight."

No one said anything for a moment. The quartermaster stood in frustrated silence, wondering whether he should move on to his list of rope, twine, nails, and other assorted things that fasten. Owain stared out the window. It wasn't just that it had been raining for two days. The rain was decidedly on the warm side. A pleasant rain that had the children out, splashing through puddles and floating little homemade boats down the swollen gutters. A very unseasonal rain.

"If the weather's anything like this out east in the Morns," said Bordeall, his voice a low rumble, "the snows'll be melting. Probably already are. If the rumors are true."

Owain grunted in response, a noise halfway between irritation and agreement. Bordeall had voiced what he had been thinking all morning. Melting snows. The passes in the Morn Mountains clear after months of being impassable. The streams and rivers choked with water and ice. Mud. An army slogging its way west. West, toward Hearne.

Rumors had been trickling in since late yesterday from a few frightened countryfolk from the far eastern reaches of the Rennet Valley. Their stories were mostly incoherent. Monsters and murderous beasts slaying people in their bed. Smoke blackening the sky from the villages in the mountains. The peculiar thing about it was that there weren't that many refugees. Just a handful. If there was an enemy army marching down the Rennet Valley, then you'd think there'd be more refugees streaming into Hearne. Whole villages full of them. Unless, of course, they were being slaughtered to the last child.

Owain shuddered. He turned from the window, his mind made up.

"Bordeall," he said.

"Sir?"

"The Gap."

"Sir?"

"It's the most defensible spot in the whole Rennet Valley. Even outnumbered. It can't be flanked, unless you ride two days into Vomaro and swing back north for another two."

"Your father held there for three weeks in the Errant Wars, if I recollect. Harth beat themselves to pieces on those slopes."

"It's time for the Guard to march."

"My thoughts exactly."

"What about the rope and twine?" said the quartermaster.

"I'm sure they'll keep in your hands," said Owain. "Let's go find ourselves a war."

The Guard rode out that afternoon. Two columns of eighty horsemen, steaming and stamping in the rain. The footmen marched behind them. Their spears angled toward the sky like a forest of impossibly straight saplings. The archers followed them, sixty strong, in looser formation. At the rear rode the men of Harlech. There were only fifty of them, led by Duke Lannaslech and his son Rane, but Owain was desperately glad to have them. He was not too proud to know that each of them were worth more than several of his Guardsmen.

Owain and Bordeall sat on their horses in the shelter of the main gate's arch. The soldiers turned as they marched by. Owain tried to look at each face as they passed by. Names flashed through his head. Fathers, husbands, brothers, and sons. Good men and scoundrels alike. They would do. They would have to do.

The Duke of Harlech nodded cheerfully at him as he rode by.

"You're most hospitable, Gawinn," he said. "A good bed, a good breakfast, and a good fight. What more could a man want?"

"Only about a thousand more soldiers," said Bordeall, but no one except Owain heard him.

"That's the lot," said Owain, as the last of the troop rode out through the gate and down the muddy road. He turned to the two soldiers standing at attention beside his horse. "Lucan, the city's yours for now. Keep an eye out for the duchies. Send the contingent from Vo on after us if they arrive anytime soon. Old Maernes and Galaestan should arrive in the morning, I hope. Both of 'em have got more common sense in their little fingers than you do in your whole skull, so treat 'em politely and listen to them, you hear me?"

"Yes, sir," said Lucan, struggling not to scowl.

"Suggest to 'em—suggest, I say—that I'd prefer they keep their men here for now, until we figure out what we're dealing with down in the Rennet Valley. No one's heard from Dolan or Vomaro. Keep a couple riders out north and south of the valley to pick up any news there might be, but on no account engage the enemy if you find him."

"Yes, sir."

"Just observe and then get out of there. Tell your men we don't want any heroes. At least, not yet. I'll send messengers back to keep you informed, once we reach the Gap. It's only a quick, half-day ride. As for you, Bridd, you're his second."

"Yes, sir," said Arodilac, for that was who the other soldier was. "But, sir, I think that—"

"You're staying here, that's an order, you understand?"

"But, sir—"

"You're in charge of keeping an eye on the castle. Keep a lookout for your, uh, uncle, but keep away from him. Far away. Don't let him see you or any of your men, if you can help it. Don't forget what I told you. He isn't precisely your uncle anymore."

"Yes, sir," said Arodilac. "I was never fond of him anyway, sir."

"Stow it, Bridd. Post a guard outside the castle walls at all time and keep out of trouble. All right, Lucan, the city's yours. Good luck."

"Thank you, sir."

Lucan snapped a salute. The sound of Owain and Bordeall's horses' hooves echoed from the cobblestones under the arch of the gate. And then they were out in the rain, past the wall and cantering after the rest of the little army as it marched away into the rain.

"Right, Bridd," said Lucan. "You heard the captain. Take three men and detail a guard duty at the castle."

"Oh, very well," said Arodilac, trudging off. "Some people have all the fun."

CHAPTER ONE HUNDRED & TWELVE
THE SHAME OF THE PRINCE

Damarkan rose up out of the desert, sudden and shimmering in the noonday sun. Declan thought it another mirage at first, another mirage in a long succession of vanishing wells, caravans, and fat men pushing carts piled high with ices and fruits and chilled wine. He was heartily sick of the desert and he was sure his horse was even more disgusted. The poor beast grumbled and hung its head as they plodded along the dusty track.

But the city did not vanish. The towers rose white and shining in the sun, waiting serenely behind the high stone walls of pale yellow. The walls looked as smooth as freshly churned butter, patted down into immense building blocks, but as Declan drew nearer, he saw that their surfaces were scarred from the years of the wind driving sand against them.

The road became populated with fellow travelers. It was a strange thing. Only an hour previously and he had been the only one on the road. A caravan of dusty mules appeared out of the desert. A child perched on a donkey laden with sacks of figs, clucking and calling encouragement to the beast. A herd of goats popped up out of nowhere. Several dogs ran careful circles around them, while the goats eyed the dogs with malevolent yellow eyes. Declan rubbed his own eyes. Perhaps he was more tired than he thought. But there were no other roads in sight. No houses. No towns huddled in among the stony cliffs. Still, the people appeared out of the desert, drifting along like the sand. The road was soon busy.

And then they were under the city wall. It loomed up above their heads. The gates stood open. Iron and wood bleached white by years of sun. Guards stood as still as stone on either side with spears in their hands. The arch of the gate curved overhead, carved with strange designs. Declan looked about him curiously once he had passed through the gate. In all of his travels he had never been to Damarkan. Even as a child over the course of years of crisscrossing the duchies of Tormay, his father had never brought them to Harth. It was too far away. It was almost a separate country, separate from the rest of Tormay.

The streets were narrower than those in Hearne. The buildings were higher, constructed of blocks of stone and flat roofs, so that each street was sunk in shadow unless the sun happened to be overhead. Bougainvillea grew everywhere he looked, climbing up walls and spilling down from trellises and over the edges of roofs in extravagant washes of red bloom. There was a quietness to the city, despite its size and the crowded streets. People walked sedately and did their business in murmurs. There was none of the bustling and shouting and yelling common in the Hearne marketplaces. Merchants did not insult and argue with their customers.

Perhaps the climate's heat requires that people act slowly, thought Declan to himself. In the cold north, people must shout and yell and generally behave like donkeys in order to keep their blood stirred. Here, the sunlight boils it for you.

He watered his horse at a stone fountain in a small square. Awnings stretched out from the sides of the houses. The ubiquitous bougainvillea spilled along the walls and dangled down in luxuriant falls. Blooms lay scattered in the street, some crushed underfoot, and the air was thick with their sweet scent.

"Pardon me," he said to a passing old man.

The old man stopped and bowed courteously.

"Can you tell me how to get to the king's palace? I am a stranger in your city."

"Assuredly. You are certainly a stranger if you do not know the way to the heart of our city. All roads in Harth lead to the palace of our most glorious Oruso Oran. However, I will show you the straightest way, for you look as if you have come a long way and need not waste any more of your journey conversing with an old man such as I."

"Which would certainly be one of the more pleasant parts of my journey."

The old man smiled and bowed again in response.

Declan had done well to ask directions; for despite the apparently square and straightforward appearances of the streets and the buildings that lined them wall by wall, the deeper he went into the city the more the streets twisted and turned until he knew that he traversed a labyrinth. The horse beneath him sighed as if to say *When will all of this be over?* and *I would appreciate a bite of oats just now.*

Declan patted the horse's neck and murmured soothingly.

The street widened and the polished ivory gates of the palace stood before him in all their splendor. Beyond them, the domes and towers of the palace rose in a mountain of white marble, peaks, crags, and spires, all topped with flags snapping in the breeze.

"Your business, sir?" said the officer at the gate.

"I've traveled here on behalf of the Lord Captain of the Guard of Hearne," said Declan. "I've word for the King of Harth."

That and the manner of Declan's bearing were enough to get him past the officer, who was still young enough to be made uneasy by a stern eye and the mention of such a notable as the Lord Captain of Hearne. They took his horse with the promise that it would be curried and fed in his absence. They also took his pack and, with the utmost tact, relieved him of his sword. The officer then handed him over to a young page who strutted along at Declan's side and sniffed in disdain at the state of his dusty clothing.

The gates opened into an immense garden plumed with peacocks and flowers and tinkling fountains and trees shadowing mossy grottoes. Everything was manicured, and here and there Declan saw white-garbed gardeners flitting about with shears and pruning hooks and rakes, dealing with errant greenery. An avenue led through the garden to steps wide enough for a troop of horsemen to have ridden up them side by side. Halfway up the steps, to the irritation of the page, a steward waited to take charge of Declan. He was even less impressed with Declan than the page had been and demanded to see his letter of introduction from Owain Gawinn, though his demand was couched in courtesy. They passed through polished hardwood doors into a vast and airy space, a hall of shadows and drifting figures and whispers. Gold and silver glimmered in sculptures, hangings of twisted metal thread, and inlaid designs in the marble walls.

"The king is in his council chambers," said the steward, "but perhaps, if luck is with you, he will shortly adjourn to the great hall and there deign to hear whatever supplicant might come before him. In the great hall, all may come before him, rich or poor."

"I'm not a supplicant," said Declan dryly. "I come with a message from the Lord Captain of Hearne, and he with the power of the regency at his beck."

"Be that as it may," said the steward, equally as dryly. "Hearne is far from Damarkan these days, and no one approaches the king in his council chambers."

The great hall was indeed great. The ceiling soared up into a mosaic of blues and whites so cunningly done that it seemed the room opened up into the sky rather than simple stone. Slender pillars rose in groves as if perfect, leafless trees grew in that place. At the far end of the room, several thrones sat empty on a raised dais. And everywhere that Declan turned, there were people. They stood patiently throughout the room, a crowd waiting in silence.

The steward ushered Declan up toward the front of the room, gently but firmly pushing his way through the crowd. As they progressed nearer to the dais, Declan noticed that the people looked wealthier and wealthier. The great hall might be open to both rich and poor, but clearly the rich found some advantage in their position. The steward's progress slowed to a struggle until he gave up in defeat, cowed into submission by an elderly lady in a tiara and possessed of a piercing stare. The steward turned, looking embarrassed.

"Perhaps, sir," he said, "we will wait here until the king chooses to appear."

And so they waited. As he stood there, Declan became aware of an ache in his back and his legs. It had been a long ride. Three days at a near gallop. Seven different horses changed at inns along the way. There was a sharper ache in his stomach. He hadn't eaten since the previous night. And then Giverny's face sprang into his mind and that was the worst ache of all. Anger filled his stomach and he swallowed hard.

Declan realized the steward was whispering to him.

". . . his Majesty or his Highness will both equally do. Do not look him in the eyes but keep your gaze fixed below his feet. On no account should a question be addressed to him. His Majesty asks the questions—he and he alone. Do not bore him, anger him, or test his credulity. Do not question his word, for even if it differs from what you hoped for, know that his wisdom is beyond yours and in it is your expectation fulfilled, though you realize it not at the time. Above all else, do not mention the Errant Wars, for his Majesty has a long memory and does not look kindly on the past."

Doubtless, the steward would have continued, even after such a beginning, but at that moment there was a commotion at the front of the hall. Doors swung open and a great many splendid personages strode in. The crowd was forced back. Declan found himself wedged between a fat man and the elderly lady in the tiara. The tiara was encrusted with emeralds, apparent now that he could afford a closer look, and he found himself wondering whether Jute would have been able to steal it without disturbing the lady. Sleight-of-hand theft had never been his forte. His talent had always been in killing people.

A trumpet sounded and a hush fell over the hall. The king of Harth had come. He was a tall man, tall with massive hands and an even more massive head, but his body had gone to fat, encouraged by the depredations of age and dissolute living. Yet, though there was a slack cast to his mouth and in his eyes, the softness was not enough to mask the hardness beneath. Silk flowed around him, and the whispering noise of its passage across the marble floor was the loudest sound in the room. The king sat down on his throne. Others sat in the grand chairs near him, but Declan did not see their faces. His attention was concentrated on the king. He could already taste the disappointment sour in his mouth. This man. On this man had Owain Gawinn pinned such hopes. Harth could field a powerful army. The biggest army in all of Tormay. It had the people and it had the treasury. But this man on the throne would never agree to such a request. Not unless there was something in it for Harth. Something more immediate than the unsubstantiated claims of a man, a boy, and a hawk.

On the dais, the court chamberlain stepped forward. He was dressed in black and carried an ivory staff.

"Silence!" said the chamberlain, his voice sharp and carrying. It was a needless thing to say, as the hall was already silent despite the crowd gathered there. "Silence, before our glorious Lord and Majesty, Oruso Oran, the ninth of his name, yet none more exalted, none more wise, none more excellent and worthy. Silence, before our king."

He pounded the staff once on the dais.

Boom!

The sound rolled through the hall.

Boom!

"Our king, the glorious, the most illustrious Oruso Oran, will now hear the grievances of his petitioners."

The staff dipped down to point in unwavering precision. A little man at the front of the crowd glanced around, his face brightening into joy. He rushed forward and fell on his knees before the dais. His words were gabbled, unintelligible to Declan at even such a short distance, but the king bent his head on his throne, intent and listening. The little man's words ran out, trickling into an arid silence. His face was hopeful and gleaming with sweat. The king spoke. His voice was dry, rasping, like the sound of sand against sand. His voice filled up the hushed room, as if the sand poured down into some vast, empty space. The crowd, which had been silent and motionless before, grew even more silent and motionless. The king's voice fell still and the little man threw his arms up in desperation, a wail bursting from his mouth. He inched forward on his knees, but before he could even reach the edge of the dais, two guards were at his side, his arms pinned, legs scrabbling uselessly beneath him.

The chamberlain's staff pointed once again.

Another petitioner fell forward on his face before the dais. A voice rose quavering, buoyed by hope. Supplication, veneration, and fear. The staff pointed again and again. Another petitioner, and then another, but still the crowd did not diminish. The mass of people around Declan were fixed, staring, and immobile. The temperature within the room crept higher and, far up on the wall, the sunlight slid across the marble with the shadows in pursuit. The day would soon be done. Another day gone. Another day closer to the spring thaw and the opening of the passes in the Morn Mountains.

Declan could not control his anger any longer. He shoved the elderly lady to one side, hard, because there was no space for her. Pushed past someone else, several someone elses, and was dimly aware of faces turning toward him in outrage. A hand plucked desperately at the back of his jacket—the steward, no doubt.

I'm the wrong sort for this, Declan thought dully to himself. I know swords and death and hunting, not words and courts and kings. His anger wearied him and he longed to be back out under the sky, away from walls and roofs and the crushing weight of this city. But then he was through the final ring of people that jealously encircled the front of the dais. Astonishment turned to outrage on the chamberlain's face. The figures sitting on the dais rose, one and all, except for the king sitting on his throne, immovable.

"Guards!" called the chamberlain, but the guards were already leaping forward.

"I'm not a supplicant!" said Declan, his voice loud with fury. The guards' hands closed on him, yanked him staggering back, but he spoke on. "I'm not a supplicant, nor one of your land! My name's Declan Farrow. I come as an emissary of the Lord Captain of the Guard of Hearne, the Sword of the Regent of Hearne, and is this how I am treated? Made to kick my heels among your common folk and their whining of goats and cheating scales?"

The guards paused, for there was sudden doubt in the chamberlain's eyes. Silence gripped the room. The king did not move on his throne, but his gaze fell on Declan. There was a remoteness in his eyes, something as distant as the long desert horizons, and though those vistas could burn with the day's heat, they could be deadly cold in the dead of night, and so were the king's eyes.

"Hearne is far from Damarkan these days," said the king.

"Take him away," said the chamberlain.

The guards renewed their hold on Declan.

"Wait!" said another voice. A man stood up from one of the lesser thrones on the dais. He was dressed in fine raiment, and on his head he bore a crown.

"Wait, my lord. I know this man as well as any can who have faced another across blades. We met in friendly battle and I deem him of utmost gentility and courtesy. Might we not hear his words on your sufferance and the good will you bear toward me?"

The king bent his head. "On the good will I bear toward you, my son, and on this alone, for my patience wears thin this day."

Eaomod, the prince of Harth, bowed to his father, and took again his seat.

"Speak your piece, man," said the chamberlain.

"I have a letter here for you, your majesty, a letter from the Lord Captain of Hearne, Owain Gawinn." Declan handed the roll of parchment to the chamberlain, who frowned, as if the touch of the thing would dirty his hands. "My Lord Gawinn requests the assistance of Harth, for when the winter snow melts in the passes of the Mountains of Morn, then through them will march an army under the command of the duke of Mizra to threaten all of Tormay."

The king stirred on his throne.

"And what does Gawinn expect of Harth?" he said.

"The aid of your sword, your majesty, for if Hearne falls, then all the duchies will fall in succession. The duke of Mizra has gathered a mighty army and his purposes are orchestrated by the Dark."

"The Dark!" The king's voice was thick with contempt. "What do I care of the Dark, a tale for fools and idle women. And what do I care for Hearne? Did not the armies of Hearne bide their time during the Errant Wars when the blood of Harth ran freely in the desert, when death plucked the flower of this land? Where was Hearne then?"

Declan bowed his head. "Old times gone by, your Majesty. I would not think to understand the choices made by dead men, but I do know that death is coming to Tormay and we shall fall at its sword unless our hand is strengthened. The courage of Harth is known in the north, your Majesty, and we would be glad of it in these coming days, for winter will soon be at an end."

"Harth has never had reason to doubt the friendship of Mizra. They have ever been courteous and mannered in their dealings with us. Harth has no reason to take up sword against them. No reason."

There was finality in his words, a closing that fell on Declan's shoulders like a heavy hand.

"Your Majesty," said Declan, stepping forward and blind in his anger to the guards that also stepped forward. "Your Majesty, I have seen his troops, men that look like men but surely are something other, driven and drawn by magic. The Dark waits in that land and its eyes look to the west, to these duchies and the death it might bring them."

"You try my patience, messenger."

"I have seen the truth, your Majesty."

"Tell Gawinn he will not have a single man of mine! Not one. And you would do well to quit my city this day!"

The chamberlain's staff slammed down on the floor. The guards moved in around Declan. Dimly, as if from a distance, he saw the prince of Harth rise from his seat. The crowd parted for the guards, and they marched him forward. He saw the steward struggling his way through the crowd but falling further and further behind, his arms gently waving as if those of a sea creature pushing futilely against the tide. The doors to the hall swung shut behind them and they were in the shadowy corridors that led away, through the palace and to the rest of the day waiting for Declan outside.

The day half gone, he thought dully to himself. I'll be able to get a few miles behind me on the road north. These past days have been wasted. I wonder if Jute and the hawk would have had better luck here?

Sunlight flashed before them and the guards halted. Declan continued down the broad sweep of steps and turned his face up toward the sun, squinting. The captain of the guard at the gate strode toward him. Behind him, he heard the patter of feet.

"Sir!" gasped the steward. He coughed, trying to inhale and speak at the same time. His face was bright red, scandalized. Declan turned away from him, wondering where his sword was. His sword and his horse. That's all he needed. "Sir! I'm shocked. I didn't realize that, that. . ." The steward ended in a splutter.

"You would do well, my lord, to be on your way in haste," said the captain. His voice was quiet.

"My things?" said Declan.

"If I may intrude?"

The voice came from further up the steps. The captain and the steward backed away, bowing. The prince of Harth's face was set and pale beneath his dark skin, but he inclined his head to Declan.

"It is indeed an honor to see you again, Declan Farrow," he said. "I treasure the memory of our match. Upon my return to Damarkan from the Autumn Fair, my old teacher, Lorcannan Nan, heard of our meeting. He guessed rightly as to who you were when I related the style of your sword-work."

"I didn't come here to discuss friendly sword-work," said Declan, his voice tight. "I came to discuss war."

The prince bowed his head in answer.

"I'm a simple man," continued Declan. "I'm not given to the hysterias that women and cityfolk seem prone to. But the Dark is gathering on the border of Tormay, held back by only the winter snows. Of this I'm sure. Harth would've been a great help in the coming war. The northern duchies of Tormay will probably fall without your army's aid. And then? Harth will fall alone."

"I think I do not doubt your word," said the prince. He paused, his throat working as if he tasted something bitter. "But I am a prince of Harth. As such, I must obey the word of the king."

Declan turned and walked away.

"I must!" called the prince after him, his voice full of anger and shame. "Do you hear me, Farrow?"

Someone brought his horse. Declan did not see who it was, for his fury made him blind. He was only aware of the creak of the saddle under him, the heat of the sun overhead, and the huge gates opening and then closing behind him.

CHAPTER ONE HUNDRED & THIRTEEN
HARLECH AND DOLAN

Early that next morning, after several hours' flight, Jute and his two companions came to the old stone manor of Lannaslech, duke of Harlech. The day was bitterly cold, but Jute did not mind and neither did the hawk or the ghost. The snow lay on the ground and there was ice in the shadows. Past the manor and beyond the forest of pine standing hunched and crooked on the slope below, the sea heaved toward a sullen, gray horizon. A man stood at the top of the manor steps. He was old and gray but stood as straight as a sapling. He smiled at their approach and bent his head in greeting.

"Welcome," he said. "You are welcome to my house."

Breakfast waited for them on a table in a room, warm with a crackling hearth. The house held a contented, sleepy sort of hush, full of years and silence. Jute felt its peace seep into him along with the warmth of the fire. Snowflakes drifted down outside the window.

"Lannaslech," said the hawk, settling on the back of a chair. "This is—"

"Jute," said the duke, nodding. "Yes, I know. The wind has been whispering of little else all morning. And you have a ghost with you too, do you not? He is welcome. Come, have breakfast."

"Oh, er, thank you, sir," said the ghost, appearing. "But I can't eat. Ghosts can't eat."

"Yes, but you can still enjoy the enjoyment of others."

They ate breakfast in a leisurely quiet, the old duke and the boy engrossed in their scones and jam, the hawk pecking politely at a slice of ham, and the ghost watching them all with melancholy appreciation.

"I have only one son," said the duke, finishing the last bite of his scone. "One son that my Arlis bore me, and he is at your service, as is every man, woman, and child of this duchy. We have always served the anbeorun, we of Harlech. It is our lot. Whether it be by life, or by death, it is one and the same to us."

"Oh, I don't know about that," said Jute, discomfited at these words.

The duke smiled. "Death is not such a hard thing when it comes in its time. Everything must have its end. How much more precious it is when spent on the behalf of a noble cause. Or a person such as yourself."

"Myself? Who am I?" Jute forked some ham onto his plate. "I'm still not sure. I opened a box, cut my hand on a knife, and everything changed. People I don't know are trying to kill me, the Dark—I never gave two thoughts about the Dark before—is chasing me, and, on top of it all, I'm supposed to be the wind."

"Which you are," said the ghost.

"I never asked for any of this. I never wanted any of this. Don't get me wrong. I don't intend to complain. It's more a problem of not really understanding. Though I suppose I've gotten used to some of it."

"And greatly appreciate the company along the way, no doubt," said the ghost.

"What we want and what we get are usually two different things," said the duke. "When you reach my age, you look back and realize that, perhaps, they were the same all the time. And what has happened, whether it be a boy cutting his finger on a knife, the birth of a foal, the blossoming of a flower on the plain of Scarpe, will all one day be seen as blindingly important, woven together with countless other threads into something that can't be seen now, from where we stand, but can be seen from some other vantage point."

"From the house of dreams," said the hawk.

"The house of dreams, aye," nodded the duke. "I wish we could see what is seen from there. Perhaps, though, that would not be wise. No matter. Tell me what you've seen for yourselves. That's what you've come for, is it not?"

They told him, in bits and pieces that gradually joined together into the whole. The hawk did a great deal of the talking, but Jute was the one who spoke of Ancalon, of the dark tower that stood there, of the strange captivity of Giverny Farrow, and of the duke of Mizra and his sceadu.

"The duke and his sceadu," said the old duke, frowning. "I wonder greatly who this fellow is, this duke, this creature of the Dark. Have you considered, old wing, whether or not he's human? The more powerful servants of the Dark change their guises easily, putting on and off faces and bodies at will. It would be better for us if we knew our enemy."

"That question has occupied my mind ever since Jute fled the dark tower," said the hawk. "I don't know the answer. There are several possibilites, and none of them reassuring. I'm reasonably certain I know one of his guises, but that isn't the same as knowing who he is. Or what he is."

"And the guise? That might prove helpful."

"Scuadimnes. The wizard who destroyed the university of Hearne."

"And the monarchy."

"Yes," said the hawk. "I suspect Scuadimnes, as terrible as he was, was only a mask that covered the true face beneath. The duke of Mizra made several remarks that hinted at this."

"When I was new to my rule," said Lannaslech, "three years after my father died, a stranger came to this land. You've heard the story, no doubt. A man without a name. He came to Harlech and built a tower without a door. A dark tower with a single window that looked out across the land. His will reached out, searching for the knots, the single thread, that would unravel the secrets of Harlech. I could feel his thirst for knowledge, a grasping and a clutching after the old words of power, seeking for the names that bind. Darkness fell on the land, and a dread took hold of my people. Harlech is not a small duchy, stretching from the mountains to the coast, but wherever I stood I could see the accursed tower. And so I summoned the lords of Harlech and we rode to the moor where the tower rose up into the dark sky. His will assailed us but we stood firm, for Harlech was our land, and her strength was ours. We pulled the tower down into ruin, but of him there was no trace. I have often considered whether that man was Scuadimnes, for even though all wizards share a similar thirst for knowledge, never has history mentioned one so willing to destroy for that which he might find. And the man in the tower sought to destroy Harlech. Perhaps simply for the sake of one word?"

"What could be worse than a sceadu?" said Jute, stirring restlessly on his chair. "If they were the first creations of—of. . ."

"Nokhoron Nozhan," said the hawk.

"If they were his first creations, what could be worse?"

"History has known men who were just as evil," said the hawk. "Individuals who sold their souls to the Dark and received great power in return. But the sceadus were terrible beings. They came from a time when the world was still young. The lord of darkness himself rode across the plains of Ranuin. His army marched behind him, unnumbered and endless. The earth shook with their passage. At his side were the sceadus. They were beautiful to look at, for they were born of starfire and the ancient tongue of the skies. But they were the lords of death, of dark magic and horror, and there was no evil that they would not do for their master. Nothing was more powerful than the sceadus, nothing save the lord of darkness himself. But Nokhoron Nozhan sleeps now in his fortress of night, as he has for hundreds of years."

"But the question isn't answered," said the duke. "Who is our enemy?" A shadow crossed his weathered face. "My ancestors came west because of a great darkness that came to power in the far east. East and across a vast ocean, so I was told, though the stories fray more and more each time they are told. A terrible darkness, and I think there were sceadus, somehow, in the tales."

"We're missing something obvious," said the hawk.

They sat for some time in silence. The ghost stared thoughtfully at the last slice of ham on the platter. Snow drifted down outside the window. A woman came and took the dishes from their table. The whisper of her footsteps faded away.

"My son Rane's wife," said the duke. "She'll rule here in my absence, for Rane and I shall ride south. She'd prefer to go to war with us, but she will have to stay and see to it that her seven sons do not fill this place with bear cubs and fox kits while we're gone, or run off to pester the ice giants. They're young still and do not yet fully understand wisdom, their grandfather's affection, or why one should not bother giants." He smiled a bit at this.

The moor was deep in snow when they left the manor of Lannaslech. They flew up into a dark gray sky, even though it was only midday. The ghost mumbled disconsolately to itself, somewhere in the folds of Jute's cloak.

"A fire on the hearth," said Jute, looking back at the house. "Food on the table and snow outside. I can't imagine anything nicer."

"You'll have it someday, if you prefer, when this is all over. Didn't Severan offer you his home? It's not far from here, further out on the headlands and beside the sea."

"When will all of this be over?"

"Things do end," said the hawk. "At least, most things do. I daresay you'll be an old man someday, with your feet on the hearth, a good supper in your belly, and smoking a pipe. These days will just be memories for you and the wind to talk over."

"And you," said Jute. "You'll be perched on a chair back, telling us what we've forgotten."

"Yes, I suppose."

Hours later, the hills of the Mearh Dun rose beneath them, huddled and sleeping beneath the snow. Smoke trailed from the chimney of a shepherd's hut tucked down in a valley. Light shone from the barn beside the hut. Jute could smell the warm scent of sheep on the wind. Sheep bedding down for the night. An old collie dreaming by the fire and the sharper, contented scent of pipe smoke. They flew on. The wind was soundless around them, for it could not exceed their speed.

"I remember something about Dolan," said the ghost, his voice near Jute's ear. "This is the duchy of Dolan, isn't it?"

"Yes," said the hawk. "From the hills of the Mearh Dun south to the Lome Forest. It's a beautiful land. A land of golden summers that linger long into the fall. It is a quiet duchy and they raise excellent horses."

"That's what it was," said the ghost. "It was the story of a horse. I think I wrote it down one day. I daresay I wrote quite a bit back then, when I was still alive. A giant of a horse who could run as fast as the wind. His name was Min the Morn. His mane was as dark as night and his eyes shone with starlight from the house of dreams. He had hooves as hard as iron. When he came to this land, there were no hills here, no valleys or dells. There was only a level plain. But Min the Morn galloped across the plain, and the hammer of his hooves broke the earth and that was how the hills and valleys of the Mearh Dun came to be. At least, that's how I've heard the story. It's true, isn't it?"

"Perfectly true," said the hawk.

They came to the town of Andolan, spiraling down through the falling snowflakes. Towers and chimneys and roofs rose up to meet them. They landed with a crunch of snow underfoot, standing in a street that opened into a small square. A castle loomed in the darkness beyond the square. It was a castle—of that there was no doubt, with its two towers rising above the roofs around it—but it was small in comparison to the regent's castle in Hearne. Small and shabby. Lights shone in its windows.

"Andolan," said the hawk in a pleased voice. "It's been many years since I've been here. They're good folks. Our friend Declan would be known well here. At least, his family would, for the duke of Dolan held the Farrows in high esteem."

"Why's that?" said Jute.

"Horses."

An archway opened through the castle wall into a courtyard deep in snow. However, there were several well-cleared paths connecting the castle with the archway, as well as a low-roofed building on one side of the courtyard.

"Stables, I imagine," said Jute, sniffing the air.

A boy exited the stable at that point, well-bundled up against the cold. He scuffed along the snowy path toward the castle and cast a curious eye at them, more at the hawk than Jute.

"Dinner's on, I s'pose," he said.

They followed him into the castle. The place bloomed with light and warmth. Fires burned on hearths and candles glowed in every hodgepodge manner of stand and chandelier. A cheerful confusion of conversation filled the air. Banging and clattering of pots and pans came from somewhere down a hallway. Most important of all, there was a wonderful smell of roasting meat.

"This way," said the boy, noticing the ghost for the first time. His eyes widened.

A brighter wash of light leapt up before them. An enormous fire crackled on an enormous hearth. Tables and their benches groaned under the weight of food and diner alike. To Jute's appreciative eye, it was not unlike an inn filled with cheerful patrons, but larger than any he'd ever seen and decorated with gorgeous old tapestries on the walls, painted portraits hung cluttered between the tapestries, and weapons arranged like fantastic sprays of iron flowers on whatever bare spots of wall were left.

"Welcome to the house of Hennen Callas."

Jute turned to find an elderly man smiling at him.

"Thank you," said Jute. "My name's Jute."

"I am Radean, steward of Lord and Lady Callas. You are welcome." His eyes drifted to the hawk on Jute's shoulder. "You and your hawk. Ah, your ghost as well. Come, let me find you a place. No one, traveler or stranger, is ever turned away from this table."

Jute found himself wedged in between a fat man and an extremely old man as bent and as withered as late summer grass. A blur of faces lined the table opposite him, cheerful, loud, and bent in enjoyment over their plates and the platters passing up and down the table. A plate appeared in front of him, as if by magic, piled high with food. Someone leaned over and poured hot ale into his mug.

"Set to, laddie," said the fat man. "You're nothing but bone. If the wind comes up, you'll blow away."

Ah, well, said the hawk in Jute's mind. *A few minutes delay won't be trouble. The Callases are famous for their hospitality. Is that duck on your plate?*

"Here," said the fat man, who seemed disturbed by Jute's skinny frame. "Try some of the parsnip casserole. And this cheese. The roast mutton's nice with mint sauce. The mint sauce is crucial. That'll fatten you up."

"Er, thanks."

"Nice mutton, that!" bawled the old man. He downed his mug of ale and slammed it onto the table. "That were my sheep. Slaughtered three yearlings fer tonight. Ain't no one raises sheep like us Hyrdes. Best sheepherders in Dolan, we are. Look now, sonny, you don't need no mint sauce to gussy it. This here mutton can stand alone."

"The mint sauce is vital," said the fat man somewhat tensely.

"You have mint sauce for brains."

"I'll ignore your manners, Cordan Hyrde," said the fat man, "as it's doubtless an excess of manure fumes have addled your wits. See here, boy: the sharpness of the mint undergirds the pungency of the mutton. It'll delight your mouth. Try it. You'll be astounded."

"The only thing pungent around here's your breath!"

"I'll try it both ways," said Jute, looking around nervously. To his amazement, no one else at the table was paying the altercation any attention. There were several other conversations being conducted at equal or even higher volumes.

"Hyrdes the best sheepherders in Dolan? Bah! You aren't fit to herd pigs."

"You call yourself a cobbler?" said the old man. "Wynn the torturer is what they should call you. Buy from Wynn if'n you enjoy screaming every time you take a step. The last time I wore one of your boots I couldn't walk for a week."

"My boots are works of art," said the fat man. "Your feet should be so lucky."

"Art?" spluttered the other. "My sheep can—!"

"Gentlemen, I trust you are enjoying your dinners? Excellent mutton, Hyrde. Can't say I've had better. By the way, Wynn, my wife enthuses about those slippers you made her. And who's our guest? You're welcome, young sir. You and your hawk."

"Er, well," said the fat man.

Jute turned. A tall man with gray hair stood there, a cup of wine in his hand. When he saw Jute's face, the man's eyes widened slightly and then he nodded.

"If you'd do me the honor of joining my wife and me at our table," he said, speaking more quietly this time. "You and your hawk."

"And ghost," said the ghost somewhat peevishly.

"Of course," said the tall man.

At the far end of the hall, a table sat on a raised dais. A chair was added for Jute, and faces along the table turned to him, politely curious.

627

"Allow me to introduce. . ." The tall man looked at Jute in question.

"My name is Jute."

Faces smiled and nodded and mouthed their own names, but Jute did not listen. His attention was caught by a lady sitting opposite him. After one quick glance at him, she turned her gaze to her plate, her face white and her lips compressed. The tall man sat down in the chair beside her.

The duke and duchess, said the hawk in Jute's mind. *Hennen and Melanor Callas.*

Conversations resumed around the table. Jute was aware of bits and pieces of talk—the price of wool in Vo, the carp in the river that had almost dragged in Vyan Sol's dog, an upcoming wedding—but he was even more painfully aware of the duchess across the table. The fork in her hand trembled, rattling against her plate.

"My dear?" said the duke, but his eyes were on Jute. "I remember you," he said, nodding. His voice was low enough that no one at the table heard him except for his wife, Jute, and the hawk. "You were at the regent's ball. When—when the darkness stood before Levoreth."

"Our Levoreth," said the duchess in a choked sort of voice. She looked up at Jute. "She was our Levoreth. Do you understand? She was our family."

"I understand," said Jute quietly.

"She was the heart of Dolan," said the hawk in an even quieter voice. He sounded sad and subdued. "She was here before the people came, before they came from the east. She loved this land even then. But she loved it even more when your towns and villages were established. She loved the life you brought."

"I miss her," said the duchess, staring in some bewilderment at the hawk. "Is she. . . is she. . .?"

"Is she dead?" said the duke, finishing the words his wife could not speak.

Jute did not answer, but his face spoke plainly enough.

"I thought as much." The duchess blinked. "I've had very bad dreams recently. If you don't mind, please excuse me, I think I will—pardon me." She got up from her chair, tried to smile at Jute, failed, and then hurried away.

"You will have twins in the spring," said the hawk. "You know that, don't you?"

"Yes." The duke drained his glass of wine. "A boy and a girl. She told us. I think we'll name the girl Levoreth." He stared glassily in front of him, not seeing Jute or the hawk any longer, not hearing the cheerful hubbub of conversation that filled the room. "There's always been a Levoreth in Dolan, and there always will be, by shadow."

"Not by shadow, I trust," said the hawk.

"No, not by shadow," said the duke. His gaze focused on the hawk. "There are old stories told about you in Dolan, master hawk. Stories that were old even when my grandfather was a child. There's only one talking hawk in all of Tormay, is there not?"

"That speaks the language of man, yes."

"The hawk and the boy who calls the wind."

"And me," mumbled the ghost. "The ghost. I wonder if I'll be remembered some day?"

The duke filled his wine glass. Candlelight gleamed on the surface of the wine and glimmered in its blood-red depths. "I don't think you came calling on a snowy night for the sake of my hospitality. There's death in your eyes. Not just Levoreth's, I wager, but the death of many more people."

"You're right," said Jute gently, feeling strangely old and sorry for the sad-looking man in front of him. He noticed that the duke's hands, wrapped around the wine glass, were calloused and worn. His cuffs and collar were frayed, and a piece of straw was caught in his hair. "I think a great many people will die before all's said and done. The Dark has come to Tormay."

"The Dark? And what does that mean for me? What does that mean for Dolan?"

"Owain Gawinn has invoked the writ of sovereignty. He requests the duchies arm every able-bodied man of age and come to Hearne as swiftly as can be. For at the first thaw in the mountains, the Dark will come marching to Hearne."

"And I fear the snow's already thawing," said the hawk.

"The writ of sovereignty?" The duke looked at Jute blankly. "That's never been invoked to the best of my knowledge. Never. Not since the Midsummer War, and when was that? Three hundred years ago? Every able-bodied man of age? What in stone's name is Gawinn thinking? I can't just pull my shepherds and farmers in from the hills. Who'll tend the sheep? Who'll look to the fields? Besides, most of 'em wouldn't last a minute in battle."

"The alternative is much worse," said Jute. "If Hearne falls, then, one day, quite soon, the Dark will be at your doorstep."

"Who are you?" said the duke angrily. "Who are you to walk into my hall with the snowflakes still melting on your shoulders and deliver such a ridiculous demand. You're younger than most of my stable lads. And I'm to lead my people into battle on the strength of your words. Look at them. They're simple folk. Happy with their lives, content with their work, their wives, and their children. They know nothing beyond the hills of Dolan. They don't want to know anything beyond these hills. And yet you want me to take their staffs and hammers and shearing clippers away and give them swords."

Jute did not say anything. The candles on the table guttered, the flames flickering and bending over like fingers pointing at him. The others sitting at the table continued their laughter and their boisterous conversation. Two serving girls bustled by with platters of roast goose. They plunked them down amidst a crash of crockery and spilled wine. Someone plunged a knife into a goose and loudly claimed victory. And yet there was only silence at the end of the table where the duke and Jute sat, with the hawk perched grim and thoughtful on the back of Jute's chair and the ghost hovering behind them.

"I almost fear if I close my eyes," said the duke, his voice suddenly quiet, "I'll open them to find myself standing at the edge of the world. Right on the top of the highest mountain of Morn, with nothing between myself and falling to my death except the wind. And you're the boy who calls the wind."

"I didn't choose it," said Jute fiercely, "but it's mine now and I must do the best I can with it. Not for myself, but for you. For all of you."

"Aye," said the duke. He shook his head and sighed. "Aye. I know. I am grateful. I don't envy you. Forgive me. Dolan is not the same these days. But, no matter. We'll make your war ours as well."

They left that same hour, though the duke offered them a place to stay the night. He stood at the door with light spilling out from behind him into the courtyard. His shadow stretched out before him, hand raised in farewell as Jute and the hawk drifted up into the sky. He was still standing there when Jute looked back down, a tiny figure limned by the light and motionless in the darkness.

"He's a decent fellow," said the ghost mournfully. "Can't blame him for not wanting to march all his men off to die. Dying isn't always pleasant, you know. We should've stayed the night. There were ghosts in that place. Sleeping, no doubt. But I could've woken them and had a nice chat."

"We must return to Hearne," said the hawk. "We've been gone long enough."

The snow tumbled down through the sky around them, nearly invisible in the darkness but obscuring anything that might be seen by virtue of the sheer number of flakes. Jute could not see a star in the sky. He couldn't see the sky at all. They flew higher up, through the darkness and the wind and the sting of the snow. They flew in blindness, but somehow, Jute knew which direction they were going. Perhaps it was the taste of the wind in his mouth. Perhaps it was the smell of the air, or the dim awareness of the land sleeping in silence beneath the snow, so far and invisible below him.

They flew higher and broke through the darkness. The stars shone overhead, studding the night with their brilliance like gems thrown across the sky by a lavish hand. It was a purply black night of such softness that the stars sparkled harder and brighter in contrast. The moon floated by in a curve of pale light. Below, and all around them, the top of the clouds glimmered in an unending landscape of ghostly luminescence.

Jute drew in his breath at the sight.

"Amazing," said the ghost. "Incredible. Never seen anything like it in my life. Or, er, in my death."

"The other side of the sky," said the hawk.

They skimmed along the top of the clouds, Jute in smiling delight and the hawk inscrutable beside him. In places, the clouds rose in towers of gray, slab upon slab of mist piled on each other in drifting disarray. In other places, the misty surface dropped away to reveal chasms and canyons. They flew over one such canyon and lightning exploded beneath them, white blinding light searing down somewhere far below to the accompaniment of a tremendous cracking shatter of thunder. The air smelled of hot iron. But though the light seared their eyes and they could not see for the brilliance of it, the night sky above them remained dark and serene and untouched.

"How much higher can we fly?" asked Jute. There was something in him that wanted to see more, to fly higher, to vanish into the sky.

"I'm not sure," said the hawk. "My old master said one could fly as far as the stars themselves, but there's danger in doing so, for the darkness grows deeper the further one goes. This is true, despite the brightness of the stars. There are silent places between the stars, lost in darkness, where the absence of light over countless centuries has left only the dark. I would not want to fly there."

"But isn't the house of dreams there as well?" said Jute, not put off by the hawk's words. "Doesn't it stand somewhere among the stars? I think I'd like to fly there and see that place."

"It isn't anywhere in particular—or, perhaps, it's nowhere in general. One can't fly there or walk there or find a ladder taller than the stars and climb there. The house of dreams is further north than north and farther than far. But it could also be quite close. Right around the next corner, as a matter of fact."

"Obviously," said the ghost from somewhere inside Jute's cloak, "you can only get there by dying. I think that's what you're trying to say. Not that I should know. I still seem to be here in Tormay."

They flew on through the night, with the moon drifting overhead across the trail of stars. The cloud tops sprawled around them, endless as the sea and, just like the sea, reflecting the moonlight back in one long swath of silver light stretching toward the invisible horizon. The stars glittered in the darkness and Jute thought he could hear the whisper of their speech as they gazed down. They had cold, clear voices, but the sounds they made seemed more akin to bells tolling from a distance rather than discernible speech. Music filled their tones, coloring it with the incomprehensible hues of starfire and time. The sounds belled through Jute's mind and trembled in the wind.

Here is fire. Here is flame. Rejoice, o thou light!
I sing the passing years. Years and moments. Moments and years.
We are born of light. We are borne by light.
See, brothers, dost thou see?
Is there not a weariness of seeing, a weariness of sight?
True. . .
But can we ever close our eyes?
True. . .
We have only the light, and the light must see and see. . .
We will rejoice!

But the wind rushed and blew Jute and the hawk along their course under the night sky, murmuring to itself, and to them, that what stars thought was all well and good, but there was a war to fight. Battles to be won. The Dark to be defeated. And then, perhaps, could they go and topple some chimneypots?

"Here!" called the hawk, his words blowing back to Jute by the wind. "I think we're somewhere over the Rennet. We must head west. However, I would prefer flying lower to ascertain."

"Here?" yelled the ghost. "What do you mean, here?"

"Would you mind not yelling in my ear?" said Jute. He had still been listening to the stars, and the sudden introduction of the ghost's voice drowned out the delicate belling tones shivering in the distance.

"I'm not yelling in your ear. Oh, I suppose I am. Sorry."

The hawk did not say anything more but dove down toward the clouds. Jute followed him, tucking his arms back against his sides and letting himself slip down the currents of the wind. Within seconds, he was plunged into a blindness of swirling gray vapor. The brilliance of the stars and the moon was gone. He was sorry of that. Snowflakes stung his face. He could not see the hawk any longer, but he could sense the bird with his mind, somewhere further below him.

"My eyes!" bawled the ghost. "I'm blind. I can't see. Help, Jute! Help me!"

"Will you stop that? You're yelling in my ear again. And if it makes you feel any better, I can't see anything either. We're flying through a cloud."

"A cloud, you say? That reminds me of a lecture I once gave when I taught the first years. My lecture was titled 'Similarities Between Cloud Formations and the Young Boy's Mind.' The audience was spellbound. You might not realize, but clouds drift. They drift, aimless, wandering, unfocused in their intent. Their material—as you well know, due to the fact that we're currently flying through a cloud—is formless and airy. They contain little of anything except a few drops of water and perhaps a few pounds of lamb's wool. A boy's mind is similar. It drifts, it wanders, the eyes gaze without focus. And, interestingly enough, if you grab a young boy about the neck and rattle his head around, water will dribble from his mouth. Just like rain."

"Fascinating," said Jute.

They broke through the bottom of the clouds then, diving down into a dark night. Jute saw the indistinct countryside far below him. The hawk was only a black spot in the darkness. Snow swirled down. The wind whistled in Jute's ear.

"Goodness gracious me," said the ghost. "Where are we now?"

The land fell away beneath them, down the slopes of the Rennet Valley. The valley, as they flew nearer, was a deep, complete darkness unbroken by even a single light. This was a peculiar thing, for the Rennet Valley was scattered with dozens of farmsteads, as well as quite a few villages along the banks of the river. Surely there should have been at least a few lights to break the darkness. A farmer milking his cows in the barn, with a lantern hung on the wall. A housewife putting up dough for the day's baking. But there were no lights in the valley.

Jute angled down sharper and silently urged the wind onward. He reveled in the speed of their descent.

Quickly now. Faster.

The wind gathered up its breath and then let out a blast that blew Jute along in a howling rush. Snowflakes whizzed by. The hawk lurched and then righted himself.

"Careful!" he called. "The wind delights in such encouragement, particularly from you. Reining him in is another matter entirely."

"Isn't this the Rennet Valley?" said Jute.

"It is. I was right, but it's the easternmost reach. How odd. I'm afraid I misjudged our direction. We're still a great distance from Hearne."

"There's no light," said Jute. "Shouldn't there something? A shepherd's fire? A lantern in a window?"

"Aye. And even a single candle so far below would be shining bright in such a night. But there's only darkness. Something's there. Something's come to this valley, and I think it is our enemy. Listen. Can you hear the echoes on the wind? A murmuring and a rustling? The clank of armor? There's an army below us, further to the west, I think. It marches in the darkness. They must have somehow made it through the Morns. I fear we have severely underestimated their resolve. This is a dreadful turn of events! We must reach Hearne as quickly as possible."

"They march without lights," said Jute. "A night without campfires, without warmth."

He shivered despite the fact that the wind and the driving snow had as little effect on him as they would have had on an ice fox snug in its den. He shut his eyes and listened. At first, he heard nothing but the rushing song of the wind. It was a keening, moaning, howling blast, almost as if the wind played some strange whistling song through a pipe of many voices. Surely there was nothing to hear other than its tune. But then he heard something else. It was blurred and diminished by the wind and the distance, but a sound nonetheless. A sound of marching, the jingle of horses' harnesses, the clatter of armor, of metal on metal. Oddly enough, however, there were no voices.

"And what does that mean?" asked the hawk, as if he had read Jute's mind.

"Magic," said Jute. "There's something in the darkness below us, something other than an army of men. Something else. Almost as if—"

"Beware!" shouted the hawk, and he abruptly dove.

Jute followed him without thinking, tucking his chin down and flying, almost falling, at dizzying speed. Lightning crashed behind them. The sound and flash deafened and blinded him. He could see nothing except a white blur tinged with red. The air smelled burnt with fire. Dimly, he became aware of the hawk shouting something else. Lightning flashed down again, and something smashed into him. The air. Sudden and as hard as a hammer. He tumbled end over end, arms flailing, losing hold of the wind. And then caught it the next second to slide, diving down and away. The air felt like it was on fire, trembling with sudden heat. Snowflakes hissed into steam. The lightning struck again and again, searching through the darkness for him. Reaching for him. Jute flew with his eyes shut, the bolts of lightning searing verticals of red on his eyelids, jarring the air around him. The snow melted into rain.

"He's hunting for us!" shouted the hawk, his voice almost inaudible in the crashing thunder. "Don't speak mind to mind! Don't speak to the wind! If you do, he'll know where you are!"

They flew through the darkness and the rain. The night surged around them, deeper and darker, torn by lightning and trembling with thunder. The wind urged them toward the west and Hearne. But it was no use.

Time and time again they sought to fly further west, and time and time again lightning flashed down from the sky, as quick as thought. The blazing branches of fire seemed like an impenetrable thicket of thorns that sprang up before them with every attempt. The darkness trembled and flickered with malevolent light. They were both silent, but the lightning seemed to find them with unerring accuracy whenever one of them veered westward. Finally, after some time, the hawk struggled through the air until he was close enough to Jute to be heard.

"It's no use," said the hawk. "The way west is closed to us."

"For now," said Jute, his voice tight with anger. He turned in the air, staring about them. He shrugged wearily. "South."

"South," said the hawk. "And then we will try again."

"West," whispered the ghost from inside Jute's cloak.

They angled away to the south then, the hawk faltering a bit on his wings, but then gaining strength as they retreated. The lightning died off, but the stormclouds remained massed behind them in their dark towers. Both of them were nearly deaf and dumb from the repeated crashing of thunder. Jute flew with his eyes shut, for they ached from all of the lightning.

And somewhere not too far away, but further and further with each passing moment, somewhere in the darkness of the valley, an army marched through the night in quick and sure step, heading west toward the sea and toward Hearne.

CHAPTER ONE HUNDRED & FOURTEEN
AN OLD SCENT

Declan crested a rise and saw the lake stretching out before him in the morning sunlight, glittering and flashing and near almost as beautiful as the sea. He missed the sea. Missed it more than the plains. He missed it more than hunting through the forests and mountains of his youth. He knew those places, particularly in the north of Tormay, like the back of his hand, knew them better than he knew his own face. The sea he did not know. But he missed it more, like a hole deep inside him that needed to be filled with blue and green and the icy depths. Declan's hand closed on the strand around his neck. The pearl was cold to the touch. He urged the horse down the slope. There was a chill in the air that had certainly not been apparent the day before. Frost gleamed on the ground and his breath misted in the air.

"Freeze, blast you," he said out loud. "Freeze and stay frozen from now until the stars fall."

It was not until midday that he came to the city of Lura, the seat of the duchy of Vomaro. Lura was really not large enough to be called a city, at least, not as large as Hearne or Damarkan or Ancalon. Lura was a town, but its people and its duke had always been a touchy lot and their town was definitely more than just a town. It was their capitol. It was obviously the finest of places, the height of fashion, architecture, art, and courtliness. Anyone other than a Vomarone would've called Lura a town, and a town was all it was in Declan's eyes, sprawling and shabby at the west end of the lake.

"Smaller than I remember," said Declan.

The horse whinnied in response, sounding equally disillusioned. It knew nothing about Lura, but it knew plenty about the fact that it had been a day and a night since it had had any oats. Grass was fine, but it grew monotonous as a diet.

Declan patted the horse's neck. "You'll be resting your hocks soon enough, you lazy bag of bones. Last time I came this way I was riding one of your better cousins. A descendant of Min the Morn, no less. At least, that's what my pa claimed."

The horse rolled a disdainful eye back at him.

A road ran along the edge of the lake. It was a lovely place, Declan had to grant that. The sunlight shone through the eucalyptus growing near the water's edge. Far out on the lake, two ketches sailed along in tandem, beating up against the wind toward the Lura docks. Their sails were white and bent gracefully to the wind.

Lura sprawled alongside the lakeshore. The houses were built in a style particular to Vomaro: steeply peaked roofs of wooden shingles atop tall walls carved with brightly painted leaves and vines and, of course, the fruit of the vine, for Vomaro had always been renowned for its wines. The lake lapped up underneath the pilings of the wharves that reached out from the town. Masts swayed in rows, their boats sleeping in their slips. The guards at the gate came to lazy attention as he rode through. They did not say anything, merely eying him insolently as he passed by.

Declan knew the way to the duke's manor. He knew it uncomfortably well, even though it had been years since he had even set foot in the duchy itself. He guided the horse through the streets, murmuring to the beast, and it stepped along eagerly, as if aware that a rest and a bag of oats were waiting up ahead.

"And then back home to Hearne," said Declan. He thought about that and then sighed. "Well, at least back to Hearne."

He twitched the collar of his cloak up more closely around his neck. Ice floated on the lake in dirty gray chunks. The wind blew through the streets, gusting against the shutters and blowing the chimney smoke into tatters that whipped away into the sky. Declan shivered, but the chill was more from a memory than the day. The duke's manor loomed at the end of the street. It was the only structure in Lura built entirely of stone.

"Name your business," said the doorkeeper. "Name it or move along. I don't have time for idle chatter." His eyes slid over Declan, weighing the cost of his clothing, his horse, the sword in the battered leather hilt rising above his shoulder. The man yawned, disdainful.

"My business is with the duke," said Declan, striving to keep his voice pleasant. "Tell him the emissary of the Lord Captain of Hearne is here with a message for the duke."

The doorkeeper might have had his own thoughts about this, but as Declan had swung down from his horse and stood a good foot taller than the man, he kept these thoughts to himself.

It was warm inside, uncomfortably warm, with fires burning on every hearth and torches flaring on every wall. The place was as he remembered it. An elegance of the past, faded velvet, wood worn dark with time, stone pillars carved like gaunt ribs rising up into the ceiling's spine.

"If you would come this way, sir."

A servant bowed and beckoned inside the hall.

But there was something different. One thing. The pearl on his neck felt even colder now than it had been, cold as ice. The smell. The smell of the place. It was a familiar smell, but it wasn't the smell his mind associated with his memory of the place. It was the scent of stone and rust, of something unbearably old and heavy beyond the capability of a man. The back of his neck prickled painfully. The pearl grew colder. Before him, the servant bowed and smiled, beckoning him forward. He could not place the smell yet, but he knew he would remember. The mind did not forget smells. Declan walked down a hall lined with loitering courtiers. Young noblemen gossiped in bored drawls, their eyes flicking at him in contempt and curiosity as he passed. Servants floated to and fro bearing trays of cool drinks. Shadows, but the heat was stifling. He snatched a goblet off a tray as it whisked by. Chilled red wine.

"The duke will see you now."

It was another servant. He hadn't even seen him approach. Declan drained the cup and handed it to the man. Doors swung open. Behind him, the courtiers momentarily hushed and glared after him.

The years had not been kind to the duke of Vomaro. At least, that's what his memory told him, for he remembered a vigorous man of hale body and a voice that snapped like a whip. He saw the same man in him who sat on the throne before him, but he was almost lost in corpulent flesh, in the sagging skin and the dull eyes that surveyed him without interest.

"The emissary from Owain Gawinn of Hearne, my lord," said someone off to the side.

"Gawinn, you say," said the duke. He shifted a bit, struggling to sit somewhat more upright but failing. "Light another candle, blast you, I can hardly see the man."

"Very well, my lord."

Candlelight flared.

"Come closer, man. Gawinn, eh? Says there's a war coming, does he now?" The candlelight glinted in the duke's eyes and Declan saw there was still life there. "I know Gawinn. Know him well. Fought in the Errant Wars with his father. Remember when we took Crushammer Ridge. Had two mounts killed beneath me. Archers, you see. Cavalry ain't the best thing when you're charging straight uphill into massed archers. Spears in front of 'em. But we didn't have any choice that day. Gawinn, good man. Both of 'em—father an' son. Good men. Do I know you? There's a familiar bit about your face. A war coming, eh? With the Dark pulling the strings? That's what he says here. That's what he says."

The duke squinted down at the unrolled parchment in his hands.

"It'll be just like old times. Old times and old ways. Call out the levies. Ride to war! Most of us'll die, no doubt, an—"

"Old times and old ways," sneered a voice. A figure moved out of the gloom. A burly young man stepped out of the shadows near the duke's chair. The strange smell sharpened. "Old ways, grandfather," said the young man.

The duke waved an unsteady hand. "My grandson Vaud, sir. Fine figure of a boy, ain't he? Sits a horse well and wields an axe at sixteen better'n most men."

"No need for us to hop when Hearne says so," said Vaud. "After all, what has Hearne done for us?"

"Eh? Well, now. True, true. There's something in what you say, my boy."

The young man bowed to the duke and then turned to look at Declan. "My grandfather is still given to the old ways, stranger. How things used to be done in Vomaro. Tradition. Old beliefs. Superstitions. The Dark! Old wives' tales."

"Here now," said the duke, roused somewhat at this. "I ain't an old wife."

"Of course not, grandfather." The young man turned back to Declan. "We don't bother with such things anymore here in Vomaro. We devote ourselves to more sensible things. The grape harvest. Last year's vintage. The price of wine, interest rates, and gold. As for your so-called trouble in Hearne, what's in it for Vomaro?"

"For you?" said Declan warily. His memory stirred, troubled by something. The scent was clearer now. He almost had it. "The safety of your land, of your borders. Freedom. Not just of Vomaro, but all of Tormay."

"Perhaps we could give you a deal on weapons," said Vaud, sneering. "Swords for five gold pieces, spears at twenty the dozen, and good mattocks for three apiece. Let no one say that Vomaro isn't willing to do her part."

And then the candlelight fell across the young man's face, revealing the heavy jaw, the gleaming eyes embedded beneath the slab of brow like pebbles, and the teeth like gravestone slabs, but much sharper. There was something other than man in that face. Declan's memory came up with the answer to the riddle of smell.

Ogre.

His skin prickled. Perhaps something of what he realized revealed itself on his face, for the young man smiled. A hideous, mocking smile. A hungry smile.

"Perhaps it would be best," said Declan, taking a step backward, "if I left the communication from Owain Gawinn in your hands for consideration at a later time."'

"Perhaps," said the young man.

"Gawinn, you say?" said the old duke peevishly. "Whyn't anyone tell me he was here? Coming for dinner, I warrant, and here me with my sleeping gown on. Steward!"

A face stared at Declan from an alcove as he turned toward the door. A fat, sleepy face peering out from under a pile of blonde curls. There was a hint of beauty still left in the face, a beauty he still remembered and cursed in his memory. But the daughter of the duke looked at him blankly with no recognition in her eyes, and Declan passed out from that house with his flesh shrinking and the smell of ogre in his nostrils. Even as he rode away through the streets of the town, his shoulders were hunched and he dared not turn around, for he felt eyes on him, and the pearl at his neck burned colder than ice.

CHAPTER ONE HUNDRED & FIFTEEN
THE GAP OF LOME

The rain did not stop. The snow on the ground had long since disappeared. The Rennet River ran swollen between her banks, and every track and path and road was churned into mud. And down the road from the east came the people. They streamed along the road that followed the valley floor toward Hearne. Wet, miserable, muddy, and frightened. They came on foot, on horseback, on mules and donkeys, on carts and wagons that rolled through mud right up to their axles. They came with their belongings piled on their backs, hauling their crying children, their cattle bellowing unhappily. They came with horrible stories of raiders and death, of towns sacked and slaughtered, of a great army marching down out of the mountains, and of fire. Always of fire.

"Fire and more fire," said Owain. "Not that I wouldn't mind to warm myself right now, but all this talk of fire leaves me feeling cold."

"A decent fire, I wouldn't say no to," said Bordeall.

Below them, at the foot of the cliffs of the Rennet Gap, ice and mud and debris choked the river. It was a surging mess of a river, eating away at its banks and threatening the collapse of the cliffs in places. They nudged their horses further off the road to stand under the dubious shelter of an oak. Rain dripped down on them. Far below in the valley, barely visible under the gray sky and rain, horsemen rode along the river road.

"Harlech," said Owain. "I did not expect them back so quickly."

They rode down to meet them, down the long switchbacks of the Gap, made even more treacherous than they normally were by the saturated earth. The fleeing people made way for them sullenly, glancing up from their misery and the mud. Oxen bawled in protest as they strained against their leads. Cartwheels turned with agonizing slowness.

"We can hold this road against a larger army," said Owain. "With the river flowing the way it is, the gorge below is impassable. They'll have to come straight up the gap in order to make the valley beyond and Hearne."

"Aye," said Bordeall. "I've been thinking on that. Archers on top of the cliff among the rocks. Spears dug in below. Horse would be worse than useless here. Slipping and sliding down these slopes. I doubt even Lannaslech's men would find it easy going. But, spears and archers, aye, and a catapult or two back behind that oak grove at the top of the ridge. A man could deal death from here."

"For a good while," said Owain.

"For a good while, and then?" Bordeall shrugged. "We all have to die someday."

They met the men of Harlech down on the valley floor. Their horses were lathered in mud and, to Owain's eyes, they were somewhat fewer in number than they had been when they had set out the previous night. The Duke of Harlech rode up, accompanied by his son Rane.

"A pleasant enough outing, Gawinn," said the Duke cheerfully. "We scouted their northern flanks. They tried to engage us now and then, but our horses are bred from better stock. At any rate, they're marching fast. Very fast. We have a strange enemy. Many of them mere men, but just as many not."

638

"What do you mean by that?"

In answer to that, Rane unlaced his saddlebag and reached within. "Let your own eyes explain, gentlemen," he said. He smiled coldly and held up a severed head.

The head appeared human at first glance, but then, on further inspection, it proved otherwise. The jaws were too large; there were too many teeth in the slackly gaping mouth. The skin was leathery and covered with a matting of bristles, and the hair, grasped in the mailed fist of the Duke's son, was a coarse stuff more akin to dog hair than human hair.

"Hmmph," said Owain. "Can't say I like the looks of him."

"They die. Just like men. There's an oddness to them, almost as if they're sleepwalking as they fight. But they die well enough."

Rane tossed the head into the mud.

"How much time do we have?" asked Owain.

"Tomorrow afternoon," said the Duke of Harlech. He turned his face up into the rain and then nodded as if the weather had confirmed what he said. "Their vanguard will reach the gap here by the afternoon. I daresay their outriders will be sniffing around long before then. Perhaps tonight."

"Time enough, but will they come down the valley? That's the question."

"They'll come. We bloodied their patrols a time or two, but they've the numbers to not mind some dead bodies on the march. Down the valley and through the gap is the fastest way to Hearne." The duke smiled slightly. "If I was their commander, I'd view you as flies, something to be squashed. A nuisance at worst."

"A nuisance with a sword," said Bordeall.

"And a nuisance we shall be," said Owain. "Gentlemen, we have about eight hours for preparation. Through the night and to the morning. Let's get to work."

The Guard set to work in good humor and enthusiasm, for Owain was wise enough to rotate them in small groups back up to the top of the gap where the field kitchen dispensed hot meals and ale. Oilcloth tents kept out the rain, and bonfires burned under the dripping trees. More important, though, Owain himself joined the work here and there, plying a shovel, swinging an axe, pausing to encourage a new recruit. The men of Harlech worked as well, as did a small contingent of mounted troops that arrived late in the evening, led by Galan Lartes, the enthusiastic nephew of Duke Lartes of Vo.

"Dig away the road until it collapses down the cliff?" said Duke's nephew. "Consider it done, my lord." And he hurried down the road to where it curved above the river far below. His soldiers hurried after him, just as cheerful as their leader. Torches flared in the darkening night. The rain hissed on the flames and pattered on the muddy ground.

Footsteps crunched behind Owain.

"Twenty soldiers from Vo? That's all?" Bordeall shook his head in disbelief. "And don't tell me they're digging with their swords. Stone the crows."

"We don't have any more shovels. And his uncle is marching to Hearne with two hundred footmen. Thule and Hull should've arrived at the city by now."

"And what of Dolan and Vomaro? What of Harth? Harth can field the biggest army in all of Tormay."

"I've no doubt of Dolan," said Owain. "Of the others I still haven't heard."

"My lord!"

Three men hurried up the road toward them.

"Civilians," said Bordeall.

"My lord," panted one of the men. He whipped off his cap and mopped at his brow. "You can't, you mustn't. . . the road, my lord!"

"Breathe, man, breathe," said Owain. "What is it that I can't?"

"My lord," said another of the three men, "you can't cut the road! We've wagons down the valley with our families an' the oxen can only pull so fast."

"You've got thirty minutes," said Owain. "Thirty minutes. Do you hear? Dump your goods, your bedsteads, your spare boots. Whip those oxen bloody! You know what comes behind you, don't you?"

"We do, my lord!"

The three men gazed at him, stricken, until he snarled at them. They turned and hurried back down the road.

"Blast it all, Bordeall. How many people are still out there?"

"I wouldn't want to say."

Owain turned and strode away, back up the road toward the top of the gap.

"We do what we have to do," he said over his shoulder.

"Nothing less, my lord."

The first attack came just past midnight. It was at the foot of the gap, where the road began to rise up through the rock. They came out of the darkness and the rain in a silent rush. A mixed contingent of Guard and Vornish soldiers were taking a breather around a fire. The last collapse in the road was almost finished. The river surged along in its torrent and its sound was enough to mask the noise of the intruders' approach. A Guardsman went down without even realizing his throat was cut. The young Vornish lord, Galan Lartes, kicked flaming embers into the face of the nearest attacker and flung himself to one side, his sword hissing free. The attack ended almost as soon as it had began. The marauders disappeared back into the night. Two of their dead were left behind.

"My horse!" said Galan. "Bring me my horse!"

"I'd advise not, my lord," said a voice. It was Rane. He strolled out of the darkness and crouched down by the fire to warm his hands. "That's what they want. Out in the night, that's their territory now."

"I suppose you're right. Still, two of theirs for one. Not bad, eh?"

"They can afford the numbers."

The men finished the last of the collapsed sections and then withdrew higher up the gap. Owain walked the road down to the bottom and then back up, inspecting the destroyed portions of the road and the fortifications dug behind each gaping collapse. Sharpened stakes protruded from the piled earth. Spearmen hid behind the earthworks, with swordsmen between them. Archers waited higher up on the slopes. It was far from perfect, but it would have to do. It was not impossible to traverse each collapse, for it merely meant descending down on the muddy face of the slope and then clambering back up, but it would greatly slow an attack. Slow them down enough for the defenders at the next higher earthworks to pour down a murderous fire of arrows. Still, numbers would tell in the end.

There were three more attacks that night. But the men were tense and ready. Each attack was driven off without difficulty or loss of life.

"They're testing us," said Bordeall. He ran his thumb along the edge of his axe. "This'll be dull by midday if I cleave enough necks."

"Examining the defenses," said the Duke of Harlech. "That's what they're doing, and that's what they would be doing if I were commanding them. Now, if you'll excuse me,

I'm going to get some sleep. Tomorrow shall be a long day." He bowed to them and walked away.

"I think I'll follow his example," said Owain. "Your father's a practical man."

"That he is," said Rane. "I've always found him so, and the best swordsman in Tormay, though some say Cullan Farrow is better. I would think it a close match."

"Cullan Farrow is dead. All his family with him, save his son Declan."

"Dead?" Rane's face went still for a moment. "That is grave news. I'd hoped the Farrows would bring their swords to our battle. They were good people. Very good people. His wife was a distant cousin of mine. But the son is still alive, you say?"

"He rode south to raise the duchies. My hope is he'll return soon with soldiers from Harth. We would profit greatly from their help."

The morning dawned bright and cold. Frost gleamed on the dead grass. The sky was a pale blue scraped so thin that it was almost devoid of color. The sun looked down with its unblinking eye, but it provided no warmth. Owain threw aside his blankets and opened the catch of his tent. One of the cooks was stoking the fire. The scent of baking bread filled the air. The Duke of Harlech stood beside the fire, warming his hands. He glanced up.

"Gawinn," he said. "I trust you slept well."

"Tolerably."

"A moment of your time?"

"Certainly, my lord," said Owain.

The duke led him to the top of the gap, a grassy knoll a little ways higher than their camp. A few old oaks stood in bent age there, but otherwise the spot afforded a good view in all directions. The walls of Hearne were visible just before the horizon, with the sea a dim line behind them. To the east, the valley fell away in curves of greens and browns, the river bending and turning as it fled the far mountains in favor of the sea.

"Can you see, there, just on the edge of sight?" The duke pointed down the valley.

"I see nothing." Owain rubbed at his eyes and squinted into the morning light. Still, he could see nothing. "Ah, fool that I am. Here." He rummaged in the pockets of his cloak. "There's a jeweler in Highneck Rise who has been experimenting with polished crystal. Most consider him crazy, but I think otherwise. He calls this a farseer."

Owain held the little crystal up to his eye and peered east. The valley swam into focus. He could see the river in startling clarity, the ice floes bobbing on the current, the broken and blackened branches of the willows. He looked farther east, over dead cornfields and meadows of dying bracken. And then, almost on the edge of where the crystal itself could aid him, he saw it.

"Burn the day!" he swore.

He saw an army marching. A dark mass flowing over the fields and slopes of the valley. Marching west in rank upon rank. Unending files of soldiers in locked and perfect step. Banners fluttered in the wind. Sunlight gleamed in countless tiny flashes upon spearheads. It was a dreadful sight, the horrible certainty in how the vast formation moved, marching as one, closer and closer with every step to where he stood. The gap, despite its height and the harsh rocky terrain of its steep slopes, felt small and defenseless. Surely that army would flow nearer and nearer and then, like a terrible tide, sweep right over them.

"Rather a lot of them, isn't there," said the duke.

"You must have the eyesight of a hawk," said Owain.

"No, but I pray the hawk will come soon, him and his boy. We need them, for it'll take more than swords to fight the Dark."

"They'll come. They're the reason we're here. I knew this day was coming, and now I truly know. But an army such as this? This is worse than I dreamed. I can't begin to estimate their number."

The duke of Harlech smiled coldly.

"Even with such great numbers, they can still die, one by one."

"If only to buy time."

Owain hurried back to the camp. His mouth tasted sour and he hunched his shoulders against the cold wind.

"Messenger! Find me a messenger!" he barked. A young boy hurried up, stiff and ridiculously proud in his new uniform. "Ride to Hearne immediately and then bring me word on the rest of the duchies. I want to know if they've arrived, how many men. Vo and Harlech I know, but I want word of the others. Don't spare your horse. Tell 'em we've sighted the enemy."

The boy nodded, wordless, and then ran off.

The sun ventured higher into the sky and the soldiers on the gap gathered at the top of the rise. They looked east, staring in silence, squinting into the morning light. There was a dreadful tension in the silence. It was not fear as fear is commonly known; rather, it was a hungry, nervous anticipation, a detestation of inaction, a desire to have the enemy already attacking, even if it meant death, for then there would no longer be this terrible wait.

The eastern approaches of the valley were soon black with the marching masses of the army. The wind blew along their path, fleeing at their advance, and it brought to those on the heights of the gap a rumbling thunder of bootsteps, of creaking armor and stepping horse. The noise sounded like the growl of some strange monster, a being more massive than giants or dragons, growing louder and louder as the wind sought to escape the valley. Storm clouds hurried along in the sky so that as the ground darkened with the approaching masses of soldiers, so did the sky. They were nearer now, much nearer.

"Shall we give these scoundrels a good beating, my lord?" Galan Lartes sauntered up to Owain's side, spear in hand. "My lads are champing at the bit. I've half a mind to ride out and tell them to hurry it up."

"Is all Vo of such good humor?" asked Owain. "Would that I had a hundred more of you here, for a cheerful heart is a brave heart."

"Aye, my lord. I think it chiefly the fine wines we make. And that we are a little duchy. We do not have the pomp of Hearne or Vomaro to put a smile on things. So we smile for no reason, and we've gotten into the habit, despite the bad weather or unwanted company."

At these words, Galan bowed mockingly to the east. Owain laughed, but as he glanced down he saw that the young man's knuckles were white as he gripped his spear.

The attack came just after noon. It came like a wave of the sea, a dark mass that surged toward them, roaring and towering ever higher. At least, it seemed so, for the morning light dimmed as if a shadow had fallen upon the sun. Arrows hissed into the wave, but they vanished like stones thrown into the sea and with just as little effect.

"Steady, men!" shouted Owain. "Hold your line! Hold!"

The wave hit the fortification with a splintering crash, a rending of metal on metal, of timbers splintering and snapping, of screams and shouts. The thin line of the defenders reeled back and then flung themselves forward, buttressed by the men of Harlech under

642

the command of the duke's son, Rane. He gave no command to his men, but they wheeled and turned with him like one living creature that bit and slashed at the flanks of the dark wave, dashing to wherever the defenders teetered on the brink of collapse. Arrows whipped down through the air from the archers higher up on the slopes. The dark wave rolled on, smashing and roaring against the fortifications. It tore away more and more, each time it returned, the ground slick with blood and mud.

"Is the sky falling as well?" said Bordeall.

He looked up, his face blanching near white. His axe was smeared with gore in his hands. Owain also looked up and thought he was going mad. It seemed as if the dark clouds overhead had been torn into bits. Little dark spots falling from the sky. Dark spots moving erratically. No, flying. They were flying.

"Birds," he said. "They're birds."

"Crows," said Bordeall.

"Archers!" shouted Owain. He motioned over one of his sergeants. "Have the archers look to the sky."

"Aye, my lord."

The man clambered up the slope to where the first line of archers crouched among the heather and the rock. Owain could dimly hear him bellowing orders over the crash and tumult of the battle. It was not a moment too soon. With a high-pitched piercing cry, as if calling with one voice, the crows fell. They dove down through the sky, through the rain, falling like spear points. The arrows met them and the sky was filled with feathers and blood, but the archers were not enough. The sound of the crows' impact was like steel on steel. Men died without seeing their death. They died with broken helms, pierced necks, and blind faces. The line faltered behind the fortification.

"Hold!" shouted Owain. "Hold the line! Lartes! Get your men up! Get your men up!"

"There's our enemy," said the duke of Harlech, pausing beside Owain in the midst of battle. His sword ran red with blood. "Look there."

Lannaslech pointed. Far beyond the surging masses of soldiers facing them, the ground down along the riverbank rose at one point. It was a gentle slope, but enough to create a rise that lay bare. The advancing army split and flowed around it. A horse and rider stood upon the rise. The rider was armored all in black, and the horse was just as black with shining coat. Its eyes seemed to gleam red, even at such a distance. There was a strange and awful stillness about the rider. A heaviness, a ponderous certainty and implacability of purpose in how that black helm stared across the distance. But then the howling wave crashed again upon their line and they had no time to consider the rider.

The line wavered, stretched, held for an agonizing handful of seconds, and then broke. It broke in death and blood and men trampled down into the wet earth. The ragged remainders retreated back up the gap, back up to the next fortifications and the fresh thin line of steel waiting there. Further down the valley, the dark horseman rode forward, and the sea of his own army drew back, keeping well clear as if they feared the rider, feared whatever face stared from behind that black helm. The horseman rode up to the first ruined fortifications and halted. The air seemed colder. The day darkened, as if there was no longer any sun behind the clouds. Both sides stood in silence, and it was a silence born of equal dread for the solitary horseman.

The silence was broken by the twang and hiss of an arrow. The arrow came from somewhere higher up on the slopes of the gap. Higher and behind Owain. His eye caught and held the shaft's flight. The arrow sped with perfect aim, straight at the rider's helm. It struck with a tremendous clang. Steel point on iron. But the rider did not move. It was as if he were carved out of stone. Immovable, unalterable, as heavy and as unshakeable as the earth itself.

Lay down thy arms.

Owain could not tell if the voice spoke out loud or whether it was only in his mind. The voice was ponderous, slow, almost whispered. A voice oddly weary with its own dreadful weight. Owain staggered and slipped down onto one knee. Around him, his men waited in tense expectation, gazing down the muddy and trampled heather at the army lapping against the bottom of the gap like the sea. Owain did not think they heard the voice.

Bid thy men lay down their arms. Let them open their hands in peace to death, for the Dark has come to Tormay. The night doth fall here. It is a night that began in long ages past, before the light shone forth, and it hath no end.

The words fell like stones, singly, in Owain's mind. Each one heavier than its predecessor until he was so heavy, so weary with their weight, that it was all he could do to keep his eyes open. Surely he should rest. A little sleep. The slopes of the gap were silent around him. There would be no noise to bother his rest.

There is a rest deeper and better than sleep. Death.

"Steady," said the duke of Harlech, standing alongside Owain.

"Can you hear him?" said Owain. He drew his shaking hand across his brow.

"Somewhat. I think he speaks only to you, but I can hear enough. I'd rather face the army before us alone than that horseman."

"There's a face behind that helm, surely," said Owain. "There must be. I feel his gaze. But maybe there's nothing there at all. Just an empty helm. Where's Jute?"

And then the earth shook beneath them. It heaved and trembled and shuddered. The muddy ground slid across itself in a whisper, then a rush, then a gathering roar. The rocks on the heights of the gap tumbled down, and the embankment above the river collapsed into the water below in a confusion of spray. There were shouts and screams and the frantic yells of men dug in behind the various fortifications as the earth fell away, plunging them to their deaths in the icy water below. The last thing Owain saw was the horseman. He sat immovable on his steed, as before, the black helm staring up at the slopes of the gap. And though the earth shook around him, he and his horse did not move at all. The horse and rider were like a statue. The sky teetered and tilted over them all like an endless expanse of frozen iron, of hammered darkness that had locked away the sun. Something struck Owain a tremendous blow on his head and he knew no more.

His skull ached. It felt as if the bone had been shattered like an eggshell. He tried to reach up a hand but could not. And then his mind cleared and Owain came back to full consciousness, coughing and gagging. The ground moved and shook beneath him. No. Not the ground. A galloping horse. He was slung over a horse, jammed down against the pommel with the mane flying in his face. Someone gripped the back of his coat with an iron hand.

"Let me up!" Owain shouted. "Blast you! Let me up!"

The horse came to an abrupt stop and Owain found himself looking into the anxious face of Arodilac Bridd.

"Bridd! What are you doing here? Let go of me, d'you hear?!"

Arodilac released his hold on the captain's coat and let him slide down to the ground. He swung down after him. Owain slowly became aware of other horsemen around them, of horses being pulled up sharply and of many eyes on him. His head hurt abominably.

"My lord," Arodilac said, "we must—"

"Don't tell me what we must do, Bridd. I distinctly remember leaving you under Lucan's command at the gate." Owain staggered then, unable to maintain standing. A hand caught him, steadied him. Arodilac. He realized, dimly, that a great many soldiers stood around them, dismounted from their horses, but none of them looked his way. They were all looking somewhere behind him. Looking back. Back toward the slopes of the Gap.

Owain turned. His eyes would not focus properly. A dim and lowering sky, full of clouds, hung over the heights of the Gap. Rain spattered down, and he wiped it from his eyes. His hand came away bloody. They were a distance away now, halfway down the valley that lay between the Gap and the meadowed slopes before the walls of Hearne. Black specks swarmed along the rocky heights in the distance. Owain fumbled in the pocket of his coat for the farseer and brought it to his eye. His vision swam and then cleared into one round window brought close. Men fighting on the top of the Gap. His men. Fighting at the last fortification at the top of the heights. A dark-armored wave crashing against the paltry steel of their swords and spears. The flag of Hearne snapping in the wind. The tiny black shapes of crows circled overhead, diving and falling. And there, there at the center of the fortifications, a tall, burly figure with axe in hand, white hair stained with blood.

"Bordeall stayed," said Owain.

"Aye, my lord," said Arodilac wretchedly. "He bade me take you away. Said he'd take my head off right there if I didn't turn and ride. No need for more of us dying, he said."

Owain looked again, screwing the farseer against his eye as if the sudden sight might bring him right to where it was. But there was no more white-haired figure swinging his axe. The dark wave broke over the fortifications, surging and raging, and then it swept past. A horseman crested the highest rise on the heights, moving slowly and without haste. A stray bit of sunlight angling down through a momentary rent in the clouds fell on the black helm. The eye-slit in the helm seemed to be staring straight at Owain over the distance. He jammed the farseer back into his pocket, his hand trembling.

"We were supposed to hold out longer," he said to no one in particular. "At least for a day. Even two." He cleared his throat, tasting blood in his mouth. "And Harlech?" he said, his voice harsh.

"They stayed as well, my lord," said one of the horsemen nearby.

"Back to Hearne, and quickly."

But Owain could not mount a horse on his own. His hands would not grasp the reins and there was no strength in his legs. Arodilac heaved him up onto his charger and then they were off in a drumming of hooves.

They came to Hearne in the late afternoon, with the horses weary under them, and the rain wavering into snow and then back to rain all through the day. It was a wet, cold, miserable ride and the walls of the city were a welcome sight. The road was slick with mud and crowded with refugees. Oxcarts and handcarts, horse-drawn wagons and wheelbarrows, people hurrying along with their lives on their back. There were herds of sheep and cattle here and there as well, lowing and baa-ing their confusion as they were chivvied along. It was a grinding welter of misery, and no one walked that muddy road but they did not look back anxiously every few minutes. With the rain and the gloom, however, there was nothing to be seen other than the phantoms of their own imaginations.

"The livestock," said Owain, waking somewhat from the near slumber he had fallen into.

"My lord?" said Arodilac.

"Confiscate their livestock and get it into the city. We'll need it for food."

The tower of the gate loomed over them. Flags flapped wetly in the rain. Torches flared within the gate and the horsemen rode under the arch. The clip-clop of hooves echoed back from the stone walls. Spear butts slammed down onto the ground as the soldiers at the gate came to attention. Owain swung down from the horse and walked across the foregate to the tower. He staggered once, but caught himself and continued on, staring in front of him and not seeing the ranks of soldiers drawn up in rigid attention. He did not see the men of Thule, Hull, and Vo. He did not see the practice ground crowded with canvas tents. His head ached. Someone took his arm, saying something, but he pushed them away. He somehow made it up the stone steps.

Owain closed the door of his study behind him and sat down behind the old oak desk. His father's desk. Rain streaked the window with gray and twilight. He tried to remember why he was there. The door opened. Someone stood at the sill. Lucan. That's who it was. Lucan, the young lieutenant. Promising lad. Must learn how to deal with subordinates, though. Doesn't understand yet what authority truly means.

"Sir?"

I've always gotten along well with the men. Probably a Gawinn trait. My father's soldiers would've followed him to the gates of Daghoron. They would've died for him to the last man.

"Sir?" said Lucan again, this time stepping forward. His face looked anxious. "Sir, are you all right? The physician will be here soon."

Owain blinked.

"Of course I'm all right," he said.

But then Lucan's face divided into two. Two faces staring at him. Two Lucans. No. Lucan and a grim, weathered old man. Galaestan. The duke of Thule. And then Maernes, the duke of Hull. Maernes said something, his mouth moving, but there was no sound. But Owain could hear the darkness chuckling. Right there. In the corner of the room.

No point to it all, Gawinn.

You might win this battle, but the war'll still be lost.

Die in the end, regardless.

Death.

And then Sibb's face was staring down at his. Sibb. Her mouth moved. He could hear her. He always could.

"Owain."

Then there was only darkness.

CHAPTER ONE HUNDRED & SIXTEEN
THE RESCUE OF HARLECH

Jute and the hawk flew out of the twilight with the rain lashing down and the sky lowering until it seemed like the clouds rested on the towers of Hearne several miles down the valley in the west. The air smelled of iron and the wind felt as cold as ice. Jute could see that the gates of the city were closed. Torches burned on top of the wall like tiny flames of fire in the darkness.

"A few minutes more," said the hawk, flying beside Jute's shoulder. "A few minutes more and we'll reach Hearne."

"We should've been there yesterday," said Jute. "What's the use of being the windlord if I can't take care of a little lightning?"

"Not all things in the sky belong to the wind. Don't forget that. Anyway, what's done is done and we can only hope our delay does not prove detrimental. Hmmph. I've had enough of being rained on and being chased around by lightning. I don't suppose I should care either way, but I wouldn't mind a nap in front of a nice fire. I must be feeling my age. Hmm. I suppose I am rather old."

"Old," said the ghost from somewhere inside Jute's cloak. "Does old mean anything to a ghost? I feel old. No, I don't. I don't feel anything."

"Look down there," said Jute.

"What?" said the hawk.

"Down there. Look to your left, beside the river."

At first, there seemed to be nothing except the river, dark with mud and flecked with ice, rushing between acres of dead and blackened cornstalks. Past the fields, the side of the valley rose in slopes of bracken. A few solitary oaks stood here and there.

"I don't see anything," said the hawk. He spoke crossly, for he did not think it proper that a boy, regardless of whether he was the windlord or not, should have better eyesight than a hawk. Particularly if he were the hawk in question.

"In the cornfields, just below us."

The hawk saw them. Men creeping through the cornstalks, crouching down to eke out what little camouflage the withered stalks could lend. Perhaps two dozen men. They were soldiers. Swords and bows were in evidence. They moved west, in the direction of Hearne, but those in the back of the group spent most of their time looking east from whence they had obviously came. The reason for their caution was not long coming. A long, drawn-out bay broke the cold night air.

"Wind preserve us!" said the hawk.

Jute felt his heart stutter. He knew that sound. A shadowhound. He looked back, twisting in the wind, trying to locate the beast. Nothing. Only more cornfields, the river, and the muddy road stretching back into the dark distances of the valley. The bay belled again, shivering through the sky.

"A shadowhound," said Jute. "But I can't see the thing. He must be after the men. Should we do something? We can't just leave them alone. Do you remember the last time we met a shadowhound?"

"We can't leave them alone?" said the ghost. "Why not? Sounds fairly straightforward to me. People like being left alone."

"Only too well," said the hawk, his voice soft. "Levoreth Callas. She had more power in her one finger than anyone in all of Tormay. I doubt we—"

"The duke of Harlech!"

"What?" said the hawk.

"That's the duke of Harlech down there."

And Jute dove down from the sky, sliding down the wind as quick as thought, flashing through the slashing rain. The hawk folded his wings and fell after him. He looked one more time to the east as he plunged after the boy. He did not see the shadowhound. He did not expect to. But further down the muddy road lying along the riverbank, he saw a troop of horsemen riding. They were no more than two miles away at most and they were riding fast. Jute and the hawk landed in a flurry of wind in the middle of the cornfield. Steel hissed free from sheaths around them.

"Hold, hold," whispered someone. "It's the hawk and his boy."

"What about the ghost?" huffed the ghost, but no one heard it.

"My lord wind," said the duke of Harlech, stepping through the cornstalks. His gray hair was matted and his face was lined with weariness. "I wasn't expecting your company, but you're very welcome. Forgive my presumption, but we're in rather a bad spot. Can you—?"

"No," said the hawk regretfully. "He can't. The wind does not answer his bidding so readily yet."

"Very well. We'll make do." The duke bowed slightly. "Your presence gladdens my heart.

"That's all fine," said Jute, embarrassed at the old man's words. "I'm sorry I can't just whistle up the wind and whisk everyone away. I'm still rather new at this. But we did see horsemen riding down the road. They're quite close."

"How many?"

"Forty, perhaps fifty at most."

"And there's barely two dozen of us," said the duke. "If we had spears, then we'd have a chance. But not with swords. Swords aren't much good against mounted horse."

"Even worse, there's a shadowhound with them." As if to underscore Jute's words, a howl rang out through the sky.

"That, I take it, is the hound you speak of?" said the duke. "I'm not familiar with this beast you speak of. Harlech has its share of strange things, but not this."

"Not a real hound of flesh and blood, but one woven from darkness and magic. I don't think swords can hurt the thing, but it can kill men well enough with its teeth."

"Horsemen closing in on us, and now this," said the duke, frowning. "A company of spearmen would be handy at the moment, or, say, a sturdy castle with a drawbridge. I'm afraid this cornfield will have to do. You're sure you can't command the wind for us?"

"Er," said Jute. "The thing is, the wind doesn't really obey me."

"Not yet," said the hawk.

"No matter." The duke shrugged. "Can't say I'm enthused about dying in the middle of a muddy cornfield, but that's not important. A magic hound?" He turned away and snapped out some orders.

The men of Harlech did not speak but fanned out in a tight half-circle facing east. The archers wiped their bowstrings dry of moisture and huddled within their cloaks, waiting and listening. The duke's son, Rane, stood at the front of the men, his sword sheathed and his face intent. The rain slashed down. The cornstalks waved under the wind's breath and pointed their blackened and slimy tips east, as if aware of that which approached.

"A magic hound," said the hawk. "Not just magic, my lord, but darkness. True darkness."

"We were cut off from our horses," said the duke. He pulled his cloak more closely about him, though it was already sodden with rain. "We held them off, halfway down the pass, until Lartes could get his men and the remaining Guard clear. Then they overran our lines as night fell. We had no choice. The horses were lost."

"What did you do?"

The duke shrugged. "The only thing we could do, other than getting slaughtered. We jumped off the cliff into the river and swam across. The night hid us and we made our way down the valley. The day brought us here, to this field, and to you."

He would've spoken more, but Rane raised his hand. They were silent then, each listening to the wind and the sounds of the evening. Faintly at first, and then more clearly, there came the drumming, thumping roll of a troop of horses galloping. The sound came louder and louder. They heard the sound of voices calling in harsh, guttural tones.

Rane said one quiet word and the archers strung their bows. The galloping sound suddenly stopped in a jingle of reins and bridles. The wind rustled nervously through the cornstalks. They were bare and tattered, but it was impossible to see very far through them. Jute strained his ears. He heard nothing except the sigh of the wind and the sullen murmur of the river. Something stirred in his memory. Something vital that he very much needed to remember. He caught hold of the wind and felt his body rise. An inch higher, one more inch, surely, and he would be able to see beyond the cornfield.

Hold, said the hawk in his mind. *The shadowhound is with the horseman. I think it is confused by what it smells. The river is choked with the bodies of the dead. The sight of you will dispel its doubt.*

Just a bit higher. Don't worry. I'll be careful.

Jute floated a few inches higher, holding the wind in his mind like a stream of water running through his fingers. He could see over the tops of the cornstalks now. There was enough moonlight, meager that it was, to see several hundred yards of the river, swift and black and rushing headlong between its banks. Beside the river was a company of horsemen. They stood quite still, the riders motionless in their saddles and the horses like statues. One horseman sat his mount somewhat removed from the others—a tall, thin form somewhat hunched over in the saddle as if he had fallen asleep. The riders were no more than dark shapes in the moonlight. One thing did move, however. Further along the road, and closer to the cornfield, a black form paced back and forth. A dog. A shadowhound. It roved across the road and onto the riverbank, its head to the ground.

"I don't like this," said the ghost from somewhere nearby in the cornstalks. "Can't we just go home?"

The memory stirred again in Jute's mind, restless and undefined. He reached for it but felt it slip away. The wind blew by with the smell of rain and the decaying corpses floating down the river, the smell of bracken, of brambleberries shriveled black on the vine, and molding cornstalks. Brambleberries. The memory surfaced again, almost coming into clarity.

Absentmindedly, Jute drifted higher. It was not even an inch. But it was enough. The shadowhound barked. The horseman standing removed from the others wheeled his mount around. A voice near the river called out a command. Jute dropped back down to the ground.

"That's torn it," said the hawk. "Well done."

"Er, yes," said the ghost. "Well done. What did he do?"

"Brambleberries," said Jute.

"You don't have to announce our presence and wave a big red flag at the same time," said the hawk. "And what do brambleberries have to do with anything?"

"Archers," said Rane quietly.

The bowmen knocked arrows to strings. The voice called again, somewhere near the cornfield. The ground shook with the thunder of hooves.

"Now," said Rane.

Arrows sliced through the air with a hissing, ripping sound that barely lasted a second. Then they hit with a punching slap. Horses screamed and whinnied in pain. Cornstalks flew through the air as steeds went down. The rain ran red with blood in the churned mud of the ground. The bowmen loosed again, not a heartbeat later. The cornfield seemed to be dissolving in front of them, shredded by arrowheads and the sharp, flailing hooves of dying horses. The voice called again from beyond the cornfield, stabbing at the air and throwing its men forward by the sheer power of its command. The line of the men of Harlech shuddered back under an onslaught of steel, but they held firm. Rane leapt from place to place, his voice hoarse and shouting, his sword like a living thing. Arrows still flew from the bowmen, but singly, as they shot past the shoulders of their own men.

"Back to the oak!" yelled Jute, catching the duke of Harlech by his arm.

"What?" The duke shook free of his clutch and swung his sword up. Steel slammed against steel. He staggered and then Rane was at his side, grim-faced and bloody, his sword an efficient, deadly blur.

"Thank you," said the duke, gasping for air.

"There's a tunnel beneath that oak," said Jute. "A tunnel that leads to Hearne."

"You're sure?"

"You must believe me!"

"Aye," said the hawk. "He's right! I recall this place now. Brambleberries. My apologies, Jute. The tunnel leads all the way to Hearne, beneath the walls and to the underbelly of the university. It's a long walk through the dark. But, more important, it could be easily defended."

"If we pull back, we'll lose men," said Rane.

"And if we stay, you'll all die!"

The hawk launched himself into the air and was lost in the rain. There was no more time to discuss the decision. There was no time to even make the decision. It was made for them, because the shadowhound attacked. A blur, a snarling howl, a rush of darkness and teeth, and the line collapsed in blood. Two men went down in quick succession. They died so swiftly that they made no sound.

"Back!" shouted the duke. "Fall back!"

The line fell back in a rush, the archers running on ahead through the cornstalks. The shadowhound leapt forward and another man died, wildly swinging his sword at the beast only to have his blade encounter darkness and vapor. The teeth stayed sharp and real enough to tear out his throat. Jute ran after the archers, overtaking them as they turned to draw and shoot. The wind shivered with the hissing of the shafts. He could hear the ghost gibbering hysterically in the folds of his cloak. He reached the edge of the cornfield.

His feet were heavy with mud. He wiped the rain from his eyes. An old oak tree towered up on the slope above them. The ground around the tree was dense with brambleberry vines, thick with withered leaves and rotting fruit. But there was no sign of a tunnel.

Where is it? snapped the hawk in his mind. *Find it or these men die! We must not lose the duke!*

Jute did not answer. He sprinted forward. The brambleberry vines caught at his pants, ripping and tearing. Where was the tunnel? It had been right here. He was sure of it. He remembered coming up out of the darkness into the sunlight, the smell of the earth, of dust and the silence left behind. It had been right here, right at the foot of the old oak. He remembered the branches now. They twisted and bent their way up into the sky. Just like these. Behind him, voices called out. He could hear Rane's hoarse shout. Arrows split the air in sharp hissing snaps like the crack of a whip. Iron crashed against iron. A hideous growl shivered through the wind, and the wind fled before it. The earth collapsed beneath him. He fell, scrabbling at the mud, and caught himself on an oak root and felt skin strip away on his palms. *Here!* He screamed inside his mind.

"Here!" he shouted. "Here! It's here!" He lost his grip on the root and slipped, tumbling down stone steps.

"He found it!" shrieked the ghost.

"To the oak tree!"

The duke of Harlech turned, his bloody sword in his hand. Lightning crashed somewhere further down the valley, driving the clouds apart. For a brief moment, the moon looked down with her pale light. She shone on the black armor of the attackers. Polished helms and hauberks, axes and swords rising and falling. The cornfield lay trampled in mud and blood. The men of Harlech retreated, fighting grimly as their line shrank with each desperate passing second. Rane fought in a blur of motion, a sword in each hand, his arms drenched in blood and his teeth bared in a fixed snarl. The shadowhound surged up from the ground. The thing came from nowhere, almost as if one instant it was mud and crushed cornstalks, the next instant a huge blot of darkness, fangs and staring eyes. An archer went down with his throat ripped out and streaming red shadows.

"To the oak tree!"

The thin line of Harlech wavered and then collapsed in on itself as the men tried to run back to the oak tree but still maintain some semblance of defense. Two more died in quick succession, one at the shadowhound's fangs and one under the swords of the attackers. Jute was almost trampled as the men dove through the opening below the tree. He scrambled away, deeper into the passage, dust in his eyes and dirt on his hands. A furious clatter of swords surged back and forth just outside the entrance. More men forced their way in. Jute could hear the voice of the duke shouting above the din.

Three archers ran toward Jute and then turned to kneel, their bows drawn and ready. Several more joined them. Part of the tunnel roof near the entrance collapsed in a sudden billow of dust and damp. More and more men crowded in, stumbling past the archers into the darkness beyond. The old duke appeared, with Rane behind him, both facing backwards. There was a lull in the clash of swords and then silence, broken only by the harsh and strained breathing of men, desperate to suck air into their lungs.

"Rats in a hole," said a voice from just outside the tunnel. There was a dreadful casualness to the voice, a dry amusement. "Hiding in the darkness. How delightful."

The voice was more than familiar. Jute knew it all too well. The thin figure in the darkness of the Silentman's dungeon. The being on the tower of Ancalon.

"The sceadu," whispered Jute.

The men around him waited in the darkness, tensed, listening to the voice. The air smelled of fear. A faint light illumined the mouth of the tunnel, a few rays of starlight brave enough to fall through the sky, past the clouds and rain, past the branches of the oak tree, past the sceadu and his hound standing there. It was not much light at all, just enough to soften the darkness and suggest the dim lines of the stone steps climbing up toward the sky.

"I smell a familar old scent here," said the sceadu. "The hawk's boy. I've had you between my teeth before, Jute. Twice now, and here is the third. Is the wind in your hand yet? Do you know the strictures of your power? Does your blood remember the starlight and from whence he who walked before you came? Or are you still just a foolish, cowardly boy? Perhaps I shall send my dog down to make your acquaintance. He has a firm grip with which to shake your hand. No, here's a better idea for you. A better death for you and these Harlech scum." The sceadu paused and then spoke again, his voice deepening. "By the hand of darkness. By the dream of darkness—"

The skin on the back of Jute's neck crawled.

"Who is this that speaks?" said the duke of Harlech. "He seems to know you from some previous, unfortunate encounter."

"Quick!" hissed Jute. "Go! Further into the tunnel as fast as you can. He's summoning up something from the Dark. I don't know what exactly, but we don't want to stay to find out."

The duke did not waste any time, but snapped out an order. Someone struck flint on tinder and they hurried off down the tunnel, led by a flickering light. Dust stirred beneath their boots. Stone and earth closed in around them. The darkness retreated before the advance of their tiny light, but then followed just as quickly on their heels. And behind them, no matter how far they went with each passing step, the voice of the sceadu whispered and grew, following them just as surely as if he walked behind them.

"By the hand of death. By the dream of death. By the hunger of death I call you."

The voice ceased and there came a strange noise. A noise of things dragging wetly through the mud, of bones shifting in the earth, a clacking of teeth, and the sound of steel rattling. And then footsteps. Many footsteps, shuffling, shambling down stone steps, down into the tunnel, down into the dark and after them. The sound of the footsteps quickened.

"Hurry," said Jute, his voice shaking.

No one needed his encouragement. The men were running now, the single flame bobbing and flickering in the hand of the man holding it. Rane came at the end of the line. He looked over his shoulder and what he saw made him stop in his tracks.

"What?" he gasped. "What's this?"

"Run!" shouted Jute. "Run, you hear me?" And he himself ran, but he did not run further down the tunnel. Instead, he ran back to Rane. "Run, blast you!"

Rane turned and fled. In the near blackness of the passageway behind them, Jute saw what Rane had seen. Points of light came closer. Cold blue light shone from eyes. It gleamed from broken teeth and shattered bones. It gilded battered armor and swords sticky with blood. The dead. The dead of Harlech who had given their lives fighting in the cornfield, fighting below the oak tree so that their friends and brothers might live. They came with ghastly faces, dragging broken limbs, dangling shattered arms, but they came, quicker and quicker. Their dead eyes were fixed on their living brothers-in-arms.

"Jute," said the ghost. "I've nothing against dead people, but these are the wrong kind. Do something. Please!"

"Wind," said Jute desperately, "are you there?"

There was no answer, except for the dreadful scraping sound of the footsteps of the dead. They were closer now, much closer. They reached for Jute with broken hands. Hunger shone in their eyes. Something beyond them in the darkness chuckled. Or maybe it was only in Jute's mind. He shouted in fury.

Shouted.

The wind came alive. From nowhere. From his own self. From within his mind. Blowing and howling out of him as if it had been waiting there all along, just on the other side of his eyes. The tunnel was full of the sky. It was full of the cold, sweet scent of the air below the stars. The wind shouted in Jute's voice. Stone shattered. Earth fell in huge and thunderous collapse. The dead were gone, swallowed up. And the wind swirled, turned, blew Jute back down the tunnel in an enormous gleeful blast. His body flipped end over end, but the wind sheltered him from the stone walls. Dimly, he heard the alarmed shouts of the men of Harlech. Weapons flying through the air, smashing against stone walls. Bodies flying. The wind laughing inside his mind.

Stop!

Why? said the wind. *Fun. I'm having fun.*

Stop. No, I mean, thank you. But you must stop. . .

Why? We can break things. We can throw stones up into the sky. Topple mountains, let the blue sky down into their roots. Blow the ocean into a fury. Shout at the stars. The wind paused, and when it spoke again, there was something almost sly about its voice. *I know the way to Daghoron. We can blow around its walls and even he will not touch you and me!*

No. You must stop now.

But this is not your place. Deep down under the dreadful earth. The heavy earth. The sky is yours. The sky!

This was true. Painfully true. Jute felt it all the way down into his bones. Sweat sprang out on his forehead. He needed to get out. Get out from under the crushing weight of stone and earth. Up into the sky. He needed the sky like a man in the desert needed a cup of water. He clenched his fist. But not now. Not now.

Not now, he said in his mind. *I'll return to the sky, but not now. Please, you must quiet yourself. For my sake.*

And the wind fell silent. Jute lay in complete darkness, stone under his face, under his hands. The air was full of dust. He could taste it in his mouth. He became aware of the quiet sounds around him of others shifting, staggering to their feet, a few groans of pain. He sat up.

"A light," said the duke of Harlech from nearby in the dark. "Someone strike a light."

Flint rasped on tinder and light bloomed bright: a small light cupped in a man's hand, but so bright that it was a shock. Faces scraped and bloody, grimed in dust, stared at Jute.

"If you ever do that again," said Rane, "give us a bit of warning, eh?" But then he grinned, so it was all right.

"Everyone accounted for?" said the duke, surveying the little group. "Eight men lost. Grief, but that's a heavy toll to keep our lives. Harlech is not so wealthy with people." He sighed and shook his head. "We must make it worthwhile. Come, Jute, you say this

653

passage leads back under the city? Let us hurry. I must admit, though, this way does not hearten me. If we can gain entrance to the city so easily, why should not others do the same?"

"Well," said Jute. "It isn't such an easy way."

"Good news and bad news in the same breath. This has been an interesting day, and I daresay it isn't over yet."

"No, it isn't. There are dangers down here, I won't deny that. But, as far as I know, they're only wards. The passage leads to the university ruins. The closer we get, the more wards we'll find. Old wards woven from before the time of the wizards' war. But I know many of them; I've been in the ruins and I've been through this tunnel. We'll be safe enough."

"Wards," said the duke with some distaste. "Bits of bone and string and old words. We don't bother with such things in Harlech. There are other ways to protect one's land. You were traveling in the other direction, weren't you?"

"What?"

"I mean, you've been through this tunnel before but only coming from the city, yes?"

"Er, yes."

"Ah," said the duke. "Still, I think we're better off down here than up there."

As the duke's words died away into the silence, a thought slowly sank through Jute's mind. The back of his neck prickled uncomfortably. Many wards were directional. They were triggered according to what direction the offending sound or movement or presence came from. That meant that a door, for example, might be benign when opened from one side. Opening it from the other side, however, could be a different story.

The fact that they were all looking at him didn't make matters any better. They were looking at him as if he, Jute, were going to lead them all to safety. As if he, Jute, had all the answers. As if getting through this tunnel would be a simple stroll led by their fearless leader, namely, Jute. A bunch of battle-hardened men deferring to a boy. Well, he wasn't a boy anymore, was he? But he certainly wasn't a man yet, either.

"Stone and shadow," muttered Jute to himself.

They found an old splintered timber on the ground, a casualty, no doubt, of the wind's enthusiasm. Proper torches were made of the wood and soon the tunnel was well lit. Jute walked back to the caved-in rubble at the end of the tunnel and stood there a while.

"Hear anything?" said Rane.

"No." Jute shook his head. "It's silent, as far as I can tell. I was worried they might try digging through, but I think there's more than just stone and earth here. The wind left something of itself as well. Some sort of binding. It's still raining up there, though, and the river is bursting its banks. But I don't hear those things. I can feel them in my mind, I suppose."

"It can be the same with tracking," said Rane. "You don't always need to hear or see the animal's prints. You can sometimes feel its passage. Rabbits and deer are easiest. The big cats are hardest."

There was no further way to stall, even though Jute was becoming more nervous about the tunnel with each passing minute. They started out with Jute and the duke in the lead, a torch burning in the duke's hand, the men treading in silence behind them, and Rane at the back of the line. Jute had warned them about being quiet and they had all nodded. The men of Harlech were hunters and trackers, and they were accustomed to silence.

"I trust the hawk is well," said the duke quietly.

"The hawk!" said Jute.

"Yes, where is the hawk?" said the ghost from inside Jute's cloak. "I miss him, even though he's a grumpy old goose."

Jute's heart sank. He had forgotten about the hawk in all of the terror and hurry. He threw his mind wide, seeking for a hint of the bird, but there was nothing. Only stone and silence and the first few whispers of wards waiting somewhere further up ahead. He could not even feel the sky. They were too deep under the earth. There was magic of some sort woven into the stones of the tunnel. Nothing dangerous or aware. It seemed to exist only to preserve the stones, but it effectively shut out whatever lay beyond the tunnel.

"I'm sure he's fine," said Jute, swallowing. "He doesn't like being away from the sky. He hates being cooped up."

And so do I. Fly well, hawk.

The torchlight wavered in front of them, revealing the fitted stones of the walls, the dusty floor, and the cobwebbed ceiling. Somewhere, far up ahead of them, was the city of Hearne. But first the tunnel and then the university ruins.

"I wish Severan was here," said Jute to himself. "I wish the hawk was here."

No one heard him except for the ghost, and it said nothing. The men of Harlech walked in silence behind him. The shadows danced along the walls beside them, married to the wavering flames of their torches.

CHAPTER ONE HUNDRED & SEVENTEEN
A KISS

Someone was whispering in his ear. It was irritating because he couldn't understand what the person was saying. He just wanted to keep on sleeping. Owain tried to turn over, shut the voice out, but he couldn't. His body wouldn't respond. It felt as if someone had shoveled earth onto him, tamped it flat, and then heaved a couple of boulders on top for good measure. He couldn't move. But he could certainly go back to sleep. He started drifting down into the darkness. Surprising how pleasant it was.

The voice whispered louder.

Something tickled his ear. A soft brush, almost like a kiss. No. Like a whispered word. Words. Words like a school of fish. Tiny fish. Yes, that was it. Fluttering into his mind. Brushing away the shadows. The words seemed to gain more clarity now. More definition. He could almost understand them. But even though the meaning stayed just out of reach, the words continued dancing through his mind. Light spilled from them. It was a dim, peaceful sort of light, almost like sunlight reaching down through water. Down into the depths. He was waking. He could not stay down in the darkness. The weight on his body lessened. Surely he could move now. Drift up to the surface. The voice spoke again and energy surged through his body. It was like a wave on the shore. Washing away the darkness.

Owain opened his eyes. He was looking at a wall, his wife's dresser heaped with clothing. The long mirror. The window was open. The one overlooking the kitchen garden. Stars shone outside in the night sky. He was home. Home in bed. He sat up, tangled in blankets. He could smell the sea, and for a moment, he thought he could hear the boom and crash of the waves far below the cliffs.

Someone spoke. He turned, certain he would see Sibb sitting in the chair in the corner, but there was no one. Just shadows. For a second, he thought he saw a dark form seated in the chair. But, no. It was a blanket folded over the back of the chair. He blinked. The battle! The enemy charging across the crest of the gap. The rain and the wind. Arrows arching down. The crows. The battle! Owain tumbled out of bed. He grabbed a pair of pants and a shirt.

"Tear it! How long have I been asleep? The moon's up." He buckled his belt on and strode to the door. "Sibb!" he yelled, flinging it open. "Sibb!"

"Hush!"

A shadow flew toward him down the hallway. The moonlight gilded Sibb's face with silver. Tears shone in her eyes.

"Hush," she said. "You'll wake the children."

Her hands touched his face.

"How long have I been out?" His voice was low and urgent.

"Nearly twenty-four hours," said Sibb. "You wouldn't wake up. Your body was as cold as ice. Your heartbeat slowed until I could no longer hear it." Her hands trembled against the line of his jaw. "There was darkness in the room, even though I tied the curtains wide. There was sunlight outside in the rain and the wind, but there was only darkness in here."

"Were you," he said, frowning, "were you just in here now, talking to me? I mean, while I was asleep?"

She looked at him, confused. "No. I was with the children. They've been having nightmares again."

"How odd." Owain shook his head. "I thought—well, no matter. I feel better now. Much better. How long have I been asleep? A day? No, don't look like that, Sibb. I must get back to my men. You know that just as well as I do."

"Owain."

"You wouldn't expect anything less of me.

"No. Go, but come back to me."

He smiled. "I always will, Sibb."

She followed him down the stairs, down into the dim candlelight of the hall. He opened the door into the night and stopped, staring. A red glow burned in the darkness. Far across the city, across the rooftops, past the twinkling lights of homes and hearths, under the starlight stabbing down from the black night sky. A flickering red glow. Watchfires at the city wall. His heart skipped a beat, quickened. Three Guardsmen snapped to attention outside the gate, spears motionless and horses standing in sleepy patience.

"Kiss me, Sibb."

She did, trying to smile, and then he was hurrying out the gate, his voice raised. A horse nickered in greeting. She heard the creak of saddles and then the quickening tattoo of hooves as the horsemen cantered down the road. Sibb stood there until the night settled back into quiet. Tears slid down her face, but she made no sound. The house was silent around her when she shut the door. Moonlight slanted through the hallway. Something crunched under her foot. A leaf of seaweed, still wet and cold in her hand. She marveled at it, wondering. The leaf smelled of the sea, and for a moment, her heart was comforted.

CHAPTER ONE HUNDRED & EIGHTEEN
THE NAME OF THE GHOST

The tunnel seemed like one long, endless stretch of night. A night in which the seconds slowed into minutes, the minutes into hours, and the hours into days. Their torchlight fell on stones and dust and cobwebs, but everywhere, around and about them, waited the shadows. The shadows walked on their heels and retreated before their advance in slow and grudging step.

"Surely," said the duke of Harlech, his voice weary, "we've walked to the sea."

Jute managed a smile. "Not yet."

The men of Harlech were silent, even through the long hours. Jute sometimes heard them whisper among themselves, but that was the exception to their closed and quiet faces. They made no noise as they walked. They were all alike, those men, tall and lean, moving like cats in the shadows behind him. Perhaps the north was a forge of ice that hammered everyone into the same semblance? The cold and the stony ground, the unrelenting winters, and the icy sea—they all conspired to bear the same children: children with ice in their blood, steel in their bones, the feel of the earth in their hearts. They grew up into men shaped by the wind.

"Hello," said the ghost. "What's that?"

"What's what?" said Jute.

The ghost materialized and drifted over to the wall. It stood there, gazing at the carvings on the face of the rock. Jute couldn't see anything out of the ordinary. This section of passage looked precisely the same as that which they had been passing through for the past several hours. The same carvings. The same dust. The duke coughed politely behind them.

"Ghost," said Jute urgently, "we don't have time to be deciphering old runes or whatever it is you're doing. We need to hurry."

"I think we should take a look at this," said the ghost.

It sounded oddly solemn, and a shiver ran down Jute's neck. He stepped forward, holding his torch high. The light illuminated the stone wall of the tunnel. There was nothing different about the wall. The stone was worked with carvings, true, but they looked no different from any other stretch of wall.

"Perhaps it'd be wise to continue," said the duke politely. "I doubt our enemy has altered his intentions in any way."

The ghost ignored him. It lifted its hand. Torchlight shone on the translucent edges of its fingers. It touched the wall.

"Here," said the ghost.

And Jute, peering closer, caught by the melancholy in the ghost's voice, saw something. A single rune. It was carved within the curve of a rose vine, hidden within a profusion of stone flowers and dusty thorns. One character. There was nothing complicated or strange about the lines of the rune, but it somehow held his eye. He immediately knew he had to know the meaning of it. Despite the urgency of the moment. Despite their need to escape the sceadu.

"What is it?" said Lannaslech. The duke stepped up beside Jute and stared at the wall. The wavering torchlight deepened the shadows in the grooves of the carved stone relief. Behind them, the other men waited in patient silence.

"This rune," said Jute. His finger wavered over the character. For some reason, he could not bring himself to touch it.

"I am not unversed in languages," said the duke, his voice quiet. "The members of my family, despite our devotion to the hunt and the art of war, are also given to study the history of words. It has always been our love, ever since Harlech was settled by my forefathers. The men of Harlech have certain obligations to the past. This rune, I think, is from the time of Siglan Cynehad, the first king of Tormay."

"Then it's very old?" said Jute.

"More than three thousand years old. I thought I knew all the characters from that time, from the language they spoke then. Mind you, what men speak has changed greatly from then to now. But this character is very strange. The nature of its composition indicates it belongs in that alphabet of runes. Of that I have no doubt, but I've never seen this particular one. I wonder if there's a man alive who would know its meaning?"

"You're right," said the ghost. "No one alive, but I'm dead and I know."

"What?" said the duke, astonished at the ghost's words. "How's that possible?"

"Because it's my name."

Jute stared at the ghost. There was an odd silence in the shadows around them. An expectant hush in the stone and dust. The carvings high on the walls, just out of reach of the torchlight, seemed to be moving closer, inching across the stone so that they could see and hear better.

The ghost sighed. "I'd forgotten, but now I remember. I carved that so very long ago. I had forgotten. I wonder what else I've forgotten?"

No one said anything, until Rane, who had been edging closer, spoke.

"What is your name?"

"My name," said the ghost, whispering more to itself than to the others, "my name was Staer Gemyndes. Yes, that was my name. I'd forgotten. I remember now."

At the ghost's words, the rune on the wall began to glow with a faint but steady light. A shiver ran down Jute's neck.

"Staer Gemyndes," said the duke, his jaw dropping. "But that's impossible. The advisor of Siglan Cynehad. The most powerful wizard ever known in history! He died thousands of years ago. How can it be? You? A mere ghost? I've nothing against ghosts, and you strike me as being an excellent fellow, but—Staer Gemyndes?"

"I know," said the ghost, sounding embarrassed. "It hardly seems plausible. It's been so long, thousands of years, did you say? I've forgotten most of who I am. I only remembered the name when I saw the rune on the wall. I'm very sorry. I wish my memory was a bit sharper."

"Even I know who you are," said Jute. He touched the rune in amazement. It felt warm. "Staer Gemyndes! Just wait until—"

But Jute didn't finish his sentence. As soon as he said the name, his fingers against the carving, the wall moved. It didn't just move. It vanished, revealing a shallow alcove. Within the alcove was a shelf, and on the shelf was a book. The ghost made a pleased sound.

"Ah, there it is. After all these years. How nice."

"What is that book?" said the duke, his voice shaking.

Jute, hearing him, knew what the book was. He did not need the ghost to say anything. He could hear Severan's voice whispering in his head. He could see the old man's face bright with longing.

"The *Gerecednes*," said the ghost.

"The *Gerecednes*!" The duke could barely manage to speak the word.

"Yes," said the ghost, sounding embarrassed. "I should've never written the thing. I'm remembering more now as we speak. I hid the book here during the construction of the university. It was becoming much too dangerous to keep the thing. The Dark was determined to get its hands on it, and I was tired of evading murder at all hours of the night. All for the sake of that book. It wouldn't have been safe to leave it in the university library, though the professors begged and pleaded with me. I couldn't destroy the thing— there was too much power in it—so I hid it here and then went north. I suppose that was when I founded the Stone Tower. I was rather tired of Hearne by that time."

"But this is fantastic," said Jute, his eyes shining. "Severan will be delighted. Don't you know he's spent his entire life trying to find this book?"

"Did you say Severan?" said the duke.

"That would be a bad idea," said the ghost, looking alarmed. "For one thing, this book'll draw the Dark like iron to a magnet. At least, once it's taken off the shelf. I wove a very powerful spell into the shelf that masks the book, but once removed—ah—I'm afraid you'd have a disaster on your hands. They want what's inside, don't you know? It's all coming back to me. That's why that villain Scuadimnes came to the university in the first place. He was trying to find the *Gerecednes*. It's not a book you just pick up and read, mind you. Most people wouldn't be able to resist picking the thing up. Once you open the book, however, you can't help but read the whole thing. It would take more than a hundred years to finish. Perhaps several hundred years. Maybe even more than that."

"What? It's that long? It doesn't look at all thick."

"It's not that," said the ghost. "Something happened when I wrote it. I can't remember exactly why. Perhaps it was due to the fact that the words I used were so old. They're almost the original language. At least, close enough to be dangerous. They don't behave the same way your modern words do, particularly when there's a lot of 'em together. They contain more truth. Once you start reading, you're caught. And, while you're reading, time slows down, er, rather dramatically. I suppose I should've just written in a different language. Not to mention the fact that some of those words are dreadfully powerful."

"Hadn't we better get a move on?" said Rane, frowning. He looked back down the tunnel, past the torchlight, as if he could somehow see through the shadows and into the distance. "The longer we stay here, the closer our enemy gets. I don't fancy another run-in with that hound and its master."

"Perfect!" said Jute.

"There's nothing perfect about it. How do you fight something that keeps on disappearing into nothing?"

"Not that," said Jute. "Don't you see? If this book truly draws the Dark, why don't we simply leave it lying on the floor here? Along comes our sceadu, he picks it up, and there! You've got him. He'll be reading for hundreds and hundreds of years. He'll be trapped. That is, if you're telling the truth, ghost."

The ghost looked at him coldly. "Of course I'm telling the truth."

After some heated discussion, they decided to try it. However, the ghost suggested that the entire group proceed a good way down the tunnel first. "It wouldn't do," it said, "to have one of you develop a sudden urge to pick the blasted book up." The duke volunteered to move the book from the shelf to the floor.

"If you don't mind," he said slowly.

They waited for him further down the tunnel, a few minutes walk. The men stood in silence. The torchlight shone on their weary faces. Rane gnawed at his lip, staring back into the darkness.

"He's taking too long," said the ghost suddenly. "Much too long. I'm very sorry."

"I'll go back," said Jute.

"No! Wait!" said the ghost, but Jute was already gone.

Jute hurried back through the passage, holding his torch high. Sweat trickled down his neck. The shadows were changing around him. They were full of menace, watching and waiting. The only sounds he could hear were the whisper of his footsteps and his heart pulsing in his blood. But somewhere beyond that, too quiet to be heard, he knew there was something else. The sceadu. Silently ghosting along through the blackness. Not needing light. Eyes blindly turning toward Jute, wherever he was. Getting closer. After a minute, he saw the duke of Harlech. The old man was standing in the middle of the passageway. He could see the book in the man's hands.

"Sir!" he said, his voice low and urgent. "Sir! Are you all right? We need to leave."

The duke did not answer. Jute stepped in front of him and saw that his eyes were fixed on the book on his hands. The book was closed, but the duke was staring at the cover. It was then that Jute heard something whispering on the edge of his mind. The book. The voice was quiet and conversational, not unlike the ghost's voice. A pleasant voice. But there was sorrow in it as well, as if it looked back over hundreds of years and found more to regret than to rejoice over. The voice spoke in words that blurred into colors and distance, into images that slowly gained clarity in Jute's mind. He stopped, caught by the voice and what he could suddenly see.

An ocean under the rising sun with light blazing on the water, shimmering in the blue depths, bursting across the sky, burning away the purple darkness of the fleeing night. A hundred ships in flight. West, always west. Sails ragged and patched, bellied out, full with the wind. The water surging white with foam against every prow. Dolphins, slick and silver, dancing between the boundary of sea and sky. Smiling their toothy grins as if to confirm the blessing of the Lady of the Sea. But there had been no land in sight for six weeks. The drinking water barrels were half empty. The bread was almost gone.

We hoped, whispered the voice in Jute's mind.

We could only hope.

The nights with a thousand thousand stars drifting in their courses above us. Shining like a thousand thousand lamps. They reflected on the darkness of the sea. Both were equally lovely, for both were equally true, like a word and the reality it describes. Night after night turned into day, and day after day turned into night. And on the last day, the wind brought us to a new land. The barren shores. Stone and dust and the hard desert light. We burned our ships under that fierce light, a light so fierce and bright that the flames leaping from the ship timbers roared up toward the sun. A reflection, like the stars drifting upon the ocean of night.

Again, the wind pointed west. Across the wastelands toward a green and pleasant land. Tormay. To a land unknown. To a land promised in dreams. The wind carried its scent across the miles and days. The dark was not there.

The dark.

The dark was not there yet.

With a shudder, Jute came out of his reverie. The duke still stood motionless in front of him, the book in his hands. Further down the corridor, right at the edge of Jute's sight, the shadows trembled. He could smell something foul in the air. Something approaching.

"Sir," said Jute. "You must put down the book. Now."

But the duke did not respond, and the darkness in the corridor drew closer. Jute could hear the sound of footsteps. He wrenched the book from the duke's hands and the man trembled. He blinked. His hand fell on his sword, but then he came awake.

"Was I?" said the duke, but he could not finish.

"Yes," said Jute. "Quickly. We have only a few seconds or we're lost."

Jute placed the book on the floor in the middle of the corridor and then, grasping Lannaslech's arm, urged the old man away. They only made it a few steps before a voice spoke behind them.

"Are you going to run forever, Jute?"

The sceadu's voice was quiet. He moved out of the shadows and into the edge of Jute's torchlight. The expressionless eyes stared at the boy and the old duke. Jute could hear Lannaslech breathing shallowly beside him. The shadowhound crouched at the sceadu's feet, a blot of darkness with the barest hint of a dog's form. There were other things behind them, things in the shadows; they did not move, but simply waited.

"No," said Jute, trying to keep his voice from trembling. "I was never running. I was just waiting for the right time."

"And this is the right time?" The sceadu's head tilted to one side, as if he sought to examine Jute from a different angle. He took a step forward. The air seemed to have gone cold in the passageway. "Death is not a difficult thing. It's an easy thing, as quick as a passing thought. That's how I've always found it. Tell me, Jute. Shall I set my beast free, or shall it be the sword?"

The shadowhound heaved itself to its feet as if in anticipation. For a dreadful moment, Jute froze. The shadowhound. He had not considered it. Presumably, it would not stop to consider a book lying on the floor. It would simply leap for his throat, and that would be the end.

The duke's sword rang free from its sheath.

"I don't doubt you let your dog do your fighting," he drawled, his voice contemptuous. "In Harlech, only the men ride to war."

A blade appeared in the sceadu's hand. The shadowhound sat back down on its haunches with a disappointed grunt.

"A Harlech lord and a whelp of an anbeorun," said the sceadu. A ghastly smile crossed his face. "I'll enjoy this."

One more step, thought Jute, trying not to turn and run.

The sceadu paused, as if he had read Jute's mind. But then he stepped forward, almost right on the book. He paused and looked down. He stooped to pick up the book. Opened it. His face froze, eyes intent on the page. Jute could hear the whisper from the book. The same voice, but stronger and clearer now. Words as clear and as pristine as the snowmelt of a mountain stream, as pure as the first edge of morning's light.

This is the Gerecednes. *Hear my words, o stranger, for they are true. I bore witness to the truth, that it might be remembered. That it might be recorded as it was once was and always shall be. My name is Staer Gemyndes.*

Jute and the duke of Harlech turned and fled away into the darkness. No one followed. Behind them, the voice whispered on and on, and it seemed it would surely have no end. The torchlight flickered and bobbed around them, a cocoon of light that kept them safe within its sphere. Dust stirred around their footsteps.

"I almost opened it," said the duke, his face white. "Almost. I think I would have if you hadn't come along. Thank you for coming back. Ever since I was a boy, I've heard of the *Gerecednes*. The first Lord Lannaslech built a library at our manor, hundreds and hundreds of years ago. Every duke since has added to it. I added quite a few during my day. My grandfather used to say that there were certain books, even certain single words, that were more powerful than an army of swords. The books of the wizards, of the ancient seafarers and the old kings, they all held secrets from the past. But the writings of Staer Gemyndes towered like an invisible mountain behind all of them. He recorded actual words of the first language, the language of Anue. He spoke with dragons. And, it was said, he was a friend of the anbeorun. To think that your ghost is one and the same. I've still half a mind to think him a liar."

"Liar or not," said Jute, "that book was real. I could feel it reaching into my mind."

"Yes." The duke sighed, and then shuddered.

They rounded a corner and found the men waiting for them. The ghost looked mournfully at Jute.

"Did you leave it?" said the ghost.

"Yes. Barely." Jute shuddered. "I could hear your voice speaking from the book, even though we didn't open it. The sceadu almost reached us, but he picked it up. How—why did you write it?"

"I'll explain one day." The ghost sighed. "I should never have written it, but perhaps it was intended to save us today? One hundred years. Two hundred, three hundred years? Perhaps more. And then what'll happen? He'll finish the book."

No one had anything to say to that. The ghost vanished into Jute's cloak. They continued on through the darkness and silence. The further they went, the more relieved Jute became. The tension in his neck relaxed and he no longer looked over his shoulder every minute. Hearne. They were nearing Hearne, and there they would be safe. At least, safe for a time.

They came to an ornately carved arch in the tunnel. Stone pillars fashioned to resemble trees on either wall rose up and joined their branches along the roof. Squirrels peered down from among the leaves. An owl regarded them gravely from its perch. A fox crouched at the foot of one tree.

"That's odd," said Jute to himself. "I don't remember this when we were escaping the wihht."

Uncertain, he stopped. The men of Harlech halted behind him. Jute took a step forward, holding his torch high. The light fell on the dusty carvings. A raven stared down from one branch. It looked dreadfully lifelike, but it was not. Could not be. He could see a chip in the stone of its beak. Jute hesitated. Perhaps it was nothing. Perhaps it was only his nerves. He needed the sky. He needed to be out from underneath all this stone.

Someone sneezed behind him.

The raven blinked its stone eyes. They focused on Jute. And the ward in the stone arch came alive before the sound of the sneeze finished. It lashed out quicker than thought, quicker than the first ray of sunlight reaching across the morning sky to the opposite end of the world. It was implacable. It was woven only to destroy. To annihilate.

Jute had even less time to react. His mind flashed open wide. It opened like a door taller than the sky and wider than the horizon. Taller and wider than the stone passage he stood motionless in. The ward slammed into him and found only sky. Only the silent emptiness with the stars watching safely from their impossible distances. The words of the ward unwove, negated, stripped the material of being down to something older than existence. But it had only the sky upon which to unleash its power. Only the sky to unmake, and the sky cannot be reduced to anything less than what it is, for the sky is only light and darkness and time. The ward flashed through Jute's mind. It did not slacken in speed or power. It was as if it sought to strike at some object in some impossibly distant place, beyond the stars.

Who made this thing? Why? What were they guarding against?

But Jute could not linger on that thought. He had only so much concentration left. He saw the duke of Harlech out of the corner of his eye. The old man stood like a statue. Torchlight shone on one side of his face. The other was lost in darkness. Light glinted on one eye. The passageway was silent behind him.

"Walk past me," said Jute, his voice barely a whisper. "All of you. Get at least fifty feet in front of me. Do it. Now. I can't hold this much longer."

He closed his eyes. The few words had almost been too much. He was not aware if the duke had heard him. He was not aware if they were walking past him. The sky filled his mind. He couldn't feel his body anymore. The ward slammed up toward the stars. It was strange. He couldn't see the spell, but he could sense it rushing through the sky. He could hear its words now. A low continuous murmur wavering on the edge of melody. There was almost beauty in it. Seconds flickered by, or perhaps they were mere hours, and still the ward surged through his mind. He could not think any longer. His body took a step forward. His boot dragged across stone. Another step. The ward howled up into the sky. Another step. And then there was only silence and darkness. He opened his eyes.

The men of Harlech stared at him, crowded into the narrow passageway. Their faces were weary, streaked with dirt and dust. Dried blood caked on Rane's forehead. The flames of the torches burned steady and motionless.

"I won't ask who sneezed," said Jute, trying to smile.

"What was that?" said the duke. "I felt something in my mind when you stopped. Something old."

"I felt it too," said Rane. "It was not friendly, whatever it was."

"It was a ward. At least, a thing similar to a ward, if a mountain lion is similar to a housecat. It's directional, so we're safe on this side of it. Quite a spot for it. Most people would be hurrying along, not expecting any wards until they neared a proper doorway or a split in the tunnel." Jute shivered. "It almost got us."

"But it didn't," said Rane. He shrugged, his hand moving to the hilt of his sword and then away. "That's the important thing. That's always the important thing."

They proceeded more cautiously from that point. Other passageways began appearing with increasing frequency. Other corridors stretched away into the impenetrable darkness from the one they followed. Doorways were cobwebbed over with dusty draperies of old spiderwebs. The stonework began to change. More carved pillars and arches supported the stone slabs of the ceiling. Gargoyles and serpents and odd, fanciful creatures perched on stone outcroppings, frozen in mid-snarl and staring down at them with blind eyes. They walked by walls carved with words in such strange and lovely flowing lines that they seemed more like flowers than characters. The duke wanted to pause there, for he was a man who loved learning, but Jute hurried him along, whispering that, sometimes, it was safer not to stare at a thing for too long. After all, it might wake up.

Jute knew they were getting closer. It wasn't from the look of where they were, even though there were things, here and there, that looked familiar. It was the murmur on the edge of his thoughts. Wards. Countless wards. The wards in the university ruins. Whispers upon whispers, voices mumbling and sighing the old words of long-dead wizards. Words guarding and watching and waiting for any intruder foolish or brave enough to try their defenses. The more Jute listened to them, the closer they got with each successive step and the more distinct the voices of the wards became. He listened with astonishment, for he had never been able to hear wards in such a way.

And that is because you become more of me, said the wind in his mind. *More of me, and me more of you. Listen with my ears and you shall hear the stars in the darkness, the sun on his trail, the ticking of time.*

The voices gained more definition until, at least with some of them, they revealed the names of their weavers as well as the words of their weaves. The names and voices fell through his mind. They spoke in dead languages, in old languages, in mixtures of known and unknown tongues, in the accents of the north and south, the rough voice of the mountains, the smooth lilt of Vo and Vomaro, the dryness of Harth.

I am Kennen the Younger of Ballantre. With my name this weave does commence. Here, is the knot. You, the wolves of Wivern Run. I call you. I hold you by my name forevermore. Bound in form, in fur, and in fang. Bound in this stone. This stone. This stone that is named thus and here. You shall tear and rend. Rip and bite. Slash and kill. Bound. I name you as you are, as you were, as you shall be. Suffer no stranger to approach. Suffer them not, o wolves of Wivern Run. Bind and bound you are.

I am Merca Vale, and I found the memory of dragon's fire hidden in the forest shadows. The sixth name of fire. So do I bind the fire in the sixth step of this staircase. Listen well, stone. Listen for the breathing of the intruder, the stranger, the enemy. Bring forth the fire.

I am Nin, the shepherd's son. I was born among the ice fields of Morn. I weave with the thirteen names of ice. To freeze, to shatter, to splinter, to reach into the darkness and steal the cold of Daghoron's shadows. Step here, stranger. Step into my weave and so stand still forever.

I am Forlana Forl, of the desert people. . .

I am Gavindre the Lame. . .

I am. . .

I. . .

"Are you all right?"

Jute blinked. He blinked again, and the tumult of voices in his head died away to a murmur. The duke of Harlech was looking at him strangely.

"I'm fine. We are getting very close, I think."

They came to a place where the passage ended and they could go no further. They stood in silence. Rane raised his torch high. The light fell on a rubble of stones, a collapse of pillars and masonry and dust. The ceiling was shattered through, revealing the dim and choked view of huge, hewn stones. A trickle of water emerged from among the rubble to flow along the floor before it disappeared down a crack.

"Well," said Rane tiredly, "I hate to say it, but this looks like a dead end."

"No." Jute knelt down and touched one of the loose stones at the edge of the rubble. He dipped his fingers in the water. He could feel something in it—a memory of how it had been, the recollection of standing silent and deep among other stones for a thousand years, edged and trimmed with plaster.

"No," he said. "This is the right place. There was a well below us when we dropped down from the floor above. This is where we came through when we fled the ruins."

"Not with all this rock here," said the duke. "Though I suppose the wind could blow through the smallest spaces."

"It came crashing down behind us. We were in a hurry, and there was something after us. Severan—a scholar, a wizard—one of the two—he said something, a spell of some sort, and the whole passage collapsed behind us."

"You did say Severan, didn't you?" The duke stared at him.

"Yes. He saved us all that day."

"And where is this Severan now?"

"I don't know."

Jute was not sure how long it took them to dig through the rubble. Hours, at least, but it seemed longer. It might have been a day. A day and a night, shifting the stones in the shadows and the meager light of the torches. It might have been longer. The air became full of dust as they moved the stones. They could taste the grit on their tongues and against their teeth. There was a whispering and a muttering all around them as more and more wards became attuned to their presence.

"And that's not the worst of them," said Jute quietly. "There are several others— three, I think—somewhere near us. They aren't making noise, but they're definitely listening to us. We don't want to wake them fully."

"Wizards and their wards," said Rane. Sweat streamed down his face as he hefted an enormous stone. "I've never liked wizards. They tamper with things. Push things out of balance. Look under rocks when they shouldn't."

"Someone has to," said his father mildly.

Jute stepped back and wiped his brow. They had made good progress. The pile of rubble was beginning to resemble a staircase. A huge staircase, of course, with teetering bits and rough steps, but definitely a staircase. It reached up to the ceiling and then continued on through the shattered slabs there into the darkness above. The men were working in a line now, handing the stones down from man to man, down the staircase to be stacked in a pile further along the passageway. The relay of stones suddenly stopped. The men standing at the top of the stairs were motionless. Dust drifted down.

"What's going on?" said the duke.

Jute could feel a shift in the air, a gentle push against his mind. Something had woken up. He ran up the stairs. His feet lightened with each step. Part of his mind called out to the wind, threading a breeze through his body so that he no longer weighed anything. He reached the top. There was barely room for him to stand. The man standing there edged over a few inches.

"Look up," said the man quietly.

The hole in the ceiling was choked with shattered slabs of stone, each bigger than the body of a man, tilted and wedged against each other. There was no way they could be shifted, unless it was with hammer and mallet. There was, however, a narrow passage through the center of them. Narrow, but surely wide enough to wriggle through. At first, Jute could see nothing except the stones and the darkness. But then he saw them. Several glimmers of light. No. It wasn't light. Just touches of luminance, hardly more than spots of color a single degree removed from the darkness. After a moment, perhaps due to his eyes adjusting more, he saw several more of the spots, and then even more.

"They weren't there before," said the man standing beside Jute. "One moment, complete darkness up there, and then they just winked on."

Jute stared at the spots of color. His mind feathered out and he closed his eyes. He could feel nothing hostile. His mind pushed out farther. There was something there. Minute touches of brilliance in his mind. A single sentence woven of ancient words looped in upon themselves. And then shattered into a thousand pieces. He knew what they were.

"Light," he whispered. "*Lig.*"

The stars came to life in the darkness. A hundred stars winking into brilliance. At least, that's what it looked like at first. But then they subsided into what they were. A hundred tiny shining stones. They shed light into the darkness and the darkness fled away. The hole in the ceiling was clearly visible now, a tangled, interwoven shambles of stone slabs and shards woven together like a giant vine leading up toward a grayer light.

"I think there's a way up," said Jute. "Up there to the right. We might be able to climb through the rocks."

"What did you do?" asked the man standing beside him.

Jute shook his head. "If the light goes out, if it changes, just say the word light out loud."

The wind stirred to life in his mind and nudged him forward. He climbed up a few feet into the wreckage of rock slabs. The wind nudged him again. He reached for a handhold, and his fingers closed on one of the tiny gleaming stones. It was smaller and thinner than a child's fingernail. He dropped it into his pocket. The wind chuckled and then subsided into satisfied stillness in his mind.

"Pass the word along to the last in line," Jute said to the man. "I want as many of those little stones as possible."

The rest of the way was easy enough. The light guided their steps, showed them handholds and footholds. The men of Harlech moved up through the stones, through the collapsed girders of granite, the tumbled pillars. They followed Jute as he threaded his way up through the spaces. The men behind him mimicked his every move, his every handhold and foothold. Rane was the last in line. As he climbed, he gathered each tiny shining stone that he could reach and placed it in his pocket. No one spoke, other than a few muttered occasions of "light." Each time the word was spoken, more of the tiny stones sprang to life around them. They shone around them, half-hidden by the slabs of fallen stone, but the light was enough to illumine their path.

Jute pulled himself up over one last slab and emerged up into a large, gloomy space. He had an impression of height and a cold, musty smell of closed-up places that had not been disturbed for a long time. The whispers of wards stirred uneasily all around him, above him, on all sides. Some were close, some were distant, but they were all familiar. He smiled. They were in the university ruins.

"Light," he said, his voice clear.

More stars came to life. Tiny stabs of radiance. But this time they were scattered all around him. A thousand bits of light lying on the floor. He was in the mosaic room.

"Come on up," Jute called down through the hole in the floor.

They all climbed up and stood around him in the cheery radiance of the room. They were a grim, stern lot, stinking of dried blood and sweat, heavy in their armor and their weapons, but they could not but smile when they looked at Jute standing among the tiny shining stones. The light shone in his eyes. Rane had collected a great many of the small stones. He handed them to Jute.

"Thank you," said the boy. He grinned. "We made it."

They emerged from the university into the dark and rainy hour before dawn. There was ice on the ground. Mioja Square lay before them. But it was a different place from what Jute had remembered. The square was crowded with tents, ramshackle huts, and lean-tos. Woodsmoke drifted up into the rain. The place was quiet for the most part, but here and there, a few solitary people crouched at fires, stirring the embers into life in preparation for their morning cooking.

"Refugees from the outlying areas," said the duke. "From the Rennet Valley and further east in the Morn Mountains. They've been pouring into the city for days. Farmers, shepherds, miners from the mountains, townsfolk." He shook his head, his face grim. "They think they've found safety here. I wish them well, but city walls can only stand for so long."

"I have no faith in walls," said Jute. "Give me the sky and the wind, and I'll feel safe enough."

"Not everyone can reach the sky."

Jute shivered. Not from the icy chill in the air, but from sudden thoughts of the wihht, of the regent and his court, the Thieves Guild, the bashers and the smashers, the Juggler, hungry days and lonely nights. The stretch of the square, the line of rooftops dim against the dark sky, the fingers of chimneys pointing up into the falling rain. He knew it all as well as the palm of his hand, but Hearne was not his home anymore.

They hurried through the streets. The city was dark around them, waiting for what the day might bring. A few lights shone in windows, but they were furtive and dim. Torches burned high up on the city wall. Jute's eyes detected the dark shapes of the Guard as they kept their watch along the parapet. Their spears were as slim as saplings, with iron heads like leaves.

"They're all looking out across the wall," he thought to himself. "Down the valley. But some should be looking within. They should watch the city."

Jute could not help himself with that thought and turned, involuntarily, to look back down the street. The rain was on the roofs and flowing in the gutters. Darkness stood in the alleys and crouched under the eaves. He wished she was here. Levoreth. He could still see her face gazing down at him. He had been safe with her. Just like with the hawk.

They reached the gates of the Guard compound. The sentries on either side came to attention, rain dripping off their helmets. An officer hurried over.

"My lord Lannaslech!" He gaped at them, stammering. "My lord. You were—were you? Where have—"

"Is your captain here?"

"In the tower."

The officer said more, but no one heard it, for the duke of Harlech was already striding past him, with Jute and Rane on his heels. The rest of the men headed in single-minded focus toward the barracks kitchen. The steps leading up to the tower were rimed with ice. Torches burned at the entrance, the flames hissing as the wind whipped rain against them. The door boomed shut behind them. There were others on the stairs: soldiers and officers from the duchies, guardsmen, servants dashing past with arms full of everything from bandages and sewing kits to lanterns and candles. Faces turned in surprise, in shock, and in delight. Voices called out to the duke, but he did not halt. The door to Owain Gawinn's study was shut. Rane knocked on it with his mailed fist.

"Enter!" shouted someone inside.

Firelight and the scent of hot ale met them. Flames burned on the hearth. Shadows swayed in the corners of the room. Owain sat at his desk, frowning down at some papers, quill in hand. He did not glance up. Someone stirred, a dark shape, in the tall-backed chair facing the desk.

"Speak your piece and then get out," said Owain, still looking down at his papers.

"It's a long road from the Rennet Gap to your hearth," said the duke of Harlech, "most of it through the dark and with dead men behind us. My feet are cold and I'm feeling my age. Now, do you have some mulled ale for us, or must I go and get it myself?"

There was a second of astonished silence, and then Owain jumped up out of his chair, shock on his face. The hawk fluttered up from the shadows beside the hearth. The ghost materialized beside him. But the biggest surprise of all was the face that popped up over the chair facing Owain's desk. Firelight fell on the man's visage, illumining the gaunt profile.

"Severan!" said Jute.

"Severan!" said the duke of Harlech.

Severan managed to look surprised, delighted, and embarrassed all at the same time. He grabbed Jute by the hand and wrung his fingers vigorously.

"Very pleased to see you again, my boy," he said. "Very pleased indeed. You can't imagine how I've been worrying ever since we parted company."

"I might say the same," said the duke of Harlech, his face grim.

"Ah, Lannaslech," said Severan, turning a bit red. "Quite a surprise seeing you here, eh? I'm afraid I—"

"I'm afraid we thought you dead these past ten years. Ten years without a word, you idiot. I didn't know what to think. Fallen down a crag in the Morns with a broken neck, dead of thirst in some sandy Harthian ruin, with your crazy dreams dried up in your sun-bleached, addled skull. Blast your overeducated hide. You could've sent word."

"Well, I, er, I must've forgot."

"Forgot!" roared the duke of Harlech. He took a step forward.

"Gentlemen," said Owain. "The important thing is—" He stopped abruptly, looking back and forth at Severan and the duke of Harlech. "Good grief. You're brothers, aren't you? May the sea take me if you aren't the mirrors of each other."

"Brothers?" said Jute.

"Yes," said Severan, even more embarrassed. "Two years apart. I'm younger, of course, thank goodness. I would've made a botch of the duchy. Ah, Rane. How are you? Everything well, I trust?"

"Of course," said his brother. "Of course he's younger. Otherwise he wouldn't be flitting about Tormay without a care in the world."

"Ten years gone should not mean much to the men of Harlech," said the hawk. He hopped up onto the back of a chair. "What are ten years but a passing day? Besides, we have much more important matters to discuss."

Severan mumbled something unintelligible, but looked relieved. His brother scowled at him. Rane's expression did not change from its typical impassivity, but he nodded in a somewhat friendly fashion at his uncle.

"That we do," said Owain, sitting back down in his chair. "My lords of Harlech, I'm grateful to have you back behind these walls. Jute, we're deep in your debt. We can ill afford to lose Lannaslech's men, given the numbers that face us. My scouts have been out all night, riding the edges of the valley. Mizra is marching up the Rennet River and will be here, I daresay, in the morning. Even though the northern duchies and Vo have brought their soldiers to Hearne's aid, we are still greatly outnumbered."

"I've something to tell you about the ghost," Jute whispered to Severan.

"What's that? The ghost? Not one of his interminable lectures, is it?"

"I'll tell you later."

A servant appeared with mugs and a pitcher of hot ale. Jute wrapped his hands around his mug and felt the warmth work its way into his fingers. He closed his eyes. The rich honey scent of the ale drifted up into his face.

"What about Harth?" asked Rane.

"Harth!" said Owain, spitting out the word as if it were a curse. "Declan Farrow rode south a week ago. We should have heard word by now, but there's been only silence. He raised Vo for us, but as for Harth and Vomaro?" He shrugged. "We'll fight without them, gentlemen. We have no other choice. The walls of this city are stout, built tall and of sturdy stone, but. . ."

Owain's voice trailed off and he stared down at the map on his desk. The flames flickered on the hearth behind him. The shadows in the room wavered in response. There was ice on the window, and beyond it, the yellow moon slid through the sky. Out of the corner of his eye, Jute thought he saw something dark crouched by the door. He blinked and there was nothing there.

". . . but," said the duke of Harlech, picking up where Owain had left off, "our enemy is more than just numbers. Much more. The Dark leads them. The walls of this city might keep out an army, if we are determined to spend our lives well, but will walls keep out the Dark? He is coming this way in sure and steady step, and we do not know him in full. Our ignorance is his strength. Our lack of knowledge could prove our downfall."

"And what of our enemy within the walls?" said the hawk.

The back of Jute's neck prickled uncomfortably. His heart lurched. He had forgotten. He had chosen to forget. The hawk fluttered over onto the back of his chair. He could smell the dry, clean scent of the bird's feathers and he felt the momentary touch of the hawk's beak at his ear. His heart slowed and steadied into peace.

"Who do you speak of?" said the duke of Harlech, his voice sharp.

There was a moment of silence. Owain stirred uncomfortably in his chair. The shadows on the walls tiptoed closer as if they made sure to hear what might be said.

"We have a bit of a problem," said Owain slowly. "Not that an enemy army marching on the city isn't problem enough. I hadn't spoken of it yet because, well, to put it bluntly, the regent is no longer the regent."

"What do you mean, man?" said the duke. "Stop talking nonsense. Nimman Botrell still rules in Hearne, doesn't he?"

"What he means to say," said Jute, "is that Botrell is dead. His body has been taken by a wihht. He might look and sound like the regent, but he is anything but."

"Goodness gracious!" Severan sat bolt upright. "No one bothered to tell me this. You speak of Nio? Curse his black heart. There are wihhts and there are wihhts. This is no ordinary wihht. No indeed." He shook his head. "He was the best of us. The quickest learner. He could intuit the words of older languages that hid behind younger words. I was three years his elder, but he probably knew more after his first year than I did after my four. The Dark caught him. A long, long line thrown out across the years, pulled in so slowly that he was probably never aware of the hook until it no longer mattered." Severan attempted to smile, but he could not. "And now he's the regent. They're one and the same. Something different."

"What do you mean?" said Owain.

"Wihhts like this one eat people. But they don't just eat them. They become them. They eat their flesh and take into themselves all the knowledge and power of their victims. They can even look like their victims if they choose. Our regent, I'm afraid, has become something with a great deal of power. Something that has been talking to the Dark for a great many years."

"Inside this city," said the duke of Harlech. He stood up abruptly, his hand moving unconsciously to the hilt of his sword. "What's stopping us from going up to the castle—that's where he is, isn't he?—and pulling the place down on top of him? I've found that evil things don't do well with a great pile of stone on top of them."

"I don't think that would work with him," said his brother.

"I have men watching the castle," said Owain. "Day and night. I'm afraid they haven't been able to get that close. Funny thing about it. The wards around the castle have become rather touchy."

"Touchy?" said Jute. "That doesn't sound good."

"The important thing is, we've still got an eye on him. The regent—hang it—whatever he is now, he hasn't stirred from the place. We'll know as soon as he makes a move."

"And then what?" said the duke.

No one had an answer for him. The fire crackled on the hearth. The duke crossed to the desk and poured himself another mug of mulled ale. He drained it in one gulp.

"Well," he said, "I'm off to see to my men. Severan, I'll speak with you later."

Rane stood up and followed him out. The door closed behind them.

"Good grief," mumbled Severan.

"I don't like fighting on two fronts," said Owain. He leaned back in his chair, frowning. "I'm a soldier. I don't know anything about magic, nor do I want to. Yet it seems we need magic to answer magic. We have the wind himself and his hawk sitting here, as well as a wizard of your repute, and yet we can't figure out how to deal with this wihht creature?"

"And the ghost," said the ghost. "Don't forget the ghost. I know plenty of magic, let me tell you."

"Perhaps, then," said the hawk, "we should send you to deal with the wihht."

"I don't know that much," said the ghost hastily. "I've forgotten a lot."

"And he isn't just this wihht!" Owain slammed his fist on the desk. "He's the Silentman. Blast Botrell's withered, greedy little soul. He's got the bloody Thieves Guild at his beck and call. The last thing I need is every basher and cutthroat in the city running amuck while we're fighting an army at the walls. Hearne will go up in flames without the enemy even setting foot within the gates."

"The enemy's already here," said the hawk.

As if to underscore Owain's words, a knock tattooed on the door, which swung open. An officer poked his head in and saluted.

"My lord Gawinn," he said. "The lieutenant of the watch and my lord the duke of Thule request your presence on the wall."

"Very well."

Owain turned in the doorway as he shrugged on his cloak.

"I trust you can think of something," he said, his gaze on Jute. His eyes were bleak. "I haven't had much faith in the fact that you are the wind. I never believed all those old stories about the anbeorun, but I do now, and it is out of desperation, Jute. I hope you don't forget that." He nodded at them, and then shut the door behind him.

"Splendid," said the ghost, rubbing its hands together. "We're all here, just like old times. I can't say I've missed any of you, but this is nice. Nice indeed."

"We have a little time," said Jute. He rose and stood by the fireplace. The heat of the flames felt delightful on his hands and face. He supposed he didn't need things like heat and food and rest anymore, but it didn't mean that they weren't enjoyable. He closed his eyes. He could feel the wind blowing outside, roaming about the stone walls, wandering through the rain, looking for him. With an effort, he opened his eyes. They were all watching him. Severan, the ghost, and the hawk. Firelight reflected from the eyes of the old man and the hawk. The ghost, however, was just a dim form in the flickering light.

"A little time," repeated Jute. "I can feel them somehow, his army, marching west. Perhaps it's the taste of the wind, or perhaps it's the feel of him. He's getting closer."

"A little time or a lot of time. It doesn't matter." Severan shuddered. "The wihht knows one of the true names of darkness. Blast Nio! You remember what he did down under the university? That was the most powerful naming I've ever seen. Incredible! I mean," he added hastily after both Jute and the hawk looked at him with surprised expressions, "truly horrific. Loathsome."

"I think, Severan," said the hawk, "you scholars sometimes forget that certain words are, in and of themselves, utterly evil. There is nothing admirable in what the creature did. And neither is there anything admirable in his knowledge."

Jute shoved his hands in his pockets, thinking hard. His fingers closed on the tiny cold fragments of stone there. He looked up at the others.

"I have an idea," he said. "It's not an excellent idea, but it's not a bad idea either. I'm afraid, though, that. . ." Here, his voice trailed off and he looked speculatively at the ghost.

"Oh?" said the ghost. "No. I know what you're about to say. Send the ghost. He can't be killed because he's already dead. Besides, if he does get killed, it won't matter because he doesn't have any friends and no one will miss him. I'm not going."

"Don't be silly," said Jute. "Of course we would miss you, but that's beside the point. You aren't going to get killed. And you won't be going alone."

"I won't?"

"Severan is going as well."

"I am?" said Severan.

"Yes, you are."

Jute's words carried the weight of the wind in them, the heavy, inexorable weight of the wind in all of its gentleness. The three others looked at him. He was only a boy of indeterminate age—perhaps fourteen years old?—standing in front of the fire. A thin boy with a shock of dark hair hanging over his forehead, his face thin and his gray eyes gazing back at them calmly. The flames traced a line of light along the edge of his form and, for a brief moment, it was as if starfire shone around him. There was something old in his eyes. Something impossibly old. The hawk nodded, partly in satisfaction and partly in sadness. The ghost said nothing. Severan leaned forward in his chair.

"All right, then," he said. "What do you want us to do?"

And Jute told them.

CHAPTER ONE HUNDRED & NINETEEN
THROUGH THE TAPESTRY

"I can't believe this," said Arodilac.

He turned and glared at Severan and the ghost. The old man glared back at him. The ghost peered around Severan's shoulder and winked at Arodilac.

"There's a war going on," said Arodilac, "and I should be on the wall with the rest of the Guard. Instead, I'm shepherding you two about while good men are dying in defense of this city."

"I didn't choose you," said Severan. "Owain Gawinn did. Besides, if it's any consolation, there's an excellent chance we'll wind up dead due to what we're about to attempt."

"Not me," said the ghost cheerfully and much too loudly. "I'm already dead."

"Shh. Keep your voice down."

"All right for you to talk," huffed the ghost. "You two can argue like cats, but when I try to say something—and I was being positive, mind you—you just tell me to pipe down. No doubt, it's due to the fact that I'm a ghost. Ghosts aren't accorded the same rights that you flesh-and-blooders have, and. . ."

"Hush," said Arodilac.

"By the way," said Severan to the ghost, "do you mind if I ask you a few questions? Jute mentioned to me, in strict confidence, of course, that your name was, uh, Staer Gemyndes. *The* Staer Gemyndes, you know, who wrote the *Gerecednes*."

"He did?" said the ghost. "Who wrote the what? I forget a lot of things from day to day, my friend, and to be honest, I can't even remember your name. Who are you again?"

"I assume you're trying to be humorous," grumbled Severan.

"Will you two please be quiet?" said Arodilac.

They were creeping along below the wall beside the castle's kitchen garden. The wall on the castle side enclosed an acre of fruit trees, berry bushes, and vegetables. The other side of the wall was an overgrown rose garden, part of the estate of Tene Tiannes. That was the side where the three found themselves.

"As long as old Tiannes doesn't let his dogs out, we're fine," said Arodilac. "I've snuck through this way dozens of times, and he only caught me once. His stable man gave me a thrashing, but I came back at night and put a badger in through his bedroom window, so it worked out fine."

"Why's that supposed to be reassuring?" said Severan. "That sounds like the beginning of a hundred years' feud."

Ivy and bramble vines grew over the wall like a waterfall of greenery. Even though the day was descending into twilight, there was enough light to see their goal. The stones of the wall beneath the ivy were crumbled in places. Arodilac began to climb.

"Easy enough for someone with young knees," said Severan. He removed a bramble from his sleeve. "You forget that I'm old enough to be your grandfather."

"You don't see me complaining," said the ghost. And with that, it faded somewhat and drifted through the wall.

"Staer Gemyndes? Hmmph."

Severan began to climb. He gritted his teeth against the pain in his joints. He was old, but the decrepitude of his body was chiefly due to the years spent sitting at desks, hunched over books, reading and writing far into the night. Being a scholar might be good for the mind, but it did no favors to the body. He sighed and then winced as a thorn caught his hand. His brother Lannaslech was older than he but still able to ride a horse all day and handle himself well in a fight.

I should've read fewer books, Severan thought to himself. I do hope he'll be all right. He and Rane. If they both die, I'll have to move back into that cold manor and rule Harlech. Not that Harlech needs a ruler. I would do a terrible job as duke.

And Jute. Please let him choose wisely this day.

"Did you say something?" said Arodilac from on top of the wall.

"No. At least, I don't think so."

Descending the other side of the wall was quicker, mainly because Severan lost his grip and fell crashing down into a bush. This made a great deal of noise. Both the ghost and Arodilac scowled at him.

"Sorry, sorry," he said.

They crouched in the shelter of some trees. The ground sloped up from where they were for about a hundred yards until it reached the castle. The space in between looked shabby. The lawns had obviously not been cut in a while. The sculpted bushes and hedges had grown shaggy. Roses and wisterias sagged from overgrown trellises.

"That's odd," said Arodilac.

"What?" said Severan. A headache was insinuating itself behind his eyes. He rubbed his forehead, but that did no good. A faint whispering buzz vibrated in his ears. Wards. Dozens of them. The castle was obviously rotten with them.

"Usually the place is streaming with light."

It was true. The castle was dark. The stone walls were gloomy with twilight. But the windows were holes of dark shadow. Arodilac took a step backward into the shelter of the trees. He had the uncomfortable feeling that something was watching them from those windows.

"Oh, pooh," said the ghost, deciding something had to be done to encourage the others. "I'm sure it'll be fine. The wihht, or whatever is in there, might kill you both. But everyone has to die. I think my old pa used to say, why put off until tomorrow what can be done today? Besides, if you do wind up getting killed in some dreadful way, it isn't such an ordeal once you're dead. Looking back on it, you'll wonder why you ever made such a fuss. Take it from me. I know."

This encouragement was received in dubious silence from the other two.

"Are you sure this thing is new?" Severan held up his hand and squinted at a ring on his finger. It was a plain-looking band of silver.

"As of a month ago. My uncle's steward gave me several when I, uh, lost my original ring. He forgot about 'em when it was returned to me."

"Maybe it's keeping me from catching on fire or whatever nasty things the castle wards do, but I'm getting a splitting headache from all the buzzing and whispering in my ears. How many wards does this place have? Good grief. Your uncle must've been paranoid beyond understanding."

"It should be all right. I wore it for weeks without any problems." Arodilac paused and then continued hesitantly. "This needs to be done, doesn't it?"

"Yes," said Severan. He slipped his hand into his pocket and touched the bag Jute had given him. He tried not to shiver. "It'll work just fine."

They crept across the grass, making their way from bush to tree to hedge, until they crouched beside the castle wall. A stone verandah jutted out several yards away. Arodilac shook his head.

"Normally," he said. "there'd be guards patrolling the grounds. There'd be lights, activity, something. A page or two, sprinting down the road with messages for Lord Whatsit or Lady Whosis. But now, there's nothing. It's as if everyone's left."

"An excellent idea," said the ghost. "Let's leave now."

Several bay windows looked out onto the verandah; with assistance from Arodilac's knife, one of them swung open. The place was silent inside and there was a stale smell in the air. A faint light straggled in through the windows, but it was hardly strong enough to do more than gleam on the glass. They stood in a long hallway that stretched away into shadows on either side. Portraits of stern-faced soldiers and dapper nobility stared down from the walls. A flight of stairs climbed up into darkness at one end of the hallway.

"Is he even here?" whispered Severan. "Is anyone here?"

The ghost sniffed the air. "Oh, something's here. Definitely. I just can't tell whether it's alive or somewhat alive. Or, for that matter, whether it's human."

They tiptoed down the hallway, past the stairs, and into a large anteroom. The ceiling soared above them. Carpet silenced the sound of their passing. A fireplace framed in marble huddled over cold ash. Another flight of stairs ascended to a balcony. A piano stood in one corner, its lid angled on an arm of silver-inlayed oak. Severan ran his finger across the wood. It was thick with dust.

The silence was heavy. The lightest and most innocent of silences is that of a baby sleeping. There is no guilt in such a silence, no regret, no sorrow, no awareness of evil. No anticipation of wickedness. As years pass, and as innocence fades with the accumulation of memories, the silence of a man can become something else. Something darker, tired, and wary. A house can behave in the same way. Wood remembers certain things. Stone has the longest memory.

"This place has some terrible memories," said the ghost. "I have some dreadful ones of my own that I wish I could forget. Why do I forget all the good things? But the ones in this place? Brr!"

"Why do you always say things like that?" Severan could feel the skin on the back of his neck prickling. "It's bad enough creeping around in here without you harping on about death and doom and all your other favorite topics. Were you like this when you were alive? I hope you realize you were the most famous wizard in all the history of Tormay."

"I don't harp," said the ghost, stung at his words. "I observe. Ghosts have a nose for memories. After all, that's primarily what we consist of. Mostly memory and a touch of magic. Regardless, something dreadful happened here. Recently."

"Dreadful? How dreadful?" Arodilac couldn't help asking.

The ghost sniffed the air, turning its head this way and that. "Oh, I'd say extremely dreadful. As far as I can tell, it involved a lot of people running around screaming unproductive things like 'Help, Help!' or 'Save me!' followed by those same people getting eaten. That's the basic gist of it. I can smell it in the walls. The stones still echo with the screams. Stone doesn't forget easily. But don't look so concerned, young Arodilac; no one's here anymore."

"No one's here? I thought you said there was someone here."

"Yes, but he just left. About thirty seconds ago."

"He?" Arodilac drew his sword. "Let's get out of here and find him! That thing, the wihht, whatever my uncle is now."

"Ah, but you're mistaken." The ghost pointed up the stairs. "He went through a door upstairs."

"So he's outside?"

"No. It isn't a normal door he went through. He's someplace else."

"The five spells of Brimwell the Lame." Severan nodded. "He built doors that allowed the user to pass through to distant places. He was a cripple and wasn't one for getting about easily. If we find the door, we can find where the wihht went."

They climbed the stairs, up into shadows that grew with every passing moment. The silence was no longer complete. Small noises insinuated themselves. The wind rattled at a windowpane. A clock ticked behind a locked door. Floorboards creaked beneath their feet.

"Here," said Arodilac, his voice quiet. "This is the door to my uncle's suite."

The rooms were grander than anything Severan had ever seen. Ceilings arched up above marble pillars. Silk drapes framed windows looking out on the moonlit gardens below. Chandeliers hung cantilevered out from the walls, dangling dozens of candles, each in cups of crystal. Everywhere there was mahogany and ivory and gold. Mirrors reflected the trio as they stood uncertainly in the middle of the room. After a moment, the ghost pointed at another door on the far side of the room. They passed through into a dark room.

"*Lig*," said Severan.

A wisp of light glimmered into being above his hand. With a flick of his wrist, he sent it drifting into the air. The light was insignificant, but it was enough to illumine the place. It was obviously a bedroom. The place smelled of dust and stale air and something else. The drapes were drawn across the windows. They looked like coffin shrouds. The ghost shivered.

"Here," it said. "In here. He left a few minutes ago."

"But where?" Arodilac looked around. "There aren't any other doors out of here."

"The doors of Brimwell the Lame don't look like normal doors. *Lig*." Severan sent another wisp of light scooting up to the ceiling. "They're spells—extremely complicated spells, of course—anchored to a physical object not intended to leave its location. The object could be small, like a hairbrush, or large, like a. . ."

"Like a tapestry?" said Arodilac.

They all stared at the tapestry on the wall. It was enormous. The fabric was woven from silk and depicted an intricate scene of buildings and soldiers and townsfolk. A king sat on his throne in the top right corner. An army of skeletons marched with spears across the bottom of the tapestry, advancing on a large building of stone and towers. Tiny flames of red silk poured from windows.

"Good grief," said Severan, peering closer. "That's Dol Cynehad, the last king of Tormay. And that's obviously the university. This must be a depiction of the Midsummer War. Priceless! I've never seen anything like this before. This needs to be studied. Look, there are some odd runes woven into the sides of these buildings. It almost looks like—"

"Dol Cynehad was very fond of onions," interrupted the ghost. "And speaking of smells, this tapestry stinks of magic."

"Onions? I suppose this might be what we're looking for. Aha! Can you sense that? There's a ward sleeping in the threads, but it isn't pointed this way. It's guarding somewhere else. Somewhere that is not this room. Yes. This is definitely what we're looking for, but how does it activate?"

Severan prodded the tapestry with one finger. It didn't feel unusual. It felt like a silk tapestry. He thought a moment, and then waved his hands in the air. Nothing happened.

"Open," he commanded. "*Vena.*"

A wooden chest on a nearby table creaked open, but the tapestry did nothing.

"Stop that," said the ghost. "You're making my ears itch."

"Perhaps the key to a spell like this has something to do with the person who uses it the most. In this case, your uncle." Severan nodded at Arodilac.

"I could've told you that," said the ghost.

"He never said anything about this to me." Arodilac touched the tapestry. "To be honest, we didn't get along all that well."

"Wait. What did you just do?"

"Nothing," said Arodilac. "What are you talking about?"

"The tapestry just moved."

"Maybe it's because he touched it," said the ghost. "I've often noticed that things move if you touch them. For instance, if you touch a blade of grass, it will invariably move to some degree. This is due to the pressure of your finger. I know that's probably a startling concept to someone with your lack of—"

"Staer Gemyndes or not, stop being a blockhead. The pattern in the tapestry moved. I saw it. The buildings shifted."

"I didn't do anything," said Arodilac. "All I did was touch the thing. See?"

He touched the tapestry again. This time, they all saw it. The buildings woven into the design began to shift around. They slid away from the center of the tapestry until the center of the hanging was an oval of blue-black thread that rippled with shadows. Arodilac snatched his hand away.

"It's alive! Did you see that?"

"It moved because of you. Is it because of who you are? A member of the Botrell family? That's logical. But I've never heard of any spell attuned to people because of what family they belonged—what's that you're wearing?"

"That? Oh, that's my ward ring. It's. . ." Arodilac's voice trailed off. He looked up, embarrassed. "My uncle had all the castle wards woven into it. He always said it was the match of his own ring."

"That's it."

Arodilac placed his hand again on the tapestry. He was acutely aware of the ring on his finger now and he thought he felt it grow warm. The buildings slid away from the center. The king on his throne in the corner of the tapestry seemed to be staring down at them.

"I suppose one of you'll have to go first," he said. "If I go through, then you might be stuck here."

"You're probably right," said Severan. "Ghost, how about you go first? You're dead already, so you'll be safe from whatever might be lurking on the other side. Perhaps you can distract it, or them, or whatever it is."

"Safe? What do you mean, safe? I think I should go last, as I'm the oldest and have experienced more of life than the two of you put together. I don't need any more experiences. So, go on. You'll thank me later. You'll find that difficulties are maturing. While you're fighting off whatever monster is chewing on your ankle, just remember that it's a learning experience. You can never place too high a value on education. Particularly the hands-on sort."

"Look," said Arodilac hastily. "Why don't you go through together? The tapestry's big enough."

Severan reached out one cautious hand and touched the tapestry. It was definitely not silk anymore. It was more like a thick, greasy vapor. He could feel it clinging to his fingertips.

"Oh, very well," he said. "Ghost, are you ready? On three. One, two, three!"

And then they were gone, both of them blurring into the tapestry and disappearing with a soft, wet sort of sound. It wasn't a pleasant thing. At least, it wasn't pleasant for Arodilac. He didn't like the sound of that noise. He didn't like the way the tapestry seemed to pull at his hand, like it wanted to swallow him up. Most of all, however, he didn't like being alone in that room. The wisps of light Severan had spelled into being were guttering out. Arodilac took a breath and stepped through the tapestry. His stomach plunged for a sickening moment. He couldn't see a thing. He stumbled forward and then felt a hand grab hold of his arm.

"Steady," said Severan.

Arodilac found himself standing on a flight of stone steps. There were stone walls on both sides and a low ceiling above his head. The steps led down into a passageway that disappeared into the dark. A torch burned in a sconce high on the wall. Behind him, at the top of the stairs, a gray wall shimmered.

"Where are we?" said Arodilac.

Severan shrugged. "I suppose somewhere in the Thieves Guild tunnels. I've never seen them before, but I've heard tales about the labyrinth the Guild has beneath the city. They use the tunnels to get quickly about the city. Some stories say the tunnels move, they rearrange themselves, though I've never seen proof of that sort of magic in anything I've read. The Silentman of the Guild is supposed to have his court hidden in the labyrinth. Mind you, the Guild didn't build these tunnels, if that's where we are. They're supposed to be from Dol Cynehad's reign."

"Actually," said the ghost, "the tunnels predate the founding of Hearne. But don't get too excited. I can't remember more than that. Moving tunnels. Wonderful. It's like we're in the belly of a snake."

Arodilac took the torch from the wall and they advanced down the tunnel. The air was cold and still. Their footsteps echoed in whispers against the stone walls. The torch did not do much more than illuminate the ground around their feet and send their shadows wavering across the nearby walls.

"Lig," said Severan, and a wisp of light rose into the air above his hand. He repeated the word and sent one of the lights floating several yards ahead of them. The other light retreated until it was well behind them. The darkness in the tunnel was so complete, however, that just past the edge of the light was a wall of utter black. It retreated before them and it advanced behind them. Severan opened the bag in his pocket and fished out a little stone.

"Lig," he said, and the stone blazed into life like a tiny star.

"You realize, of course," said the ghost, "that lig is merely a crude formulation of the original word for light? It's a weak word, in terms of power. The original word isn't just a word, it's light itself."

"Lig works for me," said Severan irritably. "I don't suppose you're going to tell me the original word, are you?"

"I can't remember," said the ghost. "At least, I can't remember right now."

"Hmmph," said Severan. "Just what I thought."

They came to a crossroads in the tunnel. Corridors branched off into the darkness. The stonework in them seemed somewhat newer, even though the cracks and corners of the ceiling were festooned with spiderwebs. The ghost sniffed the air, slowly turning in place. It pointed at the corridor on the left.

"He went this way," said the ghost, somewhat hesitantly. "And I don't think he's all that far ahead of us."

"How can you tell?" said Arodilac.

"He smells like death. Ghosts have an affinity with death because, well, we're dead. He's a wihht, so he doesn't just carry his own death with him, but all the deaths of however many people he's eaten. Dozens and dozens, I'd guess. He's a walking graveyard."

"I hope you're right."

"You might hope I'm wrong before the night's over," mumbled the ghost.

Time passed slowly, or perhaps it passed quickly. There was no way to tell down there. No windows, no clocks, just the whisper of their feet on the stone paving, the occasional halt at a crossroads or split in the passage while the ghost sniffed about. Arodilac guessed they had been walking for two hours. Severan thought it closer to five. The ghost, sounding somewhat hysterical, said it might be a whole day, and how was he to get out if they both died of starvation down there and left him all alone?

The silence and the darkness and the sensation of weight pressing down—how many tons of earth and stone were resting on the low ceiling?—began to wear on them. Shadows crept behind them in grotesque mimicry of their own movements. The darkness whispered around them in unintelligible sounds that hinted at old magic, old wards fraying into deadly fragility. The ghost walked with slower and slower steps in dread of what lay ahead. Arodilac and Severan felt it as well, and even though the cold of that place chilled their bones, sweat shone on their faces.

"What happens if it doesn't work?" said Arodilac.

"We'll be fine," said Severan, trying to smile. "This was Jute's idea, and he's not just anyone. He's an anbeorun. The stillpoint of the wind."

If it doesn't work, we'll be dead, Severan thought to himself. He glanced at Arodilac and felt a pang of regret. The lad was young. He had many years to live in front of him, not to mention that the regency of Hearne was now on his shoulders. He should never have been ordered to guide them, but he knew the castle. For himself, he was an old man. He had made his choices, good and bad, becoming so accustomed to regret that it had aged into a close friend with whom to discuss faded sorrows. Still, he didn't relish the thought of dying. He touched the stones in his pocket and shivered. Surely they were too small to bear so much hope.

They followed the ghost through the darkness, with their paltry lights illumining the stones of the passage. The dust was so thick it seemed it had lain undisturbed for hundreds of years. But in a few places, they saw the evidence of others having passed that way. Boot prints and scuff marks and, at one spot, the dark, dried splotches of what looked like blood. The ghost tiptoed in front of them, jumpy as a nervous cat as it tracked the scent of the wihht. The tunnel turned and angled and split into other passageways that yawned off into the darkness. They passed a jumble of bones, the skull leaning back against the wall and grinning with yellowed teeth at them.

"There must be rats down here," said the ghost.

"Among other things," said Severan.

The passage continued on another few yards until it opened up into a chamber. It was a large room, and their collection of lights—Severan's spelled wisps and Arodilac's torch, which was burning down to the stump in an alarming fashion—did a poor job of dispelling the darkness. They ventured across the floor toward the center of the chamber. A large stone pillar stood there, rising up to the ceiling.

"*Lig*," said Severan, sending a few more wisps of light floating into the air.

"There isn't another way out," said the ghost, sounding somewhat embarrassed. "It's a dead end. Funny. I could've sworn his trail came in here. Oh well. Shall we, er, backtrack a bit?"

"But there's no door out," said Arodilac.

"That's what I just said. Ah, youth, born deaf and dumb. How I remember it well. Not that I was ever like that, but my students were all reliably stupid." The ghost smiled kindly at Arodilac. "Don't worry. You're normal."

"No, I mean, there's no door out."

"Wind and rain above." Severan turned around, and then glanced quickly at the other walls. "The door's gone."

This news was not received well.

"What do you mean, gone? I'm a ghost. I can just float right through the wall. Watch this." The ghost bounded over to a wall and started blurring into it. Halfway in, however, with its head still visible, the ghost stopped. It pushed forward again, straining at the wall, and then sprang back.

"Blast it all," said the ghost. "This isn't supposed to happen. I'm a ghost."

"What is it?" said Severan. "A binding of air? A renunciation of sentience by stone?"

"No," groaned the ghost. "Worse. It's a rejection of ghosts. I can't believe it. Someone went to all the trouble to devise a spell that rejects ghosts. Do you know how difficult that is? And it conveniently works just as well on mice, rats, humans, and—well, everything."

"You mean we're trapped in here," said Arodilac. His voice trembled.

"We're going to die!" screamed the ghost. "We're going to starve to death, wither into dried-out corpses, husks of desiccated flesh and bone. It's going to be painful and we'll go mad in the process, like crazed skunks—oh, wait. I'm already dead. The two of you are going to die and I'll be left all alone. Captive forever. Marooned. All alone, with no one to talk to!"

"Hush," said Severan. "Things don't look good, I'll grant that, but there's always a way out. This trap was obviously built by a wizard, how many years ago, I wouldn't care to guess, but he would've left a way out. There has to be. That's the way wizards think. So we have to think in the same way."

"I'm not a wizard," said Arodilac, "but does this mean anything?"

"What?"

"The words on this pillar. At least, I think they're words. I can't read 'em."

Severan sent the wisps of light floating toward the pillar. "You're right," he said. "There's something here. Second-kingdom era, I'd wager. You see that symbol? That means stone—no, earth. Earth under stone. Or is it earth over stone? I've never seen this exact rune before. Almost like an accent, or some sort of modifier. If the lines were straighter, it'd be similar to the old-kingdom symbol for anbeorun. Sort of a star with wavy rays radiating from the center. People used to carve those on the lintels of their homes in order to invoke the protection of the anbeorun. Though that hasn't been done for hundreds of years."

"As far as you know," said the ghost. "Look here, the text is a binding of power. I'd stake my life on it, if I, er, well. . . now, if you'll just move to one side, I'll translate it for you. I used to teach classes on bindings at the Stone Tower. My lectures left my pupils spellbound."

"If we weren't trapped who knows how many feet underground in a chamber without doors or windows or even a crack in the wall, I might indulge your humor. But as it is, the more time we waste here, the fainter the wihht's trail becomes. And who knows what he's planning to do?"

"I suppose you're assuming this is all my fault?" said the ghost.

"I don't care who does it," said Arodilac. "Just translate the blasted thing!"

Severan and the ghost argued their way through each symbol. The argument ranged from early kingdom dialects and ancient Harthian alphabet modifications to the finer points of grammatical construction in the mid-kingdom poetry of Dolan. Arodilac paced back and forth, having nothing to add to the discussion. He inspected the walls with the dimming light of his torch. The stones had been hewn by a master and fit together without a single gap. He placed his hand against the wall. The stone was cold. As he stood there, it seemed as if a slight sound drifted from the wall. It was quieter than the rustle of a feather, so quiet that he almost thought his mind was playing tricks. But no—there it was again. A whispering sort of groan. Arodilac could not understand what the voice was saying, but he could sense lamentation and anger. And curiosity. A curiosity focusing on the three in the room. But as he listened more, he made out a few words.

Poor me. Poor Beneka. Poor me.

Arodilac shuddered and stepped back from the wall. There was something strangely disturbing about that voice.

"Are you almost done?" he said to the others.

Severan frowned at him. "This isn't easy. Whoever wrote this used an odd mix of ancient dialects, all shaped by the rules of old Dolani poetry. Difficult stuff to keep straight."

"Does the name Beneka mean anything to you? Something in the wall keeps on whispering it. I can't hear it all, but it sounds like 'poor Beneka—poor me' and then I don't understand the rest of it."

Severan's eyebrows shot up. He hurried over to the wall and pressed his ear against the wall. He jumped back.

"Good grief! Good gracious me. Ghost! Quick! We need to finish the translation—we need to get out of here, now!"

"What do you think I'm doing?" said the ghost. "Twiddling my nonexistent thumbs?"

"Have you ever heard of the wizard Beneka the Quick?"

"Of course. Who hasn't? Brr! A real nasty piece of work. Dropped out of studies from the Stone Tower, several years after the Midsummer War, apparently due to a pact she made with the Dark. She stole every book in the library of the duke of Hull. She drowned an entire village on the coast of Thule by calling up a storm. She kidnapped the son of the regent of Hearne and was later tracked down and captured by Dolani riders in the Morn Mountains."

"Yes, yes—and hauled back to Hearne in chains, where she had her head chopped off. Well, I'm pretty sure her ghost is trapped in the walls of this chamber, and the spell holding her is fraying around the edges. This must be her tomb. Or her prison. Either is just as bad."

"Stone and shadow!" said the ghost. "Why are we wasting time? She might get out while we're sitting around and murder us all! Do you know how many people she killed? Now, listen. It says here: Something something sea, and, er, sky—no, wind—wind and fire will meet, um, here. Meet here, to—blast this!—to give—give some stupid thing that I'd like to kick into next week!—give something to the stars. Why in the name of all that's dead would you want to give something to the stars? Let's see. . . arrive here together to—well, that's obviously saying something about doing something to the Dark. Blast it! I've forgotten my declensions. Well, this next bit here—"

"You've done an excellent job so far," interrupted Severan, "but I think I've got a more precise interpretation. If you don't mind?"

"Be my guest," said the ghost grumpily, but it looked relieved and stepped to one side.

Severan stood in front of the pillar and cleared his throat. When he spoke, it was in a measured tone, rich with poetry, with words that fell gently into the silence. The words felt right, as if the stones had been shaped by them and recognized them as a memory from hundreds and hundreds of years ago.

"Sister sea, brothers mine
Meet me here to lend your memory of stars
Gather here in concert to bind the Dark
Come here to chain her who dies not
Leave your word here to seal this place.
By dust, by tear, by breath, by candle flame.
The key is turned, the door be locked,
By name, by full and honest name."

Severan fell silent and the chamber was silent as well, but there was a sense of awakening in the shadows around them. Something waited in anticipation. The darkness watched. A whisper came to them, perhaps voiced aloud, perhaps in their minds. The voice was quiet, but there was an oddly unpleasant sort of eagerness in it as well.

Speak the name.

Speak the name and the door shall be unlocked.

The voice died away. They looked at each other. The torch in Arodilac's hand guttered into smoke and died. The shadows crept closer, as if to listen to whatever might be said.

"Did you all, er, hear that?" said the ghost. The two others nodded.

"Beneka the Quick," said Severan hesitantly. He cleared his throat and said it again, this time louder. They all looked around. The walls remained walls. No doors appeared.

"Not the right name," said the ghost. "I was wondering about that. Most wizards have two different names. The name they're given as a child and the name they take as a wizard. I daresay Beneka was her wizarding name. There's another name associated with her. Now, if I can just remember. It was in a book I once read, or perhaps a lecture I gave? Or maybe it was in a book I wrote? Yes, that's it."

"The name!" said Severan.

"Oh, right. It was, um. . . aha! Her other name was—"

"Wait," said Arodilac. "Don't say it."

"Why ever not? It's on the tip of my tongue. Here, let me just say it, and—"

"What if it's the wrong name? I mean, what if the inscription isn't referring to this Beneka person?"

"Of course it is," said the ghost. "The whole purpose of this place and the spell woven into this pillar is to lock her up until, well, until the end of time."

"Yes, but what if the name in the inscription is the name of whoever locked Beneka up?"

"Good grief," said Severan. "I think you're right. But then, that means—that means that. . ."

"That means Beneka the Quick was speaking to us!" said the ghost.

"And I wonder what would happen if we spoke her true name?" said Arodilac. "Maybe another sort of door would open, a door we wouldn't want open. So who, then, wrote the inscription?"

"Sister sea, brothers mine," repeated Severan. "Meet me here." He looked blank and scratched his head, but the ghost smiled.

"That's simple enough," said the ghost. "The anbeorun of the earth. Levoreth Callas."

The air in the chamber stirred, breathing against them with the scent of green and growing things. Their hearts lightened and stone whispered behind them. They turned to see a door forming in the wall and, without hesitation, the three hurried through. Severan was last, almost stepping on Arodilac's heels in his eagerness to leave that room. Something wept in the darkness behind him. The sound of a woman sobbing. He shivered and did not look back. The ground of the tunnel before them was scuffed with the marks of bootprints and the passing back and forth of many people. Several dozen yards further along, a torch burned on the wall.

"Do you suppose?" said Arodilac in some bewilderment. "Do you suppose the Guild uses this route, right through that wretched chamber?" He turned and gasped. "It's gone!"

They all turned, then, and saw what he meant. Behind them, the tunnel corridor stretched out straight and serene into shadows broken here and there by other torches. There was no sign of the chamber door, even though they had only taken a few steps from it.

"These tunnels move," said the ghost. "But we've the wihht's trail again. It's fainter now. Perhaps he knew we were following him and deliberately led us into that chamber? We've lost time, but this is the right direction. I'd stake my life on it."

"Well done, ghost," said Severan.

And then the way turned at right angles and turned once again, and they found themselves at a dead end. Not a dead end, for a ladder stood there, a ladder of stone steps cut into the wall. They looked at each other. Arodilac realized his hands were shaking. He took a deep breath. His sword felt oddly heavy on his back.

"He went up," said the ghost.

They began to climb.

CHAPTER ONE HUNDRED & TWENTY
THE BATTLE FOR HEARNE

The morning light was unable to break through the clouded sky. The stone walls were slick with frost. Ice floes bobbed in the Rennet River as it flowed along the edge of the city wall, hurrying toward the sea. The air smelled of iron and the first flakes of falling snow. Fog obscured the eastern reaches of the valley. Tatters and ribbons of the mist, blown by the wind, streamed up along the river toward Hearne. The wind came from far away that day, from far over the mountains, as if it fled whatever the day brought, as if it might cross the sea and find peace in the west. But there was no peace to be found that day.

"The mist hides them."

Owain Gawinn stood on top of the wall by the tower gate. The dukes of Harlech, Hull, Thule, Dolan, and Vo stood by his side. Their aides and officers remained a courteous distance away farther down the stone walk. The wind whipped at them. The flags flying above the tower fluttered and snapped. The wall was lined with ranks of soldiers, archers mostly, huddled against the mortared stones to find some protection from the wind and the occasional snow. Down below in the courtyard of the Guard, bonfires burned in smoky flaring red. Owain shrugged his cloak closer around him. He turned to face the dukes.

"This could be a hard day for Hearne, my lords. Not just for Hearne, but for all of Tormay."

"Perhaps it'll be our death, Gawinn," rumbled the duke of Thule, "but we'll die in good company, and that's not such a bad thing."

"It'd be nice to see our unwanted company," said someone else. "I don't mind war, but I dislike the waiting about."

"You shan't have to wait much longer."

Their heads turned as if one. Jute stood by the parapet a few feet down from Owain. No one had seen him arrive. His elbows were propped on the top of the stone wall and he gazed out across the valley, looking through the mist and the drizzling rain. He smiled at them and, to be truthful, none of them felt particularly reassured by the sight of him. He was only a boy. Just a boy. But then the hawk settled next to him in a flurry of wings. The wind blew past them with the scent of snow and then they all remembered quite well who this boy was.

"They aren't so far away now," said Jute. "The wind's full of their sounds, full of their marching and the hooves of their horses. The mist can't conceal them much longer. But the day is growing colder as we speak. I'm afraid the sun won't be much aid today." He sighed. "Its light would've been a great help, but there's more to the light than just the sun. We still have the wind."

"And the earth and the sea," said the hawk, though no one heard him except Jute. "Where is the sea? I wonder where the wolf is?"

"Peace," said Jute to the bird. "The wind'll be enough today." The hawk looked at him but did not answer.

It was then that the mist unraveled under the wind's touch. Silence fell on the wall, on the dukes and their officers, and on the soldiers lining the parapets. They stood as if frozen by the chill rain, staring out across the valley. Now, thanks to the wind, they could see clearly.

The valley was normally a place of cornfields and meadows. A place of low, straggling stone walls, hedgerows, and the occasional oak tree. A place of bramblevines and wheat and the Rennet River that flowed through it all. But the valley was quite different now. It was black with the army of Mizra. Company upon company of troops marched along. Rank upon rank. They were endless. They marched through the crushed cornfields, along the banks of the rushing river, across the valley slopes. Despite their numbers, they marched in unison, and the earth trembled with each bootfall. They did not move in haste, but marched stolidly along, patient and secure in the knowledge that time was on their side and that the city could only wait for them.

"Well, my lords," said Owain, his voice conversational, almost as if he was amused by the sight, "there's our foe."

"Enough of them, aren't there," said the duke of Vo. "Blast them. At any rate, we shan't want for necks to chop."

"They have no siege engines," said another of the dukes. "Unless they're trundling 'em along at the back of their lines. I can't imagine taking these walls without rams and towers. Twenty feet thick, if anything, aren't they, Gawinn?"

"But they have magic," said Jute. "Magic and the Dark. I seem to dream of Daghoron most nights." His voice was quiet now. Most of the dukes looked at him blankly, as if the name meant nothing, but the old duke of Harlech flinched. "I can see those walls in my dreams. Nokhoron Nozhan built with stone as thick as night. He knows about stones, about unmaking them, about unraveling them into nothingness. He knows about walls and you can be sure his servants will know too. They might not need siege engines for that sort of thing. All they'll need are the right words."

"Very reassuring," said the duke of Vo somewhat stiffly.

"I've rarely found the truth reassuring, my lord," said the duke of Harlech. "But it's the truth, regardless of what we think. I find comfort in that, for men are foolish and capable of thinking whatever they desire."

Owain nodded.

"Signal the archers," he said. "We'll bloody their front lines soon enough, I think. Ten minutes, no more than fifteen. No sense in waiting for them to begin the game."

A red signal pennant went up from the flagsman standing with Owain's attendant officers. Further down the wall in both directions, answering flags immediately shot up. The flagsman stood waiting at attention. The dukes stood without speaking. Across the frozen mud of the fields below the walls, the black army of Mizra marched forward, thousands upon thousands moving as one. It was like a massive wave of darkness surging forward in dreadful slow motion. The freezing rain fell down on them. It glistened on the thousands upon thousands of spearheads raised like the deadly leaves of a metal forest. It gleamed on their black armor in the gray half-light of the morning. It drummed on the endless rows of helms.

Someone swore sharply further down the wall. One of the officers among those attendant upon the dukes.

"Stone and earth!" The man pointed. "Look there!"

Far across the valley, on the southern slopes angling down to the Rennet River, a horseman came riding out of a stand of pine trees. No, not just riding. He was galloping at a tremendous pace. He was angling in front of the rightmost vanguard of the Mizran army. There were surely no more than a thousand paces between him and the closest soldier. If he continued on his course, he would be cut off from the city gates by the center vanguard. And he had yet to cross the river. The nearest bridge, a mile or so down the valley, had already been swallowed up by the advancing army. The only other bridge was below the city walls, some distance south of the gates. He would not reach it in time.

"He's not going to make it," someone said.

A dreadful silence fell on the wall. Every man there, from Owain Gawinn and the dukes on down to the lowliest soldier, stood frozen, transfixed by the sight of the horseman. He was a brilliant rider, that was for certain, and he rode a swift horse. They skimmed over the ground, mud and ice flying from the horse's hooves, its legs blurring into a desperate rhythm, urged on by the rider hunched over the streaming mane.

Jute breathed in the wind. His eyes sharpened. He could sense the hawk, tense, perched on the wall beside him, but his gaze was only on the horseman. He could see the legs of the horse reaching, reaching, the hooves hammering at the ground. He could see the rider's hands on the reins, the edge of his face half in shadow, half in the pale light. Rain on his face.

"Declan," said Jute.

Owain turned toward him, his face white, and then turned back.

"There's no place for him to go. If he makes for the bridge, he won't reach the gate. They'll cut him off. Unless, no," he said. "Don't do it, you fool!"

But Declan must have arrived at the same conclusion in Owain Gawinn's head. He did not slacken his speed, yet he nudged his mount a bit so that it aimed straight for a rise along the south bank of the river. There, the years of flow had eaten away the side of the rise until it had created a bluff of weathered granite that dropped straight down a dozen yards to the river's surface. Declan urged his steed at the bluff. The horse galloped on willingly, surging up the incline, but Jute could see the foam flecking its jaws and the staring white of its eyes. Beyond them, further down the banks on either side, the foremost ranks of soldiers marched on, drawing ever closer.

"Jute," said the hawk, but Jute had already flung himself off the wall. He caught at the wind and flew, but he knew he was already too late. Behind him, he heard Owain Gawinn shouting orders. The city gates creaked open. Somewhere in the bailey below the tower, soldiers hauled themselves into their saddles. But if Jute was too late, they were impossibly late.

Declan's horse galloped straight over the edge of the bluff, straight into thin air. He could not ride the wind like Jute, for he was only a horse. A horse made of blood and heavy flesh, desperately tired after running half the night and into the morning. He galloped into the air with all the courage of his kind. He was a horse and perhaps there was even some of the blood of Min the Morn flowing in his veins. But he was only a horse. He fell straight down into the rushing river. He was dead before he hit the water, for his heart had burst from so much courage and so much exhaustion. But he had saved his rider, if only for the moment.

Declan fell with his falling steed. He fell a bit further, thrown out of the saddle. With a tremendous splash, he plunged down into the river, disappeared, and then popped back up several yards downstream. He was coughing and choking, clawing at the water, striving for the bank. It was not so far from him now. Ice floes spun past him. He crawled up onto the bank like a dog.

Jute flew through the air as quick as a storm wind, but he still was not near. Not near enough. The soldiers were marching closer. Their black rows were full of darkness. But the ranks were splitting now, half wheeling to one side, the other wheeling in perfect counterpoint in the other direction. Through the gap rode a company of cavalry. Perfect black horses with hides as dark as midnight. Their riders wore armor that was darker still. They galloped forward, hurtling along the bank of the river, straight for Declan.

He staggered to his feet and ran. The city gates were not far away, but they were an impossible distance for a man on foot. The little troop of riders had just cleared the shadow of the gate. Declan ran on. But the horsemen of Mizra behind him were closer now. Their hooves thundered on the frozen ground. They had almost reached him. The first horseman leaned forward, spear poised.

A normal man would've died at that moment. But Declan was a Farrow. He dodged to one side, still running. The spear whistled past his shoulder. His sword hissed out of its sheath and the horse went down, hamstrung and screaming. Declan's sword described a perfect, blinding arc that eclipsed the rider's neck. He whirled, his sword a blur. Another horse crashed down. The company galloped past and wheeled, ice flying from hooves as reins were savagely wrenched to one side. They surged back toward Declan. He waited for them, his face set and his sword ready. Then he disappeared in the dark sea of their rush.

Jute could hear the ringing crash of steel on steel, horses neighing, the shouting of the cavalry. He dove down through the sky, the wind whistling in his ears. And then he saw Declan again. He was surrounded by the dead, horses and men. The ground was churned into a morass of blood and ice and mud. He fought with his back to the bulk of a dead horse. Drops of water spun through the air, spraying off the edge of his sword, flung off slashing spear tips. A rider forced his steed at the dead horse, slashing with reins and spurs to compel the beast to leap its dead peer. Declan's sword whipped through the air. But his attackers did not mind dying. They died forcing their way closer and closer to him. The horses screamed as they died, but the soldiers were strangely silent, their faces hidden behind their black helms. Three of them jumped off their steeds and advanced on Declan, their spears a sharp wall. There were too many of them. The realization was plain on Declan's face. But then the wind fell down from the sky with a triumphant, roaring blast. The wind rushed through Jute, shaped by his thoughts, his intent, his eyes. Horses and riders went flying. Ice shards hissed through the air. Bones and steel cracked, shattered, whirled away like limp straw dolls. Declan, however, crouching on the ground and staring around him, was untouched.

"Run!" yelled Jute. The wind ripped the shout from him, turned it into a roar, and hurled it through the air.

Declan ran. The clouds tumbled through the sky. The rain lashed down in every which way, whipped in one direction by the wind and then another and then another. It froze into snow in a thousand singing notes, and Jute sent them spinning through the air, slicing into the flesh of horses and men. He laughed out loud as he slid across the sky. The wind laughed with him.

Blow and break! Snap and shatter!
Shake the earth! Break the earth!
Sweep the stars from their sky!

Jute shouted, savage and exultant. The wind tumbled around him. Joy surged through him. His mind burned with it. Nothing in all of Tormay could stand before him. Nothing on the earth. Nothing in the sky. Why, he could storm the night and blow the stars from their courses. Something chuckled in the back of his thoughts. It was a nasty sort of sound, but he did not hear it.

The front lines of the army far below Jute looked as if they were mice. Rank upon rank, they stood dogged in their places, half-bent forward against the blast and blow of the wind. He laughed, a skirling cry not unlike a hunting hawk, and dove down from the clouds. The wind rushed along beside him. The first few soldiers below them wavered, staggered, and then abruptly blew away, broken and crumpled like autumn leaves. The entire front line collapsed and the soldiers tumbled away. He laughed again, the sound of it joyous and fierce and free.

Free to rush and free to fly,
Free to send the snow whirling by!
Freeze the moonlight into ice,
hurl its shards from the sky!
The sky is yours, the sky is mine!
None may gainsay you!
And none may stop me!

The wind's voice whistled in his ears. It was full of cold and joy and a dreadful love of breaking and battering and tearing and destruction. What was stone but a thing to be shattered? What were trees but things to be broken and splintered and hurled like toys? What was life but a thing to be tumbled about through the days and years?

But even as these thoughts crossed Jute's mind, something changed. The air grew heavy. The wind faltered in his grasp. The tiny toy soldiers far below him steadied in their tracks. They no longer blew about under the blast of the wind but stood firm in their places. They stood like rocks rooted deep into the earth. The wind roared, affronted at this display of defiance. It howled and snarled and hurled ice through the air, but the soldiers did not move.

The curious thing of it was that while the soldiers seemed to gain even more strength and solidity with each passing moment, the wind lost its own. It faltered and swung this way and that, bewildered and confused. Lightning broke further down the valley, flashing with light and then crashing thunder before the next second had arrived.

Turn! Turn away!

The hawk's voice was dim and distant in Jute's mind, but even over that distance there was no mistaking his urgency. But Jute did not answer him. He wavered in the sky over the valley, sinking lower and lower with the waning of the wind. His attention was fixed on the ranks of the army below him. He should have looked up, but he did not, and this was unfortunate. If he had looked up, he would have seen a darkness in the sky. A ragged, flapping darkness growing larger and larger. But he did not look up. Suddenly, a great weight struck Jute's shoulders. He tumbled down through the air. Claws and beaks bit and stabbed at him. Feathers surrounded him. Black feathers. The air was full of their stink. He could not see. There was a cawing, rasping cacophony surging around him.

Crows. Hundreds of crows. Jute could feel them clinging to his clothes. Dozens and dozens of claws found ragged purchase on his pants, his jacket, his boots, in his hair, his neck. And clinging to them where even more crows, adding more and more weight. Blood flew through the air in drops and spatters. Most of it was not his own. He was falling. He reached out for the wind but could not find it. There was nothing, only the feathers and the weight and the stink of the crows.

Jute slammed down into the ground. He could not breathe. For a moment he could not move. The earth held him fast, but then he staggered to his feet. The ground was littered with dead crows. Black feathers drifted down around him in the falling snow. The front line of soldiers stood motionless a hundred yards away. The air was rapidly turning even colder than it had been. The rain froze into snow. Snowflakes tumbled down upon the soldiers' helms and shoulders, dusting the black metal with the pristine, innocent white of the winter sky. The wind was gone.

But Jute did not spare a glance for the soldiers, though they stood there like an endless forest, their endless ranks blackening the valley. They were only soldiers. His attention was fixed on the horseman riding along the riverbank. It passed the front line of soldiers and came to a halt a dozen yards away from Jute. The horse's gaze settled on the boy, its eyes glinting red in the gloom. The rider did not move. The reins hung motionless in his gauntleted hands. The horse was enormous, but the rider was just as enormous—as if a mountain had encased itself into armor, crushed itself into the semblance of a man so that it might fit within breastplate and greaves, within hauberk and helm. The armor was forged of black iron, carved with runes that seemed to crawl upon the metal as if they were alive. The rider did not speak, but the helm stared at Jute.

Jute could not move. His body seemed to be weighted down, as if the earth pulled him down and had driven stone into him. He was part of the earth. He had always been. Who was he to think that the sky was his? Who was he to think that the wind was his, that he could fly, that he could leave the earth behind? He was only a boy, heavy with fear and empty of hopes and dreams.

Aye, thou art only a boy.

The voice struck through his mind with all the weight of stone and darkness. It was ponderous, measured, heavy with contempt. He knew the voice. It was the voice from the black tower in Ancalon. The duke of Mizra.

Thou art only a boy. Dost thou think to take thy seat amongst the powers of this world? Wouldst thou steal what can never be thine? Listen, boy, and learn wisdom. Learn from one who walked these lands when the world was young, when the darkness was full of light. Where wert thou when the mountains were formed, when their heights were carved from stone? Wert thou there when the dragons stirred in the depths? Didst thou walk upon the plains of Ranuin, where the river Elph ran down to the sea? Where wert thou when the moon rose on the world's first night? Didst thou see the starfire come alive in the darkness, when its light drew breath and began to reach out across the sky?

"No," whispered Jute. "I'm only a boy."

Aye. Only a boy.

The rider did not move, sitting in the saddle as if hewn from stone. But the horse stretched its neck forward, teeth bared and eyes glinting red. Sulfurous steam trickled from its jaws as they opened wider. There was surely no escape. The horse's teeth gleamed like sharp stones.

Snow drifted down onto Jute's shoulders, onto the dead crows, and onto the frozen ground. The snowflakes hissed into steam, though, the instant they struck the horse. On the rider, however, they rested and remained frozen. The rider's helm tilted slightly down to look at Jute. Even though the eye slit was full of shadow, he thought he saw a glimpse of something there. A trick of the half-light, perhaps a ray of light reflecting off a falling snowflake. Or maybe it was only his imagination. Whatever it was, for a second there seemed to be the suggestion of a face within the helm, eyes looking at him. And they were full of pity. Jute lurched back, his feet free. The horse's jaws snapped shut in front of his face.

"Just a boy?" he shouted in fear and fury. "A boy I might be, but am I not the wind? The sky is mine!"

Jute turned and ran. He was heavy and clumsy at first, his body weighing more than it should. He slipped in the snow. But as he ran, with each successive step, he seemed to grow lighter and lighter until his boots barely touched the ground. He skimmed over the snow. The earth pulled at him, but he was beyond it now. He was free. The wind whistled in his ear, full of delight and terror.

Don't look back, chattered the wind.

Don't look back!

Don't look back!

Of course, when he heard this, Jute had to look back. He immediately wished he hadn't. The black rider and his horse thundered along behind him at a dreadful gallop. The horse stretched out its neck low, reaching and reaching with its terrible jaws. Snow and ice flew up from its hooves as they thundered across the ground. Steam billowed from the horse's mouth in gouts. Behind the horseman, the army came to life. Rank upon rank twitched and quivered and then marched forward, quickly and quicker yet. The air shook with the rumble of their armor. The earth trembled under them. But Jute no longer ran upon the earth. He sped through the air, ascending higher as if he ran up a staircase built of sky.

Those watching from the city walls could not see Jute at first. He was only a tiny blur flashing through the air. He flickered in and out of sight through the veil of falling snow. What lay beyond him, however, while further away, was much easier to see. It looked like a dark wave rolling down the valley, advancing at a tremendous speed. The closest point was the rider galloping along behind Jute. The wave stretched back on either side of him, as if he were the tip of a spear being rushed along by the darkness. That sharp edge drew closer. Those on the wall could hear the sound now. It was a muted rumbling at first, a muttering thundering roll that grew louder and louder. The stones of the wall under their feet vibrated with it. The clouds in the sky seemed to tremble with it. And the city grew silent so that it might listen in breathless horror to that sound.

"The lad's going to make it," said Hennen Callas, leaning forward against the parapet. "He's going to make it!"

"Yes," said the duke of Harlech, "and surely his pursuers must realize that. I don't think, however, that they're showing any intention of slowing down."

"Archers, on my word," said Owain Gawinn.

The flagsman standing near him tensed at the pole, waiting for his command. The dark wave thundered closer. Jute was visible now, hurtling through the air and at a height that would bring him high above the city wall.

"Away!" said Gawinn.

The red flag shot down the pole. Instantly, as it shot down, the air was darkened with thousands of arrows launched from the wall. They rose up into the air in a hissing arc, higher and higher until they seemed to almost touch Jute in his flight. A second and third launch followed just as quickly, in deep, twanging thrums. And then the first wave of arrows slashed down from the sky and slammed into the advancing soldiers. The arrows hit with a savage rattling clatter as iron tips punched through armor. The first few lines of soldiers crumpled and a cheer went up from the wall.

"And how many dozens were shot at the rider?" said the duke of Harlech quietly. "Not a single one touched him or his steed. Not from want of skill from our archers. I fear that horseman alone, even if we felled his army to the last soldier. I daresay he'll ride unscathed by arrow or any other weapon we bring against him."

As if to add weight to the duke's words, more and more archers began targeting the galloping horseman. Arrows flew at him from all along the wall, fast and thick, slashing through the air so quickly that it was impossible to follow them with the eye. Arrows struck the rider with tremendous force but fell away, shattered, as if they had hit a rock wall. The horseman did not waver under the blows but continued on his way, unmoved in the saddle.

"Good grief," someone said. "Is the horse on fire?"

"Not the beast. The arrows!"

It was true. Every arrow that struck the horse burst into flames. From the vantage point of those on the wall, it looked as if the horse ran along with a mantle of fire streaming from its black hide. The horse was not bothered by this but seemed to gain speed, galloping on, a dreadful apparition wreathed in flames and the morning gloom. Behind it, the army marched, trampling down the bodies of their fellows slain by arrows. The arrows flew, again and again, decimating their front ranks. With each fallen soldier, though, another stepped forward to take his place.

Jute hurtled by the wall, checked himself in midair, and then angled down to land on his feet beside Owain Gawinn. His face was white and strained. Owain clapped him on the shoulder and the duke of Harlech nodded, smiling.

"Declan's safe?" But Jute answered his own question as he glanced down into the courtyard of the Guard below. The party of horsemen was clattering across the cobblestones toward the stables at that moment. Declan's lean form was visible among them. "Well, that's at least one thing that's gone right. Hawk! Where are you?"

"Here, as always," said the hawk. The bird settled onto the parapet beside Jute. "Someone has to keep their head while you're haring off bent on death."

"I'm not dead yet, am I? It was a close thing, yes, I'll admit, but I'm fine. Besides, I think I know who he is now. I'm sure of it!"

"Who?"

But before Jute could answer, the horseman answered for him. He was quite close now, perhaps only several hundred yards off. It was then that the lightning struck. With a thunderous boom, the bolt flashed down through the air and struck the horseman. White fire blinded the day. The air smelled of hot metal. The horse burst into flame. His whole body raged into fire. His eyes were shining points of molten light. Scarlet flame dripped from his mouth. The air around the horseman hissed and sizzled as snowflakes exploded into steam. Despite it all, the rider did not move but sat as if carved from stone in his saddle of fire. The reins, ribbons of flame, hung motionless from his gauntlets. The horse continued its thundering gallop across the ground on four hooves of flame.

Silence and horror fell on the wall. Even the city sprawling out behind them seemed to fall silent as well. The only sounds to be heard were the drumming tattoo of the hooves of the approaching horse and the rattling, crashing wave of the army advancing behind him.

"I know him now too," said the hawk. His voice was sad. "His name is Aeled. He is the fire that always burns. He was the eldest of the anbeorun. He burned in the darkness, in the cold spaces between the stars where the awful distances reach beyond time. He was light and warmth and the fierce sun that rose from the house of dreams. He was the captain of the four, the captain of the host that fought on the plains of Ranuin and brought Nokhoron Nozhan to ruin. And he himself has fallen into darkness now. How

691

many years ago, I do not know. I saw no sign of it in the sky. I heard nothing in the wind. The sea slept for so many long years. And now, I fear, he holds the power of the earth captive in his hands."

"And she's close now," said Jute, staring out over the wall into the falling snow. "Close indeed. She is somewhere nearby. I could feel her presence in the wind. What has he done to her? Is she broken to his will, or has she fallen into darkness as well? Whatever the answer, the earth is his to command, for it sought to hold me. He's using her. I felt as if I were turned into stone, pulled down into her domain. But look how he rides. Almost as if he would gallop right through the wall, and him without any siege weapons." Jute paused, as if he were considering his own words. The hawk hissed and flung himself into the air, beating higher and higher into the wind. Jute shouted, his voice spun into the booming of the wind and carried along the length of the wall. "Get off the wall! Get off! Now!"

But it was too late for most of those on the wall. The parapets were crowded with soldiers. The only ways down were the stairs descending on both sides of the main gates, as well as smaller stairs every several hundred yards. There was, of course, the option of jumping off the wall, but this meant falling from a very great height to the cobblestones below.

There was little response to Jute other than a few blank faces turned his way. He shouted again, throwing his voice through the wind until it rattled the windows of every house in the city. Birds exploded up into the sky, shocked from their perches under eaves and against the warmth of chimneys. Down at the docks, a flock of seagulls scattered, screeing and calling in amazement. Dogs howled in dismay in every neighborhood. The cats of the city paused wherever they were, but they did not remark on the noise, for they were already well aware of what the day was bringing.

But on the wall, hardly a soul took notice of Jute's desperate shout. Everyone stood mesmerized: ranks of archers, the Guardsmen with their pikes, the officers and attendants waiting upon the dukes, the dukes themselves. They all stared at the galloping horseman. The horse blazed with fire. It grew larger and larger with every second. Fire rimmed the horse's eye, licking against the white socket of bone. Fire raged through the air. Thunder rumbled in the clouds overhead. And within the fire, in the dreadful furnace of those flames, the black rider sat as still as stone. Closer and closer, he rode on. The ground trembled with the shock of the horse's hooves. The wall shook. The snow was melting in the sky around them as it fell. It lashed down as rain. It hissed into steam, boiling up from the molten mud as he rode past.

"Get off the wall!" screamed Jute.

Time slowed. At least, it did for Jute. A snowflake drifted past his eyes, dissolving into water as it fell. The duke of Harlech was turning toward him. Stone and shadow, but he had never realized how old the man was. The duke's eyes met his, widened as knowledge gripped him. He whirled and snapped out an order, but Jute did not hear him. The ranks of soldiers on the wall stood like statues. Far beneath the wall, beneath the city, underneath them all, the earth groaned.

I did not choose this.

The voice whispered through Jute's thoughts. A girl's voice. It was the slightest of whispers, no more noise than a leaf would make drifting down onto the damp earth. It trembled in his mind, full of sorrow.

I did not.

But then the voice was gone. Instead, there was only an impression of heat and darkness that slammed against his mind, full of malice and hatred. The day, as dark and gloomy as it was, darkened even more. It was as if the clouds had thickened their weave into the impenetrability of stone. It was as if the whole world turned under a night sky with no moon or stars, even though surely the sun still shone.

Jute threw himself off the wall. He grabbed hold of the wind and then flung it out, whipping across the top of the wall. The blast swept up hundreds of soldiers. The wind knocked them off their feet and sent them flying off the wall. It blew them end over end like so many ragdolls. The wind did not drop them, however, but wafted them down until it deposited them, not so gently, on the street below the wall. Frantically, Jute hurled the wind again, even as he mounted higher into the sky. Dukes and officers went flying this time, Owain Gawinn among them, whirling away down to the courtyard of the Guard, unscathed except for bruises and the loss of their dignity. That was all Jute had time for.

The horse glared up at him as it galloped across the ground, neck outstretched and teeth gleaming with flames. Its mane streamed out in draperies of scarlet and smoke. It was surely a giant of a horse. A monster. Even bigger than the legendary Min the Morn, the impact of whose hooves had shaped the hills of the Mearh Dun. But this horse would not shape anything unless it was destruction.

The horse and rider hit the city wall. Flame and speed and darkness collided with stone, with stone laid twenty feet in width and a hundred feet in height. The wall had been built centuries before by the master masons of Siglan Cynehad, the first king of Tormay. They had built with love and skill. Each stone had been hewn to marry its neighbor without seam. The wall had withstood wars, sieges, catapults, and the relentless depredations of weather and time. But it could not withstand this.

 The wall exploded. Flames shot up, red gouts of blinding heat, dirty with smoke and billowing dust. Chunks of rock sang viciously through the air. The ground shook as tons of stone collapsed. The wall toppled for a hundred yards in either direction. The arch over the gate collapsed, splintering the massive oak gates with a crash. The wood burst into flame with a roar. Hooves rang on stone and the horse and rider emerged from the smoke. The air shimmered around it, as if in the heat of a furnace. The rider was only a dim shape in the fierce blaze, a dark shadow of iron in the maelstrom.

A voice spoke from the fire. It echoed against the walls of the buildings still standing nearby. It was a deep and dreadful voice, a voice from nightmares and dark nights. Those who heard it found their minds full of terrible thoughts—of dead and decaying things, of hunger and desperation and the ravaging fire. The voice seemed as if it spoke within each man's mind rather than his ears.

Thou hast made thy choice, city of men. It is before thee. Behold, I hold the keys to death and darkness.

Shadows stirred behind the horseman in the shifting half-light of the flames. Figures emerged from the darkness, marching up through the wreckage of stone. Firelight glinted on spears, on helms and armor. The horse's eyes burned with fire. The rider sat motionless like stone. The voice continued, but the words were now in a strange and foreign tongue. The words echoed and trembled and shivered in the deepening darkness of the day. There was a dreadful beauty in the words, as if they were formed by a once-graceful tongue that could now speak only of death. The sound seemed as if it were woven of the shadows of starfire, though none of them understood that except for Jute and the hawk, and, perhaps, the old duke of Harlech. But deeper than the starfire was the darkness of Daghoron itself, and it was from there that those words came. The fire flickered amidst the broken stones of the wall. The soldiers behind the horseman waited in silence.

One thing might save thee. Give me the boy. Life and death stand before thee. Give me Jute and find thy salvation.

Owain Gawinn limped forward. His face was streaked with blood and dust. Sweat burned in his eyes. His whole body ached with fatigue. He tried to speak, but his throat was so dry that he found himself unable to utter a sound.

Not that it matters, he thought tiredly. We've already made our choice. We've been making the same choice for hundreds of years, haven't we? Ever since our forefathers fought and died in the forgotten lands of the east, fighting the darkness. Even before that. If the legends are true. Their children fled into the west and came to Tormay. And what will our children do? Can they flee even further into the west, beyond the sea, or will the darkness still follow them? Is death the only end?

The horse swung its head toward Owain. Its burning eyes stared as if the beast could read his mind. It advanced a step. Flame dripped down its legs and guttered among the rubble.

Choose wisely, little man.

Owain did the only thing he could do. He drew his sword.

With a sudden cheer, a rabble of Guardsmen charged forward behind him. They were not alone. The duchies charged with them: the men of Harlech, Thule, Hull, Dolan, and Vo. They came with spears and swords, with axes and maces, a line of iron and fury. A hail of arrows preceded them, snarling through the air, all aimed at the burning horseman, and all to no avail as each one exploded into fire and falling ash. The defenders of the city did not care. They charged forward over the rubble, through the falling snow in the dim light of the burning gate. They swept past Owain Gawinn and surged on toward their death. And death awaited them. A wave of black-armored soldiers marched through the gap in the ruined wall, shoulder to shoulder. The wave parted around the horseman and smashed against the advancing men of Tormay with a tremendous crash. Iron broke on iron. The line reeled back and forth, trampling the ground into blood and death. A wedge of the men of Harlech, angled behind the deadly sword of Rane, drove into the dark ranks and cut their way toward the horseman. The closer they came, however, the stiffer the opposition became until it seemed as if they cast themselves upon a stone wall that did nothing except run bright with their blood.

The horseman laughed at this. At least, those nearby thought he was the one who laughed. They could see no movement in the rider and, of course, his face was not visible behind its iron helm. But the laugh boomed out across the violent fray. It was a deep and dreadful noise, full of malice. The sound was like stones shattering, like death laughing beside the grave of a child, like cold, dead starlight. Everyone on the battlefield froze for an instant at the sound.

The horse stamped a hoof and the earth shook. The ground reeled and shuddered and quaked. Buildings collapsed. Walls cracked and fell in on themselves, bringing down roofs in shattering showers of splintered tile. Choking clouds of dust billowed out from the streets. The city walls still standing on either side of the ruined gap swayed this way and that until they collapsed outward in a thundering roar of stone.

But despite all this, despite the dead and dying and the broken bodies crushed under stone and fallen walls, the defenders surged forward undaunted. The black-armored foe met them in silence. Sword rang on sword, on helm and breastplate. Men died. They died well, fighting in ragged formation around their dukes, the Guardsmen fighting and dying to defend their city, to defend their captain, to defend their wives and families, their children. They died, cursing and spitting and calling out defiance even as more and more ranks of the enemy marched over the ruins of the walls to join the fray.

From one of the side streets, a motley assortment of fishermen and dockworkers suddenly appeared with much hollering of profanity. The court of the Guard was only blocks away from Fishgate, and it is doubtful in all the history of Hearne whether drunk fishermen have ever turned down an opportunity for a good fight. They came with boathooks, clubs, and long knives. For a heartening moment, the fishermen drove into the flank of the foe with a roar, bashing skulls and slashing throats with the same skill they brought to gutting a catch of fish. But then they broke like a wave and retreated back down their street. It was like watching the tide curling out to sea after pounding against the shore. At least, that was the thought that crossed Declan's mind when he saw them.

CHAPTER ONE HUNDRED & TWENTY-ONE
THE FISH BUTCHER'S ADVICE

Declan had almost been caught in the collapse of the wall beside the Guard tower. The troop of horsemen had been dismounting around him, the horses blowing steam and stamping on the snowy cobblestones. He swung down from his horse. He was more tired than he'd ever been. His whole body ached. His hands trembled on the saddle. He wanted nothing more than to just close his eyes and forget everything for a while. A long while. If he could only forget them all. Jute, Severan, the ghost whispering and muttering to itself, Arodilac, Giverny standing bound on a tower, the dead bodies of his parents. The sea. Liss and the sea.

The pearl pulsed into sudden, frantic life against his chest. It wanted something. It wanted him somewhere. It needed him to be somewhere. The thought surged into his mind. He had to be somewhere. He had to be not here. Not here. Get away. Move. Fast. Declan stumbled away from the horse, his hand on his chest. Someone said something to him, but he didn't hear. He was only aware of the pearl pulling at him. It pulled at him like he was caught in a riptide and had no choice but to surrender to the relentless current. He drifted across the courtyard to the street gate and the square that lay before the main city gates. The area was crowded with soldiers waiting patiently in groups divided according to duchy. Faces stared at him blankly, each man preoccupied with his own thoughts. He considered climbing the stairs to the top of the wall. He could see several of the dukes standing before the parapet. Was that Jute with them? Jute and the hawk. The pearl beat against him with a rhythm stronger than his own heart. He turned away.

It was at that moment that the wall exploded in a fury of sound and stone and flame. The explosion blew Declan backward off his feet. He skidded across the cobblestones and slammed against another body. There were shards of rock under his hands. He could taste blood in his mouth. His ears rang with the noise of it all. Shouts and screams of pain faded into silence. Dimly, he was aware of a dreadful voice that filled the quiet. Flames leapt in the darkness, behind the veil of falling snow. The voice rolled on. He could not hear it. He was only aware of the pearl. It subsided into serenity against his chest. Satisfied peace.

No, a voice said in his mind. Her voice. *The eye of the storm.*

And then the storm broke in all of its raging torment. He turned and saw the black tide of the enemy pouring in through the gap in the wall. The firelight gleamed on their armor, wet with melting snow. The firelight gleamed on their forest of spears, on the arrows flickering through the dim light, on the helms shuttering their faces. The ground shook with the stamp of their marching feet. Blades flashed in the darkness and then there was no time for anything, not even to listen for the sound of her voice again. There was no time for anything except to fight. Declan drew his sword and plunged in. The fluidity of the battle line pulled him back and forth, eddying closer to the solitary horseman standing in the gap, and then pushed farther away like driftwood on a bloody tide. He fought in a numb haze, his body weary but moving smoothly through the patterns, adapting and counter-adapting to every minute change around him. He moved through a blur of swords and faceless attackers. The snowflakes whirled around him, spattered red before they could reach the ground. Something made him glance to his right. A different sound, a new taste on the wind, perhaps the pearl hanging around his neck. He angled right, swiveling around each new attacker, administering death almost absentmindedly. It was definitely the pearl. It nudged at him insistently.

Declan smelled them before he saw them. Fishermen and dockworkers. They brought the scent of the sea with them. Salt and fish and the sweet decay of seaweed. They surged past him like a wave, yelling and cursing. He was caught up in their attack and found himself fighting at the tip of a wedge driven into the enemy's flank. A giant of a man with a cleaver in each hand and still wearing his fish scale–smeared apron roared alongside him. The cleavers blurred through the air, chopping through helms and hauberks just as quickly and as efficiently as, no doubt, they chopped through haddock. The black ranks broke before them, retreating, and then counterattacked in sudden and vicious steel. The fishermen were thrown back in a flurry of blood. They regrouped in a narrow side street leading away from the city wall. Declan found himself still beside the man with the cleavers. The fish butcher turned and grinned down at him. His breath stank of ale.

"Ain't nothing like a good fight, eh?" shouted the man. His voice boomed and carried over the sounds of the battle. He laughed, the sound as loud as the tolling of the harbor bell, and turned to holler at the others crowded around them in the street. "Another go at the bastards, right, mates?" He was answered with a cheer. The fish butcher looked down again at Declan. Something flickered behind his eyes. The sea, gray and cold. For a moment, Declan thought he could hear the rumble of the surf. The pearl pulsed against his chest.

"Straight at the horseman now," said the fish butcher quietly. "Beware the horse. Go for the rider. Take him down to earth, you hear me? Down to the earth. The fire'll burn you, but water's yours. Don't be forgetting that. Every man here'll spend their lives to get you there. To the last drop of blood." He turned and shouted. "Ready, mates! Let's have another go!"

A roar went up at his words. Declan shivered. The scent of the sea grew stronger around them, and again, he heard the pounding of the surf in his ears, louder and angrier. It was surging toward the shore. The mob drew in a breath as if one single creature, breathing in the smell of the salt waves, of seaweed and brine, of fish and the cold and silent things of the deep. Then they roared again with one voice, a great booming sound that was more like the waves crashing against the stony cliffs than something from human throats. They charged back down the street. A contingent of Thulish soldiers gave way for them in weary surprise and Declan found himself fighting alongside the fish butcher again. Black helms fell before them, cloven and bright with blood. Boathooks jabbed past his shoulders, busily gaffing the foe as if they were fish to be caught and gutted. A toothless old costermonger fought on his other side, swinging a stone mallet with both hands. For a moment, the enemy line broke before them, but then it hardened into renewed fury. They were a strange foe, those black-armored soldiers, for they fought in complete silence. They did not speak and they did not cry out in death. They had no officers yelling commands or cursing them on to greater fervor. The few faces that Declan saw, invariably of dead men who had lost their helms, were staring and slack, blank faces as expressionless as stone under the falling snow.

The wave of the fishermen and the dockworkers, the costermongers and fishbutchers—all those who made their lives on the edge of the sea—crashed again and again on the enemy line. And like the land that is worn away by the sea, their foe gave way in grudging blood, inch by inch and dead man by dead man. They were closer to the black horseman now. But new ranks of the black-armored foe marched with ringing step through the ruined walls. They pressed forward, trampling their own dead. They closed in around the horseman and pushed the attacking wedge of fishermen back, back, and further back until they were fighting under the eaves of the nearby houses.

Where's Jute? thought Declan in desperation. His sword was heavy in his grip. Far off to the left, he glimpsed Owain Gawinn fighting at the front of a flank of Guardsmen. Past them, the men of Harlech fought alongside their southern neighbors of Thule. The tall figures of Lannaslech and his son Rane were visible in the shifting shadows. The leaping flames burning along the wall and in the sprawled wreckage of the city gates cast a flickering light on the scene. Other than the fires, the day was as dark as a night without stars.

Where's Jute?

It was a question on the mind of many at that moment. It was a question that was about to be answered.

CHAPTER ONE HUNDRED & TWENTY-TWO
THE STRUGGLE IN THE HEIGHTS

Jute had been about twenty feet up in the air above the wall when it blew apart. The blast sent him cartwheeling up through the air. Shards of stone whistled past him in vicious, singing tones. He grabbed hold of the wind, wove it around him, and steadied himself. Fury flooded through him. He angled down. The horseman below him was all that existed.

"Stop!"

The hawk flew past him.

"Deal with that son of perdition later. For now, you have a more important task."

"What's more important than killing him?" said Jute.

"The darkness covering the city. Sorcery draws the storm clouds here. It weaves them together to banish the sunlight. And in this growing darkness the evil feeds and grows strong. He'll prove your master if you bring him to battle. The darkness is his element. It isn't yours. It must be dispelled or you shall be defeated. If you are defeated, then all of Tormay will fall."

Jute stared at the hawk for a moment and then flung himself up into the sky, up toward the gathering storm. The wind howled around him in delight. The hawk followed them on swift wings. The earth was forgotten. The battle raging below them was forgotten. The storm clouds grew closer and snowflakes lashed down at them. Light quaked within the clouds, as hot as molten metal, brimming with a deadly, flickering radiance. And then the lightning flashed down. It lanced down with purpose in its strike. The air cracked. Jute's eyes went blind. He spun out of the way. He was unable to see anything except the red glow of the lightning flashing before his eyes. He could smell the hot metal odor of it. The air was on fire. Another bolt struck down, and then another. They were all aimed at him. It was as if some giant archer stood above the clouds, loosing arrow after arrow.

Into the clouds, said the hawk in his mind. *Get up into the clouds and tear them apart. The longer we delay, the stronger the horseman becomes.*

Jute did not answer the hawk. All his concentration was spent on dodging the lightning bolts. They were like immense trees of searing light that grew in an instant between sky and earth, an ever-shifting forest of violence. The clouds burgeoned closer with each second as he mounted higher. But then, with a shiver of horror, he realized that the clouds were rushing down just as fast as he was flying up. They surged down in great swaths of black vapor, weaving and growing and churning. It looked to Jute as if the sky was made of stone—black stone, mottled here and there in dark gray—and that the entire mass was about to crush him to the earth. The gigantic slabs of stone slammed against each other. Lightning crashed down at him. Thunder shook the sky. He dodged and reeled, staggering up through the heights. The air around him alternately blazed with the lightning's leaping heat and then froze in the driving swirls of snow. The clouds were dreadfully close now. Molten light bloomed above him in the darkness. It was a hideous flower of heat, promising death and destruction. A fraction of a second later, the lightning flashed down at him. It was birthed so near him that he was struck deaf and blind by the proximity. He had no time to react, but the wind had already blown him to one side. Below him, though, on the edge of his mind, he felt an abrupt exclamation of pain from the hawk.

Jute had no time to bother with him, however, for he was now in the clouds. Darkness surrounded him. He could not see with his eyes, not even his own hands in front of his face. Snowflakes battered against him like a hail of rocks. He could feel blood streaming on his skin, bleeding and then freezing into ice. The currents of air buffeted him this way and that. Heat trembled into sudden and blazing life nearby and he flung himself away, cringing and waiting for the roaring thunder. Something was in the darkness with him. He could feel it somewhere close by. It was insubstantial, almost nothing at all, a vapor of thought drifting on the edge of his consciousness. Perhaps it wasn't even real. Perhaps it was only a construct of his imagination. Yet, even if it was less than real, Jute feared it more than all the lightning and thunder and the searing cold dark. The hawk was silent, and he was all alone in the storm.

Jute.

He knew the voice. It was a quiet voice, quieter than a whisper.

Little wing. Thou hast left the earth. Thou dost soar above the heights. Thou dost reach the sky, and rightly so, for all this is thine. It is thine alone and none may gainsay thee. But wither wilt thou go? Wilt thou ascend to the stars? Wilt thou ascend to the house of dreams and knock upon that silent door? No one will answer thee. No one. But I would offer thee another way. A path far from the realms of man. Set thy foot to it and thou wilt find the treasures hidden in darkness. Thou wilt find knowledge. Thou wilt find power and glory. Thou wilt set thyself on the heights of the world, and all shall bow down to thee.

The voice trailed off, quiet and patient. It waited for him in the storm. It had waited for so long. It understood patience better than the stones and the mountains, better even than the ocean that will return and return again to the shore, content to remove a single grain of sand in the certainty of its placid expectation.

The storm raged around Jute. Thunder rolled beside him, beneath him, above him, in the distance. He was no longer even sure where he was in relation to the sky. Was he flying up? Or was he hurtling straight toward the ground? Dizziness surged through him. Surely he was about to crash down into the valley below the city. The earth would shatter beneath the force of his impact. He would die. No. How do the anbeorun die?

This I can tell thee, said the voice. *I can tell thee many secrets. What dost thou wish to know? I was there when the first star was set in the dark firmament. I was there when it blazed forth into wonder and life. I was there when time began in the house of dreams. Dost thou seek such knowledge, or wouldst thou hear of other things? I can tell thee how the wind was killed. Or wouldst thou know what happened to thy brother fire? It began in the quiet, in the silence of his mind, on the edge of his dreams.*

"No!" said Jute aloud in great horror. "Don't tell me anything. I will not learn from you. Besides, I think I know what happened to the fire. I know who you are."

There are so many things waiting for thee. The heights of the world are thine, Jute, if thou wilt take a step closer. One step closer to me. One step, and I will give you everything that is in your heart.

The voice paused for a moment and then spoke again, so quiet this time that Jute almost could not hear it. *The fire need not burn forever. I will even make thee the savior of the city and its people. They will bow before thee. Thou shalt be their bulwark in wisdom and justice.*

But then Jute was no longer listening to the voice, for he had burst through the top of the clouds into sunlight. Blue sky spread out around him in an endless blaze of glory. It stretched away toward a horizon that defied even Jute's keen eyes. It was that sort of deep blue found on perfect afternoon days, when all is right with the world. In the east, however, above the undulating surface of the clouds, the sky was darkening down into shades of purple. Stars gleamed there in the gathering darkness. But where Jute floated in the air, turning and turning as if he could not see enough of the sight around him, the sun shone down in serene and dazzling brilliance. He laughed out loud with delight. The warmth of the sunlight surged through his body. The wind blew by him and its voice was glad.

We could stay here forever, you and me.

I wish that would be so, but we live for others, do we not?

The wind did not answer him. Jute took a deep breath and then plunged down into the storm clouds. He flew faster than thought, nearly as fast as the reaching rays of sunlight. He blurred into the wind and the wind was him. The clouds unraveled around him as if he had punched through a rotten weave of cloth. They sprang away in shreds and tatters of gray. They shriveled under the blast of the wind, unpicked from their knots by the relentless fingers of its breath. And the sunlight flooded on through. The storm clouds fled away in a rolling bank of darkness, hurrying away into the west.

Sunlight shone on the city of Hearne far below. From so high in the sky, Jute could see everything from the Rennet Valley east of the city to the ocean shining beyond the docks and the breakwater. What he saw made his heart falter. Sunlight flashed on a sea of black armor. The army of Mizra stretched across the valley. They darkened the earth with their numbers. They marched toward the city like an endless horde of beetles, their shiny carapaces inching closer and closer to the ruined walls. Jute could smell smoke in the air, even as high as he was. Gray plumes drifted up from the edge of the city. The sky over the city was scarred with the smoke. Fire reached up underneath it in hungry and grasping red. He could see the battle line reeling back and forth across the rubble of the ruined city wall.

Well done. The hawk soared alongside him. The bird's voice sounded tired. *It is no easy thing to say no to the master of Daghoron.*

He knows a great deal of what I wish to know. I think, now, I understand people like Severan more. The wizards and the scholars. Knowing the answer to a question is no little matter. I understand why they would be willing to devote their entire lives to such things.

Aye. Certain questions are worth dying for. The meaning of a single word could potentially change the world. But there are some questions that should never be answered.

He still sleeps, doesn't he? He isn't awake?

He sleeps and dreams. The hawk nodded.

Good. Jute shuddered. *I would not want him awake. Now, we have a battle to attend to, don't we?*

They dove down through the sky, falling to the earth like two spears. They fell faster and faster until the air flickered into color around them. Time slowed. The beams of sunlight were hard pressed to pass them by and only did so as something akin to slow, molten gold. There were people in Hearne that day who happened to look up at that moment. Some saw a great, flashing light falling from the sky. Some said it looked as if

701

shards of stars were descending to the earth. Others claimed that the sky was ripped in two by the wind and that, far beyond the void, Anue bent his gaze upon the city from the house of dreams.

Hearne grew closer. Smoke slid around them in greasy columns. Fire leapt up from the ruins of the city wall. Jute could hear the clash of battle. It was an unending din of iron on iron, of screams and yells, of the whipping hiss of arrows slashing through the air. The sky trembled with the sound of it all. Black armor marched forward in quick and clockwork rows, over the ruined wall, through the flames, and into the weary swords of the defenders. The air stank of blood and iron. Jute clove through the air like a knife. The hawk fell beside him with wings furled and beak outstretched. The wind roared along behind them, laughing and joyous. It didn't care where they went or what might happen. The wind only cared that they were blowing along at a tremendous pace. It was the wind.

CHAPTER ONE HUNDRED & TWENTY-THREE
THE RIDER'S FATE

Perhaps it was the raucous noise of the wind, or perhaps it was the sunlight that fell over the battle. Perhaps it was something entirely different, such as the whisper of someone dreaming in the darkness. Whatever it was, both the black horseman and his steed looked up. Declan looked up as well. The blue sky arched over him. He saw the tiny figure falling from the sky. Saw the even smaller figure of the hawk beside him. His sword felt lighter in his grasp.

"Now," said the fish butcher beside him. "Now's our chance. The tide's changing. It's rising, and we've work to do."

The pearl pulsed in agreement on Declan's chest. He could smell the sea again, stronger than ever before. Salt and water and the tar of ships, the sweetness of long, summer days on the shore, of anemones flowering in the dim depths. He could hear the surf roaring in his ears.

Now, Declan Farrow. The voice of Liss whispered in his mind. *Now.*

The black line in front of him dissolved in a welter of blood. He could hear the fish butcher bellowing alongside him, the cleavers hacking through armor. The fishermen surged forward around him. He was the point of their spear. Declan's sword leapt faster than thought, slamming against steel, taking life and bleeding it out on the cobblestones. The day spun sickeningly around him and there was only death under the shining sun. He was edging nearer to the black horseman now. The rider stared up at the sky, faceless behind the helm. The horse's head was lifted up as well. Flame guttered around the beast's neck.

"Jute!"

The sound was raw, violent, shivering with hatred. It echoed up into the sky. It came again, but it was the horse's mouth that moved. Flame gouted out from between its teeth. The air snapped with magic and dreadful heat. The closest ranks of enemy soldiers around the horseman stumbled away from him. Their armor seemed to glow red, as if they had been plunged into a raging furnace. Cobblestones cracked and shattered beneath the horseman.

"Jute!"

It was a scream this time. A scream ripped raw with fury from the horse's throat. There was sorcery in the sound. The voice rang out again, but this time it uttered words in some strange language. The air thickened. The light wavered around the horseman.

Hurry!

The voice of Liss was tense in Declan's mind. A soldier stumbled to his knees before him, dead before he hit the ground. Declan yanked his sword free. An axe blade caught the sunlight as it arced toward his head. He ducked. His attention was not on the enemy fighting in front of him. His gaze was locked on the dark horseman. The air trembled with the horseman's words. Something was strange about the light. It was dimming. No, it was bending. Darkness bloomed around the horseman. And Jute was diving straight down into the middle of it. Declan could see him much more clearly now. The boy's face was set and strained. The wind whipped his hair back. He was falling straight down through the air, faster and faster. The sky sparkled around him.

"Jute!"

The sound of the name rolled through the sky. The sound of it was ragged, unraveling. It was as though the speaker sought to unmake the name. Declan, fighting ever closer through the enemy ranks, saw all too clearly now who was speaking. The horse. Not the horseman. The horseman sat in silent stolidity in the saddle, head tilted back to watch Jute, but there was only passivity in the body. There was no life there. But the horse screamed its fury. Flame gushed from its throat. The air bled darkness around the horse. Declan could see its mouth working, words forming. The sound of them rolled into the air. They were a shock to all that was, like a hammer slamming against an anvil. Vision and being shook. Nothing in those words was familiar. Nothing in them even resembled a language. What the horse spoke was more ancient than that. The light was bending more. Sunlight folded in on itself. Shadows grew and warped and stretched across buildings and walls and the bodies of the dead. The battlefield seemed to subside into stillness. Soldiers moved in slow motion. They retreated and advanced as if each second had gained the duration of an hour. And then the opposing armies were no longer men but statues. Bloody and bruised statues locked in frozen combat.

But Declan was not affected. The pearl burned desperately against his skin. He could hear the waves of the sea pounding in his veins. He ran forward. His sword cut through shadows. The darkness bled around him. He stumbled over the body of a soldier, a city Guardsman from the colors of his uniform. Blank eyes stared up at the sky, already seeing something beyond it. The voice of the horse shuddered in the air. Nearer and nearer, Jute hurtled down through the sky.

And then Declan was in front of the horse. Flame burned him. The air smelled of magic. The horse's head whipped around. It lunged at him with bared teeth and bright eyes rolling in their sockets. An iron-shod hoof lashed at him. He lurched out of the way. His sword came up without him thinking, old reflexes bred into his bones. The blade slammed into the horse's side. But instead of slicing into flesh, the sword rebounded like he had smashed it against stone. Agony jarred up his arms. He couldn't feel his hands. Declan staggered back and the horse reared above him. It was a monstrous thing of darkness and fire, not resembling a horse anymore. The air around him ignited into flame. He could not breathe.

The rider. Not the horse.

Her voice was quiet in his mind, but there was desperation in it. The rider towered above Declan. The figure did not move, but still gazed up, the helm tilted back toward the sky and Jute's rapid advance. There was a strange rigidity about the rider. Declan had the dreadful thought that the black armor held a dead body, shrouded in cobwebs, dusty with stillness. The horse slashed at him with its teeth. Flame sheeted from its mouth. Declan stumbled back. One spurred boot was nearly above his head, jammed into a stirrup forged of iron. He dropped his sword and grabbed the boot. The horse bucked, jumping away from him. Declan hung onto the boot. He was knocked off his feet, but he hung on desperately. His hands were on fire. No, his whole body was on fire. The pearl pulsed cold as the ocean depths on his chest.

The horse bucked again, screaming with fury. Declan fell. He couldn't keep his feet under him any longer. His strength was gone, but his hands were still clamped around the rider's boot. He couldn't feel his fingers. He fell heavily. The rider toppled over, pulled down by Declan's weight. The enormous bulk of iron armor crashed to the ground and the horse sprang away. Declan staggered to his feet. He groped for his sword. Dimly, he was aware of the horse rearing up behind him. Its hooves were about to strike. The gaping mouth reached for him. Flames raged in the beast's ragged mane. The air shuddered with magic.

Declan's sword whipped down, slicing down quicker than thought, straight for the iron neck of the fallen horseman. No iron could stop the edge of that blade. But then the pearl stirred against his skin. A gentle touch. He stumbled, somehow, his thoughts pushed off-balance by the pearl. The point of the sword slammed down into the cobblestones, inches away from the horseman's neck. The black helmet rolled free with a clang.

"Declan."

His sister's face stared up at him from the ground. Giverny.

"The earth," she said. "Let me touch the earth."

Declan fell to his knees, blind to the horse behind him, to the iron hooves about to dash his head in. He did not hear the roar of the battle around him. He groped for the iron gauntlets and stripped them away. His sister's hands were cold in his. Earth. He stared around him wildly and then saw it, right before him. There, where his sword had dashed against the cobblestones, lay a shattered stone. Beneath the shards was the muddy earth. He pressed her fingers into the mud.

As if from far away, he could hear the horse screaming. It was a raw, ugly sound of hatred that echoed through the distance as if it sought to reach the stars or even something further beyond. And then, as Jute fell from the sky in a fury of wind, closer and closer, the horse abruptly vanished. But Declan no longer cared about any of this. He crouched on his knees over his sister. There was stillness and silence around them, though the battle raged on around them. Giverny's face was thin and white. Her eyes changed color as they gazed up at him. First an almost colorless gray that slowly deepened to brown and then a green full of darkness and depth. Declan blinked. For a moment, he thought he saw something different in his sister's eyes. Something ancient and alien. But then she was just his sister again. Almost.

"Thank you," Giverny said. Her hand clenched in the wet earth and came up with a fistful of mud. "I'm more myself now."

"No, you aren't." He felt his throat ache. "You never will be again."

"This is who I am, and yet I still remain Giverny Farrow."

Declan helped her to her feet. Her hand felt fragile in his. Her legs trembled, but as the fighting raged on around them it could not touch them, and they walked in slow and careful step away from the battle. She stopped, then, and turned.

"Look," said Giverny. "Look past the battle, past the ruins of the city wall. You'll see a thing to strengthen your heart."

At first, Declan could see nothing that gladdened him. There was only the unending fray. More and more black-armored enemy poured over the stone rubble, forcing their way into the city. The battle lines lurched across the court of the Guard, lapping up against the bloodstained stairs of the tower. It seemed as if he gazed out across a never-ending sea of clashing steel. But then he saw something. Beyond the tumbled ruins of the city wall, past the ranks of the enemy, he saw movement blurring on the far bank of the river. A troop of horsemen galloping toward the stone bridge. He was not sure of their numbers, perhaps a hundred or more, but he could see them now. The nearest flank of the enemy was not far. Surely they could hear the horsemen. Declan knew what it would sound like: the thunder of hooves on the ground, the earth shaking at their advance. But then the soldiers did hear them. The army's flank wheeled around in confusion, trying to form up a line. But they were too late. The horsemen poured across the bridge, bunching together, arrowing across the frozen ground like a spear. The tip of the spear slammed into the soldiers. The horsemen sliced through them. They galloped on, scarcely slackening in speed, cleaving their way toward the ruins of the city wall. The enemy soldiers collapsed before them. At the front of the charging cavalry, a rider was visible, hair shining near white, his lance streaming blood and his sand-colored cloak fluttering behind him like a flag in the wind. The prince of Harth.

Declan shouted out loud. He could hear others calling in sudden triumph. The deep, hoarse voice of Rane Lannaslech rallying those around him. The men of Harlech and their cousins from Dolan fighting on with renewed vigor, driving into the center line of the enemy and finding them uncertain and retreating before them. On the far right flank, the men of Vo charged forward with the fishers and the butchers of Fishgate. Owain Gawinn and his Guardsmen, buttressed by the spears of Thule and Hull, fought their way, yard by bloody yard, out of the courtyard of the Guard. The black-armored line of the enemy crumpled before them and there was only a confusion of steel and death under the cold sky.

"Don't leave me," said Giverny. Her voice was no more than a whisper, her hand weightless on his wrist. "Stay by me a while, for I'm weak still. I need time to know the earth once again."

He was obedient to her wish, though it was a hard thing for him. He wanted nothing more than to join in the battle. Surely the day was theirs. The cavalry of Harth did not slacken in their attack but cleaved through the enemy like a harvester scything down wheat. Scores fell under their lances, and the soldiers of Mizra fled before them in confusion. The ground shook under the drumming hooves of the horses of Harth. With such encouragement, the defenders of the city pressed forward in good cheer. Blood was on the ground, ice in the air, and the wind was at their backs. Arrows hissed down from the tower of the Guard and found their homes in the hearts of Mizra. The enemy broke and fled. And so it was that the prince of Harth came to the city again, his horse leaping over the tumbled stones of the wall. Owain Gawinn was there, leaning on his sword.

"My lord Gawinn," said the prince, bowing from his saddle. "Forgive my late arrival."

"You are welcome," said Owain.

"More than welcome," said another. It was the duke of Harlech. His face was lined with fatigue, but he looked warmly on the young prince. "I dread to think how this day might have ended without the aid of your lances."

They looked around them and there was nothing but the bodies of the dead thick upon the ground and the sudden quiet of the surviving defenders. The black horse was nowhere to be seen. The men of the duchies and the city stood in weary amazement. The scene was one of ghastly devastation, of broken stone and the startling view down across the valley, once blocked by the wall of the city. The slopes and meadows before them were trampled into mud and slowly reaming over with ice. A few clouds drifted by in the afternoon sky, chasing after the sun. The early moon gleamed far off over the eastern horizon. High overhead, two bright spots of reflected sunlight flew through the air, Jute and the hawk.

"Is this day ours?" said someone in disbelief. "The black horseman is gone, and his army is vanquished!"

"Aye," said Owain. And then he said it again, louder and stronger, his head raised. "Men of Tormay," he shouted. "This is our day!"

A roar went up in response to his words.

"Tormay!" he shouted, raising his sword.

"Tormay!" they roared back.

"No," whispered Giverny, staring across the battlefield. "Not yet. This is a wicked day."

But no one heard her except for Declan. Frowning, he looked across the battlefield and saw nothing except the silent wreckage of corpses and the ruins of the shattered city wall beyond. Flames guttered there in the fallen stones. He took his sister's hand in his. Her fingers were cold. The pearl laying against his chest suddenly pulsed cold as well, and his heart faltered.

CHAPTER ONE HUNDRED & TWENTY-FOUR
LENA CAPTURED

"Gotcha!"

Lena tried to run, but it was too late, and she slipped on the icy cobblestones. The man grabbed her by her hair, yanking her head back. She screamed and kicked. Her fists flailed in the air. Someone swore. The man punched her in the stomach. She couldn't breathe, and tears blurred her eyes. The street was deserted. She tried to scream again, but the man stuffed a rag in her mouth. Someone else whipped a length of rope around her wrists and knotted it tight. Another piece went around her ankles.

"That'll hold her," said a voice breathlessly. "Cor, I think she gave me a black eye."

"Shoulda ducked," said the man. He laughed. "Twenty gold coins for this scrawny bit of goods. Who'd believe it?"

"If the Silentman puts the word out for pay, let 'em pay. But quickly now. This ain't the best of days to be out, even with all the bleedin' Guard at the wall."

"Too true, too true. Twenty gold pieces. We'll be drunk for the rest of the year."

The man threw Lena over his shoulders and hurried off. Her head bounced painfully against his back. He smelled of ale. She caught a glimpse of the second man, a thin, sharp-faced fellow with a shock of graying hair. She'd seen him before. A basher, that's what he was, a basher down in the warehouse district. Snow fell from the sky, fluttering between the rows of houses and settling on the street. Lena could see it on the ground, but she could not see it in the sky. All she could see was the ground and the man's dirty boots and, if she craned her neck, the second man. He winked at her.

"Don't you fret, missy," he said. "Whatever the Silentman wants you for, it'll be painful and not so quick."

Jute. This is because of Jute. Lena's mind felt dull and tired. He was gone. Never coming back. Maybe it was time to give up.

She had been skulking and hiding for days, holing up in attics and basements, sleeping with one eye open and her hand on her knife. Three times she had run into children from the Juggler's gang. They knew all the same hiding places she knew. And, even with them, even with old friends who had stolen and starved with her and Jute in the past, she had seen the avarice in their eyes. Twenty gold coins' bounty. Twenty gold coins went a far way to overcome whatever friendship had ever existed. It had only been a matter of time. She should have left the city. But the city was all she knew. She had never been outside the walls.

And now this.

Lena lay like a trussed pig over the man's shoulder. Trussed and ready to have her throat cut. Or whatever the Silentman chose to do with her. Tears ran down her face. Snowflakes froze in her hair. The pace of the two men quickened as if the darkness and silence of the street made them nervous. Faintly, from the direction of the city gates, Lena could hear the jumbled roar of voices and then a clear, cold call of a trumpet.

"Here?" said the basher, sounding somewhat dubious.

"Aye," said the man carrying Lena. "We'll stash her and send word to the Silentman. The innkeeper knows how. One of them spell-talking things."

Lena's point of view swung as the two men turned and pushed through a door. She caught a glimpse of a sign hanging over the door, upside down to her. Despite the snow swirling down and the faded, peeling paint, she knew where they were. The last place she wanted to be. The Goose and Gold. She could smell ale and roasting meat. It was warm inside, but this was no consolation to her. She shivered, and her teeth would have chattered, no doubt, had it not been for the rag stuffed in her mouth. Faces turned her way, men at the long bar and sitting around tables. But there was not a single spark of friendliness or compassion. This was a Guild inn. These were all members of the Guild. There was no help for her here. She shut her eyes. Her captor shoved her into a chair, but she could feel his hand knotted in the collar of her shirt.

"Here, Garricky," said the man to the innkeeper. "Can you send word, quick-like, to the man himself?"

"Maybe I can, maybe I can't," said the innkeeper. He ran a dirty rag over the countertop. "What's in it for me?"

"What's in it for you? How about I don't take you out back and beat your face bloody, that's what."

"You don't have to be rude about it," said the innkeeper. "What do you have to say to him, then? It'd better be important, for he don't like being bothered, I can tell you that. Especially lately. I've heard some strange things."

"You can tell him we got the girl."

"The twenty gold coins girl?" said the innkeeper, looking greedily at Lena.

"The same."

"Right away, gentlemen. Right away." The innkeeper turned to go.

"And ale all around." The man's hand tightened on Lena's neck and he raised his voice. "A round for the house!"

A roar of delight greeted his words, but Lena's eyes were still shut, and despair filled her mind.

709

CHAPTER ONE HUNDRED & TWENTY-FIVE
RESCUING PEOPLE IS A TIME-HONORED TRADITION

The cook was sulking in the pantry, the maid was in tears, and the children were hiding in the basement. Never had the house of Owain Gawinn seen Sibb in such a state. She snapped at anyone who was foolish enough to come near. She found fault with the morning bread, she banished the dog to the garden, and she had the maid polish the silver three times before she declared herself satisfied.

Owain's absence was wearing on her. True, he had been gone many times in the past for weeks on end, but this time he was painfully near—just at the city wall—and that, in combination with his recent scrape with death, grated on Sibb. Even though their home was situated quite far from the eastern wall of the city, the tumult and din that had started in the morning was dreadfully apparent. Her nerves were frayed and she had caught herself considering packing everyone up, saddling the horses, and leaving the city. With or without Owain. The north gate was near enough, and she had cousins in Lastane. But that was ridiculous. She was a Gawinn, and Gawinns did not run.

Doubtlessly, Sibb's four children would have been gratified to know that a great deal of their mother's anxiety and irritation was due to her concern for the city's safety and, more specifically, their well-being. However, they were more preoccupied with staying out of her way and evading her swift right hand.

"Mother's in the kitchen again," said Jonas from the top of the stairs. He nudged the door open another inch to get a better look. "She sounds mad."

"She's been mad all day," said Magret.

The eldest of the four Gawinn children was perched on top of a barrel in the middle of the basement. It was a tidy basement, as far as basements go, for Sibb Gawinn did not tolerate a disorderly household. The basement was full of neatly stacked boxes and barrels and chests. Cured hams, sides of bacon, and strings of onions and garlic hung from the ceiling beams. High up on one wall, narrow rectangles of window let in whatever light could thread its way past the tangle of rose bushes growing around the front of the house. Fen sat on another barrel, her chin in her hands and her face expressionless. The two smaller boys, Bran and Ollie, chased each other around the room, clambering up and over the stacks.

"Stop that," commanded Magret. "Both of you. You're going to put your foot through something and then where'll you be? Bran! That's a wheel of cheese you're standing on. Get off. Mother will hear you if you don't stop racketing around."

Only this last threat was enough to stop the two boys. They settled on top of a chest and regarded their older sister with baleful stares.

"Hungry," announced Ollie.

"Want an onion?" said Bran.

"Yes."

Bran stood on tiptoes and managed to grab the bottom onion on a string. He tugged and the string snapped. Onions rained down.

"Stop it," said Magret. "You're horrible little boys."

"Are not!"

"You are too!"

"What if we do it ourselves?" said Jonas from the top of the stairs.

"Do what?"

"Go find Father. Mother's obviously upset, and she's obviously upset because Father's not back. We'll find him and then she'll be happy."

"Don't be silly," said Magret. "Do you remember what happened the last time you left without telling anyone?"

"But this is important." Jonas stuck his chin out. "I wouldn't mind getting spanked for this."

The two little boys stared up at him in awe. Magret jumped off her barrel and paced back and forth, scowling in thought. Fen did not stir from her perch.

"All right," said Magret finally. "We'll do it. We'll go find Father. But I'm in charge, you hear? I'm the oldest and that means I'm captain. Bran and Ollie, you stay home and take care of Mother."

"Am not," said Bran. "I'm coming too."

"Me too," said Ollie.

"No, you aren't. You're both staying here."

"I'm telling Mother," said Bran.

Magret glared at him for a moment and then sighed. "You can come. You just better behave. Ollie, you stay here."

"Telling Mother," said Ollie, his lip starting to quiver.

"Fine!" Magret threw her hands in the air in defeat. "You can come too. Stop crying! Your nose is running and you look a mess. Here, blow your nose. Don't squirm. Blow your nose, I say! All right, council of war. Now. Upstairs."

The five children gathered in the nursery and sat in a circle on the rug.

"Council is now begun," announced Magret. "Lieutenant, what do you have to say?"

"Father's at the city gate," said Jonas, "because I heard the gardener talking to the maid about it. All the Guard's there, that's what he said, right before he kissed her."

"Want my Father!" shouted Ollie.

"Be quiet," said Magret, "or I'll have you thrown in the dungeon."

Ollie shut his mouth, his eyes wide.

"Whenever Father's on duty at the city gate, he still can come home for dinner. He always does." Magret frowned. "Something must've happened to him. Something terrible. He must be in trouble. We'll have to rescue him."

They all looked at each other. Rescuing people was a time-honored tradition in all the stories they loved. It was what heroes did. It was what brave princes and soldiers did. It was what good, ordinary people did. More important, it was what Gawinns did. But having to conduct their own rescue—the first they'd ever done—was something entirely different. Bran cleared his throat uneasily.

"But how're we going to rescue him?" he said.

"We'll find out when we get there. Does that even matter?" The voice was barely a whisper. They all looked at Fen. She blushed. "After all, he's your father," said the girl.

Magret was in charge, even though Fen was older than her, because she was a Gawinn and that's what Gawinns did. They were all on strict orders to stay out of Mother's sight. Magret commanded them to dress warmly, because she thought of things like that. Cloaks, sweaters, woolen caps, and scarves. She sent Bran down to the kitchen to steal apples and bread behind the cook's back. There was no telling when they'd be back, so they had better be prepared. Jonas crept into the hall and took down the dagger of Great Uncle Bevan from the wall. He had always admired the thing and considered it vital for any rescuing they might do. He did not tell the others, however, as Bran and Ollie would want ones of their own, and there was no telling what Magret would say. Magret took the hooded lantern from the back porch. It was a small copper affair, full of oil and held with a leather wound handle. The older children knew how to use a flint and tinder (their father had seen to that), and Magret had an uneasy feeling that it might be dark later. After all, night was coming.

"All right," she said, surveying her little troop. "We're off. Downstairs and out the back door. Not a whisper. Ollie, Bran! I'm watching you. Tiptoe."

They tiptoed down the stairs, through the hall, and past the open door of the kitchen. Cook was busy with carrots and chicken and thyme and did not see or hear them. Mother was sewing in her workroom. The maid was ironing linens in the storeroom and would not have noticed a troop of cavalry galloping through. All her thoughts were on the gardener. Fen was last in line, and she closed the back door behind her. It was cold outside and a few snowflakes of snow swirled down from the gray sky. Distantly, the sound of the battle at the city wall echoed through the air, but the children paid it no heed. To them, it only sounded like thunder. They scampered across the grass, giggling with relief and delicious terror. No one saw them. They pushed through the garden gate and found themselves standing in the street running behind the Gawinn home. Magret looked back through the iron bars of the gate and something in her faltered. But then she saw the determination on the others' faces. Fen smiled at her.

"Well, no sense dragging our feet," said Magret. And, with that, the five children set off down the street.

CHAPTER ONE HUNDRED & TWENTY-SIX
WHAT FEN SAID

"Another round for the house!" roared the bigger of Lena's two captors.

He wiped his mouth and slammed his mug down on the counter. The Goose and Gold roared back in appreciation. The inn was crowded now, which was what always happened when someone began standing drinks for the customers. People surged up against the counter.

"What's the occasion, Malo?" said someone, slapping Lena's captor on the back.

"Caught me a goose," said Malo, swaying a bit on his feet. He looked around and then lowered his voice to what he thought was a conspiratorial whisper. "A golden goose. One of them gooses chock-full of gold. And the Silentman's gonna pay."

The enthusiasm around Malo dimmed at this news. People edged away, clutching their mugs of ale. The innkeeper leaned across the counter and filled Malo's mug. "Perhaps the gentlemen might care to relax in one of our rooms to wait? The, er. . . the—he's coming. I sent word through the, uh. . . He should be here very soon."

"Nonsense," said Malo. "I'm a man. He's a man. We're all men here—besides, hic!—besides my little golden goose. She ain't a man, I tell you. She ain't. I'll fight any three men of you, if you sez different."

He glared around the room, but no one met his eyes. Several people slipped out the door, and those who remained drifted away to the shadowed corners of the room. Lena sat in her chair, watching all this. For the hundredth time, she tensed against the bonds around her wrists and ankles. It was no use. They were as tight as they had been an hour ago. The front door opened and closed and two more patrons slipped out of the inn. A dusting of snow blew in through the door as they left. The room was cold, despite the fire crackling on the hearth. And with the chill in the air was fear. She could feel it, a sort of brittleness in the air that hardened in staring faces and left the innkeeper wiping the countertop in trembling and uncertain movements. Her other captor, the basher, stirred in his chair at the corner of her eye. He was a quiet man in comparison to Malo. The more dangerous of the two, in her estimation. He hadn't had any ale the entire evening but sat in his chair watching the room and watching her.

"Fool," muttered the basher.

He might have said more, but he did not, for it was at that moment that someone stepped through the doorway behind the bar. The one that led to the stairs and the cellar below. The temperature in the room seemed to drop. The innkeeper shrank away. The flames in the fireplace leapt up, crackling, but they changed in color from orange and red to a yellowish blue. The room was silent. Lena could hear the wind outside, whispering in the eaves and scratching on the windows with the icy fingertips of snowflakes.

"Good evening," said the newcomer. His voice was friendly, but there was an odd sort of vibration in the sound, as if he held himself tightly in check. "Good evening, good evening. That is, I mean to say, good evening."

He stepped forward and the light of the fireplace fell on his face. Lena's heart shuddered. The man from the tunnels. The regent. Nimman Botrell. But no, it wasn't precisely him. There was something fuller about the face, deeper about the eyes, as if there was more to him than merely Nimman Botrell.

"Someone summoned me? The mirror spoke to me. Quite urgently. It asked for the Silentman. I suppose that's me. I don't mind being bothered, but only when I don't mind, and I always mind. Being bothered makes me hungry. I really need to consult someone's memories on this. I have so many inside of me, it's like storing a library in my head. Ah, there it is. I suppose you, innkeeper, you were the one who summoned me. Some sort of Thieves Guild affair, no doubt? I've always considered the Guild a miserable collection of wretched little maggots. Cutting throats and lifting purses? Is that the best you can think of? Think higher. Think bigger. Think with your mind! I think with my mind; I've eaten quite a few, and I certainly know how to think. Why stop at one throat? Cut everyone's throat until the streets fill with blood, so deep, so swift that you must pole about in boats. Ah, what fish you might catch then in those waters, eh?"

There was no response. People sat motionless in their chairs. Malo stood unmoving at the bar. Even the fire on the hearth seemed to no longer flicker but crouched there like a statue of carved flame. The Silentman looked around the room, his head bent forward, his hands clasped behind his back. He smiled, as if he were among friends, but Lena saw the sharpness of his teeth and the madness in his eyes. Somewhere behind her, a footstep sounded furtively.

"What's this?" said the Silentman, turning. "Leaving so soon?"

"Please, if your lordship," said a plump little man near the door. "Gotta—dinner, I mean, my wife. . ."

"Wife? Dinner? Come, man. Speak up. Enunciate. Form your words with care and an appreciation for language. Now, what was it you were saying? You're going to eat your wife for dinner, was that it?"

This encouragement did nothing for the little man. It only served to plunge him further into stuttering incoherence. Sweat beaded on his face. The Silentman stepped forward, tall and stooping, not unlike a vulture leaning over its prey.

"Cat got your tongue?" he said. "Perhaps not just yet. *Catte* is the older, more precise rendition of the word. *Catte.*" He spoke the word this time with a snap in his voice. The air trembled in front of him, an odd sort of shudder that defied the eye to focus on it. Lena smelled a whiff of something strange. Scorched metal, perhaps. And then, there, on the ground before the Silentman, was a cat. A big, black cat sitting on its haunches. The Silentman nodded approvingly.

"And, of course, *tunge* is more apt than tongue," he said. "*Catte, aetbringa tunge!*"

The cat leapt forward. Lena shut her eyes as tight as she could. Her ears, however, she could not plug, for her hands were tied. Screams filled the room, screams that quickly turned into a wetter sort of moaning, an inarticulate anguish of mangled noise. The cat snarled once and then was silent.

"There," said the Silentman, "that's much better. By the way, is there anyone else who needs to leave? Any pressing engagements? Soup boiling over at home? Loved ones choking on fish bones? No? Excellent. Who was it? Ah, yes. Innkeeper, barkeep, whatever you call yourself, why was I summoned here? No, don't answer it yourself. I'll do it."

With one swift movement, the Silentman pounced on the innkeeper and grabbed him by the head. His fingers sank into the unfortunate man's skull and, with a jerk, he hoisted him off the ground to dangle kicking and squirming. The innkeeper made no sound, other than a sort of hissing exhale, as if he were a bladder deflating. And deflate

714

he did, shrinking and shriveling away until there was only a tangle of skin and cloth hanging from the Silentman's hand.

"Interesting," said the Silentman, flicking the remains off onto the floor. "Interesting and delicious, except for the aftertaste of mediocre ale. Now, you must be Malo. You've apparently captured a little girl that my—ah—predecessor was interested in collecting. Happily enough—at least, happy enough for me—I, too, am interested in the little girl."

"I caught her, my lord," said Malo, almost choking on the words.

"Like a fish?"

"There was a bounty. . ."

"Twenty pieces of gold." The Silentman surveyed Malo with a smile. "Twenty shining, round bits of metal grubbed out of the ground that will enable you to drink yourself into sodden oblivion for the rest of the year until you wake up one day with your throat cut and the remainder of your money gone. You have a shining future in front of you, my friend. Now, get out before I lose my patience. All of you. Out."

The Silentman did not raise his voice, but the room instantly emptied with a scraping of chairs and one last slam of the door. The fire on the hearth burned an even deeper blue, its reflection wavering in the windows, on the copper pots hanging on the wall, on the cracked mirror behind the bar. The Silentman's gaze settled on Lena.

"We've met before, you and I, haven't we? At least, I have memories from somebody—ah, yes, that fool Botrell—he met you. No matter. The second I walked in this room I could smell the boy on you. Jute." The Silentman seemed to tremble slightly when he uttered the name. "He's in your memories like dust in a room. By the fifth name of darkness, how I hate him. Do you know what it is to hate someone, my dear? To loathe the thought of their existence, to regard their destruction more precious than the preservation of one's own soul? I doubt it. You're young still. Jute stole my knife, you understand. He stole it from me. From who I was. I would've been someone different if it weren't for him. Very different. Every time I—ah—assume someone else, I find myself changing in odd little ways. Now, for instance, I have a tendency to talk too much, sip fine wines, and buy expensive horses. And all these memories sloshing around in my head. One hundred twenty-one different bags of memories. Most of them tedious. A few fascinating. The last one was the castle cook. All the other servants fled, after I'd eaten several of them, but the cook was too fat to make it up the stairs in a timely fashion. How he yowled. His thoughts tasted peculiar. A stew of boredom and bacon and a delicious disdain for the nobility."

"What do you want with me?" said Lena, her voice trembling.

"Want?" The Silentman smiled, showing all of his teeth. "Not a great deal, my dear. Merely everything of Jute I can rip from your memories. Every thread and shred and tatter I can tear out of you. Conversations, thefts, shared meals, beatings, pain, hungry nights, the common misery of two children without home or father or mother. I daresay this will be extremely painful for you, but rest assured that I will enjoy it to the full. That's my—how shall we call it?—my motto for the moment. Enjoy it to the full. It changes from day to day. Sometimes it's kill 'em all, or eat the thin ones last, or—"

"Nio."

The voice came from the back of the room. From the hallway leading down into the cellar. The Silentman hunched forward at the sound, his face blank as if he were rummaging through memories to discover why that name should mean anything to him. An old man stood in the hallway. A young man, anxious-looking, with a sword held

715

wavering in his hands, stood beside him. The old man's hands were cupped in front of him and something sparkled and seemed to change colors within them.

"What have you done to Nio?" said the old man.

"Nio served his purpose," said the Silentman. "He was a path we walked down, and the Dark does not return to the past. Nio is gone."

"So be it."

With one swift movement, the old man flung something into the air, bits of shattered glass or stone or something else that Lena could not determine. He uttered a single word, but the sound didn't make it past his lips, for the Silentman was even swifter than him. He snapped his fingers and time stopped. The tiny shards hung motionless in the air. The old man's face was frozen, his mouth still open. A drop of water dangled like a pearl below the faucet behind the bar counter. Lena could feel her heart poised between beats. She could not breathe. The Silentman, however, was not bound by his own spell. He stepped forward and plucked a shard from the air.

"Clever," he said, nodding. "Very clever. A stone of the farseeing mosaic from the university. Ah, yes, I remember you now. Severan. You shattered the mosaic, didn't you, when I almost had Jute in my grasp. You'll suffer for that. What fun. This day is turning out well."

The Silentman wandered around the room, chuckling and collecting tiny stones from the air. He plucked several right from Severan's outstretched fingertips.

"Begne the Lame created the mosaic to find his missing son. It took him his entire life. On the day it was finished, he went blind. And then died of grief. How appropriate. How delicious. Even a single piece of the mosaic is able to reflect the inherent truth of the spoken word. Just imagine if someone spoke the true name of—oh, I don't know—light. Was that what you were going to say? That would make quite a blaze, yes indeed. Recall, Severan, our unfortunate encounter in the university. You almost unmade me when you destroyed the mosaic. It was a painful moment. Thankfully, though, you don't know the true name of light. You never were that good of a student. Besides, there's no one alive who knows the true name of light.

"That's all of them, I trust?" The Silentman retrieved the last of the tiny stones and tucked the lot into his pocket. "Now, on to other things. Shall we discuss how I'm going to kill you all? I could indulge in tradition and flay you alive with a knife. Or, I could resurrect the thirty-three rat corpses in the walls of this inn and have them gnaw you to death. That might take too long. I could, of course, eat you myself. That's the solution I'm leaning toward, as there's obviously knowledge in your minds I could use. Thought, I'm not sure in your case, young man. You look familiar, but you don't look all that intelligent, so perhaps I'll just cut your throat. Now, so we can all enjoy this more fully, for I do enjoy the sound of screaming—there we go."

He snapped his fingers again and time resumed. Lena's heart thumped back into beat. Air whooshed into her lungs. Severan's mouth closed. His face looked gaunt and gray. The young man stepped past him, his sword raised. The Silentman smiled and opened his hand. A spot of darkness stained his palm. It drew everyone's eyes as if there was nothing else to look at in the room. It was the only thing that existed. The flames in the wall sconces and the fire on the hearth flickered and bent over, leaning toward the Silentman's hand, leaning and lengthening and thinning until the fire gave no light but was only a gray, dying thing. Everything seemed to be sliding toward that spot of darkness. It grew and spread out from the Silentman's hand. Lena could feel her chair inching across the floor. She tugged at her bonds, whimpering. There was no telling what would have happened next if something rather unexpected hadn't happened.

The front door opened.

"Excuse me," said a voice. "We're lost. Can you tell us the way to the city gate?"

"I want my mother!" announced another voice.

Even the Silentman was startled. His hand dropped to his side. There, standing at the front door, were five children. Three little boys, each with brown hair and gray eyes and the same stubborn mouths. Brothers, assuredly. A slightly older girl cast in the same mold, and another girl, blue-eyed and thin, almost ghostlike, standing behind them, with snowflakes in her pale hair. The brown-haired girl stepped forward.

"We're looking for the city gate," she said. Her voice was sturdy and self-assured.

"You are, are you?" said the Silentman, frowning a bit. "Has anyone ever warned you, little girl, about talking to strangers?"

"Of course," said the girl. "My parents say that all the time. But we're rescuing my father—ouch! Stop kicking me, Jonas!—so that doesn't matter right now."

"And who might your father be?"

The girl's chin went up. "Owain Gawinn. He's the Captain of the Guard."

"Well, well," said the Silentman. "The children of Owain Gawinn. I seem to remember that name. How interesting."

The children stared back at him, warily now, for children are not stupid, as many adults think, they themselves possessing that trait in abundance. Besides, the children were Gawinns. Jonas fingered the dagger under his cloak. On the other side of the room, Arodilac made a strangled sound of despair. Magret saw him then.

"Arodilac!" she said, her face brightening.

"Why are you here?" said Arodilac. "Of all the doors to open, you opened this one. And you, Fen, of anyone in this city, you should've been kept safe."

Fen looked at him and said nothing.

"Enough," said the Silentman, and he opened his hands.

Darkness unfolded in his grasp like a hideous flower. Petals opened, darker than a night without stars, darker than the blindness of a dead man. The darkness pulled at everything in the room. Things began to slide. Iron and stone wavered. Lena could no longer see the usual form of things, of walls and chairs and tables. Instead, everything blurred together as they frayed into nothingness. Across the room, the old man called Severan called out loud, fear on his face, but she heard no sound except for the beating of her heart. The children at the door clutched at each other as they slid across the floor. The Silentman laughed. But Fen, sprawled on the floor, reached out her hand and picked up a small stone that lay unnoticed on a chair. She stared at it in wonder. It was a beautiful little thing. Almost impossibly shiny.

Someone coughed politely in her ear.

"I just remembered something very important," whispered the ghost. "Would you mind saying a word for me? I'd say it myself, but things don't mean much when a ghost says them. If you don't mind, please repeat after me. *Leoht*."

"*Leoht*," said Fen.

And the tiny stone blazed into light. The light burned more brilliant than the sun. Even with eyes tightly shut—and Lena's were shut, her head averted—it burned red and white and then seared into something that was more than the mere negation of darkness. The light was so much older, and the darkness was merely the shadow.

717

The Silentman cried out in pain. He tried to close his hands, but it was too late. The darkness in his hands pulled greedily at the tiny stone. It sucked the thing from Fen's grasp and brought it tumbling through the air. The light fell into the darkness and the darkness could not overcome it. They all heard a dreadful shriek, as if from far away, and, when they opened their eyes, the Silentman was gone and the fire on the hearth danced cheerfully among the coals. The wihht was no more. Through a window opening to the west, Fen glanced up and saw a single star shining in the night sky.

"That was good luck," said Arodilac, his voice shaky.

"Extremely," said Severan. "If you don't mind, I need to sit down for a while."

"Not luck at all," said the ghost, drifting across the room. "That girl has an interesting way with words. Very polite and obliging, too. Dear me. Good thing I remembered that word in time."

"What a nasty man," said Magret. "I must tell Father about him. He looked familiar. I think I've seen him somewhere before."

"Never mind," said Arodilac. "He won't be coming back."

"Oh, look!" Magret hurried over to Lena. "She's tied up. Are you all right? We're rescuing people tonight. Lucky for you, isn't it?"

"Yes," managed Lena.

"We'll have to find a knife or something sharp. Jonas! That's Great Uncle Bevan's. Father'll have a fit if he finds you've taken that."

"Ah, but I've cut her cords. He'll be proud of me."

Lena was soon up and rubbing her wrists. The children surveyed her, and she surveyed the children. Presumably, they all liked what they saw, for after a moment, Magret nodded and turned to Arodilac.

"All right, then. We need to find Father. I expect you'll take us, won't you?"

"No, I will not," said Arodilac, his voice stern. "I'm taking you straight home. You've done quite enough, quite enough as it is." But then he smiled down at her. "He will be very proud."

CHAPTER ONE HUNDRED & TWENTY-SEVEN
THE FALL OF JUTE

"What is destroyed can be rebuilt," said Owain.

He leaned on his sword as he stood with the dukes and the prince of Harth in the wreckage of the city gate. On either side of them, for hundreds of yards, the walls of the city lay shattered and toppled. The unmoving forms of the dead were scattered thickly there about the ground. The small troop of cavalry from Harth stood at easy and weary attention a little distance away from the gate. Within the ruined walls, the defenders moved in slow and dazed shock, some smiling, others with blank face as they contemplated the carnage the battle had brought.

"But not our dead," said the duke of Harlech quietly. "Sons and fathers, all of them."

"No," said Owain. "Still, would our dead have us mourn them now, with such a victory fresh in our grasp?"

"My lords, while I would prefer to stay a while with you in Hearne," said the prince of Harth, swinging back up into the saddle, "I must hasten south and make amends with my own father. I fear I left his court without his leave, stealing away my cousins and his young officers. But where is the windlord? I would desire to thank him before I go."

"As would all of us," said the duke of Dolan.

"Surely I saw him but a minute ago," said the duke of Harlech. He glanced up into the sky and frowned.

It was then that fire stirred in the broken ruins of the wall not far from them. The prince of Harth's horse reared, nearly unseating him. Flames suddenly whipped and danced in the wind. A dark shape reared up from the ground. It looked somewhat like a horse. But then the flames mounted higher, obliterating what had been there before. The thing was pure darkness and flames. The air crackled with heat. The wind howled in response, dashing itself against the fire, but its fervor only caused the flames to leap higher.

A voice roared from the darkness. Flames sprang into the air, twisting and turning about themselves to shape words that echoed the voice. But the words were in no language that anyone could read. They burned bright, and the sight filled every man's mind with death, and many at that moment laid down their weapons in despair. The voice blurred into the guttural roaring of the fire, and the flames clawed their way up into the sky. The fire was enormous now, a colossus straddling the broken wall and taller than any building in the city. Wooden roofs nearby smoked and smoldered and burst into sudden flame from the proximity of that terrible heat.

The voice quieted and then said, almost conversationally, even though it reached every ear of every soldier with absolute clarity, "Hear me, ye dead. Thou art mine. By the shadow of Daghoron. By the name of Nokhoron Nozhan. Hear me now. Arise."

There was silence in the city. The wind did not stir. The tide paused upon the shore. The breath caught in a thousand throats and a thousand swords hung motionless, waiting to fall. Birds in their nests in the gardens of Highneck Rise, oblivious to battle and the cares of men, halted in their songs. And Jute, poised far overhead in the sky, waited, uncertain in his power.

With a rattling heave, the dead arose all across the battlefield. Dead soldiers of Harlech and Thule, Hull, Dolan, and Vo. The dead of the city Guard, the cold bodies of fishermen and townsfolk, the stiffening, black-armored corpses of the foe—they all arose. They clambered to their feet with shambling steps. They groped for swords and spears, whatever was at hand. Their wounds were dry and drained of blood. Blind eyes stared from broken faces. The air stank of rotting things. They advanced at a shuffle that slowly quickened into something more akin to life. The defenders of Hearne fell back in horror, for here were their friends and fellows, surely dead now, but arisen again. They fell back and their hearts were like water. The cavalry of Harth wheeled about, turning in dismay, for they were caught within the sea of dead like a small island. Their lances were no use to them, for they were trapped at a standstill. The prince of Harth was calling out, his voice sharp and clear, his sword bright in his hand, but their horses plunged and screamed in fear.

"Stand fast!" bellowed Owain Gawinn. "Stand fast, men! For Hearne, for Tormay! Stand fast, blast you!"

But the men of the Guard would not stand. Neither would most of the soldiers of the duchies. They broke and ran, overcome with the terror of what advanced. They threw down their weapons and ran away toward Mioja Square and into the side streets leading down to the sea. A few of them stayed, though, and gathered about their captain. Declan was there also, his sister standing pale and silent behind him, as well as a handful of men from Thule and Vo.

"Fancy meeting you here, guvnor," said Hoon. "I don't mind dying, particularly in your exalted company, but I don't relish turning into one o' them." He spat in the direction of the advancing dead.

"No worries, cap'n," said a voice behind them. It was Varden. The old Guardsman was leaning on a bloodstained spear. He spoke with gloomy satisfaction. "If Hoon turns into one o' them things, I'll just kill him again. It'd be a pleasure."

"Thank you, Varden," said Owain, smiling despite his weariness. "I don't know what this day holds, but we'll do our part here as well as we can. That's all that's asked of us. Farrow, I'm heartened to find you here. My lady." Here, he bowed to Giverny, his eyes full of questions. "I do not think this place is safe for—"

"Do not stray far from me," she said, interrupting him. Her voice was dry and dispassionate. "My strength is still spent, but I can secure the ground under your feet. If I were stronger, I might have been able to unmake his spell, but this is no mere wizardry we face. It is something deeper and older than mere magic. Our enemy commands the dead with the words of the first language, the words of Anue himself. But I shall do what I can. Stay close to me, and you shall at least stand against the dead."

They stared at her, all of them, even her brother, but none of them had the courage to say anything to her further. At the sharp order of Owain, the small company turned and set themselves ready. It was not a moment too soon, for the line of the dead hurled against them. They came snarling and shrieking, their voices whistling through slashed throats. The wind kicked up then, and the air seemed to be filled with fire. It was as if they were a small island of steel in a sea of death. With every enemy that fell, another stepped in to take his fellow's place. And the dead did not die easily. They died hard, if that was how it might be called, hacked to pieces, beaten down into the cobblestones, battered into the bloody ground. Even then, not all of them died.

A dreadful howling noise sounded beyond the ruined wall. It was enough to strike terror into the hearts of the defenders, and they wondered what new horror approached. The day was dreadful enough. How could they stand anything more? But the girl Giverny cried out in gladness. Something moved through the ranks of the dead, moving at great speed. As it drew closer, those around Giverny saw that the dead soldiers were being dashed and ripped and torn by a huge beast. An enormous black dog with teeth as sharp as daggers and shining silver eyes. No, not a dog. A wolf.

"Ehtan!" said Giverny.

The wolf bounded forward to her side. The men near her drew back in alarm. Declan raised his sword. His heart faltered for his sister, but she threw her arms around the wolf's neck. The wolf looked at Declan over her shoulder, his silver eyes bright. A voice flashed through his mind. A strange, rough sort of voice.

Do not trouble thy heart.

"Hawks and wolves," said Owain. His face was white with strain, smeared with blood and dirt, but he bowed courteously to the wolf. The wolf inclined his head in return and then planted himself squarely in front of Giverny.

Some distance away from them, closer to the tower of the Guard still standing amid the ruins of the city wall, the sunlight flashed on another small ring of steel drowning in the sea of dead soldiers. Owain could make out the tall figure of Rane Lannaslech, standing head and shoulders above his men. The gray hair of his father, the duke, was visible alongside him, as well as the duke of Dolan. Of Harth, he could see only dimly, far across the battlefield, a struggling knot of horsemen shrinking and shrinking within the heaving sea of the dead.

I suppose it won't be long now, Owain thought to himself. I would've liked to see Sibb and the children one more time.

The dead threw themselves forward and he no longer had time to think, but could only parry and hack and kill until the day blurred into a continuous jarring agony of steel on steel. The men alongside him fought in grim determination. The wolf leapt and slashed with his teeth, quicker than thought. Behind them, the girl stood without moving. Even though she was a slender little thing in comparison to their iron and brawn, the men had the distinct impression that it was not a girl who stood there, but a sturdy oak tree standing with its roots deep in the earth.

A sudden weight and claws dug into Owain's shoulder. He swore, staggering back.

"Listen, man," said the hawk in his ear. "Hold here. Hold fast. Every minute that you give her, she grows stronger. Her roots are going deeper. Guard her and you guard Hearne. No, you guard Tormay itself."

"What of Jute?" said Owain. "Will he just wait and watch us die?"

"Jute struggles with the darkness itself. Be assured that you would be safer battling this entire army of the dead by yourself than face what he does for one instant. Now, keep your heart strong. Hold fast!"

The hawk leapt from his shoulder back into the air and was gone. The sky darkened, and the wind blew cold. There were voices muttering in the wind, whispering words in a dead tongue that spoke of doom and despair and death. The army of the enemy rose up and there was nothing that Owain Gawinn could do except fight. Behind him, the girl still stood silent, and he could no longer see the horsemen of Harth, nor the men of Harlech. Jute was nowhere to be seen.

The thing of fire standing astride the ruined wall grew taller, flaring up into the sky. It roared forth its hate, its mouth a well of darkness, and such was the terror of that sound that men stood frozen in fear. Surely there was only darkness and it was the end of all people.

"Jute!" howled the thing. The air shimmered, as if it were about to burst into flame. "Thief! Give me what is mine!"

The wind keened in response, gathering itself and battering against the colossus of flame. The clouds tumbled by in the sky. The sun vanished, hidden in smoke or hurried to its safety beyond the sea's edge or perhaps blown out like a candle. And then Jute was there. He hurtled through the sky, wreathed in the icy air. Flames reached for him. Fire leapt up to pull him down. The sky was on fire. Darkness trembled in the thoughts of every soldier there. And even from the unblinking eyes of the dead, despair stared.

Jute darted through the fire, quicker than light. He struck with the weapons of the wind, with the force of the gale and the hammering blows of the hurricane. Ice shards flashed through the air behind him. They shattered into steam in the heart of the fire, and the fire shrieked aloud. It called out words. It called out words of unmaking, ancient words left unspoken since Nokhoron Nozhan first saw the making of the world. The words wrote themselves in the smoking darkness of that sky. And even though no living man knew that accursed language, every man felt the truth of it in his heart. Even the dead stopped in their tracks and stood in silence for the end. For there are things even deeper than death. Giverny Farrow herself, standing with the earth under her, wavered.

But Jute only flew faster. He flew faster than thought, faster than the reaching grasp of the words of the enemy. He was untouchable. He was the wind. He was the storm and the fury and the heart of the sky. Up to the stars themselves, into the vast, unbroken stretches of silence between the stars, between the awful furnaces of space—all of this was his domain.

The stars paused within their prescribed courses. Their light dimmed for a moment. The music of those spheres faltered as they stopped to gaze and wonder. No one heard the dismay in their voices in all of Tormay except, perhaps, for the hawk.

Look!

Do not look. . .

Look away. . .

Hide thine eyes. . .

And Jute struck with all the dreadful, savage power of those endless heights, the cold and silence of the sky, colder than winter's frozen heart, and more silent than the grave of death itself. He struck with the fury of the tempest and the howl of the wind that rages between the stars. He struck straight through the heart of the fire. And the fire could not stand before him. It buckled and bent. It tattered and streamed and fluttered, helpless in the wind. The towering phantasm that it had been shrank away. The darkness faded in its eyes until it was only a shadow of things once hoped for. The thing cried out. The thing that had once been the anbeorun of fire. Aeled. It was soundless now. Its mouth shaped a single word from the oldest of all languages. The language it had first spoken, long centuries before it had chosen the darkness.

Master.

But the sound was silent. And then the fire guttered out. On the battlefield, the bodies of the dead collapsed to the ground in honest death. The defenders of the city stood in weariness, dazed with surprise and doubt. There was only Jute now, triumphant in the sky. He was full of fury and delight and the wonder of his own power. The rightness of it.

Aye, said the voice in his mind. *This is how things should be.*

"I am the wind!" Jute shouted out loud.

The sound boomed through the sky like rolling thunder. It was thunder to the cowering men far below on the battlefield. It was no longer a voice. The wind howled around him in response. It blew every which way. It dashed up into the sky to shred the clouds into tatters. It careened to the east and the west, churning the sea into foam. Walls in the city collapsed. Stones flew and shattered. The bodies of the living and the dead were strewn about like a child's playthings.

Thou art the wind, said the voice. *Thou art Jute. And all this power is thine. Thou wert born for this. Thou hast conquered. Thine is the power to unravel the sky. The power to destroy.*

The voice was right. The thought grew within Jute's mind and the sky darkened. Far away, far in the eastern approaches beyond the first few stars, a window in the sky seemed to appear. It slowly opened. It was only a smudge of black in the twilight sky. A tiny smudge of black an impossible distance away. No one saw it. Not even Jute. Something lay beyond that window. Something waking. Something opening up its eyes.

The power to destroy is thine.

The wind howled in delight. It scoured the sky clean until nothing was left except Jute and the distant stars. However, there was one other. Low over the city, a single, solitary bird struggled through the power of the wind. The hawk. But even he could not last in that maelstrom. He folded his wings and dove down to the battlefield. The hawk landed in the dubious shelter of some rubble from the city wall. Even there, the wind battered everything in sight. Shards of stone hissed through the air. Something stirred on the ground next to the hawk.

"Well met, little wing."

The voice was worn thin, but the hawk would have recognized it anywhere.

"My lord Aeled," said the hawk sadly.

"Nay, no longer fire. I am spent. I have fallen, old friend." The face looked up at the bird from the ground. It seemed as if it was carved of stone, as if the flesh had been worn away by time until only bone remained. There was no sign of the duke of Mizra there, only something fading and impossibly ancient. "Perhaps I was falling all that time, when we first descended from the house of dreams. This world took hold of my heart and I wanted no other. But then, as the centuries passed, the desire grew in me to return. To go home. To return to the house of dreams. But I could not. All the knowledge of this world could not help me, thought I searched and searched. I have forgotten so many things." His voice was just a whisper now. "I did not recognize the darkness until it was too late. He snared me in my dreams. Perhaps, even now, he is waking."

"He?" said the hawk, dreading the answer.

"Save your boy before it's too late. Before he takes the path I took." Flame guttered on the stone face and there was pain in his eyes as he stared up at the hawk. "I must die, little wing, but I cannot. Will this fire never be quenched in me?"

The hawk had no answer for him, only silence. But across the battlefield and through the wind someone came walking. She was only a wisp of rain, a few snowflakes that fell in the slow curve of her face, a drift of fog off the sea. She passed between the living defenders and the dead, and no one saw her. Her steps took her unerringly to the hawk's side and it was then that he saw her.

"Lady," said the hawk.

The stone face on the ground looked up at her. A sigh of flame and smoke issued forth from his mouth.

"Sister."

The girl who had been Liss Galnes did not answer, but knelt over him. Her hand touched his face. Flames fluttered against her fingers. Tears from her eyes fell down upon his brow. They hissed into steam, and the flames guttered out and were gone. The face below her tried to smile, but it could not, and then it was only stone. Ruined stone that looked somewhat like the figure of a man asleep on the ground. She reached out her hand and caught the steam as it rose. Her fingers closed on it and there was suddenly only a single, shining jewel in her palm. Her fingers closed again and the jewel was gone. The hawk and the girl were still for a moment, staring down at the broken stone on the ground. High above them, far beyond the sky and the howling wind, the stars looked down as well.

"Lady," said the hawk again, his voice breaking.

"Courage, little wing." She smiled at him, and then she dissolved into mist.

The hawk launched himself back into the air, his wings heavy with weariness. The wind was like stone against him. It no longer knew him. He clawed his way up into the sky. He was tired. He could not think clearly. Somewhere, high above him, Jute rode upon the wind. Somewhere, up in the darkness. He could not see him. Grimly, he set his beak and flew into the wind. Even though he could not see him, he knew Jute would be at the heart of the wind's fury and dreadful joy.

The power to destroy is thine.

The hawk heard the voice and shuddered. Jute heard it too, and smiled. The power to destroy was his. The power to rend and shatter and unmake. The wind was his. He was the wind. It blew through him and it was him. He stretched out through the sky for countless miles. He could see across the breadth of the world. He blew the waves into disarray and uprooted oaks far across the eastern slopes of the Rennet Valley. He toppled walls in Hearne and he flung avalanches rumbling down the mountainsides on the reaches of Morn. He soared up to the stars and down among the habitations of men. He was everywhere, saw everything, could destroy or graciously allow life. It was all his. Everything was his.

Jute.

The voice was faint in his mind. Faint, but slowly drawing closer. He shook his head, frowning. His eyes were full of darkness, like the night sky.

Jute.

The hawk. He knew the voice now. Jute turned and saw the bird struggling through the sky toward him.

Thou dost need him no longer, said the other voice in his mind. *Thou art no longer the little wing. Thou art the wind.*

"What do you want?" Jute roared across the sky.

"Call back the wind," said the hawk. "Call back the wind. Remember who you are."

"I know who I am. I am the wind! I did not ask for this, but it is mine now. I've done everything you asked of me. I've fought your battles. I've spent my life for Tormay. I killed the lord of fire. I am the wind. I don't need you now!"

"That is not your voice that speaks," said the hawk, his voice barely audible over the howl of the wind.

"Not my voice?" shouted Jute. "Not my voice? Then whose is it?"

"You know."

"If I know, then do I need you to tell me?" The boy's voice broke into the different voices of the wind. Into the deep bass of the winter storm, into the keening shriek of the sea storm driving through a ship's rigging, into the awful depths of the mountain blast. "Do I need you? No!"

And with that final, dreadful *no*, the boy drove the hawk from him in a terrible blast of wind, blowing across the sky in a fury of power that shook the Mountains of Morn themselves down to the roots of their being. The hawk tumbled end over end, helpless before him. He was only a speck now. He fell through the sky.

As you wish. The hawk's voice was tired and failing in the boy's mind. *As you wish, little wing.*

The other voice chuckled in the boy's mind. And Jute's heart leapt in sudden pain at the sound. The sky seemed dreadfully empty now.

"Hawk!" he screamed. "Come back!"

Jute drew the wind to him, frantic and despairing. The wind came in all of its heedless power. For miles around, the wind rushed toward him, faster and faster. The hawk was borne along on it, faster than an arrow loosed from a bow. But the bird's body was limp. His wings were broken. A feather fell free from one wing and the wind hurled it along. Jute stretched out his hands for the hawk, but the feather, with its quill as sharp and as hard as iron, pierced his side. Blood streamed away into the wind. Jute felt none of it. The hawk lay in his hands.

"Remember from where you came," said the hawk, his voice a whisper. "That is what he forgot. He forgot the house of dreams. Would you forget as well?"

"No, I will not," said Jute, his eyes full of tears.

But the hawk did not answer, for his body was still.

It was said that day, by those who were there, that the wind cried out in the darkening twilight sky. It cried out with such a voice that the stars turned away and hid their faces. The sea and the earth answered back in sorrow, but there was none living who understood the language of their voices. Owain Gawinn and those standing with him saw the girl, Giverny Farrow, crumple to the ground. They ran to aid her, but she would not be comforted, though the wolf and her brother crouched beside her.

"Go find him," she said. "Out in the fields past the bridge."

They saddled horses and rode out through the ruined gate. The ground there was a trampled morass of icy mud. Several of the soldiers carried lanterns, and the light fell on the bodies of the dead, on the weapons of war, on shattered armor, on arrows standing stiff in flesh and earth like lifeless branches, on dead horses stretched out in one last frozen gallop. As they picked their way through that awful landscape, one of the soldiers cried out in surprise. A figure stumbled toward them out of the shadows. Owain thought it Jute at first, but the man was taller, a sword in his hand. He seemed a ghost, but as he drew near, the lantern light fell on the weary face of the prince of Harth. His horse walked behind with trembling step and hanging head. The prince spoke, his voice clear and courteous as it always was.

"My lords," he said. "Who do you seek among the dead?"

"Jute," said Owain.

The company clattered over the bridge with the river rushing below. That is where they found him. Jute lay on the icy ground, curled up around the wound in his side. His fingers were clenched tight on a single black feather. They bore him up and brought him to the city. Through the ruins of the city gate they rode in care and solicitude, for his face was white with pain. The soldiers of every duchy stood there in silent honor. When they set Jute down in the court of the Guard, the chief physician came and tended him. The dukes came and knelt at his pallet.

"You saved this land," said Lord Lannaslech, his voice quiet. "You, the wind."

Jute said nothing, but only clutched the feather in his hands. He did not see them. They drew back at the approach of Giverny Farrow. She crouched at his side and touched his brow.

"Jute," she said. She said nothing more than that, but stayed by his side. The wolf sat there too, as unmoving as stone, but his eyes never left Jute's face.

The moon rose higher. The wind did not blow, but through the dark streets came the sound of the sea. The soldiers, wounded and whole, slept in their tents and houses and makeshift shelters all along the ruined wall of the city. Owain Gawinn could not sleep, but paced the night away, walking back and forth on the top of the Guard tower. He looked east, but there was nothing there except for the night. In a room in the tower, Jute slept, still clutching the feather. Giverny did not sleep, but sat by his bed, her eyes on his face, the wolf crouched beside her. In a chair in the corner, Declan sprawled, having said that he would watch with her, but he had long since fallen asleep. And so, save the captain, the girl, and the wolf, all the city slept.

CHAPTER ONE HUNDRED & TWENTY-EIGHT
FAREWELLS

The next morning dawned bright. The bonfire in the court of the Guard had burned to coals. Owain walked down the steps of the tower. He found the duke of Harlech and his son Rane in the stable, talking with the prince of Harth. The prince was saddling his horse.

"What, my lord," said Owain. "Are you away so early?"

"You would be welcome in Harlech, Eaomod," said Lord Lannaslech. "Our home and hearth will always be yours for the kindness you showed Tormay. Your swords strengthened our fortunes when we thought all was lost."

"These are glad words," said the prince. "You hearten me, for though this battle is ours, all my kinsmen lie dead on the field and I alone am left. And although I would be son to all of Tormay, I am my father's son first of all, and must return to his court. I disobeyed his word and now I must go and make amends."

"No!" said Declan, stricken by his words and by his own memory of the stern king of Harth. "Surely there is time for you to tarry here in the north."

"I've been away long enough," said Eaomod quietly. "I did not leave Harth with my lord father's blessing, so I must return to hear his will."

They followed him as he walked his horse out into the yard. He swung up into the saddle.

"You will wait," said Owain, "at least, until I have you provisioned for your journey."

He turned aside and spoke with a Guardsman, sending him running to the kitchen in the tower. The soldier did not return, but Giverny came in his place, bearing a leather bag full of food. She handed it up to the prince.

"Lady," he said, bowing from the saddle, "I am honored to have seen one such as you with my own eyes. May you be blessed. May you wander in safety all your days and guard us against the designs of the Dark. Do not forget Harth, even though we have only the sands and stone and the barren desert."

"I will not forget," she said gravely.

"Is the boy well?" the prince said, somewhat hesitantly.

Giverny said nothing, though a breeze sprang up around her, stirring her hair into disarray as if it was anxious to know her answer as well. The sun shone and the clouds were gone. Light flooded the sky so that it was nearer to white than blue. The prince of Harth turned his face to the sky and it seemed that his face was eager, as if he were hungry for the light and heat of the southern sun.

"We have all come from dust, have we not?" he said. "And so we shall return."

And then he bid them treat his dead peacefully, that they would be laid in the ground side by side with the dead of the other duchies, and so honor the old blood that all of Tormay held in common. This they promised, and he then turned his horse and rode away. His steed picked his way through the rubble of the city wall and then across the battlefield. They stood and watched him go until horse and rider were a tiny black shape on the landscape that wavered and then disappeared entirely in the shimmering light of the afternoon sun.

Owain turned and saw Jute slowly descending the steps of the guard tower. Others saw him then also. A great cheer went up, unbidden and unprompted. Jute smiled, but his face was thin and white. He walked between them, limping as if his side still pained him. Many of the soldiers knelt when he drew near, and the braver ones took his hand as he passed by. Jute walked on and disappeared from sight down a street heading toward Fishgate.

"I'd follow him, if I were you," said Giverny.

She was standing beside her brother. Declan looked at her, startled.

"He has lost a great friend," said Giverny. "Let him know that he still has others. Besides, I think he's going down to the sea." She smiled.

And that was where Declan found him. Declan did not go alone, of course, but Severan and the ghost came along with him. The city streets were quiet, and the stench of smoke and fire no longer fouled the sky. Instead, the sweet scent of selia blossoms filled the air. The sun shone down and the sea sparkled before them.

"There he is," said Severan.

Jute stood at the end of the pier, staring out to sea. He turned at the sound of their footsteps on the planking.

"I used to come here all the time when I was a boy," he said. "I would sit here and dream about other lands. Dream about being a hero and fighting battles and saving a princess along the way." He sighed. "All I can dream about now is going home. But I'm not sure where that'll ever be. Or even what that really means. Hearne certainly isn't my home anymore."

"Hearne's just a city," said Declan.

"I've never been fond of cities myself," mumbled the ghost. "Too many people."

"You're always welcome to come home to Harlech with me," said Severan.

"Thank you," said Jute gravely.

He opened his hand. A black feather lay there.

"It's a little thing, isn't it. But it almost killed me. I almost wish it had."

"Don't say that," said Severan.

Jute smiled, though there were sudden tears in his eyes. "Don't worry. I am the wind, yes, but the heart of the wind is peace. *Anbeorun* means stillpoint, and that is what stands in the midst of even the worst storm. The silence and stillness of peace. The peace is stronger than the storm. I think I finally understand that now. I hope I never forget."

The four friends stared out at the sea in silence. Even the ghost had nothing to say. After a while, Jute stirred and glanced at Declan.

"She's released you," he said. "You know that, don't you?"

"I know," said Declan quietly.

The wind blew across the harbor, kicking the wave tops into foam. Seagulls flew up into the sky. Declan sat down on the end of the pier and stared out at the water. After a while, the others left and he was alone. He took out the pearl. It shone in the palm of his hand, as blue as the sky and just as full of light.

"Thank you."

Declan looked up, startled. Liss sat next to him, her legs dangling over the edge of the pier. She smiled at him. Her eyes were the same color as the pearl, blue and serene. The sunlight fell across her hair and the line of her face. The light seemed to blur through her. Declan could not speak.

"You are true, Declan Farrow. You are true in your heart and with your courage that you have freely spent for others. True to your word, this land, and your friends. I'm sorry, perhaps, for how I have used you, for now I think you would've made the same choices without my compulsion. You've done well, and I am gladdened, for even the sea has her own heart, as cold and as remote as it is." She smiled somewhat ruefully. "Keep the pearl. That story is not over yet."

"Will I see you again?" he said, finally managing words.

Liss did not answer, but she reached out and gently closed his fingers over the pearl. Her touch was as light as seafoam on his calloused hand. They looked out at the sea together in silence. The waves rolled in slow and sure confidence beneath the pier. The sunlight flashed on the water. The next time he glanced over, she was gone.

Jute left that afternoon. The Guard were drawn up in ranks on either side of the city gate. A great crowd of cityfolk filled the square, hushed and waiting. Flags snapped in the wind. Arodilac Bridd stood before the tower, looking uncomfortable in unaccustomed finery and with a thin silver circlet on his brow. The dukes and all the nobility of Hearne were gathered about him, but Owain Gawinn stood at his right hand.

"The city of Hearne is forever in your debt," said Arodilac loudly, holding himself stiff and wondering whether he was saying the right thing. He nervously eyed Owain, but the man's face was impassive. "From the days of Dol Cynehad, in the time of our forefathers, down to our own age, Tormay is beholden to the graciousness and care of the anbeorun. Though I serve the people as regent, I also serve you, my lord wind. Hearne and the regency are yours to command. I, uh, well, what I mean to say—"

"Just say thank you," muttered Owain quietly. "We don't need to hear all the other stuff. If you weren't the regent, I'd put you on guard duty."

"Thanks very much," said Arodilac, stammering a bit. He grinned and shook Jute's hand. "I'm afraid it's going to take a while to figure out this regent thing. I hope I don't make a hash of it like my uncle did. I'd much rather be on guard duty, but it can't be helped."

"Some things can't be helped," said Jute.

Some things can't be helped, whether we like them or not. We make our choices and the house of dreams directs our path. All of you chose well. You chose to fight and die. This is your land, just as much as it ever will be mine. Tormay belongs to us all, as we belong to her. And the house of dreams watches us, men and anbeorun alike. But the Dark watches as well. It watches and dreams and waits.

But Jute said none of this out loud. He only smiled as best as he could and nodded and shook hands with the dukes as they gathered about to wish him well. Finally, Jute took the reins of a horse from a waiting groom. Someone gave him a leg up and he settled into the saddle. Severan urged his own horse alongside.

"They don't expect me to fly," Jute said quietly to the old man, "do they?"

"Even the wind can ride a horse once in a while," said Severan.

"I was once bitten by a horse," said the ghost from inside a saddlebag. "It was a dreadful experience. Wait. Are you telling me we're riding horses?"

A row of trumpeters brought up their horns with a flourish. A sharp, clear blast echoed through the air. The crowd cheered. The horses set out with a jingle of bridles. A larger troop of horsemen waited for them outside the city gate. Declan sat on a tall bay at the front of the troop.

"You didn't think I'd let you lot gallivant off by yourself, did you?" he said.

729

They rode north through the day. The horsemen were all from Harlech, and the duke's son, Rane, rode with them as well. From time to time, the wind blew along their path, though it was mostly quiet, for that was how Jute felt. The wound in his side was almost healed, but it still pained him. He rode with the black feather clutched in one hand.

"Things are so much simpler now, Severan," he said.

"Aye," said the old man, smiling. "That they are."

"At least for a while," said Jute. "Tell me again about your house."

And Severan told him. It was the third time since they had left Hearne, but Severan did not mind. Even the ghost remained interested, despite a tendency to lecture them about architecture.

"It's more of a cottage than a house," said Severan, "though I can't rightly say what the distinction is between a house and a cottage. You'll know when you see it. My grandfather built it for his wife, for she was from the islands and was homesick for the sight of them. My father would have given it to my brother Lannaslech, but he would not take it. He knew I loved the place. The cottage sits at the top of a cliff overlooking the sea. Built sturdy and stout enough of stone that even the wind thinks twice before taking a blow at it. It's a cheerful thing during the winter nights to have a fire burning on the hearth. But the cottage is lonely and without any of your bustle and excitement of Hearne. And once you've grown accustomed to the sound of the wind and the sea below on the rocks, it's a silent place."

"Oh, I won't mind that," said Jute. He stirred restlessly in his saddle. His hand crept to his side and Severan saw a shadow of pain cross his face.

"Silence is nothing to be concerned about," said the ghost, who clearly was no longer paying much attention to the conversation. "I'm always happy to fill the little gaps. Why, you haven't even heard any of my celebrated lectures on cooking with magic. You'll be fascinated. There's nothing quite like roasting goat with a judicious sprinkling of powdered lightning."

"Powdered lightning!" snorted Severan. "Cooking with magic! I've heard quite a few from you, ghost, but this beats 'em all. Are you really sure you were Staer Gemyndes?"

"I'll have you know that lightning can be powdered," said the ghost. "You merely, well, you merely. . . er. . ."

"You see?" said Severan.

Jute did not say anything, and the ghost looked at him anxiously. "You don't mind, do you?" said the ghost in a low voice. "I can't help myself. It's just who I am. I'm a ghost, even if I once was Staer Gemyndes. I have to talk, otherwise I'll forget I exist and that'll be the end of me. I suppose I could just leave, if you want me to," continued the ghost miserably. "I should, shouldn't I? I'm just a ghost. You're going to have a real home now, and you don't need a ghost cluttering up the place. I might as well tell you how to make me leave. It's simple. All you have to do is—"

"No, don't tell me," said Jute. "I don't want to know. I like having you about. We're friends, don't you see?"

"Friends?" said the ghost, sounding as if it were about to burst into tears. "Friends? Do you mean it? Oh, blessed day!"

And, with that, to everyone's great surprise, the ghost was silent for a long time. It had not had a friend in hundreds of years and the thought was almost too much to bear. Besides, a happy ghost does not need to talk all the time.

They did not stop in Lastane but camped beyond the town in a hollow shielded by trees. The company built a fire and put up tents for the night. Several of them threw out baited lines in the stream that ran through the valley, and soon fish were baking in the fire. While they were eating their supper, Maernes, the duke of Hull, rode up out of the night and joined them.

"The land still tells me of visitors, when it will," he said.

He did not reproach them for avoiding his hospitality in Lastane, but sat by the fire, trading stories with the other men. Jute drowsed with a cloak wrapped around him. He fell asleep and then awoke later with a start, sure that all were gone and even Severan had left him, but the others were still sitting around the fire, talking in low voices, and he fell back asleep.

They crossed the northern fork of the Ciele River and passed on into Thule. The land grew wilder as they went. Hills interrupted the expanse of the plain, and then sudden valleys dropped down into the early shadows of afternoon. They topped a rise and before them lay the bay of Averlay. The little town shone in the late sunlight further along the curve of the shore.

"The fishermen sail from here to the Flessoray Islands," said Declan. He sat on his horse, staring down at the bay shining below them. He touched the pearl at his neck. "It takes about eight hours with a good wind."

"Let's stop here for the night," said Severan. "There's an excellent inn down by the pier. Fresh bread, fish, and featherbeds."

"I'd rather not," said Jute. "There'll be people and whispers and staring faces. I don't think I can stand much more of that."

"No, lad. We're near the border of Harlech. Folks don't ask questions up here. They won't know your face. Besides, a loaf of bread and some hot fish stew—who can turn that down?"

And so Jute agreed. To be honest, though, he was more interested in a featherbed than the food. The thought of rest, of a very long sleep, was particularly appealing.

He looked to the east and it seemed as if he could see a great distance, all the way to the Mountains of Morn themselves. They were dark and full of shadows that grew and deepened as the sun slanted further away into the west. He shivered.

"It'll always seek to return," he said, not realizing he spoke out loud. "It won't rest."

"What's that?" said Severan.

"Nothing," said Jute. "I was just thinking. It's not important. At least, not now." He took a deep breath, filling his lungs with the sweet heather scent in the air. "The hawk loved these skies. I remember now. The further north we went, the happier he was."

Severan said nothing, for this was the first time Jute had mentioned the hawk in days. He glanced over at the boy, but Jute's face was serene.

"He said the sky was deeper here," continued the boy. "I never knew what he meant, and he never bothered to explain, but I understand now."

They left Averlay early that next morning. The air was cold and clean. After a while, they topped a rise. The road angled along the top of a ridge of weathered granite, pine trees, and heather. The land stretched out in a vast sweep of purple and green and gray. Far below them, the sea shone and trembled with life.

Rane nudged his horse alongside them. "Look. Off to the west where the headlands rise up. That's where we're going. We'll have you there before nightfall."

"Home," said Severan.

"Home," said the ghost happily.

"Home," said Jute.

CHAPTER ONE HUNDRED & TWENTY-NINE
ENDINGS

Arodilac Bridd settled reluctantly into the job of ruling Hearne. He was sensible enough to listen to Owain Gawinn, and on his counsel, he married the youngest daughter of the duke of Thule. She was pretty, with the dark green eyes and brown hair that mark so many of those from Thule, and could ride a horse better than Arodilac. More importantly, she had a sharp mind and did not suffer fools gladly. With such a bride, Arodilac quickly settled down to marriage and ruling a city. He did well at both, but this was just as much his wife's due as it was his.

Owain Gawinn had stern words with his children when he got home the night after the battle. Secretly, however, he was very proud of them. They were Gawinns, through and through, even Fen. Sibb, of course, had her own words with her husband about trying to get himself killed for the second time in one week, but this was in the privacy of their bedroom. Such arguments rarely lasted long between those two and usually ended in laughter.

Owain resumed the old duties that had been carried out by every Gawinn before him. He set about building the wreckage of the Guard back into full strength. More young men would come forward to learn the arts of war and peace under his tutelage. It was during the last years of his life that a tower was constructed at the Rennet Gap, from whose heights watchmen would forevermore gaze east to wait for that which might come again someday.

The little thief girl, Lena, remained in Hearne, for that was the only home she had ever had. Little is known about the rest of her life, as she was a secretive, careful person. She probably returned to thieving. However, with the death of the Silentman, the Thieves Guild had been thrown into confusion and disarray. As Lena was a particularly clever girl, I'm sure she somehow took advantage of the opportunity. She never forgot the Gawinn children, though, and it is probably safe to say that their paths did cross again in the future.

Declan Farrow wandered about Tormay and found himself back in Hearne. He spent several weeks there, urged to stay by the new regent, who seemed to have forgotten all about the girl named Liss Galnes. Owain Gawinn, however, did not say anything in this matter. He, probably more than any other, wished to see Declan's sword and knowledge stay in the service of the city, but he also understood the restlessness in the man and could not bring himself to speak a single word in persuasion.

Declan had never felt at home within city walls before, but now it was even worse. The stone buildings and cobbled streets seemed foreign to him, as if made for a race that had never included him, and he found himself dreaming of wide-open spaces, of plains and mountains and lonely valleys, and always, of course, of the sea. Arodilac offered him a captaincy in Owain Gawinn's Guard and, with it, a manor and lands north of the city. For a moment Declan's heart leapt at the thought. To be part of the nobility. It was something he had dreamt of ever since he had been a boy, ever since he had stolen his father's sword to ride south to Vomaro and glory. But he knew that it could never be. He thanked Arodilac for the offer and left Hearne the next day.

Declan rode back into the north, that is certain. Of the rest of his life, there is much disagreement, though all agree that the painted caravans of the Farrow clan were never again seen trundling about the duchies of Tormay. Declan was the last of that blood. Some historians say that he settled in Thule and lived peaceably to an old age. Others maintain that he wandered east, across the Mountains of Morn and into the great wastes, where he was killed by those nameless things that doubtless dwell there, creatures that serve the Dark and cannot abide the race of man.

Still others write that he made his way to the coast of Harlech and from there to the Flessoray Islands. One particular legend has it that Declan Farrow lived for several years on the westernmost island of Flessoray. Usually, the island only had inhabitants during the summer when fisherfolk from other islands came to gather mussels. It is said that he built a boat, no larger than a single-masted coracle, and sailed away into the west where no man has gone before. Declan Farrow was never seen again in Tormay. Story has it that he left his sword in a cave on the island, where it was found many years later by a young fisherboy. Whatever was Declan's fate, he never did sleep without dreaming of the sea. And of the girl who had once been named Liss Galnes.

Eaomod, the prince of Harth, reached his father's court in Damarkan five days after the battle at the southern pass of the Morn Mountains. His steed died under him a day after leaving the battleground, its heart giving out from exhaustion. The prince continued on foot, walking through the days and nights across the stony landscape that comprises the terrain of the northernmost desert. When he arrived at the gates of Damarkan, he was so burnt by the sun and in such sorry straits that the city guards almost turned him back to the hovels of the poor that crowd up around that great city's walls. But he convinced them otherwise, and they allowed him through. News of the prince's arrival preceded him to his father's court, and he entered the palace amidst a great throng that gaped and cheered and called out his name. Within the palace, however, the court waited: row upon row of silked and bejeweled lords and ladies, the counselors and pet wizards of the king, and the officers of the guard.

It is not clearly recorded what was said then, but it is known that the king rose from his throne, his face black with fury and his voice thundering. The prince, his son, stood before him silent. Some stories tell that the prince was then banished from his father's court. These stories tell how he journeyed south, further even than any man had traveled before, and came to a far-off land of ice and snow where he founded a kingdom that, as far as anyone knows, still stands to this day.

Giverny Farrow disappeared from history. But she did not disappear from legend, for legend and history tend to be two very different things. Every duchy had their own stories about her and her wolf, stories of her protection and wisdom and blessing, stories of how she brought home a lost child or a lost lamb or how she routed a band of ogres. But as the centuries passed, these tales came to be believed only by children and the very wise. Of course, this did not hold true in Harlech and the north, for those people have a very long memory, and for them, history and legend tend to be the same thing.

What about the sceadu, standing in the darkness of the tunnels, deep within the earth? I'm afraid that his existence was forgotten by those who should have remembered. We can only hope that the book of the *Gerecednes* kept him spellbound for much longer than a hundred years. For even a hundred years tends to go by quite quickly. The ghost always did have a bad memory, so when he said a hundred years, we can only hope he meant a thousand years. At any rate, if the sceadu does finish reading the book someday, it'll be someone else's job to deal with him, and I don't envy them at all.

CHAPTER ONE HUNDRED & THIRTY
WHERE THE WIND WILL BLOW

On a cold, windy day in September, Giverny came walking along the heights of Lannaslech, where rock and sea and sky met in a sharp alliance that cut at the cloth of the heavens—or so the lords of Harlech have said of their sky since long ages past. The wolf Ehtan paced at her side. Far below them, at the foot of the cliffs, the sea rolled its relentless tide against the rocks, kicking up foam that misted in the air. Gulls wheeled in long, slow arcs across the sky. The girl stopped and sat on a rock to listen to their cries. She closed her eyes and turned her face up toward the pale sunlight. The wolf settled near her feet.

She spoke out loud, as was her wont, for she had not yet fallen into the easy use of spoken thought.

"I had a mother, once, though her face has faded in my mind. She hailed from this land. Did you know this, Ehtan? Sunlight, stone, and sea. And the wind over all. Harlech bears upon its cold coast the scars of each of the four stillpoints. The warmth of fire even in this thin sunlight. Stone and earth with my own marks upon them. Sister sea, restless in her sleep below. And do you hear? Listen. The whisper of my brother wind lingers in the sky here."

You need not ever lose remembrance of your mother, for you resemble her greatly—in visage and character, for she died defending her clan.

"And what if I forget I had a mother? What then?"

The wolf did not answer.

"Perhaps a mother is a small thing to forget when each stone and tree, all the nyten that draw breath, near all Tormay, leave their remembrance within my mind and clamor for my attention."

The wolf nipped her hand gently.

I will be your memory.

Sunlight gleamed and flashed on the sea far below them. A small gray warbler settled in a flurry of wings on the grass and whistled saucily at her. She whistled back, a long liquid trill of notes that soared in the air. The little bird hopped up and down in amazement.

Mistress of Mistresses!

But that was all the bird could manage. Overcome by its audacity, the warbler fluttered away into the air, wobbling at first and then gaining height until it was only a small speck skimming along the headland. Giverny laughed aloud. She whistled again and then sang.

"Blues and greens and shadows beneath—
the colors of the sea.
Breathe wind—blow the storm clouds hence
and bring my love home to me.

"Do you know this song and whence it came, memory mine? I feel it woven through the land here, like the earth breathed in and made it part of its own self. Yet I also know the song from some other, from she who was before me, Levoreth, for I remember her walking beside me and singing these words. It was on the Plain of Scarpe."

Must I remember for you your songs and fripperies?

The girl laughed again. However, the wolf raised its great head, scenting the wind.

"What is it?" she said, sobering. "Does something draw near?"

Nay. It is that which is no longer here. Do you forget why we came to Harlech?

She scrambled to her feet, remembering. Further along the headland, toward its stony height that reached out over the sea, they came to the small cottage built up against the back of a massive rock. A name sprang to the girl's mind, and she called out loud.

"Jute!"

There was no answer. The door was shut, but it opened easily enough for Giverny. Sunlight slanted in through the window on an empty room. Firewood sat neatly stacked by the hearth, though the wood was covered in cobwebs. Everywhere there was dust, and it stirred at her feet. There was nothing else in the room, only lichen growing on the walls and over the stone sills. The wolf whined at the door but would not enter.

"Ehtan." Her voice shook. "How long has it been?"

More than two hundred years have passed their way since we have stood at this door, Mistress of Mistresses. He who once lived here lives here no more. He has gone away. Who knows where and how, for he was the wind, and who can predict the wind?

Giverny wept a little, leaning on one of the sills and staring out across the headland until her tears blurred the earth and sky and sea into an endless blue, trembling and luminous with golden light. She stumbled outside and knelt on the verge of grass growing bravely on the cliff's edge. The sky was fraying into that which lay beyond it. Light filled her eyes. The cold nose of the wolf pressed against her hand.

A breeze sprang up, blowing in off the sea and full of the salt air. The grass trembled at its touch. A shadow fell on the ground there as something swooped down out of the sky. Giverny wiped her eyes and found herself staring at Jute.

"Hello," he said, grinning.

"Hello."

"Why are you crying?"

"No reason at all," said Giverny, smiling now.

A bird teetered down through the air on outstretched wings and settled onto Jute's shoulder. It was a young storm kestrel. He had feathers as dark as night, and bright blue eyes that surveyed Giverny and the wolf with interest.

"Come," said Jute, drifting up into the air. "There's a storm in the Morns, there's a fishing boat to rescue off Lastane, and it's snowing in Damarkan—the first time in four hundred years! There's so much to see."

"And there're twin foals about to be born in Andolan," said Giverny, "and bears robbing an apple orchard in Lura, and a little boy in Hearne who can't remember his way home."

"That was me, once, wasn't it?" said Jute.

They left the old cottage then. Giverny and the wolf walked at first, down along the cliffs, but then running as quick as thought, as quick as fading dreams. Jute and the kestrel swooped and dove through the air above them. The waves tumbled on the rocks below. The sky was full of light, full of the scent of the sea and the heather growing on the heights. The wind followed in their path for a while, laughing and chuckling to itself, as if eager to journey to wherever they went. After some time, though, it blew away to other places, for it was the wind.

THE END

AUTHOR'S NOTE

Thank you for reading *A Storm in Tormay*. I hope you enjoyed the story as much as I enjoyed writing it. I began working on it during a snowy Chicago winter, back in 2000, writing some days in my apartment and some days in a local coffeeshop. I wasn't sure who Jute was at first, but he began telling me more of his story as we spent more time together.

I plan on returning to Tormay in the near future. There are a great many stories waiting there that need to be told. After all, I daresay the sceadu will finish reading the poor old ghost's book one day. I'm not sure what'll happen then, but I need to find out. Fen and the Gawinn children have some stories in them. I've already been told a few of those, for those children certainly do have minds of their own. They remind me of my three boys. As for the Farrows, I recently discovered that there were some surviving Farrows (other than Giverny and Declan). If you read *A Storm in Tormay* with an eagle eye for detail, you might have stumbled on that fact. And if there are more Farrows, they'll be wanting to tell their stories as well. They always do.

Anyway, please take a moment to stop by Amazon or Barnes & Noble, or wherever you found my book, and leave a review. I greatly depend on the kindness of my readers to spread the word. Reviews are a tremendous help in that regard.

By the way, a great deal of thanks are due to those who aided me along the way with this book: Jen Ballinger for editing, Jared Blando for the map, Alexey Aparin for the cover art, and my beta readers for patiently strolling through earlier manuscripts: Rob and Sandra Kammerzell, Wayne and Jessica Collingwood, Sue McLarty, Daniel White, Dave Palshaw, Scott Mathias, Frank Troya, Jaemen Kennedy, and all the long-suffering members of the Bunn Clan (David, Michael, Jodi, Ben, Micha, Megan, and Jessica).

If you have any questions or comments (or a good pie recipe you'd like to share), please stop by my site and send me a note. Thank you again.

Sincerely,
Christopher Bunn

www.christopherbunn.com

Made in the USA
Charleston, SC
21 January 2014